The Complete N

NANCY MITFORD

PENGUIN BOOKS

PENGUIN BOOKS

UK | USA | Canada | Ireland | Australia
India | New Zealand | South Africa

Penguin Books is part of the Penguin Random House group of companies
whose addresses can be found at global.penguinrandomhouse.com.

Highland Fling first published by Thornton Butterworth 1931
Christmas Pudding first published by Thornton Butterworth 1932
Wigs on the Green first published by Thornton Butterworth 1935
Pigeon Pie first published by Hamish Hamilton 1940
The Pursuit of Love first published by Hamish Hamilton 1945
Love in a Cold Climate first published by Hamish Hamilton 1949
The Blessing first published by Hamish Hamilton 1951
Don't Tell Alfred first published by Hamish Hamilton 1960
This selection first published by Fig Tree 2011
Published in Penguin Books 2015

008

Copyright © the Estate of Nancy Mitford, 1931, 1932, 1935, 1940, 1945, 1949, 1951, 1960

Typeset by Palimpsest Book Production Limited, Falkirk, Stirlingshire
Printed and bound in Great Britain by Clays Ltd, Elcograf S.p.A.

The authorized representative in the EEA is Penguin Random House Ireland,
Morrison Chambers, 32 Nassau Street, Dublin D02 YH68

A CIP catalogue record for this book is available from the British Library

ISBN: 978-0-241-23947-6

www.greenpenguin.co.uk

MIX
Paper from
responsible sources
FSC® C018179

Penguin Random House is committed to a
sustainable future for our business, our readers
and our planet. This book is made from Forest
Stewardship Council® certified paper.

Contents

Highland Fling

To Hamish

I

Albert Gates came down from Oxford feeling that his life was behind him. The past alone was certain, the future strange and obscure in a way that it had never been until that very moment of stepping from the train at Paddington. All his movements until then had been mapped out unalterably in periods of term and holiday; there was never for him the question 'What next?' – never a moment's indecision as to how such a month or such a week would be spent. The death of his mother during his last year at Oxford, while it left him without any definite home ties, had made very little difference to the tenor of his life, which had continued as before to consist of terms and holidays.

But now he stood upon the station platform faced – not with a day or two of uncertain plans, but with all his future before him a complete blank. He felt it to be an extraordinary situation and enjoyed the feeling. 'I do not even know,' he thought, 'where I shall direct that taxicab.' This was an affectation, as he had no serious intention of telling the taxi to go anywhere else than the Ritz, as indeed a moment later he did.

On the way he pretended to himself that he was trying hard to concentrate on his future, but in fact he was, for the present, so much enjoying the sensation of being a sort of mental waif and stray, that he gave himself up entirely to that enjoyment. He knew that there would never be any danger for him of settling down to a life of idleness: the fear of being bored would soon drive him, as it had done so often in the past, to some sort of activity.

Meanwhile, the Ritz.

An hour later he was sitting in that spiritual home of Oxonian youth, drinking a solitary cocktail and meditating on his own very considerable but diverse talents, when his best friend, Walter Monteath, came in through the swing doors with a girl called Sally Dalloch.

'Albert, darling!' cried Sally, seeing him at once, 'easily the nicest person we could have met at this moment.'

'How d'you do, Sally?' said Albert getting up. 'What's the matter, why are you so much out of breath?'

'Well, as a matter of fact it's rather exciting, and we came here to find somebody we could tell about it; we've been getting engaged in a taxi.'

'Is that why Walter's face is covered with red paint?'

'Oh, darling, look! Oh, the shame of it – large red mouths all over your face. Thank goodness it was Albert we met, that's all!' cried Sally, rubbing his face with her handkerchief. 'Here, lick that. There, it's mostly off now; only a nice healthy flush left. No, you can't kiss me in the Ritz, it's always so full of my bankrupt relations. Well, you see, Albert, why we're so pleased at finding you here, we had to tell somebody or burst. We told the taximan, really because he was getting rather tired of driving round and *round* and *round* Berkeley Square, poor sweet, and he was divine to us, and luckily, there were blinds – which so few taxis have these days, do they? – with little bobbles on them and he's coming to our wedding. But you're the first *proper* person.'

'Well,' said Albert, as soon as he could get a word in, 'I really do congratulate you – I think it's quite perfect. But I can't say that it comes as an overwhelming surprise to me.'

'Well, it did to me,' said Walter; 'I've never been so surprised about anything in my life. I'd no idea women – nice ones, you know – ever proposed to men, unless for some very good reason – like Queen Victoria.'

'But I had – an excellent reason,' said Sally, quite unabashed. 'I wanted to be married to you frightfully badly. I call that a good reason, don't you, Albert?'

'It's *a* reason,' said Albert, rather acidly. He disapproved of the engagement, although he had realized for some time that it was inevitable. 'And have you two young things got any money to support each other with?' he went on.

'No,' said Walter, 'that's really the trouble: we haven't; but we think that nowadays, when everyone's so poor, it doesn't matter particularly. And, anyway, it's cheaper to feed two than one, and it's always cheaper in the end to be happy because then one's never ill or cross or bored, and look at the money being bored runs away with alone, don't you agree? Sally thinks her family might stump up five hundred a year, and I've got about that, too; then we should be able to make something out of our wedding presents. Besides, why shouldn't I do some work? If you come to think of it, lots of people do. I might bring out a book of poems in handwriting with corrections like Ralph's. What are your plans, Albert?'

'My dear . . . vague. I have yet to decide whether I wish to be a great abstract painter, a great imaginative writer, or a great psycho-analyst. When I have quite made up my mind I shall go abroad. I find it impossible to work in this country; the weather, the people and the horses militate equally against any mental effort. Meanwhile I am waiting for some internal cataclysm to direct my energies into their proper channel, whatever it is. I try not to torture myself with doubts and questions. A sidecar for you, Walter – Sally? Three sidecars, please, waiter.'

'Dear Albert, you are almost too brilliant. I wish I could help you to decide.'

'No, Walter; it must come from within. What are you both doing this evening?'

'Oh, good! Now, he's going to ask us out, which is lovely, isn't it? Sally darling, because leaving Oxford this morning somehow ran away with all my cash. So I'll tell you what, Albert, you angel, we'll just hop over to Cartier's to get Sally a ring (so lucky the one shop in London where I've an account), and then we'll come back here to dinner at about nine. Is that all right? I feel like dining here tonight and I think we'll spend our honeymoon here too, darling, instead of trailing round rural England. We certainly can't afford the Continent; besides, it's always so uncomfortable abroad except in people's houses. Drink your sidecar, ducky, and come along.'

'Cartier will certainly be shut,' thought Albert, looking at their retreating figures; 'but I suppose they'll be able to kiss each other in the taxicab again.'

At half-past nine they reappeared as breathlessly as they had left, Sally wiping fresh marks of lipstick off Walter's face and displaying upon her left hand a large emerald ring. Albert, who had eaten nothing since one o'clock, was hungry and rather cross; he felt exhausted by so much vitality and secretly annoyed that Walter, whom he regarded as the most brilliant of his friends, should be about to ruin his career by entering upon the state of matrimony. He thought that he could already perceive the signs of a disintegrating intellect as they sat at dinner discussing where they should go afterwards. Every nightclub in London was suggested, only to be turned down with:

'Not there *again* – I couldn't bear it!'

By the time they had finished their coffee Sally said that it was too early yet to go on anywhere, and that she, personally, was tired out and wanted to go home. So, to Albert's relief, they departed once more, in a taxi.

The next morning Albert left for Paris. It had come to him during the night that he wished to be a great abstract painter.

2

Two years and two weeks later Albert Gates stood on a cross-Channel steamer, watching with some depression the cliffs of Dover, which looked more than ever, he thought, like Turner's picture of them. The day was calm but mildly wet, it having, of course, begun to rain on that corner of a foreign field which is for ever England – the Calais railway station. Albert, having a susceptible stomach, was thankful for the calm while resentful of the rain, which seemed a little unnecessary in July. He stood alone and quite still, unlike the other passengers, most of whom were running to and fro collecting their various possessions, asking where they could change money and congratulating each other on the excellence of the crossing. Every mirror was besieged by women powdering their noses, an action which apparently never fails to put fresh courage and energy into females of the human species. A few scattered little groups of French people had already assumed the lonely and defiant aspect of foreigners in a strange land. Paris seemed a great distance away.

Albert remembered how once, as a child, returning from some holiday abroad, he had begun at this juncture to cry very bitterly. He remembered vividly the feelings of black rage which surged up in him when his mother, realizing in a dim way that those tears were not wholly to be accounted for by seasickness, tiredness, or even the near approach of another term at school, began to recite a dreary poem whose opening lines were:

> 'Breathes there the man with soul so dead
> Who never to himself hath said,
> "This is my own, my native land? . . ."'

She did not realize that there are people, and Albert among them, to whom their native land is less of a home than almost any other.

He thought of the journey from Calais to Paris. That, to him, was the real homecoming. Paris, the centre of art, literature and all culture! The two years that he had just spent there were the happiest of his whole life, and now the prospect of revisiting England, even for a short time, filled him with a sort of nervous misery.

Before those two years Albert had never known real contentment. Eton and Oxford had meant for him a continual warfare against authority, which to one of his highly-strung temperament was enervating in the extreme.

He had certainly some consolation in the shape of several devoted friends; but, although he was not consciously aware of it, these very friendships made too great a demand upon his nervous energy.

What he needed at that stage of his development was regular, hard and congenial work, and this he had found in Paris.

So happy had he been there that it is doubtful whether he would ever have exchanged, even for a few days, the only place where he had known complete well-being for a city which had always seemed to him cold and unsympathetic, but for two circumstances. One was that Walter and Sally had written even more persuasively than usual to beg that he would stay with them in their London flat. He had not seen them since that evening when they dined with him at the Ritz, and Walter was the one person whom he had genuinely missed and found irreplaceable.

The other circumstance – the one that really decided him – was that he had recently shown his pictures to a London art dealer of his acquaintance, who had immediately offered to give him an exhibition the following autumn. As this was a man of some influence in the London world of art, owning the particularly pleasant Chelsea Galleries where the exhibition would be held, Albert felt that here was an opportunity not to be missed. He arranged therefore to bring over his pictures immediately, intending to store them and look about for a studio where he himself could stay until the exhibition should be over, late in October. Paris was becoming hot and stuffy and he felt that a change of air would do him good. Also, he was really very much excited at the prospect of seeing Walter again.

Presently the ship approached the quay, and sailors began adjusting a gangway at the very spot where Albert stood. Inconsequently he remembered the landing of the Normans – how William the Conqueror, springing first from the boat, seized in his hands a sod of English soil. It would be hard to do that nowadays. Impossible even to be the first to land, he thought, as he was brushed from the gangway by a woman of determined features laden with hand luggage which she used as a weapon.

In the train he found himself sharing a carriage with two idiotic girls who were coming home from a term at some finishing school in Paris. They were rather obviously showing off on his account. After talking at some length of their clandestine affairs with two French officers, which appeared to consist solely in passing notes to them when visiting the Louvre on Thursday afternoons, but which they evidently regarded as the height of eroticism, they broached the subject of Art. It appeared that once a week they had spent two hours at some *atelier* drawing the death mask of Beethoven, the Venus of Milo and other better known casts in smudgy charcoal. These depressing efforts were now produced from a portfolio and pinned on to the opposite seat which was unoccupied. Albert learnt from their chatter that when a drawing was finished by a pupil at the *atelier*, 'Madame' would come round and add '*Quelques petits accents bien à leur place*'; in other words, the finishing touch. The pupil would then fix it and put it carefully away in a portfolio.

Presently one of the girls said:

'I think I must go on with my art, I might make quite a lot of money. You know, Julia once made two pounds by painting lampshades for her mother's dining-room, and I'm quite as good as she is.'

The other one remarked that she thought Art was marvellous.

They then began to play vulgar jazz tunes on a portable gramophone, a noise which Albert found more supportable than their chatter.

As the train drew near London he felt homesick and wretched. He longed to be back in his studio in Paris surrounded by his own pictures. It was a curious and rather squalid little abode, but he had been happy there and had grown attached to it. His neighbours had all been poor and friendly, and in spite of having seen practically none of his English friends and few French people of his own class for two years, he had not for a moment felt lonely.

Now he began to wish that he had never left it; the pouring rain outside the carriage and the young artists opposite him had plunged him into a state of the deepest gloom. The idea of seeing Walter again began to terrify him. Walter! How could one tell what changes a year of matrimony may not have wrought. Considering these things, Albert fell asleep in his corner.

When the train stopped at Victoria he got out drowsily, but was only half-awake until suddenly thrown into a most refreshing rage by the confiscation, from his registered luggage, of a copy of *Ulysses* which Walter had particularly asked him to procure.

'Sir!' he cried violently to the uninterested official, 'I am Albert Gates, an artist and seriously-minded person. I regard that work as literature of the highest order, not as pornography, and am bringing it to London for the enlightened perusal of my friend Monteath, one of your most notable, if unrecognized poets. Does this unutterable country, then, deny its citizens, not only the bodily comforts of decent food and cheap drink, but also the consolations of intellect?'

At this point, observing that his audience consisted of everybody on the platform except the one individual to whom he addressed himself, he followed his porter to a taxi and was soon on his way to Walter's flat in Fitzroy Square.

Driving up Grosvenor Place he was struck, as people so often are when returning from an absence abroad, by the fundamental conservatism of London. Everything looked exactly the same as it had looked the very day that he left, two years before. The streets were wet and shiny, as they had been then; the rain fell in the same heart-rending drizzle, as though it had never for a moment stopped doing so, and never would again. The same Rolls-Royces contained hard-faced fashionable women in apparently the identical printed chiffon dresses and picture-hats of two years before, fashionable, but never *chic*.

He thought how typical it is of Englishwomen that they should always elect to dress in printed materials. A passion for fussy detail without any feeling for line or shape.

'And those picture-hats which have been worn year after year, ever since the time of Gainsborough and which inevitably destroy all smartness, they seem still to be blossoming upon all heads, in this repulsive town. If ever I marry, God send it may be a woman of taste.'

Albert disliked women, his views on the sex coinciding with those of Weininger – he regarded them as stupid and unprincipled; but certain ones that he had met in Paris made up for this by a sort of worldly wisdom which amused him, and a talent for clothes, food and *maquillage* which commanded his real and ungrudging admiration.

These and other reflections continued to occupy his mind, until, looking out of the window, he saw that the taxi had already arrived in Charlotte Street. He was now seized with the miserable feeling of nervousness which always assails certain people when they are about to arrive at a strange house, even though it should belong to a dear friend of whose welcome they are inwardly assured. He began to torture himself with doubts. Suppose Walter had not received the telegram announcing the day of his arrival, and they were spending a week-end in the country? Or, worse than that – for he could easily go to an hotel if it were necessary – suppose they had really not wanted him at all, or had put off some visit on his account, or – but at this moment the taxi stopped abruptly opposite a green front door which was almost immediately opened by Walter. At the sight of his friend's welcoming face, Albert's doubts vanished completely.

'My dear!' cried Walter, 'my dear boy, my darling Albert. *How* we have been looking forward to this! Oh, how nice to see you again after all these years! Quickly! quickly – a cocktail. You must be dying for one. And here's Sally, who's been spending the whole day arranging flowers in your bedroom.'

'I do hope you won't die of discomfort here,' said Sally. 'Did Walter prepare you in the least bit for what you're going to suffer? There are no servants, my dear, except an idiot boy. You know, the sort that murders butlers in the evening papers, but he's quite sweet really, and as we haven't a butler we think it's fairly safe. Cocktail for you?'

The room into which Walter and Sally led the way was so lovely that Albert, who had half expected the usual green horror with sham eighteenth-century flower pictures, was thrown into a state of almost exaggerated rapture. For a London drawing-room it was a particularly good shape, with large windows and cheerful outlook. The walls were covered with silver tissue a little tarnished; the curtains and chair covers were of white satin, which the grime of London was rapidly turning a lovely pearl colour; the floor and ceiling were painted a dull pink. Two huge vases of white wax flowers stood one each side of the fireplace; over the mantelpiece hung a Victorian mirror, framed in large white shells and red plush. Albert, as he walked about this exquisite room, praising and admiring, felt blissfully happy; the depression which had been gathering force ever since he left his studio that morning now left him for good.

He had always experienced in Walter's company a feeling of absolute ease and lack of strain. He now found, rather to his surprise, that the presence of Sally did nothing to impair their relationship; she gave him no sensation either of intruding or of being intruded upon. Walter and Sally together seemed almost like one person, and Albert realized at once how wrong he had been to oppose their union.

'How I should like,' he said, looking at her lovely face, 'to paint a portrait of Sally.'

'Well, why not? She'd love to sit for you, I know, and we've got a room with a perfectly good north light at the back of the house. Albert, *do*.'

'My dear, impossible. I can't work in London, you know. People think it an affectation, but I assure you that it is no such thing. I might even go so far as to say that I'm incapable of working in this country at all; a question, I suppose, of nerves.'

'How like Walter,' said Sally laughing. 'Poor angel, he's quite incapable of work-ing in London, too. He gave up his last job after exactly three days.'

'Shut up, darling. You know quite well who it was that begged and implored me to leave, now don't you? Sally's father,' explained Walter, 'got me a job in a bank. I can't tell you what I suffered for three whole days. It was like a P. G. Wodehouse novel, only not funny at all, or perhaps I've no sense of humour. To begin with, I had to get up at eight every morning. One had much better be dead, you know. Then, my dear, the expense! I can't tell you what it cost me in taxis alone, not to mention the suit I had to buy – a most lugubrious black affair. There was no time to get back here for luncheon, and I couldn't go all day without seeing Sally, so we went to a restaurant which was recommended to us called "Simkins", too putting off. Sally was given some perfectly raw meat with blood instead of gravy, and naturally she nearly fainted, and she had to have brandy before I could get her out of the place. By then we were so upset that we felt we must go to the Ritz in order to be soothed, which meant more taxis. In the end we reckoned that those three days had cost me every penny of thirty pounds, so I gave it up. I can't afford that sort of thing, you know.'

'Poor Father,' said Sally, 'he's very much worried about Walter. He has a sort of notion in his head that every man ought to have some regular work to do, prefer-ably soldiering. He doesn't seem to understand about cultivating leisure at all, and he regards writing poetry as a most doubtful, if not immoral occupation.

'And he isn't as bad as your uncle Craigdalloch, who actually said in my hearing of some young man, "Ah, yes, he failed for the Army, and was chucked out of the City, so they sent him to the Slade." Just think how pleased Tonks must have been to have him!'

Walter then asked Albert how long he intended to stay.

'Can you keep me till the end of next week?'

'My dear, don't be so childish. Now that we have at last persuaded you to come, you must stay quite a month if you won't be bored. I know London in August is very unfashionable, but it would cheer us up a lot to have you, and besides, think what a boon you would be to the gossip writers!'

'Yes, indeed,' said Sally, 'poor old Peter seems to be at the end of his tether already. His page the last few days has been full of nothing but scraps of general knowledge which one assimilates quite unconsciously. I call it cheating . . . I mean, when I want to read about wild ducks sitting on their eggs at the edge of a railway line I can buy a book of natural history; but I do like gossip to *be* gossip, don't you? This paragraph about the ducks was headed, "Observed by Jasper Spengal." Well, I was quite excited; you know what a talent Jasper has for observing things he's not meant to, and then it was only the beastly old duck after all. Well, I *mean* . . . if he's come down to that sort of thing already, it will be the habits of earthworms by August, I should think.'

'So you want me to stay and have my habits noted instead?' Albert felt all his resolution slipping away. After all, it was nice to see his old friends again. It occurred to him now that he had been very lonely in Paris.

'But you'll be leaving London yourselves?'

'Not until the end of August, anyhow, then we may go to the Lido for a little.'

Walter looked rather defiantly, like a naughty child, at Sally as he said this, and she pretended not to hear. She knew quite well, and had said so already more than once, that, terribly in debt as they were, this idea of going to the Lido was quite out of the question. Sally spent much of her life trying to put a brake on Walter's wild extravagances and they had more than once been on the verge of a quarrel over the Lido question.

The Monteaths led a precarious existence. They had married in the face of much opposition from both their families, especially Sally's, who looked upon Walter as a rather disreputable, if attractive, person and an undesirable son-in-law. However, as soon as they realized that Sally was quite determined to marry him whatever happened, they had softened to the extent of settling five hundred pounds a year on her. More they could not afford. Walter had about the same, which had been left him some years previously by an uncle; they struggled along as best they could on a joint income of one thousand a year. This they supplemented from time to time by writing articles for the weekly papers and by the very occasional sale of one of Walter's rather less obscure poems.

All might have been well except for his incurable extravagance. In many ways they were extremely economical. Unlike the type of young married couple who think it essential to have a house in the vicinity of Belgrave Square and a footman, they preferred to live in a tiny flat with no servants except an old woman and a boy, both of whom came in daily. Sally did most of the cooking and all the marketing herself and rather enjoyed it.

On the other hand, Walter seemed to have a talent for making money disappear. Whenever he was on the point of committing an extravagance of any kind he would excuse himself by explaining: 'Well, you see, darling, it's so much cheaper in the end.' It was his slogan. Sally soon learnt, to her surprise and dismay, that 'it's cheaper in the end' to go to the most expensive tailor, travel first class, stay at the best hotels, and to take taxis everywhere. When asked why it was cheaper, Walter would say airily: 'Oh, good for our credit, you know!' or 'So much better for one's clothes,' or, sulkily: 'Well, it is, that's all, everybody knows it is.'

He also insisted that Sally should be perfectly turned out, and would never hear of her economizing on her dresses. The result was that during one year of married life they had spent exactly double their income, and Sally had been obliged to sell nearly all her jewellery in order to pay even a few of the bills that were pouring in, so that the idea of going to the Lido, or indeed of doing anything but stay quietly in London was, as she pointed out, quite ridiculous.

Walter, incapable always of seeing that lack of money would be a sufficient reason for giving up something that might amuse him, was inclined to be sulky about this; but Sally was not particularly worried. She generally had her own way in the end.

3

After dinner that evening, Walter said that Albert's first night in England must be celebrated otherwise than by going tamely to bed. Albert, remembering with an inward groan that Walter had always possessed an absolutely incurable taste for sitting up until daylight, submitted, tired though he was, with a good grace; and at half-past eleven they left the house in a taxi. Sally was looking particularly exquisite in a dress which quite obviously came from Patou.

Walter, explaining that it was too early as yet to go to a night club, directed the taxicab to the Savoy, where they spent a fairly cheerful hour trying to make themselves heard through a din of jazz, and taking it in turns to dance with Sally.

After this, they went to a night club called 'The Witch', Walter explaining on the way that it had become more amusing since Captain Bruiser had taken it over.

'All the night clubs now,' he told Albert, 'are run by ex-officers; in fact it is rather noticeable that the lower the night club the higher is the field rank, as a rule, of its proprietor.'

Presently they arrived in a dark and smelly mews. Skirting two overflowing dustbins they opened a sort of stable-door, went down a good many stairs in pitch darkness and finally found themselves in a place exactly like a station waiting-room. Bare tables, each with its bouquet of dying flowers held together by wire, were ranged round the walls, the room was quite empty except for a young man playing tunes out of Cochran's revue on an upright piano. Albert was horrified to see that Walter paid three pounds for the privilege of merely passing through the door into this exhilarating spot.

A weary waiter asked what they would order. A little fruit drink? Apparently no wine of any sort could be forthcoming, not even disguised in a ginger-beer bottle. They asked for some coffee but when it came it was too nasty to drink. This cost another pound. Depression began to settle upon the party, but they sat there for some time valiantly pretending to enjoy themselves.

'Let's go on soon,' said Walter, at the end of an hour, during which no other human being had entered the station waiting-room. They groped their way up the stairs and bumped into a body coming down, which proved to be that of Captain Bruiser. He asked them, in a cheerful, military voice, if they had had a good time. They replied that they had had of all times the best, and thanked him profusely for their delightful evening. He said he was sorry it had been so empty, and told them the names of all the celebrities who were there the night before.

After this, they sat for some while in a taxi, trying to decide where they should go next. The taximan was most helpful, vetoed 'The Electric Torch' on account of having as he said, 'taken some very ordinary gentlemen there earlier in the evening', and finally suggested 'The Hay Wain'. 'Major Spratt is running it now, and I hear it is very much improved.'

To 'The Hay Wain' they went. Albert felt battered with fatigue and longed for his bed. This time they approached their destination by means of a fire-escape, and when they had successfully negotiated its filthy rungs, they found themselves in a long, low, rather beautiful attic. There were rushes on the floor, pewter and wild flowers (which being dead, slightly resembled bunches of hay) on the tables, and the seats were old-fashioned oak pews, narrow, upright, and desperately uncomfortable.

A waiter, dressed in a smock which only made him look more like a waiter than ever, handed them a menu written out in Gothic lettering. Ten or twelve other people were scattered about the room, none of them were in evening dress. They all looked dirty and bored.

'Is Rory Jones singing tonight?' asked Sally.

'Yes, madam; Mr Jones will be here in a few moments.'

An hour and a half later Rory Jones did appear, but he had just come from a private party, was tired, and not a little tipsy. After singing his best known and least amusing songs for a few minutes, he staggered away, to the unrestrained fury of Major Spratt, who could be heard expressing himself outside the door in terms of military abuse.

'Let's go on, soon.'

'On,' thought Albert wearily, 'never bed?'

The next place they visited, run by a certain Colonel Bumper, was called 'The Tally-Ho' and was an enormous basement room quite full of people, noise and tobacco smoke. It appeared that champagne was obtainable here, owing to the fact that the club had been raided by the police the week before and was shortly closing down for good.

Albert thought of Paris night clubs with some regret. He felt that 'The Hay Wain' and 'The Witch' might be sufficiently depressing, but that 'The Tally-Ho' induced a positively suicidal mood – it had just that atmosphere of surface hilarity which is calculated to destroy pleasure.

'Let's go on soon,' said Walter, when they had drunk some very nasty champagne. Despite the cabman's warning, they now went to 'The Electric Torch' but found on arrival that the 'very ordinary people' had gone. Moreover the band had gone, the waiters had gone. Alone, amid piled up chairs and tables placed upside down on each other, stood the proprietor, Captain Dumps. He was crying quite quietly into a large pocket handkerchief, and never saw them come or heard them creep silently away.

After this, to Albert's ill-concealed relief, they went home. It was half-past five and broad daylight poured in at his bedroom window. He calculated with his last waking thoughts that this ecstatic evening must have cost Walter, who had insisted on paying for everything, at least twenty pounds, and he felt vaguely sorry for Sally.

4

The following afternoon at about half-past three Sally and Walter got out of bed and roamed, rather miserably, in their pyjamas.

The daily woman had come and gone, and Albert's room proved, on inspection, to be empty. After a lengthy discussion as to whether they could bring themselves to eat anything and if so, what, they made two large cups of strong black coffee, which they drank standing and in silence. Sally then announced that she felt as if she were just recovering from a long and serious illness and began to open her morning letters. 'Bills, bills, and bills! Darling, why did we hire that Daimler to go down to Oxford? There must have been trains, if you come to think of it.'

'Yes, but – don't you remember? – we hadn't an A.B.C. We couldn't look them up. Give the bill to me.' He took it from her and began to burn holes in it with his cigarette, but Sally, engrossed in a letter, did not notice.

'Who's that from?'

'Aunt Madge. Listen to it:

'*My Dearest Sally,*

'*You will no doubt have seen in the newspapers that your Uncle Craig has been appointed chairman of the mission to New South Rhodesia . . .*

'Of course I haven't! Does she imagine I have nothing better to do than read the papers?'

'Go on,' said Walter.

'Where am I? Oh, yes!

'*. . . This was all very sudden and unexpected and has caused us inconvenience in a thousand ways, but the most unfortunate part of it is that we had arranged, as usual, several large shooting parties at Dalloch Castle. I wrote and asked your father and mother if they would go up there and act as host and hostess, but Sylvia tells me that they have to pay their annual visit to Baden just then. It occurred to me that perhaps you and Walter are doing nothing during August and September, in which case, it would be a real kindness to us if you would stay at Dalloch and look after our guests. I know that this is a big thing to ask you to do and, of course, you must say no if you feel it would be too much for you. If you decide to go we will send you up in the car and you must invite some of your own friends. Dalloch will hold any amount of people.*

'*Yrs. affecly.,*

'*Madge Craigdalloch.*

'*PS. – General Murgatroyd, a great friend of your Uncle Craig's, will be there to look after the keepers, etc.*'

There was a long silence. Walter sat down rather heavily.

'Well?' said Sally.

'Well, what?'

'Shall we do it? Listen, my precious. I know it would be awful and I expect you'd simply hate it, poor sweet, and nothing to what I should, but still, facts must be faced. If we do this we shall save money for two solid months, and after that, if you like, we could probably afford to spend a little time in Paris, if we could let the flat. Albert might be able to tell us of some nice cheap hotel there.'

Walter became sulkier every minute.

'I won't stay at a cheap hotel in Paris. Paris to me means the Ritz. I'm very sorry – it's the way I'm made. Besides, it's well known to be cheaper in the end to stay at the Ritz, because otherwise one has to keep taking taxis there to see who's arrived. And I won't let the flat. It never pays to let houses, because of all the damage that is done by tenants.'

'Perhaps we could manage to have a week at the Ritz if we went to Scotland, funny creature,' she said, tickling the back of his neck.

Walter laughed and began kissing her hand, one finger at a time.

'What d'you think, then?'

'How d'you mean? What do I think?'

'Walter, you're being extremely tiresome, darling. You know quite well what I mean.'

'My precious angel, I've often noticed how clever you are at getting your own way, and if you've really made up your mind that we've got to have two months of potted hell in Scotland I suppose nothing can save us. But I should just like to say here and now, that I'm quite sure it would be cheaper in the end to go to the Lido. I know you wouldn't think so, but these economies always lead to trouble; I've seen it so often.'

'But, darling, we haven't even to pay our railway journey if we go in the car, and there can't be any expenses up there.'

'Well, mark my words. Anyhow, if we go, let's make Albert come too, then we might get some fun out of it.'

'Yes, of course, and we could ask some other chums. Jane, perhaps. It won't be too bad really, you know. Sweet darling, not to make a fuss – are you sure you don't mind terribly? Shall I ring up Aunt Madge now?' She kissed the top of Walter's head and went over to the telephone.

'Hullo? Is Lady Craigdalloch there? . . . Mrs Monteath . . . Don't wander about, Walter, it puts me off. No, don't – that's my coffee . . . Hullo, Aunt Madge? Sally speaking . . . Yes, we've just got it . . . Well, we think we'd love to . . . No, sweet of you. Can we come and see you sometime and talk it over? . . . Yes, of course, you must be frightfully. When do you go? . . . Oh, goodness what a rush for you! . . . Yes, we could be there in about half an hour . . . All right, we'll meet you there . . . No, perfect for us. Good-bye!'

Sally hung up the receiver.

'Where d'you think we've got to meet them? You'd never guess, but it's so typical of them, really. The House of Lords! So come on, my angel, and dress, because I said we'd be there in half an hour.'

Sally and Walter were perched rather uncomfortably on a red leather fireguard in the Prince's Chamber of the House of Lords. The magnificent personage, of whom they had inquired whether they could see Lord Craigdalloch, presently returned from his quest for that nobleman. 'His lordship says he may be a little time, but I will inform her ladyship that you are here. Meanwhile, would you wait a few moments?' He walked rather pompously to the other end of the room where he stood motionless.

'Well, he doesn't seem to be informing her,' said Sally, 'unless by telepathy. Still, I'm quite happy here, aren't you? Of course, it just *is* one's spiritual home, that's all. *Why* didn't I marry a peer? I'd really forgotten what a divine place it is, such ages since I've been here.'

'Like church, isn't it? I keep expecting the organ to peal forth. It rather reminds me of our wedding in some ways.'

'More like a mausoleum, really. D'you see that very old man over there?'

'I see the seven oldest living creatures, if you mean one of them.'

'The one with the greenish face over by the statue of Queen Victoria.'

'My dear, I hadn't noticed him. But how awful! Can't we help in some way? Is he dying?'

'Oh, I expect sort of vaguely he is. This place mummifies people you know, without their having to die first, and they often go on creeping about like that for years. That's why they're called Die Hards. It is a most descriptive name for them, poor old sweets. Anyway, that particular one is a great friend of Daddy's, and he disinherited his eldest son for marrying a Catholic.'

'Not really? It's rather heavenly to think such people do still exist. What happened to the son, though – was he quite broke?'

'Oh, no, not at all; the Catholic was immensely rich. So, to pay the old boy out, they took the grouse moor next to his in Scotland and started a stoat and weasel farm on it and quite soon all his grouse were eaten up by the weasels. Daddy says he never got over it – it nearly broke his heart.'

Walter looked round him for a few minutes in silence. 'I haven't seen anybody the least aristocratic-looking yet,' he remarked presently, 'except, of course, the boy friend who is by way of informing your aunt that we are here. He's a lovely man, but all the others look exactly like very old and decrepit doctors. I can imagine any of them pulling out a thermometer and saying, "Well, well, and how are we today? Put out your tongue and say 'Ah.'" Now, there is rather a spry-looking one by the door. He might be a dentist or a *masseur*. What's the muttering about in the next room?'

'Someone making a speech. Uncle Craig, most likely, as they're all trooping out. They can put up with a lot here (they have to, poor angels!), but it's only the ones who can't walk that stay and listen to Uncle Craig, and you should see the expression on their faces when they realize what they're in for – pitiful, like trapped animals!

'I heard him speak once about the peeresses in their own right who want to sit in the House of Lords. It was quite unintelligible and no wonder. His only real reason for not wanting them is that he thinks they might have to use the peers' lavatory, and, of course, he couldn't *say* that. Another time he was speaking on the Prayer Book, but somehow he got all his notes mixed up so the last half of his speech was all about new sewers for Bixton. Nobody noticed, of course, and he was able to square the reporters afterwards. Such an old duck, you know, but not exactly cut out to be a legislator.'

'It has often occurred to me to wonder, if there were a revolution tomorrow, how the mob would know which were the nobles,' said Walter. 'Personally I've always been terrified that I should be left behind when all my friends were being hurried off in the tumbrils to the echoing cry of *"A bas les aristos!"* Never mind, I shall have my turn next day when the intelligentsia is being wiped out.'

'On the contrary, my angel, you'll hang about hoping for weeks, until at last, after all your acquaintances have died gloriously in front of Buckingham Palace or the Albert Memorial, you'll be pitched into the Thames with the other *bourgeois*.'

'Of course, it just would be one's luck. Now who'd mind going to the scaffold between Lord Lonsdale and Mrs Meyrick! It would give one a social kick, you know. Think of the papers next day!

'Among others I noticed on the scaffold yesterday Walter Monteath, the poet, was wearing his favourite green tie and chatting to Lord Lonsdale. He told me that his wife was busy at the moment but hopes to attend the executions today. Picture on back page.

'But as for all those old peers, they'll have to parade up and down Piccadilly in their coronets if they want to be taken in the smart tumbrils, and even then I expect people would think they were an advertisement for something.'

At this moment the magnificent personage strolled up to where Walter and Sally were sitting and said that Lord Craigdalloch was about to speak and if they would care to follow him he would conduct them to the Strangers' Gallery, which he then proceeded to do, leading them up and down several corridors and staircases until they came to a small door, through which he pushed them into inky blackness. They groped their way to seats into which they subsided thankfully. Far below them there emerged from the gloom a sort of choked muttering.

After a few moments their eyes became more or less accustomed to the darkness and they were able to distinguish various objects – the throne, the Peeresses' Gallery, occupied by the stately figure of Lady Craigdalloch, who blew kisses to them, and two or three large tables at which some men were writing. Finally, they recognized Lord Craigdalloch. He was standing near one of the tables, and the muttering seemed to proceed from his lips. Sally was sorry, though in no way surprised, to notice that his audience consisted solely of themselves, Aunt Madge, an old bearded man seated on one of the benches with a pair of crutches just out of his reach and another stretched at full length on a red divan.

The Monteaths feverishly endeavoured to catch a few words of what their uncle was saying, but without success. As they sat straining their ears, two Frenchmen were shown into the gallery and, feeling their way to a seat, began to converse in whispers. They seemed much intrigued by the man on the divan.

'Dites donc, ce lord sur le sofa, il est saou?'

'Je dirais plutôt malade.'

'Eh bien, moi j'crois qu'il est ivre.'

'Que c'est lugubre ici.'

'Oui, rudement rasant.'

Lord Craigdalloch now raised his voice slightly and the words, 'the noble lord behind me . . .' were heard.

'The noble lord behind him has evidently slipped away,' murmured Sally, observing the rows of empty benches.

The old man with the beard now began to scrabble feverishly for his crutches, and finally, after a prolonged and unsuccessful effort to reach them, took off his watch-chain and lassoed one of them with it. He then hooked the other one with the crutch part and drew it towards him. Having planted them firmly underneath his armpits he hopped away with incredible agility, not, however, before Lord Craigdalloch had just time to say, loudly and portentously, 'My noble friend opposite.'

The departure of the only conscious member of his audience seemed now to spur him to greater vocal efforts and whole sentences could be heard at a time.

'I am convinced, m'lords, that this danger is very real. It is a very real danger.

What did Scipio Africanus say?' Here he began struggling with the notes he held in his hand, but was evidently unable to find what Scipio Africanus had said. The sleeper on the divan, subconsciously aware that something was expected of him, turned rather heavily and groaned out, ''Ear! 'ear!'

'M'lords, it has been said in another place,' continued the speaker in no way put out by this slight setback, 'that it is a very real danger. The Dukeries, m'lords, with all due respect to the noble duke behind me, are *not* to be confounded with the Fisheries. As my noble friend has so aptly remarked, it is anomalous to pretend that they are analogous . . .'

Another rather younger peer now came in, sat down opposite the divan and began to read some letters.

'*Enfin, on vient au secours du pauvre vieux.*'

'*Mais non, il n'y fait même pas attention.*'

'*Mon Dieu! Eh bien, voilà. C'est le flegme Britannique. Que voulez-vous? Dites donc, si on partait? Ce n'est pas follement gai ici.*'

'*Est-ce qu'on ôse?*'

'*Allons. Filons vite. Courage, mon ami.*'

The Frenchmen got up and left the gallery.

At last Lord Craigdalloch made his peroration, which was quite inaudible, and sat down. The man who was reading letters sprang to his feet as though fearful of interruption (a danger, however, which hardly seemed pressing as the house was empty except for the now prostrated Craigdalloch and their sleeping compeer on the sofa), and spoke rapidly and audibly:

'M'lords, I have been asked to reply to the noble lord and I wish at the outset to express the thanks of the Government to the noble lord for so readily agreeing last May to postpone his Question, in view of the position as it then stood. At that time there was some uncertainty . . .'

Here Lady Craigdalloch leant over the rail of the Peeresses' Gallery and by a series of signals gave the Monteaths to understand that she was ready to go and would meet them outside.

When, after losing their way once or twice, they at last reached the Prince's Chamber, they found her waiting there for them. A tall commanding woman with white hair and an Edwardian aspect, she had, in the days when big pale faces and Grecian features were admired to the exclusion of everything else, been considered a beauty. She had still considerable remains of looks and the unmistakable manner of one who has been courted in youth and flattered in middle-age.

'Dear Sally,' she said, embracing her niece rather voluminously, 'I knew you would like to hear your uncle's speech. It went off very well, didn't it? Always such an anxiety to the dear thing. How well you are looking, Sally. Where did you get so wonderfully sunburnt?'

'At Elizabeth Arden's, Aunt Madge.'

Lady Craigdalloch inwardly supposed that this must be one of Walter's Bright Young but Undesirable friends that she was always hearing so much about from Sally's mother. The creature probably has a villa in the South of France – so much the better, those sort of people are not wanted in England, where they merely annoy their elders and breed Socialism. In any case, she never understood this craving of the younger generation for a hideous brick-coloured complexion. If she had guessed for a moment that Sally stained hers every morning with stuff out of a bottle she would have thought her niece frankly mad.

'Craig will join us in a moment. He wishes us to begin tea without him.' She led the way down long, draughty, Gothic corridors to the tea-room, which, in contrast to other portions of the House, presented a scene of tempestuous gaiety. Several of the peers seated at the rather *intime* little tables were considerably under seventy, and one or two had relations and female friends with them whom they were entertaining with jokes and witticisms of the most abandoned description. Two bishops and some of their girl friends were fairly rollicking over a pot of tea, while the old man with crutches was being jocularly accused by the Lord Chancellor of having wiped his beard on the table-cloth, an allegation which he could hardly refute, having been caught by that dignitary in the very act. Altogether there was a spirit of goodwill and friendly banter which seemed more or less lacking elsewhere in the building.

While Walter and Sally were eating the fascinating mixed biscuits and strong tea which the nation, through the medium of Richard Coeur de Maison Lyons, provides at a slight profit for the sustenance of its administrators and their guests, Lady Craigdalloch explained in what their duties at Dalloch Castle would consist.

'You will find everything running very smoothly, I think. The servants have all been there for years and you'll have no trouble at all with them. You will, of course, give any orders for the comfort of the guests, such as, for instance, how many picnic luncheons will be required for the guns, and so on. Then, if you would meet new arrivals in the hall and show them their rooms, that sort of thing makes people feel so much more at home than if they arrive and find no host or hostess.'

'When would you like us to go up there?' asked Sally.

'Let me think. The first guests, of course, arrive on the tenth. Could you go up about the eighth? You'll find General Murgatroyd. He's there now, dear thing, fishing.'

'Is it a big party for the twelfth?'

'I think I can tell you exactly who will be there. Lord and Lady Prague – he is a great friend of your papa, Sally; very deaf, poor dear, but an extremely good shot. He married her *en secondes noces* some years ago. She was Florence Graiday. She will be a great help to you, I think, a wonderfully charming woman and so artistic. They will probably stay quite a month. They always do every year. Then a delightful young couple, the Chadlingtons. Brenda Chadlington is the daughter of a very old friend of mine. She is a most beautiful creature. The other two guns are Admiral Wenceslaus, a dear thing with only one eye; and Mr Buggins, who is, of course, secretary of the Nelson Club, a very cultured man. His wife, poor woman, is shut up, has been quite mad for years.'

'Is General Murgatroyd married?' asked Sally rather nervously. She felt that all these women might prove to be very alarming.

'No, dear, he is not. That is to say, he *was* married but unfortunately, he was obliged to divorce his wife. None of us was surprised. She was a girl from the Baker Street Bazaar, you know. She got a hold over him somehow and made him marry her. But it all happened years ago – thirty years at least, I suppose. Here comes your Uncle Craig.'

Sally kissed her uncle, who seemed genuinely pleased to see her.

'We heard your speech, Uncle Craig,' she lied, 'from the Strangers' Gallery. It was most interesting.'

'Glad you think so, my dear. One has one's duty, you know; born into a certain position and so forth. It's no use pretending that one enjoys coming here, or that it will be very pleasant going off to New South Rhodesia just when the moor has never been better. Still, as my poor father used to say, one's not only put here for enjoyment. All the same,' he added, brightening somewhat, 'Gillibrough tells me I may get the chance of shooting a lion or two and possibly some hartebeest in Rhodesia. Well, Walter, what d'you think of this place? Never been here before, eh? Finest legislative assembly in the world, you know, nothing to touch it anywhere. Made England what she is today – the House of Lords. The work that goes on here, you wouldn't believe it. There's no place like it for work, and all unpaid. And then the Socialists pretend we don't do our bit. I'll tell you one thing, Walter: the reform of the House of Lords will be the downfall of England.' He bristled at the idea, then continued more gently, 'So you two are going up to Dalloch to look after our guests for us, eh? Very kind of you, I think. Now, have you any friends of your own you'd like to ask for the shooting, eh?'

'We'd rather like to ask someone called Albert Gates, if we may, but he doesn't shoot, I'm afraid.'

'Doesn't shoot? And Walter doesn't shoot either? I can't think what all these young men are coming to. What does he do, then?'

'He studies painting, Uncle Craig.'

'An artist, is he? Well, well, how did you get to know him, then? As a matter of fact, now I come to think of it, I once knew an artist myself called Leighton – Lord Leighton. Not a bad fellow at all, really quite a decent sort of chap considering. If your friend paints he'll like being up at Dalloch: the views are really superb, wonderful colour effects, you know.'

'The old parts of the house are very paintable too,' said Lady Craigdalloch. 'Dear Mr Buggins always does some charming water-colour sketches on non-shooting days.'

'See that youngish man who's just come in, Sally?' said her uncle suddenly.

Sally saw a man of unbelievable age creeping towards them, his limbs positively shaking with palsy.

'That's Prague, he's going to be at Dalloch with you. You'd better meet him. Here, Prague! (He's very deaf so speak up, won't you?) *Prague, this is my niece, Mrs Monteath. She's going to be at Dalloch.*'

Lord Prague gave her a gouty hand and said in a quavering voice:

'You must be Johnnie's daughter, I suppose. Now, how is Johnnie?'

'*Not very well,*' screamed Sally. '*He's doing a cure at Baden.*'

'I'm very sorry to hear it. A young man like Johnnie should not be doing cures yet. Why, it's only yesterday he was my fag at Eton. Cure be damned! Little Johnnie. Yes, he was Captain of the Boats – only yesterday! Well, see you in Scotland, I hope. I must go now. They may divide on this. Coming, Craig?'

Walter and Sally, on their return home, found Albert talking to Jane Dacre, Sally's greatest and, indeed, only woman friend.

'Jane, dear, how nice to see you! Did you know Albert before? Anyhow, I'm glad to see he gave you a cocktail.'

'No, we've never met before, and in point of fact, I gave him one. He didn't seem to know where the drinks are kept.'

'I have been telling Miss Dacre about our party last night,' said Albert. 'What have you two been doing this afternoon?'

'We have been visiting the greatest legislative assembly in the world, namely, the House of Lords, and one of the legislators took such a fancy to us that he has lent us a castle and a grouse moor in Scotland for two months. And this is a perfectly true fact, believe me or not as you like, but please both come and stay and bring your guns.'

Sally explained the circumstances.

'You must both come and help us with these Pragues and Murgatroyds and people. There's an admiral with one eye and a man with a lunatic wife, but he's not bringing her because she's in a loony bin. So do come, angels, won't you?'

Albert accepted without any hesitation.

'I have never been to Scotland,' he said, 'which, for an earnest student of the Victorian era, is a very serious admission. I am happy to think that I shall soon see with my own eyes and in such charming company, that scenery of bens and braes which is so impregnated with the nineteenth century. It is also a unique chance, as I am told that no cultured people ever go there now, so much is it *démodé*.'

'I'd love to come, too,' said Jane, 'if I may let you know for certain in the morning. I shall have to ask the family – but I expect they'll be delighted. There is something so very respectable about Scotland.'

5

Jane Dacre sat in the restaurant car of the Scotch express about a month later. She had accepted Sally's invitation with great pleasure and her family's full consent, and was much looking forward to the visit, partly because she would thus avoid seeing her parents for a whole month, but chiefly because she was devoted to Walter and Sally, and rather in love with Albert.

Jane was a very ordinary sort of girl, but her character, as is so often the case with women, manifested itself by a series of contradictions and was understood by nobody. Thought by some to be exceptionally stupid, and by others brilliantly clever, she was in reality neither. She had certain talents which she was far too lazy to develop, and a sort of feminine astuteness that prevented her from saying silly things. Like many women she had taste without much intellect, her brain was like a mirror, reflecting the thoughts and ideas of her more intelligent friends and the books that she read. Although she was able to perceive originality in others, she was herself completely unoriginal. She had, however, a sense of humour, and except for a certain bitterness with which, for no apparent reason, she regarded her mother and father, the temperament of an angel.

Her attitude towards her parents was, indeed, very curious. She always spoke of them as though they were aged half-wits with criminal tendencies, whose one wish was to render her life miserable. Those of her friends who had met them never could account for this. They were charming, rather cultured people, obviously devoted to their only child, and Jane when she was actually with them seemed to return their devotion. That she was a great trial to them there could be no doubt. Men fell easily in love with her, and she was usually having an affair with some really unsuitable person. As she was most indiscreet she had acquired, among people of her parents' generation, a very bad reputation, which was hardly deserved. Up to the present she had not married, having a sort of vague idea in her head that she wished to be the wife of a genius. In the same way that some girls will not marry for love alone but must have money too, only allowing themselves to fall in love with a millionaire, so Jane thought that she could never be happy except with a really clever man; she had little intellect of her own, and needed the constant stimulus of an intellectual companion.

She intended to marry when and only when she had found the ideal person, but she was in no hurry. The idea rather bored her, and the example of her married friends (except for Walter and Sally) was, to say the least of it, unpromising.

Meanwhile, she fell in love right and left, and had many violent but short-lived love affairs, in the course of which she burnt her own fingers comparatively seldom.

The train was full of sportsmen, their wives and dogs, going North. The most depressing sight in the world, thought Jane, is a married couple travelling. The horror of it. Not only must they sleep, eat, walk, drive and go to the theatre together all their lives, but they cannot escape even in the train. It brings home to one what marriage really means more than anything else, except perhaps seeing a married couple at the bridge table. What is the terrifying chain which binds these wretched people together so inevitably? Love? Hardly, or they would look happier. Intellectual companionship? No, that certainly not; the misery on their faces is only exceeded by the boredom. Habit and convention, no doubt, aided by the natural slavishness of women. Probably they are too stupid to realize their own unhappiness. They all look terribly, terribly stupid.

As Jane glanced around, her attention was particularly attracted by one couple who seemed rather different from the rest, and yet in a way typical of them all.

The husband was an example of sporting Englishman to be seen by the dozen on every racecourse and with whom the Embassy is nightly packed. He was tall, rather burly, with a phenomenally small head, mouse-coloured hair and reddish moustache. Although possessing almost classical features he was as ugly an object as could be imagined.

His wife was more unusual looking. She was immensely long and thin, so that she appeared, as it were, out of a drawing, like an object seen in a distorting mirror. Her face, terribly thin and haggard, was completely dominated by an enormously long thin nose which turned up slightly at the very end; her large dark eyes were set close together and looked short-sighted. Her mouth was simply a red line, showing up startlingly on her dead white skin with green shadows. Jane thought that she had never seen anyone look so much like an overbred horse. She even ate like one, appearing to sniff every mouthful cautiously before she allowed herself to nibble at it, as though she might at any moment shy away from the table. Her husband behaved to her just like a groom with a nervous mare. Jane felt that he must have had difficulty in accustoming her to being handled.

She was well-dressed in an English sort of way; her tweeds were perfectly cut, and everything she wore was obviously expensive. Beautiful rings gave the uncomfortable impression of being too big for her fingers, which were abnormally thin and nervous. Her pearls were real. She wore a regimental badge of diamonds and rubies on a thick crêpe-de-chine jumper. While lacking any real *chic*, she gave an impression of genuineness and worth so unusual as to be rather pleasant. The word 'bogus' could under no circumstances have applied to her.

Jane, who was clever with her own clothes, felt annoyed with the long thin woman who, she thought, might have made more of her appearance without in any way detracting from its originality.

'And is it necessary to look as bored as that?' Jane wondered. Of course, the husband was most uninspiring, but still she might look out of the window some-times, or at her fellow-passengers instead of staring into space in that almost loopy way. Perhaps she had a hidden life of her own into which she could retire at will, or possibly she was in fact as stupid as she looked. Jane hoped for her sake that this was so.

At last she turned to her husband and said something. Only her lips moved, the expression of her face was unchanged. He nodded. Presently he gave her a cigarette and she began to blow the smoke through her nostrils like a horse in the cold weather.

Jane paid her bill and wandered back to her third-class sleeper. When she reached it she stood for a few moments in the corridor looking out of the windows at sunny fields with immense shadows of trees and hedges lying across them. The setting sun made a yellow mist over everything.

'By the time I get back to England, autumn will have begun,' she thought vaguely. Her mind was full of Albert Gates.

Jane's love affairs generally consisted of three phases. During the first phase – which lasted over a length of time varying with the number of meetings, but not often exceeding two months – she was violently in love. When away from the object of her affections she would think of him constantly in a light which gener-ally bore a very small relation to truth; when in his company she would force herself to be happy, although she was often disillusioned in little ways. The second phase was complicated, but rendered more exciting by the reciprocation of her feelings. This seldom lasted for very long, as the third phase, consisting of heartless, but determined backing out on the part of Jane, would almost immediately follow. The first and second phases were generally accompanied by shameful flirtation.

At the present moment Jane was undergoing the usual preliminary phase with regard to Albert. She had met him several times in London and thought him easily the most attractive person of her acquaintance. As she gazed out of the corridor window it occurred to her that here, most probably, was the genius for whom she had been searching for such a long time; her brain circled, as it were, round and round the subject, but she sought no conclusion and arrived at none. Presently the long thin woman passed by on her way to the first-class sleepers, followed by her husband. In motion she looked more than ever like a horse.

Jane climbed into her sleeper and lay down. She was sharing the carriage with three other women, all, luckily, unknown to each other, so there was no conversa-tion. They looked at her with some disapproval as, contrary to third-class convention, she undressed completely and put on a pair of pyjamas. She greased her face, brushed her hair and settled down for a horrible night of banging, jolting and waking up at countless stations. All the time she half thought, half dreamed of Albert, wondering if he would have arrived yet at Dalloch Castle, how long he intended to stay, and whether he was at all excited at the prospect of their meeting. Towards the morning she fell into a profound sleep.

When she woke up the train was passing through Highland scenery. Purple hills kept rising outside the carriage window and obscuring the sky. They were covered with little streams and sheep. Everything was very quiet, even the train seemed to make less noise than it had done the previous evening; the air had a peculiar quality of extreme clearness like cold water.

Jane felt, but quickly checked, a romantic tremor. She removed her gaze from the moors and began to dress. The other women were still asleep, looking like modern German pictures.

At Inverness, Jane had to change into a local train, which ambled for about an hour in rather an intimate sort of way over moors and through pine woods, stopping here and there at little toy stations. When she alighted at Dalloch Station she noticed the long thin woman of the previous night standing by the guard's van with her husband, and presumed that they must be going to the castle. Sure enough, when they had collected their luggage, which took some time because there was a great deal of it as well as two spaniels, they climbed into the motor car where Jane was already installed and introduced themselves as the Chadlingtons. She gathered from labels on their hand luggage that they were Captain and Lady Brenda Chadlington, a name she seemed vaguely to know.

'Have you stayed at Dalloch before?' asked Lady Brenda as they drove out of the station yard.

'No; you see, I don't know the Craigdallochs. Sally Monteath asked me. Have you been here before?'

'Oh, yes! Every year since I can remember. Madge Craigdalloch is my mother's greatest friend and my godmother. I can't imagine what it will be like without her and Craig, although I'm told the Monteaths are charming. What bad luck for poor Craig having to go off like that, wasn't it . . . ?'

She rambled on in the bored, uninterested voice of one who has been taught to think that any conversation is better than none. Her husband looked out of the window in silence.

6

Sally greeted them in the hall of Dalloch Castle on their arrival. She was looking lovelier than usual in a pair of pink satin pyjamas.

'Please excuse these clothes. I've just this moment woken up. We only got here last night after a most fiendish journey in the car. How tired you must all be. I've had hot-water bottles put in your beds and breakfast will be sent up at once. Shall we go upstairs?'

The Chadlingtons glanced at each other in a startled kind of way.

General Murgatroyd now appeared and was introduced to Jane. He evidently

knew the Chadlingtons very well and offered to show them their rooms, while
Sally, relieved to have got rid of them, carried off Jane to have breakfast with herself and Walter, who was still in bed.

'Let's fetch old Gates,' said Walter, 'and have a party in here.'

Sally turned on the gramophone while he went along the passage, soon to return
with Albert, who looked sleepy but cheerful in a pair of orange pyjamas. Jane
thought him more attractive even than in London.

Presently trays of delicious breakfast appeared and they all sat on the bed munching happily, except Albert who announced that he was unable to touch food in the
morning and asked the slightly astonished housemaid for a glass of Maraschino.

Jane asked if he had also travelled up in the Craigdallochs' car.

'Indeed, yes,' he replied. 'What a journey, too; all through England's green
unpleasant land, as Blake so truly calls it. My one happy moment was at Carlisle,
where we spent a night. When I opened what I supposed to be a cupboard door
in my room, I was greeted by inky blackness, through which was just visible a pile
of sordid clothes and cries of: "Well, I'm damned!" and "What impertinence!" It
was a conjugal bedroom!'

Jane laughed.

'I expect if you knew the truth it was no such thing.'

'Well, I thought of that myself, but came to the conclusion that people who
were indulging in a little enjoyable sin would probably be in better tempers. They
actually rang the bell and said very loudly to the maid so that I couldn't fail to hear:
"The person next door *keeps* coming in. Will you please lock it on this side so that
we can have some peace?" *Keeps coming in*, indeed, as though I wanted to know the
details of their squalid *ménage*. However, I had my revenge. I cleaned my teeth very
loudly every half-hour all through the night. It woke them up each time, too! I
could hear them grumbling.'

'Has all the rest of the party arrived?' asked Jane.

'All except Lord and Lady Prague. The general, whom you saw downstairs,
Admiral Wenceslaus and Mr Buggins were all here last night,' said Walter. 'We had
about half an hour's conversation with them before going to bed. Mr Buggins
seems rather nice and Sally has quite fallen for the admiral.'

'As I have for the general,' remarked Albert; 'but then I have always had a great
penchant for soldiers. It fascinates me to think how brave they must be. Sometimes
one sees them marching about in London, all looking so wonderfully brave. I
admire that. Sailors, too, must be very courageous, but somehow one doesn't feel
it in quite the same way. Perhaps the fact that they are clean-shaven makes them
more akin to oneself. This particular admiral certainly fixed upon me an extremely
fierce and penetrating eye; instinctively I thought here is the hero of many an ocean
fight, a rare old sea-dog.'

'His eye,' said Walter, 'is glass. At least, one of them is. I don't want to disillusion
you, Albert dear.'

'How fascinating!' cried Albert. 'I knew the moment I saw him that the admiral was not quite as we are. This accounts for it. How d'you think he lost it,
Walter? I suppose it hardly could have been plucked out by pirates or the Inquisi-
tion? Do you think he is sensitive about it? Will he, for instance, mind if he sees
me looking closely at him to discover which eye is which? I must find out how he

lost it. I suppose it would be tactless to ask him right out? But the general may know. I don't despair. Or Mr Buggins. I like Mr Buggins. He appears to be a man of some culture. He saw my picture "Tape Measures" reproduced in the *Studio* and was kind enough to mention it appreciatively.

'Now, my dears, I am going to dress, as I can hardly wait to begin exploring this house, which promises, in my opinion, to be very rewarding to the intelligent student of the nineteenth century. What do you intend to put on, Walter? I fear I have no tweeds, so shall be obliged to wear some trousers and a jersey. Will that be suitable, do you think?'

He picked up his black taffeta wrap and left the room.

Meanwhile, General Murgatroyd escorted the Chadlingtons to the dining-room where they made a hearty breakfast of sausages, eggs, ham and strong tea. The general, who some two hours since had eaten enough for three, kept them company with a plate of brawn. They all spoke in monosyllables, their mouths full.

'Bad luck for poor old Craig.'

'Oh, rotten.'

'When did the Monteaths get here?'

'Last night – late.'

'Anybody else?'

'Stanislas is here and Buggins.'

'Anybody else?'

'Yes; namby-pamby chap called Gates – artist or something. Came with the Monteaths.'

'Who's to come?'

'Only Floss and Prague. Coming tonight.'

'Does Monteath shoot?'

'No, nor Gates. Just as well, from the look of them.'

'What's Mrs Monteath like?'

'Oh, all right. Better than the others, I should say.'

'Pretty, isn't she?'

'Too much dolled up for me, otherwise quite handsome.'

'Finished your breakfast?'

'M'm!'

'Come and look at the river, then.'

'Wait a moment. We'll get our rods put up.'

'Not much use, too bright.'

'Oh, we might as well have a try, all the same.'

About two hours later, Jane, having bathed and changed out of her travelling clothes, wandered downstairs, where she came upon Albert, exquisitely dressed in bright blue trousers and a black sweater. He was roaming about, notebook in hand.

'My dear Jane,' he said, 'this house is unique. I am in ecstasies. Most of it seems scarcely to have been touched for the last fifty years. Nevertheless, we are only just in time. The hand of the modern decorator is already upon it. The drawing-room, alas! I find utterly ruined. Our absent hostess would appear to have that Heal *cum*

Lenigen complex so prevalent among the British aristocracy. Happily, in this case, it has been muzzled, presumably by lack of funds, but its influence is creeping over the whole house. The oak, for instance, on these stairs and in the entrance hall has been pickled – a modern habit, which one cannot too heartily deplore – and much exquisite furniture has been banished to the servants' hall, some even to the attics. On the other hand, the boudoir, stone hall, billiard- and dining-rooms appear to be quite unspoilt. Come with me, my dear.'

Albert led the way to the dining-room, where the table was being laid for luncheon. It was a huge room with dark red brocade walls and a pale blue-and-yellow ceiling covered in real gold stars. At one end there arose an enormous Gothic mantelpiece of pitch-pine. Several Raeburns and two Winterhalters adorned the walls.

'Winterhalter,' murmured Albert, 'my favourite artist. I must call your attention to this clock, made of the very cannon-ball which rolled to the feet of Ernest, fourth Earl of Craigdalloch during the battle of Inkerman. Shall we go and look at the outside of the castle? We have just time before lunch.'

They went into the garden and walked round the house, which was built in the Victorian feudal style, and rather resembled a large white cake with windows and battlements picked out in chocolate icing. Albert was thrown into raptures by its appearance.

When they returned to the front door they found Walter and the general standing on the steps.

'Ah! this house! this house!' cried Albert. 'I am enchanted by it. Good morning, General.'

'Good morning, Gates.'

'Walter, have you ever seen such a house? General, you agree, I hope, that it is truly exquisite?'

'Yes; I'm attached to the place myself. Been here, man and boy, for the last fifty years or so. Best grouse moor in the country, you know, and as good fishing as you can find between here and the Dee, I swear it is.'

'It *is* lovely,' said Jane doubtfully. 'I wonder what we shall do all day though.'

'Do? Why, my dear young lady, by the time you've been out with the guns, or flogging the river all day, you'll be too tired to do anything except perhaps to have a set or two of lawn tennis. After dinner we can always listen to Craig's wireless. I've just asked the chauffeur to fix it up.'

'I personally shall be busy taking photographs,' said Albert. 'I am shortly bringing out a small brochure on the minor arts of the nineteenth century, and although I had already collected much material for it, there are in this house some objects so unique that I shall have to make a most careful revision of my little work. I also feel it is my duty to the nation to compile a catalogue of what I find here. You write, General?'

'I once wrote a series of articles for *Country Life* on stable bedding.'

'But how macabre! Then you, I and Walter, all three, belong to the fellowship of the pen; but while you and I are in a way but tyros, I feeling frankly more at home with a paintbrush and you, most probably, with a fox's brush, Walter here is one of our latter day immortals.'

And he began to recite in a loud voice one of his friend's poems:

'Fallow upon the great black waste
And all esurient. But when
Your pale green tears are falling
Falling   and
Falling
Upon the Wapentake, there was never
So absolutely never
Such disparity.'

Walter blushed.

'*Please*, Albert.'

'My dear Walter, that is good. It is more than good – it has an enduring quality and I think will live. Do you not agree, General? You and I, Walter, will do
a great deal of work here. I have found a room with a large green table in the
centre very well lighted. It will be ideal for my purpose. Then I am hoping that
Sally will perhaps give me a few sittings. Do you think that she might be persuaded?'

'My dear, she'd adore to. Sally very much believes in having herself reproduced
in all mediums. Come on. There's the gong for lunch.'

By dinner-time that evening the whole party was assembled, Lord and Lady Prague
having arrived in a motor car soon after seven o'clock.

Sally had spent much time and thought over the arrangement of the table, feeling that it was her duty to try and make the first evening a success, and as she sat
down she thought, with some satisfaction, that she had mixed up the party rather
well. It soon became apparent, however, that the party was not mixing. Her own
task, seated between Lord Prague and Captain Chadlington, might well have
daunted a far more experienced conversationalist, the former being stone deaf and
moreover thoroughly engrossed in the pleasures of the table, while the latter
appeared to possess a vocabulary of exactly three words – 'I say!' and 'No!' – which
he used alternately. She fought a losing battle valiantly, remembering that the really
important thing on these occasions is to avoid an oasis of silence. Walter declared
afterwards that he distinctly heard her ask Lord Prague if he belonged to the London Group, and that, on receiving no answer, she then proceeded to recite *Lycidas*
to him until the end of dinner.

Jane, whose partners were Admiral Wenceslaus and Mr Buggins, courted disaster by embarking on a funny story Albert had told her about a lunatic woman with
a glass eye. She only remembered in the middle that the admiral was one-eyed and
that Mrs Buggins languished in a lunatic asylum and had to change it quickly into
a drunken man with one leg. The story lost much of its point and nobody laughed
except Walter, who choked into his soup.

Albert sat next Lady Prague, a spinsterish woman of about forty with a fat face,
thin body and the remains of a depressingly insular type of good looks. Her fuzzy
brown hair was arranged in a dusty bun showing ears which were evidently intended
to be hidden, but which insisted on poking their way out. Her skin was yellow
with mauve powder; except for this her face was quite free from any trace of *maquillage*, and the eyebrows grew at will. Her nails were cut short and unvarnished.

Albert was seized with spasms of hatred for her even before she spoke, which she did almost immediately in a loud unpleasing voice, saying:

'I didn't quite hear your name when we were introduced.'

Albert looked at her frolicking eyebrows with distaste and said very distinctly:

'Albert Memorial Gates.'

'Oh! What?'

'Albert Memorial Gates.'

'Yes. *Memorial,* did you say?'

'My name,' said Albert with some asperity, 'is Albert Memorial Gates. I took Memorial in addition to my baptismal Albert at my confirmation out of admiration for the Albert Memorial, a very great work of art which may be seen in a London suburb called Kensington.'

'Oh,' said Lady Prague crossly, 'you might as well have called yourself Albert Hall.'

'I entirely disagree with you.'

Lady Prague looked helplessly at her other neighbour, Admiral Wenceslaus, but he was talking across Jane to Mr Buggins and took no notice of her. She made the best of a bad job and turned again to Albert.

'Did I hear Mr Buggins say that you are an artist?'

'*Artiste – peintre –* yes.'

'Oh, now do tell me, I'm so interested in art, what do you chiefly go in for?'

'Go in where?'

'I mean – water-colours or oils?'

'My principal medium is what you would call oils. Gouache, tempera and prepared dung are mediums I never neglect, while my bead, straw and button pictures have aroused a great deal of criticism not by any means all unfavourable.'

'It always seems to me a great pity to go in for oils unless you're really good. Now Prague's sister has a girl who draws quite nicely and she wanted to go to Paris, but I said to her parents, "Why let her learn oils? There are too many oil paintings in the world already. Let her do water-colours. They take up much less room." Don't you agree?'

'I expect, in the case of your husband's niece, that you were perfectly right.'

'Now, do tell me, this is so interesting, what sort of things do you paint?'

'Chiefly abstract subjects.'

'Yes, I see, allegories and things like that. Art must be so fascinating, I always think. I have just been painted by Laszlo. By the way, did I see you at his exhibition? No? But I have seen you somewhere before, I know I have. It's a funny thing but I *never* forget a face – names, now I can't remember, but I never forget a face, do you?'

'So few people have faces,' said Albert, who was struggling to be polite. 'Everyone seems to have a name, but only one person in ten has a face. The old man sitting next to Sally, for instance, has no face at all.'

'That is my husband,' said Lady Prague, rather tartly.

'Then the fact must already have obtruded itself on your notice. But, take the general as an example. He hasn't got one either, in my opinion.'

'Oh, I see now what you mean,' she said brightly, 'that they are not paintable. But you surprise me. I have always been told that older people, especially men, were very paintable with all the wrinkles and lines – so much character. Now, you went, I suppose, to the Dutch exhibition?'

'I did not. I wasn't in London last spring, as a matter of fact, but even if I had been I should have avoided Burlington House as sedulously then as I should later in the summer. I regard the Dutch school as one of the many sins against art which have been perpetrated through the ages.'

'You mean . . .' She looked at him incredulously. 'Don't you *like* Dutch pictures?'

'No, nor Dutch cheese, as a matter of fact!'

'I can't understand it. I simply worship them. There was a picture of an old woman by Rembrandt. I stood in front of it for quite a while one day and I *could have sworn* she breathed!'

Albert shuddered.

'Yes, eerie, wasn't it? I turned to my friend and said: "Laura, it's uncanny. I feel she might step out of the frame any moment." Laura Pastille (Mrs Pastille, that's my friend's name) has copied nearly all the Dutch pictures in the National Gallery. For some she had to use a magnifying glass. She's very artistic. But I am amazed that you don't like them. I suppose you pretend to admire all these ugly things which are the fashion now. I expect you'll get over it in time. Epstein, for instance, and Augustus John – what d'you think about them?'

Albert contained himself with some difficulty and answered, breathing hard and red in the face, that he regarded Epstein as one of the great men of all time and would prefer not to discuss him. (General Murgatroyd, overhearing this remark, turned to Walter and asked if that 'fella Gates' were an aesthete. Walter looked puzzled and said that he hoped so, he hoped they all were. The general snorted and continued telling Captain Chadlington about how he had once played a salmon for two hours.)

Lady Prague then said: 'Why do you live in Paris? Isn't England good enough for you?' She said this rather offensively. It was evident that Albert's feelings for her were heartily reciprocated.

'Well,' he replied, 'England is hardly a very good place for a serious artist, is it? One is not exactly encouraged to use one's brain over here, you know. When I arrived from Paris this last time they would not even leave me my own copy of *Ulysses*. Things have come to a pretty pass when it is impossible to get decent literature to read.'

'*In*decent literature, I suppose you mean.'

Albert felt completely out of his depth, but to his immense relief Admiral Wenceslaus now turned upon Lady Prague the conversational gambit of, 'And where did you come from today?' thus making it unnecessary for him to answer.

Mr Buggins and Walter were getting on like a house on fire.

'Curious,' observed Mr Buggins, 'for a house party of this size in Scotland to consist entirely of Sassenachs – seven men and not one kilt among them. I have the right, of course, to wear the Forbes tartan through my maternal grandmother, but I always think it looks bad with an English name, don't you agree?' ·

'Very bad,' said Walter. 'But you could wear it as a fancy dress, I suppose?'

'The kilt, my dear sir, is not a fancy dress.'

'My wife is Scottish; her father is Lord Craigdalloch's brother.'

'Yes, of course, Johnnie. Such an interesting family, the Dallochs; one of the oldest in Scotland.'

'Really?'

'Considering that you are allied to them by marriage it surprises me that you should not be aware of that. Why, the cellars of this castle date from the tenth century. I suppose you know how it came to be built here?'

'I'm afraid I don't.'

'Well, the first Thane of Dalloch had no castle and one day when he was getting old he thought he would build himself a solid dwelling-place instead of the shieling or hut that had been his head-quarters up to then. So he went to consult a wise woman who lived in a neighbouring shieling. He told her what was in his mind and asked where would be the best place for him to build his castle. She replied, "When you find a *bike*[1] in a *birk*,[2] *busk*[3] there the *bauk*[4]."'

'The story goes that as he was walking away from the old woman's shieling he was stung by a wasp. He looked high and low for the *bike*, intending to destroy it, and presently found it in a *birk*. Instantly he recalled the witch's words. The next day he *busked* the *bauk* and soon a bonnie castle rose round the *birk*, which you can see to this very day in the cellars. To me, all these old legends are so fascinating.'

He then proceeded to tell Walter the whole history of the Dalloch family down to the present generation. Walter found it extremely dull and wondered how any-one could be bothered to remember such stuff, but he thought Mr Buggins quite a nice old bore and tried to listen intelligently.

Albert was now struggling with Lady Brenda, who was far more difficult to get on with than Lady Prague. Being a duke's daughter she was always spoken of as having so much charm. The echo of this famous charm had even reached as far as Paris, and Albert was eagerly anticipating its influence upon himself.

He was doomed to immediate disappointment, finding that besides being an unusually stupid woman she had less sex appeal than the average cauliflower; and when, in the course of conversation, he learnt that her two children were called Wendy and Christopher Robin, his last hope of being charmed vanished for ever.

She told him that Lady Craigdalloch, her godmother, was improving the whole house, bit by bit.

'This year all the oak on the staircase has been pickled. Of course, it takes time as they are not well off, but Madge has such good taste. You should have seen the drawing-room before she redecorated it: a hideous white room with nothing but Victorian furniture, bead stools and those horrible little stiff sofas. It was my mother who suggested painting it green. Of course it is really lovely now.'

'You have known the house a long time?' he asked, stifling a groan.

'Oh, yes, since I was a child. We spent our honeymoon here.'

'I hope,' said Albert, 'in the lovely bed which Sally is occupying at present. I thought when I saw it how perfect for a honeymoon.'

Lady Brenda looked horrified. Luckily at this moment Sally got up and the women left the dining-room.

As soon as the door was shut upon them, Admiral Wenceslaus monopolized the conversation, holding forth on his favourite subject: Blockade. Walter and

1. Wasps' nest.
2. Birch tree.
3. Prepare.
4. Cross beam.

Albert, who had a hazy idea that a blockade was a sort of fence behind which the white men retired when pursued by Red Indians, now learnt that, on the contrary, it is a system of keeping supplies from the enemy in times of war. The admiral explained to them, and to the table at large, that it is permissible to ration neutrals to their pre-war imports in order to prevent the enemy country from importing goods through this channel.

'Why wasn't it done from the beginning?' he bawled, in a voice which Albert felt he must have acquired when addressing his men in stormy weather from the bridge, and rolling his eye round and round. 'Was there a traitor in the Government? That's what I should like to know.'

'Hear, hear!' said Lord Prague, doubtless from force of habit, as he was, in fact, unable to hear a word.

'We had them *there*.' The admiral screwed his thumb round and round on the table as though grinding up imaginary Germans. 'And all the time our poor fellows were being blown to atoms by British shells . . .'

His speech, for it was virtually one, continued for about half an hour, and when it was finished they joined the ladies.

Albert felt disappointed. Other admirals he had met had provided excellent after-dinner company and he expected better things of the Silent Service than a lecture on Blockade.

7

After dinner the general marshalled them all into Lord Craigdalloch's study and turned on the wireless which was playing Grieg's suite from *Peer Gynt*. 'This is London calling.' (Crash! crash!) 'The Wireless Symphony Orchestra will now play "Solveig's Song".' (Crash! crash! crash!)

Albert spoke to Jane in an undertone, but he was quickly checked by a look from Lady Prague who appeared to be in a state of aesthetic rapture.

When the Grieg came to an end it was announced that Miss Sackville-West would give readings from T. S. Eliot.

'Tripe!' said the general and turned it off. He then began to arrange about the next day's shooting.

'If any of the non-shooters would like to come out tomorrow,' he said, 'it will be a good opportunity as none of the drives are very far apart and it's all easy walking. Those who don't want to come all day can meet us for lunch.'

'Jane and I would love it if we shan't be in the way,' said Sally meekly.

The general, who had taken a fancy to her, smiled benignly:

'Do you good, my dear.'

'Great,' said Albert, 'as is my distaste for natural scenery, I feel it to be my duty, as a student of the nineteenth century, to gaze just once upon the glens and bens that so entranced Royal Victoria, both as the happy wife of that industrious and illustrious prince whose name I am so proud to bear, and as his lamenting relict. I should like to see the stag stand at bay upon its native crags, the eagle cast its great shadow over the cowering grouse; I should like dearly to find a capercailzie's nest. And I feel that I could choose no more suitable day on which to witness these glories of Victorian nature than the famous twelfth, when sportsmen all over the country set forth with dog and gun to see what they can catch.'

This speech was greeted by Captain Chadlington with a sort of admiring noise in his throat which can only be transcribed as 'C-o-o-o-h.'

'Shall you come, Monteath?' asked the general, taking no notice of Albert.

'I think not, sir, thank you very much. I have rather a lot of work to do for the *Literary Times* and if everyone goes out it will be a good opportunity to get on with it.'

'Brenda and I will come, of course,' said Lady Prague briskly, 'so we shall be five extra beside the guns. Will you ring the bell, Mowbray?' The general did so. She added, with a disapproving look at Albert: 'Don't you shoot?'

'Excellently,' he replied in a threatening voice. 'With the water-pistol.'

'Perhaps you had no chance of learning when you were young; probably you have a good *natural* eye.'

The admiral looked annoyed and there was an awkward silence.

'Well, then,' said General Murgatroyd, 'that's all settled. Those who are coming out in the morning must be in the hall, suitably dressed, by ten. We shan't wait. I advise you to bring shooting-sticks.'

'What are they?' asked Albert, but his question was drowned by the overture from *William Tell* which suddenly burst upon the room.

The next day Jane came downstairs punctually at ten o'clock. Albert and Sally had apparently both found themselves unable to get up so early and had sent messages to say that they would join the guns for lunch. One of the footmen was just taking a glass of champagne to Albert's room. Jane wished that she had known this sooner; she had found it a great effort to wake up that morning herself, and was still very sleepy. She half contemplated going back to bed until luncheon time, but catching at that moment the eye of the admiral, and feeling by no means certain that it was his glass one, she lacked the moral courage to do so.

In the hall scenes of horrible confusion were going forward; a perfect regiment of men tramped to and fro carrying things and bumping into each other. They all seemed furiously angry. Above the din could be heard the general's voice:

'What the — d'you think you're doing? Get out of that! Come here, blast you!'

Lady Prague, looking like a sort of boy scout, was struggling with a strap when she caught sight of Jane.

'My dear girl,' she said taking one end of it from between her teeth, 'you can't come out in that mackintosh. Whoever heard of black on the hill? Why, it's no good at all. That scarlet cap will have to go too, I'm afraid. It's easy to see you haven't been up here before. We must alter all this.' She dived into a cupboard, and after some rummaging produced a filthy old Burberry and forced Jane to put it on. Evidently made for some portly man it hung in great folds on Jane and came nearly to her ankles.

'I don't think I'll take a mackintosh at all,' she said, rather peevishly, 'and I hardly ever wear a hat in any case, so I'll leave that behind, too.'

'As you like, my dear, of course. I think you'll be perished with cold and it will probably rain; it looks to me quite threatening. Have your own way, but don't blame me if – Hullo! we seem to be off at last.'

Jane climbed rather miserably into a sort of 'bus and sat next Lady Prague. She was disappointed that Albert had not come, having taken particular pains with her appearance that morning on his account.

The moor was about five miles away, and during the whole drive nobody spoke a word except General Murgatroyd, who continually admonished his dog, a broken-looking retriever of the name of Mons.

'Lie down, will you? No, get off that coat!' (Kick, kick, kick; howl, howl, howl.) 'Stop that noise, blast you!' (Kick, howl.)

Jane pitied the poor animal which seemed unable to do right in the eyes of its master.

When they arrived at their destination (a sort of sheep-track on the moor) they were met by two more guns who had come over from a neighbouring house to make up the numbers; and by a rabble of half-clothed and villainous-looking peasants armed for the most part with sticks. They reminded Jane of a film she had once seen called 'The Fourteenth of July'.

Their leader, an enormous man with red hair and wild eyes, came forward and addressed General Murgatroyd in a respectful, but independent manner. When they had held a short parley he withdrew, and communicated the result of it to his followers, after which they all straggled away.

Jane supposed that they were the local unemployed, soliciting alms, and felt that the general must have treated them with some tact; once aroused, she thought, they might prove ugly customers.

Presently the whole party began to walk across the moor. Jane noticed that each of the men had an attendant who carried guns and a bag of cartridges. She wondered what their mission could be: perhaps to stand by and put the wounded birds out of their pain.

After an exhausting walk of about half an hour, during which Jane fell down several times (and the general said it would be easy walking, old humbug!), they arrived at a row of little roofless buildings, rather like native huts. The first one they came to was immediately, and silently, appropriated by Lord and Lady Prague, followed by their attendant.

Jane supposed that they were allocated in order of rank and wondered which would fall to her lot.

'Better come with me, Miss Dacre,' said General Murgatroyd. It was the first time he had spoken except to swear at his dog, which he did continually, breaking the monotony by thrashing the poor brute, whose shrieks could be heard for miles across the heather.

When they reached his hut (or butt) he shouted in a voice of thunder:

'Get in, will you, and lie down.'

Jane, though rather taken aback, was about to comply when a kick from its master sent poor Mons flying into the butt, and she realized that the words had been addressed to that unfortunate and not to herself.

General Murgatroyd gave Jane his cartridge bag to sit on and paid no further attention to her. He and his attendant (the correct word for whom appeared to be *loader*) stood gazing over the top of the butt into space.

Seated on the floor, Jane could see nothing outside except a small piece of sky; she wondered why she had been made to leave her black mackintosh behind.

'I can neither see nor be seen. I expect it was that old woman's jealous spite. I don't believe she's a woman at all. She's just a very battered boy scout in disguise, and not much disguise, either.'

She began to suffer acutely from cold and cramp, and was filled with impotent rage. Eons of time passed over her. She pulled a stone out of the wall and scratched her name on another stone, then Albert's name, then a heart with an arrow through it (but she soon rubbed that off again). She knew the shape of the general's plus-fours and the pattern of his stockings by heart, and could have drawn an accurate picture of the inside of the butt blindfold, when suddenly there was an explosion in her ears so tremendous that for an instant she thought she must have been killed. It was followed by several more in quick succession, and a perfect fusillade began, up and down the line. This lasted for about twenty minutes, and Jane rather enjoyed it – 'As good as an Edgar Wallace play.'

At last it died away again, and General Murgatroyd said, 'Well, the drive's over. You can get up now, if you like.' Jane endeavoured to stand, but her legs would hardly carry her. After rubbing them for a bit she was just able to stagger out of the butt. She saw all around her the same band of peasants that had met them when they left the 'bus earlier that morning. Most of them were carrying dead grouse and picking up others.

'How kind!' she thought. 'The general has taken pity on the poor creatures and given them permission to gather the birds for their evening meal. He must really be nicer than he looks.'

Thinking of the evening meal made Jane realize that she was extremely hungry. 'Luncheon time soon, I expect.' She glanced at her watch. Only eleven o'clock! It must have stopped. Still ticking, though. Perhaps the hands had got stuck. She asked Admiral Wenceslaus the time.

'Nearly eleven, by Jove! We shall have to show a leg if we're to get in two more drives before lunch.'

Jane could hardly restrain her tears on hearing this. She sat hopelessly on a rock, while the rest of the party wandered about the heather looking for dead grouse.

When one of them found a bird he would whistle up his dog and point to the little corpse saying, 'Seek hard,' and making peculiar noises in his throat. The dog would occasionally pick it up and give it into his master's hand, but more often would sniff away in another direction, in which case its master seized it by the scruff of the neck, rubbed its nose into the bird and gave it a good walloping.

Jane began to realize the full significance of the expression 'a dog's life'.

Lady Prague, who also strode about searching for grouse, presently came up to where Jane was sitting upon her rock, and asked why she didn't help.

'Because even if I did find a bird no bribe would induce me to touch it,' said Jane rather rudely, looking at Lady Prague's bloodstained hands.

In time the birds were all collected and hung upon the back of a small pony, and the party began to walk towards the butts from which the next drive was to take place. These were dimly visible on the side of the opposite mountain, and appeared to be a great distance away.

Jane walked by herself in a miserable silence, carefully watching her feet. In spite of this she fell down continually. The others were all talking and laughing over incidents of the drive. Jane admired them for keeping up their spirits in such circumstances. Their jokes were incomprehensible to her.

'I saw you take that bird of mine, old boy, but I wiped your eye twice, you know. Ha! Ha!'

'That dog o' yours has a good nose for other people's birds. Ha! Ha!'

'D'you remember poor old Monty at that very drive last year? All he shot was a beater and a bumble-bee.'

'Ah, yes! Poor Monty, poor Monty. Ha, ha, ha!'

The walk seemed endless. They came to a river which everyone seemed able to cross quite easily by jumping from stone to stone except Jane, who lost her balance in the middle and was obliged to wade. The water was ice-cold and came to her waist, but was not at first unpleasant, her feet were hot and sore, and both her ankles were swollen. Presently, however, the damp stockings began to rub her heels and every step became agony.

When they finally reached the butts Jane felt that she was in somewhat of a quandary. With whom ought she to sit this time? She hardly liked to inflict herself on General Murgatroyd again. Lord Prague and Captain Chadlington had their wives with them, and the admiral and Mr Buggins were so very far ahead that she knew she would never have time to catch them up. She looked round rather helplessly, and saw standing near her one of the strangers who had come over for the day. As he was young and had a kind face, she ventured to ask if she might sit with him during the next drive. He seemed quite pleased and, making her a comfortable seat with his coat and cartridge bag, actually addressed her as if she were a human being. Jane felt really grateful: no one had so far spoken a word to her, except Lady Prague and General Murgatroyd, and they only from a too evident sense of duty.

The young man, whose name was Lord Alfred Sprott, asked if there was a cheery crowd at Dalloch Castle. Jane, more loyally than truthfully, said, 'Yes, a very cheery crowd.' She hoped that it was cheery where he was staying, too? He replied that it was top-hole, only a little stalking lodge, of course, but very cosy and jolly, quite a picnic. He told her some of the jolly jokes they had there. Jane, in her bemused condition, found him most entertaining; she laughed quite hysterically, and was sorry when the birds began to fly over them, putting an end to conversation.

In spite, however, of this spiritual sunshine Jane soon began to feel colder and more miserable even than before, and greatly looked forward to the next walk which might warm her up and dry her clothes.

This was not to be. While the birds were being picked up after that drive, she learnt, to her dismay, that the next one would take place from the same butts.

The wait between these two drives was interminable. Lord Alfred Sprott seemed to have come to the end of his witticisms and sat on his shooting-stick in a gloomy silence. Jane ventured one or two remarks, but they were not well received. She gathered that Lord Alfred had been shooting badly, and this had affected his spirits. She became more and more unhappy and shook all over with cold.

'I expect I shall be very ill after this,' she thought. 'I shall probably die, after lingering for some weeks; then perhaps they will be sorry.' And tears of self-pity and boredom welled up in her eyes.

When the drive was over, they all began to walk towards the hut where luncheon was prepared. They were now obliged to keep in a straight line with each other, in order to put up game for the men, who carried their guns and let them off from time to time.

'Keep up please, Miss Dacre. Keep in line, please, or you'll be shot, you know.'

Jane thought that it seemed almost uncivilized to threaten an acquaintance that she must keep up or be shot, but she said nothing and struggled, fairly successfully, not to be left behind. As the result of this further misery one tiny bird was added to the bag.

8

Nothing in this world lasts for ever. The longest morning Jane could remember was at an end and the party had assembled in a little hut for luncheon. A good fire burnt in one corner and a smell of food and peat smoke created a friendly atmosphere. Jane felt happier, especially when she saw that Sally and Albert were seated on the floor in front of the fire.

Albert looked particularly alluring in an orange crêpe-de-chine shirt open at the neck, and a pair of orange-and-brown tartan trousers, tight to the knees and very baggy round the ankles. Under one arm he carried an old-fashioned telescope of black leather heavily mounted in brass, with which, he said, when asked why he had brought it, to view the quarry. He and Lord Alfred greeted each other with unconcealed disgust; they had been at Eton and Oxford together.

Luncheon was rather a silent meal. There was not nearly enough food to go round, and everyone was busy trying to take a little more than his or her share and then to eat it quickly for fear the others should notice. (The admiral choked rather badly from trying to save time by drinking with his mouth full. Lady Prague and General Murgatroyd thumped him on the back and made him look at the ceiling, after which he recovered.) Most of the baskets in which the food was packed seemed to contain a vast quantity of apples which nobody ate at all. Some very promising-looking packages were full of *Petit-Beurre* biscuits or dry bread, and the scarcity of food was rendered all the more tantalizing by the fact that what there was of it was quite excellent. The thermos flask which should have contained coffee proved to be empty.

Lady Prague and Lord Alfred carried on a desultory conversation about their mutual relations whose name appeared to be legion.

'I hear Buzzy has sold all his hunters.'

'Yes, I heard. An absolute tragedy, you know. But I'm afraid it's . . .'

'Yes, that's what my mother says. I don't know, though, really why it should be.'

'Well, my dear, every reason if you come to think of it. But what does Eileen say about all this – ?'

'Haven't you heard?'

'No – what?'

'Eileen is staying down at Rose Dean.'

'No! Well, I must say I never, never would have thought it of her; though, mind you, I have always disliked Eileen. But really! Rose Dean – no that *is* a little too much. Then where is Looey? . . . (etc., etc.)' This was so interesting for everybody else.

When everything eatable had been consumed the general marshalled them all out of doors again. Admiral Wenceslaus was very indignant at this and said something to Jane about letting a cove finish his brandy in peace; but even he dared not mutiny and, muttering a few naval expressions, he followed the others out of the hut.

To Jane's great relief – for she was very tired and stiff – each of the women was now provided with a pony to ride. Albert walked between Jane's pony and Sally's. He looked round at the large crowd of people spread out over the moor, the ponies, dogs, and men with guns.

'We might be early settlers escaping from native tribes,' he observed. 'Led through unnatural hardships to civilization and safety by the iron will-power of one man, our beloved and sainted general. Alas, that within sight of help, his noble spirit should have flown. Poor, good old man, he will yet be enshrined in the heart of each one of us for ever.'

'Please don't laugh quite so loudly!' Lady Prague shouted to Jane and Sally, 'or all the birds will settle.'

'I wish,' said Albert, 'that I could spot an eagle or a stag with my telescope for the darling general to shoot at. He might take a fancy to me if I did. Our present lack of intimacy begins to weigh on my spirits.'

Albert searched the horizon with his telescope, but complained that, being unable to keep one eye shut, he saw nothing.

'If you ask me, I expect that's why the admiral rose from the ranks. Having only one eye, anyhow, he probably took prizes for viewing enemy craft quicker and more accurately than his shipmates. "A sail! – A sail! Ahoy!"' he cried, dancing a sort of hornpipe on the heather.

General Murgatroyd, who was beating his dog, stopped for a moment and asked Alfred Sprott if 'that fella thought the birds would be able to stand the sight of his orange shirt?' Lord Alfred grunted, he could hardly stand the sight of it himself.

'I ducked him once,' he said, 'in Mercury.'

'Good boy! Did you, then? Good for you, sir!'

'This scenery,' said Albert to Jane, 'is really most amusing. It is curious how often natural scenery belongs to one particular era. The Apennines, for instance, are purely Renaissance: Savernake was made for the age of chivalry: Chantilly and Fontainebleau for the seventeenth and eighteenth centuries: the Rhine for the Middle Ages, and so on. At other times these landscapes seem beautiful, but unreal. Scotland, as you will no doubt have noticed, was invented by the Almighty for the delectation of Victoria and Albert. Foreseeing their existence, He arranged really suitable surroundings for them, and these purple mountains and mauve streams will stand as a reminder of the Victorian age long after the Albert Memorial has turned to dust.'

'What,' asked Jane, 'would you call the landscape of today?'

Albert did not answer, but said faintly:

'Aren't we nearly there; I'm most dreadfully tired?'

Sally jumped off her pony.

'Do ride instead of me for a bit, Albert; I wanted a walk.'

General Murgatroyd could hardly contain himself when he saw Albert, his graceful figure swaying slightly from the hips, seated upon Sally's pony. He was tired himself, though nothing would have induced him to say so; if Prague could still walk so could he. Lord Prague, it may be noted, was to all intents and purposes dead, except on shooting days when he would come to life in the most astonishing manner, walking and shooting with the best. At other times he would sit in an arm-chair with his eyes shut and his hands folded, evidently keeping his strength for the next shoot. He hardly appeared able even to walk from his drawing-room to the dining-room and was always helped upstairs by his valet.

At about half a mile from their destination the horses were left behind and the party began to climb a fairly steep hill. When they reached the first butt Albert declared that he could go no farther and would stay where he was.

'That,' remarked Lord Alfred, who was passing it, 'is General Murgatroyd's butt.'

'Splendid!' And Albert, swinging himself on to the edge of it, sat there in a graceful position, his legs crossed, pretending to look through his telescope.

'Well, you'd better put on this mackintosh, Gates, that shirt would scare all the birds for miles.'

Lord Alfred went on his way feeling like the Good Samaritan.

Presently General Murgatroyd appeared with his loader. When he saw Albert he glared and muttered, but took no further notice of him and began to make his own arrangements for the drive.

'May I let off your gun, sir?' said Albert, pointing it straight into the general's face.

'Put that gun down this instant. My God! young man, I'm sure I don't know where you were brought up. When I was a kid I was sent to bed for a week because I pointed my toy pistol at the nurse.'

'I'm sorry,' said Albert, rather taken aback by his manner. 'I didn't know it was full.'

The general wiped his brow and looked round helplessly.

'You can sit on that stone,' he said, indicating one at the bottom of the butt.

'Oh, sir, please, must I sit there? I wanted to watch you. I shan't see anything from down here. Oh, please, may I stand up?'

Receiving no answer beyond a frigid stare, Albert, with a deep sigh, disposed himself upon the stone, sitting cross-legged like an idol. He then produced a slim volume from his pocket. 'I presume that you have read "The Testament of Beauty", sir?'

'Never heard of it.'

'Oh, sir, you must have heard of it. A very great poem by our Poet Laureate.'

'No, I haven't; I expect it's immoral stuff, anyway. Kipling ought to be the Poet Laureate, to my mind.'

'Alas! Philistine that I am, I must disagree with you. I cannot appreciate Sir Rudyard's writings as no doubt I should. "Lest we forget, lest *we* forget,"' he chanted. 'Have you a favourite poem, sir?'

The general remained silent, his eye on the horizon. As a matter of fact he *had* a favourite poem, but could not quite remember how it went –

> *Under the wide and starry sky*
> *Dig my grave and let me lie.*
> *Home is the hunter home from the hill,*
> *And the hunter home from the hill.*

Something more or less like that.

'You care for T. S. Eliot, sir? But no, of course, I heard you cut off the wireless last night when Mrs Nicolson was about to read us some of his poems. How I wish I could be the one to convert you!' And he began to declaim in a loud and tragic voice:

> 'We are the stuffed men, the hollow men . . .'

'Oh, *will* you be quiet? Can't you see the birds are settling?'

'I can see nothing from down here except the very *séant* pattern of your exquisite tweeds. But no matter.'

Albert read for a time in silence.

The general was breathing hard. Presently he stiffened:

'Over you! – over you, sir!' he shouted.

Albert dropped his book in a puddle and leapt to his feet, knocking the general's arm by mistake. The gun went off with a roar and a large number of birds flew over their heads unscathed.

'You blasted idiot! Why can't you sit still where I told you? Of all the damned fools I ever met –'

'I regret that I cannot stay here to be insulted,' said Albert; and he strolled out of the butt.

'Come back, will you? Blast you! Can't you see the bloody drive is beginning?'

Albert paid no attention, but walked gracefully away over the heather, telescope in hand, towards the next butt. Its occupant luckily happened to be Mr Buggins, who was rather amused by and inclined to tolerate Albert, so there were no further *contretemps*. Meanwhile, the general, infuriated beyond control, was seen to fall upon his loader and shake him violently.

When this eventful drive was over, Jane, Sally and Albert, finding themselves close to a road where the motor cars were waiting, took the heaven-sent opportunity to go home. Jane on her arrival went straight to bed, where she remained the whole of the following day, entertaining riotous parties in her bedroom. Her ankles were so swollen that it was nearly a week before she could walk without the aid of a stick.

9

Jane was enjoying herself passionately. Curiously enough, she thought, she had not fallen in love with Albert at all, but simply regarded him as a most perfect companion. Always cheerful and amusing, he was at the same time seriously intellectual and had the capacity of throwing himself heart and soul into whatever he happened to be doing. He and Jane had spent much of their time collecting together all the Victorian odds-and-ends that they could find in the house. These they assembled in the billiard-room, where Albert was now busy photographing them for a brochure which he intended to produce entitled 'Recent Finds at Dalloch Castle', and which was to form a supplement to his larger work, 'Household Art of the Nineteenth Century'.

Jane, who had up till then maintained a wholesome superiority with regard to everything Victorian, quickly smothered this feeling, and learnt from Albert really to admire the bead stools, lacquer boxes, wax flowers and albums of water-colour sketches which so fascinated him.

They practically lived in the billiard-room, hard at work the whole time, Albert making still-life compositions for his photographs, while Jane copied designs from chintzes and pieces of needlework in water-colours.

One day she was poking about in the attics trying to find more treasures for the catalogue when she noticed, poked away in a corner behind piles of furniture, a dusty glass dome. After a dangerous climb over rickety chests of drawers, derelict bedsteads and other rubbish, she managed to secure it and carry it to her bedroom, where she carefully removed the dome, which was opaque with dirt, expecting to discover some more wax fruit. Underneath it, however, she found to her amazement a representation in white wax of Jacob's Ladder. It was quite perfect. Jacob, in a sort of night-gown and an enormous beard, lay upon a floor of green plush. His head rested on a large square stone, and from just behind this rose the ladder, delicately balanced against wax clouds which billowed out of the green plush. Two angels were rather laboriously climbing on it (whether up or down it would be hard to say), while three more angels, supported by wires which rose from behind the clouds, hovered round about, twitching and quivering delightfully whenever the stand was moved.

Jane washed and replaced the dome, and then carried this treasure down to the billiard-room in great triumph. When Albert saw it his joy and delight knew no bounds.

'It is easily our most important find and shall be the frontispiece of my book!' he cried. 'I have never seen anything half so lovely. It is a poem! How can I find out the name of the artist? I must endeavour to do so without delay. But how sad, my dear, to think that this jewel should belong to people who so evidently have no feeling for beauty! It ought, of course, to occupy a place of honour in a museum. Never mind, I shall photograph it from every angle and in all lights, so that the artistic public will be able to gain some slight idea of its exquisite form, and thus share, to a certain extent, in my own emotions.'

At that moment Lady Prague was seen to pass by the open door, and Albert, longing to share his enthusiasm with somebody, rather thoughtlessly dashed out, seized her by the arm and said:

'Lady Prague, do come and see our wonderful new find. Something to cause the greatest sensation among all cultured persons – so amusing, so exquisite, so stimulating . . .'

With the naïveté of a child showing off its new toy he led her up to the dome.

She stared at it for a moment, sniffed and said rather pityingly:

'What a lot of drip you do talk. Why, that's nothing more than a particularly unattractive form of dust-trap!'

She left the room.

All the excitement died out of Albert's face and was succeeded by an expression of the deepest disgust.

'Dust-trap!' he muttered between his teeth. 'You just wait until you see the booby-trap I'm going to make for you – you viviparous old vixen!'

Walter and Sally now came in and made up for Lady Prague's lack of appreciation by an enthusiasm almost as unbounded as Albert's. They walked round and round the dome, exclaiming:

'How beautiful!' – 'How amusing!' – 'That angel's so like Lord Prague, d'you see? And, of course, Jacob just *is* the admiral with a beard!'

Walter soon retired to write a poem beginning:

> *Green plush.*
> *Admiral Jacob lay beneath a dome*
> *Of crazy glass upon green plush.*
> *And in this 'nautical' posture*
> *With angels rising from the Guinness foam*
> *The Admiral*
> *(Who was Jacob, too, out of the Bible)*
> *Fell, bucolically, asleep.*

Even Lady Brenda was quite appreciative, saying that her children would simply love it.

'It reminds me so much of a lodging-house at Westgate where we used to go for our summer holidays when we were small. Every room in it had several domes of that sort.'

Albert breathlessly asked the address of this gold mine, but Lady Brenda had forgotten it and presently left them to go out fishing.

'What a disappointing woman that is,' said Jane when she had gone. 'I noticed her particularly in the train coming up here, and somehow thought she looked rather interesting. And then, when I heard her name, I was really excited to meet her. One's always being told how charming she is – so original and cultured. But she's a perfect fool, though I must say quite nice compared to old Prague.'

'She *is* cultured in the worst sort of way,' said Albert. 'But original! Oh, dear! I had a long conversation with her yesterday after tea so I know all about her originality. I'll tell you. She has, as I had supposed that she would, a green drawing-room with flower pictures which she picked up cheap (eighteenth century, so she says). She also has a stone-coloured dining-room with a sham stone floor. On the sideboard is a model of a ship. On the walls are old maps. The lights are shaded with maps. The firescreen is a map in needlework. The chairs are covered with *petit point* which she worked herself. Her bedroom is "very modern"; that is to say, it is painted silver and stippled all over. The ceiling is of Lalique glass as is the bed. The bathroom is painted to give the impression of a submarine forest. It has portholes instead of windows. I couldn't quite understand why.

'She reads few novels, but a great many "lives" and "memoirs". Her favourite novelists are Galsworthy, Masefield, David Garnett and Maurois, she "loves modern pictures, especially flower pictures", and admires some of John's portraits, but thinks Orpen the finest living artist. She has never been to the Tate Gallery, but always means to go.

'All this she told me herself, or rather I dug it out of her. I also gathered that she goes every year to the Ascot races in one of those picture-hats and a printed dress.'

'Four of them, you mean,' said Jane.

'Very likely. She goes quite often to the Embassy Night Club, but seldom stays up later than one or two o'clock. She has a great deal of committee work when in London, mostly connected with animals. Every year she goes for three weeks to Switzerland. Captain Chadlington prefers to stay at home and kill (foxes and birds), so she always goes with her great friend, Major Lagge, chaperoned by his sister and brother-in-law. Those sort of women, I have so often noticed, never take lovers, but they have some great friend with whom they go about literally like brother and sister. It is all most peculiar and unhealthy. I think, myself, that she is a creature so overbred that there is no sex or brain left, only nerves and the herd instinct. There are many like that in English society, a sufficiently uninteresting species. I find her, in a way, beautiful.'

'Oh, yes, she is certainly that,' said Jane, 'although personally, I can't admire her very much. She has such a maddening expression. And she's really very nice, too, you know. She's been sweet to Sally and me.'

'And her husband is good-looking. But what a dreary personality he has, most uncompanionable. I suppose he will in time become a sort of Murgatroyd, although I doubt whether he will ever acquire that *joie de vivre* which so characterizes the dear general.'

'Beastly old man!'

'Ah, no, Jane! I must admit to a very great *penchant* for the general. He is so delightfully uncompromising. Yesterday I heard him say that before the War the things he hated most were Roman Catholics and Negroes, but now, he said, banging on the table, now it's Germans. I wonder what he would do if he met a Roman Catholic Negro with a German father! Dare I dress up as one and see? I could black my face, wear a rosary and Prussian boots and come in crossing myself and singing "The Watch on the Rhine" to the tune of a Negro spiritual.'

Jane laughed.

'I'm afraid you must think me rather idiotic, my dear Jane. I have been in such spirits since I came up here. I can assure you that I am quite a different person in Paris – all hard work and no play, or very little. But, after all, it is the "hols." here, as we used to say, and talking of "hols.", do help me to think out a good practical joke for Lady Prague. How I hate that old woman! Do you think she and the general – Ah! General! What a delightful surprise! I imagined that you were busy stalking those grouse again.'

'No, Gates, we are not. Very few moors can be shot over more than four times a week, you know.'

'That *must* be a relief,' said Albert sympathetically.

The general looked with some disapproval at his *matelot* clothes – a pair of baggy blue trousers worn with a blue-and-white sweater and a scarlet belt, and said severely:

'If you will be so good as to clear that mess off the table, we were going to play billiards.'

'Oh, sir, this is dreadful! You could not possibly play on the floor, I suppose? No? Well, if you'll most kindly wait for one moment while I photograph this exquisite object which Jane has found, I shall be really grateful.'

Captain Chadlington and Admiral Wenceslaus now came in. The admiral was airing his favourite topic, Blockade.

'Oh, it was a terrible scandal. Thirty thousand tons of toffee found their way through Holland alone, my dear Chadlington, and this is a most conservative estimate, worked out by my friend Jinks (whose book on the subject I have lent to your wife). Many of the Germans taken prisoner at that time by our chaps had their pockets bulging British toffee. British toffee, my dear Chadlington!'

'And then,' he added, with a catch in his voice, 'the glycerine!'

'Were their pockets bulging with that, too?' asked Captain Chadlington, who, as a prospective candidate for Parliament, was always ready to learn.

'Not their pockets. Dear me, no! Far, far worse than that – their shell-cases!'

'Oh, I say! That's disgraceful!'

'It is! Monstrous! But what I want to know is – who was the traitor? Read Page on the subject. He couldn't understand it – not a word. He couldn't make out what we were driving at. Why don't they blockade? – What on earth are you doing, Gates?'

Albert, balanced gracefully on a step-ladder, was taking a photograph of the Jacob's Ladder as seen from above.

'There,' he said, 'that's done. Now I will clear the table and you can play your little game.'

10

Jane and Albert did not stay to watch the billiards but strolled into the garden.

'I saw them playing yesterday evening,' said Albert. 'It is a curious but not a graceful game, and terribly monotonous. If it weren't such a beautiful day I should have advised you to watch them for a little, all the same: it is always interesting to see how others find their recreation. They play with ivory balls and long, tapering sticks.'

'Yes, I know,' said Jane. 'Look! there's Mr Buggins sketching.'

'How delightful. We must go and talk to him.'

Mr Buggins was sketching the old part of the house in water-colours; that is to say, he had drawn it with a pencil and was now busy colouring it in with small, rather dry brushes. It was careful work.

When he saw Albert approaching he was very much embarrassed, knowing quite well the attitude of the professional artist to the painstaking amateur; so, to cover his own confusion and to save Albert from feeling obliged to make a polite criticism of his work, he began to talk very fast about the house and its history.

'I love this part of the house, you know. That tower, and of course, the dungeons, were all that escaped the Great Fire in 1850. It is immensely old, probably eleventh century, and the walls are so thick that Lady Craigdalloch has been able to put two water-closets in the thickness alone.'

'How jolly for her!' said Albert, feeling that some remark was called for.

'Yes, very. Of course you know the history attaching to that tower?'

'No; do tell us, Mr Buggins. I was thinking that there must be some legends connected with the castle.'

Jane and Albert sat down on the grass, and Mr Buggins, clearing his throat, began his story.

'One of the Thanes of Dalloch,' he said, 'as they were then called, had a very beautiful daughter, the Lady Muscatel. Her apartment was in that tower, where she would sit all day spinning. At night, when the moon was full, she would often lean out of her window and gaze at it, and one night she was doing so when she heard from beneath her a faint noise of singing. Looking down, she beheld the handsome features of a young man of high degree, who told her that he had lost his way while out hunting.

'"Alas!" she said, "my father and brothers are from home, and I dare not open to you in their absence."

'He told her that he would not dream of trespassing on her hospitality and retired, fortified by a bottle of wine which she lowered to him in a basket.

'The next night he came again, and the next, and soon they were passionately in love with each other. But little did the unfortunate Muscatel realize that her lover was the only son of Thane McBane, head of a clan which her father was even then planning to exterminate. The warlike preparations for this raid which were going forward in the castle left the Lady Muscatel more and more to her own devices, so that one day she was able to leave her tower and go with Ronnie McBane to the nearest priest, who married them. Even so they dared not fly, but thought it better to wait until they should hear of a ship bound for France. Poor children! They knew full well that both their fathers would see them dead sooner than married (for Ronnie had by now divulged his fearful secret).

'At last Dalloch's preparations were completed and he and his men sallied forth, armed to the teeth, to wipe out the McBanes. The battle was a fearful one, but the conclusion was foregone. The unfortunate McBanes, taken unawares and overwhelmed by numbers, fought with the courage of desperation. One by one they fell, but each one that died accounted for three or four of the Dallochs. Ronnie McBane was the last to succumb, and when he did so, bleeding from forty desperate wounds, it was with the knowledge that no fewer than thirty-two of his enemies, slain by his own hand, had preceded him. It was one of the bloodiest fights in the history of the clans.

'That evening the Lady Muscatel heard sounds of merry-making in the great hall, where her father and the wild clansmen were celebrating their victory with wine and song. She went down to see what was happening and the first thing that met her eyes was Ronnie's head, horribly mutilated, on a pike. The shock proved too much for her reason and she soon became insane, wandering about the house and crying for her lost love. When her child was born neither she nor it survived many days.

'They say that at the full moon she can still be heard, wailing, wailing; and some even declare that they have seen her wan form, carrying the head of her lover.

'But surely you have heard *The Lament of the Lady Muscatel*? No? It is a beautiful ballad. Personally, I think it one of the most beautiful that Scotland has produced, although it is comparatively little known. Let me see if I can remember it.' And clearing his throat, he recited the following ballad:

The Lament of the Lady Muscatel

My lo'e he war winsome, my lo'e he war braw,[1]
Every nicht 'neath my windie he cam'.
He wad sing, oh, sae saft, till the nicht it waur o'er
I' the morn he was sadly gang ham'.

> *The pibroch i' the glen is bonny,*
> *But waley, waley, wheer's ma Ronnie?*

His e'en they were blew and his mou[2] it war red,
And his philabeg[3] cam' to the knee;
But noo ma puir Ronnie he's skaithless and deid,
Ah, wud that I a'so could dee.

> *The pibroch i' the glen is bonny,*
> *But waley, waley, wheer's ma Ronnie?*

I ganged ma gait sairly to yon branksome brae,
Wheer ma true lo'e war killed i' the ficht,
I sat on a creepy[4] and I greeted[5] the day,
And I sat greeting there till the nicht.

> *The pibroch i' the glen is bonny,*
> *But waley, waley, wheer's ma Ronnie?*

Ah, Ronnie, my true lo'e, ah, Ronnie, mine ane,
Shall I niver muir see ye ava?
I see your life's bluid poured out o'er yonder stane,
But your sperrit has flane far awa.

> *The pibroch i' the glen is bonny,*
> *But waley, waley, wheer's ma Ronnie?*

1. Brave.
2. Mouth.
3. Kilt.
4. Little stool.
5. Cried, bewailed.

They gave me your heid, Ronnie, wropped oop i' sae,[6]
And I buried it 'neath yonder saugh;[7]
For ye've left me, my Ronnie, to gang a' agley
And I niver shall see ye nae muir.

   The pibroch i' the glen is bonny,
   But waley, waley, wheer's ma Ronnie?

Ma mither she mad' me ane parritch o' kail,
And she gave me ane snood for ma heid;
But a' I can do is to greet and to wail,
Ah, Mither, I wud I were deid.

   The pibroch i' the glen is bonny,
   But waley, waley, wheer's ma Ronnie?

But e'er the sun rise, Mither, muir o'er the brae,
And e'er ane muir morrow shall dawn;
Ma heid on its pillow sae saftly I'll lay,
But ma sperrit to him will ha' flawn.

   The pilbroch i' the glen is bonny,
   But waley, waley, wheer's ma Ronnie?

There was a short silence, broken by Albert, who said:

'How beautiful, and what a touching story! We must tell it to Walter; he will be so much interested and might, I feel, write one of his charming poems round it. I think the ballad quite the finest I have ever heard.'

'I think so, too,' said Mr Buggins, who had rarely known such an appreciative audience and was greatly enjoying himself. 'To the student of medieval Scottish history it is, of course, extremely illuminating, being so full of allusions to old customs, many of which survived until quite recently.'

'Were there many allusions of that sort?' asked Albert. 'They escaped me.'

'Yes, of course, because you are not conversant with the history of those times. But take, for instance, the line: "And his philabeg cam' to the knee." This is very significant when you know, as I do, that only three clans in all Scotland wore their philabeg to the knee – that is, covering the knee: the McBanes, the Duffs of Ogle and the McFeas. Their reasons for doing so open up many aspects of clan history. The McBanes wore it to the knee in memory of Thane Angus McBane, who, when hiding from the English soldiery in some bracken was given away by the shine of his knees; his subsequent brutal treatment and shameful death will, of course, be well known to you.'

'Of course,' murmured Albert, not wishing to appear too ignorant. 'This is all so fascinating,' he added. 'Why did the two other tribes wear it to the knee?'

'The Duffs of Ogle because they used a very curious type of long bow which could only be drawn kneeling. (You will often have heard the expression: "To Duff down", meaning "to kneel".) This gave great numbers of them a sort of

6. Silk.
7. Willow tree.

housemaid's knee, so one of the Thanes gave an order that their philabegs must be made long enough for them to kneel on. The McFeas, of course, have always worn it very long on account of the old saw:

> *Should McFea show the knee,*
> *The Devil's curse upon him be.*

Am I boring you?'

'On the contrary,' said Albert, 'I am very deeply interested. I have so often wondered what the origin of "to Duff down" could be and now I know. Do tell us some more.'

'You may remember,' continued Mr Buggins, 'that one verse of the Lady Muscatel's ballad begins:

'*They gave me your heid, Ronnie, wropped oop i' sae.*

'This, of course, sounds rather peculiar – *sae*, you know, is *silk* – until you remember that only a man who had killed with his own hand in fair battle over forty warriors was entitled to have "his heid wropped oop i' sae" after his death. It was an honour that was very eagerly sought by all the clansmen and it must have consoled the Lady Muscatel in her great sorrow that she was able "to wrop her beloved's heid oop i' sae." There is a very curious legend connected with this custom.

'A young laird of Tomintoul died, they say of poison, in his bed, having only killed in his lifetime some thirty-nine warriors. His widow was distracted with grief and, although about to become a mother, she cut off his right hand, clasped it round a dirk and went herself into the thick of the fight. When she had slain one man with her husband's hand, she was able to go home and "wrop his heid oop i' sae". The Tomintouls to this day have as their family crest a severed hand with a dirk in memory of Brave Meg, as she was called. Those were strangely savage days, I often think.'

'Tell us some more,' said Jane.

'Let me see: what else can I remember? Oh, yes. The Lady Muscatel goes on to say: "I buried him 'neath yonder saugh." Up to comparatively recent times any man who had been killed by his father-in-law's clansmen was buried beneath a *saugh* (willow tree). There are some parts of Scotland where it would be impossible to find a saugh for miles that had not a grassy mound before it, telling a bloody tale. Tradition says that Ronnie's body was later exhumed and laid beside those of his wife and child in the chapel. "I sat on a creepy." A creepy was a wooden stool, often three-legged, on which women would sit to greet (or bewail) the loss of a loved one killed in the fight.'

'But was the fight always going on?' asked Albert.

'Very, very constantly. The wild clansmen were generally engaged in deadly feuds, which were often continued over many generations and were treated almost as a religion.'

'What,' asked Jane, 'is a "parritch o' kail"?'

'I am glad you mentioned that. A *parritch o' kail* is a curious and very intoxicating drink made of cabbage and oatmeal. Perhaps her mother hoped that the Lady Muscatel would drown her sorrows in it. Dear me!' he said, gathering up his painting materials, 'how I must have bored you.'

'My dear sir,' cried Albert, '*tout au contraire!* I'm entranced. But tell us one thing before you go. Have you ever seen the Lady Muscatel's ghost?'

'Alas! I have not; but Craigdalloch says that as a child he saw her constantly, sometimes looking out of the window' (he pointed to a little window in the tower) – 'but more often walking in the great corridor which leads to her apartment. He has told me that she wears a grey wimple snood (you remember that she refers to a *snood* in the ballad), and carries in one hand a sort of parcel – the "heid", no doubt, "wropped oop i' sae". She is supposed to walk when the moon is full.'

The rasping voice of Lady Prague suddenly broke in upon them, causing Albert and Mr Buggins to leap to their feet.

'Who is supposed to walk when the moon is full?'

Mr Buggins told her the story rather shortly.

'Well,' she said, 'and I suppose you believe that sort of balderdash. Tosh – bosh and nonsense! Personally, I shall believe in ghosts when I have seen one, and not before. Surely you must have noticed by now that everyone knows somebody else who has seen a ghost, but they've never seen one themselves.'

'But Craig has seen the Lady Muscatel.'

'Craig! Silly old man, he'd see anything. I expect it was really a housemaid, if you ask me.'

She blew her nose and went towards the castle.

'Such a golden nature,' said Albert pensively. 'One would hardly credit her with second sight, but still one never knows: the most unlikely people see ghosts – sometimes.'

That night Lady Prague took her bath, as she always did, before going to bed. She lay in the water for some time without washing very much; then dried herself briskly and put on a linen night-dress trimmed with crochet-lace, a pair of quilted slippers and a Chinese kimono with storks and fir-trees embroidered all over it. Thus attired, with her hair screwed into a small lump on the top of her head, and a towel and a pair of combinations over one arm, she sallied forth into the great corridor. As she did so she noticed that the lights, by some mistake, had all been put out; but she was easily able to see her way because a curtain at the other end of the corridor was drawn back and a great shaft of moonlight fell through the window on to the carpet.

Lady Prague shuffled along until she had nearly reached her bedroom door, when suddenly she stood still, rooted to the ground with terror. A female form, immensely tall and unnatural-looking, had stepped into the shaft of moonlight. In its hand was a sort of round parcel which it held out towards the paralysed peeress; then, emitting a soft but terrifying wail, vanished into the shadows. The sound of this wail seemed to unloosen Lady Prague's own tongue, and shriek upon piercing shriek resounded through the house.

Bedroom doors on every side now flew open and startled guests rushed out to the assistance of the fainting baroness. Albert, one of the first to be on the spot, quickly helped the poor lady to a chair, where she sat and rocked herself to and fro, moaning and sobbing in a distracted manner.

'What is the matter, Lady Prague?' said Albert sharply. 'Come, come, now, you must try and pull yourself together: you are hysterical, you know. What is it? Are you ill?'

'Oh, oh! oh!' said Lady Prague in a sort of moaning sing-song. 'I saw her! I saw her! I saw her!'

'Whom did you see?'

'Oh! oh! oh! I saw her! . . . Lady Muscatel! She was over by that window . . . Oh! oh! oh!'

'Fetch some water, Jane dear, will you?' said Albert. 'Now, Lady Prague, you are quite safe, you know, with us.'

'Let her talk about it,' said Mr Buggins in an undertone, 'it will do her good. How I envy you, Lady Prague: it has been the dream of my life to see someone from another world and, of all people, Muscatel. How did she look?'

'Oh! oh! oh! . . . Dreadful! . . . All in grey, with a wimple snood . . .'

'Nonsense!' said Albert, but nobody heard him.

'And she was holding a sort of parcel . . . Oh! oh! oh!'

'The heid, no doubt, "wropped oop i' sae." *How* I do envy you! She didn't speak, I suppose?'

'Oh! oh! oh! . . . Yes, she did. She did: "Ronnie! Ronnie! mine ane Ronnie!"'

'Oh, you old liar!' said Albert, under his breath.

Jane, on her way back with a glass of water, nearly tripped up over something outside Albert's bedroom. It proved on investigation to be a large bath sponge wrapped up in a silk handkerchief. Suspicions that she had already entertained as to the true identity of the Lady Muscatel now crystallized into certainty. She put the sponge into Albert's bed; then, controlling her laughter, she rejoined the others and gave the water to Lady Prague, who drank it gratefully. She appeared to be partially restored and was describing her experience in some detail, looking search-ingly at Albert as she did so.

'The worst part,' she said, 'of the whole thing was the creature's face, which I saw quite plainly in the moonlight. It was not so much mad as foolish and idiotic. Really, I assure you, the stupidest face I ever saw.'

'She has guessed,' thought Jane.

'Come, Lady Prague,' said Albert, 'not as bad as all that surely; not idiotic?'

'Perhaps *wanting,* more than idiotic, and hideous beyond belief.'

Later, when they were all returning to their rooms, and peace had descended upon the house, Jane said to Albert:

'You know, my dear, she scored in the end.'

'I'm afraid,' he replied, 'that she did.'

II

'Suddenly, just in time, I realized that he was a filthy Hun, so of course I turned my back on him and refused to shake hands. I think he noticed; anyway, I hope so. I hope he felt his position.'

General Murgatroyd looked round triumphantly. It was the end of dinner. The women had left the dining-room, and the general who had been shooting that day with the son of an old friend who had taken a neighbouring moor, was telling his experiences.

'Quite right, Murgatroyd. That's the way to treat 'em – the swine! Now, if only we had blockaded them from the very first he wouldn't have been alive today, with any luck.'

The admiral swilled off his seventh glass of port.

'Never shake hands with niggers, Catholics or Germans if I can help it,' continued the general.

Walter, knowing that Albert was an ardent pacifist and foreseeing some trouble, tried to change the conversation by asking him how his work had progressed that day; but the latter, whose face was burning, took no notice of him. Leaning towards General Murgatroyd he said in a level voice:

'Is this the way you always behave when you meet an ex-enemy, even under the roof of a mutual friend?'

'Of course – the filthy swine!' shouted the general. 'And so would you, young man, if you'd been through the last war. I think it's the most shocking thing – the way some of you young people have quite forgotten what your elders suffered in those four years.'

'We haven't exactly forgotten it,' said Albert; 'but it was never anything to do with us. It was your war and I hope you enjoyed it, that's all,' he added, losing all control over himself. 'You made it, as you are trying, by disgusting rudeness to citizens of a great and friendly nation, to make another one, trying your very hardest, too, on your own admission. But let me tell you that even when you have succeeded, even when you have brought another war upon us, it won't be any good. None of my generation will go and fight. We don't care for wars, you see. We have other things to think about.'

'Albert, *please!*' said Walter, 'don't let's talk about this any more,' he begged; but no one paid any attention to him.

Great veins stood out on the general's forehead.

'Do you mean that you would sit still and do nothing to prevent your country being invaded, governed, by a lot of filthy foreigners?'

'Really, General, I cannot feel that it would necessarily harm the country. Many of us hope in time to see, under one government, the United States of Europe, which was Napoleon's dream. The Germans are a people of undoubted culture and known for their exceptional efficiency. I dare say we should be no worse off under their administration than we are at present. If it is on sentimental grounds that you object to it, remember that for over a hundred years of undoubted prosperity England was ruled over by Germans – even German-speaking sovereigns.'

The general tried to speak, but Albert continued ruthlessly:

'People of your class notoriously enjoy wars and fighting. This is only natural. You have been educated to that end. Your very recreations consist entirely in killing things, and it is clearly more exciting to kill men than rabbits or foxes. But in future you will do well to avoid stirring up the great civilized nations against each other. That's all.'

'Quite right,' said Lord Prague, who imagined from the few words that had penetrated to his consciousness and from Albert's impassioned manner that he was reviling all foreigners. 'That is the proper spirit, Mr Gates. Down with the Huns! Down with the Frogs! Down with the Macaronis! Down with Uncle Sam! England for the English!'

Exhausted by the effort of this oration he lay back once more in his chair and closed his eyes.

Nobody paid any attention to him, and there was a long silence, accentuated by heavy breathing and the sound of the admiral gulping down his thirteenth glass of port.

At last it was broken by Mr Buggins.

'Gates is, of course, entitled to his own opinions. I can see his point of view although, naturally, it differs from my own. Being very young and very enthusiastic, he expresses himself violently and rashly and probably says a great deal more than he means. None the less, there is something to be said for his argument.

'All cultured persons are, to a certain extent, cosmopolitan. They feel at home among people of equal culture to whatever nationality they may happen to belong. I feel this very strongly myself. Italy is to me a second Fatherland; although I have no Italian blood I feel as much at home there as I do in England, having perhaps more congenial friends in Rome than I have anywhere else.

'Gates, who is an artist – may I remind you? – of recognized ability, would feel naturally more at his ease among other artists, whatever their nationality, than he would, say, in the company of English foxhunting squires.

'Artists, poets, musicians and writers are, of course, less affected by the governments under whose rule they may happen to find themselves than perhaps any other class. Therefore, it is hardly surprising if they do not greatly mind what form that government takes –'

'Then are loyalty and patriotism to count for nothing?' the general interrupted in a furious voice.

'Nothing at all!' said Lord Prague, who had opened his eyes again and appeared anxious to take part in the argument.

'Patriotism,' said Albert, 'is a virtue which I have never understood. That it should exist in any but the most primitive minds has always mystified me. I regard it as one step higher than the Chinese family worship, but it seems to me that at our stage of civilization we should have got past all that sort of thing.

'I am glad, certainly, to be English-speaking. That I regard as a very great advantage, both as a matter of convenience and also because there is no language so rich in literature. Otherwise, what is there to be proud of in this hideous island, where architecture generally vies with scenery to offend the eye and which has produced no truly great men, none to compare with, for instance, Napoleon?'

'I should have thought, my dear Gates, if I may say so, that with your strongly pacifist views you would look upon Napoleon as the most despicable of men,' said Mr Buggins.

'No, indeed; Napoleon was the greatest of all pacifists. He fought only for peace, and would have achieved what I spoke of just now – the United States of Europe, except for the jealous and pettifogging policy of certain British statesmen.'

'That, I should say, is a matter of opinion, and I doubt whether you are right,' said Mr Buggins. 'But at the same time, Gates, there is something I should like to say to you, which is, that I think you have no right to speak as you did of the men who fought in the War, sneering at them and hoping they enjoyed it, and so on. I know you did not really mean to say much, but remember that sort of thing does no good and only creates more bitterness between our two generations, as though enough did not exist already. I know that many of us seem to you narrow-minded, stupid and unproductive. But if you would look a little bit below the surface you might realize that there is a reason for this. Some of us spent four of what should have been our best years in the trenches.

'At the risk of boring I will put my own case before you.

'When the War broke out I was twenty-eight. I had adopted literature as my profession and was at that time art critic on several newspapers. I had also written and published two books involving a great deal of hard work and serious research – the first, a life of Don John of Austria, the second, an exhaustive treatise on the life and work of Cervantes. Both were well received and, encouraged by this, I was, in 1914, engaged upon an extensive history of Spain in the time of Philip II, dealing in some detail with, for instance, the art of Velásquez and El Greco, the events which led to the battle of Lepanto, the religious struggle in the Netherlands, and so on. I had been working hard at this for three years and had collected most of my material.

'On the fifth of August, 1914, whether rightly or wrongly, but true to the tradition in which I had been brought up, I enlisted in the army. Later in that year I received a commission. I will not enlarge upon the ensuing years, but I can't say that I found them very enjoyable.

'When, in 1919, I was demobilized, I found that, as far as my work was concerned, my life was over – at the age of thirty-three. I was well off financially. I had leisure at my disposal. I had my copious notes. Perhaps – no doubt, in fact – it was a question of nerves. Whatever the reason, I can assure you that I was truly incapable of such concentrated hard work as that book would have required. I had lost interest in my subject and faith in myself. The result is that I am now an oldish man, of certain culture, I hope, but unproductive, an amateur and a dilettante. I know it. I despise myself for it, but I cannot help it.

'And that, I am convinced, is more or less the story of hundreds of my contemporaries.

'Everybody knows – you are at no pains to conceal it – that the young people of today despise and dislike the men and women of my age. I suppose that never since the world began have two generations been so much at variance. You think us superficial, narrow-minded, tasteless and sterile, and you are right. But who knows what we might have become if things had been different?

'That is why I do earnestly beg of you not to speak sarcastically, as you did just now, of the men who fought in the War. Leave us, at any rate, the illusion that we were right to do so.'

'Oh, dear!' said Albert. 'How you do misunderstand me! I suppose I must express myself very badly. Of course I feel the greatest respect and admiration for the men who fought. I am only criticizing those unprincipled members of the governing classes (of all nationalities) who made it necessary for them to do so – men to whose interest it is that there should be wars. Professional soldiers, for instance, must naturally wish for war or all their work and training of years would be for nothing. Many politicians find in it a wonderful opportunity for self-aggrandizement. Certain business men make vast fortunes out of it. These are the people who are responsible. They educate the young to believe that war is right so that when they have manufactured it they are supported by all classes.

'But they ought to be regarded with the deepest distrust by their fellow citizens, instead of which they are set up as national heroes. I would have their statues removed from all public places and put where they belong – in the Chamber of Horrors – thus serving the cause both of Art and of Morals.'

He glared at the general, who returned his black looks with interest, but could not trust himself to speak.

'General Murgatroyd,' continued Albert, 'provoked this discussion by actually boasting (though I don't know how he can dare even to admit such a thing) that he is doing his best in every way to make another war. Not content with rising in his bloody profession over the dead bodies of hundreds of innocent men, he evidently continues to be a propagandist of the most insidious and dangerous type. Happily, however, mankind is beginning to realize that war is of all crimes the most degraded; and when, which will soon happen, the great majority holds that view, peace will be permanent and universal. Generals, on that rapidly approaching day, will become as extinct as the dodo, relegated to the farcical side of drama and the films.'

'Come!' exclaimed Mr Buggins, feeling that enough had now been said, 'come, Mowbray, and have a game of billiards.'

But the general, deeply incensed, retired to the study, where he listened to *Iolanthe* on the wireless and read his favourite book, *Tegetmeer on Pheasants*.

Admiral Wenceslaus, having finished the port, tottered off to bed, eye in hand, singing, 'The more we are together.'

12

After this rather acrimonious dinner, Albert, noticing that there was a very lovely full moon and that the air outside was warm and mellow, suggested to Jane that they should go out for a little walk. She thought that it would be a good idea. The evenings at Dalloch were apt to be rather boring. Lady Prague had introduced a particularly odious form of paper game, called briefly and appropriately 'Lists', which consisted in seeing who could make the longest list of boys' names, fishes, kinds of material, diseases and such things beginning with a certain letter. As Lady Prague herself always chose both the subject and the letter, and as she invariably won, it was felt, no doubt unjustly, that she sat up for hours every night with a dictionary preparing herself for the next game. The only time they had played anything else it had been at Albert's suggestion – Consequences, but this was not an unqualified success.

For the erotic Lady Prague to meet the sobered-up Admiral Wenceslaus in a bedroom, undressing; for her to say to him, 'What about it?'; for him to say to her, 'My eye!'; for the consequence to be that they had nine children in three lots of triplets; and for the world to say, 'The only compensation for regurgitation is re-assimilation,' had been considered too embarrassing to risk repetition. (Albert, accused afterwards of cheating, had hotly denied the charge.)

'I couldn't have faced "Lists" again,' said Jane as they walked away from the castle. 'Somehow, I seem to get worse and worse at it. Last night, for instance, I couldn't even think of one vegetable beginning with "c", of course – *cabbage*. It was too idiotic; all I could think of was brussels sprouts and broccoli; and I knew they were wrong.'

'Yes; indeed; it is ghastly. The diseases are the most embarrassing, though.'

'And the vices. I think it's a horrid game.'

Albert told her of the conversation that had just taken place in the dining-room and asked what her feelings were on the subject.

'Oh! the same as yours! All young people must surely agree about that except, I suppose, young soldiers, but I don't count them anyway.'

Jane had once been in love for a short time with an officer in the Guards and had looked upon the army with a jaundiced eye ever since. (She had treated him abominably.)

'Mr Buggins agrees with us, too. Of course, he had to qualify his approval with the general listening like that, but I could see exactly what he really meant. I think him so charming; at first he seemed a little tiresome with all his culture and folk-lore and good taste, but now I'm becoming very fond of him. He told us a lot about himself after dinner, but never mentioned anything about his wife. I wonder when all that happened?'

'Poor man! He looks dreadfully sad, I always think. He's the only nice one among the grown-ups here, isn't he?'

'Yes, indeed he is. I don't know what would have happened this evening if he hadn't been there. I should probably have insulted General Murgatroyd even more than I did, and then have been obliged to leave the house, the very last thing I wish to do at the moment.'

Jane suddenly began to feel embarrassed. It had come upon her lately with the certainty born of experience that Albert was falling in love with her, and now she began to think from the absent-minded way in which he spoke and his general manner that he was about to make some sort of declaration. This was the very last thing Jane wanted to happen.

She had been considering the situation and had decided that although she liked Albert more than anybody she had ever met, and although she would probably marry him in the end, she was not at present in love with him. On the other hand she did not at all want to lose him entirely, which might happen if he proposed and was refused. She was anxious for things to go on as they were at present. So she kept up a sort of barrage of rather foolish, nervous chatter.

'Do you know,' said Albert interrupting her in the middle of a sentence, and standing still, 'that I'm in love with you, Jane?'

Her heart sank.

'Are you, Albert?' she said faintly, wondering what the next move would be.

There was a silence. Albert, taking her hand, kissed her fingers one by one.

'Well?'

Jane said nothing. He took her in his arms and began kissing her face.

'Do you love me, darling?'

Jane felt frightened suddenly of committing herself to anything and said in an unnatural way:

'Albert, I don't know – I'm not sure.'

He let go of her at once, saying rather coldly: 'No, I see. Well, if you change your mind you'd better tell me, will you? Let's go on walking, it's such a lovely night.'

She thought this would be almost too embarrassing, but soon felt curiously at her ease, as though nothing had happened at all. They were in a wood of little fir trees which reminded her of a German fairy story she had been fond of as a child. She told it to Albert as they walked along. Presently they came out of the wood on to the open moor. The moon, which was enormous, shone in a perfectly empty sky; the moor looked like the sea. There was a very complete silence.

As they stood there for a moment before turning back, Jane suddenly realized with a wave of feeling how much she loved Albert. She passionately hoped now that he would take her in his arms and kiss her, but he did not do so and a strange feeling of shyness prevented her from making an opening for him.

After standing there for some time in silence they returned to the castle, talking quite naturally about everyday things. They found that all the others had gone to bed, and crept up the back stairs in complete darkness, saying good night affectionately when they reached their bedrooms.

Jane lay awake for hours that night, tingling all over with excitement and trying to concentrate on the foregoing events with some degree of calmness.

'He never said anything about marriage,' she thought. 'Probably he has no intention of marrying me: artists seldom want the extra responsibility of a wife. And then he probably has very modern ideas on the subject. No, he evidently means it to be just an *affaire*. Anyhow, tomorrow I shall tell him that I love him. Then, if he wants me to be his mistress, we can run away to Paris together when we leave here, but not before. I can't have Sally involved.'

Jane was delighted with this idea. Marriage had always seemed to her rather a dull and pompous business, but to run away to Paris as the mistress of a handsome young artist would be the height of romance, and would properly scandalize her parents and relations. (Jane's one mission in life seemed to be to alienate her family, of whom she was, if she had only realized it, extremely fond, and nobody would have been more upset or annoyed than she herself if she had succeeded.)

As she lay watching the flickering firelight she suddenly had a mental vision of Albert's good-looking face as it had appeared when he said, 'Do you love me, darling?'

'Yes! yes! yes! Albert, sweetest, I do! And I'll tell you so tomorrow.'

And Jane fell rapturously asleep.

She was awakened at a very early hour by the sound of furious voices in the hall. She knew that this indicated the departure of the shooters (or guns) for another happy day on the moors.

'But why "guns",' she thought sleepily. 'After all, one doesn't speak of people as "paint brushes" or "pens". And why does it always make them cross when they are supposed to enjoy it so enormously? Of course, they simply loathe it really, poor things, and no wonder.'

General Murgatroyd and Lady Prague came out of the front door and stood just underneath Jane's open window talking angrily.

'Young puppy, I call him! Should like to give him a good thrashing. I couldn't speak, I was so angry, and Buggins more or less stood up for him, too. But I shall certainly write to Craig and tell him the sort of thing that's happening here.'

'Yes, I should. I think of writing to Madge myself about the goings-on. All in and out of each other's bedrooms and the gramophone playing till two and three in the morning. Then, another thing is, the servants won't stand it much longer, you know – champagne for breakfast, and so on! Mind you, the Monteaths aren't so bad. It's those other two. But that young man, my dear, he's *dreadful*.'

'Don't tell me. What d'you think he said to Brenda yesterday – didn't you hear? He said: "What a drenching colour your dress is!" Poor Brenda said afterwards: "Well, I've heard of drenching a cow!"'

'Yes, she told me. Well, I dare say we shall be able to laugh at all this when it's over, but I hardly find it amusing at the present moment, personally.'

'Oh, it's too shocking! It's the downfall of England, mind you . . . Mons! will you come here.'

At this moment the others came out, and climbing into the 'bus they all roared away up the drive. Jane lay in bed shaking with laughter, but she felt rather sorry for Sally and Walter. 'Still,' she thought, 'it can't be helped. We've done nothing wrong that I know of.'

She began slowly to dress, manicured her nails, took particular pains with her face and hair, and at about eleven she strolled downstairs. She looked into the billiard-room, half hoping that Albert would be there, but it was empty. Coming back into the hall she saw Sally sitting on the bottom step of the staircase.

'Oh, my dear, I'm feeling so awful!'

Jane dashed forward, put her arm round Sally's waist and half carried her to a sofa, where she went off into a dead faint. Jane, thoroughly alarmed, called out loudly for Walter, who ran downstairs in his dressing-gown.

'Oh, God!' he said on seeing Sally. 'What! She's not . . . ?'

'She's only fainted. Pull yourself together, Walter, and fetch some brandy or something. Look, though! she's coming round now.'

Sally opened her eyes and smiled at Walter, who was rubbing her hands in a distracted sort of way. Presently she sat up and drank some brandy, which Albert, appearing from nowhere, produced in a tumbler. Walter finished what she didn't want.

'Goodness, darling, what a turn you gave me! But what on earth's the matter with you? You were as right as rain a minute ago. D'you feel better now?'

'Yes, quite better, thank you. I'll just stay here for a bit, I think . . . Walter . . .'

'Yes, my angel.'

'Promise not to be cross.'

'Yes. What?'

'No, but promise really and truly.'

'Of course I promise, funny; but what is it?'

'Well, I'm afraid this means I'm in the family way. You're not cross? You see, I've been suspecting it for some time now and hoped for the best, you know; but this is rather conclusive, isn't it. Are you terribly shocked, my sweet?'

'No, naturally not, darling precious. But how careless of us. Never mind, I think it will be rather sweet, really – I mean, the baby will. But it's too awful for you, though.'

'Oh, I don't mind. I'm rather pleased. You are divine not to be cross. It is an anxiety all the same, isn't it, because how are we ever going to clothe the poor angel? I mean, babies' clothes are always covered with lace, just like underclothes. They must be frightfully expensive. Oh, gosh!'

'Well, my treasure, you'll have to be like pregnant women in books and sit with a quiet smile on your face making little garments. It is a bit of a shock at first, isn't it, the idea of your being a pregnant woman? But I suppose one will get used to it. Will it be a boy or a girl?'

'Both, perhaps.'

'*Really*, darling!'

'I mean twins, you idiot! But if not it'll be a girl, naturally: at least, I hope so.'

'You mustn't,' said Albert. 'I read somewhere that if you have been hoping for a girl and then it turns out to be a boy, it will have a nasty, perverted nature.'

'How awful! And does the opposite hold good?'

'Yes, I believe it does.'

'Oh, poor sweet: we must be careful. We'd better say "he" and "her" alternately: you couldn't call the angel "it", could you? You know I feel quite friendly towards him already. I think she will be a great comfort to us, Walter.'

'Yes, we were needing something to draw us together. Morris will be a bond between us.'

'Oh, need it be Maurice? It's not a name I have any feeling for.'

'M-o-r-r-i-s.' He spelt it out. 'If we call him that, we might get one free for an advertisement. You never know your luck.'

'Why not Bentley, then, or Rolls?'

'No good. We couldn't afford to keep it up if we had one. Suppose the angel's a girl?'

'Minerva, and pop it. Morris Monteath: Minerva Monteath. Not at all bad.'

'Well, if we're going to do that, we'd better call her lots of things and have them all free. Minerva, Sanitas, Electrolux, Chubb, Ritz (then we could live there) Monteath. And I could think of dozens more.'

'Talking of living, where are we going to keep her: there's precious little room in the flat for him.'

'I can't think. What an awful idea!'

'I know,' said Walter, 'we can turn the cocktail chest into a cradle. My dear, what a good article for the Sunday papers:

TURN YOUR COCKTAIL CHESTS INTO CRADLES!

England Needs More Babies

and

Fewer Cocktails!

PRACTICAL and PATRIOTIC.

'No, but seriously, where do people keep their babies: one never does see them about, somehow.'

'I,' said Albert, 'am extremely shocked. I thought that when a woman discovered herself to be – well, "in an interesting condition," as they say in the papers, that she beckoned her husband into the conjugal bedroom and whispered shyly into his ear: "Baby's coming." I didn't know people went on like this, even in these days. I find it most painful and disillusioning, and shall leave you to what should, in my opinion, be your confidences. In other words, you are a pair of clowns, and I must go and work. It's my great chance, as those Murgatroyds are out for the day and I shall have the billiard table to myself. I suppose I ought to congratulate you, Sally?'

He kissed her and left the room.

Jane had expected that he would ask her to go with him, but as he did not even look in her direction she forbore from suggesting it, and went for a dreary little walk alone till luncheon time.

During the next three days Albert completely neglected Jane, who was thrown into a state almost of frenzy by his behaviour. Ever since their midnight walk she had been eagerly awaiting an opportunity to tell him that she had now changed her mind, or rather that she knew her mind and was very definitely in love with him; but the opportunity did not come and it was Albert himself who prevented it. He not only took no particular notice of her, but actually went out of his way to avoid her.

Jane's natural reaction to this treatment was to appear more than indifferent and cold towards him, whereas really she was in a perfect fever wondering what could so have altered his feelings. She began to think she must have dreamt the whole affair.

On the third morning Albert announced that he was going to begin his portrait of Sally. Jane felt that this was almost more than she could stand. Ever since Sally's announcement of her pregnancy, Albert had paid attention to no one else. He and Walter had sat with her for hours on end discussing what the baby would be like, whether it would grow up to be an artist or a writer: ('In point of fact, of course,' said Albert, 'he will probably be a well-known cricket pro.') how much Sally would suffer at the actual birth, and various other aspects of the situation; and Jane was beginning to feel if not exactly jealous, at any rate, very much left out in the cold.

The thought of them closeted together all day – Albert occupied with gazing at Sally's lovely face – was almost too much to bear. The fact that the Monteaths were completely wrapped up in each other was no consolation: it was more Albert's neglect of herself than his interest in Sally that was overwhelming her. She thought that she had never been so unhappy.

All day she avoided the billiard-room where Albert was painting. She tried to read, and write letters, but was too miserable to concentrate on anything. At luncheon Albert sat next to Sally and appeared unable to take his eyes from her face. Immediately the meal was over he carried her off to resume the sitting. Jane, too restless to remain indoors, wandered out towards the kitchen garden, where she came upon Lady Prague, with a large basket, cutting lavender. Any company seemed in her state of mind better than none and she offered to help. Lady Prague, giving her a pair of scissors, told her to cut the stalks long, and for some time they snipped away in silence. Presently Lady Prague said:

'If I were Walter Monteath I should be very much worried.'

'Why?' asked Jane, absent-mindedly.

'Well, it's rather obvious, isn't it? I mean, I don't want to make mischief, but one can't help seeing that Mr Gates is violently in love with Sally, can one? And, if you ask me, I should say that she was more interested in him than she ought to be.'

Jane's heart stood still: she thought she was going to faint. All the suspicions which she had entertained, almost without knowing it, for the last two days turned in that black moment to certainties. Others beside herself had noticed: others more qualified to judge than she was were sure of it – therefore it was true!

She muttered some excuse to Lady Prague and ran back to the house, never pausing until she had reached her own room. She lay on the bed and sobbed her heart out. This seemed to do her a great deal of good; and when she had stopped crying, and had made herself look presentable again, she felt so calm and aloof that she decided to go into the billiard-room. She told herself that she would only make things worse by sulking and that the best thing would be to behave to Albert exactly as if none of this had happened.

There was an atmosphere of concentration in the billiard-room. Albert had dragged down from some attic a curious, stiff little Victorian sofa with curly legs, upholstered in wool and bead embroidery, and had posed Sally on this in front of the window with her feet up and her head turned towards the light. He was painting with great speed and enthusiasm. Walter was writing at a table near by. Neither looked round when Jane came in. Sally, however, was delighted to see her.

'Jane, darling, where have you been all this time? We were beginning to think you must be getting off with the admiral. I hope, I'm sure, that his intentions are honourable, but don't marry him, darling. I feel he takes his eye out at night and floats it in Milton, which must look simply horrid. Anyway, I'm terribly glad you've come at last: these creatures have been just too boring and haven't thrown me a word all day. I've done nothing but contemplate that bust of the Prince Consort, and I'm terrified my poor angel will come out exactly like him – whiskers and all; because it's a well-known fact that pregnant women can influence their children's features by looking at something for too long. An aunt of mine could see from her bed a reproduction of the *Mona Lisa* and my wretched cousin is exactly like it – just that idiotic smile and muddy complexion – most depressing for her, poor thing.'

Jane laughed; but the joke about the admiral seemed unnecessary, she thought, and rather unkind considering the circumstances, forgetting that Sally was not aware of them. She wandered over to where Albert was painting and glanced at the canvas, not intending to make any comment. When she saw it, however, she was startled out of all her sulkiness into crying:

'But, surely, this isn't your style?'

'Not my usual style, no,' said Albert complacently, 'but one which, to my mind, expresses very well the personality of Sally. Do you agree?'

'Oh, Albert, it's too lovely! I can't tell you how much I admire it.' Her voice shook a little. ('Albert, Albert, darling, I do love you so much!')

The picture, which was small and square, was painted with a curious precision of detail which gave it rather a Victorian aspect, but in spite of this the general design could have been achieved at no time but the present.

'It's nearly finished already, isn't it?'

'Very nearly, which is lucky, as I leave on Thursday for Paris.'

Jane felt as though somebody had hit her very hard and very suddenly in the middle of her chest. 'Today is Tuesday . . . He goes on Thursday . . . Only one more day! Albert, oh, Albert darling! He doesn't love me, then: it's quite certain now that he doesn't; but he loves Sally, so he's running away. Lady Prague was right. But if he doesn't love me, why, why, why did he pretend to? Only one more day!'

While all these thoughts were racing through Jane's head she was talking and laughing in the most natural way. Nobody could have suspected that she was in Hell.

Lady Prague came in, followed by Mr Buggins.

'We've come to see this famous picture,' she said, walking up to it.

Albert, who hated the idea of Lady Prague criticizing his work, stood aside reluctantly.

('Only one more day!')

'How very sympathetic that is, Gates, or do I really mean *simpatica*?' said Mr Buggins. 'I feel it to be so exactly right. I can't tell you how much I admire it, really too delightful.'

'Quite pretty,' said Lady Prague, half-shutting her eyes and putting her head on one side as she had learnt to do years ago at an art school in Paris. 'The face, of course, is a little out of drawing. But it's so difficult, isn't it,' she added, with an encouraging smile. 'And when you've once started wrong it hardly ever comes right, does it? One fault, if I may say so, is that Mrs Monteath has blue eyes, hasn't she? And there you can hardly tell what colour they're meant to be, can you? But perhaps your brushes are dirty.'

('Only one more day!')

13

Jane dressed for dinner that night with unusual care, even for her. She put on a white satin dress that she had not yet worn, feeling that it was a little too smart for a Scottish house party. With it she wore a short coat to match, trimmed with white fur. She spent almost an hour making up her face and looking in the glass before going downstairs, and felt that, at any rate, she appeared at her very best. This made her feel happier until she went into the drawing-room.

Albert was talking to Sally by the fire when Jane came in. He looked up for a moment and then, not rudely but as though unintentionally, he turned his back on her.

Jane felt that she would burst into tears, but, controlling herself, she talked in a loud, high voice to Walter until dinner was announced.

She sat between Admiral Wenceslaus and Captain Chadlington. The admiral poured a torrent of facts and figures relating to the freedom of the sea into her all but deaf ears. She caught the words: 'Prize Courts . . . Foreign Office . . . Nearly two million . . . International law . . . Page . . . Permanent officials . . . Blockade.' . . . And said: 'No' . . . 'Yes' . . . and 'Not really?' from time to time in as intelligent a voice as she could muster.

When the grouse was finished she was left to the mercies of Captain Chadlington, which meant that she could indulge in her own thoughts until the end of the meal. He had given up asking what pack she hunted with in despair, and that was his only conversational gambit. Albert was sitting next to Sally again and Jane hardly even minded this. She was worn out with her emotions.

After dinner Lady Prague suggested 'Lists'. Sally said she was tired and would go to bed. Walter settled down to the piano, and Albert pleaded that he had work to do.

'Very well, if nobody wants to play we might as well go and listen to the wireless.'

'It's a wonderful programme tonight,' said the general. 'A talk on how wire-netting is made from A to B–Z, I mean – and selections from *The Country Girl*. I wouldn't miss it for anything.'

They all left the room except Walter, who was playing some Brahms, and Jane and Albert who stood by the fire laughing.

'Why are you going away so soon?' she asked him, almost against her will.

'I am wasting time here. I must return to Paris,' he said. And then, abruptly: 'Come with me. I've something to show you.'

Jane's heart thumped as she followed him into the billiard-room.

Albert shut the door and looking at her in a peculiar way, his head on one side, he said:

'Well?'

Jane put up her face to be kissed.

'Darling, Albert!'

He took her in his arms and kissed her again and again.

'Oh, Albert! I was so miserable. I thought you'd stopped loving me.'

'Yes, I know. I meant you to.'

'Oh, you monster! Why?'

'Because it was the only way for you to make up your mind. I won't be kept on a string by any woman.'

'But I'd made it up completely after that walk. Yes, it's no good shaking your head. I had, and I was going to tell you as soon as I got a chance to. Oh, *darling*, how I do love you!'

'Come and sit here.'

Jane put her head on his shoulder. She had never been so happy.

'When did you fall in love with me?'

'The first time I saw you at Sally's.'

'Did you? Fancy, I thought you seemed so bored.'

'How beautiful you are!'

'Am I?'

'Don't say "Am I?" like that, it's disgusting. Yes you are – very!'

'Oh, *good*. Albert?'

'Yes?'

'Shall I come and live with you in Paris?'

'Well, wives quite often *do* live with their husbands, you know, for a bit, anyhow.'

Jane sat up and stared at him.

'Do you want to marry me?'

'But, of course, you funny child. What d'you imagine I want?'

'I don't know. I thought you might like me to be your mistress. I never really considered marrying you.'

'Good gracious, darling! What d'you suppose I am? An ordinary seducer?'

Jane grew rather pink; it sounded unattractive, somehow, put like that.

'And may I ask if you're in the habit of being people's mistress?'

'Well, no, actually I'm not. But I should love to be yours. Albert, don't be so childish. Have you *no* modern ideas?'

'Not where you're concerned, I'm afraid.'

'I don't think I believe in marriage.'

'Now you're being childish. Anyway, why don't you?'

'Well, none of my friends have made a success of it, except Walter and Sally, and they're such very special people.'

'So are we very special people. If you can't make a success of marriage you're no more likely to make a success of living together. In any case, I insist on being married, and I'm the grown-up one here, please, remember.'

'I'm not so sure. Still I expect it would be rather nice, and I do look terribly pretty in white tulle. You'll have to meet my family, in that case, you know. You're not really going to Paris?'

'No, of course not – now. Let's stay here for a bit and then we'll go and see your parents. Will they disapprove of me?'

'I expect so, most probably,' said Jane hopefully. She had refused to marry at least two people she was quite fond of, on the grounds that her family would be certain to approve of them. 'They simply hate artists. But we need never see them once we're married.'

'I think that would be dreadful,' said Albert. 'After all, you are their only child, think how they will miss you. I shall have to spare you to them occasionally.'

'Darling, how sweet you are! Have you ever had a mistress?'

'Two.'

'Do you love me as much as them?'

'I might in time.'

'Will you love me for ever?'

'No, I shouldn't think so. It doesn't happen often.'

'Do you love me a lot?'

'Yes I do. A great lot.'

'When shall we be married?'

'After my exhibition, about the end of November.'

'Where shall we live?'

'Somewhere abroad. Paris, don't you think? I'll go back and find a flat while you're buying your trousseau, or you could come, too, and buy it there.'

'Albert, you're such a surprise to me. I should have imagined that you were the sort of person who would like to be married in the morning, and never think of a trousseau.'

'Well, my angel, you know how I hate getting up, and after all, I've got to see your underclothes, haven't I? No, I'm all for having a grand wedding I must say; one gets more presents like that, too.'

'My dear, you've never seen any wedding presents or you wouldn't call that an advantage.'

'Still, I suppose they're marketable?'

'Shall we be frightfully poor?'

'Yes, fairly poor. I have just over a thousand a year besides what I make.'

'And I've four hundred. Not too bad. Walter and Sally have to manage on a thousand between them. I must say they're generally in the deep end, though. I simply can't think what they'll do now, poor sweets. How soon shall I tell my family?'

'Not till we leave here, if I were you. You might change your mind.'

'Yes, I quite expect I shall do that. We won't tell the Murgatroyds, either, will we? Just Walter and Sally.'

'Yes, I think so.'

'How many children shall we have?'

'Ten?'

'Albert! You can consider that our engagement is at an end.'

'About four, really. Of course, you may have three lots of triplets like Lady Prague in the Consequences.'

'You do love me, don't you?'

'Yes, I do. How many more times?'

'As many as I like. You know I'm very glad I came to Scotland.'

'So am I. Come on, funny, d'you realize it's past one; we must go to bed or there'll be a hideous scandal.'

14

The days which followed were spent by Jane and Albert in a state of idyllic happiness. It was quite easy to keep their engagement a secret from all but the Monteaths as the heartier members of the house party were so seldom indoors; when there was no shooting to occupy them they would be fishing or playing tennis. The evenings were no longer brightened by the inevitable 'Lists'; nobody dared to thwart Lady Prague by refusing to play, but at least Albert, who could bear it no longer, read out a list of diseases so shocking and nauseating that the affronted peeress took herself off to the study and the game was never resumed.

One day they were all having tea in the great hall. This was an important meal for the shooters, who ate poached eggs and scones and drank out of enormous cups reminiscent of a certain article of bedroom china ware. Albert, who detested the sight of so much swilling, seldom attended it, preferring to have a cup of weak

China tea or a cocktail sent into the billiard-room, but on this occasion he had come in to ask Walter something and had stayed on talking to Jane.

'Tomorrow,' said Mr Buggins to the company at large, 'there are to be some very good Highland games at Invertochie which is about thirty miles from here. I have been talking to the general and he sees no reason why we shouldn't all go over to them. There are two cars, his own and Craig's Rolls-Royce, so there'll be plenty of room if everyone would like to come. We think it would be advisable to take a picnic luncheon which we could eat on the way at a very well-known beauty spot called the Corbie's Egg.'

There was a murmur of assent and 'That will be lovely,' from the assembled guests.

'The Corbie,' went on Mr Buggins, 'is the local name for a crow. It is not known how that particular mountain came to be called the Corbie's Egg, but the name is an ancient one: I came across it once in a sixteenth-century manuscript.'

Mr Buggins's audience began to fade away. The 'grown-ups,' as Albert called them, were frankly bored by folklore, which, it is only fair to add, was already well known to them, they had all been fellow-guests with Mr Buggins before. The others, who had not, politely listened to a long and rather dreary account of how he, personally, was inclined to think that sacrifices might have taken place on the mountain at some prehistoric date, first of human beings, then, when people were becoming more humane, of animals, and finally the whole thing having degenerated into mere superstition, of a Corbie's Egg.

'I do hope you will all come to the games,' he added rather wistfully. 'Of course, I know you don't really much like that sort of thing, but I feel that it would be a great pity for you to leave the Highlands without having seen this typical aspect of the national life. And it would make my day very much pleasanter if you came. We could all pack into the Rolls and the others could drive with the general in his Buick.'

Mr Buggins had so evidently been thinking it all out and was so pathetically anxious for them to go, that the Monteaths, Albert and Jane, who had each inwardly been planning a happy day without the grown-ups, were constrained to say that there was nothing they would enjoy so much, that they adored picnics, and could hardly wait to see the Corbie's Egg, let alone the Highland games.

'And what games do they play?' asked Albert.

'Actually, in the usual sense of the word, no games. It is what you would call in the South, sports.' (Mr Buggins identified himself so much with the North that he was apt to forget that he also was a mere Englishman. He had once seriously contemplated adding his grandmother's maiden name to his own and calling himself Forbes-Buggins.) 'The programme consists of dancing, piping, tossing the caber, and such things. The chieftains of the various neighbouring clans act as judges. It is all most interesting.'

'It must be,' said Albert. 'I long to see the chieftains.'

At dinner the subject was once more discussed at some length, and it was finally decided that the whole party should go, starting punctually at half-past twelve; and Lady Prague, who to Sally's great relief had taken upon herself all questions of housekeeping, gave the necessary orders for a picnic luncheon.

The next morning at twelve o'clock Albert had not put in an appearance, and kind Mr Buggins, knowing his customary lateness and aware that Lady Prague and General Murgatroyd wait for no man, went to his bedroom to see if he had awakened.

Albert was sitting on the edge of his bed, wearing a pair of exquisite sprigged pyjamas. A gramophone blared out 'The Ride of the Valkyries'; the whole room smelt strongly of gardenias. He stopped the gramophone and said:

'This is a great pleasure, Mr Buggins. So early, too; your energy never ceases to amaze me. I am in a state of intense excitement. Look what I received this morning from a friend in London.' He held out a Victorian glass paper-weight.

'Look into it carefully.'

Mr Buggins did so, and was immediately rewarded by the sight of Gladstone's memorable features.

'Now,' said Albert excitedly, 'turn it round just a little.'

Mr Buggins obeyed, and lo and behold! Mr Gladstone changed before his very eyes to Mr Disraeli. He made a suitable exclamation of gratified surprise.

'It is unique!' cried Albert. 'Unique in the iconography of Gladstone and Disraeli and also as a paper-weight. I regard it as a find of the greatest significance.'

'Very interesting. To what date do you think it belongs?'

'Mr Buggins, I have a theory about that paper-weight; but this, of course, is just my own idea, and must not be taken too seriously, as I am by no means an infallible authority on the subject, though it is one which I have studied deeply. You have guessed, of course, that I refer to Gabelsburgher.'

Mr Buggins had guessed no such thing, but he bowed courteously.

'In other words, I believe this paper-weight to be an original Gabelsburgher. It will, of course, be some time before I shall be able to proclaim this as an established fact. You ask what date it is? I reply that if, as I think, it is by the hand of the master, it would almost certainly have been made between the years 1875 and 1878. Gabelsburgher, as you know, came to England for the first time in '75. In '76 Elise was taken ill, in '78 he laid her remains in the Paddington cemetery and came away a broken man. Many of his best paper-weights were buried with his beloved, and from that time his work deteriorated beyond recognition. It is easy to see that this jewel belongs to his very greatest period, and I should myself be inclined to think that it was created in the March or April of '76 while Elise was still in the heydey of her youth and beauty. But, as I said just now, I am very far from infallible.'

Mr Buggins, who knew nothing and cared less about Gabelsburgher, and who heard the cars arriving at the front door, became a little restive during this speech, repeating at the end of it:

'Very interesting. I really came to tell you that we start in about ten minutes for the Highland games.'

'Ah! good gracious! I had quite forgotten!' cried Albert, leaping out of bed and seizing his black taffeta dressing-gown. 'But have no fear, I shall not be late.'

Albert, Walter, Mr Buggins, Jane and Sally went in the first car, the Craigdalloch's Rolls-Royce, and with them, as they had the most room, was packed the luncheon: one large picnic basket, two thermos flasks and several bottles of beer and whisky.

In the general's Buick, which he drove himself and which was to start a few minutes later than the Rolls, were Lady Prague, the Chadlingtons and Admiral

Wenceslaus. Lord Prague was in the apparently moribund condition which characterized him on non-shooting days, and stayed behind.

The Rolls-Royce drove along with a pleasantly luxurious motion. Mr Buggins
pointed out many places of interest as they passed through typical Highland scenery, among others the 'banksome brae' where 'Ronnie waur killed i' the ficht', and
the lodge gates of Castle Bane, let at present to some rich Americans who had
installed (Mr Buggins shook his head sadly) a cocktail bar in the chief dungeon.
Sally was much excited to hear this and wondered if it would be possible to make
their acquaintance.

'I should so *love* to see the inside of Castle Bane!' she cried. 'And I simply *worship
dungeons,* of course!'

'I believe the public are admitted every Thursday, but I will make inquiries,' said
Mr Buggins.

Presently the Rolls-Royce arrived at the Corbie's Egg, a large yellowish mountain commanding an interminable prospect of other mountains, valleys, streams
and pine woods. They all got out of the car and were induced by Mr Buggins, an
ardent picnicker, to drag the hamper, rugs, and bottles half-way up a sort of
precipice, the idea being that they would thus enjoy a slightly better view. What,
however, they gained in that respect they lost in comfort, as they were perched
on a decided slope and had some difficulty in preventing basket and bottles from
slipping down it.

Having unpacked the luncheon they waited politely for the others; but when a
quarter of an hour passed by with no signs of the Buick, Sally suggested that they
should begin. 'I'm pretty peckish,' she said, 'eating for two now, you see.' Albert
remarked that the Murgatroyds certainly would not have waited for them, and
they all fell upon the food, munching away in a happy silence.

It was only when they had quite finished and were drinking their coffee with
the delicious feeling, so rare at picnics, that even if there were any more food it
would be difficult to eat it, that Sally noticed, to her extreme horror, that there was
absolutely nothing left for the others.

She announced this fact in a voice shaking with hysteria. There was a ghastly
silence.

Mr Buggins said: 'Surely they are bringing their own,' without much conviction.

'No,' wailed Sally, 'this was for everybody.'

Another silence. Walter tried to speak, but no words came. Mr Buggins gulped
down some neat whisky and said:

'Wait a minute. We'll see what's left. Hum – yes, one leg of grouse. Three tongue
sandwiches. Look! What's this? A packet of something! Oh, dear! *Petit-Beurre*
biscuits, rather cold comfort. Fourteen apples (curious how the cook here seems
to think we are all fruitarians). No beer at all. Half a bottle of whisky. A thermos
of hot milk. Yes, this is very awkward indeed.'

Another dreadful silence descended upon them. Sally wrung her hands in despair.

'Oh, goodness, goodness me! What *are* we to do?'

Albert poured the remains of the whisky down his throat. Suddenly he shouted:

'I know, of course! The only thing we can do is to hide the picnic basket and
pretend it fell out of the car. Quick! quick! before they come!'

With shaking hands and furtive glances down the road they packed the debris of their lunch into the picnic basket, which they proceeded to hide between two large boulders. They then seized the rugs and scrambled down a precipitous slope to the motor car, explaining matters rather breathlessly to the bewildered chauffeur, who, when he grasped what they were driving at, was only too pleased to aid and abet their little plan as he had a private grudge against the general.

Hardly were all these preparations completed when the Buick bore down upon them and drew up just behind the Rolls-Royce.

General Murgatroyd was the first to get out and walked briskly up to where the guilty ones were waiting by the roadside. He looked hot and cross, his hands were covered with oil.

'How's this?' he said in a loud angry voice. 'We thought at least you'd have the lunch all ready for us by now. We've had a beastly time with a slipping clutch. Got it put right now but it's been the hell of a journey, I can tell you, and, personally, I'm ready for my food. Come on, let's get it out.'

There was a gloomy silence. At last Walter, prodded from behind by Sally, cleared his throat and said:

'I'm afraid, sir, that a rather – er – disappointing thing has happened to the lunch. Albert found that there wasn't quite enough room for his legs with the basket on the floor of the car, so we stopped and put it on to the carrier. When we arrived here we found to our dismay that it had disappeared – it must have dropped off as we drove along. We hoped that you might perhaps have come across it and picked it up. No such luck, I suppose?'

'This is damned annoying,' said the general violently. 'Who strapped it on to the carrier?'

'Albert and I did, sir.'

'Then you must have done it damned inefficiently, that's all I can say.'

He glared at Albert.

The admiral here came forward and said, not unkindly:

'Well, it can't be helped now. Let's have a drink while we're waiting.'

'Unfortunately, sir, the bottles seem to have been forgotten. I thought when I woke up this morning that Friday the thirteenth is seldom a lucky day.'

'It happens to be Friday the twelfth today, though,' said Lady Prague.

The admiral at first appeared stunned by this piece of news, but, suddenly galvanized into life, he cried:

'Forgotten! What do you mean? I saw them into the car myself. I always see to the drinks.'

'Yes, he does: I can vouch for that.' The general looked again at Albert as he spoke.

Nobody answered.

'This is all most peculiar and extremely annoying,' said Lady Prague. 'What makes it worse is that the picnic basket with fittings was Prague's silver-wedding present from the tenants – with his first wife, of course. We shall certainly have to inform the police of this loss. Meanwhile, what shall we do for luncheon?'

'If I might make a suggestion, Lady Prague,' ventured Mr Buggins timidly, 'perhaps you had better go to the Auld Lang Syne at Invertochie and have your luncheon there?'

'And what about all of you? Aren't you hungry?'

'Yes, indeed, we are starving – starving. I meant, of course, for all of us to go, but thought that if only a few can get in, owing to the large crowd which is always attracted there by the games, that you should in justice come before us, as it was partly owing to our carelessness that the basket was lost.'

'Oh, I see; yes. Well, there's no point in waiting here, we might as well push on to the Auld Lang Syne. Most inconvenient and tiresome.'

They all climbed back into the cars and when they were once more under way Albert said:

'Really, Walter, you are a sneak. Why did you say it was my legs that hadn't enough room: surely you could have chosen someone else. I'm in such disfavour with the general and I feel now that he will never look on me kindly again.'

'I'm sorry; I couldn't think of anyone else.'

'Well, there was yourself.'

'I never think of myself.'

'I suppose you all realize,' said Jane, who was tightly holding Albert's hand under the rug, 'that we are fated to eat another enormous lunch. Personally, I couldn't face a small biscuit at the moment.'

They gazed at each other in horror at this prospect, but Mr Buggins assured them that there was no need for anxiety as the hotel was certain to be full on that particular day.

'I am even rather perturbed,' he added, 'as to whether those poor hungry things will get a bite or sup.'

'I'm quite sure that Lady Prague will get a bite, and don't doubt that the admiral will somehow find a sup,' said Albert; 'but think how awful it would be if there did happen to be enough for all of us. Hadn't we better pretend to have a breakdown and let the others go on?'

'You forget it's the general behind us, who obviously knows all about cranking plugs and things: he'd see in a moment that nothing was wrong. No, we shall have to risk it.'

When they arrived at the Auld Lang Syne it presented, to their dismay, a singularly empty and welcoming appearance.

'Lunch for ten? Certainly. This way, please.'

The waiter led them through a stuffy little hall bedecked with stags' heads, up some brown linoleum stairs to the dining-room which, though empty, smelt strongly of humanity.

'No, sir; no crowd now. There has been, sir; oh, yes, but they're all to the games. Will you start with fish or soup, sir?'

At this moment the rest of the party appeared, headed by Lady Prague, who said:

'As we are in such a hurry I will order for everybody,' and took the menu card from the waiter.

'Tomato soup, roast mutton, two vegetables, rice pudding and prunes, Cheddar cheese, celery and biscuits. That will do nicely. I shall drink ginger beer. What about everybody else?'

'Whisky,' said the admiral, quickly. 'I wish I could understand what happened to those bottles.'

He looked suspiciously at Albert.

Very soon the tomato soup arrived. It tasted strongly and unnaturally of toma-toes, was hot, thick and particularly filling. Lady Prague fell upon it with relish and crumbled bread into it.

Albert, Jane, Walter, Sally and Mr Buggins never forgot that lunch. Seated in a row, their eyes fixed upon a print of the Battle of Khandi Pass (underneath which hung a key so that members of the British aristocracy portrayed there should eas-ily be recognizable), they miserably waded through the bill of fare ordered by Lady Prague.

They suffered.

First the soup, followed by enormous helpings of congealing mutton with boiled vegetables; then – except for Albert – mountains of tepid rice pudding floating about in brown prune juice and studded with the prunes. Albert firmly refused this, saying:

'It is my peculiar misfortune that from a child I have been unable to digest rice. Prunes I find so disintegrating that I seldom touch them.'

'Traitor!' whispered Jane, kicking him under the table.

'No biscuits, thank you,' said Mr Buggins; adding in a jocular voice, 'I have always been told that one should rise from a meal ready to eat a penny bun.'

'And are you ready to now?' asked Albert doubtfully.

At last the nauseating meal drew to a close, and Walter (who luckily had some money with him) was obliged to put down twenty-eight shillings for his own, Sally's, Jane's and Albert's share of the bill. This was felt by some to be the saddest moment of the day.

'My spirit is broken,' said Albert, as they walked downstairs again, 'or I should certainly bargain with the innkeeper for that exquisite aspidistra. I covet it. But I have no energy left in me for such exertions. Mr Buggins, do tell me, I have always so much wanted to know, who *was* Auld Lang Syne?'

It was past three o'clock when they arrived at the enclosure where the games were taking place. Each member of the party had to pay five shillings to go in.

'I knew it would be cheaper, in the end, to go to the Lido,' said Walter bitterly.

There was an enormous crowd in the enclosure consisting of very large strong-looking people; the men mostly wore kilts and the women dull but serviceable tweeds.

Albert bought a programme which he shared with Jane. It was printed on thin pink paper and informed them that they were about to witness:

TUG OF WAR. VAULTING WITH POLE.

PIPING. DANCING.

THROWING THE HAMMER. TOSSING THE CABER.

FOOT RACES. CYCLE RACES. RELAY TEAM RACES.

PIPING COMPETITION.

Albert began explaining this to Jane as they were separated from the others:

'"Tossing the caber". Now that will be worth seeing; the caber is Scottish for a young bull and this ancient sport was introduced into Scotland by the survivors of the Spanish Armada, who settled in many of the islands. "Throwing the hammer". Two men, I believe, are given six hammers each to throw and they see who can knock out the other one first. Dangerous, but what is that to these wild clansmen?'

'How d'you know all this?' asked Jane suspiciously.

'My dear, of course I know all about it. Don't be tiresome, but come and see for yourself.'

As they drew near to the arena their ears were greeted by a curious medley of sounds, the results of two brass bands playing different tunes, a band of bagpipes and a man walking drearily round alone, piping.

'So like *Le Pas d'Acier*,' murmured Albert, who had long entertained an unreasonable dislike for that ballet.

The arena, which was railed off from the crowd by ropes, was a large piece of flat ground like a football field. At one side of it there was a raised platform, on which sat several ancient men in kilts.

'The chieftains,' Albert explained, 'of neighbouring clans. Although they look so friendly, each in reality is fingering his dirk; their hearts are black with age-old hatreds of each other. Meanwhile, their brave clansmen are striving with might and main to win the games. Let's get up closer, I can't see anything.'

The arena presented an extraordinary spectacle of apparently meaningless activity. People seemed to be doing things quite by themselves in every available corner of the field, while, encircling the whole, about seven skinny little men in shorts were quickly cycling round and round, followed by a crowd of even skinnier little men, running. They mostly looked like Whitechapel Jews. Some girls in Highland dress and long flowing hair were dancing a fling in one corner; in another an enormous giant appeared to be balancing a tree on his chest. The tug-of-war went on the whole time, neither side gaining an inch, and the vaulting also was incessant.

'I am bitterly disappointed!' cried Albert, when he had gazed for some time upon this medley of sports. 'I had imagined that I was going to see savage Highlanders, in philabeg and bonnet, performing unheard-of feats. And what do I find? Men of more insignificant physique than myself cycling, running, jumping, and doing it rather worse than little boys at their private school sports. As for the noise, I cannot condemn it too heartily. I am suffering real physical pain and, also, I feel most dreadfully sick.'

'Well, can you wonder?' said Jane. 'Personally, I've never felt so ill in my life before. What I'm wondering, though, is how we are to account for the picnic basket being found again.'

'Oh, easily. We can say that some rough man brought it back.'

'Yes, but that's so unlikely; because how is the rough man to know whom it belongs to? Presumably, if there is an address inside, it will be that of the Prague home, as they say in films.'

'We shall have to advertise for it. Oh! the boredom of these games! I've never known anything so oppressive. And as for those *cyclistes* they make me feel positively giddy, round and round like rats in a cage. Can't we go home soon? There's Alfred Sprott! Doesn't he look awfully jolly? Let's go and embarrass him.'

Albert gracefully approached Lord Alfred, who was standing with a pretty blonde young woman.

'De-ar Alfred,' he said, placing a hand on his shoulder, 'why are you not playing in these delightful games? I remember so well the day you won *all* the sports at Eton.'

Lord Alfred turned scarlet, muttered something, and hurried away into the crowd.

'Always so *gauche*, the darling boy,' said Albert sadly. 'Here comes Mr Buggins.'

Mr Buggins was walking with a tall, oldish man in a kilt, whom he introduced as Sir Alexander McDougal.

'Sir Alexander,' he said, 'is the convener of the games this year. He has just been judging the piping competition.'

'In other words, I suppose,' said Albert, 'the producer. Well, sir, I must congratulate you. Seen as a sort of outdoor ballet these games must command the highest praise. The music, too, although at first unmelodious, seems now a very fitting background to these fantastic gestures. Charming! Charming!'

Sir Alexander walked quickly away, followed by Mr Buggins.

'Why did you say that,' asked Jane (a truthful girl), 'when you know how bored you are feeling?'

'Well, darling, I always think that any artistic endeavour, however unsuccessful, should be encouraged. These games do show a certain amount of enterprise; when looked at impartially there is a sort of pattern to be discerned in them. In time they might become most interesting and unique. Meanwhile, they are, of course, far too monotonous.'

'And do you realize,' said Walter, who, with Sally, now joined them, 'that they are still doing the very things that they were doing at ten o'clock this morning?'

'The same people?'

'The same, or others so similar to them as to be indistinguishable.'

'Don't you think,' said Sally wearily, 'that we might go home, as we're all here?'

This suggestion was felt to meet the situation quite admirably, and Walter was sent off to find Mr Buggins, while the others waited in the car.

'Sicker,' said Albert, as they finally bowled off towards Dalloch Castle, 'I have never felt.'

After dinner that evening the party assembled in the hall to take leave of Captain and Lady Brenda Chadlington, who, to nobody's very great regret, were leaving the castle for the jolly cosy little lodge where Lord Alfred Sprott and others made such a cheery crowd. When they had gone the butler came up to Lady Prague and informed her that the picnic basket had just been brought back by a rough man.

'Most peculiar,' said Lady Prague; but she let the matter rest at that.

15

Jane sat talking to Sally in her bedroom after tea. Poor Sally had spent most of the day being sick. Morris (or Minerva) was beginning to make his (or her) presence felt in no uncertain way.

'What is so unfair,' she said, 'is that I'm not only sick in the morning, which one expects to be, but sick in the afternoon and evening as well. However, I'm quite pleased we're going to have him, you know. I think a little squawking baby will be great fun, and Walter's been divine about it.'

'Albert and I are going to have four, all boys. One thing I'm *not* looking forward to is telling my family about Albert. Think of their feelings when they hear that he's an artist, who lives abroad and was sent down from Oxford. They'll blow up, that's all. Oh, how I dread it!'

Sally, who knew that Jane enjoyed nothing so much as a scene with her parents, murmured words of sympathy.

'I expect they'll be delighted when they see him. Albert gets on very well with older people. Look at Mr Buggins.'

'Yes, and look at General Murgatroyd,' said Jane quickly, frowning at the idea that they might approve of Albert. 'He's much more like Daddy than Mr Buggins is.'

'My dear Jane, how absurd you are! Two people couldn't be more different than Sir Hurbert and General Murgatroyd. Your father has a great sense of humour, for one thing, and then he's a very cultivated man. Anyhow, you shouldn't talk like that: you get all your brains from him.'

'No, indeed, I don't. I get them from my maternal grandmother, Judith Trevor. Brains often skip a generation, you know, and come out in the grandchildren. Poor Mummy and Daddy are both terribly stupid: darlings, of course, but narrow-minded and completely unintellectual.'

'I simply don't understand your attitude towards your parents, and, what's more, I believe the whole thing is a pose. Why, when you're at home you always seem to be so fond of them, and anyone can see that they adore you.'

'Think what you like, my dear Sally, you won't alter the truth. Of course, I know how charming they are and how grateful I ought to be for everything they've done, and so on, and in a way I am fond of them. We have a different outlook and that's all there is to it.'

The door opened and Walter came in with a telegram in his hand.

'Too extraordinary,' he said. 'Here's a wire from Ralph to say that he and Mrs Fairfax are coming to dinner. Can you understand it?'

Sally read it out loud:

'May Loudie and I come to dinner today? Will arrive about eight on chance of finding you.

'Ralph

'How very mysterious! Why are they in Scotland?'

'I know, so peculiar and why together? However, we shall hear all about it this evening. How pleased Albert will be to see Ralph. Do you imagine they'll be wanting to stay the night?'

'Certainly, I should think. We'll get rooms ready in case. Anyway, it's very exciting. I'm always pleased to see Ralph, myself, and Mrs Fairfax is such heaven. But I'm longing to know what it all means, aren't you?'

'What *will* the Murgatroyds think of Mrs Fairfax?'

'I expect they probably know her already. But I imagine that Ralph will be a bit of a shock to them.'

'Oh, this is going to be fun!' said Jane, and she ran off to tell Albert.

Dinner was well advanced before there was any sign of the newcomers.

As Sally had conjectured, Mrs Fairfax was well-known to all the Murgatroyds. A much-married lady, she had in turn been the wife of an English duke, an American millionaire and an Italian prince; and now, in theory, if not in fact, shared the bed of a rather depressing Colonel Fairfax. Lady Prague, in common with many of her contemporaries, still remained on bowing terms with her despite these moral lapses; as the mother of an English marquess, an American heiress and an Italian duke, Mrs Fairfax could always command a certain measure of tolerance even from the most strait-laced dowagers.

Lady Prague was in the middle of explaining to the general that dear Louisa had always been such a high-spirited girl and could, therefore, hardly be blamed for her actions. 'Not that I approve of her, of course. I don't, but somehow one forgives things to her that one couldn't put up with in others' – when the door opened and Ralph Callendar swayed into the room. He kissed Sally's hand, blew kisses to Jane and Albert, bowed to the rest of the company, and explained:

'Loudie is making up her face in the hall. She thinks that she's looking tired, but that if she is sufficiently *maquillée* everyone will think: "How painted she is!" instead of: "How aged she is!" which is naturally preferable. The angel! Here she comes!'

The door opened again to admit an immensely fat Pekinese, with bulging eyes and a rolling gait, followed by his mistress and human counterpart, Mrs Fairfax. Short and plump, waddling rather than walking, her little round face inches deep in paint, her little fat hands covered with rings, her stout little body enveloped in a sable coat, she resembled nothing so much as a rather prepossessing giant Pekinese. The moment she was inside the room she let loose a perfect flow of inconsequent chatter:

'Sally, darling, what *must* you think of us, forcing ourselves on you like this? We heard you were here quite by chance and couldn't resist coming. Florence, what a surprise! And Mowbray, too, and the admiral, and dear, nice Mr Buggins! Albert, such an age since I've seen you. Jane – looking so beautiful. What's happened to you, my dear? In love, I suppose, as usual? Well, I must say this is a delightful party. And the poor Craigdallochs are away, I hear.'

She sat down next to Walter and continued:

'Of course, I suppose you all think Ralph and I are eloping? Well, no. Though to be frank, this is the first time I've made a journey of the sort without eloping. I ran away with all my dear husbands, you know, even with poor Cosmo, though I can't remember why that was necessary. Oh, yes, of course I know, I was under age and my father said we must wait for three months. Three months! As though anyone could. So we just ran away to Paris: only for a night and it was all most innocent (dear Cosmo – so pompous!); but we were seen by several people – we took care to be, of course – and after that it was plain sailing and we were married in the rue d'Aguesso, I remember. Really, it made a vivid impression on me at the time. The Ambassador was there and poor father gave me away, and poor Cosmo took me away, dear thing, to Rome or somewhere, and it was all very different from what I had expected. And now I've shocked Florence. But what was I talking about? Oh, yes, of course. Well, Ralph and I are not eloping: merely escaping.'

'Escaping?'

'From Linda May. From the West Coast of Scotland really. You tell them about it, darling, while I get on with my fish.'

'You see,' said Ralph, shutting his pained eyes and speaking in a voice which gave the impression that he had lived a thousand tiring lives, 'Linda, the poppet, seems to have gone mad. It is a great tragedy. She invited us to go for a cruise in her yacht. She said we would go to the Islands. Naturally thinking that she meant the Greek islands, we accepted, intending to leave her quite soon for the Lido. Two days before we were to start I discovered, to my horror and amazement, that we were being taken to visit some islands on the West Coast of Scotland. Well, you know, Albert, Scotland is all right for you, but it's not my *period*. So I telephoned to Loudie and told her this agonizing news. I begged her to come straight to the Lido instead. But no, obstinate as a mule. She insisted on going with Linda. Imagine my mental sufferings faced with the prospect either of not seeing Loudie for weeks, or of facing these ghastly hardships in her company. I begged, I implored her to change her mind; and when, at last, I realized that she was absolutely bent upon going, I made the great sacrifice and accompanied her. But I did beg, didn't I, Loudie?'

'Yes, darling, you did, indeed,' she replied, with her mouth full.

'To continue: It was even more horrible than I had anticipated. The scenery – my dear Albert – forgive me if I say that the scenery made one feel physically sick whenever the eye strayed out of the porthole. I kept my curtain drawn all day and even then I couldn't help seeing those mountains sometimes – they haunted me. To make matters worse, Linda, it appears, is madly in love with a monster of a Scotsman, who came to dinner last night in his kilt. Those hairy old knees decided us. "The mountains I can bear," said Loudie. "Natives in the semi-nude at dinnertime is another matter. I leave tomorrow." Luckily the angel had her Austro-Daimler sitting at Oban, so here we are! But I tell you –'

At this moment there was a piercing shriek from Lady Prague. The Pekinese was seen to have his teeth firmly embedded in her right ankle.

'Doglet!' said Mrs Fairfax in a gently reproving voice. '*what* do I see you doing, my own? Somebody give him a piece of grouse and he'll leave go at once.'

General Murgatroyd, however, seized the dog roughly by its tail, whereupon it turned round and bit him in the hand. The general shook it off and, crimson with rage, demanded that it should instantly be destroyed.

'My little Doglet destroyed? Oh, what a dreadful idea! Such a horrid word, too. You cruel old general! Besides, a dog is always allowed his first bite, by law, isn't he?'

'First fiddlesticks! Anyhow, it's had two bites this evening – Florence and myself. The animal is not safe, I tell you.'

'"The animal", indeed! Fancy calling my Doglet "the animal"! Come here, my precious. The general isn't safe: he wants to *destroy* you. Ralph dear, be an angel and put Doglet in the car, will you, till after dinner? Thank you so much. I do hope you're not hurt, Florence?'

'Yes, Louisa, the skin *is* broken and he has torn my stocking rather badly. A new pair! Of course it doesn't signify. I must go and paint it with iodine. I only trust the animal has not got hydrophobia.'

She left the room angrily, General Murgatroyd opening the door for her with a gesture of exaggerated chivalry. Lord Prague, who had noticed nothing, went on eating.

'I'm so sorry that Doglet should have caused all this commotion,' said Mrs Fairfax. 'The angel! So unlike him! I've never known him really to lose his temper before, but you wouldn't believe how sensitive he is to dress. I ought to have remembered that pink georgette is the one material he simply cannot abide. In fact, all georgette is inclined to upset him; and dear Florence's shoes, with those long pointed toes, would drive him distracted. Poor little sweet! He'll be utterly miserable after this, I'm afraid.'

'And he'd have reason to be if I had anything to do with him,' muttered the general.

'You must find this house very interesting, Albert,' said Ralph, returning from his mission. 'So exactly your period.'

'Indeed, yes, I do,' replied Albert earnestly. 'And I would love to show you the wonderful things I have found here and collected together.'

'No, dear Albert, I think I have suffered enough during the last few days from Victorian taste crystallized by the Almighty into the extraordinary scenery with which I have recently been surrounded. Not at all my period, dear. Corbusier, now –'

Here Sally gave the signal, as they say in books, for the ladies to leave the table, and presently took Mrs Fairfax upstairs to powder her nose.

'You'll stay the night, of course?' she said.

'Alas! no, my dear. Very sweet of you, but we've taken rooms at Gleneagles for tonight. I really must push on. I should like to reach London, if possible, tomorrow, as my husband is passing through for one day on his way to America and I want to see him about being divorced, you know.'

Sally's murmured sympathy was waved aside.

'It's not been too successful, really – our marriage, I mean. I'm getting rather old for all the fuss and worry of having a husband, that's the truth. And how's yours getting on, my dear: still happy, are you? Has Walter settled down at all? I know you were rather worried about him at one time.'

'We're divinely happy,' said Sally, 'and it's wonderful being here. He hasn't a chance to spend any money and he's been working harder than I've ever known him. You know, people are too hard on Walter. Of course he gives the impression of being all over the place, but that's only because of his high spirits. And then, poor darling, he has *no* idea of the value of money, which is sometimes very annoying for me as I'm by nature rather stingy.'

'I've hardly ever met a man who has any idea of the value of money,' said Mrs Fairfax. 'It's one of the nice things about them. Now, women are nearly always mercenary creatures.'

'Oh! And, by the way, of course, I'd quite forgotten it – I'm going to have a baby.'

'Are you, Sally? Well, it does happen. Torture, my dear, but one looks lovely afterwards, which is a great consolation. I've had three, you know, and they all cut each other dead now; but they're devoted to me, specially dear Bellingham. By the way, I'm told that Potts (my second husband) has taken a house near here – Castle Bane. Dreary creature, Potts, but Héloïse is a dream. She's at the Lido now. I'm going out there really to see her. How lovely Jane was looking at dinner!'

'Yes, wasn't she? It's a great secret, so don't say I told you, but she's engaged to Albert.'

'My dear, you amaze me! Will that be a success?'

'I really don't know. They are very much in love at present; but Jane is terribly sensitive, and Albert so much wrapped up in his work that I can't help feeling there will be trouble. So long as she understands his temperament – but I'm not sure how much she does. However, even if they're happy for a year or two it's more than lots of people get out of life.'

'Yes, you're perfectly right. I've lived through it and I know. I had two years of complete happiness with Cosmo, and about eighteen months with Campo Santo, and I can tell you that it makes all the rest of one's life worth while. But I don't really advise too much chopping and changing for most people: gets one into such restless habits. I couldn't have stayed with Cosmo after . . . Well, never mind. So I thought if I can't be happy I might as well be rich, and made off with Potts. Then, of course, I was bowled over by Campo Santo in ten minutes. Well, I always think that would have lasted, only the angel died on me quite suddenly: and there he was – Campo Santo in good earnest. It was dreadfully depressing. Still, there was little Bobs to cheer me up: quite the nicest of my children. Have you seen him? He's still at Eton, the precious. He's meeting me in Venice, too, when Héloïse leaves. They can't endure each other. Not frightened about this baby, are you?'

'Well, no, not really.'

'You needn't be; nobody dies in childbirth now, my dear. It's considered quite *vieux jeu*. And it may be a consolation to you to hear that the medical profession makes an almost invariable rule of saving the mother's life in preference to that of the child if there's any doubt about it. Sick much?'

'Yes, a whole lot.'

'Excellent! A very good sign. Now can we go and collect Ralph? I think we should soon be making off.'

They found the others standing round the drawing-room fire, the 'grown-ups' having taken themselves off to the study to hear a talk on Timbuctoo. Walter had happened to be passing the door when it began, and declared that the opening words, delivered by the evidently nervous speaker in a sort of screech, had been:

'People who take their holidays abroad seldom think of Timbuctoo . . .'

'Very seldom, I should imagine,' said Albert. 'Loudie dear, I wonder if you would sing us this little song which I found in an album here? The words are by Selina Lady Craigdalloch (the genius who collected in this house so many art treasures), and the music is "By my dear friend, Lord Francis Watt". It has been my greatest wish to hear it sung by somebody ever since I found it.'

'I have often noticed,' said Ralph languidly, 'that all accompaniments between the years 1850 and 1890 were invariably written by the younger sons of dukes and marquesses. They seem to have had the monopoly – most peculiar.'

'I should love to sing it,' said Mrs Fairfax, settling herself at the piano, 'and then we must go. Where is it – here? Oh, yes . . .'

To Bxxxxxxxxxxx
————————
(Morte Poitrinaire)

She began to sing in a small, pretty voice:

> *'When my dying eye is closing,*
> *And my heart doth cease to beat;*
> *Know that I in peace reposing,*
> *Have but one, but one regret!*
>
> *Leaving you, my only treasure,*
> *Bitter is, and hard to bear,*
> *For my love can know no measure;*
> *Say then, say for me a prayer!*
>
> *Lilies, darling, on me scatter,*
> *And forget-me-nots, so blue;*
> *What can this short parting matter?*
> *We shall surely meet anew!*
>
> *We shall meet where pain and sorrow,*
> *Never more assail the breast;*
> *Where there is nor night nor morrow*
> *To disturb our endless rest.'*

'Beautiful!' cried Albert. 'And beautifully sung!'

'Well,' said Mrs Fairfax, 'a very pretty little song. You know, Ralph dear, I think that we shall *have* to be going. Unfortunately we are still in the realm of night and morrow, and if we don't soon push on to Gleneagles we shall get no rest at all.'

There was a perfect chorus of dismay, but Mrs Fairfax was adamant.

'Your figure is a dream, Ralph!' said Albert, as they followed her into the hall. 'Are you on a diet?'

'Yes, dear, most depressing. I got muscles from dancing too much, they turned into fat – *et voilà!* . . .'

'Do muscles turn into fat?'

'Of course they do. Haven't you noticed that all athletes become immense in their old age?'

'But this is very serious!' cried Albert, in a voice of horror. 'It should be brought to the notice of public schoolmasters. I myself shall give up walking and buy a little car. I sometimes walk quite a distance in Paris.'

'Nothing,' said Ralph mournfully, 'develops the muscles so much as driving. Good-bye, Albert. I hope to see you in London, dear.'

16

That night Jane found herself unable to go to sleep. Her brain was in a particularly lively condition and she tossed and turned thinking first of one thing and then of another until she felt she would go mad. 'Albert! Albert! Albert!' was the refrain.

'Shall I be happy with him in Paris? Will he be the same after we're married? Shall I interfere with his work? That, never,' she thought; 'I am far more ambitious even than he is and will help him in every possible way to achieve fame.

'If I lie quite still and breathe deeply I might manage to drop off to sleep. What shall I put on tomorrow? Not that jumper suit again. I wasn't looking so pretty today. I shan't look pretty tomorrow if I have no sleep. Perhaps if I get out of bed and walk up and down . . . Yes, now I'm feeling quite drowsy. I must write to mamma tomorrow, I haven't written for over a week. What shall I tell her? Oh, yes! the games would amuse her.'

Jane began to compose a letter in her head and was soon even more wide awake than before. She had hardly ever in her life experienced any difficulty in going to sleep and it made her furious.

'I'll stay in bed till lunch-time tomorrow to make up for this,' she thought.

After about two hours of painful wakefulness she at last fell asleep, soothed, as it were, by a delicious smell of burning which was floating in at her bedroom window and of which she was only half conscious.

Hardly, it seemed to her, had she been dozing for five minutes when she was suddenly awakened by a tremendous banging on her door, which opened a moment afterwards. The electric light blazed into her eyes as she was struggling to open them.

'What is it?' she said, very angry at being awakened in this abrupt manner when she had only just gone to sleep with so much difficulty.

The butler was standing just inside the room.

'House on fire, miss. Will you please come downstairs immediately?'

Jane sat up in bed and collected her wits about her.

'Have I time to dress?' she asked.

'No, I think not, miss; the flames are spreading very rapidly to this part of the house, and Mr Buggins wants everyone in the hall at once; he is holding a roll-call there.'

Jane leapt out of bed, put on some shoes and a coat, and taking her jewel-case from the dressing-table she ran along to Albert's room. She noticed that it was just after five o'clock.

The butler was still talking to Walter as she passed and Albert had not yet been awakened. Jane put on the light and looked at him for a moment as he lay asleep, his head on one arm, his hair in his eyes.

'How beautiful he is,' she thought as she shook him by the shoulder.

'Wake up, darling, quick! The house is on fire. We've no time even to dress; so come with me now to the hall.'

Albert stretched and got out of bed. He was wide awake and perfectly calm.

'Go back to your room,' he said, 'and throw your clothes out of the window, or you'll have nothing to go home in. I'll do the same and come along for you when I've finished.'

'What a brilliant idea!'

Jane flew back to her room and in a very short time had thrown all her possessions on to the gravel outside. Presently Albert came running down the passage and they went, hand in hand, to join the others in the hall.

'Here they are! That's everybody, then.'

Mr Buggins was cool and collected; it seemed perfectly natural that he, and not General Murgatroyd, should be taking charge of everything.

'Now,' he said in a firm voice. 'This part of the house is quite safe for the present, so as we are all here I think we might begin to save what we can.

'I must beg you all not to go upstairs again. The wing in which your bedrooms are situated is in a very dangerous position and will be the next to go. The dining-room must also, of course, be left to its fate, but we can safely collect things from the drawing-room, billiard- and smoking-rooms. I telephoned some time ago for the fire brigade, but I'm afraid it will be at least an hour before they can possibly arrive. When they come they will naturally decide for themselves where they can go; we *must* be on the safe side. The servants are all engaged with a chain of buckets in trying to prevent the garages and outhouses from catching, in which I think they may succeed. It would be useless for amateurs to attempt saving the house, the fire has much too firm a hold.'

The party dispersed into the various sitting-rooms leading out of the hall and began to work with a will.

Albert, at great personal danger, put a damp handkerchief over his mouth and dashed into the dining-room which was dense with smoke. Cutting them out of their frames with some difficulty he managed to save the portraits by Winterhalter of Selina, Lady Craigdalloch and her husband, the fourth Earl.

(The present Lady Craigdalloch was never able to forgive him this when she heard about it afterwards. It became her pet grievance.

'The dining-room,' she would say, 'was full of beautiful Raeburns, and what must the young idiot do but risk his life to save the two ugliest pictures in the house. It drives me mad.')

As he ran out of the castle to bestow the Winterhalters in a place of safety, Albert was amused to observe General Murgatroyd carrying with great care an enormous coloured print which had hung in a place of honour over the smoking-room mantelpiece. It was entitled 'The Grandest View in Europe', thus leading one to expect a view of Mont Blanc, the Doge's Palace, Chartres Cathedral or some such popular beauty spot, instead of which it depicted the back of a horse's head as it would appear to the rider, with two large grey ears sticking up in the immediate foreground. Beyond the ears could be seen a stone wall which was being negotiated with success by two horses and with no success at all by a third. Hounds running across an adjacent field gave the clue to the whole thing; a hunt was evidently in progress. 'The Grandest View in Europe' having been reverently deposited among the rapidly growing collection of objects on the lawn, its saviour trotted back to the house, bent upon rescuing the head of a moose which hung in the hall.

Admiral Wenceslaus now staggered forth with a load of miscellaneous objects, including a chronometer, a model of the *Victory* in silver, a book entitled *The*

Triumph of Unarmed Forces, which he had been trying for some time to lend to various members of the party, and several whisky bottles. Mr Buggins followed him with Prince Charlie's boot, several old family miniatures and a lock of Bothwell's hair.

Sally, looking rather green, sat tucked up on a sofa and watched these proceedings with some amusement. Albert stopped for a moment to ask her how she felt.

'Oh, quite all right, longing to help, but Walter made me promise I'd stay here.'

'D'you know how the fire started?'

'No; Haddock, the butler, says he has no idea at all. He discovered it, you know. The smoke was pouring in at his window and he says he only got some of the maids out just in time.'

When Albert went back to the house he noticed that flames were already beginning to envelop his own bedroom. Meeting Jane in the hall he kissed her hurriedly and said, 'Take care of yourself, my precious, won't you?' She was carrying the Jacob's Ladder.

He then saved his portrait of Sally and several albums containing water-colours from the billiard-room. Lady Prague was busy showing two men how to take the billiard table to pieces. They had been managing far better before she came along.

Albert and Jane made many journeys and succeeded in saving all the plush chairs, bead stools, straw boxes, wax flowers, shell photograph-frames and other nineteenth-century objects which they had collected together from various parts of the house.

(When Lady Craigdalloch, far away in Africa, had recovered from the first shock of hearing that Dalloch Castle was razed to the ground, she said that, at any rate, all the Victorian rubbish there would now have vanished for ever and that this was a slight consolation. Her horror and amazement when, on her return, she was confronted by every scrap of that 'Victorian rubbish' which had always been such a thorn in her flesh, knew no bounds.)

At last all the furniture that it was possible to move reposed on the lawn in safety, and there was nothing left to do but sit 'like Lady Airlie in the ballad', as Mr Buggins remarked, and watch the house burn down.

A ghastly early morning light illuminated the faces of Lord Craigdalloch's unfortunate guests as they sat surrounded by the salvage from his home, which looked like nothing so much as the remains of an auction sale before the buyers have removed their purchases.

Lot 1. – Fine old Jacobean oak table suitable for entrance hall. Two assegais and a waste-paper basket.

Lot 2. – Bust of the younger Pitt. Large sofa upholstered in Heal Chintz. Gong of Benares brass-work.

Lot 3. – Case of stuffed grouse in summer and winter plumage. Chippendale writing-table. Large print of Flora McDonald (etc., etc.).

Albert and Jane looked round with some amusement at the different varieties of bedroom attire displayed upon other members of the party. Sally looked lovely in crêpe-de-chine pyjamas, over which she wore a tweed coat lined with fur. Lady Prague was also wrapped in a tweed coat over a linen nightdress and a Shetland wool cardigan. She wore galoshes over her bedroom slippers. Lord Prague, who had collapsed into an armchair, was shivering in a Jaeger dressing-gown which had a sort of cape elaborately trimmed with pale blue braid, and the general stood near him in khaki pyjamas and a manly overcoat. The admiral wore a mackintosh. His bare, white and skinny legs sticking out from beneath it bore witness to the fact that Admiral Wenceslaus was a devotee of the old-fashioned, but convenient, night-shirt.

Albert went to the other side of the castle and picked up the clothes which he and Jane had thrown out of their bedroom windows. Jane and Sally, on seeing them, gave high cries of delight, and retiring behind an adjacent wardrobe they began to dress. Walter and Albert did likewise, and Albert was also able to lend a jumper and a pair of grey flannel trousers to Mr Buggins. Everybody else secretly wished that they had had sufficient forethought to throw some clothes out of the windows; the morning air was distinctly chilly.

'I've still two pairs of trousers left,' said Albert, holding in one hand the orange tartan ones he had worn upon the moor, and in the other his bright blue pair. 'Won't somebody wear them? General, can I tempt you? Lady Prague, come now! No?'

'Will you lend them to me, young man?'

'Admiral – but, of course, how very kind of you, and how lucky that I have the *matelot* ones. You will feel quite at home in them. Here is a real fisherman's jersey, too, why, you'll be thinking you are back on the dear old flagship – with "Yo! ho! ho! and a bottle of rum."'

The admiral, who seemed rather overwhelmed by the foregoing events, retired behind a zebra-skin screen to put on the trousers. He stayed there for some time, and when he finally emerged, carried his eye in his hand. Creeping up behind Lady Prague, he suddenly thrust it into her face, yelling out:

'Peep-uck-bo!'

Lady Prague uttered a piercing scream and ran away as fast as the clinging draperies of her night-dress would allow until, tripping up over her galoshes, she fell heavily on the gravel and grazed her knees rather badly. General Murgatroyd and Mr Buggins assisted her to a chair. After this she became more acid than ever.

Meanwhile the admiral again withdrew behind his screen, where he was found much later by Mr Buggins and Sally, fast asleep on the ground.

'Poor old boy,' said Sally kindly, 'it's been too much for him.'

'Humph! I think I can guess what has been too much for him.' And Mr Buggins produced from under the cast-off night-shirt three empty whisky bottles. 'Might as well leave him there,' he said. 'Got a head like a horse; he'll be all right soon.'

The whole castle was now enveloped in flames, which rose to almost double its height – a terrifying spectacle. Even more alarming was the noise, a deafening roar like the sound of huge waterfalls, broken every now and then by the crash of falling masonry. Birds and bats, fascinated by the glare, were to be seen flying to their doom; and two huge beech trees which stood near the house were completely blackened.

The little party on the lawn sat in a dazed silence, over-awed by the sight of this catastrophe.

When the firemen arrived they were far too late to save anything but some outhouses. Not to be deprived of their fun, however, they were soon playing the hose indiscriminately upon the huge flames, the beech trees and the general, who unobserved had strolled up towards the house in order to have a better view. Dripping wet and speechless with rage he rushed back to the others, and was obliged to swallow his pride and borrow Albert's tartan trousers and orange sweater. The sight of him thus attired was too much for Sally and Walter, who became perfectly hysterical with laughter which they were unable to control, and finally they had to go for a long walk in order to regain their composure.

'I wonder what the effect of all this will be on Morris-Minerva?' said Sally.

'Are you feeling all right, my own?'

'Yes, quite now, thank you, darling. Will the poor angel have red hair and a fiery nature as the result of it?'

When they got back to the others they found that quite a little crowd was collected on the lawn, constantly augmented by people from neighbouring villages, who straggled by twos and threes up the drive.

Those members of the house party who were not clothed were beginning to feel rather self-conscious. The sightseers all followed the same procedure. They stood for some time gazing at the fire, saying: 'Hoots!' – 'Wisha!' – 'Mon it's gran'!' and other unintelligible phrases of the kind, after which they had a good look at the survivors, coming up quite close and breathing heavily. They then inspected the *lares* and *penates* on the lawn, piece by piece, admiring or criticizing. Having taken their time and seen everything of interest, they sat about the place in little scattered groups and ate.

'Oh! I'm so hungry,' said Sally, breaking a long silence.

The others agreed miserably. Although it was in fact only seven o'clock they all felt as though it must at least be luncheon time. It never occurred to any of them to wonder what the next step would be, but they felt instinctively that they must now see the thing through and wait there until the last beam had fallen.

Sally asked the butler, who was busy counting silver, whether any food had been saved, but he replied that both kitchen and larder had been in flames by the time that he had discovered the fire. Lord Craigdalloch's factor came and spoke to Sally. He was in his shirt-sleeves, having been hard at work nearly from the beginning.

'Good morning, Mrs Monteath. This is a very sad business, is it not? His lordship will be most terribly upset, I'm afraid.'

'Oh! it's too dreadful. Of course, one can hardly realize yet what it means, one is only so thankful that nobody was hurt. Is the house properly insured?'

'It is insured, but I doubt whether the policy will anything like cover the loss. And then, you see, for sentimental reasons it is such a terrible tragedy. We hoped at first to be able to save Lady Muscatel's tower, but we were too late. I think, if I may say so, that you all did wonders in rescuing so much furniture. I have sent to the home farm for wagons, it must be put in safety as soon as may be. I don't like the looks of all these people: I'm sure they would think nothing of removing a few souvenirs here and there.'

Soon after half-past eight the house was a blackened ruin and the fire practically over. Walter and Mr Buggins were just discussing what they should do next, when a large old-fashioned Daimler drove up, and a middle-aged man in a very long kilt got out of it. Mr Buggins greeted him warmly and introduced him as Sir Ronald McFea.

'Should McFea show the knee?' whispered Albert to Jane. 'You see, he doesn't show it at all. Isn't it too fascinating?'

'This is a fearful thing,' said Sir Ronald. 'A fearful thing. My gillie came in just now and said Dalloch Castle had been burnt to the ground, he said. I couldn't believe it – couldn't believe it. Well, there it is. Poor old Craig. It will be a most terrible blow for him when he hears it; shouldn't wonder if it kills him – shouldn't wonder at all. He worshipped the place, every stick and stone of it. Poor old boy.

'Now, my wife says you must all come over to Castle Fea and have some breakfast. She says you must be simply starving so she's getting it ready.

'Dear, dear! it must have been a near thing, too, for hardly any of you to have saved your clothes even – and the general in fancy dress. Never mind, we shall be able to fix you up all right, I don't wonder. Hadn't you better come along now?'

Brightening somewhat at the prospect of breakfast, they accepted Sir Ronald's invitation with joy. Even the admiral stopped trying to put on Prince Charlie's boot, and staggered with the rest of them towards the Daimler, which seemed by some miracle to hold them all. Sally arranged with the factor and Haddock that the servants should be boarded out in neighbouring cottages for the present, and said that she would come back later and make plans for them.

Castle Fea, though a sufficiently welcome asylum to the dazed and hungry survivors of the fire, proved to be a perfect temple of gloom. It in no way resembled a castle, being a large square house with Gothic chimneys and a Greek portico, situated in the midst of a perfect tangle of fir trees, laurels and other evergreens which grew nearly up to its windows. Mr Buggins pointed out the ruins of the ancient fortress upon an adjacent mound.

'I should think the McFea who built this house must have shown his knee quite often,' murmured Albert as they got out of the car.

The inside of the house was, if anything, more oppressive than the outside. It was a mass of badly-stuffed animals, stained glass and imitation French and old oak furniture. The pictures were of a terrifying realism.

However, the breakfast to which the party now settled down in a grateful silence was more than excellent, and Lady McFea, an ugly, dowdy, but thoroughly nice woman, tactfully refrained from asking questions about the fire until all the poached eggs and scones had been consumed. It was indeed a heavenly meal and, when it was over, the Dalloch Castle refugees felt more able to cope with their immediate future.

Sir Ronald and Lady McFea begged that any who would care to do so should stay on at Castle Fea for a few days. Walter and Sally, after a short consultation with Mr Buggins, decided to accept this kind offer, feeling that it was more or less their duty to remain on the spot until they should hear from the Craigdallochs.

All the others, however, decided to leave by the four-thirty train for London that afternoon, and sleepers were ordered for them by telephone. These arrangements having been made, the McFeas took those who had lost their clothes upstairs, and fitted them out as best they could.

Albert and Jane found themselves alone in the drawing-room and kissed each other quite a lot. Presently Jane said in a gloomy voice:

'I suppose I shall have to go home now; what shall you do, darling?'

'Well, Mr Buggins most angelically says I can stay with him in London for as long as I like, so I think I shall do that. But hadn't I better go and see your parents fairly soon? After all, I shall have to meet them sometime, shan't I? And then we can be properly engaged if they approve of me. How far is it by train to Stow-on-the-Wold?'

'Oh, the beastly hole! don't mention it to me or I shall burst into tears. About two and a half hours, I suppose. And you needn't think they'll approve of you, darling, because they're quite certain to kick you straight out of the house.'

'Anyhow, I can but try; if I'm kicked out we'll elope. It's perfectly simple. Then I think you'd better go straight home tomorrow and more or less prepare them, and I'll come down for lunch on Thursday. If they like me I'll stay the night, and if not we'll both go back to London together. Good plan?'

'Yes, very good, I think. Sweetest!'

The rest of that day was spent in wandering about rather gloomily in the grounds of Castle Fea, and they were all quite pleased when the time came for them to say good-bye to kind Sir Ronald and his wife. The Monteaths, terribly depressed at the prospect of many more such days, waved to them from under the Gothic portico until the car was out of sight.

Jane, Albert and Mr Buggins dined together in the train that evening. At the opposite table Lord and Lady Prague, Admiral Wenceslaus and General Murgatroyd made a congenial foursome.

Albert was tired and in a very bad temper. Jane, who had never seen him like that before, felt miserable and rather resentful, but Mr Buggins was in excellent spirits, and when they confirmed his suspicion that they were engaged he ordered a bottle of champagne to celebrate the occasion. Albert insisted on reading a book between the courses which were very slow in coming.

'Albert, darling, please don't read. After all, I shan't be seeing you after tomorrow, I do think you might talk to me; besides, it's so rude.'

Albert took no notice but went on with his book, a very boring history of the Angevin kings. Mr Buggins, seeing that he was really not himself, tactfully tried to draw Jane into conversation, but she could not leave Albert alone.

'Albert, do stop reading. Mr Buggins, *isn't* it rude and disgusting of him?'

Mr Buggins felt like shaking them both, but went on quite calmly with his dinner.

'Albert, really I do think even if you must read between the courses, honestly you needn't read while you're eating. Oh, well, of course, if you prefer those beastly old Angevin kings to conversation that's one thing . . .'

At last she quite lost her temper, and snatching the book from him she threw it out of the window. Albert behaved extremely well about this, but none the less he was furious with Jane, who, in her turn, was completely miserable. They each felt that they had been stupid and childish, but rather less so than the other, and were both longing secretly to make it up.

'Isn't it a pity,' said Mr Buggins, 'for two people with as much sense of humour as you have to behave like this?'

'Well, I may have a sense of humour, I hope I have,' said Albert, 'but I see nothing funny in throwing an expensive book away like that; and, as we've paid the bill, we might as well go to our sleepers.'

'Here's my share for dinner,' said Jane, offering it to Albert, who had paid for the two of them.

'I don't want it.'

Mr Buggins got up and left them alone at their table.

'Don't be so silly, Jane.'

'Well, I'm not going to be your kept woman, thank you.'

'Oh! really! I thought that was just what you did want to be.'

'Certainly not; I happened to be in love with you and offered to be your mistress. That's quite different.'

'Exactly the same.'

'Quite different. Of course, I should have earned my own living.'

'Oh! I see. May I ask how?'

'Well, I'm not sure.'

'Nor am I; not at all sure.'

'I suppose I could be a model.'

Albert had a sudden vision of the fastidious Jane posing to a lot of half-washed French art students and burst out laughing.

'Darling, how absurd you are.'

'Well, it was horrid of you to be so cross and *horrid* of you to read, wasn't it?'

'Yes, beastly. And horrid of you to throw my book out of the window, wasn't it?'

'Yes, quite.'

'Yes, *very*.'

'Yes, very, then. Look, we're the last people left, we'd better go.'

'Well, give me a kiss.'

'Not in front of that waiter.'

'He's not looking.'

'He's coming to turn us out. We really must go.'

As Jane rolled into her sleeper she just stayed awake for long enough to think luxuriously of the contrast between her journey to Scotland three weeks ago and her present one.

'I know now for certain,' she thought, 'that I've never been really happy before.'

17

To Jane's amazement, real or pretended, her parents remained perfectly calm when she told them that she was engaged. The fact was that it had long been their greatest wish to see her married, and almost any respectable young man of reasonable fortune would have been received by them with open arms. When, the following day, Albert made his appearance, they took an immediate liking to him.

He, on his side, was very agreeably surprised. Even allowing for a good deal of exaggeration, Jane's account of her father and mother had been far from encouraging, and all the way down in the train he had been bracing himself up to meet a pair of cruel old lunatics who would probably attempt to murder him at sight. Instead of this he was greeted by two charming and good-looking people who were not, as far as he could judge, particularly put off by his appearance.

Jane took him for a little walk in the garden before lunch. 'I told them all about it,' she said, 'and they weren't nearly so horrified as I thought they would be, but I dare say they think it's a cleverer plan to pretend not to mind at first. Apparently mamma used to know your mother quite well when they were girls. She says she was a great beauty.'

'Yes, she was very beautiful.'

'But they don't know yet that you're an artist. I expect that will upset them, all right.'

'Really, darling! To hear you talk one would think you wanted them to be upset. I believe you've got a totally wrong idea of your parents, you know. I've only had a glimpse of them so far, it's true, but they seem very nice and kind – quite different from what you led me to expect.'

'Oh, well, I suppose now you're going to take their side,' said Jane pettishly. 'Anyway, there's the bell for lunch, so come along. Perhaps you'll see my point when you know them better.'

During luncheon Albert realized that, as he had always been inclined to suspect, Jane's pretended hatred of her parents was the purest affectation. She was evidently very fond of them as they were of her. He thought it a curious anomaly that a person with such a straight-forward nature as Jane seemed to him to possess should be capable of deceiving herself to this extent upon any subject, but consoled himself by thinking that marriage would bring home the real truth to her.

The Dacres did not in any way show that they knew of Jane's engagement, but behaved to Albert quite as they would have to any other visitor. They were anxious to hear every little detail of the Dalloch house party and laughed heartily at Albert's description of Lady Prague.

Encouraged by this he broached the subject of General Murgatroyd, delicately, as he imagined from what Jane had said that no officer in the British Army would be considered a fit subject for jest. Great, therefore, was his amazement when Sir Hubert Dacre cried out:

'Not really! Was Mildew Murgatroyd there? Jane, you never told me that! Well, I'm sure you got plenty of fun out of him, didn't you?'

'What did you call him, sir?' asked Albert, hardly able to believe his ears.

'Mildew Murgatroyd. They called him that in the South African War because he was so untidy and slovenly. People used to say that even his revolver was coated with mildew. Why, he's a perfect joke in the army, you know. During the last War they wouldn't have him in France at all. He was given some job in connexion with the Inland Water Transport, I believe.'

'Oh *good*!' said Albert; 'only I wish I'd known it before. I pictured him leading his men like anything, from the way he talked. He told us a most blood-curdling story about how he and twenty privates held a kopje in South Africa, alone and unaided for a fortnight.'

'Yes, and did he tell you that when the relieving force came up in answer to his urgent messages they found there wasn't a Boer for thirty miles, hadn't been the whole time, you know, except in his own imagination.'

'Oh, why didn't we know all this before!' sighed Albert.

'I hear Buggins was up there,' went on Sir Hubert. 'Such a very nice, cultivated man, and a great authority on Scottish history.'

There was a silence. Albert began to feel very much embarrassed; the end of the meal approached rapidly and he dreaded the moment when he would be left alone with Jane's father. He looked helplessly round the room for something to talk about, and presently said:

'What a lovely Richmond that is, Sir Hubert!'

'Yes, quite a pleasant picture in its way, I think. Those two children are boys, though with their long hair and frilly skirts one would rather suppose them to be girls. The one on the left is my father.'

'I see that it is painted in his earlier manner. I am inclined myself to prefer his middle period. Did Jane tell you that I was fortunate enough to be able to save two very beautiful pictures from the fire at Dalloch? Winterhalters. Is he a favourite of yours?'

'How funny,' said Lady Dacre, 'that it should be the fashion to admire these Victorian artists again after so many years.'

Albert, who rather particularly prided himself on being quite uninfluenced by such things as fashions, looked down his nose at this remark.

Lady Dacre now rose to her feet and Albert, with a sinking feeling in the pit of his stomach, was left alone with his future father-in-law.

He thought, 'Better get it over quickly,' and was beginning a beautiful and well-constructed sentence which he had made up in the train, when Sir Hubert interrupted him with:

'Have some more port?'

'Thank you, sir. The thing is,' Albert said hurriedly, forgetting all the rolling periods which he had been about to pour forth, 'Jane and I think . . . that is, we know . . . that we would like to get married.'

'Be married,' said Sir Hubert severely. 'I very much dislike the expression "to get married".'

'So do I,' replied Albert earnestly.

'Then why use it? Well, so you and Jane wish to be married, do you? And isn't this a little sudden?'

'Sudden, sir?'

'How long have you known each other?'

'Oh, for a very long time – quite six weeks altogether, and we've been engaged for nearly a fortnight.'

'Yes, I see – a perfect lifetime! And have you the means to support her?'

'I have a thousand a year, beside what I can make.'

'And what is your profession?'

Albert felt his nerve vanishing.

'If I say "artist" he will kick me out of the house. I can't face it. I shall have to tell a lie.'

'I am in business, sir.'

'What business?'

'In the city.'

'Yes; but what is your business in the city?'

'Oh, I see! Yes, I'm a pawnbroker – did I say pawnbroker? I mean, stockbroker, of course.'

Sir Hubert looked deeply disgusted.

'I'm sorry to hear that,' he said, 'although in these days people must take what work they can get. I have always felt myself – no doubt wrongly – that stockbroking is a very unproductive sort of profession. If I had a son I should have wished him to choose almost any other, and I always imagined that Jane would end by marrying a man of talent, say, a writer or an artist. However, that's neither here nor there, and I don't see that there can be much objection to your engagement. Jane is of an age to know her own mind. Personally, I should advise you to wait for a few weeks before announcing it. Let's go to the drawing-room, if you've quite finished your port.'

Albert now wished that the earth would open up and swallow him. He also felt quite furious with Jane; and as soon as they were left alone together he fell upon her, tooth and nail.

'You little idiot! We can never be married now, and it's all your fault. I can't face your father again. I must go away this instant.'

'Albert darling, what d'you mean? Was he awful to you?'

'No, he was charming; but *why* did you say he hated artists?'

'Because I'm sure he does. It's the sort of thing he always hates.'

Albert told her what had happened.

'You see,' he cried miserably, 'it's impossible for me to stay here after that!'

Jane burst into fits of laughter. She laughed and laughed. Then, she kissed Albert on the tip of his nose and ran out of the room. Presently she returned with both her parents, who were laughing so much that the tears ran down their cheeks.

The Dacres were frankly delighted at Jane's engagement. It would hardly be fair to say that they were anxious to get her off their hands, but, fond as they were of her, there was no doubt that she had lately caused them an unending amount of worry. Her constant and violent flirtations with the most curiously unsuitable people, her doubtful friends, wild behaviour and increasingly bad reputation, all these things were driving them demented, and they both felt that the only hope of steadying her lay in a happy marriage.

'I think we are very lucky,' said Sir Hubert, talking it over with his wife that night in bed. 'When you think what some of Jane's friends are like! Suppose, for instance, it had been Ralph Callendar, not very probable, I admit, but one never knows. Now this boy is of good family, has nice manners, was at Eton and all that, and at the same time he is intelligent. Jane could never have been happy with a fool. If he is a trifle affected – well, I don't know that that's such a terrible fault in a young man. Tiresome, of course, but pardonable. Altogether it seems to me quite satisfactory, far more so than I should ever have expected.'

The engagement was announced in the papers a few days later and as at that particular moment there happened to be a scarcity of news, Albert and Jane for one day vied with the Sudbury Murder Trial in holding the attention of the public.

ROMANCE OF YOUNG ARTIST AND
BARONET'S DAUGHTER.

Sequel to Fire at Dalloch Castle

blared forth on the front page of the *Daily Runner* in type only a shade smaller and less black than that used for:

Tragic Widow's Eight-Hour Ordeal
in Dock.

The gossip-writers, who have little or no use for tragic widows unless they are titled as well, gave the couple their undivided attention.

Jane was described as tall and beautiful with artistic tastes, and was credited with having designed her own bedroom at her father's house in Wilton Crescent. (In point of fact, the bedroom had not been redecorated since they bought the house.)

Much capital was made out of the fact that they had both been staying at Dalloch Castle, the beautiful and historic seat of the Earl of Craigdalloch, when it was so tragically and mysteriously burnt to the ground.

'I hear, by the way,' said one paragraph, 'that Lord and Lady Craigdalloch (she, of course, was a daughter of the late Sir Robert Barns) are shortly returning to Scotland to superintend the rebuilding of the castle. As Lady Craigdalloch is renowned for her exquisite taste, the new castle will probably be an immense improvement on the old, which was built in 1860, a bad year – as some wit is said to have remarked – for wine, women and houses.'

Albert shuddered when he read this.

'My dear Jane, I can absolutely *see* the house that she will build. It is too horrible to think of that heavenly place gone for ever, but even more horrible to imagine, rising out of its ashes, a building in the best cenotaph style. I really believe that Lady Craigdalloch would pull down the Albert Memorial if she had the chance.'

Jane received, among others, the following letters of congratulations:

Dear Jane,

Many congratulations on your engagement. I admit that it was a great surprise to me when I read it in The Times *this morning.*

My husband has been far from well since the fire. He sends good wishes.

Yrs. sincerely,

Florence Prague.

'She doesn't seem wildly enthusiastic,' said Albert, who read this over Jane's shoulder, 'but I rather think she was in love with me herself,' he added complacently.

Marlborough Club.

Dear Miss Dacre,

Congratulations.

I caught a nasty chill after the fire so please excuse this short note.

Yrs.,
Mowbray Murgatroyd.

Bachelors' Club.

Dear Miss Dacre,

Hearty congratulations. After all we went through together I shall always remember you with great affection.

What a gallant deed of yr. fiancé, saving those Winterhalters. I did not know of it until afterwards.

Yrs. sincerely,
Stanislas Wenceslaus.

Castle Fea.

Darling Jane,

I'm so glad everything has passed off all right. I was certain your parents would like Albert myself, but I know that it was an anxiety to you, feeling that they might not approve. The McFeas have been angelic to us. We leave here tomorrow as everything seems to be fixed up now. What d'you think we found yesterday among the ruins of Dalloch? The admiral's spare eye. It was hollow inside and veiny, and I can't tell you what a really nasty look it gave us! Walter insists on wearing it hanging from his watch-chain, which is so disgusting of him.

It's too awful all our things being burnt; as Walter says, it would have been cheaper in the end to go to the Lido. Still, if we had you'd never have met Albert, so it's all to the good, really.

Morris-Minerva is making my life sheer hell at the moment. I throw up quite constantly.

Best love. Come and see us soon.
Sally.

Poor Jane found that it took her the best part of that day to answer these – and some thirty-five other letters, and Albert felt himself rather neglected. When the next morning she received not thirty-five but sixty-five, he announced that he would go to Paris until this influx of congratulations was over.

'But my dear,' said Lady Dacre, 'when the letters come to an end the presents will begin, and that is much worse, because it is such an effort pretending to be grateful for absolute horrors.

'Hubert and I were discussing your plans this morning, and we think that if you want to be married in November we had better go back quite soon to Wilton Crescent. There is Jane's trousseau to be ordered, for one thing.'

'If you do that I can stay with Mr Buggins, but meanwhile I really think I had better go over to Paris for a bit. I ought to be getting rid of my present studio, and have several things that must be seen to sometime soon. I won't bother to look for a new flat yet. We can stay in an hotel after our honeymoon, until we find a nice one, but I must wind up my affairs, and this seems to be a good moment. Jane is far too much occupied to need me about the place now.'

18

Albert went to Paris meaning to stay there for a fortnight, but in a week's time he was standing outside the Dacres' front door in Wilton Crescent. Frankly, he had not enjoyed himself and had spent his time counting the hours to when he should see Jane again. This worried him a great deal. Always before he had been perfectly happy in Paris and he had expected to be so still – had thought that he would hardly miss her at all and that he might even find it quite an effort to come back to her, instead of which he found himself restless and miserable and unable to stay away. He began to realize that nothing would ever again be as it had been for him, and the realization annoyed him.

He found Jane alone in the downstairs drawing-room; she was not expecting him and flew into his arms.

'Darling sweetest,' she said after a few minutes, 'don't go away again. It was dreadful, I had to be thinking about you the whole time.'

'I got so bored with thinking about you that I had to come back.'

'Angel, did you really? I am pleased. Come and see the presents, they're simply unbelievable!' And she dragged him upstairs to a large empty room which had been set aside for the wedding presents.

'There are masses for you, too. I put them all over there. Shall we unpack them now?'

'Let's look at yours first. My dear, what a lot, though! You must know a quantity of people. But how absolutely horrible they are! What on earth shall we do with all these atrocious things? And where do people go to buy wedding presents? Is there a special shop for them, because these things are all exactly alike? Have you noticed that? Oh, look at the Lalique, and all that dreadful glass with bubbles in it! I shall burst into tears in a moment.'

'Oh, well,' said Jane, 'don't take it to heart too much. It only needs a good kick.'

'I know what we'll do,' said Albert, 'we'll have a wedding-present shoot, and get General Murgatroyd to arrange it for us. You see, the drivers can throw the things over our heads and we'll shoot at them. Then, when it's all over, we'll be photo-graphed with the bag. Haven't you any nice presents, darling?'

'Not one,' said Jane, sadly. 'Now let's open yours.'

They set to work, and soon the floor was covered with brown paper, shavings and pieces of string. Whereas Jane's presents were nearly all made of glass, Albert's seemed to consist mainly of leatherwork. Leather blotters, wastepaper baskets and note-cases were unpacked in quick succession, and lastly, a cigarette-box made out of an old book. This present, which was sent by someone he had known at Oxford, perfectly enraged Albert: it had originally contained the works of Mrs Hemans.

'My favourite poetess. Why couldn't he send me the book unmutilated? He must remember that I never smoke, in any case. Still, sweet of him to think of me.'

The maid came in with some more parcels for Jane, containing a Lalique clock from Lady Brenda ('How kind! considering we've only met her once. It will do for the shoot, too.'), a lampshade made out of somebody's last will and testament and a hideous little glass tree, growing in a china pot, from Lady Prague.

'I'm beginning to understand about wedding presents,' said Albert. 'It seems to me that they can be divided into three categories: the would-be useful, the so-called ornamental, and those that have been converted from their original purpose into something quite different, but which is seldom either useful or ornamental.'

'I think,' said Jane bitterly, 'that they can be divided into two categories: those that have been bought in a shop, which are beastly, and those that have been snatched off the mantelpiece and given to the butler to pack up, which are beastlier. Look here, Albert darling, I'm getting really sick of this wedding. I do nothing all day but thank for these revolting presents, which I would pay anybody to take away, and try on clothes I don't want. Couldn't we chuck the whole thing and be married quietly somewhere? If I have to face another two months like this I shall be ill. Really, I mean it. Please, Albert.'

'Well, darling, personally I think it would be heaven, but I must be in London for my exhibition, you know.'

'When does that open?'

'In three weeks tomorrow.'

'That gives us heaps of time to have a honeymoon and everything. Please, let's do that. Go and see about a special licence, now, this minute.'

'But, darling, listen to me . . .'

'Oh, well, if you are going to be tiresome . . .'

'Very well, I'll see what can be done, but first we must ask your parents. No, I absolutely insist on that, darling.'

Sir Hubert and Lady Dacre, as might have been expected, showed no enthusiasm at all when told of Jane's little plan.

'Don't be stupid,' said Lady Dacre scornfully, 'of course you can't do any such thing. People would say at once that Jane is going to have a baby. The presents will get better soon, I dare say: probably you won't have a great many more, and any-how, the nicest ones generally come at the end.'

'Why not advance the date a little,' suggested Sir Hubert, 'to, say, the middle of October, about a month from now? That would be much more sensible than rush-ing off in such a hurry, and after all, a month does go fairly quickly.'

Jane and Albert felt the justice of these remarks and decided that they would definitely settle on the sixteenth of October, by which time Albert's exhibition would be well begun.

'If only,' said Jane, 'when announcing a marriage, one could put, "No presents, by request," how much more bearable the life of engaged couples would become. Look what I've got to thank for now. A pair of bellows made from the timbers of the *Victory* and sent by Admiral Wenceslaus. Oh, dear!'

'Very kind of him, I think,' said her father reprovingly.

'Oh, well; yes, so it is. Very kind of all the people who send these inferior things. I only wish they wouldn't, that's all.'

'How much better it would be,' sighed Lady Dacre, 'if *everybody* would send cheques.'

'Or postal orders,' said Jane.

'Or stamps,' said Albert.

For the next week or two, Jane and Albert had to make up their minds that they would only see each other once a day. They generally dined together and sometimes went to a play, but were often too tired even for that. Presents poured in for both of them, over and above which Albert was now very busy arranging about his exhibition.

He found that he had not brought over quite enough pictures for it, and embarked on a series of woolwork designs for six chairs, based on the theme of sport in the Highlands. He also completed his 'Catalogue of Recent Finds at Dalloch' (having wired for and obtained the consent of the Craigdallochs), intending that a specimen copy should be on view at the exhibition.

With Albert thus kept so busy that anyhow he would have had no time to play with her, Jane found her own jobs far less disagreeable. As Lady Dacre had predicted, the presents she received greatly improved in quality as time went on and she found it much less boring to write letters thanking for things that she really liked. Her trousseau now became a source of great interest, especially the wedding dress, which she could not try on often enough and which was extremely lovely. As for the other things, tiring as it undoubtedly was to stand for hours every day being fitted, there was a certain excitement about the idea that by the time she began to wear them she would be a married woman, and this sustained her.

19

Walter and Sally Monteath, on their return to London, found themselves financially in a very bad way indeed. They had lost almost all their personal effects in the fire. Although they replaced these as economically as they could, it took most of their available money to do so. At this inconvenient moment the accumulated bills of months began to rain upon them, more numerous and insistent than ever before. The bank refused to allow them a further overdraft, all Sally's jewellery had long since been sold, and she began to have difficulty even in paying the household books.

Sally felt desperately ill and worried, and even Walter was obliged to give up taking taxis everywhere; but, apart from that, the situation did not appear to weigh on him at all until, one evening, he came in with some books that he was going to review and found her crying bitterly.

'Sally, darling angel! What *is* the matter?' he said, kneeling down beside her and stroking her hair. When, through her tears, she explained to him that she could bear it no longer, that she literally didn't know how to raise money for the week's books, and that she had been adding up what they owed and found it amounted to nearly a thousand pounds, Walter was enormously relieved.

'I thought something frightful must have happened,' he said. 'But if that's all you're worrying about, I can easily get some money. Why, anybody would lend us a hundred pounds or so to carry on with till our next quarter comes in. As for the bills, they can wait for years, if necessary.'

'Walter, they *can't*. Why, some of them have lawyer's letters with them already. And it's no use borrowing a hundred pounds – that won't really help us at all, permanently, I mean. Then think of Morris-Minerva. How expensive all that business will be, and how are we going to educate him, or anything?' She burst into fresh floods of tears and said wildly that she must have been mad to marry him on so little money but that she had thought they would be able to manage, and that so they would have, except for his idiotic extravagance.

Walter, who had never before in his life known Sally to utter a cross word, was amazed by this outburst and began to feel really worried. His was the sort of mentality which never apprehends an unpleasant situation until it is presented so forcibly that it can no longer be ignored. Now, for the first time, he began to see that their position was, in fact, very parlous, and he was plunged into extreme despair.

'Anyhow, darling,' he said, 'I can't have you worrying like this. Leave it all to me. I'll find a job and support you properly. I'll go out now, this minute, and find one,' he added, and seizing his hat he dashed out of the house, saying that he would come back when he had some work, and not before.

Sally felt strangely comforted by his attitude, although not very optimistic about the job. She sat by the fire and thought that, after all, these bothers were very trifling matters compared to the happiness of being married to Walter.

While she was sitting there thinking vaguely about him, there was a resounding peal on the front-door bell.

Sally remembered that the daily woman had gone home, and was half-considering whether she would sit still and pretend that everybody was out, when it occurred to her that it might be Walter, who was in the constant habit of losing his latch-key. The bell rang again, and this time Sally, almost mechanically, went to the door and opened it.

She was a little bit alarmed to see, standing in the passage, three tall bearded strangers, but was soon reassured by the unmistakably gloomy voice of Ralph Callendar which issued from behind one of the beards, and said:

'Sally, dear, I hadn't realized until this very moment that you are *enceinte*. How beautifully it suits you! Why had nobody told me?'

Sally laughed and led the way into the drawing-room. She now saw that the other men were Jasper Spengal and Julius Raynor, very efficiently disguised.

'Yes,' she said, 'but how *could* you tell? It's really very exciting, due in April. Morris, if a boy, Minerva, if a girl, and we haven't the slightest idea where she's going to live (there's no room here, as you know) or how we can afford to educate him. But Walter's out now, looking for a job. Have a cocktail: Ralph dear, be an angel and make one; the things live in that chest. But why fancy dress so early in the evening, and why haven't we been asked to the party?'

'No, dear,' said Ralph sadly, taking some bottles out of the chest. 'Not fancy dress at all – disguise.'

'Are you – not wanted by Scotland Yard for anything, I hope?'

'No, dear, curiously enough. No; we are going, simply in order to please Jasper, to the Savoy Theatre, where we shall see a Gilbert and Sullivan operette, called – what is it called, Jasper?'

'"I Gondolieri."'

'Yes, "I Gondolieri." Jasper has a new philosophy, which is that one should experience everything pleasant and unpleasant, and says that nobody ought to die until they have seen one Gilbert and Sullivan operette and one Barrie play. Last night he begged us to accompany him on these grim errands, and after much talk, we allowed ourselves to be persuaded. But as it would be impossible to explain this to all the casual acquaintances whom we might meet at the theatre, we decided to take the precaution of a disguise.

'It is one thing to see a Gilbert and Sullivan, and quite another to be seen at one. We have our unborn children to consider, not to mention our careers.

'It has taken us nearly all day, but I think the result satisfactory. To complete the illusion we intend to limp about during the *entr'acte*. Jasper, as you see, has a slight hump on one shoulder, and Julius a snub nose.

'I myself have not been obliged to go to such lengths. Nobody would ever suspect me. Even if I went undisguised, they would only say, "We didn't know Ralph had a double." Did you mention, Sally, that Walter is looking for a job?'

'Yes, poor lamb, he is.'

'He won't find one, of course. But never mind, there are worse things than poverty, though I can't for the moment remember what they are, and we'll all take it in turns to keep the baby for you. A poet of Walter's ability has no business with money troubles and jobs and nonsense like that. Are you very hard up at the moment, Sally?'

'Yes, terribly, you know. We've got such debts and then our people simply can't help. They give us more than they can afford as it is.'

'Well, then, my dear, I'll tell you what to do, straight away. Come and live with me till Christmas and let the flat to an American woman I know for twenty guineas a week. Would that help?'

'Ralph, what an angel you are! But, of course, we can't do that, and we're not really so hard up, you know, only one likes a little grumble. Anyway, who would pay twenty guineas for a tiny flat like this? What are you doing?'

'Hullo! Regent 3146,' said Ralph into the telephone, his eyes on the ceiling. 'Hullo! Mrs Swangard? Ralph here. Yes, I found you the very thing – a jewel, 65 Fitzroy Square. Belongs, you know, to the famous poet Monteath. Yes, I had the greatest difficulty . . . Oh, no, no trouble. I knew at once it would be *the* place for you. Heart of Bloomsbury . . . Oh, most fashionable, all the famous people . . . Yes, all round you, roaring away. What? I said "roaringly gay" . . . My dear, you'll be astounded when I tell you . . . only twenty guineas! A *week*, not a day.

'Wonderful, yes. Of course, they wouldn't let it to just anybody, as you can imagine . . . No . . . As soon as you like – tomorrow if you like . . . Tomorrow, then . . . Yes, I'll come round and see you about it after the play tonight . . . Yes, perfect . . . good-bye.'

'Oh, Ralph!' said Sally, almost in tears. 'How sweet you are! That means more than a hundred pounds, doesn't it, and almost at once? Think what a help it will be. That is, if she likes the flat; but perhaps she won't?'

'My dear, that woman will like just exactly what I tell her to like. So pack up and come round some time in the morning. There's quite a good-sized bedroom you can have, if you don't mind sharing my sitting-room. Oh, nonsense, darling, you'd do the same by me, as you know very well. The poor are always good to each other. Are you going to Albert's private view?' he added, as though anxious to change the subject.

'Oh, that's tomorrow, of course, I'd forgotten. Yes, we're supposed to be lunching with him first.'

'I hear he's given Jane for an engagement ring a garnet with Queen Victoria's head carved on it.'

'No! has he? Have you any idea at all what his pictures will be like?'

'Absolutely none; but Bennet, I believe, thinks well of them.'

Jasper and Julius, who had been looking at *Vogue*, now came over to the fireplace. Feeling that they had so far not quite earned their cocktails, they began to pour forth a flood of semi-brilliant conversation, mostly in Cockney, told two stories about George Moore, one about Sir Thomas Beecham, asked if there was any future for Delius, and left, taking Ralph with them.

Sally resumed her meditations. How right she had been to marry Walter after all. Nobody could have made her so happy; life with him was very nearly perfect. The same tastes, the same friends, the same sense of humour and, above all, no jealousy. She dropped happily into an almost voluptuous doze. The rain was falling outside, which made the room seem particularly warm and comfortable.

Her thoughts became more and more misty, and chased each other through her head in the most inconsequent way until they were nonsense and she was on the edge of sleep – 'When the rain is falling thickly there should be long white hands waving in it.'

Walter, finding her fast asleep on the floor, her head buried in a cushion, wondered whose were the empty cocktail glasses. He found a thimbleful of cocktail left in the shaker which he drank, and then woke up Sally by kissing her.

'It's no good, darling,' he said, 'I cannot dig, and to write gossip I'm ashamed, but I've borrowed ten pounds from Albert, and I love you dreadfully, and I'll write some articles for the Sunday papers. We'll get rich somehow. Meanwhile, I'm going to take you out to dinner at Quaglino's because you haven't been there and it might amuse you. And who's been drinking out of my cocktail glasses, I should like to know?'

'I made a hundred pounds while you were out, my angel, by letting the flat to an American friend of Ralph's from tomorrow, and Ralph says we can go and live in Gower Street while it's let; he's got a bedroom all ready for us. So what d'you think of that, sweetest?'

'Well, I think that beggars can't be choosers. If it's a load off your mind, I'm glad and, of course, it's divine of Ralph. Still, of course, really it's too bloody, because we shall never have a single minute to ourselves. You know what it is in Ralph's flat – one long party.'

'I know, darling, but it's only for six weeks, and it will be such a saving. Also, I didn't like to hurt his feelings by refusing, it was so sweet of him to think of it. As a matter of fact, we could go for some of the time to my family: they're always asking us to stay with them.'

'I believe it would be cheaper in the end,' said Walter crossly, 'to stay on here. Couldn't you telephone to Ralph and say that we've changed our minds?'

'No, darling, I couldn't. If you can't support me, somebody must, you know, and as we're both devoted to Ralph why not let it be he? We needn't really go to the family, of course; I only said that to annoy you, although I shall have to go sometime. By the way, too, remind me to tell Mother about Morris-Minerva. I'm sure I ought to have told her ages ago, because it's the sort of thing it drives her mad to hear from somebody else.

'Darling Walter. And I'm sorry I said all that about supporting me because I know you would like to be able to. And anyway, we're so much happier like this than if you had some horrid sort of job which you hated. And if we're really going to Quaglino's hadn't you better telephone for a table, my sweet?'

20

Albert had decided that the private view of his pictures should take the form of a giant cocktail party at the Chelsea Galleries, where they were being exhibited, the afternoon before they were to be opened to the public. Guests were invited from half-past three to seven, and at three o'clock Albert and Jane, supported by the Monteaths and Mr Buggins, with whom they had all been lunching, arrived at the Galleries in a state of some trepidation.

Walter and Sally, who had not seen the pictures before, gasped with amazement as they entered the room, and for several moments were left quite speechless. The pictures were indeed, at first sight, most peculiar and Albert appeared to have employed any medium but the usual. Some of them stood right out like bas reliefs, while various objects such as hair, beards, buttons and spectacles were stuck on to them. Others were executed entirely in string, newspaper and bits of coloured glass.

The first picture – *Child with Doll* – had a real doll stuck across it. The child also had real hair tied up with blue ribbons. The next on the catalogue, '*No. 2. Fire irons, formal design*', represented a poker and tongs and was executed in small pearl buttons, varying in shade from dead white to smoke-grey. This was framed in empty cotton-reels.

The most important picture in the exhibition was '*No. 15. The Absinthe Drinker*'. This was tremendously built out, the central figure – that of a woman – being in a very high relief. On her head was perched half a straw hat with black ostrich feathers. In one hand was a glass filled with *real* absinthe. This was felt by Albert himself to be his masterpiece.

The only painting in the ordinary sense of the word, was his portrait of Sally, which, hung between two huge still-lifes with surgical limbs, stuffed birds and ukuleles stuck all over them, hardly showed up to its best advantage.

Mr Buggins was rather shocked at this travesty of painting, but was nevertheless obliged to admit that there was a great deal of force in the pictures, while the Monteaths, when the first sensation of surprise had left them, pronounced themselves in raptures.

Albert was evidently in a state of nerves and hardly listened to what was said, but went from picture to picture, adjusting the feathers of *The Absinthe Drinker* at a slightly less-tipsy angle, retying one of *Child with Doll*'s hair-ribbons and borrowing Jane's comb with which to tidy its hair. Finally, he ran round combing all the hair and beards that he could find.

The others stood about rather gloomily wishing that the party would begin. Albert's nervousness had imparted itself to them and especially to Jane, who was terrified that the pictures (much as she personally admired them) might be a most dreadful failure.

If this happened, she thought selfishly, a gloom would certainly be cast over their whole wedding.

Albert, from having always before been perfectly indifferent as to what people might think of his work, now that the pictures were about to be exhibited had become almost childishly anxious for them to have a success.

The first guest appeared in the shape of Ralph, who was received with exaggerated cries of joy.

'Ralph dear, how nice of you to come so early! We *were* hoping someone would come soon. You will try and make the party go, Ralph, won't you? We're all simply terrified, and it's sure to be sticky at first, so promise to help?'

Ralph smiled sadly.

'So these are your pictures, Albert,' he said, and very slowly walked round the Gallery, carefully examining each one from various angles. Having completed the tour he went up to Albert and said earnestly, '*Go on* painting, Albert. I mean that. Go on with it and one day you will be a very considerable artist indeed. Good-bye, my dears, I must go home to bed.'

'Don't go!' they cried in disappointed voices; but he took no notice of their protestations and left the Gallery.

Albert wiped his eyes. He was more than touched and flattered by this attitude of Ralph's, and followed his friend out into the street to tell him so.

Jane broke rather an awkward silence by wondering who the next visitor would be. It was felt that Ralph had not exactly proved the life and soul of the party.

'I think this is quite awful,' said Walter. 'I'm not easily frightened myself, but the beginning of a party is always apt to upset me; and now in addition to the social fear I'm suffering, there is this enormous empty room with Albert's terrifying pictures. The whole atmosphere is painful to a degree. Not that I don't think the pictures very clever, mind you, Jane, because I do, and they will certainly cause a great sensation, but you must admit that they *are* terrifying, specially for that child. Sally, darling, I beg you won't look at it for too long, because if Morris-Minerva even faintly resembles it I shall commit infanticide on the spot.'

Sally now had a brainwave.

'Why don't we begin the cocktails?'

This brilliant idea was immediately acted upon, and when Albert came back a more cheerful atmosphere was pervading the whole place. He felt glad of a drink himself after an emotional scene with Ralph in the street.

The next arrival was Admiral Wenceslaus, who came in rather jauntily, saying:

'And don't offer me a cocktail; I never touch the things. How are you? How are you all?'

He took the cocktail which Albert was rather diffidently holding out towards him and drank it off at a single gulp.

'My dear Gates, I have brought back your trousers which I have had well pressed for you. They needed it. And also a little wedding present in the shape of a book which I thought you might read on your honeymoon. It is by an old friend of my own, Admiral Sir Bartelmass Jenks, and is entitled *The Prize Courts and Their Functions or The Truth About Blockade*. The prize courts, my dear Gates, as you know, investigate the case of ships captured in times of war . . .'

At this moment, as so often happens at parties, about twenty people all came in a lump together and the admiral, deprived of his audience, settled down to some more cocktails.

Soon the room was buzzing and humming with talk. The pictures, as Walter had foreseen, were causing a real sensation. People were, for the most part, very guarded in their criticism, asking each other rather anxiously what they thought about them.

Not so, however, Lady Prague, who, imposing but dowdy in a coat of Paisley pattern with brown fur, was accompanied by General Murgatroyd and Lady Brenda Chadlington.

She walked round the Gallery rather flat-footedly, pausing here and there to inspect the more outstanding pictures rather closely with her nose almost touching them, and then at an exaggerated distance (a trick she had learnt while visiting the Royal Academy).

When she had completed this tour she turned to Lady Brenda.

'Of course, Brenda, I expect it's my own fault, but I really think these pictures are very ugly. Not the sort of thing I should care to have in a drawing-room at all. In fact, I don't see that you could call this Art. I mean, when you think of those wonderful Dutch pictures we saw last year. These are so terribly out of drawing. And then, all that hair! Well, I suppose they're very clever, but –'

Lady Brenda said, 'Ssh! they will hear you,' and General Murgatroyd said loudly and angrily that it was another art hoax and that he was not the least taken in by it.

'If you want to see some really good pictures,' he said, 'go to the Army and Navy Stores. There's one I saw yesterday – some sheep going into a little birch wood with a mist – early morning, I should say. I think of buying it for Craig's silver wedding – silver birches, you know; makes it rather suitable.'

'Personally, I'm glad I have a sense of humour,' went on Lady Prague, warming to her subject. 'That controversy about Rima now: what I said was, "Why be angry?

Every time you want a good laugh in future you only have to go into Hyde Park and there it is!" Killing! A perfect scream!

'Ah! here's Jane. Well, my dear, congratulations on your engagement. We are just admiring your fiancé's pictures – quite pretty, aren't they? No cocktail, thank you, dear, I'm *not* very modern, I'm afraid.'

The Gallery was suddenly and surprisingly invaded by a large crowd of people dressed in the deepest mourning and carrying wreaths; among others, Jasper Spengal, who rushed up to Albert saying breathlessly:

'Such heaven, my dear! We've just been having a mock funeral. We bought a plot at the London Necropolis and we drove for miles and miles through the streets in carriages with black horses, and all the time Julius was in the coffin in grave-clothes which we bought at Harrods. And, did you know that one has grave-stockings, too? Then, when we reached our plot in the Necrop., he just pushed up the lid and walked out, and we all picked up the wreaths and ran for dear life.

'Oh, I wish you could have seen the gravediggers' faces! It was a really beautiful moment. Then we all packed into my car and Rosie's car and came on here, and we've brought the flowers for you and Jane because you are engaged. So suitable, we think,' and he laid his wreath at Albert's feet. An enormous card was tied to it, bearing the inscription:

Sweets to the Sweet. In memory of a noble life.
R.I.P.

Lady Prague, who had been drinking in every word of all this, said loudly and angrily, 'Those are the Bright Young People, no doubt. How very disgusting! Come along, Brenda, I'm going. Can I drop you anywhere, Mowbray?'

'Yes, if you happen to be passing the Marlborough . . .'

'Oh, darling!' cried Jasper. 'Did you hear what she called us? What a name! Bright Young People! Oh, how unkind to suggest that we are bright – horrid word – I see nothing bright about a funeral, anyway, do you? What a nasty old woman! I'm so – so glad she's gone!

'Now, darling, I must telephone – may I? – to the *Daily Runner* and tell them all about it: they'll just have nice time to write it up. We had six photographers and a cinematograph at the graveside, and the light has been very good today, luckily. Would you like to be photographed among the wreaths, darling? It might give quite a good boost to the exhibition.'

'I think not, Jasper, thank you so much. The Press people were here this morning and this is by way of being serious, you know, not a "freak party",' said Albert rather crossly. His nerves were on edge, and the mock funeral, which would at any other time have amused him a lot, struck him as being a painfully stupid idea.

He was thankful when they all dashed away to hear the Will read at Jasper's house, leaving the wreaths piled up underneath *The Absinthe Drinker*, especially as Jane's father and mother came in a moment later.

The Dacres, of course, thought Albert's pictures perfectly raving mad, although they were too polite to say so. They had come with every intention of buying one, but decided in whispers that they were too dreadful – even for a lavatory, so they ordered copies of 'Recent Finds at Dalloch Castle' instead. While they were doing this, they noticed that Mrs Fairfax had arrived, and Lady Dacre, remarking that she refused to shake hands with that woman, left the Gallery, taking Sir Hubert in tow.

'My dear!' said Mrs Fairfax to Albert, 'I had to come round for a moment to support you, but I am most frightfully busy. Have you heard the news? Well, I'm going to marry Cosmo again, which is lovely, because I do enjoy being a duchess when all's said and done, and now, with any luck, I shall be one for the rest of my life. You can't think what a difference it makes in shops and trains. Aren't your pictures divine? Especially the one of Florence in tweed.

'Ralph and I were furious to miss the fire, but it was lucky I went to Gleneagles, because that's where I met Cosmo again – in the swimming-bath – and we got on so well comparing notes about our various husbands and wives that we fixed it up there and then; so I must fly now and get on with my trousseau. If I have another baby, what relation will it be to Bellingham? Good-bye, darling, then. I really have to go.'

Isaac Manuel, the art critic and collector, now put in an appearance, and Albert spent nearly an hour going round the pictures with him. He was greatly soothed and comforted by the older man's intelligent appreciation of his work.

'You are very young,' he said to Albert as he was leaving, 'and your style is often crude and bombastic, but all the same, Mr Gates, I must admit that I am very favourably impressed. I have not enjoyed an afternoon so much for some time. I predict a future for you if you realize, as I can see you do, that these methods are, in themselves, far from satisfactory and only a means to an end. Keep the end always in view and you may become a very good artist indeed. I shall certainly see that you have an excellent notice in my paper, and shall most probably present one of your pictures to the Nation. Good day.'

When Albert returned to the Gallery from seeing Mr Manuel into the street, he found that everyone had gone except Jane, Sally, Walter and the admiral who appeared to have fallen asleep among the funeral wreaths, a terrifying sight as his glass eye remained open, fixed upon the ceiling in a fearful stare.

'What do you think that horrid old admiral has done?' cried Jane. 'To start with he drank so many cocktails that there weren't nearly enough to go round, and then when they were finished he got a straw from one of the wreaths and drank all the absinthe out of the glass in your picture. Sally actually saw him do it.'

'No, really that's too much,' said Albert, who couldn't help laughing all the same. 'I suppose in future I shall be obliged to fill that glass with coloured water, otherwise people will make a habit of drinking it, and you can see for yourselves how terribly the colour values are disturbed when the glass is empty.'

'Well, my dear Albert, I congratulate you,' said Walter warmly. 'The whole thing was a great success, a really good party. And everyone thought the pictures quite brilliant. Manuel was very much impressed. I heard him tell Mr Buggins that he intends to buy one for his collection, and most probably one for the Nation.'

'Clever Albert,' said Jane. 'Darling, I'm so pleased, aren't you? What's the time, by the way?'

'Past seven. We'd better go, I think. No one's likely to come now, and we'll have to be rather quick if we're really dining at eight.'

They picked up their bags, hats and other belongings and began to move towards the door, when Walter said:

'Look here! What about the admiral? He seems to have passed out completely among those lilies. We can't very well leave him like that, can we?'

Albert considered.

'No, I suppose we can't. Hadn't we better put him into a taxi and send him home? I expect we could carry him between us, Walter; or if he's too heavy I'll call the commissionaire to help.'

They advanced upon the admiral, Walter taking his shoulders and Albert his legs, and half-carried, half-dragged him to the street. Jane hailed a taxi into which they bundled him and shut the door.

'Where to, sir?'

'Oh! Walter, where does he live?'

'How should I know? I haven't an idea.'

'Well, where shall we send him?'

Silence.

'Wait a minute,' said Walter. 'Isn't there a special place somewhere for admirals? Now what *is* it called? Oh, yes! I remember, of course.'

He gave the taxi-driver half-a-crown and said:

'Take this gentleman to the Admiralty, please.'

21

The front page of next morning's *Daily Runner* was full of interest to members of the recent house party at Dalloch Castle. Jane read it, as she always did, while breakfasting in bed; and for once in her life she pored over its columns with absolutely breathless attention, reading every word, instead of merely skimming down the more sensational columns and then turning over to see if she was mentioned in the gossip page, which I regret to say was her usual method.

Today, the first paragraph which met her eye was:

AGED PEER DIES IN HARNESS

LORD PRAGUE LIFELESS IN
UPPER HOUSE

NIGHT WATCHMAN'S STORY

We regret to announce that Lord Prague, G.C.B., C.V.O., etc., was found dead late last night in the House of Lords. It is stated that his body was discovered just before midnight by Mr George Wilson, the night watchman.

Mr Wilson, when interviewed by the *Daily Runner*, said:

'I always go into the House at least once during the night to clear up any pieces of paper, orange peel, or empty bottles that happen to have been left underneath the seats. I had been tidying for some time last night when I noticed the figure of a man half-lying on one of the benches. This did not really surprise me, as the peers often sleep on late into the night after a debate. So I went up to him and said: "Twelve o'clock, m'lord. Can I get you a cup of tea?" He took no notice and, thinking he was fast asleep, I was going to let him stay there till morning when something in his attitude made me pause and look at him more closely. I then realized that he was stone dead, so I went and fetched a policeman.'

Mr Wilson was much shaken by his experience and says that although he has often known the peers to die in the corridors and refreshment rooms of the House he cannot recall one to have died in the House itself before.

Dr McGregor, who was called in by the police, said that death, which was due to heart failure, had taken place some six or seven hours previously: therefore Lord Prague must have passed away in the middle of the debate on Subsidized Potatoes (which is reported on page 13).

It was stated at an early hour this morning that Lady Prague is utterly prostrated with grief.

Lord Rainford, a cousin of the late peer, said in an interview:

'I saw Prague for a moment yesterday afternoon, and he seemed in his usual good form. It has been a terrible shock to all of us, and the loss to the Nation will be irreparable.'

DASHING MORE

Absalom More, fourth Baron Prague, was born in 1838. Educated at Eton and Sandhurst, he first distinguished himself as a boy of eighteen in the Crimea, where he earned the soubriquet of Dashing More – true to his family motto, *More to the Fore*. When peace had been declared he was warmly applauded by Queen Victoria, with whom he was always a great favourite. In 1859 he succeeded to the title on the death of his father, and in 1860 he married one of the Queen's Ladies-in-Waiting, Lady Anastasia Dalloch, daughter of the Earl of Craigdalloch, who died in 1909. In 1910 he married as his second wife, Florence, daughter of Mr Leonard Jackson of Dombey Hall, Leicestershire, who survives him. Both marriages are childless, and the peerage devolves upon a distant cousin, Mr Ivanhoe More, of Victoria Road, Kensington.

The very deepest sympathy will go out to Lady Prague, but her sorrow must needs be tempered by the thought that Dashing More died as he would have wished to die – in harness.

(Picture on the Back Page.)

Jane was entranced by this piece of news and read the paragraph over and over again. She was just about to turn to the back page for the promised picture when her eye was caught by:

THE 'BRIGHT YOUNG PEOPLE' GO TOO FAR

MOCK FUNERAL IN LONDON NECROPOLIS

NOT FUNNY – GENERAL MURGATROYD.

It is felt that the Bright Young People have had their day and that their jokes, often in the worst possible taste, should come to an end. Yesterday afternoon a 'Mock Funeral' was held in the London Necropolis at Brookwood, where a site had been purchased in the name of Mrs Bogus Bottom to hold the remains of Bogus Bottom, Esq. The funeral cortège, including six carriages full of weeping 'mourners', travelled for several miles through the London streets, often causing the traffic to be delayed while it passed, and finally boarded the special Necropolis train. At Brookwood the coffin was reverently conveyed to the graveside and was just going to be lowered carefully into the grave, when the lid opened, and Mr Julius Raynor stepped out of it, dressed as for tennis. The 'mourners' then picked up the wreaths, which were numerous and costly, and fled to waiting motor cars.

(Pictures on the Back Page.)

HEARTLESS

The *Daily Runner*, feeling that the only way to stop these heartless pranks is by means of public opinion, sent an interviewer to the following representative men and women, who have not scrupled to express their disapproval:

Miss Martha Measles (well-known novelist):

'I have never heard that it is either clever or amusing to jest with Death . . .'

Sir Holden Crane (sociologist):

'If these young people would bear more children, they would hardly have the time for such foolishness . . .'

Bishop of Burford:

'I think it most shameful, especially as I hear that many people doffed their hats to the cortège as it passed through London . . .'

Mr Southey Roberts (satirist):

'Are these people either "Bright" or "Young"? . . .'

General Murgatroyd:

'It's a damned nuisance, and not funny . . .'

It is understood that the authorities at Brookwood are taking action, and they are very anxious to know the address of Mrs Bogus Bottom.

Jane now turned to the back page and was rewarded by a photograph of Lord Prague in youth; and one of Julius Raynor, a ghastly figure dressed entirely in white, leaping from his coffin.

She then casually glanced at the middle page, where her attention was rooted by a photograph of Albert and a paragraph headed:

AMAZING FEAT OF YOUNG ARTIST

Mr Albert Gates (herewith) has astounded the art critics and half social London with his exhibition of amazing pictures (now on view at the Chelsea Galleries). They are composed in many cases round real objects stuck to the canvas, such as, for instance, eye-glasses, buttons, hats, and even surgical limbs; and are of a brilliance and novelty impossible to describe, particularly *No. 15.*, *The Absinthe Drinker*, which it is rumoured, has been bought for the Nation by Mr Isaac Manuel. Another interesting picture is entitled: *Impression of Lady P—* and is executed entirely in bits of tweed cut into small squares. This is framed in beige mackintosh.

Mr Gates, who left Oxford four years ago, and has since been studying art in Paris, is a tall, good-looking young man of a modest disposition. When a *Daily Runner* representative called on him after the private view of his pictures yesterday, he seemed unaware of the sensation his work has caused in art circles. 'I think it was quite a good party,' he said, referring to the private view.

Mr Gates recently became engaged to Miss Jane Dacre, the beautiful daughter of Sir Hubert and Lady Dacre of Stow-on-the-Wold, Gloucestershire.

Jane, on reading this, became very thoughtful. She was not at all sure that she liked this sudden blaze of fame which had come so unexpectedly upon Albert. The picture which she had framed in her mind of their married life had been imagined without this new factor. She had thought of herself as being all in all to him: his one real friend, sticking to him through thick and thin, encouraging, praising and helping. Much as she admired, or thought she admired, Albert's work herself, it had never occurred to her that he might have a real success with the critics; she had imagined that such revolutionary ideas would remain unnoticed for years, except by a few of the ultramoderns.

The telephone-bell interrupted her train of thought. She put out her hand rather absentmindedly to take off the receiver, wondering who it could be so early. Albert's voice, trembling with excitement, said:

'Have you seen the papers, darling? Yes, they're all the same. Buggins says he can't remember any exhibition to have had such notices for years and years. And I've just been talking to Isaac Manuel. He's buying *The Absinthe Drinker* for the *Tate*, my dear! and two still-lifes for himself; and he's commissioned me to fresco some rooms in his new house. What d'you think of that? So it looks as if we shall have to live in London for a bit, after all. Do you mind, darling one? Of course, I said I could do nothing until our honeymoon is over, but we may have to cut it short by a week or two, I dare say. Isn't it splendid, darling? Aren't you pleased? I never for a moment thought the English critics had so much sense, did you? Where are you lunching today? Oh, yes, I'd forgotten. Well, meet me at the Chelsea, will you, at about one? You're not feeling ill or anything, are you? Oh, I thought you sounded rather subdued, that's all. Well, good-bye. I must go round to Manuel's now.'

As Jane hung up the receiver her eyes were full of tears.

'I couldn't feel more jealous,' she thought miserably, 'if it were another woman. It's disgusting of me not to be pleased, but I can't help it.'

She began working herself up into a state of hysteria while she dressed. She saw all her dreams of Albert's struggle for fame, with herself helping and encouraging, of a tiny house in Paris only visited by a few loyal friends, and of final success in about ten years' time largely brought about by her own influence, falling to earth shattered.

Albert, with his looks, talents and new-found fame, would soon, she thought, become the centre of that semi-artistic social set which is so much to the fore in London. He would be courted and flattered, his opinions accepted, and his presence eagerly sought after: while she, instead of being his one real friend, the guiding star of his life, would become its rather dreary background. She imagined herself growing daily uglier and more boring. People would say: 'Yes, poor boy, he married her before he had met any other women. He must be regretting it now that it's too late.'

Jane, who at all times was inclined to take an exaggerated view of things, and whose nerves had been very much on edge since the fire in Scotland, was now incapable of thinking calmly or she would have realized that a few press notices, however favourable, and a commission from Sir Isaac Manuel, although very flattering to a young artist, do not in themselves constitute fame. She had a sort of wild vision of Albert as the pivot of public attention, already too busy being flattered and adulated to speak to her for more than a minute on the telephone. She imagined herself arriving at the Chelsea Galleries for their luncheon appointment and finding that he had forgotten all about her and gone off with some art critic and his wife instead.

At last Jane believed that all these things were quite true, and by the time she had finished dressing she was in a furious rage with Albert. Unable to contain herself, she wrote to him:

Darling Albert,

I have been thinking about you and me, and I can see now that we should never be happy together. You have your work, and now this tremendous success has come you won't be wanting me as well, and I think it better from every point of view to break off our engagement, so good-bye, darling Albert, and please don't try to see me any more as I couldn't bear it.

Jane.

Quickly, for fear she should change her mind, she gave this note to the chauffeur and told him to take it round at once to Mr Buggins's house.

She then went back to her bedroom and cried on the bed. She cried at first because her nerves were in a really bad state. After about half an hour she was crying for rage because Albert had not come round to see her or at least telephoned; but soon she was beyond tears, and her heart was broken.

'If he loved me he wouldn't let me go like that. This silence can only mean that he accepts: that the engagement is really broken off. Oh, God! how can I bear it? I can't go on living! I shall have to kill myself.'

The telephone-bell rang and Jane, with a beating heart, took off the receiver. 'This must be he!' It was her mother's sister asking what she wanted for a wedding present.

'China,' said Jane feverishly, 'china! china! china! Any sort of china! Thank you so much, Aunt Virginia.'

After this she felt that she had reached depths of despair which she did not even know to exist before. She sat in a sort of coma, and when the telephone-bell rang again, she knew that it could not be Albert.

But it was.

'Darling, Jane, it's a quarter-past one. Have I got to wait here for ever?'

'Oh! is it really so late? Didn't you get my note, Albert?'

'No, what note? Can't you come, then?'

'Yes, in a moment. I wrote to say I should be late, but I won't be long now.'

'Well, hurry!'

'Yes, sweetest. Oh, I do love you!'

Jane rang up Mr Buggins.

'If there's a note from me to Albert will you be an angel and burn it? Thank you so much. Yes, isn't it splendid! No. I've not seen him yet. We're lunching together so I must fly.'

Christmas Pudding

To Robert Byron

Prologue

Four o'clock on the first of November, a dark and foggy day. Sixteen characters in search of an author.

Paul Fotheringay sat in his Ebury Street lodgings looking at the presentation copies of his book, *Crazy Capers*, which had just arrived by post. He thought of the lonely evening ahead of him and wondered whether he should telephone to some of his friends, but decided that it would be of little use. They would all be doing things by now. He also thought of the wonderful energy of other people, of how they not only had the energy to do things all day but also to make arrangements and plans for these things which they did. It was as much as he could manage to do the things, he knew that he would never be able to make the plans as well. He continued sitting alone.

Walter Monteath was playing bridge with three people all much richer than himself. He was playing for more than he could afford to lose and was winning steadily.

Sally Monteath was trying on a dress for which, unless a miracle happened, she would never be able to pay. She looked very pretty in it.

Marcella Bracket was ringing up a young man and hinting, rather broadly, that he should take her out that evening.

Amabelle Fortescue was arranging her dinner-table. She wondered whether to put a divorced husband next to his first wife, and decided that it would be a good plan; they always got on famously with each other now that this was no longer a necessary or even a desirable state of things.

Jerome Field slept in his office.

Miss Monteath, nameless as yet, slept in her pram.

Bobby Bobbin, at Eton, was writing a note to an older boy.

Philadelphia Bobbin sat in her mother's drawing-room and looked at the fire. She hoped that death would prove less dull and boring than life.

Lady Bobbin tramped Gloucestershire mud and cursed the foot and mouth disease which had stopped the hunting that beautiful, open winter.

'I loved thee in life too little, I loved thee in death too well,' sang Lord Leamington Spa at a concert in aid of the Jollier Villages Movement. Later on he sang 'Fearful the death of the diver must be', and for an encore, 'Under the deodar'. Lady Leamington Spa agreed with the chairwoman of the movement that her husband had a charming voice. 'Our son is musical like his father,' she said proudly.

Squibby Almanack, the said son, sat with the three fair and slightly bald young men who were his friends at a Bach concert, in Bond Street.

Major Stanworth drove his Morris Cowley along the high road between Oxford and Cheltenham. He was on his way to the preparatory school where his little boy was having mumps rather badly.

Michael Lewes was sending out invitations for a garden party at H.B.M. Residency,

Cairo. He thanked heaven several times aloud that he was leaving the diplomatic service for good at Christmas.

The Duchess of St Neots was talking scandal with an old friend. Any single one of the things she said would have been sufficient to involve her in an action for criminal libel. Her daughter by a former marriage, Miss Héloïse Potts, was listening from an alcove where she very much hoped to remain undiscovered.

Sixteen characters in search of an author.

I

There is a certain room in the Tate Gallery which, in these unregenerate days, is used more as a passage-way towards the French pictures collected by Sir Joseph Duveen than as an objective in itself. There must be many lovers of painting who have hurried through it countless times and who would be unable to name or even to describe a single one of the flowerings of Victorian culture which hang there, so thoroughly does the human mind reject those impressions for which it has no use.

Indeed Paul Fotheringay, until, on the second day of November, he found himself sitting in this room, had been unaware of its very existence. He now observed that it was mostly hung with large and unpleasant works of the 'Every picture tells a story' school, interspersed with some rather inferior examples of pre-Raphaelitism and a few careful drawings by Ruskin. He sat on a hard and shiny bench and gave himself up to the contemplation of an elderly lady who was struggling, with but little success, to reproduce the handsome but unprepossessing features of Mrs Rossetti. For it was copying day in the Tate. Paul wondered how she managed to keep the paint so beautifully smooth. He thought it very clever of her. Whenever he had tried to express himself on canvas, the result had invariably been a mass of dirty bumps; his own particular style of course, and, he liked to think, a not unpleasing one. Nevertheless, he was perfectly aware that even if he wished to do so he was incapable of producing that oleographic smoothness which seemed to come so easily to the elderly copyist.

Soon, however, his thoughts left the exterior world and turned upon his own inward wretchedness. When a man is harassed beyond endurance through the two most important aspects of life; when the labour of months bears a bitterer fruit than that of failure; and when, at the very same moment, she whom he adores shows herself once and for all unworthy of adoration; then indeed is that man unhappy.

So thought Paul; and writhing beneath the duplicated gaze of Mrs Rossetti he considered for the hundredth time the two causes of his present depression, namely, the behaviour of his fiancée, Marcella Bracket, and the reception by the public of his first novel, *Crazy Capers*, which had been published that week. It would be difficult to say which was the more wounding. The reception accorded to his novel, indeed, appeared at first sight to have been extremely gratifying. The critics, even those of them who had been neither at Eton nor at Oxford with him, had praised it extravagantly, and with a startling unanimity; the cheque which he would eventually receive from his publisher promised to be a great deal larger than those which must so often (and so fortunately) prevent young authors from ever again putting pen to paper. The book, in fact, was an undoubted success. Nevertheless how could praise or promise of glittering gain compensate in any way to the unhappy Paul for the fact that his book, the child of his soul upon which he had expended over a year of labour, pouring forth into it all the bitterness of a bitter nature; describing earnestly, as he thought, and with passion, the subtle shades of a young man's psychology, and rising to what seemed to him an almost unbearably tragic climax with the suicide pact of his hero and heroine, had been hailed with delight on every hand as the funniest, most roaringly farcical piece of work published for years. He who had written with one goal always before him, sincere approbation from the very few, the exquisitely cultured, was now to be held up as a clown and buffoon to jeers and senseless laughter from the mob.

His eyes, fixed upon Lizzie's face, filled with tears, so that her features became blurred and her hair more woolly than ever, as he recalled with a sinking heart that one critic after another had described him as the new humorist and his book as the funniest of the month. Sadly he drew from his pocket a sheaf of press cuttings. He knew them by heart already, and to look at them again was like pressing upon the tooth that aches in the hope that after all it perhaps does not ache unbearably.

REALLY FUNNY BOOK BY NEW WRITER

A welcome contrast to the unrelieved gloom of Miss Lion's *Tragedy in a Farmyard* is provided by Paul Fotheringay, whose first novel, *Crazy Capers*, is the most amusing piece of work to be published for many months. This delicious whimsy maintains a high level of humour throughout, and should certainly find its way to the bookshelves of those who enjoy a quiet chuckle.

AMUSING FIRST NOVEL

. . . I myself paid Mr Fotheringay the very sincere tribute of laughing out loud several times over the absurd adventures of his hero, Leander Belmont . . . If *Crazy Capers* bears little or no relation to the experiences of actual life, one cannot but be grateful to its author for such a witty fantasy.

EX-UNDERGRADUATE'S DÉBUT AS HUMORIST

Paul Fotheringay's first novel, *Crazy Capers* (Fodder & Shuttlecock, 7s. 6d.) is one of the most entertaining books which it has ever been my good fortune as a reviewer to read. It reminded me sometimes of Mr Wodehouse at his funniest, and sometimes of Mr Evelyn Waugh at his most cynical, and yet it had striking originality. I could scarcely put it down, and intend to re-read it at the earliest opportunity. *Crazy Capers* is the story of a penniless young aristocrat, Lord Leander Belmont, who on leaving Oxford with a double first is unable to find any career more suited to his abilities than that of a pawnbroker's assistant . . . Lord Leander is an intensely funny character, and so is his fiancée, Clara. The last chapter, in which they attempt to commit suicide by drowning themselves in the Thames, but are unable, owing to the vigilance of the river police, to achieve anything more tragic than a mud bath, is in particular a masterpiece of humour. I laughed until I was literally driven from the room . . .

With great bitterness Paul remembered how he had written that last chapter, working through the night until he felt that he had arrived at that exact blend of tragedy and pathos for which he searched. As he wrote, the tears had poured down his cheeks. The frustration of two souls, battered beyond endurance by circumstances over which they had no control, unable even to make good their escape from a world which now held nothing for them, had seemed to him a noble, beautiful and touching theme. And nobody else had even remotely apprehended his meaning, not one person.

Putting the press cuttings back into his pocket he pulled out of it a letter which turned his thoughts towards an even more painful subject.

Paul Darling (it ran),

How sweet of you to send me a copy of Crazy Capers *– I was perfectly thrilled at the dedication, it was indeed a lovely surprise. I hope it will be a wild success, it certainly deserves to be, personally I couldn't have thought it funnier. I roared with laughter from beginning to end. I never knew you were capable of writing such a funny book. Must fly now, my sweet, as I'm going out with Eddie, so all my love and lots of kisses from*

Marcella.

P.S. – See you sometime soon.

Paul sighed deeply. That the girl whom he so distractedly adored had thus mocked his book was a wound indeed, but not a death blow; he had never, if the truth be told, entertained a very high regard for her mind. It was her unkind and neglectful conduct towards his person that was causing him so much unhappiness.

Considering her youth (she was twenty-two), Marcella Bracket had all the worst characteristics of the lion hunter developed to an extraordinary degree. She belonged to that rare and objectionable species, the intellectual snob devoid of intellect. Poets and painters were to her as earls and marquesses are to the ordinary snob; the summit of her ambition was to belong to what she considered a 'highbrow' set of people, to receive praise and adulation from the famous. Unfortunately for her, however, whilst knowing through her parents several earls and marquesses, she had not as yet managed to scrape even the most formal acquaintanceship with any great man of letters, nor had the only artist of merit to whom she was ever introduced been at all insistent that he should paint her portrait. Therefore, when poor Paul fell in love with her, which he did for some unaccountable reason at first sight, she saw in him a promising bottom rung to that particular ladder of social success which it was her ambition to climb. She even allowed him to think that they were unofficially engaged in order that she could go about with him, meeting his friends, nearly all of whom were people she had long wished to know, and at the same time picking up from him certain clichés and ideas that might be regarded as a passport to that society of which she hoped to become a member. In time, of course, she intended to marry some rich and colourless man so that she could settle down in Chelsea – a hostess; meanwhile it pleased and flattered her to feel herself the object of hopeless passion in one who had already a certain reputation for brilliance amongst the younger people.

Paul, who although he suspected something of this, only partly apprehended the situation, and moreover thought himself very much in love, was constantly plunged into a state of gloom and depression by her treatment of him. That very day, thinking thus to buy her company for the afternoon, he had invited her to luncheon at the Ritz, a luxury which he could ill afford. He had arrived there, admittedly a few moments late, to find that she was accompanied by the mindless body of Archibald ('Chikkie') Remnant. They were drinking champagne cocktails. When Paul appeared she hardly threw him a word, but continued to gossip with this moron for at least twenty minutes, after which 'Chikkie', having thrown out several unheeded hints that he would like an invitation to lunch, strolled away leaving Paul to pay for his cocktails. The meal which ensued gave him very little satisfaction; Marcella proved to be in her most irritating mood. In the intervals of ordering all the really expensive items on the menu, for it was one of her principles in life that the more you make people pay the more you can get out of them in the end, she chattered incessantly about her successes with various young men unknown to Paul. He gathered that, so far from it being her intention to spend the afternoon with him, she had planned to leave him the moment that lunch was over and go down to Heston for a flying lesson with another admirer. The feeling that he was so soon to lose her from his sight again made him cross and restless, and he was almost glad when she did finally depart in a large Bentley for her destination of loops, spins and Jupiter Wapitis. He knew quite well that by now an aerial flirtation would be in progress, for Marcella was an inveterate flirt.

Meanwhile he had come to Millbank for consolation, only to discover, as so many must have done before him, that there is in good art a quality which demands contentment if not happiness in its observer, its very harmonies serving but to accentuate disharmonies within. On the other hand, contemplation of the second-rate, by arousing the mind to a sort of amused fury, can sometimes distract it a little. Hence Mrs Rossetti. Paul felt, however, that his present unhappiness was too deeply seated to be much shaken, and that even time would be powerless against such a situation as his. There seemed to be no hope, no ray of comfort. The career for which he had longed from childhood, that of a writer, was evidently closed to him; he never wished again to face a chorus of praise uttered in such lack of comprehension. Nor could his affair with Marcella come to any more satisfactory conclusion, for although he loved her, he knew that he would always dislike her.

The copyist now came down from her high stool and began to pack up. Lights appeared, making the place look more dismal than before, and a little fog seemed to have penetrated, although outside the day had been clear and beautiful. Paul's thoughts returned to his present surroundings. He looked at his watch, which had stopped as usual, and decided that he would go home. Marcella might telephone, in which case he would like to be there – his landlady was bad at taking messages. He rose to his feet, and was about to wander towards the door when he noticed the unmistakable figure of Walter Monteath hurrying through the Turner room on his way, no doubt, to the French pictures. He looked round on hearing his name, and catching sight of Paul, said:

'Hullo, old boy, fancy seeing you here. I am pleased. Sally and I have just laughed ourselves ill over your book by the way; it is heavenly. Those policemen! Honestly, my sides ached. And the pawnbroker was divinely funny too. How did you think of it all? I'd give a lot to write a book like that, everyone's talking about it. Well, and where are you off to now?'

'I don't know,' said Paul, trying to look pleased at this praise. 'What are you doing? Can't we have a drink somewhere?'

'Yes let's. As a matter of fact, I'm just on my way to Amabelle's for a cocktail, so why don't you come along too. I know she wants to see you; she was asking about you only yesterday. If you don't mind waiting a moment while I have a look at the Puvis we'll go straight away. I've got the car outside; for once it's not being repaired at the works.'

Whilst Walter, who apparently was going to write an article on Puvis de Chavannes, was examining the picture of John the Baptist, Paul gazed at the large Manet and wished he were dead. He felt, however, that like the hero of his own book, he would be too cowardly and ineffective ever to achieve a satisfactory suicide; he was no Roman soldier to lean upon his sword.

Presently, as they drove towards Mrs Fortescue's house in Portman Square, Walter said, shouting to make himself heard above the twitterings, groanings and squeakings of his ancient motor car:

'Sally and I met your Marcella last night; she was out with that poor mut Remnant and they joined our party later. We thought she was rather a dreary old do. Whatever do you see in her, Paul?'

'Heaven knows,' said Paul, drearily.

2

Amabelle Fortescue, unlike so many members of her late profession, was an intelligent, a cultured and a thoroughly nice woman. The profession itself had, in fact, been more a result of circumstances than the outcome of natural inclination. Cast alone and penniless upon the world at eighteen by the death of her father, who had been a respectable and well-known don at Oxford, she had immediately decided, with characteristic grasp of a situation, that the one of her many talents which amounted almost to genius should be that employed to earn her bread, board and lodging. Very soon after this decision was put into practice, the bread was, as it were, lost to sight beneath a substantial layer of Russian caviare; the board, changing with the fashions of years, first took to itself a lace tablecloth, then exposed a gleaming surface of polished mahogany, and finally became transformed into a piece of scrubbed and rotting oak; while the lodging, which had originally been one indeed, and on the wrong side of Campden Hill, was now a large and beautiful house in Portman Square.

Amabelle, without apparently the smallest effort, without arousing much jealousy or even causing much scandal, had risen to the top of her trade. Then just as, at an unusually early age, she was about to retire on her savings, she had married a charming, well-known and extremely eligible Member of Parliament whom she lost (respectably, through his death) some three years later. After her marriage she became one of the most popular women in London. Her past was forgiven and forgotten by all but the most prudish, and invitations to her house were accepted with equal satisfaction by pompous old and lively young.

The house itself was one of Amabelle's most valuable assets, and its decoration, calculated as it was to suit the taste of the semi-intelligent people who were her friends, showed a knowledge of human nature as rare as it was profound. What could be more subtle, for instance, than the instinct which had prompted her to hang on the walls of her drawing-room three paintings, all by Douanier Rousseau? Her guests, on coming into this room, were put at their ease by the presence of pictures, and 'modern' pictures at that, which they could recognize at first sight. Faced by the works of Seurat, of Matisse, even of Renoir, who knows but that they might hesitate, the name of the artist not rising immediately to their lips? But at the sight of those fantastic foliages, those mouthing monkeys, there could arise no doubt; even the most uncultured could murmur: 'What gorgeous Rousseaus you have here. I always think it so wonderful that they were painted by a common customs official – abroad, of course.' And buoyed up by a feeling of intellectual adequacy, they would thereafter really enjoy themselves.

The rest of the house was just as cleverly arranged. Everything in it belonged to some category and could be labelled, there was nothing that could shock or startle. People knew without any effort what they ought to say about each picture, each article of furniture in turn. To the Victorian domes of wool flowers in the hall they cried, 'How decorative they are, and isn't it quaint how these things are coming back into fashion? I picked up such a pretty one myself at Brighton, and gave it to Sonia for a wedding present.' To the black glass bath those privileged to see it would say, 'Isn't that just too modern and amusing for words, but aren't you frightened the hot water might crack it, darling?' And to the Italian chairs and sideboards, the exquisite patina of whose years had been pickled off in deference to the modern taste for naked wood, 'How fascinating, now do tell me where you get all your lovely things?'

Amabelle's own personal charm operated in much the same way. She was clever enough only to open up, to put, as it were, on view, those portions of her mentality to which whomsoever she happened to be with could easily respond. All her life she had had before her one ambition, to be a success in the world of culture and fashion, and to this end alone her considerable talents and energy had been directed; from a child she had played to the gallery quite consciously and without much shame. If the fulfilment of this ambition brought with it the smallest degree of disappointment, she managed very successfully to conceal the fact from all but herself – herself and possibly one other, Jerome Field.

Jerome Field was Amabelle's official friend, so to speak, appointed by her to that position, and for life. Their friendship had already lasted over twenty years, and had been a most satisfactory one on both sides; for while Jerome was necessary to Amabelle's comfort and happiness, her only confidant, the one person who thoroughly understood her character and yet never questioned anything that she might do, she, supplying much of brightness and domesticity to an otherwise lonely existence, was no less indispensable to him. The fact that there had never been the smallest hint of love in their relationship (he being frankly in love with his business affairs and she with social life, and neither of them capable of any other real or lasting passion), lent it a peculiar flavour for which she at least was grateful.

On the afternoon of Paul's sad vigil in the Tate, Jerome Field took tea, as was his almost invariable custom, in the Douanier Rousseau drawing-room.

'The worst part of getting old in these days,' he said, 'seems to be that those of one's friends who are neither dead, dying nor bankrupt, are in prison. It is really most depressing, one never knows when one's own turn may not be coming. I said to my directors only today, "Now mind, if I go to the Old Bailey I don't intend to stand in the dock alone. I asked all of you to be directors on the distinct understanding that you know as well as I do how to add, subtract and even multiply, and I count on you to be equally responsible with me for any slips that are made." That shook 'em, I can tell you, especially that fat old fool, Leamington Spa; he practically asked me how long we could expect to be at large.'

'But I do hope,' said Amabelle with some anxiety, 'that you're not in immediate danger of arrest, are you? Do try and put it off till after Christmas anyhow.'

'Why, do you need me for something special at Christmas time?'

'Not more than usual, darling. I always need you as you know perfectly well. The thing is that I hope you'll come and stay with me for Christmas – I've taken a house in the country then.'

'Not in England?'

'Yes, in Gloucestershire, to be exact.'

'Good gracious, Amabelle!'

Jerome Field was one of those rare and satisfactory people who always play the exact part that would be expected of them. At this particular juncture it was obviously indicated that he should register a slightly offended amazement. He did so.

'The country in England, my dear. What a curious notion. Whatever could have made you think of such a thing? Do you say you have actually taken a house?'

Amabelle nodded.

'Have you seen it?'

She shook her head.

'How long have you taken it for, may one ask?'

'Two months. I signed the agreement today.'

'Without even seeing the house?'

'Yes, I couldn't be bothered to go all that way. The house agents seem to think it's very nice and comfortable and so on, and after all it's only for such a short time. I thought of moving in just before Christmas. The Monteaths are coming down with their baby, and naturally I want you too. I think it will be rather fun.'

'But it's such an extraordinary idea. Whatever will you do in the country for two months, at that time of year too? I'm afraid you'll be bored and wretched.'

'I don't know. After all, hundreds of people live in the country, I believe, and presumably they must occupy themselves somehow. Besides, it's patriotic not to go abroad now. I've heard you say so over and over again.'

'Abroad, yes. But there's nothing to stop you from staying in London, which would surely be more pleasant than to traipse down to Gloucestershire in this weather.'

'You're not very encouraging, are you?'

'Where is this house, anyway?'

'It's called Mulberrie Farm, and it's in the Cotswolds, near Woodford – incidentally, it's quite near Compton Bobbin, so I shall expect to have little Bobby trotting round most days, and you know how I dote on that child. Apparently Mulberrie Farm itself is very old and lovely. I'm awfully excited about it.'

'Now why, apart from the obvious attractions of young Bobby (horrid little brat) do you choose the Cotswolds of all places? Anything more dreary in winter can hardly be conceived. I dare say that Devonshire or Dorset would have been quite pleasant, but the Cotswolds – !'

'Oh, it wasn't on Bobby's account in the least, much as I shall love having him so near. I didn't even discover that he lived there until after I had signed the lease. No, I read a book about the Cotswolds once when I was waiting for a train at Oban, I don't know why, but I bought it off a book-stall. I suppose I wanted change for a pound note. Anyhow, I read it, and apparently the Cotswolds are naked, grey hills with lush valleys and Saxon churches and Elizabethan farm houses and lonely wolds, which sound so entrancing, lonely wolds, don't you agree? In fact, if I like it as much as I know I shall, I might easily buy a house there and settle down among the lonely wolds for ever.'

Jerome snorted.

'Not cross, are you darling?'

'No, of course I'm not. But, frankly, I don't think you'll enjoy yourself much.'

'Then I can come straight back here, can't I?'

'Yes, that's true.'

'There's one other reason why I don't want to be in London at present,' said Amabelle slowly. 'Michael is coming back for good at Christmas, and I can't, I can't, face all that business over again. There are limits to one's powers of endurance, you know.'

'You managed him quite all right before,' said Jerome drily.

'I'm three years older now and more easily bored by that sort of thing. Besides, Michael makes such appalling scenes and I really don't feel quite equal to them any longer.'

'Who says you'll have to feel equal to them? May I remind you, my dear, that three years at Michael's age is a lifetime, and I should think it more than doubtful that he will still be in love with you when he gets back.'

'Oh, well, if you're merely going to be disagreeable –'

At this moment Paul and Walter were announced.

3

Amabelle got up to shake hands with them and began moving tables and chairs into different positions.

'Darlings, I couldn't be more pleased to see you.'

'Let me help with that.'

'Months and months since I saw Paul last.'

'If you'd just say where you want it put.'

'All right, I can manage. There that's perfect. Now Jerome and Walter can settle down to a game of backgammon, which I know they're longing to do, while I have a little chat with Paul. Come over here to the fire, darling, and tell me a whole lot of things I'm dying to know about. First of all, was your book really meant to be funny when you wrote it? – don't answer if you'd rather not; secondly, why did you cut me dead in the Ritz today; and thirdly, who was that very repellent female you were lunching with?'

'What a clever woman you are, Amabelle,' said Paul admiringly. 'It's perfectly terrifying how nothing ever escapes those tiny yellow eyes.'

'Large green in point of fact.'

'There's nobody like you – luckily. The book was intended as a horrible tragedy, the female was my fiancée, Marcella Bracket, and the reason I cut you was that if I hadn't she would certainly have insisted on being introduced and I know just how she would bore you.'

'Oh, I see. She's a bore as well as being hideous, is she? I must say, she looks it all right.'

'I think she's maddeningly beautiful.'

'She's certainly not that, poor girl. I can see that we shall have to get you out of this.'

'I wish you could, but unfortunately I happen to be in love.'

'That won't last,' said Amabelle soothingly. 'It never does with you. As for the book, it's no good writing about the upper classes if you hope to be taken seriously. You must have noticed that by now? Station masters, my dear, station masters.'

'I know, I know. Of course, I have noticed. But you see my trouble is that I loathe station masters, like hell I do, and lighthouse keepers, too, and women with hare-lips and miners and men on barges and people in circuses; I hate them all equally. And I can't write dialect. But you must admit I had a pawnbroker in my book.'

'Yes, and such a pawnbroker – those Gibbon periods! Pawnbrokers, my dear, don't often talk like that in real life, at least, I can't imagine that they do. No wonder he was taken for a comic figure. What between your book and your young woman you seem to be in a pretty mess, poor darling.'

'I am indeed,' said Paul gloomily. He was enjoying this conversation as people can only enjoy talking about themselves.

'Though what it is you can see in her I don't know.'

'Go on saying that. Say that she's awful and hideous and stupid and unkind, you don't know what a lot of good it's doing me.'

'All right, I will, only don't cry if you can help it, there's a sweetie. I expect you'll get over her quite soon, you know; it's happened before, hasn't it? Still, of course, it must be hellish for you while it lasts, having to look at that penny bun face every day. The poor girl's certainly no oil painting.'

'Oh, I am glad to hear you talk like this, Amabelle; it's cheering me up no end. It makes things much less awful if you honestly think her plain, because perhaps one day I shall see her as you do, and then everything will be all right again.'

'Well, just you bring her round here some time and I'll tell you all about her.'

'Ha, ha, she'd bore you to death, she's the most cracking bore I've ever met.'

'Are you going to marry her?'

'No such luck. I'm not rich enough. Her mother's out to catch a guardsman for her.' To Paul the word 'guardsman' was synonymous with millionaire. 'Besides, it's not as though she cared for me in the least. She only got engaged to me because she thinks I have some clever friends she would like to meet. She's a terrific intellectual snob among other things.'

'You seem to have her pretty well sized up, don't you?'

'Oh, she's driving me mad.'

'Now, don't cry, or I shall stop talking about you. Do you intend to start another book soon?'

'What's the good of that? I only get laughed at; I don't care to be made such a fool of again, I can tell you. It has hurt me terribly – terribly. Look at these.' He drew the press cuttings from his pocket. 'They mock at me, they make fun of my sacred feelings. It's not very nice for me, is it?'

'Poor sweet.'

'It's the most appalling disappointment, I must say. All my life I have wanted to write; I love it. Now I don't know what I am going to do. It is hell – hell!'

'I should keep off fiction, if I were you. People don't understand tragedy in these days, only sentiment; and quite frankly your book was a bit melodramatic, darling, wasn't it? Now, why don't you try your hand at something else, some different form?'

'Yes, perhaps I should.'

'Biography, for instance. I've always been told that it's very good mental exercise, and it can be quite profitable into the bargain.'

'What a nice woman you are, Amabelle,' said Paul, cheering up visibly. 'Thank goodness I came to see you. I never thought of biography, but of course that's the very thing for me. Yes, but whose? May I be your Boswell, darling?'

'I believe books are still censored in England, old boy, and I don't much fancy the idea of being burnt by the public hangman, thanks awfully, just the same. No, you choose carefully some really sympathetic character – and talking of sympathetic characters, here's darling Sally. How's the mother?'

'Very well considering,' said Sally, who looked enchanting in a seal-skin tippet. 'Pleased to see you, Paul – not so pleased to see Walter at the backgammon table again. What did you promise me, darling?'

'It's all right, darling. I'm throwing doubles the whole time today. There, you see, I've got old Jerome on the run again. Backgammoned, in fact. That's a sixteen game,' he said, leaning back in his chair and putting an arm round Sally's waist. 'Anyhow, my sweet, it's hardly fair to grumble, considering that that most peculiar garment you've got on now was bought entirely out of my winnings last week, eh? So go away, or you'll spoil the luck.'

'How's my goddaughter, Sally?' asked Paul.

'Good heavens, are you going to be its godfather too?' said Amabelle. 'Whatever induced you to ask him of all people, Sally? And how many godparents does that make?'

'Altogether about twelve, I think,' said Sally vaguely. 'We thought it would be silly not to ask Paul, as he is literally the only religious maniac we know.'

'I'm not a maniac,' said Paul angrily.

'Aren't you, darling? I think you are, though.'

'Just because I happen to be a Buchanite –'

'What's that you're saying?' said Amabelle; 'I never thought an old highbrow like you would admit to such a thing. I read them in trains myself when there's nobody looking.'

'I was not,' said Paul with dignity, 'referring to the novels of John Buchan, if that is what you mean. Of course I don't read them. Buchanism is the name given to a religious sect founded by Mrs Elspeth Buchan, a Scotch and vastly superior prototype of Mrs Eddy and Mrs Besant. In fact, she started that fashion for the founding of religions by untitled married ladies which has since become almost universal. The last of her followers died in 1848, and I have constituted myself head of the N.B.M. (New Buchanite Movement). As her teachings died with her followers I am able to make up the rules as I go along, which is pleasant. When's the christening, Sally?'

'Well, if the poor little sweet is still with us then we thought next Tuesday week (suit you?), but she's most awfully ill today, she keeps on making the sort of noises Walter does after a night out, you know.'

'D'you think she's likely to live or not?' said Paul. 'Because if there's any doubt perhaps I could use your telephone, Amabelle, to call up the jewellers and see if I'm in time to stop them engraving that mug. It's such an expensive sort, and I don't want it spoilt for nothing, I must say.'

'I believe she's expected to pull through. But tell me, Paul, how could you have it engraved, we haven't even decided what her name's going to be ourselves. I want Henrietta Maria and Walter wants Dora Mildred, and we don't seem to be able to strike anything we both like.'

'It's being engraved Elspeth (after Mrs Buchan) Paula (for obvious reasons) Monteath, from her loving godfather, Paul Frederick Fotheringay.'

'Well, really, all the cheek! Walter, did you hear that?'

'Yes, I did. I'll offer you a double, Jerome. I think those names are O.K., don't you? It saves trouble if someone settles them for us, because perhaps now we shan't have to be quarrelling all day. Only I vote we use Paula, I'm not so wild about Buchanism myself.'

'Thanks, old boy, a very delicate compliment, if I may say so.'

'By the way,' said Walter, 'why Paula and not Pauline?'

'Cheaper. The thing is, you pay for engraving by the letters. I say, I do hope she lives all right, Sally.'

'So do I, you know. After all the trouble I've had, one way and another, it would be extraordinarily souring if she didn't. However, Nanny and the charlady between them are battling for her life, as they say in the papers, like mad, so I expect she will. The charlady knows all about it, too, she has lost six herself.'

'Sounds a bit of a Jonah to me, but I don't want to depress you. Anyway, I hope you won't be sparing expense in this matter. Remember that I didn't over the mug.'

'One of your own, I suppose, with the name taken out?'

'Not my name, that's left in, you see. I had "From his loving godmother, Eliza Stratford" (the Countess of Stratford, carriage folk) taken out. That came after my name, and they're putting the words "Elspeth Paula Monteath from her loving godfather" in front of it. Such a brainwave, don't you agree? And who thought it all out for me? Dear little Marcella, bless her heart.'

'We saw Marcella last night with that man Chikkie. She's a nasty piece of work, if you like. Walter finds her so repellent that he says he can only suppose he must really be in love with her.'

'I expect he is, too. Did you ask her to be Paula's godmother?'

'No, I did not.'

'That lends her a certain distinction, doesn't it? She must be the first person in London you haven't asked.'

'How careless you Protestants are of your children's souls,' said Jerome looking up from his game. 'That poor little wretch was born months ago, and there she is, still wallowing in original sin, without mentioning the horrid risk she would run if she should die before next Tuesday week – I call it a shame. Double you, Walter. What does it feel like to be a mother, Sally?'

'Childbirth,' said Sally, 'is an unpleasing process. It must be quite awful for the father who, according to Walter, suffers even more than the mother. I don't quite understand about that, but of course I take his word for it. To be honest, I should like the baby a good deal better if she wasn't the split image of Walter's Aunt Lucy; all the same I am getting quite attached to her in a sort of way, and Walter's so impressed by being a father that he's actually looking out for a job. You know, motherhood is an enormous financial asset in these days; to begin with you get pounds and pounds for publishing a photograph of a child twice or three times her age and saying she's so well-grown because of Gatebury's food, then you get more pounds for saying that no nursing mother would care to retire without her cup of Bovo, and finally I can now edit the Mothers' and Kiddies' Sunshine Page in the *Daily Runner* under my own name, so I get an extra pound a week for that. Oh, yes, the little dear is pulling her weight in the home and no mistake.'

Later that evening Paul escorted Marcella to a party given by one of her Slade friends. For Marcella, like so many girls, studied Art in her odd moments.

'It is to be a Russian party,' she told him as their taxicab threaded the mazes of S.W.14, 'in honour of Peter Dickinson, who has just come back from Moscow.'

Paul thought that under the circumstances Mr Dickinson would most probably have preferred any other sort of party, but he refrained from saying so.

'There is to be some interesting conversation,' said Marcella.

'I hope there'll be something to drink,' said Paul.

They arrived at a basement flat decorated with tasteless frescoes. All Marcella's arty friends lived in basement flats decorated with tasteless frescoes. There were hardly any chairs, but the floor was covered with the semi-recumbent forms of dirty young men in stained and spotted grey flannel trousers and dirty young women with long greasy hair. One of the young men, presumably Peter Dickinson, was holding forth when they arrived.

'Yes, I went to see the timber camps; they are fine, wonderful, a triumph of organization. A clean, healthy outdoor life, think what that must mean to these city clerks, people accustomed only to the fetid air of offices. They are as happy as little children, and in everything that they do, their work, their play, they keep always before them their wonderful ideal of communism.'

Paul thought that they sounded rather like Boy Scouts, and was unattracted by the idea. He soon wished he could go home. Marcella had disappeared almost at once accompanied by a tall young man with side-whiskers, and he saw nobody else that he knew. Although the party was by way of being Russian he could find neither vodka, caviare nor Russian cigarettes to cheer him; in fact, the only notice-able attribute of that great country was the atmosphere of dreariness and hopeless discomfort which prevailed. The chains of love, however, kept him there until past three in the morning, when Marcella appeared and announced that she was quite ready to go home. Paul felt too tired to make a scene about the young man with side-whiskers, and devoted his remaining supply of energy to finding a taxi. These are rare in S.W.14 at 3 a.m.

'How all your friends do dislike me,' said Marcella complacently as they bumped away in the ancient vehicle which he had eventually procured. 'Those Monteaths were horrid to me last night. But perhaps she's jealous, poor thing, of me being so young and pretty.'

'Sally?' said Paul. 'Sally's incapable of jealousy, I assure you. Besides, she quite honestly thinks you very plain and boring indeed,' he added in an attempt at revenge for the terrible evening he had just undergone. This reply was so unexpected that Marcella was for once quite unable to defend herself, and was quiet and affection-ate during the remaining part of the drive to Gloucester Square where she lived. She snuggled as close to Paul as the patent leather covering to the springless seats would allow, and in the hall of her house she gave him a long, hot and sticky kiss, saying, 'Anyhow, you think I'm beautiful, don't you?'

'The poor girl is admiration mad,' thought Paul. 'Apart from that she's not a bad little thing, though heaven knows how I can be in love with her.'

4

The more Paul considered the idea of writing a biography, the more it seemed to offer him an ideal medium for self-expression, and one into which he could pour his heart and soul without risk of ill-timed mockery. Even the most hardened and callous critic could scarcely shake his sides over the description of a death-bed scene that had really taken place. He felt that in this branch of literature lay his oppor-tunity to establish himself as a serious writer, and to shake off the humorous reputation which he had so unwillingly acquired. Once thus established he would surely be able to publish another novel with less danger of being misunderstood. The difficulty now before him was that of finding a suitable subject; one whose work should be thoroughly sympathetic to himself and whose outlook in life should be comprehensible to him.

He considered this problem for several days, but with no result. Those people whose lives he would have enjoyed writing, notably Maria Edgeworth, Miss Austen, Elizabeth Barrett Browning and Mrs Carlyle, seemed already to boast a formidable bibliography. Others that occurred to him, such as Dorothea Felicia Hemans, Mary Russell Mitford, and Mrs Livingstone (the mother of Dr Livingstone – I presume), presented almost insuperable difficulties in another direction, as little or nothing seemed to be known about them by anybody. It would be hard, in fact, to find exactly what he wanted, which was a woman of breeding, culture and some talent, living towards the last half of the nineteenth century, who was not already the subject of a 'life'.

At last, in despair of ever finding his ideal, he wandered into the London Library, where he began, in a desultory manner, to read through the opening pages of the *Dictionary of National Biography*. Unhelpful as it appeared to be, he waded on through the Adam brothers, Prince Adolphus Frederick, Aelfred Aethling, Anerium the Welsh poet, Bishop Baggs, Praisegod Barebones, Boate de Boot, and Bertulf. Having arrived by this weary pilgrimage of the mind as far as Beorhtric, King of the West Saxons, he was just going to abandon his search for the time being when, turning over two pages at once, his eye lit upon the name Bobbin, Lady Maria.

Lady Maria Bobbin. The only wonder was that he had never thought of her before. Here, indeed, was a life worth writing, a sermon waiting to be preached. This woman, this poet, brought up amid the conventions and restrictions of the mid-Victorian era, wife of a country squire, mother of twelve children, who found time among her manifold duties to sing in noble, deathless verse such songs as 'The Redbreast's Lament', 'Prayer of a Grecian Warrior' and 'Wales in Captivity', was surely the very heroine for whom he had been searching. There was not much information about her in the *Dictionary of National Biography*, only enough to whet Paul's appetite for more, but there was an allusion to her vast correspondence and copious journals which led him to hope that these might still be extant at her home in Gloucestershire, Compton Bobbin.

In the *Dictionary of National Biography* he discovered the following bare facts of her life:

'Lady Maria Almanack, daughter of the eighth Earl of Leamington Spa, was born in 1818, and married in 1837 Sir Josiah Bobbin, M.F.H., of Compton Bobbin, Gloucestershire. From her earliest childhood she displayed an astonishing talent for writing verse, and in 1842 her parents were foolish enough to publish her "Poems" in a quarto volume. She soon recovered from the adverse criticism which these met with, and published in 1844 "Autumnal Tints", a collection of short poems including the famous "Farewell to Mount Ida". In 1845 she had her first real success with "Elegant Elegies, Tasteful Trifles and Maidenly Melodies". The following year an epic poem, the well-known "Martyrdom in Mercia", came from her pen, and after that date, in spite of her many duties as châtelaine of Compton Bobbin and mother of twelve children, she never failed to produce an annual volume, generally far from slim, of poems, ballads, sonnets, odes or romantic plays. She was, in fact, as prolific as she was gifted a writer, for, besides her published works, she found time to conduct a vast correspondence and to keep a journal which extended into 14 volumes. This treasure is now in the possession of her descendants at Compton Bobbin. During her lifetime her works enjoyed an almost world-wide popularity, and she was intimate with many of the most famous among her contemporaries, including Meredith, Carlyle, Lord Tennyson (who often spoke of the exquisite sensibility of her writing) and Queen Victoria herself. In 1896 she died from a chill which she caught at the christening of her fiftieth descendant.'

At the end of this paragraph there was no bibliography, no hint as to how or where further information was to be sought. The mention of a journal, however, was enough to spur Paul on to further action. He returned to its shelf the *Dictionary of National Biography* and had recourse instead to *Debrett's Peerage, Baronetage and Knightage*; from which he gathered that Compton Bobbin was now held by Lady Bobbin, M.F.H., J.P., in trust for her son, Sir Roderick, a minor, her husband, the late Sir Hudson Bobbin, having been drowned in the *Lusitania* disaster. Paul needed no more information. It only remained now for him to write to the present châtelaine of Compton Bobbin and ask that he might be allowed to read the journal and letters of her predecessor. In a state of excitement and enthusiasm he returned to his rooms, where he composed the following letter:

155 Ebury Street, S.W.

Dear Madam,

I am most anxious to write a life of the late illustrious Lady Maria Bobbin, a task which, I understand, has never yet been attempted, and one which I would devote all my energy and my poor talent to completing in a manner worthy of its subject. To do this with any degree of accuracy would however be impossible without access to those of her private papers, notably the fourteen volumes of her journal, which I assume still to be in existence at Compton Bobbin. It would be most kind and gratifying to me if you would consider lending me the said volumes – or, should you very naturally object to the idea of parting, even for a space, with documents so invaluable, perhaps you would give permission for me to reside in the local hostelry that I may study them in your house, whose atmosphere must yet I feel be redolent of Her. I would naturally work at this life in entire collaboration with yourself, submitting all proofs to you before publication.

If I trouble you, please forgive me and remember that I do so in the interests of Art and to the perpetuation of a memory which must ever be sacred to you, to me, and to all lovers of Verse.

Yours sincerely,
Paul Fotheringay.

It was unfortunate that Paul, in writing this letter, had allowed himself to fall victim to the intoxication of his own style. Lady Bobbin, M.F.H., J.P., opened it together with several appeals for new hens from farmers whose old ones had been removed by Mr Reynard. She read it over twice, found herself unfamiliar with such words as hostelry, redolent and collaboration, and handed it to her secretary, saying, 'The poor chap's batty, I suppose?' The secretary, who occasionally read book reviews, said that Paul Fotheringay was a comic writer, and would be a most unsuitable person to undertake a life of Lady Maria. She was then instructed to answer his request, as well as those of the farmers, in the negative.

Meanwhile, Paul, never doubting the success of his letter, walked on air. His fingers itched to take pen in hand, to prove once and for all to those idiotic critics that he was a serious writer; and at the same time he looked forward greatly to the perusal of Lady Maria's journal, feeling that it would provide the rarest intellectual treat. He went out and bought himself a collected edition of her works, so that he might re-read some of his favourites – 'The Lament of Llywark Hen', 'Moorish Bridal Song', 'On the Death-bed of Wallace', 'To my Brother', etc., which he did with his usual appreciation of her genius. Altogether his outlook on life became far more cheerful and optimistic than it had been before he went to see Amabelle Fortescue.

Alas, how dashed were his hopes when the letter for which he had been so eagerly waiting was found to contain the following abrupt refusal in the third person:

Compton Bobbin,
Compton on the Wold,
Gloucestershire.

Lady Bobbin regrets that she is unaware of the existence of any documents at Compton Bobbin which could interest Mr Fotheringay. She cannot enter into further correspondence on this subject.

Paul was stunned by this blow.

'And then,' he said to Amabelle, to whom he had gone immediately for consolation, 'it is so rude and horrid, I feel terribly snubbed.'

'From what I've always heard of that woman I'm not in the least surprised,' said Amabelle. 'I don't want to be governessy, darling, but I do think it was a mistake for you to write off in such a very violent hurry. It would have been more sensible to find out what sort of person she was first, and what was likely to be the best method of approach.'

'Yes, I see that now. But I was so excited when I thought of the journal in fourteen volumes that my one idea was to get hold of it as soon as I possibly could.'

'It's a pity you didn't consult me, you know. Little Bobby Bobbin (Sir Roderick) is a great buddy of mine, and I'm sure he could have fixed it for you easily. After all, the journal belongs to him, doesn't it?'

'You don't think he could smuggle it out of the house for me?'

'He'd never dare to now, it wouldn't be safe. You see, Lady Bobbin is in a very strong position as far as he is concerned because she has every penny of the money, and he's terrified of getting into her bad books. She was a great heiress, a Miss Swallowfield (tea), and if old Hudson Bobbin hadn't married her the place would have gone long ago, I believe. But surely you know Bobby, don't you? Why didn't *you* ask him about it?'

'D'you mean that comic child from Eton who's always here? Of course I know him quite well, but how could I have guessed his other name was Bobbin? It's unnatural, Bobby Bobbin. Oh, dear, I do feel wretched.'

'Poor old boy, it is boring for you.'

'It's far worse than boring,' said Paul vehemently, 'it's the end of my literary career. From now onwards I am condemned to the life of a social parasite. If I can't write the life of Lady Maria I shall never set pen to paper again. She is not only my favourite poetess, but my affinity, my period, my ideal heroine. I understand her mentality, I could write the most beautiful life of her. Oh, it is too hard to bear. I tell you that since I had this idea I have thought of nothing else night and day, not even of Marcella. However, I can't despair yet, it means too much to me. I shall get inside Compton Bobbin by hook or by crook, even if I have to disguise myself as a housemaid to do it.'

Amabelle looked at him thoughtfully. There was nothing in the world she enjoyed so much as getting herself involved in other people's affairs, and she was beginning to see here a good chance to indulge in this hobby.

'Are you quite serious, Paul?'

'Yes, Amabelle. More serious than you would believe. I honestly think I could write a first-class book on Lady Maria, and I want to do it more than I've ever wanted anything.'

'Really and truly?'

'I promise you.'

'In that case, my dear, and especially if it's going to cure you of that dreary little Marcella, I think I must try to help you. I'll go down to Eton at once and call on Bobby, I expect that between us we could think out some scheme for getting you into Compton Bobbin.'

'Oh, Amabelle, if only you could,' said Paul, but he went away feeling depressed and not very hopeful.

The next day, at one o'clock punctually, Amabelle, dressed in pale beige furs, stepped out of her pale beige Rolls-Royce into the High Street of Eton, where she was met with noisy acclamations of delight by Sir Roderick Bobbin, Baronet, of Compton Bobbin, in the county of Gloucestershire.

'Cad, cad, Amabelle darling! First of all you haven't written to me once as you promised you would, and then you send me a wire only this morning to say you're coming down. If you had let me know a tiny bit sooner I could have ordered a decent lunch, but as it is I don't know what we shall get, something uneatable probably. Two days' notice in future, please, my sweet!'

'I'm sorry, duckie, I simply couldn't. I only had today free, and I must see you about something very particular. I'm sure the luncheon will be perfect, anyway, it always is. In here?'

She followed Bobby into a little old house that was half curiosity shop, half restaurant. It was stuffed so full of antiques that every step had to be taken carefully for fear of knocking down some fragile object, while interspersed among the curios were luncheon tables covered with check cloths and arty crafty earthenware. Bobby passed these by, however, and led the way up a dark and narrow staircase, hung with Indian fabrics, to a miniature room at the top of the house, where luncheon for two was laid out in front of a lattice window. A peat fire burned in the open hearth, giving off a delicious smell. The room was cosy and comfortable in the extreme, and seemed to have the very definite atmosphere, unexpected in a shop, of belonging to one particular person. This was indeed the case. Sir Roderick (who had been born with an unerring instinct for living in the greatest available comfort, and who always seemed to know exactly how that comfort could be obtained with the least amount of trouble to himself) had, by dint of showering boyish charm upon the proprietress of the shop, appropriated this room to his own use, and the objects that were strewn about it in casual disorder belonged to him.

A guitar, that he could not play (lying beside a red leather gramophone that he could and did), a tasteful edition of *A la Recherche du Temps Perdu*, the complete works of Messrs Ronald Firbank and Aldous Huxley, together with reproductions of two of Picasso's better-known aquarelles, bore testimony to the fact that young

Sir Roderick liked to associate himself with modern culture. The possessor of keen eyes, however, observing some well used bridge markers, the masterpieces of Wallace, and a positive heap of society weekly journals, might suspect that the child was in no real danger at present of overtaxing his mind.

Amabelle, who had had many opportunities of drawing her own conclusions on these matters, sat down at the table and picked up an enormous bunch of orchids that lay beside her plate. 'Are these for me? Thank you, darling, so much.' During the excellent luncheon that followed Bobby chattered incessantly, telling her with immense gusto the latest scandals from London as viewed at Eton, generally through the prejudiced eyes of son or brother to the person concerned.

'By the way, Felton's sister, the pretty one, has run away with her chauffeur – did you know?'

'Barbara Casement? Really, darling, do be careful what you say; it sounds most unlikely to me. Are you quite certain?'

'Oh, yes, rather. Felton and I saw them driving through Slough together the day before yesterday. We rocked with laughter, I must say.'

'Well, people generally do drive with their chauffeurs, it's quite usual.'

'No, I promise it's true. Felton says she never could resist a peaked cap.'

'I can't believe it – those lovely babies, she couldn't leave them.'

'Oh, heavens,' said Bobby, suddenly whispering. 'The most awful thing – I quite forgot. Felton's people are down today and they're certain to be lunching in the next room. You can hear every word. Gosh, that's just about torn it.'

'We don't hear them, though.'

'I know. They never speak, that's why. But people always hear their own name, don't they? Isn't it too ghastly – what can we do?'

'Pretend I've got a dog here called Melton.'

'Oh, what a good idea. Lie down, Melton,' he shouted. 'Stop eating my bootlaces, you little devil. There, good boy, Melton – want a drinkie water?' He made loud noises intending to imitate a dog drinking until, overcome with hysteria, he and Amabelle were forced to bury their heads in cushions to smother the sound of their giggles. Presently they ascertained from the waitress, greatly to their mutual relief, that Sir Oswald and Lady Felton and their family had left about half an hour previously.

When the bill came, Bobby said, 'You can pay that, darling, if you'd like to. I don't see why I shouldn't trade on my status as a schoolboy for as long as I possibly can. All too soon I shall be the one to pay, and that will last to the end of my life, worse luck.'

'When are you leaving Eton for good?'

'I shall trail away clasping (we hope) my little leaving book and draped in my tiny Old Etonian tie at the end of the summer half, unless, of course, the beaks should happen to find out before then that you are my dentist, darling. Such bad teeth. But I don't expect they will, I'm hardly ever unlucky.'

'Is it settled what you're going to do after that?'

'Well, Mother keeps on droning about Sandhurst, but I fully intend to go to Oxford, and I usually get my own way with the old girl in the end, you know, so I expect it will be all right.'

Presently they went for a walk. It was a beautiful day, sunny and windy; little golden leaves like small coins, earnest of a treasury to come, blew about the school yard; one of those days at Eton when Windsor Castle has all the appearance of the better type of Victorian water-colour painting, clean, clear and romantic. Specimens of the British aristocrat in embryo were to be seen on every hand running, or lounging about the place in and out of 'change'. They were hideous, pathetic little boys for the most part, with one feature, whether nose, ears, chin, Adam's apple or eyebrows outstripping its fellows which, having apparently forgotten how to grow, were overshadowed quite by their monstrous neighbour. They all stared hard at Amabelle, whose beauty was of the obvious, mature description that children always admire, and looked enviously at Bobby. He was considered a bit of a masher by the younger ones; his own contemporaries, although for the most part quite fond of him, merely thought him an extremely funny joke.

As they strolled among those playing-fields whose connexion with the Battle of Waterloo had been cause for so much facetious comment, Amabelle said:

'How about this holiday tutor you mentioned in your last letter – has your mother engaged one yet, d'you think?'

'Not yet, thank goodness,' said Bobby sulkily. 'It is a bit hard, you know. I saw my sister, Philadelphia, last Sunday, she came over with darling Aunt Loudie, and she says that Mother is still quite determined to have one who will "get me out of doors". This out of doors idea is a perfect fetish with Mamma; she quite honestly believes that there is something wrong about being under a roof unless you have to be for purposes of eating or sleeping. Last summer hols were unbelievably horrible. I was made to be out of doors from dawn till dark, and then Mother and Uncle Ernest used quite often to drag me out after dinner and make me lay traps for crayfish. Cruel and boring it was.'

'I shouldn't be surprised if that's why you have such a lovely complexion; you ought to be very glad you're not like all these spotty little wretches.'

'I know,' said Bobby with alluring archness. 'But you see, I was born with that, anyhow, it's one of my natural attributes. But do say you think this tutor business is the last straw; it's such a ghastly idea.'

'Yes, in a way. But supposing it was somebody you liked very much yourself?'

'My dear, have you met many tutors?'

'Somebody you knew already – Paul Fotheringay, for instance.'

'Of course that would be heaven. But I can't quite imagine it happening, can you?'

Amabelle then expounded her plot.

When she had finished speaking Bobby cried in tones of high delight: 'It's a divine idea! You mean that Paul shall come to Compton Bobbin disguised as my tutor so that he can read up the old girl's journal without Mother knowing. Oh, yes, it's there all right, neatly bound in red morocco – it takes up a whole shelf of the library. I rather think there are some bags full of letters, too. How marvellous you are to think of it, darling. Oh, what heavenly fun it will be!' and Bobby vaulted over some fairly low railings and back, casting off for a moment his mask of elderly roué and slipping on that of a tiny-child-at-its-first-pantomime, another role greatly favoured by this unnatural boy. 'Only it's too awful to think you won't be there, joining in the riot.'

'Don't be too sure of that,' said Amabelle darkly.

'You're not coming too by any chance, disguised as my nanny?'

If Amabelle flinched inwardly at this remark she showed no signs of it and merely said, 'But why the disguise? As a matter of fact though I shall be in your neighbourhood then, because I've taken a little house for Christmas time which can't be very far from you – Mulberrie Farm.'

'Oh, it's not true! You haven't taken Mulberrie Farm, have you? It's only two miles from us. You *are* an angel, Amabelle. I say, though, have you seen it?'

'No, why? Is it horrible?'

'No, no,' said Bobby hastily, 'quite attractive. Very comfortable and all that. Tee-hee, though, this will ginger up the hols for me top-hole, it will. Do you really think you can persuade m'tutor to recommend Paul to Mother?'

Bobby's house-master was Amabelle's first cousin and one of her greatest friends.

'I can't see why not,' said Amabelle, 'because I honestly do think that Paul will have a very good influence on you.'

'Personally I can't imagine Paul having influence over man, woman or child.'

'Anyhow, it can do no harm and may do good, as Geoffrey said when he joined the Embassy Club. And as we are here I think I might as well go in and see Maurice about it now, so good-bye, darling, try to be good, and buy yourself some sausages with that, will you?'

Amabelle, as always, had her own way, and the upshot of her visit to Eton was that Bobby's house-master, Maurice Pringle, wrote off to Lady Bobbin highly recommending one Paul Fisher as holiday tutor to her son, Roderick.

'I am not actually acquainted with this young man, but I have received from mutual friends a most glowing account of his character and attainments, and I feel certain, from what I hear, that he is in every way qualified to fill your post. I understand that he is a particularly sportsmanlike young fellow, devoted to outdoor pursuits, and at the same time (which is important), a first-class coach. Should you wish to interview him, I shall be most happy to arrange this for you . . .'

Lady Bobbin, however, who was at that time busy hunting five days a week, did not wish to waste one of them by spending it in London, and engaged Mr Fisher by return of post with no mention of an interview. She merely remarked in her letter that he would be expected to ride, shoot and play golf with 'the boy', as well as to coach him in whatever subjects Mr Pringle might think advisable, and ended up by saying that Roderick would be hunting three days a week. Paul wondered with a shudder whether he would also be obliged to participate in this unnerving sport.

The five weeks which still remained before Christmas were unpleasantly strenuous ones for Paul. His mornings were spent clinging in a frenzy of fear to the backs of ancient hirelings in the Row, mild, drowsy animals which were in his eyes monsters of fire and speed, savagely awaiting an opportunity to hurl him to his doom. His afternoons, less fraught with actual danger than with the horror of an almost equally distressing boredom, alternated between a shooting school at Richmond and golf lessons in Putney. By the evening he could hardly either stand or see. He regarded himself, however, as a martyr in the cause of Art, and this sustained him. Marcella, piqued by a sudden cessation of his advances, was now seldom off the telephone, a state of things which would have seemed unbelievably blissful two or three weeks before. But, although he still fed her loyally at the Ritz every day, he was beginning, if the truth must be known, to find her beauty less maddening and her lack of intelligence more so than formerly.

5

Walter and Sally Monteath, accompanied by Miss Elspeth Paula Monteath, now an accredited member of the Church of England, and her nanny, travelled down to Gloucestershire by train a few days before Christmas. They had temporarily solved their always-pressing money troubles by letting their flat for a few weeks, during which time they intended to live entirely at Mrs Fortescue's expense, and by selling the ancient motor car. This had from the first proved to be more in the nature of a luxury than an economy, and latterly it had cost them endless money and bother owing to what Walter was pleased to call 'Sally's incurable habit of ploughing her way through human flesh'. Walter, while showing a greater respect for life where pedestrians were concerned, was all too much addicted to tearing mudguards, headlights and other gadgets from onrushing vehicles. In fact, the sale of the car was regarded by all their friends as an undisguised blessing, and they themselves were highly relieved to see the last of it.

'Isn't this too perfect,' said Sally as she settled herself into the corner seat of a first-class carriage. 'Now, just run along and buy me all the weekly papers, will you, darling. Oh, you have already. Thanks so much. Do you realize,' she added, opening the *Tatler* and throwing a copy of the *Sketch* over to Walter, 'that from this moment we literally shan't have to put hand to pocket for six whole weeks. It's a beautiful thought. Such a comfort too that Amabelle's taken a small house, so that there'll only be her and Jerome for Christmas presents. Yes, I got them on Monday, hankies. Quite nice and very cheap.'

'I must say I rather hope they won't retaliate with diamond links and things. D'you remember the Liberty boxes?' said Walter.

Two years before, Walter and Sally, then newly married, had spent Christmas with a millionaire and his wife. On Christmas Day Sally had duly presented them with chintz handkerchief and tie boxes from Liberty, which she had chosen with some care as being suitable gifts. Slight embarrassment had been felt even by the ordinarily shameless Monteaths when they were given in return enamel waistcoat buttons, gold cigarette and vanity cases, and a handbag with a real diamond clasp.

'Oh, I'm past minding about that sort of thing now,' said Sally cheerfully. 'I'm only so thankful Elspeth Paula did well at her christening, the angel. We ought to get quite a lot for that pearl necklace, and I suppose the mugs will fetch something. I say, here's the most ghastly photo of Paul and Marcella at a night club. Do look. Aren't they exactly like deep-sea monsters! What a girl!'

They were met at Woodford station by the beige Rolls-Royce, and on the door-step of Mulberrie Farm by Amabelle herself, exquisitely turned out in that type of garment which is considered suitable for *le sport* by dressmakers of the rue de la Paix.

'Thank God you've come at least,' she said in her gloomiest voice. 'Darling Sally, looking so lovely, the angel. Oh, Paula! Isn't she sweet? Well, come in. You won't like it, but I can only hope you'll be amused by it, that's all.'

'My dear Amabelle,' cried Walter in tones of horror as he followed her into the hall, 'what a house!'

'Yes, you don't have to tell me that; I've been here now for a week, kindly remember. And do you know that from what the agents said I honestly thought it was going to be really old and attractive. They never stopped talking about its old-world charm, mullioned windows, oak beams and so on. Look at it – how could I have guessed it would be anything like this?'

'You just made the mistake,' said Walter soothingly, 'of confusing old world with olde worlde. You should have been more careful to find out whether or not there was an "e"; so much hangs on that one little letter. In any case, I must submit, with all deference, that the very name of the house, Mulberrie Farm, ought to have aroused your worst suspicions. I never heard anything so art and craft in my life, and I bet the yokels have no idea it's called that, they probably knew it as The Grange before all these inglenooks and things were put in. You must be crackie-boo, poor sweet, to go and take a house you've never even seen.'

'Don't tease her,' said Sally. 'I think it's divinely funny; just like those Paris res-taurants made for Americans that we saw on our honeymoon.'

'I think it's very beautiful, Amabelle. I didn't know so much crooked wood existed in the world. I wonder if it was the architect's wife who bored all those worm-holes in her spare time instead of knitting jumpers. Oh, I say, too, look at the way the doors open. You just pull that little string and walk in – I do call that a dainty thought. And I adore that ironwork that looks like cardboard meant to look like ironwork; a very original touch that is. Now, I think, if you don't mind me saying so, that you ought to send up to Soloman's for some rushes to strew about the floor; then, when you've hung a couple of Fortmason hams on to those hooks in the ceiling and dressed all your servants in leathern jerkins, you'll have arrived at the true atmosphere of Ye. If I think of any other homey touches I'll let you know. It's no trouble at all to me.'

'Shut up, Walter, you fool,' said Sally. 'Anyhow, I'm sure it's a very comfortable little house.'

'That's what everybody says,' wailed Amabelle. 'Personally, I could never feel comfortable in a hideous place like this. However, now we're here I suppose we must make the best of it. Sit down, angels, and you shall have some cocktails in a minute.'

Presently Walter said: 'And how d'you think you'll enjoy life in the country, Amabelle?'

'Well, it will be better now you've come, but I can't describe to you what I've suffered so far. Frankly, I doubt whether I shall be impelled to settle down here for good, which was rather my idea in taking this house, although I suppose I shall have to stay on till the end of the lease because of Jerome saying, "I told you so." The old boy was dead right, just the same.'

'Why, what's happened? You've been bored, I suppose?'

'I've nearly gone mad, that's all. Everything seems to be so queer and awful. To begin with, the lonely wolds I was so excited about are no more wolds than my hat. Ordinary fields full of mud, that's what they are. And as for their being lonely I never heard such bosh; they are covered with cows and awful staring men in filthy clothes and huge motor things which drive slowly up and down them. And in any case I think it's dangerous to go out alone here. Only yesterday I came across the bodies of two dear little rabbits which must have been killed by some lynch-maniac. It's terrifying to think there are such men wandering about. I brought the poor mites home and gave them decent burial in the garden.'

'The lynch-maniac must have been delighted when he came back for his dinner,' said Sally. She had spent her childhood in the country. Walter remarked that the amount of sadism among the lower classes was truly terrible.

'Now, listen, Sally,' went on Amabelle. 'You've lived in the country – I want you to tell me what people do all day. I simply can't find anything to occupy myself with. Your mother, for instance, what does she do?'

'Let me think now. She always seems to be extremely busy. For one thing she grows a lot of bulbs in the winter, in a dark place.'

'Don't forget to add that they always get immensely tall and thin and finally bend over like croquet hoops,' said Walter spitefully. He was not devoted to his mother-in-law.

'Be quiet. They are very pretty.'

'But that can't take up much time,' said Amabelle. 'What I want to know is how do people fill all those hours every day; there seem to be twice as many here as there are in London.'

'Mother, of course, takes a lot of exercise, walks and so on. And every morning she puts on a pair of black silk drawers and a sweater and makes indelicate gestures on the lawn. That's called Building the Body Beautiful. She's mad about it.'

'And is it really beautiful – her body, I mean?' Amabelle asked with some show of interest.

'It's all right, I think. I never really look at it much. Then, of course, she does some gardening.'

'I thought of that myself, but when I got into the garden I couldn't see anything to do. There were no flowers at all, either, only some dying chrysanthemums.'

'I think flowers are so vulgar,' said Walter. 'It sounds a nice garden to me.'

'And she orders the food every morning.'

'Oh, I could never do that, the cook would give notice at once.'

'And she's district commissioner for the Girl Guides.'

'I can't quite see myself in khaki shorts,' said Amabelle. 'I think I must be resigned to playing the gramophone and gossiping. When Jerome and Bobby arrive there'll be some bridge for you, Walter. By the way, Major Stanworth is dining here to-night.'

'Who's he?'

'A sweet man, one of my neighbours. I met him in a field yesterday opening up a dead ewe to see what she died of. It was very interesting, we made great friends at once. I expect we ought really to go and have our baths; dinner is at eight-thirty.'

Major Stanworth, whose alien presence that evening Walter and Sally had rather dreaded, turned out to be a charming person. At the beginning of dinner he seemed shy and silent, but Walter presently let loose a perfect flood of conversation by saying: 'And what was the matter with the dead ewe? I gather you were having an autopsy when Amabelle came along the other day. I hope there was no suspicion of foul play?'

Major Stanworth shook his head sadly. 'Nearly as bad, I fear,' he said; 'she was suffering from a disease known as the fluke, and once that gets among our sheep it is a knockout blow to us farmers. However, as that is the only case I have had so far I must hope for the best.'

'Oh, yes, I know,' said Walter brightly; 'fluke and mouth. I've heard of that before, but I thought only foxhounds had it.'

The major looked rather surprised, and was about to speak when Sally said, 'Don't pay any attention to Walter, he's as ignorant as a bat, poor sweet. I remember quite well when one of our farmers at home was nearly ruined by the fluke; it's a horrible scourge. Something to do with the sheep's liver, isn't it?'

'The fluke,' said Major Stanworth, sipping his sherry, 'is really a small insect. It has the most curious and interesting life history – I wonder whether you would care to hear it?'

'Indeed we would,' said Walter enthusiastically. 'I always think that one half of the world knows too little of how the other half lives.'

Thus encouraged, Major Stanworth proceeded:

'The fluke begins life as a little worm. It is born into the sheep's liver and there it reaches maturity, marries, and has an inordinate number of children,' he paused impressively, '*totally* different from itself.'

'How extraordinary,' said Amabelle.

'I don't think so at all,' said Sally. 'Look at Elspeth Paula.'

'These children,' continued the major, 'are almost immediately passed out by the sheep and find their way, as soon as may be, into the lung of – the water snail. Here they in their turn marry, reach maturity, and in due course have an inordinate number of children *totally* different from themselves.'

'What a romance!' said Walter. 'And pray where are the next wedding bells to be heard?'

'In the snail's liver. The children who were born in its lung find their way to the liver, where they reach maturity, marry, and have an inordinate number of children *totally* different from themselves, who are passed out of the snail, on to a blade of grass, and so back once more into the sheep's liver.'

'Well, I do call that a tasteful roundelay,' said Walter.

Sally choked.

'Have some fish,' said Amabelle, tactfully changing the subject. 'It is very good for the brain. I have seen it reported that Lloyd George eats great quantities of fish.'

'No fish, thank you,' said the major.

'When does your little boy begin his holidays?' asked Amabelle. Major Stanworth was a widower with an only son. His wife had died the preceding year.

'Comes back tomorrow.'

'Do you go down often and see him at his school?'

'About twice a term, you know. Unsettles the boy if one goes oftener. As a matter of fact I went down last week for the annual sports, and rather a ghastly thing happened. The father of one of the boys died in the fathers' race – just collapsed, poor chap, and died. We carried him into the gymnasium – he was a stoutish cove, too – but it was no good; he was quite dead before the doctor could get at him even.'

'What an awful thing,' said Amabelle. She was arriving at an age which no longer regards death as a funny joke.

'At my private,' said Walter, 'we had a most handy little cemetery for the fathers, just behind the cricket pav. But of course, we had a fathers' three-legged race which used to finish them off in shoals. I have even known them die at the prize-giving, from shock, I suppose, if their boys got prizes.'

'Not a bad idea that about the cemetery, what?' said the major. 'I always have said "where the oak falls, there let it lie". This poor bloke was lugged off to Suffolk in a motor hearse, I believe.'

'Why *oak*, I wonder?' said Walter. 'Why not sycamore or monkey puzzle?'

Amabelle frowned at him and asked Major Stanworth whether he had been hunting that winter.

'I have been, of course, but this beastly foot and mouth has stopped us for the present. However, Lady Bobbin tells me that if there's no fresh outbreak we should be able to start again in about ten days' time, she thinks.'

'Is Lady Bobbin a good Master?'

'Foul mouthed, very foul mouthed, you know. Scares all the young 'uns out of their wits, but she's very good with the farmers, they understand her. Do you hunt, Monteath?'

'I love it,' said Walter. 'Unfortunately, I only did it once. Before that I used to write articles in the newspapers saying that it was cruel and ought to be stopped and so on. But when I found out what jolly fun it is I gave that up in no time.'

'Oh, well done, splendid. Still, I mean to say, you couldn't really call it cruel, now, could you? Ever seen an old dog fox hunted out of covert on a fine sunny morning? Crafty old devil, he enjoys it right enough. I know he does.'

'I'm perfectly certain he doesn't,' said Walter. 'But that's not the point. The point is that I do, so I very soon stopped writing the articles and spent the money I got for them on a pair of topboots. But it was an awful waste really, because since then I've never had another opportunity to hunt.'

'Oh, but I call that good! Now, I'll tell you what, Monteath, as soon as this something foot and mouth has stopped I'll lend you a horse. Yes, yes, it would be a pleasure – I've got more than I can ride myself as it is. And besides that I'll give you a ride in the point-to-point, if you like.'

'No, thank you,' said Sally, firmly intervening. 'I've got nicely used to being married to Walter now. There was a time when I thought the only ideal state would be that of widowhood, but now, what with the shortage of marrying men and one thing and another, I'm not at all sure about it. I believe I should miss the old boy a whole heap, you know. Besides, I need a man's help with the little one. And Walter popped his riding boots last week.'

The major winked at Walter and announced that he himself was a prominent member of the husbands' union, and would see fair play. This remark scarcely seemed, in view of his own recent widowhood, to be in the best of taste, and was received in a somewhat embarrassed silence. This he broke himself by asking Amabelle how she had enjoyed her visit to old Mrs Cole that morning.

'Rather moderately, to tell you the truth,' said Amabelle. 'She looked so sweet and picturesque in her garden, feeding the chickens, that I simply had to go in; but poor old thing she is filthy, isn't she? However, that can't be her fault, because when I asked if I could send her anything from here she said she'd like some soap. So I sent some along at once, and I only hope she uses it.'

The major began to laugh.

'Are you sure it was soap she asked for?' he said.

'Quite sure. Yes, of course, what else could it have been?'

'How about soup?'

'Soup? Oh, no, it wasn't soup; it was soap all right, I'm certain.'

'Well, you're wrong. She asked for soup, as a matter of fact.'

'My dear! I mean my dear Major Stanworth, how awful, I sent soap.'

'Yes, I know you did. And the big joke is that the poor old soul thought that you had sent soup tablets, so she boiled one for her dinner. The story was all round the village this afternoon. Leverett, my cowman, told me.'

'Oh,' said Amabelle, in tones of deep dismay. 'Soup! Yes, I see. But I shall have to leave for London at once, shan't I? I couldn't stay on here after doing a thing like that. How awful!'

'Now, Mrs Fortescue, don't you worry about it. I would never have told you, only I thought it was too good a joke for you to miss.'

'I quite agree,' said Walter.

'Joke!' cried Amabelle faintly.

'Besides, I've fixed it all right for you. I went round to see her and took a couple of rabbits and told her that you were a bit hard of hearing. She was as pleased as Punch.'

'Yes, but the other people in the village must think I'm such a monster.'

'Oh, no, they're all frightfully pleased. They hate old Granny Coles like fifteen different kinds of hell because in hot weather she uses the village water supply for her garden and nobody else can get any.'

'She certainly doesn't use it for any other purpose. But it is a bit embarrassing because that's the second awful thing I've done here already.'

'What's the first?'

'The parson came to call, you see, and asked me if I would give a pound towards the bier – he said they wanted if possible to collect forty pounds for it. I said I would give five pounds, and then I thought it would be polite to take a little interest, so I asked who was going to drink all that beer. What made it worse was that he thought I was trying to be funny, and he was fearfully annoyed.'

6

Compton Bobbin is one of those houses which abound in every district of rural England, and whose chief characteristic is that they cannot but give rise, on first sight, to a feeling of depression in any sensitive observer. Nevertheless, a large, square and not unhandsome building, it bears testimony, on closer acquaintance, to the fact that it has in the past been inhabited by persons of taste and culture. But these persons have been so long dead, and the evidences of their existence have been so adequately concealed by the generations which succeeded them, that their former presence in the place is something to be supposed rather than immediately perceived. Supposed, however with some degree of certainty after a sojourn, however short, with their descendants.

It must have been, for instance, a person of taste who introduced the Chinese Chippendale mirror now hanging where only housemaids can see it in the back passage, the tails and wings of its fantastic birds sadly cracked and broken, victims of the late Sir Hudson Bobbin's addiction as a child to indoor cricket. For whom, if not for a person of taste, did Fragonard paint those pastorals, now so dirty and neglected as to be little more than squares of blackened canvas, and which must be examined in the strongest light if the grace of their composition is even faintly to emerge? They hang unnoticed in dark corners of a spare dressing-room. Again, whose were the negro slave boys in black and gold wood with which the Bobbin children have for generations terrified a new governess, and who now inhabit the big lumber-room? Whose the Hepplewhite chairs on which the servants place their underclothes at night? Whose the Venetian glass chandelier, ruined by electric wiring carelessly and locally performed, which hangs, draped in dust sheets, in the disused ballroom? Whose the enamelled snuff-boxes, whose the Waterford glass jumbled together with so much horrible junk in glass-fronted cupboards on the landing? And, oh! to whom belonged the Empire crown of blue diamonds and pink pearls, transformed in 1910, the year of her marriage, into the brooch, bracelet and two rings which now adorn the unpleasing bosom, wrist and fingers of Gloria the present Lady Bobbin?

Persons of taste there have been. The eighteenth-century statue of Apollo, hidden quite by dowdy evergreens; the domed temple on the island in the lake; the lake itself; the rococo bridge whose curious humped shapes are only permitted to appear beneath a tangle of ivy; the walled garden with its Italian gates and sundial; the classical lay-out of trees in the park; all testify to their charming and cultured existence. And after them persons some of whose taste might, not edify perhaps, but at any rate amuse. Those who bought the gay and touching little chintzes, beaded fire-screens, Stafford pottery, Berlin wool-work, gaudy flower paintings, and many strange products of a budding Empire; those who crowned a ram's head with silver and cairngorms and set it in triumph upon the mahogany sideboard. It is sad that of their possessions only the stuffiest should remain, nothing that might amuse, much that must appal. Stained glass windows, for instance, in each clouded amber pane of which leaps fierily the ruby Bobdgin, that legendary creature half unicorn half jackal from which the family (perhaps) derives its name. The hideous furniture and stuffy curtains in the dining-room, the stamped leather chairs and table in the study, the embossed wallpaper in the passages, and – let us speak of it quickly and never think of it again – the feudal fireplace with its load of heraldry in the hall. These, characteristically enough, remain, suffering in their turn and rendered even more horrible than they would otherwise appear by modern lighting, modern arrangement, and the exile to the boxroom of their jaunty fellows so patently designed to brighten their gloomy aspect.

The châtelaine of Compton Bobbin sat, a few days before Christmas, reading the *Morning Post* beneath the prancing Bobdgins. It was to her, or rather to the talent of her forebears in picking and packing the strongest brand of Indian tea, that the Bobdgins owed their continued existence, for it is hardly to be supposed that any alien purchaser of the house would have tolerated for long those active little creatures. Lady Bobbin was the type of woman best described by that single adjective so explicit of its own dreary meaning, 'plain'. As a girl she had been the greatest heiress of her time and even then nobody could find a happier epithet with which to describe her looks than 'handsome', and that to the loudly expressed mystification of those of her fellow débutantes whose faces were their fortunes. At forty-five she was tall and thin but heavy of movement, her fuzzy hair uncut, her muddy skin unaided by any condiment, and with a voice like the worst sort of loud-speaker, imitating and aggressive and perpetually at work. She was without any kind of grace, either mental or physical.

At twenty-four she had married Sir Hudson Bobbin, a weak but rather charming character. To those who knew her it was a perpetual mystery, not indeed that she had married at all, as, but for the packages of tea, it must have been; but that having married she should have produced children of such charm and beauty as were possessed by her son Roderick and her daughter Philadelphia. She herself, if she had ever considered their undoubted attractiveness, would have felt it to be profoundly unimportant. (Actually, in her eyes, Roderick was merely a tiresome little schoolboy and Philadelphia a pert and disagreeable girl.) She knew that every woman has in life two main duties, to marry well and to produce a son and heir; having achieved both it was of no consequence to her whether or not the marriage was a happy one or the heir a young man of looks and distinction. Except for one terrible period, when between the sinking of Sir Hudson in the *Lusitania* and the birth of Roderick, she had been submitted to the suspense of not knowing whether the child would indeed prove to be of the required male sex, she had never known much disquietude on the score of her family life. Her daughter, beyond the initial disappointment caused by her sex, had never interested her at all, her one wish in that direction being that Philadelphia should marry as quickly and as advantageously as possible. The only thing which afforded her a real and lasting satisfaction was her pack of foxhounds. These meant to her what husband, children or artistic expression may mean to other women; they were her vanity and her delight. A hard day's hunting was to her the most exquisite of joys, and when this happiness was rendered temporarily impossible by frost, flood, or, as at present, an outbreak of foot and mouth disease in the district, her bitterness of spirit would be beyond all bounds; she would be as one mourning the untimely loss of a beloved, shut up within herself and inaccessible to sympathy.

Philadelphia Bobbin balanced a few pieces of rather dreary holly on the frame of her great-grandmother's portrait by W. Etty.

'And now,' she said, getting down from the chair on which she had been standing and viewing without satisfaction the results of her handiwork, 'I suppose I had better go and meet this hellish tutor. God, how I do hate Christmas.'

'Don't speak like that, Philadelphia,' said Lady Bobbin sharply, looking up from her perusal of the *Morning Post*, a perusal which at present was a daily torture to her since it consisted entirely in reading about the good runs of other packs of hounds which, more fortunate than hers, were not haunted by the grim spectre of foot and mouth disease. 'May I ask what else you want to be doing at this particular moment? The truth is you never do a hand's turn for anybody except yourself – self, self, self with you, all day long. You ought to be very grateful to have a motor car of your own instead of making all this fuss when you are asked, occasionally, to do some little errand for me with it. Another time I will hire a car when Fred is away. I would much sooner do that than have all these complaints. And if you're going to be in such a disgustingly bad temper, I'll thank you to keep to yourself and not spoil Christmas for everybody else. It is a time which means a great deal to some of us, I may tell you.'

'Oh, all right,' said Philadelphia. 'I can't see that having a car is anything to be so grateful for, even the butcher's boy has one, you know. And I wasn't grumbling at having to take it out; I just hate meeting strangers, that's all. What on earth am I to talk to him about all the way from Woodford?'

'It's quite unnecessary for you to talk. I suggest that you should occupy yourself with driving rather more carefully than you usually do round those Hogrush corners. The man is being paid to teach your brother, not to talk to you, and I may say, whilst we are on this subject, that one of the chief reasons why I engaged a tutor these holidays is that I am not anxious for you to see a great deal of Roderick just at present. He is going through a very tiresome phase indeed, quite beyond himself with all this nonsense about not caring to go into the army and so on. I only hope that this tutor (who is, I understand, a sportsmanlike young fellow) will be able to make him see sense and get him out of doors a bit. You'd better go now, or you'll be late for that train – don't forget to ask if there are any packing cases for me at the station.'

Philadelphia stumped out of the room, banging the door as loudly as she dared, dragged on an old fur coat, fetched her car from the garage, and drove at a perfectly reckless speed to Woodford Station, where she found to her further annoyance that she was a quarter of an hour too early for the train. It was a clear night after a day of drenching rain, and as she sat looking through the open window of her car at a tiny new moon surrounded by twinkling stars and listening to the distant church bells practising, no doubt, their Christmas peal, her temper gradually improved. By the time that she heard the train approaching, so far off at first that the noise it made seemed almost to come from inside her own head, she was feeling quite well disposed towards the world in general. Presently the noise of the train grew much louder, then stopped altogether, and she knew that it had arrived at the next station. At last it came puffing through the tunnel, all lights and bustle. She could see people reading or sleeping behind the misted glass of the windows, and a man, probably, she thought, the tutor, taking luggage down from the rack. There was a long pause, then as the train heaved itself, groaning and creaking, towards its destination, a porter came up to the car with two suitcases, followed by a small young man who was fumbling in his pockets, no doubt for change.

'Are you Mr Fisher?' said Philadelphia. 'I'm Philadelphia Bobbin. How do you do?'

'Excuse me, miss,' said the porter; 'there are two large packing cases for her ladyship. Will you take them now?'

'No, thank you,' said Philadelphia. 'They can wait.'

'I'm so sorry you had all the bother of turning out on such a cold evening,' said Paul as they drove away.

'It doesn't matter in the least; I love driving. The chauffeur's wife is in hospital and he's gone to be with her, and Bobby went out after lunch to see an Eton friend who lives near here and he isn't back yet. I expect he's found some sort of gambling, bridge or backgammon. You know Bobby, do you?'

Paul wondered whether she was in the secret and decided that she was not. 'Yes, I have met him once or twice. Have you any more brothers and sisters?'

'No, thank goodness. I expect we should have had, only father was drowned, you see, just before Bobby was born. But on Christmas Eve all my aunts and uncles and cousins come for a week, with masses of children, so the house will be quite full.' She said this almost apologetically, as though she thought that Paul might otherwise feel bored.

'Nice uncles and aunts?'

'Oh, not too bad on the whole. Uncle Ernest Leamington Spa is rather a trial because he always has such jolly ideas for a Merry Yule, but nobody pays much attention to him.'

'Do you live down here always?' He looked at a face which seemed to him, in the faintly reflected headlights of an oncoming car, to fall very little short of perfect beauty.

'Yes, we do,' she said abruptly. 'Nobody knows how horrible it is to live in the country always, you might just as well be in prison. I hate the country.'

'Would you prefer London?'

'Well, I went to London once for the season; I was coming out, you know, and I can't say I enjoyed it very much, but there must be other sorts of life there that I should enjoy.'

'Why do you think that?'

'One knows certain things about oneself.'

'You ought to marry,' said Paul. 'Girls are always happier married, I believe.'

'So my mother tells me,' said Philadelphia drily. She looked at him as though she had remembered that he was a stranger and her brother's tutor, and said no more. Presently they separated, Paul to make his first entrance into Compton Bobbin and Philadelphia to put her car away in the garage.

When he saw her again in the drawing-room before dinner he thought that she was not really as beautiful as she had seemed to be at first. Her features were certainly very good, her eyes large and of a remarkably bright blue colour; but her hair, complexion and clothes were dull and looked uncared-for. This he thought must be due to the fact that she evidently had no idea of how to (as the French say) arrange herself. A London girl with far less to go upon in the way of looks would have made twice as good an effort. He decided that she had better be handed over to Amabelle's care as soon as possible.

As Bobby had not yet put in an appearance, Lady Bobbin said that they would not wait, and began dinner without him. Half-way through the meal he strolled into the dining-room in day clothes and said 'How *are* you?' in his most affected manner to Paul, winking at him with the eye away from Lady Bobbin. 'Sorry, mother,' he added as he took his place at the head of the table.

'Is it quite necessary to be so unpunctual for meals?' inquired Lady Bobbin in her most rasping tone of voice. 'And I think I have mentioned before that I insist upon you dressing for dinner. I can remember my dear father telling me that even when he was on one of his most strenuous safaris in the African bush he *never* omitted to dress for dinner.'

'Well, but we're not in the African bush now, are we?' said Bobby with his mouth full.

There seemed to be no reply to this piece of logic. Lady Bobbin turned to Paul with an air of effusion obviously intended to accentuate her displeasure with her son and said, 'You come here at a very unlucky moment, Mr Fisher; our hunting has been stopped by an outbreak of foot and mouth disease on the edge of my country. I am glad to say that we are allowed to hack about in this district, but of course, nothing can make up for the season being spoilt in this way, just when the weather is so beautifully open too. It is really heartbreaking. You do hunt, I fancy?'

'No, no,' said Paul, who was bent on making a good impression; 'I hack, though.'

Lady Bobbin took this to mean that the tutor had no clothes for hunting, and nodded graciously.

'And of course,' Paul went on, 'I love to see others hunt. But how rotten about the foot and mouth – so wretched for the poor cows, too.'

'What cows?'

'The ones with feet and mouths.'

'Oh, the cows,' said Lady Bobbin vaguely. 'But they're all right. The Government slaughters them at once; humanely, too. The terrible thing about it is the way it stops hunting. Of course, it's quite obvious to me that it's all done by the Bolsheviks.'

'Now, really, Mother, what do you mean by that?' said Bobby impatiently.

'Florence Prague was saying only yesterday, and I am perfectly certain she is right, that the Bolsheviks are out to do anything they can which will stop hunting. They know quite well, the devils, that every kind of sport, and especially hunting, does more to put down Socialism than all the speeches in the world, so, as they can't do very much with that R.S.V.P. nonsense, they go about spreading foot and mouth germs all over the countryside. I can't imagine why the Government doesn't take active steps; it's enough to make one believe that they are in the pay of these brutes themselves. Too bad, you know.'

'Never mind,' said Bobby, throwing a look of mock despair in the direction of Paul, who sat open-mouthed at this theory; 'the great thing is that we are allowed to hack.'

'Yes, you can hack to within a radius of five miles of Woodford. Oh, I don't fancy you will want for occupation; the golf course is in excellent order, I believe. You are very fond of golf, I hear, Mr Fisher?'

'Yes, indeed, I love nothing more than golf. In fact, I am devoted to everything in the way of open-air sports, even hiking and biking. So long as I can be out of doors, away from stuffy houses, I am perfectly happy.'

Lady Bobbin looked at him with approval. 'Then you will like the life here, Mr Fisher. It is a pity you do not hunt, but you can ride all day; there are plenty of horses to be exercised while the foot and mouth continues.'

Bobby, who hated to be ignored by anybody, even his mother, for long, now tried to ingratiate himself by asking, very politely, if everything was quite as it should be in the village.

'I'm sorry to say that we've had a good deal of trouble lately,' she answered. 'The new parson has proved far from satisfactory, far. Very high church indeed. I should not be at all surprised to find that he is in the pay of Rome, his services are nothing but lace and smells and all that nonsense about changing clothes every now and then. In fact, I have been obliged to give up going to church here at all. It is monstrous that this living is not in our gift. Why should some Oxford college choose a parson for us? I have written to the dear bishop about it, but I fear that he is powerless to intervene.'

'I say, that's too bad,' murmured Bobby, mentally resolving that he would go to church next Sunday.

'Another thing,' continued Lady Bobbin, 'which is causing me great anxiety is this new law allowing people to marry their uncles. It is a perfect scandal, I consider. Three of our women have done it already. It is really most discouraging just when one was beginning to hope and think that morals were improving in the village at last.'

'But if it's allowed by law, surely it cannot be immoral?' said Bobby, in just that reasonable tone of voice which he knew would annoy his mother most.

'It is immoral – immoral and disgusting. That sort of thing can't be made right just by passing a few laws, you know. Besides, the Church will never countenance it. The dear bishop came to lunch not long ago, and he was saying, and of course I entirely agreed with him, dear, good old man, that a measure of this kind must be the ruin of family relationships.'

'On the contrary,' said Bobby, 'I think it will ginger things up top-hole. I expect that Philadelphia already begins to look on Uncle Ernest in a new and far more fascinating light, don't you, Delphie? I must say I'm looking forward to some very matey doings this Christmas.'

'Bobby!' said his mother sharply, 'you are not to talk like that. Please get on with your food; we are all waiting for you. Silly little schoolboys like you can't be expected to understand these things, but it is unnecessary and not in the least clever to make flippant remarks about them. Mr Fisher, I am sure, will agree with me.'

'Yes, indeed I do,' said Paul fervently. 'I can't think of a single one of my aunts whom I wouldn't sooner be dead than married to.'

'That, if I may be allowed to say so, is very much beside the point, Mr Fisher. In any case, I don't feel at all certain that aunts are allowed. I rather fancy it is uncles only. Why they want to pass such filthy laws I cannot imagine, but there, it's so like the Government. They waste their time over useless and even harmful measures of that sort, and do absolutely nothing to wipe out Bolshevism. I said as much to our member, Sir Joseph Jenkins, last time he was here, and he quite agreed with me. A very sound man, Sir Joseph,' she added, turning to Paul; 'very much interested in all questions of drainage, sanitation, and so on – in fact, I believe he is nearly always chairman of drains committees in the House.'

'Ah,' said Paul.

There was a silence. Bobby began to giggle, but was fortunately able to conceal this fact from his mother, as there was a large bowl of holly on the table between them. Paul looked self-consciously into space, wondering whether or not he should mention passing angels, and Philadelphia took a second large helping of steamed pudding with hot plum jam. Presently Lady Bobbin spoke again.

'By the way, children, I went over to see Florence Prague this afternoon. She has quite recovered from that nasty little toss she took, but poor old Sagrada strained a ligament and has had to be put down.'

Bobby and Philadelphia made suitable comments upon this piece of news, and Lady Bobbin continued:

'Florence and I had a long chat about your holidays, and we agreed that as there is to be no hunt ball this winter it would be a good idea for me to give a little dance here for you both. I had been thinking of it for some time, but I thought that perhaps it would be wrong, in view of the present crisis, to spend money on pure amusement. Florence, however, says very sensibly that so long as we have neither champagne nor a proper band there could be no great harm in it, and of course it would give an immense amount of pleasure.'

'Not, I may say, to me,' remarked Bobby sourly. 'My dear Mother, I really don't know what you can be thinking of. How can you possibly have a dance without either champagne or a band?'

'Of course you can, perfectly well. There is a young man in Woodford, the butcher's son, who plays dance music very nicely; he would play all night, I am told, for thirty shillings, and I suppose even in these days everyone likes a good cider cup. The truth is, Roderick, that you are too disgustingly spoilt for words. It is perfectly sickening trying to make plans for your amusement, because one knows quite well beforehand that nothing will be right and that you will grumble unceasingly at whatever is arranged. I said so to Florence Prague this afternoon. I said: "Now, Florence, you'll see I shall get no thanks for all this from Roderick, nothing but complaints." But all the same I see no reason why, just because you happen to have these large ideas, Philadelphia and all the other young people in the neighbourhood should be deprived of their fun. I'm afraid, my boy, that you will soon find out that nowadays it's a question between taking what is offered in the way of amusement and going without it. Very few people now can afford unlimited champagne, and even if they could such extravagance would be most harmful and unpatriotic, just the very sort of thing that breeds Socialism in the country.'

Everyone now looked embarrassed. Bobby turned crimson with annoyance, but did not dare answer back, and Paul said, helpfully but tactlessly: 'Why not have champagne cocktails instead? They are very economical, because you need only buy the cheapest sort of champagne, to which you add a little brandy and sugar, and people do seem to like them most awfully.'

'No, Mr Fisher, no cocktails in this house, thank you. I regard the cocktail habit as a most pernicious and disgusting one. Besides, people get rowdy enough on champagne alone, without adding brandy to it. Why, last year, at Lady Jenkins' party, the most disgraceful things happened. I actually saw that awful Hood boy, at supper, cramming a sausage down his ear, for a bet, I suppose. Perfectly revolting, we don't want that sort of behaviour at Compton Bobbin. No, we will have good British beer and cider cup, quite sufficient for young people. Nobody need be half drunk before they can enjoy themselves, or at least I should very much hope not.'

And Lady Bobbin rose with majesty to leave the dining-room. It will be noticed that during this entire meal Philadelphia Bobbin never once opened her mouth to speak. She was a silent girl.

7

After dinner it was quite kindly indicated to Paul that he was expected to retire to the schoolroom, which he did with alacrity, most willing to exchange the physical presence of Gloria Lady Bobbin for the intellectual proximity of her predecessor. He knew that the thoughtful Bobby, who showed him the way to his appointed sanctuary, had hidden all the fourteen volumes of Lady Maria's journal and a vast quantity of her letters behind the schoolroom radiator; a spot less calculated than might, perhaps, be imagined to harm the precious documents, the central heating apparatus at Compton Bobbin never having been known to affect the temperature of the atmosphere by so much as one degree.

The moment he was alone Paul fell, with a thrill of the most exquisite antici-pation, upon his prize. The journal consisted of large manuscript volumes handsomely bound in red morocco. Lady Maria's handwriting was small but very legible, and of an extreme neatness, not one correction or erasure appearing in any of the pages that Paul looked at. After browsing indiscriminately for a while, examining the little water-colour drawings that were interspersed among the text, Paul settled down to read the fifth volume, which began with the following words:

Jan. 1st, 1878.
Another year, with its store of tribulations and sufferings, its trials and griev-ous disappointments, is now before us. Thought much last night, while listening to the New Year bells, of the Dear Dead, and was thankful for all they will have been spared. Felt how *willingly* I could join them should the Call come to me. As Mr Landor has said, so truly and so touchingly, 'I warmed both hands before the Fire of Life, it sinks, and I am ready to depart.' Thought of Dearest Papa and all his sufferings so patiently borne, and of the Loved Grave at Margate. Prayed for strength in the coming year that I and my Dear Ones may be able to bear everything that is in store for us. (N.B. – Must remember to tell Mrs Craven that the beef was overdone yesterday. It makes Josiah so very sad and angry when this is the case, and I feel that it must be *quite* unnecessary.) As I write poor Ivanhoe lies at my feet. Dear faithful beast, I fear that he may not be spared to see many more New Years; how dreary, how different this house will seem without the feeble, friendly wag of his old weatherbeaten tail . . .

Hardly had Paul read so far when Bobby came back into the room, shut the door and settled himself down by the fire in the evident anticipation of a good gossip.
'Look here, old top,' he said, 'put down great-grandmamma for a few minutes

and listen to a very natty piece of news. No, really, something too incredible is going to happen.'

'Oh, is it? What?'

'My cousin Michael Lewes is coming to stay here tomorrow for a fortnight.'

'What is there incredible about that? Your sister told me in the car that all your aunts and uncles and cousins were coming for Christmas.'

'Oh, didn't you know? Why, Michael left England three years ago and got a post in Cairo simply because of Amabelle, because she refused to marry him. She was the love of his life. He's only been home for exactly a week, and now he'll find himself in the next house to her – you must say it's pretty odd. They're bound to meet.'

'They may not.'

'Likely tale! I shall certainly make it my business to see that they do,' he added mischievously, giving Paul the benefit of that smile with which he had already launched, as it were, a thousand ships.

'Good gracious,' said Paul suddenly, forgetting to smile back and shutting up Lady Maria's journal with a bang. 'Lord Lewes. Yes, of course I remember all about it now. I'd no idea he was any relation to you though.'

'My first cousin. Father's sisters all married well, as it happens, which leaves me quite nicely connected.'

'You're a damned little snob.'

'I know; I glory in it.'

'Oh, you do, do you? Tell me some more about your cousin though. How old is he now?'

'Michael is thirty-two or -three I suppose. Amabelle's what? Nearly forty-five should you think? He was crazy about her, I believe, begged and implored her to marry him, but the old girl had too much sense to do that. And anyway she was frightfully bored by the whole affair. I don't wonder either. Michael's awfully sweet, you know, but not exactly a hero of romance.'

'What did his people think of it?' asked Paul.

'His father and mother are both dead, you know. My mother got hold of the wrong end of the stick, as she always does, and thought that poor darling Amabelle was a scheming old tart trying to lure him into her clutches. But Michael settled the whole thing himself by getting another post abroad when he saw that she was determined not to marry him.'

'D'you think he'll have got over it by now?'

'Would one ever get over being in love with Amabelle?' said Bobby sententiously. 'I doubt it. I don't imagine Michael would anyway; he took it very hard at the time; besides, he's a sentimental old thing. It's lucky you happen to be an author, Paul, my boy. This house is going to be a perfect hotbed of copy for the next week or two. Another frightfully funny thing has happened, by the way. Mamma has left cards on Amabelle. I can only suppose she has no idea it's *that* Mrs Fortescue.'

'How d'you know she has?'

'I've been over at Mulberrie Farm the whole afternoon playing bridge with Jerome and the Monteaths.'

'Oh, so that's your Eton friend. I thought as much. How does Amabelle like the country?'

'Loathes it, of course. She's so bored that she's taken to going out farming every day with old Major Stanworth. It's frightfully funny, I must say, to hear her talking about Runner Ducks and Middle Whites. Apparently she helped to *accouche* a cow yesterday.'

'I must go over and see her tomorrow. How am I going down with your mamma?' asked Paul, rather nervously, glancing at the precious journal.

'Quite O.K. so far. She likes the looks of you she told me. But for heaven's sake keep off the subject of hunting, or I know you'll put your foot in it. Oh, and by the way, she's going to talk to you about a daily programme for me this hols., so mind you arrange that we finish all the work in the morning, then we can get out after lunch and spend our afternoons at Mulberrie Farm under pretext of riding or playing golf. D'you see the idea? I'm going back there now – you coming?'

'I don't think so, thank you. Now that I am here I'm longing to get down to the journal. It looks too entrancing. Does your mother know you're going out?'

'No, of course she doesn't, you loopy old thing. What d'you suppose? I said good night to her ages ago, and what's more I've put a lay figure in my tiny bed in case she comes to look – it's been done before. Leave this window open for me, will you? – so long, then, see you in the morning.'

He jumped out of the window, and a few moments later a car was heard starting up in the road outside. Paul continued his perusal of the journal.

Jan. 3rd, 1878.

Went out in the donkey chaise accompanied by Edward and his dear children, who are here paying us a very happy visit. We took some pudding to poor old Mrs Skittle; she is not, I fear, likely to be with us much longer, poor old soul, and she herself reminded me of the country proverb, 'A green Christmas makes a fat churchyard.' This Christmas has certainly been the greenest that I can remember for years past, and Josiah says the same. (N.B. – The soup was not very warm at dinner last night; this must not occur again, as it makes darling Josiah very sad.)

   Little Hudson, darling Edward's eldest boy, looked so very pretty today in his blue dress and little pink ribbon shoes. As we approached Compton Bob-bin down the oak avenue I said to him, with a wave of my hand, 'This will be yours one day, my darling,' thinking it right that he should learn his respon-sibilities thus early in life. He looked at me earnestly for a while, clasped together his little pink hands, and said: 'Then I must be very, very good.' This reminded me so much of the dear Queen who, when first told that she was in the succession to the throne, said with charming resolution, 'I will be good.' Heaven knows that she has kept her word.

Jan. 8th, 1878.

Heard today from darling Edward, who left us on Tuesday in anticipation of this happy event that dearest Feodora has been brought to bed of a lovely little girl. This makes the fourth addition to their family. Heaven grant that in time they will have a quiverful. The news came by the telegraph, and as soon as I had imparted it to darling Josiah I went up to the nursery, where little Hudson, Mildred and Millicent sat at breakfast. I nodded to Mrs Darcy, their most excellent nurse, who was made aware by this signal of the news that I had received. I then sat down next to Hudson and said: 'Darling, the storks have brought you a little sister.' 'Where?' he cried, clapping his hands in glee. 'Does Mamma know?' At this remark Mrs Darcy and I had great difficulty in keeping our countenances.

Jan. 16th, 1878.

Alas, the little daughter born last week to Feodora passed away from us on Tuesday night. This dreadful news reached me yesterday morning by the telegraph, and for the rest of the day I was too much upset to write in my journal. Poor darling Edward, and poor, poor Feo, only a mother can guess at what she must be feeling now. Edward wrote me a dear note to say that he had been able to baptize the little one, which he did with the names Mary Ursula Christian Margaret, so I am thankful to think that the beloved little remains will be able to repose in sanctified ground. He tells me that dearest Feo is still very weak and most dreadfully sad, but beautifully resigned. She is allowed to sit up for a few hours every day and occupies herself embroidering a little shroud. How inscrutable are the ways of Providence, that He should give us this dear one to add brightness to our lives for a few days, only to take her from us in so short a space. I went up to the nursery as soon as I had received the news and found, as before, the three babies sitting at breakfast. Mrs Darcy, observing my black garments, knew the worst at once. I sat down next to baby Hudson and told him that his new sister had gone to Heaven. 'Did the storks come and fetch her away?' he asked innocently. 'No, my darling, it was the angels who took her away,' I replied.

8

The next morning after breakfast, which took place punctually at the unalluring hour of half-past eight, Lady Bobbin sent for Paul. Sleepy and rather unnerved, he found his way to her study, a room which so exactly, in every respect, resembled a man's typical smoking-room that Paul looked round for the pipe rack without which it did not seem complete. Lady Bobbin herself, dressed in a riding habit, flannel shirt and soft felt hat, looked almost human. She was one of those women who are only tidy and presentable when wearing some kind of uniform. She sat bolt upright on a hard chair and indicated another to Paul.

'I thought, Mr Fisher,' she said, tapping her booted leg briskly with a riding whip, 'that it would be a good plan if you and I together were to arrange a kind of daily programme for Roderick to carry out during the time that you are with us. I am a great believer in strict routine for young people, especially now that they have these ridiculously long holidays, and Roderick badly needs discipline, as you will very soon find out.'

Here she paused, looked at her watch, then out of the window, and finally at Paul, as though expecting him to make some comment.

'I think you are quite right. He evidently does need discipline. It seems to me that he is the sort of boy who should spend a great deal of time out in the open,' said Paul, remembering Bobby's little plan for bridge parties at Mulberrie Farm. 'Plenty of exercise and fresh air would do him a world of good, both mentally and physically; nothing like it for building character, you know. In fact,' he went on, warming to his subject, 'in all the years that I have had boys in my charge I have adhered to the motto, *Mens sana in corpore sano*. I have never found a better.'

'There is no better,' said Lady Bobbin approvingly. The tutor was making an excellent impression. 'If more young people would realize that we could do away with a great deal that is bad nowadays, and especially this unhealthy modern art, I feel certain.'

'I think we could, too.'

'Some of these artists, you know (if you could call them artists, which, personally, I don't) would be different beings after a day's hunting, do them all the good in the world, take their minds off those hideous atrocities that they pretend to like. Diseased minds, that's what they've got, diseased minds in unhealthy bodies.'

'Poor wretches,' said Paul, in tones of withering contempt.

'However, that's beside the point,' said Lady Bobbin, again looking at her watch. 'Now I had very much hoped that Roderick would be getting four or five days a week with hounds these Christmas holidays, but of course the wretched foot and mouth has stopped all that for the present (although between ourselves I have an idea that, if there are no fresh outbreaks before the new year, we shall be able to carry on just as usual in January). Luckily, however, we are not prevented from hacking on the estate, so you and he will be able to help keep the hunt horses fit. Then I shall be arranging one or two shoots for him, nothing much, you know, as we have given up rearing since my husband's death, but just rough days. Besides that there is quite a nice little golf course outside Woodford, and Major Stanworth, who is farming near here, has a squash court, so as you see there will be no lack of sport for you. Now would you be so good as to cast your eye over this piece of paper on which I have written out a daily programme for Roderick, subject, of course, to your approval, Mr Fisher.'

'Let me see, let me see,' said Paul, fixing on to his nose a pair of pince-nez through which, in fact, he could hardly see anything at all, but which he felt to be in keeping with his new character as tutor. (Amabelle had with great difficulty restrained him from making his appearance at Compton Bobbin arrayed in a platinum blonde wig, moustache and eyebrows.)

'Ah! Hum! Hem! Yes! "Breakfast at eight-thirty, work from nine to eleven, ride from eleven to one." That won't do, you know, Lady Bobbin, won't do at all, I fear. Let me see now, "luncheon at one o'clock, ride or play golf from two till four" – that's all right – "from five till seven-thirty more work or a game of squash rackets". Yes, a very excellent programme, if I may say so, but there is one thing about it which I shall be obliged to alter. We *must* have the whole morning for work.'

'Has Mr Pringle given Roderick so much to do?'

'Yes, indeed. A very great deal. I am afraid from what Mr Pringle tells me that Roderick is an idle, backward boy.'

'I know he is.'

'Mr Pringle doubts whether Roderick will pass into Sandhurst at all unless we read the whole of Horace, selections, which he has made for us, from Pliny and Virgil, the letters of Julius Caesar, the *Iliad*, most of the Greek Anthology, Gibbon's *Decline and Fall of the Roman Empire*, Burton's *Anatomy of Melancholy*, and Froude's *Essays*,' said Paul wildly, and at random. 'And besides all that he urged on me the importance of coaching Roderick thoroughly in mathematics and European history. Personally I think it seems rather a pity to pin the boy down to his lessons when he could be reaping so much benefit from fresh air and exercise, but you know what these schoolmasters are like. Besides, you must yourself be anxious for him to pass into Sandhurst, and if he is to do so with any degree of certainty we shall, I fear, be obliged to give up more time to our work than you have allowed for on this programme.'

'Very well,' said Lady Bobbin, 'I'm sure I don't wish the boy's work to suffer, and as you say I am very anxious that he should pass for Sandhurst. And that reminds me of something I wanted to mention to you – please do all that you can to persuade Roderick that he wants to go into the army. He has an absurd idea of becoming a diplomat, which I should very much dislike. I myself am a soldier's daughter and a soldier's wife –'

'So am I,' said Paul. 'At least I am a soldier's son and my mother was a soldier's wife.'

'And I particularly wish Roderick to become a soldier, to carry on the tradition in his father's regiment, so that I shall be very much obliged to you for any influence you may bring to bear in this direction. Now tell me how you intend to arrange your day, and then I must go out.'

'I fear that it will be necessary for us to work from 9 to 1 p.m. Personally, I am a great believer in morning work for young people. I think it most valuable. The whole afternoon will then be free for outdoor exercise – I am glad to hear that there are some squash courts near-by, as we shall be able to play them after it is too dark for riding or golf. We will see how the work is going, but I expect that I shall be obliged to call upon a couple of hours of his time after dinner as well.'

'I see that you intend to be very severe with Roderick, so much the better. The boy has needed a man's hand for some years. I'm afraid I have been rather inclined to spoil him myself. All right, then, we'll leave it at that. I should be obliged if you would let me know from time to time how the work is getting on.'

So saying, Lady Bobbin hurried away to the stables.

'That's grand,' said Bobby, when Paul had told him with a good deal of unseemly merriment, the results of his interview. 'I'm thankful you were quite firm about the morning work. Actually, of course, what I shall do is to tuck up on this sofa; it doesn't suit my constitution to be awake before lunch time, while you get on with great-grandmamma's journal. You might read out any juicy bits that you happen to come across. Then the moment lunch is finished we'll hack over to Mulberrie Farm. Amabelle says there is a groom who can exercise the horses for us, while we play bridge and gossip with her – I'll tell him to jolly well tire them out, too. If we get back late we'll pretend that we stopped at Woodford Manor (that's Major Stanworth's) for a game of squash and some tea. Mother will be awfully pleased. Well, thanks to you, Paul, old boy, I'm looking forward to the decentest hols. for years.' And Bobby flung himself on to the sofa, where he immediately fell asleep.

Meanwhile Paul returned to the journal, and was soon in the middle of that part of it which describes at immense length and in great detail the last weeks and hours of Sir Josiah Bobbin, who died, at the age of sixty-one, evidently from chronic over-eating.

Aug. 6th, 1878.

Spent many happy hours today in the Beloved Sick Room. I occupied some of them by reading aloud from the 'Idylls of the King', a work combining such noble sentiments with such an interesting narrative (both of which are, in my opinion, and that of Josiah, a *sine qua non* of *really great* poetry) that it is truly pleasant and edifying to read. How different from *so much* that is written in these days! My Dear One slept most of the time. He still has, I am most thankful to say, a good appetite, although so unwell, and it is by the means of constant feeding with nourishing foods that we are able to maintain his Precious Strength. It is now very late, almost midnight, the hour always consecrated to my journal. Ah! Faithful Page, to thee how many sorrows have I confided, safe in the knowledge that thou at least will never misconstrue my meaning, never repeat my secrets to a hard, uncomprehending world. Tonight I will unburden more of myself to thee, as I sit beside the Beloved Bed. For the day which is just dawning is the anniversary of the death of Dearest Mamma, who passed away when I was but an unthinking babe of four months old. Oh, cruel Fate which robbed nine little ones of their Guiding Star at such an early age, leaving them to reach maturity without a Mother's care.

At such sacred moments I sometimes think that I myself could have made a truer Wife, a more attentive Mother, if I had been less devoted to my Art. Alas! Can it be so? Would Arthur, George, Edward, Albert, Frederick and William, Alice, Julia, Maud, Eva, Louise and Beatrice have been *better* men and women, had I given up my writing? The very thought is a knife in my heart! Would darling Josiah have had a *more perfect* helpmeet but for the cultivation of my Gift? The knife turns! And yet I console myself with remembering that Nature teaches us a different, and, I hope, a truer lesson. The gentle nightingale can ever find time for the duties of her home in the intervals of charming the woodlands with her silvery note; the merry lark, soaring above the cornfields, the perky robin hopping among the evergreens, each has its little song to sing, yet is not therefore a *neglectful* Mother! And surely it has ever been thus with me? Surely I have no cause for self-reproach on that dread score? I *know* that I have not, otherwise how could I survive another moment at such a melancholy time? Sometimes it comes upon me with a fearful shudder that I am soon to be left a Widow. Widow! Hateful word, how could these fingers fashion thee? Surely I must be spared that unbearable, that fatal blow awhile? And yet I saw in the doctor's eye today a look of cruel foreboding as he said: 'Give Sir Josiah anything he likes to eat, we must not cross him now.' That word 'now', I shuddered as I heard it, nor dared to ask its meaning.

Ah! Leave, my darling, leave me not awhile,
Lonely upon this planet sere and grey;
Spare poor my heart such melancholy trial,
Lest frail my courage faint and fade away.

Forget that thou art ill and tired of woe,
Think rather of the day when first we met.
Forget the hateful burdens here below,
Sorrow, ingratitude and loss, forget!

Think only, love, upon our wedding day,
The lilies and the sunshine and the bells;
Of how, the service o'er, we drove away
To our blest honeymoon at Tunbridge Wells.

Think of our life together all these years,
The joys we've shared, the sorrows we have known;
The laughter of our children, and their tears,
The happiness of duty bravely done.

But if with longing thou art overcome
To leave forthwith this sad and tearful earth,
E'en should my heart with poignant grief be numb,
It yet would not begrudge thee Heavenly birth!

Then song of nightingales in the wet leaves
Of churchyard yews shall be thy heavy dirge;
Though for a space alone my bosom heaves,
It everlastingly with thine shall merge!

Paul recognized these as being the first verses of what later became one of Lady Maria's best known and most popular poems, 'At a Husband's Death-Bed, or The Passing of a Beloved', set to music by her son-in-law, Lord Otto Pulman, and published shortly after Sir Josiah's death. Presently he came to the following entry:

Aug. 26th, 1878.
'Tis o'er. All is over, and I a Widow. Little Hudson came to me just now as I sat by the Loved Remains in a kind of sad trance.

'Granny,' he said, in his little lisping voice, 'what is a widow, granny?'

'Alas! I am a widow, my love,' I replied.

'And granny,' went on the poor innocent, 'what is a corpse, granny?'

'Look there,' I said in awful tones, pointing to the Bed.

'But, granny, I want to see a corpse. That's only grandpa, gone to sleep.'

At this I quite broke down, and I think that the tears have done me some little good. Now I must collect my thoughts and try to recall, while it is yet fresh in my memory, every incident connected with The End.

At four o'clock, or it may have been a few minutes later, I went to my room, to rest before tea time. I removed some of my garments and lay down on the couch, and I think I must have dozed for a few moments. At any rate, I remember nothing more until I saw, with a *fearful start*, that darling Alice was standing near me, pointing with her hand towards Heaven. I realized, as soon as I observed this significant and awful gesture, that The End *must* now be very near, so hastily throwing a shawl around my shoulders I returned to the Bedside, where I found dear Arthur, George, Edward, Albert, Frederick, William, Julia, Maud, Eva, Louise and Beatrice standing around it in various attitudes of pious resignation very beautiful to see. As I approached my darling Josiah he turned over in bed, a smile of happy anticipation o'erspread his features and he spoke, not very coherently, a few words. In my agitation I thought at first that he was saying 'Bring me the oysters,' a dish to which he has ever been most partial, but of course, as dearest Edward remarked when speaking of it to me afterwards, he must really have said, 'Bury me in the cloisters,' a curious fancy as there are no cloisters in this neighbourhood. There was a long silence after this, which my Loved One broke himself. He looked darling Edward full in the face, said, very loudly, 'Pass the Port,' and fell lifeless to his pillow. Edward said immediately, in low but ringing tones, 'Safe past the Port indeed, Life's perilous journey done.' A moment later dearest Alice very reverently took my blue shawl from off my shoulders and replaced it with a black one. Then and then only did I realize that all was over, and I indeed a Widow. The *best*, the *noblest* husband that woman ever had – I can write no more at present.

Aug. 31st, 1878.
I have just returned to the house from attending My Angel's funeral. Such a long, and such a very beautiful service, how he would have rejoiced in it had he but been there to participate. Afterwards I sent for Mr Brawn, our incumbent, and spoke with him upon the subject, now most dear to my Poor Widowed Heart, that of erecting some Gothick cloisters in the churchyard as a memorial to Him. It was His dying wish. Mr Brawn, I am thankful to say, is delighted with the idea and has made one or two very feeling suggestions. He thinks, and this shows him to be a man of true sensibility, that the cloisters should have fourteen arches, one for Darling Josiah, one for myself, and one for each of our dear sons and daughters. The Dear Tomb can then repose in the middle.

The children have been very kind and considerate, and so have the poor people, who for miles around came with their little offerings of flowers, most touching. Baby Hudson's has been the only smiling face on which I have looked for days. I would hardly have it otherwise; he is mercifully too young as yet to know the dreadful anguish which he must else have felt at the loss of Such a Grandfather.

Paul read on for the rest of that day. (It was pouring wet, and even Lady Bobbin conceded, at luncheon time, that their first ride had better be postponed until slightly more reasonable weather should have set in. Bobby and Philadelphia went instead to Oxford to do some Christmas shopping, and to bring back Lord Lewes, who had telephoned to say that his car had broken down there.)

Lady Maria Bobbin, after the death of her husband, retired to a dower house in the park, where she lived for some years with her only unmarried daughter, Eva, as a companion. Her life there appeared to have been singularly uneventful, except for certain little disagreements with her daughter-in-law, Lady Feodora Bobbin, whom she too evidently detested, until, in 1888, Paul came upon the following entry:

June 3rd, 1888.

A most extraordinary and agitating event occurred this afternoon. A person of the name of Hardysides came to see me and made a proposal for dear Eva's hand. I very naturally said that I could not possibly consider this matter, and bid him good day; but the whole affair has upset me dreadfully. Supposing that Eva were in time to marry? Not Hardysides, of course, the idea is ridiculous, but supposing (which God be thanked is unlikely owing to our very retired position) that some young man of family and fortune were to make an offer for her? What could I say? For Eva's presence here is very necessary to me. If she left me, who would copy out my poems ready for the publisher? Who would order the food, arrange the flowers, attend to the linen and perform the hundred and one little odd jobs which it is a daughter's plain and joyous duty to do for her Mother? I *cannot* believe that dearest Eva would be so *base* and *selfish* as to leave me alone for the few years that remain before I join my beloved Josiah on High. Who are these Hardysides? A family with which I seem to be unacquainted. I very much hope that *no more* will be said on this subject, as these shocks are *most* injurious to my health.

June 4th, 1888.

Dearest Eva herself broached the subject of Mr Hardysides (whom she *most* improperly refers to by his christian name of Horace) during the time which I always devote to my correspondence. I kindly, but very firmly, explained my reasons for objecting to this marriage, *absurd*, *preposterous*, *unthinkable*, and indicated to the dear child that I should be much obliged if, in future, she would refrain from taking up my valuable time with such foolishness. I feel *quite tired* and done up, but I am thankful to think that this will not occur again. (It appears that Mr Hardysides is an artist, an acquaintance of dearest Feodora's, and has several times lately been to stay at Compton Bobbin. I must speak to darling Edward about this.)

June 8th, 1888.

I feel so much agitated that I can hardly even hold my pen, to communicate my feelings to *this* Sacred Page. That any child of mine should behave with such ingratitude, such selfishness, such rank inconsideration for others, and such utter lack of modesty or self-restraint, is hard to record. This Little Book has been the recipient of *many* sorrows and *some* joys, but never before has it chronicled a Deed of this description. Let the facts then speak for themselves, for who am I to judge another sinner?

This morning, as I was pondering over the proofs of my 'Peasant Children on Mount Snowdon', Eva came into my morning-room, wearing as I noticed somewhat to my surprise, a new bonnet and shawl.

'Are you going out, dearest child?' I said, intending, if this should indeed prove to be the case, to give her one or two little commissions for me in the village.

'Yes, dear Mamma,' she replied, a guilty flush o'er-spreading (and, alas! with what reason) her usually somewhat pallid cheeks. 'I have just come to acquaint you with the fact that I am now going out to be married, by special licence, to Horace Hardysides.'

I flatter myself that I maintained, on hearing these insolent words, an admirable composure.

'Then Go!' I said, in very *awful* tones, which I fear may ring in poor Eva's ears to the hour of her death. 'Go! But do not seek to return! When your Hardysides has proved himself false and unfaithful, *this* roof shall never shelter you again!'

'Mamma!' she cried imploringly, the full sense of her guilt coming over her, no doubt, for the first time.

'Go!' I reiterated. 'Pray go!'

Hesitatingly, she turned and went.

Without another word, without even so much as a glance, she left her lonely, *Widowed* Mother for the embraces of a stranger. May *he* never use *her* so! How sharper than the serpent's tooth –

I have sent in haste for dear Edward and told him to summon dear Arthur, George, Albert, Frederick and William, Alice, Julia, Maud and Louise. (Darling Beatrice is shortly expecting a happy event, and I refused to have her informed, as I fear that the shock might have *disastrous consequences* and jeopardize a little Life.) No doubt they will all, as ever, be very kind, but ah! how I long on such occasions for the guidance and wisdom of my own Sainted Josiah – I can only hope that in a very little while we shall once more be united – Above! This Happy and Dreadful thought has made me wonder how Eva will be enabled to meet her Father's eye when her day shall come – if, indeed one so selfish and untruthful be granted entrance to the Heavenly Spheres. Poor, poor misguided Child.

Later.

My darling Edward has just been round to see me. He is very much perturbed, not only upon my account, though, naturally, I am his chief preoccupation in the matter, but also because of the disgrace which poor Eva's dreadful action will have brought upon the whole Family. Dearest Feodora is immeasurably distressed (he says) and well she may be, at her share in this matter. It appears that she met this Mr Hardysides in London and asked him down to Compton Bobbin to paint a group of herself and the five eldest children. The picture was never finished, as darling Edward, when in Town, was taken to see some of the artist's works; and finding that they were most dreadfully secular and unedifying, besides being devoid of the smallest genius, whether of composition, style or design, and finding also that Mr Hardysides had a most *unsavoury* and *immoral* reputation, he gave him his immediate *congé*. Since then it would appear that the wretch has been staying in the neighbourhood in order to complete his seduction – already half begun – of poor Eva. I am saddened and amazed, and can write no more for today.

9

Lord Lewes, who arrived that evening, was the true type of Foreign Office 'young' man. (Men remain, for some reason, 'young men' longer in the Foreign Office than in any other profession.) He was tall, very correctly dressed in a style indicating the presence of money rather than of imagination, and had a mournful, thin, eighteenth-century face. His correct and slightly pompous manner combined with the absence in his speech of such expressions as 'O.K. loo', 'I *couldn't* be more amused', 'We'll call it a day', 'lousy', 'It was a riot', 'My sweetie-boo' and 'What a poodle-pie' to indicate the barrier of half a generation between himself, Paul and Bobby; a barrier which more than any other often precludes understanding, if not friendship, between young and youngish people.

He appeared, in a totally undistinguished way, however, to be a person of some culture, and since being *en poste* at Cairo, had interested himself mainly in Egyptology. He told Paul that he had recently spent much time and money on excavations, and had been rewarded, just before he had left, by finding the tomb of some early and unknown (he did not use the word 'bogus') Shepherd King, the unearthing of which had caused a certain stir amongst Egyptologists.

'Isn't it supposed to be unlucky to dig up tombs?' asked Philadelphia, who had languidly been listening to Michael's conversation.

'Who was it said that "only shallow men believe in luck"?' he replied, smiling sadly. 'Emerson, I think. In any case, it is certain that if luck exists I have had a very small share of it in my life, either before digging up poor old Papuachnas or since. Besides, I haven't kept any of the things I found for myself, not a single scarab, and I think that might make a difference, don't you?'

Paul, who had a practical side to his nature, thought that he himself would easily be able to endure the kind of lucklessness that brought with it a marquisate, a superb Adam house and fifteen thousand pounds a year. He felt sure that Michael Lewes still believed that he was in love with Mrs Fortescue; he evidently considered himself to be an unhappy person, hardly used by Fate.

'It is curious,' went on Lord Lewes, 'to consider the hold that Egyptology takes on people. Nearly everyone seems to be more or less interested in it, more so, I believe, than in any other ancient history, not excepting even that of Greece herself. The most unlikely people used to ask if they could come and see my little collection in Cairo; débutantes from London, for instance, and their mothers, people you would think had no feeling for such things.'

'It is the human interest,' said Paul. '(And I don't mean only in the case of the débutantes.) I believe most people have felt it at one time or another. Of course, it is very romantic to think of those tombs, found exactly as they were left at the beginning of the world, full of art treasures and jewels, the pill of historical research is gilded with the primitive and universal excitement of a treasure hunt. Personally, I have always thought that as a rule it is people of more imagination than intellect who feel drawn towards Egypt. Whereas the Philhellene, for instance, is less concerned with how the Greek lived than with how he *thought*, the average Egyptologist always seems to be rather too much fascinated by the little objects of everyday life which he has found, and rather too busy reconstructing the exact uses to which they were put, to look below the surface for spiritual manifestations of the age in which they were made.'

'Perhaps on the whole you may be right,' said Lord Lewes. 'One does not, however, have to look very far for such manifestations; they are all around one in that country. The Egyptian was a superb artist.'

'Ah! But for such a short time when measured by the length of his civilization. While the art was strictly formalized, I admit that it was good, almost great. Under Aknahton – correct me if I am wrong – the representational school came into being. After that, to my way of thinking, there was no more art in Egypt.'

'There, I am afraid, I cannot possibly agree with you,' said Lord Lewes with his charming smile. 'I must regard Aknahton and his artists as very wonderful reformers, and their art as some of the greatest that can be found anywhere in the world.'

'Yes, you see we have a different point of view. I cannot possibly admire purely representational art,' said Paul, thinking how few people there were so tolerant and easy to get on with. For the first time since his arrival at Compton Bobbin he found himself wishing that he had been there under slightly more creditable circumstances. It occurred to him that if Michael Lewes knew the truth he might easily regard him as quite an ordinary thief, since he was evidently a person rather lacking in humour. Lord Lewes broke in upon this train of thought by saying, after considering the matter for some moments, 'I think, you know, that the Egyptians themselves were more human than the Greeks, who always appear to have been so coldly perfect, like their own statuary, that it is difficult to credit them with the flesh and blood of ordinary human beings. "Fair Greece, sad relic of departed worth,"' he added mournfully, '"Immortal though no more, though fallen, great."'

Paul looked at him in some amazement. He had never, since his Oxford days, met anybody so fond of quoting.

'And presumably,' said Lord Lewes, 'that is how the Byzantinist must feel, otherwise I see no way to account for him. Attracted beyond words to the Archipelago itself, and repelled, I suppose, by the sheer perfection of the art which he finds there, he is obliged to search the islands for something which he thinks he can honestly admire. He ends, of course, by valuing the Byzantine quite absurdly high, far higher than its actual merit deserves.'

Paul, who was himself an ardent Byzantinist, and, like all such, extremely sensitive on the subject, was disgusted by this speech, which revealed in his opinion an intellectual dishonesty too dreadful to contemplate. He was just about to inform Lord Lewes that he was the author of a small and privately printed monograph entitled *The Byzantine Breakaway* when he remembered for the second time that evening that his position in the household was not of the most genuine, and that his name was now no longer Fotheringay but Fisher. Too angry to continue the discussion he walked quickly out of the room, saying over his shoulder to

Philadelphia, 'I'll fetch that book I said I would lend you; I particularly want to know what you think about it.'

'Nice, isn't he?' said Michael as soon as he was out of the room.

'Awfully sweet,' said Bobby.

'He's an angel, I think,' said Philadelphia dreamily.

Later Lord Lewes said to his Aunt Gloria, 'What a really charming, cultured young man, that Mr Fisher, it is a real pleasure to have made his acquaintance. I think you were so clever to find him. He is just the very person for Bobby, too; full of brains and yet most human.'

'Yes, he seems all right,' said Lady Bobbin. 'He was very much recommended to me. I only hope he will get the boy out of doors and make himself useful with Brenda Chadlington's brats. She announced today that she is bringing them again; most thoughtless and inconsiderate of her to my mind, but still – !'

Paul looked forward with no feelings of delight to his first ride to Compton Bobbin. He was, in fact, extremely terrified at the idea of it. Bobby, noticing his aversion to that form of exercise, tried to reassure him by pointing out that the distance to Mulberrie Farm was well under three miles, that it would be unnecessary for them to proceed at any pace more desperate than a walk, and that Boadicea, the mare which had been allotted to him to ride, was as quiet as any old cow; but in vain. Paul, most unfortunately for his own peace of mind, had happened to see the said mare out at exercise the day before, and had noticed in her a very different aspect from that of the ancient hireling on whose back he had spent so many painful hours jogging up and down the Rotten Row. To compare her to an old cow was simply silly. It was, in fact, only too apparent that here was a beast of pride and pedigree, who would almost certainly consider it a point of honour to cast the trembling tyro from her back. Paul knew, alas! how fatally easy, in his case, this would be; the smallest jerk, nay, even the transition between trot and canter, often proved sufficient to unseat him. He visualized with a shudder that horrid moment when everything would fly from his grip, the universe become black and roll several times round him, while the earth would suddenly rise up and bang him in the kidneys. It had happened in the soft and friendly Row and had been extraordinarily painful; what of the tarmac road, hard, black and shining like ebonite, which lay between Compton Bobbin and Mulberrie Farm? Poor Paul spent a wakeful night pondering these things, and by the morning had quite made up his mind that he would return to London sooner than court an end so sudden and unpleasing.

After breakfast, however, he felt more of a man again, and the sight of the precious red morocco volumes peeping from behind the schoolroom radiator put new courage into him. Besides, it would be a pity not to see a little more of Philadelphia. He was looking forward with some interest to hearing her verdict upon *Crazy Capers*, which he had lent her to read, saying that a friend of his had written it. Unsophisticated but intelligent, he thought, it was just possible that she might prove to be the one person who would put a proper construction on it. Possible, not likely. If she joined in the chorus of laughter he knew that he would be hurt, far more hurt than when Marcella had, who was always a hard, unimaginative little thing with a mind like a tennis ball. Meanwhile, fasting, for he felt too nervous to touch food at luncheon time, he prepared to face his ordeal.

By the most unlucky accident of fate Lady Bobbin happened to be talking to the stud groom in the stable yard when Paul and Bobby arrived there, and waited to see them mount. Paul, sadly conscious of the newness of his clothes, which had elicited roars of delight from the heartless Bobby as they left the house, stood a quaking and, no doubt, he thought bitterly, a pathetically comic figure, as he waited for Boadicea to be brought from her dark and smelly lair inside the stables.

'Cold, isn't it?' he said between chattering teeth to Lady Bobbin, who took no notice whatever of this remark. At that moment the snorting animal was led out, tossing her head from side to side in what seemed to be an ecstasy of rage and contempt, and showering little bits of froth in all directions. Paul, his unreasonable terror of horses now quite overcome by his unreasonable terror of Lady Bobbin, whose cold gimlet eye seemed to be reading his every emotion, decided that here was one of the few occasions in a man's life on which death would be preferable to dishonour, and advanced towards the mounting block with a slight swagger which he hoped was reminiscent of a French marquis approaching the scaffold. Grasping the reins and the pommel of the saddle firmly as he had been taught, he placed his left foot in the stirrup, when the animal, as indeed he had feared it probably would, began to wriggle its hind quarters away from him. When this had happened in the Row it had been his invariable custom to remove his foot from the stirrup and begin all over again. Now, however, feeling (he dared not look) that Lady Bobbin's eyes, not to mention the eyes of the stud groom, two under grooms, the stable boy, Bobby and two men who were carting away manure, were upon him, he rather lost his head and with the courage of despair gave a tremendous leap in pursuit of Boadicea's retreating back. To his immense astonishment, this piece of bravura was rewarded with complete success, and he found himself sitting fair and square in the saddle, with the stable boy placing his other foot in its appointed stirrup. Alas, he had not time to enjoy the fruits of triumph, as no sooner did the under groom, who was holding her, release Boadicea's head from his grasp than, despite Paul's frenzied tugs at the reins, she departed at a brisk trot out of the stable yard, and with a series of sickening slithers on to the tarmac road outside. Making a desperate effort, and by dint of counting out loud, one-two, one-two, Paul did manage to 'rise' in the approved Row style until he felt himself to be well out of Lady Bobbin's sight, when, abandoning all pride and self-respect, he clung with one hand to the saddle, jerked at the reins with the other and sobbed out in pitiful gasps: 'Stop, stop, dear Boadicea, whoa, whoa, Boadicea whoa, oh, please, please, stop!' The insensitive Boadicea, however, paid no attention to his pathetic cries, but continued to trot on, very nearly pulling him over from time to time by suddenly throwing her head right forward with loud and terrifying snorts. At last, when Paul felt himself to be at the end of his tether and, having long since abandoned both reins and stirrups, was looking out for a soft piece of grass on which he could hurl his aching bones, he heard another horse come up behind him, Bobby's outstretched hand seized the reins and, with a painful and alarming bump, Boadicea came to a standstill. She immediately began to eat grass at the side of the road, leaving, in the place where her head and neck had formerly been, a hideous gaping chasm. This was, for poor Paul, the last straw.

'I can't bear it, I can't bear it. I knew I should hate it. Lousy horse! Please, please let me get off and walk. Oh, what Gehenna!'

'It's all right,' said Bobby, who was laughing so much he could hardly speak. 'Oh, you did look too entrancing. I hope you'll do it again for me. No, no, don't get off, she'll walk quite quietly now as far as Amabelle's. Besides, you've got to get used to it, haven't you? But, you know, I can't think why she didn't come down, spanking along the tarmac like that. You should have taken her up on to the grass.'

'It's all very well for you to talk,' said Paul, who was still on the verge of tears; 'but I can't guide the beastly thing at all, it's as much as I can do to stay on its back.'

'My God, you looked funny,' said Bobby, rocking and guffawing. 'I'd give anything to see that again.'

Paul felt that, considering he had just been rescued from the jaws of death, he was not receiving that sympathy which was his due, and for some time he maintained a dignified silence. Presently, however, his sense of humour asserted itself, and he began to giggle too.

'I say, what will your mother have thought?' he asked rather nervously when he had recovered his breath.

'Well, by the mercy of Providence she was having a look at his horse's fetlocks when you got up, so I don't believe she noticed much. She did mutter something about "Why can't the blasted idiot wait a minute; what's all the damned hurry for?" But that doesn't mean a lot from her. No, you had a lucky escape this time, old boy. If you had let Boadicea down on the tarmac it would have been the end of Compton Bobbin and the journals for you, believe me.'

10

'One heart.'

'I double a heart.'

'Really, Sally, my sweet, don't you ride that convention to death just a little? It seems to be your one and only idea of a bid.'

'Well, I don't want to have to play the hand any more; I'd much rather you did, then there's no grumbling afterwards, you see.'

'I should have thought it would be more useful,' said Walter, ostentatiously looking at the score, 'at this stage in the proceedings, if you would show a suit.'

'Well, I've said before and I'll say again that I can't play bridge, and I don't like playing bridge. I only do it, as you know quite well, to make up a four. I think it's a horrible game, it makes everyone too bad-tempered and beastly for words – specially you, Walter darling, and you're apt to be quite nice at other times,' she added, for even when goaded to madness by Walter she always found it impossible to be unkind to him. 'Thank goodness Jerome comes tomorrow, and I shall be able to go back to my kiddies for Christmas like Mrs Culbertson.'

'Darling, now don't be sour, please, my angel. I only meant that when you are playing you might try to concentrate a tiny bit more?'

'Concentrate! My head's aching with trying to concentrate, and all the thanks I get from you are these everlasting lectures, or else you sit there looking so reproachful and swallowing every time I play a card, as though I were doing it on purpose to annoy.'

'I said a heart,' murmured Bobby, who, having a superb hand, was anxious to get on with the business and had become rather restive during this family argument.

'Well, now I've got to show a suit, have I?' said Sally.

'No, no! Of course not *now*,' cried Walter in that agony of impatience only known to the good bridge player obliged to suffer the vagaries of an absolutely incompetent partner. 'Not now, you can't. You've doubled a heart, haven't you? And you must stick at that. Paul says?'

'Two hearts,' said Paul.

'Two spades,' said Walter. 'Now, if Sally would only sometimes show a suit instead of sitting there saying double –'

'Oh, I'll show you the whole of my hand, if you go on like this,' said Sally, 'and much good may it do you!'

'Four hearts,' said Bobby with an air of finality.

'Tee-hee,' he said as Paul put down a hand with six hearts to the ace, queen and an outside ace; 'now wasn't that just too psychic of me for words. Thanks ever so much, Paul, old boy – of course, you should have given me a double rise really, shouldn't you? But still –'

'What an extraordinary lead, Sally darling. Are you in your right senses?'

'Well, in that ghastly little book you made me read it said, "never lead from an ace, queen, never lead from a king, and never lead from a doubleton, it is a rotten lead". So that's the only thing for me to do, as far as I can see.'

'That's right,' said Bobby good-naturedly, 'tell him exactly what you've got in your hand; don't mind me, will you?'

Paul wandered over to the old world inglenook where Amabelle was sitting with Elspeth Paula on her knee.

'That's right, darling, have a good gurk,' she was saying, 'makes us all feel better, that does. Isn't she a treasure? Look at those huge goggling eyes. She's going to be a one with the chaps, she is. Aren't you, sweetikin. Boo!'

A confused murmur came from the bridge table.

'Now, Sally, out with it. There's only one lead you can possibly make.'

'I don't see that. I've got six cards in my hand and I can lead any of them, can't I? Oh dear, I wish I knew.'

'Now, *think*. There's only one possible lead. Oh, my God, you are a vile player, Sally. Well, now, that makes it all very O.K. for you, Bobby, game and rub –'

The butler opened the door and announced:

'Lord Lewes, madam.'

A perfectly stunned silence fell on Amabelle's drawing-room as Michael Lewes walked into it. Amabelle herself, who hardly ever showed emotion of any sort, turned crimson and nearly dropped the baby; Paul, feeling as he had not felt since, when at Eton, he was caught by the 'beaks' in the Slough cinema, made half a movement to escape through the garden door, but decided that this would only make matters far worse and that it would be better to stay and brazen it out; and the Monteaths gave each other long glances, fraught with meaning, over their cards. Bobby alone remained unshaken and went on playing the hand in his usual brisk and businesslike style. Such was the emotion of his adversaries that he made as a result not only four hearts giving him game and rubber, but little slam as well, a fact which he was heard afterwards loudly to lament. ('You know, Paul, it was monstrous only putting me up one. After all, you had the hearts; you knew I was calling on outside cards, didn't you? I naturally imagined you had a bare rise and wanted me to go to game. It is too maddening.')

The silence was broken by a shattering gurk from Elspeth Paula.

'What *savoir faire*!' said Bobby under his breath. 'Anybody would think I was the father. No more diamonds, Sally? Yes, I thought you had – no, no, that's O.K. The rest are good on the table, aren't they? That's one hundred and twenty below, one hundred overtricks and five hundred for the rubber. Thirteen I make it.'

'How are you, Michael?' Amabelle was saying. 'Ring the bell, will you, Paul? How lovely to see you, my dear. I can't think why, but I imagined you were still abroad. You know Mr Fotheringay, do you?'

'Mr Fisher?' said Lord Lewes.

'What am I thinking of – Mr Fisher I mean, of course. And Walter and Sally you know, don't you? And this is the Monteath heiress, Miss Elspeth Paula, who was born at one of my cocktail parties.'

'Indeed she wasn't,' cried Sally indignantly.

'Well, more nearly than I care to think about; if that taxi hadn't come when it did –'

'My dear, she wasn't born till four in the morning.'

'What a cheesey time,' said Bobby. 'Well, darling, we've finished our tiny rubber and I think we'd better be going. See you all tomorrow and thanks so much for having us. Come on, Paul, to horse, to horse!'

'Where are you off to, Sally?'

'I think I'd better take baby up to her beddie-bye. Come along then, you sweet precious.'

'I'm going to see Paul on to his horse,' said Walter, chuckling. 'It sounds too good to be missed.'

Amabelle sighed. There was evidently a conspiracy to leave her alone with Lord Lewes.

'You look very well, my dear,' she said briskly, as the door shut on Walter and Sally. 'Did you enjoy yourself in Cairo?'

'No.'

'Oh, I'm sorry. I thought it all sounded so nice and interesting. I saw photos, in *The Sphere*, wasn't it, of a camp stool four thousand years old (or was it four hundred? I'm so bad at figures). Anyway, a very interesting old camp stool that you had found, and I thought how pleased you would be to find a lovely old camp stool like that,' said Amabelle desperately, making up the fire until it was a sort of burning fiery furnace.

'I shall never enjoy anything, and I shall never have a single moment's happiness in life until I can persuade you to marry me, Amabelle.'

'Oh dear. I hoped so much – I mean, surely Cairo must be full of lovely girls, isn't it. One's always reading about them, anyway. Haven't you changed your mind at all?'

'How could you imagine such a thing? No, indeed, I thought of you every moment of the day. I dreamt of you every moment of the night. I saw no beautiful girls, or if I did they looked to me like dolls stuffed with sawdust. Occasionally I came across people who knew you, they would mention your name in passing and it would go through me like a red-hot sword; if I saw in some illustrated paper a photograph of you it would make me even more wretched than I was already, and for days. Anything of beauty or of interest became intolerable because you were not there to share it with me. I tell you, you have made life very sad for me, Amabelle.'

'Dear Michael,' said Amabelle, stifling a yawn.

Curious, she thought, how some people have this devastating effect of boredom upon one. She had forgotten in three years just how much he did bore her, but the moment he had opened his mouth it had all come back to her in a wave and she was hopelessly, crushingly bored again.

'I'm so sorry, my dear,' she said.

'But I haven't come here to reproach you with that. I am here because I know, I feel quite certain that in your heart, only you won't admit it, you love me too.'

Amabelle was startled by this remark. Had she really behaved so badly as to lead him to suppose that this was the case? Or was it just his own vanity? 'Perhaps you think that because you wish it so much,' she said kindly.

'It's true, it must be true, I know it is. Only you are such an angel that you won't marry me because you think, quite mistakenly, that it would spoil my life, because you are older than I am and because of –'

'My international reputation?' Amabelle was of an age to think of reputation in these terms; in her young days a woman either had a good reputation or an international reputation, and, modern as she was in many ways, she never could quite rid her mind of these nineteenth-century *nuances*.

'Yes,' she went on, 'I admit that is partly the reason. If I didn't feel certain that you would soon be very unhappy indeed I suppose I might make the sacrifice of marrying you. But in a short time you would be miserable, your career would be ruined for one thing' (international reputations and ruined careers went hand-in-hand when Amabelle was young), 'and besides that it is important for you to have children, and I'm not Sarah, you know, though in many ways a remarkable woman. But don't you see, Michael dear, that if I *were* in love with you I shouldn't consider any of that for five minutes. I'm far too selfish. I'm not in love with you. I like you, I'm fond of you, and we have much in common. All that leads you to suppose that I'm in love with you, so now I must try and make you understand once and for all that I'm *not*. I'm *not*. And in any case I'm sick and tired to death of love. You must remember that for years it was my trade, my shop, my profession. Now I've retired, left my practice or whatever you like to call it, and I won't begin all over again. It bores me. I'm not strong enough to face the wear and tear and racket of a new love affair, with all the business of being your wife into the bargain; your relations who would come and see me, rightly as I think, to dissuade me from such a step, the sneers of the newspapers and of my own friends. Why should I be obliged to put up with all these things for something I don't even want? Because you must see, Michael, that, apart from any other consideration, if I marry you I lose instead of gaining a position. I become neither fish, flesh nor good red herring. In the case of James Fortescue it was quite different; he was an old man of the world when he married me and it was a good bargain for us both. He needed someone to keep his house, amuse his friends and be good company for himself; I needed a home and a name. We were both admirably suited, the best of friends, and, I think, very happy. I certainly was. This case is utterly different; if I married you we should each in our different way lose much of what makes life bearable, but I honestly believe that I should lose more than you would. Anyhow, Michael, I am telling the truth, I swear to you that I am, when I say that nothing would influence me, none of these worldly considerations would prevent me from marrying you tomorrow if I loved you; but I don't love you. I don't, I don't, I don't. Is it possible that perhaps now at last you understand me?'

After making this speech Amabelle fell back on the sofa with a look of utter exhaustion and there was a long silence between them.

'Then what is to become of me?' said Michael bitterly.

'Oh, my dear, really I don't know. What does become of people who have been crossed in love? I never have been myself so I can't say from experience, but I imagine that sooner or later they meet somebody else who attracts them, mentally or physically, *et violà! L'affaire est morte, vive l'affaire*. In your case let's hope it will be some nice, pretty girl who will make you very, very happy.'

'If you speak like that,' said Michael, 'it only shows that you can't understand the meaning of true love. Some people are made so that they can only love once in their lives.'

'Nobody is,' said Amabelle firmly. 'Unless, of course, they live with the person they love all their lives. Permanent and exclusive affection between married people may be possible, but nobody can remain faithful to a person they never see. As for true love, I didn't believe in that until I met Walter and Sally, but I am really beginning to be very much afraid that in their case it does exist. Maddening, because it upsets all my theories about life.'

'You promise, then, that you don't love me at all, and that no argument, no persuasion will ever induce you to marry me?'

'No, Michael, I don't love you. I never have loved you and I never shall love you, and nothing that you can say or do will ever make me marry you. And I beg you, from the bottom of my heart, if we are to remain friends, that you won't bring up this subject any more.'

'Very well. I won't speak of it again. No woman has ever been so much loved as I have loved you, none has ever been so cherished and considered as I would have cherished and considered you if you had married me. Let that pass. I promise that I will never mention this subject to you again as long as I live, if you will promise that we can go on being friends?'

'Yes, of course, Michael dear,' said Amabelle gloomily. It seemed hard that she should have been at such pains to retire from Lewes Park on purpose to avoid this very boring scene, only to find that Michael was staying in the next house to hers.

'Are you staying at Compton Bobbin?'

'I arrived yesterday.'

'How did you find out that I was here?'

'By a fortunate chance. I happened to go for a little stroll before lunch with Bobby, and just as we got on to the Stow Road a large blue Bentley drove past, and Bobby said, "Oh, look, there's Amabelle's car." Not my usual luck, it would have been more like me to have stayed here three weeks without knowing that you were in the neighbourhood at all.'

Amabelle looked pensively into the fire. She did not and never had possessed a large blue Bentley. She thought out a few pungent observations which might be made to Sir Roderick when he came for his next game of bridge.

'Bobby is a very naughty little boy; he needs a thoroughly good spanking,' she said.

'It's really amazing how much he has grown up since I was in England last,' said Michael. 'Of course, it is three years, but even so it seems like a conjuring trick. When I left he was a little boy, rather young for his age. Now he is more like a man of thirty.'

'Eton does that for them. Bobby has a peculiar character, I must say. I suppose he is the one complete egotist of this generation. It is very lucky for him, because it means that he will never, in his whole life, know the meaning of the word boredom. He will always be quite happy so long as he is with other people, because it is wildly interesting to him to watch the effect that he is producing, and their reactions to his personality. If they like him, so much the better; if not, there is the entrancing problem of how to make them. Leave him alone and he would collapse, of course; but in company, of whatever description, he is contented and amused, and always will be. Perfect from his point of view, because he will never have to be alone in his whole life presumably, and for the rare occasions when loneliness will be forced upon him he has a certain weapon of self-defence, an absolutely inexhaustible facility for sleeping.'

'Yes, I should think that sums up his character pretty well,' said Michael, who had taken no great fancy for his cousin. 'And now that we are on the subject of Bobby, what's all this mystery about his tutor? Is he Fisher or is he Fotheringay?'

'By the way, yes, I must explain that to you, because it's all my doing really. His name is Paul Fotheringay, a great friend of mine. He very much wanted to read the journal of Lady Maria Bobbin with a view to writing her life. Your aunt wouldn't hear of lending it to him, which he very politely asked if she would do, so Bobby and I between us arranged for him to come down here under another name as Bobby's tutor. You won't go and muck it all up, now will you, Michael darling?'

'Really, Amabelle, you are a baby. If you can play a trick on anybody you will. Poor Aunt Gloria; what a shame!'

'Honestly, I can't see any harm in it. In so far as anybody can have an influence over Bobby, Paul's will only be for the good, and as for the book on Lady Maria's Life and Works, I think it may be very well done and most amusing.'

'It will certainly be amusing, from what I remember of the journal,' said Michael, 'although it will probably be a case of laughing at and not with my poor great-grandmother. Philadelphia has become extraordinarily pretty since I saw her last, by the way.'

'Paul says she is so intelligent. He says she hardly ever speaks but that she has the most "heavenly instincts". I think he is falling in love with her, you know.'

Michael looked rather thoughtful on hearing this, and presently took his departure, saying, 'Good-bye then, my dear, dear friend. Please allow me to come and see you again soon. "Friendship," Lord Byron said, "is love without its wings," and that is a very consoling thought for me.'

When he had gone Amabelle went up to the nursery, where Elspeth Paula was having her evening meal.

'Oh, you cad,' she said to Sally, 'how could you have left me like that? You must have seen I didn't want to be alone with him; you are a monster, Sally darling.'

'It had to be, sooner or later,' said Sally calmly. 'Well what happened?'

'Oh, it was all most exhausting, you know, and frightfully dull. The same old arguments over and over again, just like a debate on protection *versus* free trade, each side knowing exactly what the other will say next and neither having any intention whatever of being convinced. Poor Michael, it is quite funny really when you think that probably I would have married him if he'd been at all clever about it. But instead of putting it to me as a sensible business proposition he would drag in all this talk about love the whole time, and I simply can't bear those showerings of sentimentality. Otherwise I should most likely have married him ages ago.'

'Even boring as he is?'

'Yes, I think so. One never can tell, of course. It was all this nonsense about love that put me off so much. And of course he is a cracking old bore, isn't he?'

'When I was a girl,' said Sally, 'and before I met Walter, you know, I fixed a definite price at which I was willing to overlook boringness. As far as I can remember it was twenty-five thousand pounds a year. However, nothing more than twelve seemed to offer, so I married Walter instead.'

'You have always had such a sensible outlook,' said Amabelle approvingly. 'If I had a girl I should say to her, "Marry for love if you can, it won't last, but it is a very interesting experience and makes a good beginning in life. Later on, when you marry for money, for heaven's sake let it be big money. There are no other possible reasons for marrying at all."'

Michael Lewes walked back through the moonlight to Compton Bobbin in a most curious frame of mind. During his three years' absence abroad he had persuaded himself that Amabelle really and in her heart of hearts wanted to marry him; at the same time he was convinced that if (too terrible a thought to contemplate) by any unhappy chance he should prove to be wrong and if she should definitely refuse him, in such a manner as to make him feel certain that there was no hope of her ever changing her mind, under those circumstances he would be so very unhappy that he would undoubtedly feel tempted to commit suicide. He had sincerely thought that for him the prospect of life without her would be more than he would be able to bear. And yet now, strangely enough, he felt almost as though a load had been lifted from his shoulders, happier and more light-hearted than for months.

The truth was that during those three years he had made an imaginary picture of Amabelle in his own mind which had become, the longer he was away from home, the more unlike the real woman; until, on finding himself sitting with her, holding that first interview on which he had built so many hopes, he found himself sitting beside a stranger, and the image of Amabelle in his mind was shattered for ever. The things which he said to her then had little real meaning or conviction behind them. They were speeches which he had been rehearsing to himself for three years, and out of a sort of habit, a sort of loyalty to that self which had invented them, he repeated them to her. It was with no particular feeling, except perhaps that of relief, that he received in reply a final and definite refusal. And now, it seemed that the course of his life was delightfully plain before him. Having left diplomacy, a profession of which he was heartily tired, he would settle down at Lewes Park, take his seat in the House of Lords, and marry some pretty, well-born and delightful girl, someone, in fact, not unlike his cousin, Philadelphia Bobbin. He hummed a little tune as he walked.

II

Lady Bobbin was always most particular that the feast of Christmas should be kept by herself, her family and dependents at Compton Bobbin in what she was pleased to call 'good old-fashioned style'. In her mind, always rather a muddled organ, this entailed a fusion of the Christmas customs brought to his adopted country by the late Prince Consort with those which have been invented by the modern Roman Catholic school of Sussex Humorists in a desperate attempt to revive what they suppose to have been the merrieness of England as it was before she came to be ruled by sour Protestants. And this was odd, because Germans and Roman Catholics were ordinarily regarded by Lady Bobbin with wild abhorrence. Nothing, however, could deter her from being an ardent and convinced Merrie Englander. The maypole on the village green, or more usually, on account of pouring rain, in the village hall; nocturnal expeditions to the local Druid stones to see the sun rise over the Altar Stone, a feat which it was seldom obliging enough to perform; masques in the summer, madrigals in the winter and Morris dances all the year round were organized and led by Lady Bobbin with an energy which might well have been devoted to some better cause. This can be accounted for by the fact of her having a sort of idea that in Merrie England there had been much hunting, no motor cars and that her bugbear, Socialism, was as yet unknown. All of which lent that imaginary period every attribute, in her eyes, of perfection.

But although each season of the year had its own merrie little rite it was at Christmas time that Lady Bobbin and her disciples in the neighbourhood really came into their own, the activities which she promoted during the rest of the year merely paving the way for an orgy of merrieness at Yule. Her first step in this direction was annually to summon at least thirty of the vast clan of Bobbin relations to spend the feast beneath their ancestral roof, and of these nearly twenty would, as a rule, find it convenient to obey. The remainder, even if their absence in Araby or Fair Kashmir rendered it palpably unlikely that they should accept, were always sent their invitation just the same. This was called Decent Family Feeling. Having gathered together all those of her late husband's relations who were available to come (her own had mostly died young from the rigours of tea planting in the Torrid Zone) she would then proceed to arrange for them to have a jolly Christmas. In this she was greatly helped by her brother-in-law, Lord Leamington Spa, who was also a fervent Merrie Englander, although, poor man, having been banished by poverty from his country estates and obliged to live all the year round in Eaton Square, he had but little scope for his activities in this direction.

Those who should have been Lady Bobbin's prop and mainstay at such a time, her own children, regarded the whole thing with a sort of mirthful disgust very injurious to her feelings. Nothing, however, could deter her from her purpose, and every year at Compton Bobbin the German and the Sussex customs were made to play their appointed parts. Thus the Christmas Tree, Christmas stockings and other activities of Santa Claus, and the exchange through the post of endless cards and calendars (German); the mistletoe and holly decorations, the turkeys, the boar's head, and a succession of carol singers and mummers (Sussex Roman Catholic); and the unlimited opportunity to over-eat on every sort of unwholesome food washed down with honest beer, which forms the groundwork for both schools of thought, combined to provide the ingredients of Lady Bobbin's Christmas Pudding.

On Christmas Eve, therefore, various members of the vast Bobbin family began to arrive from every corner of the British Isles. The seven sisters of the late Sir Hudson, who, be it remembered, had all married well, of course brought with them their husbands and children, and in many cases their dogs. It was noticeable that those who had married the least well came first, by train, while, as the day wore on, richer and ever richer motor cars, bedecked with larger and ever larger coronets, made stately progress down the drive; until the St Neots Rolls-Royce made its strawberry-leaved appearance, marking the end of this procession, just before dinner time.

Bobby, who for some while had been hovering round the front door, greeted this vehicle with bloodcurdling screams of delight, and rushed forward to assist from it his favourite aunt, the Duchess of St Neots and her daughter, his favourite cousin, Miss Héloïse Potts. (The duchess had been married five times, and had now settled down once more with her girlhood's husband, the Duke of St Neots, Miss Potts being the offspring of an intermediate venture with an American millionaire.)

To Paul the day was like an endless nightmare. Wherever he went he met some new, and for the most part, unsympathetic face, upon which the mutual embarrassment would become intense. Lady Bobbin, unversed in social graces, forbore to make any introductions, and Bobby spent most of the day sulking in his bedroom. His mother had instructed him to stay at home to greet his guests, the greater number of whom, however, he was pleased to consider quite unworthy of any notice.

Unluckily for himself, Paul happened to be the first down to breakfast, when, entering the dining-room with a prodigious yawn, he discovered six hungry Mackintoshes just off the midnight express from Perth. They reminded him of nothing so much as a Scotch family he had once seen on the music halls, sandwiched between some performing seals and a thin woman who gave imitations of (to him) unknown actors and actresses. The children, a son of about seventeen and three hideous girls of between ten and fourteen years old, all wore tartan woollen stockings and long tartan kilts. Lady Mackintosh was dressed in one, and Sir Alexander's reddish whiskers fell into the porridge which he ate – Paul could scarcely believe his eyes – standing up. Paul ventured a few polite remarks, inquired about their journey and observed that the weather was beautifully open, a cliché which he had learnt from Lady Bobbin, but as a family they appeared to be incapable of sustaining conversation, and he soon relapsed into that silence which they so evidently preferred. Presently Lady Bobbin came in from her early morning ride, and he was able to leave them to her hospitable ministrations.

Next to arrive were some more distant relations of Bobby's; Captain Chadlington, M.P., his wife Lady Brenda, their children Christopher Robin and Wendy, and a pack of ugly liver and white spaniels. They were being warmly congratulated by the rest of the party on Captain Chadlington's recent election to Parliament. Paul, having listened during lunch to some of his conversation, felt that it would be impossible to extend the congratulations to his electors; their choice of a representative seemed strangely unfortunate. He was evidently a young man of almost brutish stupidity, and Paul, who had hardly ever met any Conservative Members of Parliament before, was astounded to think that such a person could be tolerated for a moment at the seat of government. To hear him talking about Bolshevik Russia was a revelation to Paul, who took it for granted that Communism was now universally regarded as a high, though possibly a boring, ideal. Lady Bobbin's attitude towards it was just comprehensible, as she had evidently been out of touch with the world for years; but anybody who, being perforce in daily contact with persons of a certain intelligence, could still hold the views held by Captain Chadlington, must surely be a monster of denseness and stupidity.

Lord and Lady Leamington Spa came with their son, Squibby Almanack, whose appearance on the scene threw Paul into a fever of guilty terror since they had been at school together. He explained the situation to Bobby, who led his cousin into the schoolroom and told him the circumstances of Paul's presence in the house, upon which Squibby shook his fat sides, laughed a Wagnerian guffaw, and betook himself to the piano where he sat alone, picking out harmonious chords until it was time to dress for dinner.

Squibby Almanack was a person who belonged so exclusively to one small circle of very intimate friends that any divorce, however temporary, from that circle left him in a most pitiable condition of aimlessness and boredom. In London he was never seen anywhere unless accompanied by 'Biggy' Lennox and 'Bunch' Tarradale, the three of them forming, so to speak, a kind of modern *édition de luxe* of *Les Trois Mousquetaires*. Of this fraternity that insouciant beguiler of womanhood, Maydew Morris, provided a picturesque if only occasional fourth, a sort of d'Artagnan, who, although of very different character to the others, was drawn to them by that passion for German music which was the dominant note in all their lives. In spite of the fact that Squibby, Biggy and Bunch sought no adventures save those of the questing spirit, while the adventures of Maydew were the talk of London, they being men of words while he was in all things a man of deeds; in spite of many dissimilarities of nature, the four of them got on well together, and there were very few classical concerts and no performances of German opera at which they could not be seen sitting side by side, deep in perusal of the score. They were further made remarkable by an extraordinary physical resemblance to each other. All four were on the large side, blond and with pink and white complexions, all, with the exception of the hirsute Maydew, slightly bald and quite lacking in eyebrows. They walked with the same peculiar gait, swinging rather prominent buttocks in the manner of hockey-playing schoolgirls, and all sat listening to music (which, provided, of course, that it came from the Fatherland, was the beginning and end of their existence) with the same air of rigid concentration.

Nearly always they sat alone, dispensing with female company. Sometimes, however, by mutual consent, each would appear followed by some pretty débutante; these, with gestures of exaggerated courtesy, would be motioned into the intervening seats, presented with programmes, and then be completely ignored. Many unlucky girls were forced to subdue their very natural distaste for highbrow music for hours on end in order that they might sit in this delicious proximity to their heroes, listening with awe to the Olympian breathing and even, if lucky, occasionally brushing a heroic hand. In the case of Maydew things sometimes went further during the dark moments of The Ring, but the other three were most consistently platonic in their friendships, and were rapidly becoming the despair of matchmaking mammas. Things were indeed beginning to reach such a pitch that the more ambitious mothers of sub-débutantes were obliged to abandon Paris as an educational centre and dispatch their daughters instead to Munich, where they could be trained to endure classical music silently and, in certain cases, even intelligently. For Squibby, Biggy, Bunch and Maydew were all highly eligible young men. After one of these 'mixed' evenings each would sternly criticize the girls produced by the others. Should one of them have yawned, or even sighed a little, her immediate expulsion from her admirer's visiting list would be demanded, while too frequent crossing and uncrossing of legs would be made a cause for bitter complaint. Poor Bunch, always less fortunate in his choice than the others, because more easily beguiled by a pretty face, produced two inveterate leg crossers on consecutive nights during the Wagner season and was very severely spoken to by Biggy, who, seated on the other side of these ladies, had suffered in consequence sundry kicks and knocks, and complained that his attention had been quite abstracted from the stage during several moving moments. It is true that the climax of horror was reached by a girl friend of Maydew who, during the Rhinegold, was heard to ask in a piercing whisper what the heaps of firewood were for, what the story was all about anyway, and whether there wouldn't soon be an interval; but then a certain licence was always allowed to Maydew in matters of the heart.

When the performance was concluded the girls, if any, were obliged to stifle their cravings for food, drinks and the gay sights of the town, and were hurried away in one or two unromantically full taxis to their respective homes. (Maydew's girl, however, always lived in a different part of London from the others and had to be taken home alone.)

After this Squibby, Biggy and Bunch would foregather in Biggy's flat, where they drank strong beer and talked of music and philosophy, and where, much later if at all, they might be joined by a complacent Maydew.

These friends were so seldom separated that Christmas time, when from a sense of duty Squibby, Biggy and Bunch would rejoin their noble families, seemed to them the most inhuman of feasts. How, secretly, did they envy the unregenerate Maydew, who had departed with a Balham beauty to Berlin in order to improve his German. Squibby in particular, dreaded all the year round the Christmas house party at Compton Bobbin. This year, however, things might be more amusing; he had been fond of Paul at Eton, Bobby was now a grown-up person instead of a child; Michael Lewes, too, might prove to be pleasantly reformed. With less than his usual depression, he picked out some obscure motif from Siegfried.

★

The presence at Compton Bobbin of these people and others too numerous and boring to mention had the effect for the time being of throwing Philadelphia, Paul and Michael very much into each other's company. All three of them had a profound distaste for noise, crowds and organized pleasure, and they now spent most of their time hiding from the rest of the party. They went for long rides together every morning, Paul mounted, at his own urgent request, on an ancient cob which had long ago been turned out to enjoy a peaceful old age in the orchard, and which he found more to his liking than the aristocratic Boadicea. After dinner they would retire by mutual consent to the schoolroom and thus avoid the games of sardines, kick-the-bucket, and murders with which the others whiled away their evenings.

Bobby was now seldom to be seen; he spent most of his time giggling in corners with Miss Héloïse Potts, a pretty black-eyed little creature of seventeen who substituted parrot-like shrieks and screams of laughter for the more usual amenities of conversation, with apparently, since she was always surrounded by crowds of admiring young men, the greatest possible success. Even Squibby would often leave his beloved piano in order to enjoy her company, while at meal times her end of the table was eagerly sought after by all the men of the party, young and old, except for Paul and Michael. They, understanding neither her attraction nor her language (when she spoke at all she usually inserted the sound 'egi' after the consonants of her words, thus rendering her meaning far from clear to those unversed in this practice) would make their way with unhurried footsteps to the vacant places near Philadelphia. Indeed, everywhere else the conversation was too highly specialized to be very enjoyable. Héloïse, Bobby and their followers ended every sentence with 'egat thegi Regitz', which meant to the initiated 'at the Ritz'; Captain and Lady Brenda Chadlington, whose recent election to Parliament, actual and vicarious, had rather mounted to their heads, could speak of nothing but the P.M., S.B., L.G., the F.O., the L.C.C., the I.L.P., and their fellow M.P.s; the Mackintoshes fell upon their food in a famished silence, relieved, but very rarely, by remarks on the grouse disease; Lady Bobbin spoke to those about her of horses, hounds, and such obscure eventualities as going to ground, eating bedding, pecking while taking off, and being thoroughly well wormed; while Squibby, although quite intelligent, was apt to be a little wearisome with his musical talk or else a little exasperating with his theories on conditioned reflexes and other philosophical data.

Only Philadelphia, having no interests, talked no shop, but merely sat looking beautiful, calm and amiable, while Paul and Michael exchanged across her their cultured confidences, referring politely every now and then to her judgment. They both considered that although totally uneducated she was very far from being stupid, while the fact that what few books she had ever read had been written before the present century began gave to her mind and outlook a peculiar old-fashioned quality which Paul, at least, after the specious and metallic up-to-dateness of Marcella, found extremely restful.

As for Michael, he was consciously and most conveniently falling in love with her. For a day or two after his meeting with Amabelle he had been saddened and depressed. This was chiefly a retrospective feeling of regret for the last three years, embittered on account of what proved to have been a mere dream, a figment of his own imagination. Nature abhors a vacuum, and Michael had so extremely romantic a character that it was impossible for him not to imagine himself in love with somebody. His thoughts, therefore, turned almost immediately to his cousin Philadelphia, who, young, lovely, unsophisticated and intelligent, was clearly the sort of wife that a man in his position ought to have.

'I could never feel for her as I did for Amabelle,' he thought, as, in common with many people, he liked to believe himself only capable of loving once. 'All the same, what a charming wife she will make, and how happy I shall be with her!'

Lady Bobbin, who, with a mother's eye, saw clearly what was taking place, thought so too, as did young Sir Roderick. He had long intended that his sister should follow the example of his aunts in making a creditable alliance, and was delighted with this state of affairs. Philadelphia herself was happy in her new friends. She had a great respect for culture, and felt it to be a privilege that she was included in so many of their fascinating conversations. Of the two, however, she undoubtedly preferred Paul; Michael seemed to be rather grown up and alarming.

12

Christmas Day itself was organized by Lady Bobbin with the thoroughness and attention to detail of a general leading his army into battle. Not one moment of its enjoyment was left to chance or to the ingenuity of her guests; these received on Christmas Eve their marching orders, orders which must be obeyed to the letter on pain of death. Even Lady Bobbin, however, superwoman though she might be, could not prevent the day from being marked by a good deal of crossness, much over-eating, and a series of startling incidents.

The battle opened, as it were, with the Christmas stockings. These, in thickest worsted, bought specially for the occasion, were handed to the guests just before bedtime on Christmas Eve, with instructions that they were to be hung up on their bedposts by means of huge safety pins, which were also distributed. Lady Bobbin and her confederate, Lord Leamington Spa, then allowed a certain time to elapse until, judging that Morpheus would have descended upon the household, they sallied forth together (he arrayed in a white wig, beard and eyebrows and red dressing-gown, she clasping a large basket full of suitable presents) upon a stealthy noctambulation, during the course of which every stocking was neatly filled. The objects thus distributed were exactly the same every year, a curious and wonderful assortment including a pocket handkerchief, Old Moore's Almanack, a balloon not as yet blown up, a mouth organ, a ball of string, a penknife, an instrument for taking stones out of horses' shoes, a book of jokes, a puzzle, and, deep down in the woolly toe of the stocking, whence it would emerge in a rather hairy condition, a chocolate baby. Alas! Most of Lady Bobbin's guests felt that they would willingly have forgone these delightful but inexpensive objects in return for the night's sleep of which they were thus deprived. Forewarned though they were, the shadowy and terrifying appearance of Lord Leamington Spa fumbling about the foot of their beds in the light of a flickering candle gave most of them such a fearful start that all thoughts of sleep were banished for many hours to come.

For the lucky ones who did manage to doze off a rude shock was presently in store. At about five o'clock in the morning Master Christopher Robin Chadlington made a tour of the bedrooms, and having awoken each occupant in turn with a blast of his mouth organ, announced in a voice fraught with tragedy that Auntie Gloria had forgotten to put a chocolate baby in his stocking. 'Please might I have a bit of yours?' This quaint ruse was only too successful, and Christopher Robin acquired thereby no fewer than fourteen chocolate babies, all of which he ate before breakfast. The consequences, which were appalling, took place under the dining-room table at a moment when everybody else was busily opening the Christmas post. After this, weak but cheerful, young Master Chadlington spent the rest of the day in bed practising on his mouth organ.

By luncheon time any feelings of Christmas goodwill which the day and the religious service, duly attended by all, might have been expected to produce had quite evaporated, and towards the end of that meal the dining-room echoed with sounds of furious argument among the grown-ups. It was the duchess who began it. She said, in a clear, ringing voice which she knew must penetrate to the consciousness of Lady Bobbin:

'Yes, the day of the capitalist is over now, and a jolly good thing too.'

'May I ask,' said Lady Bobbin, rising like a trout to this remark and leaning across the projecting stomach of Lord Leamington Spa, 'why you, of all people, think that a good thing? Mind you, I don't admit that the capitalist system has come to an end, of course it hasn't, but why should you pretend to be pleased if it did? Affectation, I should call it.'

'No, not entirely affectation, Gloria darling. What I mean is that if, in a few years' time, people like us have no money left for luxuries we shall all, as a consequence, lead simpler and better lives. More fresh air, more sleep, more time to think and read. No night clubs, no Ritz, no Blue Train, less rushing about. And the result of that will be that we shall all be much happier. Don't you agree?'

Lady Bobbin, whose life was quite innocent of night clubs, the Ritz, and the Blue Train, and who had more time than she wanted in which to think and read, was not impressed by this statement. 'It has never been necessary to make a fool of oneself just because one happens to have money. There have always been plenty of decent people in the world, but unfortunately nobody ever hears about them, because they don't advertise themselves like the others. I wonder, Louisa, whether you will be quite so glad of the end of capitalism when you find yourself without the common necessities of life.'

'I don't anticipate that,' said the duchess comfortably. 'The world at present is suffering from over-production, not under-production, of the necessities of life.'

'Surely, duchess,' began Captain Chadlington ponderously, from his end of the table, feeling that now, if ever, was the time to make use of the information that he had so laboriously garnered from the P.M., the F.O., the I.L.P., S.B., L.G., and his fellow M.P.s, and to assert himself as a rising young politician. The duchess, however, took no notice of him and continued to goad Lady Bobbin.

'Think,' she said, 'how splendid it will be for our characters as a class if we are forced to lead simple, healthy lives, to look after our own children, and to earn our own bread. And then think of all the horrors that will be done away with, all those ghastly hideous country houses everywhere that will be pulled down. We shall be able to live in darling clean little cottages instead –'

'My house,' said Lady Bobbin, always quick to take offence, 'is, I hope, scrupulously kept. If you are implying –'

'Darling, don't be absurd. I only meant that they would be spiritually clean.'

'If you feel like this, Louisa,' said Lord Leamington Spa, now entering the lists with the light of battle in his eye, 'why on earth don't you act accordingly? Why not shut up Brackenhampton and live in one of the cottages there instead? I don't suppose there's anything to prevent you.'

'Nothing to prevent me, indeed!' cried the duchess. She had been waiting for this argument to be produced like a cat waiting for a mouse. 'There are nearly a hundred living souls to prevent me, that's all. D'you realize that we employ altogether ninety-eight people in the house and gardens at Brackenhampton? I can't, for no reason at all, take a step which would deprive all those old friends of work, food, even of a shelter over their heads. It would be quite unthinkable. I only say that if the whole system by which we live at present were to be changed we ourselves would all be a good deal happier than we are, and better in every way.'

Lady Bobbin said 'Pooh!' and rose to leave the table. She was trembling with fury.

The afternoon was so wet and foggy, so extremely unseasonable, in fact, that Lady Bobbin was obliged with the utmost reluctance to abandon the paper chase which she had organized. Until four o'clock, therefore, the house party was left to enjoy in peace that exquisite discomfort which can only be produced by overfed slumberings in arm-chairs. At four punctually everybody assembled in the ballroom while for nearly an hour the Woodford schoolchildren mummed. It was the Woodford schoolchildren's annual burden to mum at Christmas; it was the annual burden of the inhabitants of Compton Bobbin to watch the mumming. Both sides, however, bore this infliction with fortitude, and no further awkwardness took place until after tea, when Lord Leamington Spa, having donned once more his dressing-gown and wig, was distributing gifts from the laden branches of the Christmas Tree. This was the big moment of the day. The tree, of course, immediately caught fire, but this was quite a usual occurrence, and the butler had no difficulty in putting it out. The real crisis occurred when Lady Bobbin opened the largish, square parcel which had 'To darling Mummy from her very loving little Bobby' written on it, and which to Lady Bobbin's rage and horror was found to contain a volume entitled *The Sexual Life of Savages in Northern Melanesia*. This classic had been purchased at great expense by poor Bobby as a present for Paul, and had somehow changed places with *Tally Ho! Songs of Horse and Hound*, which was intended for his mother, and which, unluckily, was a volume of very similar size and shape. Bobby, never losing his head for an instant, explained volubly and in tones of utmost distress to his mother and the company in general that the shop must have sent the wrong book by mistake, and this explanation was rather ungraciously accepted. Greatly to Bobby's disgust, however, *The Sexual Life of Savages in Northern Melanesia* was presently consigned to the stoke-hole flames by Lady Bobbin in person.

The remaining time before dinner, which was early so that the children could come down, was spent by Bobby and Héloïse rushing about the house in a state of wild excitement. Paul suspected, and rightly as it turned out, that this excess of high spirits boded no good to somebody. It was quite obvious to the student of youthful psychology that some practical joke was on hand. He wondered rather nervously where the blow would fall.

It fell during dinner. Captain Chadlington was in the middle of telling Lady Bobbin what the P.M. had said to him about pig-breeding in the West of England when a loud whirring noise was heard under his chair. He looked down, rather startled, turned white to the lips at what he saw, sprang to his feet and said, in a voice of unnatural calm: 'Will the women and children please leave the room immediately. There is an infernal machine under my chair.' A moment of panic ensued. Bobby and Héloïse, almost too swift to apprehend his meaning, rushed to the door shrieking, 'A bomb, a bomb, we shall all be blown up,' while everyone else stood transfixed with horror, looking at the small black box under Captain Chadlington's chair as though uncertain of what they should do next. Paul alone remained perfectly calm. With great presence of mind he advanced towards the box, picked it up and conveyed it to the pantry sink, where he left it with the cold water tap running over it. This golden deed made him, jointly with Captain Chadlington, the hero of the hour. Lady Bobbin shook hands with him and said he was a very plucky young fellow and had saved all their lives, and he was overwhelmed with thanks and praise on every side. Captain Chadlington, too, was supposed to have shown wonderful fortitude in requesting the women and children to leave the room before mentioning his own danger. Only Bobby and Héloïse received no praise from anybody for their behaviour and were, indeed, more or less, sent to Coventry for the rest of the evening.

Captain Chadlington, secretly delighted to think that he was now of such importance politically that attempts were made on his life (he never doubted for a moment that this was the doing of Bolshevik agents) went off to telephone to the police. Bobby and Héloïse, listening round the corner, heard him say: 'Hullo, Woodford police? It is Captain Chadlington, M.P., speaking from Compton Bobbin. Look here, officer, there has just been an attempt to assassinate me. The Bolsheviks, I suppose. An infernal machine under my chair at dinner. Would you send somebody along to examine it at once, please, and inform Scotland Yard of what has happened?'

Lady Brenda said: 'I have always been afraid of something like this ever since Charlie made that speech against Bolshevism at Moreton-in-Marsh. Anyhow, we must be thankful that it was no worse.'

Lady Bobbin said that perhaps now the Government would do something about the Bolsheviks at last.

Lord Leamington Spa said that he didn't like it at all, which was quite true, he didn't, because on Christmas night after dinner he always sang 'The Mistletoe Bough' with great feeling and now it looked as though the others would be too busy talking about the bomb to listen to him.

Michael Lewes and Squibby Almanack dared to wonder whether it was really an infernal machine at all, but they only imparted this scepticism to each other.

The duchess said that of course it would be very good publicity for Charlie Chadlington, and she wondered – but added that perhaps, on the whole, he was too stupid to think of such a thing.

Captain Chadlington said that public men must expect this sort of thing and that he didn't mind for himself, but that it was just like those cowardly dagoes to attempt to blow up a parcel of women and children as well.

Everybody agreed that the tutor had behaved admirably.

'Where did you get it from?' Paul asked Bobby, whom he presently found giggling in the schoolroom with the inevitable Héloïse.

'A boy in my house made it for me last half; he says nobody will be able to tell that it's not a genuine bomb. In fact, it *is* a genuine one, practically, that's the beauty of it. Poor old Charlie Chad., he's most awfully pleased about the whole thing, isn't he, fussing about with those policemen like any old turkey cock. Oh! It all went off too, too beautifully, egI cegouldn't thegink egit fegunnegier, cegould yegou?'

'I think you're an odious child,' said Paul, 'and I've a very good mind to tell your mother about you.'

'That would rather take the gilt off your heroic action, though, wouldn't it, old boy?' said Bobby comfortably.

The local police, as Bobby's friend had truly predicted, were unable to make up their minds as to whether the machine was or was not an infernal one. Until this pretty point should be settled Captain Chadlington was allotted two human bulldogs who were instructed by Scotland Yard that they must guard his life with their own. A camp bed was immediately made up for one of these trusty fellows in the passage, across the captain's bedroom door, and the other was left to prowl about the house and garden all night, armed to the teeth.

'Darling,' said the duchess to Bobby, as they went upstairs to bed after this exhausting day, 'have you seen the lovely man who's sleeping just outside my room? I don't know what your mother expects to happen, but one is only made of flesh and blood after all.'

'Well, for goodness sake, try and remember that you're a duchess again now,' said Bobby, kissing his aunt good night.

13

The two children of Captain and Lady Brenda Chadlington took a tremendous fancy to Paul, and he, although in the first place had been completely put off by the fact that their names were Christopher Robin and Wendy, decided after a day or two that he would overlook this piece of affectation, which was, after all, not their own fault. He addressed them as George and Mabel (his lips refusing to utter their real names) and became very much attached to them.

'You see, it's not as though the poor things had chosen those names themselves,' he said to Bobby, 'and I should like to do what little I can to help them towards some form of self-respect. It is really tragic to see children surrounded by such an atmosphere of intellectual dishonesty. Poor George and Mabel.'

'What d'you mean?' asked Bobby, yawning. He was both bored and piqued, as Héloïse had gone off for the whole day with Squibby.

'In every respect,' went on Paul, 'they are treated as congenital half-wits by their parents. It is really shocking. They tell me,' he added disgustedly, 'that their Sussex house is called "The Cottage in the Wood". Well, I mean to say! I always refer to it as The Cedars when mentioning it to them. "The Cottage in the Wood" indeed; it's nearly as good as "Mulberrie Farm". I don't know what the English-speaking race is coming to.'

'Oh, of course, Brenda is the most affected woman in the world, we all know that, but she seems to be bringing them up quite nicely, I must say. They aren't at all spoilt or naughty.'

'They may not be. All I know is that their poor little minds are simply drowning in a welter of falsehood and pretence.'

'I s'pose you mean,' said Bobby, lighting a cigarette, 'that they are made to say their prayers and discouraged from seeing Brenda and Charlie naked in the bath. Personally, I'm rather old-fashioned about these things, too.'

'They are treated insanely. Not only are their brains being warped by constant application to the most sterile and insidiously unmoral forms of child literature – Barrie, A. A. Milne, Kenneth Grahame, Kipling, and so on – but they are being sternly repressed in every way. Just at this age when they should be opening out to life, assimilating new experiences of every sort, learning to care for truth and beauty in every form, they are subjected to constant humiliations, constant thwarting and hindering. Each little instinct has to be fought back as soon as it appears. How can they be expected to develop? Look at what happened to poor George on Christmas Day!'

'I didn't then and I should simply hate to now,' said Bobby, wondering when was the soonest that he could expect Héloïse back from her outing.

'Poor child, what could be more natural though? It was obviously the first time in his stunted little life that he had had the chance to eat as much chocolate as he really wanted. That incident told a tale of wanton cruelty.'

'Wanton greediness, I should call it. Dirty little pig.'

'As for Mabel, it is tragic to see the way she is chivvied about from pillar to post all day. "Have you washed your hands, Wendy? Did you clean your teeth? Take off your outdoor shoes. Get on with your knitting. Why haven't you brushed your hair? Put on your coat. Go for a walk." And all this, I would have you observe, to a child of inherently contemplative nature, a philosopher, probably, in the making. How *can* she develop properly? Every time she sits down to commune within herself, to think out some abstruse problem or to register some new experience, she is hounded off to perform dreary and perfunctory tasks. My heart bleeds for Mabel.'

'Wendy's the laziest little beast I know. She'd never do a thing if she were left to herself. It's pure idleness with her.'

'I entirely disagree with you, Bobby. That child has ideas and perceptions far beyond her age, and naturally they tire her out. She needs time and leisure in which to tabulate the impressions which she is always receiving from the outer world. Another thing very sad to see is the way her emotional life is threatened.'

'How d'you mean?'

'The poor child has a most distinct father-fixation, haven't you realized that? Very marked indeed.'

'Oh, nonsense, Paul; what extraordinary ideas you do have.'

'Nonsense, is it? My dear Bobby, just you notice the way she copies him in everything – she sits, walks, eats and talks exactly like him. Why, in another year or two she'll be the living image of him, always a sign of morbid affection, you know.'

'Really, you do surprise me. I suppose heredity could have nothing to do with it?' said Bobby sarcastically.

'Oh, no, nothing whatever. Nobody believes in hereditary influences nowadays. No, it's all the result of this mad passion she has, subconsciously, of course, for her father. Most dangerous.'

'Well,' said Bobby, 'I expect you know best. Anyhow, here comes one of the little cherubs, bless his tiny heart.'

'Mr Fisher,' said Christopher Robin, putting his head round the schoolroom door. 'Please will you come out with us? Mother says we must go up the drive and back before lunch.'

'*Must, must*, always that word "*must*",' sighed Paul. 'So unwholesome, so stifling. Yes, I'd like to come out with you, George. Where's Mabel, then?'

'She's just looking for still-borns in *The Times*,' said Christopher Robin. 'I'll fetch her – oh, here she comes though.' Wendy Chadlington kept a little red pocket-book in which she wrote down the number of still-born babies every day as announced in the Births column of *The Times*. This lugubrious hobby seemed to afford her the deepest satisfaction. 'Any luck today?' asked Christopher Robin casually.

'Not today. One lot of triplets though. I keep a separate page for them, and there were two still-borns yesterday. One mustn't expect too much, you know.'

'Now George and Mabel,' said Paul, 'if you are quite ready let's go, shall we? There isn't much time, really, before lunch.'

Wendy looked at Christopher Robin and they both giggled. They were not, as yet, accustomed to their new names, and thought that Paul, though both amiable and entertaining, was undoubtedly a little mad.

Paul carefully replaced a volume of Lady Maria's journal behind the radiator, a practice that had but little meaning since Lady Bobbin, for whose deception it had been invented, never came near the schoolroom by any chance.

'What story are you going to tell us today?' asked Wendy as they started out.

'Please, Mr Fisher, tell us a story about animals.'

'A true story about animals, please, Mr Fisher.'

Yesterday's 'story', a homily on the life history of eels, had not really gone with much of a swing, and it was felt that a true story would be preferable to one which he had palpably invented himself.

'Well, let me think,' said Paul. 'I don't know many stories about animals. What kind of animal?'

'Any kind. *Please*, Mr Fisher. You told us a lovely one yesterday,' said Christopher Robin encouragingly.

'I really *don't* know any,' said Paul, at his wits' end. 'Unless you'd like to hear one that I read in *Country Life* the other day. That was supposed to be true, I believe.'

'What's *Country Life*?'

'It's a paper your Aunt Gloria takes in.'

'*I* know,' said Wendy in tones of superiority, and added in a stage whisper: 'Christopher Robin can't read, you know, so of course papers aren't very interesting to him.'

'Pig,' said Christopher Robin. 'I *can* read. Anyway, *you* –'

Paul had been treated to arguments of this kind before, and hastily said: 'I'll tell you the story then, if you'll be quiet. A man was walking across a farm-yard –'

'A farmer?' asked Wendy, 'or a labourer?'

'If you interrupt I shan't go on. The man who wrote this story to *Country Life* – I don't know who he may have been – was walking across a farmyard when he saw two rats running along in front of him. He threw a stick which he had in his hand at the first rat and killed it dead. To his great surprise the second rat, instead of running away, stood quite still as though it were waiting for something. The man thought this was so odd that he went over to look at it, and when he got quite near he saw that it was stone blind and had a straw in its mouth. The rat he had killed had been leading it along by the straw, you see, and the poor blind one thought it had stopped to have a drink or something, I suppose, and was just patiently waiting there for it to go on.'

'Well?' said Wendy after a pause.

'That's the end of the story.'

'But what did the man do with the blind rat?'

'I don't know. He didn't say in *Country Life*.'

'I should have kept it for a pet,' said Christopher Robin, 'and led it about on a straw.'

'I should *love* a dear little blind rat,' said Wendy, and added in a contemplative voice: 'I sometimes wish I were blind you know, so that I needn't see my tooth water after I've spat it.'

'I know what,' said Christopher Robin, 'let's pretend you're a blind rat, Wendy. Shut your eyes, you see, and put this straw in your mouth, and I'll put the other end of it in mine, and I'll lead you along by it.'

That evening Lady Brenda said to Paul: 'I think it is so kind of you to take my wee things out for walks (I'm afraid they *must* bore you rather, don't they?) but – please don't mind me saying this – don't you think that game you taught them with the straw is perhaps just the least little bit unhygienic? Of course if the straw could be sterilized I wouldn't mind, but you see one can't be certain where it came from, and I am so frightened always of T.B. So I've strictly forbidden them to play it any more, I hope you won't be angry; it's too sweet of you to bother with them,' and with a vague smile she drifted away.

Héloïse Potts took Squibby Almanack for a ride. She did this mainly in order to annoy Bobby, because she knew that she would be fearfully bored by Squibby before the day was over. They went, in the duchess's black Rolls-Royce, to visit Bunch Tarradale, whose ancestral home, Cracklesford Castle, was some thirty miles away, in Warwickshire.

Bunch was more than pleased to see them, and quickly led off Squibby to the downstairs lavatory so that they could have a good gossip.

'Have you heard from Biggy?' said Bunch, with more than a hint of malice in his voice. 'He's in love again.'

'Not again! Who is it this time?'

'A girl called Susan Alveston. However, she's refused him, which is all to the good. Very ugly and stupid I hear she is, and only sixteen.'

'Biggy always likes them young though, doesn't he? How d'you know she's ugly and stupid?'

'He said so in his letter. He said "You might not call her strictly beautiful, but she has a most fascinating and expressive little face." That means she must be ugly, doesn't it, and all girls of sixteen are stupid. All the ones I've met are, anyhow. Besides, she must be, to refuse Biggy.'

'You seem to think that girls only have one idea in their heads, and that is to marry a lord as soon as they can.'

'Well, isn't that true?'

'*I* have my ideals,' said Squibby.

'And have you heard from Maydew?' continued Bunch. 'I had a picture postcard saying everything had turned out very satisfactorily.'

'So did I. Balham is evidently a success. What a sensible man Maydew is, to be sure, so untrammelled by feeling. It must be delightful to have a nature of that sort.' He sighed deeply. 'Anyhow, I am very glad about poor old Biggy, only I do feel that he should be more careful. One of these days he will be accepted, and how he would resent that.'

'So should we all. Do you think that perhaps my mother has now been subjected to the maddening prattle of your first cousin for long enough? Shall we relieve her?'

'Just a minute. I knew there was something else I wanted to ask you. What is all this nonsense about a quintet society?'

'Ah! Biggy has written to you about that, too, has he? Mind you, I think it's quite a good idea in some ways, only I'm afraid it's bound to be a failure if Biggy has anything to do with it. Still, I suppose one will have to join?'

'I suppose so. One must support the poor old boy, though, frankly, it seems rather a waste of his time and our money. It's so like Biggy, isn't it? He always starts these wildly unpractical schemes. As though there were not enough good concerts as it is, besides, I hate listening to music in drawing-rooms. One's always catching people's eyes.'

'He tells me we shall be able to take off our boots.'

'I always do in any case.'

'All the same, I dare say there is something to be said for it, you know,' muttered Squibby grudgingly as they went upstairs. Fond as they were of each other, these friends had a sort of underlying bitterness in their characters which made it impossible for them not to indulge sometimes in a little harmless venom; like certain brothers and sisters, they always pretended to be sceptical of any venture embarked upon by the others.

On the way home Miss Héloïse Potts took advantage of the darkness and the undoubted cold to snuggle very close to poor Squibby, who, overwhelmed by her proximity and by the kisses which soon fell upon his lips, responded in no uncertain manner and presently begged of her to marry him.

'No thanks, darling,' said Héloïse. 'I'm not old enough to marry yet. But when I am grown up I'm going to be either a duchess like Mummy or a tart like Amabelle. Nothing in between for me. Only,' she added jauntily, 'there are rather few eligible dukes about so it almost looks as though –'

14

Darling Evelyn,

How sweet, but oh, how very naughty of you to send me such lovely links, at least I s'pose it was you who sent them, wasn't it? Cartier very stupidly forgot to put in a card, but I don't know anybody else who would be likely to do such a divine thing. I just can't tell you how much I dote on them. I look at them all day and think what an angel you are to give me a present like that, although I do feel rather badly about not having sent you even a Christmas card! However, I haven't forgotten the date of your birthday, Evelyn, dear. I have had a gorgeous Christmas. I do hope you have, too. Amabelle, who has taken a house down here, gave me an evening watch (platinum with diamonds round the edge) and Auntie Loudie St Neots a pair of gold hair-brushes, rather chi-chi, but very attractive all the same, and I had altogether £60 in tips. But far, far the best of all my presents do I like your exquisite links. See you very soon, I hope. I may be in London for a few days towards the end of the holidays, in which case we might lunch or something? Anyway, mind you come trailing over to Eton some time next term, won't you?

Many more thanks for the lovely surprise.

With love from
Bobby.

Bobby folded up this letter, put it in an envelope, addressed it, and laid it in a pile of about six others, all couched in exactly identical terms.

'Think of some more people for me to write to,' he said to Paul, who was deeply engrossed in the journal.

'What sort of people?' asked Paul vaguely.

'The sort that might be taken in by a letter like this and stump up with something fairly reasonable.' He read Paul the letter.

'That's rather a good idea, isn't it?' said Paul. 'I wish I was brazen enough to do that sort of thing.'

'But I can't think of anybody else. You see, it must be someone rich, who enjoys giving presents. I won't risk taking all this trouble just to get a New Year's card back.'

'Nobody seems to enjoy giving me presents,' said Paul gloomily; 'and if they do their mothers go and burn the thing in the stoke-hole. It is hard – *The Sexual Life of Savages in Northern Melanesia* is a book I had always wanted most particularly too.'

'You can have *Tally Ho! Songs of Horse and Hound*, old boy. Here it is if you'd like it. I'm still wondering how they could have got mixed up. Do you think darling Héloïse might have had something to do with it?'

'I expect that's exactly what did happen. Thank heaven the little chatterbox isn't here any more. She gets on my nerves with her sudden shrieks and all that egi-egi.'

It was New Year's Day, and the entire house party had gone away that morning except for Lord Lewes, who remained alone and palely loitering, with the intention of very shortly laying his coronet, estates and person at the feet of his cousin, Philadelphia.

'She may be a little chatterbox,' said Bobby sourly, 'but nobody can deny that she is divinely attractive.'

'Indeed, *I* can.'

'And, as a matter of fact, I may quite likely marry her in years' and years' time,' went on Bobby, taking no notice of Paul. 'We are engaged now, if you want to know, secretly, of course.'

'My dear, she'll be married and have children before you're out of the cradle.'

'Oh, I don't expect to be her *first* husband, naturally. And you know, on second thoughts, I'm not at all sure I wouldn't rather marry Aunt Loudie. She's even more my cup of tea in many ways, and now it's allowed by law I shall consider it very seriously indeed.'

'Your mother told me most distinctly that aunts were not allowed. Only uncles, *she* said.'

'Oh, Mother! She just makes up the rules as she goes along. I dare say she's guessed my guilty passion for Aunt Loudie and thinks she can throw cold water on it from the start. If one's allowed it's quite obvious that the other would be too. I wonder where Delphie is, by the way?'

'I think I saw her go out with Michael – for a walk, I suppose.'

'That's all to the good. Splendid. I'm very pleased about that.'

'Oh, you are, are you? May one ask why?'

'Well, naturally, I'm delighted when I see Delphie going about with Michael. I'm arranging for her to marry him, you know.'

'Oh, indeed! I thought he was supposed to be in love with Amabelle?'

'Love,' said Bobby pompously, 'has little or nothing to do with a matrimonial alliance. We Bobbins never marry, we contract alliances, and all that is necessary for a successful alliance is mutual respect. Now Michael's a sentimental old thing, and he likes to imagine that his heart is broken irreparably; it gives him a certain kick, I suppose. But that needn't prevent him from wanting to marry and settle down with a family of his own. Naturally he's not *in love* with Delphie, I don't see, personally, how one could be, but she would make him an ideal wife, healthy, well-born, properly educated for that sort of position, and so on. Just the very thing he ought to be looking for.'

'Oh, damn you,' said Paul.

'Now what's the matter?'

'Well, you see, I happen to be in love with her myself.'

'Oh, no! Are you honestly? How too enthralling this is. I wish I knew what you all see in her. But that's perfect. I hope Michael has noticed; it ought to egg him on no end, oughtn't it? A little rivalry and so forth. I must drop him a hint.'

'Do be serious for one minute, Bobby.'

'I *am*, dead serious.'

'You see, I want to marry her myself.'

'You want to marry her? Poor old boy, I'm afraid that's absolutely no cop. Delphie must marry well whatever happens. We Bobbins always do. Not that I wouldn't dote on you for a brother-in-law if things were just a tiny bit different, but – you see?'

'You are a worldly little beast, Bobby,' said Paul gloomily, but without rancour.

'Yes, aren't I? It does pay so much better to be. I'm awfully sorry if you're feeling wretched about all this though, Paul dear, I am truly. I'm very fond of you, though you might not think it. Now I'll put these letters to be posted (let's hope they bring in a good fat return) and then we might ride over to Amabelle's, shall we? It's rather late, but we can always say that we stopped on the way back for a game of squash.'

At this moment Philadelphia wandered aimlessly into the room and asked what they were going to do.

'Where's Michael then?' said Bobby.

'I've no idea at all. Oh, yes, though, hasn't he gone out with Mummy to look at that old barrow he's going to excavate?'

'Why didn't you go with them?'

'I thought it would be so boring.'

'Barrows,' said Bobby severely, 'are very far from boring, let me tell you. I think you should try to take more interest in such things. You seem to live in a walking swoon.'

'Anyway, what are you doing? Can't I come too?'

'We're only going to ride over for some squash in Woodford.'

'I'll come and watch.'

'All right, do,' said Bobby, in exasperation. 'Only I warn you there won't be much to watch. It's all a blind really, this squash and riding. We're really going over to see Amabelle Fortescue at Mulberrie Farm.'

'Oh, how thrilling. You know I heard Mother talking to Auntie Loudie about her, and afterwards she forbade me ever to go near Mulberrie Farm.'

'Just you come along now then,' said Paul. 'Amabelle is longing to meet you, I know, and this is an excellent opportunity.'

On their way to the stables Bobby drew Paul aside and said: 'Now we must try and make her pay attention to that barrow, community of interests is supposed to be an essential of married happiness.'

'Damn you,' said Paul again.

They found the party at Mulberrie Farm scattered about the drawing-room in attitudes of deathlike exhaustion.

'We're awfully tired and ill today, darlings,' said Amabelle, 'but it's always lovely to see you, and I'm glad you've brought your sister at last, Bobby dear.' She lay curled up on a Knole sofa and appeared almost unable to open her eyes. Her voice had become a mere whisper, her face a grey mask on which the rouge showed up with startling intensity. Her eyelashes, which she always painted navy blue, were now no darker than the shadows beneath them. Even the tactful Bobby was hardly able to conceal the shock that her appearance had given him. Sally and Jerome lay on other sofas, their ravaged faces half buried in pillows. Walter was nowhere to be seen.

'What on earth is the matter with you all?' said Bobby, after surveying this scene for some minutes in silence. 'I know, you've been having a blind,' he added accusingly.

Amabelle, who had dropped off to sleep again, woke with a start and said, 'That's it, however did you guess? We got to bed at half-past eight this morning, if you want to know, and we should be there still if it wasn't for Sally's perfectly idiotic theory that it makes one feel better to get up for tea. I can't say I've noticed it. I couldn't possibly feel more awful myself.'

'What on earth have you been doing that could keep you up until eight-thirty; and why didn't you invite me to the ball?'

'We went to the New Year party at the Albert Hall. Sally suggested it at dinner last night, so we just bundled ourselves into fancy dress and popped up to London in the car. Oh, how I wish we hadn't, too!'

'Oh, cads!' said Bobby, and his eyes quite literally filled with tears. It was always a very real sorrow to him if he missed a party of any kind. He felt cross and resentful.

Amabelle saw this at once; she knew her little Bobby. 'Darling, you can't imagine how much we all longed for you to come,' she said quickly, 'but I simply couldn't think of taking you, for your own sake, my sweet. You must remember that it never pays to risk quarrelling with one's bread and butter, and you've got to keep in your mamma's good books, especially if you're not to be packed off to Sandhurst, eh? So don't look quite so sad, precious.'

'Oh, well, I see your point, I suppose. Actually, of course, it could have been worked quite safely; still, never mind, it's all over now. Was it lovely?'

'It was lovely,' said Sally, sitting up with an obvious effort, and powdering her nose. 'Simply grand. I got off with a miner from Lancashire, who had just absconded with the local slate club money and was having the time of his life in London on the proceeds. He was a great wit; he said the lady miners are minarets – he made that sort of joke. He was that sort of man, you see. Heavenly. And he said "I know where I've met you before, with Lady Alistair Grayson in her villa at Antibes," and I said "You can't have met me there because I don't know the old trout," and he said, "Oh, nor do I, of course. But I always read about her parties in the papers." That is the sort of man he was – very O.K. I had a great romance with him. And who Walter got off with no one knows because he vanished half-way through the party, you see, and hasn't come back yet. He must be having a gorgeous time.'

Sally rose uncertainly to her feet and staggered upstairs.

'Poor darling Sally,' said Amabelle. 'I must say she does behave well on these occasions. I admire her for it a good deal. It's really too naughty of Walter not to ring her up or something; he must know by now how much she always worries.'

'There's your groom,' said Bobby, who hated hearing about other people's troubles, and had wandered over to the window, 'galloping Paul's horse round and round that field; he is a divine man. Fielden, our groom, told Mother that he'd never known me to take so much interest in riding, or exercise the horses so thoroughly before, as I do these hols.; and of course the old girl puts it down entirely to Paul's wonderful influence. Tell us some more about that party you so kindly asked me to.'

'It was just like any other party of that sort. It had every element of discomfort and boredom and yet for no particular reason that one could see, it was divine fun. It's not often one finds English people really gay, is it? And in the Albert Hall of all places, in that odour of Sunday afternoon concerts, it is quite astonishing.'

'Who was there?'

'Everybody in the world. The improper duchess for one.'

'With Héloïse?'

'I didn't see her, but she may have been too well disguised. Jane and Albert were there, just back from Paris.'

'Were they, now?' said Paul with interest. 'And how are they? Happy?'

'Wretched, I believe. Did they expect anything else? What a silly marriage that was, to be sure.'

'Oh dear,' said Paul gloomily, 'it really is rather disillusioning. When one's friends marry for money they are wretched, when they marry for love it is worse. What is the proper thing to marry for, I should like to know?'

'The trouble is,' said Amabelle, looking at Philadelphia whom she thought surprisingly beautiful, 'that people seem to expect happiness in life. I can't imagine why; but they do. They are unhappy before they marry, and they imagine to themselves that the reason of their unhappiness will be removed when they are married. When it isn't they blame the other person, which is clearly absurd. I believe that is what generally starts the trouble.'

'I expect that's quite right,' said Paul, sighing.

'In any case,' Amabelle went on, 'the older I get the more I think it is fatal to marry for love. The mere fact of being in love with somebody is a very good reason for not marrying them, in my opinion. It brings much more unhappiness than anything else. Look at Sally. Every time Walter leaves the house for half an hour she thinks he will be run over by a bus and on an occasion like this it's impossible to guess what she must be suffering. Now, supposing she weren't in love with him, she'd be feeling ghastly now, like I am; but she wouldn't be frightfully unhappy as well, and on ordinary occasions she could enjoy her life peacefully. What does Bobby think about it?'

Bobby said, 'Just what I told you, see?' to Paul, and to Amabelle, 'I still think it's lousy of you not to have taken me last night. I shan't get over it for ages and ages. As for marriage, I fully intend to marry you, darling, when I'm a bit older and have had my fling, you know. We'll live where it's hot, shall we? and adopt four black children and be as happy as the day is long.'

'You are a fool, Bobby. I'm very glad you've brought your beautiful sister here at last,' said Amabelle. Philadelphia blushed, she was unused to being thought beautiful. 'She must come again soon, when we're not all so tired and sad. Where's Michael, by the way? Still at Compton Bobbin?'

'Oh, yes, rather,' said Bobby. 'He's gone out to look for a barrow to excavate, I believe.'

'Gosh! how boring.'

'No, no, not at all boring, you know, really. Barrow digging is a fascinating occupation.'

'Is that a car coming up the drive?' said Amabelle languidly. It was getting dark, and the sidelights of a car flashed into the room.

'Yes, it is. A huge Daimler, with Walter in it. Ha, ha, that's funny; the old boy's still in fancy dress.'

Walter came in rather sheepishly, still wearing his *matelot* clothes of the night before, and borrowed some money from Jerome to pay for the car, which was a Daimler hire. This done, he came back again, lit a cigarette and said in an exaggeratedly casual voice, 'Sally all right?'

'I suppose so; I don't imagine she's awake yet really. Did you have a good time?'

'No, lousy. Why on earth did you go away like that without me?' Walter flung himself out of the room.

'Hity-tity,' said Amabelle. 'So that's the tone, is it? Well, so long as one knows. How much did you lend him, Jerome darling?'

'A fiver,' said Jerome, who was now sitting up and reading *The Times*.

'I'll give it to you myself. It was rather a shame, I suppose, leaving him there. Still, half-past six, you know, and he hadn't been seen by anyone since midnight.'

'There are trains,' said Jerome, pursuing his own line of thought, 'and road coaches.'

'In those clothes? I hardly think he could have.'

'He had an overcoat. He must know he can't afford Daimler hires. It would have been more honest.'

'It would have been most unlike Walter. How goes the journal, Paul?'

'Grand. I'm reading the first volume now. This morning I got to where "Dearest Mamma very kindly gave me permission to go a little way into the shrubbery with Sir Josiah Bobbin, and while there he said that it would make him very happy if I should become his wife. I replied in some agitation, due to the beatings of my poor heart, that my future must be decided by dearest Mamma and dear Papa; whereupon he told me, to my immeasurable joy, that he had already solicited and obtained their consent to our union. We then went back into the drawing-room, where I was embraced by dearest Mamma, dear Papa and all my dear brothers and sisters, also by poor Aunt Agatha, who all said that they hoped I should be very very happy. It was a most touching scene, and I felt quite *faint* from joy and emotion." Isn't it exquisite?' said Paul enthusiastically. 'The account of her wedding is too perfect; I can't remember that exactly, but I'll bring it along sometime. You know, Amabelle, I think I shall be able to write something unusually good after this, thanks entirely to you and Bobby, of course.'

'Don't mention it, old boy,' said Bobby. 'Just remember me in your dedication, though. "To my friend, Sir Roderick Bobbin, Bt., great-grandson of Lady Maria, without whose help, encouragement and never failing sympathy this book could hardly have been written." Something on those lines, you know.'

Paul said nothing. He intended to dedicate the 'Life' to Philadelphia Bobbin.

15

Shortly after the New Year, foot and mouth disease vanished from the cowsheds of Gloucestershire, and the Bobbin hunt was able to resume its season. Lady Bobbin was now rarely to be seen between breakfast, at which meal she would appear booted and spurred to eat vast quantities of meaty foods, and tea-time, when she would loudly re-live the day for the benefit of Philadelphia, Paul and Michael. Her accounts of what had happened were always interspersed with bitter criticisms of the young female members of the hunt, who, according to her description of their appearance, might be supposed to come out hunting in full evening dress and with the sole idea of abstracting the attention of their men friends from the serious business on hand.

'There was Maisie Critchley, in a pink shirt and a satin stock (I know you'll hardly believe me), made up to the eyes and her hair all fuzzed out under her bowler. Perfectly disgusting. I can't imagine why she bothers to get up on a horse at all; she can't go for nuts and she spends her whole time coffee-housing with young Walters. Then, of course, he's too busy holding her horse while she makes up her face and so on to think of anything else. I don't know what the young people are coming to. Lucky thing my poor father is dead, that's what I say. It would have broken his heart to see all these goings-on.'

Paul, hoping to see some painted sirens, went to one or two meets; but the women seemed to him, young and old, to be of a uniform plainness, with hard, weather-beaten faces entirely devoid of any artificial aids to beauty. He could only suppose that Lady Bobbin, in the delirium of the chase, was subject to hallucinations which took the form of satin stocks and pretty painted faces.

Bobby, who, rather against his will, admitted to a fondness for hunting, usually accompanied his mother and stayed out most of the day; but Philadelphia, since having as a child broken nearly every bone in her body when her pony fell at a stone wall out cubbing, had no nerve left. She and Paul now spent their time between Mulberrie Farm, both Sally and Amabelle having taken a great fancy to her, and the barrow, where Michael was busily conducting excavations with the aid of four members of the local unemployed.

'That book you lent me,' she said one morning as they were walking towards the barrow; 'I finished it in bed last night. It's very sad, isn't it?'

Paul looked at her with positive rapture.

'Did you really think so?' he said incredulously.

'Yes, of course. It is dreadful – I cried at the end.'

'Oh, you *didn't*, Philadelphia?'

'Yes, I did. Why, don't you think it's very sad?'

'I do. But nobody else does, you know. They don't understand it; all the reviewers thought it was meant to be a funny book.'

'How could they? How perfectly absurd. I think it's too terrible, and wonderfully written, isn't it? Poor Leander Belmont, he was so happy at Oxford, d'you remember? And so miserable when he was working for the pawnbroker. I'm sure that must be true of certain young men. I'm sure lots of them are happy until they leave their university and then never happy any more.'

'Indeed,' said Paul eagerly, 'you are so right. I was just like that myself. I don't believe I shall ever be as happy again as I was at Oxford.'

'It is different for girls, of course. I had a dreadful childhood; I was wretched the whole time. How I longed to be grown up!'

'And now that you are grown up, is it any better?'

'Up to now I haven't thought so. I came out in London, you know, about three years ago, and went to parties, which I simply hated. I didn't like the people I met, and they didn't like me either. Since then I've just lived down here, with nothing to do and no friends, and been even more miserable than I was as a child. But I've always felt that there must be people somewhere in the world whom I could like and get on with, and I see that I was right.' She paused a moment, and then said,

'Now that you and Sally and Amabelle and Michael have all appeared in my life I'm very happy indeed. I don't know what I shall do when you all go away.' Her eyes filled with tears as she said this.

Paul felt rather annoyed at the inclusion of Michael's name in this group of superior beings.

'I've got a great secret to tell you,' he said.

'Have you? What?'

'I wrote *Crazy Capers.*'

'*You* did, Paul? Oh, how thrilling. I do feel excited to think that I know a real author at last. But how clever you must be; as clever as Michael, I should think, or even cleverer. It is a lovely book. I don't understand, though, why you wrote under another name; I should want everyone to know that I was the author if I wrote something so wonderful.'

'My real name,' said Paul, '*is* Fotheringay. Fisher was my mother's name.' And he told her why he had come to Compton Bobbin. 'Thank God I did,' he added, looking at her lovely face.

After this conversation Paul appeared in a new light to Philadelphia. She had already felt that she might fall in love with him, now she knew that she had done so. An author in disguise is a more heroic figure than a holiday tutor.

They arrived at the barrow to find Michael in his shirtsleeves, grouting about in the bottom of a hole, now about five feet deep, which had been dug by the workmen.

'We may strike the treasure at any moment now,' he cried, in a voice strangled with excitement. 'At any moment we may come upon the charred bones of the great Viking and his wives, the human ashes, surrounded by great spears and shields and gleaming gold ornaments, painted sherds and jewelled necklaces.'

Paul and Philadelphia, fired by his enthusiasm, leapt into the pit and began feverishly to dig.

'Be careful,' cried Michael, in great agitation. 'All this earth must be properly sifted. I think perhaps you had better leave it to me; you can stand on the edge there, if you like.'

This proved, however, in the bitter east wind that was blowing, to be rather a chilly occupation, and they very soon went home again.

That afternoon, coming in from a visit to Mulberrie Farm, they were met by Michael, who almost screamed, 'Come and see, come and see. I've found him; I've found the Viking with all his ornaments, great painted sherds, gold breastplates –'

'Where – where?'

'On the billiard table.'

They rushed to the billiard-room, where they found, reposing on newspaper, a small heap of earthy objects. There was a bit of bone, a square inch of what looked like broken flowerpot, some apparently meaningless pieces of metal and a tiny gold wire. These were the great skeleton, the sherds, the spears and shields, the jewelled necklaces for which Michael had so perseveringly and so expensively been searching. Such, however, is the power of an archaeological imagination that Michael himself, able to reconstruct out of these bits and pieces the objects of which they had (perhaps) originally formed a part, regarded them as a most valuable and interesting addition to modern knowledge. His gratification knew no bounds when, having dispatched his treasure to the British Museum, that revered institution graciously accepted it. (The piece of bone, however, under expert examination, proved to be not that of a Viking but of a pig.)

16

The point-to-point meeting of the South Cotswold hunt took place in some of Major Stanworth's fields. To celebrate the occasion, Amabelle gave a lunch party which consisted of the Monteaths, Major Stanworth, his little boy Adolphus and Paul. Bobby, who had, of course, been invited, was obliged, greatly to his disgust, to attend a farmers' luncheon in a large, damp and evil-smelling tent on the race-course itself. In the absence of his always cheerful rattle the party at Mulberrie Farm settled down to a meal of unrelieved gloom. Sally made no attempt to conceal her wretchedness and never for one moment stopped crying, her emotion being due to the fact that, in spite of all her efforts to prevent such a thing from happening, Major Stanworth had lent Walter one of his horses to ride in the nomination race. Nobody liked to break in upon her too evident grief with a merry remark, and her tears, though of the unobtrusive variety, stealing down her cheeks one by one instead of gushing forth in uncontrolled abandon, had a most depressing effect on the general spirits. Major Stanworth, a kindly and not insensitive soul, was perfectly well aware that poor Sally regarded him as a particularly low and evil type of murderer, and kept on making pathetic little advances to this unresponsive Niobe.

'Really, Mrs Monteath,' he said nervously, 'you need not feel in the least upset. I assure you, there is no need to worry like this. Old Foxtall, the horse that Walter is going to ride, has never put a foot wrong in his life, never. Please believe me. He may be a bit slow, but there's no safer ride in the country. Surely you must realize that I would never think of putting Walter up on one of my horses unless I knew that it was perfectly safe – would I, Mrs Fortescue?'

'No, of course not, darling,' said Amabelle, looking at him affectionately; 'but all the same, I do think it's rather dreadful for my poor Sally, and none of us are blessing you exactly, because now, you see, we shall all have to go out in this ghastly east wind to see Walter doing or dying, whereas otherwise we might have drunk our cherry brandy by the fire and imagined ourselves at the point-to-point instead. Now, Walter dear, before I forget, I mean to bet five shillings on you, not that I imagine for a moment that I shall win anything, but just for old sake's sake, don't you know.'

'Each way, or win only?' said Walter professionally. ('If you don't stop crying like this, Sally, I shall divorce you – I wish you'd try to be more controlled on these occasions; think of the women of Sparta, can't you?') It may make all the difference to my tactics when approaching the last fence. You see, if it's win only I might feel obliged to bump and bore a bit, otherwise I should probably sit tight and get a comfortable third. So make up your mind and let me know, will you?'

'That's all right, old boy,' said Paul. 'You ride a really filthy race. Above all, don't miss any opportunity to cross Captain Chadlington; he's riding a horse called Stout Unionist (out of True Blue by Brewery) and I shall die if he wins.'

'Oh, so he's back again, is he?'

'Yes, he came back for the point-to-point last night.'

'How's the Infernal Machine?'

'Grand. He's going to ask a question about it in the House.'

'I think we should be going on out,' said Amabelle, 'although a more unpleasant idea in this weather I can hardly imagine, myself! Just listen to the wind, howling down the chimney – ugh! Come on, Sally, my poor darling, I can lend you a fur coat and a nice big hankie, and we might tie hot-water bottles next to our tummies, don't you think? Very nice and pregnant we shall look, too.' She led the weeping Sally from the room.

'You'll be blind, you know, Walter, old boy, if I may say so,' remarked Paul, who had been watching Walter fill his glass with unusual abandon.

'Yes, I mean to be,' said Walter. 'I'm terrified,' he added confidentially as Major Stanworth left the room, 'never been so frightened in my life. But nothing hurts nearly so much if you're drunk, does it? I once saw a drunk man fall thirty feet, on to a stone pavement, too; he wasn't hurt a bit. Come on, then; are we all ready for the pretty spectacle of my demise? Cheer up, Sally, think of the Roman matrons, darling. Besides, you're quite attractive enough to get some more husbands, though, of course, I doubt you finding anything quite up to my form again. Have we got lots of cherry brandy in the car?'

The point-to-point course lay on the exposed and wind-swept side of a hill and the cold which assailed Amabelle's party on their arrival at this scene of action was beyond what would be thought possible by anyone not accustomed to the pleasures of rural England in winter. Walter, by now fairly drunk, got out of the car and strode about in his overcoat, accompanied by Major Stanworth, Paul and Bobby. He went down to look at the water jump, had a talk to Major Stanworth's groom, and generally behaved in what he imagined to be a professional manner. Amabelle and Sally huddled up together for warmth in the Rolls-Royce, clasping innumerable hot-water bottles and refusing to move out of it until Walter's race should begin. This was third on the programme. After the first race, at which there were many accidents, poor Sally was even further depressed by seeing the motor ambulance leave the course with its groaning load. A reserve of pride in her nature, however, prevented her from making any more scenes, and it was with a comparatively cheerful face that she went off to the paddock when the time came for Walter to mount. Amabelle still declared that nothing would drag her from the car, so Paul took Sally under his protection. He pointed out Captain Chadlington, whose ordinarily red face was now mauve from cold and harmonized unpleasingly with his racing colours of black, cerise cap and old-gold sleeves. Lady Brenda, in expensive tweeds and holding a brown leather shooting stick, was talking to friends nearby; it seemed to Sally that she was viewing her husband's approaching peril with unnatural calm.

'You can go into the paddock, if you like, Sally,' said Bobby, who was accompanied by a pretty little Jewess with thin legs and a spotted scarf.

'Oh, I shouldn't dare,' shivered Sally, 'your mother looks too forbidding today, doesn't she? Besides, Lady Prague is in there.'

At last the terrible moment came and the crowd round the paddock drew back to make a path for the horses, who jogged off with much tossing of heads and jingling of harness towards the start. They were soon lost to sight over the brow of the hill, and Walter was last seen leading the field at an uncontrolled gallop and fishing madly in the air for a stirrup with his left foot.

'Now,' said Paul, taking Sally's arm in a fatherly manner, 'where would you like to go? Shall we watch the race from the winning post or would you rather be at one of the jumps?'

'Where is he most likely to be killed?' asked Sally, her teeth chattering. She was by now in a state of utter resignation, regarding herself as a widow already; she felt, however, that she would like to be at hand to close Walter's eyes and hear his dying words, if any.

'Sally, dear, please don't be so absurd. Walter rode in several grinds at Oxford. I remember it quite well,' lied Paul, 'and he never had a scratch. I promise faithfully that he'll be all right – do stop worrying. Let's go to the last jump of all, shall we? Giles Stanworth says we can see most of the course and the finish from there.'

'Just as you like,' said Sally in a dull voice. She was wondering vaguely which of her male acquaintances she could bear to marry in the event of Walter's death.

Presently there was a murmur all over the race-course, somebody in the crowd said 'They're off,' and a distant thunder of hoofs could be heard.

'There,' said Paul triumphantly, 'what did I tell you? They're all over the first jump. Walter's among the first three; can you see? Would you like these glasses?'

'No thanks,' said Sally. 'I never can see anything but sky through them.'

'I believe Walter's bound to win, you know; all over the second jump and he's still leading. Isn't it grand. Cheer up, Sally, it'll soon be over. Now they go round that hill and we shan't see them for a minute or two.'

A voice in the crowd behind was heard to say confidentially: 'Here, photographer – I'm Sir Roderick Bobbin and that's my cousin, Lady Brenda Chadlington, in the beige hat. If you take our photographs you'll get promotion, I should think.' And a moment later, 'Oh, look, Brenda darling, we've been photographed! No, of course I won't tell him our names if you'd rather not.'

'Here they come,' said Paul excitedly. 'Walter's still leading; aren't you thrilled, darling? Over the water jump, only one more now – over that – here they come – come on, Walter – come on, old boy –'

The horses thundered towards them, Walter leading easily. They approached the last fence, rose to it, Walter for some reason lost his balance and fell heavily to earth. Six horses in rapid succession jumped into the small of his back and passed on.

'You see,' said Walter that evening, as they settled down to bridge, 'the great advantage of getting blind before point-to-points. Sober I should certainly have been killed, as it is my left knee is a little sore but otherwise I feel grand.'

'The only thing is,' said Amabelle, 'that if you'd been a shade less drunk you might easily have won the race, instead of losing my five shillings in that careless way.'

'I should like to say that it's hardly the fault of anyone here if I'm not a widow tonight,' remarked Sally coldly. Major Stanworth, who had come, as he generally did now, to spend the evening at Mulberrie Farm, looked rather uncomfortable at this remark, which he took, and with reason, to be directed at himself.

17

It seemed to Philadelphia Bobbin that there was too much going on in her life all at once, she had scarcely the time to assimilate one new impression before being faced by another, even stranger and more dazzlingly improbable than the last. She felt a smouldering resentment against fate, which had crowded three weeks of her ordinarily uneventful existence with so many and such varying excitements. How much more satisfactory if they could have been spread out over the months and years of boredom which she had hitherto been obliged to endure at Compton Bobbin. As things were, it was in the course of three short weeks that she had fallen in love, received a proposal of marriage, been precipitated into the strange and dazzling society of Amabelle, and made friends violently and passionately – 'best friends', the kind of relationship that girls of her age have usually outgrown – with Sally Monteath.

Any single one of these events would normally have kept her happy and given her food for thought over a period of months; crammed all together like this she was unable to treat them as realities, but behaved rather as though the whole thing were a play in a dream, and she the chief actress.

Philadelphia was twenty-one. She had hitherto led the flat, uninspiring life of many such girls, 'educated' by a governess (Lady Bobbin, for some reason about which she herself was none too clear, disapproved of girls' schools), sent with the same governess to Paris and Florence for six months, and then 'brought out' in London. Her mother took a house for her first season in Eaton Place and escorted Philadelphia to dances nearly every night in Pont Street, Chesham Place, Cadogan Gardens, Queen's Gate or occasionally Hyde Park Gardens or Sussex Square. Also she gave a dance for Philadelphia, for which, the Eaton Place house being too small, she hired a large and dirty mansion in Belgrave Square.

All these dances were as one dance, absolutely and completely identical. Philadelphia, self-conscious and unhappy in her printed chiffon, her pink taffeta or her white and diamanté georgette, her hair too much crimped, her nose too much powdered and her stays much too tight (her beautiful rounded body being a constant source of worry to her) would follow Lady Bobbin, or some other chaperone on duty for the evening, up stairs already crowded to their utmost capacity into the noisy, hot and overwhelming ballroom. It then became her business to make herself agreeable to the young men who danced with her, because it was essential that when she met them in similar circumstances the next night and the night after they should be willing to repeat the experience. She soon realized that to sit in that silence for which alone she felt inclined until it was time to go back to the ballroom was merely to lay up for herself a future of wall-flowerdom, which fate she thought on the whole even more embarrassing and unamusing than that of attempting, usually in vain, to interest the nonentities in whose company she found herself. It was a fate, however, from which she did not entirely escape, despite all her efforts. She had no success in London, her beauty, as produced by Lady Bobbin, never appeared to its best advantage, and in any case was not such as would appeal to the heirs of Cadogan Place, while they were unallured by those long and indifferent silences, that complete absence of small talk which Paul and Michael were later to find so intriguing. Much, indeed, as she hated sitting, an obvious failure, by the wall with her mother, or a girl friend in like case, she was very little happier when perched on the back stairs or at the supper table with some strange man. Dancing she enjoyed; she was a beautiful dancer.

If her evenings were on the whole rather depressing, her days were made positively hideous by the girls' luncheon parties to which her mother forced her to go. 'You must get to know some nice girls; besides, as we are in London, I want you to do everything you are asked to. We need never come up again.' Nearly every day, therefore, at 1.30 p.m., she would find herself in printed crêpe-de-chine, standing, finger pressed to bell marked 'Visitors', before some house in Pont Street, Chesham Place, Cadogan Gardens, Queen's Gate, Hyde Park Gardens or Sussex Square. She would be ushered into an empty L-shaped drawing-room decorated in the pre-pickled-wood-and-maps period, but brought slightly up-to-date by the presence of a waste-paper receptacle with an olde print stuck on to its plain green surface, a couple of Lalique ornaments and a pleated paper lampshade.

'I will tell Miss Joan (or Lady Felicity) that you are here, miss.' For Philadelphia, owing to early training, was one of those unfortunate people always fated to arrive a little before anybody else.

Presently Lady Joan (or Miss Felicity) would appear, and several pretty, fluffy girls in printed crêpe-de-chine and they would all go downstairs to a meal consisting of egg rissole with tomato sauce, cutlets with paper frills round the bone, hard round peas and new potatoes, followed by a pinkish jelly served in glasses with a tiny blob of cream on the top of each portion.

The conversation would run on the following lines:

'Which dance are you going to first tonight?'

'I think the Campbell-Parkers', because Archie said he'd meet me there, so I've booked up five and six with him. Besides, Lady Millicent Freke-Williams' is sure to be fearfully crowded at first.'

'I hear she's got thirty dinner parties for it.'

'I know. But I expect it will be fun later on. Which are you going to?'

'Well, I'm dining at the Freke-Williams' so I shall have to go there first, I suppose. Did you have fun last night? I was dying to get asked.'

'Yes, it was marvellous, but, my dear, the most awful thing happened. You see, Teddy asked me for number four and I said yes, and then Claud came up and said could he have number three or four because he had to go. Well, three was Johnny, and I never cut him; so I said "Yes, four. But meet me downstairs by the buffet, or else I shall be caught by Teddy." So I went to the buffet at the beginning of number four and waited for ages and Claud never came and Angela said she had just seen him leave with Rosemary, so then I dashed upstairs but Teddy had started dancing with Leila, so then, my dear, I had to pick up that awful little Jamie Trent-Pomeroy. I felt so ashamed at being seen with him. But wasn't it awful of Claud –'

Philadelphia, meanwhile, would sit in a stony silence, bored and boring, and when she had gone Lady Joan or Miss Felicity would say to her girl friends, 'Isn't she too awful. Mummy made me ask her.'

Philadelphia's one London season was from every point of view a failure, and it had never, to her great relief, been repeated. Lady Bobbin was far too much wrapped up in all her country pursuits to leave them more than once for the sake of a daughter who neither appreciated nor repaid such sacrifice. She felt that she had done all that duty demanded by the child, and could now rest on her laurels.

Philadelphia herself never had the slightest wish to repeat that particular experience, but all the same she was profoundly unhappy at Compton Bobbin. She was without occupation or interest, the days dragged by each more boring than the last, and she was beginning to think that perhaps she was never to find those people who she felt sure must exist in the world and who would prove more congenial to her than those she had met as a débutante. She longed passionately for even one friend who would not think her plain, stupid and tongue-tied.

It is hardly surprising, therefore, if she was dazed and incredulous on finding herself hailed as a beauty by Amabelle, admitted to the confidences of Sally, treated as an intellectual equal by Paul and asked in marriage by Michael, all of whom were people she felt to be not only far more intelligent and interesting than any she had met, but more thrilling even than those imaginary beings whom, in day dreams, she had longed to have as her friends.

All the attention and praise that she was now receiving had the very natural effect of making her twice as pretty and attractive as she had been before, and with Sally to help and advise her she was even acquiring a certain chic.

'You're so lucky; you've got the sort of face that can be made into anything,' said Sally one day as they sat talking in Elspeth Paula's nursery. 'It's like a sheet of white paper waiting to be drawn on – or, at least, painted. The drawing's there all right; you've got beautiful features. Fancy having real natural platinum blonde hair, too; it's incredible. You'd have a wild success in London, you know.'

'I didn't when I went there.'

'No, of course not, with all those awful debs. I mean, among people who understand what real beauty is. You must come and stay in the flat when we go back there. We can easily make up a bed for you in the bathroom, or Amabelle will put you up, and then we'll arrange some parties. Now, I've got a very good idea: why not tell your mother you want to learn drawing and come to us permanently as P.G.? Do, it would be such fun.'

'Oh, Sally, you are divine to me, only, you see, I can't draw at all.'

'That doesn't matter. It makes a wonderful excuse to be in London. I can't draw a single line, and I was at the Slade for years. My family lived in the country, too, you see, and I had to get away somehow.'

'Mummy would never let me.'

'You and Bobby seem to be very much under your mother's thumb.'

'Yes, even Bobby's frightened of her, really, although he does pretend not to be. Besides, you see, all the money we have comes from her, and that puts her in a very strong position.'

'Yes, of course, I quite see that.'

★

Michael took Philadelphia for a walk and proposed to her by the statue of Apollo. It was, like everything that Michael did, very much stage managed, very well rehearsed, supremely diplomatic and in the last degree unimaginative. Nevertheless, had he arrived at Compton Bobbin three weeks earlier it is certain that Philadelphia would have accepted him on the spot; she longed for marriage, for escape from her home, which she regarded as a prison, and from her mother, whom she detested, and she had subconsciously imbibed enough of Bobby's somewhat outspoken snobbery to be not at all averse to the idea of being a rich marchioness. Even now, had he employed any other method of approach he would probably have been successful, as Philadelphia's feelings for Paul at this stage were hardly strong enough to outweigh the obvious advantages of marriage with Michael. Besides, she liked him very much.

They went for a long walk, during which he spoke in his cultured Foreign Office voice of his life in Egypt, and before that in Paris, and of his future prospects. Philadelphia, who had a sort of blind veneration for culture and learning in all forms, thought how charming he was and how lucky it was for her that at last she knew somebody who, just occasionally, in a way that never could bore, but quite perfectly, would insert into his speech some happy little quotation that she could often recognize, from various English poets, or even, though more rarely, a few words of Latin, French or German.

'So, you see,' he said, 'I intend to leave diplomacy now. As a career it has proved a great disappointment to me, I must own.'

Philadelphia, whose ideas on the Diplomatic Service were culled exclusively from the works of Maurice Baring and Marion Crawford, said that she had always imagined a diplomat's to be the most interesting life in the world.

'In theory I suppose it must be,' said Michael, 'because you see, in theory one would be in daily contact with the most important, most intelligent people of every nation, and that would be perfect. In practice one is continually being polite to elderly ladies in amethyst brooches, and that is not quite the same thing, is it? Although, I imagine that every life has its amethyst brooch side. All the same, I am inclined now to prefer the English variety to any other, so I am going to settle down at Lewes Park for good, with, perhaps, a *pied à terre* in Westminster from which I can attend, when I wish to do so, the House of Lords. I am told that a certain amount of good work is done there, even in these days, and of course it is very necessary that a few of the younger peers should take their seats,' he added complacently.

They walked in silence for a little. Presently Michael said:

'Here we are at this very exquisite statue of Apollo – I had quite forgotten its existence. How civilized, how charming, is it not? I wonder why Aunt Gloria allows it to be hidden by all these dreary shrubs. It is a perfect example of French eighteenth-century sculpture, and I should never be surprised if it turned out to be a genuine Bouchardon. Most satisfying – most.'

With a slight effort he removed his gaze from the statue and let it rest on Philadelphia's upturned face.

'I am going to ask you a question,' he said, 'and I don't want an answer until I get back from Lewes Park on Tuesday. I expect you can guess what it is going to be?'

'No,' said Philadelphia, honestly enough.

'I want you to marry me, my dear.'

She was as though turned to stone with amazement. Now was Michael's opportunity. If he had taken advantage of her surprise and obvious emotion to make love to her, Philadelphia, young, beautiful and longing to be loved, would probably have accepted him there and then. Unfortunately he had only given rein to his emotions with the one woman who would be alienated by that particular form of courtship, and he thought that he had now learnt his lesson once and for all. Women evidently disliked to be rushed off their feet, they must have time to make up their minds, sentiment in all forms was clearly anathema to them. So instead of taking her in his arms as of course he should have done there and then, he said coldly and rather shyly: 'Don't think of answering me now; you will have plenty of time to consider the matter during the next few days and you can let me know when I return. I feel sure that you will realize how very well suited we are to each other in every way, and indeed I would do my best to make you happy.' With that he embarrassed her rather by kissing her on the forehead, and they went indoors.

Philadelphia parted from him in the hall and ran upstairs to her bedroom. Her mind was in a state of excitement and confusion. She had never had a proposal of marriage before, and she was now thinking less of how she intended to answer Michael than of what she should do immediately and whom she could tell the grand news to. Deciding, as she powdered her nose, that it would be awkward to see Michael again before his departure, which was imminent, and that she must tell Sally first of anybody, she stole downstairs by the back way, got out her little car, and drove over to Mulberrie Farm.

She found Sally wheeling the baby up and down the gravel path. 'The little monster hasn't been asleep the whole afternoon,' she said. 'No, talking doesn't keep her awake; in fact, it seems to send her off, on the contrary. Your odious brother is in there, inducing Walter to waste his time and lose his money at bridge. It *is* so naughty of him. I know he's not written his weekly article yet, and it ought to have gone off by this post at the latest. I wish the game had never been invented.'

'Then who's the fourth?' asked Philadelphia, who knew that, except during week-ends, when Jerome came down from London, poor Sally was usually dragged in, much against her will, to play.

'Giles Stanworth, of course, my dear. He's never out of the house now, you know, night or day. The poor man's quite batty about Amabelle, and he's having to earn his keep by learning contract. Walter's taken a packet off him already, I may say.'

'Isn't it funny? I can't imagine Major Stanworth in love with anybody.'

'Can't you just! You wait till tea-time and then watch the way he goes on. It's pathetic. But the really extraordinary thing is that I believe Amabelle rather fancies him too, I honestly think she does. Yesterday evening –' Sally broke off. She was a very discreet person where her friends were concerned, and decided that for the present she would keep the doings of yesterday evening to herself. 'I dare say we shall see the old girl a farmer's wife yet,' she added hastily to cover her lapse. 'What news from Compton Bobbin?'

'Michael's motoring back to Lewes after tea.'

'He is, is he? That's no great loss anyway. I shouldn't think anyone will miss him unbearably – I never notice whether he's about or not myself, do you?'

'Not much,' said Philadelphia, rather dashed by this remark. She feared that Sally would be unimpressed by her news. There was a short silence. 'He proposed to me before he left,' she said at last.

'Delphie! You don't say so? My dear, isn't that *grand*. When are you going to announce it? Oh, you lucky girl.'

'Oh, I haven't said yes. I mean I haven't given him any answer yet, you see. I'm to think it over until he comes back.'

'But of course you'll accept, won't you?'

'I hadn't thought so. I'm not in love with him.'

'My darling Delphie, you mustn't *hesitate*. Michael is a divine person. We all adore him; he's quite perfect in every way. Attractive, intelligent, everything you could want in the world. Besides just think of all that money. Why, you could afford to have ten children if you liked.'

'That would be nice,' said Philadelphia doubtfully; 'but you see I'm not in love with him.'

'Nonsense, of course you are. One couldn't help being in love with a heavenly person like that if he wanted one to be. Besides, nobody is in love with their husbands before they marry, at least I was, but that's most exceptional. It's hardly ever done. You're not fancying anyone else, by the way, are you?'

'I don't know.'

'Of course you're not.' Sally looked relieved. 'Well, that's too lovely, darling, I do congratulate you. I wonder where you'll be married, Westminster Abbey, perhaps. Shall we go and tell the others? No, no, not unless you like, of course, but I'll tell Amabelle afterwards as a great secret, can I? And you wouldn't be an angel, I suppose, and let me sell it to the press (I mean when it's all quite settled, naturally), because I could get at least a tenner for the news, do let me have it and not Bobby, please. How gorgeous of you, isn't it? I wonder what sort of ring he'll be giving you. You are a lucky girl, Delphie, I must say.'

After Sally had been working on her mind in this manner for about half an hour, Philadelphia began to regard herself quite as the future Lady Lewes, doubts and misgivings faded from her mind and she felt already a delightful new sense of her own importance. If Sally, whom she looked up to in every way, thought that it would be all right for her to marry Michael she herself would raise no further objections. Indeed, Sally had done Michael's own work for him most efficiently, and by the time that they had discussed every aspect of the wedding, from the cheering crowds outside the Abbey to the pattern of night-dress for her trousseau, Philadelphia was feeling quite romantic about him. She had some difficulty at tea-time in keeping the news to herself, and even threw out one or two hints at a mystery to which she alone had a clue, but nobody paid much attention to her. They were all busy watching the latest developments in the situation between Mrs Fortescue and Major Stanworth.

When Philadelphia returned to Compton Bobbin she found a note from Michael on the hall table.

My Dearest Philadelphia,

I couldn't find you anywhere to say good-bye. However, I shall be back again in less than a week (next Tuesday at the very latest, D.V.), and shall expect my answer then. Consider the matter very carefully, my dear, remembering that marriage is a state which, once entered into, lasts the whole of one's life. I need hardly say how much I hope that you will consent to be my wife, and I truly believe that in trusting me with your future happiness you will be putting it into reliable hands. I spoke of this before I left to Aunt Gloria. Remember, dearest Philadelphia, that if you are in any doubt as to how you should act, there can be no one so well fitted to guide and advise you as your own mother.

with love from
Michael.

This peculiar missive probably seemed less chilling to Philadelphia, who had never in her life before received a love letter, than it would have to most girls of twenty-one. On the other hand, it certainly did not arouse in her those emotions which the loved handwriting is usually supposed to evoke, and the reference to Lady Bobbin annoyed her a good deal.

Michael went to Lewes Park to settle up certain matters with his estate agent. He intended to stay there under a week. The day after he arrived, however, he caught a chill which developed into jaundice and kept him in bed for nearly a month. This circumstance very nearly altered the entire course of his life.

Before leaving Compton Bobbin he had an interview with his Aunt Gloria, during which he informed her of his intentions and hopes with regard to Philadelphia. Lady Bobbin was, of course, delighted.

'My dear Michael,' she said, almost with emotion, 'this is the best news I could possibly have. How pleased poor Hudson would have been, too. We will discuss the business side of it another time – I have to go now and speak to the huntsman about a new horse – but I may as well tell you that I have always intended to settle £2,000 a year on Philadelphia if she marries with my approval, and of course when I die she will be fairly well off. I must rush away now, so good-bye, and we meet again on Tuesday?'

'Of course she hasn't accepted me for certain yet,' said Michael with more than a touch of complacency, 'but I may say that I have little doubt that all will be well in that direction. Good-bye, then, Aunt Gloria, thank you so much for my delightful visit.'

Philadelphia herself came back from Mulberrie Farm with her mind quite made up. Sally's way of treating the whole thing as an accomplished fact had made her feel that it was so, and she only wished that Michael had not gone away and that they could begin all the exciting business, as outlined by Sally, of being engaged that very evening. She decided to answer his letter at once, begging him to return as soon as he could, and was going towards the schoolroom with this object in view when she ran into her mother.

'Oh, Philadelphia, come in here a minute. I want to speak to you. Well, darling, Michael has told me your news and I am, I need hardly say, quite delighted. It is far the best thing that could possibly have happened, and we shall be able to announce your engagement at the dance I am giving the day before Bobby goes back to Eton.'

Lady Bobbin had the somewhat unfortunate effect upon both her children of invariably provoking them to argument.

'But I haven't any intention of marrying Michael,' said Philadelphia defiantly. 'He proposed to me, certainly, but I never accepted him.'

'Then I hope that you will do so without delay,' said Lady Bobbin acidly. 'Michael spoke to me as though it was all settled.'

'He may have settled it, but I haven't.'

'You really are a very silly obstinate little girl. Michael will make you a most ideal husband. Surely you like him, don't you? What is it you have against him?'

'Yes, I like him all right, except that I think he's rather a pompous old thing,' said Philadelphia, a phrase she had borrowed from Bobby.

'Nonsense. Michael has a very proper sense of duty, of the responsibilities attached to his position in the world, and I am very glad that he has. You don't want a sort of clown and buffoon for a husband. And in any case, if you don't marry him you'll probably remain an old maid, I should think. I can't imagine that you will ever find anybody else half so suitable or so nice. And I may as well tell you, Philadelphia, while we are on this subject, that I am not obliged to settle a penny of money on you if you marry without my approval.'

'All right,' said Philadelphia sulkily, 'I'll think about it.' She left the room, tearing up Michael's letter into small pieces as she went.

In the schoolroom she found Paul, whom she had hardly seen all day.

'Your grandmother was most certainly a genius,' he said, looking up from the journal, 'although in some respects her character was not everything that could have been wished for. But her prose seems to me even to transcend her poetry in literary merit, and her metaphysical conclusions are always faultless. Listen to this now:

'One curious and very noticeable feature of the workings of a human mind is that so often it will seize upon and stress the unimportant almost to the exclusion of anything else. This it does most especially in dreams. Last night, for example, I dreamt that I was playing in the nursery with darling Julia when, suddenly seizing her teddy-bear, which I gave her yesterday and which cost me 4s. 6d. in the Baker Street Bazaar, she flung herself upon the blazing fire and was burnt to a cinder. In the dream (and this illustrates my point) I was worried far less by the extinction of poor Julia than by that of the bear, and I wandered about saying very sorrowfully, "It was a four-and-sixpenny bear".

'Funny reading that just now,' Paul went on, 'because last night I had just such a dream myself. Would you like to hear it?'

Philadelphia stifled the feeling of acute boredom which comes over those about to hear the dreams of others, and said that she would.

'Well, it was a very odd dream indeed. You and I and Michael were going down to Brighton for the wedding of the Prince Regent to Mrs Fitzherbert. We took first-class return tickets. But when we arrived at the Pavilion, where the wedding was to be held, we found that all the people there were French, and dressed in clothes of the time of Louis XIV, and Michael was very much put out by this. He said to me, loudly and angrily, "This is really too much. These people to begin with are not English, most of them don't know the Regent, even by sight, and they haven't had the common decency to dress in the proper clothes of the period. Besides, Sheridan isn't here, and Mrs Fitzherbert has gone off to the Y.W.C.A. in a rage. I don't blame her, I must say, but I do feel annoyed that we have been dragged all the way down here, first-class for nothing." So we all came straight back to London, first-class.

'Now in the whole of that dream, which was long and quite involved, I was only really impressed by one important fact, which was that we travelled first-class. I woke up with the words "first-class" on my lips, and can still, although the rest of the dream has practically faded from my mind, see most clearly in my imagination the upholstered seats with arms, clean white lace antimacassars and little views of Bath and Wells in our first-class carriage.'

'Very strange,' said Philadelphia, burning the pieces of Michael's letter. Life itself, she thought, as she went upstairs to dress for dinner, was stranger than dreams and far, far more disordered.

18

'Jerome,' said Amabelle.

Jerome looked up from his weekly, rather shamefaced, perusal of the *Tatler*.

'Yes, Amabelle?'

'I've got some news to tell you.'

'What's that, my dear?'

'I'm going to marry Giles Stanworth.'

'Oh, my God,' said Jerome, and buried his face in his hands.

'Amabelle – it isn't true, is it?' he said, a minute later; 'you don't really mean it, do you?'

'Yes, you know, it's quite true. The banns are going to be called tomorrow in the village church – not in this village, because Giles says the parson here is really a papist, but in Hogrush. It's jolly exciting, don't you think? We're being married at the beginning of February, down here. I shall wear a hat, of course, and we both hope that you'll give me away, darling.'

'I shall do no such thing.'

'Then Bobby will have to.'

'Are you off your head, Amabelle? I really never heard such scandalous nonsense in all my life. Only think of that poor man dragged up to Portman Square, out of his element, wretched, bored –'

'I don't think of it for a moment. Giles would never leave his precious farm, not even for me; besides, I shouldn't ask him to. I'm looking forward to living in the country myself.'

'My dear, you are being a little bit childish, aren't you?'

'No, darling, not in the least. However, I suppose I had better explain the situation to you quite clearly, then perhaps you'll see my point of view for once. First of all, then, I happen to be very fond of Giles, and I adore his little boy.'

'If you're so anxious to be married, why not marry Michael?'

'Because Michael bores me into fits, and I don't like being laughed at by my friends and acquaintances. People always laugh when a woman marries someone fifteen years younger than herself, quite right, too.'

'I don't understand why you want to marry at all. Aren't you happy?'

'If you would listen to me for one single minute –'

'Oh, all right, go on.'

'The real point is, old boy, that I am forty-five. You didn't know that, did you? Still, there it is. Now what happens to women like me, unattached but not unattractive women, when they are over forty-five? It's very tricky, I can tell you. They gradually begin to get taken up by boys at Oxford, who rather like being seen about with them and all that, but who really regard them as a cross between a fortune-teller, a nanny, and an interesting historical character who has somehow managed to live on until the present day. I've seen it happen over and over again, haven't you, honestly? And at about fifty-five or so people start saying, "How *wonderful* Amabelle looks for her age. Of course she must be well over seventy now, why, when I was a girl she was quite an old woman." It's an awful, and, as far as I can see, an inevitable fate, and it seems to me more dignified to retire before it overtakes one.'

'I think you are wrong,' said Jerome. 'You have been feeling depressed, I suppose, and no wonder in this ghastly house, but that is no reason for making such a terrible mistake. You'll be miserable, bored and miserable living down here always. Giles Stanworth is very nice, of course, I think he is charming, but what interests have you in common?'

'The Fluke, for one. You wouldn't believe how passionately I am interested in the Fluke. There is another fascinating disease called the staggers too, he tells me; horses have that. Then the rotation of crops –'

'Can't you be serious for one minute?' cried Jerome in exasperation. 'I see nothing to joke about in the fact that you are jeopardizing your whole future happiness for a crazy idea like this. Look here, Amabelle, if you must marry, marry me.'

'Darling Jerome, you *are* sweet. But what would Mrs Nickle say?' Mrs Nickle had been Jerome's housekeeper for twenty years. 'No, no, my dear, that would never do. Besides, strange though it may seem to you, I actually do want to marry Giles; and as nothing that you can say will stop me you might just as well look pleasant and wish me happiness.'

'I may be dense, but I still don't see the point in taking this step. It's no good pretending to me that you are passionately in love with Giles Stanworth, or anything so silly as that.'

'Actually I am rather in love with him. But that's neither here nor there. The point, as I've told you already, is that I don't want to be taken up by Oxford undergraduates.'

'I think you exaggerate the danger of these youths, the modern young man is not quite so importunate as perhaps you may imagine.'

'No, that's just it, one wouldn't mind so much if he were. It's the maiden aunt relationship that I object to more than anything.'

'You're incorrigible, Amabelle.'

'Pig-headed, you mean. Anyhow, you might wish me luck, old boy.'

'I do – I do. Oh, how bored you'll be after about six months of country life.'

'You said that before, if you remember, when I took this house. Actually I was at first, terribly bored for about a day, but since then I've enjoyed myself top-hole.'

'For a few weeks, yes. You've had people to amuse you and so on. But think of months and years on that awful farm.'

'It isn't awful at all. It's a sweet little house. I think I shall adore being a farmer's wife. I intend to have a still room and make my own face creams out of herbs, and Giles has lent me a book of syllabubs and flummery caudles and all sorts of art and craft food, and did you know before that ye rhubarbe maketh to go to ye privy? I bet you didn't.'

The news of Amabelle's engagement spread like wildfire after the banns had been read out in church the following Sunday. Bobby came round in a state of high excitement, and after kissing her repeatedly he said to Major Stanworth:

'Amabelle has always been in love with me really, of course, and that's why she's going to marry you, simply in order to live near Compton Bobbin. Darling, darling, you ought to have seen Mummy's face in church! She said afterwards, "Poor Giles, I must say I never imagined that he would end up by marrying a woman of the demi-monde, but I suppose she has got him into her clutches like so many others. It will be a finisher for him."'

Major Stanworth got rather red. Although by his own lights he was an exceptionally broadminded man, he never could quite accustom himself to hearing Amabelle's friends refer in this light-hearted way to her past.

'You heard what Mother said to Auntie Loudie,' went on the tactless child. 'You see apparently she found out somehow that I know you quite well, and she was talking it over with Auntie Loudie, who was divine as usual, and said nothing matters for boys in that sort of way, and Mother agreed with her more or less, and finally she said, "Anyhow I am told it costs £10,000 to sleep with Mrs Fortescue, so I suppose it's all right for Bobby to go over there sometimes."'

'Your mother can't know much about the state of the market in these days,' observed Amabelle drily.

'However, she said at lunch that she will receive you when you're married for Giles' sake, because she always stands by her friends in their misfortunes. It's one of her boasts, like changing for dinner in the bush – she's white all through, my mother is. And she's going to the wedding with the whole hunt, they'll meet at the church and play "gone to ground" over you on the horn and everything. It will be a riot, won't it?'

'Won't it just?' said Amabelle delightedly. 'Will you be able to get away from Eton for it, my sweet?'

'Well, I've been thinking about that. May I be best man? Then they'll simply have to give me leave.'

'No, you may not,' said Giles Stanworth.

19

'I love you, I love you, I love you, I love you, I love you, I love you, I love you, I love you,' said Paul. 'I love you. And if there were anything more to say I should say it, but there isn't, really.'

'Oh, isn't there just,' said Philadelphia rather tartly, drawing herself to the other end of the sofa and smoothing down her ruffled hair. 'Personally, I should have thought there was a good deal more that you might have said by now.'

'That only shows that you don't love me as much as I love you, my sweet poppet.'

'Yes, I do. Much more, as a matter of fact.'

'What makes you think that?'

'For one thing I've never loved anybody in my life before.'

'Nor have I.'

'What about Marcella then?'

'Oh, Marcella! She never meant a thing to me, not a thing. I thought she was rather attractive, but as for loving her –'

'And Susan and Elizabeth and Sheila and Sonia and Rosemary and Joan and Veronica?'

'Sally's been talking to you. I think it's very naughty and horrid of her. I promise you I never cared for any of those girls in the way I care for you. No other woman will ever be the same to me, you're something quite special in my life, quite apart.'

'Well, I believe you, darling, though I expect it's very silly of me to, and you must see it's a risk I'm taking. In any case, it's time we began to think of what we're going to do next.'

'Darling, don't be so practical. Everything will be all right in the end, I promise you it will, only don't fuss.'

'But I am fussing. Here we've been engaged for two whole days, and you've done nothing about it except to kiss me on the sofa and tell me lies about other girls you've been in love with.'

'But, my darling, what d'you expect me to do?'

'I expect you to take steps.'

'What steps?'

'Oh, you are maddening.'

'Yes, but really, what steps? I'm going to marry you, my precious, and that's taking a big step, I should have thought.'

'Marry me!' cried Philadelphia in despair. 'I know, so you say, but how – how – how? How are you going to tell Mother, how do you intend to support me; above all, how am I to get disengaged from Michael? You don't seem to realize that if he hadn't caught jaundice, by the mercy of Providence, he would have been back again yesterday, ring and all.'

'I can see quite plainly that you've been talking about this to Sally,' said Paul sulkily, 'and if it goes on I shall be obliged to tell your mother that as soon as her back is turned you are off like greased lightning to Mulberrie Farm. She'll soon put a stop to that.'

'Paul, darling, do you love me?'

'Yes, I do.'

'Then go and tell Mother that we're engaged.'

'I'm going to, tomorrow morning.'

'You said that yesterday.'

'I know I did. I felt so awful this morning that I simply couldn't face it. There were brains for breakfast again, and the sight of them always upsets me. But tomorrow I'm going to be brave and heroic. And you're going to write to Michael, aren't you, and I'm going to write a best-seller about your great-grandmother, and we shall be as happy as the day is long, you'll see. So give me a kiss and stop bothering, won't you?'

'No, I won't. Will you go and tell mother this evening as soon as she comes in from hunting?'

'Darling, please not. You don't know the effect your mother has on my nerves; it's positively uncanny. I shiver and shake like an aspirin leaf, whatever that may be.'

'Have a whisky and soda first.'

'That wouldn't really do. Supposing she smelt my breath, like the police in motor accidents?'

'Well, when do you intend to tell her?'

'Darling, you're not being just a shade governessy, are you? If you really want to know, I don't see very much point in telling her at all. It will only mean that I shall have to leave by the next train if I do. Imagine my position. "Oh, Lady Bobbin, by the way, my name is Fotheringay, not Fisher, and I've been here all this time under false pretences, and I've never done a stroke of work with Bobby, but instead I've been collecting material for the life you don't want me to write of Lady Maria, and I should like to marry your daughter, but as I haven't any money I should be glad if you would pay off just a few of my more pressing debts and buy me a tail coat to be married in as I've rather grown out of my old Eton one." It doesn't sound too well, you know.'

'Oh, Paul, whatever are we to do?'

'"The glory of man is in being, not in doing."'

Philadelphia burst into angry tears.

'Don't cry now, darling. Everything will be all right, you'll see.'

'Let's go and ask Amabelle what she thinks, shall we?'

'Oh, very well, if you like. Anything to stop you crying. Not that I imagine she'll be much good to us, but still –'

They found Amabelle wringing her hands in front of the drawing-room fire at Mulberrie Farm. There was a strong smell of bananas in the room.

'It's all right,' she said. 'This is not a sign of mental anguish. Giles hasn't given me the raspberry or anything like that. I've just been varnishing my nails, and I simply can't get them to dry.' And she fell to wringing her hands with even greater vigour than before. 'I wanted particularly to see you, Philadelphia. Walter and Sally left for the south of France yesterday in a wild hurry. Someone was paying for them, and the poor sweets think it will cost them nothing. Sally was miserable she couldn't say good-bye, and left a thousand messages. They're only going for a couple of weeks, but you see they won't be coming back here again as I'm off to

London myself on Saturday to buy my trousseau, dear, for the farm. I think of having corduroy trousers like the ones that Giles wears; they ought to be quite attractive. Lucky I've kept my figure, isn't it? Where's Bobby, by the way?'

'He's staying with Bunch for a shoot; he'll be back tomorrow.'

'Send him along, will you? I want to see him before I go. I don't suppose I shall get out of it under a fiver, but still. *What* it will save me in tips when that child goes to Oxford.'

'Amabelle, we really came to ask your advice about something.'

'Oh, did you just?'

'Paul and I are engaged to be married.'

'I know; Sally told me. You don't expect me to congratulate you or anything like that, do you?'

'I think you're being rather unkind; it's nearly always done, isn't it? And anyway, why not?'

'Because it is no matter for congratulations, my poor sweet. I suppose you think you are in love with each other?'

'We don't think it. We are in love,' said Paul defiantly. He had an idea of what Amabelle was going to say next.

'Then how can I possibly congratulate you? You must both know quite well that this marriage is practically an impossibility. At the best you have endless fusses and bothers in front of you; Lady Bobbin will, very naturally, refuse to give you any money. Paul has nothing but debts, you will both have to be terribly worried and unhappy for ages before you can be married, and miserably poor, probably for years, afterwards. Not a very enchanting prospect, to my mind.'

'Look how poor Walter and Sally are,' said Philadelphia. 'They couldn't be worse off, but they are the two happiest people I've ever seen.'

'Walter and Sally are very exceptional. I am inclined even to think that they are unique; anyhow, I personally have never come across another case like theirs in my life. Nothing that could happen would ever make the smallest difference to their feeling for each other. I suppose a love of that sort can be found once in a generation. I don't want to seem unkind, because I am very fond of you both, but I very much doubt whether either you or Paul has the character which is needed to sustain such a relationship – you won't believe me, of course. It's a funny thing that people are always quite ready to admit it if they've no talent for drawing or music, whereas everyone imagines that they themselves are capable of true love, which is a talent like any other, only far more rare. I don't doubt, mind you, that if Paul were an eligible young man and if you could be married in the usual way without any trouble, you would probably be quite happy. I only say that as things are it's impossible.'

'Oh, Amabelle,' cried Philadelphia, 'unkind, unkind! I thought that you at least would be able to advise us.'

'If you really want my advice here it is, but you won't like it much. Don't say a word to anybody; don't let your mother or Bobby suspect a thing, but have a lovely time together till next week, when Paul is going away in any case. Then, as soon as Michael has finished having jaundice, announce your engagement to him. Please believe me when I say that you'll be very happy with him. I know Michael so well and I feel sure of it. He'll take you for a gorgeous honeymoon, all round the world perhaps, and when you get back you'll settle down at that exquisite Lewes Park and have some nice babies, and entertain a lot, and be the best-dressed marchioness in England. I don't know how you can hesitate, I really don't.'

Philadelphia began to cry again.

'Thank you for nothing,' said Paul loudly and angrily. 'Look how you've upset my poor darling Delphie. Don't cry, my precious; you shan't marry that old bore, he'd drive you mad in a week. I thought at least you would have shown us some sympathy, Amabelle, but I suppose it's too much to expect even that. You women are all the same, a lot of blasted matchmakers, that's what you are.'

'Paul, Paul, don't be so bitter. You must have known that I of all people would take the common sense point of view. Just think for a moment; use your intelligence, my dear. You and Philadelphia have known each other for exactly three weeks. You both think, honestly I'm sure, that you are ready to undergo almost intolerable hardships over a period of years, and possibly for life, in order to be able to remain in each other's company. I say that it would be much easier, more to your mutual advantage and eventual happiness, if you could bring yourselves to part now and lead different lives. That's all.'

'Of course,' said Philadelphia, sniffing rather loudly, 'my mother would probably give us some sort of allowance once we were actually married; she'd be obliged to, really.'

'I doubt it very much,' said Amabelle; 'from what I know of your mother's character I should think it most unlikely. At present she naturally wishes you to marry Michael; when you tell her of your engagement to Paul she will be furious, and doubly so when she discovers the trick that has been played on her all this time. Think of her feelings when you tell her that he is not only not Mr Fisher, but actually that Mr Fotheringay whom she refused to have in the house!'

'Yes, that's awful, I must say,' said Paul.

'And what will happen? Angry words will pass of the sort that can never, never be forgotten, and you will find yourselves faced with the alternative of eloping on the spot and living on Paul's £300 a year' (Amabelle had an amazing faculty for knowing to a penny the incomes of her friends) 'or of staying at home and leading an incredibly drab and dreary life, more or less in disgrace with your mother, until he can make enough money to support you in moderate comfort, which, as far as I can see, will be never.'

'Oh, God!' said Paul.

'I'm sorry to be so depressing, but I say again, for heaven's sake, marry Michael. If you don't I see nothing but trouble ahead for you, my poor Philadelphia.'

'Now listen to me, Amabelle,' said Philadelphia, with unexpected firmness. 'I am not going to marry Michael, and I *am* going to marry Paul. Get that clear, and then tell me what I ought to do about it.'

Amabelle frowned. She was incapable of seeing Philadelphia's point of view, and thought that the child was being merely obstinate.

'Thank heaven I haven't got a daughter,' she said impatiently. 'However, if you really mean what you say, I consider that there is only one course open to you. Refuse Michael, giving no reason for doing so, keep all this a deadly secret (and by that I mean a secret – no hints or half-confessions to anybody, you understand) and wait for a few months while Paul finds some good, steady job. Then let Bobby go to your mother, tell her the whole story and ask her to give you enough money to be married; he is much more likely to get round her than you are, I imagine. By then she will have lost all hope of Michael as a son-in-law and may be quite anxious to get you off, even to somebody as ineligible as Paul. Only it's essential that he should first get a proper job and keep it for a few months. That seems to me your only possible hope. And of course, Paul, it goes without saying that you must give up the idea of publishing Lady Maria's life, anyhow, until you have got a good marriage settlement tucked away.'

Paul and Philadelphia looked glum. The prospect of a glamorous elopement was far more attractive to them than a course of action which necessitated on his part the daily grind of some regular job, so long and so studiously avoided by him, and on hers the indefinite continuation of her present dreary life. However, they could not but admit that this was the most sensible course to follow, and both felt immensely relieved that it would not, at present, be necessary to beard Lady Bobbin in her den.

'Thank you, dear Amabelle,' said Philadelphia. 'I think you are quite right, although it will be terrible to wait all that time. Still, it won't be so bad when you come to live here for good.'

'Of course not,' said Amabelle cheerfully. 'I'll have Paul to stay every week-end, and I expect Walter and Sally will be down sometimes, so it won't be nearly as lonely for you at Compton Bobbin as it used to be. All the same, I think you're making a terrible mistake, my dear, in refusing Michael. I shall never alter my opinion about that.'

Paul said, as they walked back to Compton Bobbin, 'I'll tell you what I'll do. My Uncle Joseph has some ghastly sort of business in the city. I'll make him give me a job, he has offered to before. I see what Amabelle means; your mother is far more likely to come round to the idea of our marriage if she thinks I have definite work. People of that generation are so extraordinary in those ways; they don't care about self-expression or any of the things that really matter. So long as one has a good solid and respectable job they are quite satisfied about one. The truth is that they have misused leisure themselves for so long that they think of it as a bad thing for anybody to have. Never mind, I will crucify myself for your sake, sweet one, on an office stool for a month or two anyway, until we see what happens. Something is sure to turn up, it always does. It's a bit souring about Lady Maria all the same. I was looking forward to publishing that.'

'Darling, I hate to think of you making such a sacrifice.'

'There's no sacrifice I wouldn't make for you, darling. Besides, the moment we're married I shall bring it out and show the world that I'm a serious writer of the front rank.'

'Paul, I do love you.'

'Darling, darling Philadelphia. How do you manage to be so heavenly with a mother like that?'

'I believe Daddy was rather sweet.'

'That accounts for it then, no doubt.'

As soon as Bobby got back from his shoot he went round to see Amabelle.

'What's all this nonsense about Paul and Delphie?' he said accusingly.

'Oh, so you know about it by now, do you? Who told you?'

'Nobody told me, but I should have to be as dense as my mother seems to be if I couldn't see with half an eye what's happening. They sit holding hands on the drawing-room sofa all day, and Delphie keeps on throwing out dark hints about how wonderful it is to be in love and all that sort of thing. It can only be a matter of moments now before Mummy tumbles to it, I should think, and then there'll be the devil to pay.'

'Didn't I know those silly children would never be able to keep it quiet? And what view do you take of the whole thing, Bobby? You needn't tell me, darling. I can guess.'

'Well, naturally, I think it's quite crazy. I only hope and pray that Delphie won't ruin her chances of marrying Michael by her idiocy, that's all. Thank heaven he's out of the way for the present. As for Paul, I really do think it's a bit hard he should behave like this after all the trouble I've taken for him.'

'I must say I agree with you for once,' said Amabelle. 'They came over yesterday to confess it all and ask my advice, and I'm afraid I was rather unkind to them. I've seen Paul wildly in love with too many people to take that very seriously, and as for Philadelphia, why at her age one is in love every other week. I gather that Michael made a mess of everything as usual. He had only to go about it with a little ordinary sense and she'd have been crazy about him by now. Really that young man, I've no patience at all with him; he behaves like a very unconvincing character in a book, not like a human being at all.'

'Yes, doesn't he. The sort of book of which the reviewers would say "the characterization is weak; the central figure, Lord Lewes, never really coming to life at all; but there are some fine descriptive passages of Berkshire scenery." What did you say to Delphie?'

'I told her she was mad not to marry Michael, and then she began to cry, and I really hadn't the heart to go on. I finally told them that if they intend to marry in spite of everything they must keep this affair a deadly secret until Paul has some satisfactory job. Of course they'll do neither the one thing nor the other. They are evidently not capable of keeping a secret, and I can no more imagine Paul in a job than a fly.'

'Good gracious, no; he'd never stick to it for a day.'

'I suppose, in point of fact, that if they did marry your mother would have to give them some sort of allowance, but it's much better that they shouldn't think so, because Paul, who must, after all, have a good idea of what poverty means, isn't likely to elope with her unless he can be fairly certain that there will be some money eventually.'

'Paul's not mercenary, you know,' said Bobby.

'Not in the least, but he's not an absolute fool either. I doubt if he'd risk such a thing, for her sake as well as his own. The worst of it is that I don't believe, apart from the money side of it, that they would be particularly happy together. They are really most unsuited. Paul needs somebody who is very strong-minded and who will manage him. Why, even that repellent girl, Marcella, would be a better wife for him. As for Philadelphia, the darling, she is obviously cut out to have money and position.'

'And I shall do my very best to see that she gets both,' said Bobby with one of his self-conscious smiles. 'What a fund of common sense you are, darling. You've cheered me up enormously. What is my line for the moment, then?'

'You must do all you can to keep this nonsense a secret from your mother. If she finds out it will be fatal. She'll probably say a lot of bitter and unkind things to both of them and as likely as not drive them straight into an elopement. If it can be kept from her I give the whole thing three months at the most before it fizzles out.'

'That ought to be easy. Paul goes away in less than a week now, when I trail back to the old col., and Mother is still out hunting most of the time. Besides, several people are coming to stay here over the week-end for this bogus dance she will insist on having. I dare say she won't notice anything much; she's been as blind as a bat so far.'

'We can only hope for the best,' said Amabelle, who was looking out of the window. 'Hullo, here comes my fiancé – whatever is he carrying? Oh, I say, isn't that rather sweet, d'you see; he's bringing two dead hens for the kitchen; he always has some exquisite present for me, the angel.'

'Well, I'll be off,' said Bobby, rather sourly; 'and I don't suppose, if you're really going to London, that I shall see you again until after you're married, which is too awful. Look here, darling, will you promise to go and choose yourself a present at Cartier? I've got an account there, so get something really nice, won't you, not a diamond hen, though, if you don't mind.'

20

The dance at Compton Bobbin was in no way a riot of joyous and abandoned merriment; it was, in fact, even more dreary an entertainment than might have been anticipated, and was long afterwards remembered by Cotswold beaux and belles as 'that frightful party at the Bobbins'. When the guests arrived, cold and dazzled after a long motor drive, they found neither the cheering strains of Terpsichore nor the sustaining draught of Bacchus awaiting them. The young man from Woodford who had been engaged to provide the former came very late indeed, so that for quite half an hour the guests stood about in uncertain groups while Paul and Squibby struggled to make the wireless work. When finally he did arrive, breathless and apologetic, having left his car upside down in a ditch, his playing proved to be of that sort which induces sleep rather than revelry by night. Lady Bobbin had remained true to her resolution that in *her* house there should be no champagne during the national crisis, and on every hand could soon be heard the groans and curses with which British youth greets the absence of any alcohol more fortifying than beer at its parties. The rare and somewhat tipsy appearances downstairs of Bobby, the duchess, and such of their intimates as were secretly invited to the cocktail bar provided by Bobby in his bedroom, merely accentuated the wretched sobriety of the other guests.

The duchess and Héloïse were staying with Bunch for this occasion, as also were Squibby, Biggy and Maydew. The two latter, however, had most ungallantly refused to attend the dance, giving as their excuse that they always felt sick in motor cars. Everybody else was quite well aware that they really wished to stay at home in order to play Brahms on two pianos. As a result of this monstrous behaviour the girls who had been invited by Bunch solely on their behalf spent the greater part of the evening sitting drearily together in the hall. This fact appeared to weigh rather on the duchess, who, as their chaperone, felt that she ought to feel some responsibility for their amusement.

'Those wretched girls,' she kept saying, in the intervals of helping Bobby to mix the cocktails, 'oughtn't I to do something about them? Shall we have them up here, darling?'

'Oh, don't let's. They look so gloomy, and there's hardly enough drink to go round as it is. Anyways, I expect they enjoy being together down there.'

'Of course they don't; they look furious, and I don't blame them either. I think it's simply odious of Biggy and Maydew to get them asked down and then stay behind like that. If I were Lady Tarradale I should be quite furious, especially as they're certain to keep her awake all night with their awful music, and she's been so wretchedly ill lately. Those poor charming girls, looking so sweet in their pink and green, too. I do feel badly about them. Do go and see if they're all right, Bobby, won't you?'

'Darling, you know they're not all right, so why bother? Besides, they're Bunch's guests, not mine. Let him look after them.'

'Bunch has got his own girl here, Sonia Beckett. You can't expect him to do more than dance about once with each of the others. Hullo, Héloïse darling. Come here, sweetest, I want to whisper. Angel, is it quite necessary for you to wander about with four young men when poor Rosemary and Laetitia have no one at all to talk to them?'

'I don't think anyone wants to talk to them,' said Héloïse; 'they're such cracking bores, aren't they? Give me a cocktail, darling, quickly. This party is quite the bloodiest I've ever been to, personally. How right Biggy and Maydew were to stay behind. I do envy them, don't you?'

'Squibby dear,' said the duchess, waving an empty glass at Bobby as she spoke, 'just tell me something. Have you seen Rosemary and Laetitia latishly? Are they all right, the sweet poppets?'

'Oh, yes,' said the heartless Squibby, 'I expect so. Sure to be. I saw them having a very jolly little chat with Lady Prague just now.'

'You don't think it would be rather nice if you went and saw how they were getting on?'

'Well, Aunt Loudie, I don't think I need. I'd much rather stay and talk to you. In any case, I've danced with both of them and they are nothing to do with me. It was Biggy and Maydew who insisted on having them asked down.'

Paul and Philadelphia spent most of the evening shut up together in the linen cupboard, bemoaning the fact that tomorrow they must be parted, and reiterating that they intended to be faithful to each other during the months to come.

'Darling, when I think,' said Philadelphia, her voice shaking, 'of all those lovely girls you go out with in London I do feel so terrified that you'll soon forget all about me.'

'I shan't do that. I tell you that you have quite a special place in my heart, and you always will have. Wherever I am I shall be thinking about you the whole time. I expect I shall go about with other girls, because it would be a mistake not to, but they won't mean anything to me really. You are, and always will be, the only woman in my life. I shall never feel about anybody as I do about you. You're perfect, to me.'

The fact that Paul had repeated this sentence, word for word, to at least three other women, did not prevent him, as he said it, from sincerely believing it to be the truth.

'But I feel terrified too,' he went on, 'that you'll decide to give me up after all and marry Michael instead. Remember, I shall never blame you in the least if you do. It would probably be much more sensible. But to me you are the only woman –'

At this juncture the duchess opened the linen cupboard door and popped her head round the corner.

'Oh, you darlings,' she said delightedly, 'I'm so glad somebody's having a lovely time. It does me good to see you. You've no idea what it's been like everywhere else, too gloomy and awful for words. Now, when you've quite finished being happy together in there we've got some cocktails in Bobby's room, so mind you come along and join us.'

She shut the door carefully and went, bursting with her news, back to Bobby.

'There they were, *locked* in each other's arms. I can't tell you how sweet they looked – the lambs. Quite frankly, I never should have thought Philadelphia had so much sense. I must ask her to stay as soon as ever we get back from Switzerland.'

'Now don't you start encouraging her,' said Bobby crossly. 'Amabelle and I are working like niggers to stop all this nonsense and make her get engaged to Michael.'

'Oh, *no*, you awful child, you can't behave like a matchmaking mamma at your age; it's not natural. For heaven's sake let the poor girl have her fun, besides, it's so good for her. Just think how pretty she's looking now. She is a different being from what she was a month ago.'

'I'm all in favour of her having as much fun as she likes,' said Bobby, 'so long as she'll be sensible and not go on with all this ridiculous talk about marriage – just think, if Michael heard about it, he might quite easily be put off for good.'

'You don't seriously want her to marry Michael, do you? He's such a fearful bore. I wouldn't allow a daughter of mine to marry him, however much she wanted to.'

'That's just very silly and naughty of you, darling Auntie Loudie, because a girl's first husband must be eligible, otherwise she will very soon go downhill altogether. Amabelle agrees with me.'

'Amabelle is so frightfully pompous in these days,' said the duchess with a hiccough. 'I can remember the time when she was just an ordinary tart (a very successful one and all that, of course) and then she really was the greatest fun. We used to go secretly to her parties and think we were being absolute daredevils, but ever since she married old James Fortescue she's been twice as much of a duchess as I am. It's a great pity, because in those days she used to be too heavenly.'

'I think she is still,' said Bobby stoutly. 'She's one of the sweetest people in the world. Look how divine she has been to the Monteaths ever since that baby was born.'

'Yes, I agree she is very sweet and kind, she always has been. I'm only saying that she's no longer such absolutely rollicking fun. In any case, I think it's absurd for her to take that line about Delphie. Why surely the child is rich enough to marry anybody she likes.'

'She's only rich so long as my mother chooses to make her an allowance.'

'Clearly. But I suppose that even darling Gloria could hardly see her own daughter starve. I don't understand what there is against Paul myself. He seems an exceptionally nice young man, good-looking, polite, everything one could want for a son-in-law.'

'Well, to begin with, if you'd really like to know, his name isn't Fisher at all.'

'Oh?'

'It's Fotheringay, Paul Fotheringay.'

'My dear, that's a much nicer name than Fisher. Most romantic, too. One of Henry VIII's wives was executed at a place called that. I remember all about it in English history.'

'Darling, I don't think you quite understand. His real name, as I said before, is Paul Fotheringay, and he is masquerading here under the alias of Fisher.'

'How divinely thrilling. Wait a moment, though, wasn't there somebody called Paul Fotheringay who wrote that screamingly funny book about pawnbrokers trying to commit suicide?'

'Yes, that's his book, *Crazy Capers*.'

'Oh, but I've never laughed so much at anything before in my life. Wait a minute while I rush to the linen cupboard – it's too bad, I haven't my copy here for him to autograph. It *was* a heavenly book. Bobby, you little monster, why ever didn't you tell me this before?'

'You see he's here in disguise really,' said Bobby, unbending a little, 'because he wants to write the life of Lady Maria. He asked Mother in a letter whether he could borrow the journal, and she wrote back awfully rudely, so then he got taken on as my tutor and ever since then he has been studying it for his book.'

'Well I should think that will be a scream,' said the duchess. 'Delphie will be mad if she doesn't marry him, but if she doesn't I shall, that's all. What I do adore is a really good sense of humour. The funny thing is that though I've liked Paul from the very beginning he never struck me as being so particularly amusing, but of course that must have been entirely my own fault. Shake up one more cocktail, won't you, Bobby, my sweet – here's Héloïse back again. Dear, what a pudding-faced young man she has got with her this time. Where can she have picked him up? Héloïse, what do you think, Philadelphia and Paul have been sitting out for more than two hours in the linen cupboard.'

'Oh, where – can I see?'

'No, certainly you can't. It's nothing whatever to do with you. I may say I'm surprised you've not been in there yourself.'

'If Maydew had come I don't doubt I should have been,' said Héloïse, 'but all the young men here seem to be so sexless. I honestly don't think I've ever been to such an awful party as this in my life. Can I introduce Mr Wainscote to you, by the way. He has been to a lot of jolly shows lately in London, and I expect he'd like a cocktail, Bobby.'

'As a matter of fact,' said Mr Wainscote, blushing, 'the rest of my party is very anxious to go home – I mean,' he added hurriedly, looking at Bobby, 'ready to leave. We have all enjoyed ourselves immensely, but we have a long cold drive before us, so I think that perhaps I should say good-bye,' and he edged out of the room sideways like a crab.

'My darling Héloïse, what an extraordinary young man,' said the duchess.

'He's not at all extraordinary,' said Héloïse, 'unless you mean extraordinarily attractive. I'm rather in love with him myself,' and she looked under long blue eyelashes at Bobby.

'No cop, old girl, you can't lead me on like that. I know you're in a temper because I haven't spoken to you the whole evening, but there's no point in making a fool of yourself just the same. Have another cegocktegail?'

'I degon't megind egif egI dego,' said Héloïse, happily settling herself on the edge of the bed. 'Now run along downstairs, Mother, if you don't mind, because I want to kiss Bobby.'

'All right, I'll go and see how Rosemary and Laetitia are getting on. Have a lovely time, and don't be too long.'

Shortly after this, Bobby himself came downstairs, and revolted by the sights and sounds of cheerlessness which greeted his eyes, thoughtfully turned out the electric light at the main, thus breaking up the party. By the flickering rays of the only candle that Compton Bobbin possessed, coats were found, *adieux* were said, and, grumbling to the last, the flower of Gloucestershire man and maidenhood climbed into their Morris Cowleys and drove away.

This *contretemps* postponed but did not avert Lady Bobbin's furious upbraiding of Bobby and Philadelphia, who, having disappeared at the first dance on the programme, had never been seen again mingling with their guests.

'I know it's all Louisa's fault,' she said angrily, 'and I'm damned if I'll go on having that woman to the house. I'm sick and tired of her rudeness, and as for that little— Héloïse, I'd much sooner neither of you had any more to do with her.'

Paul and Philadelphia parted the next day with tears and promises of eternal fidelity. Their farewells were rendered slightly more bearable than they would otherwise have been by the fact that Aunt Loudie, having given them the only moral support they had as yet received, had promised that she would invite Philadelphia to stay in London as soon as she herself should return from Switzerland.

'See you very soon, my darling,' said Paul, as they stood on Woodford platform waiting for his train.

'Yes, darling. And mind you write to me.'

'Of course I will, every day. And mind you do, too. Take care of yourself, my precious, and don't worry too much. Everything will come all right in the end, you'll see.'

'I don't know,' said Philadelphia, miserably.

'Now come on,' said Bobby impatiently as the train came to a standstill, 'jump in, Paul – good-bye, Delphie, come and see me at Eton some time, old girl. Don't let them forget to send on my letters and parcels. Good-bye – good-bye.'

To Philadelphia, left alone on the cold, wet and empty platform, it seemed as though all happiness had come to an end. She cried so much that she could hardly see to drive her car home.

Paul and Bobby lounged luxuriously in their first-class carriage (it was one of Bobby's talents that he could always travel first-class on a third-class ticket), and argued as to whether they should lunch at the Ritz or the Berkeley, and what film they should go to afterwards. At Oxford they got out and bought all the illustrated papers. Paul felt agreeably sentimental and wretched, but he was glad, on the whole, to be going back to London. The only drawback was that he had promised Philadelphia to look for work, a pastime that he detested, and worse still, to do work if he found it. Much would he have preferred to settle down in a desultory manner to his life of Lady Maria Bobbin. However, he put these unpleasant thoughts from him without any difficulty and was soon deep in perusal of the *Tatler*.

Philadelphia wandered about Compton Bobbin like a lost soul. She could find no comfort in her situation. It was typical, she thought again, of the malignant spirit which apparently controlled her destiny to cram just one month of her life with fascinating people and events, only to remove them all in a single day, leaving in their place a few memories to make everything seem flatter, more dreary than before. Paul had gone, Sally and Walter had gone for ever, Amabelle would not, it appeared, be back before Easter – her plans for a country wedding had been altered; she now intended to get married quietly in London as soon as the lambing season should be over and go to her villa on the Riviera for the honeymoon.

Philadelphia found herself once more without any occupation or interests, and for the rest of that day she sat before the fire in an arm-chair, assailed by the ghastly boredom only known to those who live in the country but have no love for country pursuits, and no intellectual resources on which they can fall back. And in the clutches of that boredom, too boring even to describe, she remained during the weeks to come. She would get up in the morning as late as she dared, and read the papers over and over again, hoping to pass the time until luncheon. In the afternoon she would go for a little walk, and when she came in from that would sit or wander aimlessly about the house, waiting for tea. After tea she would perhaps try to read some improving work suggested to her by Michael, or, more often, play canfield on the schoolroom table (if this comes out it means that he loves me and I shall marry him) until it was time to have her bath and change for dinner. The evenings were occupied with wireless, to which Lady Bobbin was devoted. And so the days dragged on, from one meal to the next. Poor Philadelphia hardly employed the best methods with which to fight depression, but it is difficult to know, under the circumstances, what else she could have done. Her education had not fitted her for study, and in any case, like most women, she was only really interested in personalities. When she received a letter from Paul it would colour a whole day, and she would spend hours reading, re-reading and answering it; but he wrote at the most irregular intervals. Like most people who write for a living he hated writing letters, and moreover seldom had any notepaper in his lodgings.

Michael, on the other hand, wrote from his bed of jaundice nearly every day. Although his letters were, in tone, more those of a father than a lover, he evidently quite regarded himself as engaged to Philadelphia, and she was too indolent, and too much afraid of bringing matters to a climax to disillusion him. Besides, she rather enjoyed receiving and answering his letters, Lady Bobbin also assumed that the engagement was to be announced as soon as Michael recovered.

Meanwhile, Paul was leading his usual happy-go-lucky existence in London. He obtained, without much difficulty, a 'job' in his uncle's office. The uncle having flatly refused to give him work, was quite glad to let him sit for a few hours every day in the office, at a pound a week, so that he might obtain that background of respectability which was to prove such a valuable factor in influencing Lady Bobbin. He still loved Philadelphia very much, and wanted nothing more than to marry her, but he felt that since several months must now elapse before it would be in any way feasible to ask her mother's consent, he might as well pass those months as pleasantly as he could. With this end in view he went, a few days after his arrival in London, to a fancy-dress party given in a tiny flat off the Brompton Road. On entering the room, which was a seething mass of travesty, the togas of ancient Rome and the beards of Elizabethan England rubbing against the talc wings of modern fairyland, he was immediately greeted with cries of enthusiasm by Marcella Bracket.

'Here's darling Paul. Oh, how cross I am with you. Where have you been all this time? I've done nothing but ring you up for weeks. You might have sent me a Christmas card, you ogre.'

Paul tried to ignore the girl, he really tried hard. Nevertheless, before the night was over he had abjectly apologized for his neglect of her during the past month, and had finally found himself with her in his arms, her large painted mouth pressed to his as of yore.

The next day he woke up with a bad headache and a worse conscience.

'This is really terrible,' he thought, 'I must pull myself together. How can I, how can I be behaving in this caddish manner whilst poor little Philadelphia is shut up in that dreary house with no one to speak to but Lady Bobbin, and she out hunting all day. It is beginning to look as if Amabelle were right in saying that I have no talent for true love. I am evidently incapable of being faithful to one person. All the same, I do love Philadelphia far, far the best, although Marcella seems to have this extraordinary effect on me.'

And he resolved never to see Marcella again. That determined young woman, however, was not easily to be put off. She had just suffered a serious reverse in her own love affairs, and it suited her very well to have Paul hanging around her once more. Paul, on the other hand, lonely, worried and very much attracted by Marcella, did not require a great deal of encouragement, and at the end of a fortnight they were inseparable.

21

As soon as Michael was allowed to move again he returned by train to Compton Bobbin to arrange about his wedding. No doubts whatever had crossed his mind as to Philadelphia's attitude towards him, and he travelled as far as London with perfect serenity. On his way through London he took the opportunity to lunch with Amabelle, and she immediately put him in possession of all the facts with regard to Paul and Philadelphia, once more giving it as her opinion that the whole affair was a piece of childish nonsense.

'Everything will be quite all right,' she said, 'if you do as I tell you. First of all, you'd better go round to Cartier this afternoon and buy her a lovely ring and some other little present as well, one of those diamond bracelets for instance. I should give her the bracelet when you arrive, but keep the ring for a day or two to give her when she has been really nice to you – it will seem more romantic like that. Be very sweet and sympathetic, of course, but perfectly firm, make her feel she is definitely engaged to you; and if by any chance she should mention Paul, take up the attitude of being surprised and pained but ready to forgive just this once. I should try to keep off the subject for as long as you can, though. I think you will find that, what with the boredom of her present existence and her fear of you (she regards you with a good deal of wholesome awe, you know), she will be beside you on the altar steps in no time. That's what you really do want, I suppose?'

'Yes, yes,' said Michael, adding uncertainly: 'Poor child, I only hope I shall be able to make her happy. You know, Amabelle, that it is you who will always be the love of my life, don't you?'

'Nonsense, my dear, of course you'll make her happy. You two are cut out for each other, obviously. As for Paul, I'm very fond of him myself, but all the same I feel perfectly certain that she would be wretched with him; he has far too weak a character to marry a girl of her sort. He needs something really hard-boiled. Why, at this very moment he is having an affair with that awful Marcella Bracket, whom he actually dislikes – I've no patience with him sometimes, I must say.'

Michael looked very much relieved. 'Then he's not in love with Philadelphia at all?'

'I tell you the whole thing is nonsense from beginning to end, and it's the greatest mercy that you are about again and can put a stop to it. All the same, I believe that in his queer way he does love Philadelphia, only he hasn't the strength of mind to get rid of the Bracket. Now, Michael, dear, you must be off. My last words to you are be firm and don't forget the diamond bracelet. It ought to work wonders for you.'

Michael followed this advice to the letter. Immediately on leaving Portman Square, he went to Cartier, where he bought a large and beautiful emerald ring and a diamond bracelet of magnificent proportions. With these in his pocket he caught the 4.45 from Paddington, arriving at Compton Bobbin just in time to dress for dinner.

He was met by his Aunt Gloria with the news that Philadelphia had gone to bed with a headache.

'In that case,' he said, 'I think I will go up and see her for a moment,' and before Lady Bobbin, gratified but somewhat scandalized at such haste, had time to utter a half-hearted protest, he had run up the stairs and was knocking at Philadelphia's bedroom door.

It would be idle to pretend that Philadelphia was not pleased to see him. The boredom and depression of the last few weeks had been such that she was ready to welcome with delight any new face, anybody from the outer world. With the greatest reluctance she had forced herself to avoid him by pretending to be ill, feeling in some obscure way that loyalty to Paul demanded this gesture, and when Michael came up to see her immediately on his arrival she was more touched and pleased than she cared to admit.

He sat on the edge of her bed and talked of this and that, cheerfully and without embarrassment, looking most attractively pale and thin from his recent illness. Presently, having made no mention whatever of an engagement, he said: 'Now I must have my bath, or I shall be late for Aunt Gloria, and you ought to go to sleep if you're not very well, so I will say good night. But first of all put out your hand and shut your eyes, darling.' Philadelphia did so, and he snapped the diamond bracelet on to her wrist.

The diamond is a stone possessed for the female mind, however unsophisticated, of curious psychological attributes. Philadelphia looked at the sparkling flowers on her wrist and forgot that she had been about to announce her betrothal to another. She flung her arms round Michael's neck in an access of childlike pleasure and cried: 'Oh, the lovely bracelet. Thank you, thank you, darling Michael. You are sweet to me.'

Amabelle's love potion had done its work for the moment. Its effect, however, wore off sadly during the night, and the next morning, very early, at about six o'clock, Philadelphia woke up tormented with agonies of self-reproach.

'Paul, my darling, darling Paul,' she wept into her pillow. 'I won't lose you; they shan't bribe me like this. I will never give you up, never, as long as I live.' She flung the offending bracelet, which gleamed beneath her bedside lamp, into the farthest corner of the room, sobbing bitterly. After a while she pulled herself together and began to consider her position. The idea had come to her that if she should stay any longer at Compton Bobbin now that Michael had arrived, she would inevitably find herself engaged to him. She knew that she was too weak to offer, alone and unsupported, any real resistance; and she dreaded beyond words the idea of those frightful scenes with her mother which would certainly ensue if she did. If she was ever to escape, now and now only, was the time. It would be her last opportunity. She must go, at once, to Paul.

Having taken this decision she began very quickly to dress. Better leave the house before anybody was about. She slipped downstairs, feeling like an escaping criminal, took the key of the garage from the hall table, climbed out of the schoolroom window into the cold, dark morning air, and by seven o'clock was well on the road to London in her little car. She would be in time to have breakfast with Paul before he left for his office. Poor darling, how he must hate working in such a place; it was wonderful to think of him doing it for her sake. Everything would be all right when she was with him, and she would be safe again. The idea of seeing him so soon filled her with nervous excitement.

Shortly after nine o'clock she drove up to the house in Ebury Street where Paul had rooms. Her heart beat in great thumps as she rang the front door bell. For an eternity there was no answer; at last, however, the door was opened by an elderly woman who held in one hand a bucket of soapy water. She looked at Philadelphia with hostility and said, in reply to her question, 'Mr Fotheringay has not been called yet.' Philadelphia hesitated. She felt cold and dazed after her long drive.

'I must see him, though,' she said at last. 'It is very important. I am his sister. Please will you show me the way to his room?'

The woman shrugged her shoulders. 'Mr Fotheringay is on the first floor, but he gave orders that he was not to be called. You must please yourself,' she said, and falling to her knees she began scrubbing the linoleum on the floor.

Philadelphia went upstairs timidly. She knocked several times on the first door that she came to, and finally, receiving no answer, she turned the handle and walked in. The room was evidently a sitting-room, and at first sight seemed to be empty, although the electric light was burning. Suddenly, however, it was empty no more, for she realized with a start that Paul himself lay on the sofa, fully dressed.

In certain emergencies the human brain neglects to register such subsidiary emotions as that of surprise. To Philadelphia, overstrung, hysterical, and worn out by her long and fasting drive, it seemed quite natural that Paul should be lying on his sofa instead of in his bed, that he should still be wearing evening dress at nine o'clock in the morning, and that although he was fast asleep the electric light should be turned on, shining full in his face. A person of more experience might have been prepared for what followed; Philadelphia only felt an overpowering relief that she had found him again. Everything must be all right now, it seemed.

'Paul,' she said, leaning over him. 'Darling. Wake up.'

No answer. No movement. No sound in the room but that of his thick, heavy and regular breathing. She touched him rather shyly on the arm. 'Please wake up, Paul.' She shook him gently. She shook him really hard. 'Paul, don't be so unkind to me. You must wake up. I've come so far to see you. Please, please, my darling.'

At last he half-opened his eyes, looked at her as though from a great distance, and said in a thick voice: 'For God's sake, leave me alone. I told them not to call me,' after which he turned over deliberately and once more lay motionless.

'Paul, you must speak to me,' she cried, shaking now with angry sobs, and losing all self-control she began to hit him on the chest until he opened his eyes again. This time he seemed to recognize her. He took one of her hands in his and said with a great effort, 'Go away, darling, I'm drunk.' After that neither tears nor protestations could move him.

Philadelphia went slowly down the stairs. That was the end. She must get back to Michael, who would never treat her so. She felt sick and faint now, and was blinded by her tears. The woman who had let her in was scrubbing the front door steps. Philadelphia passed her quickly, aware of curious looks, got into her car and drove down the street until she thought she must be out of sight. Then, oblivious of passers-by, she stopped and cried until she could cry no more. After that she began to think of what she should do next. In spite of her unhappiness she realized that to drive home at once in her present condition would be impossible; she must have something to eat first, and a rest. Whom did she know in London? Her Aunt Loudie was in Switzerland, Sally was almost certainly still on the Riviera. Amabelle – she would be kind. She started up the engine of the car and, after getting lost several times, for she did not know her way about London, she found herself at last outside Amabelle's house. She rang the front door bell; there was no answer. She rang again, and presently a red-faced footman appeared still struggling into his coat.

'Can I see Mrs Fortescue, please?'

'Mrs Fortescue has not been called yet.'

Philadelphia was trying to decide what she should say next when she found that the door had been rudely shut in her face. Such terrible things had happened to her already that this incident, which on any ordinary occasion would have caused her unspeakable mortification, seemed quite unimportant. She even sat in her car this time without bothering to move on while she considered what her next step should be. Sally was her last remaining hope, if she was back from the Riviera all would be well. She drove to Fitzroy Square. 'Please, God, let her be there please, please.' This time the door was opened immediately by a fat and smiling charlady.

'Yes, Mrs Monteath came back last night. Will you come this way, please.'

'Thank you, God, thank you, thank you.'

She took Philadelphia up to the first floor flat, opened the door of it with a special key and precipitated her into a large, light bedroom, where Sally and Walter Monteath were sitting up in bed eating their breakfast.

'A young lady to see you, ma'am.'

'Philadelphia darling!' cried Sally in a loud and cheerful voice.

Philadelphia opened her mouth to say something and then fell to the floor in a dead faint.

When she recovered consciousness she was lying in the bed herself, and Sally was sponging her face with cold water while the charwoman looked on. Walter was nowhere to be seen.

'There, darling,' said Sally, 'you lie quite still and don't worry about anything.'

'I'm so sorry,' said Philadelphia, 'to be such a bother.'

'Don't be silly. Are you feeling all right now?'

'Yes, perfect. I expect I'm rather hungry really, that's why I fainted.'

'Poor sweet. Mrs Crumpit will make you some breakfast at once. You didn't motor all the way up this morning, did you?'

'Yes, I did.'

'Good gracious. Walter thought you had by the look of the car.'

Philadelphia felt warm, happy and contented. She was in no hurry to tell her story, and Sally did not ask any more questions, but went off to help Mrs Crumpit in the kitchen. Presently she came back with a most delicious breakfast. While Philadelphia was eating this the telephone bell rang in the next room and Walter's voice could be heard answering it.

'Hullo – yes? Oh, hullo, Amabelle – my dear, she's in our bed, quite all right – she appeared about half an hour ago and fainted away. Gave us an awful fright, but she's eating breakfast now. What? I don't know. I've no idea. Oh, very well, we'll keep her here for the present then. Right you are, Amabelle. Good-bye.'

'You seem to have caused a perfect uproar,' he said, coming into the bedroom. 'Apparently Michael has been telephoning to Amabelle from Compton Bobbin half out of his mind, and she tried to get on to Paul, but there was no answer; and then by a stroke of luck it occurred to her that we might know something about you. Michael is on his way to London now. I must go and have my bath. See you later.'

'Do tell me all about it,' said Sally as he shut the door. 'I'm eaten with curiosity.'

'Well, you see, Michael arrived at home last night and gave me a diamond bracelet.'

'Darling, how gorgeous.'

'And I simply hadn't the courage to tell him about Paul. I couldn't face the scene with Mother; you don't know how terrifying she can be. But I thought that if I went to Paul straight away everything would be all right. I thought it was my only chance. So I got up very early this morning –'

'You must have.'

'And drove up here and went straight to Paul's house, and when I got there,' she said, her voice shaking, 'he was lying on the sofa looking too awful, and he wouldn't speak to me or even bother to open his eyes.'

'Blind, I suppose,' said Sally with the wisdom of experience.

'Yes, he was. At last when I had shaken him for ages all he said was, "Go away – I'm drunk." Sally, I never knew people got drunk in the morning?'

'I expect he had a jolly old hangover,' said Sally. 'What did you do then?'

'As soon as I realized what was the matter I went to Amabelle's, because I thought you were still abroad, but she hadn't been called and the footman was rude to me, so I came here on the chance that I might find you.'

'You've been crying, haven't you?'

'Well, of course. It's so terrible to think that all this time I've been in love with a drunkard.'

'Paul's not a drunkard, my dear; that's absurd. All men get blind sometimes, but they don't expect their girl friends to call at nine in the morning as a rule.'

'Anyway, it's all over between us now. I couldn't bear to see him again after that.'

'Couldn't you?'

'Never. It was too horrible. He could never have done such a thing if he had really loved me. Michael couldn't behave like that; he does love me, I know, and I shall be frightfully happy with him now.'

'I never doubted that you would be happy with Michael,' said Sally in a dry voice. 'For one thing, you weren't at any time properly in love with Paul. He was the first person who had ever made love to you and you fell for him; but that doesn't count.'

'Oh, Sally, you don't understand. I adored him right up to this morning more than anyone in the world. You couldn't go on being in love with somebody after a thing like that had happened, could you?'

'But of course you could. That sort of thing doesn't make a scrap of difference if you really love somebody. When I think of all the times I've put Walter to bed absolutely paralytic with drink! You weren't a bit in love with Paul, my sweet, and you've realized it, that's all. And I think it's a mercy you have, myself, because you are entirely unsuited to each other in every way. You would both have been miserably unhappy. Now, you'll be able to marry that divine Michael and have a really enviable life. Don't cry, darling, but have some more coffee and then I'll lend you some rouge. You mustn't be looking pale for Michael when he comes.'

Two days later Paul read in *The Times* that a marriage had been arranged and would shortly take place between the Marquis of Lewes and Philadelphia, only daughter of Lady Bobbin and the late Sir Hudson Bobbin, of Compton Bobbin, Gloucestershire.

With a sigh, whether of sadness or of relief will never be known, he settled down to write the first chapter of his *Life and Works of Lady Maria Bobbin*.

Wigs on the Green

To Peter

'That man is by nature a buffoon and that his best work is done in an antic, is a theory which gentlemen of leisure and high spirits will find very comforting.'

A. F. Wedgwood

I

'No, I'm sorry,' said Noel Foster, 'not sufficiently attractive.'

He said this in unusually firm and final accents, and with a determination which for him was rare he hung up his office telephone receiver. He leant back in his chair. 'That's the last time,' he thought. Never again, except possibly in regard to the heiresses he now intended to pursue, would he finish long and dreary conversations with the words, 'Not sufficiently attractive.'

Now that he was leaving the office for good he felt himself in no particular hurry to be off. Unlike other Friday evenings he made no dash for the street; on the contrary he sat still and took a long gloating look round that room which for the last two years had been his prison. With the heavenly knowledge that he would never see them again he was able to gaze in perfect detachment at the stained-glass windows (a cheerful amber shade, full of bubbles too, just like champagne), and the old oak furnishing – which made such a perfectly delightful setting for the charms of Miss Clumps the pretty typist, Miss Brisket the plain typist, and Mr Farmer the head clerk. This amiable trio had been his fellow prisoners for the last two years; he most sincerely hoped never to see any of them again. He said goodbye to them cordially enough, however, took his hat and his umbrella, and then, rich and free, he sauntered into the street.

He had not yet had time since good fortune had befallen him to leave his dreary lodging in Ebury Street, and as a matter of habit returned to it now. He then rang up Jasper Aspect. This he did knowing perfectly well that it was a mistake of the first order. Poor young men who have just received notice of agreeable but moderate legacies can do nothing more stupid than to ring up Jasper Aspect. Noel, who had been intimate with Jasper for most of his life, was aware that he was behaving with deplorable indiscretion, nevertheless some irresistible impulse led him to the telephone where the following conversation took place:

'Hullo Jasper?'

'My dear old boy, I was just going to ring you up myself.'

'Oh, what are you doing tonight?'

'I thought it would be exceedingly agreeable to take a little dinner off you.'

'All right, I wanted to see you; where shall we dine – how about Boulestins? Meet you there at eight?'

'Look here, I haven't got any money, you know.'

'That's all right,' said Noel. He would keep his glorious news until such time as he could see the incredulity and disgust which would no doubt illumine Jasper's honest countenance when it was broken to him. Jasper now once more proclaimed his inability to pay, was once more reassured and rang off.

'This is all exceedingly mysterious,' he said when they met.

'Why?' said Noel.

'Well, my dear old boy, it isn't every day of the week one can get a free meal off you, let alone an expensive one like this is going to be. Why did you choose me for the jolly treat? I find it very puzzling indeed.'

'Oh! I wanted to see you. I want your advice about one or two things actually, and after all one must eat somewhere, so why not here?' And fishing for his handkerchief he produced, as though by accident, and replaced with nonchalance, a roll of ten pound notes.

Jasper's expression did not change however, as Noel had hopefully anticipated that it would. He merely ordered another champagne cocktail. When it came he said, 'Well, here's to the Scrubs old boy, hope you'll find it comfy there, you can come and see me sometimes in between terms, I'm never at all up-stage about my jail-bird friends.'

'I don't know what you mean,' said Noel, coldly.

'Don't you? Well it's fairly obvious that you've got the skates on, isn't it? And I suppose you want me to help you get away with the dough. Now I suggest that we should go fifty-fifty on it, and do a bunk together. That suit you?'

'No.'

'First of all you had better tell me frankly if you are wanted. I've been wanted in Paris, and not wanted anywhere else, for simply ages, there's nothing I don't know on the subject of wanting.'

'My dear old boy,' said Noel, comfortably. 'I'm afraid you've got hold of the wrong end of the stick.'

'But you came to me for advice.'

'Yes, I did, I thought you might be able to put me in touch with some rich girl who would like to marry me.'

'That's a good one I'm bound to say. To begin with, if I was lucky enough to know any rich girls can you see me handing them out to you? And to go on with, I shouldn't think the girl is born who would like to marry you.'

'Oh! nonsense, girls will marry anybody. Besides, I'm a pretty attractive chap you know.'

'Not very. Anyhow, let me tell you something. Courting heiresses is an exceedingly expensive occupation. You didn't give me time just then to count exactly how much you have managed to extract from the till, but I'm pretty sure it wasn't enough to finance a racket of that sort. Why, you don't know what these girls run you in for, nights out, lunches, orchids, week-ends to all parts of the Continent; that's not the beginning, I've been through it, I know what I'm talking about. I suppose the worst part of it,' he went on, warming to his subject, 'is the early-morning telephoning. The precious little poppet, buried in lace pillows, likes to have a nice long cosy chat between 9 and 10 a.m., she doesn't realize that you, meanwhile, are shivering half-way up your landlady's staircase with an old woman scrubbing the linoleum round your feet. And what's the end of it all? When she marries her Rumanian prince she may remember to ask you to be one of those pretty young gentlemen who leave the guests to find their own pews at weddings. It's all fearfully dismal I can tell you.'

'How you do talk,' said Noel admiringly. 'Just like a book. I wonder you don't write one.'

'I shall, when I'm thirty. Nobody ought to write books before they're thirty. I hate precocity. Now then, out with it, Noel, how did you get all that cash?'

'Well, if you really want to know, an aunt of mine has died. She has left me some money.'

'That's just an ordinary lie, of course. Legacies never happen to people one knows. It's like seeing ghosts or winning the Irish Sweep, one never meets the people who have, only people who know people who have. So how much did she leave you?'

'Three thousand three hundred and fourteen pounds.'

'Just say that again.'

'Three thousand three hundred and fourteen pounds.'

'Did I hear you say three thousand three hundred and fourteen pounds?'

'You did.'

'Honest to God?'

'Honest to God.'

'D'you think the aunt was in full possession of her faculties when she made that will?'

'There's no doubt that she was.'

'Such a very odd sum. Well now, Noel, my dear old boy, you have my warmest congratulations. And what about the fourteen pounds?'

'What about them?'

'Hadn't it occurred to you that three thousand three hundred pounds rolls off the tongue much easier without that niggly little fourteen tacked on to it? Sounds more really, I should have said – the fourteen rather spoils it. Actually fourteen pounds is the exact sum I owe my landlady by a curious coincidence.'

'Oh, it is is it?' said Noel in a voice of boredom. 'Now shall I tell you what I said to myself when the lawyer rang me up about all this? I said, no cash presents to any of the boys, and that I keep to, so lay off will you?'

'That was exceedingly sensible of you. So now you intend to devote the whole of this little nest-egg to the pursuit of heiresses?'

'I should very much like to find a nice girl and marry her, if that's what you mean.'

'It's such a fearful gamble. Much better put the money on a horse and be out of your misery at once.'

'I'm not in any misery at all. I intend to lead a soft, luxurious life for the next six months or so, at the rate of six thousand six hundred and twenty-eight pounds a year.'

'And after that a soft uxorious life at an even better rate. I'm bound to say it's quite a pleasing outlook – only you don't know any heiresses.'

'Not at present. I thought perhaps you did.'

'Pass the brandy, old boy.'

'In that case,' said Noel, summoning the waiter. 'I'll have my bill, please – in that case I think I shall have to be going. I've watched you drinking that very expensive brandy for quite long enough.'

'Hold on,' said Jasper in an aggrieved tone of voice, 'give a chap time to think, I've just had an idea – pass the brandy, old boy.' He helped himself, carelessly splashing the brandy into his glass. 'The Jolly Roger,' he said.

'What Jolly Roger?'

'It's a public-house in Chalford where I once stayed when I was shooting the moon. Pretty little place, pretty little barmaid, I remember – Minnie or Winnie or some name like that.'

'Thanks, I know plenty of pretty little barmaids myself. It's not what I'm looking for at present. I think I shall have to be going.'

'Suppose you allow me to finish what I was saying.'

'I beg your pardon.'

'About a mile from Chalford village are the lodge gates of Chalford Park, and there lives the girl whom I believe to be England's largest heiress – Eugenia Malmains. I couldn't make a pass at her then because she was under the age of consent; it was about four years ago. She must be quite seventeen by now though. Nobody knows anything about her because she lives with her grandparents who are batty – she's fairly batty herself I believe.'

'That's nothing. She couldn't be battier than the girls one meets about the place in London. I don't think it sounds worth investigating, but I might go down to the pub for a week-end sometime – where is Chalford?'

'About ten miles away from Rackenbridge, that's the station. Best train in the day is the 4.45 from Paddington.'

'Well, many thanks, old boy. See you before long, I hope.'

'I hope so. Thank you very much for my good dinner.'

They spoke with nonchalance. Neither, however, was the least deceived as to the other's intentions, nor was Noel at all surprised when, arriving at Paddington next day to catch the 11.50 to Rackenbridge, he saw Jasper waiting for him on the platform.

Sadly he lent the requisite pound for Jasper's ticket, drearily he followed him into a first-class luncheon car. Poor young men who have just received notice of agreeable but moderate legacies should know better than to ring up Jasper Aspect.

'I've no one to blame but myself,' thought Noel, gloomily.

2

'Britons, awake! Arise! oh, British lion!' cried Eugenia Malmains in thrilling tones. She stood on an overturned wash-tub on Chalford village green and harangued about a dozen aged yokels. Her straight hair, cut in a fringe, large, pale-blue eyes, dark skin, well-proportioned limbs and classical features, combined with a certain fanaticism of gesture to give her the aspect of a modern Joan of Arc.

She was dressed in an ill-fitting grey woollen skirt, no stockings, a pair of threadbare plimsolls, and a jumper made apparently out of a Union Jack. Round her waist was a leather belt to which there was attached a large bright dagger.

Noel Foster and Jasper Aspect were taking a short walk round the village waiting for 'them' to open. The true amateur of bars, be it noted, is seldom content to drink his beer in his own hotel, where he may have it in comfort at any hour; he is always restlessly awaiting the glorious moment when some other 'they' shall be available. This is called pub-crawling, a sport much indulged in by gentlemen of the leisured classes.

Suddenly they came upon the godlike apparition of Eugenia Malmains on her wash-tub. They gasped.

'That's the girl we want,' said Jasper suddenly, 'that's Eugenia. I didn't recognize her at first. I'm bound to say she's become exceedingly beautiful since I was here, but she's evidently quite batty just like I told you. Still you can't have everything in this life. D'you mind if I make a pass at her too, old boy?'

'Yes I do, you're not to,' said Noel peevishly, 'and anyway shut up. I want to hear what she's saying.'

'The Union Jack Movement is a youth movement,' Eugenia cried passionately, 'we are tired of the old. We see things through their eyes no longer. We see nothing admirable in that debating society of aged and corrupt men called Parliament which muddles our great Empire into wars or treaties, dropping one by one the jewels from its crown, casting away its glorious colonies, its hitherto undenied supremacy at sea, its prestige abroad, its prosperity at home, and all according to each vacillating whim of some octogenarian statesman's mistress –'

At this point a very old lady came up to the crowd, pushed her way through it and began twitching at Eugenia's skirt. 'Eugenia, my child,' she said brokenly, 'do get off that tub, pray, please get down at once. Oh! when her ladyship hears of this I don't know what will happen.'

'Go away Nanny,' said Eugenia, who in the rising tide of oratory seemed scarcely aware that she had been interrupted. 'How could anyone,' she continued, 'feel loyalty for these ignoble dotards, how can the sacred fire of patriotism glow in any breast for a State which is guided by such apathetic nonentities? Britons, I beseech you to take action. Oh! British lion, shake off the nets that bind you.' Here the old lady again plucked Eugenia's skirt. This time however, Eugenia turned round and roared at her, 'Get out you filthy Pacifist, get out I say, and take your yellow razor gang with you. I will have free speech at my meetings. Now will you go of your own accord or must I tell the Comrades to fling you out? Where are my Union Jackshirts?' Two hobbledehoys also dressed in red, white and blue shirts here came forward, saluted Eugenia and each taking one of the nanny's hands they led her to a neighbouring bench where she sat rather sadly but unresistingly during the rest of the speech.

'We Union Jackshirts,' remarked Eugenia to the company at large, 'insist upon the right to be heard without interruption at our own meetings. Let the Pacifists' – here she gave her nanny a very nasty look – 'hold their own meetings, we shall not interfere with them at all, but if they try to break up our meetings they do so at their own risk. Let me see, where had I got to – oh! yes. Patriotism is one of the primitive virtues of mankind. Allow it to atrophy and much that is valuable in human nature must perish. This is being proved today, alas, in our unhappy island as well as in those other countries, which, like ourselves, still languish 'neath the deadening sway of a putrescent democracy. Respect for parents, love of the home, veneration of the marriage tie, are all at a discount in England today, society is rotten with vice, selfishness, and indolence. The rich have betrayed their trust, preferring the fetid atmosphere of cocktail bars and night clubs to the sanity of a useful country life. The great houses of England, one of her most envied attributes, stand empty – why? Because the great families of England herd together in luxury flats and spend their patrimony in the divorce courts. The poor are no better than the rich, they also have learnt to put self before State, and satisfied with the bread and circuses which are flung to them by their politicians, they also take no steps to achieve a better spirit in this unhappy land.'

'The girl's a lunatic but she's not stupid,' said Jasper.

'My friends, how can we be saved? Who can lift this country from the Slough of Despond in which she has for too long wallowed, to a Utopia such as our corrupt rulers have never pictured, even in their wildest dreams? He who aims highest will reach the highest goal, but how can those ancient dipsomaniacs reach any goal at all? Their fingers are paralysed with gout – they cannot aim; their eyesight is impeded with the film of age – they see no goal. The best that they can hope is that from day to day they may continue to creep about the halls of Westminster like withered tortoises seeking to warm themselves in the synthetic sunlight of each other's approbation.'

'I'm liking this,' said Jasper, 'my father's brother is an M.P.'

'How then, if a real sun shall arise, arise with a heat which will shrivel to cinders all who are not true at heart? How if a real Captain, a man, and not a tortoise, shall appear suddenly at their adulterous bedsides, a cup of castor oil in the one hand, a goblet of hemlock in the other, and offer them the choice between ignominy and a Roman death?

'Britons! That day is indeed at hand. There is a new spirit abroad, a new wine that shall not be poured into those ancient bottles. Britons are at last coming to their senses, the British lion is opening his mouth to roar, the attitude of mind which we call Social Unionism is going to save this country from her shameful apathy. Soon your streets will echo 'neath the tread of the Union Jack Battalions, soon the day of jelly-breasted politicians shall be no more, soon we shall all be living in a glorious Britain under the wise, stern, and beneficent rule of Our Captain.'

'Hooray,' cried Jasper, clapping loudly at this stirring peroration, 'Hear! hear! splendid!' The villagers turned and looked at him in amazement. Eugenia gave him a flashing smile.

'Now, Britons,' she continued, 'do you wish to ask any questions? If so I will devote ten minutes to answering them.'

The yokels stood first on one foot and then on the other. Finally one of them removed a straw from his mouth and remarked that they had all enjoyed Miss Eugenia's speech very much, he was sure, and how was His Lordship's hay-fever?

'Better, thank you,' said Eugenia politely, 'it always goes away in July, you know.' She looked disappointed. 'No more questions? In that case I have an announcement to make. Anyone wishing to join our Union Jack Movement can do so by applying to me, either here or at Chalford House. You are asked to pay ninepence a month, the Union Jack shirt costs five shillings, and the little emblem is sixpence. Would any of you care to join up now?'

The yokels immediately began to fade away. Already they paid two shillings a year to Lady Chalford towards the Conservative funds, and twopence a week for the Nursing Association; they failed, therefore, to see why any more of their hard-earned money should be swallowed up by the Malmains family. Jasper and Noel, on the other hand, snatched at this heaven-sent opportunity to ingratiate themselves with the heiress. They sprang forward and announced in chorus that they were anxious to be recruited. Eugenia's face lit up with a perfectly radiant smile.

'Oh, good,' she said, coming down from her tub. She then began hitching up her skirt, disclosing underneath it a pair of riding breeches, from the pocket of which she produced two recruiting cards and a fountain-pen. 'You sign here – see? You have to promise that you will obey the Captain in all things and pay ninepence.'

'I promise,' said Jasper.

'It's all very well,' said Noel, 'I suppose that's O.K., but look here, who is the Captain? Is he a nice chap? Couldn't I promise to obey him in most things? He might want me to do something very peculiar, mightn't he?'

Eugenia looked at him with lowering brow, fingering her dagger. 'You had better be careful,' she said gloomily. 'That is no way to speak of the Captain.'

'I'm awfully sorry,' said Noel, nervously eyeing the weapon. 'I'll never do it again. Right then, here's my ninepence.'

'Lend me a bob, old boy,' said Jasper.

'Sorry, old boy,' said Noel.

'Don't be a cad, you swine,' said Jasper, kicking him gently on the shin.

'Here, don't kick me,' said Noel.

Eugenia looked from one to the other. Her sympathies were clearly with Jasper. 'Are you perhaps unemployed?' she asked him, 'because if you are it's only fourpence.'

'Am I unemployed? Is unemployed my middle name? Lend me fourpence, old boy.'

'Sorry, old boy.'

'I will lend you fourpence,' said Eugenia suddenly, 'but you will have to pay me back soon, because what I really came down for this afternoon was to buy two twopenny bars at the village shop.'

'Bars of what?'

'Chocolate, of course.'

On hearing this Noel was naturally obliged to produce fourpence for Jasper. Eugenia then persuaded him to pay for both their Union Jack shirts and little emblems as well. He thought that Fate, as usual, was being wonderful to Jasper, who was quite obviously top boy in Eugenia's estimation, and who now capped all by suggesting that they should repair to the village shop in search of twopenny bars. While Noel paid for the bars he realized that the credit for them was going to Jasper. He decided that he must return this old-man-of-the-sea to London as soon as might be.

'I've never seen you before, do you live near here?' Eugenia asked Noel, as they all emerged, munching twopenny bars, from the village shop.

'No, we don't, we are just staying at the Jolly Roger for a few weeks, or at least that is to say *I* am staying for a few weeks. My friend, Mr Aspect here, has to leave tomorrow, quite early. It is very unfortunate.'

'Don't you believe it,' said Jasper shortly, 'not now I've met you, I'm not leaving. No such thing.'

'Oh! good,' said Eugenia, 'it would really be too sad if you had to go, just when you've joined the Movement and everything. You're the type of young men I need in this village, keen, active, energetic.'

'That's me,' said Jasper.

'Besides, you won't be busy doing other things all day. I have some wonderful members in my detachment, but, of course, they are all working boys, except my two Union Jackshirt defenders you saw just now dealing with that old female Pacifist. I thought they did it very bravely; she would have razored them up for twopence, no tricks are too filthy for that gang, it seems. Yes, what we need here is educated people of leisure like yourselves, for canvassing and platform work. That's why I'm so particularly glad you're staying on.'

'I suppose you are Eugenia Malmains?' said Jasper. 'I used to see you riding about the village here years ago when you were under the age of – quite a kid you know. You lived alone with your grandparents then.'

'I still do, worse luck.'

'Always down here? Don't you ever go to London?'

'No, you see, T.P.O.F. (that's what I always call my grandmother, it stands for The Poor Old Female) says that nobody would speak to us in London if we did go. T.P.O.M. (The Poor Old Male, that's my grandfather) used to go up to the House of Lords, before he had his stroke. As he was stone deaf it didn't matter so much whether people spoke to him or not. It wouldn't matter to me a bit, either, because I know the comrades at the Union Jack House would speak to me. T.P.O.F. has got a bee in her bonnet about it.'

'Do you want to go?'

'Of course I want to. I should see the Captain if I did, besides, I could march with the Union Jack Battalions.'

'Who is the Captain?'

'Captain Jack, founder of the Social Unionist Movement and Captain of the Union Jackshirts,' said Eugenia, throwing up her hand in a salute.

'Why don't you marry and get away from here?'

'Thank you, I am wedded to the Movement though. Oh! bother, here comes Nanny again, I must go.' She put her hands to her mouth and called, on two peculiar notes, 'Vivian Jack-son.' A small black horse without saddle or bridle came trotting up to her, accompanied by an enormous mastiff. 'This is Vivian Jackson, my horse,' she explained. 'My dog is called the Reichshund, after Bismarck's dog you know. Good-bye.' She swung herself on to the horse's back, gave it a resounding smack on one side of its neck, and galloped away in the direction of Chalford Park.

'Thank God for our English eccentrics,' said Jasper. 'Come on, old boy, they must be open by now.'

3

'What's the news?' asked Noel. He came into the garden of the Jolly Roger feeling hot and grumpy after a long walk. Noel, when in the country, always took large doses of fresh air and exercise. He believed in looking after his health. Jasper, who believed in having a good time, sat smoking cigarettes and reading the morning papers, which, it seemed, could be expected to arrive in that remote village, together with the one post, at any hour between 10 a.m. and 4 p.m.

'Another body has been found in another trunk and two fearfully pretty Janes turned up here late last night. It appears that they intend to stay several days – just what we needed.'

'I don't see why,' said Noel petulantly. 'We've got Eugenia.'

'Don't you just? Well it's like this old boy, the more the merrier. You can't have enough of a good thing. Many hands make light work. And so on. Rather nice about the body too, the one in the trunk I mean. In fact I'm very suited by this place altogether.'

'Are you?'

'I am. I also had three minutes' conversation with Eugenia before Nanny got at us. Enchanting girl, I quite expect I shall marry her.'

'Jasper, old boy, there's something I must say to you. It's not very easy for me, but I've known you long enough, I hope, to be able to speak my mind to you.'

'That's quite all right, old boy, don't you worry. I've got some money coming in any day now – I shan't be touching you for another penny I promise you.'

Noel sighed deeply. He might have foreseen that this old-man-of-the-sea would be hard to shake off.

'So what had Eugenia to say for herself?' he asked with some irritation.

'A lot more about how we are governed by octogenarian statesmen's mistresses. I'm bound to say it's a shaking thought, isn't it?'

'Which are octogenarians, the statesmen or their mistresses?'

'Oh, I see. I must remember to ask her that some time. Whichever it is they must certainly be got rid of. Ignominy or a Roman death for them. Good – here's the beer at last – some for you, old boy? Two more beers please miss, and put all that down to room 6, will you?'

'Room 8,' said Noel. His room was 6.

'Oh, dear, now you're going to be mean,' said Jasper. 'Put two down to room 6 and one down to room 8, and put the newspapers down to room 6 – no good old boy, you'll have to read about the trunk sooner or later you know. I must say I hate all this cheese-paring.'

'So do I,' said Noel eagerly. 'Tell you what, Jasper, I'll give you this for your fare back to London and pay your bill here when you've gone. How's that?'

'Exceedingly generous of you,' said Jasper, tucking thirty shillings into his note-case and settling down to more grisly details of the trunk murders.

Later that day he remarked to Noel; 'I say, there's something very queer indeed about those new Janes. First of all they've signed the book here as Miss Smith and Miss Jones, both of Rickmansworth. Likely tale. Then they've taken a private sitting-room, which strikes me as odd. But the oddest thing of all is that the Miss Jones one spent her whole afternoon in the orchard picking ducal coronets out of her drawers and night-dresses. Bit fishy, the whole business I'm thinking.'

'How d'you know they were ducal coronets?'

'My dear old boy, I know a ducal coronet when I see it. You forget that my grandfather is a duke.'

'Not a proper one.'

'I imagine that proper is just what he isn't anything else but. Not much chance for impropriety when one has been binned-up for thirty-five years, eh?'

'That's just it. I don't count dukes that are binned-up same way I don't count bankrupt dukes.'

'Well, I mean, count him or not as you like. I'm sure he doesn't mind.'

'Go on telling me about Miss Jones's drawers, won't you?'

'As soon as I made quite sure she was picking some kind of monogram out of them (I couldn't see as well as I should have liked, through the hedge) I legged it upstairs to her bedroom, number 4, opposite the bath, and it's full of ducal coronets wherever you look. On the brushes and combs even, the whole place is a regular riot of strawberry leaves. And the jewels she's got lying about on her dressing-table! I managed to find two quid in cash as well, in the pocket of an old mackintosh – shouldn't think she'll miss it.'

'You must be quite nicely off for cash now.'

'Mm. But isn't it extraordinary about Miss Jones. Is she an absconding duchess or a duchess's absconding ladies' maid or what? Anyway, I'll stand you a drink at the Rose Revived. Eugenia should be round before long and I promised we'd meet her outside the twopenny-bar shop.'

Eugenia, however, was in the middle of a gruelling interview with The Poor Old Female, her grandmother, who had come to hear something of her recent activities.

'My child, I cannot have you running round the village like a kitchen-maid,' T.P.O.F. was saying, sadly rather than angrily, 'talking to strangers, worse than that, accepting sweets from them. Besides, I hear that you have been riding that pony of yours astride again – you are not a baby any more, my dear, and young ladies should not ride in that way. What must the village people think of you? I blame nurse for all this and I blame myself; I suppose I can hardly blame you, Eugenia. After all, your mother was a wicked sinful woman, and bad blood always comes out sooner or later.'

'I'm not bad at all,' said Eugenia, sullenly. 'I never do sins, and I would gladly lay down my life for the Captain.'

Lady Chalford, who vaguely supposed that Eugenia must be referring to the Deity, looked embarrassed. Religious fervour was, in her eyes, almost as shocking as sexual abandon, and quite likely to be associated with it. Many of the most depraved women whom she had known in her social days had been deeply and ostentatiously religious.

She went to church herself, of course, feeling it a patriotic duty so to do, but she had no personal feelings towards God, whom she regarded as being, conjointly with the King, head of the Church of England. However, if the girl was really obsessed by religion, a tendency which Lady Chalford had never noticed in her before, and which she presumed to be of recent origin, it might yet be possible to save her from following in her mother's steps. Lady Chalford considered whether or not it would be advisable to call in the parson. Meanwhile she forced herself to say rather shyly, 'The Captain was always obedient to those in authority. Try to follow His example, Eugenia.'

'I don't agree at all,' was the reply. 'The Captain's ideas are most revolutionary, most, and he doesn't have to obey anyone, being a Leader.'

Lady Chalford knew herself to be unfitted for a theological argument on these lines. She decided that the parson would have to be called in.

'Give unto Caesar the things that are Caesar's,' she said vaguely. 'I suppose if you follow Him you won't come to much harm. But pray don't let me hear of you careering about the village and speaking to strange men, or you will end as your mother did.'

'How did she?' asked Eugenia, with passionate interest. Lady Chalford refused to be trapped in this manner. It was not a subject which she considered suitable for discussion, still less suitable for the ears of a young lady whom it concerned so intimately. The ugly word 'divorce' would have to be spoken, even uglier words understood. Sooner or later, of course, Eugenia must be informed, but the news would surely come best from the child's own husband, if Fate were sufficiently kind to provide her with one. Lady Chalford was haunted by sad forebodings on this subject, no nice man, she felt sure, would wish to marry the daughter of Eugenia's mother; different propositions were more likely to be made.

'Go to your room now until dinner-time. I am extremely vexed with you.'

'Stupid old female,' Eugenia muttered under her breath. She obeyed, however. Indeed, until the Social Unionists had come to fill the void of boredom that was her life, she had always obeyed her grandparents in everything. It had never occurred to her to do otherwise.

So Jasper and Noel awaited her in vain outside the twopenny-bar shop. They were not, however, left without any distraction. Hardly had they taken up a position on Ye Olde Stocks (which had been placed on the village green by some enthusiastic lover of the countryside in about 1890, and had since constituted a lure for Americans) than the Misses Smith and Jones appeared in search of aspirins, soap, and a daily paper. The first two were procurable, the last was not. Miss Smith and Miss Jones emerged from the village shop loudly bewailing this fact. Jasper saw and took his opportunity.

'Do let me lend you my *Daily Mail*,' he said, addressing himself to the ducal Miss Jones while comprising in his glance the rather more luscious-looking Miss Smith.

'Oh, thank you, that is very kind,' said Miss Smith. Miss Jones almost snatched at the paper. She then began to race through its pages while Miss Smith looked eagerly over her shoulder. They seemed to be searching for some particular piece of news.

'Second body in trunk is on the middle page,' said Jasper quietly. 'The missing ladies are on page eight.'

Horror appeared on the faces of Miss Smith and Miss Jones. 'What missing ladies?' asked Miss Smith in a shaking voice.

'The ones the police suspect of being in more trunks,' said Jasper, looking at them with a thoughtful expression. They appeared very much relieved by this. 'Will you have a cigarette?'

Miss Smith took one. Miss Jones did not smoke. They continued, in a desultory way, to examine the paper, but apparently failing to find anything of interest in it they gave it back to Jasper.

'As we all appear to be using the same bathroom and so on, and so forth,' he said, 'supposing we introduce ourselves. I am Jasper Aspect and this is Noel Foster, who is down here in order to have a complete rest. He has been far from well lately, thoroughly run down.'

Noel gave Jasper a look which, if looks could kill, would have killed him. Too late, the harm was now done. Of no avail to expostulate or deny, the impression had duly been made and registered of a boring hypochondriac. Once more he cursed himself for letting Jasper join in this adventure. Alone he could have stood up to each situation as it arose, cutting quite a romantic figure. Jasper was always just too quick for him. He ground his teeth and thought of vengeance, after all his was the upper hand financially.

It appeared that Miss Smith was called Poppy. She seemed to like Jasper and expressed sympathy for Noel, whose appearance probably failed to attract her. Miss Jones did not vouchsafe her name, neither did she join in the conversation which followed, but stood tapping long white fingers on her bag, as though anxious to get away.

Miss Smith asked how long Jasper was stopping at the Jolly Roger.

'I expect we shall be here for some weeks. I am engaged upon research work in the neighbourhood, of a delicate and interesting nature, and Noel has his cure. He has had a very sad time lately – the aunt with whom he lived died suddenly.'

Miss Smith regretted. Noel raged inwardly. From now onwards he was stamped as a delicate young man who had always lived with his aunt, a woman whom actually he had seen about four times in his life.

'And you,' continued Jasper, 'how long shall you be here?'

It appeared that Miss Smith felt herself suited by Chalford, but that Miss Jones did not. 'My friend,' said Miss Smith, rather nervously, 'er – Miss Jones here, finds the Jolly Roger so very uncomfortable. The bath isn't built in, as you have probably noticed, and she is not used to sharing a bathroom with other people. The beds, too, are rather hard.'

'I didn't know that Rickmansworth was noted for its sybarites,' said Jasper.

'Rickmansworth?' said Miss Smith vaguely – then pulling herself together, 'Oh, Rickmansworth you mean? Where we come from? Is a liking for the ordinary comforts of life limited within geographic boundaries? I never heard it.'

'The Jolly Roger is fitted with more than the ordinary comforts of life. The place is clean, the food eatable, the beer extraordinarily good, while as for the bath it is often quite nice and warm you know, and now that, as I see, you have bought some soap, we shall all be able to have a good wash in it.'

Miss Jones shuddered. Opening her mouth for the first time she remarked in a sort of high wail that she was going to grease her face and lie down for a bit. She then walked quickly away. Jasper noticed, on the fourth finger of Miss Smith's left hand, a palpable wedding-ring of small diamonds. He was not displeased, and suggested that they should take a stroll together.

It was now that Noel, wandering gloomily by himself, ran into Mrs Lace, the Local Beauty.

4

Every country neighbourhood has its local beauty, and Chalford provided no exception to this rule. Anne-Marie Lace, however, was not quite the usual type of faded fluffy little woman whose large blue eyes attract a yearly-diminishing troop of admirers at the covert side or on the tennis court. She was lacking in any sporting accomplishments; she was intellectually pretentious; she was ambitious, and she was really beautiful. It was her tragedy that she was born, bred and married in the country.

In London, with her looks and energetic will to please, she could undoubtedly have made an entrance into that sort of society which she longed for, the semi-intellectual society which is much photographed and often spoken of in the newspapers. Even in the vicinity of Chalford, wretchedly narrow as was the field it had to offer, she was something of a star, and indeed was known to the gentry for many miles around as 'the beautiful Mrs Lace'. She had the satisfaction of knowing that most of the women disliked her, while their husbands, loutish boors whom she despised, thought her lovely but much too highbrow. This was satisfactory, still more so was the whole-hearted adulation which was laid at her feet by some ten or twelve rather weedy youths, who formed every summer a kind of artistic colony in thatched cottages near Rackenbridge. They supposed her to be rich, ate quantities of free meals beneath her roof, and painted incompetent little pictures of her in the most extravagant poses. They also helped to design her clothes which were always an endless topic of local conversation as she never could resist appearing at everyday functions in elaborate fancy dress. The black velvet, fur hat and ear-rings of a Russian Grand Duchess, the livid greens and yellows of a Bakst ballet dancer, taffeta bustle and Alexandra fringe, Mandarin tunic and trousers, making each its appearance on some most inappropriate occasion aroused each in turn, among tweeded local ladies, a storm of discussion and criticism, the repercussions of which reached Mrs Lace, by no means displeasing her.

Nevertheless Mrs Lace was a thoroughly discontented woman, neither her house, her husband nor her children afforded her any satisfaction. The house, Comberry Manor, had belonged to the parents of Major Lace and was very nondescript. In vain did she beg that she might redecorate it to her own taste, thus giving expression to the aesthetic side of her nature by painting every wall white and having all the furniture pickled.

Major Lace refused to spend a penny in that direction; he liked his house very well as it was, so poor Mrs Lace was obliged to confine her activities to the bathroom, which she papered entirely with pictures out of *Vogue*, curtaining it with oilcloth. This she did with her own hands, under the supervision of an artistic young man from Rackenbridge called Mr Leader.

Her husband was considered by Anne-Marie and her satellites to be a terrible drag upon his exquisite wife. In fact, he was a nice, simple, ordinary man, with few ideas beyond the suitable mating of his prize Jersey cows. He was no longer in love with Anne-Marie, but still took her at her own valuation, was proud of her beauty, and considered that she was the very glass of fashion and the mould of form. This did not, however, ensure him making the requisite allowances for her artistic temperament, often he irritated her profoundly when she was in one of her moods, by saying, 'Don't be ratty, old girl,' and stumping off to his cowsheds. She would long on such occasions to pay him back with secret infidelities, but the Rackenbridge young men, whilst only too ready to profess undying love for her, were idle fellows and never seemed to contemplate adultery.

As a result, little Caroline and little Romola both had tow-coloured hair, moon-shaped faces, and pale-blue eyes like the Major, and were, like him, stolid unimaginative personalities. They were a great disappointment to their mother.

As soon as Mrs Lace heard, by means of Major Lace's old governess who lived in one of his cottages and was a great gossip, that four people, all of them quite young, had come to stay at the Jolly Roger, she nipped round to have a look at the visitors' book. The Jolly Roger was in many ways rather superior to the ordinary village inn, it had a reputation for good English cooking, cleanliness, and an adequate cellar, and was for this reason visited every now and then by quite notable people. Authors, actors, antiquarians, and distinguished members of various professions came there, and their names were treasured by Mr Birk, the landlord, but although Anne-Marie always kept an eye on the book, she found that the guests were usually too old, or their visits too short for them to be of much use to her. Today the signatures seemed more promising. It is true that she had never heard either of Noel Foster or of the Rickmansworth sybarites; on the other hand Jasper Aspect's name was a name with which she was acquainted. She instantly planned to go home and change her clothes which were at present of the Paris-Plage variety. Mr Aspect, a well-known figure in society circles, was probably tired of sophistication and would be more likely to take an interest in simplicity and rural charm. Her Austrian-Tyrolean peasant's dress would meet the case exactly. Delighted with the subtlety of this reasoning she hurried away in the direction of Comberry. On the village green, however, she met Noel, decided to waste no time, and weighed-in with an old conversational gambit.

'Excuse me,' she said, 'have you seen two rather sweet children in a donkey-cart?'

Noel had not. This was to have been expected, considering that, as Mrs Lace very well knew, the said children were at home playing in the garden, where they had been all day.

'Oh! the monkeys,' she continued playfully, 'you can't imagine how frightening it is to have a family. They do most awfully unnerving things. Where in the world can *les petites méchancetés* have got to now?'

And she flapped her eyelids at Noel, who remarked, as indeed he was meant to, that she did not look old enough to have a family.

'Me? I'm terribly old. Actually I was married more or less out of the nursery.' She sighed, and opening her eyes to their full extent she looked at the ground. Poor kid, poor exquisite little creature, trapped into the drudgery of marriage before she knew anything about life and love. Noel's most chivalrous instincts were aroused, he thought her extremely beautiful, far more to his taste than Miss Smith, Miss Jones, or Eugenia. He felt thankful that, for once, Jasper was nowhere about.

'Who are you?' asked Mrs Lace prettily. 'Perhaps you were dropped by magic on to our village green. Anyway, I hope you won't vanish again into a little puff of smoke. *Espérons que non*. Promise you won't do that.'

Noel promised. He then went back with her to Comberry Manor, where he was given cowslip wine, and told a very great deal about Mrs Lace.

She was happily married, she said, to a handsome man called Hubert Lace, who was an old darling, but fearfully jealous, selfish, greedy and mean. These unpleasant words were not named, but served up with a frothing sauce of sugary chatter. As the old darling was also slightly half-witted he could naturally have no sympathy for Anne-Marie's artistic leanings, and she was therefore obliged to wrap herself up in her garden, her children, and the consolations of the intellect. Noel assumed from the fact that her name, as she told him, was Anne-Marie, from the slightly foreign accent and curious idiom in which she spoke, and from her general appearance, that she was not altogether English. He was wrong, however.

For the first twenty years of her life she had lived in a country vicarage and been called Bella Drage. Being an imaginative and enterprising girl she had persuaded her father to send her to Paris for a course of singing lessons. He scraped together enough money for her to have six months there, after which she came back Anne-Marie by name and Anne-Marie by nature. Shortly after this metamorphosis had occurred she met Hubert Lace, who was enslaved at the Hunt Ball by her flowing dress, Edwardian coiffure and sudden, if inaccurate, excursions into the French language. He laid heart and fortune at her feet. Bella Drage was shrewd enough to realize that she was unlikely to do better for herself, not sufficiently shrewd to foresee an unexpected vein of obstinacy in the Major which was to make him perfectly firm in his refusal to live anywhere but at Comberry. She now knew that her ambition of entertaining smart Bohemians in London could never be realized while she was still married to him. It was one of her favourite daydreams to envisage the death of Hubert, gored perhaps by a Jersey bull or chawed up by one of those Middle White pigs, who, their energies having been directed by a fad of the Major's towards fields of cabbages rather than the more customary trough, were apt to behave at times with a fearful madness of demeanour. After the funeral and a decent period of mourning, an interesting young widow would then take London by storm. The idea of divorce never occurred to her as an alternative to the demise of poor Hubert. Early upbringing in the parsonage had not been without its influence upon her and Mrs Lace was at heart a respectable little person.

None of these truths made themselves apparent to Noel. He beheld, as he was meant to behold, a vivid vital creature living in unsuitable surroundings, a humming bird in a rusty cage, a gardenia in a miry bog, a Mariana of the Moated Grange. Eugenia faded into unreality, Miss Smith and Miss Jones might never have been born for all he cared. Jasper could now retire into his proper place as a penniless sycophant, Noel had at last gone one better than him, and found by his own unaided efforts a pearl among women.

They talked and talked over the cowslip wine and Noel began to realize that his pearl was as cultivated as she was beautiful. She was a student of obscure Restoration poetry and early French ballads, so she told him, knew Proust by heart (expressing a pained surprise when he owned that he had only read *Swann's Way*, and that in English), also D. H. Lawrence, Strindberg, Ibsen, which last two she preferred to read in French.

In painting, her taste, it appeared, was catholic. Primitives, Dutch and Italian Renaissance, the English School, French impressionists, Surréalistes, all was grist that came to her mill; in music her exquisite sensibilities were apparent. She only cared for Bach, Brahms, and Beethoven. Wagner was to her a mere ugly noise, Chopin a sentimental tinkle. She told him that she was born out of her proper time, she could only have been contented in the eighteenth century – this boisterous age, these machine-made nineteen-thirties said nothing to her, she found herself bored, bewildered, and unhappy.

Noel was enchanted. Never before, he thought, had he met a beautiful woman who was at the same time a natural aesthete. He drank a great quantity of cowslip wine and went back to the Jolly Roger, feeling rather sick, but apart from that, tremendously elated.

He joined Jasper in the dining-room. Dinner, Mr Birk told him reproachfully, had been ready for some time. Jasper handed him a note which had just arrived from Eugenia, it was addressed to Union Jackshirt Aspect and Union Jackshirt Foster.

Hail! The filthy old female Pacifist my grandmother has shut me up in my room because I was seen talking to you. She misuses me and tramples upon me as for many years France has misused and trampled upon Germany. It does not signify. Germany has now arisen and I shall soon arise and my day shall dawn blood red. Terrible must be the fate of the enemies of Social Unionism, so let the poor old female beware. I will meet you both tomorrow outside the twopenny-bar shop at four o'clock exactly.

Yours in
Social Unionism,
EUGENIA MALMAINS.

This document was adorned with a Swastika, Union Jack, and Skull and Crossbones, all carefully drawn in black ink.

'She's a fine girl,' said Jasper, with his mouth full. 'I hope to marry her yet. Tell you what, Noel old boy, I'm in love.'

Noel was profoundly irritated by this statement, which took all the wind out of his own sails.

'So am I,' he said.

'Good egg,' said Jasper. They both went on eating in silence for a bit.

'My Miss Smith,' said Jasper, 'is a dangerous good armful. She wriggles in an exceedingly delicious way when you kiss her. I'm fearfully in love.'

Noel thought that there was no point in mentioning that he had not so far kissed his beloved. He wondered now why on earth this was, and supposed that the girl, while perfect in other ways, must be lacking in initiative. 'My girl is called Anne-Marie,' he said, 'Anne-Marie Lace, she is wonderful.'

'How did you pick her up?' asked Jasper with interest.

'We met,' said Noel haughtily, 'on the village green; she was looking for her children.'

'And does she wriggle when you kiss her?'

'Not exactly. She is a most fascinating creature, a natural highbrow. We had a long discussion on art and literature.'

'Sounds a cracking old bore,' said Jasper, 'if there's one thing I can't abide it is culture in women. Miss Smith reads the *Strand Magazine* and hates foreigners. That's all I found out about her intellect, but there's nothing I can't tell you about her physiological reactions. Darling Miss Smith, I love her like hell, Oh, gee – do I love Miss Smith.'

Noel felt jealous. It began to look as though Jasper loved Miss Smith more than he, Noel, loved Mrs Lace. This was extremely boring for Noel, and he wished more than ever that Jasper was back in London.

'You wait until you see Anne-Marie,' he said crossly. 'I should think she'll make that Miss Smith of yours look like a – like a – well, like a twopenny bar.'

'That's right,' said Jasper, 'Miss Smith looks to me like a twopenny bar looks to Eugenia, and I'm sure you can't say fairer than that.'

'What strikes one most particularly about Anne-Marie is her wonderfully original appearance. Her beauty is something different from what we are used to. I suppose it is that she belongs to her environment so exquisitely, she borrows nothing from your smart London women.'

'Yes, I see, a great hulking dairy-maid with apple cheeks. Not my type at all, I'm bound to say.'

'Oh! far from that,' said Noel, with a superior smile, 'if anything you would call her exotic. Very pale and delicate looking, with a rare quality that hardly seems to belong to our generation. A *Dame aux Camélias*, if you like.'

'Tubercular is she?' said Jasper. 'You be careful, old boy.'

5

Next day the mystery of Miss Jones's strawberry leaves was solved. Jasper brought the morning papers into Noel's bedroom just before luncheon-time and showed him with glee the large photographs of Miss Jones which appeared in of all them under such headings as 'It should have been her Wedding day', 'Orangeade instead of Orange Blossom' or 'Earl's fatherless daughter's misfortune'. The captions underneath announced, with hysteria, or with dignity, according to the calibre of the newspaper, that Lady Marjorie Merrith, whose marriage to the Duke of Dartford was to have taken place that very day, had been obliged to postpone it indefinitely, as she had been stricken with an attack of scarlet-fever and would therefore be in quarantine for the next six weeks; she was doing as well as could be expected. Lady Marjorie, they went on to say, was the daughter of the Countess of Fitzpuglington and of the late Earl, whose tragic death in the *Titanic* disaster left his wife a widow ere she was a mother, and his only child an orphan at birth.

'She looks all right, considering,' said Noel. He felt even more stupid than usual, having sat up with Jasper until five o'clock that morning talking about love.

'Considering what?'

'Considering she has scarlet-fever.'

'Scarlet-fever my bottom. Try and pull yourself together old boy. How can I help you if you won't help yourself at all? Could you listen to me intelligently for a few minutes, all this is really most interesting from our point of view. You see what has obviously happened – either she can't take the Duke or the Duke can't take her (doesn't matter which) so they decided, or she decided off her own bat, that the only way to break it off at the eleventh hour would be for her to have some illness with a long quarantine. Good. The interesting part from our point of view is this – next, possibly, to Eugenia Malmains, Lady Marjorie Merrith (Miss Jones) is the greatest heiress in England. I believe it's something fabulous how rich she is. Now here are we, two old bums, with two enormous fortunes dangling in front of our noses. Ours for the asking and God knows we need 'em.'

'What makes you suppose they are ours for the asking?'

'In the case of Eugenia I should have thought it was obvious. She would marry anybody to get away from T.P.O.F. In the case of Lady M. we have a powerful ally in the Rebound. Fantastic what a girl will do on the Rebound. But what I want you to understand now is that we must sketch out a plan of action – it's no good both going for both, that would only end in neither getting either. So we must choose which we want. Now I thought of giving you first choice on condition that you go on financing this racket.'

'I absolutely refuse to lend you another penny, if that's what you're driving at.'

Jasper sighed. 'If you don't,' he said, reluctantly, 'I shall be forced to stay on here insolvent, which would be awkward for you under the circumstances, and make a pass at Mrs Lace.'

Noel saw the force of this argument. Jasper had, before now, broken up many a happy love affair. 'As a matter of fact old boy,' he said, in a conciliatory tone of voice, 'I was only joking. I like to have you here, it would be awfully dull all alone.'

'Thanks,' said Jasper, 'just choose your girl then will you? I'm rather anxious to get on with the work in hand.'

'My head aches,' said Noel. 'Let me go to sleep again please.'

'You can, as soon as you've chosen. Now, think well, I can't have you changing your mind about this later. Eugenia is richer, more beautiful and madder, Miss Jones is better dressed, more presentable and I should say on the whole lousier. Which will you have?'

'You don't seem to remember that I'm in love already,' said Noel with simple dignity.

'Oh, cut it out. I'm fearfully in love myself. Do you suppose I am going to let that stand in my way? Not likely. There are times, my dear old boy, when love has got to take its proper place as an unethical and anti-social emotion, and this is one of them. Come on, now choose?'

'I will have Eugenia,' Noel muttered into his bed-clothes, 'anything for a quiet life.'

'A quiet life is the last thing you are likely to enjoy with that girl, still have it your own way of course. I shall now go and tee myself up *"très snob pour le sport"* and pursue the elusive Lady Marjorie. I wonder if she's about yet – never knew a girl to be so bedridden, goes to bed early, gets up late, and lies down most of the day with her face greased.'

Noel called out after him that he did not want any luncheon, and once more composed himself for sleep.

*

Ten minutes later Jasper, contrary to all his plans, was kissing Miss Smith at the bottom of the garden.

'Darling Miss Smith,' he said, 'do you know that I'm madly in love with you?'

'Darling Mr Aspect, are you really? I call that sweet of you.'

'Darling Miss Smith, could one be told who you are?'

'Why do you want to know?'

'Because it happens to interest me.'

'Well, I'm a lot of different things. At the present time I seem to be just a confidante.'

'To Lady Marjorie?'

'Oh! you know that now, do you? Yes, I'm her confidante. When Marge goes mad in white satin with flowers in her hair, I go mad in white linen with straws in my hair (literary allusion), that's what we're up to at the present moment.'

'Yes, I suppose so. Who is your husband?'

'He's called Anthony St Julien, I'm called Poppy St Julien. Call me Poppy if you want to.'

'Thanks, you're Miss Smith to me though. Where is Anthony St Julien now?'

'Having a cocktail somewhere before lunch I should guess.'

'Does he know that Poppy St Julien has been kissing Jasper Aspect under a willow tree, so early in the morning?'

'He does not. Nor, if he did, would he care,' said Mrs St Julien.

'Good heavens, is the man an eel? Now tell me all about the heroine.'

'She's just a heroine you know.'

'In what way so heroic?'

'I mean, she's not ordinary like you and me. One must either regard her as a monstrosity of selfishness or else as a heroine. To me she's a heroine. Her gloves are always so much cleaner than anybody else's, an attribute which I admire.'

'Yes, I see. So why didn't she marry the Duke?'

'You never can tell with Marge why she does this, that or the other. Her mind doesn't work in any comprehensible channels. She just decided to chuck the whole thing the day before yesterday, and then we came down here.'

'Some people don't know when they're lucky,' said Jasper.

'That's what I told her. Marge, I said, in three days' time from now, if you take my advice, you'll be a duch. It's not necessary to look upon that as an end in itself, but think what a useful stepping-stone to all the things one would really like to be – a double duch, for instance, awfully *chic*, you can't be a double duch without being an ordinary one first can you? Then think how enjoyable to be a dowager duch, or even a divorced duch.'

'Or even a dear old duch,' said Jasper.

'But it was all no good, she hardly even listened to me. It appears that romance is what she's after now, or some such nonsense – the girl's been reading trash I suppose. So she left the classical notes on her pincushion, one for Osborne Dartford and one for her mamma, and she fondly imagines that they won't find out where we are hiding, so you won't tell anyone who would matter will you?'

'I won't.'

'And don't let anyone see that we are – well – you know –'

'Walking out you mean?'

'Mm.'

'Why not?'

'Because Anthony St Julien might get to hear of it.'

'I thought you said he wouldn't mind?'

'He wouldn't mind at all, quite the contrary, he'd be pleased. He wants to divorce me on account of he dotes on a débutante.'

'Boy must be batty,' said Jasper. 'If I had a lovely wife like you I'd never go near débutantes.'

'I say, you are sweet.'

'I'm not sweet at all, only sane. So you don't like the idea of being divorced by Anthony St Julien?'

'Of course I don't, why should I? It's most unusual for ladies to be divorced you know, and besides I shouldn't have any money to live on.'

'Why doesn't Anthony Dirty Sweep St Julien let you divorce him?'

'Because it appears that débutantes don't like marrying divorced gentlemen. You see, she won't be a co-respondent herself, and she won't let him take a lady to Brighton either.'

'Sounds like a whist drive,' said Jasper. 'Winning lady moves up, and the losing gentleman moves down. I think your husband is a cad, Miss Smith, if there's one sort of chap I do hate it's a cad.'

'Thank you,' said Poppy St Julien, 'you are really sweet.'

'Sweet's my middle name. Good morning Miss Jones, how did you sleep?'

'Wretchedly, thank you,' said Lady Marjorie, 'You should feel my bed.'

'Oh! I say, I'd like to later on. You know, you must be a real princess, old girl.'

'Are we on old girl terms?'

'Perhaps you're right,' said Jasper. 'By the way, there's a whole heap about you in the papers this morning, orangeade instead of orange blossom. Have you seen it?'

'Yes thanks, I have.'

'I don't think I quite approve of all this careless casting away of dukes you know, dear.'

'Thank you so much. It's immaterial to me what you think about my private affairs. And pray don't call me "dear".'

There was a short silence. Jasper would have liked to get down in good earnest to his conquest of Miss Jones, but felt himself most unaccountably hampered by the presence of Miss Smith. He was very much disgusted by this weakness, and feared that it might indicate the presence of a real emotion.

'Where's your friend?' asked Mrs St Julien.

'Noel? He's doing badly. He's gone and fallen in love with a local beauty, poor old boy.'

'Talking about local beauties,' said Mrs St Julien, 'I've got a mysterious cousin who must live somewhere in this neighbourhood. She's called Eugenia Malmains and nobody has ever clapped eyes on her as far as I know – I thought I'd try and see her while I'm down here.'

'Nothing easier,' said Jasper. 'If you will be outside the twopenny-bar shop this afternoon at four o'clock exactly, I will introduce to you your cousin Eugenia Malmains.'

*

The day was very hot and breathless. Jasper, Noel, and the two ladies sat beneath a large lime tree on the village green and found little to say to each other. Jasper, who had a great many subjects in common with Mrs St Julien, when alone with her, and who could, he felt sure, have made a most pleasing impression on Lady Marjorie under the same circumstance, found it strangely difficult to deal with the two of them together. The presence of Noel, too, rather cramped his style. Lady Marjorie and Mrs St Julien made desultory conversation, while Jasper bided his time, and Noel silently considered where, when, and how, he should make a declaration to Mrs Lace.

At four o'clock, exactly, Eugenia arrived, swinging down the village street with the gait of a triumphant goddess, and closely followed by Vivian Jackson and the Reichshund. 'Hail!' she cried, throwing up her arm in the Social Unionist salute.

'Snow,' replied Noel, laughing immoderately at this very poor joke.

Eugenia regarded him with lowering brow. 'Union Jackshirt Foster,' she said sternly, 'beware, I have had to speak to you once before. If you continue to be facetious at the expense of our Movement I shall be obliged to degrade you before the comrades. In fact I will cut off all your buttons with my own dagger.'

'Quite right,' said Jasper 'Ignominy or a Roman death for Union Jackshirt Foster. Miss Eugenia, I want to introduce you to your cousin Mrs St Julien, and to Lady Marjorie Merrith. They are staying at the Jolly Roger like us.'

'Hail!' said Eugenia. She saluted each in turn and then shook hands. 'I am very pleased to see you here. We are badly in need of members for a women's branch in this village, perhaps you would help me to organize one?'

'Of course we will,' said Poppy. She was attracted by her cousin.

'Union Jackshirt Aspect,' Eugenia went on, 'I have brought you a message from T.P.O.F. She says that your poor grandfather was one of her greatest friends and she wishes to meet you. Would it be convenient for you to take tea at Chalford House today?'

'Perfectly convenient,' said Jasper. 'I accept with pleasure.'

'Perhaps my cousin would care to come?'

'Thank you, I should like to,' said Poppy St Julien.

Eugenia then rather half-heartedly invited the others. She evidently hoped that they would refuse, which they did. Noel had arranged to visit Mrs Lace at tea-time; Lady Marjorie said that she must grease her face and lie down for a bit.

So the three of them set forth, with Vivian Jackson and the Reichshund trotting at their heels.

'Is it far?' asked Mrs St Julien.

'Oh! no,' Eugenia replied. Her cousin was not much reassured. Eugenia walked with effortless strides, giving the impression that twenty miles to her would be the merest stroll. Quite soon, however, they came upon the lodge gates of Chalford Park, which were large and beautiful, and surmounted by a marble arch of baroque design. The two lodges, one on each side, were small round temples. Inside the park there was an atmosphere of unreality. They advanced up an avenue of elm trees which hung in the sleepy air like large green balloons. The surface of the drive, although in perfect repair, was faintly tinged with mossy green; it was evident that wheeled traffic seldom passed that way.

'Are we approaching the palace of the Sleeping Beauty?' Jasper murmured.

'You will see the house from the top of this rise,' said Eugenia. She looked a little anxious, as though hoping so much that they would like it. She need not have worried. The house, when it appeared to view, presented the most beautiful vision that could be imagined. Built, in the Palladian style, of pale pink marble, it consisted of a central dome flanked by two smaller ones, to which it was connected by gleaming colonnades. The whole thing was raised above the level of the drive, and approached in the front by a huge twisted marble staircase. Beyond the house there lay a gleaming lake, beyond that again a formal garden of clipped yews, grass and statuary, and in the background of this picture was the pale but piercing blue of a far-distant landscape.

'Good heavens,' said Jasper, when the power of speech returned to him.

'Do you think it beautiful?' said Eugenia. 'I do. I think it is the most beautiful house in the world, but then, of course, I have seen few others.'

'I have never, in any country, seen one to beat it,' said Poppy.

They began to walk slowly towards it.

'Under the Social Unionist régime,' said Jasper, 'your Captain should make a law that all really beautiful houses must be preserved and occupied. It is much the most horrible feature of this age that so many are being destroyed, allowed to stand derelict, or, worst of all, handed over to the proletariat and turned into postcard counters and ice-cream booths. That is too ignoble. Beautiful houses ought to be a setting for beautiful women, their lovers, and perhaps a few frail, but exquisite little children.'

Eugenia looked at him reprovingly. 'Under our régime,' she said, 'women will not have lovers. They will have husbands and great quantities of healthy Aryan children. I think you forget the teachings of our Captain, Union Jackshirt Aspect.'

Poppy St Julien said, 'I don't know a thing about politics, but I'm sure Hitler must be a wonderful man. Hasn't he forbidden German women to work in offices and told them they never need worry about anything again, except arranging the flowers? How they must love him.'

'They do,' said Eugenia. '*Heil Hitler!* Cousin Poppy St Julien, you must be enrolled as a Union Jackshirt at once. It costs ninepence a month, the Union Jack shirt is five shillings, and sixpence for the little emblem. Here we are.'

Vivian Jackson and the Reichshund followed them up the twisted marble staircase, but when they had reached the top a word from Eugenia made them turn round and trot down it again. 'Stay there,' she said, over her shoulder, and ushered Poppy and Jasper into a huge domed room, so blue that it might have been a pool in some Mediterranean lagoon, and they fishes swimming in it.

Across its azure immensity sat Lady Chalford waiting to dispense tea out of a golden tea-pot of exquisite design. She looked rather like Whistler's portrait of his mother.

6

If Lady Chalford was like a relic from a forgotten age, a museum-piece of great antiquity, it was not because her years were heavy so much as that her speech, her dress, and her outlook, had remained unaltered since before the War. Nineteen fourteen had marked the evening of her days when she should have been yet in her prime.

The world calamity, however, had little or nothing to do with this decline, having been far eclipsed in her eyes by the disastrous marriage made by her only son; while to her, his death in 1920 from wounds received the day before the Armistice, was a lesser disaster than the fact of his divorce. It made no difference in the eyes of his parents that Lord Malmains had divorced his wife; her shame was his, and theirs, and furthermore the heiress to their lands and titles had the tainted blood of an adulteress in her veins. No such thing had ever happened before in the Malmains family, throughout history no shadow of disgrace had ever fallen upon the proud ambitious heads whose likenesses now stared down from pink brocade walls in Lord Chalford's portrait gallery.

Since the disaster Lady Chalford had never set foot outside her park gates. Lord Chalford, protected by an armour of total deafness, had, until recently laid low by a stroke, performed his duties as a legislator most punctiliously, but when in London he had always stayed at his club, the almost unearthly beauties of Malmains Palace, in Cheyne Walk, having now been hidden from all human eyes, except those of the caretaker, for sixteen long years.

Eugenia had been handed over to her grandparents at the age of three, after her father's death. They could never forgive her for what her mother had been, and regarded the poor child with suspicion, which became tempered, however, as she grew older with a sort of sorrowful affection. Luckily, her appearance made things easier for them, Malmains women were all large blonde goddesses, and her looks bore no relation to those of their sinful daughter-in-law. Now that she had reached the age of seventeen she presented a problem with which poor Lady Chalford wrestled miserably. What was to be done with her? Of no use to give her a London season, how should any respectable mother invite, any decent young man propose, to the Child of Scandal. (Lady Chalford, it will be observed, was a trifle pessimistic in her estimate of modern London Society's attitude towards heiresses.) And yet Eugenia must marry, Chalford House and the barony of Malmains which she would in due course inherit from her grandfather must have an heir.

Haunted night and day by these problems, Lady Chalford had been constrained to question Eugenia with regard to the two young strangers whom she had so indiscreetly spoken to on the village green. Had they been suitable friends for the child they would surely have waited to be presented before addressing a young lady, yet, might it be that they had been brought by the hand of a far-seeing Providence to Chalford? She was disposed to consider that such had been the case when she learnt that one of them was Mr Jasper Aspect, grandson, she reassured herself with Debrett, yes, sure enough, grandson of her old friend, Driburgh, and child of that enchantingly pretty little Lady Venetia. Her delight knew no bounds, at last somebody of her own kind, somebody whom she could consult on equal terms, was at hand. Her thoughts sprang happily forward, even should he wish to marry Eugenia the match would be a perfectly suitable one, the Aspects although far from rich, were an old family of unimpeachable antecedents.

Lady Chalford's pleasure at seeing Jasper was greatly, however, surpassed by that which she felt when she realized Poppy's identity. Here was a member of her own family, a married woman and a woman of the world at that; Poppy would certainly be able to advise her what were the best measures to take for her granddaughter's future happiness. She would be able now to talk without the reservations which would have been imposed upon her if she were discussing the case with a gentleman. For the first few moments indeed she did not at all realize the good fortune which had befallen her. She was immensely annoyed with Eugenia for bringing two visitors when only one had been expected. There were a cup and plate too few, another chair must be drawn up. Eugenia's reluctance to invite Marjorie and Noel now became comprehensible, Lady Chalford would fuss herself almost ill over such an incident. When at last they were settled, however, she declared herself overjoyed to see Poppy.

'Agatha's granddaughter,' she cried, embracing her. 'When I was ten years old Agatha and I were inseparable. I remember so well that we both had plum-coloured merino dresses with beautiful brass buttons, the size of pennies, down the front of the bodices. When my poor great-uncle died Mamma cut the brass buttons off mine, I was very much displeased by this, having hoped for a proper mourning such as grown-up people had, and besides, I was fond of those buttons – the dress was never much without them. At nineteen Aggie was a most beautiful girl. We went to the same drawing-room and everyone was talking of her beauty. I never shall forget her as a bride. Everybody loved her. Poor Driburgh was so madly in love with her that we feared he should kill himself when she married your dear grandfather. And at twenty-two she was dead. I remember that I heard the news a week after I became engaged myself, and it seemed to take away all my happiness. I think now that she was perhaps fortunate to die so young and still so happy. I am very glad that you have come to see me, my dear child.'

Poppy was moved by this tribute to her grandmother, who, up to now had seemed a most shadowy figure.

'Also I am very much pleased to meet you, Mr Aspect. How is poor dear Driburgh?'

'I believe he is perfectly happy,' said Jasper. 'My mother goes to see him fairly often.'

'Of course Peersmont is a wonderful place,' said Lady Chalford, referring to that lunatic asylum, which, as its name denotes, is kept exclusively for the use of insane peers. 'I often think to myself where should we be without it? To know that our loved ones, in their great trouble, are so perfectly cared for, that indeed is much. You know, I suppose, that it is not at all far from here, in fact I think you ought to visit your dear grandfather. I will be happy to send you over in one of my motor cars if you should wish to do so.'

Jasper thanked her and said he would be glad to avail himself of her kindness. He then began to ask many questions about Chalford House, but was obliged to be content with the vaguest of information, Lady Chalford evidently noticed its beauties no more than the air she breathed.

After tea, however, she said that as Jasper appeared to be so much interested in it, Eugenia might show him the other rooms and the pictures, so long as they were suitably chaperoned by Nanny.

'I wish to have a little talk with dear Poppy,' she said, and presently she conducted Mrs St Julien upstairs to a small boudoir decorated in the Edwardian manner. It was pink and white, like a sugar cake, with white lace over pink satin in panels on the walls. There were two exquisitely comfortable *chaise-longues* upholstered in white brocade edged with pink silk rosebuds, several small pink satin armchairs, each with a blue muslin beribboned cushion, and a quantity of occasional tables covered with albums, photographs of ladies with tremendous eyebrows in straw boaters, and bric-à-brac of every description. Poppy thought she had never seen anything so pretty and so feminine in her life.

During the little talk that followed, Lady Chalford poured out all her misgivings over the future of Eugenia into Poppy's sympathetic ear. 'You see how it is,' she said, 'dear Poppy. Now what should you advise me to do with the poor child?'

'Personally I should be inclined to take her out in London,' said Poppy. 'Everything is so changed there, since the War, and people are by no means as strict as they were.'

'My dear, that may well be the case in certain circles,' said Lady Chalford stiffly. 'Among my own friends, however, and those people with whom I should wish my granddaughter to visit, I am convinced that she would never be received. And even if, out of charity or friendship for me, people did invite her to their houses, it would still be most painful to me. What pleasure could I derive, for instance, from taking the child of a divorced woman to Court? The scandal nearly killed both my husband and myself at the time; with Eugenia making a début in London we must continually be reminded of it. To begin with, neither of us has set foot inside Malmains Palace since the last day of that terrible trial. And then consider what anxiety I should feel in chaperoning her. Eugenia is the child of a bad, wicked woman, never forget that. No, I assure you that it would be impossible for me to take her out in London. My only wish is that she may marry as soon as may be. But whom? This Mr Aspect, now, what should you say are his intentions?'

'Oh, I'm sure he thinks of her as a child,' said Poppy. 'She is so young, isn't she, and young for her age at that. I shouldn't marry her off just yet, Lady Chalford. I think that would be a mistake if I may say so. Why don't you entertain for her down here? Give a garden party, for instance, and perhaps a ball later on, in the autumn. There must be some nice young people in the neighbourhood?'

Lady Chalford considered for a little while and then said: 'This seems to me, dear Poppy, a most excellent plan. I will mention it to my husband this evening, and if he agrees we will give a garden party for the child next month. Now you must promise that you will stay down here and help me, little Poppy. I have not entertained for many years, and we shall want it to be gay. Darling Aggie had the greatest talent for organizing picnics and such things; I vividly remember one enchanting expedition she arranged to a wishing-well, when I wished that I might marry that handsome Mr Howard (I was very young then). But I told my wish to Effie Cholmondely, so of course it never could come true. And then there were always the theatricals at Christmas time. How would it be if we combined something of that sort with our garden party? A pageant, for example – I am told they are tremendously popular nowadays? Then all you young people could take part in it.'

'I think that's a splendid idea,' said Poppy.

'Very well then, we'll see what can be arranged. By the way, where is your husband, my dear?'

Poppy considered it on the whole discreet to say that her husband was delayed in London on business, but that she was expecting him to join her at the Jolly Roger in a few days' time.

'My friend, Marjorie Merrith, is there and her maid,' she went on, feeling secure in the assumption that Lady Chalford was no reader of the illustrated daily Press.

'Ah! yes,' said Lady Chalford, 'bring her to see me some time. Poor dear Puggie (her father) was a great friend of my darling Malmains. But, dearest child, is it not rather adventurous for you two young women to be staying quite alone in a country inn? Of course I know the Jolly Roger is a very respectable sort of place, but even so, I feel that it is hardly suitable. Would you not both prefer to move in here until your husband arrives?'

Poppy however, deciding in her own mind that freedom was preferable to comfort, made excuses which Lady Chalford accepted graciously enough. Soon after this Jasper and Eugenia appeared, having finished their tour of the house.

'I think we should be going now,' Poppy said.

When they had left Lady Chalford made her way to her husband's bedroom, and shouting down his ear-trumpet informed him that Poppy was a dear child with wonderfully red lips who reminded her vividly of darling Aggie. 'I only fear,' she added, 'that she may be rather unconventional in some of her habits. She evidently walked home quite alone with young Mr Aspect. I wonder whether I ought to encourage Eugenia in this friendship.' Lord Chalford made no comment. He lay, as always, on his back, staring at the beautiful plaster ceiling high above his bed. Lady Chalford invariably consulted him before taking any decision.

'Perhaps really,' she went on, 'I ought not to invite her here again, perhaps I should give up all idea of this garden party and pageant.'

She sighed, knowing quite well that to do so would be beyond her power. Now that it had once made its appearance that young gay face must often be seen at Chalford House. It had brought a happiness into her life which she had not known for sixteen years, the happiness of talking freely, cosily, and at length to another woman.

Eugenia walked back to the Jolly Roger with her friends. Her animals came too.

Poppy said: 'I think your grandmother is a perfect angel.'

'She is,' said Eugenia, 'I'm fond of the poor old female myself, but I can never forget that she has treated me really very badly. She wouldn't let me go to school, you see, and the result is that I hardly know any Greek at all. I did manage to learn Latin, with the clergyman at Rackenbridge but only after making the most fearful fuss. She never wanted me to.'

'I doubt whether you would have learnt much Greek at school, judging by the perfect illiteracy of the schoolgirls I have met,' said Jasper.

'Then I wanted to go and study National Socialism in Germany, but she stopped me doing that too. She is a great trial to me, the poor old female.'

Poppy told them about the projected garden party, and Lady Chalford's idea of having a pageant at the same time, upon which Eugenia flew into a state of excitement.

'Don't you see,' she cried, 'that this is a most wonderful opportunity for having a grand Social Unionist rally. All the comrades (the Union Jackshirt Comrades, I mean) for miles round, can act in the pageant and help us in every way; they'd love it. Then we will make the people pay to come in and like that will earn a lot of money for the funds.'

'That wasn't quite your grandmother's idea, you know,' said Poppy doubtfully.

'No, of course not, but there's no reason why T.P.O.F. should ever find out, she's very easy to deceive in such ways. I say, the Comrades will be pleased. Union Jackshirt Aspect, I shall count on your support in this matter.'

'You shall have it,' said Jasper.

In the garden of the Jolly Roger they found Noel, who, accompanied by Mrs Lace, was gloomily awaiting their arrival. Noel would have preferred to keep his find to himself for a little longer, but Mrs Lace, having wheedled out of him the true identities of Miss Smith and Miss Jones, absolutely insisted upon meeting them. Lady Marjorie, however, was still reposing on her bed.

The introductions having been effected Mrs Lace became extremely gushing towards Poppy, and waved her hips at Jasper in a most inviting fashion, much to poor Noel's apprehension. Eugenia she evidently regarded as a mere child, beneath her notice. Jasper took an immediate dislike to her, and rudely went on discussing the pageant with Poppy as though they were alone together.

'A pageant?' cried Mrs Lace, when after listening eagerly to them for a few minutes she had gathered what they were talking about. 'In Chalford Park? But this is unheard of. Nobody in the neighbourhood has seen Chalford House since the div – for years and years,' she emended, looking at Eugenia.

'I have never seen it although I live so near. How too exciting. You must be sure and give me a good part in the pageant,' she added archly, 'because I studied acting in Paris, you know, under the great Bernhardt.'

'The great Bottom,' said Jasper, in a loud aside to Poppy.

The others felt that he had gone too far, and Poppy, who was a kind little person, quickly said that of course Mrs Lace must have the chief part.

'You must let me help you with the clothes too,' Mrs Lace went on, looking at Jasper from beneath her eyelashes, 'my nanny and I between us could easily run them up on the sewing-machine, and at Rackenbridge there is a dressmaker who is quite competent. We might get her to help us cheap if it's for charity. I am sure Mr Aspect would design some beautiful dresses for us.'

'What on earth do you suppose I am?' asked Jasper, highly indignant. 'A pansy dress designer, eh?' Jasper felt that in thus discouraging Mrs Lace he was, as far as Noel was concerned, singing for his supper; he did not perhaps yet quite realize that she was the kind of woman who thrives on kicks and blows.

'If you want actors for crowd scenes and so on I can round up the Women's Institute and put you in touch with every sort of person,' she went on, perfectly unmoved.

It was by now apparent that Mrs Lace was one of those people whose energies, whilst often boring, are occasionally indispensable. Poppy and Jasper recognized though they deplored this fact. Noel sat in a kind of admiring trance.

'Now,' said Mrs Lace briskly, 'we must all lay our heads together and decide what period this pageant is to be.'

'A Pageant of Social Unionism,' said Eugenia at once, 'the March on Rome, the Death of Horst Wessel, the Burning of the Reichstag, the Presidential Election of Roosevelt.'

'Very nice, but don't you think perhaps a trifle esoteric?' said Jasper.

Mrs Lace looked scornfully at Eugenia. 'Pageants,' she said, 'must be historical. Now I suggest Charles I and Henrietta Maria's visit to Chalford – it actually happened, you know. They came to Chalford Old Manor, a perfect little Tudor ruin on the edge of the park.'

Jasper observed that a perfect ruin was a contradiction in terms.

Eugenia vetoed the suggestion of Charles I. 'You can't have Charles and Henrietta Maria at a Social Unionist rally,' she said. 'Cromwell and Mrs Cromwell, if you like – the first Englishman to have the right political outlook.'

'Nobody ever heard of Mrs Cromwell appearing in a pageant,' said Noel. 'It would be simply absurd. Do for goodness' sake stick to the ordinary pageant characters – Edward I, Florence Nightingale, Good Queen Bess, Hengist and Horsa, the Orange Girl of Old Drury, William Rufus, Sir Philip Sidney, or Rowena, otherwise you'll find yourselves getting into a fearful muddle.'

'Oh! I don't agree with you at all,' said Mrs Lace, thinking thus to curry favour with Jasper. 'Do let's be original, whatever happens.'

Poppy, seeing that the discussion was about to become acrimonious, put an end to it by reminding the others that the idea of a pageant had originated with Lady Chalford, and that therefore it would be a matter of ordinary politeness to let her choose its period. Eugenia said that she must now return home as T.P.O.F. would scold her for going to Chalford with the others if it were found out. '*Heil Hitler!*' she cried, and swinging herself on to the back of Vivian Jackson she galloped away.

'Poor little thing, what a bore she is with her stupid Movement,' said Mrs Lace spitefully.

'Oh, dear, how I do disagree with you,' said Jasper. 'Personally I can't imagine a more fascinating girl. If all débutantes were like that I should never be away from Pont Street during the summer months.'

'Such awful clothes,' said Mrs Lace angrily.

'Are they? I really hadn't noticed. In the face of such staggering beauty I suppose little details of that sort are likely to escape one.'

'And all that Social Unionist nonsense.'

'Nonsense, is it?' cried Jasper. 'Perhaps you are not aware, Madam, that Social Unionism is now sweeping the world as Liberalism swept the world of the eighteenth century. You call it nonsense – in spite of the fact that millions of people are joyfully resigning themselves to its sway. Pray now let us have an attack on the principles of Social Unionism delivered from a standpoint of sense.'

Mrs Lace did not take refuge in silence as a lesser woman might have done. She tossed her head and pronounced that when you find schoolgirls like Eugenia going mad about something you can be pretty sure that it is nonsense.

'I'm afraid I don't follow your argument. On the contrary, I believe that Eugenia belongs to a new generation which is going to make a new and better and a cleaner world for old back numbers like you and me to end our days in.'

Mrs Lace winced at this, but returned gallantly to the charge. 'I am sure we must be very well off as we are. Why do you want to have a lot of changes in the Government of this country?'

'My dear good Mrs Lace, you must have been keeping company with the local

Conservative M.P. Captain Chadlington, I believe, has the honour of representing this part of the world (and a more congenital half-wit never breathed).'

Mrs Lace was not altogether displeased by this allegation. Captain Chadlington and his wife, Lady Brenda, constituted, in fact, a peak of social ambition which she had recently conquered.

'Well?' she said, 'and then?'

'I suppose that poor baboon has been telling you that we are very well off as we are? Very well off, indeed! I don't ask you to look at the unemployment figures which are a commonplace. I do point to the lack of genius to be found in the land, whether political, artistic, or literary. I point with scorn to our millionaires, who, not daring to enjoy their wealth, cower in olde worlde cottages, and hope that no one will suspect them of being rich; to the city man grubbing his ill-gotten money in the hopes of achieving this dreary aim, and unable to take an interest in anything but market prices or golf; to the aristocrats who, as Eugenia truly says, prefer the comfort of a luxury flat to the hardship of living on their own land; to the petty adulteries, devoid of passion, which are indulged in by all classes, and to the cowardly pacifism which appears to be the spirit of the age. Nothing grand, nothing individual, nothing which could make anybody suppose that the English were once a fine race, brave, jolly and eccentric. So I say that we need a new spirit in the land, a new civilization, and it is to the Eugenias of this world that I look for salvation. Perhaps that new spirit is called Social Unionism, in any case let us leave no stone unturned. Our need is desperate, we must hail any movement which may relight the spark of vitality in this nation before it is too late, anything which may save us from the paralysing squalor, both mental and moral, from which we are suffering so terribly at present. Germany and Italy have been saved by National Socialism; England might be saved by Social Unionism, who can tell? Therefore I say, "*Heil Hitler!*" "*Viva il Duce!*", and "Miss" – Miss, I'll have another beer, please.'

7

Lady Marjorie Merrith leant back in the bath that was, so disturbingly, not built in, and covered her smooth white arms with lacy sleeves of soap.

'You must admit that it's tiresome of them,' she said to Poppy who, faithful to her role of confidante, was perched on a chair beside the bath. 'After all, I particularly said in both my notes that any communications would be forwarded by my bank, and besides, they could easily have found out where we are by now, if they had really wanted to. I do think they might show some sign of life – makes it so awkward for me. What is my next move?'

'Really, darling, you must decide these things for yourself. It all depends on whether or not you want to marry Osborne – which is it?'

Marjorie said with petulance that she didn't know. 'I ran away,' she continued angrily, 'to find romance, and I have only found this disgusting bath.'

'Well, I don't know what you expect. There are two quite presentable young men staying in this very hotel, much more than you could have hoped for.'

'I don't like them.'

'I never shall understand how you could have left that gorgeous wedding dress.'

'Well, you know, I have an idea that the fashions will be far prettier next winter. What d'you suppose poor Mummy is doing with the presents?'

'Keeping them, of course. After all the engagement isn't broken off in *The Times*, remember; you've got scarlet-fever. I must say I take off my hat to your mother for thinking of that, it lasts six weeks you know, and at the end of that time, if you want to, you will be able to break off your engagement without the smallest scandal. People are far too busy laying each other out in Venice at this time of year to think about your affairs. The duke is evidently playing for time; you won't have to make up your mind until the hospital trains begin arriving at Victoria after the hols.'

'Yes, but now what,' said Lady Marjorie, running in some more hot water. She yelled to make herself heard above the noise, 'I can't stay in this lousy hole all the summer.'

'I can't see why not.'

'It's not quite my dish, darling, now is it?'

'When you come to think of it this pub isn't at all uncomfortable, and you couldn't fail to find the local life wildly entertaining if only you would throw yourself into it more.'

'I can't do that you see. I don't like any of the people, except, of course, Eugenia.'

'Hate them then. Do you a lot of good. You've never hated anyone in your life, or loved anyone either. You don't know the meaning of real emotion, and that's why you can't make up your mind about the duke.'

'I love you,' said Lady Marjorie.

'Well, I think perhaps you do,' said Poppy, 'there's nothing radically wrong with your nature, darling, but your upbringing and environment, so far, have been lousy. I never met anybody more unfitted to cope with the ordinary contingencies of life – especially the emotional side of it.'

'Would you marry Osborne?'

'I've told you a thousand times. These vague romantic impulses won't do anybody any good, and least of all yourself, it's not as though you had any real reason for breaking it off. If I were you I should go straight home and say you're sorry.'

'I don't exactly mean would you marry him if you were me. I mean would you marry him if you were you?'

'Well, I suppose I would. He's a duke, and I should have a diamond tiara, very nice.'

'But if he wasn't a duke?'

'My darling Marge, the whole thing about Osborne is that he *is* a duke. People can't be divorced from their status in life like that. You might as well say if George Robey wasn't an actor, or if Hitler wasn't a Führer. They just wouldn't be Hitler or George Robey, that's all.'

'No I suppose they wouldn't. Then we stay here do we?'

'Oh! let's. I tell you this village is a highly interesting place just at present. Besides, I'm enjoying my flip with Mr Aspect a whole heap.'

'Poppy.'

'Mm.'

'Aren't you still in love with Anthony?'

'Oh – in love. I don't really know. I'm extremely angry with him at present, but as for love –'

'Does he want to marry the girl do you think?'

'God knows what Anthony wants, ever. If he doesn't marry her I can promise you that he'll be eating out of my hand again in a few months' time. He always comes drearily trundling back to me after these little incidents. But this time I don't feel at all certain that I'll take him back. I believe it would be better to make a clean break at last. Sometimes I think I really can't stand it any longer. You see, supposing he comes back now, fearfully penitent, and rather sweet as he always is, the whole routine will be certain to start again before long. About the beginning of next season, I should think, he will be falling for some awful little débutante, and she'll have to be in my house morning, noon, and night, with me always about the place as a suitable chaperone. The girl will hate me, because the poor little fool will suppose that I am the only obstacle to her eternal happiness, and I shall be bored into fits by her idiotic chatter. If only he would choose rather more companionable ones I might be able to bear it, or if he would have a straightforward affair with a married woman in her own house – these sentimental attachments to little girls in mine are so humiliating. Really, now I come to think of it, I'm absolutely sick and tired of Anthony St Julien.'

'Poor sweet. And you're still in love with him, aren't you?' said Lady Marjorie, slowly emerging from her bath into the towel which Poppy was holding out for her.

'I suppose I am, really. I've got into the habit of being in love with him, and you know how hard it is breaking oneself of habits.'

Jasper and Noel meanwhile were sitting in the bar drinking beer, which they fondly supposed would give them an appetite for the joint of beef whose luscious odours were at that very moment floating about the passage, stairs, and landing of the Jolly Roger.

'Jasper, old boy,' said Noel, who was in a particularly expansive mood, 'I really think you might have been nicer to Anne-Marie. She was most awfully upset after you had pitched into her like that over Social Unionism the other day. I told her you didn't mean a word of what you said, but that you would always take up any standpoint for the sake of an argument.'

'And that's not strictly true either. I believe a great deal of what I said, and if I were in any way politically minded, which I'm not, I should most certainly join the Social Unionist Movement.'

'You have, old boy.'

'Splendid, so I have. So have you. Fine girl, Eugenia. Incidentally you're not making much headway with your bride-to-be, are you?'

'I've decided that Eugenia can keep,' said Noel carelessly. 'She doesn't look much like a marrying girl to me at present, a few months one way or the other won't make all that difference, and in any case I'm potty about Anne-Marie. Don't you agree that she is an exquisite beauty?'

'She's all right,' said Jasper. 'Too bitchy for me though. And why full evening dress at tea-time?'

'It wasn't full evening dress you idiot, it was a little beach frock.'

'Well, I reckon we must be a hundred good miles from the nearest beach.'

'You don't seem to understand, Jasper. That child never has any fun, never goes to Venice or the South of France like other girls of her age. So, in order to make her life seem more interesting she has to make believe all the time, poor darling.'

'Like Mrs Thompson you mean?'

'I've a very good mind to take her off to Cannes with me next week.'

'My dear old boy, now, for God's sake don't lose your head. There's the husband remember.'

'You don't have to remind me,' said Noel, moodily. 'And from what I hear I should think he's the divorcing kind too. Sounds a perfect swine. Poor little Anne-Marie, you have no idea what that child has to put up with.'

'Oh, well, you can have lots of fun down here. Just think of the pageant, garden party, and Grand Social Unionist rally, it will be a perfect riot. Besides, like this you can keep an eye on Eugenia, which seems to me an exceedingly important feature from your point of view, eh what?

'I say, old boy,' he added, half rising in his seat and staring out of the window, 'just come here and take a look at these two chaps would you?' Noel looked without much interest. Two excessively ordinary men in tweed coats and grey flannel trousers stood outside the Jolly Roger. Two suitcases, which clearly belonged to them, were being removed from a hired car by the boot-boy, and deposited in the hall.

'This pub will be overflowing soon,' remarked Noel, in a bored kind of voice.

'Private detective agents,' said Jasper.

'Good heavens! Jasper, do you really think so?'

'I know it.'

'How?'

'By the look of them for one thing. Nobody looks quite so obtrusively ordinary as private detective agents. Besides I'm practically certain the left-hand one is the chap who used to shadow poor little Marigold. She got awfully chummy with him after a bit, allowed him to keep a charcoal brazier inside her garden gate when the weather got bad, and promised to stay at home all Christmas Day so that he could spend it with his kiddies. He liked her a lot after that.'

'Who can they be after down here?'

'That's what I propose to find out, it's an exceedingly important point because you see it might be any one of us.'

'I don't see why.'

'Well, my dear old boy, just consider the situation for a moment. Major Lace, to begin with yourself, may well be feeling jealous; Mr St Julien would be only human if he was wondering why his wife came to this unlikely place; the Duke of Dartford is probably not uninterested in getting the low-down on Lady Marjorie's behaviour here, while it is not beyond the bounds of possibility that my Uncle Bradenham may be beginning to guess at the authorship of certain blackmailing letters which he receives from time to time (only when I am on my beam ends, of course, and anyway the old miser jolly well ought to make me a decent allowance).'

'This is too fearful,' said Noel. 'What are we to do?'

'I'm going to send for the girls, warn them about these dicks, and evolve some plan of action.'

Jasper sent a note up to Poppy's room, with the boots, who had finished carrying luggage. In it he requested that she and Lady Marjorie should join him in the bar as soon as they were up and dressed.

'You'd better come along Marge,' said Poppy, as her friend began to demur at this suggestion. 'I told you before, you must join in the life here unless you want to die of boredom.'

'I shall probably be rude to Mr Aspect.'

'That's all right, he'll give as good as he gets. Don't you worry about him.'

'Good morning,' said Jasper, as they walked into the bar a few minutes later. 'What's yours?'

'What's what?' said Lady Marjorie.

'I meant to say that as we are having the unexpected pleasure of your company, my dear lady (running a bit short of face cream, I suppose?) what can we offer you in the shape of a drink? You so rarely assume a vertical position in these days that I imagine you to be in need of alcoholic support when you do.'

'Thank you,' said Lady Marjorie coldly. 'I have been brought up to regard drinking in between meals as a very middle-class habit.'

'I see, you prefer to get sozzled in the dining-room, I suppose. What's yours, Miss Smith?'

Poppy said she would like a glass of sherry, and after this had duly been procured Jasper proceeded to impart his news.

'Now the point is,' he said, 'that they may be after any one of us, and it would really be a good thing if we could find out which. The sooner the better in fact, so what we must have now is a little intelligent cooperation. I suggest that after luncheon today Miss Smith here, Noel, and myself, should each go for a long walk in different directions. Lady Marjorie, having lost, it appears, the use of her legs, had better spread a pot of "Ponds" over her face and resume horizontality. Now, private detective agents always behave in a pathetically obvious way, and whichever one of us it is that they are after will certainly find him or herself shadowed by these boys. However fast, however tirelessly one walks, it is impossible to shake them off. On the other hand, if they stay around here we can set our minds at rest. It will only mean that old Dartford is keeping an eye on those gold and diamond hair brushes, and so on.'

'How dare you go into my bedroom?' said Lady Marjorie, with cold fury.

'My dear lady, I didn't have to go into it. The door happened to be wide open and I was positively blinded by the flashing of gems which came from your dressing-table. Why, I nearly fell down the stairs.'

Poppy giggled at this.

Lady Marjorie gave her a reproving look, and saying: 'I think you are a very rude and badly brought-up young man, Mr Aspect, and I think all this nonsense about detectives is simply childish,' she left the bar.

'That's all right,' said Jasper. 'We can count on her for complete immobility during the afternoon – lend her your face cream, Miss Smith, in case she's run out, would you? What about you then, are you falling in with my scheme?'

Poppy said that it was all rather Phillips Oppenheim, but she supposed there could be no harm in it.

They arranged, after a good deal of talk, that Jasper should wander round to Comberry Manor at about four o'clock, and pay a call on Mrs Lace.

Poppy had already promised that she would take tea with Lady Chalford in order to discuss the garden party and pageant, so she would stick to that plan. This would leave Noel to await Eugenia, who was to be at the twopenny-bar shop as usual.

'Common sense demands that we should begin by allaying any possible suspicion until we see how the land lies,' said Jasper. 'For instance, if I go to Comberry Manor, they will be put off the scent as far as Noel and Mrs Lace are concerned –'

'But there is nothing,' Noel interrupted. 'I mean I have only seen Mrs Lace about three times in my life.'

'Still, you're mad about the girl, and intend to see her a good deal more in future. By this time next week there's no knowing what won't have happened, eh, old boy? To continue, Miss Smith can go with the utmost propriety and visit her second cousin four times removed, or whatever it is, neither could there be any harm in Noel smoking a pipe on the village green, or in Lady Marjorie's virginal cultivation of beauty, a pursuit in which, as everybody knows, she constantly indulges. I consider, ladies and gentlemen, that it is exceedingly important for us to find out which pole these boys are barking up. Once we know that we shall doubtless be able to thwart them at every turn.'

8

It was another day of intense heat, the sky was deep indigo, the shadows beneath the trees were black. No birds sang, and the landscape quivered slightly. Poppy, as she walked towards Chalford House, felt extremely contented. She was at her best in hot weather, it suited her and made her feel energetic. This was the first summer she had spent in England for some years, and she thought that nowhere abroad had she seen such beautiful days. The little coppice through which the drive passed just after the lodge gates was very dark, and smelt deliciously of leaf-mould, and the hot bark of trees. Chalford House itself, lying in a dancing haze of heat, looked like three enormous pink pearls upon a green velvet cushion. Eugenia now came into the picture, riding lazily upon a sleeping Vivian Jackson, and bound, no doubt, for the twopenny-bar shop.

'T.P.O.F. is expecting you,' she cried. 'Hail and farewell, cousin Poppy St Julien.'

'Hail and farewell, Eugenia,' said Poppy smiling. A moment later she turned and shouted over her shoulder, 'Noel is waiting for you on the village green.'

Lady Chalford received her with an almost touching cordiality. 'Dear child,' she cried, 'I have been thinking of you a great deal since Thursday – it is a very happy thing for me that you have come to Chalford. Why, I have not seen one of my relations since our tragedy – sixteen years ago. You must tell me a great deal of news – first of all, how is your dear mother?'

Poppy said that her dear mother was very well. She did not mention the painful fact that they had not been on speaking terms since Poppy's marriage to Anthony St Julien. Lady Chalford then proceeded to inquire after innumerable collaterals, mentioning aunts, uncles, and cousins, of whose existence Poppy was, in many cases, hardly herself aware.

'Dear child,' Lady Chalford said, when Poppy was unable to throw any light on the health, happiness, or even the whereabouts of two of her own father's first cousins, 'you seem to be, as a family, sadly *décousu*, if I may say so.'

The old lady evidently carried in her head a vast family tree; not a birth, a death, or a marriage among the remotest of her connexions seemed ever to have escaped her notice. Poppy thought it a sad thing that her extraordinary prejudice against so normal an eventuality as the fact of a divorce should have caused her to be shut away for ever from the world. She was evidently a woman who possessed an unusual capacity for affection and interest in the lives of other people.

They began to talk about the garden party, Lady Chalford producing a list of those neighbours who had been invited to her son's coming-of-age ball in 1912. 'I expect it must be a little out of date now,' she said, smiling. 'I must try and get it revised before the invitations are sent. There is no hurry really.' She then suggested a date for the party in about three weeks' time. 'Will that give you long enough to get up a little pageant, dear?'

'Oh! yes,' said Poppy, 'if we get to work straight away. Will you settle a subject for the pageant? As soon as that is fixed we can get on with it.'

'I was thinking about that before you came,' said Lady Chalford. 'Now two monarchs, with their wives, are known to have visited Chalford, so we shall be able to repeat actual history itself. They were Charles I and Henrietta Maria, who came to the Old Manor, and George III and Queen Charlotte. They came to see Chalford House when it was finally completed, and I incline myself towards reproducing their visit, for this reason. We still have, in the stables here, George III's own coach, and I thought it would be very interesting to use that for the scene of his arrival. Those acting the parts of King George and Queen Charlotte could get into the coach somewhere behind the kitchen garden, drive round the park and then up to the house – if you will come to this window, dear, I will show you exactly how it can be arranged.' She led Poppy forward and began pointing out various landmarks and a route for the coach. Poppy, however, was paying no attention to her. For, standing in the middle of the drive, looking up at Chalford House, were two excessively ordinary men in tweed jackets and grey flannel trousers. Poppy gazed at them for a moment, thunderstruck, then inadvertently cried out, 'Oh! Anthony, you dirty swine!' Lady Chalford turned towards her in amazement. Putting an arm round her waist she said, 'Dear Poppy, you are very white. Come and lie down for a little, it is the heat – you should never have walked all the way from the village. I will send at once for my motor car to take you home again.'

The local beauty looked out of her drawing-room window and saw Jasper Aspect coming towards the house. He ignored the drive, which twisted and turned among rhododendron bushes like a snake in its death agony (a late Victorian arrangement calculated to make the grounds seem more spacious), and strode carelessly over lawn and flower-beds alike, until, reaching the front door, he gave a tremendous peal to the bell. Mrs Lace meanwhile had escaped to her bedroom. She was delighted by this very unexpected turn of circumstance; she thought Jasper far more attractive than the too-obviously infatuated Noel, but had rather given up hope of his conquest since their meeting at the Jolly Roger. Telling her maid that she would be down in a moment, she hastily proceeded to change her clothes, and her face. Anne-Marie Lace was one of those women who alternate in appearance between the very extremes of squalor and smartness; when she was alone she could never be bothered to brush her hair, varnish her nails, or powder her nose; when in company she was always excessively well turned out. Having now arranged herself to her own satisfaction, she came into the drawing-room so quietly that Jasper who, more from habit than interest, was reading a letter he had found on the writing-table, gave a guilty start. Mercifully, however, Mrs Lace appeared to notice nothing, and greeted him with effusion.

'This is nice of you,' she cried, '*enchantée de vous voir*,' and she proceeded to sweep about the room in a highly theatrical manner, patting up cushions and tidying away books and newspapers with a variety of stunning gestures. These antics put Jasper in mind of some actress who is left alone on the stage for a few moments after the curtain has gone up.

'That's better now,' she said, smiling at him with wide-opened eyes, 'my little darlings have been romping in here, and you know how children upset everything in a room. Won't you sit down and have a cigarette?' She lit one for him, which gave her another excuse for some highly theatrical gestures.

'Now,' she said, 'we can have a nice cosy gossip. There are so many things I have been longing to ask you, but you weren't very kind to me last time we met.'

'Ah! but we were talking politics then,' said Jasper, as though to imply that more personal topics were now about to be broached. 'But what is it you wanted to ask me?'

'To begin with, what exactly persuaded you and Noel to come down to poor dead-alive old Chalford? That naughty Noel is always so vague about it when I ask him.'

'I expect he is,' said Jasper.

'You know, Mr Aspect, I am very fond of Noel and I'm afraid he is the tiniest little bit in love with me, but –'

'But what?' Jasper thought that in his whole career he had never had sex appeal thrown at his head more deliberately or with less effect. He was profoundly unattracted by Mrs Lace, and decided that it would be a generous and inexpensive gesture if he made a present of her to Noel, lock, stock and barrel.

Mrs Lace continued, 'Well, I don't think I could ever fall for someone like Noel, although he's most awfully sweet, isn't he?'

'Why couldn't you fall for him?'

'I suppose it's because he is so – so indefinite.'

'Perhaps it may be difficult for him, in the circumstances, to be very definite,' said Jasper, wrapping up Mrs Lace in a brown paper parcel, as it were, before handing her over, once and for all, to his friend.

'How do you mean?'

'Perhaps his position, at the moment, is a bit equivocal.'

Mrs Lace wrinkled her forehead and gazed inquiringly at Jasper.

'But, of course, you have guessed long ago.'

'I should very much like to know for certain,' said Mrs Lace, who naturally had no idea at all of Jasper's meaning.

'It is impossible, without a breach of confidence, to tell you everything. The most that I am permitted to say is that if you think you have an idea of whom he really is, you are probably right.'

'Oh!' cried Mrs Lace. She said no more; her brain was in a turmoil. After all, she thought with wild exhilaration, Miss Smith was not Miss Smith, neither was Miss Jones Miss Jones; on the contrary, they were both well-known figures in London Society. Why then should not the name of 'Noel Foster' also conceal some thrilling identity?

'I can see that, of course, you know quite well,' said Jasper, smiling. 'Those famous features are not so easy to disguise, are they? And now, dear Mrs Lace, one word of warning. Don't let the – don't let him see that you know. He is down here with the express intention of avoiding publicity, formality, and all the tedious attributes of his position, and if his identity were to be found out, even by the lady whom he – (do you mind if I am frank with you?) whom he so passionately admires, he would leave at once. It would be better if neither of us were to speak of this again, even to each other, and, of course, I rely upon your absolute discretion as far as the outside world is concerned. Should his whereabouts be discovered we should have journalists and photographers behind every tree, and these few short weeks of privacy which he so badly needs would be ruined for him.'

'I will keep his secret locked in my heart for ever,' whispered Mrs Lace, her eyes shining.

'And now the time has come for me to fulfil my errand,' said Jasper, looking furtively over his shoulder and lowering his voice, 'where can the – where can my friend see you for a while alone and without fear of interruption.'

Mrs Lace, her colour heightening, considered. At last she said, 'In Chalford Park, not so very far from the Old Manor, there is a small lake on whose shores a pink and white temple stands. It is almost entirely overgrown with ivy, honeysuckle and amaryllis, and is concealed from view by the wild-rose bushes which surround it. Nobody ever goes there.'

'Ah! happy Noel,' cried Jasper gallantly. 'With how much envy do I contemplate his lot. Will you, then, be there tomorrow afternoon at three o'clock punctually, and when you hear the hooting of an owl answer with the cry of a woodpecker if you are certain that the coast is clear?'

'Yes, you can count upon it,' said Mrs Lace. Unversed in ornithology she resolved that at dinner she would learn from Major Lace, who was, the cry of the wood-pecker.

Jasper now rose and, with a courtly gesture, he kissed her hand prior to taking his leave. At that moment, however, Major Lace could be heard banging about in the hall, and Anne-Marie, who enjoyed showing off her friends to him, begged Jasper to stay a few moments. 'He always complains if people leave as soon as he comes in.'

Major Lace, it appeared, had been attending a sale of pedigree cows. His usually good-humoured face was clouded with extreme bad temper, as he had, during the sale, turned over by mistake two pages of the catalogue instead of one, and had thus been misled as to the cow for which he was bidding. He bought the wrong one for an exorbitant price only to discover that his purchase was totally lacking in that desirable piece of anatomy – the udder.

'It appears that this brute is well known at sales,' he cried angrily. 'They've been hawking her round the country for months in the hope of finding some mug who would buy her. Chap next to me said, "Why the hell have you bought that cow, Lace?" I said, "Why not? Good cow, good pedigree, heavy record." "Some mistake there, Lace," he said, "her pedigree is all right, but she'll never have a record. Brute is bagless." Then I found out what I'd done, see, turned over two pages of the b— catalogue at once. There was such a glare, you know.'

'Very easy thing to do,' said Jasper sympathetically.

'Damned stupid of me all the same. I should have taken a good look at the brute, then it would never have happened. Bagless she is, absolutely bagless. Have a whisky and soda, Aspect?'

Jasper liked Major Lace. When they had drunk several whiskies he accompanied him round his cow-byres and pigsties and they exchanged dirty stories. Major Lace, who had a jolly, bawdy mind, thought that Jasper was distinctly a cut above Anne-Marie's usual friends, and was soon restored to a good temper.

As for Mrs Lace she slept but little that night. She was tormented with curiosity to know more about Noel, and quite unable to see how this could be achieved. She racked her brains, trying to recall the physiognomy of some royal person who might remotely resemble him. Then it occurred to her that he was perhaps a film star of enormous fame. In any case, he was clearly not unworthy of her chariot wheels, and this thought did much to restore her peace of mind.

No sooner had Jasper left the Jolly Roger and walked off in the direction of Comberry Manor, than Noel began to fall into a shocking state of restlessness. He cursed himself bitterly for consenting to any arrangement whereby Jasper was to enjoy a prolonged tête-à-tête with Mrs Lace; the full horror of the jealous torments he himself would be condemned to endure had not assailed him until the moment when he saw Jasper swinging jauntily down the village street. Dreadful thoughts now came to discomfort him. Jasper was notorious as a seducer of women, and had never shown himself averse to scoring off an old friend if the occasion presented; moreover, Mrs Lace had already shown an obvious predilection for him. Worst of all, she had by no means succumbed, as yet, to Noel's own blandishments, and he greatly feared that she found him uninteresting. He sat gloomily biting his nails, once indeed so desperate did he feel that he started up and made a move to pursue Jasper, but remembering that it was of the utmost importance to find out the motives of the two detectives, and having no wish to cut a jealous figure of fun in the eyes of Jasper and Mrs Lace, he forced himself to remain where he was. He hung about the village in a terrible state of nerves, trying to console himself with the consideration of Jasper's alleged love for Poppy St Julien and his own slight financial hold over Jasper. Neither of these facts afforded him much reassurance.

Presently Eugenia appeared on the scene and talked to him for a little while, but she seemed disappointed not to have found Jasper, whom she evidently regarded as a more satisfactory Social Unionist than Noel. She then busily set to work arranging an empty cottage, whose key she had wheedled out of her grandfather's estate agent, as a Union Jackshirt head-quarters for Chalford and district. Exquisite Chippendale furniture, smuggled away from Chalford House, was being pushed and banged into rooms and through doorways several sizes too small for it. Two or three of the Comrades were working like beavers at this task, while Eugenia stood by to encourage and occasionally to lend her own not inconsiderable weight. Her nanny also hovered round with a duster, flicking at the pieces which were already in place, and muttering to herself about what her ladyship would say if she knew of such goings on. When the head-quarters were ready (that is, when all the furniture had been forced into position, regardless of chips and knocks, and the rooms had been hung with life-size photographs of Hitler, Mussolini, Roosevelt and the Captain), Eugenia mounted a particularly fragile and valuable settee, which bent beneath her weight, and announced that there was to be a public ceremony for the opening of Chalford's new head-quarters the following Wednesday at 3.30 p.m.

'Well, how was it?' asked Noel, in an agony of suspense, 'did you like Anne-Marie – did she like you – what did you talk about – how did you hit it off together?'

'We got on like a house on fire,' said Jasper. 'Fine girl, Mrs Lace.' Noel almost groaned out loud. Jasper saw at once what a state of mind he was in, and found it not unamusing. 'Come and have a drink at the New Moon,' he said, deciding to prolong the agony for a bit. 'They ought to be open any minute now.'

'What a perfectly delightful husband she has too,' he continued, as they nestled up against the bar while waiting for their beer. 'A really charming man. He told me some exceedingly funny stories. I expect I shall be seeing a great deal of him in the future.'

Noel found this news far from reassuring. He knew that Jasper always made a point of being on most friendly terms with husbands.

Jasper now changed the subject lightly. He asked whether Noel had met Eugenia, how she was, and what she had been up to. 'Have a jolly afternoon yourself?' he inquired. 'Any sign of the dicks? No? They certainly weren't following me either. Looks like it's one of those Janes they're after. I wonder which?'

They now gulped their beer in silence. Noel had a dozen questions on the tip of his tongue, and racked his brain to think of some way in which he could word them without appearing ridiculous. He looked quite pathetic, as though he might burst into tears at any minute.

Presently Jasper threw him a crumb of comfort.

'Mrs Lace talked a lot about you,' he said.

Noel looked overjoyed for a moment, but this expression soon gave way to one of apprehension. He felt it more than likely that the conversation as directed by Jasper might have been on extremely unflattering lines, uncertain as he was of Mrs Lace's attitude towards himself. He rather expected that he would be thrown into a pit of despair by Jasper's next remark. Bracing himself as for a physical shock he took a large gulp of beer and said: 'Oh! really, what did she say?'

The crumb of comfort, however, was most unexpectedly succeeded by the contents of a whole baker's shop.

'Mrs Lace is nuts about you, old boy. She can't think of anything else.'

Noel still suspected a trap. Walking warily, he said: 'I don't believe she is at all. She never shows it when she is with me, anyway.'

'My dear old boy, you are such a shocking bad psychologist. Can't you realize that Mrs Lace is one of those shy, retiring little women who must have all the running made for them? Haven't you noticed, for one thing, how reserved she is?'

Even the love-blinded Noel had not quite noticed this. He was only too prepared, however, to believe it.

'Never mind,' continued Jasper, 'I think everything should be all right now. I've done a lot of work for you today, old boy. You should be grateful to me.'

'What work?' asked Noel, dubiously.

'To begin with I praised you up to the skies, said you had an exceedingly noble character, and so on. But what is even more important, I made an assignation for you.'

'Not with Anne-Marie?'

'Who else? You are to meet her in a place where you will be quite undisturbed for as long as you wish – a romantic place, a place which might have been (probably was) designed for lovers' meetings. There she will be awaiting your declaration at three o'clock tomorrow afternoon.'

'Where is it then?' cried Noel, who was duly thrown, as Jasper had intended that he should be, into a fever of excited anticipation. 'Quickly, tell me, Jasper, where?'

Jasper did not reply. He appeared to have gone off into a reverie and sat gazing into the middle distance, a dreamy expression on his face.

'Jasper – where is this place, damn you?'

'By the way, old boy,' said Jasper, suddenly coming back to earth again, 'I could do with ten pounds.'

'I dare say you could,' said Noel.

There was a long silence.

'Oh, I see,' said Noel peevishly, 'blackmail?'

'I say, hold on old boy, that's not a very polite word is it? Supposing we called it commission? After all, a chap must live you know.'

'I really can't see why,' said Noel.

Presently however, he pulled out a cheque-book and proceeded with bad grace to scribble a cheque for ten pounds. He then screwed it up in a ball and threw it at Jasper's head. Jasper smoothed it out carefully and read it. 'It's exceedingly untidy,' he said, 'but I dare say it will do.

'Temple by lake near Chalford Old Manor. You approach it hooting like an owl to prove *bona fide*; if all is O.K. Mrs Lace replies with a merry laugh. Let's go back to our pub, shall we, and find out what those girls have been up to all the afternoon.'

Lady Marjorie and Mrs St Julien, however, made no further appearance that evening. They dined, as usual, in their private sitting-room, but after dinner they did not, as was their custom, wander out into the garden to breathe the cool night air before going to bed. They remained in their sitting-room, and were evidently talking nineteen to the dozen. Jasper spent much of his evening with his ear glued to the keyhole, thus balking the detectives who were wandering about like ghosts, apparently with the same intention.

When, very much later than usual, Mrs St Julien retired to her own room, she was slightly startled to notice a figure tucked up comfortably in her bed. It was Jasper's.

'Quite all right,' he said. 'Those boys saw me go into Lady Marjorie's room – I went in there first and then climbed round by the window. Pathetically easy to deceive, dicks are, and as it's you they're after it can't matter to her.'

Poppy St Julien sat down on the chair in front of her dressing-table and looked at him severely. 'Now I wonder how you happen to know it's me they're after – it almost looks as though you must have been listening to my conversation with Marge just now.'

'That's right,' said Jasper, rearranging the pillows so that his head should be on a higher level.

'You appear very ignorant of ordinary social conventions.'

'Perhaps I prefer to ignore them.'

Poppy began to brush her hair.

'I thought,' said Jasper, 'by your tone of voice just now, that you seemed to be upset by Anthony St Julien's behaviour. I am sorry.'

Poppy continued to brush her hair.

'He also prefers to ignore social conventions, it seems.'

'He does,' said Poppy gloomily; 'but there's some excuse for him, poor sweet. He's in love.'

'So am I in love.'

'So you say. But you are such a liar, aren't you? And I wish you wouldn't drop cigarette ash into my bed.'

'Give me an ash-tray then would you, darling Miss Smith? That soap-dish would do. Thanks awfully. Will you marry me?'

'Don't be silly.'

'Silly's my middle name. I asked you a question, however, and should like an answer.'

'Please leave my room.'

'Don't be governessy.'

'I want to undress.'

'Undress then.'

'Oh! damn you,' said Poppy.

'Now look here, Miss Smith darling,' said Jasper, 'do be sensible and listen to me for a minute. Anthony St Julien is an eel and he doesn't want you any more because he lusts after strange débutantes, I am not an eel and I do want you, and I will never leave you for anybody else as long as I live. Now if you marry me everyone will be pleased, Anthony St Julien, his débutante, the detectives, and me. Doesn't it seem an easy way to give pleasure all round?'

'You can't keep me,' said Poppy, 'in the comfort to which I have been accustomed.'

'Same to you, my angel.'

'I dare say, but wives aren't expected to keep their husbands.'

'I never could see why not. It seems so unfair.'

'Not at all. The least the chaps can do is to provide for us financially when you consider that we women have all the trouble of pregnancy and so on.'

'Well, us boys have hang overs don't we? Comes to the same thing in the end.'

'Anyway, the fact remains that I can't keep you and you can't keep me. You ought to be marrying Marge.'

'I know. I would like a shot if I thought there was the smallest chance. Is there?'

'None whatever.'

'There you are. I knew there wasn't. Why raise my hopes? You see, looks like it'll have to be you after all, darling Miss Smith. I can't say I mind much. You are most awfully pretty you know.'

'Jolly kind of you to say so,' said Poppy, yawning. She began to undress.

9

The opening ceremony of Chalford head-quarters happened to fall upon the same day as that of a cocktail party for which Mrs Lace had sent out invitations. As the one entertainment was billed to take place at 3.30 p.m. and the other not until six o'clock, it was evident that both could easily be attended. Anne-Marie's party was ostensibly inaugurated to set in motion the machinery of the pageant. An organizing committee was to be elected and the allocation of minor rôles to be considered (the chief parts, those of George III and Queen Charlotte, had already been snapped up by Mrs Lace for herself and Noel). Actually all this was unnecessary. Jasper and Eugenia between them were getting on perfectly well with the arrangements, but it provided that for which Mrs Lace had been long-ing, namely, an excuse to show off to the neighbourhood her newly acquired friends and lover.

It was, of course, rather annoying to her that she would be obliged to preserve Marjorie's incognito, and to refrain from whispered conjectures as to the identity of Noel; on the other hand, she considered that not even the assumed names of Foster and Jones entirely hid their intrinsic presentability, while Mr Aspect and Mrs St Julien were good fat fishes for her net. Besides, could she not look forward to that glorious day when she would be in the superior position of having 'known all along'? When Chalford learnt at last what greatness it had been harbouring in the shape of Noel, Chalford would see Mrs Lace in a dramatic light. People would be saying to each other: 'You remember, last summer. He was staying at the Jolly Roger and called himself Noel Foster, and that was when he fell in love with her. And now, only think of it, they have eloped together. Of course one always knew she wouldn't stay for long in this out-of-the-way place, the amazing thing is that she should ever have married such a dull bore –'

Even supposing that this dream of elopement which now filled her days should never come true, it would be known that Mrs Lace had been the love of Noel's life, and that although, for political or other reasons, he was unable to marry her, he still sent her a dried rose-leaf in a crested box once a year.

She decided that she would always thereafter dress herself in deepest mourning for her widowed heart. It would be wonderful, too, whispering to her intimates: 'I made him go back. He wished to give up all for me, but I could not allow that. He must have his career, do his duty, live his life. It is far better so. If I had allowed him to do as he wished he might have learnt in time to hate me; like this our love is fresh, eternal. No, my heart is broken, but I regret nothing.' Mrs Lace's imagina-tion, which was vivid, ran away with her like this all the time.

The party was also intended to provide an opportunity of showing Noel that he was not the only pebble on Mrs Lace's beach; superfluous gesture, as poor Noel was already too firmly convinced that to see was to desire her. To this end the artistic Mr Leader and his colleagues were invited over from Rackenbridge, that local Athens which had, up to now, provided Anne-Marie with all her cultured conquests.

The great day dawned with thunder in the air, and soon after breakfast there was thunder in the Laces' drawing-room as well. Major Lace, filling up his pipe before setting out to examine a sick cow, remarked casually:

'Isn't it your binge today, Bella?'

Anne-Marie winced at this. She objected to the use of her real name, despised the word 'binge', and considered that Major Lace ought to have known as well as she did that it was *the* great day.

'I have asked a few people round at cocktail-time,' she said, in her society voice. 'Perhaps that's what you're thinking of?'

'Splendid! I thought it was today all right. I ran into old George Wilkins yesterday at the Show, and told him to be sure and come along. Lucky thing I happened to remember about it. Why, he'll simply be the life and soul of a party like that.'

Anne-Marie froze on hearing this news. Then she flew into a passion. She refused to have Mr Wilkins at her party, he was quite unsuitable, an odious man, stupid and loutish. She hated him. She hated his red face, and Hubert knew that perfectly well, and Hubert had only asked him out of spite, in order to spoil everything for her. Everything. She burst into tears.

Major Lace listened to these recriminations with an expression of bewilderment which was by degrees succeeded by one of intense disgust on his kind round face.

'You're such a little snob, my dear,' he said, as soon as he was able to get a word in, 'I know what you're thinking, that those new grand friends of yours won't like poor old George Wilkins – eh? Well, as it happens you're wrong there, because I'm prepared to bet a large sum that they will. He's the most amusing fellow I've ever come across, and what's more, everybody likes old Wilkins – except you.'

'I'm not a snob,' cried Mrs Lace, angrily. 'If I were a snob should I be friends with penniless artists like Leslie Leader? On the contrary, many people would think I was too much the other way – not particular enough. It is not snobbish to demand certain qualities in one's acquaintances – and personally I prefer to mix with people of culture. I dislike vulgarity of mind. However, all this is beside the point. I shall be delighted for you to invite Mr Wilkins any other time. At this particular party it will be quite impossible to have him.'

'Why?'

'For the reasons I have given you. He is an unsuitable person, so *unsoigné* too. And for another thing, Leslie Leader would leave the house if he came. He absolutely hates him.'

'Dear, dear, does he now? Mr Leader goes up in my estimation. I never thought that white slug had the guts to hate anybody. Still I think I should risk it, rather awkward to put Leader off at the last minute like this.'

'Naturally there will be no question of doing that. I am going to ring up Mr Wilkins now this minute and tell him you have made a mistake.'

'Anne-Marie, you can do that if you like, but I warn you that I shan't turn up at your blasted party unless Wilkins does,' said Major Lace, setting his jaw.

'Nonsense, Hubert, of course you'll have to come. It would look very odd if you didn't, and besides, who's to mix the cocktails?'

'I don't give a damn who mixes the cocktails. Leader can mix them.'

'You know he can't; he's teetotal.'

'He would be. Anyway if I'm to come Wilkins must come, you can take it or leave it old girl.' So saying, Major Lace stumped off to his cow-byres.

Mrs Lace spent much of the morning in tears of rage. During luncheon she uttered no word, a fact which Major Lace apparently never noticed, as he went on as usual, chatting about John's disease, and the tubercular content of a pint of milk. He did not mention Mr Wilkins or the party, and the moment he had swallowed his food he went off again. Arrangements for the party occupied Anne-Marie's afternoon, but gave her little satisfaction. Even the arrival of Mr Leader, who came, as he had promised that he would, to decorate her drawing-room with whitewashed brambles and cellophane, failed to improve her temper.

While she was changing her dress, however, her spirits began to rise, and by the time that the first guests had appeared she became positively gay once more. She enjoyed entertaining more than anything else on earth, and was, considering her inexperience, a good enough hostess, unflagging in her zeal to please.

Neighbour after neighbour now arrived, husbands, wives, daughters, and an occasional son home on leave or down from Oxford. They were all jolly friendly, dull people, and were suitably startled by Anne-Marie's silver *lamé* cocktail-trousers and heavy make-up. The young men from Rackenbridge struck, she considered, exactly the right note of Bohemian *négligé* in their shrimp trousers and 'Aertex' shirts open at the neck. The scene, in fact, was now set for the entry of Mrs Lace's new friends. Anxiously she began to keep one eye on the drive, and for a whole hour she played Pagliacci, chatting and laughing with a breaking heart. For the new friends did not appear.

When finally they did turn up, fearfully late, and accompanied by a stockingless Eugenia, they all seemed to be in the last stages of exhaustion. 'We are quite worn out, you see,' Jasper explained politely, 'by Eugenia's party. It was an absolute riot from beginning to end. We think she is a genius: Eugenia, Eugenius, E.U.G.E.N.I.A. Eugenia.'

'It was too lovely,' said Lady Marjorie, who appeared far less languid than usual. She had colour in her cheeks and her eyes shone. 'But why didn't you come, Mrs Lace; you can't imagine what a lovely party it was.'

'We sang Jackshirt hymns for hours outside the head-quarters,' said Poppy. '"Onward Union Jackshirts" – D'you know that one; shall we teach it you, another time perhaps? Then we went for a wonderful march with a band playing and we each carried a Union Jack. Marge and I have both joined up. The Comrades were heaven, so beautiful-looking.'

They all fell into chairs and fanned themselves. Poppy and Marjorie looked anything but smart London ladies, calculated to impress local housewives. Eugenia, her eye suddenly lighting upon Mr Leader pointed him out to Poppy, saying in a stage whisper, 'He's a well-known Pacifist. Shall we give him Union Jackshirt justice?'

'Not now,' Poppy whispered back, 'we're all much too tired.'

A sort of blight now began to fall on Mrs Lace's party. It was dreadful for her because nobody was behaving in the way she had planned they should. Most of the neighbours had gone home to their early dinners and those that remained formed little knots in the garden, talking to each other about sport or to Major Lace about the iniquities of the Milk Marketing Board. The Rackenbridge young men hung round the bar eating and drinking all they could lay their hands on, while her new friends were being in no way wonderful, but merely lay about the place in attitudes of extreme debility.

'We are so tired,' they reiterated apologetically, 'you should have seen what a distance we marched, it was terrible. In this heat too, whew!'

Poppy, who had a conscience about these things, did whisper in Jasper's ear that she thought they should mingle a bit more. Jasper replied, 'Mingle then,' but nothing happened.

Mrs Lace brought up Mr Leader and introduced him all round, saying, 'It was Leslie who did these wonderful decorations for me. He is a Surréaliste you know.'

Poppy said, politely, 'Oh! how interesting. Aren't you the people who like intestines and pulling out babies' eyes?'

Jasper said that he had once written a play, the whole action of which took place inside Jean Cocteau's stomach. 'Unfortunately I sold the film rights,' he added, 'otherwise you could have had them. The film was put on in Paris and many people had to leave the Jockey Club and stop being Roman Catholics because of it. I was pleased.'

Eugenia looked gloomily at Mr Leader, and said in a menacing voice, 'You should see the inside of the new Social Unionist head-quarters.'

'It's even more exciting than the inside of Jean Cocteau's stomach,' added Jasper.

After these sallies conversation died, and poor Mr Leader presently wandered away. Noel now lay back and put a newspaper over his face – nobody could have supposed, to see him, that he was madly in love with his hostess, nor were her guests at all likely to go home with the impression that between these two people was undying romance. Mrs Lace looked at him in despair.

Worse things, however, were to befall her. Presently the hated Mr Wilkins, looking even less *soigné* than usual, and covered with white dust, was shepherded into the room by Major Lace, who rubbed his hands together saying, 'Here's dear old George at last – broke down twice on the way! Still, better late than never, eh! George? I thought that was your old bag of nails heard rattling up the drive. Cocktail or whisky and soda, eh?'

'I absolutely love that man's appearance,' Lady Marjorie whispered to Poppy.

'He certainly has a very whimsical face,' Poppy agreed.

At this juncture Mrs Lace was called away from the room to speak on the telephone. One of the neighbours had left a dust-coat behind and would call for it the following day. 'We loved your party,' she added. 'It was too bad we had to leave so early.' Mrs Lace agreed that it was too bad, promised to keep the dust-coat quite safely, and returned to the drawing-room, where an extremely painful sight met her eyes.

Mr Wilkins was seated on a sofa between Mrs St Julien and Lady Marjorie who were both doubled up with laughter. Mr Aspect, and the nameless but exalted

Noel, crouching on the floor beside them, also appeared to be highly amused, whilst Major Lace stood over the whole group with the expression of a conjurer who has just produced from his sleeve some enchanting toy.

'And have you heard about the man who went into W. H. Smith?' Mr Wilkins was saying.

'No,' they cried, in chorus.

'He said to the girl behind the counter, "Do you keep stationery?" And she said, "No, I always wriggle."'

Roars of laughter greeted this story.

'And do you know about the man who was had up by the police?'

'No.'

'They said, "Anything you say will be held against you." He said, "*Anything* I say will be held against me?" and they said, "Yes," and he said, "Right oh, then, Greta Garbo."'

As Mrs Lace gazed with disgust upon this scene, she was approached by Mr Leader, who, looking as if he had a bad smell under his nose, came up to say good-bye.

'I will walk down the garden with you,' she said, glad of any excuse to take her away from hateful Mr Wilkins and his success.

'Dear, lovely Anne-Marie,' said Mr Leader, putting his hand on her arm, 'do explain your new friends to me – what is the point of them? You always used to tell me how much you dislike that sort of person, rich, smart, idle and stupid,' he spoke reproachfully.

'You don't quite understand,' said poor Mrs Lace. 'They are delightful really, only today they seem different. If you talked to them alone you wouldn't think them at all stupid.'

'My dear, they must be stupid if they have joined the Social Unionist party.'

'Oh! I think that's all a joke.'

'Social Unionism is no joke. It is a menace to the life's work of those who, like myself, love peace and wish all men equal. Surely, Anne-Marie, you cannot in two short weeks have forgotten all our wonderful ideals?'

'Oh! no,' said Anne-Marie, 'it's not that. But it is always interesting to meet new people, don't you think so, to try and get a view of life from their angle? And Noel Foster is, in many ways, very exceptional. The others are nice, but he is something different from what I have ever known. I can't explain why, you must meet him again, more quietly and see for yourself.'

'No thank you,' said Mr Leader, 'I have seen enough of him this afternoon.'

'I wondered,' Mrs Lace went on, 'whether all of you at Rackenbridge would help us with the pageant? We want various groups of people to undertake the different episodes, nothing is quite settled yet though.'

Mr Leader said he would think it over. 'I must say good-bye now, you wonderful creature. Don't forget that you are the greatest inspiration any man could have, and never waste your friendship on somebody who may be unworthy of such a gift.'

Mrs Lace could have kicked him for not making this pretty compliment in the hearing of Noel. She felt it to be utterly wasted among the dank laurels at the bottom of the garden.

When she got back to the house she found that all her guests had departed, with the exception of Mr Wilkins and his still admiring claque.

'Here's Anne-Marie,' said Noel, affectionately. 'Come over here and talk to us for a bit. You've been a hostess for long enough.'

'Oh! yes,' cried Poppy, making room for her on the sofa. 'We want you, we want to tell you all the things we've been fixing up for the pageant.'

'Ah! the pageant,' Mrs Lace felt happier. What mattered it that her cocktail party had not been all she had hoped when she still had the pageant glowing on her horizon? She reminded herself that she and Noel were to play the parts of Queen Charlotte and George III. Together they would drive through cheering crowds, bowing to right and to left of them, a cynosure for all eyes, in the beautiful and historic coach that Lady Chalford was lending on that occasion.

This picture was constantly in Anne-Marie's mind; she thought about it nearly the whole time. How sweet and pretty she would look in her charming head-dress, how handsome the appearance of Noel in wig and uniform; how evident to all observers their great love for each other. In after days those who had seen them would be saying, 'What a pity we didn't know then who he really was. I suppose we might have guessed from the grace and ease with which he acknowledged the cheers. Of course, they were deeply in love, nobody could have failed to realize that. How romantic it all is!'

Perhaps their photograph would appear in the newspapers, a photograph in which Noel would be gazing at her, a whole wealth of love in his eyes. There was no end to the intoxicating vista of possibilities which stretched out before Anne-Marie when she began to think about the pageant.

What was Poppy saying now? 'Yes, it was Marge's idea. She is clever to have thought of it, and it's all quite settled. Mr Wilkins is going to be George III! He has promised he will at last, but we had to go down on our hands and knees to persuade him, didn't we, Mr Wilkins? And that will make the pageant a most wonderful success because no two people have ever looked so much alike as Mr Wilkins and George III; had you noticed it? Now you know we shall have to be getting back to Chalford because it's fearfully late and our dinner will be ready. We have loved the party, specially meeting Mr Wilkins. Thank you so much for it, and for introducing us to Mr Wilkins, it was heavenly of you. Good-bye Mr Wilkins, see you tomorrow then, at about one.'

Major Lace could not understand why his wife cried herself to sleep that night. He supposed that she must be in the family way again.

10

Next day at the usual hour Noel pushed his way, hooting from time to time, through the undergrowth which surrounded his trysting-place. As he heard no answering cry, he presumed that Anne-Marie had been unable to come. He found her lying, however, a little crumpled heap of despondency, on the steps of the temple, and very soon she was sobbing her heart out on Noel's shoulder.

'Darling, I really can't see that it matters as much as all that,' he said, when at last he had realized the reason for all this misery. 'Of course it would have been fun to do it together, and it is sweet of you to mind, but you know, Lady Marjorie is quite right, Mr Wilkins is the living double of George III. Rather clever of her to notice I thought.'

'Oh! you don't understand,' sobbed Mrs Lace. 'I'm not so stupid as to make all this fuss over an old pageant, although I had been looking forward to acting with you quite particularly.'

'Then what is it, my darling?' said Noel, who was getting rather bored with this scene.

'I'm so dreadfully, dreadfully unhappy.'

'Darling, why?'

'You're so unkind to me. I feel I can't bear it any longer.'

'Unkind?'

'All the secrecy.'

'What secrecy?'

Mrs Lace had now, more or less, recovered her composure. She knew that she looked pretty when she cried, so long as the crying only lasted a little while. Therefore, at the psychological moment she usually stopped. She did so now, and proceeded to comb her hair and powder her nose, peeping from beneath dewy eyelashes at Noel from time to time. There was an expression on his face which she interpreted as a warning not to go too far. In actual fact he was merely reminding himself that all women like an occasional good cry; it was a tax which lovers had to pay. He hoped that she would cut it short, meanwhile steeling himself to endurance.

'You see, darling,' she went on presently, 'it is rather cruel, the way you never tell me anything about yourself.'

Typical grievance, thought Noel. 'My darling,' he said, 'there really isn't much to tell. The history of my life up to date is extremely dull, believe me.'

'The smallest things about you are interesting to me,' said Anne-Marie, passionately.

'Well,' said Noel, with that bright facetiousness which was such an unattractive feature of his mind, 'shall we begin at the beginning? I was born of poor but honest parents –'

'Where?'

'Where was I born? I don't know exactly, it was somewhere in the Balkans. My father, you see, was an archaeologist, and he and my mother spent the first years of their married life wandering about in that part of the Continent. I know she had a bad time when I was born, as I was premature, and they could not get hold of a proper doctor for ages. They were both so vague, always.'

'Yes, I see. So then where were you educated?'

'In England, of course. After the War broke out circumstances compelled my parents to settle down at Hampton Court, and I went to a private school and to Eton in the ordinary way. They did want to send me to some foreign university, but there were various complications and in the end I went to Oxford.'

'And your parents – did they never go back?'

'No. After the War they said they were too old (they had married rather late in life). Besides, things had become so changed then, they preferred to stay on at Hampton Court. Now they are both dead.'

This conversation seemed to confirm suspicions which were already forming in Mrs Lace's mind. Noel was obviously the rightful king of some Ruritania, preparing in the solitude of an English village for the *coup d'état* which should restore to him his throne. Any day now the courier might arrive and announce that the time was ripe, the people and the regiments in a proper frame of mind to welcome him back to the land of his fathers. Those two strange men whom she had noticed hanging about the Jolly Roger were doubtless members of his personal bodyguard. Her total ignorance of central European politics and geography, coupled with an imaginative nature, enabled her to treat this conjecture as though it were a solid fact; she did not have the smallest misgiving about it from the first moment of its inception.

'What made you think of coming down here?' she asked, boldly.

Noel looked embarrassed. It would be difficult for him to explain his exact motives for coming to Chalford. He wondered whether Mrs Lace had spoken about this to Jasper, and if so what impression she had received from him. In order to be on the safe side, he muttered vaguely, 'Oh, I don't know, just waiting for something to turn up.'

The courier. The news from his Capital. 'And how long will it be before that happens? How much longer do you expect to be here?'

'Just as long as I can go on seeing you every day, darling Anne-Marie.'

'I wish you would take me away from here,' she cried, passionately.

Noel frowned. He had been anticipating some such development to this conversation. 'My dear,' he said, in a matter-of-fact voice, 'Whatever would your husband say if I did?'

'He would divorce me, and I shouldn't care a pin.'

'My darling Anne-Marie,' said Noel, kissing her hand and holding it in his, 'I must explain to you, I should have explained before – that I am not in a position to marry anybody. If I were, it would be my dream of dreams to marry you. But, for many reasons this is not possible, alas! You must take my word for it, dearest.'

Now for the storm, he thought, now for half an hour of hysterical reproaches. He knew exactly what would be said, he had heard it all before. 'To you I have been nothing except an agreeable summer holiday's diversion, but to me you are life itself,' and so on. It would take all his tact at the end of it to keep things on their old footing, as he very much hoped he would succeed in doing. For he still thought that Mrs Lace was a wildly attractive young woman.

There was a pause, during which he could feel the storm gathering. Metaphorically speaking, he cowered, putting up his coat collar. But to his enormous surprise and relief no storm broke. Mrs Lace encircled his neck with her arms and whispered in his ear, 'I quite understand, my own angel; don't let's think of this any more. We must be happy together whilst happiness is still possible, and try to forget that the day is at hand when we must part, perhaps for ever. And when that day does come, let us be brave and hide, from the world at any rate if not from each other, our broken hearts.'

Noel could hardly believe his ears. He thought that Mrs Lace was by far the most remarkable woman he had ever met.

'I always told you she was something out of the ordinary,' he said to Jasper that evening, after repeating the whole conversation for his benefit. They were on the best of terms now, Noel feeling so much gratitude for Jasper's surprisingly loyal intervention in this affair that he had forgiven and forgotten the piece of blackmail which had ensued. Ever since that afternoon when Jasper had been to see Anne-Marie she had shown a perfectly stupendous love for Noel, he felt that it would have taken weeks of diffident courtship on his part to produce such a result.

Jasper watched the situation developing itself with fiendish amusement, and could not resist telling Poppy what he had done.

'Oh! I say, poor Mrs Lace,' she said, laughing, 'anyway, I don't suppose she believed a word of it.'

'Didn't she just? Well then, why is she being so nice to Noel all of a sudden? She would hardly look at him before.'

'That's true. I think it's awfully funny, but awfully unkind of you, Jasper.'

'Not at all. The girl's having a fine time, and so is Noel. I think it was exceedingly nice of me, especially as I could have had her myself by raising a finger, and she's quite a cup of tea you know.'

'Really, Jasper, you are outrageous. Pass me the soap-dish, will you?'

Next time they were all together Poppy could not resist treating Noel with exaggerated deference for the benefit of Mrs Lace.

As for Anne-Marie, her dreams became daily more extravagant. She saw herself now as the central figure of an impending tragedy. The farewell scene – Noel booted and spurred, and glittering with decorations, kissing her good-bye in the moonlight while an equerry, holding two horses, awaited him at a discreet distance. 'Keep this ring and wear it always, it was my mother's.' He would tuck her little glove (or handkerchief, she had better order some new ones) into his belt, and gallop away, leaving her in a dead faint. Dreary weeks would follow, during which she would scan the papers for news of his triumph. Then, much later on, the wedding. Anne-Marie, drawn as by a magnet to his capital, would be standing in the crowd while Noel rode in state to marry some royal princess of an unexampled hideosity. His eye would light upon her as she stood there heavily veiled, and pierce her disguise. He would turn deathly pale and bite his lip until the blood came, to hide its quivering. Then, regaining his composure with a kingly gesture, he would ride on amid the huzzas of the populace. At that moment the assassin would draw his weapon, quick as thought she would throw herself before him, and stop the bullet with her own body, to die a few minutes later in the arms of Noel. As he closed her eyes he would pluck from his bosom, and pin to hers, the highest Order that was his to bestow. An alternative. Perhaps in the hour of his triumph he would send for her and install her in some gorgeous palace, joined to his own by an underground tunnel. She would be his good genius, guiding him with her wonderful feminine intuition through the quagmire of internal and international politics. The statesmen of all countries would bow before her and solicit her good offices with the king, and when she died her strange life would be written in several different languages. In fact, there was no end to these interesting possibilities.

The day after his scene with Mrs Lace, Noel was obliged to go to London. His lawyer wanted to see him; a visit to his dentist was becoming necessary. Jasper suggested that as he was going anyway, he should use the opportunity to buy some little present for Anne-Marie.

'I've never known it do much harm at this stage in the proceedings,' he said, 'and after all, you're simply stiff with cash old boy aren't you?'

Noel said it was no thanks to Jasper if he was. He thought the idea a good one, however, and when he had finished all his business and eaten his luncheon he went to a pawnshop and bought a small but pretty aquamarine set in a ring. The price, as the jeweller told him, was extremely reasonable, and this was because the market had been flooded ever since the sale of the Russian Imperial jewels, which had included several parures of this stone.

When he slipped his present on to Anne-Marie's finger he said, to make it seem more romantic, 'This ring, my beloved, once shone upon the finger of an Empress, but she wasn't half as beautiful as you.'

'An Empress!' cried Mrs Lace. 'How wonderful!'

Meanwhile arrangements for the pageant were going ahead in good earnest. It had been settled that the inhabitants of the Jolly Roger, Mrs Lace, Eugenia and her Comrades of the Chalford Branch, were to be responsible between them for providing all the clothes and for the opening scene, in which George III would arrive and be welcomed to Chalford House. After this, George and Charlotte, surrounded by their courtiers, were to mount a small platform on which there would await them two thrones, and here they would remain whilst the other scenes, consisting of salient events of the reign, were enacted on the lawn before them. These episodes were being entrusted by Eugenia to various neighbouring branches of Social Unionists, each branch to be responsible for one episode. (Mr Leader and his friends, having learnt that the pageant was in aid of the Social Unionist funds, had politely intimated to Mrs Lace that they would be unable to help.)

Rehearsals for the first scene had already begun. Mrs Lace, having resigned herself to the dismal necessity of driving with Mr Wilkins, was greatly cheered when Jasper promised her that Noel, taking the part, and wearing the actual clothes of the Lord Chalford of the day, should receive them at the front door, help her from the coach and arm her to the platform, where he would then present an address of welcome. Eugenia, as the Prince of Wales, Poppy as Fanny Burney, and Lady Marjorie as the Duchess of Devonshire, would also be there to greet them with billowing curtsies. Mrs Lace felt that after all there would now be even greater opportunities for interplay of flirtatious gestures between herself and Noel than if they had arrived together in the coach, and was happy. Jasper, when the first rehearsal was over, told Poppy that in the minds of those who saw the pageant horrid scandals would be associated with the hitherto unsullied name of Queen Charlotte.

Lady Chalford had invited Jasper to write and produce the pageant on the grounds of his grandfather's well-remembered talent for composing Valentines. Jasper was finding the job anything but agreeable, each decision in turn seemed to give offence to somebody, while Eugenia plagued him unmercifully, insisting that he must introduce a strong Social Unionist interest.

'My dear child, I don't see how I can,' he said, in despair. 'I mean, think for yourself, what have George III and Social Unionism in common? Not one single thing.'

'And what about the Glory of England?' cried Eugenia, in a grandiose voice.

'Glory of bottoms. The ordinary person simply remembers George III by the fact that he went mad and lost America. That's all he's ever supposed to have done for England, poor old boy.'

'I can't help it,' said Eugenia, 'If we are having a Grand Social Unionist rally and pageant, Social Unionism has got to come into it somehow.'

Jasper tore his hair.

Next day Eugenia appeared very early at the Jolly Roger having spent a sleepless night in the throes of composition. As soon as Jasper was up she handed him a document, which ran as follows:

SPEECH BY GEORGE III

Hail! and thanks for all your good wishes, we are happy to be among our loyal Aryan subjects of Chalford and district. In our speech today we thought we would tell you of a very curious prophetic dream which we had last night. We dreamt that by degrees this, our glorious country, will begin to sink into the slush and slime of a decaying democracy. America, as we are sure you must have all noticed with horror, is already tainted with the disease, and we expect we shall soon have to be kicking her out of our glorious Empire; but even this wonderfully foreseeing action on our part won't make any difference in the long run. Nothing can save our country from a contagion which is to sweep the earth. Never mind, Britons, do not despair, for in our dream we foresaw that when you shall have been plunged into the darkest night, governed (if one can use such a word) by a pack of disastrous old ladies who ought to have been dead for years, a new day will dawn, the old ladies will be forced to retire to their unhallowed beds, and their place at Westminster will be taken by young and victorious Comrades. In those days, the streets will ring with the cry of youths who will march, each carrying his little banner, towards the fulfilment of a Glorious Britain. A new spirit, the spirit of Social Unionism will be abroad in the land, vitality will flow back into her withered veins, hateful democracy will die the death. We will now all sing the Social Unionist Hymn, 'Land of Union Jackshirts, Mother of the Flag'.

'What d'you think of it?' asked Eugenia, anxiously.

'It's a fine speech,' said Jasper, who had evidently got some beer up his nose and was choking into a handkerchief.

When Mr Wilkins saw it he said that it was very good but much too long for him to learn by heart.

'Oh! you must try,' said Eugenia. 'It would spoil a speech like that if you read it. Learn one sentence every day – you've got heaps of time.'

'I'll try,' said Mr Wilkins, good-naturedly.

'I'm hoping,' continued Eugenia, 'that you will join the Social Unionist party. You are asked to pay ninepence a month, the Union Jack shirt costs five shillings and the little emblem sixpence. When you have signed on you will be able to use the head-quarters as much as you like. I hope to arrange for instruction in boxing and other Social Unionist sports there soon, and we shall be having a social every Tuesday evening as well. So do join up.'

'Anything to please you, Miss Eugenia, but I'm afraid I don't know much about it at present. Wait a minute, though, is it against foreigners and the League of Nations, because if so I'll join with pleasure. Damned sewers.'

Mr Wilkins had spent several years tea-planting in Ceylon where 'sewer' is apparently a usual term of opprobrium.

'It is,' said Eugenia, earnestly. 'Some of us think of sterilizing all foreigners, you know, but I'm not sure our Captain would go quite as far as that.'

'That's the stuff to feed the troops! Well done! just what they need. I think Hitler's a splendid fellow too, although I'm not sure he doesn't carry things a shade far sometimes. I mean, shoot up the chaps as much as you like, but don't kill their wives at breakfast – eh?'

'When shooting is in progress,' said Eugenia, coldly, 'the woman's duty is to retire to her proper place, the bedroom. If she interferes in men's business she must put up with a man's fate.'

'There's something in what you say, by Jove; women are a damned sight too fond of poking their noses into things that are none of their business, these days specially. Look here, I'm joining up; what did you say I owe you?'

'Ninepence a month, the Union Jack shirt costs five shillings, and sixpence for the little emblem. You sign here – see?'

Jasper's embarrassment as pageant producer reached a climax when Poppy came to him and said, 'Look here, darling, Marge wants to know whether she can't be Queen Charlotte instead of Mrs Lace. Do say "Yes".'

'No, really, I don't think she can,' said Jasper, 'and anyway why does she want to be, all of a sudden like this?'

'Well, she didn't want me to tell you, but I suppose I shall have to. The fact is, you see, she's keen on Mr Wilkins, and so of course she quite naturally wants to drive in the coach with him.'

'Darling Miss Smith, you'll have to tell her to be sensible. Tell her she can make eyes at him on the platform as much as she likes (she had better take a lesson in amorous gestures from Mrs Lace), but I don't see how the whole works can be altered now.'

'Oh, dear! Oh, dear! Marge will be simply furious. She is used to getting her own way in life.'

'All I can say is that she must be furious for once. Why, it's as much as my place is worth to tell Mrs Lace she can't be Queen Charlotte – Noel would stop paying my expenses down here most likely, if I did, and you don't want me to go straight back to London, I suppose! No, my angel, I'm sorry but it's quite out of the question. Tell you what I will do though, if you like.'

'What's that?'

'I'll give you a good bite on the back of your neck.'

'No, thank you,' said Poppy, 'I'm a mass of bruises as it is.'

The question, however, was by no means dropped, Lady Marjorie herself coming to the charge, hotly supported by Eugenia.

'Is this to be a Great Social Unionist rally, or not?' the latter demanded furiously, 'because if it is, it stands to reason that we must keep the best parts for Union Jackshirts. Mrs Lace is not only not one of us, she is a well-known friend of Pacifists – in fact, it would never surprise me if she should turn out to be a Pacifist spy. How absurd then to insist that she shall be the one to drive along hailed by Social Union-ist cheers.'

'I dare say, but you should have thought of all this sooner,' said Jasper, with some irritation, 'before it was settled. Personally, I don't give a damn who plays which part, and I wish you were all at the bottom of the sea, anyway, but you might remember that wretched old Local Beauty is slaving herself to death over your dresses, and if she wants to take the part of the least attractive queen in history, I should have thought it would be a matter of ordinary decency to let her. In any case you must arrange it among yourselves, I absolutely refuse to make any such suggestion to her.'

'Oh, well, I see your point,' said Lady Marjorie, good-temperedly, 'I'll ask her myself at the committee meeting tomorrow.'

Mrs Lace, however, when approached was perfectly firm. She listened calmly while the suggestion was being made, and then said that it was too unlucky, but Queen Charlotte's dress was now finished, and could never be altered to fit Lady Marjorie, as there were no means of letting out the seams on the hips and round the waist. Marjorie, who had never been spoken to in such a way before, was more surprised than angry, and took her defeat with the greatest of good humour. Poppy and Eugenia were furious, and said afterwards that Mrs Lace was a spiteful cat, and Poppy said at the time to Mrs Lace that as she looked exactly like Queen Charlotte, she was quite right to keep the part. Unfortunately, owing to its target's total ignorance of English history, this Parthian shaft went wide of the mark.

Noel and Jasper, who seldom met these days, over a quiet glass at the Rose Revived, made a point of doing so now, and agreed together that women were impossible everywhere, except in what Eugenia had referred to as their proper place. Noel no longer took Mrs Lace's side on every subject; feeling quite certain, as he now did, of her great love for him, he was able to adopt a high-handed attitude towards her, and was by no means inclined to jeopardize all future relations with Eugenia Malmains on her account.

Mrs Lace, on her part, secure in the knowledge of her own romantic situation, felt that she could now alienate dukes' ex-fiancées and earls' granddaughters with the most perfect indifference. She carried her head in the air and permitted herself the luxury of being extremely disagreeable to everybody except Noel.

II

Meanwhile the two detectives continued to ply their lugubrious trade. They appeared to ignore the necessity for repose, and the inhabitants of the Jolly Roger were continually being startled by their appearance in the most unexpected places. They would jump out from dark corners like sinister Jack-in-the-Boxes, at all times of the day and night. It was most unnerving. Finally, Jasper made a heroic if unsuccessful attempt to win their confidence. He stood them drink after drink at the bar. Their heads proved to be of the ox-like variety; and although they unbent after the fourth whisky sufficiently to admit to their profession, and made after the seventh some startling disclosures as to the present tendencies of modern London society, human ingenuity and liberality could push them no further than this. The two things which Poppy was so anxious to find out, namely, whether Anthony St Julien himself was employing them or whether it was the mother of his débutante, and how much or how little they knew of her relationship with Jasper, remained locked in their own bosoms. The end of the matter was that the detectives were obliged to carry Jasper upstairs to bed, where he lay, fully clothed and staring at the electric light bulb until far on into the next day.

'Never mind,' he said to Poppy, when he had more or less recovered from the attack of alcoholic poisoning which ensued, 'I am on exceedingly good terms with them now, which is always something. The worst of it is that I rather think I told them about us being engaged. Would that matter, do you suppose?'

'I don't know,' said Poppy. 'I don't think it was very clever of you and anyway we're not.'

'Oh! aren't we? I thought we were?'

'Not at all,' said Poppy. 'You might bear in mind the fact that I have a perfectly good husband already, would you?'

'Perfectly good strikes me as an euphemism. Besides, it's quite obvious to any thinking man that you are heading for the divorce courts at present.'

'That's no reason for wanting to marry you,' said Poppy, 'and anyway I hope you always take very good care to come in through Marge's room. You do, now don't you, Jasper?'

'I do when I remember. That sort of thing is so awfully easy to forget.'

'I'd be very much obliged if you would bear it in mind all the same. After all, I've only got to hold out for long enough and Anthony St. Julien will be forced to let me divorce him. Then we shall be on clover.'

'Only so-so. Remember what awful times the innocent party has before the absolute, with the King's Proctor breathing down its neck every night. I often think one should look at every side of a question before settling upon a course of action. However, I see you are admitting our engagement; that's always something.'

'Indeed, I am not.'

'Now I have thought out a very good scheme whereby we might yet be able to raise some money to live on. We will go and see my grandfather, who is binned-up in an asylum near here. He may fall for you (it seems to run in the family), and come across with the goods. You never know.'

'If he's binned-up he won't have any goods to come across with, will he?' said Poppy.

'That's just where you're wrong, little Miss Know-all. You see, my grandfather is in a very special kind of bin, for lunatic peers only, and it has quite different rules from the ordinary sort. It was endowed by some rich old peeress in 1865 who was clearly insane herself; she had it built on the exact plans of the House of Lords, so that the boys should feel at home, and she made up the rules as she went along. I once got hold of a copy of them, feeling it might come in handy – here we are.' He pulled a bundle of typescript out of his pocket. 'I'll read you out the bits that matter,' he said. 'First of all there's a sort of preface, pointing out that madness is an infliction which can befall any one of us, from the most humble to the most noble, and that therefore it is quite possible even for peers of the realm to be attacked by this distressing malady. The old girl goes on to say that for too long it has been a disgraceful scandal, a blot on the name of England, that such quantities of these poor, good old men should, through no fault of their own, have been allowed to perish in the hateful and unrefined atmosphere of the common mad-house. This scandal apparently weighed on her mind to such a degree that she spent most of her time visiting the poor good old men and trying to ease their lot by reading to them, teaching them poker work and other useful and profitable occupations, and providing them, as far as the regulations of their bins permitted, with those little luxuries which do so much to make life worth living. "I feel," she says, "and our dear Queen has been gracious enough to approve of my sentiments on this subject, that the *most* one can do for gentlemen who have so *faithfully* served their Sovereign and their Country, but who through the inscrutable visitation of Providence have been rendered unable, not only to continue such service, but to enjoy any of the amenities of life, and worse yet are cut off from the society of their *loved* ones and of those of their fellow peers upon whom the infliction has *not yet* fallen, can never be too much." And so on and so forth. Now – are you listening, Miss Smith – here is the rule on which I build my hopes, Rule 6.

'"In order that these unhappy noblemen should be enabled to preserve that measure of self-respect which their birth should guarantee, but of which circumstances too often conspire to rob them, the inhabitants of Peersmont shall be entitled, under this foundation, to the full and entire control of one half of their incomes during life, and to the full and entire disposal, by testament, of one half of their fortune after death."

'That's quite plain, isn't it? You see she made up all these rules for the place and they were ratified by Act of Parliament. Now I happen to know that the old boy, my grandfather, is worth over a million altogether, and he is a complete miser, so it stands to reason that if he has been controlling, say £25,000 a year for the thirty years that he has spent at Peersmont, he must now be worth a tidy penny. On the other hand, it is like squeezing blood out of a stone to get any of it. I know my poor mother has been going to see him for years and has never managed to extract a penny. Uncle Bradenham is a miser too, it's a family trait.'

'Doesn't sound all that hopeful,' said Poppy.

'It's pretty hopeless I can tell you, that's why I've never bothered to go and see the old boy before. All the same, there can be no harm in trying, and it would be quite funny to see over Peersmont. Lady Chalford keeps on offering to lend me her car whenever I want it, so I vote we go over there one day this week and try our luck, eh?'

'K.O.,' said Poppy indifferently.

Jasper went to see Lady Chalford about the pageant, as indeed he did most days, and asked whether he could borrow the car. They were on very good terms; she thought him a delightful young man, and made no secret of her wish that he should ally himself to her family by marrying Eugenia; Jasper, on his side, was getting very much attached to the old lady.

'By all means,' she said, 'I shall be enchanted to lend you the car. Yes, take Poppy with you; it will do poor Driburgh good to see her pretty face. Now which day had you thought of going? Tomorrow? Very well then, I shall tell the gardener that he is to pick a really first-class bunch of grapes and some peaches for you to give dear Driburgh from me with very many messages. I shall be very anxious to have an account of how you find him.'

Jasper was pleased to hear this. First-class grapes and peaches were a long-felt want at the Jolly Roger, where the strawberries were over and the raspberries were becoming decidedly squashy.

'Should he seem to be more or less himself,' Lady Chalford continued, little suspecting that such black thoughts lurked in the mind of her young friend, 'my dear husband and I would be most happy to receive him here some time. Now I wonder, for instance, if the curator would permit him to come over to see the pageant. Anyhow, I leave it in your hands, Mr Aspect, to do as you think best.'

Lady Chalford then spoke of the pageant. 'You have all been most kind. I am more grateful to you than I can say for relieving me of any trouble in this matter. It would have been far beyond my powers to organize a thing of this sort, living as I have for so long in seclusion. That dear little woman, Mrs Lace now – so clever of you to find her. She tells me that she knows all the neighbours for miles around. I have asked her to revise my list so that we can send out the invitations. My husband's agent will then look through it for me and tell me all about the people, so that I can be quite sure that I shall ask nobody who it would be unsuitable for my little Eugenia to meet. One cannot be too careful, of course. Mrs Lace herself is, he tells me, the daughter of a rural dean, and Lace I know to be a much-respected name in these parts; the family has lived at Comberry for a hundred years or more and Major Lace is a lay rector. I am perfectly contented for Eugenia to make friends with them, quite suitable people. Now, tell me, when is dear Poppy's husband expected down here?'

12

Poppy and Jasper bowled across the sixteen odd miles of rural England which lay between Chalford and Peersmont in an ancient maroon-coloured Rolls-Royce, the one concession made by Lord and Lady Chalford to the age of progress. Instead of being carried along in an almost recumbent position, seeing nothing except gleaming paint-work, as in modern cars, they sat bolt upright and enjoyed a full view of the summer landscape. The inside of the car smelt rather musty and the upholstery was hidden under holland covers.

The countryside looked extremely beautiful, covered as it was with alternate acres of golden corn, dark-green woods and lemon-coloured stubble dotted with stooks of corn. The heat was intense. Poppy said how sad it made her feel when she thought that in a very few years' time these lovely lonely stretches would probably be covered with mean little jerry-built houses.

'Think of Sussex,' she said with a shiver, 'how agreeable it would be if England could become much poorer, smaller, inconspicuous among nations and civilized once more.'

'Becoming poorer won't necessarily make her more civilized,' said Jasper. 'Civilization is dependent on one economic factor and that is extreme inequalities of wealth. The inevitable advent of Socialism, whether national or international, will be the fatal blow to what is left of our civilization.'

'If that is your view I am surprised that you should have joined Eugenia's party, which is obviously a form of national Socialism, isn't it?'

'I prefer national Socialism to the other sort, it is so much more romantic. Besides, I am inclined to think that the Western civilization we know needs putting out of its agony as soon as possible. It is old and tired, the dark ages are practically upon us anyhow, and I should prefer that they march in with trumpet and flag than that they should creep upon us to the tap of the typewriter. I am at heart, I suppose, a Nihilist.'

'I don't know what that is,' said Poppy.

'No! But then you are a girl with a very limited outlook, aren't you?'

'I'm not.'

'Oh! yes, you are. Like most women you only care about personalities, things don't interest you.'

'That's simply not true. I'm fearfully interested in things – I absolutely long for a sable coat.'

'Don't be flippant, it irritates me.'

'Well, it's a fact,' said Poppy, defiantly, 'and I should be quite happy for ever if I had one.'

'Really! women are extraordinary.'

'All the same darling, you do love me, don't you?'

'I'm bound to say I do. But I should love you a great deal more if you were my intellectual equal.'

'As I'm always telling you – you ought to marry Marge. She speaks four languages.'

'As I'm always telling you, there's nothing would suit me better, but you're so idle, you never take any kind of steps to arrange it for me.'

'Too late now, she's nuts about Mr Wilkins – simply nuts. You can't imagine how she dotes on that man.'

'More than you dote on me?'

'Much more. He's literally the only chap she has ever been keen on you see, so she thinks him perfect. She has nothing else to compare him with.'

'I'm bound to say it has made a great difference to her. She is quite civil to me now instead of biting my head off whenever I speak as she did at first. Love is an exceedingly remarkable thing, in some ways. So what is she going to do about it?'

'Well, I believe she has written to Osborne to tell him definitely that their engagement is off – she was keeping him on a string before, like Nellie Bly and the fly you know. I say, look at that little white house. I wouldn't mind living there, would you?'

'And what are her intentions towards Mr Wilkins?'

'Strictly honourable. She's decided to wait a fortnight, and then propose to him if he hasn't done anything about it by then. I'm sure he won't have, he's obviously a man of no imagination or initiative.'

'Of course she's an exceedingly horizontal girl,' said Jasper in a contemplative voice. 'All the same, I should say that Mr Wilkins is a lucky chap.'

'Oh! he is indeed.'

'What's she worth?'

'She's fabulously rich. Her father left something like three million, I believe.'

'Makes me sick,' said Jasper, 'you see that definitely shows I must be a Nihilist, otherwise why should I be engaged to the only poor girl in the parish.'

'You're not engaged. And there's still Eugenia,' said Poppy.

'Eugenia's a fine girl, but it's you I'm in love with, darling Miss Smith.'

'Good,' said Poppy, bouncing over to his side of the car and putting her arm round his waist. 'Hullo! there's something hard and bulging in your pocket – what is it?'

'I had an idea that, as we are unlikely to get anything out of my old man, it might be a good plan to translate this visit into terms of hard cash at the earliest opportunity. There's a chap on the *Evening Banner* who will give me £50 for a photograph of grandfather – you see they've only got one of him taken seventy years ago in his Fauntleroys and as he's bound to die soon they'll be needing a more recent one for the obituary. So I brought this "Kodak" along (they are very strictly forbidden in Peersmont). I found it in Mrs Lace's house the first time I went there and thought it might come in handy.'

When they arrived at Peersmont village they stopped at a public-house and had what Poppy described afterwards as a fairly delicious but really rather disgusting lunch, over which they sat for such an immoderate length of time that it was already past four o'clock when they set forth, again in the Rolls-Royce, for the asylum. They drove through a grim Victorian medieval gateway flanked on either side by huge black walls, on the top of which were a double row of revolving spikes. Inside, the grounds were dank with conifers, in the midst of which there suddenly appeared the towers and spires of the Houses of Parliament, looking strangely uncomfortable in their rustic setting. The chauffeur drew up without any hesitation at the Peers' entrance, when the door of the car was immediately flung open by a policeman, who asked their business.

'The Duke of Driburgh?' said Jasper casually.

'I believe His Grace is in the House at present,' replied the policeman, 'would you kindly step this way and I will tell the curator that you are here. What name, please?'

He led them across the courtyard towards what should have been the House of Commons but which was, it appeared, the residential part of the asylum. The curator sat in a little Gothic room tremendously decorated with wood carvings, and received them warmly. He was a charming young man.

'The Duke of Driburgh?' he said, when Jasper had explained who he was. 'Splendid! The duke will be most awfully pleased to see you, I know. But look here, the House is sitting at the moment, can you wait until it rises? It won't be more than another half-hour at the outside, there is very little business today. In fact I would send for him at once except that he happens to be deputizing for our Lord Chancellor, Lord Rousham, who is on the sick-list again – no, nothing at all serious I am glad to say. He has just nipped up to the top of a big elm tree and is building himself a nest there. We don't stop him nowadays, one is never supposed to stop them doing harmless things of that sort. He won't catch a chill in this warm weather and the others like to watch how the nest is getting along. Rather fun for them really.'

'How interesting,' said Jasper. 'And has my grandfather any little hobbies of that sort?'

'Nothing in the least spectacular. He is fond of building and reads a great deal of Rider Haggard. A few bricks and a bucket of white paint keep him happy for hours, he thinks the paint is mortar you see. But he has never had an outburst since he came here, he is very easy from my point of view.'

'What was he shut up for?' said Jasper, 'I have often wondered, but it happened years before I was born, and has been kept very dark in the family ever since.'

'I'm not absolutely certain myself – I could look it up in the records for you though. Let me see' – he opened a drawer and took out of it a card-index – 'A.B.C.D. Driburgh. Here we are. Oh, yes, of course, I remember now. He was shooting over his estate and something annoyed him – the birds were going in the wrong direction or something like that. Anyway the result was that he deliberately shot a gamekeeper and three beaters straight off, two left-and-rights. Curious little nerve storm, he always seems quite sane here. A very leading figure in the political line, you know.'

'And what are his political opinions?' asked Poppy with a slight giggle, which was hastily checked as the curator gave her a severe look. She gathered that jokes about the inmates and their eccentricities were not much encouraged.

'The duke is an out-and-out Tory and anti-White Paper man.'

'But I imagine they are all that?' said Jasper.

'My dear sir, you are very much mistaken. We have comparatively few reactionary peers, the majority here are moderate Baldwinites; among the Liberals there are some extremely advanced thinkers, and besides that we can boast no fewer than four Communists and two Scottish Nationalists.'

An electric bell now rang twice on the curator's table.

'House up,' he said, 'even sooner than I had expected. Come along with me will you and I'll find the duke for you. By the way, that object in your pocket – it's not a camera, is it?'

'No indeed,' said Jasper, 'I am more than a little deaf and it is an instrument to assist my hearing.'

The curator blushed. 'I am so sorry,' he said. 'I was obliged to ask you, as cameras are most strictly forbidden here.'

'Naturally,' said Jasper.

The curator now led them out on to the terrace which, like its prototype at Westminster, overhung a sheet of water and was covered with dainty tea-tables. Trooping on to it from another entrance was a throng of funereal-looking and for the most part ancient gentlemen. As they emerged some of them formed little groups animated with earnest conversation, while others made straight for the tea-tables, loudly ordering vanilla ices, crumpets, raspberry jam or sausages and mash.

'Ah! Duke,' said the curator. Breaking into one of the groups he buttonholed a tall, rather paunchy but handsome old man and conducted him towards the place where Jasper and Poppy stood waiting. 'Here are two visitors to see you, your grandson Mr Aspect, and Mrs St Julien.'

'My boy,' said the duke, in tones of exaggerated emotion. His watery eyes brimmed over and a large tear splashed the pavement. He took hold of Jasper's arm in two places and shook it up and down with vigour. 'My boy. Very good of you to come and see your old grandfather. Not many of my descendants can be bothered to these days.'

The curator slipped away.

The duke then greeted Poppy with a courtly bow and conducted them both to an adjacent table. When they were seated Jasper said, 'My *fiancée*,' indicating Poppy.

'Yes, yes, I suppose so,' said the duke. 'Charming little lady. I always used to think, in my younger days, that it takes a lot to beat a pretty widow, and you are a very pretty widow my dear, if I may be permitted to say so.' He pressed his foot gently on Poppy's underneath the table. She gave him an inviting smile, whereupon he proceeded to hold her hand as well. 'And when are you going to be married may I ask – lucky fella,' he said, turning towards Jasper, but firmly retaining Poppy's hand.

'That's just what we wanted to discuss with you sir,' said Jasper, 'because we would do nothing without your approval naturally. As soon as Mrs St Julien consented to become my wife I said we must come over and ask for your blessing. We are staying at Chalford you see.'

'Upon my soul, that was very polite and considerate of you, young man,' cried the duke heartily. 'Not one of my own children ever bothered about a thing like that, I'm most extremely touched. Charming little lady too, charming. So what are you up to these days, Jasper my boy – soldier, sailor, candle-stick maker, or what, eh?'

'Well, at the moment I'm out of work,' said Jasper. 'A gentleman of leisure you might say.' He was not very sure how this news would be received. Other elderly persons of his acquaintance were always trying to chivvy him into jobs of extraordinary uncongeniality. He need have had no qualms, the duke was delighted.

'That's damned good news, by Jove,' he said, 'damned good. Why I do believe you're the only one of my grandsons who is not in trade. I hate trade, it's not suitable for a gentleman. Gentlemen, my grandsons, should have leisure and plenty of it, I hate all this hurrying about, getting up early in the morning to sell motor cars and such nonsense. Bradenham's sons all do it, most inconsiderate of them, in my opinion. It lets down the traditions of a fine old family. Gentlemen should go into politics, that's their duty – to govern the country, it's the only thing they're fit for anyway.'

'What are your politics, my boy?'

'I'm an out-and-out anti-White Paper Tory,' said Jasper advisedly.

'Splendid. I can see that we shall get on famously. And you don't stand for Parliament?'

'I can't afford to,' said Jasper, who was longing to bring the conversation round to the subject of money.

'Quite right. Nobody can afford to get mixed up with that rabble in the Commons, it's the greatest mistake, believe me. If you wait long enough they're bound to give you a peerage, always do in the end, and then you'll be able to come here. This is the only legislative assembly that's worth two pins these days, I assure you.'

There was a silence, while Jasper racked his brains to think of the most pleasing terms in which a request for money could be couched. The duke, however, relieved him of the necessity by saying, 'Only wish I could do something for you, my boy, pay off your debts or make you an allowance, but there it is – I hope you understand the situation. I expect I am poorer than you are, if anything.'

Jasper looked at Poppy and raised his eyes to heaven.

'We landowners,' continued the duke, 'are very hard hit in these days. Ever since finance bills have been taken out of our hands, in the Lords, the country has gone from bad to worse. We have had one Socialist government after another, I don't know which are more Socialistic, the Labour people or these milk-and-water White-Paper, lily-livered, black-hearted, so-called Conservatives. It's a scandal. They take half your income away before you have a chance of getting at it, and the other half shortly afterwards. Hard times for millionaires these are, I can tell you. Then you know my expenses here' (he lowered his voice) 'are very heavy – very. Why, a pot of tea costs sixpence and I must say I do like to have a crumpet with it some-times – fourpence! Rank profiteering of course. However, tell you what I'll do, my boy. I'll send up to my bank and find out if I haven't got some little trinket there that this charming lady would accept as a wedding present.'

'Oh! thank you so much, you are kind,' said Poppy sweetly. Jasper, envisaging a seed-pearl locket, merely scowled.

At this moment a slight commotion broke out the other side of the terrace. Two liveried attendants sprang forward and led away between them a young man of untidy appearance who was gesticulating wildly. The other peers seemed totally uninterested by this occurrence.

'That's Gunnersbury,' said the duke, 'dreadful fellow. A shocking Socialist you know.'

'Poor thing, he seems to be in a great stew,' said Poppy.

'All the Labour peers are very much upset at the moment, it's about a bill of theirs we flung out last week. They called it the Toll of the Roads or some such nonsense and they kept us up until four o'clock one morning talking the most utter gibberish you can possibly imagine. It appears that every year a few thousand totally unimportant persons are killed on the roads, and that lunatic Gunnersbury, sup-ported by some squeamish asses on the Labour benches, brought in a bill to abolish all motor transport. These Socialists put a perfectly exaggerated value on human life, you know. Ridiculous. As I said in my speech, what on earth does it matter if a few people are killed, we're not at war are we? We don't need 'em for cannon fodder? Then what earthly good do they do to anybody? Kill 'em on the roads by all means, they come off the unemployment figures and nobody is likely to be any the wiser.'

'I see your point,' said Jasper. 'So I suppose you had a fairly heated debate?'

'Very heated indeed. However, we Tories won the day – we always do, of course, there's some sense talked in this place let me tell you. All the same, these Labour fellows are a perfect curse, forever bringing in some ludicrous bill or other, and then making the dickens of a fuss because they are in the minority here. Damned good thing for the country if they are, I should say. That blasted fool Lord Williams now, red-hot Communist if you please, brought in a bill the other day to try and substitute dandelions for strawberry leaves on our coronets and rabbit skins for ermine on our robes. Anybody would think the poor chap wasn't quite right in the head, the way he goes on.'

The duke then took them for a short stroll in the park, which was dank and gloomy. During the course of it, however, Jasper managed to obtain several promising snapshots of his grandfather as well as an interesting study of Lord Rousham, who, peeping over the edge of his nest as they passed, began to pelt them with orange-peel, chattering wildly to himself.

'Wonderful fellow, Rousham,' said the duke, hardly bothering even to look up, 'he can turn his hand to anything, you know. That's a first-class nest he has made. They tell me it is entirely lined with pieces of the India Report. Of course we miss him in the House just now, but I bet you he is doing good work up there all the same.'

Presently they were joined by the curator, who had come to inform Jasper that all visitors must be outside the park by six o'clock.

'That'll be in ten minutes' time,' he said. 'Why don't you come again and take the duke out? We always allow it in the case of the moderate ones. There is an excellent tuckshop in the village and they love to go there, it makes a nice change for them.'

'I'll do that one day,' said Jasper. 'I had thought of taking him over to see Lady Chalford as I know she would be pleased. And by the way, there is to be a garden party and pageant at Chalford House next Wednesday week, and she asked me to find out whether you would care to come over for it, and bring any of the peers with you?'

The curator accepted this invitation with pleasure, and so, when it was put to him, did the Duke of Driburgh. After this, Poppy and Jasper, feeling more exhausted than if they had spent the day with a small boy at his private school, mounted their Rolls-Royce and drove away.

13

The artistic young men of Rackenbridge found themselves a good deal inconvenienced by Mrs Lace's preoccupation in her new love affair. Their hearts were perhaps less affected than their stomachs, the emotions of those young men had never been much shaken by any petticoat, but up to now they had always been able to count on Comberry Manor and its chatelaine for such agreeable amenities as free meals and pocket-money during the summer. This year a gloomy change had come about. The colony had already been at Rackenbridge for over a month, but as yet not one single picture, photograph, piece of pottery or hand-woven linen had been commissioned by their patroness, nor had she introduced to the studios, as she usually did, any gullible visitors. Almost worse than this trade depression was the fact that practically no invitations to meals at Comberry were now being issued. The artistic young men were getting tired of scrambled eggs and sardines eaten off studio floors, they longed to sit up to a table and attack a joint.

This state of affairs was rightly laid at Noel's door. As well as providing a complete distraction from the ordinary routine of her life he had shaken Mrs Lace in the belief that her friends were geniuses. He assured her that in London they were perfectly unknown, and his attitude towards their work, too, was distressing. For instance, after glancing at Mr Forderen's series of photographs entitled 'Anne-Marie in some of her exquisite moods' which, when they were first taken a year before had caused the greatest enthusiasm in Rackenbridge, he had remarked quite carelessly that she ought to have her photograph taken by some proper photographer.

'Don't you see,' Anne-Marie had said, 'that these pictures represent, not me but my moods, this one, for instance, "pensive by firelight", don't you think it rather striking?'

'No I don't,' said Noel, whose own mood that day was not of the sunniest. 'It is nothing but an amateurish snapshot of you looking affected. Frankly, I see no merit in any of them whatever, and as I said before, all those young aesthetes at Rackenbridge strike me as being fearfully 1923, and bogus at that.'

As a result of this conversation the series was removed from the walls of Anne-Marie's drawing-room, from whence it had long revolted Major Lace, and consigned to those of a downstairs lavatory. Here it was duly observed by poor Mr Forderen on the occasion of the cocktail party.

Under the stress of these circumstances Rackenbridge abandoned the petty jealousies which usually marred its peace, and decided with unanimity upon a course of action. Mr Leader, who, up till now had been the envied but acknowledged favourite at Comberry Manor, was deputized to woo Mrs Lace away from her Philistine lover or, if this should not prove feasible, to point out at any rate that her old friends were entitled to some small part of her time and attention. To this end Mr Leader sent a little note accompanied by an offering of honey in a handmade jar, in which he begged Mrs Lace to keep a midnight assignation with him at a spot well known to them both, a little green knoll surmounted by a giant oak tree. He knew his Anne-Marie well enough to be convinced that whereas she might easily refuse to see him alone if he called in the ordinary way at six o'clock, the prospect of tearful scenes by moonlight would be beyond her powers to resist. Sure enough, at the very stroke of twelve o'clock she crept from her conjugal bed, leaving Major Lace to the company of his own tremendous snores which, as she well knew, nothing short of an earthquake could disturb. Throwing a chiffon wrap over her chiffon nightdress she floated away to join Mr Leader at his oak tree.

As she approached he took a graceful step forward, throwing out both his hands and cried, 'Beautiful Swan!' hoping thus to evoke romantic memories of a time when he and she were known in Rackenbridge as 'Leader and the Swan'. 'You look more lovely than I have ever seen you tonight. Are you a denizen of this earth, you wonderful creature, or do you come to us from another sphere!'

Anne-Marie, arranging herself upon the greensward, assumed a classical pose and gazed up at him with sombre eyes.

'I have com,' she said, her foreign accent more than usually stressed. 'It was dangerrous and de*ef* feecult, but I have com. What ees it that you want – *que veux-tu mon ami?*'

'Everything,' said Mr Leader, moodily, 'or nothing.'

Anne-Marie leant back and waited for the passionate outburst which she hoped was coming; she was not disappointed. Mr Leader, assuming the attitude which had proved so successful when he as Hamlet and she as Ophelia had taken Rackenbridge by storm two years previously, began to accuse her of unfaithfulness, not to individuals, but to the deathless cause of Art. He told her that she alone could provide inspiration to those who loved her so earnestly, that no good work had been done at Rackenbridge that year, or could ever be done again until she should consent to shine like a star in their midst once more. As individuals they could bear her loss even if it killed them, as artists it was their duty to recall her to hers. Mr Leader spoke in this strain for some time, during which Anne-Marie wept and enjoyed it all very much, and particularly wished that Noel could have heard. When at last she had an opportunity to speak she said that those to whom she meant so much must make a tremendous effort to understand her now. She explained that she was probably one of the world's great lovers, and her love for Noel would be accounted in days to come as one of history's greatest loves.

'You must remember,' she said, gazing at the moon which hung over them like a large melon, 'that love, if it is to be worth while, is always tragic, always demands immense sacrifice. Otherwise it is of no value. I will sacrifice everything to it ruthlessly: my husband, my children, my reputation, even all of you my friends, you and your wonderful work must go to feed the flames which light its altar. *Je n'en peux rien, que voulez-vous. C'est plus fort que la mort.*'

'How wonderful,' said Mr Leader, gloomily contrasting in his mind scrambled eggs and sardines with the very satisfying quality of Mrs Lace's food; 'but, dear Anne-Marie, can he be worthy of your exquisite intellect? We all greatly fear that he is not.'

'That may be so,' she said, complacently, 'but that is neither here nor there. What is intellect, compared with passion? I tell you that I love him, he occupies my time, my thoughts, my very soul – there is no room in my life for anybody else at the moment. When he is gone, as go he must, I may come back to all of you, an empty hollow husk; life will hold no more for me, but I shall at least have loved and made the great sacrifice, and I shall struggle on to the end, living for my memories.'

Her voice trailed away into a sob. Mr Leader, in the face of so much fortitude, and so much grief, found no words with which to suggest that a few free meals and one or two of the usual small commissions would be a great boon to himself, and his companions. He assured Anne-Marie that when her hour of sorrow should come she would find loving friends at Rackenbridge ready and anxious to pour balm into her wounds. Before he could enlarge upon this theme, Anne-Marie, whose trailing chiffon afforded but little warmth, and who was blue with cold, was floating back to that excellent circulation which, in her eyes, constituted Major Lace's chief virtue as a husband. Mr Leader sadly set forth on the long tramp to Rackenbridge.

One o'clock in the morning. The village of Chalford was sleeping soundly when a flickering light appeared in the sky and presently became a steady crimson glow. A reflection of it shone into Jasper's room, so he got up, very sleepy, and went out on to the green, looking to see where it could come from. In doing so he ran into Mr Leader, who was walking quickly towards Rackenbridge.

'Oh, hullo!' said Jasper, 'what is it, a house or a haystack?'

Mr Leader merely gave him a nasty look and hurried away.

Jasper, turning a corner of the village street, saw that Eugenia's Social Unionist head-quarters were a mass of flames. He felt sorry for Eugenia, he knew that she would be very much upset by this disaster. As it was a pretty sight, and he now felt fairly wide awake, he stayed to watch it blaze. Presently the others appeared, having been woken up by the smell of burning.

'Jolly little bonfire, isn't it?' said Jasper, putting his arm round Poppy's waist. 'Nothing we can do would be of any use, luckily. Hullo! here are the Comrades, rotten luck for them I must say.'

The Comrades marched up in formation, but seeing that no human effort would avail to extinguish that furnace, they indulged in a little community singing to keep up their spirits in the face of this setback to their cause.

Lady Marjorie, by the light of the flames, observed Mr Wilkins and with a little cry of excitement she streaked off in his direction.

'Wonderful, what love will do for a girl,' observed Jasper. 'I can't think when she finds time to grease her face nowadays; I suppose it will seize up soon, like a motor car. Hullo! here come the Laces to see the fun – good-bye, Noel. What did I say? This village is a perfect hotbed of romance, isn't it, darling Miss Smith?' He kissed her ear. 'Oh, God! there are the detectives again; come on, let's bunk shall we? I'm sick of the sight of them.'

'Yes, in a way,' said Poppy. 'The only thing is, if they are still here it must mean that they haven't got any evidence on us.'

'I can't imagine why you don't hand out the dope and let the old boy divorce you if he wants to. It would save a lot of trouble.'

'Feminine caution, I suppose,' said Poppy. She was a good deal in love with Jasper, but not sure that she wanted to marry him. Certain aspects of his nature seemed far from satisfactory.

'He is such a fearful pickpocket, you know,' she said, in a burst of confidence to Marjorie. 'I can't leave my bag lying about for a moment.'

'Goodness knows how much he's had out of mine,' said Marjorie.

'Funny how customs have changed,' said Poppy. 'I'm sure in our mothers' day ladies didn't fall in love with thieves.'

Early next morning, Eugenia, on Vivian Jackson, came thundering down to the village at a hard gallop. Having inspected the still smouldering ruins of her head-quarters, she went round to the Jolly Roger, where she found Jasper and Noel eating breakfast in their pyjamas.

'It is a nuisance,' was all she said, but Jasper thought she had been crying. He plied her with sausages and she became more cheerful.

'Of course, it must be the work of Pacifists,' she said, with her mouth full, 'and you may be quite sure that I am going to sift this affair thoroughly. Wait until I have run them to earth, the brutal yellows financed by Jews too, no doubt.'

'Talking of Pacifists,' said Jasper, suddenly, 'whom do you think I saw last night hurrying away from your head-quarters just after the fire must have started? Dear little Mr Leader. He was behaving in a highly suspicious manner, I thought.'

Eugenia made that gesture which usually accompanies a snapping of the fingers. It was one she was very fond of, but as her hands were soft and babyish she seldom achieved a satisfactory crack. On this occasion it was completely absent.

'Mr Leader,' she cried, 'how mad of me, I had forgotten all about him. Of course, when we have a nest of filthy yellows in our midst, we need look no further afield. Very well, I shall act immediately.'

'What are you going to do?'

'I will send the Comrades to fetch him along,' said Eugenia. 'Terrible shall be the fate of the enemies of Social Unionism. In fact, I think I will arrange for the Comrades to seize him this very afternoon, while he is working in his *studio*.' (She pronounced the word with infinite contempt.) 'He is probably laughing up his sleeve by now, thinking that nobody will ever find out who is the author of that foul crime. They can bind and gag him, and bring him to a quiet place I know of in Chalford Park, where I will court-martial him at the drumhead.'

'And if he is found guilty?'

'If,' cried Eugenia, tossing her head, 'there is no "if". He *shall* be found guilty and Oh, boy! will I have him beaten up? Terrible shall be the fate –'

Jasper, however, with some difficulty restrained her from putting such extreme proposals into practice. He explained that the time was not yet ripe for a blood-bath in Chalford, that such a proceeding would do infinite harm to her cause and that if she carried it out she would get herself into serious trouble with the Comrades at the London head-quarters. Those men of iron, he hinted, might easily degrade her from her position of patrol leader and remove her little emblem if she drew down upon them the unwelcome publicity that would follow such a step. It was this last argument which persuaded Eugenia to leave the whole matter in Jasper's hands.

'If he really did it, I think perhaps some small punishment is coming to him,' said Jasper, 'but it is absolutely essential that we should hear what he has to say for himself.'

'That's why we must have a trial,' said Eugenia, 'and you can't have a trial unless he is gagged and bound first. He is far too cunning and cowardly to put his head into the lion's den of his own accord.'

'We must consider it carefully,' said Jasper, 'there are probably ways and means.'

In the end, Lady Marjorie, whose passion for Mr Wilkins had brought her down from her high horse, and revealed her as a most surprisingly good-natured creature, allowed herself to be used as a decoy. She sent a note to Mrs Lace asking her to tea at the Jolly Roger. 'We hope *so* much that you will be able to come, Yours sincerely, Marjorie Merrith. P.S. We wanted to invite also that charming Mr Leader whom we met at your cocktail party, but cannot find out where he lives. Could you very kindly give him the message for us?'

'Very good indeed,' said Jasper, when this composition was submitted to him, 'I particularly like the use of the royal "We".'

Anne-Marie was pleased with her invitation. It was the first occasion on which she had been asked, except by Noel, to anything which was unconnected with the pageant, and privately she thought it was high time. Also she was pleased that Mr Leader had been included, and not her dreary husband. She had wished for some time that the Jolly Roger should make overtures to Rackenbridge. It would be so nice, she thought, if their inhabitants were to be merged into one Society for the Admiration of Mrs Lace. Besides, truth to tell, Noel's demeanour during the last few days had been slightly disquieting – he had seemed preoccupied and lacking in ardour. It would be an excellent stimulant for him to catch a glimpse of Mr Leader's breaking heart.

In fact, Noel was worrying. It was not his nature to live as Jasper did, from one day to another, picking up by fair means or foul enough cash for the needs of the moment and being dragged out of the bankruptcy courts about once every three years by protesting relations. He had always admired Jasper for this mode of life, envying the ease with which he could get something for nothing, and his eternal serenity, but was quite unable, at the last resort, to imitate him. His mother was a Scotchwoman and he, although hardly burdened with moral scruples, had inherited from her a care for the future. How often now did he curse himself for letting Jasper know of his legacy. This mad idea of pursuing unknown heiresses (he forgot that it had originated, in a moment of exaltation, from himself), would never have come to anything but for Jasper. When the first glow of excitement had died down he would have taken a cheap little holiday, perhaps in Spain, and then have returned to his job, happy in the extra security afforded him by the possession of a small capital. In time he would doubtless have achieved a partnership in his firm.

Under these circumstances it was specially irritating to observe that Jasper pursued, with great cheerfulness, his usual policy of living in the present. To see that jolly face one might suppose that there was no such thing as a day after tomorrow.

Noel, for his part, enjoyed nothing, not even his affair with Anne-Marie; he was tormented by the thought that his aunt's legacy was being frittered away with nothing to show for it, never considering that a happy time might be set off against the more material advantages which money can secure. He sent for his pass-book, and was overwhelmed with misery and self-reproach when he found that in one way and another four hundred pounds of his money had disappeared.

Nobody could fail to notice the gloom which enveloped him after this discovery and all put different constructions upon it. Jasper thought he had probably been gambling on the Stock Exchange; Poppy, that Mrs Lace was being tough to him; and Eugenia, that he had written an article for *The Union Jack* which had been turned down. This continually happened to her.

Mrs Lace begged in vain for his confidence. It was obvious in her mind that he must have received ill news from his own country, perhaps the regiments were proving unexpectedly loyal to the usurper, or could it be that Communism presented a greater menace than had at first been feared. She spent much of her time poring over her little girl's map of Europe and hazarding many a guess, but always ended up in a state of mystification. She was sadly deficient in general knowledge and was wont to declare that politics, and especially foreign politics were dreadfully boring compared to art and literature. Her reading of the newspapers was confined to the gossip columns, news about film stars, and such easily assimilated items of information as the birth in Dumfries-shire of a two-headed blackbird.

Noel was most unhelpful. If she threw out some hint such as 'I often think that it would be both interesting and enjoyable to visit the Balkans,' he would merely say, 'What an extraordinary idea, darling. It's a frightfully expensive journey, and nothing to do when you get there. I should have thought the South of France was more your dish.' At first, Mrs Lace felt herself to have been insulted by this remark; did he then suppose her to be a mere foolish butterfly searching for pleasure? Later on, however, having pondered over his words, she read another meaning into them. Perhaps, although unable to take his beloved with him to his own kingdom, he had it in mind to install her in some gorgeous villa on the Riviera, where he could visit her when on holiday. She felt that an arrangement of this description would suit her very well, as she was partial both to dagoes and sunbathing. She wondered whether it would be too much to ask for a flat in Paris as well.

Mrs Lace had some difficulty in luring Mr Leader to the Jolly Roger. He felt instinctively that these new people who had come to upset the whole summer would be unlikely to accept him at his own valuation and he very much objected to the company of anybody who might prove to be his intellectual superior. In the end, Mrs Lace managed to persuade him that he had better come with her by hinting that he might be commissioned to design dresses for the pageant, which surely would not go against his conscience so long as he was well paid. He saw the force of this argument, and besides, it was not really in his nature to resist free food.

When they arrived at the Jolly Roger they found the party already sitting round a tea-table in the garden. It consisted of Marjorie, Poppy, Eugenia, Jasper and Mr Wilkins. Noel was not there, having been obliged to go to London for the day. Mrs Lace was annoyed by his absence but concealing the fact she sat down beside Jasper. There was no chair for poor Mr Leader, who was obliged to fetch one for himself out of the parlour. Poppy and Lady Marjorie then made him sit between them, and asked him, with every demonstration of friendliness, why he and his friends had not undertaken an episode in the pageant.

'Our political principles forbid,' said Mr Leader. 'Thank you, I like it very weak, with no milk or sugar, also we are busy men.'

'So busy,' said Eugenia, coming straight to the charge, 'that you still haven't been to see the inside of our Social Unionist head-quarters.'

'Not yet,' said Mr Leader.

'Did you know that they have been burnt down?' she inquired, staring at him with eyes like enormous blue headlamps.

'Have they really? I say, bad luck.'

'Thank you, we don't want your sympathy, we want to know what you were doing the night before last?'

Mrs Lace looked anxiously at Mr Leader.

'Really, I have no idea at all. What were you doing yourself?'

'Don't be impertinent,' said Eugenia, stiffly. 'It is curious, is it not, that you, a well-known Pacifist, should have been observed retreating guiltily from the scene of incendiarism shortly after the fire began. How do you explain this coincidence?'

Mr Leader silently waited for Anne-Marie to provide his alibi. Anne-Marie did no such thing. She was far from anxious that Noel on the one hand, or Major Lace on the other, should know of her midnight rendezvous. If it were to be disclosed at this table, Noel would certainly hear it from Jasper, and Major Lace from Mr Wilkins. She could not take the risk.

'Answer,' said Eugenia, sternly, 'and answer truthfully. Lies shall not avail you here.'

Mrs Lace now turned to Jasper, and said, 'How absurd. That child's passion for play-acting is great fun of course, but doesn't it make her behave in rather a baby-ish way sometimes?'

'If Eugenia suspects a chap of burning down her head-quarters,' said Jasper, 'I think it is only fair to them both that he should be questioned and given a chance to clear himself. After all, he was behaving rather suspiciously that night. What have you to say, Leader?'

Mr Leader held his peace.

'As I thought,' remarked Eugenia, 'Van der Lubbe, I always felt that here was no Dimitroff.'

At this insult Mr Leader got up and left the party.

Mrs Lace, if she felt inclined to follow her friend, who after all had stood by her with some courage, made no move to do so. She must, whatever the cost, keep on good terms with Eugenia until the Grand Social Unionist rally, pageant and garden party was over. Not for any loyalty was she going to sacrifice her chance of riding in that coach.

She now chattered gaily about many things, supplementing her remarks with a wealth of gestures, and presently asked Jasper why that naughty Noel had gone to London so suddenly.

'That is a state secret,' said Jasper.

She looked at him significantly, and then, lowering her voice, she said, 'How goes it?'

'Only too well,' said Jasper.

'He tells me nothing.'

'He is afraid – of spoiling things for you.'

'This silence is hard to bear.'

'A woman's lot is often hard. You must have courage.'

'When will he have to leave?'

'¿Quien sabe?'

Mrs Lace wondered whether Lady Marjorie and Mrs St Julien were in the secret, not that it would help her much if they were. She would never be able to worm anything out of them, even if pride permitted her to make the attempt.

'I wonder,' she said to Jasper, still in an undertone, 'if you would write down his motto for me. I thought of having some little memento made for him, a little keepsake, and I should like to have his motto engraved on it.'

'Certainly,' said Jasper, who had been finding out one or two things from Mr Wilkins of late. He took the paper and pencil that she offered and wrote. 'Bella, Horrida Bella.' Over these words he drew a crown of exaggerated dimensions. Mrs Lace folded the paper carefully and placed it in her bag. She thought it a wonder-fully romantic coincidence that her own name should be incorporated in the royal motto of Noel's ancestors.

'By the way,' said Poppy, breaking in on these confidences, 'I have been meaning for ages to ask you whether you have made out that list of neighbours for Cousin Maud Chalford? I think she is depending on it, and the invitations must be sent during the next day or two, because the time really is getting rather short.'

Lady Marjorie asked Mr Wilkins if he wasn't living for the pageant and Mr Wilkins said that he supposed he was.

'I can't wait,' said Lady Marjorie.

'But I'm afraid you'll have to,' said Mr Wilkins, who liked to stress the obvious.

'The list is quite ready,' said Mrs Lace. 'I brought it with me so that Eugenia can give it to Lady Chalford without any more delay.'

'Do let me see,' said Lady Marjorie. 'Oh, good! Wilma Alexander. Of course, I forgot that she lives near here – the Faircombes too. I say, Poppy, there are masses of people we know on this list, will it matter, d'you think?'

'I don't suppose they'll recognize us in our fancy dresses.'

'Well, it can't be helped if they do. I really can't live the whole rest of my life in disguise on account of Osborne.' She went on perusing the list.

'The episodes are all arranged for, now,' Jasper told Mrs Lace. 'Each branch of Social Unionism in the county is responsible for one. There will be nearly three hundred Comrades acting, as far as I can make out, for whom we have to provide clothes. We shall have to call a committee meeting to discuss it.

'Then Miss Trant, the organist, has had a wonderful idea. She thinks we should have an Olde Englyshe Fayre going on at the same time, and she is arranging Maypole dances and art needlework stalls and so on.'

'Oh! surely,' said Mrs Lace, 'Olde Englyshe things are rather a bore, aren't they? I should have thought that we want to keep an eighteenth-century spirit? Why not a Regency Rout for example?'

'We like Olde Englyshe best,' said Jasper, 'because it is so wonderfully funny. Besides, a pageant must be kept thoroughly lowbrow or it loses all character.'

'Miss Trant is being very kind and helpful. She is so sweet,' said Poppy. 'Do you know her?'

Mrs Lace had spent the eight years of her married life patronizing Miss Trant, whom she regarded as a stupid, common little woman, second only in dreariness to Mr Wilkins. There seemed no end to the pin-pricks which poor Mrs Lace was doomed to endure.

Eugenia, who had sat in silence, munching a twopenny bar, since the departure of Mr Leader, now said she must be off. She hailed Vivian Jackson, who appeared from nowhere, took Mrs Lace's list of the neighbours, kicked up the Reichshund, who was snoring in the sun; and, still munching, she trotted away. That evening Mr Leader was dragged from his bed by masked men wearing Union Jack shirts and flung into an adjacent duck pond. As the weather was extremely hot he took no chill and suffered nothing worse than a little mortification and the loss of his *eau-de-nil* pyjama trousers. Nobody else witnessed the affair and Mr Leader did not take any legal or other steps. Nevertheless, the seed was sown of an active resentment against Social Unionism and his treacherous enchantress, Mrs Lace.

14

Lady Chalford sent her motor car to the Jolly Roger with a message that she wished to see Mrs St Julien and Mr Aspect on a matter of extreme importance, and would be greatly obliged if they would come to Chalford House immediately. The car would wait to take them. They entered it with some trepidation, feeling very much like naughty children and wondering which particular enormity had been found out.

When they arrived however, their minds were set at rest on this score; T.P.O.F. was in an almost hysterical mood, but not on account of anything they had done.

'Dear child, dear Mr Aspect,' she said, waving the list of neighbours at them, 'I need your advice, a really dreadful thing has happened – I don't know when I have felt so much upset. On reading this list I am horrified and disgusted to see that there is nobody on it (not a single soul) whom I could possibly ask inside my house. Do you know that when I had been through it twice I could scarcely believe that there was not some mistake, so I sent for my husband's agent and he assured me that it is perfectly accurate, every family for miles round is mentioned on it. I had no idea that we lived in such a shocking neighbourhood.'

'Really,' said Poppy, with interest, 'why, whatever is the matter with them all?'

'The matter?' said Lady Chalford, in a voice of bewilderment, 'the matter is that none of them are respectable. I really cannot understand it. Since I stopped going out of course some of the houses have changed hands, but for all that a great many are still occupied by the same families as the ones I used to know quite well, and who were ordinary decent people like you or me. Since those days the most shocking, distressing things seem to have taken place.'

'What sort of things?'

'My dear, you may well ask. I tell you this list has upset me more than I can say. Take any name from it at random – they are all alike, they all have some sort of cloud hanging over them. Take for instance the first name, the Alexanders. The late Lord Alexander, my dear husband's closest friend for many years, has been succeeded at Bruton Park by his eldest son, Lord Bruton whom, as a child, I often held in my arms. Now, what do I learn? This unfortunate young man has been trapped into marriage with a woman years older than himself, a woman from the variety stage; what is called, I believe, a *cabaret* artiste.'

Poppy gave half a look in Jasper's direction and they both checked a giggle. Trapped into marriage was hardly the expression to use of Lord Alexander, who was well known to have pursued his lovely wife over three continents before she would make up her mind to marry him.

'But you know,' said Poppy, 'Wilma Alexander is awfully respectable and the sweetest person in the world. You'd love her. They are as happy as kings and she is quite wrapped up in Bertie and the children.'

'My dear, I am prepared to believe anything you tell me about this Lady Alexander, but I have no intention of inviting her to my house. She may, for all I know, be a most excellent wife and mother, such women sometimes are. But the fact remains that she could never be a suitable friend for a young girl like Eugenia. I don't want you to think that I am being unduly particular however, so I am now going to read out a few more examples from this unsavoury document.' Lady Chalford adjusted her spectacles and continued, 'Here we have the Hon. Adrian and Mrs Duke; Mrs Duke, it appears, is the divorced wife of a colonel, so these two people are in fact living together adulterously.'

'Dodo wasn't divorced,' said Poppy, 'she divorced her husband, who was a perfect brute to her.'

'I am surprised that you should think it makes any difference. "Till death us do part", is the vow. If her husband was cruel to her she could apply for a separation and live in decent retirement for the rest of her life. Pray, my dear, do not interrupt me. Here we have Mr John Shipton, grandson of a man who was publicly accused, in his clubs, of cheating at billiards. I well remember the incident, which caused a great deal of unpleasantness at the time; he was, of course, obliged to leave the country. Now, although it is not the fault of this Mr Shipton that he was born into such a family, and although he may be most respectable himself, I cannot risk inviting him here. Bad blood usually comes out sooner or later, and it is impossible to be over careful where a young girl like dearest Eugenia is concerned. Sir Archibold and Lady Faircombe, poor things, have a divorced daughter who runs a dress-shop in London – not very nice, is it? Major Montgomerie's son was expelled from Eton – in my day when such a disgrace fell upon a family it was usual for them to go and settle in some colony. Mr Newman's mother was half German and my husband very rightly refuses to have anyone of German extraction inside the house. Lord George Fairbrother is a well-known drunkard and people say that General Parsley had to leave his regiment on account of gambling debts. I won't bore you with any further accounts of such dreadful people, there are dozens of them on this paper and I can assure you that it is one long sordid tale of vice, drunkenness and gaming too terrible to think about. I'm sure I don't know what it is that has come over this unfortunate neighbourhood; anybody might suppose it had been cursed.'

It was now quite evident to Poppy and Jasper that Lady Chalford could not be right in the head; her long seclusion, they supposed, had affected her sanity. She must be humoured.

Poppy said, gently, 'What a dreadful state of affairs, Cousin Maud. Now, you must tell us what you would like us to do about the pageant and garden party on the sixteenth.'

'That is exactly what I have been so worried about,' said Lady Chalford, pathetically. 'After all the trouble you have taken I don't wish you to be disappointed, and Eugenia, poor child, has set her heart on this pageant. I think her Scouts or Guides or Comrades or whatever she calls them have all been working very hard too, and I am particularly glad to see that she is doing something for the village at last. I never used to be able to make her feel the smallest interest until she joined this Movement, whatever it is. So, taking all that into consideration, I have decided that, although it would be out of the question now to entertain my neighbours at a garden party, there is no reason why the pageant should not take place. We will throw open the park on that day, charging a small sum for charity, and like this your time will not have been wasted, and my little Eugenia will not be disappointed.'

'That is much the best plan,' said Poppy, soothingly.

'But, alas! now I am as far as ever from solving the future of my poor little grandchild.'

'She is very young,' said Jasper, 'and I expect you will find that her future will arrange itself quite satisfactorily.'

Lady Chalford gave him a searching look. She seemed about to say something, but refrained.

As he walked home with Poppy through Chalford Park, Jasper said: 'The poor old female is evidently as stupid as an owl and as blind as a bat. She thinks I'm going to marry Eugenia and what's more she likes the idea. Somehow I shouldn't have imagined, from what I know of her moral standards, that I was at all her dish, quite the contrary.'

'Perhaps her estate agent doesn't know much about you yet.'

'Maybe. I'm bound to say I think she has some exceedingly odd views on the subject of social relationships. She ostracizes all the chaps that have had tough luck, like being caught out cheating at billiards or having lousy husbands, whereas one knows she wouldn't mind a scrap if they did really wicked things like grinding down the poor. I believe that our generation has far better ethical values than hers had; we see the chaps we like, even if they are hell, and avoid the ones we don't. It's the only sensible criterion, don't you agree, Miss Smith?'

'You can't talk about ethical values and moral standards,' said Poppy, bitterly, 'because you don't know the meaning of such things.'

'I'm a nicer guy than you seem to think,' said Jasper, carelessly. 'I never do anybody much harm, and I'm loyal to my friends when it comes to the point.'

'I don't notice you being specially loyal to the wretched Noel.'

'That's where you're wrong. Nobody understands about me and Noel; ours is a very complicated relationship which began nearly twenty years ago when we were new boys together at our private. It is chiefly based on the fact that Noel expects a certain type of treatment from me, he would be very much put out if he got any other. The truth is that he gets a great deal of vicarious pleasure out of my evil doings. For instance, he likes having me down here, enjoys my company and so on; but what he positively adores is the feeling that he is forced to keep me here by the most unprincipled blackmail on my part. It wouldn't be a quarter the satisfaction to him if I were to pay for myself like any ordinary person, because then I shouldn't be living up to his conception of my character.'

'I suppose that's one way of looking at it,' said Poppy, doubtfully.

'Besides, think what a wonderfully good turn I did him with that old Local Beauty. Why, the girl was gunning for me, you know, as hard as she could, but after half an hour's conversation with me she turned right about and started gunning for Noel instead, and from that day to this she has never looked back once. No, you can't pretend that I'm disloyal.'

'I shouldn't call it a sign of loyalty to throw anyone into the arms of that awful, affected, pretentious Mrs Lace.'

'Bella, Horrida Bella? I think she's quite a cup of tea. But the point is, you don't know the old boy like I do. The only love that counts for a row of pins from his point of view is the hopeless sort. As soon as a girl begins to be able to sit in the same room with him he sheers off. If the old L.B., or Local Beauty, had still been after me, he would still have been mad about her, as it is, he is cooling down wonderfully. Darling Miss Smith, now you might as well admit that I am a loyal guy.'

'All right, my poppet, don't make such a to-do. I expect even you have got a few good qualities, everybody has. I was only suggesting that, judged by the usual standards, you are a bit of a burglar.'

'Oh! well,' said Jasper gloomily, 'if that's all – a chap has got to live somehow you know, it's one long struggle to survive in one's environment. But look here, why don't you marry me? I'll promise to give up being a burglar and work for my living some other way – how about that?'

'We'll see,' said Poppy. 'I don't really approve of marriage, you know. I think settlements are the thing to go for, these days.'

'Why did you marry Anthony St Julien?'

'How stupid you are. A girl must marry once, you can't go on being called Miss – Miss all your life, it sounds too idiotic. All the same, marriage is a great bore – chap's waistcoats lying about in one's bedroom, and so on. It gets one down in time. Hullo! Look! here come Eugenia and Vivian Jackson. Hail!' she cried.

'Hail, Union Jackshirts!' Eugenia trotted up to them and dismounted, sending Vivian Jackson about his business with a tremendous whack on the hind-quarters, 'have you been to see T.P.O.F.? She was in an awful stew when I left.'

'We have,' said Poppy, 'and she's calmed down again nicely.'

'Yes,' said Eugenia anxiously, 'but what did you arrange?'

'It's all right. There's to be no tee-d up garden party, but the pageant is to take place just the same, with a small charge for admission.'

'Oh! good,' said Eugenia, greatly relieved. 'That makes it all the easier for us to have our Grand S.U. rally. I must begin to see about the posters and leaflets – I thought we might distribute some Social Unionist hymns and propaganda while we are about it.'

'T.P.O.F. seems quite enthusiastic about Union Jackshirtism.'

'Yes, she thinks it's the Women's Institute and she's all for it. Keeps on saying how pleased she is that I do something for the village at last. Nanny's the one who hates it so much. I'm always afraid she's going to tell on me, the old Pacifist.'

'I shouldn't think she'd do that.'

'She'd better not, unless she wants to be beaten up by the Comrades.'

There was a pause in the conversation. Eugenia began to hum, as she often did, the tune of '*Deutschland Deutschland Uber Alles!*' to which she sang the substituted words, 'Union Jackshirts Up and At 'Em, Push their faces in the mud!'

Presently Jasper said: 'Poppy and I were just talking about getting married.'

'To whom?'

'To each other, dear.'

Eugenia looked at them severely. 'If cousin Poppy St Julien had the true principles of Social Unionism at heart she would return to her husband and present him with several healthy male children.'

'Darling Eugenia,' cried Poppy, 'he wouldn't like that a bit. Why, when I think of all the trouble I've taken –'

'Is your husband an Aryan?'

'I really don't quite know what an Aryan is.'

'Well, it's quite easy. A non-Aryan is the missing link between man and beast. That can be proved by the fact that no animals, except the Baltic goose, have blue eyes.'

'How about Siamese cats?' said Jasper.

'That's true. But Siamese cats possess, to a notable degree, the Nordic virtue of faithfulness.'

'Indeed they don't,' said Poppy. 'We had one last summer and he brought back a different wife every night. Even Anthony was quite shocked.'

Eugenia was in no way put out. 'I know, they may not be faithful to non-Aryan cats,' she said, 'why should they be? But they love their Nordic owners, and even go for long walks with them.'

'So your definition of an Aryan is somebody who will go for long walks with other Aryans? Come on now, Miss Smith, does Anthony St Julien go for long walks with you or is he the missing link?'

'Union Jackshirt Aspect,' said Eugenia sharply, 'no levity, please.' She turned to Poppy and said, 'If your husband is an Aryan you should be able to persuade him that it is right to live together and breed; if he is a filthy non-Aryan it may be your duty to leave him and marry Jackshirt Aspect. I am not sure about this, we want no immorality in the Movement . . .'

'It's quite all right,' said Jasper, 'you can take it from me that Anthony St Julien is a very low type, there is nothing of the Baltic goose about him.'

Eugenia paid no attention. 'I have just been to see Union Jackshirt Foster and was obliged to speak to him about his association with Mrs Lace. It may, of course, be perfectly innocent, but it causes much talk in the village, so my Comrades tell me. It must come to an end therefore; at best it gives the Pacifists a peg on which they may hang libellous statements about the party to which Union Jackshirt Foster belongs, at worst he may be luring her away from her duty as the wife and mother of Aryans.'

'Well, well, what a governessy little thing it is,' said Jasper. 'So what had Union Jackshirt Foster to say for himself?'

'His statement was neither satisfactory nor convincing,' replied Eugenia, 'in fact, I shall be obliged to write a request for his formal resignation from the Movement tonight.'

'I don't know which is the worse, you or T.P.O.F.'

'This country must be purged of petty vice before it can be fit to rule the world,' cried Eugenia. She remounted Vivian Jackson and galloped away.

'That's a fine girl,' said Jasper. 'If she had been born twenty years sooner she would have been a suffragette.'

15

Jasper and Noel sat in the bar, deserted by their womenkind who were at Comberry Manor trying on dresses for the pageant. They drank quantities of beer and talked about themselves, the conversation having opened in a tone of extreme cordiality. It appeared that Noel was now rather uncomfortably involved in the affair Lace; Anne-Marie, having abandoned that philosophical serenity which he had found so unusual and so admirable, had recently embarked upon a series of painful scenes. Major Lace, too, according to his wife, was both jealous and suspicious, and trouble was to be anticipated from that quarter.

'Of course I was a fool to imagine it,' Noel said drearily, 'but she honestly did seem a bit different from other girls. I must try and remember another time that they are all the same in the end.'

'The great thing about women,' said Jasper, 'is that they have a passion for getting relationships cut and dried. It seems to be their first object in life. If they are having an ordinary love affair they can't be happy until they have turned it into a romance of the till-death-us-do-part description, while matrimony, even in these days, is never as far as it might be from the back of their minds. They are wonderfully adept at herding chaps into that particular pen, no method is too dishonest which achieves that end. If they are themselves unmarried they pretend that their mother has forbidden them to see one, if married that the husband is getting jealous, until, maddened by all these restrictions, one ends by proposing. Of course neither mother nor husband would have the smallest idea that anything unusual was going on if the little darlings weren't continually dropping dark hints. Oh! what maddening creatures. I do envy people whose tastes lie in any other direction. All the same,' he added, 'I'm bound to say that my Miss Smith seems exceptional in that respect.'

'Don't you believe it,' said Noel, cheerfully, 'she's just leaving a side door open in case she can persuade that husband of hers to take her back.'

'Blast you,' said Jasper gloomily. He had long suspected as much himself.

'Anyway,' continued Noel, 'she has one great advantage – she does at least realize that you can't afford to marry. I wish to goodness I could convince Anne-Marie the same about me – that ring was a bad tactical error on my part, ever since I gave it to her she seems to suppose that I am vastly rich. Why, what on earth do you think she suggested this morning? That I should buy a villa for her in the south of France, if you please, and install her there as my mistress! The girl must be wrong in the head.'

Jasper giggled. 'I think that's funny.'

'It's not funny for me,' said Noel, 'I'm getting too much tied up altogether and it's damned tiresome I can tell you. As soon as this pageant is over I'm jolly well going to cut and run.'

'Where to?'

'Back to my old job at Fruel's again, I suppose,' said Noel drearily, 'as I seem to have ratted all these heiresses I shall be obliged to go on working for my living.' As he said these words a horrid vision rose before his eyes of Miss Brisket the plain typist, Miss Clumps the pretty one, and the ferret eyes and astute nose of Mr Farmer the head clerk. They were framed in olde oake and stained glass, and looked like demons in hell waiting to torment him.

Jasper's voice recalled him to earth. 'Actually,' it was saying, 'I don't think you'll be going back to Fruel's.'

'Oh? Why not?'

'Because when I was up in London the other day I went round to New Broad Street and had a chat with Sir Percy. I explained to him that I am really in many ways more suited to that particular line of business than you are, and do you know he quite saw my point – quite. Charming and intelligent man, Sir Percy. He told me that you had left for good this time. I begin work on the first of next month.'

Noel paled. The vision which had seemed so devilish a moment ago recurred to him with a strangely altered aspect. Miss Brisket, Miss Clumps and Mr Farmer, in their old-world setting, now appeared as angels of light, singing to welcome the pilgrims of the night.

'Jasper,' he said bitterly, 'I always knew you were the biggest swine I knew, but I never knew quite what a swine you were until now.'

'My dear old boy,' said Jasper, in pained surprise, raising his eyebrows very high, 'now don't let's have any ill feeling about this, please. You had definitely resigned, hadn't you? As jobs go it's a good job, and it seemed only sensible to keep it in the family, so to speak. Honestly, old boy, I'm most exceedingly sorry that you are upset about this, but I'm bound to say I don't see what you're complaining of.'

'All right,' said Noel suddenly, 'as you've got my job and as you're welcome to my share of Mrs Lace, you can't do me any more dirt, so I can stop paying your bills in this lousy hole. That's one comfort. Here, miss! Put all these beers down to room 8, will you?'

For once in his life Jasper was left with nothing to say.

After this Noel began taking steps to find himself work. He stayed on at Chalford because he was infected with the general excitement over the pageant, and besides London at the moment was hot and empty of influential people. So he wrote letters. He felt that it was useless to hope for an invitation to resume his old position in the office of Fruel and Grimthorpe; after the barbed shafts which had doubtless been inserted into the mind of Sir Percy Fruel by Jasper, an application there would only be made at the risk of a colossal snub. Noel therefore wrote to his three uncles, all of whom occupied good positions in the world of finance. He explained that he was wasting his time in a stockbroker's office, it was an occupation which he felt gave him too little scope for his talents. He would prefer some job where he could make use of his languages and his rather special knowledge of central European conditions. If Jasper can bluff his way through life, he thought, as he wrote this, so should I be able to. The uncles, he knew, rightly regarded him as a young man who, while lacking in brilliance, could be relied upon to execute anything he might be given to do with steady industry. They had for years deprecated his friendship with the notorious Mr Aspect and might be very much inclined to assist him to a job abroad, far from that malign influence. Noel also thought that once away from Chalford it would be no bad thing to put the German ocean between himself and Mrs Lace for a time. Whilst awaiting developments however, he continued to dally with that lady, to whose attractions he was perhaps not quite so insensible as he liked to imagine.

'How very mysterious,' said Poppy, who, accompanied by Jasper, had just returned from a rehearsal of the Chalford group's episode. It was the last but one before the pageant and had been a heavy failure. 'How very mysterious, here's an enormous parcel for me. It is strange, as nobody knows I'm here, except I suppose Anthony, and he wouldn't be likely to send me a parcel.'

'No, only a writ,' said Jasper.

'So queer,' Poppy continued. 'It's not my birthday or anything either, besides, nobody gets a post here ever, except the detectives.' She pulled at its brown paper wrapping, 'Why, it's just like a very heavy hat box, registered too. I simply don't understand it.'

When at last she had made a hole in the brown paper, which was of a particularly tough brand, a neat wooden box was revealed, clearly needing hammer and chisel to open it. Jasper, who was by now almost as curious as Poppy, went off and borrowed these implements from Mr Birk.

'It's exactly the sort of box my wedding presents used to arrive in,' said Poppy, hovering round while Jasper bashed away at it. 'Somebody always used to injure themselves opening them, and then one would plough one's way through oceans of shavings in order to reveal some awful little glass inkstand. How I used to cry when I was engaged.'

'I'm not surprised. Marriage with old missing link St Julien can't have been a very pretty future for a nice Nordic girl like you to contemplate.'

'Hullo!' said Poppy, 'so what did I tell you? Oceans of shavings. How like old times – now for the inkpot.'

Inside the shavings was a large red leather case.

'Whoever sent this wasn't going to risk having their precious inkpot broken.'

Inside the large red leather case was a large diamond tiara.

Poppy and Jasper blinked. They looked at each other and looked again at the tiara and neither spoke. After a few minutes Poppy placed it carefully on the hall table and removing her gaze from it with some reluctance she began to search once more among the shavings. This she did in the purely mechanical manner of one whose reflexes have been conditioned to a particular reaction on the receipt of diamond tiaras. She soon found what she was looking for, a visiting-card. The name engraved upon it was the name of Jasper's grandfather, and on it was written in pencil, 'To a very charming little lady from an old friend, who hopes that soon he may boast a more intimate relationship.'

Jasper took it from her and read it in his turn.

'Good,' he said comfortably, 'now we really shall be able to be married.'

Poppy, who was trying on the tiara in front of a looking-glass, said, 'Why?'

'On the proceeds, silly.'

'Proceeds of what? I don't somehow think I intend to sell my tiara,' said Poppy, 'if that's what you mean.' She twisted her head about to make it sparkle. 'Really, it suits me a treat, doesn't it?'

'Remember you are going to be a poor man's wife, you can't afford these expensive treats.'

'Yes, but if I stay with Anthony St Julien I can afford them easily.'

'Well, I'm bound to say that's pretty cool. If you stay with Anthony St Julien it is to be hoped you will be sufficiently honourable to hand over that tiara.'

'To whom, pray?'

'To me, of course. After all, the old boy sent it along as a wedding present for me, didn't he?'

'I don't agree at all. Just read that card again and show me one single mention either of you or of a wedding on it. I might possibly return it to the duke, but it has nothing to do with you.'

'Here look,' said Jasper, holding up the card, '"who hopes he may soon boast a more intimate relationship with her." How about that?'

'I hope the duke has honourable intentions,' said Poppy carelessly. She picked up the tiara and put it back into its case, and then, still holding it, she walked through the hall, 'Mr Birk!' she called.

Mr Birk appeared from his parlour.

'Could I borrow your car now, at once? I want to go to the bank at Rackenbridge.'

'Yes, by all means, Miss Smith.'

'It's after five now,' said Jasper, 'banks shut at three, you know, dear.' Mr Birk looked from one to the other. Poppy said to him, 'I have got a piece of jewellery here that I am very anxious to see safely locked up, Mr Birk. Do you think there is any way I could get hold of the bank manager?'

'Yes, certainly, Miss Smith. As it happens the manager is my wife's brother – I will drive you into Rackenbridge myself, and see to it. I'm sure he will do anything to oblige you. If you will wait a moment I will go and start the car.'

'Thank you very much,' said Poppy, 'I will come round to the garage with you.' A few minutes later she could be seen driving off in the direction of Rackenbridge, still clutching the precious red leather case.

That Jane has learnt a thing or two since she has been down here, thought Jasper, with some admiration. He turned automatic steps towards the bar where he was met by Mrs Birk.

'Excuse me troubling you, sir,' she said, 'but here is your account for last week. Mr Foster told us that yours is to be kept separate as from last Thursday.'

'Oh! yes, thanks,' said Jasper. The bill seemed to him enormous. He read the items, recognized with a sigh that they were correct, and wrote out a cheque for the amount, which he handed airily to Mrs Birk.

'A double whisky, please,' he added.

16

The countryside for many miles round Chalford was now made hideous by enormous posters, carefully printed out by hand in black ink, which for weeks past had occupied the leisure hours of Eugenia and her Comrades, and which combined a little discreet propaganda with the announcement that a Grand Social Unionist Rally, Pageant, Garden Party and Olde Englyshe Fayre would take place at Chalford House. The gates would be open at 2.30 p.m. on the Wednesday following, entrance 1s. Eugenia pointed out to Jasper the true *chic* of these posters which lay in the fact that no two were alike.

'Oh really, aren't they?' said Jasper, 'but I thought they looked exactly the same – anyway, they all seem to have a picture of King Kong on them.'

'How stupid you are,' said Eugenia, angrily fingering her dagger, 'can't you see that's a Union Jackshirt Comrade handing on the torch of Social Unionism to the youth of Britain? They all have that, I mean that the wording of each is different, according to where it is to be hung. Haven't you read the one outside the Jolly Roger for instance?'

'I didn't read it,' said Jasper, 'because I was too busy admiring King – I mean the Union Jackshirt Comrade.'

'Well, you should. It refers to the decadence of high society in these post-War days, pointing out that its members are no longer of any value to the community as they possess neither moral sense nor political integrity. That's meant for all of you.'

'Oh, thanks, I'm sure,' said Jasper.

'The posters in Rackenbridge speak of the yellow hand of the Pacifist incendiaries, and how the fate of Van der Lubbe will surely o'ertake all enemies to the Social Unionist cause. There is one on Major Lace's big cowshed comparing our agricultural policy with that of jelly-breasted Tory politicians, and explaining that agriculture will be nationalized under the régime and farmers allowed no longer to muddle about in their own way. The one on the vicarage wall says that whereas religion has failed so notably in this country Social Unionism will soon be here to take its place, the one on Mr Isaac's house promises that all Jews will be sent to live in Jerusalem the Golden with milk and honey blest, and the one on Lord Alexander's park gates has information with regard to the obsolete nature of hereditary legislation.'

'I expect you must be making yourself most wonderfully popular in these parts.'

'What is popularity?' cried Eugenia with contempt. 'What is life itself compared to The Flag? The Comrades are simply thrilled for Wednesday. I can't tell you,' she went on, 'how splendidly they have arranged everything. Seven big charabancs full of Union Jackshirts are expected, and they are all coming over for the dress-rehearsal on Monday as well. Those who aren't actually performing are going to dress up in the proper clothes of the period and help swell the cheering for George III. Oh, bother! it is really too bad we have got to have Mrs Lace in that coach.'

'Never mind, you will have to concentrate on Mr Wilkins, he seems to be quite an enthusiastic member now.'

'Yes, that's one comfort. I'm going to ask him if he will wear his little emblem on his robes, after all George III was a sort of prophet, wasn't he?'

'Quite batty, I believe,' said Jasper.

'Miss Trant has been wonderful,' continued Eugenia, 'I can't think what we should have done without her to help us. She has managed to hire a hundred Dolly Varden and a hundred Dresden Shepherd costumes for only half a crown each, and she is organizing the tea. I must go now and write out post-cards to remind all branches concerned that the dress-rehearsal will be at 2 p.m. on Monday, not 3 as originally settled. Oh! you do think it's going to be a success Union Jackshirt Aspect, don't you?'

'I am certain that it will prove a highly entertaining afternoon,' said Jasper. She trotted away on her little black horse. 'Yes, Mr Birk?'

'So sorry to trouble you,' said Mr Birk. He held in his hand a cheque, which Jasper had no difficulty in recognizing as the one with which he had paid Mrs Birk some days previously. 'This has been sent back R/D,' said Mr Birk, 'there must be some mistake.'

Jasper took it, glanced at it casually and said, 'Oh, I see, a small misunderstanding no doubt. How stupid of my bank, I suppose I shall have to go and send a telegram to that fool of a manager.'

He strolled away in the direction of the post office, where he sent a telegram to his sister, urging her to wire him ten pounds, signing it 'S.O.S. Jasper'. He felt low. Poppy still pursued her plan of keeping him on tenterhooks so that he had no idea whether she also was emotionally committed or not. The detectives had left Chalford, vanishing as suddenly and as mysteriously as they had appeared, and this seemed to be worrying her. 'It looks as though they have the evidence they wanted,' she said. 'We were mad not to be more careful.' Jasper thought that there could be nothing in the world so depressing as financial troubles coupled with emotional uncertainty. He very much hoped, incidentally, that his sister would not have gone abroad yet.

Noel now accentuated Jasper's sufferings by suddenly assuming the demeanour of excessive cheerfulness. He boasted continually of wonderful jobs which his uncles were going to find for him on the Continent. They had, in fact, written to him quite kindly on this subject, and he was expecting any day to hear more definitely from one or other of them.

Hopeful of this he kept Mrs Lace at bay with vague but interesting promises, an achievement which was not at the moment very difficult, as all her thoughts and energies were concentrated on the pageant. So engrossed was she with dreams of the great day near at hand that she never noticed the unusual behaviour of the Rackenbridge young men. Mr Leader cut her in the High Street one morning, Mr Forderen had not even answered a letter in which she had invited him to photograph her in some eighteenth-century moods. It did not occur to her to conclude from these and other omens that Rackenbridge might be making its own plans for Wednesday afternoon.

The day before the pageant broke in a downpour which was perfectly solid and had every appearance of being the sort that lasts for a week at least.

'Set in for wet,' said Mr Birk cheerfully, whistling between his teeth. The weather forecast in the *Daily Mail* supported him in this dreary prophecy; 'Further outlook uncertain,' it said.

Poppy, Marjorie, Jasper and Noel herded together in the parlour for company, gazed at the drifting sheets of rain and wondered whether it would be giving too much trouble to ask Mrs Birk to substitute a fire for the ferns and crinkly paper in the fireplace. Early in the afternoon Eugenia and Mrs Lace joined them and they all gloomed together. The labour of weeks, the excited expectation as it seemed of a lifetime, were being balked of an object before their very eyes; they felt hopelessly dejected.

'There is the squash court,' Eugenia muttered, without much conviction. Besides, the dress-rehearsal, which had taken place the day before, had been an utter failure in every respect, and everyone had been unanimous in deciding that it was essential to have another, but, of course, this was now impossible.

Conversation progressed in snatches, by common consent all pretended to take it for granted that tomorrow would be fine.

'Mr Wilkins must remember to take off his hat, or bow, or something to the cheering populace. He sat right back and one couldn't see him at all.'

'I thought he was just wonderful,' said Lady Marjorie.

'Besides, I think he ought to sit on the left-hand side, so that he can get out first and hand out Mrs Lace.'

'Noel is handing me out,' said Mrs Lace.

'Eugenia, if you can remember, do tell the coachman to drive at foot's pace, after all, we must try and make the arrival really impressive, it is far the most important episode. To my mind everything depends on how that goes off.'

'Didn't you think the platform looked rather bare? I thought it might be hung with flags or something to cheer it up a bit.'

'Union Jacks,' said Eugenia, 'I will see to that.'

'The first messenger must be very strictly told not to approach the platform until little Margaret Cooper has finished presenting her bouquet to Queen Charlotte. All that part was so fearfully rushed yesterday.'

'I think myself that we ought to have the Morris dancing first, before the episodes begin.'

'That's not a bad plan, but if we do we mustn't forget to tell Miss Trant.'

'And Mr Wilkins.'

'Oh, this rain!'

'You know the episodes do vary frightfully. I thought the Boston Tea Party was a pretty good flop myself.'

'Well, of course it was. None of the principals turned up for it you see and Miss Trant had to read all their parts in turn, so I suppose it was bound to be rather dreary.'

'Anyway it was exactly like *Alice in Wonderland* – and always will be.'

'Who is responsible for the Boston Tea Party?'

'The Barton branch,' said Eugenia, 'and I had a letter this morning from their leader saying that their charabanc broke down on the way here. It will be mended by tomorrow. I say, Union Jackshirt Aspect, can't you make Mr Wilkins speak up in the: "Leave our great Empire then, vile democrats" speech at the Boston T.P. It is a frightfully important speech and he mumbled it dreadfully.'

'I thought he was just wonderful,' said Lady Marjorie. 'Oh, dear! how divine he looked in his robes too.'

'Oh, this rain!'

'One thing,' said Eugenia, 'if it rains an inch tomorrow we do get £100 out of the insurance.' Jasper had arranged this transaction, gaining a small commission for himself in the process. 'We'll get that anyhow,' he said, 'it is going to be measured in the schoolmaster's rain gauge and I thought of nipping round there with a small watering can some time during the day.'

'You know, Jasper, something must be done about Nelson's arm, so that it doesn't show. Yesterday one could see it under the pinned-up sleeve all the time, it did look so idiotic.'

'Yes, and why does Nelson limp and pretend to be deaf? Gross overacting, I call it.'

'Of course the whole Nelson episode is a bit unsatisfactory. For instance, was Lady Hamilton really so matey with George III? I have a sort of idea she was never received at Court at all, and anyway he was batty by then.'

'Nobody will know that.'

'Well, I dare say, but I'm sure everyone knows she wasn't at Nelson's deathbed. There is a very famous picture of it for one thing.'

'She isn't *meant* to be in it,' cried Jasper despairing, 'I've told her time and again to keep off. She quite ruins the "Kiss me, Hardy" bit.'

'Oh! but what happened yesterday was that Hardy never turned up, and as somebody had to kiss the old boy, Lady Hamilton did seem to be the obvious person.'

'It appears she's nuts about him, in real life, I mean. Miss Trant told me.'

'Anyway, I saw a letter in the *Sunday Times* saying it was really Kismet, Hardy.'

'I don't care, Hardy kissed him all right. Everybody knows that.'

'Oh, this rain!'

'Didn't you think the bit where Wolfe recites Gray's "Elegy" to his troops dragged rather? I suppose it couldn't be pruned at all?'

'And Napoleon on board the *Bellerophon* looked exactly like the "Wounding of Nelson at the Canary Islands". I told you it would.'

'It struck me that Napoleon was blind, anyway.'

'Well, I don't know where he found anything to drink, I never did.'

'The ennobling of Pitt was nice,' said Eugenia. 'I must tell the Comrades to cheer like anything for that. Had Pitt been alive today he would have been a Social Unionist, of course. So would Fox.'

'Oh, this rain!'

'By the way,' said Eugenia, 'one of the old carriage horses has gone quite lame since yesterday, so we are going to use Vivian Jackson instead. He is awfully pleased, the darling, he loves to be in on things.'

The rain continued all the evening without a break. It poured and poured. At tea-time the telegram Jasper had sent his sister returned to him, 'Gone abroad, whereabouts not known'.

'Oh, dear,' he said gloomily, 'it never rains but it pours. I suppose when cheques begin coming back on one it is quite natural for telegrams to follow suit. I say old boy, lend me ten pounds.'

'Sorry, old boy.'

'Darling Miss Smith,' he said, much later in the evening, 'are you going to marry me or aren't you? I should be glad to know soon.'

'Why?'

'Because if not I think I shall bunk after the pag.'

'Where to?'

'Uruguay.'

'Oh, I wouldn't do that.'

'Then marry me.'

'I will tell you tomorrow,' said Poppy, 'after the pageant is over – if it ever takes place at all. Oh, this rain!'

Jasper wondered why he found it impossible to borrow ten pounds from Poppy. He had never been troubled by such diffidence before in his relations with women. Poor little Marigold, indeed, had once been left in pawn in a Paris hotel where he had found it impossible to pay the bill, and for all he knew she was still there. He could not quite imagine himself meting out such treatment to Poppy.

'Good night, darling,' he said, 'oh, this rain!'

There was but little sleep in the Jolly Roger that night, the weather was too much on everybody's mind. Some composed themselves for rest with their curtains drawn back so that they could observe from their beds the smallest change, others tried to forget their anxiety by shutting the windows, but soon found themselves making continual pilgrimages to open them again. At 2 a.m. the rain suddenly stopped and except for the regular dripping of trees there was no sound. The sky could not be seen, or any stars, there was a profound darkness. Shortly before five o'clock advancing daylight revealed that the village was wrapped in an opaque white mist. At eight o'clock this began to clear, and by nine a hot sun was pouring down its rays on to the steamy fields. It was a perfect summer day.

17

It was a perfect summer day. Morning sun blazed into the windows of the Jolly Roger, but quite failed to awaken the occupants. As soon as they felt perfectly confident that this fine weather was an indisputable fact, they had all made up for a wakeful night by sinking into happy, carefree slumber. The more the sun shone the sounder they slept. It was not until nearly eleven o'clock, when Eugenia and Vivian Jackson appeared on Chalford green, that they were finally aroused by a hideous din, compounded of shouting, neighing, and the cracking of a whip. Sleepy faces appeared, one by one, in four windows.

'Hail! and arise, Union Jackshirt Comrades!' cried Eugenia. 'I don't know how you could still be in bed on such a day – I myself have been out since dawn. There is much work for all to do in Chalford Park – I command you, as your district leader, to follow me there without delay.' She dragged Vivian Jackson's head right round, whereupon he reared twice and gave several tremendous buck-jumps, after which he galloped away, while Eugenia, sitting like a rock, sang at the top of her voice, 'Land of Union Jackshirts, Mother of the Flag'.

Poppy was the first to be ready. She abandoned her usual post in the battle of the bathroom, having had the wily idea that it might be possible to take a hot, deep bath in Chalford House whilst dressing for the pageant. She came downstairs delighted at having thus stolen a march on the others. On the hall table she saw, for the first time since she had been at the Jolly Roger, a letter addressed to herself. And, what was more, addressed in the once loved and always familiar handwriting of Anthony St Julien. She felt a little giddy as she opened it.

It was, for him, a long letter, four pages of writing which began by being small and neat and which ended up large and untidy. In it he suggested that Poppy should return to him at once. He said that his house was getting very uncomfortable, the cook had given notice and the housemaid, although he reminded her daily, either could not or would not send the loose covers to be cleaned. He considered too, that the weekly books were over large. He then went on to say, towards the end of the second page, that no other woman would ever mean much in his life, and that if she was prepared to let bygones be bygones he would be glad to welcome her home again. No direct reference to the detectives or the débutante. Poppy wondered what she would do. Anthony St Julien was, after all, her husband, and she loved her little house in Chapel Street. She did not have to close her eyes in order to visualize her drawing-room with its trellis wallpaper, red plush curtains and satinwood furniture. It would be much harder to leave a dwelling to which she was singularly devoted, than a husband for whom devotion was now a thing of the past. In a position in which many women would be weighing an old loyalty against a new passion, she found herself wondering whether it would be possible to smuggle her writing-table out of the house, should she decide to throw in her lot with Mr Aspect. This indecision in no way troubled her, she felt sure that once the Grand Union Jackshirt Pageant and Garden Party was over she would with certainty know her own mind.

Noel also found a letter that morning. It was from one of the uncles and informed him that he should go to London as soon as might be, when an interview would be arranged for him with a Viennese banker who might be feeling disposed to offer him employment. He immediately sent off a telegram to the uncle saying that he would be in London the following day.

When all were ready, they packed into the motor car which kind Mr Birk had placed at their disposal, and were driven to Chalford Park. In and around the house a state of chaos reigned, it was hard to imagine that things would ever straighten themselves out. Workmen, Social Unionists, the Women's Institute and a multitude of reporters were falling over each other outside, whilst inside, Miss Trant and Mrs Lace were engaged in a battle royal over dressing-rooms. Fourteen large bedrooms had been placed at their disposal for this purpose by Lady Chalford, and Mrs Lace was insisting that she would need, in order to dress those appearing in the Chalford episode, at least seven. As she was responsible for dressing twenty people, and as Miss Trant was expecting to have at least two hundred on her hands, it was felt that Mrs Lace's demands were disproportionate. Finally, after a long and enraged argument, Mrs Lace was persuaded to make do with three rooms only. These she now proceeded to deck out with finery, laying dresses all over the beds and chairs, and covering the tables with accessories. Jasper and Poppy wandered in to have a look, and concluded that Mrs Lace had sat for too long at the feet of the Rackenbridge young men. Her ideas on dressing up were very modern.

'I rather think,' said Jasper, in one of his loud asides, 'that these American-cloth kirtles, cardboard wigs and cellophane fichus are going to look very peculiar alongside the two hundred Dolly Varden and Dresden Shepherd dresses hired by darling Miss Trant from the Oxford costumier.'

'I say, they are ugly,' murmured Poppy, 'have I really got to wear this monstrosity of a wig?'

'It's your own fault, darling, you wouldn't take the trouble to get a dress for yourself and now you are at the mercy of Rackenbridge taste. Serves you right too.'

Lady Marjorie looked quite wild with excitement and ran about looking for Mr Wilkins, saying, 'I can't wait, I can't wait.' Mr Wilkins, however, had not yet appeared on the scene.

The morning passed in a flash.

Lady Chalford, who was thoroughly enjoying the unwonted bustle, begged that everybody would stay on for a cold luncheon, to which she had already invited the curator of Peersmont and his charges. The years seemed to have rolled away from her on this occasion; she looked like a young woman as she greeted her old friend the Duke of Driburgh and those two of his colleagues considered by the curator as suitable candidates for the day's outing.

The duke, however, slipped away from her side as soon as he decently could and made a bee-line for Poppy, whom he embarrassed considerably with his attentions. When luncheon-time came he manoeuvred that she should sit next him, kept his knee clamped against hers during the entire meal and held her hand between the courses. When she tried to thank him for the tiara he ogled her fearfully and dropped a few mysterious hints.

'How is Lord Rousham?' she asked, to change the subject.

'Off his diet, I am sorry to say. Won't eat anything now, except the coco-nuts and bits of suet we put out for the tits. Gunnersbury is busy making a nesting box for him, meddling old idiot, he always has fussed over housing conditions, and so on. I've no patience with his silly Socialistic ideas; if a man likes to build his own nest, let him. Trade Unions have been the downfall of this country you mark my words, young lady.'

After luncheon the duke led Poppy into the recess of a window and proposed marriage to her.

'But you're married already, Duke,' she cried, in order to gain time. There was a wild look in his eye which she did not altogether like.

'Ah, you think I am old-fashioned, behind the times, eh, what? But I have been getting very modern in my outlook lately I can assure you, and I understand that nowadays it is perfectly usual to be engaged while one is still married. Damned sensible idea. Now I suggest that we should give old Maud all the evidence she wants and then we could nip round to a registry office. What do you say to that, little lady? There are lots more pretty toys hanging on the tree where that tiara came from, you know.'

'That will be lovely,' said Poppy, 'and now, Duke –'

'Call me Adolphus.'

'And now, Adolphus, I am really rather busy. If you will excuse me I think I should be going. But I will see you again soon.'

'And for good, little lady, for good,' cried the amorous Adolphus, leering after her.

Poppy, who had nothing whatever to do for at least another hour (they had lunched early and very quickly), escaped next door into the library, where she could hide herself from her admirer behind jutting-out bookcases. She was rather pleased to see that the daily papers were there, neatly arranged on a large round leather-topped table, and taking up *The Times* she began to glance through it in a desultory manner. Almost the first thing to meet her eye was the name of Anthony St Julien's débutante heading the list of marriage announcements; the girl was engaged to a well-known polo player.

Poppy now understood the eagerness with which Anthony St Julien wanted her back again; she felt sorry for him, but at the same time considered that his behaviour was unnecessarily crude. He might have waited for a day or two. At the same time she was rather grateful to him for having been so caddish, as now, whatever course she should decide to take, she would be not treating him otherwise than as he deserved. Her thoughts once more turned towards the writing-table. It was rather heavy, but she and Jasper between them could probably carry it out in the middle of the night.

Presently she was sought out by Lady Marjorie, who looked quite ghoulishly hideous in mauve panniers of American-cloth over a skirt of bright silver mackintosh. The wire-netting wig made for her by Mrs Lace had proved too small and very painful to wear, so she had cast it away, and borrowed instead a Dolly Varden one from Miss Trant. This was of very untidy white horse-hair, which stood up in a fuzzy aureole round her head; a corkscrew curl fell behind one ear, and became more of a corkscrew and less of a curl at every step she took. The wig was rather too large for Lady Marjorie and her own dark hair strayed out behind, in spite of innumerable hairpins.

'Gosh!' said Poppy, trying not to look horrified at this apparition, 'dressed already?'

'There's no need to be, for ages yet, but I wanted to get it over. I'm really too excited to sit still and wait.'

'I had to hide in here,' said Poppy, 'because that awful old duke pounced me. In fact, he went so far as to propose marriage.'

'Hity-tity, awful old duke indeed. When I think of the way you always go on to me about Osborne. So I suppose you have accepted with pleasure – do I congratulate you, darling?'

'My darling Marge – *that* old duke?'

'Nonsense. He's a very nice old duke, much nicer than that mountain of pomposity you want me to marry. Darling, do I look all right?'

'Lovely, darling.'

'That's good. Because – you know – Mr Wilkins. I wanted to look quite my best on his account, the angel. Oh, dear! it does seem hard I can't drive in the coach with him.'

'Never mind, I really think you have a better chance of getting off with him like this, because you'll be sitting next him for hours on the platform, and when the episodes are over, Noel is going to escort the Local Beauty round the Olde Eng-lyshe Fayre. That'll be your big opportunity.'

'Oh, I am excited! I keep feeling quite cold and shivery. The Social Unionists ought to be here any minute now in their charabancs. Do come and dress, Poppy, I feel too shy to go and look for Mr Wilkins by myself.'

Presently, to the accompaniment of Union Jackshirt songs, cheers and yells, the Comrades began to arrive. They appeared to be in the wildest of good spirits as they were shepherded by their district leaders into Miss Trant's dressing-rooms, where they proceeded to cover their Union Jack shirts with cotton brocade coats and sateen breeches, or cotton brocade panniers and sateen skirts, according to their sex. Made-up jabots of cheap lace were tied round their necks and frills of it sewn to their sleeves, but these did not fit very well and in most cases a few inches of red, white and blue were to be seen poking out. Jasper, hot and perspiring in one of Mrs Lace's artistic rubber suits, was taking his duties as producer with the utmost seriousness. He dashed about, a grubby piece of paper in one hand and megaphone in the other, admonishing the various district leaders and trying to make sure that all the groups had arrived upon the scene. Finally he stood on a chair and addressed them all through his megaphone.

'Now, boys,' he said, 'there are one or two little things I wish to mention. The dress-rehearsal on Monday did not go off too well. Nobody was dressed, and you could hardly have called it a rehearsal. However, that's not going to stop us from doing splendidly this afternoon. Now, I want you all to try and enter into the spirit of the age – remember, you are in the eighteenth century from now on. When the coach drives up with King George and Queen Charlotte in it, I want you all to be lining the drive – give them a good rousing cheer, don't yell and don't give the Social Unionist salute. Let a few words be audible: 'God bless His Majesty'; 'Long live the House of Hanover'; 'Queen Charlotte for ever', and so on, and as the coach passes, fall on one knee. Those of you whose wigs are not sewn on to your hats might snatch them off, the hats, I mean, and wave them. Another important point – remember, you will have plenty of time to get into your places for the episodes while the King and Queen are alighting and hearing speeches of welcome. On Monday you all scrambled far too much; there was an appalling muddle. Now I will read over the list of the episodes again in their proper order, as I want to get it all clear:

'Arrival of George III and Queen Charlotte (Union Jackshirt Wilkins and Mrs Lace).

'Speech of Welcome by Lord Chalford (Union Jackshirt Noel Foster).

'Answering speech by George III.

'Pause, for Morris dancing.

'First messenger arrives announcing the victory of Wolfe over French Pacifists at Quebec.

'*First Episode*: Wolfe, while reading Gray's "Elegy in a Country Churchyard" to his troops, is hit by a stray bullet and dies on a heap of straw. Rackenbridge brass band plays the "Dead March in Saul".

'Messenger arrives announcing the doings at the Boston Tea Party. Speech by George III "Leave our Great Empire then, vile democrats," etc.

'*Second Episode*: The Burghers of Boston, with halters round their necks, pour their tea on the ground and drink illicit whisky instead. Rackenbridge brass band does *not* play the "Dead March in Saul", (as it did on Monday) but "Little Brown Jug Don't I Love Thee".

'Messenger arrives announcing that Clive and Warren Hastings have disgraced themselves in India.

'*Third Episode*: Clive and Warren Hastings, seated on an elephant, are surrounded by Nautch girls – (by the way, I hope the hind legs is here this afternoon, Miss Trant had to be them on Monday – Ah! Union Jackshirt Pierpont, good). Rackenbridge brass band plays "In a Persian Garden".

'Pause, for the ennobling of Pitt. Rackenbridge brass band plays "For he's a jolly good fellow".

'Messenger arrives announcing the French Revolution. Rackenbridge brass band plays "Mademoiselle from Armentières".

'Another messenger arrives announcing the wounding of Nelson at the Canary Islands and his naval victory over French Pacifists.

'Speech by George III. "God blew His breath and they were scattered", etc.

'*Fourth Episode*: Nelson, his telescope pressed to his blind eye, and staring at Lady Hamilton with his other one, has his arm blown off. Rackenbridge brass band plays "Every nice girl loves a sailor, every nice girl loves a tar". Tableau of Lady Hamilton in one of her attitudes.

'Messenger arrives announcing Death of Nelson.

'*Fifth Episode*: Nelson dying on a heap of straw, Hardy kisses him. Speech by Nelson, "It is a far, far better thing I do", etc. Nelson dies saying, "Look after pretty witty Emmie". Rackenbridge brass band plays the "Dead March in Saul" again.

'Final tableau: "The Exile of Napoleon".

'Rackenbridge brass band plays "God save the King".

'I hope that is all quite clear to you now,' said Jasper, rather hoarsely, as he jumped down from his chair.

Meanwhile, the neighbourhood was turning up in force. Had T.P.O.F. only known it, her change of plans was to avail her nothing, and the very people whose presence beneath her roof was so obnoxious to her were all busily paying their shillings at the park gates. They were not only eager to enjoy this pageant, the advertisements of which had been so strangely worded, but most of them had long been immensely curious to see Eugenia, the unknown heiress, and the by now almost legendary beauties of Chalford House. Large shining cars therefore sailed up the drive one after another, to be directed by Comrades to a rather soggy parking-place where they disgorged the infamous *élite* of the neighbourhood. They all laughed and chattered together, crying out that the house was a dream and wondering whether they should meet Eugenia; the weight of shame lay lightly upon their shoulders – they would have been surprised if they knew the violence of Lady Chalford's feelings about them.

The hour of three was near at hand. Mrs Lace, resplendently 1927 in her gilded American-cloth dress and wig of paper-clips, had long ago disappeared with Mr Wilkins to a place behind the kitchen-garden, where the royal coach awaited them. The party of welcomers was gracefully posed round the front door, ready to greet the Sovereign and his Consort with elegant bows and curtsies; Beau Brummels, Scarlet Pimpernels and Lady Teezles lined the drive for as far as the eye could see, all agog to make a loyal eighteenth-century demonstration. The crowd of onlookers had assumed proportions such as nobody had dared to hope for.

A hush of expectation fell upon all.

'Something awful is going to happen,' said Jasper, nervously. 'I know it.'

At last thrilling cheers were heard, the coach was evidently on its way. A shudder of excitement swept the crowd, all necks were craned to see the great arrival, all breaths were drawn in to swell the cheering which was coming ever nearer. Suddenly it wavered, lost heart and stopped. A noise like thunder was heard instead, punctuated by horrible thin shrieks, and the next moment the coach came crashing into sight with horses at full gallop and evidently quite out of control. Mrs Lace, screaming loudly, was attempting to throw herself out of a window, and was being forcibly restrained from doing so by Mr Wilkins. Both their wigs had fallen off.

The crowd now took to its heels. It seemed as though nothing could save coach and horses from being dashed to pieces against Chalford House when suddenly, Mr Wilkins, having thrown Mrs Lace on to the floor, climbed out through the window and up on to the coachman's seat, where he wrenched the reins from the trembling and inefficient hands of Lady Chalford's ancient groom. In the nick of time he managed to drag Vivian Jackson and his colleague up onto the grass. The coach, after rocking frantically for a moment, overturned, and both horses were brought to a standstill. The Comrades now dashed forward; with ready hands they dragged forth the hysterical Mrs Lace, and carried away the groom on an improvised stretcher – he appeared to be suffering from concussion. Lady Marjorie, beside herself with love and admiration, implored her hero to tell her that he was still alive, which he did very heartily; Eugenia sobbed on the neck of her horse, 'Darling, darling Vivian Jackson, you must never frighten me like that again, you might have been killed. Are you sure you're all right?' She felt his legs one after the other and presently led him away to his loose-box.

'Funny thing,' said Mr Wilkins to Jasper, 'a chap who lives at Rackenbridge – forget his name – caused all the trouble. He sprang out of the crowd waving a yellow flag at the horses, extraordinary stupid thing to do, you know; why, they might easily have bolted.'

Mrs Lace was taken into Chalford House. Her golden gown was split in several places and her wig quite ruined but her person was unscathed. She indulged in a comforting exhibition of hysteria until Major Lace gave her a good shaking, after which she restored her face, borrowed a cotton-wool wig from kind Miss Trant, and resumed her place at the side of Mr Wilkins.

Meanwhile the pageant was proceeding as though nothing out of the way had happened. Mr Wilkins, perfectly unmoved by his shaking, remembered his speeches better than ever before and went through his royal part as to the manner born.

The Social Unionists gave him a rousing welcome as he mounted the platform. 'G.E.O.R.G.E! We want George!' they cried.

Lady Marjorie stood beside him, her horse-hair locks quivering, her heart thumping, her cheeks flushed. She also wanted George.

It was all an enormous success. The episodes went off without a single hitch and nobody seemed to notice the fact that Jasper had ignored historical truth to a degree unprecedented even in pageantry. The most popular scenes of all were just those with the smallest foundation in fact.

Social Unionists and the public alike shouted themselves to a frenzy when, a messenger arriving to tell George III that Louis of France had been razored up by Marxist non-Aryans, the English monarch observed sadly, 'Alas! my poor brother!'

The episodes were to have been brought to an end by a tableau representing Napoleon on board the *Bellerophon*, but at the last moment Eugenia had vetoed this, as it had suddenly occurred to her that, even though Napoleon was a dirty foreigner, he was nevertheless somebody's Leader. They ended therefore, rather pointlessly, with the Death of Nelson, which was not altogether a success from Jasper's point of view, as both Hardy and Lady Hamilton made an unseemly rush to kiss the expiring admiral. The public, however, appeared to enjoy it.

After this the Rackenbridge brass band struck up the tune of 'Onward, Christian Soldiers', to which the Social Unionists, standing at attention, sang their hymn.

> 'Onward, Union Jackshirts
> Fight for England's fame.
> Fight and die for England,
> Saving her from shame.
> When foreigners make grimaces,
> Stamp them in the mud,
> Jump upon their faces,

Cover them with blood.
Onward, Union Jackshirts
Fight for England's fame,
Fight and die for England,
Saving her from shame.

'Onward, Union Jackshirts
England shall win through.
England shall rise greater,
Thanks to Jackshirts true.
Junket fronts shall quiver,
We shall give them more
Reasons to shiver
Than they had before.
Onward, etc.

'Fight with shell and bullet,
Fight with castor oil,
Fight with pen and paper,
Fight, Oh Jackshirts loyal.
Fight the loathly Pacifist,
Fight the junket breast,
Make them feel the Jackshirt's fist,
Make them howl for rest.
Onward, Union Jackshirts
Foreigners you'll whack.
Fight and die for England
And the Union Jack.'

After this another unrehearsed incident took place. There was a moment's pause while George III prepared to descend from the platform for his inspection of the Olde Englyshe Fayre. The Comrades, who had completely entered into the spirit of the thing, were crowding round him cheering themselves hoarse, when suddenly and most unexpectedly they were attacked from the rear by quantities of horrible-looking men dressed as the *sansculottes* of Revolutionary France and wearing yellow caps on their heads. 'We want peace! we want peace!' they cried, scattering white feathers in every direction.

'We will fight
Red, White and Blue
'Cos we are yellow
Through and through
We'll have a crack
At Captain Jack
Because we think
His heart is black.

'Kill Social Unionism!' and they fell upon the defenceless Comrades with life pre-
servers, knuckledusters, potatoes stuffed with razor blades, bicycle bells filled with
shot, and other primitive, but effective, weapons. The Social Unionists, who were
not only unarmed, but also sadly hampered by their full-bottomed coats, ill-fitting
breeches and the wigs, which in many cases fell right over their eyes, impeding
their vision, were at first utterly overcome by the enemy. Many were laid out,
others, less fortunate, were carried away to a distant part of the estate where
atrocities too horrible to name were perpetrated upon their persons. Mrs Lace was
dragged to the lake and there was soundly ducked more than once by masked, but
vaguely familiar assailants.

Eugenia, meanwhile, had gone into the house to fetch a sunshade for her grandmother. On hearing the din of battle she rushed out again, to be confronted by an
appalling scene of carnage. The Social Unionists, in small, scattered groups, were
defending themselves bravely enough, but to no avail. They were completely
disorganized, and it was clear that the Pacifists must win the day, unless something
quite unforeseen should happen to turn the tide of war against them.

It happened. Like a whirlwind, Eugenia Malmains dashed into the fray, seizing
a Union Jack from off the platform she held it high above her head and with loud
cries she rallied the Comrades to her. The Pacifists fell back for a second in amazement, never had they seen so large, so beautiful, or so fierce a woman. That second
was their undoing. They returned ferociously enough to the charge, but from now
onwards the fight began to go against them. The Social Unionists, all rallying to
Eugenia, presented at last a united front. Led by her, they shouted their fighting
cry: 'We defend the Union Jack.'

> 'We will whack
> And we will smack,
> And we will otherwise attack
> All traitors to the Union Jack.
> For we defend the Union Jack.'

and charged again and again into the ranks of the enemy, which were gradually
falling away before their determined onslaught. The cowardly Pacifists, armed to
the teeth though they were, could stand up to the Jackshirts' fists no longer. They
began to retire in extreme confusion, which ended in an utter rout. They fled,
leaving in possession of the Comrades a battlefield on which were scattered a
quantity of white wigs, white feathers and wounded men.

'How wonderfully realistic that was,' said Lady Chalford, appreciatively. 'One
might almost believe that some of those poor fellows were actually hurt.' She
surveyed the scene through her lorgnettes, and addressed the Duke of Driburgh,
who stood at her side. 'Mr Aspect,' she continued, 'has evidently inherited all your
talent for writing, my dear Driburgh – I have never forgotten the pretty Valentines
you composed so charmingly in those days.'

'Very kind of you, my dear,' said the Duke. 'I presume that what we have just
witnessed is the Battle of Waterloo, with your dear little Eugenia in the part of
Boadicea, such a clever notion.'

The Social Unionists, in spite of their wounds (and hardly one had escaped injury) now went quite mad with excitement. They hoisted Eugenia upon their shoulders and carried her, with loud cheers, to the platform, from which point of vantage she made a stirring speech. She urged that all who had witnessed this cowardly attack upon the peaceful Social Unionists should join their party without more ado. 'We are your only safeguard against Pacifism in its most brutal form,' she cried; 'do you want your streets to run with blood, your wives to be violated and your children burnt to death? No? Then join the Union Jack defenders here and now –' She pointed to her tattered flag, saying that in time it would surely be one of the most honoured relics of the Movement. She told the Comrades that their scars were honourable scars, received on a great occasion and in defence of a great cause. Their names would go down to history, she said, and become famous; they would boast in after years to their children and their children's children that they had been privileged to fight beneath the Union Jack in the Battle of Chalford Park.

This speech was received with the utmost enthusiasm, not only by the Comrades themselves but by members of the public, many of whom now hastened to become recruited to the Social Unionist party, Eugenia herself pinning the little emblem to their bosoms. Such Pacifists as had fallen into their enemies' hands were presently led away and treated to enormous doses of 'Ex-Lax', the 'Delicious Chocolate Laxative', which was the only substitute for castor oil to be found in Nanny's medicine-chest.

The victims of Pacifist atrocities now began to stagger back one by one. They told hair-raising tales of the treatment which they had received, and were hailed as martyrs and heroes by Eugenia, who wrote their names down in a small exercise book. When their wounds had been dressed, and the more serious cases had been put to bed in Lady Chalford's spare rooms (her ladyship having by this time retired, fatigued by the day's excitements, to her own), Eugenia, at Jasper's suggestion, led a contingent of Social Unionists to the cellar, and several cases of vintage champagne were carried on to the lawn.

The Olde Englyshe Fayre from now on became more like an Olde Englyshe Orgy. An enormous bonfire was made, on which Karl Marx and Captain Chadlington (the local Conservative Member of Parliament) were burnt together in effigy amid fearful howls and cat-calls from the Comrades. 'Down with the Pacifists! Down with the Communists! Down with non-Aryans! Down with the Junket-fronted National Government! We defend the Union Jack, we will whack and we will smack and we will otherwise attack all traitors to the Union Jack –'

Everybody danced with everybody else, some people even danced alone, certain sign of a good party, while the Rackenbridge brass band moaned out 'Night and Day', its latest number, for hours on end. The visitors from Peersmont became as drunk as the lords they were, and, each with a pretty girl on his arm, refused to budge when the curator said that it was time to go home. Lady Marjorie and Mr Wilkins disappeared together for a while; when they rejoined the throng of merry-makers it was to dance a jig and announce their engagement. The Comrades cheered and sang their Union Jackshirt songs until they could cheer and sing no more, and it was not before one o'clock in the morning that they finally packed themselves into their charabancs and drove away, hoarse but happy.

Silence at last fell upon the park. Under a full moon Poppy and Jasper staggered hand in hand towards the Jolly Roger. In spite of their extreme exhaustion they still went on talking over the events of that sensational afternoon.

'Did you adore the fight?' asked Poppy; 'I did. I dug my heel into a fallen Pacifist's face – remind me to tell Eugenia that, by the way. It ought to give me a leg up in the Movement. And what were you up to? I never saw you.'

'No,' said Jasper, 'because I was hiding underneath the platform all the time. I can't bear being hurt.'

'Darling Jasper, you never let one down for a moment, do you?'

'Are you going to marry me?'

'Honestly, I don't see how I can help it. It would seem a bit wasteful not to keep you about the place, considering that you are the only person I've ever met who makes me laugh all the time without stopping.'

'Good,' said Jasper, 'we'll sell the tiara then, shall we?'

'Yes, darling!'

'And go to Uruguay next week?'

'No, darling. I shouldn't fancy that – fuzzy wuzzies aren't at all my dish!'

18

A large luncheon-table was prepared in the Iolanthe room at the Savoy. There were a great many glasses on it and a huge bouquet of orchids, while several champagne bottles in buckets of ice completed an atmosphere of extreme gaiety. The room next door was also thrown open and a cocktail bar here awaited the assembling of the guests. All was now in readiness for the wedding luncheon-party of Mr Wilkins and Lady Marjorie Merrith, who were busy uttering nuptial vows in the presence of their nearest and dearest at the Caxton Hall, Westminster.

The first guest strayed into Iolanthe and thence into the next room, where she refused a cocktail which was pressed upon her by several waiters, but fell with healthy appetite upon the salted almonds and potato crisps. It was Eugenia, who, having given T.P.O.F. the slip, had found her way to London by an early train, and from thence to the Union Jack House, where she had spent a blissful morning with Comrades of the London branch. Her eyes still sparkled from excitement at the memory of her reception. The Captain had himself granted her an interview, warmly thanked her for all the work she had done on behalf of the Movement and had finally, as a token of gratitude, plucked, like the pelican, his own little emblem from his own bosom and pinned it, still warm, upon hers. When she had left the great man, tears of emotion streaming from her eyes, the Comrades had clustered round her and had made her give her own account of the now epic Battle of Chalford Park. After this they had made much of her, fed her on sausage rolls and twopenny bars, given her a special cheer and salute, and had all promised to visit the Chalford Branch in the nearest of futures.

As Eugenia was still wearing her usual costume of Union Jack shirt, old grey woollen skirt, belt complete with dagger, and bare legs and head, she cut a suffi-ciently incongruous figure in the sophisticated atmosphere of a large hotel. The waiters stared at her in astonishment and she returned their glances quite unabashed; she was lacking in the nervousness which many a young girl might have felt while spending her first day in London.

Presently Mrs Lace came trailing in, wearing clothes reminiscent of the riding habit of a widowed queen-empress. She also had been unable to attend the marriage ceremony, having spent her morning in a frenzied rush round the shops. Eugenia had already seen her that day, they had come up from Rackenbridge by the same train, the Laces travelling first-class and Eugenia third.

'Oh! how are you?' said Mrs Lace. For the hundredth time she took in the details of Eugenia's attire with a kind of disgusted satisfaction, disgust that one so rich should put her money to so little use, satisfaction that Eugenia would certainly never rival herself as the best-dressed woman in the Cotswolds. Eugenia, who could not understand the significance of her glances, thought that Anne-Marie was looking more grumpy than usual today. Presently, gathering up her velvet train, Anne-Marie sauntered to a looking-glass, where she rearranged her silver fox to its best advantage and pinned to it a couple of gardenias which she took out of a thick white paper bag. She looked at herself with her head on one side and her lips pursed as though she were about to whistle, after which she swayed back to the side of Eugenia, who was happily browsing in a basket of crystallized fruits.

'Cold, isn't it?' said Mrs Lace, in her foreign accent. In truth, she was not feeling quite happy about her black velvet, furs and feathers; the day being a particularly hot one in late September, she was beginning to wonder whether she was not rather unsuitably dressed for it. 'Cold, isn't it?'

'No,' said Eugenia, with her mouth full.

'I always think these autumn days singularly deceptive, they look so warm, but one has to be very careful, *le fond de l'air est cru.*'

'It's perfectly boiling today,' said Eugenia, scornfully. 'I don't know what those foreign words mean I'm afraid. Under the régime people will talk English or hold their tongues.'

'My dear child, how ridiculous you are. Régime itself is a French word, you know.'

'Oh! no, it's not,' said Eugenia, 'it has become anglicized long ago by the Comrades.'

Jasper and Noel now came in. Jasper flung his arms round Eugenia's neck. 'You simply can't have any idea how pleased I am to see you, darling,' he cried, 'I never thought you would make it.'

'Nor did I,' said Eugenia. 'Luckily T.P.O.F. is ill in bed, so she will never know, unless that old yellow Pacifist of a nanny tells her. I rode to the station on Vivian Jackson and had to leave him tethered there all day, the poor angel.'

'Well, and what have you been up to since we left?'

'Oh! nothing much, it's been fairly dull down there (you heard we made a hundred and eighty-six pounds for the Movement, I suppose?) But today has been wonderful. I was able to keep a non-Aryan family from getting into my carriage at Oxford simply by showing them my little emblem and drawing my dagger at them and I can't tell you what a morning I've had with the Comrades at the Union Jack House – Oh, boy!'

'Come next door and let's hear about it,' said Jasper, mischievously, leaving Noel to a tête-à-tête with Mrs Lace.

Noel was now wondering whether he had ever really been in love with her at all. Good manners, however, demanded that he should keep up the fiction, so he kissed her hand, gazed passionately into her eyes and murmured that he was happy to be with her again.

'*Moi aussi je suis contente*,' said Mrs Lace, with a mournful look. She felt that her black velvet, if rather sweaty in such weather, at least assisted her to present a highly romantic appearance. 'How are things going with you, *mon cher*?' She had been cheated out of her great renunciation scene at Chalford, perhaps she would be able to enact it here and now.

'I am rather worried,' said Noel, snatching at any opportunity to talk about himself as opposed to themselves. The others could not now be long in coming, until they did, the conversation must be kept on a safe level. He cursed Jasper for leaving them together, typical piece of spitefulness. 'I am doubtful now whether I shall get that appointment in Vienna I told you of. My uncle, who has some influence there, is still trying hard to get it for me, and General von Pittshelm, an old friend of my parents, is pulling certain strings, I believe. All the same, it seems fairly hopeless – so much stands in the way.'

On hearing this Mrs Lace felt thankful that things had gone no farther between herself and Noel. She had begun to think during the calm, dull weeks which had succeeded the pageant that the penniless heir to a throne, which he was unlikely ever to ascend, would be a poor exchange for the solid comforts of the Lace home, although he might provide a sweet romance to while away a boring summer. It behoved her to be discreet.

'You never came to say good-bye to me,' she murmured, plaintively.

'Darling, it wasn't possible. If you only knew –'

'I think I do. We must say good-bye here, then, I suppose. In public. It seems hard.'

'But I shall come to Chalford again awfully soon, you know.'

'It can never be the same. My husband – he knows something of our romance and suspects more. I have had a terrible time since you left.'

'I say, not really? Is he – will he – I mean he hasn't got anything on us, has he?'

'My husband,' said Mrs Lace, grandiloquently, 'will forgive me everything. He has a noble character and moreover he loves me to distraction.'

'Thank heaven!' said Noel, 'I mean – you know, darling, that I would love to carry you right away from Chalford for ever, but it isn't possible in the circumstances. I am much too poor. Besides, I could never have taken you from your children; the thought of them would have come between us in the end. All the same, I shall love you for ever; you will always be the love of my life.'

'And you,' said Mrs Lace, 'of mine.'

She looked up at him with her sideways glance that she supposed to be so alluring, and thought, as she used to think when he first came to Chalford, that his was an unromantic appearance. 'More like a stockbroker than a king,' she thought.

'If you should ever happen to be passing through Vienna,' he was saying, 'you must look me up, if I go, and we will do the night clubs together if there are any, although I hear it is far from gay there now. A friend of mine who has just come back from there tells me that he is off to North Wales in search of amorous adventure – been reading Caradoc Evans, I suppose.

'Ah!' he cried, greatly relieved, 'here come the others at last.'

A buzz of lively conversation could be heard approaching down the corridor. Mrs Lace took up a position by the window, twitching at her fox. She opened her eyes very wide and assumed an expression of romantic gloom.

The door burst open. Lady Marjorie, radiant and beautiful in white crêpe-de-chine with a huge black hat, appeared hand in hand with Mr Wilkins. She looked the very picture of happiness. Mr Wilkins looked the same as usual, except for his smart grey suit and buttonhole of a red carnation. Immediately after them came Lady Fitzpuglington, escorted by a well-known statesman and followed by a flock of smart and glittering young people, which included Poppy St Julien.

Lady Fitzpuglington, considering what her feelings must have been on the subject, had behaved extraordinarily well to Marjorie over this marriage. She had made three earth-shaking scenes about it, after which, seeing that nothing she could say would avail to alter the girl's determination, she had given way with a good grace, merely stipulating that the wedding itself should be kept absolutely private, in order that the Duke of Dartford's feelings might be spared as far as possible.

'There's nothing to be done,' she told her brother. 'Marjorie is of age and madly in love, therefore nothing I can say or do will stop her. We must make the best of a bad job and be thankful that divorce is such an easy matter in these days. Poor Mr Wilkins, of course, doesn't want to marry her in the least, but there it is, poor man. Now, if Puggie had only taken my advice and left her a minor until the age of forty, how different it would all have been. We should at least have had some hold over the little idiot then.'

Her ladyship's brother did not reply. He thought that the unlucky Fitzpuglington, floating as he had been, a six months' corpse in the Atlantic when his daughter was born, might be excused for having failed to provide against her passion for Mr Wilkins. Lady Fitzpuglington was noted in the family as being an adept at loading her own responsibilities upon the shoulders of other people.

Mrs Lace noticed that the ladies of the party were not curtsying to Noel – even his hostess had not greeted him. She found this puzzling. Surely in London he did not preserve his incognito. Also she was very much annoyed when she saw that the other young women present were every bit as pretty as she. She thought their clothes excessively boring, however. They were all of the plainly tailored variety, consisting of little suits or crêpe-de-chine dresses covered by thin woollen coats. Mrs Lace only cared for fancy dress. She wished, all the same, that she had put on something a trifle cooler, she was boiled in her riding habit.

'I say, darling,' whispered one of the pretty ladies to Marjorie, 'is that a fortune-teller over by the window, or what? And who is that lovely mad-looking girl with no hat?'

Major Lace now appeared. He had been best man to his friend and had only just got away from the registry office. Mrs Lace, for once in her life, was pleased to see her husband. In all this large gay crowd nobody was paying any attention to her; she almost felt that she would be glad to be back in Chalford again where she was the undisputed belle.

'Are you going to marry Union Jackshirt Aspect?' Eugenia asked Poppy.

'Yes darling, I am, isn't it wonderful. My husband was rather tiresome about it at first, but now he's really behaving quite well and I think, with any luck, he ought to let me divorce him.'

'Why?' asked Eugenia.

'Well, it's not usual for ladies to be divorced, you know, my sweet, and the old boy has always been a great one for etiquette. Those detectives were never anything to do with him at all, just down there for a hol. we found out afterwards. Awfully funny, really, when one thinks of it. Will you come to my wedding, Eugenia?'

'I will, and we'll have a Social Unionist guard of honour, if you like. I hope you will be very happy, Cousin Poppy St Julien, and continue to work for the Cause after your marriage.'

At luncheon Jasper and Noel sat one on each side of Mrs Lace.

'By the way old boy,' Jasper said to Noel, leaning across her, 'I don't want that job of yours any more. Poppy and I got forty thousand pounds for the tiara, you know, and I think of standing for Parliament or something like that as soon as the divorce is over. It occurred to me that if your Viennese business doesn't come off as you hope, you might care to go back to Fruel's. Sir Percy seems quite anxious to have you there again. I went to see him yesterday about a few investments I am making.'

'Too kind of you,' said Noel.

Faint suspicions, shadowy doubts which had long been gathering in Mrs Lace's mind were thus rudely confirmed. She would not, however, allow her brain to take in the full-portent of all this until she was safely in her first-class carriage, alone with Major Lace. Then she cried and cried. Major Lace supposed that she was in the family way again. She was.

Afterwards, Jasper said to Noel, 'Was it tactless of me to mention Fruel's like that? It occurred to me, too late, that perhaps you would really feel safer if she thought you were abroad?'

'She seems just about as ready to wind it all up as I am. I do think girls are queer.'

'Perhaps she has found out something to your discredit.'

'I don't suppose any such thing,' said Noel, peevishly.

'Bit tired of you perhaps?'

'Certainly not. The girl is madly in love with me, madly, but the husband has been cutting up rough and all that, and naturally she can't face leaving the children.'

'That must be a great relief for you, old boy.'

After luncheon the elder statesman made a speech proposing the health of bride and bridegroom. It was a long speech with rather poor jokes distributed like sugar plums here and there. Lady Marjorie replied to it, as Mr Wilkins was too bashful. She said that it was fearfully kind of everybody to give her a second lot of wonderful wedding presents so soon after having the first ones returned. The second ones were much the nicest, too. She was fearfully happy, she said, inconsequently, and indeed this was apparent to all beholders. She hoped that everybody would come to her house-warming party when she and Mr Wilkins had returned from their honeymoon and settled in Carlton House Terrace, where she had bought a house. 'In fact, you can all come and stay if you like,' she added, 'as we shall have quantities of spare rooms.'

'Good,' said Jasper, '"where I drinks I sleeps" has always been my favourite motto.'

Eugenia was now called upon, and leapt to her feet without the smallest diffidence, amid ringing cheers. She said that she was sure nobody could grudge any amount of gorgeous wedding presents to such a heavenly person as Lady Marjorie, or to such a brave Union Jackshirt as Mr Wilkins. In any case they certainly took with them on their honeymoon any amount of good wishes from herself and all the members of the Chalford Branch. As for the spare rooms, she said, it was to be hoped that they would soon be quite filled up with healthy little Aryan babies. The company then rose at her suggestion and sang:

> 'Land of Union Jackshirts,
> Mother of the Flag.'

Two days later Noel was back once more in the office of Fruel and Grimthorpe. Miss Brisket, Miss Clumps and Mr Farmer sat as of old in their appointed places. Noel was just coming to the end of a long telephone conversation. 'No, I'm sorry,' he was saying, in a firm and final voice, 'not sufficiently attractive.'

Pigeon Pie

To Phyllis Blake, Margaret Candler
and, of course, to the
Wonderful Old Songster
of Kew Green himself
I dedicate this book.

I hope that anybody who is kind enough to read it in a second edition will remember that it was written before Christmas 1939. Published on 6 May 1940 it was an early and unimportant casualty of the real war which was then beginning.

Nancy Mitford, Paris 1951

I

Sophia Garfield had a clear mental picture of what the outbreak of war was going to be like. There would be a loud bang, succeeded by inky darkness and a cold wind. Stumbling over heaps of rubble and dead bodies, Sophia would search with industry, but without hope, for her husband, her lover and her dog. It was in her mind like the End of the World, or the Last Days of Pompeii, and for more than two years now she had been steeling herself to bear with fortitude the hardships, both mental and physical, which must accompany this cataclysm.

However, nothing in life happens as we expect, and the outbreak of the great war against Hitlerism certainly did not happen according to anybody's schedule except possibly Hitler's own. In fact, Sophia was driving in her Rolls-Royce through one of those grey and nondescript towns on the border between England and Scotland when, looking out of the window, she saw a man selling newspapers; the poster which he wore as an apron had scrawled upon it in pencil the words WAR BEGUN. As this was on the thirty-first of August, 1939, the war which had begun was the invasion of Poland by Germany; the real war, indeed, did begin more pompously, if not more in accordance with preconceived ideas, some four days later. There was no loud bang, but Mr Chamberlain said on the wireless what a bitter blow it had been for him, and then did his best to relieve the tension by letting off air-raid sirens. It sounded very nice and dramatic, though a few citizens, having supposed that their last hour was at hand, were slightly annoyed by this curious practical joke.

Sophia's war began in that border town. She felt rather shivery when she saw the poster, and said to Rawlings, her chauffeur, 'Did you see?' and Rawlings said, 'Yes, m'lady, I did.' Then they passed by a hideous late-Victorian church, and the whole population of the town seemed to be occupied in propping it up with sandbags. Sophia, who had never seen a sandbag before, began to cry, partly from terror and partly because it rather touched her to see anybody taking so much trouble over a church so ugly that it might have been specially made for bombs. Further along the road in a small, grey village, a band of children, with labels round their necks and bundles in their arms, were standing by a motor-bus. Most of them were howling. Rawlings volunteered the remark that he had never expected to see refugees in England, that Hitler was a red swine, and he would like to get his hands on him. At a garage where they stopped for petrol the man said that we could never have held up our heads if we hadn't finished it now.

When they got to Carlisle, Sophia decided that she must go on by train to London. She had been on the road already for ten hours, and was miserably stiff, but having arranged to help with the evacuation of mothers and children, she was due at a school in the Commercial Road at eight o'clock the following morning. Accordingly, she told Rawlings to stay the night at Carlisle, and she herself boarded the London train. There were no sleepers, the train was full of drunken soldiers, and it was blacked out. Some journeys remain in the memory as a greater nightmare even than bad illness; this was to be one of them. Sophia was lucky to secure a seat, as people were standing in the corridors; she did so, however, sharing the carriage with a Scotch officer, his very young wife, a nasty middle-aged lady and several sleeping men. The nasty lady and the officer's wife both had puppies with them, which surprised Sophia. She had wrenched herself away from her own Milly that morning, unwilling to have an extra object of search among the rubble and corpses. Soon total darkness descended, and fellow-passengers became mere shadowy forms and voices assuming ghost-like proportions.

The officer's wife went to the lavatory, and the little officer said confidentially to Sophia, 'We were only married on Saturday, and she's verra upset,' which made Sophia cry again. She supposed she was going to spend the war in rivers of tears, being an easy crier. The nasty lady now said that it seemed foolish to go to war for Poland, but nobody bothered to take up the point.

'You mark my words,' she said, 'this will mean a shilling on the income tax.'

Whether or not it be true that drowning persons are treated to a cinematograph show of their past lives, it is certainly a fact that during fiendish journeys undertaken with no cheerful object in view most people's thoughts are inclined to take on that drowning aspect either with regard to past or future events. Sophia, achingly tired, but unable to go to sleep, began to re-enact in her mind scenes from her past life.

The only child of a widowed peer, who could write his name, Maida Vale, but little else, she had seen London for the first time at the age of eighteen. An aunt had then taken her out in the world. She fell under the influence of Maurice Baring's novels, her ideal hero was a suave, perhaps slightly bald, enormously cultivated diplomat. Gentlemen of this description did not abound at the balls she went to, and the callow youths of twenty who did, were a source of disillusionment to her. She was not shy and she had high spirits, but she was never a romper and therefore never attained much popularity with the very young. At the end of her first London season, she went to a large house party for Goodwood, and here one of her fellow-guests was Luke Garfield. He had just left the diplomatic service to go into the City. His very pompous, cultivated manner, excellent clothes, knowledge of foreign affairs and slight baldness gave him prestige in the eyes of Sophia, and he became her hero. On the other hand, Luke saw at once that her charm and unusual looks would be invaluable to him in his career, and in so far as he was capable of such a warm-blooded emotion, he fell in love with the girl. He proposed to her the following November, after she had poured out tea for him in her aunt's drawing-room. His pinstripe trousers and perfect restraint seemed to her quite ideal, the whole scene could have come out of 'Cat's Cradles', and was crowned for her by Luke's suggestion that their honeymoon should be spent in Rome where he had recently been *en poste*.

How soon she began to realize that he was a pompous prig she could not remember. He was a sight-seeing bore, and took her the Roman rounds with a dutiful assiduity, and without ever allowing her to sit on a stone and use her eyes. Her jokes annoyed and never amused him; when she said that all the sights in Rome were called after London cinemas, he complained that she was insular, facetious and babyish. She was insular, really; she loved England and never thought abroad was worth the trouble it took getting there. Luke spoke Italian in such a dreadfully affected way that it embarrassed her to hear him.

It was on her honeymoon in Rome that she first met Rudolph Jocelyn. He made no great impression on her, being the antithesis of what she then so much admired. He was not bald, suave, or in any sense of the word a diplomat. On the contrary, he had a shock of tow-coloured hair, spoke indistinctly, dressed badly, and was always in a great hurry. Luke disapproved of him; he said that Jocelyn's journalistic activities were continually getting the Embassy in trouble with the Italians. Besides, he kept low company and looked disreputable, and the fact that he spoke Italian like a native, and two dialects as well, failed to endear him to Luke. Some months later Sophia heard that he had mobilized the Italian army in a moment of light-heartedness; his newspaper splashed the martial news, and Rudolph Jocelyn was obliged to abandon journalism as a career.

Sophia had a happy character and was amused by life; if she was slightly disillusioned she was by no means unhappy in her marriage. Luke was as cold as a fish and a great bore; soon however she began to regard him as a great joke, and as she liked jokes she became quite fond of him when, which happened soon, she fell out of love with him. Also she saw very little of him. He left the house before she was properly awake in the morning, returning only in time to dress for dinner, then they dined out. Every Saturday to Monday they stayed with friends in the country. Sophia often spent weeks at a time with her father, in Worcestershire or Scotland. Luke seemed to be getting very rich. About twice a week he obliged her to entertain or be entertained by insufferably boring business people, generally Americans. He explained that this must be regarded as her work so she acquiesced meekly, but unfortunately she was not very good at her work, as Luke never hesitated to tell her. He said that she treated the wives of these millionaires as if they were cottage women and she a visiting duchess. He said they were unused to being treated with condescension by the wives of much poorer men, who hoped to do business with their husbands. Sophia could not understand all this; she thought she was being wonderful to them, but they seemed to her a strange species.

'I simply don't see the point of getting up at six all the time you are young and working eighteen hours a day in order to be a millionaire, and then when you are a millionaire still getting up at six and working eighteen hours a day, like Mr Holst. And poor Mrs Holst, who has got up at six too all these years, so that now she can't sleep on in the morning, only has the mingiest little diamond clip you ever saw. What does it all mean?'

Luke said something about big business and not tying up your capital. Mr Holst was the head of the firm of which Luke's was the London office, and the Holst visits to England were a nightmare for Sophia. She was obliged to see a great deal of Mrs Holst on these occasions and to listen by the hour to her accounts of their early struggles as well as to immense lectures on business ethics.

'Lady Sophia,' Mrs Holst would say, fingering her tiny diamond clip, 'I hope that you and Sir Luke fully realize that Mr Holst has entrusted his good name – for the good of the business, Lady Sophia, is the good name of Mr Holst, and in fact Mr Holst has often said to me that Mr Holst's business is Mr Holst – well, as I was saying, this good name is entrusted into Sir Luke's keeping and into your keeping, Lady Sophia. I always say a business man's wife should be Caesar's wife. As I have told you, Lady Sophia, Mr Holst worked for twenty hours a day for thirty years to build up this business. Often and often I have heard him say "My home is my office and my office is my home" and that, Lady Sophia, is the profound truth. Now, as I was saying . . .' and so it went on.

Sophia, who was never able to get it out of her head that the City was a large room in which a lot of men sat all day doing sums, and who was of course quite unable to distinguish between stockbrokers, billbrokers, bankers and jobbers, found these lectures almost as incomprehensible as the fact that Mrs Holst should take so much interest in her husband's profession when it had only produced, for her, such a wretched little diamond clip. Sophia loved jewels, she had fortunately inherited very beautiful ones of her own from her mother, and Luke, who was not at all mean, often added to them when he had brought off a deal.

The train stopped. The Scotch officer, his wife, the nasty lady and their puppies all got out. It was one o'clock in the morning. The carriage then filled up, from the corridor which was packed, with very young private soldiers. They were very drunk, singing over and over again a dirty little song about which bits of Adolph they were going to bring back with them. They all ended by passing out, two with their heads in Sophia's lap. She was too tired to remove them, and so they lay snoring hot breath on to her for the rest of the journey.

Her thoughts continued. After some years of marriage Luke had joined the Boston Brotherhood, one of those new religions which are wafted to us every six months or so across the Atlantic. At first she had suspected that he found it very profitable in the way of deals with other Brothers; presently however he became earnest. He inaugurated week-end parties in their London house, which meant a hundred people to every meal, great jolly queues waiting outside the lavatories, public confessions in the drawing-room, and quiet times in the housemaid's cupboard. Sophia had not been very ladylike about all this, and in fact had played a double game in order to get the full benefit of it. She allowed people to come clean all over her, and even came clean herself in a perfectly shameless way, combing the pages of Freud for new sins with which to fascinate the Brotherhood. So, of course, they loved her. It was just at this time that everything in Sophia's life began to seem far more amusing because of Rudolph Jocelyn whom she had fallen in love with. He came to all the week-end parties, tea parties, fork luncheons and other celebrations of the newest Christianity, and Luke disliked him as much as ever but endured him in a cheery Brotherly way, regarding him no doubt as a kind of penance, sent to chasten, as well as a brand to be snatched from the burning. Brothers, like Roman Catholics, get a bonus for souls.

Sophia and Rudolph loved each other very much. This does not mean that it had ever occurred to them to alter the present situation, which seemed exactly to suit all parties; Rudolph was unable to visualize himself as a married man, and Sophia feared that divorce, re-marriage and subsequent poverty would not bring out the best in her character. As for Luke, he took up with a Boston Brotherly soulmate called Florence, and was perfectly contented with matters as they stood. Florence, he realized, would not show to the same advantage as Sophia when he was entertaining prospective clients; Sophia might not be ideally tactful with their wives, but she did radiate an atmosphere of security and of the inevitability of upper-class status quo. Florence, however saintly, did not. Besides that, Luke was hardly the kind of man to favour divorce. Middle-aged, rather fat and very rich, he would look ridiculous, he knew, if his wife ran away with a poor, handsome and shabby young man. Let it be whispered too that Luke and Sophia, after so many years, were really rather attached to each other.

As she sat in the train reviewing her past life, Sophia felt absolutely certain that it was now over and done with. It lay behind her, while she, with every revolution of the wheels, was being carried towards that loud bang, those ruins, corpses and absence of loved ones. She had been taken very much unawares by the war, staying with her father in a remote part of Scotland where telephone and radio were unknown, and where the newspapers were often three days late. Now in the blacked-out train crowded with soldiers, she was already enveloped by it. The skies of London were probably dark by now with enemy planes, but apprehension was of so little use that she concentrated upon the happiness of her past life. The future must look after her in its own way. She became drowsy, and her mind filled with images. The first meet she ever went to, early in the morning with her father's agent. She often remembered this, and it had become a composite picture of all the cub-hunting she had ever done, the autumn woods and the smell of bonfires, dead leaves and hot horses. Riding home from the last meet of a season, late in the afternoon of a spring day, there would be primroses and violets under the hedges, far far away the sound of a horn, and later an owl. The world is not a bad place, it is a pity to have to die. But, of course, it is only a good place for a very few people. Think of Dachau, think of China, and Czechoslovakia and Spain. Think of the distressed areas. We must die now, and there must be a new world. Sophia went to sleep and only woke up at Euston. She went to the station hotel, had a bath, and arrived at the Commercial Road at exactly eight o'clock. Of the day which followed she had afterwards but little recollection. The women from London were wonderful, their hostesses in the country extremely disagreeable. It was a sad business.

When it was over Sophia went to bed and slept for thirteen hours.

2

She got up in time for luncheon. There had been no loud bang, the house was not in ruins, and when she rang her bell Greta, her German maid, appeared.

'Oh Greta, I thought you would have gone.'

'Gone, Frau Gräfin?'

Arguments and persuasion from Sophia failed to prevent Greta from calling her this.

'Back to Germany.'

'Oh no, Frau Gräfin; Sir Luke says there will be no war. Our good Führer will not make war on England.'

Sophia was rather bored. She had never liked Greta and had not expected to find her still there. She asked whether Sir Luke was in, and was told yes, and that he had ordered luncheon for four. It was a very hot day, and she put on a silk dress which, owing to the cold summer, she had hitherto been unable to wear.

Rudolph was in the drawing-room making a cocktail.

'I say, have you seen Florence? God has guided her to dye her hair.'

'No – what colour – where is she?'

'Orange. Downstairs,' he said, pulling Sophia towards him with the hand which did not hold the cocktail shaker, and kissing her. 'How are you?'

'Very pleased to see you, my darling. It seemed a long time.'

Florence appeared, followed by Luke. Her hair, which had been brown, was indeed a rich marmalade, and she was rather smartly dressed in printed crêpe-de-chine, though the dress did not look much when seen near Sophia's.

'Have a drink,' said Rudolph, pouring them out. Florence gave him a tortured, jolly smile, and said that drinking gave her extraordinarily little pleasure nowadays. Luke, who hated being offered drinks in his own house, refused more shortly. 'Lunch is ready,' he said.

They went downstairs.

'Has the war begun?' asked Sophia, wondering who could have ordered soup for luncheon, and seeing in this the God-guided hand of Florence. She guessed that Florence was staying in the house.

'No,' said Rudolph. 'I don't know what we're waiting for.'

'My information is,' said Luke, at which Rudolph gave a great wink, because Luke so often used those words and his information was so often not quite correct, 'my information is that Our Premier (his voice here took on a reverent note) is going to be able to save the peace again. At a cost, naturally. We shall have to sacrifice Poland, of course, but I hear that the Poles are in a very bad way, rotten with Communism, you know, and they will be lucky to have Herr Hitler to put things right there. Then we may have to give him some colony or other, and of course a big loan.'

'What about the Russian pact?' said Rudolph.

'Means nothing – absolutely nothing. Herr Hitler will never allow the Bolsheviks into Europe. No, I don't feel any alarm. We have no quarrel with Germany that Our Premier and Herr Hitler together cannot settle peacefully.'

Sophia said shortly, 'Well, if they do, and there isn't a revolution here as the result, I shall leave this country for ever and live somewhere else, that's all. But I won't believe it.'

Then, remembering from past experience that such conversations were not only useless but also led to ill-feeling, she changed the subject. She had never been so near parting from Luke as at the time of Munich, when, in his eyes, Our Premier had moved upon the same exalted sphere as Brother Bones, founder of the Boston Brotherhood, and almost you might say, God. His information then had been that the Czechs were in a very bad way, rotten with Communism, and would be lucky to have Herr Hitler to put things right. It also led him to believe that universal disarmament would follow the Munich agreement, and that the Sudetenland was positively Hitler's last territorial demand in Europe. Carlyle has said that identity of sentiment but difference of opinion are the known elements of pleasant dialogue. The dialogue in many English homes at that time was very far from pleasant.

'Then a silly old welfare-worker came up to a woman with eight coal-black children and said, "You haven't got a yellow label, so you can't be pregnant," and the woman said, "Can't I? Won't the dad be pleased to hear that now?" And when we got to the village green the parson was waiting to meet us, and he looked at the pregnant ladies and said, very sadly, "To think that *one man* is responsible for all this." It's absolutely true.'

Rudolph watched her with admiration. He enjoyed Sophia's talent for embroidering on her own experiences, and the way she rushed from hyperbole to hyperbole, ending upon a wild climax of improbability with the words 'It's absolutely true.' According to Sophia, she could hardly move outside her house without encountering the sort of adventure that only befalls the ordinary person once in a lifetime. Her narrative always had a basis of truth, and this was an added fascination for Rudolph who amused himself by trying to separate fact from fiction.

'Darling Sophia,' he said, as she came to the end of a real tour de force about her father, whom she had left, she said, blackening the pebbles of his drive which he considered would be particularly visible from the air, 'I know what your job will be in the war – taking German spies out to luncheon and telling them what you believe to be the truth. When you look them in the eye and say "I promise it's absolutely true", they'll think it's gospel because it'll be so obvious that you do yourself. The authorities will simply tell you the real truth, and you'll do the rest for them.'

'Oh, Rudolph, what a glamorous idea!'

She took Florence upstairs. Florence wriggled a good deal which she always did if she felt embarrassed, and in spite of her conscious superiority in the moral sphere she often felt embarrassed with Sophia. Presently she said in a loud, frank voice, 'I hope it's all right, Sophia. I'm staying here.'

'Oh, good. I hope you're comfortable. If you want any ironing done, just tell Greta.'

Florence said she required extraordinarily little maiding, but this did not for a moment deceive Sophia, who had been told by Greta, in a burst of confidence, that Fraulein Turnbull gave more trouble than three of the Frau Gräfin.

Florence now drew a deep breath, always with her the prelude to an outburst of Christianity, and said that the times were very grave and that it made her feel sad to see people pay so little attention to their souls as Sophia and Rudolph.

'We don't think our rotten little souls so important as all that.'

'Ah but you see it isn't only your souls. Each person has a quantity of other souls converging upon his – that's what makes this life such a frightfully jolly adventure. In your case, Sophia, with your looks and position, you could influence directly and indirectly hundreds – yes, hundreds of people. Think how exciting that would be.'

Sophia saw that she was in for a sermon, and resigned herself. She knew from sad experience that to answer back merely encouraged the Brotherhood to fresh efforts.

'You know, dear, Luke feels it very much. It hurts him when you talk as you did at lunch, flippantly and with exaggeration. I wish you could realize how much happier it makes one to be perfectly truthful, even in little ways. Truth is a thing that adds so greatly to the value of human relationships.'

'Some,' said Sophia carelessly. 'Now it adds to the value of my relationship with Rudolph to tell more and funnier lies. He likes it.'

'I wonder if that sort of relationship is of much value. Personally the only people I care to be very intimate with are the ones you feel would make a good third if God asked you out to dinner.'

Sophia wished that Florence would not talk about the Almighty as if his real name was Godfrey, and God was just Florence's nickname for him.

'Oh, God would get on with Rudolph,' she said.

Florence smiled her bright, crucified smile, and said that she was sure there was good material in Rudolph if one knew where to look for it. Then she wriggled about and said, very loudly, 'Oh, Sophia, how much happier it would be for you, and for those about you, if you would give your sins to God. I feel there would be, oh! such a gay atmosphere in this house if you could learn to do just that.'

'Only one sin, Florence, such a harmless one. I don't steal, I honour my father, I don't covet, and I don't commit murder.'

'Perhaps flippancy is the worst sin of all.'

'I'm not flippant but I'm not religious and I never will be, not if I live to a hundred. It's a matter of temperament, you know.'

This was a false step. Florence now embarked on a rigmarole of bogus philosophy which no power short of an explosion could have stopped. Poor Sophia lay back and let it flow, which it did until the men came into the drawing-room, when Florence gave Luke a flash of her white and even teeth which all too clearly said 'I have failed again.'

'I'm just going up for a little quiet time,' she said. 'I'll be ready in half an hour.' She and Luke played golf on Saturday afternoons.

'I'm just going down for a little quiet time and I'll be ready in about half an hour,' said Rudolph, picking up the *Tatler*. When he got back, he said, 'Come along, Sophia, I'm taking you to the local A.R.P. office to get a job.'

'There won't be any war,' said Luke comfortably, as he settled down to his *Times*.

Sophia and Rudolph strolled out into the sunshine.

'Let's go to Kew,' said Sophia.

'Yes, we will when you have got your job.'

'Oh darling, oh dear, do I have to have a job?'

'Yes, you do, or I shall be through with you. You know that I think it's perfectly shameful the way you haven't done any training the last few months. Now you must get on with it quickly. There is only one justification for people like you in a community, and that is that they should pull their weight in a war. The men must fight and the women must be nurses.'

'Darling, I couldn't be a nurse. Florence has a first aid book and I looked inside and saw a picture of a knee. I nearly fainted. I can't bear knees, I've got a thing about them. I don't like ill people, either, and then I'm not so very strong, I should cockle. Tell you what – could I be a précis writer at the Foreign Office?'

'There haven't been précis writers at the Foreign Office since Lord Palmerston. Anyway, you couldn't work in a Government Department, you're far too mooney. If you can't bear knees and don't like ill people, you can scrub floors and wash up for those that can and do. Now here we are, go along and fix yourself up.'

Sophia found herself in a large empty house, empty, that is, of furniture, but full of would-be workers. She had to wait in a queue before being interviewed by a lady at a desk. The young man in front of her announced that he was a Czech, and not afraid of bombs. The lady said nor are British women afraid of bombs, which Sophia thought was going too far. She gave the young man an address to go to, and turned briskly to Sophia.

'Yes?' she said.

Sophia felt the shades of the prison-house closing in on her. She explained that she would do full-time voluntary work, but that she had no qualifications. For one wild moment of optimism she thought that the lady was going to turn her down. After looking through some papers, she said, however, 'Could you do office work in a First Aid Post?'

'I could try,' said Sophia doubtfully.

'Then take this note to Sister Wordsworth at St Anne's Hospital First Aid Post. Thank you. Good day.'

Rudolph was in earnest conversation with a German Jew when she came out. On hearing that she was fixed up, he said that she might have a holiday before beginning her job. 'You can go to St Anne's tomorrow,' he said. 'I'm taking you down to Kew now.'

They sat on a bench at the end of the ilex avenue and stared at Syon House across the river. Sophia asked Rudolph what he planned to do, now that the war had begun.

'I hope for a commission, of course,' he said; 'failing that I shall enlist.'

'Somebody who knows all those languages could get a job at home – I mean not a fighting job. Perhaps it is your duty to do that,' she said hopefully.

'Can't help my duty; I'm going to fight Germans in this war – not Nazis, mind you, Germans. I mean huns.'

Sophia agreed with him really. The huns must be fought.

'How strange everything seems now that the war is here,' she said. 'I suppose it is unreal because we have been expecting it for so long now, and have known that it must be got over before we can go on with our lives. Like in the night when you want to go to the loo and it is miles away down a freezing cold passage and yet you know you have to go down that passage before you can be happy and sleep again. We are starting down it now. Oh, darling, I wish it was over and we were back in bed. What shall I do when you've gone?'

'Don't you anticipate,' said Rudolph severely; 'you never have, so don't begin now. You are the only person I know who lives entirely in the present, it is one of the attractive things about you.'

'If you are killed,' said Sophia, paying no attention.

'You are one of those lucky women with two strings to their bow. If I am killed, there is always old Luke.'

'Yes, but the point is I shall have such an awful grudge against Luke, don't you see? I do so fearfully think the war is the result of people like him, always rushing off abroad and pretending to those wretched foreigners that England will stand for anything. Cracking them up over here, too; Herr Hitler this, and Herr von Ribbentrop that, and bulwarks against Bolshevism and so on. Of course, the old fellow thought he was making good feeling, and probably he never even realized that the chief reason he loved the Germans was because they buttered him up so much. All those free rides in motors and aeroplanes.'

'You can't blame him,' said Rudolph, 'he never cut any ice over here, but as soon as he set foot in Germany he was treated as a minor royalty or something. Of course it was lovely for him. Why, Berlin has been full of people like that for years. The Germans were told to make a fuss of English people, so of course masses of English stampeded over there to be made a fuss of. But it never occurred to them that they were doing definite harm to their own country; they just got a kick out of saying "mein Führer" and being taken round in Mercedes-Benzes. All the same they weren't directly responsible for the war. Old Luke is all right, he's a decent old fellow at heart. I feel quite happy leaving you in his hands. I believe he's getting over the Brotherhood, too, you'll see.'

As they strolled across Kew Green to get a taxi, an unearthly yelp announced to them that they had been observed by Sophia's godfather, Sir Ivor King, and sure enough, there he was, the old fellow, waving a curly, butter-coloured wig at them out of his bedroom window. He invited them to come in for a cup of tea.

This faintly farcical old figure was the idol of the British race, and reigned supreme in the hearts of his fellow-countrymen, indeed of music lovers all over the world, as the King of Song. In his heyday, he had been most famous as a singer of those sexy ballads which were adored by our grandparents, and for which most of us have a secret partiality. He was unrivalled, too, in opera. The unique quality of his voice was the fact that it could reach higher and also lower notes than have ever been reached before by any human being, some of which were so high that only bats, others so low that only horses, could hear them. When he was a very young man studying in Germany, his music teacher said to him, 'Herr King, you shall make, with that voice of yours, musical history. I hope I may live to hear you at your zenith.'

The prophecy came true. Ivor King was knighted at an early age, he made a large fortune, gained an unassailable position and the nickname by which he was always known, 'The King of Song', largely on the strength of this enormous range of voice. Largely, but not solely. A lovable and very strong personality, a genial quality of good fellowship, and latterly his enormous age, had played their part, and combined with his magnificent notes to make him not only one of the best known but also one of the best loved men of several successive generations. Among particular achievements he was the only man ever to sing the name part in the opera *Norma*, the script of which had been re-written especially for him, and re-named *Norman*.

The King of Song had toured the world, and particularly the Empire, dozens of times and these tours were indeed like royal progresses. In very remote parts of Africa the natives often mistook him for Queen Victoria's husband, and it was universally admitted that he had done more towards welding the Empire in the cultural sphere than any other individual. Quite bald, although with a marvellous selection of wigs, and finally quite toothless, he still maintained a gallant fight against old age, although some two years previously he had succumbed to the extent of giving a final farewell concert at the Albert Hall. He had then retired to a charming house on Kew Green, which he named Vocal Lodge, and devoted himself to botany; in the pursuit of this science, however, he was more keen than lucky.

'She wore a wreath of roses the day that first we met,' he chanted, cutting a seed cake. It was what the most vulgar of the many generations which had passed over his head would call his signature tune, and he sang it in a piercing soprano.

Sophia poured out tea, and asked after his Lesbian irises.

'They were not what they seemed,' he said, 'wretched things. I brought the roots all the way from Lesbos, as you know, and when they came up, what were they? Mere pansies. Too mortifying. And now I'm the air-raid warden for Kew Gardens, in a tin hat – and it will be years before I visit Greece again. It may be for years, and it may-hay be for ever. As you will note, the war has found me in excellent voice. I am singing at the Chiswick Town Hall tonight to our local decontamination squads. Such dear boys and girls. And let me darkly hint at a more exalted engagement in the not-too-too-far-off future. I was trying to decide, when I saw you on the Green, whether I should go to my interview with some Important Personages as a blond or a brunette. I think I favour the butter-coloured curls,' he said, taking off his wig and revealing beneath a head of egg-like baldness.

Sophia and Rudolph were quite used to this, for the King's wigs were as much off as on, and there was never any kind of pretence about them being his own luxuriant hair.

'Yes, I have always liked that one,' said Sophia, 'it softens your features. What important personages?'

'Ah,' said the old singer, 'I can keep a secret. What are you up to, Rudolph? I haven't seen you since the Munich crisis. I may tell you that, having heard that you were doing the Italian broadcast from the B.B.C., I switched on the wireless to listen. Well, I said to Magdalen Beech, poor Rudolph sounds very ill – then we discovered that it was the dear late Pope, and not Rudolph at all.'

Sir Ivor was a fervent Roman Catholic. For a short time, many years ago, he had been married to a woman so pious and so lavish with Sir Ivor's money that she had posthumously been made a Papal Duchess and was accorded the unique honour of being buried in the Vatican gardens. Lady Beech was her sister.

'Now you can tell me something,' said Sophia, glancing at the Sargent portrait, in brown velvet and lace, of Duchess King which hung over the chimneypiece. 'I had a letter from Lady Beech saying what a pity, as we must all so soon be dead, that we shouldn't all be going on to the same place afterwards. What really happens to us heretics, darling old gentleman?'

'Darling pretty young lady, you pop straight on to a gridiron and there you baste to eternity.'

'Baste?' said Sophia.

'Baste. Whenever I have time, perhaps say once in a million years, I will bring you a drop of water on the end of my finger. Apart from this, your pleasures will be few and simple.'

'What I'm wondering is,' said Rudolph, 'how much you and Lady Beech will enjoy such purely Catholic society for so uninterrupted a spell?'

At dinner that night, Luke's information was that a huge scheme of appeasement, world-wide in its implications, was even now being worked out. He said the wretched Socialists were not making things easy for Our Premier, but that he was too big a man and the scheme too big a scheme to be thwarted by pinpricks in Parliament. Parliament and the Press might have to be got rid of for a time whilst Our Premier and Herr Hitler rearranged the world. In any case, there would be no war. The next morning poor Luke was so wretched that Sophia felt quite sorry for him. He really seemed astounded that Herr Hitler should be prepared to risk all those wonderful swimming-pools in a major war.

When the Prime Minister's speech and hoax air-raid warning were over, Sophia went round to report at the First Aid Post. Here, in a large garage under St Anne's Hospital, cold, damp and dirty, pretty Sister Wordsworth was bringing order out of confusion. She really seemed pleased to engage Sophia, in spite of her lack of qualifications, and told her that she could come every day from one to seven. The work was simple. Sophia was to sit behind a partition of sacking, labelled Office, to answer the telephone, count the washing and do various odd jobs. In the case of raids, Sister Wordsworth assured her that while she might have to see knee joints, she would have no intimate contact with them.

Henceforward Sophia's life was sharply divided in two parts, her life behind the gas-proof flap of the First Aid Post and her own usual unhampered life outside. Sometimes she rather enjoyed her sacking life, sometimes she felt that she could hardly endure it. The cold stuffy atmosphere got on her nerves, she was unaccustomed to sitting still for hours on end, and what work there was to do, such as counting washing, she did not do very well. On the other hand, she liked all the people in the Post, and habit once having gripped her, as it does so soon in life, she became quite resigned and regarded the whole thing completely as a matter of course.

3

Rather soon after the war had been declared, it became obvious that nobody intended it to begin. The belligerent countries were behaving like children in a round game, picking up sides, and until the sides had been picked up the game could not start.

England picked up France, Germany picked up Italy. England beckoned to Poland, Germany answered with Russia. Then Italy's Nanny said she had fallen down and grazed her knee, running, and mustn't play. England picked up Turkey, Germany picked up Spain, but Spain's Nanny said she had internal troubles, and must sit this one out. England looked towards the Oslo group, but they had never played before, except little Belgium, who had hated it, and the others felt shy. America, of course, was too much of a baby for such a grown-up game, but she was just longing to see it played. And still it would not begin.

The party looked like being a flop, and everybody was becoming very much bored, especially the Americans who are so fond of blood and entrails. They were longing for the show, and with savage taunts, like boys at a bull-baiting from behind safe bars, they urged that it should begin at once. The pit-side seats for which they had paid so heavily in printer's ink were turning out to be a grave disappointment; they sat in them, chewing gum, stamping their feet and shouting in unison, 'This war is phoney.'

Week after week went by. People made jokes about how there was the Boer War, and then the Great War, and then the Great Bore War. They said Hitler's

secret weapon was boredom. Sophia hoped it was. She had long cherished a conviction that Hitler's secret weapon was an aerial torpedo addressed to Lady Sophia
Garfield, 98 Granby Gate, S.W., and she very much preferred boredom.

Sophia had two friends in the Cabinet. They were called Fred and Ned, and as a
matter of fact while Fred was in the Cabinet, Ned had not yet quite reached that
sixth form of politicians and was only in the Government, but Sophia could not
distinguish between little details like that, and to her they were 'My friends in the
Cabinet'. She often dined with the two of them and found these evenings very
enjoyable because, although they both had young and pretty wives, it seems that
the wives of Cabinet Ministers race, so to speak, under different rules from ordinary
women, and never expect to see their husbands except in bed if they share one. So
Sophia had Fred and Ned to herself on these occasions. As she liked both male and
female company, but did not much like it mixed, this arrangement suited her nicely.

They took her to dine at the Carlton, and talked a great deal about the political
prospects of their various acquaintances, and it was talk which Sophia was very
much accustomed to, because it had begun years ago, when she was a young married woman taking Fred and Ned out to tea at the Cockpit; only then it had been
a question of Pop and coloured waistcoats, and the Headmaster in those days had
delivered his harangues in Chapel instead of on the floor of the House. She told
them all about her Post, and Ned wrote things down in a notebook, and promised
that A.R.P. should be reconstructed on the exact lines suggested by Sophia. She
knew from experience how much that meant. Then Fred asked her if Luke was in
the Tower yet, and this annoyed her because, while it was one thing to say to
Rudolph in the privacy of Kew Gardens that Luke was an awful old Fascist, it was
quite another to have Fred, that ardent upholder of Munich, being facetious about
him; so she turned on poor Fred with great vigour, and gave him a brisk résumé
of the achievements of the National Government. She very nearly made him cry,
and was just coming nicely into her stride over the National Liberals, of whom
Fred was one, when Ned came loyally to his rescue saying 'Ah, but you haven't
heard of Fred's wonderful scheme, all his own idea, for fixing Dr Goebbels.' And
he proceeded to outline the scheme.

It appeared that Fred's idea, his own unaided brainwave, was to invite Sir Ivor
King, the King of Song, to conduct a world-wide campaign of songful propaganda.

'Harness his personality, as it were,' Fred explained, warming to his subject, 'to
our cause. He's the only chap who could bring it off, and it would be wicked not
to use him – why, he is one of our great natural advantages, you might say, like –
well, coal, or being an island. They've got nobody to touch him over there. Now
my idea is that he should give out a special news bulletin every day, strongly fla-
voured with propaganda, of course, followed by a programme of song. See the
point? People will switch on to hear him sing (the first time for two years, you
know), and then they won't be able to help getting an earful of propaganda. We'll
have him singing with the troops, singing with the air force, singing with the navy,
jolly, popular stuff which the listeners all over the world can join in. You know how
people like roaring out songs when they know the words. Besides, the man in the
street has a great respect for old Ivor, great.'

According to Fred, he and the man in the street were as one, which was strange, considering that, except for the High Street, Windsor and The Turl, he had hardly ever been in a street.

'When you say listeners all over the world can join in, you mean English listeners?' said Sophia. She wanted to get the thing straight.

'By no means,' said Fred, eagerly, 'because, you see, the strength of this scheme is that it will be world-wide. I confess that, to begin with, I forgot that it's not everybody who can speak English. Then of course I remembered that there are Chinks and Japs and Fuzzy Wuzzies and Ice Creamers and Dagoes, and so on. Ah! but we can overcome that difficulty. Is there any reason why he shouldn't learn to make those extraordinary sounds which they think of as music? Of course not. No. The old chappie is full of brains and enterprise – take on anything we ask him to, you bet.' And Fred began to give what he thought an excellent imitation of un-English music, nasal sounds of a painful quality. A county family who were dining at the next table told each other that this could not be the Minister for Propaganda, after all. Ned beat two forks together as an accompaniment, and they assured each other that neither was that the Member (so promising, such a career before him) for East Wessex.

'The old King is coming to my office tomorrow. I am seeing him myself,' Fred continued, when this horrid cacophony came to an end.

'He will be wearing his curly, butter-coloured wig,' said Sophia.

'We must see that he has a black one made. Don't want any Aryan nonsense in my scheme – I always think Propaganda is awfully un-English, anyway, but what I say, if you have it at all, for the Lord's sake have it good. And, by the way, Sophie, this is all most fearfully hush-hush, you know. Leakage and all that – not a word to Luke or anybody. The element of surprise is vital to the scheme.'

'I see, the old gentleman is your answer to Hitler's secret weapon.'

'I wouldn't go quite so far as that, but I can tell you we are expecting some pretty fruity results. I mean it's a world-wide scheme you see, not just a pettifogging little affair confined to England. And by the way,' he got out a notebook, 'I must remember to tell the police they had better keep an eye on the chap. Think what a coup for the Huns if he got bumped off or anything; I should never get over it.'

Sophia rang up her enemy. Olga Gogothsky (née Baby Bagg) had been her enemy since they were both aged ten. It was an intimate enmity which gave Sophia more pleasure than most friendships; she made sacrifices upon its altar and fanned the flames with assiduity.

'Hullo, my darling Sophie,' Olga purred, in the foreign accent which she had cultivated since just before her marriage and which was in striking contrast with the Eton and Oxford tones (often blurred by drink but always unmistakable) of Prince Gogothsky. 'Yes, I have been back a fortnight; such a journey, darling. And where did you go for the summer? Just quietly with dear Lord Maida Vale? Delicious. Me? Oh, poor little me, I had a very banal time with Pauline Mallory you know, the poetess, in her villa at Antibes. Crowds and crowds of people, parties, nothing else. You can imagine how that palled on me, dearest. Happily my beloved old Ambassador was there. He has her little villa, in the garden, and there he writes his memories. He is sweet enough to say that I inspire him in his work; he read it to me – so interesting, and written, how can I express it, with such art. The old days at the Montenegrin court – so picturesque. You can imagine. Then Baroness von Bülop was a great friend of his, and he told me some fascinating things about her and her beautiful aunt which were rather too *intime* for cold, cold print. Well, what else – oh yes, Torchon was painting my portrait – he sees me as a Turkish slave girl which is very interesting because when Fromenti cast my horoscope he said that is what I used to be in one of my former lives. (In the Sultan's harem, I was his favourite wife.) Besides all this, I managed to get in a little writing, so you see my time was not quite wasted after all.'

Olga's writing was an interesting phenomenon, rather like the Emperor's new clothes. She let it be known that she was a poetess, and whenever, which was often, her photograph appeared in the illustrated press, the caption underneath would announce that very soon a slender volume might be expected from her pen. Sometimes even the subject-matter would be touched upon: 'Princess Serge Gogothsky, who is at present engaged upon a series of bird studies in verse.'

'This beautiful visitor to our shores is a lady of great talent. The long epic poem on Savonarola from her pen will soon be ready for publication,' and so on.

Once, for several weeks on end, Olga sat alone every evening at a special table at the Café Royal and wrote feverishly upon sheets of foolscap which she tore up, with an expression of agony on her face, just before closing time. Her work always seemed to be in progress rather than in print.

Sophia asked what she was doing as war work.

'Dearest, I must tell you that it's a secret. However, when you hear that I have an appointment under the Government, that I have to undertake great responsibilities, and that I may often be called out in the middle of the night without any idea of where I am to go, you may guess the kind of thing it is. More I cannot say.'

'Sounds to me like a certified midwife,' said Sophia crossly. It was really too much if old Baby Bagg was going to assume the rôle of beautiful female spy, while she herself had drearily admitted to working in a First Aid Post, all boredom and no glamour. Olga lied with such accomplishment that there were some people who believed in her tarradiddles, and Sophia had often been told what a talent for verse, what a delightful touch the Princess had.

'No, darling – what a charming joke, by the way, I must remember to tell my dear Chief. No, not a midwife. Though I'm sure it must be far far more exhausting, my Chief is a regular slave driver.'

'Oh, you have a Chief?'

'I only wish I could tell you Who it is. But there must be no leakage. What a wonderful man to work with – what magnetism, what finesse and what a brain! I must allow I am fortunate to be with him, and then the work is fascinating, vital. What if it does half kill me? There, I mustn't talk about myself. Tell me, what are you doing in this cruel war?'

Sophia said that she too had an important job under the Government.

'Really, my darling, have you? A First Aid Post, or something like that, I suppose?'

'Ah well, that's only what I tell people, actually of course it is an excellent blind for my real work. I wonder you don't adopt this idea, say you are working in a canteen, for instance. I'll forget what you've just told me if you like, and spread it round about the canteen!'

'Delicate little me!' cried Olga, 'in a canteen! But darling, who would ever believe such an unlikely thing – they would at once suspect goodness knows what. Well, dearest, I see the Chief waiting for me in his great car with the flag and priority notices, I shall feel quite important as we whirl away to Whitehall. I must fly, darling. Good-bye. I will visit you very soon in your little First Aid Post. Good-bye.'

Sophia then telephoned to her friend, Mary Pencill.

'Now, Mary, listen. You've got to come and work in my First Aid Post,' she said. 'It's perfect heaven. You can't think what heaven Sister Wordsworth is.'

'No, thank you, Sophie. I don't intend to work for this war in any way. I don't approve of it, you see.' Mary belonged to the extreme Left.

'Gracious, just like Luke. He doesn't approve of it either, nor does Florence. You are in awful company. So why are you in this awful company?'

'I can't help it if Luke happens to be right for once. It's sure to be for the wrong reasons if he is. All I know is that everything decent and worth supporting has been thrown away – Spain, Czechoslovakia, and now we're supposed to be fighting for the Poles, frightful people who knout their peasants. Actually, of course, it's simply the British Empire and our own skins as usual.'

'I'm fond of my skin,' said Sophia, 'and personally I think the British Empire is worth fighting for.'

'You can't expect me to think so. Why, look at our Government. Your friends Fred and Ned, for instance, are just as bad as Hitler, exactly the same thing. What is the use of fighting Hitler when there are people like Ned and Fred here? We should do some cleaning up at home first.'

'Anyway, it's Hitler and Stalin now, don't forget the wedding bells.'

Mary had gone P.O.U.M., so she grudgingly conceded this point. 'Ned and Fred are practically the same people as Hitler and Stalin,' she said.

'I never heard anything so silly. Poor Fred and Ned. Well, I mean the proof of the pudding is in the eating. Just suppose now that the Ministry of Information had forgotten to tell us we had been beaten, and one day in Harrods we saw a little crowd gathering, and when we went to look it was Hitler and Stalin. Think how we should scream.'

'I expect you would.'

'So would you. Now, my point is, I often see Fred and Ned in Harrods, and I don't scream at all, I just say "Hullo duckie" or something. See the difference?'

'No, Sophia,' said Mary disapprovingly, 'I'm afraid you don't understand the principle.' She loved Sophia but thought her incurably frivolous.

'Another thing,' she said; 'why have you left the Left Book Club?'

'Darling, I only joined to please you.'

'That's no answer.'

'Well, if you want to know it's because the books are left.'

'Sophia!'

'I don't mean because they are Left and I can't get Evelyn Waugh or any of the things I want to read. I mean because they are left lying about the house. Ordinary libraries like Harrods take them away when one has finished with them. I don't want the place cluttered up with books, so I have left. See?'

'Really, your life is bounded by Harrods.'

'Yes, it is rather. I had rather a horrid dream, though, about its being full of parachutists; my life is slightly bounded by them now, to tell you the truth, I think they are terrifying.'

'Nonsense, they would be interned.'

'That's what Luke says. Still, the idea of those faces floating past one's bedroom window is rather unpleasant, you must admit.'

'By the way, I saw Rudolph last night coming out of the Empire with that foreign woman.'

'Who?'

'The one who always wears star-spangled yashmaks.'

'Oh, you mean Olga Gogothsky; she's no more foreign than you or me – although she does pretend to have Spanish blood, I believe.'

'Really – Government or Franco?'

'Baby Bagg. You must remember her at dances.' Sophia was only fairly pleased to hear that Olga had been out with Rudolph, who had announced that he was going to play bridge at his club.

'Anyhow, she looks too stupid.'

'She has just told me that she has got an important job under the Government, I simply must find out what it is.'

'First Aid Post, probably,' said Mary. 'You haven't told me yet what you do in yours?'

'Well, it sounds rather lugubrious but I absolutely love it. I have an indelible pencil, you see, and when people are brought in dying and so on, I write on their foreheads.'

'Good gracious me, what do you write?'

'M for male and F for female, according to which they are, and a number. That's for the Ministry of Pensions. Then, for the doctor, how many doses of morphia and castor oil and so on they have had.'

'What an awful idea. What happens if you get a negro – or a neanderthal type with a very low forehead? You can't always count on having high, smooth, white brows, you know, like Luke's.'

'Try not to be facetious, darling, it's quite serious. Then I put their jewels into dainty little chintz bags made out of Fortmason remnants.'

'When you say you do all this, what exactly do you mean?'

'Well, darling, I should do it if there was a raid. It's rather like private theatricals, you know what I mean. "It'll be all right on the night" kind of idea. The worse the dress rehearsal, the better the show, and so on.'

Mary became very scornful and said it was the stupidest job she had ever heard of. 'Jewels,' she said, 'in chintz bags. Writing M and F. Really, Sophia, I give up.'

Sophia said it was better than doing nothing like Mary, and they rang off, each in a huff.

When Sophia saw Rudolph she said she had heard that he had been seen out with a duck-billed platypus disguised as a Sultana. (Olga's rather long, turned-up nose was considered to be one of her great attractions.)

'Yes, my little Puss-puss,' he said, 'I did take the alluring Princess to a movie what time you went whoring round with your Cabinet puddings.'

'I thought you told me you were going to play bridge at your club?'

'So I was, until I met Olga.'

'But where did you meet her?'

'At my club.'

'Rudolph, what a story.'

'Well, I did. She came along in a taxi after I had telephoned to her.'

'Oh. What was she like?'

'Cracking bore, as usual. Talked about nothing but herself. I had to hear the whole story of how Serge blighted her life by refusing to allow her self-expression on the films. As though one didn't know that the old boyar would allow her to do anything which brought in the roubles.'

'She was always having tests,' said Sophia.

'And they were lousy. Well, then of course she is having all those books dedicated to her and pictures painted of her, and so on. But she has abandoned these activities for a very important job under the Government. First Aid Post, I guess. Chap in my club, a doctor, gave her her first aid exam. He said, "Now Princess, if you found a man with a badly broken leg and you had no splint or bandage, what would you do?' and she said, "Take my drawers off and tie the leg to my leg." So of course he passed her.'

Sophia saw that she must look out. She knew very well that when a man is thoroughly disloyal about a woman, and at the same time begins to indulge in her company, he nearly always intends to have an affair with that woman. The disloyalty is in itself a danger signal. She would not have supposed that Olga was exactly to Rudolph's taste, but these things do not follow any known rules and you never can tell.

'Beastly fellow,' she said. 'I see you're in love with her.'

'Rather,' said Rudolph. 'I see you're jealous.'

'Rather.' Sophia got up and rang the bell for the cocktail things. 'I say, darling, by the way, you know Florence?'

'Yes, I'm in love with her too, of course?'

'Very likely. Anyhow, you know she lives with us now. Well, I believe she must be nicer than we thought she was, because, whatever do you think? She keeps a pigeon in her bedroom.'

'Does she now? I thought she kept Luke.'

'No, no, darling, I've often told you. Anyway, there it is, she keeps this terribly nice pigeon.'

'Whatever for?'

'I expect it is her friend. I would love to have a sweet pigeon for a friend, but I must say I never would have thought it of Florence, she doesn't strike one as an animal lover. Milly doesn't like her at all.'

'I call it very queer,' said Rudolph. 'Do you think it might have some religious significance?'

'It's a pigeon, not a dove.'

'Florence wouldn't know the difference. That's it, I expect she is keeping it to let loose over Brother Bones's head next time she sees him.'

'Or maybe she saved its life. Mr Stone, in our Post, you know, has to keep down the London pigeons in peace time, and he says it's awfully difficult because wherever you put your trap some old lady always pops her head out of a window and sets up a screeching about it and calls in the police and so on. However early in the morning, it's always just the same. So the result is that London's pigeons are not really kept down very much, as you may note. Perhaps Florence saw this one in a trap (they get up very early in the Brotherhood, you know), and promised not to let it loose again if she might have it. I like her much better for it, actually.'

Florence now came into the room. She told Sophia that Luke had been guided to ask a hundred people to dinner the next day to talk about Moral Rearmament. 'It's to meet this friend of ours, Heatherley Egg,' she said. (Florence always introduced new people into her conversation with the word 'this'. 'This woman I met in the bus' or 'This cousin of my father's'. It was a habit which maddened Sophia.) 'I have arranged the whole thing,' Florence continued; 'gold chairs and food and so on are all ordered. I just looked in here to say how much we hope you will come to it, as I feel sure you will be interested. Heatherley Egg has just arrived from the States, and he will tell us what the President said to him about Moral Rearmament. Just the two of them (the three, I should say, because of course, there was a Third present) talked it over for nearly five minutes, and Heth says – well, you must hear it from his own lips tomorrow evening. There will be members of the Brotherhood from all, yes, I am happy to say, all the European countries.'

Sophia and Rudolph hurriedly explained that they had a very long-standing engagement for the following evening. Florence looked a bit crucified and said how strange it must seem to live in a perpetual whirl of thoughtless gaiety.

'I call a hundred people to dinner a pretty good whirl, personally.'

Florence said she must go as she had this First Aid lecture.

'It was her book I saw that awful old knee joint in.'

Sophia went to the telephone and dialled a number. 'You know I really admire her for doing the first aid course, I never would have expected it, like the pigeon, and dyeing her hair. It all shows how I underestimated Florence.' She rang up Vocal Lodge and asked Sir Ivor whether she and Rudolph might dine with him the next day. 'There is a Brotherhood orgy here, and we can't take it.'

'Yes, Sophie, my darling, you may, but you must be nice to the Gogothskys who are coming, and not make poor dear Olga cry like you did last time. Promise? All right, eight o'clock then, I have to be at my post by ten.'

'Thank goodness for that,' said Sophia to Rudolph when she had rung off. 'People from every European country, think of it. I mean the whole point of the war is one doesn't have to see foreigners any more. And as for what the President said to Heth – horrors!'

The Russians marched into Poland on the very day of Florence's party. Luke was stunned by this practical demonstration of Russo-German solidarity.

'Herr Hitler told me himself that his life's work was to lead a crusade against Bolshevism.'

'Then you ought to have smelt a rat at once,' said Sophia unkindly.

'But he was so earnest about it. He said over and over again that Bolshevism was the greatest force for evil the world has ever known.'

'Of course I don't want to say I told you so, darling, but there's never been a pin to put between the Communists and the Nazis. The Communists torture you to death if you're not a worker, and the Nazis torture you to death if you're not a German. If you are they look at your nose first. Aristocrats are inclined to prefer

Nazis while Jews prefer Bolshies. An old bourgeois like yourself, Luke, should keep your fingers out of both their pies.'

Luke must have been quite distracted. He did not even protest, as he usually did, when Sophia called him a bourgeois, that the Garfields were an old Saxon family dating back to before the Conquest. Which, as Sophia would very justly observe, did not affect the matter one way or another.

'And let me tell you,' she went on, 'if you continue to believe everything those foreigners in Germany said to you, you are in for some very nasty shocks, old boy. They have told a lot of people a lot of things not strictly speaking true, and most of us are beginning to get wise. The day they said they would never use gas against civilians every First Aid Post in London let down its gas-proof flaps, and we have all stifled ever since.'

Poor Luke passed his hand over his smooth, white forehead and looked sad. Sophia was sorry that she had been so beastly to him, and said, 'Darling, are you excited for your party tonight?'

'I am not a baby to be excited for a party. It will, I hope, be interesting. Mr Egg appears to have seen the President.'

So Rudolph was right, and Luke was getting bored with the Brotherhood. She wondered whether it was a religion which took a great hold on people, and whether it would leave the poor fellow with an uneasy conscience for the rest of his life.

Brothers and Sisters now began flocking into the house. They all looked very much alike and might easily, had there not been a hundred of them, have been brothers and sisters indeed. The girls were all dressed in simple little tub frocks with a bastard Tyrolean flavour, they wore no hats or stockings, and quite a lot of grimy toes poked their way out of sandals. They were sunburnt, their foreheads were wrinkled, and their hair and lips were very thin. The young men, of whom there were quantities, appeared at first sight to be extremely well dressed, but their suits were too broad at the shoulder, too slim in the hips, and not made of quite the very best stuff – in fact, they would not stand up to close examination. They answered to names like Heth for Heatherley, Ken for Kennerley, and Win for Winthrop, and spoke with Hollywood accents. They were sunburnt, and when you first looked at them, immensely handsome, like the suits. Their eyes and teeth were blue. The cosmopolitan element in this party was not in evidence, and Sophia thought Florence must have meant Americans from every country in Europe, until she heard a gabble of foreign languages. She concluded that the Brotherhood, like Hollywood, places its own stamp on all nationalities, as it certainly confers a particular type of looks, of clothes, and that 'If this is pleasure give me pain' expression which is permanently on all the faces of its adherents. There was not one soul in uniform.

Rudolph, however, when he arrived to take Sophia down to Kew was resplendent in the full fig of the Wessex Guards.

'I kept it secret for a surprise for you,' he said; 'wait till you see my coat, though, lined with scarlet.'

'Well, you do look pretty,' said Sophia approvingly. Before the war, she had often thought of seeing him in uniform for the first time, and had supposed that she would cry. Now she simply felt delighted. Indeed Rudolph, unusually well shaved, looked handsome and soldierly, an example, she felt, to the brothers. War psychology, so incomprehensible during peace time, already had her in its grip.

Florence introduced Mr Egg to them. 'Heatherley, this is Sophia Garfield. Rudolph, this is Heatherley.' Brotherhood manners were like that. 'Sophia, you must wait a moment while Heth tells us what the President said to him. He's just going to now.' She got up on a chair and clapped her hands. 'Silence everybody, please. Heatherley is going to tell us what the President said about Moral Rearmament.'

Silence fell at once, and all faces were turned towards Heatherley who was scrambling on to the chair.

'Well, folks,' he said impressively, 'I went to see the President.' Pause. 'We were alone together, just the three of us, you understand. The President is a busy man.' Pause. 'Well, he said to me.' An impressive pause. Heatherley looked all round the room, and finally continued, 'He said "I think Moral Rearmament is a very very fine idea."'

There was a prolonged and reverent silence, broken by Florence who said, 'I always think it is so important to hear the exact words when a man like that makes a statement like that. Thank you, Heth; personally I shall treasure this little scene.'

The Gogothskys were already at Vocal Lodge when Sophia and Rudolph arrived. Olga, greatly to Sophia's delight, for she made a mental collection of Olga's clothes, was wearing a snood. A bit of it came round and fastened under her chin like a beard and she looked, as no doubt she felt, very Slav. The Prince, a huge jolly drunken fellow whom everybody liked, was dressed in Air Force blue; he announced that he was on leave from his balloon, Blossom. It was evident that Blossom had made a man of him. Hitherto his life had been spent trailing about after Olga, making, in return for her considerable income, the small and rather unreal (as he was a British subject), but in his wife's eyes, invaluable, contribution of princedom. Now he was bronzed, clean, fairly well shaven, and apparently quite sober. He and Rudolph slapped each other on the back, compared uniforms and were very gay.

'You managed to get away from your Chief,' Sophia said to Olga, her eyes feasting on the snood.

'He heard of my sorrow and begged me to take some leave,' said Olga reproachfully.

'Sorrow?' said Rudolph. 'Why, you are looking a bit widowed, come to think of it. What's up?'

'My relations in Poland –'

'Didn't know you had any,' said Sophia sceptically.

'Didn't you, darling? Yes, indeed, my great-great-great-grandmother was a Paczinska, and I fear my poor cousins must have fallen into Bolshevik hands. You know what that meant in Russia – they were given over to their peasantry to do as they liked with.' Olga gave a tremendous shudder.

Sophia said there must be something wrong somewhere. If the Duchess of Devonshire, for instance, was handed over to the peasantry to do as they liked with, they would no doubt put her in the best bedroom and get her a cup of tea. 'If the peasantry are really such demons,' she said, 'whose fault is that, pray?'

'But I saw in the papers that the Bolshies are going in on purpose to protect you White Russians,' said old Ivor, rather puzzled.

Serge Gogothsky had been brought up in England, and had spent most of his life here. He must, therefore, have been well accustomed to the national ignorance on the subject of foreign affairs, but this was too much even for him. He gave a sort of warbling roar, and jumped about the room like an agonized Petrushka explaining the historical and geographical position of White Russia.

'All right, keep your hair on,' said the old singer, taking his off and adjusting a curl. 'Have another drink.'

This panacea for all ills was accepted, and peace reigned once more until Rudolph tactlessly observed that he was not so enthusiastic about Europe being over-run by the murderous Muscovites as Hitler seemed to be. The Prince once more became very much excited, and said that if the Allies had assisted the White Russians at the end of the last war and enabled them to reinstate the Romanoffs, none of this would have happened.

'What nonsense. The Romanoffs were just as likely to get imperial ideas as Uncle Joe any day of the week. You Asiatics should be kept out of Europe, that's what it is.'

'Keep your hairs on, dears, and let's have dinner,' said Sir Ivor, who only enjoyed joking conversations of an esoteric kind.

During dinner Sophia noticed that Olga was drooping her eyelids a good deal at Rudolph who seemed not to be disliking it. She cast about for means of retaliation (upon Rudolph, Olga she could always deal with very easily) but saw none to hand. The old gentleman would hardly bring conviction as a stalking horse, and the trouble with Serge was that the smallest encouragement too often led to rape. A tremendous dip of the offending eyelids stung Sophia into action and she turned to Olga with a sweet smile and asked how Savonarola was getting along. She always reserved this question for very special occasions.

'Dearest, there is a war on, you know. Sometimes, however, I do manage to do a little scribbling, busy as I am my poetry simply forces its way on to paper. Last night, during a lull, I read some of my sonnets to the Chief. He says they remind him of Elizabeth Browning's Sonnets to the Portuguese.'

'From,' said Rudolph. 'Who is your Chief?'

Olga gave a great swoop of the eyelids, and said that her job, which was very important, and her Chief, who was very very famous, had to be kept very very secret.

'Bet Haw-Haw knows them,' said Rudolph. 'I suppose you are one of those pin-money lovelies I am always reading about, eh? Come clean now, aren't you?'

'By the way, dears, I have a new job,' said Ivor.

Sophia wrestled with temptation. She longed to take Olga down a peg by being in the know; the old gentleman was just going to tell them himself, so where would be the harm? On the other hand, Fred had begged her to be careful. She decided to wait and see what Ivor said. Meanwhile the conversation flowed on.

Rudolph said, 'I suppose you are a wonderful old spy in a wonderful new wig. I suppose that's what Olga is really, a beautiful female spy, worming her way into the hearts of careless young officers like Serge and me.' Olga, who liked to be taken very seriously, was not pleased. She drooped her eyelids at the Empire *dessus de table* instead of at Rudolph, and Sophia relaxed once more.

'Talking of jobs, you should see Sophia's Post,' went on Rudolph, who, entirely against her orders, was always popping in and out of it. 'Serge, old boy, here's a tip for you – the first thing that strikes the eye is a notice, written out in wobbling capitals by our Sophia, which says, "Never give a drink to a patient marked H." See the form, you old mujik, the great thing is never by any chance let yourself be marked H. Farther on, however, you come to notices with arrows attached, also written by our little friend, and therefore extremely unprofessional in appearance, saying, "Males remove underclothing here", "Females remove underclothing here", and these lead, quite logically, to the midwifery department. I had no idea the Borough Councils were such realists.'

'It's called the Labour Ward,' said Sophia; 'don't listen to him, he has no business to come prying round my Post.'

'The Labour Ward has to be seen to be believed,' said Rudolph; 'it's a kind of dog kennel, and the only furnishings are a cradle and a pair of woolly boots. If I were a lady I should bag not having a baby there, I must say, raid or no raid.'

'Poor Sister Wordsworth can't get anybody to take charge of it, did I tell you?' said Sophia, falling happily into talking shop. 'You see, it's awfully dull just sitting and looking at the cradle all day, they prefer the Treatment Room.'

'But the real thrill is the Hospital Museum,' went on Rudolph. 'It's next door to the Labour Ward – very suitable really, as exhibit A is a bottle containing pre-natal Siamese twins. You should come along one day, Serge, and take a load of the ulcerated stomachs. I promise nobody shall mark you H, and there's a pub up the street.'

'You've none of you taken any interest in my new job,' said the King of Song peevishly.

'Darling Ivor, how beastly of us. Come clean, then. What is it?'

'I'm to go down to Torquay with our evacuated orchids.'

4

Sophia sat by her telephone at the Post, and tried not to long for an air raid. On the one or two occasions when she had lifted up the receiver and had heard, instead of the Medical Officer of Health wishing to speak to Sister Wordsworth, 'This is the Southern Control Centre. Air raid warning Yellow,' she had experienced such an unhealthy glow of excitement that she felt she might easily become a raid addict, or take to raids in the same way that people do to drugs, and for much the same reason. Her life outside the Post had ceased to be much fun, for Rudolph, after looking almost too pretty in his uniform for about a week, was now paying the penalty attached to such prettiness in a training camp on the East Coast.

Inside the Post she made up things to keep her occupied, as people do who lie for weeks in bed not particularly ill. She looked a great deal at her watch, knitted, read Macaulay's *History of England*, wrote quantities of unnecessary letters for the first time since she was a girl, and chatted to Sister Wordsworth. Finally, as a last resort, there was the wireless. Sophia hated the wireless. It seemed to her to be a definite and living force for evil in the land. When she turned it on, she thought of the women all over England in lonely little houses with their husbands gone to the war, sick with anxiety for the future. She saw them putting their children to bed, their hearts broken by the loneliness of the evening hours, and then, for company, turning on the wireless. What is the inspiration which flows to them from this, the fountain-head, as it must seem to them, of the Empire? London, with all its resources of genius, talent, wit, how does London help them through these difficult times? How are they made to feel that England is not only worth dying for but being poor for, being lonely and unhappy for? With great music, stirring words and sound common sense? With the glorious literature, nobly spoken, of our ancestors? Not at all. With facetiousness and jazz.

Chatting to Sister Wordsworth was her favourite occupation. This young and pretty creature turned out to be a remarkable person in many ways. Before the war, she had been a health visitor, and Sophia, who knew but little of such matters, discovered that this was a profession which required the combination of a really impressive training with such virtues as tact, knowledge of human nature, sense of humour, and a complete lack of pretentiousness. Sister Wordsworth's charming, rather hearty manner was that of a schoolgirl, deceptively young, but she was a nurse, certified midwife, and trained psychologist, and furthermore, had an extensive knowledge of law. Week after week she kept close upon a hundred idle people in that Post contented, on good terms with each other, and in so far as she could invent things for them to do, busy. Of course, there were troubles and difficulties. A German Jew had come to the Post as a voluntary worker; after two days the nurses had sent a deputation to Sister Wordsworth saying that they could not work in the same building as a Prussian spy, and she was obliged to send him to the next Post in the district where it was to be hoped that a more tolerant spirit prevailed. Sophia had been greatly tickled by this, and had wished that a few Prussians could have had a look at their prototype. She asked why he was supposed to be a spy. It seemed that he had spent half an hour reading the notices which were displayed everywhere in the Post, and which pertained to such things as the horrid fate of patients marked H, hot-water bottles to be filled at certain specified hours, the quantity of sterilized instruments to be kept handy, and so on. Sophia, who had written most of them out herself, could not believe that the High Command in Berlin would find its path greatly smoothed by such information. Still, as Fred had remarked when she told him about it, 'You can't be too careful, and after all, we are at war with the Germans.' Fred had a wonderful way of hitting nails on the head.

Today it was a Sunday, and all was very quiet in the Post. Sister Wordsworth was out, the wireless programme absolutely impossible, and the workmen who generally made life hideous with their bangings were able, unlike the personnel of the Post, to take Sundays off. Sophia did her knitting. She was a bad, slow knitter, and the sleeves of anything she made were always too short. She listened dreamily to a conversation which was going on beyond the sacking partition. Three of the nurses were discussing a certain foreign Royal Family with an inaccuracy astonishing as to every detail. It all sounded rather cosy and delicious, and Sophia would have liked to join in. One of the penalties, however, attached to immunity from knee-joints was that she was incarcerated in the office. The people in the

Treatment Room had lovely gossips, but the day would come when they would have knees as well; in order to avoid the knees, she was obliged to forgo the gossips.

St Anne's Hospital First Aid Post

Darling, darling, darling, darling,

I say, Florence's bird is house-trained, I saw her letting it out of the window like a dog last thing at night. I only saw this because I happened to be in that loo which isn't blacked out, with the light off, of course, and I heard a great flapping and Florence's window opening, so I was guided to look out. As there is a moon, I saw it quite clearly streaking off to do its business with a most determined look on its face. I waited for ages, but it didn't come back. What d'you suppose it does, peck on the window, or coo or what? Well, I should love to have a terribly nice, pretty faithful house-trained pigeon, what with missing Milly and so on, and I said so this morning to Florence, but she gave me a simply horrid look, so perhaps she thought I was laughing at her or something which indeed I wasn't. Really I am getting quite attached to Florence, and it's nice for Luke having her around, with me here such a lot, gives him something else to think about besides the Income Tax. Poor old thing, he looks fearfully tucked up about that, and of course it must be hell paying all those seven and sixes for a war you don't believe in much. Besides, he feels quite torn in two between his heroes, Our Premier and Herr Hitler, now they don't tread the same path any longer.

Darling, how is camp life, and do you miss me? Florence quite misses you, you know, perhaps she is in love with you. She keeps on coming into my room to ask what your address is, and what battalion you have joined, and how long you will be training, and who your commanding officer is and all sorts of things. I expect you'll get a balaclava for Christmas; she is knitting one for some lucky fellow, but I think he must be one of those African pigmies with a top knot by the shape of it.

Oh dear, I do love you, love from your darling

Sophia.

PS. Olga is really putting on a most peculiar act. She lunched alone at the Ritz yesterday in a black wig, a battle bowler and her sables, and pretended not to know any of her friends. Half-way through lunch a page-boy (she had bribed him no doubt) brought her a note, and she gave a sort of shriek, put a veil over the whole thing, battle bowler and all, and scrammed. So now of course everyone knows for certain she is a beautiful female spy. Poor old Serge has been dismissed his Blossom because he passed out and so did it; I hear they looked too indecent lying side by side in the Park.

As Sophia finished her letter Sister Wordsworth came in.

'Oh, Lady Sophia,' she said, 'I forgot to tell you that a friend of yours came to see me yesterday morning. She is joining the Post tomorrow for the night shift, full time. It is lucky as we are so very short-handed on that shift.'

'A friend of mine – what's she called?'

'Miss – I have it written down here, wait a minute – oh, yes, Miss Turnbull.'

'Gracious,' said Sophia, 'you surprise me. I never would have thought it of Florence. She hasn't said a word about it to me. Can I go now?'

'Yes, do. I shall be here the whole evening.'

Sophia found herself, for the first time since the beginning of the war, dining alone with Luke. It struck her that he wanted to have an intimate conversation with her, but did not quite know how to begin. Sophia would have been willing to help him; she was feeling quite soft towards Luke these days, he looked so ill and unhappy, but intimate conversations, except very occasionally with Rudolph, were not much in her line.

Luke began by saying that he was going back to the Foreign Office.

'How about your business?'

'There isn't any,' he said shortly, 'and I must tell you, my dear Sophia, that you and I are going to be very much poorer.'

'So I supposed. Well, you must decide what we ought to do. We could move into the garage at the back of the house very easily, and I could manage with a daily maid, or none at all. I should probably have to work shorter hours at the Post in that case.'

Luke, who was always put out by Sophia's apparent indifference to the advantages his money had brought her, shook his head impatiently. 'We shall be forced to make various radical economies by the very fact of there being a war. I shall not travel as I used to, we shall not entertain, there will be no question of any shooting or fishing, and you I presume will not be wanting much in the way of new clothes. There is absolutely no need to reduce our standard of living any further for the present. Besides, I should think it very wrong to send away any servants.'

'Except Greta,' said Sophia. 'I wish to goodness we could get rid of her. I simply hate having a German about the place, and so do the others. Mrs Round keeps on saying to me, "Not to be able to talk world politics in one's own servants' hall is very upsetting for all of us." I'm sure it must be. And yet I haven't the heart to put her in the street, poor thing. It's all my own fault, I never liked her but I was too lazy to give her notice, you know how it is.'

'Better keep her on for a time, now she is here.'

'Oh yes, I know. We must really.'

They ate on in a polite and not very comfortable silence.

Luke said presently, 'Sophia, I hope you don't object to Florence staying on here.'

'Of course not.'

'She is very poor, you know. I don't know what would become of her unless we could help her.'

Sophia's eyebrows went up. She thought that the Brotherhood must really be improving Luke's character. Hitherto he had despised, disliked and mistrusted people for no better reason than that they were poor.

'Well then, of course we must help her,' she said warmly. 'I wonder – perhaps she would think it awful cheek if I offered to give her my silver-fox coat. I never wear it now, and I know they are not fashionable, but it is extremely warm.'

'That is very good of you, my dear Sophia, and I am sure if you were guided to share it with her she would be only too happy to accept.'

Sophia stifled the temptation to say that she would arrange for it to come clean at Sketchley's first.

'I'm very glad Florence is here to keep you company when I'm at the Post,' she said; 'actually she has joined the Post too now, did you know, but our shifts only overlap by about an hour. It's really very good of her; she is going to do a twelve-hour night shift, simply horrible I should think.'

'Florence is, of course, one of the people who believed, as I did, that Herr Hitler and Our Premier between them could make a very wonderful thing of world relationships. Like me, she is bitterly disillusioned by Herr Hitler's treacherous (yes, it is the only word) treacherous behaviour to Our Premier. But like me, she feels that this cruel war is not the proper solution, it can only cause a deterioration in world affairs and will settle nothing. People who think as we do are ploughing a lone furrow just now, you know, Sophia.'

'What I can't see is why you think that the behaviour of the Germans has been any worse, or different, during the past few months from what it always is. Anybody who can read print knows what they are like, cruel and treacherous, they have always been the same since the days of the Roman Empire. I can't see why we have to wait for Government Blue Books and White Papers to tell us all this – oh well,' she said, 'what's the good of talking about it now? I really do feel awfully sorry for you, Luke, as you have so many friends over there and thought everything was going to be rosy.'

'Don't misunderstand me,' said Luke, earnestly, 'I consider that Herr Hitler has treated Our Premier most outrageously. At the same time, I feel that if the British people had gone all out for moral rearmament and real appeasement, things need never have reached this pass.'

'The British people indeed, that's a good one, I must say. However, it's now quite obvious to any thinking man that our lot in life is to fight the Huns about once in every twenty years. I'm beginning to consider having a baby; we shall need all we can muster to cope with the 1942 class in 1960, who, if there is anything in heredity, will be the most awful brutes.'

Luke, who belonged to the 'We have no quarrel with the German people' school of thought, looked wistful, and presently went off to his smoking-room,

Rudolph wrote:

It is exactly like one's private here. One of the masters gave us bayonet drill this morning – this is how it goes:

'The first thing we 'ave got to consider is wot are the parts of a soldier? First you 'ave the 'ead. Now, the 'ead of a soldier is covered with a tin 'at, so it ain't of no good to go sloshing it with a bay'net becos all yer gits is a rattle. Wot 'ave we next – the throat, and the throat is a very different proposition. Two inches of bay'net there, and yer gits the wind-pipe and the jugular. Very good. Next we comes to wot yer might call the united dairies. A soldier's dairies are well covered with ammunition pouches and for this reason should be left alone, and also becos a very little lower down yer gits the belly. Now it only requires three inches of bayonet in the belly, twist it well, and out they comes, liver and lights and all. Etc. (I spare you the rest of the anatomical analysis.) Now, when pursuing a retreating enemy, you

should always make a jab for 'is kidneys becos it will then go in like butter and
come out like butter. When the — is wounded, you should kneel on 'is chest and
bash his face with the butt end, thus keeping the bay'net ready in case you want it
to jab at some other — with. You've got to 'ate the —s or yer won't git nowhere
with them.' (Tremendous pantomime.) If it wasn't so heavenly, I might easily have
felt sick.

How are you? If you ask me, I think Florence is more of a beautiful female spy
than Olga; I call all this bird-life extremely suspicious. I shall be having some leave
soon and intend to conduct a rigid investigation in Flossie's bedroom. Meanwhile
you be on the look-out for suspicious behaviour – cameras, for instance, people
lurking on the stairs, false bottoms to trunks and all the other paraphernalia.

I don't get along without you very well.

Love and xxxx Rudolph.

5

The newspapers suddenly awoke from the wartime hibernation and were able to
splash their pages with a story which all their readers could enjoy. The idol of the
British people, the envy of all civilized nations, the hero of a thousand programmes,
The Grand Old Gentleman of Vocal Lodge, in short none other than the famous
King of Song, Sir Ivor King himself, had been found brutally done to death in the
Pagoda at Kew Gardens. Here was a tale to arouse interest in the bosoms of all
but the most hardened cynics, and indeed the poor old man's compatriots, as they
chewed their bacon and eggs the following morning, were convulsed with rather
delicious shudders. The naked corpse, they learnt, surmounted by that beloved
old bald head, had been mutilated and battered with instruments ranging from
the bluntness of a croquet mallet to the sharpness of a butcher's knife. This treatment had rendered the face unrecognizable, and only the cranium had been left
untouched. His clothes had been removed and there was no trace of them, but his
favourite wig, dishevelled and bloodstained, was found, late in the evening, by two
little children innocently playing on Kew Green. Those lucky ones among the
breakfasting citizens who subscribed to the *Daily Runner* began their day with

WIGLESS HEAD ON KEW PAGODA,
HEADLESS WIG ON GREEN

Later, when they issued forth into the streets it was to find that the placards of
the evening papers had entirely abandoned 'U-Boat Believed Sunk', 'Nazi Planes
Believed Down', 'Hitler's Demands', 'Stalin's Demands', and the reactions of the
U.S.A., and were devoting themselves to what soon became known as the Wig
Outrage. 'Wig on Green Sensation, Latest.' 'Pagoda Corpse – Foul Play?' 'Wig
Mystery, Police Baffled.'

When the inquest was held, the police were obliged to issue an appeal to the great crowds that were expected, begging them to stay at home in view of the target which they would present to enemy bombers. In spite of this warning, the Wig Inquest was all too well attended, and the Wig Coroner had a few words to say about this generation's love of the horrible. Indeed, Chiswick High Road had the aspect of Epsom Heath at Derby Day's most scintillating moment.

It would be difficult to do better, for an account of the Wig Inquest than to switch over, as they say on the wireless, to the columns of the *Evening Runner*:

INQUEST ON WIG MURDER
VALET'S STATEMENT
ONLY CURLED LAST WEEK
WAS MURDERED MAN THE KING OF SONG?

The 'colonel's lady and Judy O'Grady' fought for places at the inquest today on the body, which was found last Friday in Kew Pagoda, and which is presumed to be that of Sir Ivor King, 'the King of Song'. The body was so extensively mutilated that a formal identification was impossible, although Mr Larch, Sir Ivor's valet, swore that he would recognize that particular cranium anywhere as belonging to the 'King'.

HIS MASTER'S VOICE

Giving evidence, Mr Larch, who showed signs of great emotion, said that Sir Ivor had left Vocal Lodge to go up to London at two o'clock on Friday afternoon. He had seemed rather nervous and said that he had to keep a very important appointment in town, but that he would be back in time to change for a local sing-song he had promised to attend after tea. His master's voice, said Mr Larch, had been in great demand with A.R.P. organizations, and Mr Larch thought that what with so much singing, and the evacuations in the Orchid House, Sir Ivor had been looking strained and tired of late. By tea-time he had not returned. Mr Larch did not feel unduly worried. 'Sir Ivor had the temperament of an artiste, and was both unpunctual and vague, sometimes spending whole nights in the Turkish bath without informing his staff that he intended to sleep out.'

HIS FAVOURITE WIG

'When the children brought in the wig,' went on Mr Larch, 'I thought it was eerie, as it was his favourite wig; we only had it curled last week, and he would never have thrown it away. Besides, I knew he had no spare with him. I immediately notified the police.' Here Mr Larch broke down and had to be assisted out of the court.

Mr Smith, taxi-driver, said that the old person first of all told him to go to the Ritz, but stopped him at Turnham Green and was driven back to the gates of Kew Gardens where he paid the fare, remarking that it was a fine day for a walk. He was singing loudly in a deep tenor all the while, and seemed in excellent spirits.

A Very High Note

Mr Jumont, a gardener at Kew Gardens, said that he was manuring the rhododendrons when he heard the 'King' go past on a very high note.

The Coroner: 'Did you see him?'

Mr Jumont: 'No, sir. But there was no mistaking that old party when he was singing soprano. Besides, this was his favourite song, "When I am dead, my dearest".' (Music by the Marchioness of Waterford.)

At these words there was a sensation, and hardly a dry eye in court. Some fashionably dressed ladies were sobbing so loudly that the Coroner threatened to have them evicted unless they could control themselves.

Continuing his evidence, Mr Jumont said that Sir Ivor seemed to be walking in the direction of the Pagoda, the time being about 3 p.m.

A Wonderful Thatch

Mr Bott, another employee at Kew Gardens, told how he had found the body. Just before closing time he noticed some blood stains and one or two blond curls at the foot of the Pagoda, then saw that the Pagoda door, which is always kept locked, stood ajar. He went in, and a trail of blood on the stairs led him to the very top where the sight which met his eyes was so terrible that he nearly swooned. 'More like a butcher's shop it was, and it gave me a nasty turn.'

Coroner: 'Did it seem to you at the time that this might be the body of Sir Ivor King?'

Mr Bott: 'No, sir. For one thing the old gentleman (who, of course, I knew very well by sight) always seemed to have a wonderful thatch, as you might say, for his age, but the only thing I could clearly see about the individual on the Pagoda was that he hadn't a hair to his name.'

Mr Bott said, in answer to further questioning, that it had never occurred to him Sir Ivor King's hair might have been a wig.

One or two more witnesses having been examined, the Coroner's jury, without retiring, returned a verdict of murder by person or persons unknown.

The Coroner said there was an overwhelming presumption that the corpse was that of Sir Ivor King.

Next day, the *Daily Runner*, in its column of pocket leading articles called BRITAIN EXPECTS, in which what Britain generally Expects is a new Minister for Agriculture, had a short paragraph headed:

Mourn the King of Song

A very gallant and loved old figure has gone from our midst. Mourn him. But remember that he now belongs to the past. It is our duty to say that in the circumstances of his death there may be more than meets the eye. One of our Cabinet Ministers may be guilty of negligence. If so, we should like to see a statement made in Parliament.

Our grief must not blind us to *his* fault. For remember that *we* belong to the future.

There was more than met the eye. Sure enough, the very next day it was learned from reliable sources that the King of Song had been a trump-card in the hand of the Government. He had, in fact, been about to inaugurate, in conjunction with the B.B.C., Ministry of Information, and Foreign Office, the most formidable campaign of Propaganda through the medium of Song that the world has ever seen. The British and French Governments, not only they, but democrats everywhere, had attached great importance to the scheme. They had estimated that it would have a profound effect upon neutral opinion, and indeed might well bring America into the war, on one side or another. Without the King of Song to lead it, this campaign would fall as flat as a pancake, no other living man or woman having the requisite personality or range of voice to conduct it. It must, therefore, necessarily be abandoned. Thus his untimely and gruesome end constituted about as severe a blow to the Allied cause as the loss of a major engagement would have done.

The horrid word Sabotage, the even horrider word Leakage, were now breathed, and poor Fred, who was given no credit for having conceived the idea, was universally execrated for not having delivered it. In the same way that the First Lord of the Admiralty is held responsible for the loss of a capital ship, so the death of Sir Ivor was laid at poor Fred's door. He made a statement in the House that mollified nobody, and Britain Expected every morning that he would resign. Britain did not expect it more than poor Fred expected that he would have to; however, in the end he got off with a nasty half-hour at No. 10. It was now supposed that the King of Song had been liquidated by German spies who had fallen into Kew Gardens in parachutes, and Sophia said 'I told you so' to Luke, and hardly dared look out of her bedroom window any more.

Sophia was really upset by the whole business. She had loved her old godfather, and having always seen a great deal of him she would miss him very much. On the other hand, it cannot be denied that she found a certain element of excitement in her near connexion with so ghastly and so famous a murder – especially when, the day after the inquest, Sir Ivor's solicitor rang her up and told her, very confidentially, that Vocal Lodge and everything in it had been left to her. She had also inherited a substantial fortune and a jet tiara.

Sophia now considered herself entitled to assume the gratifying rôle of mourner in chief. She took a day off from the Post, instructed Rawlings to fill up the car with a month's ration of petrol, and drove round to the Brompton Oratory. Here she spent an hour with a high dignitary of the Roman Church arranging for a Requiem Mass to be held at the Oratory. The dignitary was such a charmer, and Sophia was so conscious of looking extremely pretty in her new black hat, that she cast about for ways of prolonging the interview. Finally she handed over a large sum of money so that masses could be sung in perpetuity for the old gentleman's soul; and when she remembered the eternal basting to which he had so recently condemned her, she considered that this was a high-minded and generous deed on her part. This transaction over, she made great efforts to edge the conversation round to her own soul, but the dignitary, unlike Florence, seemed completely uninterested in so personal a subject, and very soon, with tact and charm but great firmness, indicated to her that she might go. Sophia, as she drove away, reflected that whatever you might say about Popery it is, at least, a professional religion, and shows up to a great advantage when compared with such mushroom growths as the Boston Brotherhood.

On her way to Vocal Lodge she went to pick up Lady Beech who had consented to accompany her on her sad pilgrimage. She was to meet the solicitor there, see Sir Ivor's servants and make various arrangements connected with her legacy. Lady Beech lived in Kensington Square. She was evidently determined to take the fullest advantage of Sophia's petrol ration, for, when the car drew up at her front door, she was already standing on the steps beside an enormous object of no particular shape done up in sacking.

'Very late,' she said. 'Most unlike you. I know, darling, that you won't mind taking this little bed to Heal's on our way.'

This rather delayed matters. It became evident, during the course of the drive, that Lady Beech very much wished that Vocal Lodge had been left to her instead of to Sophia.

'Oh, darling, what a pity,' said Sophia; 'silly old gentleman not to think of it. Of course I'm going to give it to the Nation, don't you think that's right, really? To be kept exactly as it is, a Shrine of Song, and I am giving some of the money he left to keep it up. He left nearly a quarter of a million, you know, so I am going to build an Ivor King Home of Rest for aged singers, and an Ivor King Concert Hall as well. Don't you think he'd be pleased?'

'Very wonderful of you, my dear,' said Lady Beech gloomily. 'Tell me, now, had it occurred to you what a very much more interesting gift to the Nation Vocal Lodge would be if somebody lived in it – I mean somebody rather cultivated, with rather exquisite taste? She could preserve the spirit of the place, don't you see? Like those châteaux on the Loire which have their original families living in them.'

Sophia said she had just the very person in mind, an old governess of her own, who was extremely cultivated and had perfectly exquisite taste. Lady Beech sighed deeply.

When they arrived at Vocal Lodge, Sophia was closeted for some time, first with the solicitor and then with Sir Ivor's servants, whom she begged to stay on there for the rest of their lives if it suited them. Larch took her upstairs and showed her all Sir Ivor's wigs laid out on his bed, rather as it might have been a pilgrimage to view the body. He was evidently, like Sophia, divided between genuine sorrow and a feeling of self-importance.

'The Press, m'lady,' he said with relish, 'awful they've been. Nosing round every-where and taking photos. And the lies they tell, I don't know if you saw, m'lady, they said cook had been with Sir Ivor ten years. It's not a day more than seven.'

'I know,' said Sophia. 'I can't go outside the house for them. Why, look at all the cars which have followed us down here.' And indeed there had been a perfect fleet, greatly incommoded, Sophia was glad to think, by the roundabout and, to them, surely rather baffling journey via Heal's.

Lady Beech meanwhile had not been idle. It was quite uncanny what a lot of Sir Ivor's furniture, books, knick-knacks and even cooking utensils had been lent him by Lady Beech. The house was really nothing but a loan collection. She had, with great forethought, provided herself with two packets of labels, stick-on and tie-on, and by the time Sophia had finished her business, these appeared like a sort of snow-storm, scattered throughout all the rooms.

'Darling, I have just labelled a few little things of my own which dear Ivor had borrowed from me from time to time,' she said, putting a sticky one firmly on to the giant radiogram as she spoke.

'Very sensible, darling.' Sophia secured the jet tiara, an object which she had coveted from childhood. 'Good-bye, then, Larch,' she said. 'Keep the wigs, won't you, and we'll send them to the Ivor King Home of Rest. The aged singers are sure to need them, and I feel it's just what *he* would have liked.' Larch evidently thought that this idea was full of good feeling, and held open the door of the car with an approving look.

They motored back to London in silence. Sophia loved Lady Beech and would have done almost anything for her, but she knew that it would be useless to present Vocal Lodge to the Nation if Lady Beech was always to be there, sighing at whatever visitors might venture in.

St Anne's Hospital First Aid Post

Darling Rudolph darling,

Well, the Memorial Service, I mean Requiem Mass. Did you see the photograph of Luke and me with the glamorous Mgr? I thought it was quite pretty. The object behind us in silver foxes was Florence in my ex-ones. You never saw anything like the crowds outside the Oratory, and inside there were people all over the statues. When we arrived at the front pew reserved for us, who do you think was in it dressed as what? Of course Olga as a Fr. widow. You should have just seen the looks darling Lady Beech gave her. She would keep singing just like one doesn't in Papist churches, and Serge was crying out loud into a huge black-edged handkerchief, fancy at eleven in the morning, but I believe it's really because of his Blossom they say he can't stop.

As we all came down the aisle Olga threw back her veil, and, supported by Fred, gave plucky little smiles to right and left. I forgot to say poor Fred turned up late, looking too guilty and hoping nobody would recognize him, and of course Hamish insisted on bringing him all the way up to our pew where there wasn't room, and after fearful whisperings Luke had to give up his place to the Minister. Then on the way out Olga felt faint so that she could cling to him as you will note if you see the Tatler.

The whole of the stage world was there, of course, as well as all of us. Just think how old Ivor would have enjoyed it. What waste we couldn't have had it while he was alive, can't you see him choosing which wig he would wear? But you know, funny as it was in many ways I couldn't help feeling awfully sad, especially when we got outside again and saw those huge silent mournful crowds. There's no doubt the dear old creature was a sort of figurehead, and I suppose there can hardly be a soul in England who hasn't heard that – let's face it – slightly cracking voice. I thought The Times put it very nicely when it said that the more that golden voice was tinged with silver, the more we loved it. I hope those fiends of parachutists killed him quickly before he knew anything about it – they think so at Scotland Yard because of no cry being heard and no sign of a struggle.

As soon as Fred had shaken off Olga she came floating up to us in her veil and began hinting that she knew more than she cared to reveal about Ivor's death. I'm afraid I was rather rude to her but really I'm getting tired of Olga in the rôle of beautiful female spy – it's becoming a bore. I've just sent her a telegram saying 'Proceed John o' Groats and await further instructions. F.69.' Hope she proceeds, that's all. Darling, what a heavenly idea that Floss might be a B.F.S. – so teasing for Olga if she were. Now get some leave soon and we'll proceed to her bedroom and investigate.

Love my darling from your darling

Sophia.

PS. Did I tell you Luke is proceeding to America on a very secret mission for the F.O.? Fancy choosing that old Fascist. I must get him some Horlick's malted tablets for the 100 hours in an open boat which will almost certainly be his fate – I keep advising him to go rowing on the Serpentine to get his hand in. So here I shall be, left all alone with Florrie and her gang, isn't it terrifying for me? Should you say Heatherley and Winthrop are ones too?

6

Sophia was now designated by the newspapers as 'Wig Heiress'. The reporters pursued her from the pillars of her own front door to the Post, where Sister Wordsworth finally routed them with a hypodermic needle, in an effort to find out how she intended to dispose of her legacy. As she refused to make any statement, they invented every kind of thing. Ninety-eight Granby Gate was for sale, and Sir Luke and Lady Sophia Garfield would take up their residence at Vocal Lodge. They were only going to use it as a summer residence. They were going to pull it down and build a block of flats. (The Georgian Group, wrapped in dreams of Federal Union, stirred in its sleep on hearing this, and groaned.) They were shutting it up to avoid the rates. They were digging for victory among the Lesbian Irises. Only the truth was not told.

Luke, who really hated publicity, even when it took the form of a beautiful studio portrait of Sophia in *Vogue*, because, he said, it did him harm in the City, became very restive, and speeded up his arrangements for leaving England. Sophia spent a busy day shopping for him. Her heart smote her for not having been much nicer to him, as it did periodically, so she tried to atone in Harrods' man's shop, and he left England fully equipped as a U-boat victim. Florence saw him off at his front door and presented him with the balaclava helmet, but Sophia, who accompanied him to the station, threw it out of the taxi window explaining that there was a proper machine-made one in his valise. She kissed him good-bye on the platform to the accompaniment of magnesium flares which, rather to her disappointment (because although she always looked like an elderly negress in them, she liked to see photographs of herself in the papers), were prevented by the

Ministry of Information from bearing any fruit. Luke's mission was a very secret one. As a final parting present she gave him a pocket Shakespeare to read, she explained, on the desert island where his open boat would probably deposit him.

'And if you hear a loud bang in the night,' she added, as the train drew out of the station, 'don't turn over and go to sleep again.'

'Luke hates jokes and hates the war,' she said to Mary Pencill who was also on the platform, seeing off one of Trotsky's lieutenants, 'so isn't he lucky to be going to America where they have neither?'

Mary carried Sophia off to her flat when the train had gone, and they had a long and amicable talk during which they managed to avoid the subject of politics. Sophia, who was considered absolutely red by those supporters of Munich, apologists for Mussolini and lovers of Franco, Fred and Ned, was apt to feel the truest of blue Tories when in the presence of Mary whose attitude of suspicion and obstruction always annoyed her.

'Still writing on foreheads?' Mary inquired when they were settled down in front of her gas stove.

'It's all very well for you to laugh, just wait until you've got a crushed tongue and slight oozing hæmorrhage like one of the patients we had in yesterday – you'll be only too glad to have me writing on your forehead.'

'How d'you mean, yesterday? Was there an air raid – I never noticed a thing.'

'Darling, you are so dense. Practice of course. The telephone bell rings, and I answer it and it says "Southern Control speaking. Practice air raid warning Red, expect casualties." Then, some time later, a lot of unhappy-looking people are brought in out of the street in return for threepence and a cup of tea. They are labelled with a description of their injuries, then we treat them, at least the nurses do, and I write on their foreheads and take them up to the canteen for their cup of tea.'

'With their foreheads still written on?'

'Well, they get threepence, don't they? First of all, we used to practise on each other, but then Mr Stone very sensibly pointed out what a shambles it would be if there were a real raid and real casualties were brought in and found all the personnel tied up in Thomas's splints, and so on. Think of it! So they work on this other scheme now; it seems much more professional too.'

'Well, all I can say is, if there's a raid I hope I shall be allowed to die quietly where I am.'

'Don't be defeatist, darling,' said Sophia.

The next day Sophia, looking, she thought, really very pretty and wearing another new black hat, went off to the Horse Guards Parade where, in the presence of a large crowd, of the microphone and of cinematographers, she handed over to Fred, who accepted it on behalf of the Nation, a cardboard model of Vocal Lodge, the Shrine of Song.

Fred made a very moving speech. He spoke first, of course, about Sophia's enormously generous action, until she hardly knew where to look. He went on to say that the Shrine of Song would be a fitting memorial to one whose loss was irreparable both to Britain and to the whole world of art; the loss of a beloved citizen and venerated artist.

'And we must remember,' he went on, warming to his work, 'that Death never has the last word. When we think of the King of Song, when we pay our pious pilgrimage to Vocal Lodge, it is not of Death that we must think but of that wonderful old spirit which is still watching over us, merged with the eternal Spirit of Patriotism. The work he would have done, had he lived to do it, will now be left undone. But will it? Those who loved him – and they were not confined to this country, mind you, they mourn as we mourn in palaces and cottages the world over – those who loved him know that before he died he had intended literally to devote every breath in his body to an Ideal. He knew that if our cause is lost there will be no Song left in the world, no Music, no Art, no Joy. Lovers of music everywhere, yes and inside Germany too, will remember that the greatest singer of our time, had he not died so prematurely, was going to give his all in the struggle for Freedom. Many an Austrian, many a Czech, many a Pole, and even many a German will think of this as he plays over the well-loved gramophone records, fearful of the creeping feet behind his windows, yet determined once more to enjoy, come what may, that Golden Voice. The cause of such a man, they will think, as they listen to those immortal trills, to that historic bass, and of such an artist, must be indeed the Cause of Right. Who can tell but that the King of Song will not finally accomplish more in death than he, or any other mortal man, could ever accomplish in life.

'Oh Death! Where is thy sting? Oh Grave! Where is thy victory?'

This speech, which was extremely well received, put Fred back on his feet again with everybody except that irascible fellow who indicates daily to Britain what she should Expect.

'We learn,' he wrote the following day, 'that Vocal Lodge has been presented to the Nation to be kept as a Shrine of Song. How do we learn this news, of Empire-wide interest? Through the columns of a free Press? No! A Minister of the Crown withholds it from the public in order to announce it himself in a speech. Praise Lady Sophia Garfield, who gives. The clumsy mismanagement of the whole affair is not her fault. Examine the record of this Minister. It is far from good. We should like to see him offer his resignation forthwith and we should like to see his resignation accepted.'

However, all the other newspapers as well as Fred's colleagues thought that it was first-class stuff and that he had more or less atoned for so carelessly mislaying the King. He was extremely grateful to Sophia who had given him the opportunity for turning Sir Ivor's death to such good account. He and Ned took her out to dinner, fed her with oysters and pink champagne, and stayed up very late indeed.

Sophia, when at last she got home, was surprised and bored, as well as rather startled, to find Greta in her bedroom. She never allowed anybody to wait up for her. Greta seemed very much upset about something, her face was swollen with tears and it was several moments before she could speak.

'Oh Frau Gräfin, don't let them send me back to Germany – they will, I know it, and then in a camp they will put me and I shall die. Oh, protect me, Frau Gräfin.'

'But Greta, don't be so absurd. How can anybody send you back to Germany? We are at war with the Germans, so how could you get there? You might have to be interned here in England if you didn't pass the tribunal, you know, but I will come with you and speak to the Magistrate and I'm sure it will be quite all right. Now go to bed and don't worry any more.'

Greta seemed far from being reassured. She shivered like a nervous horse and went on moaning about the horrors of German concentration camps and how she would certainly be sent to one, unless an even worse fate was in store for her.

'You've been reading the White Paper,' said Sophia impatiently. 'And it should make you realize how very, very lucky you are to be in England.'

'Oh, please protect me,' was all Greta replied to this felicitous piece of propaganda. 'They are coming for me; it may be tonight. Oh please, Frau Gräfin, may I sleep in your bathroom tonight?'

'Certainly not. Why, you have got Mrs Round in the very next room, and Rawlings next door to that. Much safer than being in my bathroom, and besides, I want to have a bath. Now, Greta, pull yourself together and go to bed. You have been upset by poor Sir Ivor's death, and so have we all. We must just try to forget about it, you see. Good night, Greta.'

Greta clutched Sophia's arm, and speaking very fast she said, 'If I tell you something about Sir Ivor, may I sleep in your bathroom? He is –' Her voice died away in a sort of moan, her eyes fixed upon the doorway. Sophia looked round and saw Florence standing there.

'Well, that's all now, Greta. Good night,' Sophia said. Greta slunk out past Florence, who did not give her a glance but told Sophia that she had come in search of an aspirin.

'I had to go off duty, my head ached so badly.'

'Oh, what bad luck. Would a Cachet Fèvre do as well? I've just been having such a scene with Greta; she has got it into her head that somebody is going to take her back to Germany, silly fool. I wish to goodness somebody would, I'd give anything to get rid of her.'

Florence said it was always a mistake to have foreign servants, thanked her for the Cachet Fèvre, and went upstairs. Sophia had rather been expecting that now Luke had gone perhaps Florence would be moving too, but she showed no signs of such an intention. However, the house was large, and they very rarely met, besides, she did not exactly dislike Florence; it was more that they had so little in common.

St Anne's Hospital First Aid Post

My own darling Rudolph,

Florence has joined the Post, did I tell you, and it really is rather a joke. All those terribly nice cosy ladies who have such fun with the Dowager Queen of Ruritania and whether she had Jewish blood, and whether the Crown Princess will ever have a baby and so on, are simply withered up by Flo who says she finds extraordinarily little pleasure in gossiping nowadays. They had rather fun for a time, coming clean and sharing and being guided and so on, but they never really got into it. The last straw was that Miss Edwards said she simply couldn't tell fortunes any more when Florence was there because of the atmosphere, and Miss Edwards' fortunes were the nicest thing in the Post, we all had ours done every day.

Anyhow, it seems that last night the nurses went to Sister Wordsworth in a body and said that although of course Florence is very, very charming and they all liked her very, very, very much, they really couldn't stick her in the Treatment Room another moment. Sister Wordsworth is wonderful, she never turned a hair. She sent for Florence at once and asked her if, as a great favour, she would consent to take charge of the Maternity Ward, which is that little dog kennel, you know, by the Museum, with a cradle and a pair of woolly boots. As it happens, Florence is very keen on obstetrics and she was delighted. So all is honey again and the Dowager Queen of Ruritania and Miss Edwards reign supreme. Sister Words-worth says the head A.R.P. lady in these parts is a pillar of the Brotherhood, and sent Florence with such a tremendous recommendation that she can never be sacked however much of a bore she is.

Heatherley and Winthrop have also joined as stretcher-bearers, in fact the Brother-hood seems to be doing pretty well, just like I never thought it would. I wonder if Heth isn't a bit in love with Florence, there was a form which looked awfully like his on the half-landing when I got back late from the 400 a day or two ago. I was too terrified to look again, so I ran up to my room and locked myself in. Probably it was my imagination.

Love my darling, when are you going to have some leave,
Sophia.

The telephone bell rang and Sophia answered it. 'Southern Control speaking. Practice RED, expect casualties.' This meant that 'casualties' would be arriving from the street. She ran up to the canteen to warn Sister Wordsworth, who was having tea.

'Thank you, Lady Sophia. Now would you go and ring up the doctor?' said Sister Wordsworth. 'If you hurry, you will catch him at his home address. He said he would like to come to the next practice we have here.'

Sophia ran downstairs again. On her way back to the office she nearly collided with Heth and Winthrop who were carrying a stretcher.

'Casualties already!' she said, and as she was going on she noticed that the 'casualty' under the rugs on the stretcher was her own maid, Greta. For a moment she felt surprised, and then she thought that Florence must have asked Greta to do it; probably they were short of casualties. Greta was far too superior to be bribed by threepence and a cup of tea. She had a sort of bandage over her mouth, and had evidently been treated for 'crushed tongue', a very favourite accident at St Anne's. She seemed to have something in her eye, or at any rate it was winking and rolling in a very horrible way.

Sophia, as she went to the telephone, giggled to herself. 'Typical of them,' she thought, 'to treat the wretched woman for crushed tongue when really she is half blinded by a grit in the eye. Let's hope they'll take it out and give her a cup of tea soon.' As the practice got into full swing Sophia became very busy and forgot the incident. She never saw Greta again.

7

The sensation which was caused by the supposed murder of Sir Ivor King, the King of Song, at a time so extremely inconvenient to the British Government, had scarcely subsided when the old singer turned up, wig and all, in Germany. It happened on the very day that Vocal Lodge was opened to the public, a ceremony which, at the request of the A.R.P., was unadvertised, and which therefore consisted of Sophia, in a simple little black frock, dispensing cocktails to Fred, in his pinstripes, and a few other friends. The house was rather bare of furniture, owing to Lady Beech. Hardly had Fred arrived when he was called to the telephone; white to the lips he announced that he had had news which compelled him to leave for the office at once.

The German Press and Radio were jubilant. The old gentleman, it seemed, was visiting that music-loving country with the express purpose of opening there a world-wide anti-British campaign of Propaganda allied to Song. This campaign, it was considered, would have a profound effect on neutral opinion, and indeed might well bring America into the war, on one side or another. He was received like a king in Germany, the Führer sending his own personal car and bodyguard to meet him at the airport, and he celebrated his first evening in Berlin by singing 'Deutschland über Alles' on the radio in a higher and then in a lower key than it had ever been sung before.

Lord Haw-Haw succeeded him at the microphone, and in his inimitable accents announced that the Lieder König was too tired to sing any more that evening but that listeners should prepare for his first full programme of Song-Propaganda in two days' time at 6.30 p.m. on the thirty-one meter band.

'You must all be most anxious to hear,' continued Lord Haw-Haw, '*how* the Lieder König came to our Fatherland. (He himself will be telling you *why* he came.) Your English police, it seems, never realized that the body found on the Pagoda at Kew Gardens was, in fact, the body of a wigless pig. Had they not jumped so quickly to conclusions, had they not assumed, as, of course, they were intended to assume, that these bleeding lumps of meat did constitute the mangled body of the Lieder König, they would not, I expect, have been in such a hurry to bury them. There must be many housewives, whose husbands are at present behind the lines in France, flirting with the pretty French demoiselles, and to whom your Minister of War, Mr Horribleisha, has not yet paid their pathetically small allowances, who would have been only too glad to dispose of these lumps of pig. For bacon is extremely scarce in England now, and is indeed never seen outside the refrigerators of the wealthy.

'Again I ask, where is the *Ark Royal*?

'Here are the stations Hamburg, Bremen and D x B, operating on the thirty-one metre band. Thank you for your attention. Our next news in English will be broadcast from Reichsender Hamburg and station Bremen at 11.15 Greenwich mean time.'

For a day or two the English newspapers assured their readers that the loyal old 'King' was really reposing in his Catholic grave, and that the Germans must be making use of gramophone records, made before the war had begun, in order to perpetrate a gigantic hoax. Alas! The 'King' only had to give his first full-length broadcast for this theory to collapse. Nobody but himself could say 'Hullo dears! Keep your hairs on' in quite that debonair tone of voice.

'I have come to Germany,' he went on, 'with the express intention of lending my services to the Fatherland, and this I do partly because I feel a debt of gratitude to this great country, this home of music where many years ago my voice was trained, but chiefly because of my love of Slavery. I have long been a member of the English Slavery Party, an underground movement of whose very existence most of you are unaware but which is daily increasing in importance. It is my intention to give bulletins of news and words of encouragement to that Party, sandwiched between full programmes of joyous song in which I hope you will all join.

> 'Land of dope you're gory
> And very much too free,
> The workers all abhor thee,
> And long for slavery.'

After bellowing out a good deal more of this kind of drivel, the 'King' told a long story about an English worker who, having been free to marry a Jewess (a thing which, of course, could never happen in Germany), had been cheated out of one and sixpence by his brother-in-law.

'Now here is a word of advice to my brothers of the Slavery Party. Burn your confidential papers and anything that could incriminate you at once. Those of you who have secret stores of castor oil, handcuffs and whips waiting for the great dawn of Slavery, bury them or hide them somewhere safe. For Eden was seen entering the Home Office at 5.46 Greenwich mean time this afternoon, and presently the Black-and-Tans are to conduct a great round-up in the homes of the suspects. For the benefit of my non-British listeners, let me explain that the Black-and-Tans are Eden's dreaded police, so called because those of them that are not negroes are Mayfair playboys, the dregs of the French Riviera. They are a brutal band of assassins, and those who fall foul of them vanish without any trace.'

Now the sinister thing about all this was that Mr Eden really had entered the Home Office at 5.46 on the afternoon in question. How could they have known it in Berlin at 6.30? The Ministry of Information decided to suppress so disquieting a fact for the present.

By the next morning, of course, every single window of the newly constituted Shrine of Song had been broken. Lady Beech having removed all her own furniture, books, knick-knacks and kitchen utensils in three large vans, there was fortunately nothing much to damage, except the 'King's' tatty striped wallpapers. Larch and his fellow-domestics gave notice at once, and fled from the Shrine of Shame as soon as they could.

Poor Sophia felt that she had been made a fool of, and wished the beastly old fellow dead a thousand times. She communicated this sentiment to the many reporters by whom she was once more surrounded, but unfortunately, once crystallized into hard print, it did not redound entirely to her credit considering that she was the 'King's' heiress. The dignitary of the Roman Catholic Church, too, was very much displeased at having been bamboozled into allowing a Requiem Mass to be sung for the soul of a pig. Indeed Roman Catholics all over the world were aghast at the 'King's' treachery, the more so as they had always hitherto felt great pride that one so distinguished should be a co-religionist, had regarded his enormous fame as being a feather in the cap of Holy Mother Church herself, and had never forgotten the pious deeds of his late wife, the posthumous Duchess King. At last Papist feeling became so strong on the subject that the Pope, bowing before the breeze, removed the body of the posthumous Duchess from its distinguished resting-place in the Vatican gardens, and had it re-interred in the Via della Propaganda. When a German note was presented to him on the subject, he gave it as an excuse that the younger cardinals were obliged to learn bicycling on account of the petrol shortage, and were continually falling over her grave. Equally furious and disillusioned were music lovers and fans of the 'King' in the whole civilized world. His gramophone records and his effigy were burnt in market towns all over England, his wigs were burnt on Kew Green, whilst in London his songs were burnt by the public hangman.

But the person who really caught the full blast of the storm was poor Fred. He hurried round to No. 10, and did not spend anything like half an hour there, but only just so long as it took him to write a letter beginning 'My dear Prime Minister' and to hand over his Cabinet key. He was succeeded at the Ministry by Ned, to Ned's delight hardly veiled. The *Daily Runner* unkindly printed extracts from the 'Oh! Death! where is thy sting' speech, and crowed over Fred's resignation, but was not the least bit pleased over Ned's appointment, and suggested that it was a case of out of the frying-pan into the fire.

Fred and Sophia dined together very sadly at the Hyde Park Hotel. Ned would not risk being seen in such discredited company and kept away, and probably he was wise because, as they went into dinner, they were ambushed and subjected to withering fire by about ten press photographers. Fred could no longer afford oysters or pink champagne, so they had smoked salmon and claret instead.

He was intensely gloomy altogether. 'My career is over,' he said.

Sophia told him, 'Nonsense, think of Lord Palmerston,' but there was not much conviction in her voice.

The next day she heard that he had taken over Serge's Blossom.

St Anne's Hospital First Aid Post

Oh, darling Rudolph, who ever would have thought it of the old horror?

I must say there is one comfort to be got out of the whole business and that is the broadcasts. Aren't they heaven? I can't keep away from them, and Sister Wordsworth has had to alter all the shifts here so that nobody shall be on the road during them. I can't ever go out in the evening because of the 10.45 one – the 6.30 I get here before I leave.

Poor Fred sometimes sneaks round, when he can get away from his Blossom, and we listen together after dinner. His wife simply can't stand it, and I don't blame her when you think of the thousands a year it is costing them. Certainly it comes hardest on Fred, but I look a pretty good fool too what with the Requiem Mass, Shrine of Song, and so on.

It was fortunate about Olga being a plucky Fr. widow you must say, and being photographed with Fred, otherwise how she would have crowed. I hear she was just about to proceed to John o' Groats when she guessed it was me and now she's furious so I must think up some more things to do to her. Perhaps you could think as you're in love with her – do.

What else can I tell you? Oh yes, Greta has left, isn't it lucky? She came round here to lend a hand with a practice and hasn't been back since and apparently her luggage has all gone so I suppose she just walked out on me. I'm very pleased, I really hated having a German in the house especially as she used to be so keen on all the Nazi leaders, she gave me the creeps you know. So now Mrs Round can talk world-politics in her own servants' hall again.

Here everything is just the same. Florence, Heatherley and Winthrop hardly ever leave the Maternity ward at all nowadays. I can't imagine how they squash into that tiny room. They seem to be for ever fetching food from the Canteen. I believe Brothers eat twice what ordinary people do. Anyhow they don't hurt anyone by being there, and Miss Edwards is back on the top of her form again telling the most heavenly fortunes, and isn't it funny she says she can see the same thing in all our hands, like before a railway accident, and it is SOMETHING QUEER UNDER YOUR FEET. *Thank goodness not over your head because then I should have known it was parachutists and died of fright. She thinks perhaps this place is built over a plague spot, but Mr Stone says it must be the Main Drain and I suppose there are some pretty queer things in that all right.*

I must fly home now because the old wretch is going to sing Camp Songs (concentration camp, I suppose) at 8 for an extra treat.

Love and xxx from
Sophia.

PS. There is a water pipe here which makes a noise exactly like those crickets on the islands at Cannes. Much as I hate abroad, you can hardly count Cannes and it was a heavenly summer, do you remember, when Robin lent the Clever Girl for the Sea Funeral of a Fr. solicitor from Nice and the coffin bobbed away and came up on the bathing beach at Monte Carlo. I wish it was now. Darling.

Henceforward the doings of the Lieder König were a kind of serial story, which appeared day by day on the front pages of the newspapers, quite elbowing out the suave U-boat commanders, the joy of French poilus at seeing once more the kilt, and the alternate rumours that there would, or would not, be bacon rationing, which had so far provided such a feast of boredom at the beginning of each day. He soon became the only topic of conversation whenever two or more Englishmen met together, while the sale of wireless sets in London were reported to have gone up fifty per cent, and a hundred people of the name of King applied to change it by deed poll. His programmes were a continual treat, especially for collectors of musical curiosities, as, for instance, when he sang the first act from *La Bohème*, '*Tes petites mains sont gelées*,' etc., twice through with Frau Goering, each taking alternately the male and female parts. It was after this that he suddenly gave an account of the Prime Minister walking in St James's Park that very morning, with a list of all the birds he saw and exactly what they were doing; and although the birds, owing to the autumnal season, were behaving with absolute propriety, and therefore nobody need feel embarrassed on that score, the mere fact of such accurate knowledge having reached Berlin so quickly was disquieting to the authorities. On another occasion he sang through an entire act of *Pelléas et Mélisande*, taking all the parts himself; as a tour de force this was pronounced unique and even *The Times* musical critic was obliged to admit that the Lieder König had never, within living memory, been in better voice. A touching incident occurred some days later when Herr Schmidt, the Lieder König's music teacher, who had prophesied all those years ago in Düsseldorf that Herr King's voice would make musical history, was brought to the microphone. He was now 108 and claimed to be the oldest living music teacher. His broadcast, it is true, was not very satisfactory and sounded rather like someone blowing bubbles, but the Lieder König paid a charming tribute to the old fellow. He said that as all his success in life had been due to the careful training which he had received from Herr Schmidt, a German, he was so happy that he had the opportunity of helping the Fatherland in its time of difficulty. He and his teacher were then decorated by Herr von Ribbentrop, speaking excellent English, with the Order of the Siegfried Line, third class.

Always at the end of his concerts the Lieder König announced succulent pieces of good cheer for the English Slavery Party. Soon, according to his information, vast concentration camps would spring into being all over England, to be filled with Churchill, Eden and other Marxist – here he corrected himself – Liberals, Jews and plutocrats.

Soon the benevolent rule of National Socialism would stretch across the seas to every corner of the British and French Empires, harnessing all their citizens to the tyrant's yoke, and removing the last vestiges of personal freedom. Soon all nations of the world would be savouring the inestimable advantages of Slavery.

'Here are the Reichsender Bremen, stations Hamburg and D x B operating on the thirty-one metre band. This is the end of the Lieder König's talk in English.'

8

Sophia was dressing to go out to dinner with Fred, Ned and Lady Beech. She took a good deal of trouble always with her appearance, but especially when she was going to be seen in the company of Lady Beech, whose clothes were the most exquisite in London and whom it was not possible in that respect to outshine. Sophia had not attempted to replace Greta and was beginning to realize what an excellent maid that boring German had been; on this occasion she could not find anything she wanted, nor was Elsie, the housemaid, very much help to her.

Sophia was a very punctual character, with the result that she often found herself waiting for people, and indeed must have spent several weeks of her life, in all, waiting for Rudolph. On this occasion Fred and she arrived simultaneously and first, in spite of the many setbacks in her bedroom. He ordered her a drink and muttered in her ear that Ned was behaving as if he had been in the Cabinet all his life. It seemed anyhow that he felt himself firmly enough in the saddle after three Cabinet meetings to be able once more to consort with those victims of circumstances, Fred and Sophia. But of course Fred in the uniform pertaining to his Blossom was hardly at all reminiscent of Fred in the pin-stripe trousers of his disgrace; he looked already brown and healthy and seemed to have grown quite an inch.

Lady Beech appeared next, wonderful in sage green and black with ostrich feathers and a huge emerald laurel leaf. Sophia felt at once extremely dowdy.

'You are lucky,' she said, 'the way you always have such heavenly things. I do wish I were you.'

'Child!' said Lady Beech, deprecatingly.

Very late the Minister himself galloped up to them complaining loudly that he had been kept at No. 10. As his own house happened to be No. 10 Rufford Gate, there was a pleasing ambiguity about this excuse. They went in to dinner.

Fred and Ned were very partial to Lady Beech. She was the only link they had with culture, and Fred and Ned were by no means so insensible to things of the mind as they appeared to be. At school and at Oxford they had been clever boys with literary gifts and a passion for the humanities; it was only their too early excursion into politics which had reduced their intellectual capacity once more to that of the private school. The poor fellows still felt within them a vague yearning towards a higher plane of life, and loved to hear Lady Beech discourse, in polished accents now sadly unfamiliar, of Oscar, Aubrey, Jimmy, Algernon, Henry, Max, Willie, Osbert and the rest. They could talk to her, too, of those of their contemporaries whose lives had taken a more intellectual turn than their own, for Lady Beech is as much beloved by the present as she was by a past generation of artists and writers. Another thing which endeared her to them was the fact that she, unlike anybody else, called them Sir Frederick and Lord Edward and, instead of telling them her opinion of The Situation, flatteringly deferred to theirs. It made them feel positively grown up. She liked them, too; they were such pretty, polite young men, and she particularly liked oysters and pink champagne. When, on this occasion, they suggested that a little white wine would be suitable because of the income tax, and the fact that poor Fred had so little income left to tax, she sighed very dreadfully indeed and they good naturedly reverted to pre-war rations for that evening. The dinner having been ordered to her entire satisfaction, Lady Beech turned to Ned with her usual opening gambit of, 'Tell me, Lord Edward.' This was really rather horrid of her as, hitherto, it had always been, 'Tell me, Sir Frederick.'

'Tell me what you think will happen?'

Ned opened his napkin and said cheerfully, 'Oh gracious, I don't know. Nothing much, I don't expect.'

'Ah! You mean there will be no allied offensive for the moment?'

'Hullo, there's Bob! Well, now, Lady Beech, you won't quote me, will you? I never said that, you know. But between ourselves, quite between, well I rather expect we shall all go bumbling along as we are doing until we have won the war – or lost it, of course.'

'Should you say there was quite a good possibility of that?'

'Of what?'

'Of our losing the war?'

'Oh quite a good chance, oh Lord yes. Mind you, of course, we're bound to win really, in the end, we always do. All I say is it may be a long business, the way we're setting about it. Well, Fred, so how's the balloon these days, eh?'

'Up and down, you know. It's rather like playing a salmon, getting her down. I enjoy it. Frankly I enjoy it more than – oh well, it's a healthy outdoor life.'

'Should you say,' asked Lady Beech, 'that the balloons are of much use?'

'I'm told none whatever,' said Ned in his loud jolly voice.

'Ah!' she looked searchingly at Fred who was quite nettled.

'That's entirely a matter of opinion,' he said crossly. 'I should think myself they are a jolly sight more use than – oh well. Anyway, it's a healthy outdoor life for the lads who do it, which is more than you can say for – well, some other kinds of lives.'

'Do you think you can keep off the parachutists?' said Sophia. 'They are the only thing I mind. Give me bombs, gas, anything you like. It's the idea of those sinister grey-clad figures, with no backs to their heads, slowly floating past one's bedroom window like snowflakes that gives me the creeps.'

'They would not be grey-clad,' Ned assured her. 'If they come at all, which is very unlikely (not that the balloons would stop them) they will be dressed as Guards' officers.'

'Lean out of your window and break their legs with a poker as they go by,' suggested Fred.

Lady Beech now broke the ice by saying, 'I was listening to my poor old brother-in-law on the wireless before I came out.'

Everybody had, of course, been dying to begin on this topic but none of the others had liked to, Sophia because of poor Fred, poor Fred because he knew that Lady Beech was the 'King's' sister-in-law, and Ned because, although the least sensitive person in the world, he did feel it was perhaps hardly for him to do so, having made such good capital out of Sir Ivor's defection.

Lady Beech went on, 'He was giving a concert of Mozart, and I must tell you that it was perfectly exquisite. Schumann herself could not have given such an ideal rendering of '*Voi che sapete*' – I never heard such notes, never.'

'Yes, the old beast can sing,' Fred muttered gloomily.

'I wonder what he feels like,' said Sophia. 'I mean, when he thinks of all of us he must be rather sad. He did so love jokes, too, and I don't suppose he gets many of them, or at any rate people to share them with.'

'It is so strange,' said Lady Beech, 'oh, it is so strange! As you know, I was very intimate indeed with him, and I should have said that he had a particularly strong love of his country, and of his own people. He was so attached to you, darling, and to all his friends – I think I may add, to me.' She sighed. The disposition of Vocal Lodge, although it had proved to be premature, still rankled a little with her. 'Well, there it is. I shall never understand it, never, it seems to me that it can't be true, and yet – tell me, Lord Edward, is it possible that he is doing this with some motive that we know nothing about?'

'I couldn't say. I suppose the old buffer gets well paid, what?'

'Oh, you don't know Ivor if you think that would have anything to do with it. He never cared the least bit for money. He had far too much of it for his needs. Why should he want more?'

'I put it down to a morbid love of publicity,' said Fred. He could not speak without bitterness of the wrecker of his career.

'But he would have had publicity under your scheme, Sir Frederick, and with it love and praise instead of hatred and contempt.'

'Depends which way you look at it. I expect he gets love and praise in Germany all right.'

'I can't believe that that is much comfort to him. He never cared for Germany as far as I knew; he certainly never sang there. I should have said he cared for nothing, these last years, but his garden. He was even neglecting his voice in order to be able to work longer hours among his cabbages. I reproached him for it.'

'Perhaps they promised him a whole mass of Lesbian Irises.'

'Perhaps they caught him and tortured him until he said he would sing for them.'

'Ah, now that I think is very probably the explanation,' said Lady Beech with mournful satisfaction. 'And curiously enough, just the one that had occurred to me. Terrible, terrible. What should you say they do to him, Lord Edward?'

'Oh, really, I don't know much about these things. Thumbscrew, I suppose, then there was the rack, the boot and the *peine forte et dur*, but I always think a night-light under the sole of the foot would be as good as anything.'

'Do stop,' said Sophia, putting her fingers in her ears. She could never bear to hear of tortures.

'Actually I wonder if he would do it with such gusto if he had the thumbscrew hanging over him, so to speak. I mean he does get the stuff off his chest as if he really enjoyed it – eh?'

'You forget,' said Lady Beech, 'that Ivor was nothing if not an artist. Once he began to sing he would be certain to do it well, whatever the circumstances. That he could not help.'

'Oh, poor old gentleman,' said Sophia, 'it would really have been better for him to have died on Kew Pagoda all along.'

'Very, very much better,' said Lady Beech. 'Now, tell me, Lord Edward (I am changing the subject to one hardly less painful) supposing, I say *supposing* anybody had a very small sum of money to invest, what should you yourself advise doing with it? I don't mean speaking as a Member of the Cabinet; I just want your honest advice.'

'Personally,' said Ned, brightening up, 'I should put it on a horse. I mean, a sum like that, the sort of sum you describe, is hardly worth saving, is it? Why not go a glorious bust on Sullivan in the 3.30 tomorrow?'

'You wouldn't say that if you knew how unlucky I am, would he, child?' she said to Sophia; 'but what I really wanted to know about is these defence loans, to buy or not to buy? I thought you could advise me.'

Ned gave a guilty jump and said the defence loans were just the very thing for her. 'I bought a certificate for my little nipper today,' he said, 'but the little blighter wanted it in hard cash. Couldn't blame the kid either – I mean, of course, at that age. In fifteen years he'll be glad – if he's not dead. Well,' he looked importantly at his watch, 'I must be getting back to No. 10.'

'Child,' said Lady Beech, 'have you got Rawlings with you? No? Then perhaps Lord Edward will escort me to a bus.'

Fred and Sophia decided to make a night of it. They went to several very gay restaurants and then to a night club. Here, many hours after they had left the Carlton, Fred talked about his Ideals. It seemed that, at night, as he watched his Blossom careering about among the stars, Ideals had come to Fred, and he had resolved, should he ever again achieve Cabinet rank, that he would be guided by them.

'I used to go on, you know, from day to day, doing things just as they came without any purpose in my life. But now it will be different.'

Sophia had heard this kind of talk before; it sounded horribly as though the Brotherhood was claiming another victim. Apparently however, this time it was Federal Union, and Fred expounded its theories to her at great length.

'So what d'you think of it?' he said when he had finished.

'Well, darling, I didn't quite take it in. I feel rather deliciously muzzy to tell you the truth, you know the feeling, like that heavenly anaesthetic they give you nowadays.'

'Oh.' Fred was disappointed.

'Tell me again, darling, and I'll listen more carefully.'

He told her.

'Well, if it means the whole world is going to be ruled by the English, I'm all for it.'

'Oh no, it's not like that at all; I must have explained it badly.'

He began again, taking enormous trouble.

Presently someone Sophia knew came up to their table. Sophia was feeling extremely vague. She introduced Fred as Sir Frederick Union. After this he took her home.

9

The Lieder König had just finished one of his Pets' Programmes. These were a terrible thorn in the side of the authorities, who considered that all the other pieces in his repertoire were exceedingly harmless, although the news which was thrown in at the end always included some item proving that the German Secret Service arrangements for transmitting facts to Berlin had ours beat by about twelve hours, and this certainly did tease the M.I. rather. But the Pets' Programmes were a definite menace. Playing upon the well-known English love of animals the wily Hun provided this enormous treat for the pets of the United Kingdom.

'Bring your Bow-wow, your Puss-puss, your Dickie-bird, your Moo-cow, your Gee-gee, your Mousie and your three little fishes to the radio. Or, take the radio out to the stables if your pets cannot be brought indoors. For those raising hens on the battery system these concerts should prove profitable indeed – few hens can resist laying an egg after hearing the Lieder König. The real object of these programmes is not, however, a mercenary one, the object is to bring joy to the hearts of dumb creatures, too many of whom spend a joyless life without song. There is no need for your pets to belong to this category any more; bring them all to the radio and see what pleasure you will give them. The Lieder König himself, who can sing so high that bats can hear him, and so low that buffaloes can, is here expressly to minister to your dumb ones, and bring them strength through joy.'

The old gentleman then came to the radio and gave first a little talk about the muddle of animal A.R.P. in London. Few dogs and no cats, he said, carried gas masks, and gas-proof cages for birds and mice were the exception rather than the rule. The animal First Aid Posts were scandalously few and ill equipped. The evacuation scheme had not been a success, and many mothers of dogs had fetched their little ones home rather than unselfishly bear the parting for their sakes. 'I dedicate this concert to the animal evacuees in strange homes,' he said, 'may they think of England and stay away from London until this stupid war is over. Here in Germany you hardly ever see a pet; all the dogs are at the West Wall, and the rest are nobly playing their part, somewhere.' He then delivered a series of shrieks and groans which certainly did have an uncanny effect upon any animals who happened to listen in. Dogs and cats joined in the choruses, horses danced upon their hind legs, and dickie-birds went nearly mad with joy. Mice crept out of their holes to listen, while in the country the radio on these occasions proved such a magnet to frogs and snails and slugs that many people thankfully used it as a trap for small garden pests. The authorities at the Zoo had gramophone records made to cheer up their charges during the black-out, and Ming, the panda, would soon eat no food until one of them was played to her.

The results of all this can readily be imagined. On the day after one of these concerts Members of Parliament would be inundated by a perfect flood of letters from sentimental constituents demanding instant cessation of hostilities against our fellow animal-lovers, the Germans. In fact, the Pets' Programme did more for the enemy cause over here than all the broadcasts by Lord Haw-Haw, all the ravings of the Slavery Party's organ, *The New Bondsman*, and all the mutterings of Bloomsbury's yellow front put together.

'If the pets all over the world,' concluded the Lieder König, 'were to rise up as one pet and demand peace, peace we should have.'

'Here are the Reichsender Bremen, stations Hamburg and D x B operating on the thirty-one metre band. The Lieder König wishes to thank all pets for listening. The next Pets' Concert will be on Tuesday next at 9.45.'

Sophia and Fred, who had dined with her, had been listening, for the benefit of those returned evacuees, Milly and Abbie. Sophia had sent for Milly, against her better judgment, because she did not get along without her very well, and also for protection from the parachutists. She was a French bulldog, as clever as she was beautiful, and Abbie was her daughter. Abbie's blood was mixed, Milly having thrown herself away upon a marmalade Don Juan, one spring morning in Westminster Abbey, but she was very sweet and the apple of Fred's eye. When the Pets' Programme was over, they took their leave, Sophia going a little way up the Square with them in order to give Milly a run after her emotional experience. When they got back, Milly galloped upstairs and burrowed her way under Sophia's quilt until she came to where the hot-water bottle was, when she flopped at once into a snoring sleep.

Sophia followed more slowly. She had a pain which had not been improved by her excursion into the cold. When she reached her bathroom she looked for the Cachets Fèvre, but presently remembered that she had given the box to Florence, and went up the next flight of stairs to Florence's bedroom. She knocked on the door without much expecting any reply: when there was none, she went in.

She had not seen the room since Florence had occupied it, and was quite shocked to see how much it had been subdued. Pretty and frilly as it was, like any room done up by Sophia, Florence had done something intangible to it by her mere presence, and it was looking frightful. The dressing-table, exquisite with muslin, lace, roses and blue bows, like a ball dress in a dream, and which was designed to carry an array of gold-backed brushes, bottles, pots of cream and flagons of scent, was bare except for one small black brush and a comb which must have originally been meant for a horse's mane. The Aubusson carpet had its pattern of lutes and arrows, with more roses and blue bows, completely obscured by two cheap-looking suitcases. A pair of stays and a gas-mask case had been thrown across the alluring bed cover, puckered with pink velvet and blue chiffon. Sophia, who herself wore a ribbon suspender-belt, looked in horrified fascination at the stays. 'No wonder Florence is such a queer shape,' she thought, picking them up, 'she will never be a glamour girl in stays like that, and how does she get into them?' She held them against her own body but could not make out which bit went where; they were like medieval armour. As she put them back on the bed she saw that the gas-mask carrier contained a Leica camera instead of a gas mask, and she thought it was simply horrible of Florence never to have taken a photograph of Milly with it. The pigeon, in its cage, was dumped on a beautiful satinwood table, signed by Sheraton; considering how much Florence was supposed to love it, she might have provided it with a larger cage. The poor thing was shuffling up and down miserably. Sophia stroked its feathers with one finger through the wire netting, and remembered a beautiful Chippendale birdcage for sale in the Brompton Road. She might give it to Florence for Christmas, but Florence seemed so very indifferent to pretty objects. Perhaps, she thought, the bird wants to go out. She opened the cage, took it in her hands, stroked it for a while, and put it out of the window, just too late, evidently, for it made a mess on her skirt.

When she had shut the window and wiped her skirt, Sophia felt an impulse to tidy up; it was really too annoying of Elsie, the housemaid, to leave the room in such a mess. She put away the stays and gasmask case, and then took hold of a hatbox, intending to take it upstairs to the boxroom, but although, as she did so, the top opened, revealing that it was quite empty inside, it was so heavy that she could hardly lift it, so she gave up the idea. Really, her pain was quite bad and she must find the cachets. She opened a few drawers, but they were all full of papers. Then she remembered that there were some shelves in the built-in cupboard so she opened that.

In the part of the cupboard which was meant for dresses stood Heatherley Egg.

Sophia's scream sounded like a train going through a tunnel. Then she became very angry indeed.

'Stupid,' she said, 'to frighten me like that. Anyway, what's the point of waiting in Florence's cupboard – she's on duty, doesn't come off till six.'

Heatherley slid out into the room and gripped her arm. 'Listen,' he said, 'we have got to get this straight.'

'Oh, don't let's bother,' said Sophia, who had lost interest now that she had recovered from her fright. 'God knows I'm not a prude, and Florence's private life has nothing to do with me. Live in her cupboard if you like to; I don't care.'

'See here, Sophia, you can't get away with that. Now, sit down; we have to talk this over.'

'You haven't seen some Cachets Fèvre anywhere, have you? I lent her a box and, of course, she didn't bring them back; people never do, do they? It doesn't matter to speak of, I must go to bed. Well, good night, Heatherley. What about breakfast? Do you like it in your own cupboard, or downstairs?'

She went towards the door.

'Oh, no you don't!' said Heatherley, in quite a menacing sort of voice, very different from his usual transatlantic whine. 'You can't fool me that way, Sophia. Very clever, and I should have been quite taken in, but I happened to watch you through the keyhole. Those bags have false bottoms, haven't they, the gasmask contains a camera, doesn't it, and there are code signals sewn into the stuffing of those stays. Eh?'

'Are there, how simply fascinating! Is that why they are so bumpy? Do go on!'

'Quite an actress, aren't you, and I might easily have believed you if you hadn't sent off the pigeon with a phoney message.'

'The dear thing asked to go out.'

'Yes, knowing how stupid you are, Sophia, I might have believed that everything had passed over your head, but you can't laugh off that pigeon. So come clean now; you've known the whole works since Greta disappeared, haven't you?'

'What works? Darling Heth, do tell me; it does sound such heaven.'

'As you know so much already, I guess I better had, too, tell you everything. Florence, of course, as you are no doubt aware, is a secret agent, working under a pseudonym, and with a false American passport. Her real name is Edda Eiweiss and she is the head of the German espionage in this country.'

'You don't say so! Good for Florence,' said Sophia. 'I never thought she would have had the brains.'

'Gee, Florence is probably the cleverest, most astute and most daring secret agent alive today.'

'Do go on. What are you? Florence's bottle-washer?'

'Why no, not at all. I am engaged in counter-espionage on behalf of the Allied Governments, but Florence, of course, believes that I am one of her gang. Now, what I want to know is, are you employed by anybody, or are you on your own?'

'But neither,' said Sophia, opening her eyes very wide.

'Sophia, I want an answer to my question, please. I have laid my cards on the table; let's have a look at yours.'

'Oh, on my own, of course,' said Sophia. As Heatherley seemed to be crediting her with these Machiavellian tactics it would be a pity to undeceive him.

'I thought so. Now, Sophia, I need your help. A woman's wits are just what I lack, so listen carefully to me. I have found out a great deal, but not all, about the

German system of espionage. By November tenth, I shall have all the facts that will enable the Government to round up the entire corps of spies at present operating in this country. On that day we can catch the gang, Florence and her associates, but not before. Will you come in on this with me, Sophia?' He clutched her shoulders and stared with his light blue eyes into her face. 'Before you answer, let me tell you that it is difficult and dangerous work. You risk death, and worse, if you undertake it, but the reward, to a patriotic soul, is great.'

'Rather, of course I will.' Sophia was delighted. She, and not Olga, was now up to the neck in a real-life spy story.

'Understand, you must take all your orders from me. One false step might render useless my work of months.'

'Yes, yes.'

'And not act on your own initiative at all?'

'No, no.'

'Sophia, you are a brave woman and a great little patriot. Shake.' They shook.

'Can I ask you a question?'

'Go right ahead.'

'Well, what happened to Greta in the end?'

'What did she say to you?' asked Heatherley, with a searching look.

'I don't understand.'

'What did she say when you saw her in the Post on that stretcher?'

'Well, but she couldn't speak. She had a sort of bandage on her tongue, you see.'

'Sophia,' Heatherley's voice again took on that horrid rasping tone, 'you promised to be perfectly frank with me. Come clean now, what was she doing with her eyes?'

'Oh, her eyes. Yes, she must have had a great grit in one of them, I should imagine. She was blinking like mad; I had quite forgotten.'

'She was winking out a message to you in Morse Code. What was that message, Sophia? No double crossing –'

'My dear Heatherley, however should I know?'

'You don't know Morse Code?'

Sophia saw that she might just as well have admitted to an Ambassador of the old school that she knew no French. She decided that as she did long to be a counter-spy with Heatherley and that as she could quite quickly learn the Morse Code (she knew that stupid-looking Girl Guides managed to do so) there would be no harm in practising a slight deception.

'Semaphore perfect,' she said airily. 'But I must confess my Morse needs brushing up. And anyhow, if you remember, I was running to the telephone when I passed you in that dark passage and had no time at all to see what Greta was winking about. She was such a bore, anyway, I never could stick her. So what happened to her after that?'

Heatherley pursed his lips. 'I'm afraid, my dear Sophia, that it was not very pleasant,' he said. 'You must remember that my job is counter-espionage, that I have to suppress my own personal feelings rigidly, and that very very often I am obliged to do things which are obnoxious to me.'

'Like in Somerset Maugham's books?'

'Just like – I am glad you appreciate my point. Well, it seems that Florence wasn't feeling any too sure about Greta, who was, of course, one of her corps, and was particularly anxious that Greta should not come up before the Aliens' tribunal as she would probably have made mistakes and given them all away, Florence and the rest of them. Also her papers were not foolproof. So, at Florence's bidding, of course, Winthrop and I carried her on the stretcher, just as you saw her, gagged and bound, and put her into the main drain which flows, as you may not know, under the First Aid Post.'

Sophia screamed again. Heatherley went on, 'Yes, my dear Sophia, counter-espionage is a dangerous, disagreeable profession. I should like you to remember this and be most careful, always, how you act. It is absolutely necessary for you to trust me and do exactly what I say on every occasion. We are in this together now, remember, you and I.'

Sophia did not so much care about being in anything with Heatherley, and hoped that all this would not lead to being in bed with him; she seemed to remember that such things were part of the ordinary day's work of beautiful female spies. On the other hand, she felt that she would, if necessary, endure even worse than death in order to be mixed up in this thrilling real-life spy drama. The horrible end of poor Greta served to show that here was the genuine article. Fancy. The main drain. Sophia shuddered. No wonder Miss Edwards saw something queer going on under her feet.

'Now, Sophia, I hope you realize,' Heatherley said, 'that whatever happens you are not to tell a living soul about all this. You and I are watched day and night by unseen eyes. These are evil things that we are fighting – yes, evil, and very clever. The telephone, to this house and to the Post, is tapped by Florence's men; our letters are read and our movements followed. We may have got away with this conversation simply by daring to hold it here, in the heart of the enemy country; on the other hand, we may not. As you leave this room, masked men may seize upon us and carry us, on stretchers, to the fate which befell you know who. Of course, if you were to go to anybody in authority with this tale, the gang would know it, and would disperse like a mist before the sun – at the best my work of months would be destroyed, at the worst you and I would suffer the supreme penalty. I may tell you that the War Office and Scotland Yard are watching over us in their own way, and I have secret means of communicating with them. By the tenth of November, as I told you before, I shall have all the evidence I need, and then the whole lot can be rounded up. Meanwhile, you and I, Sophia, must be a team. Now you should go back to your room; this conversation has already lasted too long. I shan't be able to speak to you like this again until all is over, SO REMEMBER.'

Heatherley squeezed back into his cupboard, and Sophia, highly elated and with her pain quite forgotten, skipped off and slid down the banisters to her own landing. They had evidently got away with that conversation all right, as no masked men pounced out on her and she was soon in bed, kicking Milly off the warm patch which she wanted for her own feet.

IO

When Sophia awoke the next day, she had the same feeling with which, as a child, she had greeted Christmas morning, or the day of the Pantomime. A feeling of happy anticipation. At first, and this also was like when she was little, she could not even remember what it was all about; she simply knew that something particularly lively was going to happen.

Elsie, the housemaid, called her and put a breakfast tray in front of her on which there were coffee, toast and butter, and a nice brown boiled egg, besides a heap of letters and *The Times*. Sophia had woken up enough to remember that she was now a glamorous female spy; she put on a swansdown jacket, sat up properly, and admonished Milly for refusing to go downstairs.

'Drag her,' she said to Elsie. Elsie dragged, and they left the room with a slow, shuffling movement, accompanied by the bedside rug.

The letters looked dull; Sophia began on her egg, and was attacking it with vigour when she saw that something was written on it in pencil. Not hard-boiled, she hoped. Not at all. The writing was extremely faint, but she could make out the word AGONY followed by 22.

Sophia was now in agony, for this must be, of course, a code. She knew that spies and counter-spies had the most peculiar ways of communicating with each other, winking in Morse and so on; writing on eggs would be everyday work for them. She abandoned the delicious egg, done so nicely to a turn, and rolled her eyes round the pink ceiling with blue clouds of her bedroom while she tried the word AGONY backwards and forwards and upside down. She made anagrams of the letters. She looked at the egg in her looking-glass bed-post, but all in vain. She would have to get hold of the Chief at once, but how was she to do that? Impossible to send Elsie upstairs with instructions to see if Mr Egg was still in Miss Turnbull's cupboard, if so, Lady Sophia's compliments and would he step downstairs. In any case he was unlikely to have remained in the cupboard all night, and Florence's bed, a narrow single one, would not harbour any but impassioned lovers with the smallest degree of comfort. This, she somehow felt, Florence and Heatherley were not.

Elsie now returned with Milly, who once more dived under the eiderdown, and, with a piercing snore, resumed her slumbers.

'Did she do anything?'

'Yes, m'lady.'

'Good girl. Would you be very kind,' said Sophia, 'and go and ask Miss Turnbull if she would give me Mr Egg's telephone number. Say I'm short of a man for to-night.'

Florence, who had only come off duty at six, was displeased at being woken up. She was understood by Elsie to say that Mr Egg had gone to Lympne for the day, and had her ladyship remembered that there was to be a Brotherhood meeting at 98 that evening.

Sophia saw that she had been rather dense. Of course she might have realized that if Heth had been available to see her there would have been no need for him to write on her egg. Then she saw light.

'He, Egg, is in agony, because he is unable 2 see me before 2 night.' Sophia turned to her breakfast with a happy appreciation both of its quality and of her own brilliance.

She picked up *The Times* and read about the Pets' Programme. It seemed to have fallen very flat with the musical critic. 'Not with Milly though.' Then, without looking at the war news, which she guessed would be dull, she turned to the front page and read, as she always did, the agony column. She usually found one or two advertisements that made her feel happy, and today there was a particularly enjoyable one. 'Poor old gentleman suffering from malignant disease would like to correspond with pretty young lady. Box 22 *The Times*.'

When Sophia had finished laughing she became quite wistful. She always called Sir Ivor the poor old gentleman, and he called her the pretty young lady. If only he were not being a dreadful old traitor in Berlin, she would have cut the advertisement out and sent it to him. 'I never should have expected to miss him as much as I do, but the fact is there are certain jokes which I can only share with him. Funny thing too,' she thought, 'suffering from malignant disease, just what he is. National Socialism.' She cut out the advertisement and put it in her jewel case, deciding that if she ever had the opportunity to do so, through neutrals, she would send it to Sir Ivor in the hopes of making him feel small. Her blood boiled as she thought again of his treachery and of the programme of Camp songs, which was exactly similar to one he had given before the Chief Scout some months previously, and which had included that prime and perennial favourite:

> There was a bee i ee i ee,
> Sat on a wall y all y all y all y all,
> It gave a buzz y wuz y wuz y wuz y wuz,
> And that was all y all y all y all y all.

Sir Ivor and Dr Goebbels between them had altered the words of this classic to:

> The British E i ee i ee,
> Sat on a wall y all y all y all y all,
> Like Humpty Dumpt y ump ty ump ty ump ty ump,
> It had a fall y all y all y all y all.

So queer it seemed, and so horrible, that somebody who had had the best that England can give should turn against her like that. Sir Ivor had received recognition of every kind, both public and private, from all parts of the British Empire, of his great gifts. Had he been one of those geniuses who wither in attics, it would have been much more understandable. Sophia got out of bed, and while her bath was running in she did a few exercises in order to get fit for the dangers and exactions of counter-espionage.

On the way to St Anne's, Sophia bought a Manual of Morse Code which she fully intended to learn that day. When she arrived however she found, greatly to her disgust, that, as it was Thursday, there was a great heap of clean washing to be counted.

She supposed that she must have a brain rather like that of a mother bird who, so the naturalists tell us, cannot count beyond three; counting the washing was her greatest trial. There would be between twenty and thirty overalls to be checked and put away in the nurses' pigeonholes in the 'dressing-room' which was a sacking partition labelled, rather crudely, Female. Now Sophia, with an effort of concentration, could stagger up to twelve or thirteen; having got so far the telephone bell would ring, somebody would come and ask her a question, or her own mind would stray in some new direction. Then she would have to begin all over again.

It generally took her about an hour before she could make the numbers tally twice, and even then it was far from certain that they were correct. On this occasion she made them alternately twenty-five and twenty-eight, so she assumed the more optimistic estimate to be the right one, and stowed them away in their pigeonholes. She was longing to tell Sister Wordsworth about Greta and the main drain, but of course that would never do. She did ask Mr Stone whether the drain really flowed underneath the First Aid Post and could she see it, to which he replied that it did, and that she could, but in his opinion she would not enjoy such an experience.

'Rats,' he said. Sophia thought of Greta and shuddered. 'As a matter of fact,' he went on, 'some fellows are going down there this evening to have a look round. I expect you could go with them if you like.'

Sophia asked what time, and when she was told at half-past ten, she declined the offer. It would require a bigger bribe than the main drain to get her back to St Anne's when her work there was finished.

She spent the rest of the day learning Morse Code, partly because she wished to be a well equipped counter-spy and partly (and this spurred her to enormous industry) so that she could wink at Olga in it the next time they met. There was a photograph of Olga in that week's *Tatler* wearing a black velvet crinoline with a pearl cross, and toying with a guitar, beneath which was written the words, 'This Society beauty does not require a uniform for her important war work.'

Sophia, thinking of this, redoubled her efforts of dot and dash. But she found it far from easy, even more difficult than counting overalls, though the reward of course was greater. She sat, winking madly into her hand looking-glass, until she was off duty, by which time she knew the letters A, B and C perfectly, and E and F when she thought very hard. The opportunity for showing off her new accomplishment came that evening. She had gone on duty at the Post earlier than usual, as Sister Wordsworth wanted to go out; leaving it correspondingly early, she was on her way home when she remembered that her house would be full of Brothers. So she looked in at the Ritz. Here the first person she saw was Rudolph, and sitting beside him was a heaving mass of sables which could only conceal the beautiful Slavonic person of La Gogothska herself, in the uniform, so to speak, of her important war-work.

'Hullo, my darling,' said Rudolph, fetching a chair for her. 'You're off very early. I'm dining with you tonight, though you may not know it. Elsie said I could, and she's telling your cook.'

'Good,' said Sophia, without listening much. Her eyes were fixed upon Olga and she was working away with concentration.

'What are you making those faces at me for?' said Olga crossly.

'Dear me,' said Sophia, 'how disappointing. It was just a bet I had with Fred. I betted him sixpence that you were in the secret service, he was so positive you couldn't be, and I said I could prove it. Well, I have proved it, and I have lost sixpence, that's all.'

'What do you mean?'

'Well, darling, I was just telling you, in Morse Code, to proceed to the ladies' cloakroom, and are you proceeding? No. Have you made any excuse for not doing so? No. Therefore, as you evidently don't know Morse Code which is a _sine qua non_ for any secret agent, you can't be that beautiful female spy we all hoped you were.' Actually, of course, Sophia had only been winking out, and with great trouble at that, A, B and C.

Olga said, 'Nonsense. Morse Code is never used in this war; it's completely out of date. Why, what would be the use of it?' and she gave a theatrically scornful droop of the eyelids.

'Well, as a matter of fact, dear, it would be a very great deal of use indeed under certain circumstances. Supposing one happened to be gagged, for an example, it would be possible to wink out messages to the bystanders which, if they understood Morse, would save one's life.'

'Gagged,' said Olga, shrugging her shoulders. 'Gagged indeed. Bystanders! Darling, you have been reading Valentine Williams, I suppose. Let me tell you that in real life the secret service is very different from what the outside public, like you, imagine it to be. Gagged! No, really, I must tell the Chief that.'

'Do,' said Sophia. 'He'll roar, I should think. Naturally, I don't know much about these things. Well, then, what shall I do with the sixpence?'

'I'll tell you when the war is over. Are you working very hard in your little First Aid Post? Poor Olga is overwhelmed with work. Figure to yourselves, last night I was up till six – even the Chief with his iron constitution was half dead. I had to keep on making cups of black coffee for him, and even so he fell asleep twice. Of course, the responsibility is very wearing, especially for the Chief – if things went wrong, it doesn't bear thinking of, what would happen. My knowledge of Russian, however, is standing us in good stead.'

Olga had learnt Russian when she was courting Serge, to but little avail so far as he was concerned, as he did not know a word of it. However, as she had taken the name of Olga, broken her English accent, and in other ways identified herself with the great country of Serge's forbears, she rather liked to be able to sing an occasional folk-song from the Steppes in its original tongue. She felt that it put the finishing touches to her part of temperamental Slav.

'I wonder they don't send you to Russia. I hear they find it very difficult to get reliable information.'

'Darling, it would be certain death.'

'Oh, yes, I forgot. You would be handed over to the grandchildren of Serge's grandfather's peasantry, wouldn't you? Very unpleasant. But couldn't you go disguised as a member of the proletariat in no silk stockings and drab clothes? I could give you lots of hints. You share a room with about seven other people and their bulldogs if they have any, and you have no pleasures of any kind. I really think, speaking Russian as you do, that you ought to volunteer.'

'Far, far too dangerous. The Chief would never let me. I may of course have to go abroad later – to Egypt, Turkestan or Waziristan perhaps, but Russia is entirely out of the question.'

'I call it very cowardly of you,' said Sophia, 'your country should come first. Well, good-bye, I must be going,' and she winked out rather inaccurately A, B and C. 'I'm sure the Chief would raise your screw if you knew a bit of Morse,' she said, and got up to go, followed by Rudolph who quite shamelessly left Olga to pay for the drinks.

'Think how rich she must be with all that spying,' he said happily, and kissed Sophia a great deal in the taxi. 'Darling, heavenly to see you. I've got a fortnight's leave.'

'What were you doing with Baby Bagg?'

'Just met her in the Ritz.'

'After you had telephoned to tell her to go there, I suppose.'

'Well, darling, in point of fact, I do feel rather intrigued about Olga's job. I have a sort of feeling that there may be more in that little woman than meets the eye, and I must say she's remarkably secretive. Now if you were a beautiful female spy, my own precious poppet, we should all know all about it in two days. For one thing of course, you would never be able to resist telling funny stories about your Chief. But Olga is as close as an oyster. I must have another go at her before my leave comes to an end.'

Sophia was very much nettled by the unfairness of all this. Had she told a single funny story about her Chief? Had she not been a counter-spy for a whole day without hinting a word of it to anybody? Of course, she had been about to take Rudolph into her confidence; now nothing would induce her to do so. She would pay him out for being so horrid to her. Besides he must be broken of this new predilection for Olga; it was becoming a bore.

'Yes, do,' she said; 'have another go at her. Have it now, won't you – much more convenient for me actually because I want to dine with Heatherley.'

'Heatherley? You don't mean Egg? You don't mean that fearful red-headed brute who told us what the President said? Darling Sophia – besides, you're dining with me, you said you would. I haven't seen you for weeks.'

'Darling, I'm terribly sorry, but I haven't seen Heth all day and there are masses of things I want to talk over with him.'

Rudolph said no more. He stopped the cab, got out into the street, told the man to go on to Granby Gate, hailed another cab going in the opposite direction, jumped into it and disappeared.

Sophia minded rather. She had been pleased to see Rudolph, and excited at the idea of spending an evening with him, more pleased and more excited even than she generally was when she had been separated from him for some time, but he must be taught a lesson. It was quite bad enough for him not to say that he was coming on leave, and to let her find him sitting at the Ritz with Olga. But to have him comparing her in a denigrating manner with that pseudo-Muscovite was altogether intolerable. Women are divided into two categories: those who can deal with the men they are in love with, and those who cannot. Sophia was one of those who can.

When she arrived at her house she found a merry meeting of the Brotherhood was in full and joyous progress. Brothers and Sisters were overflowing from all the reception rooms, and the downstairs lavatory was in constant use. A large photograph of Brother Bones was propped up on the drawing-room piano with a bunch of lilies in front of it, for it was the Brother's birthday. Sophia hurried into the lift, and going to the top floor she got the key of her bedroom from Elsie, who had instructions always to lock it on these occasions against the quiet-timers. Sophia had a very hot bath and changed her clothes. Then she went to look for Heth. It was rather a long search, ending in the coal-hole where he was in earnest converse with one of the thin-haired young ladies. Being members of the Brotherhood they were, of course, not at all abashed at being found in such curious circumstances; they merely showed their gums.

Sophia beckoned to Heatherley and whispered in his ear, 'There will be dinner for two in my small sitting-room in about half an hour. I hope you will join me there.'

Heatherley accepted at once. There was always, at these meetings, a large brotherly buffet-meal in the dining-room for which the food was always ordered by Florence, was cold, of the fork variety, non-alcoholic, and very dull. Sophia had an exquisite cook and a pretty taste in food herself, and Luke's wine was not to be sniffed at.

Exactly at the appointed time Heatherley tried the door of the small sitting-room. It was locked. Sophia knew all about the Brothers by now. They would come into her room, and brightly assuring her that she did not disturb them, begin an all-in wrestling match with their souls. She had told Florence that meetings could only take place at 98 Granby Gate, on condition that the Brothers were neither to use the lift nor be guided to force open any doors which they might find locked.

Heatherley announced himself, upon which Sophia let him in. Dinner was waiting on a hot plate, and they helped themselves. Sophia thought he looked like Uriah Heap, and wished she had a more attractive counter-spy to work with, somebody, say, like the ruthless young German in *The Thirty-Nine Steps*; it was impossible to take much pleasure in the company of Heth. How fortunate she loved her work for its own sake (and that of Olga).

With an alluring smile she gave him some soup.

'What was agony 22 for?' she said.

'I don't know what you're talking about.'

'The word, or letters, or code, or whatever it was you wrote on my egg, of course. I took ages trying to decode it, and I wondered if I had the right solution.'

'On your egg?' Heatherley put down his soup-spoon and looked completely blank.

'Yes, yes. Think. Of course it must have been you. This morning I had a boiled egg for breakfast, and written on the shell, in pencil, it had agony 22.'

'Sophia, now, why would I write on your egg when I could so easily call you, come round and see you, or leave a note for you here?'

Why indeed? Sophia felt that she had been a fool.

'Well, you said that we must be so careful, that our letters would be opened, and our telephone tapped –'

'If your telephone can be tapped, so could your egg be. No, Sophia, we need to be very, very careful, but there's no sense in writing on eggs, no sense at all, when we can meet all we want to both at the Post and in this house.'

'Anyway, what is our next move? I want to start work,' said Sophia, to change the painful subject.

'I was just coming to that.' Heatherley paused and seemed to consider her. 'How are your nerves?' he said. 'Pretty good? Fine. I have a very delicate job that I wish to entrust to you, delicate, and it may be dangerous. Are you game?'

'Oh, yes, Heatherley, I think so.'

'O.K. Well, presently, when you have quite finished your dinner, I want you to go back to the Post.'

Sophia was not pleased. She had spent eight hours in the Post that day, and had left, as she always did, with a feeling of immense thankfulness and relief. The idea of going back there after dinner did not appeal to her at all.

Heatherley went on, 'You are to make a list of all the nurses there on night duty. Then I want a copy of every word that is written on the notice-board. When you have done that, go to the Regal Cinema and pin an envelope containing the copy to the second stall in the third row on the left-hand side of the centre gangway. You can give me the list of the nurses tomorrow; that is less important. One last word of instruction – on no account take a taxi, that might be fatal. You will be safe enough if you walk it.'

'Well, really,' said Sophia, 'that is far sillier than writing on eggs. Why can't whoever is going to the third stall in the second row walk into the Post and see for himself what is written on the notice-board?'

'Sophia.' Heatherley gave a fish-like look which for a moment, and until she remembered it was only old Heth, quite struck a chill into her heart. 'Are you, or are you not going to help me in clearing out a nest of dangerous spies? Let me tell you that Florence communicates with the rest of her gang by means of that notice-board. My friend cannot go to the Post himself, it would be as much as his life is worth to venture near it. If I were seen to be in communication with him, I too would have short shrift, but it is of vital importance that he should know what is on the board tonight. I can't get away from this Brotherhood meeting without arousing Florence's suspicions, but I thought I had seen a way of fixing things. I thought you would go for me.'

'Oh, all right, Heth, I will. I only meant it sounded rather silly, but I see now that it has to be done. Have some apple flan.'

II

Now although Sophia supposed herself to be such a keen and enthusiastic spy, she had not really the temperament best suited to the work. It was not in her nature, for instance, to relish being sent out on a cold and foggy evening, after she had had her bath and changed her clothes, in order to do an apparently pointless job for somebody who could quite well do it for himself. Obviously if Heatherley could be closeted for ages in the coal-hole, if he could dine for more than an hour behind a locked door, he could easily escape from the house without Florence or anybody else noticing that he had gone, and do his own dreary work. So she determined that somehow or another she would wriggle out of going, but of course without annoying her Chief as she had not the least intention of being excluded from the delights of counter-espionage, and this might well happen should she be caught out disobeying orders. Sophia was very good at not doing things she disliked, and soon her plans were laid. She remembered that, exasperated by her long and unequal struggle with the overalls, she had herself, that very evening, written out a notice to the effect that those nurses who wanted to have their overalls sorted when they came back from the wash, should write their names clearly both on the overalls themselves and on their pigeonholes so that Sophia should know where to put them. When she had pinned this to the board, there had been no other notice there, and she had been particularly pleased, thinking that more attention would be paid to it on this account. Now a notice written out by Sophia could not, in the nature of things, contain Florence's secret instructions to her corps of spies. Sophia therefore decided that she would explain to Heatherley that there had been nothing on the notice-board; impossible to make a copy of nothing, so she had done no more about it. That disposed of the notice-board. As for the list of nurses on night duty, she could find that out from Sister Wordsworth's ledger in the morning. And in order to make perfectly certain of not seeing Heatherley before she arrived at the Post she decided to go immediately after breakfast to Phyllis Earle and have her hair done.

As soon as she had reached these comfortable decisions, and with the prospect now of a delicious evening with *Caroline of England* in her warm bed, she became extremely nice, indeed almost flirtatious to Heatherley during the rest of their meal together. When it was over, and Heth had enjoyed brandy and a huge cigar (unlike Florence he did not despise his creature comforts at all), she went upstairs most cheerfully, put on her fur coat with its pretty, scarlet-lined hood, and then was shepherded by a quite unusually genial Heth, through a few Brothers who had finished eating, to the front door.

'I'm afraid it's rather foggy,' he said, peering out with his pale eyes into a solid curtain of fog.

'All the better. I am less likely to be followed,' said Sophia.

'And cold.'

'Ssh. Think of our cause, dear Heatherley.'

'You understand that on no account must you take a taxi,' he reminded her. A more competent spy, she thought, would have seen the impossibility of walking more than two steps in her high-heeled velvet sandals. Anyhow, what did the man think she was, for heaven's sake, a marathon walker?

'No taxi, no indeed.' She stepped gaily into the fog.

'Sophia, you're wonderful.'

'No! No! Good-bye! Good-bye!'

Heatherley shut the front door. Sophia waited a moment and then she went down the area steps, let herself in at the back door and took off her shoes. The servants were in the servants' hall with the wireless blazing away, the back-stairs were pitch dark, and Sophia, using her torch, crept up them and hoped that she would not fall over Heatherley and his girl friend, quiet-timing. They could hardly have got there yet, she thought. On the first floor a door led from the back-stairs into the ballroom, a room which was used about twice a year for parties, and otherwise kept shut up, with dust sheets. She was rather surprised to notice, through the cracks of the door, that the lights were on. Wonderful how the quiet-timers seep into everything. She crept to the door and looked through the keyhole. What she saw turned her to stone.

In a group quite near the door stood Florence, Heatherley, Winthrop, a microphone, and Sir Ivor King, the Lieder König.

'I reckon,' Heatherley was saying, 'that she will be gone an hour at the very least, in this fog. Five minutes to the Post, ten minutes to copy out the notices, three-quarters of an hour to the Regal and back. And this is a very conservative estimate, I may add, for the fog is thick outside, and I have not allowed for her stopping to talk to anybody at the Post. So you see there is no danger, and we have ample time for everything. If the servants should happen to hear us, they will only think we have switched on the radio and old Ivor is coming over the air better than usual. But they will surely be listening to him themselves downstairs.'

Florence was looking cross. 'I still think it was perfectly stupid of you to tell her anything at all.'

'Say, we've talked all this over before, haven't we? She was wise to everything already, and it was a choice between making her think she was in on the racket, or taking her for a ride. If we had adopted the latter course, the police would have been rubbering round this house and the First Aid Post, and we should have been in a regular spot. Another thing, how would I have got her away this evening if she hadn't been told the works, or some of them – as it is she's just eating out of my hand, will do anything I order her to.'

'Yes, there's something in that,' said Florence grudgingly.

'I tell you,' Heth continued, 'I shall be glad when this business is over and we can do a bunk. I'm not so wild about the inspection of the drain tonight; it may mean they are on to something, or it may be just a routine affair. Either way, I don't like it.'

'In one minute it will be a quarter of,' said Winthrop. He took up a position in front of the microphone, gazing at his wrist-watch. The others fell silent.

'Germany calling, Germany calling,' Winthrop said, with a very slight German accent and in an entirely different voice from his usual one. 'Here is the Lieder König who is going to give you one of his inimitable programmes of Song Propaganda, so popular with lovers of song and also with lovers of propaganda the world over. The Lieder König.'

Sir Ivor stepped smartly to the microphone. Sophia saw that, out of deference no doubt to the taste of his employers, he was wearing an Aryan wig of metallic brilliance; each curl was like a little golden spring. He raised his voice in song, 'Kathleen Mavourneen the Grey Dawn is breaking,' then he gave a short news bulletin, during the course of which he exactly described that evening's Low cartoon, and also reminded his listeners that Sir Kingsley Wood was due to visit three aerodromes in Yorkshire the following day.

Then Winthrop spoke. 'The Lieder König thinks you would like to know certain facts which have come our way recently. In your great, free, British Empire, in the colony of Kenya, to be exact, there are two honest, thrifty, industrious German farmers, Herr Bad and Herr Wangel. These worthy men have been dragged away from their homes, for no better reason than that they were German-born, and put into the local prison. The prison is a wretched hut, the beds in it are unbearably hard, and the central heating hardly works at all. The prisoners are only allowed baths twice a week. But the worst scandal is the food which is offered to these Germans. Let me read out the bill of fare, considered by your Government as being sufficient for two grown men.

'Breakfast. A liquid supposed to be coffee, some milk substitute, two lumps of beet sugar, pseudo-eggs and a loaf of brackish bread.

'Luncheon. A so-called veal and ham pie, things which look like potatoes and beans, crab-apple pudding, cheese which is full of mites.

'Tea. Tea (a nerve tonic indispensable to the decadent English, but which we Germans despise).

'Dinner. A thin soup, fish, which is well known in these parts to cause leprosy. The leg of some sheep which had had to be killed, turnips and beetroot such as one feeds to cattle.

'There was no tin of biscuits by their beds in case they woke up hungry in the night.

'When you hear that things like this can happen in your great, vaunted, rich Empire perhaps you will demand that your statesmen, who can allow two honest and unoffending farmers to be so treated, should stop worrying over the scum of Polish cities in luxurious concentration camps, and should be a little bit more concerned about the beam in their own eye, for a change.

'Ask Mr Churchill, where is the *Ark Royal*?

'Here is the Lieder König again.'

'Well,' said Sir Ivor, 'I hope you have all been as much shocked as I have by the brutal ill-treatment of Herr Bad and Herr Wangel. And now I am going to sing an old favourite, "Under the Deodar".'

He did so, and wound up his programme with 'Fearful the Death of the Diver Must Be, walking alone, walking alone, walking alone in the Dehehehe-he-he-pths of the Sea', a song of which both he and his admirers were extremely fond, as, at the word 'depths', his voice plumbed hitherto uncharted ones, and any seals or hippos who might happen to be around would roar in an agony of appreciation. 'Good night, dears,' said the old König, 'keep your hairs on. By the way, where *is* the *Ark Royal*?'

'This ends,' said Winthrop, resuming his place at the microphone, 'our programme of Song-Propaganda in English, arranged and sung by the Lieder König.

'Here are the Reichsender Bremen, stations Hamburg and D x B, operating on the thirty-one metre band. I have a special announcement for my English listeners. There will be a Pets' Programme tomorrow from station D x B at 9.30 Greenwich mean time.'

'Now we must scram,' said Heatherley, 'we can always wait in the Maternity Ward if the drain inspection is not finished.'

They all, including the old gentleman, began to struggle into anti-gas clothing. Sophia waited no longer. She flew upstairs to her bedroom and locked herself in, dumbfounded by what she had seen.

Her mind was in a whirl. If Heatherley, who pretended to be an American counter-spy, was really a German spy, perhaps the 'King of Song' was pretending to be a German spy, but was really an English counter-spy? Was he in the pay of the gang, or merely hoaxing them; was he perhaps longing, but unable, to get a message through to the outside world or was he only too anxious that his shameful secret should be kept? Was he neither spy nor counter-spy, but just a poor old gentleman who got a taste of the thumbscrew twice a day? She wondered, irrelevantly, whether he had seen in the newspapers the pæans of praise followed by the dirges of disillusionment which had so prominent a place in them. Suddenly she remembered that advertisement in *The Times*: 'Poor old gentleman suffering from malignant disease would like to correspond with pretty young lady.' Perhaps he did want to correspond with the pretty young lady, perhaps in fact, it was he who had written on her egg 'Agony (column, box) 22', and who had sent in the advertisement. But if he could do all this, surely he could equally well write to her, to Rudolph, or even to poor Fred directly.

Sophia felt that life had become very complicated all of a sudden. She wished she were more versed in the intricacies of spying, and she very much wished that she could remember more about what had happened in the limited number of spy stories which she had read at various times (generally, of course, on journeys, and how often does one remember anything read on journeys?) At what stage, for instance, does the beautiful heroine abandon her lone trail and call in the heavy hand, large boots and vacant faces of The Yard? She rather thought not until the whole plot had been brilliantly unmasked, except for a few unimportant details, by the glamorous amateur spy herself. This was a point of view which appealed to Sophia, who had to consider Rudolph and Olga as well as King and Country. She went to sleep, having decided on a policy of watchful waiting.

The next day, when Sophia arrived at her First Aid Post, she found an atmosphere of subdued but horrified excitement. She immediately concluded that something untoward had happened at the Theatre; the nurses were always retailing awful atrocities they had witnessed there, and by Theatre they did not at all mean, as anybody else would have, the play; the 'He' of these entertainments was not Tom Walls, but the Surgeon, the 'She' not Hermione Baddeley but the Patient; in short, 'the Theatre' was not the Gaiety but St Anne's Hospital Operating Theatre. The dramas enacted there alternated, as at the Grand Guignol in Paris, between gruesome tragedy and roaring farce. Sophia supposed that a dead man must have come to life; the reverse, which too often happened, could never have caused such a stir.

Nurses were standing about in little groups, whispering, their eyes as round as marbles. Even Sister Wordsworth and Mr Stone, whom Sophia found in the office, were looking quite concerned.

'Don't tell Lady Sophia, she wouldn't like it,' said kind Sister Wordsworth, remembering about the knees.

'What?' said Sophia. 'But of course you must tell me. I am so curious, I have the most curious nature in the world. If you don't tell, I shan't get a wink of sleep, or give you one minute's peace until you have. So please, dear Sister Wordsworth.'

Of course they were dying to tell her really. It seemed that, during the drain inspection of the previous night, something too horrible had been found down there, brought up, carried through the Post (dripping, my dear, the smell), and taken to the Hospital mortuary. Sophia began to guess what this object might be, and sure enough, it was the body of a young woman, bound and gagged, and with its face completely gnawed away by rats. Greta.

'But how on earth could it have got there?' she asked, in a shaking voice.

'Why, poor Lady Sophia looks as white as a sheet. I told you we shouldn't tell her. Sit down here, my dear, and have a cup of tea.'

'They say it must have been washed down from much higher up. Nothing to do with this place at all.'

'I should hope not indeed,' said Sophia. 'We should never get another outside patient for practices if they thought they were going to be popped down the main drain when we had finished with them.'

'Outside patient – what an idea. Whatever made you think of that? Well, here's your tea, drink it up, and you'll feel better. We all think it was so clever of Miss Edwards, the way she saw something queer under our feet. I'm longing to have my fortune done again, now that there isn't any more.'

Sophia, however, was beginning to think that there was something very queer indeed, no less a thing than the head-quarters of Florence's gang and the hide-out of Sir Ivor King himself; otherwise, why did they hold their broadcast in her ballroom on the night of the drain inspection? Why did they all work so assiduously at the Post? She had seen a plan of the hospital and knew that underneath the garage there were vast cellars and tunnels, as well as the main drain, no doubt admirably suited to Florence's purpose. A more convenient place, in fact, it would be hard to imagine, a place where people wander in and out at all hours, often bandaged and on stretchers, or disguised in the sinister uniform of the decontamination squad. Could anything be more ideal? Then if, for any reason, the Post became temporarily unsuitable for their purposes, as it had done the previous evening during the drain inspection, they could repair, with their old ally (or victim) to Granby Gate, and under the guise of Brothers could hold their meetings and conduct their broadcasts there. Florence might not be a glamour girl, but she seemed to be a most efficient spy. Sophia hoped that this would all be a lesson to Luke, and that he would, in future, investigate the antecedents of his soulmates before introducing them into the home.

12

Luke wrote an extremely entertaining letter from America. The change of scene had evidently done him good; he appeared to be in high spirits, and to have cast off the gloom in which he had been enveloped before leaving England.

He said that, having always heard from Mary Pencill that America was the one truly democratic country in the world, quite free from class distinction of any kind, it had seemed to him rather odd that the talk should run almost entirely on such subjects as how charming the late Lady Fort William used to be. 'Another topic which is nearly always introduced, sooner or later, is what do the English think of America? When I reply that, although most Englishmen have heard of America, not one in ten actually believes in it, they seem almost incredulous.' He also said that they were quite indignant at what seemed to them to be the boring progress of the war, and that on the whole, he thought, they hoped that Germany would win. They hoped this, of course, in the kind of irresponsible, guilty way a child hopes the house will catch fire. 'They have a juvenile point of view and in particular an extreme love of sensation.' He had nearly finished his work, he said, and would soon be home. Had had an interesting time, but was looking forward to being back in England again; he would be flying home by clipper. No mention of Florence, Herr Hitler, or the Brotherhood, and in fact Luke's journey to the New World would seem to have readjusted his perspective as regards the Old.

The news that her husband's return was imminent put an altered complexion on things for Sophia, who realized that she must hurry up with her unmasking activities. Luke was already much disliked owing to his well-known sympathies of the last few years, and it would be extremely awkward for him if a nest of spies were to be found lodged in his house while he himself was there. If, on the other hand, they were tracked down and handed over to justice, by means of the great brilliance and deep cunning of his wife while he was engaged in work of national importance abroad, it would be quite a different affair, and could reflect only to his credit.

Sophia decided that she must immediately find out where the King of Song was hiding, or being hidden, and get into communication with that treacherous and venal (or, alternatively, loyal and disinterested) old body. She felt that even if the former adjectives proved to be correct, he would not have lost all his affection for his godchild; she could not somehow imagine him handing her over to Heatherley, the drain and thumbscrew. If really on the side of England all along, he would be only too glad to be assisted from the clutches of his captors. She hoped he would not prove to be drugged, like Van der Lubbe, but supposed that he would hardly be in such good voice if so. The more she thought of it, the more she felt certain that he must be underneath the First Aid Post, and that one clue to his whereabouts lay in the snacks which Florence and Heatherley carried from the canteen in such quantities. Their appetites had become quite a joke with the nurses. The Maternity Ward was too small to hide a mouse, but next door to that was the Hospital Museum, a huge, half dark vault, of a most sinister shape and size. The manhole which led to the main drain was in Mr Stone's little office, so they would not be able to use that; investigation, she felt, should be made in the Museum.

She also decided that it was no longer possible for her to blaze a lone trail through the jungle of spies and counter-spies that her life had now become. After all, she had a lot of valuable counter-espionage work to her credit; the brilliant piece of feminine intuition which had prevented her from leaving the house on Heatherley's bogus errand, as many a lesser woman might have done, having led to the sensational discoveries that the King of Song was still in this country, that Heatherley Egg, far from being a counter-spy, was a counter-counter-spy, and that Winthrop, if not Heatherley himself, was a German. In *The Thirty-Nine Steps*, even Scudder, who, like her, preferred to work on his own, had finally bequeathed his little black notebook to an accomplice; Sophia had no black notebook: all the more necessary that she should have an accomplice. At any moment she might be drained, and then nobody would ever know that she had been a beautiful female spy all along. It was a dreadful prospect.

The choice of an accomplice lay between Fred and Rudolph, and while Rudolph probably had more initiative and more spare time at present, she really favoured

Fred on account of his being so much more under her thumb. There was quite good reason, knowing what she did of Fred's character, to hope that in his eyes she would be the Chief; Fred was used to Chiefs, and in fact had never yet been without one during the whole of his life. Rudolph, as she very well knew, would order her about or ignore her, just as it suited him; besides, it would give her the most intense pleasure, as well as serving him right for flirting with Olga, to leave Rudolph out of all this until she could point to the fruits of her activities in the shape of at least three prisoners in the Tower. Having therefore, quite decided upon Fred, to the point of lifting the receiver of her telephone to ring him up, she suddenly remembered the main drain and the possible fate of inept counter-spies. Fred had a young and lovely wife who seemed to be devoted to the idea of him; he also had two fat babies. Rudolph had nothing but a perfectly horrible sister who had often been very rude to Sophia. She rang up Rudolph.

Rudolph was by now bored to death with Olga and her long stories about a job and a Chief that too palpably did not exist. On the other hand, she having been the cause of his break with Sophia, he had felt himself obliged to haunt her company. When he realized that he was being summoned back into the fold he made no secret of his delight.

'Serge came round this morning to horse-whip me,' he said; 'wasn't it fascinating? It seems that he bought a horse-whip at Fortnum's on Olga's account, and he turned up here with it very early, about nine. He hadn't been to bed at all (there's a new place called The Nut-house, we'll go tonight). The porter telephoned up to my room and said, "There's a gentleman in sporting kit, wants to see you most particular," so I had him sent up with my breakfast, and in comes old Voroshilov, furling and unfurling a great whip; I felt quite giddy. So I ordered some drinks and he sat on my bed and told me that Olga bumps up his allowance every time he horse-whips anybody for making a pass at her, because she read somewhere that this was the form in Imperial Russia. Then he told me all about his Blossom. He simply loved his Blossom, apparently he never loved any other creature so much in his life. He says it was grossly unfair, the way they dismissed him; he only passed out because she passed out first and he couldn't think of anything else to do, with her lying there so flat and dead looking, and the idea of her being in the charge of poor Fred makes him quite sick. I should think he feels quite sick, quite often actually, because he is busy drinking himself to death – he was, anyway, of course, so it doesn't make all that difference. Still, it's rather dreadful to see the poor old tartar so sad and low; he used to be such a jolly old drunk, but he was crying like anything; he has only just gone. When do I see you, shall I come round now or meet you at the Post?'

'No, neither. I don't want to be seen seeing you, you see.'

'Why ever not?'

'Well, I can't explain for the present.'

'Good heavens, Sophia, is Luke cutting up rough?'

'Luke's not back yet, and you know quite well he never cuts up rough. I will meet you at the Ritz in half an hour.'

'You'll be seen seeing me there all right. However,' said Rudolph quickly, not wishing her, as in her present eccentric mood she easily might, to change her mind, 'meet you there, darling; good-bye.'

Sophia smiled to herself. That evening spent with Heatherley instead of with Rudolph had been wonderfully productive of results, one way and another.

When she arrived at the Ritz, Rudolph was already there reading an early edition of an evening paper. He stood up to greet her, hardly raising his eyes from the paper. Sophia sat down beside him, then, remembering what she was, she bobbed up again in order to see that nobody was lurking behind her chair and that there was no microphone underneath it.

'Walking round your chair for luck?' said Rudolph, still reading.

'Put that paper down, darling. I've got a very great deal to tell you.'

'Go ahead.'

'Stop reading, then.'

'I can read and listen to you quite well.'

'Probably you can. But I can't talk to you while you're reading. Darling, really you are rude. You might have been married to me for years.'

'To all intents and purposes I have.'

'That's very rude, too. Thank heavens I have Luke to fall back on.'

'Poor old Luke. You always talk about him as if he were a lie-low.'

'So he is, and it's a jolly nice thing to be. The more I see of you, the more I like Luke, as somebody said about dogs. Rudolph now, please don't let's quarrel. Put that paper down and talk to me.'

Rudolph did so with bad grace. They were both by now thoroughly out of temper with each other.

'Well, what is it?'

'Darling, now listen. You know about me being beautiful?'

'You're all right.'

'No, Rudolph, please say I'm beautiful; it's part of the thing.'

'I suppose you're going to tell me you're a beautiful female spy?'

'In a way, I was.'

'Yes, I'm quite sure you were. And that you have a Chief, but you don't feel happy about his loyalty, so you're really working on your own, and the War Office and Scotland Yard haven't got an inkling of what you're up to because you're blazing a lone trail, but soon there will be sensational revelations, and you will be a national heroine. Oh God! women are bores in wars.' Rudolph returned to his paper.

Sophia left the Ritz in a great temper, and went straight to her Post where she had lunch alone at the canteen. It was much too late now to ring up Fred; he would be with his Blossom; she would have to make investigations on her own after all.

13

Sophia had wondered why the canteen was so empty, and when she got downstairs she found the reason was that the Post was in the throes of a major practice. This event had been canvassed with great excitement for the past few days, and nothing but Sophia's preoccupation with other matters could have put it out of her mind. As soon as she arrived, she was engulfed in it. Not only did the Southern Control hiss into her ear 'Practice Red, expect casualties', not only did casualties covered with 'wounds' of the most lugubrious description appear in shoals – these things had often happened before and been regarded as part of everyday work – today was made memorable by the fact that a real (not practice) Admiral was scheduled to escort a real (not practice) Royal Princess round the Post to see it at work.

Sophia immediately saw that if she was ever going to conduct investigations, this would be the time. Heatherley and Winthrop were on continual stretcher duty and would not be able to leave the Treatment Room for a moment, except to carry 'cases' upstairs to the Hospital. Only Florence was unemployed; this must be remedied. Sophia went into the Treatment Room in search of Sister Wordsworth. It was a hive of industry; dressings and splints were laid out in quantities, and the instruments were all getting a double dose of sterilization, as though the royal eye were fitted with a microscopic lens which would enable it to note, with disapproval, fast-gathering clouds of streptococci. Sister Wordsworth stood surveying the scene.

Sophia said, 'Can I speak to you a moment?' and suggested that if everything was supposed to be in progress exactly as though there had been a real raid, surely Florence ought to be sent a practice pregnancy. Sister Wordsworth saw the force of this argument, and taking hold of the next woman 'patient' who appeared, she bundled her into the Labour Ward.

'Sixty-five if she's a day,' she said in a loud cheerful aside. 'I should think it will be a very difficult delivery. Have the forceps handy, Sister Turnbull, and plenty of hot water.' Florence looked very peevish indeed, and prepared to do as she was told with a bad grace.

At this moment the real Princess appeared, and jokes were forgotten.

As soon as H.R.H. had seen her office, and gone through into the Treatment Room, Sophia summoned up all her courage and left her chair by the telephone. If it rang while she was gone, Sister Wordsworth would never forgive her; this would have to be risked, among other things. She ran down a back passage to the Hospital Museum. The door was locked but she had Sister Wordsworth's master-key, with which she opened it. Florence was standing in the Labour Ward, the door of which was at right angles to that of the Museum; she appeared to be leaning over her aged victim, and her back was turned on Sophia who slipped into the Museum carefully, shutting the door behind her. Then, shaking with terror, she switched on her electric torch and crept down the main avenue between the glass cases. She passed the pre-natal Siamese twins, fearful little withered white figures, unnaturally human and with horrible expressions of malignity on their faces. She passed the diseased hearts and decayed livers, and reached the case of brains with tumours on them. Then her heart stood still. On the floor beneath the brains, shining in the light of her torch like a golden wire, was a springy butter-coloured curl which could only have come from one source. The horrified curiosity felt by Robinson Crusoe when he saw the footstep of Man Friday, the ecstasy and joy of Madame Curie when at last she had a piece of radium, were now experienced with other and more complex sensations by Sophia. For a minute or two she almost choked with excitement; then, recovering herself, she followed in the direction in which (so far as a curl can be said to point) it pointed. Under the large intestines another one winked out a welcome, under the ulcerated stomachs was a third. The passage ended with a case of bladders against the wall, and under this was a curl. Very gingerly Sophia pushed the case. It moved. She put down her torch and lifted the case away from the wall. Behind it there was a door. As she opened this door she knew that she must be the bravest woman in the world. As a child, if she had been extremely frightened of something, she used to remind herself that she was descended from Charles II, and this had sustained her. She now invoked this talisman, to but little avail. The Merry Monarch had lived too long ago, and blankets the adult Sophia knew to have more than one side. In any case, even if his blood did flow in her veins, she thought, the worst terrors he had faced were Roundheads and death on the block, or, later in life, highwaymen who would have been easily charmed by a guinea and a royal joke. A Hospital Museum with its grisly exhibits, the darkness, the main drain, possible rats and creeping spies, were a test of nerves which might well break down the resistance of a man far braver than Charles II had ever shown himself to be.

She was now faced by a long flight of stone stairs leading, she supposed, to some fearful dungeons. She went down them, and then down a short passage at the end of which was another door which she opened. Sitting in quite a cheerful little room with an electric fire was the old gentleman himself.

'Darling,' he cried, 'what has happened – are they all caught? How did you get here? Where are the police?'

'Ssh,' said Sophia, her knees turning to jelly. 'I am all alone. I came down from the Post.'

'But my darling child, this is terrible, so terribly dangerous. You must go back at once. But just listen carefully to me. They – (do you know who I mean, Florence and the others?)'

Sophia nodded. 'Yes, I know about them being spies; go on.'

'They have got some scheme on foot which I must find out. They are putting it into execution next Friday, in three days' time. It is something devilish; I have half guessed what, but I must know for certain. Apart from that, I know everything about the German spies in this country. Now I want you to tell the police where I am and all about Florence and co., so that they can be watched. But I also want them to wait before rounding up the gang until six o'clock on Friday evening. It, whatever it is, will happen at ten o'clock that night, so if I don't know all by six, I probably never shall. Anyhow, I don't dare leave it until later. Now quickly go back. If they find you here they will put us both in the main drain, and all my work will have been wasted. Go, go. Be careful now. Good-bye till we meet again, my dearest. Good-bye.'

Something in the old King's manner terrified Sophia. He looked at her, she thought, as if he never expected to see her again in life; he spoke with the abruptness and irritation of a badly frightened man. She turned and fled back, up the stairs to the Museum; here, with shaking hands, she put back the case of bladders as she had found it against the door. Then she crept through the medical curiosities and out again into the Post. The door of the Labour Ward was shut this time and the coast seemed clear. She ran as fast as she could to the office, collapsed into her chair and felt extremely faint; she held her head between her knees for a few moments until the giddiness had passed off. She longed for brandy, which she knew to be unobtainable.

The Royal inspection was still in progress; indeed, although it seemed to her like several days, Sophia had only been away from the office for ten minutes, and very fortunately the telephone bell had not rung once during this time. It did so now, 'Southern Control speaking, practice White.' Sophia decided that she was not temperamentally suited to the profession, which she had so gaily chosen, of secret agent; she was not nearly brave enough. Her teeth were still chattering, her hand was trembling so much that she could hardly lift the telephone receiver. She would blaze her lone trail no longer, that evening the whole affair was going to be placed before Scotland Yard, and her responsibility would be at an end. This comforting resolution greatly strengthened her nerves; a large, red-faced policeman would be more stimulating than brandy and she would insist on having one to watch over her until Friday. She wondered if she could persuade him to sleep in her bathroom, and thought that nothing could give her so much happiness.

Sister Wordsworth now made a cheerful reappearance, having just seen the Princess out to her car. She said that everything had gone off perfectly. Sister Turnbull's patient, it seemed, had come through her dangerous and unusual experience as easily as if she had been twenty instead of sixty (twin boys, Neville and Nevile, after the Blue Book), and was now with all the other patients enjoying a nice cup of tea in the canteen. The Princess had been charming and had amazed everybody, royal persons always being assumed to be half-witted, deaf and dumb until they have given practical proof to the contrary, by asking quite intelligent questions. The Admiral had winked at several of the nurses, and had been bluff, honest-to-God, hearty and all other things that are expected of seafaring men. In the short, everybody had been pleased and put into a satisfied frame of mind, and the Post rang with the rather loud chatter which is induced by great relief from strain. Sophia, joining with the others, almost forgot her nightmare experiences in the Museum.

When the time came for her to go home, however, she felt that she really could not face the terrors of the black-out and walk, as she generally did. She was feeling frightened again, and the idea of masked men waiting to boo out at her from behind sandbags was too unnerving. So she telephoned for a taxi. As she got into it, she wondered whether she really ought to go straight to Scotland Yard before going home. After some hesitation she decided that she felt too tired and dirty. Dinner and especially a bath were necessary before she could undertake such an expedition; besides, it was quite possible that she might even persuade some fatherly inspector to go and see her, in comfort, at Granby Gate, which would be much nicer.

She took a whisky and soda to her bedroom, undressed slowly before the fire, and wrapped herself in her dressing-gown; then she sat for a time sipping the whisky. She felt very much restored, and presently went to turn on her bath. Sitting on the edge of it was Heatherley.

Sophia huddled into her dressing-gown, paralysed with terror. She had a remote feeling of thankfulness that she had put on the dressing-gown; as her bathroom led out of her bedroom and had no other entrance she very often did not. Heatherley had an extremely disagreeable, not to say alarming expression on his face, and she was far too much unnerved to reproach him for being in her bathroom, or indeed to say anything.

He stood up and barked at her, and any doubts left in her mind as to his being a German were removed.

'You were seen this afternoon, coming out of the Hospital Museum. What were you doing there?'

Sophia felt like a rabbit with a snake. 'Oh, nothing much,' she said. 'I always think those Siamese twins are rather little duckies, don't you?'

She saw that this had teased Heatherley and it occurred to her that he did not know about her finding the King of Song. She rather supposed that if he had even guessed at such a thing, she would by now be going for a swim down the drain. 'Pull yourself together, you're descended from Charles II, aren't you?' Sophia was enough of a snob to feel that this equivocal connexion put her on a superior footing to Heatherley whether he was American or German, neither country having, so far as she could remember, existed in Charles II's day. 'Now do you agree,' she babbled on, playing for time, 'that Charles II was far the most fascinating of all our Kings?'

'I'm afraid I have not come here to discuss Charles II. I have come to inform you upon two subjects. First, you should know that I am not, as you supposed, a counter-spy.'

'Hun or Yank?' asked Sophia. A spasm of intense rage crossed Heatherley's face. She was beginning positively to enjoy the interview.

'I am the head of the German espionage system in this country. My name is Otto von Eiweiss. Florence is Truda von Eiweiss, my wife. *Heil Hitler.*'

'Your wife!' said Sophia, 'goodness me, all this time I've been thinking you fancied her!'

'Secondly,' went on Heth, taking no notice of her but trembling with anger, 'Truda and I think you know too much. We think you have been prying into affairs which do not concern you. We also think that you might soon begin to prattle of these affairs to your friends, who, although they all belong to that decadent class which we National Socialists most despise, might in their turn (purely by accident, of course, they are too soft and stupid to have any purpose in life) harm us with their talk. So, in order to make certain that none of this shall happen, we have taken your bulldog, Millicent, into protective custody, as we have noticed that in your unnatural English way you seem to love her more than anything else. In three days' time, if you behave exactly as we tell you, she will be back once more under your eiderdown, but otherwise –'

'Quilt,' Sophia corrected him mechanically. She despised the word eiderdown. Then, suddenly realizing what he meant, 'My bulldog, Millicent – Milly? You fearful brute,' and she forgot all about Charles II and what fun it was to tease Heth, and went for him tooth and nail.

Heatherley warded off her bites and scratches with humiliating ease, and twisting one of her arms in schoolboy fashion, he continued, 'Now, be quite quiet, and listen to me.'

'Ow, this hurts; let me go.'

'Are you going to be quiet? Good. Now I shall continue our little chat. The bulldog, Millicent, as I was just remarking, is in protective custody.'

'Where?'

'I shall not divulge.'

'Has she had her dinner at six?'

'If her dinner-time is punctually at six she most probably has. She was removed from your house at six-thirty precisely.'

'Oh! Where is she, please?'

'It is no concern of yours where she is.'

'You brutish Hun, of course it is a concern of mine. In this weather. She will catch cold, she will get bronchitis. These dogs have frightfully weak chests. Savage – kaffir – fuzzy wuzzy – you –'

'To call me all these things will not advance the cause of Millicent, very far from it. She is now in my power, and you had better be nice to me.' Heatherley leant towards her with a horrible leer.

'I shall tell Florence about you coming into my bathroom when I have nearly nothing on,' she said. This shot appeared to have gone home. Heatherley looked quite disconcerted.

'The bulldog,' he said, after a pause, 'will be returned to you in perfectly good condition so long as you have been obedient to us and stuck not only to the letter but also to the spirit of our instructions. Otherwise, I regret to inform you that not only will she be vivisected for several hours and then put, as Greta was put, still alive, into the main drain, but that, long before you can act, you also will have ceased to live.'

'Devil. I must say I shouldn't care to be you, after you are dead. Would you like to hear what will happen to you? Well, you'll lie on a gridiron to eternity and baste – do you hear me, B A S T E.'

'Instead of abusing me, and threatening me with the out-worn superstitions of a decadent religion, it will be better for you to listen to what I have to say.

'For the next three days and nights either Florence, or Gustav, whom you know as Winthrop, or I myself will be watching you like lynxes; you will never be out of the sight of one or other. Florence will take night duty and sleep in your room. Gustav and I will take turns by day. If you make the smallest sign to anybody, or convey any message to the outside world, we shall know it, and within half an hour the bulldog Millicent will be wishing she had never been born.'

'How do you mean Florence will sleep in my room? There's only one bed.'

'It is a very large one. You can take the choice between sharing it with Florence and having another bed made up in your room.'

'Ugh!' Sophia shuddered. Then she rang the bell, and feeling uncommonly foolish, went into her bedroom, where she told Elsie that she had been suffering from nightmares, and that Miss Turnbull had very kindly consented to sleep in her room.

'Oh, and Elsie, tell Mrs Round that I have taken Milly to the vet, to be wormed, will you? She'll be about three days.'

'Yes, m'lady. We were all wondering where Milly had got to.'

When Elsie had gone, Heatherley came out of the bathroom and said, 'One last word. I warn you that you had better act in good faith. It will not avail you to do such things as, for instance, write notes in invisible ink on match-boxes, for we shall act on the very smallest suspicion. Your telephone here is cut; please do not have it mended. It will be the safest from your point of view, and that of your bulldog, if you were to see nobody at all except the personnel at the Post. Of them, I may tell you that ninety per cent are members of my corps, and will assist in keeping you under observation. Miss Wordsworth received last night in an omni-bus a *piqûre* that will incapacitate her for a week at least.'

'I see, you are white slavers as well as everything else.'

'Mr Stone, as you are aware, has gone away on holiday. You will sit alone in the office, and either Gustav or myself will often sit there with you. When you think you are quite alone, one of us will be watching you through a rent in the hessian.'

Sophia lay awake all night. Florence did not, it is true, snore so loudly or so incessantly as Milly, nor was her face so near to Sophia's as Milly's generally became during the course of a night. What she did was to give an occasional rather sinister little 'honk' which was far more disturbing. But in any case Sophia would probably have lost her sleep. There seemed to be no way out of the quandary in which she found herself, look at it how she would. Even supposing that she was anxious to sacrifice Milly to the common good, which she was not, very, it seemed to her that she would only have time to give one hysterical shout before she was herself over-powered, gagged, and put down the drain, or, if in the street, liquidated in some other way. Then her secret, like Scudder's, would die with her, for it was too late now to begin keeping a black notebook. The prospect was discouraging.

She turned about miserably racking her brains until she was called, when the sight of Florence sitting up in bed, and disposing of an enormous breakfast, quite put her off her own. For a moment she forgot her troubles in the fascination of seeing how Florence fixed herself into the stays, but with so many so much weight-ier affairs on her mind, Sophia hardly got the best advantage from this experience. For one thing she was tortured by wondering who would give Milly her morning run and whether she would do all she should. If she was being kept, like the old gentleman, underneath the Post, there was unlikely to be such a thing as a bit of grass for her, unless some kind of subterranean weed grew beside the main drain. Then there was the question of food.

She had sent Florence to Coventry. Florence, she considered, having lived with her all these months and accepted her fur cape, only to repay by kidnapping Milly, had proved herself to be outside the pale, what Lord Haw-Haw calls 'not public school'. Sophia would not and could not speak to her, so she would have to discuss Milly's diet-sheet with Heatherley, and meanwhile she decided that she would take a dinner for her in a parcel when she went to the Post.

She and Florence spent a dismal morning together in Harrods, where, whenever Sophia saw somebody she knew, Florence threatened her with the barrel of a gun which she kept in her bag; after this they went off, still in silence and rather early, to the Post. Sophia was clutching a damp parcel of minced meat which she depos-ited in the Labour Ward when they arrived, and hoped for the best. She thought it was a gesture rather like that made by primitive Greek peasants who are supposed to put out, in some sacred spot, little offerings of food for the god Pan.

Heatherley's predictions were correct. Sister Wordsworth was off duty, ill, Mr Stone was away on a week's holiday, and Sophia sat alone in the office. Heatherley and Winthrop took it in turns to watch over her, and the first thing she saw when she came in was a dreadful, unwinking, pale blue eye pressed against a tear in the sacking. There was nothing to be done, nothing whatever. She felt quite sick, and the hours dragged away slowly. Even Macaulay's *History of England* held no more charms for her, the landing of the Prince of Orange among the rude fisher-folk of

Torquay with a background of ghostly future villas was a painted scene which could not have much interest for one who sat on such a powder-barrel as she did. The question uppermost in her mind now was 'What is going to happen on Friday?' but the more she thought, the less she could form an opinion. Perhaps it was only that on that day Florence and her corps of spies were leaving the country; she felt, however, that it was something far more sinister. The assassination of some public man, for instance; although it was difficult to think of any public man whose assassination would not greatly advance the Allied cause, and the same objection, multiplied by about twelve hundred, would, of course, apply to blowing up the Houses of Parliament. In Sophia's opinion, this would no longer even be an aesthetic disaster, since they had been subjected to the modish barbarism of pickling.

That evening Fred dined with her, a long-standing engagement. She was told that she could choose which of her three chaperons should attend her on this occasion, and chose Heatherley. He was the one she hated the most, because she was quite certain it was he who had thought of abducting Milly, and she hoped to be able to tease him by talking about Germany with Fred and at him. Unfortunately this did not work out very well. A Fred racked with ideals, and in the grip of Federal Union, was quite a different cup of tea from the old, happy-go-lucky Fred who used to join with her in blasting abroad, its food, its manners, its languages, its scenery, and the horrible time one had getting there.

'I can't see eye to eye with you, my dear Sophia,' he said pompously, when she thought she had worked him up to better things. 'I think of all foreigners, even Germans, in quite a different light now. To me they are our brothers in Union. Whatever happens, don't you see, we must finish the war with a great glow of love in our hearts – the punishment we are giving them should be quite in the spirit of "this hurts me more than it does you".'

Heatherley gave a loathsome snigger.

'I beg your pardon? Of course, Mr Egg, as you come from the United States of America, you can tell us all about Federal Union from experience. I am sure you must think highly of it?'

'It works very badly over there, and would be quite useless in Europe. In Europe you have one Power so far in advance of all the rest that ethical sense as well as common sense would put the other countries in complete submission to its dictates.'

'Yes, that's what I always say,' said Sophia, 'but, of course, it will be an awful bore having to rule over those fiendish foreigners, and I rather doubt if we can be bothered. Perhaps we could make the French do it for us.'

Heatherley smiled in a superior way. He seemed far too comfortable to please Sophia and she greatly feared that his plans, whatever they were, must be maturing satisfactorily for him. She made no attempt to communicate in any way with Fred, knowing that, quite alone and uninterrupted, it would have taken her a good hour to explain the whole matter to him. Fred liked to get to the bottom of things, to ask a hundred questions and to write a great deal in his notebook; his particular temperament rendered such devices as tapping on his leg in Morse Code (even had Sophia been sufficiently expert to do so) much worse than useless. She very wisely left the whole thing alone.

The evening was not a great success. Fred asked where Milly was, and when told about the vet, reminded Sophia that she and Abbie had been wormed together less than two months before. He went on to tell her what a strain it was on a dog's inside, asking what evidence she had of Milly's worms, until poor Sophia could have screamed. Then they listened to the King of Song, but he was not really much in form. At the end of his programme, however, there was a drop of comfort for Sophia when he sang, very distinctly, 'Milly is my darling, my darling, my darling, Milly is my darling, the young bow wow dear,' after which she heard, or thought she heard, a rumbling snore. If Milly was with the old gentleman that would be nice for both of them, and especially, of course, for the old gentleman. At last Fred took his leave, after which Heatherley escorted Sophia, who was by now very sleepy in spite of all her cares, to join Florence in her bedroom.

This was the end of the first day.

14

The next morning Sophia, having enjoyed, from sheer exhaustion, an excellent night's rest, awoke feeling more resolute. She had often heard that the Germans are the stupidest people in the world; when she remembered this and also the fact that, until she had found out that they were spies, she had always looked upon Florence, Heatherley and Winthrop as being the greatest bores she knew, it seemed to her that it should be possible to outwit Truda, Otto and Gustav, even if they were three to one against her. She stayed in bed until it was time to go to St Anne's, thinking very hard.

Clearly the first thing to be done was to write out a concise report of her situation, and this she must keep handy in case she had an opportunity, unobserved, of giving it to some reliable person. Hatred of Heatherley, even more than fear, lent her courage and cunning, and when she had been at the Post a little while, she put down her handkerchief over a stump of pencil on the table. Presently she picked up both handkerchief and pencil and went off to the lavatory, the only place where she could be out of sight of the unholy trinity, one of whose members followed her to its very door. Here she wrote, very quickly, on her handkerchief, 'Spies. Milly and Ivor King imprisoned below Post. Tell police but act carefully. I am watched. No joke.' She had to waste valuable space and time in saying 'no joke' because she knew that if this missive should happen to reach any of her friends they would be sure to think it was one and act accordingly. The trouble now was to think of somebody to give it to, as, although she felt certain that Heatherley was bluffing when he said that nearly all the nurses were his fellow-spies, she did not know any of them well enough, now that Sister Wordsworth was away, to be positive beyond doubt of their integrity. She thought that if, by the next day, nothing else had turned up, she would, as a last resort, give the handkerchief to one of them; meanwhile she hoped for luck.

The sister in charge of the Treatment Room brought a Mrs Twitchett into the office. She was one of those fat women whose greatly over-powdered faces look like plasticine, and whose bosoms, if pricked, would surely subside with a loud bang and a gust of air. The sister introduced her to Sophia, saying that she had already been taken on at the local A.R.P. head-quarters as a part-time worker for St Anne's; Sophia's business was to note down all particulars on the card index.

'Emma Twitchett,' she wrote, '144 The Boltons. Qualifications, First Aid, Home Nursing and Gas Certificates. Next of kin, Bishop of the Antarctic. Religion, The Countess of Huntingdon's Connexion.'

Here Sophia looked up sharply and saw, what in her preoccupation had not hitherto dawned on her, that Emma Twitchett was none other than Rudolph. For the first moment of crazy relief she thought that he must know everything and have come to rescue her, Milly and Sir Ivor. Then she realized that this could not be the case. He was merely bored and lonely without her, and was hoping that he would get back into favour by means of an elaborate joke. It was absolutely important to prevent him from giving himself away in the office, while under the impression that they were alone. Sophia was only too conscious of the eye in the hessian. As soon as she had scribbled down Mrs Twitchett's particulars, she hurried him out into the Post.

Although it could not be said that Sophia had hitherto proved herself to be a very clever or successful counter-spy, she now made up for all her former mistakes by perfectly sensible behaviour. The luck, of which she had been so hopeful, had come her way at last and she did not allow it to slip through her fingers. She conducted Mrs Twitchett, as she always did new people, round the Post, chatting most amicably. She was careful to omit nothing, neither the rest room upstairs, the canteen, the ladies' cloakroom nor the room with the nurses' lockers. She hoped that Rudolph would notice, and remember afterwards, how Winthrop, without giving himself the trouble to dissimulate his movements, was following them closely during this perambulation. Sophia was only too thankful that it was Winthrop who, she estimated, was about half as intelligent as Heatherley. At last she took Mrs Twitchett to the exit and showed her out, saying 'Very well then, that will be splendid; tomorrow at twelve. Oh yes, of course,' she said rather hesitatingly and shyly, 'Yes, naturally, Mrs Twitchett, I'll lend you mine.' She took out her handkerchief and offered it to Rudolph with a smile. 'No, of course, bring it back any time. I have another in my bag; it's quite all right. Good, then, see you tomorrow; that will be very nice. So glad you are coming; we are rather short-handed, you know.'

She went back without even glancing at Winthrop who was hovering about inside the Post, and who followed her to the office. Then she sat for a while at her table trembling very much and expecting that any moment she would be summoned to the drain, but as time went on and nothing had happened, she took up her knitting. If she had a certain feeling of relief that, at any rate, she had been able to take a step towards communication with the outside world, she was also tortured with doubts as to whether Rudolph would ever see what was written on the handkerchief and whether, if he did, he would not merely say that women were bores in wars. Olga had certainly queered the pitch for her rivals in the world of espionage as far as Rudolph was concerned. Also, if he did have the luck to read and the sense to follow her directions, would he be in time? He must hurry; she felt sure that after tomorrow any action which might be taken would be too late to save Milly and the old gentleman, certainly too late to catch

Florence. Tomorrow was what the posters call zero hour. The rest of that day dragged by even more horribly slowly than the preceding one, and there was no sign from Rudolph. She could not help half expecting that he would have got some kind of a message through to her; when seven o'clock arrived and there was nothing, she was bitterly disappointed. Heatherley conducted her home in a taxi, dined with her and never let her out of his sight until Florence was ready to take charge of her. Sophia did not sleep a single wink; she lay strenuously willing Rudolph to read her handkerchief.

On the morning of the third and last day, Sophia would have been ready to construe anything which seemed at all mysterious into a code message from Rudolph. But nothing of the sort came her way. She eagerly scanned her egg for a sign of calligraphy, however faint; it was innocent, however, of any mark. The agony column of *The Times* was equally unproductive, nor had Milly contributed to the dog advertisements; there was not even a mention of French bulldogs. Her morning post consisted of nothing more hopeful than *Harrods' Food News*. In fact, it became obvious to Sophia that Rudolph had never read her SOS at all, or if he had that he did not believe in it. Two large tears trickled down her cheeks. She decided that if nothing had materialized to show that Rudolph was helping by four o'clock, she would abandon Milly and the old gentleman to death and worse in the main drain, and dash out of the Post on the chance of finding a policeman before she too was liquidated.

Having made up her mind to some definite action, she felt happier. She jumped out of bed, dressed in a great hurry and led poor Florence, who suffered a good deal from fallen arches, round and round Kensington Gardens for two hours at least.

When Sophia arrived at the Post, accompanied by a limping Florence, the first person she saw was Mrs Twitchett. Her doubts were dispersed in a moment and great was her relief. Rudolph must certainly be working on her side; it would be unnatural for anybody to go to the trouble of dressing up like that, twice, for a joke. Mrs Twitchett was busily employed in the Labour Ward, but found time, when Sophia came down from her luncheon at the canteen, to go round to the office and give back the borrowed handkerchief. Sophia put it away in her bag without even looking at it.

'So kind of you,' said Mrs Twitchett. 'I have had it washed and ironed for you, of course. And now you must forgive me if I run back to the Labour Ward. I am in the middle of a most fascinating argument with Sister Turnbull about umbilical cords. Thank you again, very much, for the handkerchief.'

Rudolph's disguise was perfect, and Sophia did not feel at all nervous that Florence would see through it; he had, in his time, brought off much more difficult hoaxes, and she herself had not seen who it was yesterday until he began to make a joke of the card index.

Presently Sophia gave a loud sniff, rummaged about in her bag and pulled out the handkerchief. Rudolph really did seem to have had it washed and ironed, unless it was a new one. Slowly she spread it out, gave it a little shake and blew her nose on it. The letters 'O.K.' were printed in one corner, so that was all right. She began to do her knitting. An almost unnatural calm seemed to have descended on the

Post. Several people, as well as Sister Wordsworth, were on the sick list, and the personnel were so depleted that it was not even possible to hold the usual practice in the Treatment Room. The wireless, joy of joys, was out of order. One nurse came in and asked Sophia for a clean overall in which to go to the theatre, and Sophia felt guilty because she had known that this girl's own overall was lost in the wash and she ought to have sent a postcard about it to the laundry. As she got a clean one out of the general store, she assured the girl that she had done so and was eagerly awaiting the reply. It seemed that today was to be a gala at the theatre, with two cerebral tumours and a mastoid. This nurse had been looking forward to it all the week. Sophia helped her with her cap, and she dashed away to her treat, singing happily.

Sophia felt very restless, and wandered into the Treatment Room where, done out of the ordinary practice, the nurses, in an excess of zeal, were giving each other bed pans. Further on, in the Labour Ward, Sister Turnbull and Mrs Twitchett sat on the floor counting over the contents of the poison cupboard. Mrs Twitchett was enlarging on the most horrid aspects of childbirth. Then Sophia went back to the office, and hour upon hour went by with absolutely nothing happening until she thought she would scream.

Suddenly, just before it was time for her to go off duty, all the lights went out. This was always happening at the Post; nevertheless Sophia found herself under the table before she had time consciously to control her actions. A moment later she heard Winthrop push his way through the sacking curtain and he began to flash a powerful torch round the office, evidently looking for her. In one more minute he must see her. Sophia experienced a spasm of sick terror, like a child playing a too realistic game of hide and seek, and then, almost before she had time to remember that this was no game at all, two more torches appeared in the doorway, and, by the light of Winthrop's which was now flashed on to them, she could see Mrs Twitchett, accompanied by the reassuring form of a tin-hatted policeman. For a few moments the office resembled the scene of a gangster play in which it is impossible to discover what is happening; however, when the shooting and scuffling was over, she saw Winthrop being led away with gyves upon his wrists, and this gave her great confidence.

'Sophia, where are you?' shouted Rudolph.

Sophia crawled out from under her table feeling unheroic, but relieved.

'Good girl,' he said. 'You all right?'

He took her hand, and together they ran through the Post, which seemed to be quite full of men with torches, shouting and running, towards the Museum. This was also full of policemen. They went past the Siamese twins, past the brains and came to where the case of bladders lay in pieces on the floor; beyond it the door stood open. Framed in the doorway, with the light behind him making an aura of his golden hair, stood the old gentleman with Milly in his arms.

'We've got Winthrop all right,' said Rudolph, 'what about your two?'

Sophia was busy kissing Milly, who showed enthusiasm at the sight of her owner.

'She looks a little bit all eyes,' she said; 'otherwise quite well. Oh, Milly, I do love you.'

'Florence and Heatherley have scuttled themselves in the main drain,' said Sir Ivor, 'and I could do with a whisky and soda, old dears.'

15

Rudolph had only just been in time. He confessed that when he first read Sophia's message on the handkerchief he had felt excessively bored. Every woman in London seemed to have some secret service activity on hand. Then he remembered that Sophia's manner had been rather queer, and that, although she must have known who Mrs Twitchett was, she had not given him so much as a wink, even when they were outside the Post. She was looking white and strained and anxious, and the circumstance of her having the handkerchief ready to give him was peculiar. Finally there was something about the way she had worded her message that made him think this was, after all, no silly joke, but an affair which called for some investigation.

Accordingly, when he had divested himself of his Twitchett personality and was once more respectable in uniform, he hurried round to Scotland Yard with the handkerchief which he showed, rather deprecatingly, to Inspector McFarlane. The Inspector, however, so far from laughing at him, was exceedingly interested. He told Rudolph that for a long time now the authorities had suspected that the old 'King' was broadcasting in this country; that furthermore, Scotland Yard was on the track of three dangerous spies, the leaders of a large and well organized gang who were known to be in London and who so far could not be located. Quite a lot had been discovered about their activities, but nobody had any idea who they might be or where to find them. Rudolph told him about Florence, of how he had jokingly suggested that she was really a spy, and of the pigeon in her bedroom, and the Inspector, who was quite interested to hear all this, said that the Boston Brotherhood, or any such cranky society, and an American accent would provide an admirable smokescreen for clever spies. He also said that the gang he was looking for certainly used pigeons, two of which had been shot down over the Channel quite recently.

The long and the short of it was that the Inspector told his two best men that they must somehow penetrate into the cellars of St Anne's. He advised Rudolph on no account to make any attempt at communicating with Sophia until they knew more, as her life might easily be endangered if he did.

'By the way,' he said, glancing once again at the handkerchief, 'who is Milly?'

'Milly,' said Rudolph angrily, for this made him look a fool, 'since you ask me, is a blasted bitch.'

'A friend of Lady Sophia's?'

'You misunderstand me, Inspector. No, her French bulldog. She is potty about the wretched animal, and certainly if anyone wanted to get Sophia into his power an infallible way would be by kidnapping Milly.'

'I see. So my men must look out (unless the whole thing is a joke) for Sir Ivor King and a French bulldog. If it should prove to be a joke, you must in no way distress yourself, Mr Jocelyn. In wartime we are bound to explore every avenue, whether it is likely to be productive of results, or not. Every day we follow up false clues, and think ourselves lucky if something turns out to be genuine once in a hundred times. I am very grateful to you for coming round, and will let you know of course if there are any developments.'

Rudolph went to the Ritz from Scotland Yard, and here he saw Olga, who was telling quite a little crowd of people that she was hot-foot on the track of a gang of dangerous spies, and soon hoped to be able, single-handed, to deliver them over to justice. Mary Pencill was also there, assuring her admirers that Russia's interest in Finland was only that of a big brother, not, she said, that she held any brief for the present ruler of Russia, who had shown his true colours the day he accepted the overtures of Hitler.

In the middle of the night, Inspector McFarlane sent for Rudolph to go and see him. He had some news. One of his men had actually seen the King of Song in his subterranean cubby-hole; not only that, he had managed to hold a short whispered conversation with him. Sir Ivor told him that the gang had now entirely dispersed with the exception of Florence, Heatherley and Winthrop. Florence was planning to leave for Germany, taking Sir Ivor with her, the following day at 8 p.m. An hour later, a time fuse, which was already in one of the cellars, would go off, setting in motion an elaborate network of machinery connected with the whole drainage system of London. Every drain would be blown up, carrying with it, of course, hundreds of buildings and streets; the confusion and loss of life would be prodigious, the more so as none of the bombs would explode simultaneously, and people hurrying to safety from one part of the town to another would find themselves in the middle of fresh explosions. London would lie a total wreck, and prove an easy prey for the fleet upon fleet of aeroplanes which would now pour over it, dropping armed parachutists. Taking advantage of the city's disorganization, and led by Heatherley and Winthrop, they would soon be in possession of it. London would be destroyed and in enemy hands, the war as good as lost.

'So, you see,' remarked the Inspector, 'it was just as well that you did not treat Lady Sophia's message as a joke. Oh, and by the way, Sir Ivor has the dog with him. He says her snoring gets on his nerves.'

'I'm not surprised. What anybody wants to have a dog like that for – !'

The Inspector told Rudolph that he had better become Mrs Twitchett again and go to the Post. Like this he would be able to keep an eye on Florence and also to reassure Sophia, whose nerves, if nothing were done to relieve her anxiety, might give way, greatly to the detriment of the Inspector's plans. He wanted to leave the gang undisturbed until nearly the last minute, as it was important that no message should get through to Berlin which would prevent the now eagerly awaited arrival of the parachutists. The War Office was seething with arrangements for their reception.

Everything went off beautifully except that the fusing of the lights, a pure accident, had enabled Florence and Heatherley to dive into the main drain before they could be arrested. It had happened just as the Inspector's men were pouring into the Post through the ordinary entrance and also by means of the drain, and had momentarily caused some confusion.

'We should have preferred to catch them alive,' said the Inspector, 'but there it is.'

Sophia was rather pleased; the idea of Florence as Mata Hari in her silver foxes was repugnant to her, and besides, it would have been embarrassing for Luke. Far better like this.

Presently the air was filled with Dracula-like forms descending slowly through the black-out. These young fellows, the cream of the German army, met with a very queer reception. Squads of air-raid wardens, stretcher-bearers, boy scouts, shop assistants and black-coated workers awaited them with yards and yards of twine, and when they were still a few feet from the earth, tied their dangling legs together. Trussed up like turkeys for the Christmas market, they were bundled into military lorries and hurried away to several large Adam houses which had been commandeered for the purpose. Soon all the newspapers had photographs of them smoking their pipes before a cheery log fire, with a picture of their Führer gazing down at them from the chimneypiece. Sir Ivor King went several times to sing German folk songs with them, a gesture that was much appreciated by the great British public who regarded them with a sort of patronizing affection, rather as if they were members of an Australian cricket team which had come over here and competed, unsuccessfully, for the Ashes.

16

Sophia was not acclaimed as a national heroine. The worthy burghers of London, who should have been grateful to her, were quite displeased to learn that, although their total destruction had in fact been prevented, this had been done in such an off-hand way, and with so small a margin of time to spare. Sophia was criticized, and very rightly so, for not having called in Scotland Yard the instant she had first seen Florence letting a pigeon out of her bedroom window. Had the full story of her incompetence emerged, had the facts about Milly seen the light of day, it is probable that the windows of 98 Granby Gate would have shared the fate of those at Vocal Lodge, which were now being mended, in gratitude and remorse, at the expense of all the residents of Kew Green. Actually, Sophia was damned with faint praise in the daily press, and slightly clapped when she appeared on the News Reels.

In any case, the King of Song had now soared to such an exalted position in the hearts of his fellow-countrymen that there would hardly have been room for any-body else. Wherever he showed his face in public, even in the Turkish bath, he was snatched up and carried shoulder high; the taxi he had modestly hired to take him from the Ritz, where he had spent the night after being rescued, to Vocal Lodge, was harnessed with laurel ropes to a team of A.T.S., who dragged him there through dense, hysterical crowds. The journey took two and a half hours. He arrived at Vocal Lodge simultaneously with Lady Beech's three van-loads of furniture which she was most thoughtfully re-lending him. Larch, overcome with shame at the recollection of his own Peter-like behaviour, was sobbing on the doorstep; the glaziers were still at work on the windows, and in fact, the whole place was so disorganized that Sir Ivor got back into the taxi, very much hoping that it would be allowed to return under its own steam. The taximan, however, glad of the opportunity to save petrol, signalled to the local decontamination squad who seized the ropes and dragged it back to the Ritz. This journey, owing to the fact that the decontamination squad was in full gas-proof clothing and service masks, took three and a half hours, and one of them died of heart failure in the bar soon after the arrival.

All the secrets of the German espionage system were now as an open book to the astute old singer, who had had the opportunity of looking through many secret documents during the course of his captivity and had committed everything of importance to memory. Not for nothing had he the reputation of being able to learn a whole opera between tea and dinner. Codes, maps of air bases, army plans, naval dispositions, all were now in the hands of the M.I.; while the arrangements for the occupation of England, perfect to every detail, were issued in a White Paper, much to the delight of the general public.

It was universally admitted that Sir Ivor had played his cards brilliantly. When Winthrop, alias Gustav, had approached him, shortly before the outbreak of war, with the offer of a huge sum if he would lend his services to Germany, he had seen at once that here was a wonderful opportunity to help his country. He had accepted, partly, as he told Winthrop, because he needed the money, and partly because he was a firm believer in slavery. Then, very cleverly, he had resisted the temptation to communicate with Scotland Yard before disappearing; had he done so, the Eiweisses, through certain highly-placed officials now languishing in the Tower, would inevitably have found out, and the 'murder' of the old gentleman would have been one indeed.

The Eiweisses, close friends of Hitler, had been preparing their position since the Munich *putsch* of 1923, and as Heatherley Egg and Florence Turnbull were quite well-known citizens of the United States, and the most trusted lieutenants of Brother Bones. They were known to be bores, on both sides of the Atlantic; more sinister attributes had never been suspected, least of all by the worthy Brother himself. In the end they seemed to have been undone by a sort of childish naïveté. Sir Ivor could always dispel, as soon as they arose, any doubts of his *bona fides* by talking to them of his old music teacher at Düsseldorf, of the German Christmas which he loved so much, of the duel he had fought as a student, and his memories of the old beer cellar. He aroused a nostalgia in their souls for the Fatherland, and thus he lulled any suspicions which they might otherwise have had. Picture the delight with which his fellow-citizens now learnt of his duplicity. The old music teacher (long since dead, the broadcast, like the duet with Frau Goering, had been a hoax) was really a Polish Jew, the 'King' detested beer, he had never spent a Christmas in Germany, and the scar on his temple, which, so he had told the von Eiweisses, was the result of a duel, had really been acquired in a bicycling accident many years ago when he had toured the Isle of Wight with the posthumous Duchess and Lady Beech, in bloomers.

As for Rudolph, while everybody admitted the value of his work, nobody could forbear to smile; the public took him to their hearts as a sort of Charley's Aunt, and he soon figured in many a music-hall joke. His colonel sent for him and drew his attention to the rule that officers should not appear in mufti during wartime.

Sophia gave a dinner party in honour of the King of Song and of Luke's safe return from America. It was a large party. The guests included Lady Beech, Fred and Ned and their wives, Mary Pencill, Sister Wordsworth, the Gogothskas, Rudolph, a girl called Ruth whom Luke had met on the clipper and who was now staying in Florence's room at 98 Granby Gate, and, of course, the King of Song himself in the very wig which had been found by the innocent gambollers of Kew Green, and which he had borrowed for the evening from the Scotland Yard museum of horrors.

Olga arrived late enough to be certain of being last, but not so late that dinner would have been started without her. Years of practice enabled her to hit off the right moment. She was in the uniform of her important war work, and wore a small tiara which she had bought back from the American who had bought it from Serge's father. It bore historic associations, having belonged, so she alleged, to Catharine the Great, one of whose lovers one of Serge's ancestors, of course, had been. Sophia had once caused very bad feeling by asking whether the diamonds were yellow with age or whether Catharine the Great had been disappointed in Serge's ancestor. Olga now made herself the centre of attention by the announcement that she was leaving almost at once for Kurdistan, on a very important mission.

'Tomorrow,' she said, 'I go down to Suffolk to say adieu to Moushka; early next week I leave.'

Moushka was old Mrs Bagg. In Olga's pre-Russian days she had been known as Mummy, which had been all right for the mother of Baby Bagg. Princess Olga Gogothsky required a Moushka. Serge, on the other hand, always called his parents Pa and Ma; but then he pronounced his own name, as did all his friends, like that stuff of which schoolgirls' skirts are made. Olga gave it a very different sound – 'Sairgay'.

'I suppose, now that Sophia has caught all the spies in London, there is nothing much left for you to do here,' said Rudolph, loyally.

'Spies!' The Princess gave a scornful twist to her lips as though spies were enormously beneath her attention, nowadays. 'No, I have important business to do there, for my Chief, with the Kahns.'

Nobody asked who the Kahns were.

Serge was in the seventh heaven. It seemed that, by dint of enlisting under an assumed name and as a private, he had managed to get back to his Blossom. Determined not to lose his love a second time, he was now on the water-waggon, but even this experiment had not damped his spirits, and he appeared to be the happiest living Russian.

Fred and Ned had once more reversed positions. Ned had proved to be even more of a failure at the Ministry than Britain had expected he would, and there had been, the day before Sophia's dinner, a Cabinet purge during which Ned was sent off to try his luck in another place. As we do not yet live under a totalitarian régime, this other place was, of course, that English equivalent of the grave, the House of Lords. Meanwhile, Fred, reinstated in both popular and Ministerial esteem by the triumphant return of Sir Ivor King, was back at his old job. This exchange was, luckily, to the satisfaction of both parties. Ned's wife had for some time been making his nights hideous with her complaints and assertions that at her age (she was nearly thirty) it was quite unheard of not to be a peeress and made her look ridiculous, while Fred had never taken to Blossom with Serge's ardour and had really been hankering after that Cabinet key all the time.

Fred and Sir Ivor were soon discussing the campaign of Song Propaganda which was to be launched the following week.

'We must especially concentrate, of course, on bigger and better Pets' Programmes than ever before,' said the Minister.

'You're joking!'

'What? Indeed I am not.'

'Of course the Pets' Programmes were simply put in to tease the Germans,' said Sir Ivor, 'and I also hoped they would show people here that the whole thing was bogus.'

'Then you very much underestimated our English love for dumb animals,' Fred replied pompously. 'Let me tell you that the Pets' Programmes were the only ones the Government were really worried about – why, every man, woman and dog in the whole country listened to those wretched programmes. You should have seen, for instance, how much Abbie and Milly enjoyed them. They never missed one. Why, entirely owing to you, there is now a Pets' League of Peace and Slavery, with literally thousands of members. The Pets wear awful little badges and pay half-a-crown. They had a mammoth meeting last week in the Dell at Hyde Park.'

'We'll soon alter that,' said the old gentleman. 'I will start a Society for Patriotic Pets and make them pay five bob.'

'Please will you two come in to dinner.'

Sophia sat between the King of Song and Luke, because, as she explained, she had not yet had a word with Luke since his return. 'We shall have to have the Clipper,' she said in an undertone to her godfather, who quite understood. They had it. After a bit they were able to leave Luke and Ruth having it together, with Lady Beech, who, like the Athenians, loved new things, lending an occasional ear. The pink sunrise, the pink sunset, the next pink sunrise and the food.

Sophia asked Sir Ivor about Agony 22, but he was quite as much in the dark about the great egg mystery as Heatherley had been.

'Come now, pretty young lady,' he said. 'How could I get at your egg?'

'I know, but in spy stories people seem to manage these things.'

Ned here chimed in with the news that many eggs nowadays have things written on them.

'I expect there is a farm called Agony, and that egg was laid in 1922,' he said.

'But why should there be a farm called Agony?'

'You never can tell; farms are called some very queer things. When I was Under-Secretary for Agriculture –'

'By the way, Sophie, you must be feeling a bit easier on the subject of parachutists, eh?' asked Fred. Anything to stop Ned from telling about when he was Under-Secretary for Agriculture.

'Well, yes, but there's such an awful new horror; I think of nothing else. I read in some paper that the Germans are employing midget spies, so small that they can hide in a drawer, and the result is I simply daren't look for a hanky nowadays.'

'Don't worry; we've caught nearly all of them. The Government are issuing an appeal tomorrow for old dolls' houses to keep them in.'

Lady Beech, having heard the Clipper out to the last throb of its engines, now collected a few eyes, for she liked general conversation, leant across the table, and said to her brother-in-law, 'Tell me, Ivor, dear, what sort of a life did you have under the First Aid Post?'

'Oh yes,' said all the others, 'do tell us how it was.'

'Spiffing,' said the old Edwardian. 'They fitted up a Turkish bath for me, and I spent hours of every day in that. Then one member of the gang (I expect you would remember him, Sophie, a stretcher-bearer called Wolf) used to be a hair-dresser on one of those liners, and he brushed my – er – scalp in quite a special way, to induce baby growth. And by jingo he induced it!' And sure enough Sir Ivor snatched off his wig and proudly exhibited some horrible little bits of white fluff. 'After all these years,' he said. 'I was stone bald at thirty, you know; the man must be a genius. He is now in the Tower and I am making an application at the Home Office to be allowed to visit him once a week, for treatment. It is all I ask in return for my, not inconsiderable, services.'

'Tell me, Ivor, did you not feel most fearfully anxious when the weeks passed and you had no communication with the outside world?'

'Rather not. I know how stupid Germans are, you see – felt certain they would give themselves away sooner or later, and sure enough they did and everything was O.K. just as I always guessed it would be.'

'Bit touch and go?' said Luke.

'Keep your hair on,' said the old Singer. 'A miss is as good as a mile, ain't it?'

The Pursuit of Love

To Gaston Palewski

I

There is a photograph in existence of Aunt Sadie and her six children sitting round the tea-table at Alconleigh. The table is situated, as it was, is now, and ever shall be, in the hall, in front of a huge open fire of logs. Over the chimney piece plainly visible in the photograph hangs an entrenching tool, with which, in 1915, Uncle Matthew had whacked to death eight Germans one by one as they crawled out of a dug-out. It is still covered with blood and hairs, an object of fascination to us as children. In the photograph Aunt Sadie's face, always beautiful, appears strangely round, her hair strangely fluffy, and her clothes strangely dowdy, but it is unmistakably she who sits there with Robin, in oceans of lace, lolling on her knee. She seems uncertain what to do with his head, and the presence of Nanny waiting to take him away is felt though not seen. The other children, between Louisa's eleven and Matt's two years, sit round the table in party dresses or frilly bibs, holding cups or mugs according to age, all of them gazing at the camera with large eyes opened wide by the flash, and all looking as if butter would not melt in their round pursed-up mouths. There they are, held like flies, in the amber of that moment – click goes the camera and on goes life; the minutes, the days, the years, the decades, taking them further and further from that happiness and promise of youth, from the hopes Aunt Sadie must have had for them, and from the dreams they dreamed for themselves. I often think there is nothing quite so poignantly sad as old family groups.

When a child I spent my Christmas holidays at Alconleigh, it was a regular feature of my life, and, while some of them slipped by with nothing much to remember, others were distinguished by violent occurrences and had a definite character of their own. There was the time, for example, when the servants' wing caught fire, the time when my pony lay on me in the brook and nearly drowned me (not very nearly, he was soon dragged off, but meanwhile bubbles were said to have been observed). There was drama when Linda, aged ten, attempted suicide in order to rejoin an old smelly Border Terrier which Uncle Matthew had had put down. She collected and ate a basketful of yew-berries, was discovered by Nanny and given mustard and water to make her sick. She was then 'spoken to' by Aunt Sadie, clipped over the ear by Uncle Matthew, put to bed for days and given a Labrador puppy, which soon took the place of the old Border in her affections. There was much worse drama when Linda, aged twelve, told the daughters of neighbours, who had come to tea, what she supposed to be the facts of life. Linda's presentation of the 'facts' had been so gruesome that the children left Alconleigh howling dismally, their nerves permanently impaired, their future chances of a sane and happy sex life much reduced. This resulted in a series of dreadful punishments, from a real beating, administered by Uncle Matthew, to luncheon upstairs for a week. There was the unforgettable holiday when Uncle Matthew and Aunt Sadie went to Canada. The Radlett children would rush for the newspapers every day hoping to see that their parents' ship had gone down with all aboard; they yearned to be total orphans – especially Linda, who saw herself as Katy in *What Katy Did*, the reins of the household gathered into small but capable hands. The ship met with no iceberg and weathered the Atlantic storms, but meanwhile we had a wonderful holiday, free from rules.

But the Christmas I remember most clearly of all was when I was fourteen and Aunt Emily became engaged. Aunt Emily was Aunt Sadie's sister, and she had brought me up from babyhood, my own mother, their youngest sister, having felt herself too beautiful and too gay to be burdened with a child at the age of nineteen. She left my father when I was a month old, and subsequently ran away so often, and with so many different people, that she became known to her family and friends as the Bolter; while my father's second, and presently his third, fourth, and fifth wives, very naturally had no great wish to look after me. Occasionally one of these impetuous parents would appear like a rocket, casting an unnatural glow upon my horizon. They had great glamour, and I longed to be caught up in their fiery trails and be carried away, though in my heart I knew how lucky I was to have Aunt Emily. By degrees, as I grew up, they lost all charm for me; the cold grey rocket cases mouldered where they happened to fall, my mother with a major in the South of France, my father, his estates sold up to pay his debts, with an old Rumanian countess in the Bahamas. Even before I was grown up much of the glamour with which they had been surrounded had faded, and finally there was nothing left, no foundation of childish memories to make them seem any different from other middle-aged people. Aunt Emily was never glamorous but she was always my mother, and I loved her.

At the time of which I write, however, I was at an age when the least imaginative child supposes itself to be a changeling, a Princess of Indian blood, Joan of Arc, or the future Empress of Russia. I hankered after my parents, put on an idiotic face which was intended to convey mingled suffering and pride when their names were mentioned, and thought of them as engulfed in deep, romantic, deadly sin.

Linda and I were very much preoccupied with sin, and our great hero was Oscar Wilde.

'But what did he *do*?'

'I asked Fa once and he roared at me – goodness, it was terrifying. He said: "If you mention that sewer's name again in this house I'll thrash you, do you hear, damn you?" So I asked Sadie and she looked awfully vague and said: "Oh, duck, I never really quite knew, but whatever it was was worse than murder, fearfully bad. And, darling, don't talk about him at meals, will you?"'

'We must find out.'

'Bob says he will, when he goes to Eton.'

'Oh, good! Do you think he was worse than Mummy and Daddy?'

'Surely he couldn't be. Oh, you are so lucky, to have wicked parents.'

This Christmas-time, aged fourteen, I stumbled into the hall at Alconleigh blinded by the light after a six-mile drive from Merlinford station. It was always the same every year, I always came down by the same train, arriving at tea-time, and always found Aunt Sadie and the children round the table underneath the entrenching tool, just as they were in the photograph. It was always the same table and the same tea-things; the china with large roses on it, the tea-kettle and the silver dish for scones simmering over little flames – the human beings of course were getting imperceptibly older, the babies were becoming children, the children were growing up, and there had been an addition in the shape of Victoria now aged two. She was waddling about with a chocolate biscuit clenched in her fist, her face was smothered in chocolate and was a horrible sight, but through the sticky mask shone unmistakably the blue of two steady Radlett eyes.

There was a tremendous scraping of chairs as I came in, and a pack of Radletts hurled themselves upon me with the intensity and almost the ferocity of a pack of hounds hurling itself upon a fox. All except Linda. She was the most pleased to see me, but determined not to show it. When the din had quieted down and I was seated before a scone and a cup of tea, she said:

'Where's Brenda?' Brenda was my white mouse.

'She got a sore back and died,' I said. Aunt Sadie looked anxiously at Linda.

'Had you been riding her?' said Louisa, facetiously. Matt, who had recently come under the care of a French nursery governess, said in a high-pitched imitation of her voice: '*C'était, comme d'habitude, les voies urinaires.*'

'Oh, dear,' said Aunt Sadie under her breath.

Enormous tears were pouring into Linda's plate. Nobody cried so much or so often as she; anything, but especially anything sad about animals, would set her off, and, once begun, it was a job to stop her. She was a delicate, as well as a highly nervous child, and even Aunt Sadie, who lived in a dream as far as the health of her children was concerned, was aware that too much crying kept her awake at night, put her off her food, and did her harm. The other children, and especially Louisa and Bob, who loved to tease, went as far as they dared with her, and were periodically punished for making her cry. *Black Beauty, Owd Bob, The Story of a Red Deer*, and all the Seton Thompson books were on the nursery index because of Linda, who, at one time or another, had been prostrated by them. They had to be hidden away, as, if they were left lying about, she could not be trusted not to indulge in an orgy of self-torture.

Wicked Louisa had invented a poem which never failed to induce rivers of tears:

> A little, houseless match, it has no roof, no thatch,
> It lies alone, it makes no moan, that little, houseless match.

When Aunt Sadie was not around the children would chant this in a gloomy chorus. In certain moods one had only to glance at a match-box to dissolve poor Linda; when, however, she was feeling stronger, more fit to cope with life, this sort of teasing would force out of her very stomach an unwilling guffaw. Linda was not only my favourite cousin, but, then and for many years, my favourite human being. I adored all my cousins, and Linda distilled, mentally and physically, the very essence of the Radlett family. Her straight features, straight brown hair and large blue eyes were a theme upon which the faces of the others were a variation; all pretty, but none so absolutely distinctive as hers. There was something furious about her, even when she laughed, which she did a great deal, and always as if forced to against her will. Something reminiscent of pictures of Napoleon in youth, a sort of scowling intensity.

I could see that she was really minding much more about Brenda than I did. The truth was that my honeymoon days with the mouse were long since over; we had settled down to an uninspiring relationship, a form, as it were, of married blight, and, when she had developed a disgusting sore patch on her back, it had been all I could do to behave decently and treat her with common humanity. Apart from the shock it always is to find somebody stiff and cold in their cage in the morning, it had been a very great relief to me when Brenda's sufferings finally came to an end.

'Where is she buried?' Linda muttered furiously, looking at her plate.

'Beside the robin. She's got a dear little cross and her coffin was lined with pink satin.'

'Now, Linda darling,' said Aunt Sadie, 'if Fanny has finished her tea why don't you show her your toad?'

'He's upstairs asleep,' said Linda. But she stopped crying.

'Have some nice hot toast, then.'

'Can I have Gentleman's Relish on it?' she said, quick to make capital out of Aunt Sadie's mood, for Gentleman's Relish was kept strictly for Uncle Matthew, and supposed not to be good for children. The others made a great show of exchanging significant looks. These were intercepted, as they were meant to be, by Linda, who gave a tremendous bellowing boo-hoo and rushed upstairs.

'I wish you children wouldn't tease Linda,' said Aunt Sadie, irritated out of her usual gentleness, and followed her.

The staircase led out of the hall. When Aunt Sadie was beyond earshot, Louisa said: 'If wishes were horses beggars would ride. Child hunt tomorrow, Fanny.'

'Yes, Josh told me. He was in the car – been to see the vet.'

My Uncle Matthew had four magnificent bloodhounds, with which he used to hunt his children. Two of us would go off with a good start to lay the trail, and Uncle Matthew and the rest would follow the hounds on horseback. It was great fun. Once he came to my home and hunted Linda and me over Shenley Common. This caused the most tremendous stir locally, the Kentish week-enders on their way to church were appalled by the sight of four great hounds in full cry after two little girls. My uncle seemed to them like a wicked lord of fiction, and I became more than ever surrounded with an aura of madness, badness, and dangerousness for their children to know.

The child hunt on the first day of this Christmas visit was a great success. Louisa and I were chosen as hares. We ran across country, the beautiful bleak Cotswold uplands, starting soon after breakfast when the sun was still a red globe, hardly over the horizon, and the trees were etched in dark blue against a pale blue, mauve, and pinkish sky. The sun rose as we stumbled on, longing for our second wind; it shone, and there dawned a beautiful day, more like late autumn in its feeling than Christmas-time.

We managed to check the bloodhounds once by running through a flock of sheep, but Uncle Matthew soon got them on the scent again, and, after about two hours of hard running on our part, when we were only half a mile from home, the baying slavering creatures caught up with us, to be rewarded with lumps of meat and many caresses. Uncle Matthew was in a radiantly good temper, he got off his horse and walked home with us, chatting agreeably. What was most unusual, he was even quite affable to me.

'I hear Brenda has died,' he said. 'No great loss I should say. That mouse stank like merry hell. I expect you kept her cage too near the radiator, I always told you it was unhealthy, or did she die of old age?'

Uncle Matthew's charm, when he chose to turn it on, was considerable, but at that time I was always mortally afraid of him, and made the mistake of letting him see that I was.

'You ought to have a dormouse, Fanny, or a rat. They are much more interesting than white mice – though I must frankly say, of all the mice I ever knew, Brenda was the most utterly dismal.'

'She was dull,' I said, sycophantically.

'When I go to London after Christmas, I'll get you a dormouse. Saw one the other day at the Army and Navy.'

'Oh, Fa, it *is* unfair,' said Linda, who was walking her pony along beside us. 'You know how I've always longed for a dormouse.'

'It *is* unfair' was a perpetual cry of the Radletts when young. The great advantage of living in a large family is that early lesson of life's essential unfairness. With them I must say it nearly always operated in favour of Linda, who was the adored of Uncle Matthew.

Today, however, my uncle was angry with her, and I saw in a flash that this affability to me, this genial chat about mice, was simply designed as a tease for her.

'You've got enough animals, miss,' he said, sharply. 'You can't control the ones you have got. And don't forget what I told you – that dog of yours goes straight to the kennel when we get back, and stays there.'

Linda's face crumpled, tears poured, she kicked her pony into a canter and made for home. It seemed that her dog Labby had been sick in Uncle Matthew's business-room after breakfast. Uncle Matthew was unable to bear dirtiness in dogs, he flew into a rage, and, in his rage, had made a rule that never again was Labby to set foot in the house. This was always happening, for one reason or another, to one animal or another, and, Uncle Matthew's bark being invariably much worse than his bite, the ban seldom lasted more than a day or two, after which would begin what he called the Thin End of the Wedge.

'Can I bring him in just while I fetch my gloves?'

'I'm so tired – I can't go to the stables – do let him stay just till after tea.'

'Oh, I see – the thin end of the wedge. All right, this time he can stay, but if he makes another mess – or I catch him on your bed – or he chews up the good furniture (according to whichever crime it was that had resulted in banishment), I'll have him destroyed, and don't say I didn't warn you.'

All the same, every time sentence of banishment was pronounced, the owner of the condemned would envisage her beloved moping his life away in the solitary confinements of a cold and gloomy kennel.

'Even if I take him out for three hours every day, and go and chat to him for another hour, that leaves twenty hours for him all alone with nothing to do. Oh, why can't dogs read?'

The Radlett children, it will be observed, took a highly anthropomorphic view of their pets.

Today, however, Uncle Matthew was in a wonderfully good temper, and, as we left the stables, he said to Linda, who was sitting crying with Labby in his kennel:

'Are you going to leave that poor brute of yours in there all day?'

Her tears forgotten as if they had never been, Linda rushed into the house with Labby at her heels. The Radletts were always either on a peak of happiness or drowning in black waters of despair; their emotions were on no ordinary plane, they loved or they loathed, they laughed or they cried, they lived in a world of superlatives. Their life with Uncle Matthew was a sort of perpetual Tom Tiddler's ground. They went as far as they dared, sometimes very far indeed, while sometimes, for no apparent reason, he would pounce almost before they had crossed the boundary. Had they been poor children they would probably have been removed from their roaring, raging, whacking papa and sent to an approved home, or, indeed, he himself would have been removed from them and sent to prison for refusing to educate them. Nature, however, provides her own remedies, and no doubt the Radletts had enough of Uncle Matthew in them to enable them to weather storms in which ordinary children like me would have lost their nerve completely.

2

It was an accepted fact at Alconleigh that Uncle Matthew loathed me. This violent, uncontrolled man, like his children, knew no middle course, he either loved or he hated, and generally, it must be said, he hated. His reason for hating me was that he hated my father; they were old Eton enemies. When it became obvious, and obvious it was from the hour of my conception, that my parents intended to doorstep me, Aunt Sadie had wanted to bring me up with Linda. We were the same age, and it had seemed a sensible plan. Uncle Matthew had categorically refused. He hated my father, he said, he hated me, but, above all, he hated children, it was bad enough to have two of his own. (He evidently had not envisaged so soon having seven, and indeed both he and Aunt Sadie lived in a perpetual state of surprise at having filled so many cradles, about the future of whose occupants they seemed to have no particular policy.) So dear Aunt Emily, whose heart had once been broken by some wicked dallying monster, and who intended on this account never to marry, took me on and made a life's work of me, and I am very thankful that she did. For she believed passionately in the education of women, she took immense pains to have me properly taught, even going to live at Shenley on purpose to be near a good day school. The Radlett daughters did practically no lessons. They were taught by Lucille, the French governess, to read and write, they were obliged, though utterly unmusical, to 'practise' in the freezing ballroom for one hour a day each, their eyes glued to the clock, they would thump out the 'Merry Peasant' and a few scales, they were made to go for a French walk with Lucille on all except hunting days, and that was the extent of their education. Uncle Matthew loathed clever females, but he considered that gentlewomen ought, as well as being able to ride, to know French and play the piano. Although as a child I rather naturally envied them their freedom from thrall and bondage, from sums and science, I felt, nevertheless, a priggish satisfaction that I was not growing up unlettered, as they were.

Aunt Emily did not often come with me to Alconleigh. Perhaps she had an idea that it was more fun for me to be there on my own, and no doubt it was a change for her to get away and spend Christmas with the friends of her youth, and leave for a bit the responsibilities of her old age. Aunt Emily at this time was forty, and we children had long ago renounced on her behalf the world, the flesh, and the devil. This year, however, she had gone away from Shenley before the holidays began, saying that she would see me at Alconleigh in January.

On the afternoon of the child hunt Linda called a meeting of the Hons. The Hons was the Radlett secret society, anybody who was not a friend to the Hons was a Counter-Hon, and their battle-cry was 'Death to the horrible Counter-Hons.' I was a Hon, since my father, like theirs, was a lord.

There were also, however, many honorary Hons; it was not necessary to have been born a Hon in order to be one. As Linda once remarked: 'Kind hearts are more than coronets, and simple faith than Norman blood.' I'm not sure how much we really believed this, we were wicked snobs in those days, but we subscribed to the general idea. Head of the hon. Hons was Josh, the groom, who was greatly beloved by us all and worth buckets of Norman blood; chief of the horrible Counter-Hons was Craven, the gamekeeper, against whom a perpetual war to the knife was waged. The Hons would creep into the woods, and hide Craven's steel traps, let out the chaffinches which, in wire cages without food or water, he used as bait for hawks, give decent burial to the victims of his gamekeeper's larder, and, before a meet of the hounds, unblock the earths which Craven had so carefully stopped.

The poor Hons were tormented by the cruelties of the countryside, while, to me, holidays at Alconleigh were a perfect revelation of beastliness. Aunt Emily's little house was in a village; it was a Queen Anne box; red brick, white panelling, a magnolia tree and a delicious fresh smell. Between it and the country were a neat little garden, an ironwork fence, a village green and a village. The country one then came to was very different from Gloucestershire, it was emasculated, sheltered, over-cultivated, almost a suburban garden. At Alconleigh the cruel woods crept right up to the house; it was not unusual to be awoken by the screams of a rabbit running in horrified circles round a stoat, by the strange and awful cry of the dog-fox, or to see from one's bedroom window a live hen being carried away in the mouth of a vixen; while the roosting pheasant and the waking owl filled every night with wild primeval noise. In the winter, when snow covered the ground, we could trace the footprints of many creatures. These often ended in a pool of blood, a mass of fur or feathers, bearing witness to successful hunting by the carnivores.

On the other side of the house, within a stone's throw, was the Home Farm. Here the slaughtering of poultry and pigs, the castration of lambs and the branding of cattle took place as a matter of course, out in the open for whoever might be passing by to see. Even dear old Josh made nothing of firing, with red-hot irons, a favourite horse after the hunting season.

'You can only do two legs at a time,' he would say, hissing through his teeth as though one were a horse and he grooming one, 'otherwise they can't stand the pain.'

Linda and I were bad at standing pain ourselves, and found it intolerable that animals should have to lead such tormented lives and tortured deaths. (I still do mind, very much indeed, but in those days at Alconleigh it was an absolute obsession with us all.)

The humanitarian activities of the Hons were forbidden, on pain of punishment, by Uncle Matthew, who was always and entirely on the side of Craven, his favourite servant. Pheasants and partridges must be preserved, vermin must be put down rigorously, all except the fox, for whom a more exciting death was in store. Many and many a whacking did the poor Hons suffer, week after week their pocket-money was stopped, they were sent to bed early, given extra practising to do; nevertheless they bravely persisted with their discouraged and discouraging activities. Huge cases full of new steel traps would arrive periodically from the Army and Navy Stores, and lie stacked until required round Craven's hut in the middle of the wood (an old railway carriage was his head-quarters, situated, most inappropriately, among the primroses and blackberry bushes of a charming little glade); hundreds of traps, making one feel the futility of burying, at great risk to life and property, a paltry three or four. Sometimes we would find a screaming animal held in one; it would take all our reserves of courage to go up to it and let it out, to see it run away with three legs and a dangling mangled horror. We knew that it then probably died of blood-poisoning in its lair; Uncle Matthew would rub in this fact, sparing no agonizing detail of the long drawn-out ordeal, but, though we knew it would be kinder, we could never bring ourselves to kill them; it was asking too much. Often, as it was, we had to go away and be sick after these episodes.

The Hons' meeting-place was a disused linen cupboard at the top of the house, small, dark, and intensely hot. As in so many country houses the central-heating apparatus at Alconleigh had been installed in the early days of the invention, at enormous expense, and was now thoroughly out of date. In spite of a boiler which would not have been too large for an Atlantic liner, in spite of the tons of coke which it consumed daily, the temperature of the living-rooms was hardly affected, and all the heat there was seemed to concentrate in the Hons' cupboard, which was always stifling. Here we would sit, huddled up on the slatted shelves, and talk for hours about life and death.

Last holidays our great obsession had been childbirth, on which entrancing subject we were informed remarkably late, having supposed for a long time that a mother's stomach swelled up for nine months and then burst open like a ripe pumpkin, shooting out the infant. When the real truth dawned upon us it seemed rather an anticlimax, until Linda produced, from some novel, and read out loud in ghoulish tones, the description of a woman in labour.

'Her breath comes in great gulps – sweat pours down her brow like water – screams as of a tortured animal rend the air – and can this face, twisted with agony, be that of my darling Rhona – can this torture-chamber really be our bedroom, this rack our marriage-bed? "Doctor, doctor," I cried, "do something" – I rushed out into the night' – and so on.

We were rather disturbed by this, realizing that too probably we in our turn would have to endure these fearful agonies. Aunt Sadie, who had only just finished having her seven children, when appealed to, was not very reassuring.

'Yes,' she said, vaguely. 'It is the worst pain in the world. But the funny thing is, you always forget in between what it's like. Each time, when it began, I felt like saying, "Oh, now I can remember, stop it, stop it." And, of course, by then it was nine months too late to stop it.'

At this point Linda began to cry, saying how dreadful it must be for cows, which brought the conversation to an end.

It was difficult to talk to Aunt Sadie about sex; something always seemed to prevent one; babies were the nearest we ever got to it. She and Aunt Emily, feeling at one moment that we ought to know more, and being, I suspect, too embarrassed to enlighten us themselves, gave us a modern textbook on the subject.

We got hold of some curious ideas.

'Jassy,' said Linda one day, scornfully, 'is obsessed, poor thing, with sex.'

'Obsessed with sex!' said Jassy, 'there's nobody so obsessed as you, Linda. Why if I so much as look at a picture you say I'm a pygmalionist.'

In the end we got far more information out of a book called *Ducks and Duck Breeding.*

'Ducks can only copulate,' said Linda, after studying this for a while, 'in running water. Good luck to them.'

This Christmas Eve we all packed into the Hons' meeting-place to hear what Linda had to say – Louisa, Jassy, Bob, Matt, and I.

'Talk about back-to-the-womb,' said Jassy.

'Poor Aunt Sadie,' I said. 'I shouldn't think she'd want you all back in hers.'

'You never know. Now rabbits eat their children – somebody ought to explain to them how it's only a complex.'

'How can one *explain* to *rabbits?* That's what is so worrying about animals, they simply don't understand when they're spoken to, poor angels. I'll tell you what about Sadie though, she'd like to be back in one herself, she's got a thing for boxes and that always shows. Who else – Fanny, what about you?'

'I don't think I would, but then I imagine the one I was in wasn't very comfortable at the time you know, and nobody else has ever been allowed to stay there.'

'Abortions?' said Linda with interest.

'Well, tremendous jumpings and hot baths anyway.'

'How *do* you know?'

'I once heard Aunt Emily and Aunt Sadie talking about it when I was very little, and afterwards I remembered. Aunt Sadie said: "How does she manage it?" and Aunt Emily said: "Skiing, or hunting, or just jumping off the kitchen table."'

'You are so lucky, having wicked parents.'

This was the perpetual refrain of the Radletts and, indeed, my wicked parents constituted my chief interest in their eyes – I was really a very dull little girl in other respects.

'The news I have for the Hons today,' said Linda, clearing her throat like a grown-up person, 'while of considerable Hon interest generally, particularly concerns Fanny. I won't ask you to guess, because it's nearly tea-time and you never could, so I'll tell you straight out. Aunt Emily is engaged.'

There was a gasp from the Hons in chorus.

'Linda,' I said, furiously, 'you've made it up.' But I knew she couldn't have.

Linda brought a piece of paper out of her pocket. It was a half-sheet of writing-paper, evidently the end of a letter, covered with Aunt Emily's large babyish handwriting, and I looked over Linda's shoulder as she read it out:

'. . . not tell the children we're engaged, what d'you think darling, just at first? But then suppose Fanny takes a dislike to him, though I don't see how she could, but children are so funny, won't it be more of a shock? Oh, dear, I can't decide. Anyway, do what you think best, darling, we'll arrive on Thursday, and I'll telephone on Wednesday evening and see what's happened. All love from Emily.'

Sensation in the Hons' cupboard.

3

'But why?' I said, for the hundredth time.

Linda, Louisa, and I were packed into Louisa's bed, with Bob sitting on the end of it, chatting in whispers. These midnight talks were most strictly forbidden, but it was safer, at Alconleigh, to disobey rules during the early part of the night than at any other time in the twenty-four hours. Uncle Matthew fell asleep practically at the dinner-table. He would then doze in his business-room for an hour or so before dragging himself, in a somnambulist trance, to bed, where he slept the profound sleep of one who has been out of doors all day, until cockcrow the following morning, when he became very much awake. This was the time for his never-ending warfare with the housemaids over wood-ash. The rooms at Alconleigh were heated by wood fires, and Uncle Matthew maintained, rightly, that if these were to function properly, all the ash ought to be left in the fireplaces in a great hot smouldering heap. Every housemaid, however, for some reason (an early training with coal fires probably) was bent on removing this ash altogether. When shakings, imprecations, and being pounced out at by Uncle Matthew in his paisley dressing-gown at 6 a.m., had convinced them that this was not really feasible, they became absolutely determined to remove, by hook or by crook, just a little, a shovelful or so, every morning. I can only suppose they felt that like this they were asserting their personalities.

The result was guerrilla warfare at its most exciting. Housemaids are notoriously early risers, and can usually count upon three clear hours when a house belongs to them alone. But not at Alconleigh. Uncle Matthew was always, winter and summer alike, out of his bed by 5 a.m., and it was then his habit to wander about, looking like Great Agrippa in his dressing-gown, and drinking endless cups of tea out of a thermos flask, until about seven, when he would have his bath. Breakfast for my uncle, my aunt, family, and guests alike, was sharp at eight, and unpunctuality was not tolerated. Uncle Matthew was no respecter of other people's early morning sleep, and after five o'clock one could not count on any, for he raged round the house, clanking cups of tea, shouting at his dogs, roaring at the housemaids, cracking the stock whips which he had brought back from Canada on the lawn with a noise greater than gunfire, and all to the accompaniment of Galli-Curci on his gramophone, an abnormally loud one, with an enormous horn, through which would be shrieked 'Una voce poco fà' – 'The Mad Song' from *Lucia* – 'Lo, here the gen-tel lar-ha-hark' – and so on, played at top speed, thus rendering them even higher and more screeching than they ought to be.

Nothing reminds me of my childhood days at Alconleigh so much as those songs. Uncle Matthew played them incessantly for years, until the spell was broken when he went all the way to Liverpool to hear Galli-Curci in person. The disillusionment caused by her appearance was so great that the records remained ever after silent, and were replaced by the deepest bass voices that money could buy.

'Fearful the death of the diver must be,
Walking alone in the de-he-he-he-he-epths of the sea'
or 'Drake is going West, lads.'

These were, on the whole, welcomed by the family, as rather less piercing at early dawn.

'Why should she want to be married?'

'It's not as though she could be in love. She's forty.'

Like all the very young we took it for granted that making love is child's play.

'How old do you suppose he is?'

'Fifty or sixty I guess. Perhaps she thinks it would be nice to be a widow. Weeds, you know.'

'Perhaps she thinks Fanny ought to have a man's influence.'

'Man's influence!' said Louisa. 'I forsee trouble. Supposing he falls in love with Fanny, that'll be a pretty kettle of fish, like Somerset and Princess Elizabeth – he'll be playing rough games and pinching you in bed, see if he doesn't.'

'Surely not, at his age.'

'Old men love little girls.'

'And little boys,' said Bob.

'It looks as if Aunt Sadie isn't going to say anything about it before they come,' I said.

'There's nearly a week to go – she may be deciding. She'll talk it over with Fa. Might be worth listening next time she has a bath. You can, Bob.'

Christmas Day was spent, as usual at Alconleigh, between alternate bursts of sunshine and showers. I put, as children can, the disturbing news about Aunt Emily out of my mind, and concentrated upon enjoyment. At about six o'clock Linda and I unstuck our sleepy eyes and started on our stockings. Our real presents came later, at breakfast and on the tree, but the stockings were a wonderful *hors d'œuvre* and full of treasures. Presently Jassy came in and started selling us things out of hers. Jassy only cared about money because she was saving up to run away – she carried her post office book about with her everywhere, and always knew to a farthing what she had got. This was then translated by a miracle of determination as Jassy was very bad at sums, into so many days in a bed-sitting-room.

'How are you getting on, Jassy?'

'My fare to London and a month and two days and an hour and a half in a bed-sitter, with basin and breakfast.'

Where the other meals would come from was left to the imagination. Jassy studied advertisements of bed-sitters in *The Times* every morning. The cheapest she had found so far was in Clapham. So eager was she for the cash that would transform her dream into reality, that one could be certain of picking up a few bargains round about Christmas and her birthday. Jassy at this time was aged eight.

I must admit that my wicked parents turned up trumps at Christmas, and my presents from them were always the envy of the entire household. This year my mother, who was in Paris, sent a gilded birdcage full of stuffed hummingbirds which, when wound up, twittered and hopped about and drank at a fountain. She also sent a fur hat and a gold and topaz bracelet, whose glamour was enhanced by the fact that Aunt Sadie considered them unsuitable for a child, and said so. My father sent a pony and cart, a very smart and beautiful little outfit, which had arrived some days before, and been secreted by Josh in the stables.

'So typical of that damned fool Edward to send it here,' Uncle Matthew said, 'and give us all the trouble of getting it to Shenley. And I bet poor old Emily won't be too pleased. Who on earth is going to look after it?'

Linda cried with envy. 'It *is* unfair,' she kept saying, 'that you should have wicked parents and not me.'

We persuaded Josh to take us for a drive after luncheon. The pony was an angel and the whole thing easily managed by a child, even the harnessing. Linda wore my hat and drove the pony. We got back late for the Tree – the house was already full of tenants and their children; Uncle Matthew, who was struggling into his Father Christmas clothes, roared at us so violently that Linda had to go and cry upstairs, and was not there to collect her own present from him. Uncle Matthew had taken some trouble to get her longed-for dormouse and was greatly put out by this; he roared at everybody in turns, and ground his dentures. There was a legend in the family that he had already ground away four pairs in his rages.

The evening came to a climax of violence when Matt produced a box of fireworks which my mother had sent him from Paris. On the box they were called *pétards*. Somebody said to Matt: 'What do they do?' to which he replied: *'Bien, ça pète, quoi?'* This remark, overheard by Uncle Matthew, was rewarded with a first-class hiding, which was actually most unfair, as poor Matt was only repeating what Lucille had said to him earlier in the day. Matt, however, regarded hidings as a sort of natural phenomenon, unconnected with any actions of his own, and submitted to them philosophically enough. I have often wondered since how it was that Aunt Sadie could have chosen Lucille, who was the very acme of vulgarity, to look after her children. We all loved her, she was gay and spirited and read aloud to us without cease, but her language really was extraordinary, and provided dreadful pitfalls for the unwary.

'Qu'est-ce que c'est ce custard, qu'on fout partout?'

I shall never forget Matt quite innocently making this remark in Fuller's at Oxford, where Uncle Matthew had taken us for a treat. The consequences were awful.

It never seemed to occur to Uncle Matthew that Matt could not know these words by nature, and that it would really have been more fair to check them at their source.

4

I naturally awaited the arrival of Aunt Emily and her future intended with some agitation. She was, after all, my real mother, and, greatly as I might hanker after that glittering evil person who bore me, it was to Aunt Emily that I turned for the solid, sustaining, though on the face of it uninteresting relationship that is provided by motherhood at its best. Our little household at Shenley was calm and happy and afforded an absolute contrast to the agitations and tearing emotions of Alconleigh. It may have been dull, but it was a sheltering harbour, and I was always glad to get back to it. I think I was beginning dimly to realize how much it all centred upon me; the very time-table, with its early luncheon and high tea, was arranged to fit in with my lessons and bedtime. Only during those holidays when I went to Alconleigh did Aunt Emily have any life of her own, and even these breaks were infrequent, as she had an idea that Uncle Matthew and the whole stormy set-up there were bad for my nerves. I may not have been consciously aware of the extent to which Aunt Emily had regulated her existence round mine, but I saw, only too clearly, that the addition of a man to our establishment was going to change everything. Hardly knowing any men outside the family, I imagined them all to be modelled on the lines of Uncle Matthew, or of my own seldom seen, violently emotional papa, either of whom, plunging about in that neat little house, would have been sadly out of place. I was filled with apprehension, almost with horror, and, greatly assisted by the workings of Louisa's and Linda's vivid imaginations, had got myself into a real state of nerves. Louisa was now teasing me with *The Constant Nymph*. She read aloud the last chapters, and soon I was dying at a Brussels boarding-house, in the arms of Aunt Emily's husband.

On Wednesday Aunt Emily rang up Aunt Sadie, and they talked for ages. The telephone at Alconleigh was, in those days, situated in a glass cupboard half-way down the brilliantly lighted back passage; there was no extension, and eavesdropping was thus rendered impossible. (In later years it was moved to Uncle Matthew's business-room, with an extension, after which all privacy was at an end.) When Aunt Sadie returned to the drawing-room she said nothing except: 'Emily is coming tomorrow on the 3.5. She sends you her love, Fanny.'

The next day we all went out hunting. The Radletts loved animals, they loved foxes, they risked dreadful beatings in order to unstop their earths, they read and cried and rejoiced over Reynard the Fox, in summer they got up at four to go and see the cubs playing in the pale-green light of the woods; nevertheless, more than anything in the world, they loved hunting. It was in their blood and bones and in my blood and bones, and nothing could eradicate it, though we knew it for a kind of original sin. For three hours that day I forgot everything except my body and my pony's body; the rushing, the scrambling, the splashing, struggling up the hills, sliding down them again, the tugging, the bucketing, the earth, and the sky. I forgot everything, I could hardly have told you my name. That must be the great hold that hunting has over people, especially stupid people; it enforces an absolute concentration, both mental and physical.

After three hours Josh took me home. I was never allowed to stay out long or I got tired and would be sick all night. Josh was out on Uncle Matthew's second horse; at about two o'clock they changed over, and he started home on the lathered, sweating first horse, taking me with him. I came out of my trance, and saw that the day, which had begun with brilliant sunshine, was now cold and dark, threatening rain.

'And where's her ladyship hunting this year?' said Josh, as we started on a ten-mile jog along Merlinford road, a sort of hog's back, more cruelly exposed than any road I have ever known, without a scrap of shelter or windscreen the whole of its fifteen miles. Uncle Matthew would never allow motor cars, either to take us to the meet or to fetch us home; he regarded this habit as despicably soft.

I knew that Josh meant my mother. He had been with my grandfather when she and her sisters were girls, and my mother was his heroine, he adored her.

'She's in Paris, Josh.'

'In Paris – what for?'

'I suppose she likes it.'

'Ho,' said Josh, furiously, and we rode for about half a mile in silence. The rain had begun, a thin cold rain, sweeping over the wide views on each side of the road; we trotted along, the weather in our faces. My back was not strong, and trotting on a side-saddle for any length of time was agony to me. I edged my pony on to the grass, and cantered for a bit, but I knew how much Josh disapproved of this, it was supposed to bring the horses back too hot; walking, on the other hand, chilled them. It had to be jog, jog, back-breaking jog, all the way.

'It's my opinion,' said Josh at last, 'that her ladyship is wasted, downright wasted, every minute of her life that she's not on a 'oss.'

'She's a wonderful rider, isn't she?'

I had had all this before from Josh, many times, and could never have enough of it.

'There's no human being like her, that I've ever seen,' said Josh, hissing through his teeth. 'Hands like velvet, but strong like iron, and her seat – ! Now look at you, jostling about on that saddle, first here, then there – we shall have a sore back to-night, that's one thing certain we shall.'

'Oh, Josh – trotting. And I'm so tired.'

'Never saw her tired. I've seen 'er change 'osses after a ten-mile point, get on to a fresh young five-year-old what hadn't been out for a week – up like a bird – never know you had 'er foot in your hand, pick up the reins in a jiffy, catch up its head, and off over a post and rails and bucking over the ridge and furrow, sitting like a rock. Now his lordship (he meant Uncle Matthew) he can ride, I don't say the contrary, but look how he sends his 'osses home, so darned tired they can't drink their gruel. He can ride all right, but he doesn't study his 'oss. I never knew your mother bring them home like this, she'd know when they'd had enough, and then heads for home and no looking back. Mind you, his lordship's a great big man, I don't say the contrary, rides every bit of sixteen stone, but he has great big 'osses and half kills them, and then who has to stop up with them all night? Me!'

The rain was pouring down by now. An icy trickle was feeling its way past my left shoulder, and my right boot was slowly filling with water, the pain in my back was like a knife. I felt that I couldn't bear another moment of this misery, and yet I knew I must bear another five miles, another forty minutes. Josh gave me scornful looks as my back bent more and more double; I could see that he was wondering how it was that I could be my mother's child.

'Miss Linda,' he said, 'takes after her ladyship something wonderful.'

At last, at last, we were off the Merlinford road, coming down the valley into Alconleigh village, turning up the hill to Alconleigh house, through the lodge gates, up the drive, and into the stable yard. I got stiffly down, gave the pony to one of Josh's stable boys, and stumped away, walking like an old man. I was nearly at the front door before I remembered, with a sudden leap of my heart, that Aunt Emily would have arrived by now, with HIM. It was quite a minute before I could summon up enough courage to open the front door.

Sure enough, standing with their backs to the hall fire, were Aunt Sadie, Aunt Emily, and a small, fair, and apparently young man. My immediate impression was that he did not seem at all like a husband. He looked kind and gentle.

'Here is Fanny,' said my aunts in chorus.

'Darling,' said Aunt Sadie, 'can I introduce Captain Warbeck?'

I shook hands in the abrupt graceless way of little girls of fourteen, and thought that he did not seem at all like a captain either.

'Oh, darling, how wet you are. I suppose the others won't be back for ages – where have you come from?'

'I left them drawing the spinney by the Old Rose.'

Then I remembered, being after all a female in the presence of a male, how dreadful I always looked when I got home from hunting, splashed from head to foot, my bowler all askew, my hair a bird's nest, my stocking a flapping flag, and, muttering something, I made for the back stairs, towards my bath and my rest. After hunting we were kept in bed for at least two hours. Soon Linda returned, even wetter than I had been, and got into bed with me. She, too, had seen the Captain, and agreed that he looked neither like a marrying nor like a military man.

'Can't see him killing Germans with an entrenching tool,' she said, scornfully.

Much as we feared, much as we disapproved of passionately as we sometimes hated Uncle Matthew, he still remained for us a sort of criterion of English man-hood; there seemed something not quite right about any man who greatly differed from him.

'I bet Uncle Matthew gives him rat week,' I said, apprehensive for Aunt Emily's sake.

'Poor Aunt Emily, perhaps he'll make her keep him in the stables,' said Linda with a gust of giggles.

'Still, he looks rather nice to know, and, considering her age, I should think she's lucky to get anybody.'

'I can't wait to see him with Fa.'

However, our expectations of blood and thunder were disappointed, for it was evident at once that Uncle Matthew had taken an enormous fancy to Captain Warbeck. As he never altered his first opinion of people, and as his few favourites could commit nameless crimes without doing wrong in his eyes, Captain Warbeck was, henceforward, on a good wicket with Uncle Matthew.

'He's such a frightfully clever cove, literary you know, you wouldn't believe the things he does. He writes books and criticizes pictures, and whacks hell out of the piano, though the pieces he plays aren't up to much. Still, you can see what it would be like, if he learnt some of the tunes out of the *Country Girl*, for instance. Nothing would be too difficult for him, you can see that.'

At dinner Captain Warbeck sitting next to Aunt Sadie, and Aunt Emily next to Uncle Matthew, were separated from each other, not only by four of us children (Bob was allowed to dine down, as he was going to Eton next half), but also by pools of darkness. The dining-room table was lit by three electric bulbs hanging in a bunch from the ceiling, and screened by a curtain of dark-red jap silk with a gold fringe. One spot of brilliant light was thus cast into the middle of the table, while the diners themselves, and their plates, sat outside it in total gloom. We all, naturally, had our eyes fixed upon the shadowy figure of the fiancé, and found a great deal in his behaviour to interest us. He talked to Aunt Sadie at first about gardens, plants, and flowering shrubs, a topic which was unknown at Alconleigh. The gardener saw to the garden, and that was that. It was quite half a mile from the house, and nobody went near it, except as a little walk sometimes in the summer. It seemed strange that a man who lived in London should know the names, the habits, and the medicinal properties of so many plants. Aunt Sadie politely tried to keep up with him, but could not altogether conceal her ignorance, though she partly veiled it in a mist of absent-mindedness.

'And what is your soil here?' asked Captain Warbeck.

Aunt Sadie came down from the clouds with a happy smile, and said, triumphantly, for here was something she did know, 'Clay.'

'Ah, yes,' said the Captain.

He produced a little jewelled box, took from it an enormous pill, swallowed it, to our amazement, without one sip to help it down, and said, as though to himself, but quite distinctly, 'Then the water here will be madly binding.'

When Logan, the butler, offered him shepherd's pie (the food at Alconleigh was always good and plentiful, but of the homely schoolroom description) he said, again so that one did not quite know whether he meant to be overheard or not, 'No, thank you, no twice-cooked meat. I am a wretched invalid, I must be careful, or I pay.'

Aunt Sadie, who so much disliked hearing about health that people often took her for a Christian Scientist, which, indeed, she might have become had she not disliked hearing about religion even more, took absolutely no notice, but Bob asked with interest, what it was that twice-cooked meat did to one.

'Oh, it imposes a most fearful strain on the juices, you might as well eat leather,' replied Captain Warbeck, faintly, heaping onto his plate the whole of the salad. He said, again in that withdrawn voice:

'Raw lettuce, anti-scorbutic,' and, opening another box of even larger pills, he took two, murmuring, 'Protein.'

'How delicious your bread is,' he said to Aunt Sadie, as though to make up for his rudeness in refusing the twice-cooked meat. 'I'm sure it has the germ.'

'What?' said Aunt Sadie, turning from a whispered confabulation with Logan ('ask Mrs Crabbe if she could quickly make some more salad').

'I was saying that I feel sure your delicious bread is made of stone-ground flour, containing a high proportion of the germ. In my bedroom at home I have a picture of a grain of wheat (magnified, naturally) which shows the germ. As you know, in white bread the germ, with its wonderful health-giving properties, is eliminated – extracted, I should say – and put into chicken food. As a result the human race is becoming enfeebled, while hens grow larger and stronger with every generation.'

'So in the end,' said Linda, listening all agog, unlike Aunt Sadie, who had retired into a cloud of boredom, 'Hens will be Hons and Hons will be Hens. Oh, how I should love to live in a dear little Hon-house.'

'You wouldn't like your work,' said Bob. 'I once saw a hen laying an egg, and she had a most terrible expression on her face.'

'Only about like going to the lav,' said Linda.

'Now, Linda,' said Aunt Sadie, sharply, 'that's quite unnecessary. Get on with your supper and don't talk so much.'

Vague as she was, Aunt Sadie could not always be counted on to ignore everything that was happening around her.

'What were you telling me, Captain Warbeck, something about germs?'

'Oh, not germs – the germ –'

At this point I became aware that, in the shadows at the other end of the table, Uncle Matthew and Aunt Emily were having one of their usual set-tos, and that it concerned me. Whenever Aunt Emily came to Alconleigh these tussles with Uncle Matthew would occur, but, all the same, one could see that he was fond of her. He always liked people who stood up to him, and also he probably saw in her a reflection of Aunt Sadie, whom he adored. Aunt Emily was more positive than Aunt Sadie, she had more character and less beauty, and she was not worn out with childbirth, but they were very much sisters. My mother was utterly different in every respect, but then she, poor thing, was, as Linda would have said, obsessed with sex.

Uncle Matthew and Aunt Emily were now engaged upon an argument we had all heard many times before. It concerned the education of females.

Uncle Matthew: 'I hope poor Fanny's school (the word school pronounced in tones of withering scorn) is doing her all the good you think it is. Certainly she picks up some dreadful expressions there.'

Aunt Emily, calmly, but on the defensive: 'Very likely she does. She also picks up a good deal of education.'

Uncle Matthew: 'Education! I was always led to suppose that no educated person ever spoke of notepaper, and yet I hear poor Fanny asking Sadie for notepaper. What is this education? Fanny talks about mirrors and mantelpieces, handbags and perfume, she takes sugar in her coffee, has a tassel on her umbrella, and I have no doubt that, if she is ever fortunate enough to catch a husband, she will call his father and mother Father and Mother. Will the wonderful education she is getting make up to the unhappy brute for all these endless pinpricks? Fancy hearing one's wife talk about notepaper – the irritation!'

Aunt Emily: 'A lot of men would find it more irritating to have a wife who had never heard of George III. (All the same, Fanny darling, it is called writing-paper you know – don't let's hear any more about the note, please.) That is where you and I come in, you see, Matthew, home influence is admitted to be a most important part of education.'

Uncle Matthew: 'There you are –'

Aunt Emily: 'A most important, but not by any means the most important.'

Uncle Matthew: 'You don't have to go to some awful middle-class establishment to know who George III was. Anyway, who was he, Fanny?'

Alas, I always failed to shine on these occasions. My wits scattered to the four winds by my terror of Uncle Matthew, I said, scarlet in my face:

'He was king. He went mad.'

'Most original, full of information,' said Uncle Matthew, sarcastically. 'Well worth losing every ounce of feminine charm to find that out, I must say. Legs like gateposts from playing hockey, and the worst seat on a horse of any woman I ever knew. Give a horse a sore back as soon as look at it. Linda, you're uneducated, thank God, what have you got to say about George III?'

'Well,' said Linda, her mouth full, 'he was the son of poor Fred and the father of Beau Brummel's fat friend, and he was one of those vacillators you know. "I am his Highness's dog at Kew, pray tell me, sir, whose dog are you?"' she added, inconsequently. 'Oh, how sweet!'

Uncle Matthew shot a look of cruel triumph at Aunt Emily. I saw that I had let down the side and began to cry, inspiring Uncle Matthew to fresh bouts of beastliness.

'It's a lucky thing that Fanny will have £15,000 a year of her own,' he said, 'not to speak of any settlements the Bolter may have picked up in the course of her career. She'll get a husband all right, even if she does talk about lunch, and *en*velope, and put the milk in first. I'm not afraid of that, I only say she'll drive the poor devil to drink when she has hooked him.'

Aunt Emily gave Uncle Matthew a furious frown. She had always tried to conceal from me the fact that I was an heiress, and, indeed, I was one only until such time as my father, hale and hearty and in the prime of life, should marry somebody of an age to bear children. It so happened that, like the Hanoverian family, he cared for women only when they were over forty; after my mother had left him he had embarked upon a succession of middle-aged wives whom even the miracles of modern science were unable to render fruitful. It was also believed, wrongly, by the grown-ups that we children were ignorant of the fact that my mamma was called the Bolter.

'All this,' said Aunt Emily, 'is quite beside the point. Fanny may possibly, in the far future, have a little money of her own (though it is ludicrous to talk of £15,000). Whether she does, or does not, the man she marries may be able to support her – on the other hand, the modern world being what it is, she may have to earn her own living. In any case she will be a more mature, a happier, a more interested and interesting person if she –'

'If she knows that George III was a king and went mad.'

All the same, my aunt was right, and I knew it and she knew it. The Radlett children read enormously by fits and starts in the library at Alconleigh, a good representative nineteenth-century library, which had been made by their grandfather, a most cultivated man. But, while they picked up a great deal of heterogeneous information, and gilded it with their own originality, while they bridged gulfs of ignorance with their charm and high spirits, they never acquired any habit of concentration, they were incapable of solid hard work. One result, in later life, was that they could not stand boredom. Storms and difficulties left them unmoved, but day after day of ordinary existence produced an unbearable torture of ennui, because they completely lacked any form of mental discipline.

As we trailed out of the dining-room after dinner, we heard Captain Warbeck say:

'No port, no, thank you. Such a delicious drink, but I must refuse. It's the acid from port that makes one so delicate now.'

'Ah – you've been a great port drinker, have you?' said Uncle Matthew.

'Oh, not me, I've never touched it. My ancestors –'

Presently, when they joined us in the drawing-room, Aunt Sadie said: 'The children know the news now.'

'I suppose they think it's a great joke,' said Davey Warbeck, 'old people like us being married.'

'Oh, no, of course not,' we said, politely, blushing.

'He's an extraordinary fella,' said Uncle Matthew, 'knows everything. He says those Charles II sugar casters are only a Georgian imitation of Charles II, just fancy, not valuable at all. Tomorrow we'll go round the house and I'll show you all our things and you can tell us what's what. Quite useful to have a fella like you in the family, I must say.'

'That will be very nice,' said Davey, faintly, 'and now I think, if you don't mind, I'll go to bed. Yes, please, early morning tea – so necessary to replace the evaporation of the night.'

He shook hands with us all, and hurried from the room, saying to himself: 'Wooing, so tiring.'

'Davey Warbeck is a Hon,' said Bob as we were all coming down to breakfast next day.

'Yes, he seems a terrific Hon,' said Linda, sleepily.

'No, I mean he's a real one. Look, there's a letter for him, The Hon. David Warbeck. I've looked him up, and it's true.'

Bob's favourite book at this time was Debrett, his nose was never out of it. As a result of his researches he was once heard informing Lucille that *'les origines de la famille Radlett sont perdues dans les brumes de l'antiquité.'*

'He's only a second son, and the eldest has got an heir, so I'm afraid Aunt Emily won't be a lady. And his father's only the second Baron, created 1860, and they only start in 1720, before that it's a female line.' Bob's voice was trailing off. 'Still –' he said.

We heard Davey Warbeck, as he was coming down the stairs, say to Uncle Matthew:

'Oh no, that couldn't be a Reynolds. Prince Hoare, at his very worst, if you're lucky.'

'Pig's thinkers, Davey?' Uncle Matthew lifted the lid of a hot dish.

'Oh, yes please, Matthew, if you mean brains. So digestible.'

'And after breakfast I'm going to show you our collection of minerals in the north passage. I bet you'll agree we've got something worth having there, it's supposed to be the finest collection in England – left me by an old uncle, who spent his life making it. Meanwhile, what'd you think of my eagle?'

'Ah, if that were Chinese now, it would be a treasure. But Jap I'm afraid, not worth the bronze it's cast in. Cooper's Oxford, please, Linda.'

After breakfast we all flocked to the north passage, where there were hundreds of stones in glass-fronted cupboards. Petrified this and fossilized that, blue-john and lapis were the most exciting, large flints which looked as if they had been picked up by the side of the road, the least. Valuable, unique, they were a family legend. 'The minerals in the north passage are good enough for a museum.' We children revered them. Davey looked at them carefully, taking some over to the window and peering into them. Finally, he heaved a great sigh and said:

'What a beautiful collection. I suppose you know they're all diseased?'

'Diseased?'

'Badly, and too far gone for treatment. In a year or two they'll all be dead – you might as well throw the whole lot away.'

Uncle Matthew was delighted.

'Damned fella,' he said, 'nothing's right for him, I never saw such a fella. Even the minerals have got foot-and-mouth, according to him.'

5

The year which followed Aunt Emily's marriage transformed Linda and me from children, young for our ages, into lounging adolescents waiting for love. One result of the marriage was that I now spent nearly all my holidays at Alconleigh. Davey, like all Uncle Matthew's favourites, simply could not see that he was in the least bit frightening, and scouted Aunt Emily's theory that to be too much with him was bad for my nerves.

'You're just a lot of little crybabies,' he said, scornfully, 'if you allow yourselves to be upset by that old cardboard ogre.'

Davey had given up his flat in London and lived with us at Shenley, where, during term-time, he made but little difference to our life, except in so far as a male presence in a female household is always salutary (the curtains, the covers, and Aunt Emily's clothes underwent an enormous change for the better), but, in the holidays, he liked to carry her off, to his own relations or on trips abroad, and I was parked at Alconleigh. Aunt Emily probably felt that, if she had to choose between her husband's wishes and my nervous system, the former should win the day. In spite of her being forty they were, I believe, very much in love; it must have been a perfect bore having me about at all, and it speaks volumes for their characters that never, for one moment, did they allow me to be aware of this. Davey, in fact was, and has been ever since, a perfect stepfather to me, affectionate, understanding, never in any way interfering. He accepted me at once as belonging to Aunt Emily, and never questioned the inevitability of my presence in his household.

By the Christmas holidays Louisa was officially 'out', and going to hunt balls, a source of bitter envy to us, though Linda said scornfully that she did not appear to have many suitors. We were not coming out for another two years – it seemed an eternity, and especially to Linda, who was paralysed by her longing for love, and had no lessons or work to do which could take her mind off it. In fact, she had no other interest now except hunting, even the animals seemed to have lost all charm for her. She and I did nothing on non-hunting days but sit about, too large for our tweed suits, whose hooks and eyes were always popping off at the waist, and play endless games of patience; or we lolled in the Hons' cupboard, and 'measured'. We had a tape-measure and competed as to the largeness of our eyes, the smallness of wrists, ankles, waist and neck, length of legs and fingers, and so on. Linda always won. When we had finished 'measuring' we talked of romance. These were most innocent talks, for to us, at that time, love and marriage were synonymous, we knew that they lasted for ever, to the grave and far, far beyond. Our preoccupation with sin was finished; Bob, back from Eton, had been able to tell us all about Oscar Wilde, and, now that his crime was no longer a mystery, it seemed dull, unromantic, and incomprehensible.

We were, of course, both in love, but with people we had never met; Linda with the Prince of Wales, and I with a fat, red-faced, middle-aged farmer, whom I some-times saw riding through Shenley. These loves were strong, and painfully delicious; they occupied all our thoughts, but I think we half realized that they would be superseded in time by real people. They were to keep the house warm, so to speak, for its eventual occupant. What we never would admit was the possibility of lovers after marriage. We were looking for real love, and that could only come once in a lifetime; it hurried to consecration, and thereafter never wavered. Husbands, we knew, were not always faithful, this we must be prepared for, we must understand and forgive. 'I have been faithful to thee, Cynara, in my fashion' seemed to explain it beautifully. But women – that was different; only the lowest of the sex could love or give themselves more than once. I do not quite know how I reconciled these sentiments with the great hero-worship I still had for my mother, that adulterous doll. I suppose I put her in an entirely different category, in the face that launched a thousand ships class. A few historical characters must be allowed to have belonged to this, but Linda and I were perfectionists where love was concerned and did not ourselves aspire to that kind of fame.

This winter Uncle Matthew had a new tune on his gramophone, called 'Thora'. 'I live in a land of roses,' boomed a deep male voice, 'but dream of a land of snow. Speak, speak, SPEAK to me, Thora'. He played it morning, noon, and night; it suited our mood exactly, and Thora seemed the most poignantly beautiful of names.

Aunt Sadie was giving a ball for Louisa soon after Christmas, and to this we pinned great hopes. True, neither the Prince of Wales nor my farmer was invited, but, as Linda said, you never could tell in the country. Somebody might bring them. The Prince might break down in his motor car, perhaps on his way to Badminton; what could be more natural than that he should while away the time by looking in on the revelry?

'Pray, who is that beautiful young lady?'

'My daughter Louisa, sir.'

'Ah, yes, very charming, but I really meant the one in white taffeta.'

'That is my youngest daughter Linda, Your Royal Highness.'

'Please present her to me.'

They would then whirl away in a waltz so accomplished that the other dancers would stand aside to admire. When they could dance no more they would sit for the rest of the evening absorbed in witty conversation.

The following day an A.D.C., asking for her hand –

'But she is so young!'

'His Royal Highness is prepared to wait a year. He reminds you that Her Majesty the Empress Elizabeth of Austria was married at sixteen. Meanwhile, he sends this jewel.'

A golden casket, a pink and white cushion, a diamond rose.

My daydreams were less exalted, equally improbable, and quite as real to me. I imagined my farmer carrying me away from Alconleigh, like young Lochinvar, on a pillion behind him to the nearest smith, who then declared us man and wife. Linda kindly said that we could have one of the royal farms, but I thought this would be a great bore, and that it would be much more fun to have one of our own.

Meanwhile, preparations for the ball went forward, occupying every single member of the household. Linda's and my dresses, white taffeta with floating panels and embroidered bead belts, were being made by Mrs Josh, whose cottage was besieged at all hours to see how they were getting on. Louisa's came from Reville, it was silver lamé in tiny frills, each frill edged with blue net. Dangling on the left shoulder, and strangely unrelated to the dress, was a large pink silk over-blown rose. Aunt Sadie, shaken out of her accustomed languor, was in a state of exaggerated preoccupation and worry over the whole thing; we had never seen her like this before. For the first time, too, that any of us could remember, she found herself in opposition to Uncle Matthew. It was over the following question: The nearest neighbour to Alconleigh was Lord Merlin; his estate marched with that of my uncle, and his house at Merlinford was about five miles away. Uncle Matthew loathed him, while, as for Lord Merlin, not for nothing was his telegraphic address Neighbourtease. There had, however, been no open breach between them; the fact that they never saw each other meant nothing, for Lord Merlin neither hunted, shot, nor fished, while Uncle Matthew had never in his life been known to eat a meal in anybody else's house. 'Perfectly good food at home,' he would say, and people had long ago stopped asking him. The two men, and indeed their two houses and estates afforded an absolute contrast. Alconleigh was a large, ugly, north-facing, Georgian house, built with only one intention, that of sheltering, when the weather was too bad to be out of doors, a succession of bucolic squires, their wives, their enormous families, their dogs, their horses, their father's relict, and their unmarried sisters. There was no attempt at decoration, at softening the lines, no apology for a façade, it was all as grim and as bare as a barracks, stuck upon the high hillside. Within, the keynote, the theme, was death. Not death of maidens, not death romantically accoutred with urns and weeping willows, cypresses and valedictory odes, but the death of warriors and of animals, stark, real. On the walls halberds and pikes and ancient muskets were arranged in crude patterns with the heads of beasts slaughtered in many lands, with the flags and uniforms of bygone Radletts. Glass-topped cases contained, not miniatures of ladies, but miniatures of the medals of their lords, badges, penholders made of tiger's teeth, the hoof of a favourite horse, telegrams announcing casualties in battle, and commissions written out on parchment scrolls, all lying together in a timeless jumble.

Merlinford nestled in a valley of south-westerly aspect, among orchards and old mellow farmhouses. It was a villa, built at about the same time as Alconleigh, but by a very different architect, and with a very different end in view. It was a house to live in, not to rush out from all day to kill enemies and animals. It was suitable for a bachelor, or a married couple with one, or at most two, beautiful, clever, delicate children. It had Angelica Kauffman ceilings, a Chippendale staircase, fur-niture by Sheraton and Hepplewhite; in the hall there hung two Watteaus; there was no entrenching tool to be seen, nor the head of any animal.

Lord Merlin added continually to its beauties. He was a great collector, and not only Merlinford, but also his houses in London and Rome flowed over with treas-ures. Indeed, a well-known antique dealer from St James's had found it worth his while to open a branch in the little town of Merlinford, to tempt his lordship with choice objects during his morning walk, and was soon followed there by a Bond Street jeweller. Lord Merlin loved jewels; his two black whippets wore diamond necklaces designed for whiter, but not slimmer or more graceful necks than theirs. This was a neighbour-tease of long standing; there was a feeling among the local gentry that it incited the good burghers of Merlinford to dishonesty. The neighbours were doubly teased, when year after year went by and the brilliants still sparkled on those furry necks intact.

His taste was by no means confined to antiques; he was an artist and a musician himself, and the patron of all the young. Modern music streamed perpetually from Merlinford, and he had built a small but exquisite playhouse in the garden, where his astonished neighbours were sometimes invited to attend such puzzlers as Cocteau plays, the opera 'Mahagonny', or the latest Dada extravagances from Paris. As Lord Merlin was a famous practical joker, it was sometimes difficult to know where jokes ended and culture began. I think he was not always perfectly certain himself.

A marble folly on a nearby hill was topped with a gold angel which blew a trumpet every evening at the hour of Lord Merlin's birth (that this happened to be 9.20 p.m., just too late to remind one of the BBC news, was to be a great local grievance in years to come). The folly glittered by day with semi-precious stones, by night a powerful blue beam was trained upon it.

Such a man was bound to become a sort of legend to the bluff Cotswold squires among whom he lived. But, although they could not approve of an existence which left out of account the killing, though by no means the eating, of delicious game, and though they were puzzled beyond words by the aestheticism and the teases, they accepted him without question as one of themselves. Their families had always known his family, and his father, many years ago, had been a most popular M.F.H.; he was no upstart, no new rich, but simply a sport of all that was most normal in English country life. Indeed, the very folly itself, while considered absolutely hideous, was welcomed as a landmark by those lost on their way home from hunting.

The difference between Aunt Sadie and Uncle Matthew was not as to whether Lord Merlin should or should not be asked to the ball (that question did not arise, since all neighbours were automatically invited), but whether he should be asked to bring a house party. Aunt Sadie thought he should. Since her marriage the least wordly of women, she had known the world as a girl, and she knew that Lord Merlin's house party, if he consented to bring one, would have great decorative value. She also knew that, apart from this, the general note of her ball would be utter and unrelieved dowdiness, and she became aware of a longing to look once more upon young women with well-brushed hair, London complexions, and Paris clothes. Uncle Matthew said: 'If we ask that brute Merlin to bring his friends, we shall get a lot of aesthetes, sewers from Oxford, and I wouldn't put it past him to bring some foreigners. I hear he sometimes has Frogs and even Wops to stay with him. I will not have my house filled with Wops.'

In the end, however, as usual, Aunt Sadie had her way, and sat down to write:

Dear Lord Merlin,

We are having a little dance for Louisa, etc . . .

while Uncle Matthew went gloomily off, having said his piece, and put on 'Thora'.

Lord Merlin accepted, and said he would bring a party of twelve people, whose names he would presently submit to Aunt Sadie. Very correct, perfectly normal behaviour. Aunt Sadie was quite agreeably surprised that his letter, when opened, did not contain some clockwork joke to hit her in the eye. The writing-paper did actually have a picture of his house on it, and this she concealed from Uncle Matthew. It was the kind of thing he despised.

A few days later there was another surprise. Lord Merlin wrote another letter, still jokeless, still polite, asking Uncle Matthew, Aunt Sadie and Louisa to dine with him for the Merlinford Cottage Hospital Ball. Uncle Matthew naturally could not be persuaded, but Aunt Sadie and Louisa went. They came back with their eyes popping out of their heads. The house, they said, had been boiling hot, so hot that one never felt cold for a single moment, not even getting out of one's coat in the hall. They had arrived very early, long before anyone else was down, as it was the custom at Alconleigh always to leave a quarter of an hour too soon when motoring, in case there should be a puncture. This gave them the opportunity to have a good look round. The house was full of spring flowers, and smelt wonderful. The hot-houses at Alconleigh were full of spring flowers too, but somehow they never found their way into the house, and certainly would have died of cold if they had. The whippets did wear diamond necklaces, far grander ones than Aunt Sadie's, she said, and she was forced to admit that they looked very beautiful in them. Birds of paradise flew about the house, quite tame, and one of the young men told Louisa that, if she came in the daytime, she would see a flock of multi-coloured pigeons tumbling about like a cloud of confetti in the sky.

'Merlin dyes them every year, and they are dried in the linen cupboard.'

'But isn't that frightfully cruel?' said Louisa, horrified.

'Oh, no, they love it. It makes their husbands and wives look so pretty when they come out.'

'What about their poor eyes?'

'Oh, they soon learn to shut them.'

The house party, when they finally appeared (some of them shockingly late) from their bedrooms, smelt even more delicious than the flowers, and looked even more exotic than the birds of paradise. Everybody had been very nice, very kind to Louisa. She sat between two beautiful young men at dinner, and turned upon them the usual gambit:

'Where do you hunt?'

'We don't,' they said.

'Oh, then why do you wear pink coats?'

'Because we think they are so pretty.'

We all thought this dazzlingly funny, but agreed that Uncle Matthew must never hear of it, or he might easily, even now, forbid the Merlinford party his ball.

After dinner the girls had taken Louisa upstairs. She was rather startled at first to see printed notices in the guest rooms:

OWING TO AN UNIDENTIFIED CORPSE IN THE CISTERN VISITORS ARE REQUESTED NOT TO DRINK THE BATH WATER.

VISITORS ARE REQUESTED NOT TO LET OFF FIREARMS, BLOW BUGLES, SCREAM OR HOOT, BETWEEN THE HOURS OF MIDNIGHT AND 6 A.M.

and, on one bedroom door:

MANGLING DONE HERE

But it was soon explained to her that these were jokes.

The girls had offered to lend her powder and lipstick, but Louisa had not quite dared to accept, for fear Aunt Sadie would notice. She said it made the others look simply too lovely.

As the great day of the Alconleigh ball approached, it became obvious that Aunt Sadie had something on her mind. Everything appeared to be going smoothly, the champagne had arrived, the band, Clifford Essex's third string, had been ordered, and would spend the few hours of its rest in Mrs Craven's cottage. Mrs Crabbe, in conjunction with the Home Farm, Craven, and three women from the village who were coming in to help, was planning a supper to end all suppers. Uncle Matthew had been persuaded to get twenty oil-stoves, with which to emulate the caressing warmth of Merlinford, and the gardener was preparing to transfer to the house every pot-plant that he could lay his hands on. ('You'll be dyeing the White Leghorns next,' said Uncle Matthew, scornfully.)

But, in spite of the fact that the preparations seemed to be going forward without a single hitch, Aunt Sadie's brow was still furrowed with anxiety, because she had collected a large house party of girls and their mammas, but not one single young man. The fact was that those of her own contemporaries who had daughters were glad to bring them, but sons were another matter. Dancing partners, sated with invitations at this time of the year, knew better than to go all the way down to Gloucestershire to a house as yet untried, where they were by no means certain of finding the warmth, the luxury and fine wines which they looked upon as their due, where there was no known female charmer to tempt them, where they had not been offered a mount, and where no mention had been made of a shoot, not even a day with the cocks.

Uncle Matthew had far too much respect for his horses and his pheasants to offer them up to be messed about by any callow unknown boy.

So here was a horrible situation. Ten females, four mothers and six girls, were advancing from various parts of England, to arrive at a household consisting of four more females (not that Linda and I counted, still, we wore skirts and not trousers, and were really too old to be kept all the time in the schoolroom) and only two males, one of whom was not yet in tails.

The telephone now became red-hot, telegrams flew in every direction. Aunt Sadie abandoned all pride, all pretence that things were as they should be, that people were asked for themselves alone, and launched a series of desperate appeals. Mr Wills, the vicar, consented to leave Mrs Wills at home, and dine, *en garçon*, at Alconleigh. It would be the first time they had been separated for forty years. Mrs

Aster, the agent's wife, also made the same sacrifice, and Master Aster, the agent's son, aged not quite seventeen, was hurried off to Oxford to get himself a ready-made dress suit.

Davey Warbeck was ordered to leave Aunt Emily and come. He said he would, but unwillingly, and only after the full extent of the crisis had been divulged. Elderly cousins, and uncles who had been for many years forgotten as ghosts, were recalled from oblivion and urged to materialize. They nearly all refused, some of them quite rudely – they had, nearly all, at one time or another, been so deeply and bitterly insulted by Uncle Matthew that forgiveness was impossible.

At last Uncle Matthew saw that the situation would have to be taken in hand. He did not care two hoots about the ball, he felt no particular responsibility for the amusement of his guests, whom he seemed to regard as an onrushing horde of barbarians who could not be kept out, rather than as a group of delightful friends summoned for mutual entertainment and joyous revelry. But he did care for Aunt Sadie's peace of mind, he could not bear to see her looking so worried, and he decided to take steps. He went up to London and attended the last sitting of the House of Lords before the recess. His journey was entirely fruitful.

'Stromboli, Paddington, Fort William, and Curtley have accepted,' he told Aunt Sadie, with the air of a conjurer producing four wonderful fat rabbits out of one small wine-glass.

'But I had to promise them a shoot – Bob, go and tell Craven I want to see him in the morning.'

By these complicated devices the numbers at the dinner-table would now be even, and Aunt Sadie was infinitely relieved, though inclined to be giggly over Uncle Matthew's rabbits. Lord Stromboli, Lord Fort William, and the Duke of Paddington were old dancing partners of her own; Sir Archibald Curtley, Librarian of the House, was a well-known diner-out in the smart intellectual world, he was over seventy and very arthritic. After dinner, of course, the dance would be another matter. Mr Wills would then be joined by Mrs Wills, Captain Aster by Mrs Aster, Uncle Matthew and Bob could hardly be counted on as partners, while the House of Lords contingent were more likely to head for the bridge table than for the dancing floor.

'I fear it will be sink or swim for the girls,' said Aunt Sadie, dreamily.

In one way, however, it was all to the good. These old boys were Uncle Matthew's own choice, his own friends, and he would probably be polite to them; in any case they would know what he was like before they came. To have filled the house with strange young men would, she knew, have been taking a great risk. Uncle Matthew hated strangers, he hated the young, and he hated the idea of possible suitors for his daughters; Aunt Sadie saw rocks ahead, but this time they had been circumnavigated.

This then is a ball. This is life, what we have been waiting for all these years, here we are and here it is, a ball, actually going on now, actually in progress round us. How extraordinary it feels, such unreality, like a dream. But, alas, so utterly different from what one had imagined and expected; it must be admitted, not a good dream. The men so small and ugly, the women so frowsty, their clothes so messy and their faces so red, the oil-stoves so smelly, and not really very warm, but, above all, the men, either so old or so ugly. And when they ask one to dance (pushed to it, one cannot but suspect, by kind Davey, who is trying to see that we have a good time at our first party), it is not at all like floating away into a delicious cloud, pressed by a manly arm to a manly bosom, but stumble, stumble, kick, kick. They balance, like King Stork, on one leg, while, with the other, they come down, like King Log, on to one's toe. As for witty conversation, it is wonderful if any conversation, even of the most banal and jerky description, lasts through a whole dance and the sitting out. It is mostly: 'Oh, sorry – oh, my fault,' though Linda did get as far as taking one of her partners to see the diseased stones.

We had never learnt to dance, and, for some reason, we had supposed it to be a thing which everybody could do quite easily and naturally. I think Linda realized there and then what it took me years to learn, that the behaviour of civilized man really has nothing to do with nature, that all is artificiality and art more or less perfected.

The evening was saved from being an utter disillusionment by the Merlinford house party. They came immensely late, we had all forgotten about them in fact, but, when they had said how do you do to Aunt Sadie and taken the floor, they seemed at once to give the party a new atmosphere. They flourished and shone with jewels, lovely clothes, brilliant hair and dazzling complexions; when they danced they really did seem to float, except when it was the Charleston, and that, though angular, was so accomplished that it made us gasp with admiration. Their conversation was quite evidently both daring and witty, one could see it ran like a river, splashing, dashing, and glittering in the sun. Linda was entranced by them, and decided then and there that she would become one of these brilliant beings and live in their world, even if it took her a lifetime to accomplish. I did not aspire to this. I saw that they were admirable, but they were far removed from me and my orbit, belonging more to that of my parents; my back had been towards them from that day Aunt Emily had taken me home, and there was no return – nor did I wish for it. All the same, I found them fascinating as a spectacle, and, whether I sat out with Linda or stumped round the room with kind Davey, who, unable to persuade any more young men to take us on, gave us an occasional turn himself, my eyes were glued to them. Davey seemed to know them all quite well, and was evidently great friends with Lord Merlin. When he was not being kind to Linda and me, he attached himself to them, and joined in their accomplished chatter. He even offered to introduce us to them, but, alas, the floating panels of taffeta, which had seemed so original and pretty in Mrs Josh's cottage, looked queerly stiff beside their printed chiffons, so soft and supple; also, our experiences earlier in the evening had made us feel inferior, and we begged him not to.

That night in bed, I thought more than ever of the safe sheltering arms of my Shenley farmer. The next morning Linda told me that she had renounced the Prince of Wales.

'I have come to the conclusion,' she said, 'that Court circles would be rather dull. Lady Dorothy is a lady-in-waiting and look at her.'

6

The ball had a very unexpected sequel. Lord Fort William's mother invited Aunt Sadie and Louisa to stay at their place in Sussex for a hunt ball, and, shortly afterwards, his married sister asked them to a shoot and an Infirmary Ball. During this visit, Lord Fort William proposed to Louisa and was accepted. She came back to Alconleigh a fiancée, to find herself the centre of attention there for the first time since the birth of Linda had put her nose for ever out of joint. This was indeed an excitement, and tremendous chats took place in the Hons' cupboard, both with and without Louisa. She had a nice little diamond ring on her fourth finger, but was not as communicative as we could have wished on the subject of Lord (John now to us, but how could we remember that?) Fort William's lovemaking, retiring, with many blushes, behind the smoke-screen of such things as being too sacred to speak of. He soon appeared again in person, and we were able to observe him as an individual, instead of part, with Lord Stromboli and the Duke of Paddington, of a venerable trinity. Linda pronounced the summing-up. 'Poor old thing, I suppose she likes him, but, I must say, if he was one's dog one would have him put down.' Lord Fort William was thirty-nine, but he certainly looked much more. His hair seemed to be slipping off backwards, like an eiderdown in the night, Linda said, and he had a generally uncared-for middle-aged appearance. Louisa, however, loved him, and was happy for the first time in her life. She had always been more frightened of Uncle Matthew than any of the others, and with good reason; he thought she was a fool and was never at all nice to her, and she was in heaven at the prospect of getting away from Alconleigh for ever.

I think Linda, in spite of the poor old dog and the eiderdown, was really very jealous. She went off for long rides by herself, and spun more and more fantastic daydreams; her longing for love had become an obsession. Two whole years would have to be made away with somehow before she would come out in the world, but oh the days went dragging by. Linda would flop about in the drawing-room, playing (or beginning and then not finishing) endless games of patience, sometimes by herself, sometimes with Jassy, whom she had infected with her own restlessness.

'What's the time, darling?'

'Guess.'

'A quarter to six?'

'Better than that.'

'Six!'

'Not quite so good.'

'Five to?'

'Yes.'

'If this comes out I shall marry the man I love. If this comes out I shall marry at eighteen.'

If this comes out – shuffle – if this comes out – deal. A queen at the bottom of the pack, it can't come out, begin again.

*

Louisa was married in the spring. Her wedding dress, of tulle frills and sprays of orange blossom, was short to the knee and had a train, as was the hideous fashion then. Jassy got very worked up about it.

'So unsuitable.'

'Why, Jassy?'

'To be buried in, I mean. Women are always buried in their wedding dresses, aren't they? Think of your poor old dead legs sticking out.'

'Oh, Jassy, don't be such a ghoul. I'll wrap them up in my train.'

'Not very nice for the undertakers.'

Louisa refused to have bridesmaids. I think she felt that it would be agreeable, for once in her life, to be more looked at than Linda.

'You can't think how stupid you'll look from behind,' Linda said, 'without any. Still, have it your own way. I'm sure we don't want to be guyed up in blue chiffon, I'm only thinking what would be kinder for you.'

On Louisa's birthday John Fort William, an ardent antiquarian, gave her a replica of King Alfred's jewel. Linda, whose disagreeableness at this time knew no bounds, said that it simply looked like a chicken's mess. 'Same shape, same size, same colour. Not my idea of a jewel.'

'I think it's lovely,' said Aunt Sadie, but Linda's words had left their sting all the same.

Aunt Sadie had a canary then, which sang all day, rivalling even Galli-Curci in the pureness and loudness of its trills. Whenever I hear a canary sing so immoderately it recalls that happy visit, the endless flow of wedding presents, unpacking them, arranging them in the ballroom with shrieks of admiration or of horror, the hustle, the bustle, and Uncle Matthew's good temper, which went on, as fine weather sometimes does, day after unbelievable day.

Louisa was to have two houses, one in London, Connaught Square, and one in Scotland. Her dress allowance would be three hundred a year, she would possess a diamond tiara, a pearl necklace, a motor car of her own and a fur cape. In fact, granted that she could bear John Fort William, her lot was an enviable one. He was terribly dull.

The wedding day was fine and balmy, and, when we went in the morning to see how Mrs Wills and Mrs Josh were getting on with the decorations, we found the light little church bunchy with spring flowers. Later, its well-known outlines blurred with a most unaccustomed throng of human beings, it looked quite different. I thought that I personally should have liked better to be married in it when it was so empty and flowery and full of the Holy Ghost.

Neither Linda nor I had ever been to a wedding before, as Aunt Emily, most unfairly we thought at the time, had been married privately in the chapel at Davey's home in the North of England, and we were hardly prepared for the sudden transformation on this day of dear old Louisa, of terribly dull John, into eternal types of Bride and Bridegroom, Heroine and Hero of romance.

From the moment when we left Louisa alone at Alconleigh with Uncle Matthew, to follow us in the Daimler in exactly eleven minutes, the atmosphere became positively dramatic. Louisa, enveloped from head to knee in tulle, sat gingerly on the edge of a chair, while Uncle Matthew, watch in hand, strode up and down the hall. We walked, as we always did, to the church, and arranged ourselves in the family pew at the back of it, from which vantage point we were able to observe with fascination, the unusual appearance of our neighbours, all tricked out in their best. The only person in the whole congregation who looked exactly as usual was Lord Merlin.

Suddenly there was a stir. John and his best man, Lord Stromboli, appearing like two jack-in-the-box from nowhere, stood beside the altar steps. In their morning coats, their hair heavily brilliantined, they looked quite glamorous, but we hardly had time to notice this fact before Mrs Wills struck up 'Here comes the Bride', with all the stops out, and Louisa, her veil over her face, was being dragged up the aisle at double quick time by Uncle Matthew. At this moment I think Linda would gladly have changed places with Louisa, even at the cost – the heavy cost – of being happy for ever after with John Fort William. In what seemed no time at all Louisa was being dragged down the aisle again by John, with her veil back, while Mrs Wills nearly broke the windows, so loud and triumphant was her 'Wedding March'.

Everything had gone like clockwork, and there was only one small incident. Davey slipped out of the family pew almost unobserved, in the middle of 'As pants the hart' (Louisa's favourite hymn) and went straight to London, making one of the wedding cars take him to Merlinford station. That evening he telephoned to say that he had twisted his tonsil, singing, and had thought it better to go imme- diately to Sir Andrew Macpherson, the nose, throat, and ear man, who was keeping him in bed for a week. The most extraordinary accidents always seemed to overtake poor Davey.

When Louisa had gone away and the wedding guests had left Alconleigh, a sense of flatness descended upon the house, as always happens on these occasions. Linda then became plunged into such despairing gloom that even Aunt Sadie was alarmed. Linda told me afterwards that she thought a great deal about killing herself, and would most likely have done so had the material difficulties not been so great.

'You know what it is,' she said, 'trying to kill rabbits. Well, think of *oneself*!'

Two years seemed an absolute eternity, not worth ploughing through even with the prospect (which she never doubted, just as a religious person does not doubt the existence of heaven) of blissful love at the end of it. Of course, this was the time when Linda should have been made to work, as I was, all day and hard, with no time for silly dreaming except the few minutes before one went to sleep at night. I think Aunt Sadie dimly perceived this fact, she urged her to learn cooking, to occupy herself in the garden, to be prepared for confirmation. Linda furiously refused, nor would she do jobs in the village, nor help Aunt Sadie in the hundred and one chores which fall to the lot of a country squire's wife. She was, in fact, and Uncle Matthew told her so countless times every day, glaring at her with angry blue eyes, thoroughly bloody-minded.

Lord Merlin came to her rescue. He had taken a fancy to her at Louisa's wed- ding, and asked Aunt Sadie to bring her over to Merlinford some time. A few days later he rang up. Uncle Matthew answered the telephone, and shouted to Aunt Sadie, without taking his mouth away from the receiver:

'That hog Merlin wants to speak to you.'

Lord Merlin, who must have heard, was quite unmoved by this. He was an eccentric himself, and had a fellow feeling for the idiosyncrasies of others. Poor

Aunt Sadie, however, was very much flustered, and, as a result, she accepted an invitation which she would otherwise most probably have refused, to take Linda over to Merlinford for luncheon.

Lord Merlin seemed to become immediately aware of Linda's state of mind, was really shocked to discover that she was doing no lessons at all, and did what he could to provide some interests for her. He showed her his pictures, explained them to her, talked at length about art and literature, and gave her books to read. He let fall the suggestion, which was taken up by Aunt Sadie, that she and Linda should attend a course of lectures in Oxford, and he also mentioned that the Shakespeare Festival was now in progress at Stratford-on-Avon.

Outings of this kind, which Aunt Sadie herself very much enjoyed, soon became a regular feature of life at Alconleigh. Uncle Matthew scoffed a bit, but never interfered with anything Aunt Sadie wanted to do; besides, it was not so much education that he dreaded for his daughters, as the vulgarizing effect that a boarding-school might have upon them. As for governesses, they had been tried, but none had ever been able to endure for more than a few days the terror of Uncle Matthew's grinding dentures, the piercing, furious blue flash of his eyes, the stock whips cracking under their bedroom windows at dawn. Their nerves, they said, and made for the station, often before they had had time to unpack enormous trunks, heavy as though full of stones, by which they were always accompanied.

Uncle Matthew went with Aunt Sadie and Linda on one occasion to a Shakespeare play, *Romeo and Juliet*. It was not a success. He cried copiously, and went into a furious rage because it ended badly. 'All the fault of that damned padre,' he kept saying on the way home, still wiping his eyes. 'That fella, what's 'is name, Romeo, might have known a blasted papist would mess up the whole thing. Silly old fool of a nurse too, I bet she was an R.C., dismal old bitch.'

So Linda's life, instead of being on one flat level plain of tedium, was now, to some extent, filled with outside interests. She perceived that the world she wanted to be in, the witty, sparkling world of Lord Merlin and his friends, was interested in things of the mind, and that she would be able to shine in it only if she became in some sort educated. The futile games of patience were abandoned, and she sat all day hunched up in a corner of the library, reading until her eyes gave out. She often rode over to Merlinford, and, unbeknownst to her parents, who never would have allowed her to go there, or indeed anywhere, alone, left Josh in the stable yard where he had congenial friends, and chatted for hours with Lord Merlin on all sorts of subjects. He knew that she had an intensely romantic character, he foresaw much trouble ahead, and he continually urged upon her the necessity for an intellectual background.

7

What could possibly have induced Linda to marry Anthony Kroesig? During the nine years of their life together people asked this question with irritating regularity, almost every time their names were mentioned. What was she after, surely she

could never possibly have been in love with him, what was the idea, how could it
have happened? He was admittedly very rich, but so were others and surely the
fascinating Linda had only to choose? The answer was, of course, that, quite simply, she was in love with him. Linda was far too romantic to marry without love
and indeed I, who was present at their first meeting and during most of their courtship, always understood why it had happened. Tony, in those days, and to
unsophisticated country like us, seemed a glorious and glamorous creature. When
we first saw him, at Linda's and my coming-out ball, he was in his last year at
Oxford, a member of Bullingdon, a splendid young man with a Rolls-Royce, plenty
of beautiful horses, exquisite clothes, and large luxurious rooms, where he entertained on a lavish scale. In person he was tall and fair, on the heavy side, but with
a well-proportioned figure; he had already a faint touch of pomposity, a thing which
Linda had never come across before, and which she found not unattractive. She
took him, in short, at his own valuation.

What immediately gave him great prestige in her eyes was that he came to the
ball with Lord Merlin. It was really most unlucky, especially as it happened that he
had only been asked at the eleventh hour, as a stopgap.

Linda's ball was not nearly such a fiasco as Louisa's had been. Louisa, a married
London lady now, produced a lot of young men for Aunt Sadie's house party, dull,
fair Scotch boys mostly, with nice manners; nothing to which Uncle Matthew could
possibly take exception. They got on quite well with the various dull dark girls
invited by Aunt Sadie, and the house party seemed to 'go' very nicely, though Linda
had her head in the air, saying they were all too impossibly dreary for words. Uncle
Matthew had been implored by Aunt Sadie for weeks past to be kind to the young
and not to shout at anybody, and he was quite subdued, almost pathetic in his wish
to please, creeping about as though there were an invalid upstairs and straw in the
street.

Davey and Aunt Emily were staying in the house to see me come out (Aunt
Sadie had offered to bring me out with Linda and give us a London season together,
an offer which was most gratefully accepted by Aunt Emily) and Davey constituted
himself a sort of bodyguard to Uncle Matthew, hoping to stand as much as possible between him and the more unbearable forms of irritation.

'I'll be simply wonderful to everybody, but I won't have the sewers in my business-
room, that's all,' Uncle Matthew had said, after one of Aunt Sadie's prolonged
exhortations, and, indeed, spent most of the week-end (the ball was on a Friday
and the house party stayed on until Monday) locked into it, playing '1812' and the
'Haunted Ballroom' on the gramophone. He was rather off the human voice this
year.

'What a pity,' said Linda, as we struggled into our ball dresses (proper London
ones this time, with no floating panels), 'that we are dressing up like this, and looking so pretty, and all for those terrible productions of Louisa's. Waste, I call it.'

'You never know in the country,' I said, 'somebody may bring the Prince of
Wales.'

Linda shot me a furious look under her eyelashes.

'Actually,' she said, 'I am pinning great hopes on Lord Merlin's party. I'm sure
he'll bring some really interesting people.'

Lord Merlin's party arrived, as before, very late, and in very high spirits. Linda immediately noticed a large, blond young man in a beautiful pink coat. He was dancing with a girl who often stayed at Merlinford called Baby Fairweather, and she introduced him to Linda. He asked her to dance the next, and she abandoned one of Louisa's Scotch boys, to whom she had promised it, and strutted off with him in a quick one-step. Linda and I had both been having dancing lessons, and, if we did not exactly float round the room, our progress was by no means so embarrassing as it had been before.

Tony was in a happy mood, induced by Lord Merlin's excellent brandy, and Linda was pleased to find how well and easily she was getting on with this member of the Merlinford set. Everything she said seemed to make him laugh; presently they went to sit out, she chattered away, and Tony roared with laughter. This was the royal road to Linda's good books; she liked people who laughed easily more than anything; it naturally did not occur to her that Tony was a bit drunk. They sat out the next dance together. This was immediately noticed by Uncle Matthew, who began to walk up and down in front of them, giving them furious looks, until Davey, observing this danger signal, came up and hurried him away, saying that one of the oil-stoves in the hall was smoking.

'Who is that sewer with Linda?'

'Kroesig, Governor of the Bank of England, you know; his son.'

'Good God, I never expected to harbour a full-blooded Hun in this house – who on earth asked him?'

'Now, Matthew dear, don't get excited. The Kroesigs aren't Huns, they've been over here for generations, they are a very highly respected family of English bankers.'

'Once a Hun always a Hun,' said Uncle Matthew, 'and I'm not too set on bankers myself. Besides, the fella must be a gate-crasher.'

'No, he's not. He came with Merlin.'

'I knew that bloody Merlin would start bringing foreigners here sooner or later. I always said he would, but I didn't think even he would land one with a German.'

'Don't you think it's time somebody took some champagne to the band?' said Davey.

But Uncle Matthew stumped down to the boiler-room, where he had a long soothing talk with Timb, the odd man, about coke.

Tony, meanwhile, thought Linda ravishingly pretty, and great fun, which indeed she was. He told her so, and danced with her again and again, until Lord Merlin, quite as much put out as Uncle Matthew by what was happening, firmly and very early took his party home.

'See you at the meet tomorrow,' said Tony, winding a white scarf round his neck.

Linda was silent and preoccupied for the rest of the evening.

'You're not to go hunting, Linda,' said Aunt Sadie, the next day, when Linda came downstairs in her riding-habit, 'it's too rude, you must stay and look after your guests. You can't leave them like that.'

'Darling, darling Mummy,' said Linda, 'the meet's at Cock's Barn, and you know how one can't resist. And Flora hasn't been out for a week, she'll go mad. Be a love and take them to see the Roman villa or something, and I swear to come back early. And they've got Fanny and Louisa after all.'

It was this unlucky hunt that clinched matters as far as Linda was concerned. The first person she saw at the meet was Tony, on a splendid chestnut horse. Linda herself was always beautifully mounted, Uncle Matthew was proud of her horsemanship, and had given her two pretty, lively little horses. They found at once, and there was a short sharp run, during which Linda and Tony, both in a somewhat showing-off mood, rode side by side over the stone walls. Presently, on a village green, they checked. One or two bounds put up a hare, which lost its head, jumped into a duckpond, and began to swim about in a hopeless sort of way. Linda's eyes filled with tears.

'Oh, the poor hare!'

Tony got off his horse, and plunged into the pond. He rescued the hare, waded out again, his fine white breeches covered with green muck, and put it, wet and gasping, into Linda's lap. It was the one romantic gesture of his life.

At the end of the day Linda left the hounds to take a short cut home across country. Tony opened a gate for her, took off his hat, and said:

'You are a most beautiful rider, you know. Good night, when I'm back in Oxford I'll ring you up.'

When Linda got home she rushed me off to the Hons' cupboard and told me all this. She was in love.

Given Linda's frame of mind during the past two endless years, she was obviously destined to fall in love with the first young man who came along. It could hardly have been otherwise; she need not, however, have married him. This was made inevitable by the behaviour of Uncle Matthew. Most unfortunately Lord Merlin, the one person who might perhaps have been able to make Linda see that Tony was not all she thought him, went to Rome the week after the ball, and remained abroad for a year.

Tony went back to Oxford when he left Merlinford, and Linda sat about waiting, waiting, waiting for the telephone bell. Patience again. If this comes out he is thinking of me now this very minute – if this comes out he'll ring up tomorrow – if this comes out he'll be at the meet. But Tony hunted with the Bicester, and never appeared on our side of the country. Three weeks passed, and Linda began to feel in despair. Then one evening, after dinner, the telephone bell rang; by a lucky chance Uncle Matthew had gone down to the stables to see Josh about a horse that had colic, the business-room was empty, and Linda answered the telephone herself. It was Tony. Her heart was choking her, she could scarcely speak.

'Hullo, is that Linda? It's Tony Kroesig here. Will you come to lunch next Thursday?'

'Oh! But I should never be allowed to.'

'Oh, rot,' very impatiently, 'several other girls are coming down from London – bring your cousin if you like.'

'All right, that will be lovely.'

'See you then – about one – 7 King Edward Street, I expect you know the rooms. Altringham had them when he was up.'

Linda came away from the telephone trembling, and whispered for me to come quick to the Hons' cupboard. We were absolutely forbidden to see young men at any hour unchaperoned, and other girls did not count as chaperons. We knew quite well, though such a remote eventuality had never even been mooted at

Alconleigh, that we would not be allowed to have luncheon with a young man in his lodgings with any chaperon at all, short of Aunt Sadie herself. The Alconleigh standards of chaperonage were medieval; they did not vary in the slightest degree from those applied to Uncle Matthew's sister, and to Aunt Sadie in youth. The principle was that one never saw any young man alone, under any circumstances, until one was engaged to him. The only people who could be counted on to enforce this rule were one's mother or one's aunts, therefore one must not be allowed beyond the reach of their ever-watchful eyes. The argument, often put forward by Linda, that young men were not very likely to propose to girls they hardly knew, was brushed aside as nonsense. Uncle Matthew had proposed, had he not? to Aunt Sadie, the very first time he ever saw her, by the cage of a two-headed nightingale at an Exhibition at the White City. 'They respect you all the more.' It never seemed to dawn upon the Alconleighs that respect is not an attitude of mind indulged in by modern young men, who look for other qualities in their wives than respectability. Aunt Emily, under the enlightened influence of Davey, was far more reasonable, but, of course, when staying with the Radletts, I had to obey the same rules.

In the Hons' cupboard we talked and talked. There was no question in our minds but that we must go, not to do so would be death for Linda, she would never get over it. But how to escape? There was only one way that we could devise, and it was full of risk. A very dull girl of exactly our age called Lavender Davis lived with her very dull parents about five miles away, and once in a blue moon, Linda, complaining vociferously, was sent over to luncheon with them, driving herself in Aunt Sadie's little car. We must pretend that we were going to do that, hoping that Aunt Sadie would not see Mrs Davis, that pillar of the Women's Institute, for months and months, hoping also that Perkins, the chauffeur, would not remark on the fact that we had driven sixty miles and not ten.

As we were going upstairs to bed, Linda said to Aunt Sadie, in what she hoped was an offhand voice, but one which seemed to me vibrant with guilt:

'That was Lavender ringing up. She wants Fanny and me to lunch there on Thursday.'

'Oh, duck,' said Aunt Sadie, 'you can't have my car, I'm afraid.'

Linda became very white, and leant against the wall.

'Oh, please, Mummy, oh please do let me, I do so terribly want to go.'

'To the Davises,' said Aunt Sadie in astonishment, 'but, darling, last time you said you'd never go again as long as you lived – great haunches of cod you said, don't you remember? Anyhow, I'm sure they'll have you another day, you know.'

'Oh, Mummy, you don't understand. The whole point is, a man is coming who brought up a baby badger, and I do so want to meet him.'

It was known to be one of Linda's greatest ambitions, to bring up a baby badger.

'Yes, I see. Well, couldn't you ride over?'

'Staggers and ringworm,' said Linda, her large blue eyes slowly filling with tears.

'What did you say, darling?'

'In their stables – staggers and ringworm. You wouldn't want me to expose Flora to that.'

'Are you sure? Their horses always look so wonderful.'

'Ask Josh.'

'Well, I'll see. Perhaps I can borrow Fa's Morris, and if not, perhaps Perkins can take me in the Daimler. It's a meeting I must go to, though.'

'Oh, you are kind, you are kind. Oh, do try. I do so long for a badger.'

'If you go to London for the season you'll be far too busy to think of a badger. Good night then, ducks.'

'We must get hold of some powder.'

'And rouge.'

These commodities were utterly forbidden by Uncle Matthew, who liked to see female complexions in a state of nature, and often pronounced that paint was for whores and not for his daughters.

'I once read in a book that you can use geranium juice for rouge.'

'Geraniums aren't out at this time of year, silly.'

'We can blue our eyelids out of Jassy's paint-box.'

'And sleep in curlers.'

'I'll get the verbena soap out of Mummy's bathroom. If we let it melt in the bath, and soak for hours in it, we shall smell delicious.'

'I thought you loathed Lavender Davis.'

'Oh, shut up, Jassy.'

'Last time you went you said she was a horrible Counter-Hon, and you would like to bash in her silly face with the Hons' mallet.'

'I never said so. Don't invent lies.'

'Why have you got your London suit on for Lavender Davis?'

'Do go away, Matt.'

'Why are you starting already, you'll be hours too early.'

'We're going to see the badger before luncheon.'

'How red your face is, Linda. Oh, oh you do look so funny!'

'If you don't shut up and go away, Jassy, I swear I'll put your newt back in the pond.'

Persecution, however, continued until we were in the car and out of the garage yard.

'Why don't you bring Lavender back for a nice long cosy visit?' was Jassy's parting shot.

'Not very Honnish of them,' said Linda, 'do you think they can possibly have guessed?'

We left our car in the Clarendon yard, and, as we were very early, having allowed half an hour in case of two punctures, we made for Elliston & Cavell's ladies' room, and gazed at ourselves, with a tiny feeling of uncertainty, in the looking-glasses there. Our cheeks had round scarlet patches, our lips were the same colour, but only at the edges, inside it had already worn off, and our eyelids were blue, all out of Jassy's paint-box. Our noses were white, Nanny having produced some powder with which, years ago, she used to dust Robin's bottom. In short, we looked like a couple of Dutch dolls.

'We must keep our ends up,' said Linda, uncertainly.

'Oh, dear,' I said, 'the thing about me is, I always feel so much happier with my end down.'

We gazed and gazed, hoping thus, in some magical way, to make ourselves feel less peculiar. Presently we did a little work with damp handkerchiefs, and toned our faces down a bit. We then sallied forth into the street, looking at ourselves in every shop window that we passed. (I have often noticed that when women look at themselves in every reflection, and take furtive peeps into their hand looking-glasses, it is hardly ever, as is generally supposed, from vanity, but much more often from a feeling that all is not quite as it should be.)

Now that we had actually achieved our objective, we were beginning to feel horribly nervous, not only wicked, guilty and frightened, but also filled with social terrors. I think we would both gladly have got back into the car and made for home.

On the stroke of one o'clock we arrived in Tony's room. He was alone, but evidently a large party was expected, the table, a square one with a coarse white linen cloth, seemed to have a great many places. We refused sherry and cigarettes, and an awkward silence fell.

'Been hunting at all?' he asked Linda.

'Oh, yes, we were out yesterday.'

'Good day?'

'Yes, very. We found at once, and had a five-mile point and then –' Linda suddenly remembered that Lord Merlin had once said to her: 'Hunt as much as you like, but never talk about it, it's the most boring subject in the world.'

'But that's marvellous, a five-mile point. I must come out with the Heythrop again soon, they are doing awfully well this season, I hear. We had a good day yesterday, too.'

He embarked on a detailed account of every minute of it, where they found, where they ran to, how his first horse had gone lame, how, luckily, he had then come upon his second horse, and so on. I saw just what Lord Merlin meant. Linda, however, hung upon his words with breathless interest.

At last noises were heard in the street, and he went to the window.

'Good,' he said, 'here are the others.'

The others had come down from London in a huge Daimler, and poured, chattering, into the room. Four pretty girls and a young man. Presently some undergraduates appeared, and completed the party. It was not really very enjoyable from our point of view, they all knew each other too well. They gossiped away, roared with laughter at private jokes, and showed off; still, we felt that this was Life, and would have been quite happy just looking on had it not been for that ghastly feeling of guilt, which was now beginning to give us a pain rather like indigestion. Linda turned quite pale every time the door opened, I think she really felt that Uncle Matthew might appear at any moment, cracking a whip. As soon as we decently could, which was not very soon, because nobody moved from the table until after Tom had struck four, we said good-bye, and fled for home.

The miserable Matt and Jassy were swinging on the garage gate.

'So how was Lavender? Did she roar at your eyelids? Better go and wash before Fa sees you. You have been hours. Was it cod? Did you see the the badger?'

Linda burst into tears.

'Leave me alone, you horrible Counter-Hons,' she cried, and rushed upstairs to her bedroom.

Love had increased threefold in one short day.

*

On Saturday the blow fell.

'Linda and Fanny, Fa wants you in the business-room. And sooner you than me by the look of him,' said Jassy, meeting us in the drive as we came in from hunting. Our hearts plunged into our boots. We looked at each other with apprehension.

'Better get it over,' said Linda, and we hurried to the business-room, where we saw at once that the worst had occurred.

Aunt Sadie, looking unhappy, and Uncle Matthew, grinding his teeth, confronted us with our crime. The room was full of blue lightning flashing from his eyes, and Jove's thunder was not more awful than what he now roared at us:

'Do you realize,' he said, 'that, if you were married women, your husbands could divorce you for doing this?'

Linda began to say no they couldn't. She knew the laws of divorce from having read the whole of the Russell case off newspapers with which the fires in the spare bedrooms were laid.

'Don't interrupt your father,' said Aunt Sadie, with a warning look.

Uncle Matthew, however, did not even notice. He was in the full flood and violence of his storm.

'Now we know you can't be trusted to behave yourselves, we shall have to take certain steps. Fanny can go straight home tomorrow, and I never want you here again, do you understand? Emily will have to control you in future, if she can, but you'll go the same way as your mother, sure as eggs is eggs. As for you, miss, there's no more question of a London season now – we shall have to watch you in future every minute of the day – not very agreeable, to have a child one can't trust – and there would be too many opportunities in London for slipping off. You can stew in your own juice here. And no more hunting this year. You're damned lucky not to be thrashed; most fathers would give you a good hiding, do you hear? Now you can both go to bed, and you're not to speak to each other before Fanny leaves. I'm sending her over in the car tomorrow.'

It was months before we knew how they found out. It seemed like magic, but the explanation was simple. Somebody had left a scarf in Tony Kroesig's rooms, and he had rung up to ask whether it belonged to either of us.

8

As always, Uncle Matthew's bark was worse than his bite, though, while it lasted, it was the most terrible row within living memory at Alconleigh. I was sent back to Aunt Emily the next day, Linda waving and crying out of her bedroom window: 'Oh, you *are* lucky, not to be me' (most unlike her, her usual cry being 'Isn't it lovely to be lovely *me*'); and she was stopped from hunting once or twice. Then relaxation began, the thin end of the wedge, and gradually things returned to normal, though it was reckoned in the family that Uncle Matthew had got through a pair of dentures in record time.

Plans for the London season went on being made, and went on including me. I heard afterwards that both Davey and John Fort William took it upon themselves to tell Aunt Sadie and Uncle Matthew (especially Uncle Matthew) that, according to modern ideas, what we had done was absolutely normal, though, of course, they were obliged to own that it was very wrong of us to have told so many and such shameless lies.

We both said we were very sorry, and promised faithfully that we would never act in such an underhand way again, but always ask Aunt Sadie if there was something we specially wanted to do.

'Only then, of course, it will always be no,' as Linda said, giving me a hopeless look.

Aunt Sadie took a furnished house for the summer near Belgrave Square. It was a house with so little character that I can remember absolutely nothing about it, except that my bedroom had a view over chimney-pots, and that on hot summer evenings I used to sit and watch the swallows, always in pairs, and wish sentimentally that I too could be a pair with somebody.

We really had great fun, although I don't think it was dancing that we enjoyed so much as the fact of being grown up and in London. At the dances the great bar of enjoyment was what Linda called the chaps. They were terribly dull, all on the lines of the ones Louisa had brought to Alconleigh; Linda, still in her dream of love for Tony, could not distinguish between them, and never even knew their names. I looked about hopefully for a possible life-partner, but, though I honestly tried to see the best in them, nothing remotely approximating to my requirements turned up.

Tony was at Oxford for his last term, and did not come to London until the end of the season.

We were chaperoned, as was to be expected, with Victorian severity. Aunt Sadie or Uncle Matthew literally never let us out of the sight of one or the other; as Aunt Sadie liked to rest in the afternoon, Uncle Matthew would solemnly take us off to the House of Lords, park us in the Peeresses' Gallery, and take his own forty winks on a back bench opposite. When he was awake in the House, which was not often, he was a perfect nuisance to the Whips, never voting with the same party twice running; nor were the workings of his mind too easy to follow. He voted, for instance, in favour of steel traps, of blood sports, and of steeplechasing, but against vivisection and the exporting of old horses to Belgium. No doubt he had his reasons, as Aunt Sadie would remark, with finality, when we commented on this inconsistency. I rather liked those drowsy afternoons in the dark Gothic chamber, fascinated by the mutterings and antics that went on the whole time, and besides, the occasional speech one was able to hear was generally rather interesting. Linda liked it too, she was far away, thinking her own thoughts. Uncle Matthew would wake up at tea-time, conduct us to the Peer's dining-room for tea and buttered buns, and then take us home to rest and dress for the dance.

Saturday to Monday was spent by the Radlett family at Alconleigh; they rolled down in their huge, rather sick-making Daimler; and by me at Shenley, where Aunt Emily and Davey were always longing to hear every detail of our week.

Clothes were probably our chief preoccupation at this time. Once Linda had been to a few dress shows, and got her eye in, she had all hers made by Mrs Josh, and, somehow, they had a sort of originality and prettiness that I never achieved, although mine, which were bought at expensive shops, cost about five times as much. This showed, said Davey, who used to come and see us whenever he was in London, that either you get your clothes in Paris or it is a toss-up. Linda had one particularly ravishing ball-dress made of masses of pale grey tulle down to her feet. Most of the dresses were still short that summer, and Linda made a sensation whenever she appeared in her yards of tulle, very much disapproved of by Uncle Matthew, on the grounds that he had known three women burnt to death in tulle ball-dresses.

She was wearing this dress when Tony proposed to her in the Berkeley Square summer-house at six o'clock on a fine July morning. He had been down from Oxford about a fortnight, and it was soon obvious that he had eyes for nobody but her. He went to all the same dances, and, after stumping round with a few other girls, would take Linda to supper, and thereafter spend the evening glued to her side. Aunt Sadie seemed to notice nothing, but to the whole rest of the débutante world the outcome was a foregone conclusion, the only question being when and where Tony would propose.

The ball from which they had emerged (it was in a lovely old house on the east side of Berkeley Square, since demolished) was only just alive, the band sleepily thump-thumped its tunes through the nearly empty rooms; poor Aunt Sadie sat on a little gold chair trying to keep her eyes open and passionately longing for bed, with me beside her, dead tired and very cold, my partners all gone home. It was broad daylight. Linda had been away for hours, nobody seemed to have set eyes on her since supper-time, and Aunt Sadie, though dominated by her fearful sleepiness, was apprehensive, and rather angry. She was beginning to wonder whether Linda had not committed the unforgivable sin, and gone off to a night club.

Suddenly the band perked up and began to play 'John Peel' as a prelude to 'God Save the King'; Linda, in a grey cloud, was galloping up and down the room with Tony; one look at her face told all. We climbed into a taxi behind Aunt Sadie (she never would keep a chauffeur up at night), we splashed away past the great hoses that were washing the streets, we climbed the stairs to our rooms, without a word being spoken by any of us. A thin oblique sunlight was striking the chimney-pots as I opened my window. I was too tired to think, I fell into bed.

We were allowed to be late after dances, though Aunt Sadie was always up and seeing to the household arrangements by nine o'clock. As Linda came sleepily downstairs the next morning, Uncle Matthew shouted furiously at her from the hall:

'That bloody Hun Kroesig has just telephoned, he wanted to speak to you. I told him to get the hell out of it. I don't want you mixed up with any Germans, do you understand?'

'Well, I am mixed up,' said Linda, in an offhand, would-be casual voice, 'as it happens I'm engaged to him.'

At this point Aunt Sadie dashed out of her little morning-room on the ground floor, took Uncle Matthew by the arm, and led him away. Linda locked herself into her bedroom and cried for an hour, while Jassy, Matt, Robin, and I speculated upon further developments in the nursery.

There was a great deal of opposition to the engagement, not only from Uncle Matthew, who was beside himself with disappointment and disgust at Linda's choice, but also quite as much from Sir Leicester Kroesig. He did not want Tony to marry at all until he was well settled in his career in the City, and then he had hoped for an alliance with one of the other big banking families. He despised the landed gentry, whom he regarded as feckless, finished and done with in the modern world, he also knew that the vast, the enviable capital sums which such families undoubtedly still possessed, and of which they made so foolishly little use, were always entailed upon the eldest son, and that very small provision, if any, was made for the dowries of daughters. Sir Leicester and Uncle Matthew met, disliked each other on sight, and were at one in their determination to stop the marriage. Tony was sent off to America, to work in a bank house in New York, and poor Linda, the season now being at an end, was taken home to eat her heart out at Alconleigh.

'Oh, Jassy, darling Jassy, lend me your running-away money to go to New York with.'

'No, Linda. I've saved and scraped for five years, ever since I was seven, I simply can't begin all over again now. Besides I shall want it for when I run away myself.'

'But, darling, I'll give it you back, Tony will, when we're married.'

'I know men,' said Jassy, darkly.

She was adamant.

'If only Lord Merlin were here,' Linda wailed. 'He would help me.' But Lord Merlin was still in Rome.

She had 15s. 6d. in the world, and was obliged to content herself with writing immense screeds to Tony every day. She carried about in her pocket a quantity of short, dull letters in an immature handwriting and with a New York postmark.

After a few months Tony came back, and told his father that he could not settle down to business or banking or think about his future career at all, until the date for his marriage had been fixed. This was quite the proper line to take with Sir Leicester. Anything that interfered with making money must be regulated at once. If Tony, who was a sensible fellow, and had never given his father one moment's anxiety in his life, assured him that he could be serious about banking only after marriage, then married he must be, the sooner the better. Sir Leicester explained at length what he considered the disadvantages of the union. Tony agreed in principle, but said that Linda was young, intelligent, energetic, that he had great influence with her, and did not doubt that she could be made into a tremendous asset. Sir Leicester finally gave his consent.

'It might have been worse,' he said, 'after all, she is a lady.'

Lady Kroesig opened negotiations with Aunt Sadie. As Linda had virtually worked herself into a decline, and was poisoning the lives of all around her by her intense disagreeableness, Aunt Sadie, secretly much relieved by the turn things had taken, persuaded Uncle Matthew that the marriage, though by no means ideal, was inevitable, and that, if he did not wish to alienate for ever his favourite child, he had better put a good face on it.

'I suppose it might have been worse,' Uncle Matthew said doubtfully, 'at least the fella's not a Roman Catholic.'

9

The engagement was duly announced in *The Times*. The Kroesigs now invited the Alconleighs to spend a Saturday to Monday at their house near Guildford. Lady Kroesig, in her letter to Aunt Sadie, called it a week-end, and said it would be nice to get to know each other better. Uncle Matthew flew into a furious temper. It was one of his idiosyncrasies that, not only did he never stay in other people's houses (except, very occasionally, with relations), but he regarded it as a positive insult that he should be invited to do so. He despised the expression 'week-end', and gave a sarcastic snort at the idea that it would be nice to know the Kroesigs better. When Aunt Sadie had calmed him down a bit, she put forward the suggestion that the Kroesig family, father, mother, daughter Marjorie, and Tony, should be asked instead if they would spend Saturday to Monday at Alconleigh. Poor Uncle Matthew, having swallowed the great evil of Linda's engagement, had, to do him justice, resolved to put the best face he could on it, and had no wish to make trouble for her with her future in-laws. He had at heart a great respect for family connexions, and once, when Bob and Jassy were slanging a cousin whom the whole family, including Uncle Matthew himself, very much disliked, he had turned upon them, knocked their heads together sharply, and said:

'In the first place he's a relation, and in the second place he's a clergyman, so shut up.'

It had become a classical saying with the Radletts.

So the Kroesigs were duly invited. They accepted, and the date was fixed. Aunt Sadie then got into a panic, and summoned Aunt Emily and Davey. (I was staying at Alconleigh anyhow, for a few weeks' hunting.) Louisa was feeding her second baby in Scotland, but hoped to come south for the wedding later on.

The arrival at Alconleigh of the four Kroesigs was not auspicious. As the car which had met them at the station was heard humming up the drive, every single light in the whole house fused – Davey had brought a new ultra-violet lamp with him, which had done the trick. The guests had to be led into the hall in pitch darkness, while Logan fumbled about in the pantry for a candle, and Uncle Matthew rushed off to the fuse box. Lady Kroesig and Aunt Sadie chatted politely about this and that, Linda and Tony giggled in the corner, and Sir Leicester hit his gouty foot on the edge of a refectory table, while the voice of an invisible Davey could be heard, apologizing in a high wail, from the top of the staircase. It was really very embarrassing.

At last the lights went up, and the Kroesigs were revealed. Sir Leicester was a tall fair man with grey hair, whose undeniable good looks were marred by a sort of silliness in his face; his wife and daughter were two dumpy little fluffy females. Tony evidently took after his father, and Marjorie after her mother. Aunt Sadie, thrown out of her stride by the sudden transformation of what had been mere voices in the dark into flesh and blood, and feeling herself unable to produce more topics of conversation, hurried them upstairs to rest, and dress for dinner. It was always considered at Alconleigh that the journey from London was an experience involving great exhaustion, and people were supposed to be in need of rest after it.

'What is this lamp?' Uncle Matthew asked Davey, who was still saying how sorry he was, still clad in the exiguous dressing-gown which he had put on for his sun-bath.

'Well, you know how one can never digest anything in the winter months.'

'I can, damn you,' said Uncle Matthew. This, addressed to Davey, could be interpreted as a term of endearment.

'You think you can, but you can't really. Now this lamp pours its rays into the system, your glands begin to work, and your food does you good again.'

'Well don't pour any more rays until we have had the voltage altered. When the house is full of bloody Huns one wants to be able to see what the hell they're up to.'

For dinner, Linda wore a white chintz dress with an enormous skirt, and a black lace scarf. She looked entirely ravishing, and it was obvious that Sir Leicester was much taken with her appearance – Lady Kroesig and Miss Marjorie, in bits of georgette and lace, seemed not to notice it. Marjorie was an intensely dreary girl, a few years older than Tony, who had failed so far to marry, and seemed to have no biological reason for existing.

'Have you read *Brothers*?' Lady Kroesig asked Uncle Matthew, conversationally, as they settled down to their soup.

'What's that?'

'The new Ursula Langdok – *Brothers* – it's about two brothers. You ought to read it.'

'My dear Lady Kroesig, I have only ever read one book in my life, and that is *White Fang*. It's so frightfully good I've never bothered to read another. But Davey here reads books – you've read *Brothers*, Davey, I bet.'

'Indeed, I have not,' said Davey, petulantly.

'I'll lend it to you,' said Lady Kroesig, 'I have it with me, and I finished it in the train.'

'You shouldn't,' said Davey, 'read in trains, ever. It's madly wearing to the optic nerve centres, it imposes a most fearful strain. May I see the menu, please? I must explain that I'm on a new diet, one meal white, one meal red. It's doing me so much good. Oh, dear, what a pity. Sadie – oh, she's not listening – Logan, could I ask for an egg, very lightly boiled, you know. This is my white meal, and we are having saddle of mutton I see.'

'Well, Davey, have your red meal now and your white meal for breakfast,' said Uncle Matthew. 'I've opened some Mouton Rothschild, and I know how much you like that – I opened it specially for you.'

'Oh, it is too bad,' said Davey, 'because I happen to know that there are kippers for breakfast, and I do so love them. What a ghastly decision. No! it must be an egg now, with a little hock. I could never forgo the kippers, so delicious, so digestible, but, above all, so full of proteins.'

'Kippers,' said Bob, 'are brown.'

'Brown counts as red. Surely you can see that.'

But when a chocolate cream, in generous supply, but never quite enough when the boys were at home, came round, it was seen to count as white. The Radletts often had cause to observe that you could never entirely rely upon Davey to refuse food, however unwholesome, if it was really delicious.

Aunt Sadie was making heavy weather with Sir Leicester. He was full of boring herbaceous enthusiasms, and took it for granted that she was too.

'What a lot you London people always know about gardens,' she said. 'You must talk to Davey, he is a great gardener.'

'I am not really a London person,' said Sir Leicester, reproachfully. 'I work in London, but my home is in Surrey.'

'I count that,' Aunt Sadie said, gently but firmly, 'as the same.'

The evening seemed endless. The Kroesigs obviously longed for bridge, and did not seem to care so much for racing demon when it was offered as a substitute. Sir Leicester said he had had a tiring week, and really should go to bed early.

'Don't know how you chaps can stand it,' said Uncle Matthew, sympathetically. 'I was saying to the bank manager at Merlinford only yesterday, it must be the hell of a life fussing about with other blokes' money all day, indoors.'

Linda went to ring up Lord Merlin, who had just returned from abroad. Tony followed her, they were gone a long time, and came back looking flushed and rather self-conscious.

The next morning, as we were hanging about in the hall waiting for the kippers, which had already announced themselves with a heavenly smell, two breakfast trays were seen going upstairs, for Sir Leicester and Lady Kroesig.

'No, really, that beats everything, dammit,' said Uncle Matthew, 'I never heard of a *man* having breakfast in bed before.' And he looked wistfully at his entrenching tool.

He was slightly mollified, however, when they came downstairs, just before eleven, all ready to go to church. Uncle Matthew was a great pillar of the church, read the lessons, chose the hymns, and took round the bag, and he liked his household to attend. Alas, the Kroesigs turned out to be blasted idolaters, as was proved when they turned sharply to the east during the creed. In short, they were of the company of those who could do no right, and sighs of relief echoed through the house when they decided to catch an evening train back to London.

'Tony is Bottom to Linda, isn't he?' I said, sadly.

Davey and I were walking through Hen's Grove the next day. Davey always knew what you meant, it was one of the nice things about him.

'Bottom,' he said sadly. He adored Linda.

'And nothing will wake her up?'

'Not before it's too late, I fear. Poor Linda, she has an intensely romantic character, which is fatal for a woman. Fortunately for them, and for all of us, most women are madly *terre à terre*, otherwise the world could hardly carry on.'

Lord Merlin was braver than the rest of us, and said right out what he thought. Linda went over to see him and asked him.

'Are you pleased about my engagement?' to which he replied:

'No, of course not. Why are you doing it?'

'I'm in love,' said Linda proudly.

'What makes you think so?'

'One doesn't think, one knows,' she said.

'Fiddlesticks.'

'Oh, you evidently don't understand about love, so what's the use of talking to you.'

Lord Merlin got very cross, and said that neither did immature little girls understand about love.

'Love,' he said, 'is for grown-up people, as you will discover one day. You will also discover that it has nothing to do with marriage. I'm all in favour of you marrying soon, in a year or two, but for God's sake, and all of our sakes, don't go and marry a bore like Tony Kroesig.'

'If he's such a bore, why did you ask him to stay?'

'I didn't ask him. Baby brought him, because Cecil had 'flu and couldn't come. Besides, I can't guess you'll go and marry every stopgap I have in my house.'

'You ought to be more careful. Anyhow, I can't think why you say Tony's a bore, he knows everything.'

'Yes, that's exactly it, he does. And what about Sir Leicester? And have you seen Lady Kroesig?'

But the Kroesig family was illuminated for Linda by the great glow of perfection which shone around Tony, and she would hear nothing against them. She parted rather coldly from Lord Merlin, came home, and abused him roundly. As for him, he waited to see what Sir Leicester was giving her for a wedding present. It was a pigskin dressing-case with dark tortoiseshell fittings and her initials on them in gold. Lord Merlin sent her a morocco one double the size, fitted blonde tortoiseshell, and instead of initials, LINDA in diamonds.

He had embarked upon an elaborate series of Kroesig teases of which this was to be the first.

The arrangements for the wedding did not go smoothly. There was trouble without end over settlements. Uncle Matthew, whose estate provided a certain sum of money for younger children, to be allocated by him as he thought best, very naturally did not wish to settle anything on Linda, at the expense of the others, in view of the fact that she was marrying the son of a millionaire. Sir Leicester, however, refused to settle a penny unless Uncle Matthew did – he had no great wish to make a settlement in any case, saying that it was against the policy of his family to tie up capital sums. In the end, by sheer persistence, Uncle Matthew got a beggarly amount for Linda. The whole thing worried and upset him very much, and confirmed him, if need be, in his hatred of the Teutonic race.

Tony and his parents wanted a London wedding, Uncle Matthew said he had never heard of anything so common and vulgar in his life. Women were married from their homes; he thought fashionable weddings the height of degradation, and refused to lead one of his daughters up the aisle of St Margaret's through a crowd of gaping strangers. The Kroesigs explained to Linda that, if she had a country wedding, she would only get half the amount of wedding presents, and also that the important, influential people, who would be of use, later, to Tony, would never come down to Gloucestershire in the depth of winter. All these arguments were lost on Linda. Since the days when she was planning to marry the Prince of Wales she had had a mental picture of what her wedding would be like, that is, as much like a wedding in a pantomime as possible, in a large church, with crowds both outside and in, with photographers, arum lilies, tulle, bridesmaids, and an enormous choir singing her favourite tune, 'The Lost Chord'. So she sided with the Kroesigs against poor Uncle Matthew, and, when fate tipped the scales in their favour by putting out of action the heating in Alconleigh church, Aunt Sadie took a London house, and the wedding was duly celebrated with every circumstance of publicized vulgarity at St Margaret's.

What with one thing and another, by the time Linda was married, her parents and her parents-in-law were no longer on speaking terms. Uncle Matthew cried without restraint all through the ceremony; Sir Leicester seemed to be beyond tears.

IO

I think Linda's marriage was a failure almost from the beginning, but I really never knew much about it. Nobody did. She had married in the face of a good deal of opposition; the opposition proved to have been entirely well founded, and, Linda being what she was, maintained, for as long as possible, a perfect shop-front.

They were married in February, had a hunting honeymoon from a house they took at Melton, and settled down for good in Bryanston Square after Easter. Tony then started work in his father's old bank, and prepared to step into a safe Conservative seat in the House of Commons, an ambition which was very soon realized.

Closer acquaintance with their new in-laws did not make either the Radlett or the Kroesig families change their minds about each other. The Kroesigs thought Linda eccentric, affected, and extravagant. Worst of all, she was supposed not to be useful to Tony in his career. The Radletts considered that Tony was a first-class bore. He had a habit of choosing a subject, and then droning round and round it like an inaccurate bomb-aimer round his target, ever unable to hit; he knew vast quantities of utterly dreary facts, of which he did not hesitate to inform his companions, at great length and in great detail, whether they appeared to be interested or not. He was infinitely serious, he no longer laughed at Linda's jokes, and the high spirits which, when she first knew him, he had seemed to possess, must have been due to youth, drink, and good health. Now that he was grown up and married he put all three resolutely behind him, spending his days in the bank house and his evenings at Westminster, never having any fun or breathing fresh air: his true self emerged, and he was revealed as a pompous, money-grubbing ass, more like his father every day.

He did not succeed in making an asset out of Linda. Poor Linda was incapable of understanding the Kroesig point of view; try as she might (and in the beginning she tried very hard, having an infinite desire to please) it remained mysterious to her. The fact is that, for the first time in her life, she found herself face to face with the bourgeois attitude of mind, and the fate often foreseen for me by Uncle Matthew as a result of my middle-class education had actually befallen her. The outward and visible signs which he so deprecated were all there – the Kroesigs said notepaper, perfume, mirror, and mantelpiece, they even invited her to call them Father and Mother, which, in the first flush of love, she did, only to spend the rest of her married life trying to get out of it by addressing them to their faces as 'you', and communicating with them by postcard or telegram. Inwardly their spirit was utterly commercial, everything was seen by them in terms of money. It was their barrier, their defence, their hope for the future, their support for the present, it raised them above their fellowmen, and with it they warded off evil. The only mental qualities that they respected were those which produced money in substantial quantities, it was their one criterion of success, it was power and it was glory. To say that a man was poor was to label him a rotter, bad at his job, idle, feckless, immoral. If it was somebody whom they really rather liked, in spite of this cancer, they could add that he had been unlucky. They had taken care to insure against this deadly evil in many ways. That it should not overwhelm them through such cataclysms beyond their control as war or revolution they had placed huge sums of money in a dozen different countries; they owned ranches, and estancias, and South African farms, an hotel in Switzerland, a plantation in Malaya, and they possessed many fine diamonds, not sparkling round Linda's lovely neck to be sure, but lying in banks, stone by stone, easily portable.

Linda's upbringing had made all this incomprehensible to her; for money was a subject that was absolutely never mentioned at Alconleigh. Uncle Matthew had no doubt a large income, but it was derived from, tied up in, and a good percentage of it went back into, his land. His land was to him something sacred, and, sacred above that, was England. Should evil befall his country he would stay and share it, or die, never would the notion have entered his head that he might save himself, and leave old England in any sort of lurch. He, his family, and his estates were part of her and she was part of him, for ever and ever. Later on, when war appeared to be looming upon the horizon, Tony tried to persuade him to send some money to America.

'What for?' said Uncle Matthew.

'You might be glad to go there yourself, or send the children. It's always a good thing to have –'

'I may be old, but I can still shoot,' said Uncle Matthew, furiously, 'and I haven't got any children – for the purposes of fighting they are all grown up.'

'Victoria –'

'Victoria is thirteen. She would do her duty. I hope, if any bloody foreigners ever got here, that every man, woman, and child would go on fighting them until one side or the other was wiped out. Anyhow, I loathe abroad, nothing would induce me to live there, I'd rather live in the gamekeeper's hut in Hen's Grove, and, as for foreigners, they are all the same, and they all make me sick,' he said, pointedly, glowering at Tony, who took no notice, but went droning on about how clever he had been in transferring various funds to various places. He had always remained perfectly unaware of Uncle Matthew's dislike for him, and, indeed, such was my uncle's eccentricity of behaviour, that it was not very easy for somebody as thick-skinned as Tony to differentiate between Uncle Matthew's behaviour towards those he loved and those he did not.

On the first birthday she had after her marriage, Sir Leicester gave Linda a cheque for £1,000. Linda was delighted and spent it that very day on a necklace of large half pearls surrounded by rubies, which she had been admiring for some time in a Bond Street shop. The Kroesigs had a small family dinner party for her, Tony was to meet her there, having been kept late at his office. Linda arrived, wearing a very plain white satin dress cut very low, and her necklace, went straight up to Sir Leicester, and said: 'Oh, you were kind to give me such a wonderful present – look –'

Sir Leicester was stupefied.

'Did it cost all I sent you?' he said.

'Yes,' said Linda. 'I thought you would like me to buy one thing with it, and always remember it was you who gave it to me.'

'No, dear. That wasn't at all what I intended. £1,000 is what you might call a capital sum, that means something on which you expect a return. You should not spend it on a trinket which you wear three or four times a year, and which is most unlikely to appreciate in value. (And, by the way, if you buy jewels, let it always be diamonds – rubies and pearls are too easy to copy, they won't keep their price.) But, as I was saying, one hopes for a return. So you could either have asked Tony to invest it for you, or, which is what I really intended, you could have spent it on entertaining important people who would be of use to Tony in his career.'

These important people were a continual thorn in poor Linda's side. She was always supposed by the Kroesigs to be a great hindrance to Tony, both in politics and in the City, because, try as she might, she could not disguise how tedious they seemed to her. Like Aunt Sadie, she was apt to retire into a cloud of boredom on the smallest provocation, a vague look would come into her eyes, and her spirit would be absent itself. Important people did not like this; they were not accustomed to it; they liked to be listened and attended to by the young with concentrated deference when they were so kind as to bestow their company. What with Linda's yawns, and Tony informing them how many harbour-masters there were in the British Isles, important people were inclined to eschew the young Kroesigs. The old Kroesigs deeply deplored this state of affairs, for which they blamed Linda. They saw that she did not take the slightest interest in Tony's work. She tried to at first but it was beyond her; she simply could not understand how somebody who already had plenty of money could go and shut himself away from God's fresh air and blue skies, from the spring, the summer, the autumn, the winter, letting them merge into each other unaware that they were passing, simply in order to make more. She was far too young to be interested in politics, which were anyhow, in those days before Hitler came along to brighten them up, a very esoteric amusement.

'Your father was cross,' she said to Tony, as they walked home after dinner. Sir Leicester lived in Hyde Park Gardens, it was a beautiful night, and they walked.

'I don't wonder,' said Tony, shortly.

'But look, darling, how pretty it is. Don't you see how one couldn't resist it?'

'You are so affected. Do try and behave like an adult, won't you?'

The autumn after Linda's marriage Aunt Emily took a little house in St Leonard's Terrace, where she, Davey and I installed ourselves. She had been rather unwell, and Davey thought it would be a good thing to get her away from all her country duties and to make her rest, as no woman ever can at home. His novel, *The Abrasive Tube*, had just appeared, and was having a great success in intellectual circles. It was a psychological and physiological study of a South Polar explorer, snowed up in a hut where he knows he must eventually die, with enough rations to keep him going for a few months. In the end he dies. Davey was fascinated by Polar expeditions; he liked to observe, from a safe distance, how far the body can go when driven upon thoroughly indigestible foodstuffs deficient in vitamins.

'Pemmican,' he would say, gleefully, falling upon the delicious food for which Aunt Emily's cook was renowned, 'must have been so bad for them.'

Aunt Emily, shaken out of the routine of her life at Shenley, took up with old friends again, entertaining for us, and enjoyed herself so much that she talked of living half the year in London. As for me, I have never, before or since, been happier. The London season I had with Linda had been the greatest possible fun; it would be untrue and ungrateful to Aunt Sadie to deny that; I had even quite enjoyed the long dark hours we spent in the Peeresses' gallery; but there had been a curious unreality about it all, it was not related, one felt, to life. Now I had my feet firmly planted on the ground. I was allowed to do what I liked, see whom I chose, at any hour, peacefully, naturally, and without breaking rules, and it was wonderful to bring my friends home and have them greeted in a friendly, if somewhat detached manner, by Davey, instead of smuggling them up the back stairs for fear of a raging scene in the hall.

During this happy time I became happily engaged to Alfred Wincham, then a young don at, now Warden of, St Peter's College, Oxford. With this kindly scholarly man I have been perfectly happy ever since, finding in our home at Oxford that refuge from the storms and puzzles of life which I had always wanted. I say no more about him here; this is Linda's story, not mine.

We saw a great deal of Linda just then; she would come and chat for hours on end. She did not seem to be unhappy, though I felt sure she was already waking from her Titania-trance, but was obviously lonely, as her husband was at his work all day and at the House in the evening. Lord Merlin was abroad, and she had, as yet, no other very intimate friends; she missed the comings and goings, the cheerful bustle and hours of pointless chatter which had made up the family life at Alconleigh. I reminded her how much, when she was there, she had longed to escape, and she agreed, rather doubtfully, that it was wonderful to be on one's own. She was much pleased by my engagement, and liked Alfred.

'He has such a serious, clever look,' she said. 'What pretty little black babies you'll have, both of you so dark.'

He only quite liked her; he suspected that she was a tough nut, and rather, I must own, to my relief, she never exercised over him the spell in which she had entranced Davey and Lord Merlin.

One day, as we were busy with wedding invitations, she came in and announced:

'I am in pig, what d'you think of that?'

'A most hideous expression, Linda dear,' said Aunt Emily, 'but I suppose we must congratulate you.'

'I suppose so,' said Linda. She sank into a chair with an enormous sigh. 'I feel awfully ill, I must say.'

'But think how much good it will do you in the long run,' said Davey, enviously, 'such a wonderful clear-out.'

'I see just what you mean,' said Linda. 'Oh, we've got such a ghastly evening ahead of us. Some important Americans. It seems Tony wants to do a deal or something, and these Americans will only do the deal if they take a fancy to me.

Now can you explain that? I know I shall be sick all over them, and my father-in-law will be so cross. Oh, the horror of important people – you are lucky not to know any.'

Linda's child, a girl, was born in May. She was ill for a long time before, and very ill indeed at her confinement. The doctors told her that she must never have another child, as it would almost certainly kill her if she did. This was a blow to the Kroesigs, as bankers, it seems, like kings, require many sons, but Linda did not appear to mind at all. She took no interest whatever in the baby she had got. I went to see her as soon as I was allowed to. She lay in a bower of blossom and pink roses, and looked like a corpse. I was expecting a baby myself, and naturally took a great interest in Linda's.

'What are you going to call her – where is she, anyway?'

'In Sister's room – it shrieks. Moira, I believe.'

'Not Moira, darling, you can't. I never heard such an awful name.'

'Tony likes it, he had a sister called Moira who died, and what d'you think I found out (not from him, but from their old nanny)? She died because Marjorie whacked her on the head with a hammer when she was four months old. Do you call that interesting? And then they say we are an uncontrolled family – why even Fa has never actually murdered anybody, or do you count that beater?'

'All the same, I don't see how you can saddle the poor little thing with a name like Moira, it's too unkind.'

'Not really, if you think. It'll have to grow up a Moira if the Kroesigs are to like it (people always grow up to their names I've noticed) and they might as well like it because frankly, I don't.'

'Linda, how can you be so naughty, and, anyway, you can't possibly tell whether you like her or not, yet.'

'Oh, yes I can. I can always tell if I like people from the start, and I don't like Moira, that's all. She's a fearful Counter-Hon, wait till you see her.'

At this point the Sister came in, and Linda introduced us.

'Oh, you are the cousin I hear so much about,' she said. 'You'll want to see the baby.'

She went away and presently returned carrying a Moses basket full of wails.

'Poor thing,' said Linda indifferently. 'It's really kinder not to look.'

'Don't pay any attention to her,' said the Sister. 'She pretends to be a wicked woman, but it's all put on.'

I did look, and, deep down among the frills and lace, there was the usual horrid sight of a howling orange in a fine black wig.

'Isn't she sweet,' said the Sister. 'Look at her little hands.'

I shuddered slightly, and said:

'Well, I know it's dreadful of me, but I don't much like them as small as that; I'm sure she'll be divine in a year or two.'

The wails now entered on a crescendo, and the whole room was filled with hideous noise.

'Poor soul,' said Linda. 'I think it must have caught sight of itself in a glass. Do take it away, Sister.'

Davey now came into the room. He was meeting me there to drive me down to Shenley for the night. The Sister came back and shooed us both off, saying that Linda had had enough. Outside her room, which was in the largest and most expensive nursing home in London, I paused, looking for the lift.

'This way,' said Davey, and then, with a slightly self-conscious giggle: '*Nourri dans le sérail, j'en connais les détours.* Oh, how are you, Sister Thesiger? How very nice to see you.'

'Captain Warbeck – I must tell Matron you are here.'

And it was nearly an hour before I could drag Davey out of this home from home. I hope I am not giving the impression that Davey's whole life was centred round his health. He was fully occupied with his work, writing, and editing a literary review, but his health was his hobby, and, as such, more in evidence during his spare time, the time when I saw most of him. How he enjoyed it! He seemed to regard his body with the affectionate preoccupation of a farmer towards a pig – not a good doer, the small one of the litter, which must somehow be made to be a credit to the farm. He weighed it, sunned it, aired it, exercised it, and gave it special diets, new kinds of patent food and medicine, but all in vain. It never put on so much as a single ounce of weight, it never became a credit to the farm, but, somehow, it lived, enjoying good things, enjoying its life, though falling victim to the ills that flesh is heir to, and other, imaginary ills as well, through which it was nursed with unfailing care, with concentrated attention, by the good farmer and his wife.

Aunt Emily said at once, when I told her about Linda and poor Moira:

'She's too young. I don't believe very young mothers ever get wrapped up in their babies. It's when women are older that they so adore their children, and maybe it's better for the children to have young unadoring mothers and to lead more detached lives.'

'But Linda seems to loathe her.'

'That's so like Linda,' said Davey. 'She has to do things by extremes.'

'But she seemed so gloomy. You must say that's not very like her.'

'She's been terribly ill,' said Aunt Emily. 'Sadie was in despair. Twice they thought she would die.'

'Don't talk of it,' said Davey. 'I can't imagine the world without Linda.'

II

Living in Oxford, engrossed with my husband and young family, I saw less of Linda during the next few years than at any time of my life. This, however, did not affect the intimacy of our relationship, which remained absolute, and, when we did meet, it was still as though we were seeing each other every day. I stayed with her in London from time to time, and she with me in Oxford, and we corresponded regularly. I may as well say here that the one thing she never discussed with me was the deterioration of her marriage; in any case it would not have been necessary, the whole thing being as plain as relations between married people can ever be. Tony was, quite obviously, not good enough as a lover to make up, even at first, for his shortcomings in other respects, the boredom of his company and the mediocrity of his character. Linda was out of love with him by the time the child was born, and, thereafter, could not care a rap for the one or the other. The young man she had fallen in love with, handsome, gay, intellectual, and domineering, melted away upon closer acquaintance, and proved to have been a chimera, never to have existed outside her imagination. Linda did not commit the usual fault of blaming Tony for what was entirely her own mistake, she merely turned from him in absolute indifference. This was made easier by the fact that she saw so little of him.

Lord Merlin now launched a tremendous Kroesig-tease. The Kroesigs were always complaining that Linda never went out, would not entertain, unless absolutely forced to, and did not care for society. They told their friends that she was a country girl, entirely sporting, that if you went into her drawing-room she would be found training a retriever with dead rabbits hidden behind the sofa cushions. They pretended that she was an amiable, half-witted, beautiful rustic, incapable of helping poor Tony, who was obliged to battle his way through life alone. There was a grain of truth in all this, the fact being that the Kroesig circle of acquaintances was too ineffably boring; poor Linda, having been unable to make any headway at all in it, had given up the struggle, and retired to the more congenial company of retrievers and dormice.

Lord Merlin, in London for the first time since Linda's marriage, at once introduced her into his world, the world towards which she had always looked, that of smart bohemianism; and here she found her feet, was entirely happy, and had an immediate and great success. She became very gay and went everywhere. There is no more popular unit in London society than a young, beautiful, but perfectly respectable woman who can be asked to dinner without her husband, and Linda was soon well on the way to having her head turned. Photographers and gossip writers dogged her footsteps, and indeed one could not escape the impression, until half an hour of her company put one right again, that she was becoming a bit of a bore. Her house was full of people from morning till night, chatting. Linda, who loved to chat, found many congenial spirits in the carefree, pleasure-seeking London of those days, when unemployment was rife as much among the upper as the lower classes. Young men, pensioned off by their relations, who would sometimes suggest in a perfunctory manner that it might be a good thing if they found some work, but without seriously helping them to do so (and, anyhow, what work was there for such as they?) clustered round Linda like bees round honey, buzz, buzz, buzz, chat, chat, chat. In her bedroom, on her bed, sitting on the stairs outside while she had a bath, in the kitchen while she ordered the food, shopping, walking round the park, cinema, theatre, opera, ballet, dinner, supper, night clubs, parties, dances, all day, all night – endless, endless, chat.

'But what do you suppose they talk about?' Aunt Sadie, disapproving, used to wonder. What, indeed?

Tony went early to his bank, hurrying out of the house with an air of infinite importance, an attaché case in one hand and a sheaf of newspapers under his arm. His departure heralded the swarm of chatterers, almost as if they had been waiting round the street corner to see him leave, and thereafter the house was filled with them. They were very nice, very good-looking, and great fun – their manners were perfect. I never was able, during my short visits, to distinguish them much one from another, but I saw their attraction, the unfailing attraction of vitality and high spirits. By no stretch of the imagination, however, could they have been called 'important', and the Kroesigs were beside themselves at this turn of affairs.

Tony did not seem to mind; he had long given up Linda as hopeless from the point of view of his career, and was rather pleased and flattered by the publicity which now launched her as a beauty. 'The beautiful wife of a clever young M.P.' Besides, he found that they were invited to large parties and balls, to which it suited him very well to go, coming late after the House, and where there were often to be found not only Linda's unimportant friends, with whom she would amuse herself, but also colleagues of his own, and by no means unimportant ones, whom he could buttonhole and bore at the bar. It would have been useless, however, to explain this to the old Kroesigs, who had a deeply rooted mistrust of smart society, of dancing, and of any kind of fun, all of which led, in their opinion, to extravagance, without compensating material advantages. Fortunately for Linda, Tony at this time was not on good terms with his father, owing to a conflict of policies in the bank; they did not go to Hyde Park Gardens as much as when they were first married, and visits to Planes, the Kroesig house in Surrey, were, for the time being, off. When they did meet, however, the old Kroesigs made it clear to Linda that she was not proving a satisfactory daughter-in-law. Even Tony's divergence of views was put down to her, and Lady Kroesig told her friends, with a sad shake of the head, that Linda did not bring out the best in him.

Linda now proceeded to fritter away years of her youth, with nothing whatever to show for them. If she had had an intellectual upbringing the place of all this pointless chatter, jokes, and parties might have been taken by a serious interest in the arts, or by reading; if she had been happy in her marriage that side of her nature which craved for company could have found its fulfilment by the nursery fender; things being as they were, however, all was frippery and silliness.

Alfred and I once had an argument with Davey about her, during which we said all this. Davey accused us of being prigs, though at heart he must have known that we were right.

'But Linda gives one so much pleasure,' he kept saying, 'she is like a bunch of flowers. You don't want people like that to bury themselves in serious reading; what would be the good?'

However, even he was forced to admit that her behaviour to poor little Moira was not what it should be. (The child was fat, fair, placid, dull, and backward, and Linda still did not like her; the Kroesigs, on the other hand, adored her, and she spent more and more time, with her nanny, at Planes. They loved having her there, but that did not stop them from ceaseless criticism of Linda's behaviour. They now told everybody that she was a silly society butterfly, hard-hearted neglecter of her child.)

Alfred said, almost angrily:

'It's so odd that she doesn't even have love affairs. I don't see what she gets out of her life, it must be dreadfully empty.'

Alfred likes people to be filed neatly away under some heading that he can understand; careerist, social climber, virtuous wife and mother, or adulteress.

Linda's social life was completely aimless; she simply collected around her an assortment of cosy people who had the leisure to chat all day; whether they were millionaires or paupers, princes or refugee Rumanians, was a matter of complete indifference to her. In spite of the fact that, except for me and her sisters, nearly all her friends were men, she had such a reputation for virtue that she was currently suspected of being in love with her husband.

'Linda believes in love,' said Davey, 'she is passionately romantic. At the moment I am sure she is, subconsciously, waiting for an irresistible temptation. Casual affairs would not interest her in the least. One must hope that when it comes it will not prove to be another Bottom.'

'I suppose she is really rather like my mother,' I said, 'and all of hers have been Bottoms.'

'Poor Bolter!' said Davey, 'but she's happy now, isn't she, with her white hunter?'

Tony soon became, as was to be expected, a perfect mountain of pomposity, more like his father every day. He was full of large, clear-sighted ideas for bettering the conditions of the capitalist classes, and made no bones of his hatred and distrust of the workers.

'I hate the lower classes,' he said one day, when Linda and I were having tea with him on the terrace of the House of Commons. 'Ravening beasts, trying to get my money. Let them try, that's all.'

'Oh, shut up, Tony,' said Linda, bringing a dormouse out of her pocket, and feeding it with crumbs. 'I love them, anyway I was brought up with them. The trouble with you is you don't know the lower classes and you don't belong to the upper classes, you're just a rich foreigner who happens to live here. Nobody ought to be in Parliament who hasn't lived in the country, anyhow part of their life – why, my old Fa knows more what he's talking about, when he does talk in the House, than you do.'

'I have lived in the country,' said Tony. 'Put that dormouse away, people are looking.'

He never got cross, he was far too pompous.

'Surrey,' said Linda, with infinite contempt.

'Anyhow, last time your Fa made a speech, about the Peeresses in their own right, his only argument for keeping them out of the House was that, if once they got in, they might use the Peers' lavatory.'

'Isn't he a love?' said Linda. 'It's what they all thought, you know, but he was the only one who dared to say it.'

'That's the worst of the House of Lords,' said Tony. 'These backwoodsmen come along just when they think they will, and bring the whole place into disrepute with a few dotty remarks, which get an enormous amount of publicity and give people the impression that we are governed by a lot of lunatics. These old peers ought to realize that it's their duty to their class to stay at home and keep quiet. The amount of excellent, solid, necessary work done in the House of Lords is quite unknown to the man in the street.'

Sir Leicester was expecting soon to become a peer, so this was a subject close to Tony's heart. His general attitude to what he called the man in the street was that he ought constantly to be covered by machine-guns; this having become impossible, owing to the weakness, in the past, of the great Whig families, he must be doped into submission with the fiction that huge reforms, to be engineered by the Conservative party, were always just round the next corner. Like this he could be kept quiet indefinitely, as long as there was no war. War brings people together and opens their eyes, it must be avoided at all costs, and especially war with Germany, where the Kroesigs had financial interests and many relations. (They were originally a Junker family, and snobbed their Prussian connexions as much as the latter looked down on them for being in trade.)

Both Sir Leicester and his son were great admirers of Herr Hitler: Sir Leicester had been to see him during a visit to Germany, and had been taken for a drive in a Mercedes-Benz by Dr Schacht.

Linda took no interest in politics, but she was instinctively and unreasonably English. She knew that one Englishman was worth a hundred foreigners, whereas Tony thought that one capitalist was worth a hundred workers. Their outlook upon this, as upon most subjects, differed fundamentally.

12

By a curious irony of fate it was at her father-in-law's house in Surrey that Linda met Christian Talbot. The little Moira, aged six, now lived permanently at Planes; it seemed a good arrangement as it saved Linda, who disliked housekeeping, the trouble of running two establishments, while Moira was given the benefit of country air and food. Linda and Tony were supposed to spend a couple of nights there every week, and Tony generally did so. Linda, in fact, went down for Sunday about once a month.

Planes was a horrible house. It was an overgrown cottage, that is to say, the rooms were large, with all the disadvantages of a cottage, low ceilings, small windows with diamond panes, uneven floorboards, and a great deal of naked knotted wood. It was furnished neither in good nor in bad taste, but simply with no attempt at taste at all, and was not even very comfortable. The garden which lay around it would be a lady water-colourist's heaven: herbaceous borders, rockeries, and water-gardens were carried to a perfection of vulgarity, and flaunted a riot of huge and hideous flowers, each individual bloom appearing twice as large, three times as brilliant as it ought to have been and if possible of a different colour from that which nature intended. It would be hard to say whether it was more frightful, more like glorious Technicolor, in spring, in summer, or in autumn. Only in the depth of winter, covered by the kindly snow, did it melt into the landscape and become tolerable.

One April Saturday morning, in 1937, Linda, with whom I had been staying in London, took me down there for the night, as she sometimes did. I think she liked to have a buffer between herself and the Kroesigs, perhaps especially between herself and Moira. The old Kroesigs were by way of being very fond of me, and

Sir Leicester sometimes took me for walks and hinted how much he wished that it had been me, so serious, so well educated, such a good wife and mother, whom Tony had married.

We motored down past acres of blossom.

'The great difference,' said Linda, 'between Surrey and proper, real country, is that in Surrey, when you see blossom, you know there will be no fruit. Think of the Vale of Evesham, and then look at all this pointless pink stuff – it gives you quite a different feeling. The garden at Planes will be a riot of sterility, just you wait.'

It was. You could hardly see any beautiful, pale, bright, yellow-green of spring, every tree appeared to be entirely covered with a waving mass of pink or mauve tissue-paper. The daffodils were so thick on the ground that they too obscured the green, they were new varieties of a terrifying size, either dead white or dark yellow, thick and fleshy; they did not look at all like the fragile friends of one's childhood. The whole effect was of a scene for musical comedy, and it exactly suited Sir Leicester, who, in the country, gave a surprisingly adequate performance of the old English squire. Picturesque. Delightful.

He was pottering in the garden as we drove up, in an old pair of corduroy trousers, so much designed as an old pair that it seemed improbable that they had ever been new, an old tweed coat on the same lines, secateurs in his hand, a depressed Corgi at his heels, and a mellow smile on his face.

'Here you are,' he said, heartily. (One could almost see, as in the strip advertisements, a bubble coming out of his head – thinks – 'You are a most unsatisfactory daughter-in-law, but nobody can say it's our fault, we always have a welcome and a kind smile for you.') 'Car going well, I hope? Tony and Moira have gone out riding, I thought you might have passed them. Isn't the garden looking grand just now, I can hardly bear to go to London and leave all this beauty with no one to see it. Come for a stroll before lunch – Foster will see to your gear – just ring the front-door bell, Fanny, he may not have heard the car.'

He led us off into Madame Butterfly-land.

'I must warn you,' he said, 'that we have got rather a rough diamond coming to lunch. I don't know if you've ever met old Talbot who lives in the village, the old professor? Well, his son, Christian. He's by way of being rather a Communist, a clever chap gone all wrong, and a journalist on some daily rag. Tony can't bear him, never could as a child, and he's very cross with me for asking him today, but I always think it's as well to see something of these Left-wing fellows. If people like us are nice to them they can be tamed wonderfully.'

He said this in the tone of one who might have saved the life of a Communist in the war, and, by this act, turned him, through gratitude, into a true blue Tory. But in the first world war Sir Leicester had considered that, with his superior brain, he would have been wasted as cannon fodder, and had fixed himself in an office in Cairo. He neither saved nor took any lives, nor did he risk his own, but built up many valuable business contacts, became a major and got an O.B.E., thus making the best of all worlds.

So Christian came to luncheon, and behaved with the utmost intransigence. He was an extraordinarily handsome young man, tall and fair, in a completely different way from that of Tony, thin and very English-looking. His clothes were outrageous – he wore a really old pair of grey flannel trousers, full of little round moth-holes in the most embarrassing places, no coat, and a flannel shirt, one of the sleeves of which had a tattered tear from wrist to elbow.

'Has your father been writing anything lately?' Lady Kroesig asked, as they sat down to luncheon.

'I suppose so,' said Christian, 'as it's his profession. I can't say I've asked him, but one assumes he has, just as one assumes that Tony has been banking something lately.'

He then planted his elbow, bare through the rent, onto the table between himself and Lady Kroesig and swivelling right round to Linda, who was on his other side, he told her, at length and in immense detail, of a production of *Hamlet* he had seen lately in Moscow. The cultured Kroesigs listened attentively, throwing off occasional comments calculated to show that they knew *Hamlet* well – 'I don't think that quite fits in with my idea of Ophelia', or 'But Polonius was a very old man', to all of which Christian turned an utterly deaf ear, gobbling his food with one hand, his elbow on the table, his eyes on Linda.

After luncheon he said to Linda:

'Come back and have tea with my father, you'd like him,' and they went off together, leaving the Kroesigs to behave for the rest of the afternoon like a lot of hens who have seen a fox.

Sir Leicester took me to his water-garden, which was full of enormous pink forget-me-nots, and dark-brown irises, and said:

'It is really too bad of Linda, little Moira has been so much looking forward to showing her the ponies. That child idolizes her mother.'

She didn't, actually, in the least. She was fond of Tony and quite indifferent to Linda, calm and stolid and not given to idolatry, but it was part of the Kroesigs' creed that children should idolize their mothers.

'Do you know Pixie Townsend?' he asked me, suddenly.

'No,' I said, which was true, nor did I then know anything about her. 'Who is she?'

'She's a very delightful person.' He changed the subject.

Linda returned just in time to dress for dinner, looking extremely beautiful. She made me come and chat while she had her bath – Tony was reading to Moira upstairs in the night nursery. Linda was perfectly enchanted with her outing. Christian's father, she said, lived in the smallest house imaginable, an absolute contrast to what Christian called the Kroesighof, because, although absolutely tiny, it had nothing whatever of a cottage about it – it was in the grand manner, and full of books. Every available wall space was covered with books, they lay stacked on tables and chairs and in heaps on the floor. Mr Talbot was the exact opposite of Sir Leicester, there was nothing picturesque about him, or anything to indicate that he was a learned man, he was brisk and matter-of-fact, and had made some very funny jokes about Davey, whom he knew well.

'He's perfect heaven,' Linda kept saying, her eyes shining. What she really meant, as I could see too clearly, was that Christian was perfect heaven. She was dazzled by him. It seemed that he had talked without cease, and his talk consisted of variations upon a single theme – the betterment of the world through political change. Linda, since her marriage, had heard no end of political shop talked by Tony and his friends, but this related politics entirely to personalities and jobs. As the persons all seemed to her infinitely old and dull, and as it was quite immaterial to her whether they got jobs or not, Linda had classed politics as a boring subject, and used to go off into a dream when they were discussed. But Christian's politics did not bore her. As they walked back from his father's house that evening he had taken her for a tour of the world. He showed her Fascism in Italy, Nazism in Germany, civil war in Spain, inadequate Socialism in France, tyranny in Africa, starvation in Asia, reaction in America, and Right-wing blight in England. Only the U.S.S.R., Norway, and Mexico came in for a modicum of praise.

Linda was a plum ripe for shaking. The tree was now shaken, and down she came. Intelligent and energetic, but with no outlet for her energies, unhappy in her marriage, uninterested in her child, and inwardly oppressed with a sense of futility, she was in the mood either to take up some cause, or to embark upon a love affair. That a cause should now be presented by an attractive young man made both it and him irresistible.

13

The poor Alconleighs were now presented with crises in the lives of three of their children almost simultaneously. Linda ran away from Tony, Jassy ran away from home, and Matt ran away from Eton. The Alconleighs were obliged to face the fact, as parents must sooner or later, that their children had broken loose from control and had taken charge of their own lives. Distracted, disapproving, worried to death, there was nothing they could do; they had become mere spectators of a spectacle which did not please them in the least. This was the year when the parents of our contemporaries would console themselves, if things did not go quite as they hoped for their own children, by saying: 'Never mind, just think of the poor Alconleighs!'

Linda threw discretion, and what worldly wisdom she may have picked up during her years in London society, to the winds; she became an out-and-out Communist, bored and embarrassed everybody to death by preaching her new-found doctrine, not only at the dinner-table, but also from a soap-box in Hyde Park, and other equally squalid rostra, and finally, to the infinite relief of the Kroesig family, she went off to live with Christian. Tony started proceedings for divorce. This was a great blow to my aunt and uncle. It is true that they had never liked Tony, but they were infinitely old-fashioned in their ideas; marriage, to their way of thinking, was marriage, and adultery was wrong. Aunt Sadie was, in particular, profoundly shocked by the light-hearted way in which Linda had abandoned the little Moira. I think it all reminded her too much of my mother, and that she envisaged Linda's future from now on as a series of uncontrollable bolts.

Linda came to see me in Oxford. She was on her way back to London after having broken the news at Alconleigh. I thought it was really very brave of her to do it in person, and indeed, the first thing she asked for (most unlike her) was a drink. She was quite unnerved.

'Goodness,' she said. 'I'd forgotten how terrifying Fa can be – even now, when he's got no power over one. It was just like after we lunched with Tony; in the business-room just the same, and he simply roared, and poor Mummy looked miserable, but she was pretty furious too, and you know how sarcastic she can be. Oh, well, that's over. Darling, it's heaven to see you again.'

I hadn't seen her since the Sunday at Planes when she met Christian, so I wanted to hear all about her life.

'Well,' she said, 'I'm living with Christian in his flat, but it's very small, I must say, but perhaps that is just as well, because I'm doing the housework, and I don't seem to be very good at it, but luckily he is.'

'He'll need to be,' I said.

Linda was notorious in the family for her unhandiness, she could never even tie her own stock, and on hunting days either Uncle Matthew or Josh always had to do it for her. I so well remember her standing in front of a looking-glass in the hall, with Uncle Matthew tying it from behind, both the very picture of concentration, Linda saying: 'Oh, now I see. Next time I know I shall be able to manage.' As she had never in her life done so much as make her own bed, I could not imagine that Christian's flat could be very tidy or comfortable if it was being run by her.

'You are horrid. But oh how dreadful it is, cooking, I mean. That oven – Christian puts things in and says: "Now you take it out in about half an hour." I don't dare tell him how terrified I am, and at the end of half an hour I summon up all my courage and open the oven, and there is that awful hot blast hitting one in the face. I don't wonder people sometimes put their heads in and leave them in out of sheer misery. Oh, dear, and I wish you could have seen the Hoover running away with me, it suddenly took the bit between its teeth and made for the lift shaft. How I shrieked – Christian only just rescued me in time. I think housework is far more tiring and frightening than hunting is, no comparison, and yet after hunting we had eggs for tea and were made to rest for hours, but after housework people expect one to go on just as if nothing special had happened.' She sighed.

'Christian is very strong,' she said, 'and very brave. He doesn't like it when I shriek.'

She seemed tired I thought and rather worried, and I looked in vain for signs of great happiness or great love.

'So what about Tony – how has he taken it?'

'Oh, he's awfully pleased, actually, because he can now marry his mistress without having a scandal, or being divorced, or upsetting the Conservative Association.'

It was so like Linda never to have hinted, even to me, that Tony had a mistress.

'Who is she?' I asked.

'Called Pixie Townsend. You know the sort, young face, with white hair dyed blue. She adores Moira, lives near Planes, and takes her out riding every day. She's a terrific Counter-Hon, but I'm only too thankful now that she exists, because I needn't feel in the least bit guilty – they'll all get on so much better without me.'

'Married?'

'Oh, yes, and divorced her husband years ago. She's frightfully good at all poor Tony's things, golf and business and Conservatism, just like I wasn't, and Sir Leicester think's she's perfect. Goodness, they'll be happy.'

'Now, I want to hear more about Christian, please.'

'Well, he's heaven. He's a frightfully serious man, you know, a Communist, and so am I now, and we are surrounded by comrades all day, and they are terrific Hons, and there's an anarchist. The comrades don't like anarchists, isn't it queer? I always thought they were the same thing, but Christian likes this one because he threw a bomb at the King of Spain; you must say it's romantic. He's called Ramón, and he sits about all day and broods over the miners at Oviedo because his brother is one.'

'Yes, but, darling, tell about Christian.'

'Oh, he's perfect heaven – you must come and stay – or perhaps that wouldn't be very comfortable – come and see us. You can't think what an extraordinary man he is, so detached from other human beings that he hardly notices whether they are there or not. He only cares for ideas.'

'I hope he cares for you.'

'Well, I think he does, but he is very strange and absent-minded. I must tell you, the evening before I ran away with him (I only moved down to Pimlico in a taxi, but running away sounds romantic) he dined with his brother, so naturally I thought they'd talk about me and discuss the whole thing, so I couldn't resist ringing him up at about midnight and saying: "Hullo, darling, did you have a nice evening, and what did you talk about?" and he said: "I can't remember – oh, guerrilla warfare, I think."'

'Is his brother a Communist too?'

'Oh, no, he's in the Foreign Office. Fearfully grand, looks like a deep-sea monster – you know.'

'Oh, that Talbot – yes, I see. I hadn't connected them. So now what are your plans?'

'Well, he says he's going to marry me when I'm divorced. I think it's rather silly, I rather agree with Mummy that once is enough, for marriage, but she says I'm the kind of person one marries if one's living with them, and the thing is it would be bliss not to be called Kroesig any more. Anyway, we'll see.'

'Then what's your life? I suppose you don't go to parties and things now, do you?'

'Darling, such killing parties, you can't think – he won't let us go to ordinary ones at all. Grandi had a dinner-dance last week, and he rang me up himself and asked me to bring Christian, which I thought was awfully nice of him actually – he always has been nice to me – but Christian got into quite a temper and said if I couldn't see any reason against going I'd better go, but nothing would induce him to. So in the end, of course, neither of us went, and I heard afterwards it was the greatest fun. And we mayn't go to the Ribs or to . . .' and she mentioned several families known as much for their hospitality as for their Right-wing convictions.

'The worst of being a Communist is that the parties you may go to are – well – awfully funny and touching, but not very gay, and they're always in such gloomy places. Next week, for instance, we've got three, some Czechs at the Sacco and Vanzetti Memorial Hall at Golders Green, Ethiopians at the Paddington Baths, and the Scotsboro' boys at some boring old rooms or other. You know.'

'The Scotsboro' boys,' I said. 'Are they really still going? They must be getting on.'

'Yes, and they've gone downhill socially,' said Linda, with a giggle. 'I remember a perfectly divine party Brian gave for them – it was the first party Merlin ever took me to so I remember it well, oh, dear, it was fun. But next Thursday won't be the least like that. (Darling, I am being disloyal, but it is such heaven to have a chat after all these months. The comrades are sweet, but they never chat, they make speeches all the time.) But I'm always saying to Christian how much I wish his buddies would either brighten up their parties a bit or else stop giving them, because I don't see the point of sad parties, do you? And Left-wing people are always sad because they mind dreadfully about their causes, and the causes are always going so badly. You see, I bet the Scotsboro' boys will be electrocuted in the end, if they don't die of old age first, that is. One does feel so much on their side, but it's no good, people like Sir Leicester always come out on top, so what can one do? However, the comrades don't seem to realize that, and, luckily for them, they don't know Sir Leicester, so they feel they must go on giving these sad parties.'

'What do you wear at them?' I asked, with some interest, thinking that Linda, in her expensive-looking clothes, must seem very much out of place at these baths and halls.

'You know, that was a great tease at first, it worried me dreadfully, but I've discovered that, so long as one wears wool or cotton, everything is all right. Silk and satin would be the blunder. But I only ever do wear wool and cotton, so I'm on a good wicket. No jewels, of course, but then I left them behind at Bryanston Square, it's the way I was brought up but I must say it gave me a pang. Christian doesn't know about jewellery – I told him, because I thought he'd be rather pleased I'd given them all up for him, but he only said: "Well, there's always the Burma Jewel Company." Oh, dear, he is such a funny man, you must meet him again soon. I must go, darling, it has so cheered me up to see you.'

I don't quite know why, but I felt somehow that Linda had been once more deceived in her emotions, that this explorer in the sandy waste had seen only another mirage. The lake was there, the trees were there, the thirsty camels had gone down to have their evening drink; alas, a few steps forward would reveal nothing but dust and desert as before.

A few minutes only after Linda had left me to go back to London, Christian and the comrades, I had another caller. This time it was Lord Merlin. I liked Lord Merlin very much, I admired him, I was predisposed in his favour, but I was by no means on such intimate terms with him as Linda was. To tell the real truth he frightened me. I felt that, in my company, boredom was for him only just round the corner, and that, anyhow, I was merely regarded as pertaining to Linda, not existing on my own except as a dull little don's wife. I was nothing but the confidante in white linen.

'This is a bad business,' he said, abruptly, and without preamble, though I had not seen him for several years. 'I'm just back from Rome, and what do I find – Linda and Christian Talbot. It's an extraordinary thing that I can't ever leave England without Linda getting herself mixed up with some thoroughly undesirable character. This is a disaster – how far has it gone? Can nothing be done?'

I told him that he had just missed Linda, and said something about her marriage with Tony having been unhappy. Lord Merlin waved this remark aside – it was a disconcerting gesture and made me feel a fool.

'Naturally she never would have stayed with Tony – nobody expected that. The point is that she's out of the frying-pan into an empty grate. How long has it been going on?'

I said I thought it was partly the Communism that had attracted her.

'Linda has always felt the need of a cause.'

'Cause,' he said, scornfully. 'My dear Fanny, I think you are mixing up cause with effect. No, Christian is an attractive fellow, and I quite see that he would provide a perfect reaction from Tony, but it is a disaster. If she is in love with him he will make her miserable, and, if not, it means she has embarked upon a career like your mother's, and that, for Linda, would be very bad indeed. I don't see a ray of comfort anywhere. No money either, of course, and she needs money, she ought to have it.'

He went to the window, and looked across the street at Christ Church gilded by the westerly sun.

'I've known Christian,' he said, 'from a child – his father is a great friend of mine. Christian is a man who goes through the world attached to nobody – people are nothing in his life. The women who have been in love with him have suffered bitterly because he has not even noticed that they are there. I expect he is hardly aware that Linda has moved in on him – his head is in the clouds and he is always chasing after some new idea.'

'This is rather what Linda has just been saying.'

'Oh, she's noticed it already? Well, she is not stupid, and, of course, at first it adds to the attraction – when he comes out of the clouds he is irresistible, I quite see that. But how can they ever settle down? Christian has never had a home, or felt the need for one; he wouldn't know what to do with it – it would hamper him. He'll never sit and chat to Linda, or concentrate upon her in any way, and she is a woman who requires, above all things, a great deal of concentration. Really it is too provoking that I should have been away when this happened, I'm sure I could have stopped it. Now, of course, nobody can.'

He turned from the window and looked at me so angrily that I felt it had all been my fault – actually I think he was unaware of my presence.

'What are they living on?' he said.

'Very little. Linda has a small allowance from Uncle Matthew, I believe, and I suppose Christian makes something from his journalism. I hear the Kroesigs go about saying that there is one good thing, she is sure to starve.'

'Oh, they do, do they?' said Lord Merlin, taking out his notebook, 'can I have Linda's address, please, I am on my way to London now.'

Alfred came in, as usual unaware of exterior events and buried in some pamphlet he was writing.

'You don't happen to know,' he said to Lord Merlin, 'what the daily consumption of milk is in the Vatican City?'

'No, of course not,' said Lord Merlin, angrily, 'Ask Tony Kroesig, he'll be sure to. Well, good-bye, Fanny, I'll have to see what I can do.'

What he did was to present Linda with the freehold of a tiny house far down Cheyne Walk. It was the prettiest little doll's house that ever was seen, on that great bend of the river where Whistler had lived. The rooms were full of reflections of water and full of south and west sunlight; it had a vine and a Trafalgar balcony. Linda adored it. The Bryanston Square house, with an easterly outlook, had been originally, dark, cold, and pompous. When Linda had had it done up by some decorating friend, it had become white, cold, and tomblike. The only thing of beauty that she had possessed was a picture, a fat tomato-coloured bathing-woman, which had been given her by Lord Merlin to annoy the Kroesigs. It had annoyed them, very much. This picture looked wonderful in the Cheyne Walk house, you could hardly tell where the real water-reflections ended and the Renoir one began. The pleasure which Linda derived from her new surroundings, the relief which she felt at having once and for all got rid of the Kroesigs, were, I think, laid by her at Christian's door, and seemed to come from him. Thus the discovery that real love and happiness had once more eluded her was delayed for quite a long time.

I4

The Alconleighs were shocked and horrified over the whole Linda affair, but they had their other children to think of, and were, just now, making plans for the coming out of Jassy, who was as pretty as a peach. She, they hoped, would make up to them for their disappointment with Linda. It was most unfair, but very typical of them, that Louisa, who had married entirely in accordance with their wishes and had been a faithful wife and most prolific mother, having now some five children, hardly seemed to count any more. They were really rather bored by her.

Jassy went with Aunt Sadie to a few London dances at the end of the season, just after Linda had left Tony. She was thought to be rather delicate, and Aunt Sadie had an idea that it would be better for her to come out properly in the less strenuous autumn season, and, accordingly, in October, took a little house in London into which she prepared to move with a few servants, leaving Uncle Matthew in the country, to kill various birds and animals. Jassy complained very much that the young men she had met so far were dull and hideous, but Aunt Sadie took no notice. She said that all girls thought this at first, until they fell in love.

A few days before they were to have moved to London Jassy ran away. She was to have spent a fortnight with Louisa in Scotland, had put Louisa off without telling Aunt Sadie, had cashed her savings, and, before anybody even knew that she was missing, had arrived in America. Poor Aunt Sadie received, out of the blue, a cable saying: 'On way to Hollywood. Don't worry. Jassy.'

At first the Alconleighs were completely mystified. Jassy had never shown the smallest interest in stage or cinema, they felt certain she had no wish to become a film star, and yet, why Hollywood? Then it occurred to them that Matt might know something, he and Jassy being the two inseparables of the family, and Aunt Sadie got into the Daimler and rolled over to Eton. Matt was able to explain everything. He told Aunt Sadie that Jassy was in love with a film star called Gary Coon (or Cary Goon, he could not remember which), and that she had written to Hollywood to ask him if he were married, telling Matt that if he proved not to be she was going straight out there to marry him herself. Matt said all this, in his wobbling half grown-up, half little-boy voice, as if it were the most ordinary situation imaginable.

'So I suppose,' he ended up, 'that she got a letter saying he's not married and just went off. Lucky she had her running away money. What about some tea, Mum?'

Aunt Sadie, deeply preoccupied as she was, knew the rules of behaviour and what was expected of her, and stayed with Matt while he consumed sausages, lobsters, eggs, bacon, fried sole, banana mess, and a chocolate sundae.

As always in times of crisis, the Alconleighs now sent for Davey, and, as always, Davey displayed a perfect competence to deal with the situation. He found out in no time that Cary Goon was a second-rate film actor whom Jassy must have seen when she was in London for the last parties of the summer. He had been in a film then showing called *One Splendid Hour*. Davey got hold of the film, and Lord Merlin put it on his private cinema for the benefit of the family. It was about pirates, and Cary Goon was not even the hero, he was just a pirate and seemed to have nothing in particular to recommend him; no good looks, talent, or visible charm, though he did display a certain agility shinning up and down ropes. He also killed a man with a weapon not unlike the entrenching tool, and this, we felt, may have awakened some hereditary emotion in Jassy's bosom. The film itself was one of those of which it is very difficult for the ordinary English person, as opposed to the film fan, to make head or tail, and every time Cary Goon appeared the scene had to be played over again for Uncle Matthew, who had come determined that no detail should escape him. He absolutely identified the actor with his part, and kept saying:

'What does the fella want to do that for? Bloody fool, he might know there would be an ambush there. I can't hear a word the fella says – put that bit on again, Merlin.'

At the end he said he didn't think much of the cove, he appeared to have no discipline and had been most impertinent to his commanding officer. 'Needs a haircut! and I shouldn't wonder if he drinks.'

Uncle Matthew said how-do-you-do and good-bye quite civilly to Lord Merlin. He really seemed to be mellowing with age and misfortune.

After great consultations it was decided that some member of the family, not Aunt Sadie or Uncle Matthew, would have to go to Hollywood and bring Jassy home. But who? Linda, of course, would have been the obvious person, had she not been under a cloud and, furthermore, engrossed with her own life. But it would be no use to send one bolter to fetch back another bolter, so somebody else must be found. In the end, after some persuasion ('madly inconvenient just now that I have started this course of *piqûres*') Davey consented to go with Louisa – the good, the sensible Louisa.

By the time this had been decided, Jassy had arrived in Hollywood, had broadcast her matrimonial intentions to all and sundry, and the whole thing appeared in the newspapers, which devoted pages of space to it, and (it was a silly season with nothing else to occupy their readers) turned it into a sort of serial story. Alconleigh now entered upon a state of siege. Journalists braved Uncle Matthew's stock-whips, his bloodhounds, his terrifying blue flashes, and hung around the village, penetrating even into the house itself in their search for local colour. Their stories were a daily delight. Uncle Matthew was made into something between Heathcliff, Dracula, and the Earl of Dorincourt; Alconleigh a sort of Nightmare Abbey or House of Usher; and Aunt Sadie a character not unlike David Copperfield's mother. Such courage, ingenuity, and toughness were displayed by these correspondents that it came as no surprise to any of us when, later on, they did so well in the war. 'War report by So-and-So –'

Uncle Matthew would then say:

'Isn't that the damned sewer I found hiding under my bed?'

He greatly enjoyed the whole affair. Here were opponents worthy of him, not jumpy housemaids, and lachrymose governesses with wounded feelings, but tough young men who did not care what methods they used so long as they could get inside his house and produce a story.

He also seemed greatly to enjoy reading about himself in the newspapers and we all began to suspect that Uncle Matthew had a hidden passion for publicity. Aunt Sadie, on the other hand, found the whole thing very distasteful indeed.

It was thought most vital to keep it from the press that Davey and Louisa were leaving on a voyage of rescue, as the sudden surprise of seeing them might prove an important element in influencing Jassy to return. Unfortunately, Davey could not embark on so long and so trying a journey without a medicine chest, specially designed. While this was being made they missed one boat, and, by the time it was ready, the sleuths were on their track – this unlucky medicine chest having played the same part that Marie Antoinette's *nécessaire* did in the escape to Varennes.

Several journalists accompanied them on the crossing, but did not reap much of a reward, as Louisa was prostrated with seasickness and Davey spent his whole time closeted with the ship's doctor, who asserted that his trouble was a cramped intestine, which could easily be cured by manipulation, rays, diet, exercises, and injections, all of which, or resting after which, occupied every moment of his day.

On their arrival in New York, however, they were nearly torn to pieces, and we were able, in common with the whole of the two great English-speaking nations, to follow their every move. They even appeared on the newsreel, looking worried and hiding their faces behind books.

It proved to have been a useless trip. Two days after their arrival in Hollywood Jassy became Mrs Cary Goon. Louisa telegraphed this news home, adding, 'Cary is a terrific Hon.'

There was one comfort, the marriage killed the story.

'He's a perfect dear,' said Davey, on his return. 'A little man like a nut. I'm sure Jassy will be madly happy with him.'

Aunt Sadie, however, was neither reassured nor consoled. It seemed hard luck to have reared a pretty love of a daughter in order for her to marry a little man like a nut, and live with him thousands of miles away. The house in London was cancelled, and the Alconleighs lapsed into such a state of gloom that the next blow, when it fell, was received with fatalism.

Matt, aged sixteen, ran away from Eton, also in a blaze of newspaper publicity, to the Spanish war. Aunt Sadie minded this very much, but I don't think Uncle Matthew did. The desire to fight seemed to him entirely natural, though, of course, he deplored the fact that Matt was fighting for foreigners. He did not take a particular line against the Spanish reds, they were brave boys and had had the good sense to bump off a lot of idolatrous monks, nuns, and priests, a proceeding of which he approved, but it was surely a pity to fight in a second-class war when there would so soon be a first-class one available. It was decided that no steps should be taken to retrieve Matt.

Christmas that year was a very sad one at Alconleigh. The children seemed to be melting away like the ten little nigger boys. Bob and Louisa, neither of whom had given their parents one moment of disquiet in their lives, John Fort William, as dull as a man could be, Louisa's children, so good, so pretty, but lacking in any sort of originality, could not make up for the absence of Linda, Matt, and Jassy, while Robin and Victoria, full as they were of jokes and fun, were swamped by the general atmosphere, and kept themselves to themselves as much as possible in the Hons' cupboard.

Linda was married in the Caxton Hall as soon as her divorce was through. The wedding was as different from her first as the Left-wing parties were different from the other kind. It was not exactly sad, but dismal, uncheerful, and with no feeling of happiness. Few of Linda's friends, and none of her relations except Davey and me were there; Lord Merlin sent two Aubusson rugs and some orchids but did not turn up himself. The pre-Christian chatters had faded out of Linda's life, discouraged, loudly bewailing the great loss she was in theirs.

Christian arrived late, and hurried in, followed by several comrades.

'I must say he is wonderful-looking,' Davey hissed in my ear, 'but oh, bother it all!'

There was no wedding breakfast, and, after a few moments of aimless and rather embarrassed hanging about in the street outside the hall, Linda and Christian went off home. Feeling provincial, up in London for the day and determined to see a little life, I made Davey give me luncheon at the Ritz. This had a still further depressing effect on my spirits. My clothes, so nice and suitable for the George, so much admired by the other dons' wives ('My dear, where did you get that lovely tweed?'), were, I now realized, almost bizarre in their dowdiness; it was the floating panels of taffeta all over again. I thought of those dear little black children, three of them now, in their nursery at home, and of dear Alfred in his study, but just for the moment this thought was no consolation. I passionately longed to have a tiny fur hat, or a tiny ostrich hat, like the two ladies at the next table. I longed for a neat black dress, diamond clips and a dark mink coat, shoes like surgical boots, long crinkly black suède gloves, and smooth polished hair. When I tried to explain all this to Davey, he remarked, absent-mindedly:

'Oh, but it doesn't matter a bit for you, Fanny, and, after all, how can you have time for *les petits soins de la personne* with so many other, more important things to think of.'

I suppose he thought this would cheer me up.

Soon after her marriage the Alconleighs took Linda back into the fold. They did not count second weddings of divorced people, and Victoria had been severely reprimanded for saying that Linda was engaged to Christian.

'You can't be engaged when you're married.'

It was not the fact of the ceremony which had mollified them, in their eyes Linda would be living from now on in a state of adultery, but they felt the need of her too strongly to keep up a quarrel. The thin end of the wedge (luncheon with Aunt

Sadie at Gunters) was inserted, and soon everything was all right again between them. Linda went quite often to Alconleigh, though she never took Christian there, feeling that it would benefit nobody were she to do so.

Linda and Christian lived in their house in Cheyne Walk, and, if Linda was not as happy as she had hoped to be, she exhibited, as usual, a wonderful shop-front. Christian was certainly very fond of her, and, in his way, he tried to be kind to her, but, as Lord Merlin had prophesied, he was much too detached to make any ordinary woman happy. He seemed, for weeks on end, hardly to be aware of her presence; at other times he would wander off and not reappear for days, too much engrossed in whatever he was doing to let her know where he was or when she might expect to see him again. He would eat and sleep where he happened to find himself – on a bench at St Pancras' station, or just sitting on the doorstep of some empty house. Cheyne Walk was always full of comrades, not chatting to Linda, but making speeches to each other, restlessly rushing about, telephoning, typewriting, drinking, quite often sleeping in their clothes, but without their boots, on Linda's drawing-room sofa.

Money troubles accrued. Christian, though he never appeared to spend any money, had a disconcerting way of scattering it. He had few, but expensive amusements, one of his favourites being to ring up the Nazi leaders in Berlin, and other European politicians, and have long teasing talks with them, costing pounds a minute. 'They can never resist a call from London,' he would say, nor, unfortunately, could they. At last, greatly to Linda's relief, the telephone was cut off, as the bill could not be paid.

I must say that Alfred and I both liked Christian very much. We are intellectual pinks ourselves, enthusiastic agreers with the *New Statesman*, so that his views, while rather more advanced than ours, had the same foundation of civilized humanity, and he seemed to us a great improvement on Tony. All the same, he was a hopeless husband for Linda. Her craving was for love, personal and particular, centred upon herself; wider love, for the poor, the sad, and the unattractive, had no appeal for her, though she honestly tried to believe that it had. The more I saw of Linda at this time, the more certain I felt that another bolt could not be very far ahead.

Twice a week Linda worked in a Red bookshop. It was run by a huge, perfectly silent comrade, called Boris. Boris liked to get drunk from Thursday afternoon, which was closing day in that district, to Monday morning, so Linda said she would take it over on Friday and Saturday. An extraordinary transformation would then occur. The books and tracts which mouldered there month after month, getting damper and dustier until at last they had to be thrown away, were hurried into the background, and their place taken by Linda's own few but well-loved favourites. Thus for *Whither British Airways?* was substituted *Around the World in Forty Days*, *Karl Marx, the Formative Years* was replaced by *The Making of a Marchioness*, and *The Giant of the Kremlin* by *Diary of a Nobody*, while *A Challenge to Coal-Owners* made way for *King Solomon's Mines*.

Hardly would Linda have arrived in the morning on her days there, and taken down the shutters, than the slummy little street would fill with motor cars, headed by Lord Merlin's electric brougham. Lord Merlin did great propaganda for the shop, saying that Linda was the only person who had ever succeeded in finding him *Froggie's Little Brother* and *Le Père Goriot*. The chatters came back in force, delighted to find Linda so easily accessible again, and without Christian, but sometimes there were embarrassing moments when they came face to face with comrades. Then they would buy a book and beat a hasty retreat, all except Lord Merlin, who had never felt disconcerted in his life. He took a perfectly firm line with the comrades.

'How are you today?' he would say with great emphasis, and then glower furiously at them until they left the shop.

All this had an excellent effect upon the financial side of the business. Instead of showing, week by week, an enormous loss, to be refunded from one could guess where, it now became the only Red bookshop in England to make a profit. Boris was greatly praised by his employers, the shop received a medal, which was stuck upon the sign, and the comrades all said that Linda was a good girl and a credit to the Party.

The rest of her time was spent in keeping house for Christian and the comrades, an occupation which entailed trying to induce a series of maids to stay with them, and making sincere, but sadly futile, efforts to take their place when they had left, which they usually did at the end of the first week. The comrades were not very nice or very thoughtful to maids.

'You know, being a Conservative is much more restful,' Linda said to me once in a moment of confidence, when she was being unusually frank about her life, 'though one must remember that it is bad, not good. But it does take place within certain hours, and then finish, whereas Communism seems to eat up all one's life and energy. And the comrades are such Hons, but sometimes they make me awfully cross, just as Tony used to make one furious when he talked about the workers. I often feel rather the same when they talk about us – you see, just like Tony, they've got it all wrong. I'm all for them stringing up Sir Leicester, but if they started on Aunt Emily and Davey, or even on Fa, I don't think I could stand by and watch. I suppose one is neither fish, nor good red herring, that's the worst of it.'

'But there is a difference,' I said, 'between Sir Leicester and Uncle Matthew.'

'Well, that's what I'm always trying to explain. Sir Leicester grubs up his money in London, goodness knows how, but Fa gets it from his land, and he puts a great deal back into the land, not only money, but work. Look at all the things he does for no pay – all those boring meetings. County Council, J.P., and so on. And he's a good landlord, he takes trouble. You see, the comrades don't know the country – they didn't know you could get a lovely cottage with a huge garden for 2s. 6d. a week until I told them, and then they hardly believed it. Christian knows, but he says the system is wrong, and I expect it is.'

'What exactly does Christian do?' I said.

'Oh, everything you can think of. Just at the moment he's writing a book on famine – goodness! it's sad – and there's a dear little Chinese comrade who comes and tells him what famine is like, you never saw such a fat man in your life.'

I laughed.

Linda said, hurriedly and guiltily:

'Well, I may seem to laugh at the comrades, but at least one does know they are doing good not harm, and not living on other people's slavery like Sir Leicester, and really you know I do simply love them, though I sometimes wish they were a little more fond of chatting, and not quite so sad and earnest and down on everybody.'

15

Early in 1939, the population of Catalonia streamed over the Pyrenees into the Roussillon, a poor and little-known province of France, which now, in a few days, found itself inhabited by more Spaniards than Frenchmen. Just as the lemmings suddenly pour themselves in a mass suicide off the coast of Norway, knowing neither whence they come nor whither bound, so great is the compulsion that hurls them into the Atlantic, thus half a million men, women, and children suddenly took flight into the bitter mountain weather, without pausing for thought. It was the greatest movement of population, in the time it took, that had ever hitherto been seen. Over the mountains they found no promised land; the French government, vacillating in its policy, neither turned them back with machine-guns at the frontier, nor welcomed them as brothers-in-arms against Fascism. It drove them like a herd of beasts down to the cruel salty marshes of that coast, enclosed them, like a herd of beasts, behind barbed-wire fences, and forgot all about them.

Christian, who had always, I think, had a half-guilty feeling about not having fought in Spain, immediately rushed off to Perpignan to see what was happening, and what, if anything, could be done. He wrote an endless series of reports, memoranda, articles, and private letters about the conditions he had found in the camps, and then settled down to work in an office financed by various English humanitarians with the object of improving the camps, putting refugee families in touch again, and getting as many as possible out of France. This office was run by a young man who had lived many years in Spain called Robert Parker. As soon as it became clear that there would not be, as at first was expected, an outbreak of typhus, Christian sent for Linda to join him in Perpignan.

It so happened that Linda had never before been abroad in her life. Tony had found all his pleasures, hunting, shooting, and golf, in England, and had grudged the extra days out of his holiday which would have been spent in travelling; while it would never have occurred to the Alconleighs to visit the Continent for any other purpose than that of fighting. Uncle Matthew's four years in France and Italy between 1914 and 1918 had given him no great opinion of foreigners.

'Frogs,' he would say, 'are slightly better than Huns or Wops, but abroad is unutterably bloody and foreigners are fiends.'

The bloodiness of abroad, the fiendishness of foreigners had, in fact, become such a tenet of the Radlett family creed that Linda set forth on her journey with no little trepidation. I went to see her off at Victoria, she was looking intensely English in her long blond mink coat, the *Tatler* under her arm, and Lord Merlin's morocco dressing-case, with a canvas cover, in her hand.

'I hope you have sent your jewels to the bank,' I said.

'Oh, darling, don't tease, you know how I haven't got any now. But my money,' she said with a self-conscious giggle, 'is sewn into my stays. Fa rang up and begged me to, and I must say it did seem quite an idea. Oh, why aren't you coming? I do feel so terrified – think of sleeping in the train, all alone.'

'Perhaps you won't be alone,' I said. 'Foreigners are greatly given, I believe, to rape.'

'Yes, that would be nice, so long as they didn't find my stays. Oh, we are off – good-bye, darling, do think of me,' she said, and, clenching her suède-covered fist, she shook it out of the window in a Communist salute.

I must explain that I know everything that now happened to Linda, although I did not see her for another year, because afterwards, as will be shown, we spent a long quiet time together, during which she told it all to me, over and over again. It was her way of re-living happiness.

Of course the journey was an enchantment to her. The porters in their blue overalls, the loud, high conversations, of which, although she thought she knew French quite well, she did not understand a single word, the steamy, garlic-smelling heat of the French train, the delicious food, to which she was summoned by a little hurried bell, it was all from another world, like a dream.

She looked out of the window and saw chateaux, lime avenues, ponds, and villages exactly like those in the *Bibliothèque Rose* – she thought she must, at any moment, see Sophie in her white dress and unnaturally small black pumps cutting up goldfish, gorging herself on new bread and cream, or scratching the face of good, uncomplaining Paul. Her very stilted, very English French, got her across Paris and into the train for Perpignan without a hitch. Paris. She looked out of the window at the lighted dusky streets, and thought that never could any town have been so hauntingly beautiful.

A strange stray thought came into her head that, one day, she would come back here and be very happy, but she knew that it was not likely, Christian would never want to live in Paris. Happiness and Christian were still linked together in her mind at this time.

At Perpignan she found him in a whirl of business. Funds had been raised, a ship had been chartered, and plans were on foot for sending six thousand Spaniards out of the camps to Mexico. This entailed an enormous amount of staff work, as families (no Spaniard would think of moving without his entire family) had to be reunited from camps all over the place, assembled in a camp in Perpignan, and taken by train to the port of Cette, whence they finally embarked. The work was greatly complicated by the fact that Spanish husbands and wives do not share a surname. Christian explained all this to Linda almost before she was out of the train; he gave her an absent-minded peck on the forehead and rushed her to his office, hardly giving her time to deposit her luggage at an hotel on the way and scouting the idea that she might like a bath. He did not ask how she was or whether she had had a good journey – Christian always assumed that people were all right unless they told him to the contrary, when, except in the case of destitute, coloured, oppressed, leprous, or otherwise unattractive strangers, he would take absolutely no notice. He was really only interested in mass wretchedness, and never much cared for individual cases, however genuine their misery, while the idea that it is possible to have three square meals a day and a roof and yet be unhappy or unwell, seemed to him intolerable nonsense.

The office was a large shed with a yard round it. This yard was permanently full of refugees with mountains of luggage and quantities of children, dogs, donkeys, goats, and other appurtenances, who had just struggled over the mountains in their flight from Fascism, and were hoping that the English would be able to prevent them being put into camps. In certain cases they could be lent money, or given railway tickets enabling them to join relations in France and French Morocco, but the vast majority waited hours for an interview, only to be told that there was no hope for them. They would then, with great and heart-breaking politeness, apologize for having been a nuisance and withdraw. Spaniards have a highly developed sense of human dignity.

Linda was now introduced to Robert Parker and to Randolph Pine, a young writer who, having led a more or less playboy existence in the South of France, had gone to fight in Spain, and was now working in Perpignan from a certain feeling of responsibility towards those who had once been fellow soldiers. They seemed pleased that Linda had arrived, and were most friendly and welcoming, saying that it was nice to see a new face.

'You must give me some work to do,' said Linda.

'Yes, now what can we think of for you?' said Robert. 'There's masses of work, never fear, it's just a question of finding the right kind. Can you speak Spanish?'

'No.'

'Oh, well, you'll soon pick it up.'

'I'm quite sure I shan't,' said Linda doubtfully.

'What do you know about welfare work?'

'Oh, dear, how hopeless I seem to be. Nothing, I'm afraid.'

'Lavender will find her a job,' said Christian, who had settled down at his table and was flapping over a card index.

'Lavender?'

'A girl called Lavender Davis.'

'No! I know her quite well, she used to live near us in the country. In fact she was one of my bridesmaids.'

'That's it,' said Robert, 'she said she knew you, I'd forgotten. She's wonderful, she really works with the Quakers in the camps, but she helps us a great deal too. There's absolutely nothing she doesn't know about calories and babies' nappies, and expectant mummies, and so on, and she's the hardest worker I've ever come across.'

'I'll tell you,' said Randolph Pine, 'what you can do. There's a job simply waiting for you, and that is to arrange the accommodation on this ship that's going off next week.'

'Oh, yes, of course,' said Robert, 'the very thing. She can have this table and start at once.'

'Now look,' said Randolph. 'I'll show you. (What delicious scent you have, Après l'Ondée? I thought so.) Now here is a map of the ship – see – best cabins, not such good cabins, lousy cabins, and battened down under the hatches. And here is a list of the families who are going. All you have to do is to allocate each family its cabin – when you have decided which they are to have, you put the number of the cabin against the family – here – you see? And the number of the family on the cabin here, like that. Quite easy, but it takes time, and must be done so that when they arrive on the boat they will know exactly where to go with their things.'

'But how do I decide who gets the good ones and who is battened? Awfully tricky, isn't it?'

'Not really. The point is it's a strictly democratic ship run on republican principles, class doesn't enter into it. I should give decent cabins to families where there are small children or babies. Apart from that do it any way you like. Take a pin if you like. The only thing that matters is that it should be done, otherwise there'll be a wild scramble for the best places when they get on board.'

Linda looked at the list of families. It took the form of a card index, the head of each family having a card on which was written the number and names of his dependants.

'It doesn't give their ages,' said Linda. 'How am I to know if there are young babies?'

'That's a point,' said Robert. 'How is she to?'

'Quite easy,' said Christian. 'With Spaniards you can always tell. Before the war they were called either after saints or after episodes in the life of the Virgin – Anunciación, Asunción, Purificación, Concepción, Consuelo, etc. Since the Civil War they are called Carlos after Charlie Marx, Frederigo after Freddie Engels, or Estalina (very popular until the Russians let them down with a wallop), or else nice slogans like Solidaridad-Obrera, Libertad, and so on. Then you know the children are under three. Couldn't be simpler, really.'

Lavender Davis now appeared. She was indeed the same Lavender, dowdy, healthy, and plain, wearing an English country tweed and brogues. Her short brown hair curled over her head, and she had no make-up. She greeted Linda with enthusiasm, indeed, it had always been a fiction in the Davis family that Lavender and Linda were each other's greatest friends. Linda was delighted to see her, as one always is delighted to see a familiar face, abroad.

'Come on,' said Randolph, 'now we're all here let's go and have a drink at the Palmarium.'

For the next weeks, until her private life began to occupy Linda's attention, she lived in an atmosphere of alternate fascination and horror. She grew to love Perpignan, a strange little old town, so different from anything she had ever known, with its river and broad quays, its network of narrow streets, its huge wild-looking plane trees, and all around it the bleak vine-growing country of the Roussillon bursting into summery green under her very eyes. Spring came late and slowly, but when it came it was hand-in-hand with summer, and almost at once everything was baking and warm, and in the villages the people danced every night on concrete dancing floors under the plane trees. At week-ends the English, unable to eradicate such a national habit, shut up the office and made for Collioure on the coast, where they bathed and sunbathed and went for Pyrenean picnics.

But all this had nothing to do with the reason for their presence in these charming surroundings – the camps. Linda went to the camps nearly every day, and they filled her soul with despair. As she could not help much in the office owing to her lack of Spanish, nor with the children, since she knew nothing about calories, she was employed as a driver, and was always on the road in a Ford van full of supplies, or of refugees, or just taking messages to and from the camps. Often she had to sit and wait for hours on end while a certain man was found and his case dealt with; she would quickly be surrounded by a perfect concourse of men talking to her in their heavy guttural French. By this time the camps were quite decently organized; there were rows of orderly though depressing huts, and the men were getting regular meals, which, if not very appetizing, did at least keep body and soul together. But the sight of these thousands of human beings, young and healthy, herded behind wire away from their womenfolk, with nothing on earth to do day after dismal day, was a recurring torture to Linda. She began to think that Uncle Matthew had been right – that abroad, where such things could happen, was indeed unutterably bloody, and that foreigners, who could inflict them upon each other, must be fiends.

One day as she sat in her van, the centre, as usual, of a crowd of Spaniards, a voice said:

'Linda, what on earth are you doing here?'

And it was Matt.

He looked ten years older than when she had last seen him, grown up, in fact, and extremely handsome, his Radlett eyes infinitely blue in a dark-brown face.

'I've seen you several times,' he said, 'and I thought you had been sent to fetch me away so I made off, but then I found out you are married to that Christian fellow. Was he the one you ran away from Tony with?'

'Yes,' said Linda. 'I'd no idea, Matt. I thought you'd have been sure to go back to England.'

'Well, no,' said Matt. 'I'm an officer, you see – must stay with the boys.'

'Does Mummy know you're all right?'

'Yes, I told her – at least if Christian posted a letter I gave him.'

'I don't suppose so – he's never been known to post a letter in his life. He is funny, he might have told me.'

'He didn't know – I sent it under cover to a friend of mine to forward. Didn't want any of the English to find out I was here, or they would start trying to get me home. I know.'

'Christian wouldn't,' said Linda. 'He's all for people doing what they want to in life. You're very thin, Matt, is there anything you'd like?'

'Yes,' said Matt, 'some cigarettes and a couple of thrillers.'

After this Linda saw him most days. She told Christian, who merely grunted and said: 'He'll have to be got out before the world war begins. I'll see to that,' and she wrote and told her parents. The result was a parcel of clothes from Aunt Sadie, which Matt refused to accept, and a packing-case full of vitamin pills from Davey, which Linda did not even dare to show him. He was cheerful and full of jokes and high spirits, but then there is a difference, as Christian said, between staying in a place because you are obliged to, and staying there because you think it right. But in any case, with the Radlett family, cheerfulness was never far below the surface.

The only other cheerful prospect was the ship. It was only going to rescue from hell a few thousand of the refugees, a mere fraction of the total amount, but, at any rate, they would be rescued, and taken to a better world, with happy and useful future prospects.

When she was not driving the van Linda worked hard over the cabin arrangements, and finally got the whole thing fixed and finished in time for the embarkation.

All the English except Linda went to Cette for the great day, taking with them two M.P.s and a duchess, who had helped the enterprise in London and had come out to see the fruit of their work. Linda went over by bus to Argelès to see Matt.

'How odd the Spanish upper classes must be,' she said, 'they don't raise a finger to help their own people, but leave it all to strangers like us.'

'You don't know Fascists,' Matt said, gloomily.

'I was thinking yesterday when I was taking the Duchess round Barcarès – yes, but why an English duchess, aren't there any Spanish ones, and, come to that, why is it nothing but English working in Perpignan? I knew several Spaniards in London, why don't they come and help a bit? They'd be awfully useful. I suppose they speak Spanish.'

'Fa was quite right about foreigners being fiends,' said Matt, 'upper-class ones are, at least. All these boys are terrific Hons, I must say.'

'Well, I can't see the English leaving each other in the lurch like this, even if they did belong to different parties. I think it's shameful.'

Christian and Robert came back from Cette in a cheerful mood. The arrangements had gone like clockwork, and a baby which had been born during the first half-hour on the ship was named Embarcación. It was the kind of joke Christian very much enjoyed. Robert said to Linda:

'Did you work on any special plan when you were arranging the cabins, or how did you do it?'

'Why? Wasn't it all right?'

'Perfect. Everybody had a place, and made for it. But I just wondered what you went by when you allocated the good cabins, that's all.'

'Well, I simply,' said Linda, 'gave the best cabins to the people who had *Labrador* on their card, because I used to have one when I was little and he was such a terrific ... so sweet, you know.'

'Ah,' said Robert, gravely, 'all is now explained. *Labrador* in Spanish happens to mean labourer. So you see under your scheme (excellent by the way, most democratic) the farm hands all found themselves in luxury while the intellectuals were battened. That'll teach them not to be so clever. You did very well, Linda, we were all most grateful.'

'He was such a sweet Labrador,' said Linda dreamily. 'I wish you could have seen him. I do miss not having pets.'

'Can't think why you don't make an offer for the *sangsue*,' said Robert.

One of the features of Perpignan was a leech in a bottle in the window of a chemist's shop, with a typewritten notice saying: SI LA SANGSUE MONTE DANS LA BOUTEILLE IL FERA BEAU TEMPS. SI LA SANGSUE DESCEND – L'ORAGE.'

'It might be nice,' said Linda, 'but I can't somehow imagine her getting fond of one – too busy fussing about the weather all day, up and down, up and down – no time for human relationships.'

16

Linda never could remember afterwards whether she had really minded when she discovered that Christian was in love with Lavender Davis, and, if so, how much. She could not at all remember her emotions at that time. Certainly wounded pride must have played a part, though perhaps less so with Linda than it would have many women, as she did not suffer from much inferiority feeling. She must have seen that the past two years, her running away from Tony, all now went for nothing – but was she stricken at the heart, was she still in love with Christian, did she suffer the ordinary pangs of jealousy? I think not.

All the same, it was not a flattering choice. Lavender had seemed for years and years, stretching back into childhood, to epitomize everything that the Radletts considered most unromantic: a keen girl guide, hockey player, tree climber, head girl at her school, rider astride. She had never lived in a dream of love; the sentiment was, quite obviously, far removed from her thoughts, although Louisa and Linda, unable to imagine that anybody could exist without some tiny spark of it, used to invent romances for Lavender – the games mistress at her school or Dr Simpson of Merlinford (of whom Louisa had made up one of her nonsense rhymes – 'He's doctor and king's proctor too, and she's in love with him but he's in love with you'). Since those days she had trained as a nurse and as a welfare worker, had taken a course of law and political economy, and, indeed, might have done it all, Linda saw only too well, with the express intention of fitting herself to be a mate for Christian. The result was that in their present surroundings, with her calm assured confidence in her own ability, she easily outshone poor Linda. There was no competition, it was a walkover.

Linda did not discover their love in any vulgar way – surprising a kiss, or finding them in bed together. It was all far more subtle, more dangerous than that, being quite simply borne in upon her week after week that they found perfect happiness in each other, and that Christian depended entirely on Lavender for comfort and encouragement in his work. As this work now absorbed him heart and soul, as he thought of nothing else and never relaxed for a moment, dependence upon Lavender involved the absolute exclusion of Linda. She felt uncertain what to do. She could not have it out with Christian; there was nothing tangible to have out, and, in any case, such a proceeding would have been absolutely foreign to Linda's character. She dreaded scenes and rows more than anything else in the world, and she had no illusions about what Christian thought of her. She felt that he really rather despised her for having left Tony and her child so easily, and that, in his opinion, she took a silly, light-hearted, and superficial view of life. He liked serious, educated women, especially those who had made a study of welfare, especially Lavender. She had no desire to hear all this said. On the other hand she began to think that it would be as well for her to get away from Perpignan herself before Christian and Lavender went off together, as it seemed to her most probable that they would, wandering off hand in hand to search for and relieve other forms of human misery. Already she felt embarrassed when she was with Robert and Randolph, who were obviously very sorry for her and were always making little manoeuvres to prevent her noticing that Christian was spending every minute of the day with Lavender.

One afternoon, looking idly out of the window of her hotel bedroom, she saw them walking up the Quai Sadi Carnot together, completely absorbed, utterly contented in each other's company, radiating happiness. Linda was seized by an impulse and acted on it. She packed her things, wrote a hasty letter to Christian saying that she was leaving him for good, as she realized that their marriage had been a failure. She asked him to look after Matt. She then burnt her boats by adding a post-script (a fatal feminine practice), 'I think you had much better marry Lavender'. She bundled herself and her luggage into a taxi and took the night train for Paris.

The journey this time was horrible. She was, after all, very fond of Christian, and as soon as the train had left the station, she began to ask herself whether she had not in fact behaved stupidly and badly. He probably had a passing fancy for Lavender, based on common interests, which would fade away as soon as he got back to London. Possibly it was not even that, but simply that he was obliged, for his work, to be with Lavender all the time. His absent-minded treatment of Linda was, after all, nothing new, it had begun almost as soon as he had got her under his roof. She began to feel that she had done wrong to write that letter.

She had her return ticket, but very little money indeed, just enough, she reckoned, for dinner on the train and some food for the next day. Linda always had to translate French money into pounds, shillings, and pence before she knew where she was with it. She seemed to have about 18s. 6d. with her, so there could be no question of a sleeper. She had never sat up all night in a train, and the experience appalled her; it was like some dreadful feverish illness, when the painful hours drag by, each one longer than a week. Her thoughts brought her no comfort. She had torn up her life of the past two years, all that she had tried to put into her relationship with Christian, and thrown it away like so much waste-paper. If this was to be the outcome why had she ever left Tony, her real husband for better for worse, and her child? That was where her duty had lain, and well she knew it. She thought of my mother and shuddered. Could it be that she, Linda, was from now on doomed to a life that she utterly despised, that of a bolter?

And in London what would she find? A little empty, dusty house. Perhaps, she thought, Christian would pursue her, come and insist that she belonged to him. But in her heart she knew that he would not, and that she did not, and that this was the end. Christian believed too sincerely that people must be allowed to do as they wish in life, without interference. He was fond of Linda, she knew, but disappointed in her, she also knew; he would not himself have made the first move to separate, but would not much regret the fact that she had done so. Soon he would have some new scheme in his head, some new plan for suffering mortals, any mortals, anywhere, so long as there were enough of them and their misery was great. Then he would forget Linda, and possibly also Lavender, as if they had never been. Christian was not in passionate quest of love, he had other interests, other aims, and it mattered very little to him what woman happened to be in his life at a given moment. But in his nature, she knew, there was a certain ruthlessness. She felt that he would not forgive what she had done, or try to persuade her to go back on it, nor, indeed, was there any reason why he should do so.

It could not be said, thought Linda, as the train pursued its way through the blackness, that her life so far had been a marked success. She had found neither great love nor great happiness, and she had not inspired them in others. Parting with her would have been no death blow to either of her husbands; on the contrary, they would both have turned with relief to a much preferred mistress, who was more suited to them in every way. Whatever quality it is that can hold indefinitely the love and affection of a man she plainly did not possess, and now she was doomed to the lonely, hunted life of a beautiful but unattached woman. Where now was love that would last to the grave and far beyond? What had she done with her youth? Tears for her lost hopes and ideals, tears of self-pity in fact, began to pour down her cheeks. The three fat Frenchmen who shared the carriage with her were in a snoring sleep, she wept alone.

Sad and tired as Linda was, she could not but perceive the beauty of Paris that summer morning as she drove across it to the Gare du Nord. Paris in the early morning has a cheerful, bustling aspect, a promise of delicious things to come, a positive smell of coffee and croissants, quite peculiar to itself.

The people welcome a new day as if they were certain of liking it, the shopkeepers pull up their blinds serene in the expectation of good trade, the workers go happily to their work, the people who have sat up all night in night clubs go happily to their rest, the orchestra of motor car horns, of clanking trams, of whistling policemen tunes up for the daily symphony, and everywhere is joy. This joy, this life, this beauty did not underline poor Linda's fatigue and sadness, she felt it but was not of it. She turned her thoughts to old familiar London, she longed above all for her own bed, feeling as does a wounded beast when it crawls home to its lair. She only wanted to sleep undisturbed in her own bedroom.

But when she presented her return ticket at the Gare du Nord she was told, furiously, loudly, and unsympathetically, that it had expired.

'Voyons, madame – le 29 Mai. C'est aujourd'hui le 30, n'est-ce pas? Donc – !' Tremendous shruggings.

Linda was paralysed with horror. Her 18s. 6d. was by now down to 6s. 3d., hardly enough for a meal. She knew nobody in Paris, she had absolutely no idea what she ought to do, she was too tired and too hungry to think clearly. She stood like a statue of despair. Her porter, tired of waiting beside a statue of despair, deposited the luggage at its feet and went grumbling off. Linda sank onto her suitcase and began to cry; nothing so dreadful had ever happened to her before. She cried bitterly, she could not stop. People passed to and fro as if weeping ladies were the most ordinary phenomenon at the Gare du Nord. 'Fiends! Fiends!' she sobbed. Why had she not listened to her father, why had she ever come to this bloody abroad? Who would help her? In London there was a society, she knew, which looked after ladies stranded at railway stations; here, more likely, there would be one for shipping them off to South America. At any moment now somebody, some genial-looking old woman might come up and give her an injection, after which she would disappear for ever.

She became aware that somebody was standing beside her, not an old lady, but a short, stocky, very dark Frenchman in a black Homburg hat. He was laughing.

Linda took no notice, but went on crying. The more she cried the more he laughed. Her tears were tears of rage now, no longer of self-pity.

At last she said, in a voice which was meant to be angrily impressive, but which squeaked and shook through her handkerchief:

'*Allez-vous en.*'

For answer he took her hand and pulled her to her feet.

'*Bonjour, bonjour,*' he said.

'*Voulez-vous vous en aller?*' said Linda, rather more doubtfully, here at least was a human being who showed signs of taking some interest in her. Then she thought of South America.

'*If faut expliquer que je ne suis pas,*' she said, '*une esclave blanche. Je suis la fille d'un très important lord anglais.*'

The Frenchman gave a great bellow of laughter.

'One does not,' he said in the early perfect English of somebody who has spoken it from a child, 'have to be Sherlock Holmes to guess that.'

Linda was rather annoyed. An Englishwoman abroad may be proud of her nationality and her virtue without wishing them to jump so conclusively to the eye.

'French ladies,' he went on, 'covered with *les marques extérieurs de la richesse* never never sit crying on their suitcases at the Gare du Nord in the very early morning, while *esclaves blanches* always have protectors, and it is only too clear that you are unprotected just now.'

This sounded all right, and Linda was mollified.

'Now,' he said, 'I invite you to luncheon with me, but first you must have a bath and rest and a cold compress on your face.'

He picked up her luggage and walked to a taxi.

'Get in, please.'

Linda got in. She was far from certain that this was not the road to Buenos Aires, but something made her do as he said. Her powers of resistance were at an end, and she really saw no alternative.

'Hotel Montalembert,' he told the taxi man. 'Rue du Bac. *Je m'excuse, madame,* for not taking you to the Ritz, but I have a feeling for the Hotel Montalembert just now, that it will suit your mood this morning.'

Linda sat upright in her corner of the taxi, looking, she hoped, very prim. As she could not think of anything pertinent to say she remained silent. Her companion hummed a little tune, and seemed vastly amused. When they arrived at the hotel, he took a room for her, told the liftman to show her to it, told the *concierge* to send her up a *café complet*, kissed her hand, and said:

'*A tout à l'heure* – I will fetch you a little before one o'clock and we will go out to luncheon.'

Linda had her bath and breakfast and got into bed. When the telephone bell rang she was so sound asleep that it was a struggle to wake up.

'*Un monsieur qui demande, madame.*'

'*Je descends tout de suite,*' said Linda, but it took her quite half an hour to get ready.

17

'Ah! You keep me waiting,' he said, kissing her hand, or at least making a gesture of raising her hand towards his lips and then dropping it rather suddenly. 'That is a very good sign.'

'Sign of what?' said Linda. He had a two-seater outside the hotel and she got into it. She was feeling more like herself again.

'Oh, of this and that,' he said, letting in the clutch, 'a good augury for our affair, that it will be happy and last long.'

Linda became intensely stiff, English, and embarrassed, and said, self-consciously:

'We are not having an affair.'

'My name is Fabrice – may one ask yours?'

'Linda.'

'Linda. *Comme c'est joli*. With me, it usually lasts five years.'

He drove to a restaurant where they were shown, with some deference, to a table in a red plush corner. He ordered the luncheon and the wine in rapid French, the sort of French that Linda frankly could not follow, then, putting his hands on his knees, he turned to her and said:

'*Allons, racontez, madame.*'

'*Racontez* what?'

'Well, but of course, the story. Who was it that left you to cry on that suitcase?'

'He didn't. I left him. It was my second husband and I have left him for ever because he has fallen in love with another woman – a welfare worker, not that you'd know what that is, because I'm sure they don't exist in France. It just makes it worse, that's all.'

'What a very curious reason for leaving one's second husband. Surely with your experience of husbands you must have noticed that falling in love with other women is one of the things they do? However, it's an ill wind, and I don't complain. But why the suitcase? Why didn't you put yourself in the train and go back to Monsieur the important lord, your father?'

'That's what I was doing until they told me that my return ticket had expired. I only had 6s. 3d., and I don't know anybody in Paris, and I was awfully tired, so I cried.'

'The second husband – why not borrow some money from him? Or had you left a note on his pillow – women never can resist these little essays in literature, and they do make it rather embarrassing to go back, I know.'

'Well, anyhow he's in Perpignan, so I couldn't have.'

'Ah, you come from Perpignan. And what were you doing there, in the name of heaven?'

'In the name of heaven we were trying to stop you Frogs from teasing the poor Epagnards,' said Linda with some spirit.

'E-spa-gnols! So we are teasing them, are we?'

'Not so badly now – terribly at the beginning.'

'What were we supposed to do with them? We never invited them to come, you know.'

'You drove them into camps in that cruel wind, and gave them no shelter for weeks. Hundreds died.'

'It is quite a job to provide shelter, at a moment's notice, for half a million people. We did what we could – we fed them – the fact is that most of them are still alive.'

'Still herded in camps.'

'My dear Linda, you could hardly expect us to turn them loose on the countryside with no money – what would be the result? Do use your common sense.'

'You should mobilize them to fight in the war against Fascism that's coming any day now.'

'Talk about what you know and you won't get so angry. We haven't enough equipment for our own soldiers in the war against Germany that's coming – not any day, but after the harvest, probably in August. Now go on telling me about your husbands. It's so very much more interesting.'

'Only two. My first was a Conservative, and my second is a Communist.'

'Just as I guessed, your first is rich, your second is poor. I could see you once had a rich husband, the dressing-case and the fur coat, though it is a hideous colour, and no doubt, as far as one could see, with it bundled over your arm, a hideous shape. Still, *vison* usually betokens a rich husband somewhere. Then this dreadful linen suit you are wearing has ready-made written all over it.'

'You are rude, it's a very pretty suit.'

'And last year's. Jackets are getting longer you will find. I'll get you some clothes – if you were well dressed you would be quite good-looking, though it's true your eyes are small. Blue, a good colour, but small.'

'In England,' said Linda, 'I am considered a beauty.'

'Well, you have points.'

So this silly conversation went on and on, but it was only froth on the surface. Linda was feeling, what she had never so far felt for any man, an overwhelming physical attraction. It made her quite giddy, it terrified her. She could see that Fabrice was perfectly certain of the outcome, so was she perfectly certain, and that was what frightened her. How could she, Linda, with the horror and contempt she had always felt for casual affairs, allow herself to be picked up by any stray foreigner, and, having seen him only for an hour, long and long and long to be in bed with him? He was not even good-looking, he was exactly like dozens of other dark men in Homburgs that can be seen in the streets of any French town. But there was something about the way he looked at her which seemed to be depriving her of all balance. She was profoundly shocked, and, at the same time, intensely excited.

After luncheon they strolled out of the restaurant into brilliant sunshine.

'Come and see my flat,' said Fabrice.

'I would rather see Paris,' said Linda.

'Do you know Paris well?'

'I've never been here before in my life.'

Fabrice was really startled.

'Never been here before?' He could not believe it. 'What a pleasure for me, to show it all to you. There is so much to show, it will take weeks.'

'Unfortunately,' said Linda, 'I leave for England tomorrow.'

'Yes, of course. Then we must see it all this afternoon.'

They drove slowly round a few streets and squares, and then went for a stroll in the Bois. Linda could not believe that she had only just arrived there, that this was still the very day which she had seen unfolding itself, so full of promise, through her mist of morning tears.

'How fortunate you are to live in such a town,' she said to Fabrice. 'It would be impossible to be very unhappy here.'

'Not impossible,' he said. 'One's emotions are intensified in Paris – one can be more happy and also more unhappy here than in any other place. But it is always a positive source of joy to live here, and there is nobody so miserable as a Parisian in exile from his town. The rest of the world seems unbearably cold and bleak to us, hardly worth living in.' He spoke with great feeling.

After tea, which they had out of doors in the Bois, he drove slowly back into Paris. He stopped the car outside an old house in the rue Bonaparte, and said, again:

'Come and see my flat.'

'No, no,' said Linda. 'The time has now come for me to point out that I am *une femme sérieuse*.'

Fabrice gave his great bellow of laughter.

'Oh,' he said, shaking helplessly, 'how funny you are. What a phrase, *femme sérieuse*, where did you find it? And if so serious, how do you explain the second husband?'

'Yes, I admit that I did wrong, very wrong indeed, and made a great mistake. But that is no reason for losing control, for sliding down the hill altogether, for being picked up by strange gentlemen at the Gare du Nord and then immediately going with them to see their flat. And please, if you will be so kind as to lend me some money, I want to catch the London train tomorrow morning.'

'Of course, by all means,' said Fabrice.

He thrust a roll of banknotes into her hand, and drove her to the Hotel Mont-alembert. He seemed quite unmoved by her speech, and announced he would come back at eight o'clock to take her out to dinner.

Linda's bedroom was full of roses, it reminded her of when Moira was born.

'Really,' she thought with a giggle, 'this is a very penny-novelettish seduction, how can I be taken in by it?'

But she was filled with a strange, wild, unfamiliar happiness, and knew that this was love. Twice in her life she had mistaken something else for it; it was like seeing somebody in the street who you think is a friend, you whistle and wave and run after him, and it is not only not the friend, but not even very like him. A few minutes later the real friend appears in view, and then you can't imagine how you ever mistook that other person for him. Linda was now looking upon the authentic face of love, and she knew it, but it frightened her. That it should come so casually, so much by a series of accidents, was frightening. She tried to remember how she had felt when she had first loved her two husbands. There must have been strong and impelling emotion; in both cases she had disrupted her own life, upset her parents and friends remorse-lessly, in order to marry them, but she could not recall it. Only she knew that never before, not even in dreams, and she was a great dreamer of love, had she felt anything remotely like this. She told herself, over and over again, that tomorrow she must go back to London, but she had no intention of going back, and she knew it.

Fabrice took her out to dinner and then to a night club, where they did not dance, but chatted endlessly. She told him about Uncle Matthew, Aunt Sadie and Louisa and Jassy and Matt, and he could not hear enough, and egged her on to excesses of exaggeration about her family and all their various idiosyncrasies.

'*Et* Jassy – *et* Matt – *alors, racontez.*'

And she recounted, for hours.

In the taxi on their way home she refused again to go back with him or to let him come into the hotel with her. He did not insist, he did not try to hold her hand, or touch her at all. He merely said:

'*C'est une résistance magnifique, je vous félicite de tout mon cœur, madame.*'

Outside the hotel she gave him her hand to say good night. He took it in both of his and really kissed it.

'*A demain,*' he said, and got into the taxi.

'*Allô – allô.*'

'Hullo.'

'Good morning. Are you having breakfast?'

'Yes.'

'I thought I heard a coffee-cup clattering. Is it good?'

'It's so delicious that I have to keep stopping, for fear of finishing it too quickly. Are you having yours?'

'Had it. I must tell you that I like very long conversations in the morning, and I shall expect you to *raconter des histoires.*'

'Like Schéhérazade?'

'Yes, just like. And you're not to get that note in your voice of "now I'm going to ring off", as English people always do.'

'What English people do you know?'

'I know some. I was at school in England, and at Oxford.'

'No! When?'

'1920.'

'When I was nine. Fancy, perhaps I saw you in the street – we used to do all our shopping in Oxford.'

'Elliston & Cavell?'

'Oh, yes, and Webbers.'

There was a silence.

'Go on,' he said.

'Go on, what?'

'I mean don't ring off. Go on telling.'

'I shan't ring off. As a matter of fact I adore chatting. It's my favourite thing, and I expect you will want to ring off ages before I do.'

They had a long and very silly conversation, and, at the end of it, Fabrice said:

'Now get up, and in an hour I will fetch you and we will go to Versailles.'

At Versailles, which was an enchantment to Linda, she was reminded of a story she had once read about two English ladies who had seen the ghost of Marie Antoinette sitting in her garden at the Little Trianon. Fabrice found this intensely boring, and said so.

'*Histoires,*' he said, 'are only of interest when they are true, or when you have made them up specially to amuse me. *Histoires de revenants*, made up by some dim old English virgins, are neither true nor interesting. *Donc plus d'histoires de revenants, madame, s'il vous plaît.*'

'All right,' said Linda, crossly. 'I'm doing my best to please – you tell me a story.'

'Yes, I will – and this story is true. My grandmother was very beautiful and had many lovers all her life, even when she was quite old. A short time before she died she was in Venice with my mother, her daughter, and one day, floating up some canal in their gondola, they saw a little palazzo of pink marble, very exquisite. They stopped the gondola to look at it, and my mother said: "I don't believe anybody lives there, what about trying to see the inside?"

'So they rang the bell, and an old servant came and said that nobody had lived there for many, many years, and he would show it to them if they liked. So they went in and upstairs to the *salone*, which had three windows looking over the canal and was decorated with fifteenth-century plaster work, white on a pale blue background. It was a perfect room. My grandmother seemed strangely moved, and stood for a long time in silence. At last she said to my mother:

'"If, in the third drawer of that bureau there is a filigree box containing a small gold key on a black velvet ribbon, this house belongs to me."

'And my mother looked, and there was, and it did. One of my grandmother's lovers had given it to her years and years before, when she was quite young, and she had forgotten all about it.'

'Goodness,' said Linda, 'what fascinating lives you foreigners do lead.'

'And it belongs to me now.'

He put up his hand to Linda's forehead and stroked back a strand of hair which was loose:

'And I would take you there tomorrow if –'

'If what?'

'One must wait here now, you see, for the war.'

'Oh, I keep forgetting the war,' said Linda.

'Yes, let's forget it. *Comme vous êtes mal coiffée, ma chère.*'

'If you don't like my clothes and don't like my hair and think my eyes are so small, I don't know what you see in me.'

'*Quand même j'avoue qu'il y a quelquechose,*' said Fabrice.

Again they dined together.

Linda said: 'Haven't you any other engagements?'

'Yes, of course. I have cancelled them.'

'Who are your friends?'

'*Les gens du monde.* And yours?'

'When I was married to Tony, that is, my first husband, I used to go out in the *monde*, it was my life. In those days I loved it. But then Christian didn't approve of it, he stopped me going to parties and frightened away my friends, whom he considered frivolous and idiotic, and we saw nothing but serious people trying to put the world right. I used to laugh at them, and rather long for my other friends, but now I don't know. Since I was at Perpignan perhaps I have become more serious myself.'

'Everybody is getting more serious, that's the way things are going. But, whatever one may be in politics, right, left, Fascist, Communist, *les gens du monde* are the only possible ones for friends. You see, they have made a fine art of personal relationships and of all that pertains to them – manners, clothes, beautiful houses, good food, everything that makes life agreeable. It would be silly not to take advantage of that. Friendship is something to be built up carefully, by people with leisure, it is an art, nature does not enter into it. You should never despise social life – *de la haute société* – I mean, it can be a very satisfying one, entirely artificial of course, but absorbing. Apart from the life of the intellect and the contemplative religious life, which few people are qualified to enjoy, what else is there to distinguish man from the animals but his social life? And who understand it so well and who can make it so smooth and so amusing as *les gens du monde*? But one cannot have it at the same time as a love affair, one must be whole-hearted to enjoy it, so I have cancelled all my engagements.'

'What a pity,' said Linda, 'because I'm going back to London tomorrow morning.'

'Ah yes, I had forgotten. What a pity.'

'*Allô – allô.*'

'Hullo.'

'Were you asleep?'

'Yes, of course. What's the time?'

'About two. Shall I come round and see you?'

'Do you mean now?'

'Yes.'

'I must say it would be very nice, but the only thing is, what would the night porter think?'

'*Ma chère*, how English you are. *Eh bien; je vais vous le dire – il ne se fera aucune illusion.*'

'No, I suppose not.'

'But I don't imagine he's under any illusion as it is. After all, I come here for you three times every day – you've seen nobody else, and French people are quite quick at noticing these things, you know.'

'Yes – I see –'

'*Alors, c'est entendu – à tout à l'heure.*'

The next day Fabrice installed her in a flat, he said it was *plus commode*. He said, 'When I was young I liked to be very romantic and run all kinds of risks. I used to hide in wardrobes, be brought into the house in a trunk, disguise myself as a footman, and climb in at the windows. How I used to climb! I remember once, half-way up a creeper there was a wasps' nest – oh the agony – I wore a Kestos *soutien-gorge* for a week afterwards. But now I prefer to be comfortable, to follow a certain routine, and have my own key.'

Indeed, Linda thought, nobody could be less romantic and more practical than Fabrice, no nonsense about him. A little nonsense, she thought, would have been rather nice.

It was a beautiful flat, large and sunny, and decorated in the most expensive kind of modern taste. It faced south and west over the Bois de Boulogne, and was on a level with the tree-tops. Tree-tops and sky made up the view. The enormous windows worked like the windows of a motor car, the whole of the glass disappearing into the wall. This was a great joy to Linda, who loved the open air and loved to sunbathe for hours with no clothes on, until she was hot and brown and sleepy and happy. Belonging to the flat, belonging, it was evident, to Fabrice, was a charming elderly *femme de ménage* called Germaine. She was assisted by various other elderly women who came and went in a bewildering succession. She was obviously most efficient, she had all Linda's things out of her suitcase, ironed and folded away, in a moment, and then went off to the kitchen, where she began to prepare dinner. Linda could not help wondering how many other people Fabrice had kept in this flat; however, as she was unlikely to find out, and, indeed, had no wish to know, she put the thought from her. There was no trace of any former occupant, not so much as a scribbled telephone number or the mark of a lipstick anywhere to be seen; the flat might have been done up yesterday.

In her bath, before dinner, Linda thought rather wistfully of Aunt Sadie. She, Linda, was now a kept woman and an adulteress, and Aunt Sadie, she knew, wouldn't like that. She hadn't liked it when Linda had committed adultery with Christian, but he, at least, was English, and Linda had been properly introduced to him and knew his surname. Also, Christian had all along intended to marry her. But how much less would Aunt Sadie like her daughter to pick up an unknown, nameless foreigner and go off to live with him in luxury. It was a long step from lunching in Oxford to this, though Uncle Matthew would, no doubt, have considered it a step down the same road if he knew her situation, and he would disown her for ever, throw her out into the snow, shoot Fabrice, or take any other violent action which might occur to him. Then something would happen to make him laugh, and all would be well again. Aunt Sadie was a different matter. She would not say very much, but she would brood over it and take it to heart, and wonder if there had not been something wrong about her method of bringing up Linda which had led to this; Linda most profoundly hoped that she would never find out.

In the middle of this reverie the telephone bell rang. Germaine answered it, tapped on the bathroom door, and said:

'*M. le duc sera légèrement en retard, madame.*'

'All right – thank you,' said Linda.

At dinner she said:

'Could one know your name?'

'Oh,' said Fabrice. 'Hadn't you discovered that? What an extraordinary lack of curiosity. My name is Sauveterre. In short, *madame*, I am happy to tell you that I am a very rich duke, a most agreeable thing to be, even in these days.'

'How lovely for you. And, while we are on the subject of your private life, are you married?'

'No.'

'Why not?'

'My fiancée died.'

'Oh, how sad – what was she like?'

'Very pretty.'

'Prettier than me?'

'Much prettier. Very correct.'

'More correct than me?'

'*Vous – vous êtes une folle, madame, aucune correction. Et elle était gentille – mais d'une gentillesse, la pauvre.*'

For the first time since she knew him, Fabrice had become infinitely sentimental, and Linda was suddenly shaken by the pangs of a terrible jealousy, so terrible that she felt quite faint. If she had not already recognized the fact, she would have known now, for certain and always, that this was to be the great love of her life.

'Five years,' she said, 'is quite a long time when it's all in front of you.'

But Fabrice was still thinking of the fiancée.

'She died much more than five years ago – fifteen years in the autumn. I always go and put late roses on her grave, those little tight roses with very dark green leaves that never open properly – they remind me of her. *Dieu, que c'est triste.*'

'And what was her name?' said Linda.

'Louise. *Enfant unique du dernier Rancé.* I often go and see her mother, who is still alive, a remarkable old woman. She was brought up in England at the court of the Empress Eugénie, and Rancé married her in spite of that, for love. You can imagine how strange everybody found it.'

A deep melancholy settled on them both. Linda saw too clearly that she could not hope to compete with a fiancée who was not only prettier and more correct than she was, but also dead. It seemed most unfair. Had she remained alive her prettiness would surely, after fifteen years of marriage, have faded away, her correctness have become a bore; dead, she was embalmed for ever in her youth, her beauty, and her *gentillesse*.

After dinner, however, Linda was restored to happiness. Being made love to by Fabrice was an intoxication, quite different from anything she had hitherto experienced.

('I was forced to the conclusion,' she said, when telling me about this time, 'that neither Tony nor Christian had an inkling of what we used to call the facts of life. But I suppose all Englishmen are hopeless as lovers.'

'Not all,' I said, 'the trouble with most of them is that their minds are not on it, and it happens to require a very great deal of application. Alfred,' I told her, 'is wonderful.'

'Oh, good,' she said, but she sounded unconvinced I thought.)

They sat until late looking out of the open window. It was a hot evening, and, when the sun had gone, a green light lingered behind the black bunches of the trees until complete darkness fell.

'Do you always laugh when you make love?' said Fabrice.

'I hadn't thought about it, but I suppose I do. I generally laugh when I'm happy and cry when I'm not, I am a simple character, you know. Do you find it odd?'

'Very disconcerting at first, I must say.'

'But why – don't most women laugh?'

'Indeed they do not. More often they cry.'

'How extraordinary – don't they enjoy it?'

'It is nothing to do with enjoyment. If they are young they call on their mothers, if they are religious they call on the Virgin to forgive them. But I have never known one who laughed except you. *Mais qu'est-ce que vous voulez, vous êtes une folle.*'

Linda was fascinated.

'What else do they do?'

'What they all do, except you, is to say: *"Comme vous devez me mépriser."'*

'But why should you despise them?'

'Oh, really, my dear, one does, that's all.'

'Well, I call that most unfair. First you seduce them, then you despise them, poor things. What a monster you are.'

'They like it. They like grovelling about and saying *"Qu'est-ce que j'ai fait? Mon Dieu, hélas Fabrice, que pouvez-vous bien penser de moi? O, que j'ai honte."* It's all part of the thing to them. But you, you seem unaware of your shame, you just roar with laughter. It is very strange. *Pas désagréable, il faut avouer.'*

'Then what about the fiancée,' said Linda, 'didn't you despise her?'

'*Mais non, voyons,* of course not. She was a virtuous woman.'

'Do you mean to say you never went to bed with her?'

'Never. Never would such a thing have crossed my mind in a thousand thousand years.'

'Goodness,' said Linda. 'In England we always do.'

'*Ma chère, c'est bien connu, le côté animal des anglais.* The English are a drunken and an incontinent race, it is well known.'

'They don't know it. They think it's foreigners who are all those things.'

'French women are the most virtuous in the world,' said Fabrice, in the tones of exaggerated pride with which Frenchmen always talk about their women.

'Oh, dear,' said Linda, sadly. 'I was so virtuous once. I wonder what happened to me. I went wrong when I married my first husband, but how was I to know? I thought he was a god and that I should love him for ever. Then I went wrong again when I ran away with Christian, but I thought I loved him, and I did too, much much more than Tony, but he never really loved me, and very soon I bored him, I wasn't serious enough, I suppose. Anyhow, if I hadn't done these things, I shouldn't have ended up on a suitcase at the Gare du Nord and I would never have met you, so, really, I'm glad. And in my next life, wherever I happen to be born, I must remember to fly to the boulevards as soon as I'm of marriageable age, and find a husband there.'

'*Comme c'est gentil,*' said Fabrice, '*et, en effet,* French marriages are generally very very happy you know. My father and mother had a cloudless life together, they loved each other so much that they hardly went out in society at all. My mother still lives in a sort of afterglow of happiness from it. What a good woman she is!'

'I must tell you,' Linda went on, 'that my mother and one of my aunts, one of my sisters and my cousin, are virtuous women, so virtue is not unknown in my family. And anyway, Fabrice, what about your grandmother?'

'Yes,' said Fabrice, with a sigh. 'I admit that she was a great sinner. But she was also *une très grande dame,* and she died fully redeemed by the rites of the Church.'

18

Their life now began to acquire a routine. Fabrice dined with her every night in the flat – he never took her out to a restaurant again – and stayed with her until seven o'clock the following morning. '*J'ai horreur de coucher seul,*' he said. At seven he would get up, dress, and go home, in time to be in his bed at eight o'clock, when his breakfast was brought in. He would have his breakfast, read the newspapers, and, at nine, ring up Linda and talk nonsense for half an hour, as though he had not seen her for days.

'Go on,' he would say, if she showed any signs of flagging. '*Allons, des histoires!*'

During the day she hardly saw him. He always lunched with his mother, who had the first-floor flat in the house where he lived on the ground floor. Sometimes he took Linda sight-seeing in the afternoon, but generally he did not appear until about half-past seven, soon after which they dined.

Linda occupied her days buying clothes, which she paid for with great wads of banknotes given her by Fabrice.

'Might as well be hanged for a sheep as a lamb,' she thought. 'And as he despises me anyway it can't make very much difference.'

Fabrice was delighted. He took an intense interest in her clothes, looked them up and down, made her parade round her drawing-room in them, forced her to take them back to the shops for alterations which seemed to her quite unnecessary, but which proved in the end to have made all the difference. Linda had never before fully realized the superiority of French clothes to English. In London she had been considered exceptionally well dressed, when she was married to Tony; she now realized that never could she have had, by French standards, the smallest pretensions to *chic*. The things she had with her seemed to her so appallingly dowdy, so skimpy and miserable and without line, that she went to the Galeries Lafayette and bought herself a ready-made dress there before she dared to venture into the big houses. When she did finally emerge from them with a few clothes, Fabrice advised her to get a great many more. Her taste, he said, was not at all bad, for an Englishwoman, though he doubted whether she would really become *élégante* in the true sense of the word.

'Only by trial and error,' he said, 'can you find out your *genre*, can you see where you are going. *Continuez, donc, ma chère, allez-y. Jusqu'à présent, ça ne va pas mal du tout.*'

The weather now became hot and sultry, holiday, seaside weather. But this was 1939, and men's thoughts were not of relaxation but of death, not of bathing-suits but of uniforms, not of dance music but of trumpets, while beaches for the next few years were to be battle and not pleasure grounds. Fabrice said every day how much he longed to take Linda to the Riviera, to Venice and to his beautiful chateau in the Dauphine. But he was a reservist, and would be called up any day now. Linda did not mind staying in Paris at all. She could sunbathe in her flat as much as she wanted to. She felt no particular apprehensions about the coming war, she was essentially a person who lived in the present.

'I couldn't sunbathe naked like this anywhere else,' she said, 'and it's the only holiday thing I enjoy. I don't like swimming, or tennis, or dancing, or gambling, so you see I'm just as well off here sunbathing and shopping, two perfect occupations for the day, and you, my darling love, at night. I should think I'm the happiest woman in the world.'

One boiling hot afternoon in July she arrived home wearing a new and particularly ravishing straw hat. It was large and simple, with a wreath of flowers and two blue bows. Her right arm was full of roses and carnations, and in her left hand was a striped bandbox, containing another exquisite hat. She let herself in with her latchkey, and stumped, on the high cork soles of her sandals, to the drawing-room.

The green venetian blinds were down, and the room was full of warm shadows, two of which suddenly resolved themselves into a thin man and a not so thin man – Davey and Lord Merlin.

'Good heavens,' said Linda, and she flopped down on to a sofa, scattering the roses at her feet.

'Well,' said Davey, 'you do look pretty.'

Linda felt really frightened, like a child caught out in some misdeed, like a child whose new toy is going to be taken away. She looked from one to the other. Lord Merlin was wearing black spectacles.

'Are you in disguise?' said Linda.

'No, what do you mean? Oh, the spectacles – I have to wear them when I go abroad, I have such kind eyes you see, beggars and things cluster round and annoy me.'

He took them off and blinked.

'What have you come for?'

'You don't seem very pleased to see us,' said Davey. 'We came, actually, to see if you were all right. As it's only too obvious that you are, we may as well go away again.'

'How did you find out? Do Mummy and Fa know?' she added, faintly.

'No, absolutely nothing. They think you're still with Christian. We haven't come in the spirit of two Victorian uncles, my dear Linda, if that's what you're thinking. I happened to see a man I know who had been in Perpignan, and he mentioned that Christian was living with Lavender Davis –'

'Oh good,' said Linda.

'What? And that you had left six weeks ago. I went round to Cheyne Walk and there you obviously weren't, and then Mer and I got faintly worried to think of you wandering about the Continent, so ill suited (we thought, how wrong we were) to look after yourself, and at the same time madly curious to know your whereabouts and present circumstances, so we put in motion a little discreet detective work, which revealed your whereabouts – your circumstances are now as clear as daylight, and I, for one, feel most relieved.'

'You gave us a fright,' said Lord Merlin, crossly. 'Another time, when you are putting on this Cléo de Mérode act, you might send a postcard. For one thing, it is a great pleasure to see you in the part, I wouldn't have missed it for worlds. I hadn't realized, Linda, that you were such a beautiful woman.'

Davey was laughing quietly to himself.

'Oh, goodness, how funny it all is – so wonderfully old-fashioned. The shopping! The parcels! The flowers! So tremendously Victorian. People have been delivering cardboard boxes every five minutes since we arrived. What an interest you are in one's life, Linda dear. Have you told him he must give you up and marry a pure young girl yet?'

Linda said disarmingly: 'Don't tease, Dave. I'm *so* happy you can't think.'

'Yes, you look happy I must say. Oh, this flat is such a joke.'

'I was just thinking,' said Lord Merlin, 'that, however much taste may change, it always follows a stereotyped plan. Frenchmen used to keep their mistresses in *appartements*, each exactly like the other, in which the dominant note, you might say, was lace and velvet. The walls, the bed, the dressing-table, the very bath itself were hung with lace, and everything else was velvet. Nowadays for lace you substitute glass, and everything else is satin. I bet you've got a glass bed, Linda?'

'Yes – but –'

'And a glass dressing-table, and bathroom, and I wouldn't be surprised if your bath were made of glass, with goldfish swimming about in the sides of it. Goldfish are a prevailing motif all down the ages.'

'You've looked,' said Linda sulkily. 'Very clever.'

'Oh, what heaven,' said Davey. 'So it's true! He hasn't looked, I swear, but you see it's not beyond the bounds of human ingenuity to guess.'

'But there are some things here,' said Lord Merlin, 'which do raise the level, all the same. A Gauguin, those two Matisses (chintzy, but accomplished) and this Savonnerie carpet. Your protector must be very rich.'

'He is,' said Linda.

'Then, Linda dear, could one ask for a cup of tea?'

She rang the bell, and soon Davey was falling upon *éclairs* and *mille feuilles* with all the abandon of a schoolboy.

'I shall pay for this,' he said, with a devil-may-care smile, 'but never mind, one's not in Paris every day.'

Lord Merlin wandered round with his tea-cup. He picked up a book which Fabrice had given Linda the day before, of romantic nineteenth-century poetry.

'Is this what you're reading now?' he said. '"*Dieu, que le son du cor est triste au fond des bois.*" I had a friend, when I lived in Paris, who had a boa constrictor as a pet, and this boa constrictor got itself inside a French horn. My friend rang me up in a fearful state, saying: "*Dieu, que le son du boa est triste au fond du cor.*" I've never forgotten it.'

'What time does your lover generally arrive?' said Davey, taking out his watch.

'Not till about seven. Do stay and see him, he's such a terrific Hon.'

'No, thank you, not for the world.'

'Who is he?' said Lord Merlin.

'He's called the Duke of Sauveterre.'

A look of great surprise, mingled with horrified amusement, passed between Davey and Lord Merlin.

'Fabrice de Sauveterre?'

'Yes. Do you know him?'

'Darling Linda, one always forgets, under that look of great sophistication, what a little provincial you really are. Of course we know him, and all about him, and, what's more, so does everyone except you.'

'Well, don't you think he's a terrific Hon?'

'Fabrice,' said Lord Merlin with emphasis, 'is undoubtedly one of the wickedest men in Europe, as far as women are concerned. But I must admit that he's an extremely agreeable companion.'

'Do you remember in Venice,' said Davey, 'one used to see him at work in that gondola, one after another, bowling them over like rabbits, poor dears?'

'Please remember,' said Linda, 'that you are eating his tea at this moment.'

'Yes, indeed, and so delicious. Another *éclair*, please, Linda. That summer,' he went on, 'when he made off with Ciano's girl friend, what a fuss there was, I never shall forget, and then, a week later, he *plaqué*'d her in Cannes and went to Salzburg with Martha Birmingham, and poor old Claud shot at him four times, and always missed him.'

'Fabrice has a charmed life,' said Lord Merlin. 'I suppose he has been shot at more than anybody, and, as far as I know, he's never had a scratch.'

Linda was unmoved by these revelations, which had been forestalled by Fabrice himself. Anyhow, no woman really minds hearing of the past affairs of her lover, it is the future alone that has the power to terrify.

'Come on, Mer,' said Davey. 'Time the *petite femme* got herself into a *négligée*. Goodness, what a scene there'll be when he smells Mer's cigar, there'll be a *crime passionel*, I shouldn't wonder. Good-bye, Linda darling, we're off to dine with our intellectual friends, you know, will you be lunching with us at the Ritz tomorrow? About one, then. Good-bye – give our love to Fabrice.'

When Fabrice came in he sniffed about, and asked whose cigar. Linda explained.

'They say they know you?'

'*Mais bien sûr – Merlin, tellement gentil, et l'autre Warbeck, toujours si malade, le pauvre. Je les connaissais à Venise.* What did they think of all this?'

'Well, they roared at the flat.'

'Yes, I can imagine. It is quite unsuitable for you, this flat, but it's convenient, and with the war coming –'

'Oh, but I love it, I wouldn't like anything else half so much. Wasn't it clever of them, though, to find me?'

'Do you mean to say you never told anybody where you were?'

'I really didn't think of it – the days go by, you know – one simply doesn't remember these things.'

'And it was six weeks before they thought of looking for you? As a family you seem to me strangely *décousu*.'

Linda suddenly threw herself into his arms, and said, with great passion:

'Never, never let me go back to them.'

'My darling – but you love them. Mummy and Fa, Matt and Robin and Victoria and Fanny. What is all this?'

'I never want to leave you again as long as I live.'

'Aha! But you know you will probably have to, soon. The war is going to begin, you know.'

'Why can't I stay here? I could work – I could become a nurse – well, perhaps not a nurse, actually, but something.'

'If you promise to do what I tell you, you may stay here for a time. At the beginning we shall sit and look at the Germans across the Maginot Line, then I shall be a great deal in Paris, between Paris and the front, but mostly here. At that time I shall want you here. Then somebody, we or the Germans, but I am very much afraid the Germans, will pour across the line, and a war of movement will begin. I shall have notice of that *étape*, and what you must promise me is that the very minute I tell you to leave for London you will leave, even if you see no reason for doing so. I should be hampered beyond words in my duties if you were still here. So you will solemnly promise, now?'

'All right,' said Linda. 'Solemnly. I don't believe anything so dreadful could happen to me, but I promise to do as you say. Now will you promise that you will come to London as soon as it's all over and find me again. Promise?'

'Yes,' said Fabrice. 'I will do that.'

Luncheon with Davey and Lord Merlin was a gloomy meal. Preoccupation reigned. The two men had stayed up late and merrily with their literary friends, and showed every sign of having done so. Davey was beginning to be aware of the cruel pangs of dyspepsia, Lord Merlin was suffering badly from an ordinary straightforward hangover, and, when he removed his spectacles, his eyes were seen to be not kind at all. But Linda was far the most wretched of the three, she was, in fact, perfectly distracted by having overheard two French ladies in the foyer talking about Fabrice. She had arrived, as, from old habits of punctuality drummed into her by Uncle Matthew she always did, rather early. Fabrice had never taken her to the Ritz, she thought it delightful, she knew she was looking quite as pretty, and nearly as well dressed, as anybody there, and settled herself happily to await the others. Suddenly she heard, with that pang which the heart receives when the loved one's name is mentioned by strangers:

'And have you seen Fabrice at all?'

'Well, I have, because I quite often see him at Madame de Sauveterre's, but he never goes out anywhere, as you know.'

'Then what about Jacqueline?'

'Still in England. He is utterly lost without her, poor Fabrice, he is like a dog looking for its master. He sits sadly at home, never goes to parties, never goes to the club, sees nobody. His mother is really worried about him.'

'Who would ever have expected Fabrice to be so faithful? How long is it?'

'Five years, I believe. A wonderfully happy *ménage*.'

'Surely Jacqueline will come back soon.'

'Not until the old aunt has died. It seems she changes her will incessantly, and Jacqueline feels she must be there all the time – after all, she has her husband and children to consider.'

'Rather hard on Fabrice?'

'*Qu'est-ce que vous voulez?* His mother says he rings her up every morning and talks for an hour –'

It was at this point that Davey and Lord Merlin, looking tired and cross, arrived, and took Linda off to luncheon with them. She was longing to stay and hear more of this torturing conversation, but, eschewing cocktails with a shudder, they hurried her off to the dining-room, where they were only fairly nice to her, and frankly disagreeable to each other.

She thought the meal would never come to an end, and, when at last it did, she threw herself into a taxi and drove to Fabrice's house. She must find out about Jacqueline, she must know his intentions. When Jacqueline returned would that be the moment for her, Linda, to leave as she had promised? War of movement indeed!

The servant said that M. le Duc had just gone out with Madame la Duchesse, but that he would be back in about an hour. Linda said she would wait, and he showed her into Fabrice's sitting-room. She took off her hat, and wandered restlessly about. She had been here several times before, with Fabrice, and it had seemed, after her brilliantly sunny flat, a little dismal. Now that she was alone in it she began to be aware of the extreme beauty of the room, a grave and solemn beauty which penetrated her. It was very high, rectangular in shape, with grey boiseries and cherry-coloured brocade curtains. It looked into a courtyard and never could get a ray of sunshine, that was not the plan. This was a civilized interior, it had nothing to do with out-of-doors. Every object in it was perfect. The furniture had the severe lines and excellent proportions of 1780, there was a portrait by Lancret of a lady with a parrot on her wrist, a bust of the same lady by Bouchardon, a carpet like the one in Linda's flat, but larger and grander, with a huge coat of arms in the middle. A high carved bookcase contained nothing but French classics bound in contemporary morocco, with the Sauveterre crest, and open on a map table lay a copy of Redouté's roses.

Linda began to feel much more calm, but, at the same time, very sad. She saw that this room indicated a side of Fabrice's character which she had hardly been allowed to apprehend, and which had its roots in old civilized French grandeur. It was the essential Fabrice, something in which she could never have a share – she would always be outside in her sunny modern flat, kept away from all this, kept rigidly away even if their liaison were to go on for ever. The origins of the Radlett family were lost in the mists of antiquity, but the origins of Fabrice's family were not lost at all, there they were, each generation clutching at the next. The English, she thought, throw off their ancestors. It is the great strength of our aristocracy, but Fabrice has his round his neck, and he will never get away from them.

She began to realize that here were her competitors, her enemies, and that Jacqueline was nothing in comparison. Here, and in the grave of Louise. To come here and make a scene about a rival mistress would be utterly meaningless, she would be one unreality complaining about another. Fabrice would be annoyed, as men always are annoyed on these occasions, and she would get no satisfaction. She could hear his voice, dry and sarcastic:

'Ah! *Vous me grondez, madame?*'

Better go, better ignore the whole affair. Her only hope was to keep things on their present footing, to keep the happiness which she was enjoying day by day, hour by hour, and not to think about the future at all. It held nothing for her, leave it alone. Besides, everybody's future was in jeopardy now the war was coming, this war which she always forgot about.

She was reminded of it, however, when, that evening, Fabrice appeared in uniform.

'Another month I should think,' he said. 'As soon as they have got the harvest in.'

'If it depended on the English,' said Linda, 'they would wait until after the Christmas shopping. Oh, Fabrice, it won't last very long, will it?'

'It will be very disagreeable while it does last,' said Fabrice. 'Did you come to my flat today?'

'Yes, after lunching with those two old cross-patches I suddenly felt I wanted to see you very much.'

'*Comme c'est gentil,*' he looked at her quizzically, as though something had occurred to him, 'but why didn't you wait?'

'Your ancestors frightened me off.'

'Oh, they did? But you have ancestors yourself I believe, *madame*?'

'Yes, but they don't hang about in the same way as yours do.'

'You should have waited,' said Fabrice, 'it is always a very great pleasure to see you, both for me and for my ancestors. It cheers us all up.'

Germaine now came into the room with huge armfuls of flowers and a note from Lord Merlin, saying:

'Here are some coals for Newcastle. We are tottering home by the ferry-boat. Do you think I shall get Davey back alive? I enclose something which might, one day, be useful.'

It was a note for 20,000 francs.

'I must say,' said Linda, 'considering what cruel eyes he has, he does think of everything.'

She felt sentimental after the occurrences of the day.

'Tell me, Fabrice,' she said, 'what did you think the first moment you ever saw me?'

'If you really want to know, I thought: *"Tiens, elle ressemble à la petite Bosquet."*'

'Who is that?'

'There are two Bosquet sisters, the elder, who is a beauty, and a little one who looks like you.'

'*Merci beaucoup*,' said Linda. '*J'aimerais autant ressembler à l'autre.*'

Fabrice laughed. '*Ensuite, je me suis dit, comme c'est amusant, le côté démodé de tout ça –*'

When the war, which had for so long been pending, did actually break out some six weeks later, Linda was strangely unmoved by the fact. She was enveloped in the present, in her own detached and futureless life, which, anyhow, seemed so precarious, so much from one hour to another: exterior events hardly impinged on her consciousness. When she thought about the war it seemed to her almost a relief that it had actually begun, in so far as a beginning is the first step towards an end. That it had begun only in name and not in fact did not occur to her. Of course, had Fabrice been taken away by it her attitude would have been very different, but his job, an intelligence one, kept him mostly in Paris, and, indeed, she now saw rather more of him than formerly, as he moved into her flat, shutting up his own and sending his mother to the country. He would appear and disappear at all sorts of odd moments of the night and day, and, as the sight of him was a constant joy to Linda, as she could imagine no greater happiness than she always felt when the empty space in front of her eyes became filled by his form, these sudden apparitions kept her in a state of happy suspense and their relationship at fever point.

Since Davey's visit Linda had been getting letters from her family. He had given Aunt Sadie her address and told her that Linda was doing war work in Paris, providing comforts for the French army, he said vaguely, and with some degree of truth. Aunt Sadie was pleased about this, she thought it very good of Linda to work so hard (all night sometimes, Davey said), and was glad to hear that she earned her keep. Voluntary work was often unsatisfactory and expensive. Uncle Matthew thought it a pity to work for foreigners, and deplored the fact that his children were so fond of crossing the oceans, but he also was very much in favour of war work.

He was himself utterly disgusted that the War Office were not able to offer him the opportunity of repeating his exploit with the entrenching tool, or, indeed, any job at all, and he went about like a bear with a sore head, full of unsatisfied desire to fight for his King and country.

I wrote to Linda and told her about Christian, who was back in London, had left the Communist party and had joined up. Lavender had also returned; she was now in the A.T.S.

Christian did not show the slightest curiosity about what had happened to Linda, he did not seem to want to divorce her or to marry Lavender, he had thrown himself heart and soul into army life and thought of nothing but the war.

Before leaving Perpignan he had extricated Matt, who, after a good deal of persuasion, had consented to leave his Spanish comrades in order to join the battle against Fascism on another front. He went into Uncle Matthew's old regiment, and was said to bore his brother officers in the mess very much by arguing that they were training the men all wrong, and that, during the battle of Ebro, things had been done thus and thus. In the end his colonel, who was rather brighter in the head than some of the others, hit upon the obvious reply, which was, 'Well anyway, your side lost!' This shut Matt up on tactics, but got him going on statistics – '30,000 Germans and Italians, 500 German planes', and so forth – which were almost equally dull.

Linda heard no more about Jacqueline, and the wretchedness into which she had been thrown by those few chance words overheard at the Ritz were gradually forgotten. She reminded herself that nobody ever really knew the state of a man's heart, not even, perhaps specially not, his mother, and that in love it is actions that count. Fabrice had no time now for two women, he spent every spare moment with her and that in itself reassured her. Besides, just as her marriages with Tony and Christian had been necessary in order to lead up to her meeting with Fabrice, so this affair had led up to his meeting with her: undoubtedly he must have been seeing Jacqueline off at the Gare du Nord when he found Linda crying on her suitcase. Putting herself in Jacqueline's shoes, she realized how much preferable it was to be in her own: in any case it was not Jacqueline who was her dangerous rival, but that dim, virtuous figure from the past, Louise. Whenever Fabrice showed signs of becoming a little less practical, a little more nonsensical, and romantic, it was of his fiancée that he would speak, dwelling with a gentle sadness upon her beauty, her noble birth, her vast estates, and her religious mania. Linda once suggested that, had the fiancée lived to become a wife, she might not have been a very happy one.

'All that climbing,' she said, 'in at other people's bedroom windows, might it not have upset her?'

Fabrice looked intensely shocked and reproachful and said that there never would have been any climbing, that, where marriage was concerned, he had the very highest ideals, and that his whole life would have been devoted to making Louise happy. Linda felt herself rebuked, but was not entirely convinced.

All this time Linda watched the tree-tops from her window. They had changed, since she had been in the flat, from bright green against a bright blue sky, to dark green against a lavender sky, to yellow against a cerulean sky, until now they were black skeletons against a sky of moleskin, and it was Christmas Day. The windows could no longer be opened until they disappeared, but, whenever the sun did come out, it shone into her rooms, and the flat was always as warm as toast. On this Christmas morning Fabrice arrived, quite unexpectedly, before she was up, his arms full of parcels, and soon the floor of her bedroom was covered with waves of tissue paper through which, like wrecks and monsters half submerged beneath a shallow sea, appeared fur coats, hats, real mimosa, artificial flowers, feathers, scent, gloves, stockings, underclothes, and a bulldog puppy.

Linda had spent Lord Merlin's 20,000 francs on a tiny Renoir for Fabrice: six inches of seascape, a little patch of brilliant blue, which she thought would look just right in his room in the rue Bonaparte. Fabrice was the most difficult person to buy presents for, he possessed a larger assortment of jewels, knick-knacks, and rare objects of all kinds than anybody she had ever known. He was delighted with the Renoir, nothing, he said, could have pleased him more, and Linda felt that he really meant it.

'Oh, such a cold day,' he said. 'I've just been to church.'

'Fabrice, how can you go to church when there's me?'

'Well, why not.'

'You're a Roman Catholic, aren't you?'

'Of course I am. What do you suppose? Do you think I look like a Calvinist?'

'But then aren't you living in mortal sin? So what about when you confess?'

'*On ne précise pas*,' said Fabrice, carelessly, 'and in any case, these little sins of the body are quite unimportant.'

Linda would have liked to think that she was more in Fabrice's life than a little sin of the body, but she was used to coming up against these closed doors in her relationship with him, and had learnt to be philosophical about it and thankful for the happiness that she did receive.

'In England,' she said, 'people are always renouncing each other on account of being Roman Catholics. It's sometimes very sad for them. A lot of English books are about this, you know.'

'*Les Anglais sont des insensés, je l'ai toujours dit.* You almost sound as if you want to be given up. What has happened since Saturday? Not tired of your war work, I hope?'

'No, no, Fabrice. I just wondered, that's all.'

'But you look so sad, *ma chérie*, what is it?'

'I was thinking of Christmas Day at home. I always feel sentimental at Christmas.'

'If what I said might happen does happen and I have to send you back to England, shall you go home to your father?'

'Oh, no,' said Linda, 'anyway, it won't happen. All the English papers say we are killing Germany with our blockade.'

'*Le blocus*,' said Fabrice, impatiently, '*quelle blague! Je vais vous dire, madame, ils ne se fichent pas mal de votre blocus.* So where would you go?'

'To my own house in Chelsea, and wait for you to come.'

'It might be months, or years.'

'I shall wait,' she said.

The skeleton tree-tops began to fill out, they acquired a pinkish tinge, which gradually changed to golden-green. The sky was often blue, and, on some days,

Linda could once more open her windows and lie naked in the sun, whose rays by now had a certain strength. She always loved the spring, she loved the sudden changes of temperature, the dips backward into winter and forward into summer, and, this year, living in beautiful Paris, her perceptions heightened by great emotion, she was profoundly affected by it. There was now a curious feeling in the air, very different from and much more nervous than that which had been current before Christmas, and the town was full of rumours. Linda often thought of the expression '*fin de siècle*'. There was a certain analogy, she thought, between the state of mind which it denoted and that prevailing now, only now it was more like '*fin de vie*'. It was as though everybody around her, and she herself, were living out the last few days of their lives, but this curious feeling did not disturb her, she was possessed by a calm and happy fatalism. She occupied the hours of waiting between Fabrice's visits by lying in the sun, when there was any, and playing with her puppy. On Fabrice's advice she even began to order some new clothes for the summer. He seemed to regard the acquisition of clothes as one of the chief duties of woman, to be pursued through war and revolution, through sickness, and up to death. It was as one who might say, 'Whatever happens the fields must be tilled, the cattle tended, life must go on.' He was so essentially urban that to him the slow roll of the seasons was marked by the spring *tailleurs*, the summer *imprimés*, the autumn *ensembles*, and the winter furs of his mistress.

On a beautiful windy blue and white day in April the blow fell. Fabrice, whom Linda had not seen for nearly a week, arrived from the front looking grave and worried, and told her that she must go back to England at once.

'I've got a place for you in the aeroplane,' he said, 'for this afternoon. You must pack a small suitcase, and the rest of your things must go after you by train. Germaine will see to them. I have to go to the Ministère de la Guerre, I'll be back as soon as possible, and anyhow in time to take you to Le Bourget. Come on,' he added, 'just time for a little war work.' He was in his most practical and least romantic mood.

When he returned he looked more preoccupied than ever. Linda was waiting for him, her box was packed, she was wearing the blue suit in which he had first seen her, and had her old mink coat over her arm.

'*Tiens,*' said Fabrice, who always at once noticed what she had on, 'what is this? A fancy-dress party?'

'Fabrice, you must understand that I can't take away the things you have given me. I loved having them while I was here, and while they gave you pleasure seeing me in them, but, after all, I have some pride. *Je n'étais quand même pas élevée dans un bordel.*'

'*Ma chère*, try not to be so middle-class, it doesn't suit you at all. There's no time for you to change – wait, though –' He went into her bedroom, and came out again with a long sable coat, one of his Christmas presents. He took her mink coat, rolled it up, threw it into the waste-paper basket, and put the other over her arm in its place.

'Germaine will send your things after you,' he said. 'Come now, we must go.'

Linda said good-bye to Germaine, picked up the bulldog puppy, and followed Fabrice into the lift, out into the street. She did not fully understand that she was leaving that happy life behind her for ever.

19

At first, back in Cheyne Walk, she still did not understand. The world was grey and cold certainly, the sun had gone behind a cloud, but only for a time: it would come out again, she would soon once more be enveloped in that heat and light which had left her in so warm a glow, there was still much blue in the sky, this little cloud would pass. Then, as sometimes happens, the cloud, which had seemed at first such a little one, grew and grew, until it became a thick grey blanket smothering the horizon. The bad news began, the terrible days, the unforgettable weeks. A great horror of steel was rolling over France, was rolling towards England, swallowing on its way the puny beings who tried to stop it, swallowing Fabrice, Germaine, the flat, and the past months of Linda's life, swallowing Alfred, Bob, Matt, and little Robin, coming to swallow us all. London people cried openly in the buses, in the streets, for the English army which was lost.

Then, suddenly one day, the English army turned up again. There was a feeling of such intense relief, it was as if the war were over and won. Alfred and Bob and Matt and little Robin all reappeared, and, as a lot of French soldiers also arrived, Linda had a wild hope that Fabrice might be with them. She sat all day by the telephone and when it rang and was not Fabrice she was furious with the unlucky telephoner – I know, because it happened to me. She was so furious that I dropped the receiver and went straight round to Cheyne Walk.

I found her unpacking a huge trunk, which had just arrived from France. I had never seen her looking so beautiful. It made me gasp, and I remembered how Davey had said, when he got back from Paris, that at last Linda was fulfilling the promise of her childhood, and had become a beauty.

'How do you imagine this got here?' she said, between tears and laughter. 'What an extraordinary war. The Southern Railway people brought it just now and I signed for it, all as though nothing peculiar were happening – I don't understand a word of it. What are you doing in London, darling?'

She seemed unaware of the fact that half an hour ago she had spoken to me, and indeed bitten my head off, on the telephone.

'I'm with Alfred. He's got to get a lot of new equipment and see all sorts of people. I believe he's going abroad again very soon.'

'Awfully good of him,' said Linda, 'when he needn't have joined up at all, I imagine. What does he say about Dunkirk?'

'He says it was like something out of the *Boy's Own* – he seems to have had a most fascinating time.'

'They all did, the boys were here yesterday and you never heard anything like their stories. Of course they never quite realized how desperate it all was until they got to the coast. Oh, isn't it wonderful to have them back. If only – if only one knew what had happened to one's French buddies –' She looked at me under her eyelashes, and I thought she was going to tell me about her life, but, if so, she changed her mind and went on unpacking.

'I shall have to put these winter things back in their boxes really,' she said. 'I simply haven't any cupboards that will hold them all, but it's something to do, and I like to see them again.'

'You should shake them,' I said, 'and put them in the sun. They may be damp.'

'Darling, you are wonderful, you always know.'

'Where did you get that puppy?' I said enviously. I had wanted a bulldog for years, but Alfred never would let me have one because of the snoring.

'Brought him back with me. He's the nicest puppy I ever had, so anxious to oblige, you can't think.'

'What about quarantine, then?'

'Under my coat,' said Linda, laconically. 'You should have heard him grunting and snuffling, it shook the whole place, I was terrified, but he was so good. He never budged. And talking of puppies, those ghastly Kroesigs are sending Moira to America, isn't it typical of them? I've made a great thing with Tony about seeing her before she goes, after all I am her mother.'

'That's what I can't ever understand about you, Linda.'

'What?'

'How you could have been so dreadful to Moira.'

'Dull,' said Linda. 'Uninteresting.'

'I know, but the point is that children are like puppies, and if you never see puppies, if you give them to the groom or the gamekeeper to bring up, look how dull and uninteresting they always are. Children are just the same – you must give them much more than their life if they are to be any good. Poor little Moira – all you gave her was that awful name.'

'Oh, Fanny, I do know. To tell you the truth I believe it was always in the back of my mind that, sooner or later, I should have to run away from Tony, and I didn't want to get too fond of Moira, or to make her too fond of me. She might have become an anchor, and I simply didn't dare let myself be anchored to the Kroesigs.'

'Poor Linda.'

'Oh, don't pity me. I've had eleven months of perfect and unalloyed happiness, very few people can say that, in the course of long long lives, I imagine.'

I imagined so too. Alfred and I are happy, as happy as married people can be. We are in love, we are intellectually and physically suited in every possible way, we rejoice in each other's company, we have no money troubles and three delightful children. And yet, when I consider my life, day by day, hour by hour, it seems to be composed of a series of pin-pricks. Nannies, cooks, the endless drudgery of housekeeping, the nerve-racking noise and boring repetitive conversation of small children (boring in the sense that it bores into one's very brain), their absolute incapacity to amuse themselves, their sudden and terrifying illnesses, Alfred's not infrequent bouts of moodiness, his invariable complaints at meals about the pudding, the way he will always use my tooth-paste and will always squeeze the tube in the middle. These are the components of marriage, the wholemeal bread of life, rough, ordinary, but sustaining; Linda had been feeding upon honey-dew, and that is an incomparable diet.

The old woman who had opened the door to me came in and said was that everything, because, if so, she would be going home.

'Everything,' said Linda. 'Mrs Hunt,' she said to me, when she had gone. 'A terrific Hon – she comes daily.'

'Why don't you go to Alconleigh,' I said, 'or to Shenley? Aunt Emily and Davey would love to have you, and I'm going there with the children as soon as Alfred is off again.'

'I'd like to come for a visit some time, when I know a little more what is happening, but at the moment I must stop here. Give them my love though. I've got such masses to tell you, Fanny, what we really need is hours and hours in the Hons' cupboard.'

After a great deal of hesitation Tony Kroesig and his wife, Pixie, allowed Moira to go and see her mother before leaving England. She arrived at Cheyne Walk in Tony's car, still driven by a chauffeur in uniform not the King's. She was a plain, stodgy, shy little girl, with no echo of the Radletts about her; not to put too fine a point on it she was a real little Gretchen.

'What a sweet puppy,' she said, awkwardly, when Linda had kissed her. She was clearly very much embarrassed.

'What's his name?'

'Plon-plon.'

'Oh. Is that a French name?'

'Yes it is. He's a French dog, you see.'

'Daddy says the French are terrible.'

'I expect he does.'

'He says they have let us down, and what can we expect if we have anything to do with such people.'

'Yes, he would.'

'Daddy thinks we ought to fight with the Germans and not against them.'

'M'm. But Daddy doesn't seem to be fighting very much with anybody, or against anybody, or at all, as far as I can see. Now, Moira, before you go I have got two things for you, one is a present and the other is a little talk. The talk is very dull, so we'll get that over first, shall we?'

'Yes,' said Moira, apathetically. She lugged the puppy on to the sofa beside her.

'I want you to know,' said Linda, 'and to remember, please, Moira (stop playing with the puppy a minute and listen carefully to what I am saying) that I don't at all approve of you running away like this, I think it most dreadfully wrong. When you have a country which has given you as much as England has given all of us, you ought to stick to it, and not go wandering off as soon as it looks like being in trouble.'

'But it's not my fault,' said Moira, her forehead puckering. 'I'm only a child and Pixie is taking me. I have to do what I'm told, don't I?'

'Yes, of course, I know that's true. But you'd much rather stay, wouldn't you?' said Linda, hopefully.

'Oh no, I don't think so. There might be air-raids.'

At this Linda gave up. Children might or might not enjoy air-raids actually in progress, but a child who was not thrilled by the idea of them was incomprehensible to her, and she could not imagine having conceived such a being. Useless to waste any more time and breath on this unnatural little girl. She sighed and said:

'Now wait a moment and I'll get your present.'

She had in her pocket, in a velvet box, a coral hand holding a diamond arrow, which Fabrice had given her, but she could not bear to waste anything so pretty on this besotted little coward. She went to her bedroom and found a sports wristwatch, one of her wedding presents when she had married Tony and which she had never worn, and gave this to Moira, who seemed quite pleased by it, and left the house as politely and unenthusiastically as she had arrived.

Linda rang me up at Shenley and told me about this interview.

'I'm in such a temper,' she said, 'I must talk to somebody. To think I ruined nine months of my life in order to have that. What do your children think about air-raids, Fanny?'

'I must say they simply long for them, and I am sorry to say they also long for the Germans to arrive. They spend the whole day making booby-traps for them in the orchard.'

'Well that's a relief anyhow – I thought perhaps it was the generation. Actually of course, it's not Moira's fault, it's all that bloody Pixie – I can see the form only too clearly, can't you? Pixie is frightened to death and she has found out that going to America is like the children's concert, you can only make it if you have a child in tow. So she's using Moira – well, it does serve one right for doing wrong.' Linda was evidently very much put out. 'And I hear Tony is going too, some Parliamentary mission or something. All I can say is what a set.'

All through those terrible months of May, June, and July, Linda waited for a sign from Fabrice, but no sign came. She did not doubt that he was still alive, it was not in Linda's nature to imagine that anyone might be dead. She knew that thousands of Frenchmen were in German hands, but felt certain that, had Fabrice been taken prisoner (a thing which she did not at all approve of, incidentally, taking the old-fashioned view that, unless in exceptional circumstances, it is a disgrace), he would undoubtedly manage to escape. She would hear from him before long, and, meanwhile, there was nothing to be done, she must simply wait. All the same, as the days went by with no news, and as all the news there was from France was bad, she did become exceedingly restless. She was really more concerned with his attitude than with his safety – his attitude towards events and his attitude towards her. She felt sure that he would never be associated with the armistice, she felt sure that he would want to communicate with her, but she had no proof, and, in moments of great loneliness and depression, she allowed herself to lose faith. She realized how little she really knew of Fabrice, he had seldom talked seriously to her, their relationship having been primarily physical while their conversations and chat had all been based on jokes.

They had laughed and made love and laughed again, and the months had slipped by with no time for anything but laughter and love. Enough to satisfy her, but what about him? Now that life had become so serious, and, for a Frenchman, so tragic, would he not have forgotten that meal of whipped cream as something so utterly unimportant that it might never have existed? She began to think, more and more, to tell herself over and over again, to force herself to realize, that it was probably all finished, that Fabrice might never be anything for her now but a memory.

At the same time the few people she saw never failed when talking, as everybody talked then, about France, to emphasize that the French 'one knew', the families who were 'bien', were all behaving very badly, convinced Pétainists. Fabrice was not one of them, she thought, she felt, but she wished she knew, she longed for evidence.

In fact, she alternated between hope and despair, but as the months went by without a word, a word that she was sure he could have sent if he had really wanted to, despair began to prevail.

Then, on a sunny Sunday morning in August, very early, her telephone bell rang. She woke up with a start, aware that it had been ringing already for several moments, and she knew with absolute certainty that this was Fabrice.

'Are you Flaxman 2815?'

'Yes.'

'I've got a call for you. You're through.'

'*Allô – allô?*'

'Fabrice?'

'*Oui.*'

'Oh! Fabrice – *on vous attend depuis si longtemps.*'

'*Comme c'est gentil. Alors, on peut venir tout de suite chez vous?*'

'Oh, wait – yes, you can come at once, but don't go for a minute, go on talking, I want to hear the sound of your voice.'

'No, no, I have a taxi outside, I shall be with you in five minutes. There's too much one can't do on the telephone, *ma chère, voyons –*' Click.

She lay back, and all was light and warmth. Life, she thought, is sometimes sad and often dull, but there are currants in the cake and here is one of them. The early morning sun shone past her window on to the river, her ceiling danced with water-reflections. The Sunday silence was broken by two swans winging slowly upstream, and then by the chugging of a little barge, while she waited for that other sound, a sound more intimately connected with the urban love affair than any except the telephone bell, that of a stopping taxicab. Sun, silence, and happiness. Presently she heard it in the street, slowly, slower, it stopped, the flag went up with a ring, the door slammed, voices, clinking coins, footsteps. She rushed downstairs.

Hours later Linda made some coffee.

'So lucky,' she said, 'that it happens to be Sunday, and Mrs Hunt isn't here. What would she have thought?'

'Just about the same as the night porter at the Hotel Montalembert, I expect,' said Fabrice.

'Why did you come, Fabrice? To join General de Gaulle?'

'No, that was not necessary, because I have joined him already. I was with him in Bordeaux. My work has to be in France, but we have ways of communicating when we want to. I shall go and see him, of course, he expects me at midday, but actually I came on a private mission.'

He looked at her for a long time.

'I came to tell you that I love you,' he said, at last.

Linda felt giddy.

'You never said that to me in Paris.'

'No.'

'You always seemed so practical.'

'Yes, I suppose so. I had said it so often and often before in my life, I had been so romantic with so many women, that when I felt this to be different I really could not bring out all those stale old phrases again, I couldn't utter them. I never said I loved you, I never *tutoyé*'d you, on purpose. Because from the first moment I knew that this was as real as all the others were false, it was like recognizing somebody – there, I can't explain.'

'But that is exactly how I felt too,' said Linda, 'don't try to explain, you needn't, I know.'

'Then, when you had gone, I felt I had to tell you, and it became an obsession with me to tell you. All those dreadful weeks were made more dreadful because I was being prevented from telling you.'

'How ever did you get here?'

'*On circule*,' said Fabrice, vaguely. 'I must leave again tomorrow morning, very early, and I shan't come back until the war is over, but you'll wait for me, Linda, and nothing matters so much now that you know. I was tormented, I couldn't concentrate on anything, I was becoming useless in my work. In future I may have much to bear, but I shan't have to bear you going away without knowing what a great love I have for you.'

'Oh, Fabrice, I feel – well, I suppose religious people sometimes feel like this.'

She put her head on his shoulder, and they sat for a long time in silence.

When he had paid his visit to Carlton Gardens they lunched at the Ritz. It was full of people Linda knew, all very smart, very gay, and talking with the greatest flippancy about the imminent arrival of the Germans. Had it not been for the fact that all the young men there had fought bravely in Flanders, and would, no doubt, soon be fighting bravely again, and this time with more experience, on other fields of battle, the general tone might have been considered shocking. Even Fabrice looked grave, and said they did not seem to realize –

Davey and Lord Merlin appeared. Their eyebrows went up when they saw Fabrice.

'Poor Merlin has the wrong kind,' Davey said to Linda.

'The wrong kind of what?'

'Pill to take when the Germans come. He's just got the sort you give to dogs.'

Davey brought out a jewelled box containing two pills, one white and one black.

'You take the white one first and then the black one – he really must go to my doctor.'

'I think one should let the Germans do the killing,' said Linda. 'Make them add to their own crimes and use up a bullet. Why should one smooth their path in any way? Besides, I back myself to do in at least two before they get me.'

'Oh, you're so tough, Linda, but I'm afraid it wouldn't be a bullet for me, they would torture me, look at the things I've said about them in the *Gazette*.'

'No worse than you've said about all of us,' Lord Merlin remarked.

Davey was known to be a most savage reviewer, a perfect butcher, never sparing even his dearest friends. He wrote under several pseudonyms, which in no way disguised his unmistakable style, his cruellest essays appearing over the name Little Nell.

'Are you here for long, Sauveterre?'

'No, not for long.'

Linda and Fabrice went in to luncheon. They talked of this and that, mostly jokes. Fabrice told her scandalous stories about some of the other lunchers known to him of old, with a wealth of unlikely detail. He spoke only once about France, only to say that the struggle must be carried on, everything would be all right in the end. Linda thought how different it would have been with Tony or Christian. Tony would have held forth about his experiences and made boring arrangements for his own future, Christian would have launched a monologue on world conditions subsequent to the recent fall of France, its probable repercussions in Araby and far Cashmere, the inadequacy of Pétain to deal with such a wealth of displaced persons, the steps that he, Christian, would have taken had he found himself in his, the Marshal's, shoes. Both would have spoken to her exactly, in every respect, as if she had been some chap in their club. Fabrice talked to her, at her, and for only her, it was absolutely personal talk, scattered with jokes and allusions private to them both. She had a feeling that he would not allow himself to be serious, that if he did he would have to embark on tragedy, and that he wanted her to carry away a happy memory of his visit. But he also gave an impression of boundless optimism and faith, very cheering at that dark time.

Early the next morning, another beautiful, hot, sunny morning, Linda lay back on her pillows and watched Fabrice while he dressed, as she had so often watched him in Paris. He made a certain kind of face when he was pulling his tie into a knot, she had quite forgotten it in the months between, and it brought back their Paris life to her suddenly and vividly.

'Fabrice,' she said. 'Do you think we shall ever live together again?'

'But of course we shall, for years and years and years, until I am ninety. I have a very faithful nature.'

'You weren't very faithful to Jacqueline.'

'Aha – so you know about Jacqueline, do you? *La pauvre, elle était si gentille – gentille, élégante, mais assommante, mon Dieu! Enfin,* I was immensely faithful to her and it lasted five years, it always does with me (either five days or five years). But as I love you ten times more than the others that brings it to when I am ninety, and, by then, *j'en aurai tellement l'habitude –'*

'And how soon shall I see you again?'

'*On fera la navette.*' He went to the window. 'I thought I heard a car – oh yes, it is turning round. There, I must go. *Au revoir,* Linda.'

He kissed her hand politely, almost absent-mindedly, it was as if he had already gone, and walked quickly from the room. Linda went to the open window and leaned out. He was getting into a large motor car with two French soldiers on the box and a Free French flag waving from the bonnet. As it moved away he looked up.

'*Navette – navette –*' cried Linda with a brilliant smile. Then she got back into bed and cried very much. She felt utterly in despair at this second parting.

20

The air-raids on London now began. Early in September, just as I had moved there with my family, a bomb fell in the garden of Aunt Emily's house in Kent. It was a small bomb compared with what one saw later, and none of us were hurt, but the house was more or less wrecked. Aunt Emily, Davey, my children, and I, then took refuge at Alconleigh, where Aunt Sadie welcomed us with open arms, begging us to make it our home for the war. Louisa had already arrived there with her children, John Fort William had gone back to his regiment and their Scottish home had been taken over by the Navy.

'The more the merrier,' said Aunt Sadie. 'I should like to fill the house, and, besides, it's better for rations. Nice, too, for your children to be brought up all together, just like old times. With the boys away and Victoria in the Wrens, Matthew and I would be a very dreary old couple here all alone.'

The big rooms at Alconleigh were filled with the contents of some science museum and no evacuees had been billeted there, I think it was felt that nobody who had not been brought up to such rigours could stand the cold of that house.

Soon the party received a very unexpected addition. I was upstairs in the nursery bathroom doing some washing for Nanny, measuring out the soap-flakes with wartime parsimony and wishing that the water at Alconleigh were not so dreadfully hard, when Louisa burst in.

'You'll never guess,' she said, 'in a thousand thousand years who has arrived.'

'Hitler,' I said, stupidly.

'Your mother, Auntie Bolter. She just walked up the drive and walked in.'

'Alone?'

'No, with a man.'

'The Major?'

'He doesn't look like a major. He's got a musical instrument with him and he's very dirty. Come on, Fanny, leave those to soak –'

And so it was. My mother sat in the hall drinking a whisky-and-soda and recounting in her birdlike voice with what incredible adventures she had escaped from the Riviera. The major with whom she had been living for some years, always having greatly preferred the Germans to the French, had remained behind to collaborate, and the man who now accompanied my mother was a ruffianly looking Spaniard called Juan, whom she had picked up during her travels, and without whom, she said, she could never have got away from a ghastly prison camp in Spain. She spoke of him exactly as though he were not there at all, which produced rather a curious effect, and indeed seemed most embarrassing until we realized that Juan understood no word of any language except Spanish. He sat staring blankly into space, clutching a guitar and gulping down great draughts of whisky. Their relationship was only too obvious, Juan was undoubtedly (nobody doubted for a moment, not even Aunt Sadie) the Bolter's lover, but they were quite incapable of verbal exchange, my mother being no linguist.

Presently Uncle Matthew appeared, and the Bolter told her adventures all over again to him. He said he was delighted to see her, and hoped she would stay as long as she liked, he then turned his blue eyes upon Juan in a most terrifying and uncompromising stare. Aunt Sadie led him off to the business-room, whispering, and we heard him say:

'All right then, but only for a few days.'

One person who was off his head with joy at the sight of her was dear old Josh.

'We must get her ladyship up on to a horse,' he said, hissing with pleasure.

My mother had not been her ladyship since three husbands (four if one were to include the Major), but Josh took no account of this, she would always be her ladyship to him. He found a horse, not worthy of her, in his eyes, but not an absolute dud either, and had her out cub-hunting within a week of her arrival.

As for me it was the first time in my life that I had found myself really face to face with my mother. When a small child I had been obsessed by her and the few appearances she had made had absolutely dazzled me, though, as I have said, I never had any wish to emulate her career. Davey and Aunt Emily had been very clever in their approach to her, they, and especially Davey, had gradually and gently and without in any way hurting my feelings, turned her into a sort of joke. Since I was grown up I had seen her a few times, and had taken Alfred to visit her on our honeymoon, but the fact that, in spite of our intimate relationship, we had no past life in common put a great strain upon us and these meetings were not a success. At Alconleigh, in contact with her morning, noon, and night, I studied her with the greatest curiosity, apart from anything else she was, after all, the grandmother of my children. I couldn't help rather liking her. Though she was silliness personified there was something engaging about her frankness and high spirits and endless good nature. The children adored her, Louisa's as well as mine, and she soon became an extra unofficial nurserymaid, and was very useful to us in that capacity.

She was curiously dated in her manner, and seemed still to be living in the 1920s. It was as though, at the age of thirty-five, having refused to grow any older, she had pickled herself, both mentally and physically, ignoring the fact that the world was changing and that she was withering fast. She had a short canary-coloured shingle (windswept) and wore trousers with the air of one still flouting the conventions, ignorant that every suburban shopgirl was doing the same. Her conversation, her point of view, the very slang she used, all belonged to the late twenties, that period now deader than the dodo. She was intensely unpractical, foolish, and apparently fragile, and yet she must have been quite a tough little person really, to have walked over the Pyrenees, to have escaped from a Spanish camp, and to have arrived at Alconleigh looking as if she had stepped out of the chorus of *No, No, Nanette*.

Some confusion was caused in the household at first by the fact that none of us could remember whether she had, in the end, actually married the Major (a married man himself and father of six) or not, and, in consequence, nobody knew whether her name was now Mrs Rawl or Mrs Plugge. Rawl had been a white hunter, the only husband she had ever lost respectably through death, having shot him by accident in the head during a safari. The question of names was soon solved, however, by her ration book, which proclaimed her to be Mrs Plugge.

'This Gewan,' said Uncle Matthew, when they had been at Alconleigh a week or so, 'what's going to be done about him?'

'Well, Matthew dulling,' she larded her phrases with the word darling, and that is how she pronounced it. 'Hoo-arn saved my life, you know, over and over again, and I can't very well tear him up and throw him away, now can I, my sweet?'

'I can't keep a lot of dagoes here, you know.' Uncle Matthew said this in the same voice with which he used to tell Linda that she couldn't have any more pets, or if she did they must be kept in the stables. 'You'll have to make some other arrangements for him, Bolter, I'm afraid.'

'Oh, dulling, keep him a little longer, please, just a few more days, Matthew dulling,' she sounded just like Linda, pleading for some smelly old dog, 'and then I promise I'll find some place for him and tiny me to go to. You can't think what a lousy time we had together, I must stick to him now, I really must.'

'Well, another week if you like, but it's not to be the thin end of the wedge, Bolter, and after that he must go. You can stay as long as you want to, of course, but I do draw the line at Gewan.'

Louisa said to me, her eyes as big as saucers: 'He rushes into her room before tea and lives with her.' Louisa always describes the act of love as living with. 'Before tea, Fanny, can you imagine it?'

'Sadie, dear,' said Davey. 'I am going to do an unpardonable thing. It is for the general good, for your own good too, but it is unpardonable. If you feel you can't forgive me when I've said my say, Emily and I will have to leave, that's all.'

'Davey,' said Aunt Sadie in astonishment, 'what can be coming?'

'The food, Sadie, it's the food. I know how difficult it is for you in wartime, but we are all, in turns, being poisoned. I was sick for hours last night, the day before Emily had diarrhoea, Fanny has that great spot on her nose, and I'm sure the children aren't putting on the weight they should. The fact is, dear, that if Mrs Beecher were a Borgia she could hardly be more successful – all that sausage mince is poison, Sadie. I wouldn't complain if it were merely nasty, or insufficient, or too starchy, one expects that in the war, but actual poison does, I feel, call for comment. Look at the menus this week – Monday, poison pie; Tuesday, poison burger steak; Wednesday, Cornish poison –'

Aunt Sadie looked intensely worried.

'Oh, dear, yes, she is an awful cook, I know, but Davey, what can one do? The meat ration only lasts about two meals, and there are fourteen meals in a week, you must remember. If she minces it up with a little sausage meat – poison meat (I do so agree with you really) – it goes much further, you see.'

'But in the country surely one can supplement the ration with game and farm produce? Yes, I know the Home Farm is let, but surely you could keep a pig and some hens? And what about game? There always used to be such a lot here.'

'The trouble is Matthew thinks they'll be needing all their ammunition for the Germans, and he refuses to waste a single shot on hares or partridges. Then you see Mrs Beecher (oh, what a dreadful woman she is, though of course, we are lucky to have her) is the kind of cook who is quite good at a cut off the joint and two veg., but she simply hasn't an idea of how to make up delicious foreign oddments out of little bits of nothing at all. But you are quite, absolutely right, Davey, it's not wholesome. I really will make an effort to see what can be done.'

'You always used to be such a wonderful housekeeper, Sadie dear, it used to do me so much good, coming here. I remember one Christmas I put on four and a half ounces. But now I am losing steadily, my wretched frame is hardly more than a skeleton and I fear that, if I were to catch anything, I might peter out altogether. I take every precaution against that, everything is drenched in T.C.P., I gargle at least six times a day, but I can't disguise from you that my resistance is very low, very.'

Aunt Sadie said: 'It's quite easy to be a wonderful housekeeper when there are a first-rate cook, two kitchen-maids, a scullery-maid, and when you can get all the food you want. I'm afraid I am dreadfully stupid at managing on rations, but I really will try and take a pull. I'm very glad indeed that you mentioned it, Davey, it was absolutely right of you, and of course, I don't mind at all.'

But no real improvement resulted. Mrs Beecher said 'yes, yes' to all suggestions, and continued to send up Hamburger steaks, Cornish pasty, and shepherd pie, which continued to be full of poison sausage. It was very nasty and very unwholesome, and, for once, we all felt that Davey had not gone a bit too far. Meals were no pleasure to anybody and a positive ordeal to Davey, who sat, a pinched expression on his face, refusing food and resorting more and more often to the vitamin pills with which his place at the table was surrounded – too many by far even for his collection of jewelled boxes – a little forest of bottles, vitamin A, vitamin B, vitamins A and C, vitamins B3 and D, one tablet equals two pounds of summer butter – ten times the strength of a gallon of cod-liver oil – for the blood – for the brain – for muscle – for energy – anti this and protection against that – all but one bore a pretty legend.

'And what's in this, Davey?'

'Oh, that's what the panzer troops have before going into action.'

Davey gave a series of little sniffs. This usually denoted that his nose was about to bleed, pints of valuable red and white corpuscles so assiduously filled with vitamins would be wasted, his resistance still further lowered.

Aunt Emily and I looked up in some anxiety from the rissoles we were sadly pushing round our plates.

'Bolter,' he said, severely, 'you've been at my Mary Chess again.'

'Oh, Davey dulling, such a tiny droppie.'

'A tiny drop doesn't stink out the whole room. I'm sure you have been pouring it into the bath with the stopper out. It is a shame. That bottle is my quota for a month, it is too bad of you, Bolter.'

'Dulling, I swear I'll get you some more – I've got to go to London next week, to have my wiggie washed, and I'll bring back a bottle, I swear.'

'And I very much hope you'll take Gewan with you and leave him there,' growled Uncle Matthew. 'Because I won't have him in this house much longer, you know. I've warned you, Bolter.'

Uncle Matthew was busy from morning to night with his Home Guard. He was happy and interested and in a particularly mellow mood, for it looked as if his favourite hobby, that of clocking Germans, might be available again at any moment. So he only noticed Juan from time to time, and, whereas in the old days he would have had him out of the house in the twinkling of an eye, Juan had now been an inmate of Alconleigh for nearly a month. However, it was beginning to be obvious that my uncle had no intention of putting up with his presence for ever and things were clearly coming to a head where Juan was concerned. As for the Spaniard himself, I never saw a man so wretched. He wandered about miserably, with nothing whatever to do all day, unable to talk to anybody, while at meal-times the disgust on his face fully equalled that of Davey. He hadn't even the spirit to play his guitar.

'Davey, you must talk to him,' said Aunt Sadie.

My mother had gone to London to have her hair dyed, and a family council was gathered in her absence to decide upon the fate of Juan.

'We obviously can't turn him out to starve, as the Bolter says he saved her life, and, anyhow, one has human feelings.'

'Not towards Dagoes,' said Uncle Matthew, grinding his dentures.

'But what we can do is to get him a job, only first we must find out what his profession is. Now, Davey, you're good at languages, and you're so clever, I'm sure if you had a look at the Spanish dictionary in the library you could just manage to ask him what he used to do before the war. Do try, Davey.'

'Yes, darling, do,' said Aunt Emily. 'The poor fellow looks too miserable for words at present, I expect he'd love to have some work.'

Uncle Matthew snorted.

'Just give me the Spanish dictionary,' he muttered. 'I'll soon find the word for "get out".'

'I'll try,' said Davey, 'but I can guess what it will be I'm afraid. G for gigolo.'

'Or something equally useless, like M for matador or H for hidalgo,' said Louisa. 'Yes. Then what?'

'Then B for be off,' said Uncle Matthew, 'and the Bolter will have to support him, but not anywhere near me, I beg. It must be made perfectly clear to both of them that I can't stand the sight of the sewer lounging about here any longer.'

When Davey takes on a job he does it thoroughly. He shut himself up for several hours with the Spanish dictionary, and wrote down a great many words and phrases on a piece of paper. Then he beckoned Juan into Uncle Matthew's business-room and shut the door.

They were there a short time, and, when they emerged, both were wreathed in happy smiles.

'You've sacked him, I hope?' Uncle Matthew said, suspiciously.

'No, indeed, I've not sacked him,' said Davey, 'on the contrary, I've engaged him. My dears, you'll never guess, it's too absolutely glamorous for words, Juan is a cook, he was the cook, I gather, of some cardinal before the Civil War. You don't mind I hope, Sadie. I look upon this as an absolute lifeline – Spanish food, so delicious, so unconstipating, so digestible, so full of glorious garlic. Oh, the joy, no more poison-burger – how soon can we get rid of Mrs Beecher?'

Davey's enthusiasm was fully justified, and Juan in the kitchen was the very greatest possible success. He was more than a first-class cook, he had an extraordinary talent for organization, and soon, I suspect, became king of the local black market. There was no nonsense about foreign dishes made out of little bits of nothing at all; succulent birds, beasts, and crustaceans appeared at every meal, the vegetables ran with extravagant sauces, the puddings were obviously based upon real ice-cream.

'Juan is wonderful,' Aunt Sadie would remark in her vague manner, 'at making the rations go round. When I think of Mrs Beecher – really, Davey, you were so clever.'

One day she said: 'I hope the food isn't too rich for you now, Davey?'

'Oh no,' said Davey. 'I never mind rich food, it's poor food that does one such an infinity of harm.'

Juan also pickled and bottled and preserved from morning till night, until the store cupboard, which he had found bare except for a few tins of soup, began to look like a pre-war grocer's shop. Davey called it Aladdin's Cave, or Aladdin for short, and spent a lot of his time there, gloating. Months of tasty vitamins stood there in neat rows, a barrier between him and that starvation which had seemed, under Mrs Beecher's régime, only just round the corner.

Juan himself was now a very different fellow from the dirty and disgruntled refugee who had sat about so miserably. He was clean, he wore a white coat and hat, he seemed to have grown in stature, and he soon acquired a manner of great authority in his kitchen. Even Uncle Matthew acknowledged the change.

'If I were the Bolter,' he said, 'I should marry him.'

'Knowing the Bolter,' said Davey, 'I've no doubt at all that she will.'

Early in November I had to go to London for the day, on business for Alfred, who was now in the Middle East, and to see my doctor. I went by the eight o'clock train, and, having heard nothing of Linda for some weeks, I took a taxi and drove straight to Cheyne Walk. There had been a heavy raid the night before, and I passed through streets which glistened with broken glass. Many fires still smouldered, and fire engines, ambulances, and rescue men hurried to and fro, streets were blocked, and several times we had to drive quite a long way round. There seemed to be a great deal of excitement in the air. Little groups of people were gathered outside shops and houses, as if to compare notes; my taxi-driver talked incessantly to me over his shoulder. He had been up all night, he said, helping the rescue workers. He described what he had found.

'It was a spongy mass of red,' he said, ghoulishly, 'covered with feathers.'

'Feathers?' I said, horrified.

'Yes. A feather bed, you see. It was still breathing, so I takes it to the hospital, but they say that's no good to us, take it to the mortuary. So I sews it in a sack and takes it to the mortuary.'

'Goodness,' I said.

'Oh, that's nothing to what I have seen.'

Linda's nice daily woman, Mrs Hunt, opened the door to me at Cheyne Walk.

'She's very poorly, ma'am, can't you take her back to the country with you? It's not right for her to be here, in her condition. I hate to see her like this.'

Linda was in her bathroom, being sick. When she came out she said:

'Don't think it's the raid that's upset me. I like them. I'm in the family way, that's what it is.'

'Darling, I thought you weren't supposed to have another baby.'

'Oh, doctors! They don't know anything, they are such fearful idiots. Of course I can, and I'm simply longing for it, this baby won't be the least like Moira, you'll see.'

'I'm going to have one too.'

'No – how lovely – when?'

'About the end of May.'

'Oh, just the same as me.'

'And Louisa, in March.'

'Haven't we been busy? I do call that nice, they can all be Hons together.'

'Now, Linda, why don't you come back with me to Alconleigh? Whatever is the sense of stopping here in all this? It can't be good for you or the baby.'

'I like it,' said Linda. 'It's my home, and I like to be in it. And besides, somebody might turn up, just for a few hours you know, and want to see me, and he knows where to find me here.'

'You'll be killed,' I said, 'and then he won't know where to find you.'

'Darling Fanny, don't be so silly. There are seven million people living in London, do you really imagine they are all killed every night? Nobody is killed in air-raids, there is a great deal of noise and a great deal of mess, but people really don't seem to get killed much.'

'Don't – don't –' I said. 'Touch wood. Apart from being killed or not it doesn't suit you. You look awful, Linda.'

'Not so bad when I'm made up. I'm so fearfully sick, that's the trouble, but it's nothing to do with the raids, and that part will soon be over now and I shall be quite all right again.'

'Well, think about it,' I said, 'it's very nice at Alconleigh, wonderful food –'

'Yes, so I hear. Merlin came to see me, and his stories of caramelized carrots swimming in cream made my mouth water. He said he was preparing to throw morality to the winds and bribe this Juan to go to Merlinford, but he found out it would mean having the Bolter too and he couldn't quite face that.'

'I must go,' I said uncertainly. 'I don't like to leave you, darling, I do wish you'd come back with me.'

'Perhaps I will later on, we'll see.'

I went down to the kitchen and found Mrs Hunt. I gave her some money in case of emergency, and the Alconleigh telephone number, and begged her to ring me up if she thought there was anything I could do.

'She won't budge,' I said. 'I've done all I can to make her, but it doesn't seem to be any good, she's as obstinate as a donkey.'

'I know, ma'am. She won't even leave the house for a breath of air, sits by that telephone day in day out playing cards with herself. It ain't hardly right she should sleep here all alone in my opinion, either, but you can't get her to listen to sense. Last night, ma'am, whew! it was terrible, walloping down all night, and those wretched guns never got a single one, whatever they may tell you in the papers. It's my opinion they must have got women on those guns, and, if so, no wonder. Women!'

A week later Mrs Hunt rang me up at Alconleigh. Linda's house had received a direct hit and they were still digging for her.

Aunt Sadie had gone on an early bus to Cheltenham to do some shopping, Uncle Matthew was nowhere to be found, so Davey and I simply took his car, full of Home Guard petrol, and drove to London, hell for leather. The little house was an absolute ruin, but Linda and her bulldog were unhurt, they had just been got out and put to bed in the house of a neighbour. Linda was flushed and excited, and couldn't stop talking.

'You see,' she said. 'What did I tell you, Fanny, about air-raids not killing people. Here we are, right as rain. My bed simply went through the floor, Plon-plon and I went on it, most comfortable.'

Presently a doctor arrived and gave her a sedative. He told us she would probably go to sleep and that when she woke up we could drive her down to Alconleigh. I telephoned to Aunt Sadie and told her to have a room ready.

The rest of the day was spent by Davey in salvaging what he could of Linda's things. Her house and furniture, her beautiful Renoir, and everything in her bedroom was completely wrecked, but he was able to rescue a few oddments from the splintered, twisted remains of her cupboards, and in the basement he found, untouched, the two trunks full of clothes which Fabrice had sent after her from Paris. He came out looking like a miller, covered with white dust from head to foot, and Mrs Hunt took us round to her own little house and gave us some food.

'I suppose Linda may miscarry,' I said to Davey, 'and I'm sure it's to be hoped she will. It's most dangerous for her to have this child – my doctor is horrified.'

However, she did not, in fact she said that the experience had done her a great deal of good, and had quite stopped her from feeling sick. She demurred again at leaving London, but without much conviction. I pointed out that if anybody was looking for her and found the Cheyne Walk house a total wreck they would be certain at once to get into touch with Alconleigh. She saw that this was so, and agreed to come with us.

21

Winter now set in with its usual severity on those Cotswold uplands. The air was sharp and bracing, like cold water; most agreeable if one only goes out for short brisk walks or rides, and if there is a warm house to go back to. But the central-heating apparatus at Alconleigh had never been really satisfactory and I suppose that by now the pipes, through old age, had become thoroughly furred up – in any case they were hardly more than tepid. On coming into the hall from the bitter outside air one did feel a momentary glow of warmth; this soon lessened, and gradually, as circulation died down, one's body became pervaded by a cruel numbness. The men on the estate, the old ones that is, who were not in the army, had no time to chop up logs for the fires; they were occupied from morning till night, under the leadership of Uncle Matthew, in drilling, constructing barricades and blockhouses, and otherwise preparing to make themselves a nuisance to the German army before ending up as cannon-fodder.

'I reckon,' Uncle Matthew would say proudly, 'that we shall be able to stop them for two hours – possibly three – before we are all killed. Not bad for such a little place.'

We made our children go out and collect wood, Davey became an assiduous and surprisingly efficient woodman (he had refused to join the Home Guard, he said he always fought better out of uniform), but, somehow, they produced only enough to keep the nursery fire going, and the one in the brown sitting-room, if it was lit after tea, and, as the wood was pretty wet, this really got warm only just when it was time to tear oneself away and go up the freezing stairs to bed. After dinner the two armchairs on each side of the fire were always occupied by Davey and my mother. Davey pointed out that it would be more trouble for everybody in the end if he got one of his chills; the Bolter just dumped herself down. The rest of us sat in a semicircle well beyond the limits of any real warmth, and looked longingly at the little flickering yellow flames, which often subsided into sulky smoke. Linda had an evening coat, a sort of robe from head to foot, of white fox lined with white ermine. She wrapped herself in this for dinner, and suffered less than we others did. In the daytime she either wore her sable coat and a pair of black velvet boots lined with sable to match, or lay on the sofa tucked up in an enormous mink bedspread lined with white velvet quilting.

'It used to make me so laugh when Fabrice said he was getting me all these things because they would be useful in the war, the war would be fearfully cold he always said, but I see now how right he was.'

Linda's possessions filled the other females in the house with a sort of furious admiration.

'It does seem rather unfair,' Louisa said to me one afternoon when we were pushing our two youngest children out in their prams together. We were both dressed in stiff Scotch tweeds, so different from supple flattering French ones, in woollen stockings, brogues, and jerseys, knitted by ourselves, of shades carefully chosen to 'go with' though not 'to match' our coats and skirts. 'Linda goes off and has this glorious time in Paris, and comes back covered with rich furs, while you and I – what do we get for sticking all our lives to the same dreary old husbands? Three-quarter-length shorn lamb.'

'Alfred isn't a dreary old husband,' I said loyally. But of course I knew exactly what she meant.

Aunt Sadie thought Linda's clothes too pretty.

'What lovely taste, darling,' she would say when another ravishing garment was brought out. 'Did that come from Paris too? It's really wonderful what you can get there, on no money, if you're clever.'

At this my mother would give tremendous winks in the direction of anybody whose eye she might happen to catch, including Linda herself. Linda's face would then become absolutely stony. She could not bear my mother; she felt that, before she met Fabrice, she had been heading down the same road herself, and she was appalled to see what lay at the end of it. My mother started off by trying a 'let's face it, dear, we are nothing but two fallen women' method of approach to Linda, which was most unsuccessful. Linda became not only stiff and cold, but positively rude to the poor Bolter, who, unable to see what she could have done to offend, was at first very much hurt. Then she began to be on her dignity, and said it was great nonsense for Linda to go on like this; in fact, considering she was nothing but a high-class tart, it was most pretentious and hypocritical of her. I tried to explain Linda's intensely romantic attitude towards Fabrice and the months she had spent with him, but the Bolter's own feelings had been dulled by time, and she either could not or would not understand.

'It was Sauveterre she was living with, wasn't it?' my mother said to me, soon after Linda arrived at Alconleigh.

'How do you know?'

'Everybody knew on the Riviera. One always knew about Sauveterre somehow. And it was rather a thing, because he seemed to have settled down for life with that boring Lamballe woman; then she had to go to England on business and clever little Linda nabbed him. A very good cop for her, dulling, but I don't see why she has to be so high-hat about it. Sadie doesn't know, I quite realize that, and of course wild horses wouldn't make me tell her, I'm not that kind of a girl, but I do think, when we're all together, Linda might be a tiny bit more jolly.'

The Alconleighs still believed that Linda was the devoted wife of Christian, who was now in Cairo, and, of course, it had never occurred to them for a moment that the child might not be his. They had quite forgiven her for leaving Tony, though they thought themselves distinctly broadminded for having done so. They would ask her from time to time what Christian was doing, not because they were interested, but so that Linda shouldn't feel out of it when Louisa and I talked about our husbands. She would then be obliged to invent bits of news out of imaginary letters from Christian.

'He doesn't like his Brigadier very much,' or,

'He says Cairo is great fun, but one can have enough of it.'

In point of fact Linda never got any letters at all. She had not seen her English friends now for so long, they were scattered in the war to the ends of the earth, and, though they might not have forgotten about Linda, she was no longer in their lives. But, of course, there was only one thing she wanted, a letter, a line even, from Fabrice. Just after Christmas it came. It was forwarded in a typewritten envelope from Carlton Gardens with General de Gaulle's stamp on it. Linda, when she saw it lying on the hall table, became perfectly white. She seized it and rushed up to her bedroom.

About an hour later she came to find me.

'Oh, darling,' she said, her eyes full of tears. 'I've been all this time and I can't read one word. Isn't it torture? Could you have a look?'

She gave me a sheet of the thinnest paper I ever saw, on which were scratched, apparently with a rusty pin, a series of perfectly incomprehensible hieroglyphics. I could not make out one single word either, it seemed to bear no relation to handwriting, the marks in no way resembled letters.

'What can I do?' said poor Linda. 'Oh, Fanny.'

'Let's ask Davey,' I said.

She hesitated a little over this, but feeling that it would be better, however intimate the message, to share it with Davey than not to have it all, she finally agreed.

Davey said she was quite right to ask him.

'I am very good at French handwriting.'

'Only you wouldn't laugh at it?' Linda said, in a breathless voice like a child.

'No, Linda, I don't regard it as a laughing matter any longer,' Davey replied, looking with love and anxiety at her face, which had become very drawn of late. But when he had studied the paper for some time, he too was obliged to confess himself absolutely stumped by it.

'I've seen a lot of difficult French writing in my life,' he said, 'and this beats them all.'

In the end Linda had to give up. She went about with the piece of paper, like a talisman, in her pocket, but never knew what Fabrice had written to her on it. It was cruelly tantalizing. She wrote to him at Carlton Gardens, but this letter came back with a note regretting that it could not be forwarded.

'Never mind,' she said. 'One day the telephone bell will ring again and he'll be there.'

Louisa and I were busy from morning to night. We now had one nanny (mine) between eight children. Fortunately they were not at home all the time. Louisa's two eldest were at a private school, and two of hers and two of mine went for lessons to a convent Lord Merlin had most providentially found for us at Merlinford. Louisa got a little petrol for this, and she and I or Davey drove them there in Aunt Sadie's car every day. It can be imagined what Uncle Matthew thought of their arrangement. He ground his teeth, flashed his eyes, and always referred to the poor good nuns as 'those damned parachutists'. He was absolutely convinced that whatever time they could spare from making machine-gun nests for other nuns, who would presently descend from the skies, like birds, to occupy the nests, was given to the seduction of the souls of his grandchildren and great nieces.

'They get a prize you know for anybody they can catch – of course you can see they are men, you've only got to look at their boots.'

Every Sunday he watched the children like a lynx for genuflections, making the sign of the Cross, and other Papist antics, or even for undue interest in the service, and when none of these symptoms was to be observed he was hardly reassured.

'These Romans are so damned artful.'

He thought it most subversive of Lord Merlin to harbour such an establishment on his property, but only really what one might expect of a man who brought Germans to one's ball and was known to admire foreign music. Uncle Matthew had most conveniently forgotten all about 'Una voce poco fa', and now played, from morning to night, a record called 'The Turkish Patrol', which started piano, became forte, and ended up pianissimo.

'You see,' he would say, 'they come out of a wood, and then you can hear them go back into the wood. Don't know why it's called Turkish, you can't imagine Turks playing a tune like that, and of course there aren't any woods in Turkey. It's just the name, that's all.'

I think it reminded him of his Home Guard, who were always going into woods and coming out of them again, poor dears, often covering themselves with branches as when Birnam Wood came to Dunsinane.

So we worked hard, mending and making and washing, doing any chores for Nanny rather than actually look after the children ourselves. I have seen too many children brought up without nannies to think this at all desirable. In Oxford, the wives of progressive dons did it often as a matter of principle; they would gradually become morons themselves, while the children looked like slum children and behaved like barbarians.

As well as looking after the clothes of our existing families we also had to make for the babies we were expecting, though they did inherit a good deal from brothers and sisters. Linda, who naturally had no store of baby clothes, did nothing of all this. She arranged one of the slatted shelves in the Hons' cupboard as a sort of bunk, with pillows and quilts from spare bedrooms, and here, wrapped in her mink bedspread, she would lie all day with Plon-plon beside her, reading fairy stories. The Hons' cupboard, as of old, was the warmest, the one really warm place in the house. Whenever I could I brought my sewing and sat with her there, and then she would put down the blue or the green fairy book, Anderson or Grimm, and tell me at length about Fabrice and her happy life with him in Paris. Louisa sometimes joined us there, and then Linda would break off and we would talk about John Fort William and the children. But Louisa was a restless busy creature, not much of a chatter, and, besides, she was irritated to see how Linda did absolutely nothing, day after day.

'Whatever is the baby going to wear, poor thing,' she would say crossly to me, 'and who is going to look after it, Fanny? It's quite plain already that you and I will have to, and really, you know, we've got enough to do as it is. And another thing, Linda lies there covered in sables or whatever they are, but she's got no money at all, she's a pauper – I don't believe she realizes that in the least. And what is Christian going to say when he hears about the baby, after all, legally his, he'll have to bring a suit to illegitimize it, and then there'll be such a scandal. None of these things seem to have occurred to Linda. She ought to be beside herself with worry, instead of which she is behaving like the wife of a millionaire in peacetime. I've no patience with her.'

All the same, Louisa was a good soul. In the end it was she who went to London and bought a layette for the baby. Linda sold Tony's engagement ring at a horribly low price, to pay for it.

'Do you never think about your husbands?' I asked her one day, after she had been talking for hours about Fabrice.

'Well, funnily enough, I do quite often think of Tony. Christian, you see, was such an interlude, he hardly counts in my life at all, because, for one thing, our marriage lasted a very short time, and then it was quite overshadowed by what came after. I don't know, I find these things hard to remember, but I think that my feelings for him were only really intense for a few weeks, just at the very beginning. He's a noble character, a man you can respect, I don't blame myself for marrying him, but he has no talent for love.

'But Tony was my husband for so long, more than a quarter of my life, if you come to think of it. He certainly made an impression. And I see now that the thing going wrong was hardly his fault, poor Tony, I don't believe it would have gone right with anybody (unless I happened to meet Fabrice) because in those days I was so extremely nasty. The really important thing, if a marriage is to go well, without much love, is very very great niceness – *gentillesse* – and wonderful good manners. I was never *gentille* with Tony, and often I was hardly polite to him, and, very soon after our honeymoon, I became exceedingly disagreeable. I'm ashamed now to think what I was like. And poor old Tony was so good-natured, he never snapped back, he put up with it all for years and then just ambled off to Pixie. I can't blame him. It was my fault from beginning to end.'

'Well, he wasn't very nice really, darling. I shouldn't worry yourself about it too much, and look how he's behaving now.'

'Oh, he's the weakest character in the world, it's Pixie and his parents who made him do that. If he'd still been married to me he would have been a Guards officer by now, I bet you.'

One thing Linda never thought about, I'm quite sure, was the future. Some day the telephone bell would ring and it would be Fabrice, and that was as far as she got. Whether he would marry her, and what would happen about the child, were questions which not only did not preoccupy her, but which never seemed to enter her head. Her mind was entirely on the past.

'It's rather sad,' she said one day, 'to belong, as we do, to a lost generation. I'm sure in history the two wars will count as one war and that we shall be squashed out of it altogether, and people will forget that we ever existed. We might just as well never have lived at all, I do think it's a shame.'

'It may become a sort of literary curiosity,' Davey said. He sometimes crept, shivering, into the Hons' cupboard to get up a little circulation before he went back to his writing. 'People will be interested in it for all the wrong reasons, and collect Lalique dressing-table sets and shagreen boxes and cocktail cabinets lined with looking-glass and find them very amusing. Oh good,' he said, peering out of the window, 'that wonderful Juan is bringing in another pheasant.'

(Juan had an invaluable talent, he was expert with a catapult. He spent all his odd moments – how he had odd moments was a mystery, but he had – creeping about the woods or down by the river armed with this weapon. As he was an infallible shot, and moreover, held back by no sporting inhibitions, that a pheasant or a hare should be sitting or a swan the property of the King being immaterial to Juan, the results of these sallies were excellent from the point of view of larder and stock-pot. When Davey really wanted to relish his food to the full he would recite, half to himself, a sort of little grace, which began: 'Remember Mrs Beecher's tinned tomato soup.'

The unfortunate Craven was, of course, tortured by these goings on, which he regarded as little better than poaching. But his nose, poor man, was kept well to the grindstone by Uncle Matthew, and, when he was not on sentry-go, or fastening the trunks of trees to bicycle-wheels across the lanes to make barricades against tanks, he was on parade. Uncle Matthew was a byword in the county for the smartness of his parades. Juan, as an alien, was luckily excluded from these activities, and was able to devote all his time to making us comfortable and happy, in which he very notably succeeded.)

'I don't want to be a literary curiosity,' said Linda. 'I should like to have been a living part of a really great generation. I think it's too dismal to have been born in 1911.'

'Never mind, Linda, you will be a wonderful old lady.'

'You will be a wonderful old gentleman, Davey,' said Linda.

'Oh, me? I fear I shall never make old bones,' replied Davey, in accents of the greatest satisfaction.

And, indeed, there was a quality of agelessness about him. Although he was quite twenty years older than we and only about five years younger than Aunt Emily, he had always seemed much nearer to our generation than to hers, nor had he altered in any respect since the day when he had stood by the hall fire looking unlike a captain and unlike a husband.

'Come on, dears, tea, and I happen to know that Juan has made a layer-cake, so let's go down before the Bolter gets it all.'

Davey carried on a great meal-time feud with the Bolter. Her table manners had always been casual, but certain of her habits, such as eating jam with a spoon which she put back into the jam-pot, and stubbing out her cigarette in the sugar-basin, drove poor Davey, who was very ration-conscious, to a frenzy of irritation, and he would speak sharply to her, like a governess to a maddening child.

He might have spared himself the trouble. The Bolter took absolutely no notice whatever, and went on spoiling food with insouciance.

'Dulling,' she would say, 'whatever does it matter, my perfectly divine Hoo-arn has got plenty more up his tiny sleeve, I promise you.'

At this time there was a particularly alarming invasion scare. The arrival of the Germans, with full paraphernalia of airborne troops dressed as priests, ballet dancers, or what you will, was expected from one day to the next. Some unkind person put it about that they would be the doubles of Mrs Davis, in W.V.S. uniform. She had such a knack of being in several places at once that it already seemed as if there were a dozen Mrs Davises parachuting about the countryside. Uncle Matthew took the invasion very seriously indeed, and one day he gathered us all together, in the business-room and told us in detail the part that we were expected to play.

'You women, with the children, must go to the cellar while the battle is on,' he said, 'there is an excellent tap, and I have provisioned you with bully-beef for a week. Yes, you may be there several days, I warn you.'

'Nanny won't like that,' Louisa began, but was quelled by a furious look.

'While we are on the subject of Nanny,' Uncle Matthew said, 'I warn you, there's to be no question of cluttering up the roads with your prams, mind, no evacuation under any circumstances at all. Now, there is one very important job to be done, and that I am entrusting to you, Davey. You won't mind it I know, old boy, if I say that you are a very poor shot – as you know, we are short of ammunition, and what there is must, under no circumstances, be wasted – every bullet must tell. So I don't intend to give you a gun, at first, anyhow. But I've got a fuse and a charge of dynamite (I will show you, in a moment), and I shall want you to blow up the store cupboard for me.'

'Blow up Aladdin,' said Davey. He turned quite pale. 'Matthew, you must be mad.'

'I would let Gewan do it, but the fact is, though I rather like old Gewan now, I don't altogether trust the fella. Once a foreigner always a foreigner in my opinion. Now I must explain to you why I regard this as a most vital part of the operations. When Josh and Craven and I and all the rest of us have been killed there is only one way in which you civilians can help, and that is by becoming a charge on the German army. You must make it their business to feed you – never fear, they'll do so, they don't want any typhus along their lines of communication – but you must see that it's as difficult as possible for them. Now that store cupboard would keep you going for weeks, I've just had a look at it; why, it would feed the entire village. All wrong. Make them bring in the food and muck up their transport, that's what we want, to be a perfect nuisance to them. It's all you'll be able to do, by then, just be a nuisance, so the store cupboard will have to go, and Davey must blow it up.'

Davey opened his mouth to make another observation, but Uncle Matthew was in a very frightening mood and he thought better of it.

'Very well, dear Matthew,' he said, sadly, 'you must show me what to do.'

But as soon as Uncle Matthew's back was turned he gave utterance to loud complaints.

'No, really, it is too bad of Matthew to insist on blowing up Aladdin,' he said. 'It's all right for him, he'll be dead, but he really should consider us a little more.'

'But I thought you were going to take those black and white pills,' said Linda.

'Emily doesn't like the idea, and I had decided only to take them if I were arrested, but now I don't know. Matthew says the German army will have to feed us, but he must know as well as I do that if they feed us at all, which is extremely problematical, it will be on nothing but starch – it will be Mrs Beecher again, only worse, and I can't digest starch especially in the winter months. It is such a shame. Horrid old Matthew, he's so thoughtless.'

'Well, but, Davey,' said Linda, 'how about us? We're all in the same boat, but we don't grumble.'

'Nanny will,' said Louisa with a sniff, which plainly said, 'and I wish to associate myself with Nanny.'

'Nanny! She lives in a world of her own,' said Linda. 'But we're all supposed to know why we're fighting, and, speaking for myself, I think Fa is absolutely right. And if I think that, in my condition –'

'Oh, you'll be looked after,' said Davey, bitterly, 'pregnant women always are. They'll send you vitamins and things from America, you'll see. But nobody will bother about me, and I am so delicate, it simply won't do for me to be fed by the German army, and I shall never be able to make them understand about my inside. I know Germans.'

'You always said nobody understood as much about your inside as Dr Meyerstein.'

'Use your common sense, Linda. Are they likely to drop Dr Meyerstein over Alconleigh? You know perfectly well he's been in a camp for years. No, I must make up my mind to a lingering death – not a very pleasant prospect, I must say.'

Linda took Uncle Matthew aside after that, and made him show her how to blow up Aladdin.

'Davey's spirit is not so frightfully willing,' she said, 'and his flesh is definitely weak.'

There was a certain coldness between Linda and Davey for a little while after this, each thought the other had been quite unreasonable. It did not last, however. They were much too fond of each other (in fact, I am sure that Davey really loved Linda most in the world) and, as Aunt Sadie said, 'Who knows, perhaps the necessity for these dreadful decisions will not arise.'

So the winter slowly passed. The spring came with extraordinary beauty, as always at Alconleigh, with a brilliance of colouring, a richness of life, that one had forgotten to expect during the cold grey winter months. All the animals were giving birth, there were young creatures everywhere, and we now waited with longing and impatience for our babies to be born. The days, the very hours, dragged slowly by, and Linda began to say 'better than that' when asked the time.

'What's the time, darling?'

'Guess.'

'Half-past twelve?'

'Better than that, a quarter to one.'

We three pregnant women had all become enormous, we dragged ourselves about the house like great figures of fertility, heaving tremendous sighs, and feeling the heat of the first warm days with exaggerated discomfort.

Useless to her now were Linda's beautiful Paris clothes, she was down to the level of Louisa and me in a cotton smock, maternity skirt, and sandals. She abandoned the Hons' cupboard, and spent her days, when it was fine weather, sitting by the edge of the wood, while Plon-plon, who had become an enthusiastic, though unsuccessful, rabbiter, plunged panting to and fro in the green mists of the undergrowth.

'If anything happens to me, darling, you will look after Plon-plon,' she said. 'He has been such a comfort to me all this time.'

But she spoke idly, as one who knows, in fact, that she will live for ever, and she mentioned neither Fabrice nor the child, as surely she would have done had she been touched by any premonition.

Louisa's baby, Angus, was born at the beginning of April. It was her sixth child and third boy, and we envied her from the bottom of our hearts for having got it over.

On the 28th May both our babies were born – both boys. The doctors who said that Linda ought never to have another child were not such idiots after all. It killed her. She died, I think, completely happy, and without having suffered very much, but for us at Alconleigh, for her father and mother, brothers and sisters, for Davey and for Lord Merlin a light went out, a great deal of joy that never could be replaced.

At about the same time as Linda's death Fabrice was caught by the Gestapo and subsequently shot. He was a hero of the Resistance, and his name has become a legend in France.

I have adopted the little Fabrice, with the consent of Christian, his legal father. He has black eyes, the same shape as Linda's blue ones, and is a most beautiful and enchanting child. I love him quite as much as, and perhaps more than, I do my own.

The Bolter came to see me while I was still in the Oxford nursing home where my baby had been born and where Linda had died.

'Poor Linda,' she said, with feeling, 'poor little thing. But, Fanny, don't you think perhaps it's just as well? The lives of women like Linda and me are not so much fun when one begins to grow older.'

I didn't want to hurt my mother's feelings by protesting that Linda was not that sort of woman.

'But I think she would have been happy with Fabrice,' I said. 'He was the great love of her life, you know.'

'Oh, dulling,' said my mother, sadly. 'One always thinks that. Every, every time.'

Love in a Cold Climate

To Lord Berners

Part One

I am obliged to begin this story with a brief account of the Hampton family, because it is necessary to emphasize the fact once and for all that the Hamptons were very grand as well as very rich. A glance at Burke or at Debrett would be quite enough to make this clear, but these large volumes are not always available, while the books on the subject by Lord Montdore's brother-in-law, Boy Dougdale, are all out of print. His great talent for snobbishness and small talent for literature have produced three detailed studies of his wife's forebears, but they can only be read now by asking a bookseller to get them at second hand. (The bookseller will put an advertisement in his trade paper *The Clique*, 'H. Dougdale, any by'. He will be snowed under with copies at about a shilling each, and will then proudly inform his customer that he has 'managed to find what you want', implying hours of careful search on barrows, dirt cheap, at 30s. the three.) *Georgiana Lady Montdore and Her Circle, The Magnificent Montdores* and *Old Chronicles of Hampton*, I have them beside me as I write, and see that the opening paragraph of the first is:

'Two ladies, one dark, one fair, both young and lovely, were driving briskly towards the little village of Kensington on a fine May morning. They were Georgiana, Countess of Montdore and her great friend Walburga, Duchess of Paddington, and they made a delightfully animated picture as they discussed the burning question of the hour – should one, or should one not, subscribe to a parting present for poor, dear Princess Lieven?'

This book is dedicated, by gracious permission, to Her Royal Highness the Grand Duchess Peter of Russia, and has eight full-page illustrations.

It must be said that when this terrible trilogy first came out it had quite a vogue with the lending library public.

'The family of Hampton is ancient in the West of England, indeed Fuller, in his *Worthies*, mentions it as being of stupendous antiquity.'

Burke makes it out just a shade more ancient than does Debrett, but both plunge back into the mists of medieval times, from which they drag forth ancestors with P. G. Wodehouse names, Ugs and Berts and Threds, and Walter Scott fates. 'His Lordship was attainted – beheaded – convicted – proscribed – exiled – dragged from prison by a furious mob – slain at the Battle of Crécy – went down in the White Ship – perished during the third crusade – killed in a duel.' There were very few natural deaths to record in the early misty days. Both Burke and Debrett linger with obvious enjoyment over so genuine an object as this family, unspoilt by the ambiguities of female line and deed poll. Nor could any of those horrid books which came out in the nineteenth century, devoted to research and aiming to denigrate the nobility, make the object seem less genuine. Tall, golden-haired barons, born in wedlock and all looking very much alike, succeeded each other at Hampton, on lands which had never been bought or sold, until, in 1770, the Lord Hampton of the day brought back, from a visit to Versailles, a French bride, a Mademoiselle de Montdore. Their son had brown eyes, a dark skin and presumably, for it is powdered in all the pictures of him, black hair. This blackness did not persist in the family; he married a golden-haired heiress from Derbyshire and the Hamptons reverted to their blue and gold looks, for which they are famous to this day. The son of the Frenchwoman was rather clever and very worldly; he dabbled in politics and wrote a book of aphorisms. A great and life-long friendship with the Regent procured him, among other favours, an earldom. His mother's family having all perished during the Terror in France, he took her name as his title. Enormously rich, he spent enormously; he had a taste for French objects of art and acquired, during the years which followed the Revolution, a splendid collection of such things, including many pieces from the royal establishments, and others which had been looted out of the Hôtel de Montdore in the rue de Varenne. To make a suitable setting for this collection he then proceeded to pull down, at Hampton, the large plain house that Adam had built for his grandfather, and to drag over to England stone by stone (as modern American millionaires are supposed to do) a Gothic French château. This he assembled round a splendid tower of his own designing, covered the walls of the rooms with French panelling and silks, and set it in a formal landscape which he also designed and planted himself. It was all very grand and very mad, and in the between-wars period of which I write, very much out of fashion. 'I suppose it is beautiful,' people used to say, 'but frankly I don't admire it.'

This Lord Montdore also built Montdore House in Park Lane and a castle on a crag in Aberdeenshire. He was really much the most interesting and original character the family ever produced, but no member of it deviated from a tradition of authority. A solid, worthy, powerful Hampton can be found on every page of English history, his influence enormous in the West of England and his counsels not unheeded in London.

The tradition was carried on by the father of my friend Polly Hampton. If an Englishman could be descended from the gods it would be he, so much the very type of English nobleman that those who believed in aristocratic government would always begin by pointing to him as a justification of their argument. It was generally felt, indeed, that if there were more people like him the country would not be in its present mess, even Socialists conceding his excellence, which they could afford to do since there was only one of him and he was getting on. A scholar, a Christian, a gentleman, finest shot in the British Isles, best-looking Viceroy we ever sent to India, a popular landlord, a pillar of the Conservative party, a wonderful old man, in short, who nothing common ever did or mean. My cousin Linda and I, two irreverent little girls whose opinion makes no odds, used to think that he was a wonderful old fraud, and it seemed to us that in that house it was Lady Montdore who really counted. Now Lady Montdore was for ever doing common things and mean and she was intensely unpopular, quite as much disliked as her husband was loved, so that anything he might do that was considered not quite worthy of him, or which did not quite fit in with his reputation, was immediately laid at her door. 'Of course she made him do it.' On the other hand I have often wondered whether without her to bully him and push him forward and plot and intrigue for him and 'make him do it', whether in fact, without the help of those very attributes which caused her to be so much disliked, her thick skin and ambition and boundless driving energy, he would ever have done anything at all noteworthy in the world.

This is not a popular theory. I am told that by the time I really knew him, after they got back from India, he was already old and tired out and had given up the struggle, and that, when he was in his prime, he had not only controlled the destinies of men but also the vulgarities of his wife. I wonder. There was an ineffectiveness about Lord Montdore which had nothing to do with age; he was certainly beautiful to look at, but it was an empty beauty like that of a woman who has no sex appeal, he looked wonderful and old, but it seemed to me that, in spite of the fact that he still went regularly to the House of Lords, attended the Privy Council, sat on many committees, and often appeared in the Birthday Honours, he might just as well have been made of wonderful old cardboard.

Lady Montdore, however, was flesh and blood all right. She was born a Miss Perrotte, the handsome daughter of a country squire of small means and no particular note, so that her marriage to Lord Montdore was a far better one than she could reasonably have been expected to make. As time went on, when her worldly greed and snobbishness, her terrible relentless rudeness, had become proverbial, and formed the subject of many a legendary tale, people were inclined to suppose that her origins must have been low or transatlantic, but, in fact, she was perfectly well-born and had been decently brought up, what used to be called 'a lady'; so that there were no mitigating circumstances, and she ought to have known better.

No doubt her rampant vulgarity must have become more evident and less controlled with the years. In any case her husband never seemed aware of it, and the marriage was a success. Lady Montdore soon embarked him upon a public career, the fruits of which he was able to enjoy without much hard work since she made it her business to see that he was surrounded by a horde of efficient underlings, and though he pretended to despise the social life which gave meaning to her existence, he put up with it very gracefully, exercising a natural talent for agreeable conversation and accepting as his due the fact that people thought him wonderful.

'Isn't Lord Montdore wonderful? Sonia, of course, is past a joke, but he is so brilliant, such a dear, I do love him.'

People liked to pretend that it was solely on his account that they ever went to the house at all, but this was great nonsense because the lively quality, the fun of Lady Montdore's parties had nothing whatever to do with him, and, hateful as she may have been in many ways, she excelled as a hostess.

In short, they were happy together and singularly well suited. But for years they suffered one serious vexation in their married life; they had no children. Lord Montdore minded this because he naturally wanted an heir, as well as for more sentimental reasons. Lady Montdore minded passionately. Not only did she also want an heir, but she disliked any form of failure, could not bear to be thwarted, and was eager for an object on which she could concentrate such energy as was not absorbed by society and her husband's career. They had been married nearly twenty years, and quite given up all idea of having a child when Lady Montdore began to feel less well than usual. She took no notice, went on with her usual occupations and it was only two months before it was born that she realized she was going to have a baby. She was clever enough to avoid the ridicule which often attaches to such a situation by pretending to have kept the secret on purpose, so that instead of roaring with laughter, everybody said, 'Isn't Sonia absolutely phenomenal?'

I know all this because my uncle Davey Warbeck has told me. Having himself for many years suffered, or enjoyed, most of the distempers in the medical dictionary he is very well up in nursing-home gossip.

The fact that the child, when it was born, turned out to be a daughter, never seems to have troubled the Montdores at all. It is possible that, as Lady Montdore was under forty when Polly was born, they did not at first envisage her as an only child and that by the time they realized that they would never have another they loved her so much that the idea of her being in any way different, a different person, a boy, had become unthinkable. Naturally they would have liked to have a boy, but only if it could have been as well as, and not instead of, Polly. She was their treasure, the very hub of their universe.

Polly Hampton had beauty, and this beauty was her outstanding characteristic. She was one of those people you cannot think of except in regard to their looks, which in her case were unvarying, independent of clothes, of age, of circumstances, and even of health. When ill or tired she merely looked fragile, but never yellow, withered or diminished; she was born beautiful and never, at any time when I knew her, went off or became less beautiful, but on the contrary her looks always steadily improved. The beauty of Polly and the importance of her family are essential elements of this story. But, whereas the Hamptons can be studied in various books of reference, it is not much use turning to old *Tatlers* and seeing Polly as Lenare, as Dorothy Wilding saw her. The bones of course are there, hideous hats, old-fashioned poses cannot conceal them, the bones and the shape of her face are always perfection. But beauty is more, after all, than bones, for while bones belong to death and endure after decay, beauty is a living thing; it is, in fact, skin deep, blue shadows on a white skin, hair falling like golden feathers on a white smooth forehead, it is embodied in the movement, in the smile and above all in the regard of a beautiful woman. Polly's regard was a blue flash, the bluest and most sudden thing I ever saw, so curiously unrelated to the act of seeing that it was almost impossible to believe that those opaque blue stones observed, assimilated, or did anything except confer a benefit upon the object of their direction.

No wonder her parents loved her. Even Lady Montdore, who would have been a terrible mother to an ugly girl, or to an eccentric, wayward boy, had no difficulty in being perfect to a child who must, it seemed, do her great credit in the world and crown her ambitions; literally, perhaps, crown. Polly was certainly destined for an exceptional marriage – was Lady Montdore not envisaging something very grand indeed when she gave her the name Leopoldina? Had this not a royal, a vaguely Coburg flavour which might one day be most suitable? Was she dreaming of an Abbey, an altar, an Archbishop, a voice saying, 'I, Albert Edward Christian George Andrew Patrick David take thee, Leopoldina'? It was not an impossible dream. On the other hand nothing could be more purely English, wholesome and unpretentious than 'Polly'.

My cousin Linda Radlett and I used to be borrowed, from a very early age, to play with Polly, for, as so often happens with the parents of only children, the Montdores were always much preoccupied with her possible loneliness. I know that my own adopted mother, Aunt Emily, had the same feeling about me and would do anything rather than keep me alone with her during the holidays. Hampton Park is not far from Linda's home, Alconleigh, and she and Polly, being more or less of an age, each seemed destined to become the other's greatest friend. For some reason, however, they never really took to each other much, while Lady Montdore disliked Linda, and as soon as she was able to converse at all pronounced her conversation 'unsuitable'. I can see Linda now, at luncheon in the big dining-room at Hampton (that dining-room in which I have, at various times in my life, been so terrified that its very smell, a bouquet left by a hundred years of rich food, rich wine, rich cigars and rich women, is still to me as the smell of blood is to an animal), I can hear her loud sing-song Radlett voice, 'Did you ever have worms, Polly? I did, you can't imagine how fidgety they are. Then, oh the heaven of it. Doctor Simpson came and wormed me. Well you know how Doc. Simp. has always been the love of my life – so you do see –'

This was too much for Lady Montdore and Linda was never asked to stay again. But I went for a week or so almost every holidays, packed off there on my way to or from Alconleigh as children are, without ever being asked if I enjoyed it or wanted to go. My father was related to Lord Montdore through his mother. I was a well-behaved child and I think Lady Montdore quite liked me, anyhow she must have considered me 'suitable', a word which figured prominently in her vocabulary, because at one moment there was a question of my going to live there during the term, to do lessons with Polly. When I was thirteen, however, they went off to govern India, after which Hampton and its owners became a dim, though always alarming, memory to me.

2

By the time the Montdores and Polly returned from India I was grown-up and had already had a season in London. Linda's mother, my Aunt Sadie (Lady Alconleigh), had taken Linda and me out together, that is to say we went to a series of débutante dances where the people we met were all as young and as shy as we were ourselves, and the whole thing smelt strongly of bread and butter; it was quite unlike the real world, and almost as little of a preparation for it as children's parties are. When the summer ended Linda became engaged to be married, and I went back to my home in Kent, to another aunt and uncle, Aunt Emily and Uncle Davey, who had relieved my own divorced parents of the boredom and the burden of bringing up a child.

I was finding it dull at home, as young girls do when, for the first time, they have neither lessons nor parties to occupy their minds, and then one day into this dullness fell an invitation to stay at Hampton in October. Aunt Emily came out to find me, I was sitting in the garden, with Lady Montdore's letter in her hand.

'Lady Montdore says it will be rather a grown-up affair, mostly "young married people", she says, but she particularly wants you as company for Polly. There will be two young men for you girls, of course. Oh what a pity it happens to be Davey's day for getting drunk. I long to tell him, he'll be so much interested.'

There was nothing for it, however, but to wait; Davey had quite passed out and his stertorous breathing could be heard all over the house. My uncle's lapses into insobriety had no vice about them, they were purely therapeutic. The fact is he was following a new régime for perfect health, much in vogue at that time, he assured us, on the Continent.

'The aim is to warm up your glands with a series of jolts. The worst thing in the world for the body is to settle down and lead a quiet little life of regular habits; if you do that it soon resigns itself to old age and death. Shock your glands, force them to react, startle them back into youth, keep them on tip-toe so that they never know what to expect next, and they have to keep young and healthy to deal with all the surprises.'

Accordingly he ate in turns like Gandhi and like Henry VIII, went for ten-mile walks or lay in bed all day, shivered in a cold bath or sweated in a hot one. Nothing in moderation. 'It is also very important to get drunk every now and then.' Davey, however, was too much of a one for regular habits to be irregular otherwise than regularly, so he always got drunk at the full moon. Having once been under the influence of Rudolf Steiner he was still very conscious of the waxing and waning of the moon, and had, I believe, a vague idea that the waxing and waning of the capacity of his stomach coincided with its periods.

Uncle Davey was my one contact with the world; not the world of bread-and-butter misses but the great wicked world itself. Both my aunts had renounced it at an early age so that for them its existence had no reality, while their sister, my mother, had long since disappeared from view into its maw. Davey, however, had a modified liking for it, and often made little bachelor excursions into it from which he would return with a bag of interesting anecdotes. I could hardly wait to have a chat with him about this new development in my life.

'Are you sure he's too drunk, Aunt Emily?'

'Quite sure, dear. We must leave it until tomorrow.'

Meanwhile, as she always answered letters by return of post, she wrote and accepted. But the next day, when Davey reappeared looking perfectly green and with an appalling headache ('Oh, but that's splendid don't you see, such a challenge to the metabolism. I've just spoken to Dr England and he is most satisfied with my reaction') he was rather doubtful whether she had been right to do so.

'My darling Emily, the child will die of terror, that's all.' He was examining Lady Montdore's letter. I knew quite well that what he said was true, I had known it in my heart ever since Aunt Emily had read me the letter, but nevertheless I was determined to go; the idea had a glittering fascination for me.

'I'm not a child any longer, Davey,' I said.

'Grown-up people have died of terror at Hampton before now,' he replied. 'Two young men for Fanny and Polly indeed! Two old lovers of two of the old ladies there if I know anything about it. What a look, Emily! If you intend to launch this poor child in high society you must send her away armed with knowledge of the facts of life, you know. But I really don't understand what your policy is. First of all you take care that she should only meet the most utterly innocuous people, keep her nose firmly to Pont Street – quite a point of view, don't think I'm against it for a moment – but then all of a sudden you push her off the rocks into Hampton and expect that she will be able to swim.'

'Your metaphors, Davey – it's all those spirits,' Aunt Emily said, crossly for her.

'Never mind the spirits and let me tell poor Fanny the form. First of all, dear, I must explain that it's no good counting on these alleged young men to amuse you, because they won't have any time to spare for little girls, that's quite certain. On the other hand who is sure to be there is the Lecherous Lecturer, and as you are probably still just within his age group there's no saying what fun and games you may not have with him.'

'Oh, Davey,' I said, 'you are dreadful.'

The Lecherous Lecturer was Boy Dougdale. The Radlett children had given him this name after he had once lectured at Aunt Sadie's Women's Institute. The lecture, it seemed (I was not there at the time), had been very dull, but the things the lecturer did afterwards to Linda and Jassy were not dull at all.

'You know what secluded lives we lead,' Jassy had told me when next I was at Alconleigh. 'Naturally, it's not very difficult to arouse our interest. For example, do you remember that dear old man who came and lectured on the Toll Gates of England and Wales? It was rather tedious, but we liked it – he's coming again, Green Lanes this time. Well, the Lecherous Lecturer's lecture was Duchesses, and of course, one always prefers people to gates. But the fascinating thing was after the lecture he gave us a foretaste of sex, think what a thrill. He took Linda up on to the roof and did all sorts of blissful things to her; at least, she could easily see how they would be blissful with anybody except the Lecturer. And I got some great sexy pinches as he passed the nursery landing. Do admit, Fanny.'

Of course, my Aunt Sadie had no inkling of all this; she would have been perfectly horrified. Both she and Uncle Matthew always had very much disliked Mr Dougdale, and, when speaking of the lecture, she said it was exactly what she would have expected, snobbish, dreary and out of place with a village audience, but she had such difficulty filling up the Women's Institute programme month after month, in that remote district, that when he had himself written and suggested coming she had thought 'Oh, well –!' No doubt she supposed that her children called him the Lecherous Lecturer for alliterative rather than factual reasons, and indeed with the Radletts you never could tell. Why, for instance, would Victoria bellow like a bull and half kill Jassy whenever Jassy said, in a certain tone of voice, pointing her finger with a certain look, 'Fancy'? I think they hardly knew why themselves.

When I got home I told Davey about the lecturer, and he had roared with laughter, but said I was not to breathe a word to Aunt Emily or there would be an appalling row, and the one who would really suffer would be Lady Patricia Dougdale, Boy's wife.

'She has enough to put up with as it is,' he said, 'and besides, what would be the good? Those Radletts are clearly heading for one bad end after another, except that for them nothing ever will be the end. Poor dear Sadie just doesn't realize what she has hatched out, luckily for her.'

All this had happened a year or two before the time of which I am writing, and the name of Lecturer for Boy Dougdale had passed into the family language, so that none of us children ever called him anything else, and even the grown-ups had come to accept it, though Aunt Sadie, as a matter of form, made an occasional vague protest. It seemed to suit him perfectly.

'Don't listen to Davey,' Aunt Emily said, 'he's in a very naughty mood. Another time we'll wait for the waning moon to tell him these things, he's only really sensible when he's fasting, I've noticed. Now we shall have to think about your clothes, Fanny. Sonia's parties are always so dreadfully smart. I suppose they'll be sure to change for tea? Perhaps if we dyed your Ascot dress a nice dark shade of red that would do? It's a good thing we've got nearly a month.'

Nearly a month was indeed a comforting thought. Although I was bent on going to this house party, the very idea of it made me shake in my shoes with fright, not so much as the result of Davey's teasing as because ancient memories of Hampton now began to revive in force, memories of my childhood visits there and of how little, really, I had enjoyed them. Downstairs had been so utterly terrifying. It might be supposed that nothing could frighten somebody accustomed, as I was, to a downstairs inhabited by my uncle Matthew Alconleigh. But that rumbustious ogre, that eater of little girls, was by no means confined to one part of his house. He raged and roared about the whole of it, and indeed, the safest place to be in as far as he was concerned was downstairs in Aunt Sadie's drawing-room, since she alone had any control over him. The terror at Hampton was of a different quality, icy and dispassionate, and it reigned downstairs. You were forced down into it after tea, frilled up, washed and curled, when quite little, or in a tidy frock when older, into the Long Gallery, where there would seem to be dozens of grown-ups, all usually playing bridge. The worst of bridge is that out of every four people playing it one is always at liberty to roam about and say kind words to little girls.

Still, on the whole, there was not much attention to spare from the cards, and we could sit on the long white fur of the polar bear in front of the fireplace, looking at a picture book propped against its head, or just chatting to each other until welcome bedtime. It quite often happened, however, that Lord Montdore, or Boy Dougdale if he was there, would give up playing in order to amuse us. Lord Montdore would read aloud from Hans Andersen or Lewis Carroll and there was something about the way he read that made me squirm with secret embarrassment; Polly used to lie with her head on the bear's head, not listening, I believe, to a single word. It was far worse when Boy Dougdale organized hide-and-seek or sardines, two games of which he was extremely fond, and which he played in what Linda and I considered a 'stchoopid' way. The word stupid, pronounced like that, had a meaning of its own in our language when we (the Radletts and I) were little; it was not until after the Lecturer's lecture that we realized that Boy Dougdale had not been stupid so much as lecherous.

When bridge was in progress we would at least be spared the attention of Lady Montdore, who, even when dummy, had eyes for nothing but the cards, but if by chance there should not be a four staying in the house she would make us play racing demon, a game which has always given me an inferiority feeling because I do pant along so slowly.

'Hurry up, Fanny – we're all waiting for that seven, you know. Don't be so moony, dear.'

She always won by hundreds, never missing a trick. She never missed a detail of one's appearance, either, the shabby old pair of indoor shoes, the stockings that did not quite match each other, the tidy frock too short and too tight, grown out of in fact – it was all chalked up on the score.

That was downstairs. Upstairs was all right, perfectly safe, anyhow, from intrusion, the nursery being occupied by nurses, the schoolroom by governesses, and neither being subject to visits from the Montdores who, when they wished to see Polly, sent for her to go to them. But it was rather dull, not nearly as much fun as staying at Alconleigh. No Hons' cupboard, no talking bawdy, no sallies into the woods to hide the steel traps or to unstop an earth, no nests of baby bats being fed with fountain-pen fillers in secret from the grown-ups, who had absurd ideas about bats, that they were covered with vermin, or got into your hair. Polly was a withdrawn, formal little girl, who went through her day with the sense of ritual, the poise, the absolute submission to etiquette of a Spanish Infanta. You had to love her, she was so beautiful and so friendly, but it was impossible to feel very intimate with her.

She was the exact opposite of the Radletts who always 'told' everything. Polly 'told' nothing and if there were anything to tell it was all bottled up inside her. When Lord Montdore once read us the story of the Snow Queen (I could hardly listen, he put in so much expression) I remember thinking that it must be about Polly and that she surely had a glass splinter in her heart. What did she love? That was the great puzzle to me. My cousins and I poured out love on each other, on the grown-ups, on a variety of animals, and above all on the characters (often historical or even fictional) with whom we were IN love. There was no reticence and we all knew everything there was to know about each other's feelings for every other creature, whether real or imaginary. Then there were the shrieks. Shrieks of laughter and happiness and high spirits which always resounded through Alconleigh, except on the rare occasions when there were floods. It was shrieks or floods in that house, usually shrieks. But Polly did not pour or shriek, and I never saw her in tears. She was always the same, always charming, sweet and docile, polite, interested in what one said, rather amused by one's jokes, but all without exuberance, without superlatives, and certainly without any confidences.

Nearly a month then to this visit about which my feelings were so uncertain. All of a sudden, not only not nearly a month but now, today, now this minute, and I found myself being whirled through the suburbs of Oxford in a large black Daimler. One mercy, I was alone, and there was a long drive, some twenty miles, in front of me. I knew the road well from my hunting days in that neighbourhood. Perhaps it would go on nearly for ever. Lady Montdore's writing-paper was headed Hampton Place, Oxford, station Twyfold. But Twyfold, with the change and hour's wait at Oxford which it involved, was only inflicted upon such people as were never likely to be in a position to get their own back on Lady Montdore, anybody for whom she had the slightest regard being met at Oxford. 'Always be civil to the girls, you never know whom they may marry' is an aphorism which has saved many an English spinster from being treated like an Indian widow.

So I fidgeted in my corner, looking out at the deep intense blue dusk of autumn, profoundly wishing that I could be safe back at home or going to Alconleigh or indeed anywhere rather than to Hampton. Well-known landmarks kept looming up, it got darker and darker, but I could just see the Merlinford road with its big signpost. Then in a moment, or so it seemed, we were turning in at lodge gates. Horrors! I had arrived.

3

A scrunch of gravel; the motor car gently stopped, and exactly as it did so the front door opened, casting a panel of light at my feet. Once inside, the butler took charge of me, removed my nutria coat (a coming-out present from Davey), led me through the hall, under the great steep Gothic double staircase up which rushed a hundred steps, half-way to heaven, meeting at a marble group which represented the sorrows of Niobe, through the octagonal antechamber, through the green drawing-room and the red drawing-room into the Long Gallery where, without asking it, he pronounced my name very loud and clear and then abandoned me.

The Long Gallery was, as I always remember it being, full of people. On this occasion there were perhaps twenty or thirty; some sat round a tea table by the fire while others, with glasses instead of cups in their hands, stood watching a game of backgammon. This group was composed, no doubt, of the 'young married' people to whom Lady Montdore had referred in her letter. In my eyes, however, they seemed far from young, being about the age of my own mother. They were chattering like starlings in a tree, did not break off their chatter when I came in, and when Lady Montdore introduced me to them, merely stopped it for a moment, gave me a glance and went straight on with it again. When she pronounced my name, however, one of them said:

'Not by any chance the Bolter's daughter?'

Lady Montdore paused at this, rather annoyed, but I, quite used to hearing my mother referred to as the Bolter – indeed nobody, not even her own sisters, ever called her anything else – piped up 'Yes'.

It then seemed as though all the starlings rose in the air and settled on a different tree, and that tree was me.

'The Bolter's girl?'

'Don't be funny – how could the Bolter have a grown-up daughter?'

'Veronica – do come here a minute – do you know who this is? She's the Bolter's child, that's all –!'

'Come and have your tea, Fanny,' said Lady Montdore. She led me to the table and the starlings went on with their chatter about my mother in 'eggy-peggy', a language I happened to know quite well.

'Egg-is shegg-ee reggealleggy, pwegg-oor swegg-eet? I couldn't be more interested, considering that the very first person the Bolter ever bolted with was Chad, wasn't it, darling? Lucky me got him next, but only after she had bolted away from him again.'

'I still don't see how it can be true. The Bolter can't be more than thirty-six, I know she can't. Roly, you know the Bolter's age, we all used to go to Miss Vacani's together, you in your tiny kilt, poker and tongs on the floor, for the sword dance. Can she be more than thirty-six?'

'That's right, bird-brain, just do the sum. She married at eighteen, eighteen plus eighteen equals thirty-six, correct? No?'

'Yes. Steady on though, what about the nine months?'

'Not nine, darling, nothing like nine, don't you remember how bogus it all was and how shamingly huge her bouquet had to be, poor sweet? It was the whole point.'

'Veronica's gone too far as usual – come on, let's finish the game.'

I had half an ear on this riveting conversation and half on what Lady Montdore was saying. Having given me a characteristic and well-remembered look, up and down, a look which told me what I knew already, that my tweed skirt bulged behind and why had I no gloves (why, indeed, left them in the motor no doubt, and how would I ever have the courage to ask for them?), she remarked in a most friendly way that I had changed more in five years than Polly had, but that Polly was now much taller than me. How was Aunt Emily? And Davey?

That was where her charm lay. She would suddenly be nice just when it seemed that she was about to go for you tooth and nail, it was the charm of a purring puma. She now sent one of the men off to look for Polly.

'Playing billiards with Boy, I think,' and poured me out a cup of tea.

'And here,' she said, to the company in general, 'is Montdore.'

She always called her husband Montdore to those she regarded as her equals, but to border-line cases such as the estate agent or Dr Simpson he was Lord Montdore, if not His Lordship. I never heard her refer to him as 'my husband', it was all part of the attitude to life that made her so generally unbeloved, a determination to show people what she considered to be their proper place and keep them in it.

The chatter did not continue while Lord Montdore, radiating wonderful oldness, came into the room. It stopped dead, and those who were not already standing up, respectfully did so. He shook hands all round, a suitable word for each in turn.

'And this is my friend Fanny? Quite grown-up now, and do you remember that last time I saw you we were weeping together over the Little Match Girl?'

Perfectly untrue, I thought. Nothing about human beings ever had the power to move me as a child. Black Beauty now –!

He turned to the fire, holding his large, thin white hands to the blaze, while Lady Montdore poured out his tea. There was a long silence in the room. Presently he took a scone, buttered it, put it in his saucer, and turning to another old man said, 'I've been wanting to ask you –'

They sat down together, talking in low voices, and by degrees the starling chatter broke loose again.

I was beginning to see that there was no occasion to feel alarmed in this company, because as far as my fellow guests were concerned, I was clearly endowed with protective colouring; their momentary initial interest in me having subsided I might just as well not have been there at all, and could keep happily to myself and observe their antics. The various house parties for people of my age that I had been to during the past year had really been much more unnerving, because there I knew that I was expected to play a part, to sing for my supper by being, if

possible, amusing. But here, a child once more among all these old people, it was
my place to be seen and not heard. Looking round the room I wondered vaguely
which were the young men Lady Montdore had mentioned as being specially
invited for Polly and me. They could not yet have arrived as certainly none of
these were the least bit young, all well over thirty I should have said and probably
all married, though it was impossible to guess which of the couples were husbands
and wives, because they all spoke to each other as if they all were, in voices and
with endearments which, in the case of my aunts, could only have meant that it
was their own husbands they were addressing.

'Have the Sauveterres not arrived yet, Sonia?' said Lord Montdore coming up
for another cup of tea.

There was a movement among the women. They turned their heads like dogs
who think they hear somebody unwrapping a piece of chocolate.

'Sauveterres? Do you mean Fabrice? Don't tell me Fabrice is married? I couldn't
be more amazed.'

'No, no, of course not. He's bringing his mother to stay, she's an old flame of
Montdore's – I've never seen her, and Montdore hasn't for quite forty years. Of
course, we've always known Fabrice, and he came to us in India. He's such fun, a
delightful creature. He was very much taken up with the little Ranee of Rawalpur,
in fact they do say her last baby –'

'Sonia –!' said Lord Montdore, quite sharply for him. She took absolutely no
notice.

'Dreadful old man the Rajah, I only hope it was. Poor creatures, it's one baby
after another, you can't help feeling sorry for them, like little birds you know. I used
to go and visit the ones who were kept in purdah and of course they simply worshipped me, it was really touching.'

Lady Patricia Dougdale was announced. I had seen the Dougdales from time to
time while the Montdores were abroad because they were neighbours at Alconleigh
and although my Uncle Matthew by no means encouraged neighbours, it was
beyond even his powers to suppress them altogether and prevent them from turning up at the meets, the local point-to-points, on Oxford platform for the 9.10 and
Paddington for the 4.45, or at the Merlinford market. Besides, the Dougdales had
brought house parties to Alconleigh for Aunt Sadie's dances when Louisa and Linda
came out and had given Louisa, for a wedding present, an antique pin cushion,
curiously heavy because full of lead. The romantic Louisa, making sure it was
curiously heavy because full of gold, 'somebody's savings don't you see?' had ripped
it open with her nail scissors, only to find the lead, with the result that none of her
wedding presents could be shown for fear of hurting Lady Patricia's feelings.

Lady Patricia was a perfect example of beauty that is but skin deep. She had
once had the same face as Polly, but the fair hair had now gone white and the white
skin yellow, so that she looked like a classical statue that has been out in the weather,
with a layer of snow on its head, the features smudged and smeared by damp. Aunt
Sadie said that she and Boy had been considered the handsomest couple in London,
but of course that must have been years ago, they were old now, fifty or something,
and life would soon be over for them. Lady Patricia's life had been full of sadness
and suffering, sadness in her marriage and suffering in her liver. (Of course, I am
now quoting Davey.) She had been passionately in love with Boy, who was younger

than she, for some years before he had married her, which it was supposed that he had done because he could not resist the relationship with his esteemed Hampton family. The great sorrow of his life was childlessness, since he had set his heart on a quiverful of little half-Hamptons, and people said that the disappointment had almost unhinged him for a while, but that his niece Polly was now beginning to take the place of a daughter, he was so extremely devoted to her.

'Where is Boy?' Lady Patricia said when she had greeted, in the usual English way of greeting, the people who were near the fire, sending a wave of her gloves or half a smile to the ones who were further off. She wore a felt hat, sensible tweeds, silk stockings and beautifully polished calf shoes.

'I do wish they'd come,' said Lady Montdore, 'I want him to help me with the table. He's playing billiards with Polly – I've sent word once, by Rory – oh, here they are.'

Polly kissed her aunt and kissed me. She looked round the room to see if any-body else had arrived to whom she had not yet said 'How do you do?' (she and her parents, as a result, no doubt, of the various official positions Lord Montdore had held, were rather formal in their manners) and then turned back again to me.

'Fanny,' she said, 'have you been here long? Nobody told me.'

She stood there, rather taller now than me, embodied once more, instead of a mere nebulous memory of my childhood, and all the complicated feelings that we have for the human beings who matter in our lives came rushing back to me. My feelings for the Lecturer came rushing back too, uncomplicated.

'Ha!' he was saying, 'here, at last, is my lady wife.' He gave me the creeps, with his curly black hair going grey now, and his perky, jaunty little figure. He was shorter than the Hampton women, about an inch shorter than Lady Patricia, and tried to make up for this by having very thick soles to his shoes. He always looked horribly pleased with himself, the corners of his mouth turned up when his face was in repose, and if he was at all put out they turned up even more in a profoundly irritating smile.

Polly's blue look was now upon me, I suppose she also was rediscovering a person only half remembered, quite the same person really, a curly little black girl, Aunt Sadie used to say, like a little pony which at any moment might toss its shaggy mane and gallop off. Half an hour ago I would gladly have galloped, but now I felt happily inclined to stay where I was.

As we went upstairs together Polly put her arm round my waist saying, with obvious sincerity, 'It's too lovely to see you again. The things I've got to ask you! When I was in India I used to think and think about you – do you remember how we both had black velvet dresses with red sashes for coming down after tea and how Linda had worms? It does seem another life, so long ago. What is Linda's fiancé like?'

'Very good-looking,' I said, 'very hearty. They don't care for him much at Alcon-leigh, any of them.'

'Oh, how sad. Still, if Linda does – fancy, though, Louisa married and Linda engaged already! Of course, before India we were all babies really, and now we are of marriageable age, it makes a difference, doesn't it.'

She sighed deeply.

'I suppose you came out in India?' I said. Polly, I knew, was a little older than I was.

'Well, yes I did, I've been out two years, actually. It was all very dull, this coming-out seems a great great bore – do you enjoy it, Fanny?'

I had never thought about whether I enjoyed it or not, and found it difficult to answer her question. Girls had to come out, I knew. It is a stage in their existence just as the public school is for boys, which must be passed before life, real life, could begin. Dances are supposed to be delightful; they cost a lot of money and it is most good of the grown-ups to give them, most good, too, of Aunt Sadie to have taken me to so many. But at these dances, although I quite enjoyed going to them, I always had the uncomfortable feeling that I missed something, it was like going to a play in a foreign language. Each time I used to hope that I should see the point, but I never did, though the people round me were all so evidently seeing it. Linda, for instance, had seen it clearly but then she had been successfully pursuing love.

'What I do enjoy,' I said, truthfully, 'is the dressing up.'

'Oh, so do I! Do you think about dresses and hats all the time, even in church? I do too. Heavenly tweed, Fanny, I noticed it at once.'

'Only it's bagging,' I said.

'They always bag, except on very smart little thin women like Veronica. Are you pleased to be back in this room? It's the one you used to have, do you remember?'

Of course I remembered. It always had my name in full, 'The Honble Frances Logan', written in a careful copperplate on a card on the door, even when I was so small that I came with my nanny, and this had greatly impressed and pleased me as a child.

'Is this what you're going to wear tonight?'

Polly went up to the huge red four-poster where my dress was laid out.

'How lovely – green velvet and silver, I call that a dream, so soft and delicious, too.' She rubbed a fold of the skirt against her cheek. 'Mine's silver lamé, it smells like a bird cage when it gets hot but I do love it. Aren't you thankful evening skirts are long again? But I want to hear more about what coming-out is like in England.'

'Dances,' I said, 'girls' luncheon parties, tennis if you can, dinner parties to go to, plays, Ascot, being presented. Oh, I don't know, I expect you can just about imagine.'

'And all going on like the people downstairs?'

'Chattering all the time? Well, but the downstairs people are old, Polly. Coming-out is with people of one's own age, you see.'

'They don't think they're old a bit,' she said, laughing.

'Well –' I said, 'all the same, they are.'

'I don't see them as so old myself, but I expect that's because they seem young beside Mummy and Daddy. Just think of it, Fanny, your mother wasn't born when Mummy married, and Mrs Warbeck was only just old enough to be her bridesmaid. Mummy was saying so before you came. No, but what I really want to know about coming-out here is what about love? Are they all always having love affairs the whole time? Is it their one and only topic of conversation?'

I was obliged to admit that this was the case.

'Oh, bother. I felt sure, really, you would say that – it was so in India, of course, but I thought perhaps in a cold climate –! Anyway, don't tell Mummy if she asks you, pretend that English débutantes don't bother about love. She is in a perfect fit because I never fall in love with people; she teases me about it all the time. But 'it isn't any good because if you don't, you don't. I should have thought, at my age, it's natural not to.'

I looked at her in surprise, it seemed to me highly unnatural, though I could well understand not wanting to talk about such things to the grown-ups, and specially not to Lady Montdore if she happened to be one's mother. But a new idea struck me.

'In India,' I said, 'could you have fallen in love?' Polly laughed.

'Fanny darling, what do you mean? Of course I could have, why not? I just didn't happen to, you see.'

'White people?'

'White or black,' she said, teasingly.

'Fall in love with blacks?' What would Uncle Matthew say?

'People do, like anything. You don't understand about Rajahs, I see, but some of them are awfully attractive. I had a friend there who nearly died of love for one. And I'll tell you something, Fanny. I honestly believe Mamma would rather I fell in love with an Indian than not at all. Of course there would have been a fearful row, and I should have been sent straight home, but even so she would have thought it quite a good thing. What she minds so much is the not at all. I know she's only asked this Frenchman to stay because she thinks no woman can resist him. They could think of nothing else in Delhi – I wasn't there at the time, I was in the hills with Boy and Auntie Patsy, we did a heavenly, heavenly trip – I must tell you about it but not now.'

'But would your mother like you to marry a Frenchman?' I said. At this time love and marriage were inextricably knotted in my mind.

'Oh, not marry, good gracious no. She'd just like me to have a little weakness for him, to show that I'm capable of it – she wants to see if I'm like other women. Well, she'll see. There's the dressing-bell – I'll call for you when I'm ready, I don't live up here any more, I've got a new room over the porch. Heaps of time, Fanny, quite an hour.'

4

My bedroom was in the tower, where Polly's nurseries had been when she was small. Whereas all the other rooms at Hampton were classical in feeling the tower rooms were exaggeratedly Gothic, the Gothic of fairy-story illustrations; and in this one the bed, the cupboards and the fireplace had pinnacles, the wallpaper was a design of scrolls and the windows were casements. An extensive work of modernization had taken place all over the house while the family was in India, and looking round I saw that in one of the cupboards there was now a tiled bathroom.

In the old days I used to sally forth, sponge in hand, to the nursery bathroom, which was down a terrifying twisting staircase, and I could still remember how cold it used to be outside in the passages, though there was always a blazing fire in my room. But now the central heating had been brought up to date and the temperature everywhere was that of a hothouse. The fire which flickered away beneath the spires and towers of the chimney piece was merely there for show, and no longer to be lighted at 7 a.m., before one was awake, by a little maid scuffling about like a mouse. The age of luxury was ended and that of comfort had begun. Being conservative by nature I was glad to see that the decoration of the room had not been changed at all, though the lighting was very much improved, there was a new quilt on the bed, the mahogany dressing-table had acquired a muslin petticoat and a triple looking-glass and the whole room and bathroom were close-carpeted. Otherwise everything was exactly as I remembered it, including two large yellow pictures which could be seen from the bed, Caravaggio's 'The Gamesters' and 'A Courtesan' by Raphael.

As I dressed for dinner I passionately wished that Polly and I could have spent the evening together upstairs, supping off a tray, as we used to do, in the schoolroom. I was dreading this grown-up dinner ahead of me because I knew that, once I found myself in the dining-room seated between two of the old gentlemen downstairs, it would no longer be possible to remain a silent spectator, I should be obliged to try and think of things to say. It had been drummed into me all my life, especially by Davey, that silence at meal times is anti-social.

'So long as you chatter, Fanny, it's of no consequence what you say, better recite out of the ABC than sit like a deaf mute. Think of your poor hostess, it simply isn't fair on her.'

In the dining-room, between the man called Rory and the man called Roly, I found things even worse than I had expected. The protective colouring, which had worked so well in the drawing-room, was now going on and off like a deficient electric light. I was visible. One of my neighbours would begin a conversation with me, and seem quite interested in what I was telling him when, without any warning at all, I would become invisible and Rory and Roly were both shouting across the table at the lady called Veronica, while I was left in mid-air with some sad little remark. It then became too obvious that they had not heard a single word I had been saying but had all along been entranced by the infinitely more fascinating conversation of this Veronica lady. All right then, invisible, which really I much preferred, able to eat happily away in silence. But no, not at all, unaccountably visible again.

'Is Lord Alconleigh your uncle then? Isn't he quite barmy? Doesn't he hunt people with bloodhounds by full moon?'

I was still enough of a child to accept the grown-ups of my own family without a question, and to suppose that each in their own way was more or less perfect, and it gave me a shock to hear this stranger refer to my uncle as quite barmy.

'Oh, but we love it,' I began, 'you can't imagine what fun –' No good. Even as I spoke I became invisible.

'No, no, Veronica, the whole point was he brought the microscope to look at his own –'

'Well, I dare you to say the word at dinner, that's all,' said Veronica, 'even if you know how to pronounce it which I doubt, it's too shame-making, not a dinner thing at all –' And so they went on backwards and forwards.

'I couldn't think Veronica much funnier, could you?'

The two ends of the table were quieter. At one Lady Montdore was talking to the Duc de Sauveterre, who was politely listening to what she said but whose brilliant, good-humoured little black eyes were nevertheless slightly roving, and at the other Lord Montdore and the Lecturer were having a lovely time showing off their faultless French by talking in it across the old Duchesse de Sauveterre to each other. I was near enough to listen to what they were saying, which I did during my periods of invisibility, and though it may not have been as witty as the conversation round Veronica it had the merit of being, to me, more comprehensible. It was all on these lines:

Montdore: 'Alors le Duc de Maine était le fils de qui?'

Boy: 'Mais, dites donc mon vieux, de Louis XIV.'

Montdore: 'Bien entendu, mais sa mère?'

Boy: 'La Montespan.'

At this point the duchess, who had been munching away in silence and not apparently listening to them, said, in a loud and very disapproving voice,

'*Madame* de Montespan.'

Boy: 'Oui – oui – oui, parfaitement, Madame la Duchesse.' (In an English aside to his brother-in-law, 'The Marquise de Montespan was an aristocrat you know, they never forget it.')

'Elle avait deux fils d'ailleurs, le Duc de Maine et le Comte de Toulouse et Louis XIV les avait tous deux légitimés. Et sa fille a épousé le Régent. Tout cela est exacte, n'est-ce pas, Madame la Duchesse?'

But the old lady, for whose benefit this linguistic performance was presumably being staged, was totally uninterested in it. She was eating as hard as she could, only pausing in order to ask the footman for more bread. When directly appealed to she said 'I suppose so.'

'It's all in Saint-Simon,' said Boy, 'I've been reading him again and so must you, Montdore, simply fascinating.' Boy was versed in all the court memoirs that had ever been written, thus acquiring a reputation for great historical knowledge.

'You may not like Boy, but he does know a lot about history, there's nothing he can't tell you.' All depending on what you wanted to find out. The Empress Eugénie's flight from the Tuileries, yes, the Tolpuddle Martyrs' martyrdom, no. The Lecturer's historical knowledge was a sublimation of snobbery.

Lady Montdore now turned to her other neighbour, and everybody else followed suit. I got Rory instead of Roly, which was no change as both by now were entirely absorbed in what was going on on the other side of the table, and the Lecturer was left to struggle alone with the duchess. I heard him say:

'Dans le temps j'étais très lié avec le Duc de Souppes, qu'est-ce qu'il est devenu, Madame la Duchesse?'

'How, you are a friend to that poor Souppes?' she said, 'he is such an annoying boy.'

Her accent was very strange, a mixture of French and Cockney.

'Il habite toujours ce ravissant hôtel dans la rue du Bac?'

'I suppose so.'

'Et la vieille duchesse est toujours en vie?'

But his neighbour was now quite given over to eating and he never got another word out of her. She read the menu over and over again. She craned to see what the next dish looked like, when plates were given round after the pudding she touched hers and I heard her say approvingly to herself,

'Encore une assiette chaude, très – très bien.'

She was loving her food.

I was loving mine, too, especially now that the protective colouring was in perfect order again, and indeed continued to work for the rest of the evening with hardly another break-down.

I thought what a pity it was that Davey could not be here for one of his overeating days. He always complained that Aunt Emily never really provided him with enough different dishes on these occasions to give his metabolism a proper shock.

'I don't believe you understand the least bit what I need,' he would say, crossly for him. 'I've got to be giddy, exhausted from over-eating if it's to do me any good – that feeling you have after a meal in a Paris restaurant is what we've got to aim at, when you're too full to do anything but lie on your bed like a cobra for hours and hours, too full even to sleep. Now there must be a great many different courses, to coax my appetite – second helpings don't count, I must have them anyway – a great many different courses of really rich food, Emily dear. Naturally, if you'd rather, I'll give up the cure, but it seems a pity, just when it's doing me so much good. If it's the house books you're thinking of you must remember there are my starvation days. You never seem to take them into account at all.'

But Aunt Emily said the starvation days made absolutely no difference to the house books and that he might call it starvation but anybody else would call it four square meals.

Some two dozen metabolisms round this table were getting a jolly good jolt I thought, as the meal went on and on. Soup, fish, pheasant, beefsteak, asparagus, pudding, savoury, fruit. Hampton food, Aunt Sadie used to call it, and indeed it had a character of its own which can best be described by saying that it was like mountains of the very most delicious imaginable nursery food, plain and wholesome, made of first-class materials, each thing tasting strongly of itself. But, like everything else at Hampton, it was exaggerated. Just as Lady Montdore was a little bit too much like a countess, Lord Montdore too much like an elder statesman, the servants too perfect and too deferential, the beds too soft and the linen too fine, the motor cars too new and too shiny and everything too much in apple-pie order, so the very peaches there were too peach-like. I used to think when I was a child that all this excellence made Hampton seem unreal compared with the only other houses I knew, Alconleigh and Aunt Emily's little house. It was like a noble establishment in a book or a play, not like somebody's home, and in the same way the Montdores, and even Polly, never quite seemed to be real flesh-and-blood people.

By the time I was embarked on a too peach-like peach I had lost all sense of fear, if not of decorum, and was lolling about as I would not have dared to at the beginning of dinner, boldly looking to right and left. It was not the wine, I had only had one glass of claret and all my other glasses were full (the butler having paid no attention to my shakes of the head) and untouched; it was the food, I was reeling drunk on food. I saw just what Davey meant about a cobra, everything was stretched to its capacity, and I really felt as if I had swallowed a goat. I knew that my face was scarlet, and looking round I saw that so were all the other faces, except Polly's.

Polly, between just such a pair as Rory and Roly, had not made the least effort to be agreeable to them, though they had taken a good deal more trouble with her than my neighbours had with me. Nor was she enjoying her food. She picked at it with a fork, leaving most of it on her plate, and seemed to be completely in the clouds, her blank stare shining, like the ray from a blue lamp, in the direction of Boy, but not as though she saw him really or was listening to his terribly adequate French. Lady Montdore gave her a dissatisfied look from time to time, but she noticed nothing. Her thoughts were evidently far away from her mother's dinner table, and after a while her neighbours gave up the struggle of getting yes and no out of her, and, in chorus with mine, began to shout backchat at the lady called Veronica.

This Veronica was small and thin and sparkling. Her bright gold hair lay on her head like a cap, perfectly smooth with a few flat curls above her forehead. She had a high bony nose, rather protruding pale blue eyes, and not much chin. She looked decadent I thought, my drunkenness putting that clever grown-up word into my mind, no doubt, but all the same it was no good denying that she was very, very pretty and that her clothes, her jewels, her make-up and her whole appearance were the perfection of smartness. She was evidently considered to be a great wit, and as soon as the party began to warm up after a chilly start it revolved entirely round her. She bandied repartee with the various Rorys and Rolys, the other women of her own age merely giggling away at the jokes but taking no active part in them, as though they realized it would be useless to try and steal any of her limelight, while the even older people who surrounded the Montdores at the two ends of the table kept up a steady flow of grave talk, occasionally throwing an indulgent glance at 'Veronica'.

Now that I had become brave I asked one of my neighbours to tell me her name, but he was so much surprised at my not knowing it that he quite forgot to answer my question.

'Veronica?' he said, stupefied. 'But surely you know Veronica?'

It was as though I had never heard of Vesuvius. Afterwards I discovered that her name was Mrs Chaddesley Corbett and it seemed strange to me that Lady Montdore, whom I had so often been told was a snob, should have only a Mrs, not even an Hon. Mrs, to stay, and treat her almost with deference. This shows how innocent, socially, I must have been in those days, since every schoolboy (every Etonian, that is) knew all about Mrs Chaddesley Corbett. She was to the other smart women of her day as the star is to the chorus and had invented a type of looks as well as a way of talking, walking, and behaving which was slavishly copied by the fashionable set in England for at least ten years. No doubt the reason why I had never heard her name before was that she was such miles, in smartness, above the callow young world of my acquaintance.

It was terribly late when at last Lady Montdore got up to leave the table. My aunts never allowed such long sitting in the dining-room because of the washing-up and keeping the servants from going to bed, but that sort of thing simply was not considered at Hampton, nor did Lady Montdore turn to her husband, as Aunt Sadie always did, with an imploring look and a 'not too long, darling?' as she went, leaving the men to their port, their brandy, their cigars and their traditional dirty stories, which could hardly be any dirtier, it seemed to me, than Veronica's conversation had become during the last half hour or so.

Back in the Long Gallery some of the women went upstairs to 'powder their noses'. Lady Montdore was scornful.

'I go in the morning,' she said, 'and that is that. I don't have to be let out like a dog at intervals, thank goodness – there's nothing so common, to my mind.'

If Lady Montdore had really hoped that Sauveterre would exercise his charm on Polly and fill her mind with thoughts of love, she was in for a disappointment. As soon as the men came out of the dining-room, where they had remained for quite an hour ('This English habit,' I heard him say, 'is terrible'), he was surrounded by Veronica and her chorus and never given a chance to speak to anybody else. They all seemed to be old friends of his, called him Fabrice and had a thousand questions to ask about mutual acquaintances in Paris, fashionable foreign ladies with such unfashionable English names as Norah, Cora, Jennie, Daisy, May, and Nellie.

'Are all Frenchwomen called after English housemaids?' Lady Montdore said, rather crossly, as she resigned herself to a chat with the old duchess, the ground round Sauveterre having clearly settled down for good. He seemed to be enjoying himself, consumed, one would say, by some secret joke, his twinkling eyes resting with amusement rather than desire on each plucked and painted face in turn, while in turn, and with almost too obvious insincerity, they asked about their darling Nellies and Daisies. Meanwhile, the husbands of these various ladies, frankly relieved, as Englishmen always are, by a respite from feminine company, were gambling at the other end of the long room, playing, no doubt, for much higher stakes than they would have been allowed to by their wives and with a solid, heavy masculine concentration on the game itself, undisturbed by any of the distractions of sex. Lady Patricia went off to bed; Boy Dougdale began by inserting himself into the group round Sauveterre but finding that nobody there took the slightest notice of him, Sauveterre not even answering when he asked about the Duc de Souppes, beyond saying evasively, 'I see poor Nina de Souppes sometimes,' he gave up, a hurt, smiling look on his face. He came and sat with Polly and me and showed us how to play backgammon, holding our hands as we shook the dice, rubbing our knees with his, generally behaving, I thought, in a stchoopid and lecherous way. Lord Montdore and one or two other very old men went off to play billiards; he was said to be the finest billiards player in the British Isles.

Meanwhile poor Lady Montdore was being subjected to a tremendous inter-rogation by the duchess, who had relapsed, through a spirit of contradiction perhaps, into her native tongue. Lady Montdore's French was adequate, but by no means so horribly wonderful as that of her husband and brother-in-law, and she was soon in difficulties over questions of weights and measures; how many hectares in the park at Hampton, how many metres high was the tower, what would it cost, in francs, to take a house boat for Henley, how many kilometres were they from Sheffield? She was obliged to appeal the whole time to Boy, who never failed her of course, but the duchess was not really very much interested in the answers, she was too busy cooking up the next question. They poured out in a relentless torrent, giving Lady Montdore no opportunity whatever to escape to the bridge table as she was longing to do. What sort of electric-light machine was there at Hampton, what was the average weight of a Scotch stag, how long had Lord and Lady Montdore been married ('*tiens!*'), how was the bath water heated, how many hounds in a pack of foxhounds, where was the Royal Family now? Lady Montdore was undergoing the sensation, novel to her, of being a rabbit with a snake. At last she could bear it no more and broke up the party, taking the women off to bed very much earlier than was usual at Hampton.

5

As this was the first time I had ever stayed away in such a large, grand grown-up house party I was rather uncertain what would happen about breakfast, so before we said goodnight I asked Polly.

'Oh,' she said vaguely, 'nine-ish, you know', and I took that to mean, as it meant at home, between five and fifteen minutes past nine. In the morning, I was woken up at eight by a housemaid who brought me tea with slices of paper-thin bread and butter, asked me 'Are these your gloves, miss, they were found in the car?' and then, after running me a bath, whisked away every other garment within sight, to add them no doubt to the collection she had already made of yesterday's tweed suit, jersey, shoes, stockings and underclothes. I foresaw that soon I should be appearing downstairs in my gloves and nothing else.

Aunt Emily never allowed me to take her maid on visits as she said it would spoil me in case later on I should marry a poor man and have to do without one; I was always left to the tender mercies of housemaids when I went away from home.

So by nine o'clock I was bathed and dressed and quite ready for some food. Curiously enough, the immense dinner of the night before, which ought to have lasted me a week, seemed to have made me hungrier than usual. I waited a few minutes after the stable clock struck nine, so as not to be the first, and then ventured downstairs, but was greatly disconcerted in the dining-room to find the table still in its green baize, the door into the pantry wide open and the men-servants, in striped waistcoats and shirt sleeves, engaged upon jobs which had nothing to do with an approaching meal, such as sorting out letters and folding up the morning papers. They looked at me, or so I imagined, with surprise and hostility. I found them even more frightening than my fellow guests, and was about to go back to my bedroom as quick as I could when a voice behind me said,

'But it's terrible, looking at this empty table.'

It was the Duc de Sauveterre. My protective colouring was off, it seemed, by morning light, in fact he spoke as if we were old friends. I was very much surprised, more so when he shook my hand, and most of all when he said, 'I also long for my porridge, but we can't stay here, it's too sad, shall we go for a walk while it comes?'

The next thing I knew I was walking beside him, very fast, running almost to keep up, in one of the great lime avenues of the park. He talked all the time, as fast as he walked.

'Season of mists,' he said, 'and mellow fruitfulness. Am I not brilliant to know that? But this morning you can hardly see the mellow fruitfulness, for the mists.'

And indeed there was a thin fog all round us, out of which loomed great yellow trees. The grass was soaking wet, and my indoor shoes were already leaking.

'I do love,' he went on, 'getting up with the lark and going for a walk before breakfast.'

'Do you always?' I said.

Some people did, I knew.

'Never, never, never. But this morning I told my man to put a call through to Paris, thinking it would take quite an hour, but it came through at once, so now I am at a loose end with time on my hands. Do I not know wonderful English?'

This ringing-up of Paris seemed to me a most dashing extravagance. Aunt Sadie and Aunt Emily only made trunk calls in times of crisis, and even then they generally rang off in the middle of a sentence when the three-minute signal went; Davey, it is true, spoke to his doctor in London most days, but that was only from Kent, and in any case Davey's health could really be said to constitute a perpetual crisis. But Paris, abroad!

'Is somebody ill?' I ventured.

'Not exactly ill, but she bores herself, poor thing. I quite understand it, Paris must be terrible without me, I don't know how she can bear it. I do pity her, really.'

'Who?' I said, curiosity overcoming my shyness, and indeed it would be difficult to feel shy for long with this extraordinary man.

'My fiancée,' he said, carelessly.

Alas! Something had told me this would be the reply; my heart sank and I said dimly,

'Oh! How exciting! You are engaged?'

He gave me a sidelong whimsical look.

'Oh, yes,' he said, 'engaged!'

'And are you going to be married soon?'

But why, I wondered, had he come away alone, without her? If I had such a fascinating fiancé I would follow him everywhere, I knew, like a faithful spaniel.

'I don't imagine it will be very soon,' he said gaily. 'You know what it is with the Vatican, time is nothing to them, a thousand ages in their sight are like an evening gone. Do I not know a lot of English poetry?'

'If you call it poetry. It's a hymn, really. But what has your marriage got to do with the Vatican, isn't that in Rome?'

'It is. There is such a thing as the Church of Rome, my dear young lady, which I belong to, and this Church must annul the marriage of my affianced – do you say affianced?'

'You could. It's rather affected.'

'My inamorata, my Dulcinea (brilliant?) must annul her marriage before she is at liberty to marry me.'

'Goodness! Is she married already?'

'Yes, yes, of course. There are very few unmarried ladies going about, you know. It's not a state that lasts very long with pretty women.'

'My Aunt Emily doesn't approve of people getting engaged when they are married. My mother is always doing it and it makes Aunt Emily very cross.'

'You must tell your dear Aunt Emily that in many ways it is rather convenient. But all the same, she is quite right, I have been a fiancé too often and far too long and now it is time I was married.'

'Do you want to be?'

'I am not so sure. Going out to dinner every night with the same person, this must be terrible.'

'You might stay in?'

'To break the habit of a lifetime is rather terrible too. The fact is, I am so accustomed now to the engaged state that it's hard to imagine anything different.'

'But have you been engaged to other people before this one?'

'Many many times,' he admitted.

'So what happened to them all?'

'Various unmentionable fates.'

'For instance, what happened to the last one before this?'

'Let me see. Ah, yes – the last one before this did something I couldn't approve of, so I stopped loving her.'

'But can you stop loving people because they do things you don't approve of?'

'Yes, I can.'

'What a lucky talent,' I said, 'I'm sure I couldn't.'

We had come to the end of the avenue and before us lay a field of stubble. The sun's rays were now beginning to pour down and dissolve the blue mist, turning the trees, the stubble, and a group of ricks into objects of gold. I thought how lucky I was to be enjoying such a beautiful moment with so exactly the right person and that this was something I should remember all my life. The duke interrupted these sentimental reflections, saying,

> 'Behold how brightly breaks the morning,
> Though bleak our lot our hearts are warm.

Am I not a perfect mine of quotations? Tell me, who is Veronica's lover now?'

I was once more obliged to confess that I had never seen Veronica before, and knew nothing of her life. He seemed less astounded by this news than Roly had been, but looked at me reflectively, saying,

'You are very young. You have something of your mother. At first I thought not, but now I see there is something.'

'And who do you think Mrs Chaddesley Corbett's lover is?' I said. I was more interested in her than in my mother at the moment, and besides all this talk about lovers intoxicated me. One knew, of course, that they existed, because of the Duke of Monmouth and so on, but so near, under the very same roof as oneself, that was indeed exciting.

'It doesn't make a pin of difference,' he said, 'who it is. She lives, as all those sort of women do, in one little tiny group or set, and sooner or later everybody in that set becomes the lover of everybody else, so that when they change their lovers it is more like a Cabinet reshuffle than a new government. Always chosen out of the same old lot, you see.'

'Is it like that in France?' I said.

'With society people? Just the same all over the world, though in France I should say there is less reshuffling on the whole than in England, the ministers stay longer in their posts.'

'Why?'

'Why? Frenchwomen generally keep their lovers if they want to because they know that there is one infallible method of doing so.'

'No!' I said, 'Oh, do tell.'

I was more fascinated by this conversation every minute.

'It's very simple. You must give way to them in every respect.'

'Goodness!' I said, thinking hard.

'Now, you see, these English *femmes du monde*, these Veronicas and Sheilas and Brendas, and your mother too though nobody could say she stays in one little set, if she had done that she would not be so *déclassée*, they follow quite a different plan. They are proud and distant, out when the telephone bell rings, not free to dine unless you ask them a week before – in short, *elles cherchent à se faire valoir*, and it never never succeeds. Even Englishmen, who are used to it, don't like it after a bit. Of course, no Frenchman would put up with it for a day. So they go on reshuffling.'

'They're very nasty ladies, aren't they?' I said, having formed that opinion the night before.

'Not at all, poor things. They are *les femmes du monde, voilà tout*, I love them, so easy to get on with. Not nasty at all. And I love *la mère* Montdore, how amusing she is, with her snobbishness. I am very very much for snobs, they are always so charming to me. I stayed with them in India, you know. She was charming and Lord Montdore pretended to be.'

'Pretended?'

'That man is made up of pretence, like so many of these stiff old Englishmen. Of course, he is a great great enemy of my country – dedicated to the undoing of the French empire.'

'Why?' I said, 'I thought we were all friends now.'

'Friends! Like rabbits and snakes. I have no love for Lord Montdore but he is rather clever. Last night after dinner he asked me a hundred questions on partridge shooting in France. Why? You can be very sure he had some reason for doing so.'

'Don't you think Polly is very beautiful?' I said.

'Yes, but she also is rather a riddle to me,' he replied. 'Perhaps she is not having a properly organized sex life. Yes, no doubt it is that which makes her so dreamy. I must see what I can do for her – only there's not much time.' He looked at his watch.

I said primly that very few well brought up English girls of nineteen have a properly organized sex life. Mine was not organized at all, I knew, but I did not seem to be so specially dreamy.

'But what a beauty, even in that terrible dress. When she has had a little love she may become one of the beauties of our age. It's not certain, it never is with Englishwomen. She may cram a felt hat on her head and become a Lady Patricia Dougdale, everything depends on the lover. So this Boy Dougdale, what about him?'

'Stupid,' I said, meaning, really, 'stchoopid'.

'But you are impossible, my dear. Nasty ladies, stupid men – you really must try and like people more or you'll never get on in this world.'

'How d'you mean, get on?'

'Well, get all those things like husbands and fiancés, and get on with them. They are what really matter in a woman's life, you know.'

'And children?' I said.

He roared with laughter.

'Yes, yes, of course, children. Husbands first, then children, then fiancés, then more children – then you have to live near the Parc Monceau because of the nannies – it's a whole programme having children, I can tell you, especially if you happen to prefer the Left Bank, as I do.'

I did not understand one word of all this.

'Are you going to be a Bolter,' he said, 'like your mother?'

'No, no,' I said. 'A tremendous sticker.'

'Really? I'm not quite sure.'

Soon, too soon for my liking, we found ourselves back at the house.

'Porridge,' said the duke, again looking at his watch.

The front door opened upon a scene of great confusion, most of the house party, some in tweeds and some in dressing-gowns, were assembled in the hall, as were various outdoor and indoor servants, while a village policeman, who in the excitement of the moment had brought his bicycle in with him, was conferring with Lord Montdore. High above our heads, leaning over the balustrade in front of Niobe, Lady Montdore, in a mauve satin wrap, was shouting at her husband:

'Tell him we must have Scotland Yard down at once, Montdore. If he won't send for them I shall ring up the Home Secretary myself. Most fortunately, I have the number of his private line. In fact, I think I'd better go and do it now.'

'No, no, my dear, please not. An Inspector is on his way, I tell you.'

'Yes, I dare say, but how do we know it's the very best Inspector? I think I'd better get on to my friend, I think he'd be hurt with me if I didn't, the dear thing. Always so anxious to do what he can.'

I was rather surprised to hear Lady Montdore speak so affectionately of a member of the Labour Government, this not being the attitude of other grown-ups, in my experience, but when I came to know her better I realized that power was a positive virtue in her eyes and that she automatically liked those who were invested with it.

My companion, with that look of concentration which comes over French faces when a meal is in the offing, did not wait to hear any of this. He made a bee-line for the dining-room, but although I was also very hungry indeed after my walk, curiosity got the better of me and I stayed to find out what it all meant. It seemed that there had been a burglary during the night and that nearly everybody in the house, except Lord and Lady Montdore, had been roundly robbed of jewels, loose cash, furs and anything portable of the kind that happened to be lying about. What made it particularly annoying for the victims was that they had all been woken up by somebody prowling in their rooms, but had all immediately concluded that it must be Sauveterre, pursuing his well-known hobby, so that the husbands had merely turned over with a grunt, saying, 'Sorry, old chap, it's only me, I should try next door,' while the wives had lain quite still in a happy trance of desire, murmuring such words of encouragement as they knew in French. Or so, at least, they were saying about each other, and when I passed the telephone box on my way upstairs to change my wet shoes I could hear Mrs Chaddesley Corbett's bird-like twitters piping her version of the story to the outside world. Perhaps the Cabinet changes were becoming a little bit of a bore after all and these ladies did rather long, at heart, for a new policy.

The general feeling was now very much against Sauveterre, whose fault the whole thing clearly was. It became positively inflamed when he was known to have had a good night's rest, to have got up at eight to telephone to his mistress in Paris and then to have gone for a walk with that little girl. ('Not the Bolter's child for nothing,' I heard somebody say bitterly.) The climax was reached when he was seen to be putting away a huge breakfast of porridge and cream, kedgeree, eggs, cold ham, and slice upon slice of toast covered with Cooper's Oxford. Very un-French, not at all in keeping with his reputation, unsuitable behaviour too, in view of the well-known frailty of his fellow guests. Britannia felt herself slighted by this foreigner, away with him! And away he went, immediately after breakfast, driving hell-for-leather to Newhaven to catch the boat for Dieppe.

'Castle life,' explained his mother, who placidly stayed until quite late on Monday, 'always annoys Fabrice and makes him nervous, poor boy.'

6

The rest of that day was rather disorganized. The men finally went off shooting, very late, while the women stayed at home to be interviewed by various Inspectors on the subject of their lost possessions. Of course, the burglary made a wonderful topic of conversation, and indeed, nobody spoke of anything else.

'I couldn't care less about the diamond brooch, after all, it's well insured and now I shall be able to have clips instead, which will be far and away smarter. Veronica's clips always make me miserable, every time I see her, and besides, that brooch used to remind me of my bogus old mother-in-law too much. But I couldn't think it more hateful of them to have taken my fur tippet. Burglars never seem to realize one might feel the cold. How would they like it if I took away their wife's shawl?'

'Yes, it is a shame. I'm in a terrible do about my bracelet of lucky charms – no value to anybody else – really – too too sick-making. Just when I had managed to get a bit of hangman's rope, Mrs Thompson too, did I tell you? Roly will never win the National now, poor sweet.'

'With me it's Mummy's little locket she had as a child. I can't think why my ass of a maid had to go and put it in, she never does as a rule.'

These brassy ladies became quite human as they mourned their lost trinkets, and now that the men were out of the house they suddenly seemed very much nicer. I am speaking of the Veronica chorus, for Mrs Chaddesley Corbett herself, in common with Lady Montdore and Lady Patricia, was always exactly the same whatever the company.

At tea-time the village policeman reappeared with his bicycle, having wiped the eye of all the grand detectives who had come from London in their shiny cars. He produced a perfect jumble-sale heap of objects which had been discarded by the burglars under a haystack, and nearly all the little treasures were retrieved, with high cries of joy, by their owners. As the only things which now remained missing were jewels of considerable value, and as these were felt to be the business of the Insurance Companies, the party continued in a much more cheerful atmosphere. I never heard any of the women mention the burglary again though their husbands droned on rather about underwriters and premiums. There was now, however, a distinctly noticeable current of anti-French feeling. The Norahs and Nellies would have had a pretty poor reception if any of them had turned up just then, and Boy, if it was possible for him to have enough of a duchess, must have been having enough of this one, since all but he fled from the machine-gun fire of questions, and he was obliged to spend the next two days practically alone with her.

I was hanging about as one does at house parties, waiting for the next meal; it was not yet quite time to dress for dinner on Sunday evening. One of the pleasures of staying at Hampton was that the huge Louis XV map table in the middle of the Long Gallery was always covered with every imaginable weekly newspaper neatly laid out in rows and rearranged two or three times a day by a footman, whose sole occupation this appeared to be.

I seldom saw the *Tatler* and *Sketch*, as my aunts would have thought it a perfectly unwarranted extravagance to subscribe to such papers, and I was greedily gulping down back numbers when Lady Montdore called to me from a sofa where, ever since tea, she had been deep in talk with Mrs Chaddesley Corbett. I had been throwing an occasional glance in their direction, wondering what it could all be about and wishing I could be a fly on the wall to hear them, thinking also that it would hardly be possible for two women to look more different. Mrs Chaddesley Corbett, her bony little silken legs crossed and uncovered to above the knee, perched rather than sat on the edge of the sofa. She wore a plain beige kasha dress which must certainly have been made in Paris and certainly designed for the Anglo-Saxon market, and smoked cigarette after cigarette with a great play of long thin white fingers, flashing with rings and painted nails. She did not keep still for one moment though she was talking with great earnestness and concentration.

Lady Montdore sat well back on the sofa, both her feet on the ground. She seemed planted there, immovable and solid, not actually fat, but solid through and through. Smartness, even if she had sought after it, would hardly be attainable by her in a world where it was personified by the other, and had become almost as much a question of build, of quick and nervous movements, as of actual clothes. Her hair was shingled, but it was grey and fluffy, by no means a smooth cap; her eyebrows grew at will, and when she remembered to use lipstick and powder they were any colour and slapped on anyhow, so that her face, compared with that of Mrs Chaddesley Corbett, was as a hayfield is to a lawn, her whole head looking twice as large as the polished little head beside her. All the same she was not disagreeable to look at. There was a healthiness and liveliness about her face which lent it a certain attraction. Of course, she seemed to me, then, very old. She was, in fact, about fifty-eight.

'Come over here, Fanny.'

I was almost too much surprised to be alarmed by this summons and hurried over, wondering what it could all be about.

'Sit there,' she said, pointing to a needlework chair, 'and talk to us. Are you in love?'

I felt myself becoming scarlet in the face. How could they have guessed my secret? Of course I had been in love for two days now, ever since my morning walk with the Duc de Sauveterre. Passionately, but as indeed I realized hopelessly, in love. In fact, the very thing that Lady Montdore had intended for Polly had befallen me.

'There you are, Sonia,' said Mrs Chaddesley Corbett triumphantly, tapping a cigarette with nervous violence against her jewelled case and lighting it with a gold lighter, her pale blue eyes never meanwhile leaving my face. 'What did I tell you? Of course she is, poor sweet, just look at that blush, it must be something quite new and horribly bogus. I know, it's my dear old husband. Confess, now! I couldn't mind less, actually.'

I did not like to say that I still, after a whole week-end, had no idea at all which of the many husbands present hers might be, but stammered out as quick as I could. 'Oh, no no, not anybody's husband, I promise. Only a fiancé, and such a detached one at that.'

They both laughed.

'All right,' said Mrs Chaddesley Corbett, 'we're not going to worm. What we really want to know, to settle a bet is, have you always fancied somebody ever since you can remember? Answer truthfully, please.'

I was obliged to admit that this was the case. From a tiny child, ever since I could remember, in fact, some delicious image had been enshrined in my heart, last thought at night, first thought in the morning. Fred Terry as Sir Percy Blakeney, Lord Byron, Rudolph Valentino, Henry V, Gerald du Maurier, blissful Mrs Ashton at my school, Steerforth, Napoleon, the guard on the 4.45, image had succeeded image. Latterly it had been that of a pale pompous young man in the Foreign Office who had once, during my season in London, asked me for a dance, had seemed to me the very flower of cosmopolitan civilization, and had remained the pivot of existence until wiped from my memory by Sauveterre. For that is what always happened to these images. Time and hateful absence blurred them, faded them but never quite obliterated them until some lovely new broom image came and swept them away.

'There you are you see,' Mrs Chaddesley Corbett turned triumphantly to Lady Montdore. 'From kiddie-car to hearse, darling, I couldn't know it better. After all, what would there be to think about when one's alone, otherwise?'

What indeed? This Veronica had hit the nail on the head. Lady Montdore did not look convinced. She, I felt sure, had never harboured romantic yearnings and had plenty to think about when she was alone, which, anyhow, was hardly ever.

'But who is there for her to be in love with, and if she is, surely I should know it?' she said.

I guessed that they were talking about Polly, and this was confirmed by Mrs Chaddesley Corbett saying,

'No, darling, you wouldn't, you're her mother. When I remember poor Mummy and her ideas on the subject of my ginks –'

'Now Fanny, tell us what you think. Is Polly in love?'

'Well, she says she's not, but –'

'But you don't think it's possible not to be fancying someone? Nor do I.'

I wondered. Polly and I had had a long chat the night before, sprawling on my bed in our dressing-gowns, and I had felt almost certain then that she was keeping something back which she would half have liked to tell.

'I suppose it might depend on your nature?' I said, doubtfully.

'Anyhow,' said Lady Montdore, 'there's one thing only too certain. She takes no notice of the young men I provide for her and they take no notice of her. They worship *me*, of course, but what is the good of that?'

Mrs Chaddesley Corbett caught my eye and I thought she gave me half a wink. Lady Montdore went on,

'Bored and boring. I can't say I'm looking forward to bringing her out in London very much if she goes on like this. She used to be such a sweet easy child, but her whole character seems to have changed now she is grown-up. I can't understand it.'

'Oh, she's bound to fall for some nice chap in London, darling,' said Mrs Chaddesley Corbett. 'I wouldn't worry too much if I were you. Whoever she's in love with now, if she is in love, which Fanny and I know she must be, is probably a kind of dream and she only needs to see some flesh-and-blood people for her to forget about it. It so often happens, with girls.'

'Yes, my dear, that's all very well, but she was out for two years in India you know. There were some very attractive men there, polo and so on, not suitable of course, I was only too thankful she didn't fall in love with any of them, but she could have, it would not have been unnatural at all. Why, poor Delia's girl fell in love with a Rajah, you know.'

'I couldn't blame her less,' said Mrs Chaddesley Corbett. 'Rajahs must be perfect heaven, all those diamonds.'

'Oh no, my dear – any English family has better stones than they do. I never saw anything to compare with mine when I was there. But this Rajah was rather attractive, I must say, though of course Polly didn't see it, she never does. Oh dear, oh dear! Now if only we were French; they really do seem to arrange things so very much better. To begin with, Polly would inherit all this instead of those stupid people in Novia Scotia, so unsuitable – can you imagine Colonials living here – and to go on with we should find a husband for her ourselves, after which he and she would live partly at his place, with his parents, and partly here with us. Think how sensible that is. The old French tart was telling me the whole system last night.'

Lady Montdore was famous for picking up words she did not quite understand and giving them a meaning of her own. She clearly took the word tart to mean old girl, trout, body. Mrs Chaddesley Corbett was delighted, she gave a happy little squeak and rushed upstairs saying that she must go and dress for dinner. When I came up ten minutes later she was still telling the news through bathroom doors.

After this Lady Montdore set out to win my heart, and, of course, succeeded. It was not very difficult, I was young and frightened, she was old and grand and frightening, and it only required an occasional hint of mutual understanding, a smile, a movement of sympathy to make me think I really loved her. The fact is that she had charm, and since charm allied to riches and position is almost irresistible, it so happened that her many haters were usually people who had never met her or people she had purposely snubbed or ignored. Those whom she made efforts to please, while forced to admit that she was indefensible, were very much inclined to say, '. . . but all the same she has been very nice to me and I can't help liking her'. She herself, of course, never doubted for one moment that she was worshipped, and by every section of society.

Before I left Hampton on Monday morning Polly took me up to her mother's bedroom to say good-bye. Some of the guests had left the night before, the others were leaving now, all rolling away in their huge rich motor cars, and the house was like a big school breaking up for the holidays. The bedroom doors we passed were open revealing litters of tissue paper and unmade beds, servants struggling with suitcases and guests struggling into their coats. Everybody seemed to be in a struggling hurry all of a sudden.

Lady Montdore's room, I remembered it of old, was enormous, more like a ballroom than a bedroom, and was done up in the taste of her own young days when she was a bride; the walls were panelled in pink silk covered with white lace, the huge wickerwork bed on a dais had curtains of pink shot-silk. The furniture was white with fat pink satin upholstery outlined in ribbon roses. Silver flower vases stood on all the tables, and there were many photographs in silver frames, mostly of royal personages, with inscriptions cordial in inverse ratio to the actual importance of the personage, reigning monarchs having contented themselves with merely a Christian name, an R, and perhaps a date, while ex-Kings and Queens, Archduchesses and Grand Dukes had scattered Dearest and Darling Sonia and Loving all over their trains and uniform trousers.

In the middle of all this silver and satin and silk, Lady Montdore cut rather a comic figure drinking strong tea in bed among masses of lace pillows, her coarse grey hair frizzed out and wearing what appeared to be a man's striped flannel pyjama top under a feathered wrap. The striped pyjamas were not the only incongruous touch in the room. On her lacy dressing-table with its big, solid silver looking-glass and among her silver and enamel brushes, bottles and boxes, with their diamond cypher, were a black Maison Pearson hair brush and a pot of Pond's cold cream, while dumped down in the middle of the royalties were a rusty nail-file, a broken comb and a bit of cotton wool. While we were talking, Lady Montdore's maid came in and with much clicking of her tongue was about to remove all these objects when Lady Montdore told her to leave them as she had not finished.

Her quilt was covered with newspapers and opened letters and she held *The Times* neatly folded back at the Court Circular, probably the only part of it she ever looked at, since news, she used to say, can always be gleaned, and far more entertainingly too, from those who make it. I think she felt it comfortable, rather like reading prayers, to begin the day with Mabell, Countess of Airlie having succeeded the Lady Elizabeth Motion as lady-in-waiting to the Queen. It indicated that the globe was still revolving in accordance with the laws of nature.

'Good morning, Fanny dear,' she said, 'this will interest you, I suppose.'

She handed me *The Times* and I saw that Linda's engagement to Anthony Kroesig was announced at last.

'Poor Alconleighs,' she went on, in tones of deep satisfaction. 'No wonder they don't like it! What a silly girl, well, she always has been in my opinion. No place.

Rich, of course, but banker's money, it comes and it goes and however much of it there may be it's not like marrying all this.'

'All this' was a favourite expression of Lady Montdore's. It did not mean all this beauty, this strange and fairy-like house set in the middle of four great avenues rushing up four artificial slopes, the ordered spaces of trees and grass and sky seen from its windows, or the joy given by the treasures it contained, for she was not gifted with an aesthetic sense and if she admired anything at all it was rather what might be described as stockbroker's picturesque. She had made herself a little garden in the park, copied from one she had seen at a Chelsea flower show, in which rambler roses, forget-me-nots, and cypress trees were grouped round an Italian well-head, and here she would often retire to see the sunset. 'So beautiful it makes me want to cry.' She had all the sentimentality of her generation, and this sentimentality, growing like a green moss over her spirit, helped to conceal its texture of stone, if not from others at any rate from herself. She was convinced that she was a woman of profound sensibility.

'All this', on her lips, meant position allied to such solid assets as acres, coal mines, real estate, jewels, silver, pictures, incunabula, and other possessions of the sort. Lord Montdore owned an almost incredible number of such things, fortunately.

'Not that I ever expected poor little Linda to make a suitable marriage,' she went on. 'Sadie is a wonderful woman, of course, and I'm devoted to her, but I'm afraid she hasn't the very smallest idea how to bring up girls.'

Nevertheless, no sooner did Aunt Sadie's girls show their noses outside the schoolroom than they were snapped up and married, albeit unsuitably, and perhaps this fact was rankling a little with Lady Montdore, whose mind appeared to be so much on the subject.

The relations between Hampton and Alconleigh were as follows. Lady Montdore had an irritated fondness for Aunt Sadie, whom she half admired for an integrity which she could not but recognize and half blamed for an unworldliness which she considered out of place in somebody of her position; she could not endure Uncle Matthew and thought him mad. Uncle Matthew, for his part, revered Lord Montdore, who was perhaps the only person in the world whom he looked up to, and loathed Lady Montdore to such a degree that he used to say he longed to strangle her. Now that Lord Montdore was back from India, Uncle Matthew continually saw him at the House of Lords and on the various county organizations which they both attended, and he would come home and quote his most banal remark as if it were the utterance of a prophet – 'Montdore tells me –', Montdore says –'. And that was that, useless to question it; what Lord Montdore believed on any subject was final in the eyes of my uncle.

'Wonderful fella, Montdore. What I can't imagine is how we ever got on without him in this country all those years. Terribly wasted, among the blackamoors, when he's the kind of fella we need so badly here.'

He even broke his rule about never visiting other people's houses in favour of Hampton. 'If Montdore asks us I think we ought to go.'

'It's Sonia who asks us,' Aunt Sadie would correct him, mischievously.

'The old she-wolf. I shall never know what can have come over Montdore to make him marry her. I suppose he didn't realize at the time how utterly poisonously bloody she is.'

'Darling – darling –!'

'Utterly bloody. But if Montdore asks us I think we should go.'

As for Aunt Sadie, she was always so vague, so much in the clouds, that it was never easy to know what she really thought of people, but I believe that though she rather enjoyed the company of Lady Montdore in small doses, she did not share my uncle's feelings about Lord Montdore, for when she spoke of him there was always a note of disparagement in her voice.

'Something silly about his look,' she used to say, though never in front of Uncle Matthew, for it would have hurt his feelings dreadfully.

'So that's Louisa and poor Linda accounted for,' Lady Montdore went on. 'Now you must be the next one, Fanny.'

'Oh no,' I said. 'Nobody will ever marry me.' And indeed I could not imagine anybody wanting to, I seemed to myself so much less fascinating than the other girls I knew, and I despised my looks, hating my round pink cheeks and rough curly black hair which never could be made to frame my face in silken cords, however much I wetted and brushed it, but would insist on growing the wrong way, upwards, like heather.

'Nonsense. And don't you go marrying just anybody, for love,' she said. 'Remember that love cannot last, it never never does, but if you marry all this it's for your life. One day, don't forget, you'll be middle-aged and think what that must be like for a woman who can't have, say, a pair of diamond earrings. A woman of my age needs diamonds near her face, to give a sparkle. Then at meal times, sitting with all the unimportant people for ever and ever. And no motor. Not a very nice prospect, you know. Of course,' she added as an afterthought, 'I was lucky, I had love as well as all this, but it doesn't often happen, and when the moment comes for you to choose, just remember what I say. I suppose Fanny ought to go now and catch her train – and when you've seen her off, will you find Boy please and send him up here to me, Polly? I want to think over the dinner party for next week with him. Good-bye, then, Fanny – let's see a lot of you now we're back.'

On the way down we ran into Boy.

'Mummy wants to see you,' said Polly, gravely posing, her blue look upon him. He put his hand to her shoulder and massaged it with his thumb.

'Yes,' he said, 'about this dinner party, I suppose. Are you coming to it, old girl?'

'Oh, I expect so,' she said. 'I'm out now, you know.'

'I can't say I look forward to it very much. Your mother's ideas on *placement* get vaguer and vaguer. The table last night was totally mad, the *duchesse* is still in a temper about it! Sonia really shouldn't have people at all if she doesn't intend to treat them properly.'

A phrase I had often heard on the lips of my Aunt Emily, with reference to animals.

7

Back at home I was naturally unable to talk of anything but my visit. Davey was much amused and said he had never known me so chatty.

'But my dear child,' he said, 'weren't you petrified? Sauveterre and the Chaddesley Corbetts –! Far worse even than I had expected.'

'Well yes, at first I thought I'd die. But nobody took any notice of me really except Mrs Chaddesley Corbett and Lady Montdore –'

'Oh! And what notice did they take, may I ask?'

'Well, Mrs Chaddesley Corbett said Mummy bolted first of all with Mr Chaddesley Corbett.'

'So she did,' said Davey, 'that boring old Chad, I'd quite forgotten. But you don't mean to say Veronica told you so? I wouldn't have thought it possible, even of her.'

'No, I heard her tell, in eggy-peggy.'

'I see. Well then, what about Sonia?'

'Oh, she was sweet to me.'

'She was, was she? This is indeed sinister news.'

'What is sinister news?' said Aunt Emily, coming in with her dogs. 'It's simply glorious out, I can't imagine why you two are stuffing in here on such a heavenly day.'

'We're gossiping about this party you so unwisely allowed Fanny to go to. And I was saying that if Sonia has really taken a fancy to our little one, which it seems she has, we must look out for trouble, that's all.'

'What trouble?' I said.

'Sonia's terribly fond of juggling with people's lives. I never shall forget when she made me go to her doctor. I can only say he very nearly killed me; it's not her fault if I'm here today. She's entirely unscrupulous, she gets a hold over people much too easily with her charm and her prestige and then forces her own values on them.'

'Not on Fanny,' Aunt Emily said, with confidence, 'look at that chin.'

'You always say look at Fanny's chin but I never can see any other signs of her being strong-minded. Those Radletts make her do whatever they like.'

'You'll see,' said Aunt Emily. 'Siegfried is quite all right again by the way, he's had a lovely walkies.'

'Oh, good,' said Davey. 'Olive oil's the thing.'

They both looked affectionately at the Pekingese, Siegfried.

But I wanted to get some more interesting gossip out of Davey about the Hamptons. I said coaxingly,

'Go on Dave, do go on telling about Lady Montdore. What was she like when she was young?'

'Exactly the same as she is now.'

I sighed. 'No, but I mean what did she look like?'

'I tell you, just the same,' said Davey. 'I've known her ever since I was a little tiny boy and she hasn't changed one scrap.'

'Oh, Davey –' I began. But I left it at that. It's no good, I thought, you always come up against this blank wall with old people, they always say about each other that they have never looked any different, and how can it be true? Anyway, if it is true, they must have been a horrid generation, all withered or blowsy, and grey at the age of eighteen, knobbly hands, bags under the chin, eyes set in a little map of wrinkles, I thought crossly, adding up all these things on the faces of Davey and Aunt Emily as they sat there, smugly thinking that they had always looked exactly the same. Quite useless to discuss questions of age with old people, they have such peculiar ideas on the subject. 'Not really old at all, only seventy,' you hear them saying, or 'quite young, younger than me, not much more than forty'. At eighteen this seems great nonsense, though now, at the more advanced age which I have reached, I am beginning to understand what it all meant because Davey and Aunt Emily in their turn seem to me to look as they have looked ever since I knew them first, when I was a little child.

'Who else was there,' asked Davey, 'the Dougdales?'

'Oh, yes. Isn't the Lecturer stchoopid?'

Davey laughed. 'And lecherous?' he said.

'No, I must say not actually lecherous, not with me.'

'Well, of course, he couldn't be with Sonia there, he wouldn't dare. He's been her young man for years, you know.'

'Don't tell me!' I said, fascinated. That was the heaven of Davey, he knew everything about everybody, quite unlike my aunts, who, though they had no special objection to our knowing gossip, now that we were grown-up, had always forgotten it themselves, being totally uninterested in the doings of people outside their own family. 'Davey! How could she?'

'Well, Boy is very good-looking,' said Davey, 'I should say rather, how could he? But as a matter of fact, I think it's a love affair of pure convenience, it suits them both perfectly. Boy knows the Gotha by heart and all that kind of thing, he's like a wonderful extra butler, and Sonia on her side gives him an interest in life. I quite see it.'

One comfort, I thought, such elderly folk couldn't do anything, but again I kept it to myself because I knew that nothing makes people crosser than being considered too old for love, and Davey and the Lecturer were exactly the same age, they had been at school together. Lady Montdore, of course, was even older.

'Let's hear about Polly,' said Aunt Emily, 'and then I really must insist on you going out of doors before tea. Is she a real beauty, just as we were always being told, by Sonia, that she would be?'

'Of course she is,' said Davey, 'doesn't Sonia always get her own way?'

'So beautiful you can't imagine,' I said. 'And so nice, the nicest person I ever met.'

'Fanny is such a hero-worshipper,' said Aunt Emily, amused.

'I expect it's true though, anyway, about the beauty,' said Davey, 'because, quite apart from Sonia always getting what she wants, Hamptons do have such marvellous looks, and after all, the old girl herself is very handsome. In fact, I see that she would improve the strain by giving a little solidity – Montdore looks too much like a collie dog.'

'And who is this wonderful girl to marry?' said Aunt Emily. 'That will be the next problem for Sonia. I can't see who will ever be good enough for her.'

'Merely a question of strawberry leaves,' said Davey, 'as I imagine she's probably too big for the Prince of Wales, he likes such tiny little women. You know, I can't help thinking that now Montdore is getting older he must feel it dreadfully that he can't leave Hampton to her. I had a long talk about it the other day with Boy in the London Library. Of course, Polly will be very rich – enormously rich, because he can leave her everything else – but they all love Hampton so much, I think it's very sad for them.'

'Can he leave Polly the pictures at Montdore House? Surely they must be entailed on the heir?' said Aunt Emily.

'There are wonderful pictures at Hampton,' I butted in. 'A Raphael and a Caravaggio in my bedroom alone.'

They both laughed at me, hurting my feelings rather.

'Oh, my darling child, country-house bedroom pictures! But the ones in London are a world-famous collection, and I believe they can all go to Polly. The young man from Nova Scotia simply gets Hampton and everything in it, but that is an Aladdin's Cave, you know, the furniture, the silver, the library – treasures beyond value. Boy was saying they really ought to get him over and show him something of civilization before he becomes too transatlantic.'

'I forget how old he is,' said Aunt Emily.

'I know,' I said, 'he's six years older than me, about twenty-four now. And he's called Cedric, like Lord Fauntleroy. Linda and I used to look him up when we were little to see if he would do for us.'

'You would, how typical,' said Aunt Emily. 'But I should have thought he might really do for Polly – settle everything.'

'It would be too much unlike life,' said Davey. 'Oh, bother, talking to Fanny has made me forget my three o'clock pill.'

'Take it now,' said Aunt Emily, 'and then go out please, both of you.'

From this time on I saw a great deal of Polly. I went to Alconleigh, as I did every year, for some hunting, and from there I often went over to spend a night or two at Hampton. There were no more big house parties, but a continual flow of people, and in fact the Montdores and Polly never seemed to have a meal by themselves. Boy Dougdale came over nearly every day from his own house at Silkin, which was only about ten miles away. He quite often went home to dress for dinner and came back again to spend the evening, since Lady Patricia it seemed was not at all well, and liked to go to bed early.

Boy never seemed to me quite like a real human being and I think this is because he was always acting some part. Boy the Don Juan alternated with Boy the Old Etonian, squire of Silkin, and Boy the talented cosmopolitan. In none of these parts was he quite convincing. Don Juan only made headway with very unsophisticated women, except in the case of Lady Montdore, and she, whatever their relationship may have been in the past, had come to treat him more as a lady companion or private secretary than as a lover. The squire played cricket in a slightly arch manner with village youths, and lectured village women, but never seemed like a real squire, for all his efforts, and the talented cosmopolitan gave himself away whenever he put brush to canvas or pen to paper.

He and Lady Montdore were much occupied, when they were in the country, with what they called 'their art', producing enormous portraits, landscapes and still lifes by the dozen. In the summer they worked out of doors, and in the winter they installed a large stove in a north-facing bedroom and used it as a studio. They were such great admirers of their own and each other's work that the opinion of the outside world meant but little to them. Their pictures were always framed and hung about their two houses, the best ones in rooms and the others in passages.

By the evening Lady Montdore was ready for some relaxation.

'I like to work hard all day,' she would say, 'and then have agreeable company and perhaps a game of cards in the evening.'

There were always guests for dinner, an Oxford don or two with whom Lord Montdore could show off about Livy, Plotinus and the Claudian family, Lord Merlin, who was a great favourite of Lady Montdore and who published her sayings far and wide, and the more important county neighbours, strictly in turns. They seldom sat down fewer than ten people; it was very different from Alconleigh.

I enjoyed these visits to Hampton. Lady Montdore terrified me less and charmed me more, Lord Montdore remained perfectly agreeable and colourless, Boy continued to give me the creeps and Polly became my best-friend-next-to-Linda.

Presently Aunt Sadie suggested that I might like to bring Polly back with me to Alconleigh, which I duly did. It was not a very good time for a visit there since everybody's nerves were upset by Linda's engagement, but Polly did not seem to notice the atmosphere, and no doubt her presence restrained Uncle Matthew from giving vent to the full violence of his feelings while she was there. Indeed, she said to me, as we drove back to Hampton together after the visit, that she envied the Radlett children their upbringing in such a quiet, affectionate household, a remark which could only have been made by somebody who had inhabited the best spare room, out of range of Uncle Matthew's early morning gramophone concerts, and who had never happened to see that violent man in one of his tempers. Even so, I thought it strange, coming from Polly, because if anybody had been surrounded by affection all her life it was she; I did not yet fully understand how difficult the relations were beginning to be between her and her mother.

8

Polly and I were bridesmaids at Linda's wedding in February, and when it was over I motored down to Hampton with Polly and Lady Montdore to spend a few days there. I was grateful to Polly for suggesting this, as I remembered too well the horrible feeling of anti-climax there had been after Louisa's wedding, which would certainly be ten times multiplied after Linda's. Indeed, with Linda married, the first stage of my life no less than of hers was finished, and I felt myself to be left in a horrid vacuum, with childhood over but married life not yet beginning.

As soon as Linda and Anthony had gone away Lady Montdore sent for her motor car and we all three huddled on to the back seat. Polly and I were still in our bridesmaids' dresses (sweet-pea tints, in chiffon) but well wrapped up in fur coats and each with a Shetland rug wound round our legs, like children going to a dancing class. The chauffeur spread a great bearskin over all of us and put a foot warmer under our silver kid shoes. It was not really cold, but shivery, pouring and pouring with rain as it had been all day, getting dark now. The inside of the motor was like a dry little box, and as we splashed down the long wet shiny roads, with the rain beating against the windows, there was a specially delicious cosiness about being in this little box and knowing that so much light and warmth and solid comfort lay ahead.

'I love being so dry in here,' as Lady Montdore put it, 'and seeing all those poor people so wet.'

She had done the journey twice that day, having driven up from Hampton in the morning, whereas Polly had gone up the day before, with her father, for a last fitting of her bridesmaid's dress and in order to go to a dinner-dance.

First of all we talked about the wedding. Lady Montdore was wonderful when it came to picking over an occasion of that sort, with her gimlet eye nothing escaped her, nor did any charitable inhibitions tone down her comments on what she had observed.

'How extraordinary Lady Kroesig looked, poor woman! I suppose somebody must have told her that the bridegroom's mother should have a bit of everything in her hat – for luck perhaps. Fur, feathers, flowers and a scrap of lace – it was all there and a diamond brooch on top to finish it off nicely. Rose diamonds – I had a good look. It's a funny thing that these people who are supposed to be so rich never seem to have a decent jewel to put on – I've often noticed it. And did you see what mingy little things they gave poor Linda? A cheque – yes, that's all very well but for how much, I wonder? Cultured pearls, at least I imagine so, or they would have been worth quite £10,000, and a hideous little bracelet. No tiara, no necklace, what will the poor child wear at Court? Linen, which we didn't see, all that modern silver and a horrible house in one of those squares by the Marble Arch. Hardly worth being called by that nasty German name, I should say. And Davey tells me there's no proper settlement – really, Matthew Alconleigh isn't fit to have children if that's all he can do for them. Still, I'm bound to say he looked very handsome coming up the aisle, and Linda looked her very best too, really lovely.'

I think she was feeling quite affectionately towards Linda for having removed herself betimes from competition, for although not a great beauty like Polly she was certainly far more popular with young men.

'Sadie, too, looked so nice, very young and handsome, and the little thing's so puddy.' She pronounced the word pretty like that.

'Did you see our dessert service, Fanny? Oh, did she, I'm glad. She could change it, as it came from Goodes, but perhaps she won't want to. I was quite amused, weren't you, to see the difference between our side of the church and the Kroesig side. Bankers don't seem to be much to look at – so extraordinarily unsuitable having to know them at all, poor things, let alone marry them. But these sort of people have got megalomania nowadays, one can't get away from them. Did you notice the Kroesig sister? Oh, yes, of course, she was walking with you, Fanny. They'll have a job to get her off!'

'She's training to be a vet,' I said.

'First sensible thing I've heard about any of them. No point in cluttering up the ballrooms with girls who look like that, it's simply not fair on anybody. Now Polly, I want to hear exactly what you did yesterday.'

'Oh – nothing very much.'

'Don't be so tiresome. You got to London at about twelve, I suppose?'

'Yes, we did,' said Polly, in a resigned voice. She would have to account for every minute of the day, she knew, quicker to tell of her own accord than to have it pumped out of her. She began to fidget with her bridesmaid's wreath of silver leaves. 'Wait a moment,' she said, 'I must take this off, it's giving me a headache.'

It was twisted into her hair with wire. She tugged and pulled at it until finally she got it off and flung it down on the floor.

'Ow,' she said, 'that did hurt! Well yes then, let me think. We arrived. Daddy went straight to his appointment and I had an early luncheon at home.'

'By yourself?'

'No, Boy was there. He'd looked in to return some books, and Bullitt said there was plenty of food so I made him stay.'

'Well then, go on. After luncheon?'

'Hair.'

'Washed and set?'

'Yes, naturally.'

'You'd never think it. We really must find you a better hairdresser. No use asking Fanny I'm afraid, her hair always looks like a mop.'

Lady Montdore was becoming cross, and, like a cross child, was seeking to hurt anybody within reach.

'It was quite all right until I had to put that wreath on it. Well then, tea with Daddy at the House, rest after tea, dinner you know about, and bed,' she finished in one breath. 'Is that all?'

She and her mother seemed to be thoroughly on each other's nerves, or perhaps it was having pulled her hair with the wreath that made her so snappy. She flashed a perfectly vicious look across me at Lady Montdore. It was suddenly illuminated by the headlights of a passing motor. Lady Montdore neither saw it nor, apparently, noticed the edge in her voice and went on,

'No, certainly not. You haven't told me about the party yet. Who sat next to you at dinner?'

'Oh, Mummy, I can't remember their names.'

'You never seem to remember anybody's name, it is too stupid. How can I invite your friends to the house if I don't know who they are?'

'But they're not my friends, they were the most dreadful, dreadful bores you can possibly imagine. I couldn't think of one thing to say to them.'

Lady Montdore sighed deeply.

'Then after dinner you danced?'

'Yes. Danced, and sat out and ate disgusting ices.'

'I'm sure the ices were delicious. Sylvia Waterman always does things beautifully. I suppose there was champagne?'

'I hate champagne.'

'And who took you home?'

'Lady Somebody. It was out of her way because she lives in Chelsea.'

'How extraordinary,' said Lady Montdore, rather cheered up by the idea that some poor ladies have to live in Chelsea. 'Now who could she possibly have been?'

The Dougdales had also been at the wedding and were to dine at Hampton on their way home; they were there when we arrived, not having, like us, waited to see Linda go away. Polly went straight upstairs. She looked tired and sent a message by her maid to say that she would have her dinner in bed. The Dougdales, Lady Montdore, and I dined, without changing, in the little morning-room where they always had meals if there were fewer than eight people. This room was perhaps the most perfect thing at Hampton. It had been brought bodily from France and was entirely panelled in wood carved in a fine, elaborate pattern, painted blue and white; three cupboards matched three French windows and were filled with eighteenth-century china. Over cupboards, windows and doorways were decorative paintings by Boucher, framed in the panelling.

The talk at dinner was of the ball which Lady Montdore intended to give for Polly at Montdore House.

'May Day, I think,' she said.

'That's good,' said Boy, 'it must either be the first or the last ball of the season, if people are to remember it.'

'Oh, not the last, on any account. I should have to invite all the girls whose dances Polly had been to, and nothing is so fatal to a ball as too many girls.'

'But if you don't ask them,' said Lady Patricia, 'will they ask her?'

'Oh, yes,' said Lady Montdore shortly, 'they'll be dying to have her. I can pay them back in other ways. But, anyhow, I don't propose to take her about in the débutante world very much (all those awful parties, S.W. something), I don't see the point of it. She would become quite worn out and meet a lot of unsuitable people. I'm planning to let her go to not more than two dances a week, carefully chosen. Quite enough for a girl who's not very strong. I thought later on, if you'll help me, Boy, we could make a list of women to give dinners for my ball. Of course, it must be perfectly understood that they are to ask the people I tell them to; can't have them paying off their own friends and relations on me.'

After dinner, we went back to the Long Gallery. Boy settled down to his petit-point while we three women sat with idle hands. He had a talent for needlework, had hemstitched some of the sheets for the Queen's doll's house and had covered many chairs at Silkin and at Hampton. He was now making a fire-screen for the Long Gallery which he had designed himself in a sprawling Jacobean pattern, the theme of it was supposed to be flowers from Lady Montdore's garden, but these flowers really looked more like horrid huge insects. Being young and deeply prejudiced it never occurred to me to admire his work. I merely thought how too dreadful it was to see a man sewing and how hideous he looked, his grizzled head bent over the canvas, into which he was deftly stitching various shades of khaki. He had the same sort of thick coarse hair as mine and I knew that the waves in it, the little careless curls (boyish) must have been carefully wetted and pinched in before dinner.

Lady Montdore had sent for paper and a pencil in order to write down the names of dinner hostesses. 'We'll put down all the possible ones and then weed,' she said. But she soon gave up this occupation in order to complain about Polly, and though I had already heard her on the subject when she had been talking with Mrs Chad-desley Corbett, the tone of her voice was now much sharper and more aggrieved.

'One does everything for these girls,' she said, 'everything. You wouldn't believe it, perhaps, but I assure you I spend quite half my day making plans for Polly – appointments, clothes, parties and so on. I haven't a minute to see my own friends, I've hardly had a game of cards for months. I've quite given up my art – in the middle of that nude girl from Oxford, too – in fact, I devote myself entirely to the child. I keep the London house going simply for her convenience. I hate London in the winter, as you know, and Montdore would be quite happy in two rooms without a cook (all that cold food at the club), but I've got a huge staff there eating their heads off, entirely on her account. You'd think she'd be grateful, at least, wouldn't you? Not at all. Sulky and disagreeable, I can hardly get a word out of her.'

The Dougdales said nothing. He was sorting out wools with great concentration, and Lady Patricia lay back, her eyes closed, suffering, as she had suffered for so long, in silence. She was looking more than ever like some garden statue, her skin and her beige London dress exactly the same colour, while her poor face was lined with pain and sadness, the very expression of antique tragedy.

Lady Montdore went on with her piece, talking exactly as if I were not there.

'I take endless trouble so that she can go and stay in nice houses, but she never seems to enjoy herself a bit, she comes home full of complaints and the only ones she wants to go back to are Alconleigh and Emily Warbeck. Both pure waste of time! Alconleigh is a madhouse – of course, I love Sadie, everybody does, I think she's wonderful, poor dear, and it's not her fault if she has all those eccentric children – she must have done what she can – but they are their father over again. No more need be said. Then I like the child to be with Fanny and one has known Emily and Davey all one's life – Emily was our bridesmaid and Davey was an elf in the very first pageant I ever organized – but the fact remains, Polly never meets anybody there, and if she never meets people how can she marry them?'

'Is there so much hurry for her to marry?' said Lady Patricia.

'Well, you know, she'll be twenty in May, she can't go on like this for ever. If she doesn't marry what will she do, with no interests in life, no occupation? She doesn't care for art or riding or society. She hardly has a friend in the world – oh, can you tell me how Montdore and I came to have a child like that – when I think of myself at her age. I remember so well Mr Asquith saying he had never met anybody with such a genius for improvisation –'

'Yes, you were wonderful,' said Lady Patricia, with a little smile. 'But after all, she may be slower at developing than you were, and, as you say, she's not twenty yet. Surely it's rather nice to have her at home for another year or two?'

'The fact is,' replied her sister-in-law, 'girls are not nice, it's a perfectly horrid age. When they are children, so sweet and puddy, you think how delightful it will be to have their company later on, but what company is Polly to Montdore or to me? She moons about, always half cross and half tired, and takes no interest in any mortal thing, and what she needs is a husband. Once she is married we shall be on excellent terms again, I've so often seen it happen. I was talking to Sadie the other day and she agreed, she says she has had a most difficult time lately with Linda – Louisa, of course, was never any trouble, she had a nicer character and then she married straight out of the schoolroom. One thing you can say about the Radletts, no delay in marrying them off, though they might not be the sort of marriages one would like for one's own child. A banker and a dilapidated Scotch peer – still, there it is, they are married. What can be the matter with Polly? So beautiful and no B.A. at all.'

'S.A.,' said Lady Patricia faintly, 'or B.O.'

'When we were young none of that existed, thank goodness. S.A. and B.O., perfect rubbish and bosh – one was a beauty or a *jolie-laide* and that was that. All the same, now they have been invented I suppose it is better if the girls have them, their partners seem to like it, and Polly hasn't a vestige, you can see that. But how differently,' she said with a sigh, 'how differently life turns out from what we expect! Ever since she was born, you know, I've worried and fussed over that child, and thought of the awful things that might happen to her – that Montdore might die before she was settled and we should have no proper home, that her looks would go (too beautiful at fourteen I feared), or that she would have an accident and spend the rest of her days in a spinal chair – all sorts of things, I used to wake up in the night and imagine them, but the one thing that never even crossed my mind was that she might end up an old maid.'

There was a rising note of aggrieved hysteria in her voice.

'Come now, Sonia,' said Lady Patricia rather sharply, 'the poor girl is still in her teens. Do wait at least until she has had a London season before you call her an old maid – she'll find somebody she likes there soon enough you can be quite sure.'

'I only wish I could think it, but I have a strong feeling she won't, and that what's more they won't like her,' said Lady Montdore, 'she has no come-hither in her eye. Oh, it is really too bad. She leaves the light on in her bathroom night after night too, I see it shining out –'

Lady Montdore was very mean about modern inventions such as electric light.

9

As her mother had predicted, summer came and went without any change in Polly's circumstances. The London season duly opened with a ball at Montdore House which cost £2,000, or so Lady Montdore told everybody, and was certainly very brilliant. Polly wore a white satin dress with pink roses at the bosom and a pink lining to the sash (touches of pink as the *Tatler* said), chosen in Paris for her by Mrs Chaddesley Corbett and brought over in the bag by some South American diplomat, a friend of Lady Montdore's, to save duty, a proceeding of which Lord Montdore knew nothing and which would have perfectly horrified him had he known. Enhanced by this dress, and by a little make-up, Polly's beauty was greatly remarked upon, especially by those of a former generation, who were all saying that since Lady Helen Vincent, since Lily Langtry, since the Wyndham sisters (according to taste), nothing so perfect had been seen in London. Her own contemporaries, however, were not so greatly excited by her. They admitted her beauty but said that she was dull, too large. What they really admired were the little skinny goggling copies of Mrs Chaddesley Corbett which abounded that season. The many dislikers of Lady Montdore said that she kept Polly too much in the background, and this was hardly fair because, although it is true to say that Lady Montdore automatically filled the foreground of any picture in which she figured, she was only too anxious to push Polly in front of her, like a hostage, and it was not her fault if she was forever slipping back again.

On the occasion of this ball many of the royalties in Lady Montdore's bedroom had stepped from their silver frames and come to life, dustier and less glamorous, poor dears, when seen in all their dimensions; the huge reception rooms at

Montdore House were scattered with them, and the words Sir or Ma'am could be heard on every hand. The Ma'ams were really quite pathetic, you would almost say hungry-looking, so old, in such sad and crumpled clothes, while there were some blue-chinned Sirs of dreadfully foreign aspect. I particularly remember one of them because I was told that he was wanted by the police in France and not much wanted anywhere else, especially not, it seemed, in his native land where his cousin, the King, was daily expecting the crown to be blown off his head by a puff of east wind. This Prince smelt strongly, but not deliciously, of camellias, and had a *fond de teint* of brilliant sunburn.

'I only ask him for the sake of my dear old Princess Irene,' Lady Montdore would explain if people raised their eyebrows at seeing him in such a very respectable house. 'I never shall forget what an angel he was to Montdore and me when we were touring the Balkans (one doesn't forget these things). I know people do say he's a daisy, whatever that may be, but if you listen to what everybody says about everybody you'll end by never having anybody, and besides, half these rumours are put about by anarchists, I'm positive.'

Lady Montdore loved anybody royal. It was a genuine emotion, quite disinterested, since she loved them as much in exile as in power, and the act of curtsying was the consummation of this love. Her curtsies, owing to the solid quality of her frame, did not recall the graceful movement of wheat before the wind. She scrambled down like a camel, rising again backside foremost like a cow, a strange performance, painful it might be supposed to the performer, the expression on whose face, however, belied this thought. Her knees cracked like revolver shots but her smile was heavenly.

I was the only unmarried woman to be asked to dine at Montdore House before the dance. There was a dinner party of forty people with a very grand Sir and Ma'am indeed, on account of whom everybody was punctual to the minute, so that all the guests arrived simultaneously and the large crowd in Park Lane was rewarded by good long stares into the queueing motor cars. Mine was the only cab.

Upstairs a long wait ensued, without cocktails, and even the most brassy people, even Mrs Chaddesley Corbett, began to twitter with nerves, as though they were being subjected to an intolerable strain; they stood about piping stupidities in their fashionable voices. At last the butler came up to Lord Montdore and murmured something, upon which he and Lady Montdore went down into the hall to receive their guests, while the rest of us, directed by Boy, formed ourselves into a semi-circle. Very slowly Lady Montdore led this tremendous Sir and Ma'am round the semi-circle, making presentations in the tone of voice, low, reverent but distinct, which my aunts used for responses in church. Then, arm through exalted arm, the four of them moved off, still in slow motion, through the double doors into the dining-room, leaving the rest of us to sort ourselves out and follow. It all went like clockwork.

Soon after dinner, which took a long time and was Hampton food at its climax, crest and top, people began to arrive for the ball. Lady Montdore in gold lamé, and many diamonds, including her famous pink diamond tiara, Lord Montdore, genial, noble, his long thin legs in silk stockings and knee-breeches, the Garter round one of them, its ribbon across his shirt front and a dozen miniatures dangling on his chest, and Polly in her white dress and her beauty, stood shaking hands at the top of the stairs for quite an hour and a very pretty sight it was to see the people streaming past them. Lady Montdore, true to her word, had invited very few girls and even fewer mammas. The guests were therefore neither too young nor too old to decorate but were all in their glittering prime.

Nobody asked me to dance. Just as no girls had been invited to the ball so also were there very few young men except such as were firmly attached to the young married set, but I was quite happy looking on, and since there was not a soul I knew to see me, no shame attached to my situation. All the same I was delighted when the Alconleighs, with Louisa and Linda and their husbands, Aunt Emily and Davey, who had been dining together, appeared, as they always did at parties, nice and early. I became assimilated into their cheerful group and we took up a position, whence we could have a good view of the proceedings, in the picture gallery. This opened into the ballroom on one hand and the supper-room on the other, there was a great deal of coming and going and at the same time never any crowd so that we could see the dresses and jewels to their best advantage. Behind us hung a Correggio St Sebastian, with the usual Buchmanite expression on his face.

'Awful tripe,' said Uncle Matthew, 'fella wouldn't be grinning, he'd be dead with all those arrows in him.'

On the opposite wall was the Montdore Botticelli which Uncle Matthew said he wouldn't give 7s. 6d. for, and when Davey showed him a Leonardo drawing he said his fingers only itched for an india-rubber.

'I saw a picture once,' he said, 'of shire horses in the snow. There was nothing else, just a bit of broken-down fence and three horses. It was dangerous good – Army and Navy. If I'd been a rich man I'd have bought that – I mean you could see how cold those poor brutes must have felt. If all this rubbish is supposed to be valuable, that must be worth a fortune.'

Uncle Matthew, who absolutely never went out in the evening, let alone to balls, would not hear of refusing an invitation to Montdore House, though Aunt Sadie, who knew how it tormented him to be kept awake after dinner, and how his poor eyes would turn back to front with sleepiness, had said,

'Really, darling, as we are between daughters, two married, and two not yet out, there's no occasion whatever for us to go if you'd rather not. Sonia would understand perfectly – and be quite glad of our room, I dare say.'

But Uncle Matthew had gloomily replied, 'If Montdore asks us to his ball it is because he wants to see us there. I think we ought to go.'

Accordingly, with many groans, he had squeezed himself into the knee-breeches of his youth, now so perilously tight that he hardly dared sit down, but stood like a stork beside Aunt Sadie's chair, and Aunt Sadie had got all her diamonds out of the bank and lent some to Linda and some to Aunt Emily and even so had quite a nice lot left for herself, and here they were chatting away happily enough with their relations and with various county figures who came and went, and even Uncle Matthew seemed quite amused by it all until a dreadful fate befell him, he was made to take the German Ambassadress to supper. It happened like this, Lord Montdore, at Uncle Matthew's very elbow, suddenly exclaimed in horror,

'Good heavens, the German Ambassadress is sitting there quite alone.'

'Serve her right,' said Uncle Matthew. It would have been more prudent to have held his tongue. Lord Montdore heard him speak, without taking in the meaning of his words, turned sharply round, saw who it was, seized him by the arm and said,

'My dear Matthew, just the very man – Baroness von Ravensbrück, may I present my neighbour, Lord Alconleigh? Supper is quite ready in the music room – you know the way, Matthew.'

It was a measure of Lord Montdore's influence over Uncle Matthew that my uncle did not then and there turn tail and bolt for home. No other living person could have persuaded him to stay and shake hands with a Hun, let alone take it on his arm and feed it. He went off, throwing a mournful backward glance at his wife.

Lady Patricia now came and sat by Aunt Sadie and they chatted, in rather a desultory way, about local affairs. Aunt Sadie, unlike her husband, really enjoyed going out so long as it was not too often, she did not have to stay up too late, and she was allowed to look on peacefully without feeling obliged to make any conversational effort. Strangers bored and fatigued her; she only liked the company of those people with whom she had day-to-day interests in common, such as country neighbours or members of her own family, and even with them she was generally rather absent-minded. But on this occasion it was Lady Patricia who seemed half in the clouds, saying yes and no to Aunt Sadie and what a monstrous thing it was to let the Skilton village idiot out again specially now it was known what a fast runner he was since he had won the asylum 100 yards.

'And he's always chasing people,' Aunt Sadie said indignantly.

But Lady Patricia's mind was not on the idiot. She was thinking, I am sure, of parties in those very rooms when she was young, and how much she had worshipped the Lecturer, and what agony it had been when he had danced and flirted, she knew, with other people, and how perhaps it was almost sadder for her that now she could care about nothing any more but the condition of her liver.

I knew from Davey ('Oh, the luck,' as Linda used to say, 'that Dave is such an old gossip, poor simple us if it weren't for him!') that Lady Patricia had loved Boy for several years before he had finally proposed to her, and had indeed quite lost hope. And then how short-lived was her happiness, barely six months before she had found him in bed with a kitchen-maid.

'Boy never went out for big stuff,' I once heard Mrs Chaddesley Corbett say, 'he only ever liked bowling over the rabbits, and now, of course, he's a joke.'

It must be hateful, being married to a joke.

Presently she said to Aunt Sadie, 'When was the first ball you ever came to, here?'

'It must have been the year I came out, in 1906, I well remember the excitement of actually seeing King Edward in the flesh and hearing his loud foreign laugh.'

'Twenty-four years ago, fancy,' said Lady Patricia, 'just before Boy and I were married. Do you remember how, in the war, people used to say we should never see this sort of thing again, and yet look! Only look at the jewels.'

Presently, as Lady Montdore came into sight, she said,

'You know, Sonia really is phenomenal. I'm sure she's better-looking and better-dressed now than she has ever been in her life.'

One of those middle-aged remarks I used to find incomprehensible. It did not seem to me that Lady Montdore could be described either as good-looking or as well-dressed; she was old and that was that. On the other hand nobody could deny that on occasions of this sort she was impressive, almost literally covered with great big diamonds, tiara, necklace, earrings, a huge Palatine cross on her bosom, bracelets from wrist to elbow over her suède gloves, and brooches wherever there was possible room for them. Dressed up in these tremendous jewels, surrounded by the exterior signs of 'all this', her whole demeanour irradiated by the superiority she so deeply felt in herself, she was, like a bull-fighter in his own ring, an idol in its own ark, the reason for and the very centre of the spectacle.

Uncle Matthew, having made his escape from the Ambassadress with a deep bow expressive of deep disgust, now came back to the family party.

'Old cannibal,' he said, 'she kept asking for more fleisch. Can't have swallowed her dinner more than an hour ago – I pretended not to hear, wouldn't pander to the old ogress, after all, who won the war? And what for, I should like to know? Wonderful public-spirited of Montdore to put up with all this foreign trash in his house – I'm blowed if I would. I ask you to look at that sewer!' He glared in the direction of a blue-chinned Sir who was heading for the supper-room with Polly on his arm.

'Come now, Matthew,' said Davey, 'the Serbs were our allies you know.'

'Allies!' said Uncle Matthew, grinding his teeth. The word was as a red rag to a bull and naughty Davey knew this and was waving the rag for fun.

'So that's a Serb, is it? Well, just what one would expect, needs a shave. Hogs, one and all. Of course, Montdore only asks them for the sake of the country. I do admire that fella, he thinks of nothing but his duty – what an example to everybody!'

A gleam of amusement crossed Lady Patricia's sad face. She was not without a sense of humour and was one of the few people Uncle Matthew liked, though he could not bring himself to be polite to Boy, and gazed furiously into space every time he passed our little colony, which he did quite often, squiring royal old ladies to the supper-room. Of his many offences in the eyes of Uncle Matthew, the chief was that, having been A.D.C. to a general in the war, he was once discovered by my uncle sketching a château behind the lines. There must clearly be something wrong about a man who could waste his time sketching, or indeed, undertake the duties of an A.D.C. at all, when he might be slaughtering foreigners all day.

'Nothing but a blasted lady's maid,' Uncle Matthew would say whenever Boy's name was mentioned. 'I can't stick the sewer. Boy indeed! Dougdale! What does it all mean? There used to be some perfectly respectable people called Blood at Silkin in the Old Lord's time. Major and Mrs Blood.'

The Old Lord was Lord Montdore's father. Jassy once said, opening enormous eyes, 'He *must* have been old', upon which Aunt Sadie had remarked that people do not remain the same age all their lives, and he had no doubt been young in his time just as one day, though she might not expect it, Jassy herself would become old.

It was not very logical of Uncle Matthew so exaggeratedly to despise Boy's military record, and was just another example of how those he liked could do no wrong and those he disliked no right, because Lord Montdore, his great hero, had never in his life heard the cheerful sound of musketry or been near a battle; he would have been rather elderly to have taken the field in the Great War, it is true, but his early years had vainly offered many a jolly fight, chances to hack away at native flesh, not to speak of Dutch flesh in that Boer war which had provided Uncle Matthew with such radiant memories, having given him his first experience of bivouac and battle.

'Four days in a bullock waggon,' he used to tell us, 'a hole as big as your fist in my stomach, and maggoty! Happiest time of my life. The only thing was one got rather tired of the taste of mutton after a bit, no beef in that campaign, you know.'

But Lord Montdore was a law unto himself, and had even got away with the famous Montdore Letter to the *Morning Post* which suggested that the war had gone on long enough and might be brought to an end, several months before the cowardly capitulation of the Hun had made this boring adjournment necessary. Uncle Matthew found it difficult to condone such spoiling of sport but did so by saying that Lord Montdore must have had some good reason for writing it which nobody else knew anything about.

My thoughts were now concentrated upon the entrance to the ballroom door, where I had suddenly perceived the back of somebody's head. So he had come after all. The fact that I had never thought he would (such a serious character) had in no way mitigated my disappointment that he had not; now, here he was. I must explain that the image of Sauveterre, having reigned in my hopeless heart for several months, had recently been ousted and replaced by something more serious, with more reality and promise.

The back of a head, seen at a ball, can have a most agitating effect upon a young girl, so different from the backs of other heads that it might be surrounded by a halo. There is the question, will he turn round, will he see her, and if so will he merely give a polite good-evening or invite her to dance? Oh, how I wished I could have been whirling gaily round in the arms of some fascinator instead of sitting with my aunts and uncles, too obviously a wallflower. Not that it mattered. There were a few moments of horrible suspense before the head turned round, but when it did he saw me, came straight over, said good-evening more than politely, and danced me away. He thought he would never get here, it was a question of borrowed, but mislaid, knee-breeches. Then he danced with Aunt Emily, again with me, and with Louisa, having engaged me to have supper after that.

'Who is that brute?' said Uncle Matthew, grinding his teeth as my young man went off with Louisa, 'why does he keep coming over here?'

'He's called Alfred Wincham,' I said, 'shall I introduce him to you?'

'For pity's sake, Fanny!'

'What an old Pasha you are,' said Davey. And indeed, Uncle Matthew would clearly have preferred to keep all his female relations in a condition if not of virginity at any rate of exaggerated chastity, and could never bear them to be approached by strange men.

When not dancing I went back and sat with my relations. I felt calmer now, having had two dances and the promise of supper, and was quite happy to fill in the time by listening to my elders as they conversed.

Presently Aunt Sadie and Aunt Emily went off to have supper together; they always liked to do this at parties. Davey moved up to sit next to Lady Patricia and Uncle Matthew stood by Davey's chair, sleeping on his feet as horses can, patiently waiting to be led back to his stable. 'It's this new man Meyerstein,' Davey was saying. 'You simply must go to him, Patricia, he does it all by salt elimination. You skip in order to sweat out all the salt in your organism, and eat saltless meals, of course. Too disgusting. But it does break down the crystals.'

'Do you mean skip with a skipping-rope?'

'Yes, hundreds of times. You count. I can do three hundred at a go, as well as some fancy steps, now.'

'But isn't it horribly tiring?'

'Nothing tires Davey – fella's as strong as a bull,' said Uncle Matthew, opening one eye.

Davey cast a sad look at his brother-in-law and said that of course it was desperately tiring, but well worth it for the results.

Polly was now dancing with her uncle, Boy. She did not look radiant and happy as such a spoilt darling should at her coming-out ball, but tired and pinched about the mouth, nor was she chattering away like the other women.

'I shouldn't care for one of my girls to look like that,' Aunt Sadie said, 'you'd think she had something on her mind.'

And my new friend Mr Wincham said, as we danced round before going to supper, 'Of course she's a beauty, I quite see that she is, but she doesn't attract me, with that sulky expression, I'm sure she's very dull.'

I began to deny that she was either sulky or dull when he said 'Fanny' to me, the first time he ever had, and followed this up with a lot of things which I wanted to listen to very carefully so that I could think them over later on, when I was alone.

Mrs Chaddesley Corbett shouted at me, from the arms of the Prince of Wales, 'Hullo, my sweet! What news of the Bolter? Are you still in love?'

'What's all this?' said my partner, 'Who is that woman? Who is the Bolter? And is it true that you are in love?'

'Mrs Chaddesley Corbett,' I said. I felt that the time was not yet ripe to begin explaining about the Bolter.

'And how about love?'

'Nothing,' I said, rather pink, 'just a joke.'

'Good. I should like you to be on the verge of love but not yet quite in it. That's a very nice state of mind, while it lasts.'

But of course, I had already dived over that verge and was swimming away in a blue sea of illusion towards, I supposed, the islands of the blest, but really towards domesticity, maternity and the usual lot of womankind.

A holy hush now fell upon the crowd as the Royals prepared to go home, the very grand Royals serene in the knowledge that they would find the traditional cold roast chicken by their beds, not the pathetic Ma'ams and sinister Sirs who were stuffing away in the supper-room as if they were far from sure they would ever see so much food again, nor the gay young Royals who were going to dance until morning with little neat women of the Chaddesley Corbett sort.

'How late they have stayed, what a triumph for Sonia,' I heard Boy saying to his wife.

The dancers divided like the Red Sea forming a lane of bowing and curtsying subjects, down which Lord and Lady Montdore conducted their guests.

'Sweet of you to say so, Ma'am. Yes, at the next Court. Oh, how kind of you.'

The Montdores came back into the picture gallery, beaming happily and saying, to nobody in particular,

'So simple, so easy, pleased with any little thing one can do for them, such wonderful manners, such a memory. Astounding how much they know about India, the Maharajah was amazed.'

They spoke as though these Princes are so remote from life as we know it that the smallest sign of humanity, the mere fact even that they communicated by means of speech, was worth noting and proclaiming.

The rest of the evening was spent by me in a happy trance, and I remember no more about the party as such. I know that I was taken back to the Goring Hotel, where we were all staying, at five o'clock on a fine May morning by Mr Wincham who had clearly shown me, by then, that he was not at all averse to my company.

10

So Polly was now 'out' in London society, and played her part during the rest of the season, as she had at the ball, with a good enough grace, the performance only lacking vitality and temperament to make it perfect. She did all the things her mother arranged for her, went to the parties, wore the clothes and made the friends that Lady Montdore thought suitable and never branched out on her own or gave any possible cause for complaint. She certainly did nothing to create an atmosphere of fun, but Lady Montdore was perhaps too much employed herself in that very direction to notice that Polly, though good and acquiescent, never for one moment entered into the spirit of the many entertainments they went to. Lady Montdore enjoyed it all prodigiously, appeared to be satisfied with Polly, and was delighted with the publicity that, as the most important and most beautiful débutante of the year, she was receiving. She was really too busy, in too much of a whirl of society while the season was going on, to wonder whether Polly was being a success or not; when it was over they went to Goodwood, Cowes, and Scotland, where no doubt among the mists and heather she had time to take stock of the situation. They vanished from my life for many weeks.

By the time I saw them again, in the autumn, their relationship was back to what it had been before and they were clearly very much on each other's nerves. I was now living in London myself, Aunt Emily having taken a little house in St Leonard's Terrace for the winter. It was a happy time in my life, as presently I became engaged to Alfred Wincham, the same young man whose back view had so much disturbed me at the Montdore ball. During the weeks that preceded my engagement I saw a great deal of Polly. She would telephone in the morning.

'What are you up to, Fanny?'

'Aching,' I would reply, meaning aching with boredom, a malaise from which girls, before national service came to their rescue, were apt to suffer considerably.

'Oh, good. So can I bend you to my will? You can't think how dull, but if you are aching anyway? Well then, I've got to try on that blue velvet hat at Madame Rita, and go and fetch the gloves from Debenhams – they said they would have them today. Yes, but the worst is to come – I couldn't possibly bend you to have luncheon with my Aunt Edna at Hampton Court and afterwards to sit and chat while I have my hair done? No, forget I said anything so awful – anyway, we'll see. I'll be round for you in half an hour.'

I was quite pliable. I had nothing whatever to do and enjoyed bouncing round London in the big Daimler, while Polly went about the business which is demanded of a beauty. Although society, at present, had no attractions for her, she was very much interested in her own appearance and would never, I think, have given up bothering about it as Lady Patricia had.

So we went to Madame Rita, and I tried on all the hats in the shop while Polly had her fitting, and wondered why it was that hats never seemed to suit me, something to do with my heather-like hair perhaps, and then we drove down to Hampton Court where Polly's old great-aunt, the widow of a general, had an apartment. She sat all day dealing out cards to herself as she waited for eternity.

'And yet I don't believe she aches, you know,' said Polly.

'I've noticed,' I said, 'that married ladies and even widows never ache. There is something about marriage that seems to stop it for good, I wonder why?'

Polly did not answer. The very word marriage always shut her up like a clam, it was a thing that had to be remembered in her company.

The afternoon before my engagement was to be announced in *The Times*, Aunt Emily sent me round to Montdore House to tell the news. It is not at all my nature to be one of those who 'drop in', I like to be invited by people to their houses at a given time, so that when I arrive they are expecting me and have made their dispositions accordingly, but I saw Aunt Emily's point when she said that, after all Lady Montdore's kindness to me, and considering that Polly was such a very great friend, I could hardly allow them to become aware of my engagement by reading it casually, in the paper.

So round I went, trembling rather. Bullitt, the butler, always frightened me into a fit. He was like Frankenstein's monster and one had to follow his jerky footsteps as though through some huge museum before arriving at the little green room, the only room in the house which did not seem as if it had been cleared ready for a reception, in which they always sat. Today, however, the front door was opened by a footman of more human aspect, and, furthermore, he told me the good news that Her Ladyship had not yet come in but Lady Polly was there alone, so off we trudged and presently discovered her amid the usual five o'clock paraphernalia of silver kettle on flame, silver teapot, Crown Derby cups and plates and enough sugary food to stock a pastrycook's shop. She was sitting on the arm of a chair reading the *Tatler*.

'Heavenly *Tatler* day,' she said, 'it really does help with the aching. I'm in and Linda's in, but not you this week. Faithful of you to come, I was just wishing somebody nice would – now we can have our tea.'

I was uncertain how she would take my engagement, I had in fact never spoken to her of Alfred since I had begged her to get him asked to the ball, she always seemed so much against young men or any talk of love. But when I told her the news she was enthusiastic and only reproached me with having been so secretive.

'I remember you made me ask him to the ball,' she said. 'But then you never mentioned him again, once.'

'I didn't dare to talk about it,' I said, 'in case – well – it really was of too much importance.'

'Oh, I do understand that. I'm so glad you were longing for it before he asked you, I never believe in the other sort, the ones who have to make up their minds, you know. How lucky you are, oh, fancy being able to marry the person you love. You don't know your luck.' Her eyes were full of tears, I saw. 'Go on,' she said. 'Tell everything.'

I was rather surprised at this show of feeling, so unusual with Polly, but in my selfish state of great new happiness did not pause to consider what it might mean. Besides, I was, of course, longing to tell.

'He was terribly nice to me at your ball, I hadn't a bit expected that he would come to London for it because for one thing, knee-breeches. I knew how he wouldn't have any, and then he's so busy always and hates parties, so you can imagine when I saw him I was all excited. Then he asked me to dance, but he danced with old Louisa too and even Aunt Emily so I thought, oh, well, he doesn't know anybody else, it must be that. So then he took me to supper and said he liked my dress and he hoped I'd go and see him at Oxford, and then he said something which showed he'd remembered a conversation we had had before. You know how encouraging that always is. After that he asked me to Oxford, twice, once he had a luncheon party and once he was alone, but in the holidays he went to Greece. Oxford holidays are terribly long, you know. Not even a postcard, so I thought it was all off. Well, on Thursday I went to Oxford again and this time he proposed to me and look –' I said, showing a pretty old ring, a garnet set in diamonds.

'Don't say he had it on him like in *The Making of a Marchioness*,' said Polly.

'Just like, except that it's not a ruby.'

'Quite the size of a pigeon's egg though. You are lucky.'

Lady Montdore now appeared. She bustled in still wearing her outdoor clothes and seemed unusually mellow.

'Ah! The girls!' she said, 'talking balls, I suppose, as usual! Going to the Gravesends' tonight, Fanny? Give me some tea, I'm quite dead, such an afternoon with the Grand Duchess, I've just dropped her at Kensington Palace. You'd never believe that woman was nearly eighty, she could run us all off our feet you know, and such a dear, so human, one doesn't mind what one says to her. We went to Woollands to get some woollens – she does feel the cold. Misses the double windows so she tells me.'

It must have been rather sad for Lady Montdore (though with her talent for ignoring disagreeable subjects she probably never even realized the fact) that friendship with royal personages only ever began for her when their days of glory were finished. Tsarskoe-Selo, Schönbrunn, the Quirinal, Kotrocheny Palace, Miramar, Laecken and the island of Corfu had never known her, unless among an enormous crowd in the state apartments. If she went to a foreign capital with her husband she would, of course, be invited to official receptions, while foreign rulers who came to London would attend her big parties, but it was all very formal. Crowned heads may not have had the sense to keep their crowns but they were evidently not too stupid to realize that give Lady Montdore an inch and she would take an ell. As soon as they were exiled, however, they began to see her charm, and another kingdom gone always meant a few more royal habitués at Montdore House; when they were completely down-and-out and had got through whatever money they had managed to salt away, she was allowed to act as lady-in-waiting and go with them to Woollands.

Polly handed her a cup of tea and told her my news. The happy afterglow from her royal outing immediately faded, and she became intensely disagreeable.

'Engaged?' she said. 'Well, I suppose that's very nice. Alfred what did you say? Who is he? What is that name?'

'He's a don, at Oxford.'

'Oh, dear, how extraordinary. You don't want to go and live at Oxford, surely? I should think he had better go into politics and buy a place – I suppose he hasn't got one by the way? No, or he wouldn't be a don, not an English don at least, in Spain of course, it's quite different – dons are somebody there, I believe. Let's think – yes, why shouldn't your father give you a place as a wedding present? You're the only child he's ever likely to have. I'll write to him at once – where is he now?'

I said vaguely that I believed in Jamaica, but did not know his address.

'Really, what a family! I'll find out from the Colonial Office and write by bag, that will be safest. Then this Mr Thing can settle down and write books. It always gives a man status if he writes a book, Fanny, I advise you to start him off on that immediately.'

'I'm afraid I haven't much influence with him,' I said uneasily.

'Oh, well, develop it dear, quick. No use marrying a man you can't influence. Just look what I've done for Montdore, always seen that he takes an interest, made him accept things (jobs, I mean) and kept him up to the mark, never let him slide back. A wife must always be on the look-out, men are so lazy by nature, for example, Montdore is forever trying to have a little nap in the afternoon, but I won't hear of it, once you begin that, I tell him, you are old, and people who are old find themselves losing interest, dropping out of things and then they might as well be dead. Montdore's only got me to thank if he's not in the same condition as most of his contemporaries, creeping about the Marlborough Club like dying flies and hardly able to drag themselves as far as the House of Lords. I make Montdore walk down there every day. Now, Fanny dear, the more I think of it, the more it seems to me quite ridiculous for you to go marrying a don, what does Emily say?'

'She's awfully pleased.'

'Emily and Sadie are hopeless. You must ask my advice about this sort of thing, I'm very glad indeed you came round, we must think how we can get you out of it. Could you ring him up now and say you've changed your mind, I believe it would be kindest in the long run to do it that way.'

'Oh, no, I can't.'

'Why not, dear? It isn't in the paper yet.'

'It will be tomorrow.'

'That's where I can be so helpful. I'll send for Geoffrey Dawson now and have it stopped.'

I was quite terrified. 'Please –' I said, 'oh, please not!'

Polly came to my rescue. 'But she wants to marry him, Mummy, she's in love, and look at her pretty ring!'

Lady Montdore looked, and was confirmed in her opposition. 'That's not a ruby,' she said, as if I had been pretending it was. 'And as for love I should have thought the example of your mother would have taught you something – where has love landed her? Some ghastly white hunter. Love indeed – whoever invented love ought to be shot.'

'Dons aren't a bit the same as white hunters,' said Polly. 'You know how fond Daddy is of them.'

'Oh, I dare say they're all right for dinner, if you like that sort of thing. Montdore does have them over sometimes, I know, but that's no reason why they should go marrying people. So unsuitable, megalomania, I call it. So many people have that, nowadays. No, Fanny, I'm very much distressed.'

'Oh, please don't be,' I said.

'However, if you say it's settled, I suppose there's no more I can do, except to try and help you make a success of it. Montdore can ask the Chief Whip if there's something for you to nurse, that will be best.'

It was on the tip of my tongue to say that what I hoped to be nursing before long would be sent by God and not the Chief Whip, but I restrained myself, nor did I dare to tell her that Alfred was not a Tory.

The conversation now turned upon the subject of my trousseau, about which Lady Montdore was quite as bossy though less embarrassing. I was not feeling much interest in clothes at that time, all my thoughts being of how to decorate and furnish a charming little old house which Alfred had taken me to see after placing the pigeon's egg on my finger, and which, by a miracle of good luck, was to be let.

'The important thing, dear,' she said, 'is to have a really good fur coat, I mean a proper, dark one.' To Lady Montdore, fur meant mink; she could imagine no other kind except sable, but that would be specified. 'Not only will it make all the rest of your clothes look better than they are but you really needn't bother much about anything else as you need never take it off. Above all, don't go wasting money on underclothes, there is nothing stupider – I always borrow Montdore's myself. Now for evening a diamond brooch is a great help, so long as it has good big stones. Oh, dear, when I think of the diamonds your father gave that woman, it really is too bad. All the same, he can't have got through everything, he was enormously rich when he succeeded, I must write to him. Now, dear, we're going to be very practical. No time like the present.'

She rang for her secretary and said my father's address must be found out.

'You could ring up the Under Secretary for the Colonies with my compliments, and will you make a note that I will write to Lord Logan tomorrow.'

She also told her to make a list of places where linen, underclothes, and house furnishings could be obtained at wholesale prices.

'Bring it straight back here for Miss Logan when it is ready.'

When the secretary had gone, Lady Montdore turned to Polly and spoke to her exactly as if I had gone too, and they were alone. It was a habit she had, and I always found it very embarrassing, as I never quite knew what she expected me to do, whether to interrupt her by saying good-bye, or simply to look out of the window and pretend that my thoughts were far away. On this occasion, however, I was clearly expected to wait for the list of addresses, so I had no choice.

'Now, Polly, have you thought of a young man yet, for me to ask down on the third?'

'Oh, how about John Coningsby?' said Polly, with an indifference which I could plainly see must be maddening to her mother. Lord Coningsby was her official young man, so to speak. She invited him to everything, and this had greatly pleased Lady Montdore to begin with since he was rich, handsome, agreeable and an 'eldest son', which meant in Lady Montdore's parlance the eldest son of a peer (never let Jones or Robinson major think of themselves for one moment as eldest sons). Too soon, however, she saw that he and Polly were excellent friends and would never be anything else, after which she regretfully lost all interest in him.

'Oh, I don't count John,' she said.

'How d'you mean you don't count him?'

'He's only a friend. Now, I was thinking in Woollands – I often do have good ideas in shops – how would it be to ask Joyce Fleetwood.'

Alas, the days when I, Albert Edward Christian George Andrew Patrick David, was considered to be the only person worthy of taking thee, Leopoldina, must have become indeed remote if Joyce Fleetwood was to be put forward as a substitute. Perhaps it was in Lady Montdore's mind that, since Polly showed no inclination to marry an established, inherited position, the next best thing would be somebody who might achieve one by his own efforts. Joyce Fleetwood was a noisy, self-opinionated young Conservative M.P. who had mastered one or two of the drearier subjects of debate, agriculture, the Empire, and so on, and was always ready to hold forth upon them in the House. He had made up to Lady Montdore who thought him much cleverer than he really was; his parents were known to her, they had a place in Norfolk.

'Well, Polly?'

'Yes, why not?' said Polly. 'It's a shower-bath when he talks, but do let's, he's so utterly fascinating, isn't he?'

Lady Montdore now lost her temper and her voice got quite out of control. I sympathized with her really, it was too obvious that Polly was wilfully provoking her.

'It's perfectly stupid to go on like this.'

Polly did not reply. She bent her head sideways and pretended to be deeply absorbed in the headlines, upside-down, of the evening paper which lay on a chair by her mother. She might just as well have said out loud, 'All right, you horrible vulgar woman, go on, I don't care, you are nothing to me,' so plain was her meaning.

'Please listen when I speak to you, Polly.'

Polly continued to squint at the headlines.

'Polly, will you please pay attention to what I'm saying?'

'What were you saying? Something about Mr Fleetwood?'

'Let Mr Fleetwood be, for the present. I want to know what, exactly, you are planning to do with your life. Do you intend to live at home and go mooning on like this for ever?'

'What else can I do? You haven't exactly trained me for a career, have you?'

'Oh, yes, indeed I have. I've trained you for marriage which, in my opinion (I may be old-fashioned), is by far the best career open to any woman.'

'That's all very well, but how can I marry if nobody asks me?'

Of course, that was really the sore point with Lady Montdore, nobody asking her. A Polly gay and flirtatious, surrounded by eligible suitors, playing one off against the others, withdrawing, teasing, desired by married men, breaking up her friends' romances, Lady Montdore would have been perfectly happy to watch her playing that game for several years if need be, so long as it was quite obvious that she would finally choose some suitably important husband and settle down with him. What her mother minded so dreadfully was that this acknowledged beauty should appear to have no attraction whatever for the male sex. The eldest sons had a look, said, 'Isn't she lovely?' and went off with some chinless little creature from Cadogan Square. There had been three or four engagements of this sort lately which had upset Lady Montdore very much indeed.

'And why don't they ask you? It's only because you give them no encouragment. Can't you try to be a little jollier, nicer with them, no man cares to make love to a dummy, you know, it's too discouraging.'

'Thank you, but I don't want to be made love to.'

'Oh, dear, oh, dear! Then what is it you do want?'

'Leave me alone Mother, please.'

'To stay on here, with us, until you are old?'

'Daddy wouldn't mind a bit.'

'Oh, yes he would, make no mistake about that. Not for a year or two perhaps, but in the end he would. Nobody wants their girl to be hanging about for ever, a sour old maid, and you'll be the sour kind, that's too obvious already, my dear, wizened-up and sour.'

I could hardly believe my ears; could this be Lady Montdore speaking, in such frank and dreadful terms, to Polly, her beautiful paragon, whom she used to love so much that she was even reconciled to her being a daughter and not an heir? It seemed to me terrible, I went cold in my very backbone. There was a long and deeply embarrassing silence, broken by Frankenstein's monster who jerked into the room and said that the King of Portugal was on the telephone. Lady Montdore stumped off and I seized the opportunity to escape.

'I hate her,' said Polly, kissing me good-bye. 'I hate her, and I wish she were dead. Oh, Fanny, the luck of not being brought up by your own mother – you've no idea what a horrible relationship it can be.'

'Poor Polly,' I said, very much upset. 'How sad. But when you were little it wasn't horrible?'

'Always, always horrible. I've always hated her from the bottom of my heart.'

I did not believe it.

'She isn't like this the whole time?' I said.

'More and more. Better make a dash for it, love, or you'll be caught again. I'll ring up very soon –'

II

I was married at the beginning of the Christmas vacation, and when Alfred and I returned from our honeymoon we went to stay at Alconleigh while our little house in Oxford was being got ready. This was an obvious and convenient arrangement

as Alfred could go into Oxford every day for his work, and I was at hand to super-
vise the decoration of the house, but, although Alconleigh had been a second home
to me from my babyhood, it was not without misgivings that I accepted Aunt
Sadie's invitation to take my husband there for a long visit, at the very outset of
our married life. My Uncle Matthew's likes and dislikes were famous for their
violence, for the predomination of the latter over the former, and for the fact that
he never made the slightest attempt to conceal them from their object; I could see
that he was already prejudiced against poor Alfred. It was an accepted fact in the
family that he loathed me; furthermore he also hated new people, hated men who
married his female relations, hated and despised those who did not practise blood
sports. I felt there was but little hope for Alfred, especially as, culmination of horror, 'the fella reads books'.

True, all this had applied to Davey when he had first appeared upon the scene,
engaged to Aunt Emily, but Uncle Matthew had taken an unreasoning fancy to
Davey from the very beginning, and it was not to be hoped that such a miracle
could repeat itself. My fears, however, were not entirely realized. I think Aunt Sadie
had probably read the riot act before our arrival; meanwhile I had been doing my
best with Alfred. I made him have his hair cropped like a guardsman, explained to
him that if he must open a book he should do so only in the privacy of his bedroom,
and specially urged great punctuality at meal times. Uncle Matthew, as I told him,
liked to get us all into the dining-room at least five minutes before the meal was
ready. 'Come on,' he would say, 'we'll go and sit in.' And in the family would sit,
clasping hot plates to their bosoms (Aunt Sadie had once done this, absent-mindedly,
with a plate of artichoke soup), all eyes upon the pantry door.

I tried to explain these things to Alfred, who listened patiently though uncom-
prehendingly. I also tried to prepare him for the tremendous impact of my uncle's
rages, so that I got the poor man, quite unnecessarily, into a panic.

'Do let's go to the Mitre,' he kept saying.

'It may not be too bad,' I replied, doubtfully.

And it was not, in the end, too bad at all. The fact is that Uncle Matthew's tremendous and classical hatred for me, which had begun when I was an infant and
which had cast a shadow of fear over all my childhood, had now become more
legend than actuality. I was such an habitual member of his household, and he
such a Conservative, that this hatred, in common with that which he used to nur-
ture against Josh, the groom, and various other old intimates, had not only lost its
force but I think had, with the passage of years, actually turned into love; such a
lukewarm sentiment as ordinary avuncular affection being of course foreign to his
experience. Be that as it may, he evidently had no wish to poison the beginning of
my married life, and made quite touching efforts to bottle up whatever irritation
he felt at Alfred's shortcomings: his unmanly incompetence with his motor car,
vagueness over time and fatal disposition to spill marmalade at breakfast. The fact
that Alfred left for Oxford at nine o'clock, only returning in time for dinner, and
that we spent Saturday to Monday of every week in Kent with Aunt Emily, made
our visit just endurable to Uncle Matthew, and, incidentally to Alfred himself, who
did not share my unquestioning adoration for all members of the Radlett family.

The Radlett boys had gone back to their schools, and my cousin Linda, whom
I loved best in the world after Alfred, was now living in London, expecting a baby,

but, though Alconleigh was never quite the same without her, Jassy and Victoria were at home (none of the Radlett girls went to school) so the house resounded as usual with jingles and jangles and idiotic shrieks. There was always some joke being run to death at Alconleigh and just now it was headlines from the *Daily Express* which the children had made into a chant and intoned to each other all day.

Jassy: '*Man's* long *agony* in a lift-*shaft.*'

Victoria: '*Slowly crushed* to *death* in a *lift.*'

Aunt Sadie became very cross about this, said they were really too old to be so heartless, that it wasn't a bit funny, only dull and disgusting, and absolutely forbade them to sing it any more. After this they tapped it out to each other, on doors, under the dining-room table, clicking with their tongues or blinking with their eyelids, and all the time in fits of naughty giggles. I could see that Alfred thought them terribly silly, and he could hardly contain his indignation when he found out that they did no lessons of any sort.

'Thank heaven for your Aunt Emily,' he said. 'I really could not have married somebody quite illiterate.'

Of course, I too thanked heaven more than ever for dear Aunt Emily, but at the same time Jassy and Victoria made me laugh so much, and I loved them so much, that it was impossible for me to wish them very different from what they were. Hardly had I arrived in the house than I was lugged off to their secret meeting-place, the Hons' cupboard, to be asked what IT was like.

'Linda says it's not all it's cracked up to be,' said Jassy, 'and we don't wonder when we think of Tony.'

'But Louisa says, once you get used to it, it's utter utter utter blissikins,' said Victoria, 'and we do wonder, when we think of John.'

'What's wrong with poor Tony and John?'

'Dull and old. Come on then Fanny – tell.'

I said I agreed with Louisa, but refused to enter into details.

'It is unfair, nobody ever tells. Sadie doesn't even know, that's quite obvious, and Louisa is an old prig, but we did think we could count on Linda and you. Very well then, we shall go to our marriage beds in ignorance, like Victorian ladies, and in the morning we shall be found stark staring mad with horror and live sixty more years in an expensive bin, and then perhaps you'll wish you had been more helpful.'

'Weighted down with jewels and Valenciennes costing thousands,' said Victoria. 'The Lecturer was here last week and he was telling Sadie some very nice sexy stories about that kind of thing – of course, we weren't meant to hear but you can just guess what happened, Sadie didn't listen and we did.'

'I should ask the Lecturer for information,' I said. 'He'd tell.'

'He'd show. No thank you very much.'

Polly came over to see me. She was pale and thinner, had rings under her eyes and seemed quite shut up in herself, though this may have been in contrast with the exuberant Radletts. When she was with Jassy and Victoria she looked like a swan, swimming in the company of two funny little tumbling ducks. She was very fond of them. She had never got on very well with Linda, for some reason, but she loved everybody else at Alconleigh, especially Aunt Sadie, and was more at her ease with Uncle Matthew than anybody I ever knew, outside his own family circle. He, for his part, bestowed on her some of the deference he felt for Lord

Montdore, called her Lady Polly, and smiled every time his eyes fell on her beautiful face.

'Now children,' said Aunt Sadie, 'leave Fanny and Polly to have a little chat, they don't want you all the time, you know.'

'It is unfair – I suppose Fanny's going to *tell* Polly now. Well, back to the medical dictionary and the Bible. I only wish these things didn't look quite so sordid in cold print. What we need is some clean-minded married woman, to explain, but where are we to find her?'

Polly and I had a very desultory little chat, however. I showed her photographs of Alfred and me in the South of France, where we had been so that he could meet my poor mother the Bolter, who was living there now with a nasty new husband. Polly said the Dougdales were off there next week as Lady Patricia was feeling the cold so dreadfully that winter. She told me also that there had been a huge Christmas party at Hampton and that Joyce Fleetwood was in disgrace with her mother for not paying his bridge debts.

'So that's one comfort. We've still got the Grand Duchess, poor old thing. Goodness she's dull – not that Mummy seems to think so. Veronica Chaddesley Corbett calls her and Mummy Ma'am and Super-Ma'am.'

I did not like to ask if Polly and her mother were getting on any better, and Polly volunteered nothing on that subject, but she looked, I thought, very miserable. Presently she said she must go.

'Come over soon and bring Alfred.'

But I dreaded the impact of Lady Montdore upon Alfred even more than that of Uncle Matthew, and said he was too busy but I would come alone sometime.

'I hear that she and Sonia are on very bad terms again,' Aunt Sadie said when Polly had driven off.

'The hell-hag,' said Uncle Matthew, 'drown her if I were Montdore.'

'Or he might cut her to pieces with nail scissors like that French duke the Lecherous Lecturer was telling you all about, Sadie, when you weren't listening and we were.'

'Don't call me Sadie, children, and don't call Mr Dougdale the Lecherous Lecturer.'

'Oh, dear. Well, we always do behind your backs so you see it's bound to slip out sometimes.'

Davey arrived. He had come to stay for a week or so for treatment at the Radcliffe Infirmary. Aunt Emily was becoming more and more attached to all her animals and could seldom now be persuaded to leave them, for which, on this occasion, I was thankful, since our Sundays in Kent really were an indispensable refuge to Alfred and me.

'I met Polly in the drive,' Davey said, 'we stopped and had a word. I think she looks most dreadfully unwell.'

'Nonsense,' said Aunt Sadie, who believed in no illness except appendicitis. 'There's nothing wrong with Polly, she needs a husband, that's all.'

'Oh! How like a woman!' said Davey. 'Sex, my dear Sadie, is not a sovereign cure for everything, you know. I only wish it were.'

'I didn't mean sex at all,' said my aunt, very much put out by this interpretation. Indeed, she was what the children called 'against' sex, that is to say it never entered into her calculations. 'What I said, and what I meant, was she needs a husband. Girls of her age, living at home, are hardly ever happy and Polly is a specially bad case because she has nothing whatever to do, she doesn't care for hunting, or parties, or anything much that I can see, and she doesn't get on with her mother. It's true that Sonia teases and lectures her and sets about it all the wrong way, she's a tactless person, but she is perfectly right, you know. Polly needs a life of her own, babies, occupations, and interests – an establishment, in fact – and for all that she must have a husband.'

'Or a lady of Llangollen,' said Victoria.

'Time you went to bed, miss, now off you go both of you.'

'Not me, it's not nearly my bedtime yet.'

'I said both of you, now begone.'

They dragged themselves out of the room as slowly as they dared and went upstairs, stamping out 'Man's long agony' on the bare boards of the nursery passage so that nobody in the whole house could fail to hear them.

'Those children read too much,' said Aunt Sadie. 'But I can't stop them. I honestly believe they'd rather read the label on a medicine bottle than nothing at all.'

'Oh, but I love reading the labels of medicine bottles,' said Davey, 'they're madly enjoyable, you know.'

12

The next morning when I came down to breakfast I found everybody, even the children, looking grave. It seemed that by some mysterious local tom-tom Aunt Sadie had learnt that Lady Patricia Dougdale had died in the night. She had suddenly collapsed, Lord Montdore was sent for, but by the time he could arrive she had become unconscious, and an hour later was dead.

'Oh, poor Patricia,' Aunt Sadie kept saying, very much upset, while Uncle Matthew, who cried easily, was mopping his eyes as he bent over the hot plate, taking a sausage, or in his parlance, a 'banger', with less than his usual enthusiasm.

'I saw her only last week,' he said, 'at the Clarendon Yard.'

'Yes,' said Aunt Sadie, 'I remember you told me. Poor Patricia, I always liked her so much, though of course, all that about being delicate was tiresome.'

'Well, now you can see for yourself that she was delicate,' said Davey triumphantly. 'She's dead. It killed her. Doesn't that show you? I do wish I could make you Radletts understand that there is no such thing as imaginary illness. Nobody who is quite well could possibly be bothered to do all the things that I, for instance, am obliged to, in order to keep my wretched frame on its feet.'

The children began to giggle at this, and even Aunt Sadie smiled because they all knew that so far from it being a bother to Davey it was his all-absorbing occupation, and one which he enjoyed beyond words.

'Oh, of course, I know you all think it's a great great joke, and no doubt Jassy and Victoria will scream with laughter when I finally do conk out, but it's not a joke to me, let me tell you, and a liver in that state can't have been much of a joke to poor Patricia, what's more.'

'Poor Patricia, and I fear she had a sad life with that boring old Lecturer.'

This was so like Aunt Sadie. Having protested for years against the name Lecturer for Boy Dougdale she was now using it herself, it always happened; very soon no doubt we should hear her chanting 'Man's long agony'.

'For some reason that I could never understand, she really loved him.'

'Until lately,' said Davey. 'I think for the past year or two it has been the other way round, and he had begun to depend on her, and then it was too late, she had stopped bothering about him.'

'Possibly. Anyway, there it is, all very sad. We must send a wreath, darling, at once. What a time of year – it will have to come from Oxford, I suppose – oh, the waste of money.'

'Send a wreath of frog spawn frog spawn frog spawn, lovely lovely frog spawn it is my favourite thing,' sang Jassy.

'If you go on being so silly, children,' said Aunt Sadie, who had caught a look of great disapproval on Alfred's face, 'I shall be obliged to send you to school, you know.'

'But can you afford to?' said Victoria. 'You'd have to buy us plimsolls and gym tunics, underclothes in a decent state and some good strong luggage. I've seen girls going off to school, they are covered with expensive things. Of course, we long for it, pashes for the prefects and rags in the dorm. School has a very sexy side you know, Sadie – why, the very word "mistress", Sadie, you know –'

But Aunt Sadie was not really listening; she was away in her cloud and merely said,

'Mm, very naughty and silly, and don't call me Sadie.'

Aunt Sadie and Davey went off to the funeral together. Uncle Matthew had his Bench that day, and particularly wanted to attend in order to make quite sure that a certain ruffian, who was to come up before it, should be committed to the Assizes, where, it was very much to be hoped, he would get several years and the cat. One or two of Uncle Matthew's fellow beaks had curious, modern ideas about justice and he was obliged to carry on a strenuous war against them, in which he was greatly assisted by a retired Admiral of the neighbourhood.

So they had to go to the funeral without him, and came back in low spirits.

'It's the dropping off the perches,' said Aunt Sadie. 'I've always dreaded when that begins. Soon we shall all have gone – oh well, never mind.'

'Nonsense,' Davey said, briskly. 'Modern science will keep us alive, and young, too, for many a long day yet. Patricia's insides were a terrible mess – I had a word with Dr Simpson while you were with Sonia and it's quite obviously a miracle she didn't die years ago. When the children have gone to bed I'll tell you.'

'No, thank you,' said Aunt Sadie, while the children implored him to go then and there with them to the Hons' cupboard and tell.

'It is unfair, Sadie doesn't want to hear the least bit, and we die to.'

'How old was Patricia?' said Aunt Sadie.

'Older than we are,' said Davey. 'I remember when they married she was supposed to be quite a bit older than Boy.'

'And he was looking a hundred in that bitter wind.'

'I thought he seemed awfully cut up, poor Boy.'

Aunt Sadie, during a little graveside chat with Lady Montdore, had gathered that the death had come as a shock and surprise to all of them, that, although they had known Lady Patricia to be far from well, they had no idea that she was in immediate danger; in fact, she had been greatly looking forward to her trip abroad the following week. Lady Montdore, who resented death, clearly thought it most inconsiderate of her sister-in-law to break up their little circle so suddenly, and Lord Montdore, devoted to his sister, was dreadfully shaken by the midnight drive with a deathbed at the end of it. But surprisingly enough, the one who had taken it hardest was Polly. It seemed that she had been violently sick on hearing the news, completely prostrated for two days, and was still looking so unwell that her mother had refused to take her to the funeral.

'It seems rather funny,' said Aunt Sadie, 'in a way. I'd no idea she was so particularly devoted to Patricia, had you, Fanny?'

'Nervous shock,' said Davey. 'I don't suppose she's ever had a death so near to her before.'

'Oh, yes she has,' said Jassy. 'Ranger.'

'Dogs aren't exactly the same as human beings, my dear Jassy.'

But to the Radletts they were exactly the same, except that to them dogs on the whole had more reality than people.

'Do tell about the grave,' said Victoria.

'Not very much to tell, really,' said Aunt Sadie. 'Just a grave, you know, lots of flowers and mud.'

'They'd lined it with heather,' said Davey, 'from Craigside. Poor Patricia, she did love Scotland.'

'And where was it?'

'In the graveyard, of course, at Silkin – between the Wellingtonia and the Blood Arms, if you see where I mean. In full view of Boy's bedroom window, incidentally.'

Jassy began to talk fast and earnestly.

'You will promise to bury me here, whatever happens, won't you, won't you, there's one exact place I want, I note it every time I go to church, it's next door to that old lady who was nearly a hundred.'

'That's not our part of the churchyard – miles away from grandfather.'

'No, but it's the bit I want. I once saw a dear little dead baby vole there. Please please please don't forget.'

'You'll have married some sewer and gone to live in the Antipodes,' said Uncle Matthew who had just come in. 'They let that young hog off, said there was no evidence. Evidence be damned, you'd only got to look at his face to see who did it, afternoon completely wasted, the Admiral and I are going to resign.'

'Then bring me back,' said Jassy, 'pickled. I'll pay, I swear I will. Please, Fa, you must.'

'Write it down,' said Uncle Matthew, producing a piece of paper and a fountain-pen, 'if these things don't get written down they are forgotten. And I'd like a deposit of ten bob please.'

'You can take it out of my birthday present,' said Jassy, who was scribbling away with great concentration. 'I've made a map like in *Treasure Island*,' she said. 'See?'

'Yes, thank you, that's quite clear,' said Uncle Matthew. He went to the wall, took his master-key from his pocket, opened a safe, and put in the piece of paper. Every room at Alconleigh had one of these wall-safes, whose contents would have amazed and discomfited the burglar who managed to open them. Aunt Sadie's jewels, which had some very good stones, were never kept in them, but lay glittering about all over the house and garden, in any place where she might have taken them off and forgotten to put them on again, on the downstairs wash-basin, by the flower-bed she had been weeding, sent to the laundry pinning up a suspender. Her big party pieces were kept in the bank. Uncle Matthew himself possessed no jewels and despised all men who did. (Boy's signet ring and platinum and pearl evening watch-chain were great causes for tooth-grinding.) His own watch was a large loudly ticking object in gun-metal, tested twice a day by Greenwich mean time on a chronometer in the business-room, and said to gain three seconds a week. This was attached to his key-ring across his moleskin waistcoat by an ordinary leather bootlace, in which Aunt Sadie often tied knots to remind herself of things.

The safes, nevertheless, were full of treasures, if not of valuables, for Uncle Matthew's treasures were objects of esoteric worth, such as a stone quarried on the estate and said to have imprisoned for two thousand years a living toad; Linda's first shoe; the skeleton of a mouse regurgitated by an owl; a tiny gun for shooting bluebottles; the hair of all his children made into a bracelet; a silhouette of Aunt Sadie done at a fair; a carved nut; a ship in a bottle; altogether a strange mixture of sentiment, natural history, and little objects which from time to time had taken his fancy.

'Come on, do let's see,' said Jassy and Victoria, making a dash at the door in the wall. There was always great excitement when the safes were opened, as they hardly ever were, and seeing inside was considered a treat.

'Oh! The dear little bit of shrapnel, may I have it?'

'No, you may not. It was once in my groin for a whole week.'

'Talk about death,' said Davey. 'The greatest medical mystery of our times must be the fact that dear Matthew is still with us.'

'It only shows,' said Aunt Sadie, 'that nothing really matters the least bit so why make these fearful efforts to keep alive?'

'Oh, but it's the efforts that one enjoys so much,' said Davey, and this time he was speaking the truth.

13

I think it was about a fortnight after Lady Patricia's funeral that Uncle Matthew stood, after luncheon, outside his front door, watch in hand, scowling fiercely, grinding his teeth and awaiting his greatest treat of all the year, an afternoon's chubb fuddling. The Chubb Fuddler was supposed to be there at half-past two.

'Twenty-three and a quarter minutes past,' Uncle Matthew was saying furiously, 'in precisely six and three-quarter minutes the damned fella will be late.'

If people did not keep their appointments with him well before the specified time he always counted them as being late, he would begin to fidget quite half an hour too soon, and wasted, in this way, as much time as people do who have no regard for it, besides getting himself into a thoroughly bad temper.

The famous trout stream that ran through the valley below Alconleigh was one of Uncle Matthew's most cherished possessions. He was an excellent dry-fly fisherman, and was never happier, in and out of the fishing-season, than when messing about the river in waders and inventing glorious improvements for it. It was the small boy's dream come true. He built dams, he dug lashers, he cut the weed and trimmed the banks, he shot the herons, he hunted the otters, and he restocked with young trout every year. But he had trouble with the coarse fish, especially the chubb, which not only gobble up the baby trout but also their food, and they were a great worry to him. Then, one day, he came upon an advertisement in *Exchange and Mart*. 'Send for the Chubb Fuddler.'

The Radletts always said that their father had never learnt to read, but in fact he could read quite well, if really fascinated by his subject, and the proof is that he found the Chubb Fuddler like this all by himself. He sat down then and there and sent. It took him some time, breathing heavily over the writing-paper and making, as he always did, several copies of the letter before finally sealing and stamping it.

'The fella says here to enclose a stamped and addressed envelope, but I don't think I shall pander to him, he can take it or leave it.'

He took it. He came, he walked along the river bank, and sowed upon its waters some magic seed, which soon bore magic fruit, for up to the surface, flapping, swooning, fainting, choking, thoroughly and undoubtedly fuddled, came hundreds upon hundreds of chubb. The entire male population of the village, warned beforehand and armed with rakes and landing-nets, fell upon the fish, several wheelbarrows were filled and the contents taken off to be used as manure for cottage gardens or chubb pie, according to taste.

Henceforward chubb fuddling became an annual event at Alconleigh, the Fuddler appearing regularly with the snowdrops, and to watch him at his work was a pleasure which never palled. So here we all were, waiting for him, Uncle Matthew pacing up and down outside the front door, the rest of us just inside on account of the bitter cold but peering out of the window, while all the men on the estate were gathered in groups down at the river's edge. Nobody, not even Aunt Sadie, wanted to miss a moment of the fuddling except, it seemed, Davey, who had retired to his room saying,

'It isn't madly me, you know, and certainly not in this weather.'

A motor car was now heard approaching, the scrunch of wheels, and a low, rich hoot, and Uncle Matthew, with a last look at his watch, was just putting it back in his pocket when down the drive came, not at all the Chubb Fuddler's little Standard, but the huge black Daimler from Hampton Park containing both Lord and Lady Montdore. This was indeed a sensation! Callers were unknown at Alconleigh, anybody rash enough to try that experiment would see no sign of Aunt Sadie or the children, who would all be flat on the floor out of sight, though Uncle Matthew, glaring most embarrassingly, would stand at a window in full view, while they were being told 'not at home'. The neighbours had long ago given it up as a bad job. Furthermore, the Montdores, who considered themselves King and Queen of the neighbourhood, never called, but expected people to go to them, so from every point of view it seemed most peculiar. I am quite sure that if anybody else had broken in upon the happy anticipation of an afternoon's chubb fuddling Uncle Matthew would have bellowed at them to 'get out

of it', possibly even have hurled a stone at them. When he saw who it was, however, he had one moment of stunned surprise and then leapt forward to open
the door of the motor, like a squire of olden times leaping to the stirrup of his
liege lord.

The hell-hag, we could all see at once, even through the window, was in a dreadful state. Her face was blotchy and swollen as from hours of weeping, she seemed
perfectly unaware of Uncle Matthew and did not throw him either a word or a
look as she struggled out of the car, angrily kicking at the rug round her feet, she
then tottered with the gait of a very old woman, legs all weak and crooked, towards
the house. Aunt Sadie, who had dashed forward, put an arm round her waist and
took her into the drawing-room, giving the door a great 'keep-out, children' bang.
At the same time Lord Montdore and Uncle Matthew disappeared together into
my uncle's business-room; Jassy, Victoria and I were left to goggle at each other
with eyes like saucers, struck dumb by this extraordinary incident. Before we had
time to begin speculating on what it could all mean, the Fuddler drove up, punctual
to the very minute.

'Damned fella,' Uncle Matthew said afterwards, 'if he hadn't been so late we
should have started by the time they arrived.'

He parked his little tinpot of a motor in line with the Daimler, and bustled, all
happy smiles, up to the front door. At his first visit he had gone modestly up the
back drive, but the success of his magic had so put Uncle Matthew on his side that
he had told him, in future, to come to the front door, and always gave him a glass
of port before starting work. He would no doubt have given him Imperial Tokay
if he had had any.

Jassy opened the door before the Fuddler had time to ring and then we all hung
about while he drank his port, saying 'Bitter, isn't it?' and not quite knowing what
to be at.

'His Lordship's not ill, I hope?' he said, surprised no doubt not to have found
my uncle champing up and down as usual, his choleric look clearing suddenly into
one of hearty welcome as he hurried to slap the Fuddler's back and pour out his
wine.

'No no, we think he'll be here in a moment. He's busy.'

'Not so like His Lordship to be late, is it?'

Presently a message came from Uncle Matthew that we were to go down to the
river and begin. It seemed too cruel to have the treat without him, but the fuddling
had, of course, to be concluded by daylight. So we shivered out of the house, into
the temporary shelter of the Fuddler's Standard and out again into the full blast
of a north wind which was cutting up the valley. While the Fuddler sprinkled his
stuff on the water we crept back into his car for warmth and began to speculate
on the reason for the extraordinary visit now in progress. We were simply dying
of curiosity.

'I guess the Government has fallen,' said Jassy.

'Why should that make Lady Montdore cry?'

'Well, who would do all her little things for her?'

'There'd soon be another lot for her to fag – Conservatives this time perhaps.
She really likes that better.'

'D'you think Polly is dead?'

'No no, they'd be mourning o'er her lovely corpse, not driving about in motor cars and seeing people.'

'Perhaps they've lost all their money and are coming to live with us,' said Victoria. This idea cast a regular gloom, seeming as it did rather a likely explanation. In those days, when people were so rich and their fortunes so infinitely secure, it was quite usual for them to think that they were on the verge of losing all their money, and the Radlett children had always lived under the shadow of the workhouse, because Uncle Matthew, though really very comfortably off with about £10,000 a year gross, had a financial crisis every two or three years and was quite certain in his own mind that he would end up on parish relief.

The Fuddler's work was done, his seed was sown and we got out of the motor with our landing-nets. This was a moment that never failed to thrill, the river banks were dotted with people all gazing excitedly into the water and very soon the poor fish began to squirm about the surface. I landed a couple of whales and then a smaller one, and just as I was shaking it out of the net a well-known voice behind me, quivering with passion, said,

'Put it back at once, you blasted idiot – can't you see it's a grayling, Fanny? O my God, women – incompetent – and isn't that my landing-net you've got there? I've been looking for it all over the place.'

I gave it up with some relief. Ten minutes at the water's edge was quite enough in that wind. Jassy was saying 'Look, look, they've gone', and there was the Daimler crossing the bridge, Lord Montdore sitting very upright in the back seat, bowing a little from side to side, almost like royalty. They overtook a butcher's van and I saw him lean forward and give the driver a gracious salute for having got out of the way. Lady Montdore was hardly visible, bundled up in her corner. They had gone, all right.

'Come on, Fanny,' said my cousins, downing tools, 'home, don't you think? Too cold here,' they shouted at their father, but he was busy cramming a giant chubb in its death throes into his hare pocket, and took no notice.

'And now,' said Jassy, as we raced up the hill, 'for worming it all out of Sadie.'

It was not, in fact, necessary to do any worming, Aunt Sadie was bursting with her news. She was more human and natural with her younger children than she had ever been with the elder ones. Her attitude of awe-inspiring vagueness, alternating with sudden fits of severity, which had combined with Uncle Matthew's rages to drive Louisa and Linda and the boys underground, so that their real lives were led in the Hons' cupboard, was very much modified with regard to Jassy and Victoria. She was still quite as vague, but never very severe, and far more companionable. She had always been inclined to treat her children as if they were all exactly the same age, and the younger ones were now benefiting from the fact that Louisa and Linda were married women who could be spoken to, and in front of, without reserve.

We found her and Davey in the hall, she was quite pink with interest, and as for Davey he was looking as much excited as if he had developed some fascinating new symptom.

'Come on,' said the children, question-marks all over their faces. 'Tell.'

'You'll never believe it,' said Aunt Sadie, addressing herself to me, 'Polly Hampton has informed her poor mother that she is going to marry Boy Dougdale. Her uncle, if you please! Did you ever hear such a thing? The wretched Patricia, not cold in her grave –'

'Well,' said Jassy, aside, 'cooling in this weather –'

'Miserable old man!' Aunt Sadie spoke in tones of deep indignation and was clearly a hundred per cent on Lady Montdore's side. 'You see, Davey, how right Matthew has been about him all these years?'

'Oh, poor Boy, he's not so bad,' Davey said, uncomfortably.

'I don't see how you can go on standing up for him after this, Davey.'

'But Sadie,' said Victoria. 'How can she marry him if he's her uncle?'

'Just exactly what I said. But it seems, with an uncle by marriage, that you can. Would you believe that anything so disgustingly dreadful could be allowed?'

'I say,' said Jassy. 'Come on, Dave.'

'Oh, no dear, thank you. Marry one of you demons? Not for any money!'

'What a law!' said Aunt Sadie, 'whenever was it passed? Why, it's the end of all family life, a thing like that.'

'Except it's the beginning for Polly.'

'Who told Lady Montdore?' Of course, I was fascinated. This key-piece of the jigsaw made everything quite clear, and now I could not imagine how I could ever have been so stupid as to have missed it.

'Polly told her,' said Aunt Sadie. 'It happened like this. They hadn't seen Boy since the funeral because he caught a bad cold at it and stayed indoors – Sonia got an awful cold there too and still has it, but he had spoken to Sonia every day on the telephone, as he always does. Well, yesterday they both felt a bit better and he went over to Hampton with the letters he'd had about poor Patricia from Infantas and things, and they had a good gloat over them, and then a long discussion about what to put on the tombstone. It seems they more or less settled on "She shall not grow old as we that are left grow old".'

'Stupid!' said Jassy. 'She had grown old already!'

'Old! A few years older than me,' said Davey.

'Well –!' said Jassy.

'That's enough, miss. Sonia says he seemed terribly low and unhappy, talking about Patricia and what she'd always been to him, and how empty the house seems without her – just what you'd expect after twenty-three years or something. Miserable old hypocrite! Well, he was supposed to stay for dinner, without dressing, because of his cold. Sonia and Lord Montdore went upstairs to change, and when Sonia came down again she found Polly, still in her day clothes, sitting on that white rug in front of the fire. She said, "What are you doing, Polly? it's very late. Go up and dress. Where's Boy then?" Polly got up and stretched herself and said, "He's gone home and I've got something to tell you. Boy and I are going to be married!" At first, of course, Sonia didn't believe it, but Polly never jokes as you know, and she very soon saw she was in deadly earnest, and then she was so furious she went sort of mad – how well I can understand that – and rushed at Polly and boxed her ears, and Polly gave her a great shove into an arm-chair and went upstairs. I imagine that Sonia was perfectly hysterical by then; anyway, she rang for her maid who took her up and put her straight to bed. Meanwhile, Polly dressed, came down again and calmly spent the evening with her father without saying a single word about it all to him, merely telling him that Sonia had a headache and wouldn't dine. So this morning poor Sonia had to tell him, she said it was terrible, because he so adores Polly. Then she tried to ring up Boy but the wretched coward has gone away, or pretends to have, leaving no address. Did you ever hear such a story?'

I was speechless with interest. Davey said,

'Personally, and speaking as an uncle, the one I feel for over all this is the unhappy Boy.'

'Oh, no, Davey, nonsense. Just imagine the Montdores' feelings – while they were trying to argue her out of it this morning she told them she'd been in love with him since before they went to India, when she was a little girl of fourteen.'

'Yes, very likely, but how do we know he wanted her to be in love with him? If you ask me I don't suppose he had the very faintest idea of it.'

'Come now, Davey, little girls of fourteen don't fall in love without any encouragement.'

'Alas, they do,' said Jassy, 'look at me and Mr Fosdyke. Not one word, not one kindly glance has he ever thrown me, and yet he is the light of my life.'

Mr Fosdyke was the local M.F.H.

I asked if Lady Montdore had had an inkling of all this before, knowing really quite well that she had not, as everything always came straight out with her and neither Polly nor Boy would have had one moment's peace.

'Simply no idea at all, it was a complete bolt from the blue. Poor Sonia, we know she has her faults but I can't think she has deserved this. She said Boy had always been very kind about taking Polly off her hands when they were in London, to the Royal Academy and so on, and Sonia was pleased because the child never seemed to have anybody to amuse her. Polly wasn't a satisfactory girl to bring out, you know. I'm very fond of her myself, I always have been, but you could see that Sonia was having a difficult time in many ways. Oh, poor Sonia, I do feel – now children, will you please go up and wash your fishy hands before tea?'

'This is the very limit, you're obviously going to say things while we're away. What about Fanny's fishy hands, then?'

'Fanny's grown-up, she'll wash her hands when she feels like it. Off you go.'

When they were safely out of the room she said, in horror, to Davey and me,

'Just imagine, Sonia, who had completely lost control of herself (not that I blame her), sort of hinted to me that Boy had once been her own lover.'

'Darling Sadie, you are such an innocent,' Davey said, laughing. 'It's a famous famous love affair which everybody except you has known all about for years. I sometimes think your children are right and you don't know the facts of life.'

'Well, all I can say is, I'm thankful I don't. How perfectly hateful. Do you think Patricia knew?'

'Of course she did and she was only too glad of it. Before his affair with Sonia began, Boy used to make Patricia chaperone all the dismal little débutantes that he fancied, and they would sob out broken hearts on her shoulder, and beg her to divorce him, very last thing he wanted, naturally. She had a lot of trouble with him, you know.'

'I remember a kitchen-maid,' Aunt Sadie said.

'Oh yes, it was one thing after another before Sonia took him on, but she had some control over him and Patricia's life became much easier and more agreeable, until her liver got so bad.'

'All the same,' I said, 'we know he still went for little girls, because look at Linda.'

'Did he?' said Aunt Sadie, 'I have sometimes wondered – Ugh! What a man! How you can think there's anything to be said for him, Davey, and how can you pretend he hadn't the faintest idea Polly was in love with him? If he made up to Linda like that, of course he must have done the same with her.'

'Well, Linda's not in love with him, is she? He can't be expected to guess that because he strokes the hair of a little girl when she's fourteen she's going to insist on marrying him when she grows up. Bad luck on a chap I call it.'

'Davey, you're hopeless! And if I didn't know quite well that you're only teasing me I should be very cross with you.'

'Poor Sonia,' said Davey. 'I feel for her, her daughter and her lover at a go – well, it often happens but it can't ever be very agreeable.'

'I'm sure it's the daughter she minds,' said Aunt Sadie, 'she hardly mentioned Boy, she was moaning and groaning about Polly, so perfectly beautiful, being thrown away like that. I should be just the same, I couldn't bear it for any of mine – that old fellow, they've known all their lives, and it's worse for her, Polly being the only one.'

'And such a treasure, so much the apple of their eye. Well, the more I see of life the more profoundly thankful I am not to have any children.'

'Between two and six they are perfect,' said my aunt, rather sadly I thought, 'after that I must say they are a worry, the funny little things. Then another horror for Sonia is wondering what went on all those years between Polly and Boy. She says last night she couldn't sleep for thinking of times when Polly pretended to have been to the hairdresser and obviously hadn't – that sort of thing – she says it's driving her mad.'

'It needn't,' I said firmly. 'I'm quite sure nothing ever happened. From various things I can remember Polly saying to me, I'm quite sure her love for the Lecturer must always have seemed hopeless to her. Polly's very good, you know, and she was very fond of her aunt.'

'I dare say you're right, Fanny. Sonia herself said that when she came down and found Polly sitting on the floor she thought at once "the girl looks as if she had been making love", and said she'd never seen her look like that before, flushed, her eyes simply huge and a curl of tousled hair hanging over her forehead – she was absolutely struck by her appearance, and then Polly told her –'

I could so well imagine the scene, Polly sitting, it was a very characteristic attitude with her, on the rug, getting up slowly, stretching, and then carelessly and gracefully implanting the cruel banderillas, the first movement of a fight that could only end in death.

'What I guess,' I said, 'is that he stroked a bit when she was fourteen and she fell in love then without him having any idea of it. Polly always bottles things up, and I don't expect anything more happened between them until the other evening.'

'Simply too dreadful,' said Aunt Sadie.

'Anyhow, Boy can't have expected to get engaged there and then, or he wouldn't have had all that talk about the Infanta's letter and the gravestone, would he?' said Davey. 'I expect what Fanny says is true.'

'You've been telling things – it is unfair – Fanny's hands are still foully fishy.' The children were back, out of breath.

'I do wonder what Uncle Matthew and Lord Montdore talked about in the business-room,' I said. I could not imagine such a tale being unfolded between those two, somehow.

'They topicked,' said Aunt Sadie. 'I told Matthew afterwards, I've never seen anybody so angry. But I haven't told you yet what it was that Sonia really came about. She's sending Polly here for a week or two.'

'No!' we all cried in chorus.

'Oh, the utter fascination!' said Jassy. 'But why?'

'Polly wants to come, it was her idea, and Sonia can't endure the sight of her for the present, which I can well understand. I must say I hesitated at first, but I am very fond of that little girl, you know, I really love her, and if she stays at home her mother will have driven her into an elopement within a week. If she comes here we might be able to influence her against this horrible marriage – and I don't mean you, children. You'll please try and be tactful for once in your lives.'

'I will be,' said Jassy, earnestly, 'it's dear little Vict. you must speak to, there's no tack in her, and personally I think it was a great mistake ever to have told her at all – ow – help – help – Sadie, she's killing me –'

'I mean both of you,' said Aunt Sadie, calmly, taking no notice whatever of the dog-fight in progress, 'you can talk about the chubb at dinner, that ought to be a safe subject.'

'What?' they said, stopping the fight, 'she's not coming today?'

'Yes, she is. After tea.'

'Oh, what a thrill. Do you think the Lecturer will have himself carried into the house dressed up as a sack of wood?'

'They shan't meet under my roof,' Aunt Sadie said firmly. 'I promised Sonia that, but of course, I pointed out that I can't control what Polly does elsewhere, I can only leave that to her own sense of what is in good taste, while she is staying with me.'

14

Polly soon made it clear that Aunt Sadie need have no misgivings about her behaviour while at Alconleigh. Her self-possession was complete, the only exterior indication that her life was at a crisis being an aura of happiness which transformed her whole aspect. Nothing she said or did was at all out of the usual or could have led anybody to suppose that she had recently been involved in scenes of such intensity, and it was obvious that she held no communication of any sort with Boy. She never went near the telephone, she did not sit all day scribbling letters, received very few, and none, so the children informed me, with a Silkin postmark; she hardly ever left the house and then only to get a breath of air with the rest of us, certainly not in order to go for long solitary walks which might end in lovers' meetings.

Jassy and Victoria, romantic like all the Radletts, found this incomprehensible and most disappointing. They had expected to be plunged into an atmosphere of light opera, and had supposed that the Lecturer would hang, sighing but hopeful, about the precincts, that Polly would hang, sighing but expectant, out of a moonlit window, to be united, and put on the first stage of their journey to Gretna Green, by the ingenuity and enterprise of their two young friends.

They lugged a mattress and stocks of food into the Hons' cupboard in case Boy wanted to hide there for a day or two. They had thought of everything, so they informed me, and were busy making a rope ladder. But Polly would not play.

'If you have any letters for the post, Polly, you know what I mean, a letter – we could easily run down to the village with it on our bikes.'

'Darling, you are kind, but they'll go just as quickly if I put them on the hall table, won't they?'

'Oh, of course, you can do that if you like, but everybody will read the envelope and I just thought – Or any messages? There's a telephone in the village post office, rather public, but you could talk in French.'

'I don't know French very well. Isn't there a telephone here?'

'Oh, it's a brute, extensions all over the place. Now there's a hollow tree in the park quite big enough for a man to hide in – quite dry and comfy – shall we show you?'

'You must, one day. Too cold to go out today, I think.'

'You know there's a frightfully nice little temple in a wood the other side of the river, would you like us to take you there?'

'Do you mean Faulkner's Folly, where they have the meets? But, Jassy, I know it quite well, I've often seen it. Very pretty.'

'What I really mean is the key is kept under a stone, and we could show you exactly where so that you could go inside.'

'There's nothing to see inside except cobwebs,' I said, 'it was never finished, you know.'

Jassy made a furious face at me. 'Tackless,' she muttered.

'Let's go there next summer, darlings,' said Polly, 'for a picnic. I can't enjoy anything out of doors in this weather, my eyes water too much.'

The children slouched away, discouraged.

Polly exploded with laughter. 'Aren't they too heavenly? But I don't really see the point of making all these great efforts to spend a few minutes with Boy in freezing cold temples, or to write to him about nothing at all when very soon I shall be with him for the whole rest of my life. Besides, I don't want to annoy Lady Alconleigh when she is being such an angel to have me here.'

Aunt Sadie herself, while applauding Polly's attitude, which relieved her of any need to worry, found it most unnatural.

'Isn't it strange,' she said, 'you can see by looking at her that she is very happy, but if it weren't for that nobody could guess that she was in love. My girls always get so moony, writing reams all day, jumping when the telephone bell rings and so on, but there's none of that with Polly. I was watching her last night when Matthew put *Che Gelida Manina* on the gramophone, she didn't look a bit sentimental. Do you remember what an awful time we had with Linda when Tony was in America – never out of floods?'

But Polly had been brought up in a harder school for the emotions than had the

Radletts, with a mother determined to find out everything that was in her mind and to mould her very thoughts to her own wishes. One could only admire the complete success with which she had countered both of these aims. Clearly her character had a steely quality incomprehensible to my cousins, blown hither and thither as they were upon the winds of sentiment.

I managed to have a few long talks alone with Polly at this time, but it was not very easy. Jassy and Victoria hardly left us for a single minute, so frightened were they of missing something; furthermore, they were shameless eavesdroppers, while hair-brushing chats at bedtime were ruled out by the fact of my so recent marriage. Mercifully the children went riding every day, when an hour or so of peace could be counted on; there was no hunting just then because of foot-and-mouth disease.

Gradually the whole thing came out. Polly's reserve, it is true, never really broke down, but every now and then the landscape was illuminated and its character exposed to view by flashes of startling frankness. It all seemed to have been very much as we had thought. For instance, I said to her something about when Boy proposed and she replied, quite carelessly,

'Oh, Boy never proposed to me at all, I don't think he ever would have, being that kind of a person – I mean, so wonderfully unselfish and thinking that it matters for me not being left things in wills and all that rubbish. Besides, he knows Mummy so well and he knew just what a hullaballoo she would make – he couldn't face it for me. No no, I always realized that I should have to do the proposing, and I did. It wasn't very difficult.'

So Davey was right, no doubt. The idea of such a marriage would never have entered the Lecturer's head if it had not been put there by Polly herself. After that it would clearly have been beyond flesh and blood to resist such a prize, greatest beauty and greatest heiress of her generation, potential mother of the children, the little half-Hamptons, he had always longed for. He could never have said no once it all lay at his feet waiting to be pocketed.

'After all, I've loved him ever since I can remember. Oh, Fanny – isn't being happy wonderful?'

I felt just the same myself and was able to agree with all my heart. But her happiness had a curiously staid quality, and her love seemed less like the usual enchanted rapture of the young girl, newly engaged, than a comfortable love of old establishment, love which does not need to assert itself by continually meeting, corresponding with and talking about its object, but which takes itself, as well as his response, for granted. The doubts and jealousies which can be so painful and make a hell almost of a budding love affair did not seem to have occurred to Polly, who took the simple view that she and Boy had hitherto been kept apart by one insuperable barrier, and that this barrier having been removed, the path to lifelong bliss lay at their feet.

'What can it matter if we have a few more weeks of horrid waiting when we are going to live together all the rest of our lives and be buried in the same grave?'

'Fancy being buried in the same grave with the Lecturer,' Jassy said, coming into my bedroom before luncheon.

'Jassy, I think it's too awful the way you listen at doors.'

'Don't tease, Fan, I intend to be a novelist (child novelist astounds the critics), and I'm studying human nature like mad.'

'I really ought to tell Aunt Sadie.'

'That's it. Join the revereds, now you are married, just like Louisa. No, but seriously Fanny, think of sharing a grave with that old Lecturer, isn't it disgusting? And anyway, what about Lady Patricia?'

'Well, she's nice and snug in one all to herself, lined with heather. She's quite all right.'

'I think it's shocking.'

Meanwhile, Aunt Sadie was doing what she could to influence Polly, but as she was much too shy to speak to her directly on such intimate subjects as sex and marriage she used an oblique method of letting fall an occasional reflection, hoping that Polly would apply it to her own particular case.

'Always remember, children, that marriage is a very intimate relationship, it's not just sitting and chatting to a person, there are other things, you know.'

Boy Dougdale, to her, was physically repulsive, as I think he generally was to those women who did not find him irresistible, and she thought that if Polly could be brought to a realization of the physical aspect of marriage she might be put off him for good.

As Jassy very truly observed, however, 'Isn't Sadie a scream, she simply doesn't realize that what put Polly on the Lecturer's side in the first place must have been all those dreadful things he did to her, like he once tried to with Linda and me, and that now what she really wants most in the world is to roll and roll and roll about with him in a double bed.'

'Yes, poor Sadie, she's not too hot on psychology,' said Victoria. 'Now I should say the only hope of curing Polly's uncle-fixation is to analyse her. Shall we see if she'd let us try?'

'Children, I absolutely forbid you to,' I said firmly, 'and if you do I promise I'll tell Aunt Sadie about the eavesdropping, so there.'

I knew what dreadful questions they would ask Polly and that as she was rather prim she would be shocked and angry. They were very much taken up at this time with the study and practice of psycho-analysis. They got hold of a book on the subject ('Elliston's library, would you believe it?') and several days of peace ensued while they read it out to each other in the Hons' cupboard, after which they proceeded to action.

'Come and be analysed,' was their parrot cry. 'Let us rid you of the poison that is clogging your mental processes, by telling you all about yourselves. Now, suppose we begin with Fa, he's the simplest proposition in the house.'

'What d'you mean, simple?'

'ABC to us. No no, not your hand you dear old thing, we've grown out of palmistry ages ago, this is science.'

'All right, let's hear it.'

'Well, so then you're a very straightforward case of frustration – wanted to be a gamekeeper, were obliged to be a lord – followed, as is usual, by the development of over-compensation so that now you're a psycho-neurotic of the obsessive and hysterical type engrafted on to a paranoid and schizoid personality.'

'Children, you are not to say these things about your father.'

'Scientific truths are nothing to object to, Sadie, and in our experience everybody enjoys learning about themselves. Would you care for us to test your intelligence level with an ink blot, Fa?'

'What's that?'

'We could do it to you all in turn and mark you if you like. It's quite easy, you show the subject an ordinary blot of ink on white paper, and, according to the picture it makes for each individual (you understand what I mean, does it look like a spider, or the Himalayas, everybody sees something different), a practised questioner can immediately assess his intelligence level.'

'Are you practised questioners?'

'Well, we've practised on each other and all the Joshes and Mrs Aster. And we've noted the results in our scientific notebook, so come on.'

Uncle Matthew gazed at the blot for a while and then said that it looked to him very much like an ordinary ink blot, and reminded him of nothing so much as Stephens' Blue-Black.

'It's just as I had feared,' said Jassy, 'and shows a positively sub-human level – even Baby Josh did better than that. Oh, dear, sub-human, that's bad –'

Jassy had now overstepped the boundary in the perpetual game of Tom Tiddler's Ground that she played with her father. He roared at her in a sudden rage and sent her to bed. She went off chanting 'paranoid *and* schizoid, paranoid *and* schizoid' which had taken the place of 'Man's long agony'. She said to me afterwards, 'Of course, it's rather grave for all of us because, whether you believe in heredity or environment, either way we are boiled, shut up here with this old sub-human of a father.'

Davey now decided that it would be only kind to go over and see his old friend Lady Montdore, so he rang her up and was invited to luncheon. He stayed until after tea, and by good luck when he got back Polly was lying down in her bedroom, so he was able to tell all.

'She is in a rage,' he said, 'a rage. Simply frightening. She has taken what the French call a *coup de vieux*; she looks a hundred. I wouldn't care to be hated by anyone as much as she hates Boy. After all, you never know, there may be something in Christian Science; evil thoughts and so on, directed at us with great intensity, may affect the body. How she hates him. Just imagine, she has cut out the tapestry he made for that fire-screen, quite roughly, with a pair of scissors, and the screen is still there in front of the fire with an enormous hole in it. It gave me quite a shock.'

'Poor Sonia, how like her, somehow. And what does she feel about Polly?'

'She mourns her, and she's pretty cross with her, too, for being so underhand and keeping it a secret all these years. I said, "You really couldn't expect that she would tell you?" but she didn't agree. She asked me a lot of questions about Polly and her state of mind. I was obliged to say that her state of mind is not revealed to me, but that she is looking twice as pretty as before, if possible, so it can therefore be presumed that she is happy.'

'Yes, you can always tell by that, with girls,' said Aunt Sadie. 'If it weren't for that I wouldn't have thought she cared a bit, one way or the other. What a strange character she must have, after all.'

'Not so strange,' said Davey. 'Many women are rather enigmatic, and very few laugh when they are happy and cry when they are sad to the extent that your children do, my dear Sadie, nor do we all see everything in black and white. Life is over-simplified at Alconleigh, it's part of the charm and I'm not complaining, but you mustn't suppose that all human beings are exactly like Radletts, because it is not so.'

'You stayed very late.'

'Poor Sonia, she's lonely. She must be, dreadfully, if you come to think of it. We talked about nothing else, too, round and round the subject, every aspect of it. She asked me to go over and see Boy to find out if there's any hope of his giving up the idea and going abroad for a bit. She says Montdore's lawyer has written and told him that the day Polly marries him she will be completely cut out of her father's will and also Montdore will stop Patricia's allowance, which he was intending to give Boy for his life. Even so, she fears they will have enough to live on, but it might shake him, I suppose. I didn't promise to go, but I think perhaps I will, all the same.'

'Oh, but you must,' said Jassy. 'There's us to consider.'

'Children, do stop interrupting,' said Aunt Sadie. 'If you can't hold your tongues you will have to leave the room when we are having serious conversations – in fact,' she said, becoming strict all of a sudden, just as she used to be when Linda and I were little, 'I think you'd better go now. Go on, off with you.'

They went. As they reached the door Jassy said in a loud aside,

'This labile and indeterminate attitude to discipline may do permanent damage to our young psychology. I really think Sadie should be more careful.'

'Oh, no, Jassy,' Victoria said, 'after all, it's our complexes that make us so fascinating and unusual.'

When they had shut the door Davey said rather seriously,

'You know, Sadie, you do spoil them.'

'Oh, dear,' said Aunt Sadie, 'I'm afraid so. It comes of having so many children. One can force oneself to be strict for a few years, but after that it becomes too much of an effort. But Davey, do you honestly imagine it makes the smallest difference when they are grown-up?'

'Probably not to your children, demons one and all. But look how well we brought up Fanny.'

'Davey! You were never strict,' I said, 'not the least bit. You spoilt me quite completely.'

'Yes, now that's true,' said Aunt Sadie. 'Fanny was allowed to do all sorts of dreadful things – especially after she came out. Powder her nose, travel alone, go in cabs with young men – didn't she once go to a night club? Fortunately for you, she seems to have been born good, though why she should have been, with such parents, is beyond me.'

Davey told Polly that he had seen her mother but she merely said,

'How was Daddy?'

'In London, House of Lords, something about India. Your mother doesn't look at all well, Polly.'

'Temper,' said Polly, and left the room.

Davey's next visit was to Silkin. 'Frankly, I can't resist it.' He bustled off in his little motor car on the chance of finding the Lecturer at home. He still refused to come to the telephone, giving out that he was away for a few weeks, but all other evidence pointed to the fact that he was living in his house, and indeed this now proved to be the case.

'Puzzled and lonely, and gloomy, poor old boy, and he's still got an awful cold he can't get rid of. Sonia's evil thoughts, perhaps. He has aged, too. Says he has seen nobody since his engagement to Polly – of course, he has cut himself off at Silkin but he seems to think that the people he has run into, at the London Library and so on, have been avoiding him as if they already knew about it. I expect it's really because he's in mourning – or perhaps they don't want to catch his cold – anyway, he's fearfully sensitive on the subject. Then he didn't say so, but you can see how much he is missing Sonia – naturally, after seeing her every day all these years. Missing Patricia too, I expect.'

'Did you talk quite openly about Polly?' I asked.

'Oh, quite. He says the whole thing originated with her, wasn't his idea at all.'

'Yes, that's true. She told me that herself.'

'And if you ask me, it shocks him dreadfully. He can't resist it, of course, but it shocks him, and he fully expects to be a social outcast as the result. Now that would have been the card for Sonia to have played, if she had been clever enough to foresee it all. Too late once the words were spoken, of course, but if she could have warned Boy what was likely to happen and then rubbed in about how that would finish him for ever in the eyes of society, I think she might have stopped it. After all he's frightfully social, poor chap. He would hate to be ostracized. As a matter of fact, though I didn't say so to him, people will come round in no time once they are married.'

'But you don't really think they will marry?' said Aunt Sadie.

'My dear Sadie, after ten days in the same house with Polly, I don't doubt it for one single instant. What's more, Boy knows he's in for it all right whether he likes it or not – and of course he half likes it very much indeed. But he dreads the consequences, not that there'll be any. People have no memory about that sort of thing, and after all, there's nothing to forget except bad taste.'

'*Détournement de jeunesse?*'

'It won't occur to the ordinary person that Boy could have made a pass at Polly when she was little, we would never have thought of it except for what he did to Linda. In a couple of years nobody outside the family will even remember what all the fuss was about.'

'I'm afraid you're right,' said my aunt. 'Look at the Bolter! Ghastly scandal after ghastly scandal, elopements, horse-whippings, puts herself up as a prize in a lottery, cannibal kings – I don't know what all – headlines in the papers, libel actions, and yet she only has to appear in London and her friends queue up to give parties for her. But don't encourage Boy by telling him. Did you suggest he might chuck it and go abroad?'

'Yes, I did, but it's no good. He misses Sonia, he is horrified in a way by the whole thing, hates the idea of his money being stopped, though he's not penniless himself, you know, he's got an awful cold and is down in the dumps, but at the same time you can see that the prospect dazzles him, and as long as Polly makes all the running, I bet you he'll play. Oh, dear, fancy taking on a new young wife at our age – how exhausting. Boy, too, who is cut out to be a widower, I do pity him.'

'Pity him indeed! All he had to do was to leave little girls alone.'

'You're so implacable, Sadie. It's a heavy price to pay for a bit of cuddling – I wish you could see the poor chap –!'

'Whatever does he do with himself all the time?'

'He's embroidering a counterpane,' said Davey, 'it's his wedding present for Polly. He calls it a bedspread.'

'Oh, really!' Aunt Sadie shuddered. 'He is the most dreadful man! Better not tell Matthew – in fact, I wouldn't tell him you've been over at all. He nearly has a fit every time he thinks of Boy now, and I don't blame him. Bedspread indeed!'

15

Soon after this Polly announced to Aunt Sadie that she would like to go to London the following day, as she had an appointment there with Boy. We were sitting alone with Aunt Sadie in her little room. Although it was the first time that Polly had mentioned her uncle's name to anybody at Alconleigh, except me, she brought it out not only without a tremor of self-consciousness but as though she spoke of him all and every day. It was an admirable performance. There was a pause. Aunt Sadie was the one who blushed and found it difficult to control her voice, and when at last she replied it did not sound natural at all, but hard and anxious.

'Would you care to tell me what your plans are, Polly?'

'Please – to catch the 9.30 if it's convenient.'

'No, I don't mean your plans for tomorrow, but for your life.'

'You see, that's what I must talk about, with Boy. Last time I saw him we made no plans, we simply became engaged to be married.'

'And this marriage, Polly dear – your mind is made up?'

'Yes, quite. So I don't see any point in all this waiting. As we are going to be married whatever happens, what can it matter when? In fact, there is every reason why it should be very soon now. It's out of the question for me to go and live with my mother again and I can't foist myself on you indefinitely. You've been much too kind as it is.'

'Oh, my darling child, don't give that a thought. It never matters having people here so long as Matthew likes them. Look at Davey and Fanny, they're in no hurry to go, they know quite well we love having them.'

'Oh, yes, I know, but they are family.'

'So are you, almost, and quite as welcome as if you were. I have got to go to London in a few weeks, as you know, for Linda's baby, but that needn't make any difference to you, and you must stay on for as long as ever you like. There'll be Fanny, and when Fanny goes there are the children – they worship you, you are their heroine, it's wonderful for them having you here. So don't think about that again. Don't, for heaven's sake, rush into marriage because you think you have nowhere to live, because for one thing it's not the case at all, since you can live here, and anyhow, it could never be a sufficient reason for taking such a grave step.'

'I'm not rushing,' said Polly. 'It's the only marriage I could ever have made, and if it had continued to be impossible I should have lived and died a spinster.'

'Oh, no you wouldn't,' said Aunt Sadie, 'you've no idea how long life goes on and how many many changes it brings. Young people seem to imagine that it's over in a flash, that they do this thing, or that thing, and then die, but I can assure you they are quite wrong. I suppose it's no good saying this to you, Polly, as I can see your mind is made up, but since you have the whole of your life before you as a married woman why not make the most of being a girl? You'll never be one again. You're only twenty. Why be in such a hurry to change?'

'I hate being a girl, I've hated it ever since I grew up,' said Polly, 'and besides, do you really think a lifetime is too long for perfect happiness? I don't.'

Aunt Sadie gave a profound sigh.

'I wonder why it is that all girls suppose the married state to be one of perfect happiness? Is it just clever old Dame Nature's way of hurrying them into the trap?'

'Dear Lady Alconleigh, don't be so cynical.'

'No no, you are quite right, I mustn't be. You've settled upon your future and nothing anybody can say will stop you, I'm sure, but I must tell you that I think you are making a terrible mistake. There, I won't say another word about it. I'll order the car for the 9.30, and will you be catching the 4.45 back or the 6.10?'

'Four forty-five please. I told Boy to meet me at the Ritz at one – I sent him a postcard yesterday.'

And by a miracle the said postcard had lain about all day on the hall table without either Jassy or Victoria spotting it. Hunting had begun again, and although they were only allowed out three times a fortnight the sheer physical exhaustion which it induced did a great deal towards keeping their high spirits within bounds. As for Uncle Matthew, who went out four days a week, he hardly opened an eye after tea-time, but nodded away standing up in his business-room, with the gramophone blaring his favourite tunes. Every few minutes he gave a great jump and rushed to change the needle and the disc.

That evening, before dinner, Boy rang up. We were all in the business-room listening to *Lakmé* on the gramophone, new records which had just arrived from the Army and Navy Stores. My uncle ground his teeth when the temple bells were interrupted by a more penetrating peal, and gnashed them with anger when he heard Boy's voice asking for Polly, but he handed her the receiver and pushed up a chair for her with the old-fashioned courtesy which he used towards those he liked. He never treated Polly as if she were a very young person and I believe he was really rather in awe of her.

Polly said 'Yes? Oh? Very well. Good-bye' and hung up the receiver. Even this ordeal had done nothing to shake her serenity.

She told us that Boy had changed the rendezvous, saying he thought it was pointless to go all the way to London, and suggesting the Mitre in Oxford as a more convenient meeting-place.

'So perhaps we could go in together, Fanny darling.'

I was going, anyhow, to visit my house.

'Ashamed of himself,' said Davey, when Polly had gone upstairs. 'Doesn't want to be seen. People are beginning to talk. You know how Sonia can never keep a secret, and once the Kensington Palace set gets hold of something it is all round London in a jiffy.'

'Oh, dear,' said Aunt Sadie, 'but if they are seen at the Mitre it will look far worse.'

I feel rather worried, I only promised Sonia they shouldn't meet here, but ought I to tell her? What do you think?'

'Shall I go over to Silkin and shoot the sewer?' said Uncle Matthew, half asleep.

'Oh, no, darling, please don't. What do you think, Davey?'

'Don't you worry about the old she-wolf – good Lord, who cares a brass button for her?'

If Uncle Matthew had not hated Boy so much he would have been quite as eager as his daughters were to aid and abet Polly in any enterprise that would fly in the face of Lady Montdore.

Davey said, 'I wouldn't give it a thought. It so happens that Polly has been perfectly open and above-board about the whole thing – but suppose she hadn't told you? She's always going into Oxford with Fanny, isn't she? I should turn the blind eye.'

So in the morning Polly and I motored to Oxford together, and I lunched, as I often did, with Alfred at the George. (If I never mention Alfred in this story it is because he is so totally uninterested in other human beings and their lives that I think he was hardly aware of what was going on. He certainly did not enter into it with fascination like the rest of us. I suppose that I and his children and perhaps an occasional clever pupil seem real to him, but otherwise he lives in a world of shadows and abstract thought.)

After luncheon I spent a freezing, exhausting, and discouraging hour in my little house, which seemed hopelessly haunted by builders. I noted, with something like despair, that they had now made one of the rooms cosy, a regular home from home, with blazing fire, stewing tea, and filmstars on the walls. As far as I could see they never left it at all to ply their trade, and indeed, I could hardly blame them for that, so terrible were the damp and cold in the rest of the house. After a detailed inspection with the foreman which merely revealed more exposed pipes and fewer floor-boards than last time I had been there, I went to the window of what was supposed to be my drawing-room to fortify myself with the view of Christ Church, so beautiful against the black clouds. One day, I thought (it was an act of faith), I would sit by that very window, open wide, and there would be green trees and a blue sky behind the college. I gazed on, through glass which was almost opaque with dirt and whitewash, forcing myself to imagine that summer season, when, battling their way down the street, the east wind in their faces, Polly and the Lecturer appeared to view. It was not a happy picture, but that may have been the fault of the climate. No aimless dalliance hand in hand beneath warm skies for poor English lovers who, if circumstances drive them to making love out-of-doors, are obliged to choose between the sharp brisk walk and the stupefying stuffiness of the cinema. They stumped on out of my sight, hands in pockets, heads bowed, and plunged, one would have said, in gloom.

Before going home I paid a visit to Woolworth's, having been enjoined by Jassy to get her a goldfish bowl for her frog spawn. She had broken hers the day before and had only got the precious jelly to the spare-room bath just in time, she said, to save it. Alfred and I were obliged to use the nursery bathroom until Jassy got a new bowl. 'So you see how it's to your own advantage, Fanny, not to forget.'

Once inside Woolworth's I found other things that I needed, as one always does, and presently I ran into Polly and Boy. He was holding a mouse-trap, but I think it was shelter from the wind that they really sought.

'Home soon?' said Polly.

'Now, d'you think?' I was dead tired.

'Do let's.'

So we all three went to the Clarendon Yard, where our respective motor cars were waiting. The Lecturer still had a terrible cold, which made him most unappetizing, I thought, and he seemed very grumpy. When he took my hand to say good-bye he gave it no extra squeeze, nor did he stroke and tickle our legs when tucking us up in the rug, which he would certainly have done had he been in a normal state, and when we drove off he just walked gloomily away with no backward glance, jaunty wave or boyish shake of the curls. He was evidently at a low ebb.

Polly leaned forward, wound up the window between us and the chauffeur and said,

'Well, everything's settled, thank goodness. A month from today if I can get my parents' consent – I shall still be under age, you see. So the next thing is a tussle with Mummy. I'll go over to Hampton tomorrow if she's there and point out that I shall be of age in May, after which she won't be able to stop me, so hadn't she better swallow the pill and have done with it. They won't be wanting to have birthday celebrations for me now since in any case Daddy is cutting me off with a shilling.'

'Do you think he really will?'

'As if I cared! The only thing I mind about is Hampton and he can't leave me that even if he wants to. Then I shall say "Do you intend to put a good face on it and let me be married in the chapel (which Boy terribly wants for some reason, and I would rather like it, I must say), or must we sneak off and be done in London?" Poor Mummy. Now I'm out of her clutches I feel awfully sorry for her in a way. I think the sooner it's over the better for everybody.'

Boy, it was clear, was still leaving all the dirty work to Polly. Perhaps his cold was sapping his will-power, or perhaps the mere thought of a new young wife at his age was exhausting him already.

So Polly rang up her mother and asked if she could lunch at Hampton the following day and have a talk. I thought it would have been more sensible to have had the talk without the additional strain imposed by a meal, but Polly seemed unable to envisage a country house call which did not centre round food. Perhaps she was right, since Lady Montdore was very greedy and therefore more agreeable during and after meals than at other times. In any case, this is what she suggested; she also told her mother to send a motor as she did not like to ask the Alconleighs for one two days running. Lady Montdore said very well, but that she must bring me. Lord Montdore was still in London and I suppose she felt she could not bear to see Polly alone. Anyhow, she was one of those people who always avoid a *tête-à-tête* if possible, even with their intimates. Polly said to me that she herself had just been going to ask if I could come too.

'I want a witness,' she added, 'if she says yes in front of you she won't be able to wriggle out of it again later.'

Poor Lady Montdore, like Boy, was looking very much down; not only old and ill (like Boy, she was still afflicted with Lady Patricia's funeral cold which seemed to have been a specially virulent germ), but positively dirty. The fact that she had never, at the best of times, been very well-groomed, had formerly been offset by her flourish and swagger, radiant health, enjoyment of life, and the inward assurance of superiority bestowed upon her by 'all this'. These supports had been cut away by her cold as well as by the simultaneous defection of Polly, which must have taken much of the significance out of 'all this', and of Boy, her constant companion, the last lover, surely, that she would ever have. Life, in fact, had become sad and meaningless.

We began luncheon in silence. Polly turned her food over with a fork, Lady Montdore refused the first dish, while I munched away rather self-consciously alone, enjoying the change of cooking. Aunt Sadie's food, at that time, was very plain. After a glass or two of wine, Lady Montdore cheered up a bit and began to chat. She told us that the dear Grand Duchess had sent her such a puddy postcard from Cap d'Antibes, where she was staying with other members of the Imperial family. She remarked that the Government really ought to make more effort to attract such important visitors to England.

'I was saying so only the other day to Ramsay,' she complained. 'And he quite agreed with me, but of course, one knows nothing will be done, it never is in this hopeless country. So annoying. All the Rajahs are at Suvretta House again – the King of Greece has gone to Nice – the King of Sweden has gone to Cannes and the young Italians are doing winter sports. Perfectly ridiculous not to get them all here.'

'Whatever for,' said Polly, 'when there's no snow?'

'Plenty in Scotland. Or teach them to hunt, they'd love it, they only want encouraging a little.'

'No sun,' I said.

'Never mind. Make it the fashion to do without sun and they'll all come here. They came for my ball and Queen Alexandra's funeral – they love a binge, poor dears. The Government really ought to pay one to give a ball every year, it would restore confidence and bring important people to London.'

'I can't see what good all these old royalties do when they are here,' said Polly.

'Oh, yes, they do, they attract Americans and so on,' said Lady Montdore, vaguely. 'Always good to have influential people around you know, good for a private family and also good for a country. I've always gone in for them myself and I can tell you it's a very great mistake not to. Look at poor dear Sadie, I've never heard of anybody important going to Alconleigh.'

'Well,' said Polly, 'and what harm has it done her?'

'Harm! You can see the harm all round. First of all the girls' husbands' – on this point Lady Montdore did not lean, suddenly remembering no doubt her own situation in respect of daughters' husbands, but continued, 'Poor Matthew has never got anything, has he – I don't only mean jobs, but not even a V.C. in the war and goodness knows he was brave enough. He may not be quite cut out to be a Governor, I grant you that, especially not where there are black people, but don't tell me there's nothing he could have got, if Sadie had been a little cleverer about it. Something at Court, for instance. It would have calmed him down.'

The idea of Uncle Matthew at Court made me choke into my pancake, but Lady Montdore took no notice and went on,

'And now I'm afraid it will be the same story with the boys. I'm told they were sent to the very worst house at Eton because Sadie had nobody to advise her or help her at all when the time came for them to go there. One must be able to pull strings in life, everything depends on that in this world, I'm afraid, it's the only way to be successful. Luckily for me, I like important people best and I get on with them like a house on fire, but even if they bored me I should have thought it my duty to cultivate them, for Montdore's sake.'

When we had finished our meal and installed ourselves in the Long Gallery, the butler brought in a coffee tray which Lady Montdore told him to leave. She always had several cups of strong black coffee. As soon as he had gone she turned to Polly and said sharply, 'So what is it you want to say to me?'

I made a half-hearted attempt to go, but they both insisted on me staying. I knew they would.

'I want to be married in a month from now,' said Polly, 'and to do that I must have your consent as I'm not of age until May. It seems to me that as it is only a question of nine weeks, when I shall marry anyhow, you might as well agree and get it over, don't you think?'

'I must say that's very puddy – your poor aunt – when the breath has hardly left her body.'

'It doesn't make the slightest difference to Aunt Patricia whether she has been dead three months or three years so let's leave her out of it. The facts are what they are. I can't live at Alconleigh much longer, I can't live here with you, hadn't I better start my new life as soon as possible?'

'Do you quite realize, Polly, that the day you marry Boy Dougdale your father is going to alter his will?'

'Yes, yes, yes,' said Polly impatiently, 'the times you've told me!'

'I've only told you once before.'

'I've had a letter about it, Boy has had a letter about it. We know.'

'I wonder whether you also know that Boy Dougdale is a very poor man? They lived, really, on Patricia's allowance, which, of course, in the ordinary way your father would have continued during Boy's lifetime. That will also stop if he marries you.'

'Yes. It was all in the letters.'

'And don't count on your father changing his mind because I've no intention of allowing him to.'

'I'm quite sure you haven't.'

'You think it doesn't matter being poor, but I wonder if you realize what it is like.'

'The one who doesn't realize,' said Polly, 'is you.'

'Not from experience I'm glad to say, but from observation I do. One's only got to look at the hopeless, dreary expression on the faces of poor people to see what it must be.'

'I don't agree at all, but anyhow, we shan't be poor like poor people. Boy has £800 a year, besides what he makes from his books.'

'The parson here and his wife have £800 a year,' said Lady Montdore. 'And look at their faces –!'

'They were born with those – I did better, thanks to you. In any case, Mummy, it's no good going on and on arguing about it, because everything is as much settled as if we were married already, so it's just pure waste of time.'

'Then why have you come? What do you want me to do?'

'First, I want to have the wedding next month, for which I need your consent, and then I also want to know what you and Daddy prefer about the actual marriage ceremony itself – shall we be married here in the chapel or shall I go off without you to London for it? We naturally don't want anybody to be there except Fanny and Lady Alconleigh, and you, if you'd care to come. I must say I would love to be given away by Daddy –'

Lady Montdore thought for a while, and finally said, 'I think it is quite intolerable of you to put us in this position and I shall have to talk it over with Montdore, but frankly, I think that if you intend to go through with this indecent marriage at all costs, it will make the least talk if we have it here, and before your birthday. Then I shan't have to explain why there are to be no coming-of-age celebrations, the tenants have begun asking about that already. So I think you may take it that you can have the marriage here, and next month, after which, you incestuous little trollop, I never want to set eyes on either you or your uncle again, as long as I live. And please don't expect a wedding present from me.'

Tears of self-pity were pouring down her cheeks. Perhaps she was thinking of the magnificent parure in its glass case against which, had things been otherwise, so many envious noses would have been pressed during the wedding reception at Montdore House. 'From the Bride's Parents.' Her dream of Polly's wedding, long and dearly cherished, had ended in a sad awakening indeed.

'Don't cry, Mummy, I'm so very very happy.'

'Well, I'm not,' said Lady Montdore, and rushed furiously from the room.

16

Exactly one month later, Davey, Aunt Sadie and I drove over to Hampton together for the wedding, our ears full of the lamentations of Jassy and Victoria who had not been invited.

'Polly is a horrible Counter-Hon and we hate her,' they said, 'after we made our fingers bleed over that rope ladder, not to speak of all the things we would have done for her, smuggling the Lecturer up to the Hons' cupboard, sharing our food with him – no risk we wouldn't have taken to give them a few brief moments of happiness together, only they were too cold-blooded to want it, and now she doesn't even ask us to the wedding. Do admit, Fanny.'

'I don't blame her for a single minute,' I said, 'a wedding is a very serious thing, naturally she doesn't want gusts of giggles the whole way through it.'

'And did we gust at yours?'

'I expect so, only it was a bigger church and more people, and I didn't hear you.'

Uncle Matthew on the other hand was asked, and said that nothing would induce him to accept.

'Wouldn't be able to keep my hands off the sewer,' he said. 'Boy!' he went on, scornfully, 'there's one thing, you'll hear his real name at last, just note it down for me please, I've always wanted to know what it is, to put in a drawer.'

It was a favourite superstition of Uncle Matthew's that if you wrote somebody's name on a piece of paper and put it in a drawer, that person would die within the year. The drawers at Alconleigh were full of little slips bearing the names of those whom my uncle wanted out of the way, private hates of his and various public figures such as Bernard Shaw, de Valera, Gandhi, Lloyd George, and the Kaiser, while every single drawer in the whole house contained the name Labby, Linda's old dog. The spell hardly ever seemed to work, even Labby having lived far beyond the age usual in Labradors, but he went hopefully on, and if one of the characters did happen to be carried off in the course of nature he would look pleased but guilty for a day or two.

'I suppose we must all have heard his name when he married Patricia,' Aunt Sadie said, looking at Davey, 'but I can't remember it, can you? Though I have an idea it was one of those surnames, Stanley, or Norman. Such a thousand thousand years ago. Poor Patricia, what can she be thinking now?'

'Was she married in the chapel at Hampton too?' I said.

'No, in London, and I'm trying to remember where. Lord Montdore and Sonia were married in the Abbey, of course. I well remember that, because Emily was a bridesmaid and I was so furiously jealous, and my Nanny took me, but outside because Mamma thought we would see more like that than if we were stuck away behind a tomb. It was like a royal wedding, almost. Of course, I was out by the time Patricia married – St Margaret's, Westminster, I think – yes, I'm nearly sure it was. I know we all thought she was awfully old for a white wedding, thirty or something terrible.'

'But she was beautiful,' said Davey.

'Very much like Polly, of course, but she never had that something extra, what-ever it is, that makes Polly such a radiant beauty. I only wish I knew why these lovely women have both thrown themselves away on that old Lecturer – so unnat-ural.'

'Poor Boy,' said Davey, with a deeply sympathetic sigh.

Davey, who had been in Kent with Aunt Emily since finishing his cure, had come back to Alconleigh in order to be best man. He had accepted, so he said, for poor Patricia's sake, but really, I think, because he longed to go to the wedding; he also very much enjoyed the excuse it gave him to bustle about between Silkin and Hampton and see for himself all that was going on in those two stricken homes.

Polly had gone back to Hampton. She had taken no steps whatever towards getting a trousseau, and as the engagement and wedding were to be announced simultaneously in *The Times*, 'took place very quietly, owing to deep mourning at Hampton Park' (all these little details arranged by Davey), she had no letters to write, no presents to unpack, and none of the business that usually precedes a wedding. Lord Montdore had insisted that she should have an interview with his lawyer, who came all the way from London to explain to her formally that every-thing hitherto set aside in her father's will, for her and her children, that is to say Montdore House, Craigside Castle and their contents, the property in Northum-berland with its coal mines, the valuable and extensive house property in London, one or two docks and about two million pounds sterling would now all go to her father's only male heir, Cedric Hampton. In the ordinary course of events, he would merely have inherited Hampton itself and Lord Montdore's titles, but as the result of this new will, Cedric Hampton was destined to be one of the five or six richest men in England.

'And how is Lord Montdore taking it?' Aunt Sadie asked Davey when he brought back this news from Hampton, via a visit to Boy at Silkin.

'Quite impossible to say. Sonia is wretched, Polly is nervous, but Montdore is just as usual. You couldn't guess that anything out of the ordinary was happening to him.'

'I always knew he was an old stick. Had you realized he was so rich, Davey?'

'Oh, yes, one of the very richest.'

'Funny when you think how stingy Sonia is, in little ways. How long d'you imagine he'll keep it up, cutting off Polly, I mean?'

'As long as Sonia is alive. I bet you she won't forgive, and, as you know, he is entirely under her thumb.'

'Yes. So what does Boy say to living with a wife, on £800 a year?'

'Doesn't like it. He talks of letting Silkin and to go to live somewhere cheap, abroad. I told him he'll have to write more books. He doesn't do so badly with them, you know, but he is very low, poor old fellow, very.'

'I expect it will do him good to get away,' I said.

'Well, yes,' said Davey expressively. 'But –'

'I do wonder what Cedric Hampton is like.'

'So do we all – Boy was talking about it just now. It seems they don't really know where he is even. The father was a bad lot and went to Nova Scotia, fell ill there and married his nurse, an elderly Canadian woman, who had this one child, but he (the father) is dead and nothing more is known except the bare fact that there is this boy. Montdore gives him some small allowance, paid into a Canadian bank every year. Don't you think it's very odd he hasn't taken more interest in him, considering he will have his name and is the only hope of this ancient family being carried on?'

'Probably he hated the father.'

'I don't believe he ever knew him. They are quite a different generation – second cousins once removed – something like that. No, I put it down to Sonia, I expect she couldn't bear the idea of Hampton going away from Polly and pretended to herself that this Cedric did not really exist – you know what a one she is for shutting her eyes to things she doesn't like. I should imagine she'll be obliged to face up to him now, Montdore is sure to want to see him under these new circumstances.'

'Sad, isn't it, the idea of some great lumping colonial at Hampton!'

'Simply tragic!' said Davey. 'Poor Montdores, I do feel for them.'

Somehow, the material side of the business had never been fully borne in upon me until Davey went into these facts and figures, but now I realized that 'all this' was indeed something tremendous to be so carelessly thrown into the lap of a total stranger.

When we arrived at Hampton, Aunt Sadie and I were shown straight into the chapel, where we sat alone. Davey went off to find Boy. The chapel was a Victorian building among the servants' quarters. It had been constructed by the 'old lord', and contained his marble effigy in Garter robes with that of Alice, his wife, some

bright stained glass, a family pew designed like a box at the opera, all red plush
with curtains, and a very handsome organ. Davey had engaged a first-class organist from Oxford, who now regaled us with some Bach preludes. None of the
interested parties seemed to have bothered to take a hand in any of the arrangements. Davey had chosen all the music and the gardener had evidently been left
to himself with the flowers, which were quite overwhelming in their magnificence,
the exaggerated hot-house flowers beloved of all gardeners, arranged with typical
florist's taste. I began to feel dreadfully sad. The Bach and the flowers induced
melancholy, besides, look at it as you would, this marriage was a depressing business.

Boy and Davey came up the aisle, and Boy shook hands with us. He had evidently
got rid of his cold, at last, and was looking quite well; his hair, I noticed, had received
the attention of a damp comb to induce little waves and a curl or two, and his
figure, not bad at all, especially from behind, was set off by his wedding clothes.
He wore a white carnation, and Davey a red one. But though he was in the costume
of a bridegroom, he had not the spirit to add this new part to his repertory with
any conviction and his whole attitude was more appropriate to a chief mourner.
Davey even had to show him where to stand, by the altar steps. I never saw a man
look so hopeless.

The clergyman took up his position, a very disapproving expression on his face.
Presently a movement at our left indicated that Lady Montdore had come into the
family pew, which had its own entrance. It was impossible to stare, but I could not
resist a glance and saw that she looked as if she were going to be sick. Boy also
glanced, after which his back view became eloquent of a desire to slink in beside
her and have a good long gossip. It was the first time he had seen her since they
had read the Infanta's letters together.

The organist from Oxford stopped playing Bach, which he had been doing with
less and less interest during the last few minutes, and paused. Looking round, I
saw that Lord Montdore was standing at the entrance to the chapel. He was impas-
sive, well-preserved, a cardboard earl, and might have been about to lead his
daughter up the aisle of Westminster Abbey to marry the King of England for all
that could be read into his look.

'O Perfect Love, All Human Thought Transcending' rang out, sung by an invisible choir in the gallery. And then, up the aisle, one large white hand on her father's
arm, dispelling the gloomy embarrassment which hung like a fog in the chapel,
came Polly, calm, confident, and noble, radiating happiness. Somehow, she had got
herself a wedding dress (did I recognize a ball dress of last season? No matter) and
was in a cloud of white tulle and lilies-of-the-valley and joy. Most brides have difficulty with their expression as they go to the altar, looking affected, or soulful, or,
worst of all, too eager, but Polly simply floated along on waves of bliss, creating
one of the most beautiful moments I have ever experienced.

There was a dry, choking sound on our left, the door of the family pew was
slammed, Lady Montdore had gone.

The clergyman began to intone the wedding service. 'Forasmuch,' and so on.
'Who giveth this woman to be married to this man?' Lord Montdore bowed, took
Polly's bouquet from her and went into the nearest pew.

'Please say after me, "I, Harvey, take thee, Leopoldina".' A look from Aunt Sadie.

It was soon over. One more hymn, and I was left alone while they all went behind a screen to sign the register. Then the burst of Mendelssohn and Polly floated out again as she had come, only on the arm of a different well-preserved old man.

While Polly and Boy changed into their going-away things we waited in the Long Gallery to say good-bye and see them off. They were motoring to the Lord Warden at Dover for the night, and going abroad the following day. I half expected that Polly would send for me to go upstairs and chat, but she did not, so I stayed with the others. I think she was so happy that she hardly noticed if people were with her or she was alone; perhaps she really preferred the latter. Lady Montdore put in no further appearance, Lord Montdore talked to Davey, congratulating him upon an anthology he had recently published, called *In Sickness and in Health*. I heard him say that, to his mind, there was not quite enough Browning, but that apart from that it would all have been his own choice.

'But Browning was so healthy,' objected Davey. The stress throughout the book was upon sickness.

A footman handed round glasses of champagne. Aunt Sadie and I settled down, as one always did, somehow, at Hampton, to a prolonged scrutiny of *Tatler*, *Sketch*, and *Bystander*, and Polly took so long that I even got on to *Country Life* before she appeared. Through my happy haze of baronets' wives, their children, their dogs, their tweeds and their homes, or just their huge faces, wave of hair on the forehead held by a diamond clip, I was conscious that the atmosphere in the Long Gallery, like that in the chapel, was one of embarrassment and gloom. When Boy reappeared, I saw him give a puzzled glance at the fire-screen with its jagged hole and then, as he realized what had happened to it, he turned his back on the room, and stood gazing out of the window. Nobody spoke to him. Lord Montdore and Davey sipped champagne, having exhausted the topic of the anthology, in silence.

At last Polly came in wearing her last year's mink coat and a tiny brown hat. Though the cloud of tulle had gone the cloud of joy still enveloped her, she was perfectly unselfconscious, hugged her father, kissed us all, including Davey, took Boy by the arm and led him to the front door. We followed. The servants, looking sad, and the older ones sniffing, were gathered in the hall, she said good-bye to them, had some rice thrown over her, rather half-heartedly, by the youngest house-maid, got into the big Daimler, followed, very half-heartedly, by Boy, and was driven away.

We said good-bye politely to Lord Montdore and followed suit. As we went up the drive I looked back. The footmen had already shut the front door, and it seemed to me that beautiful Hampton, between the pale spring green of its lawns and the pale spring blue of the sky, lay deserted, empty and sad. Youth had gone from it and henceforward it was to be the home of two lonely old people.

Part Two

I

My real life as a married woman, that is to say life with my husband in our own house, now began. One day I went to Oxford and a miracle seemed to have taken place. There was paper on all the walls of my house, the very paper I had chosen, too, and looking even prettier than I had hoped it would, the smell of cheap cigarettes, cement, stewed tea, and dry rot had gone, and in its place there was a heavenly smell of new paint and cleanliness, the floor boards were all smooth and solid, and the windows so clean that they seemed to be glassless. The day was perfect, spring had come and my home was ready; I felt too happy for words. To set the seal upon this happiness, the wife of a professor had called, her card and her husband's two cards had carefully been put by the workmen on a chimneypiece: Professor and Mrs Cozens, 209 Banbury Road. Now, at last, I was a proper grownup married lady on whom people called. It was very thrilling.

I had at this time a romantic but very definite picture in my mind of what life was going to be like in Oxford. I imagined a sort of Little Gidding, a community of delightful, busy, cultivated people, bound together by shared intellectual tastes and by their single-minded exertions on behalf of the youth entrusted to their care. I supposed that the other wives of dons would be beautiful, quiet women, versed in all the womanly arts but that of coquetry, a little worn with the effort of making a perfection of their homes at the same time as rearing large families of clever children, and keeping up with things like Kafka, but never too tired or too busy for long, serious discussions on subjects of importance, whether intellectual or practical. I saw myself, in the daytime, running happily in and out of the houses of these charming creatures, old houses with some important piece of architecture framed in the windows as Christ Church was in mine, sharing every detail of their lives, while the evenings would be spent listening to grave and scholarly talk between our husbands. In short I saw them as a tribe of heavenly new relations, more mature, more intellectual Radletts. This happy intimacy seemed to be heralded by the cards of Professor and Mrs Cozens. For one moment the fact that they lived in the Banbury Road struck a note of disillusionment, but then it occurred to me that of course the clever Cozenses must have found some little old house in that unpromising neighbourhood, some nobleman's folly, sole reminder of long-vanished pleasure grounds, and decided to put up with the Banbury Road for the sake of its doorways and cornices, the rococo detail of its ceilings and the excellent proportions of its rooms.

I never shall forget that happy, happy day. The house at last was mine, the workmen had gone, the Cozens had come, the daffodils were out in the garden, and a blackbird was singing fit to burst its lungs. Alfred looked in and seemed to find my sudden rush of high spirits quite irrational. He had always known, he said, that the house would be ready sooner or later, and had not, like me, alternated between faith and black moods of scepticism. As for the Cozenses, in spite of the fact that I realized by now that one human being, in Alfred's eyes, was exactly the same as another, I did find his indifference with regard to them and their cards rather damping.

'It's so terrible,' I wailed, 'because I can't return the call, our cards haven't come yet. Oh, yes, they are promised for next week, but I long to go now, this very minute, don't you see?'

'Next week will do quite well,' Alfred said, shortly.

Soon an even more blissful day dawned; I woke up in my own bed in my own bedroom, done up in my own taste and arranged entirely to suit me. True, it was freezing cold and pouring with rain on this occasion, and, since I had as yet no servant, I was obliged to get up very early and cook Alfred's breakfast, but I did not mind. He was my own husband, and the cooking took place in my own kitchen; it all seemed like heaven to me.

And now, I thought, for the happy sisterhood on which I had pinned my hopes. But alas, as so often happens in life, this turned out rather differently from what I had expected; I found myself landed with two sisters indeed, but they were very far removed from the charming companions of my dream. One was Lady Montdore and the other was Norma Cozens. At this time I was not only young, barely twenty, but extremely simple. Hitherto all human relationships had been with members of my family or with other girls (schoolfellows and débutantes) of my own age, they had been perfectly easy and straightforward and I had no idea that anything more complicated could exist; even love, with me, had followed an exceptionally level path. I supposed, in my simplicity, that when people liked me I ought to like them back as much, and that whatever they expected of me, especially if they were older people, I was morally bound to perform. In the case of these two, I doubt if it ever occurred to me that they were eating up my time and energy in a perfectly shameless way. Before my children were born I had time on my hands and I was lonely. Oxford is a place where social life, contrary to what I had imagined, is designed exclusively for celibate men, all the good talk, good food and good wine being reserved for those gatherings where there are no women; the whole tradition is in its essence monastic, and as far as society goes wives are quite superfluous.

I should never have chosen Norma Cozens to be an intimate friend, but I suppose that her company must have seemed preferable to hours of my own, while Lady Montdore did at least bring a breath of air which, though it could not have been described as fresh, had its origins in the great world outside our cloister, a world where women do count for something more than bed-makers.

Mrs Cozens' horizon also extended beyond Oxford, though in another direction. Her maiden name was Boreley, and the Boreley family was well known to me, since her grandfather's huge 1890 Elizabethan house was situated not far from Alconleigh and they were the new rich of the neighbourhood. This grandfather, now Lord Driersley, had made his money in foreign railroads, he had married into the landed gentry and produced a huge family, all the members of which, as they grew up and married, he settled on estates within easy motoring distance of Driersley Manor; they, in their turns, became notable breeders, so that the Boreley tentacles had spread by now over a great part of the West of England and there seemed to be absolutely no end of Boreley cousins, aunts, uncles, brothers, and sisters and their respective in-laws. There was very little variety about them; they all had the same cross, white guinea-pig look, thought alike, and led the same sort of lives, sporting, country lives; they seldom went to London. They were respected by their neighbours for their conformity to the fashion of the day, for their morals, for their wealth, and for their excellence at all kinds of sport. They did everything that they ought to do in the way of sitting on Benches and County Councils, walking hound puppies and running Girl Guides, one was an M.P., another an M.F.H. In short, they were pillars of rural England. Uncle Matthew, who encountered them on local business, loathed them all, and they were collectively in many drawers under the one name, Boreley, I never quite knew why. However, like Gandhi, Bernard Shaw, and Labby the Labrador, they continued to flourish, and no terrible Boreley holocaust ever took place.

My first experience of Oxford society, as the wife of a junior don, was a dinner party given in my honour by the Cozenses. The Waynflete Professor of Pastoral Theology was the professor of Alfred's subject, and was, therefore, of importance in our lives and an influence upon Alfred's career. I understood this to be so without Alfred exactly putting it into words. In any case I was of course anxious that my first Oxford appearance should be a success, anxious to look nice, make a good impression, and be a credit to my husband. My mother had given me an evening dress from Mainbocher which seemed specially designed for such an occasion; it had a white pleated chiffon skirt, and black silk jersey top with a high neck and long sleeves, which was tucked into a wide, black, patent-leather belt. Wearing this with my only jewel, a diamond clip sent by my father, I thought I was not only nicely, but also suitably, dressed. My father, incidentally, had turned a deaf ear to Lady Montdore's suggestion that he should buy me a place, and had declared himself to be too utterly ruined even to increase my allowance on my marriage. He did, however, send a cheque and this pretty jewel.

The Cozenses' house was not a nobleman's folly. It was the very worst kind of Banbury Road house, depressing, with laurels. The front door was opened by a slut. I had never seen a slut before but recognized the genus without difficulty as soon as I set eyes on this one. Inside the hall Alfred and I and the slut got rather mixed up with a large pram. However, we sorted ourselves out and put down our coats, and then she opened a door and shot us, without announcing our names, into the terrible Cozens' drawing-room. All this to the accompaniment of shrill barking from four Border terriers.

I saw at once that my dress would not do. Norma told me afterwards, when pointing out the many fearful gaffes which I was supposed to have made during the course of the evening, that as a bride I would have been expected to wear my wedding dress at our first dinner party. But, even apart from that blunder, a jersey top, however Parisian, was obviously unacceptable for evening wear in high Oxford society. The other women present were either in lace or marocain, décolleté to the waist behind, and with bare arms. Their dresses were in shades of biscuit, and so were they. It was a cold evening following upon a chilly day. The Cozenses' hearth was not laid for a fire, but had a piece of pleated paper in the grate. And yet these naked ladies did not seem to be cold; they were not blue and goosey as I should have been, nor did they shiver. I was soon to learn that in donnish circles the Oxford summer is considered to be horribly hot, and the Oxford winter nice and bracing, but that no account is taken of the between seasons or of the findings of the thermometer; cold is never felt. Apart from there being no fire, the room was terribly cheerless. The hard little sofa, the few and hard little arm-chairs were upholstered in a cretonne of so dim and dismal a pattern that it was hard to imagine anybody, even a Boreley, actually choosing it, to imagine them going into a shop, taking a seat, having cretonnes thrown over a screen one after another and suddenly saying, all excited, 'That's the very thing for me – stop!' The lights were unshaded and held in chromium-plated fittings, there was no carpet on the floor, just a few slippery rugs, the walls were of shiny cream paint, and there were no pictures, objects, or flowers to relieve the bareness.

Mrs Cozens, whose cross, creased Boreley face I recognized from my hunting days, greeted us heartily enough, and the Professor came forward with a shadow of Lord Montdore's manner, an unctuous geniality which may have originated with the Church, though his version of it was as that of a curate to Lord Montdore's cardinal. There were three other couples to whom I was introduced, all dons and their wives. I was perfectly fascinated to see these people among whom I was henceforward to live. They were ugly and not specially friendly, but no doubt, I supposed, very brilliant.

The food at dinner, served by the slut in a gaunt dining-room, was so terrible that I felt deeply sorry for Mrs Cozens, thinking that something must have gone wrong. I have had so many such meals since then that I do not remember exactly what it was; I guess, however, that it began with tinned soup and ended with dry sardines on dry toast, and that we drank a few drops of white wine. I do remember that the conversation was far from brilliant, a fact which, at the time, I attributed to the horrible stuff we were trying to swallow, but which I now know was more likely to have been due to the presence of females; dons are quite used to bad food but become paralysed in mixed company. As soon as the last sardine tail had been got down, Mrs Cozens rose to her feet, and we went into the drawing-room, leaving the men to enjoy the one good item of the whole menu, excellent vintage port. They only reappeared just before it was time to go home.

Over the coffee, sitting round the pleated paper in the fireplace, the other women talked of Lady Montdore and Polly's amazing marriage. It seemed that, while their husbands all knew Lord Montdore slightly, none of them knew Lady Montdore, not even Norma Cozens, though, as a member of an important county family, she had been inside Hampton once or twice to various big functions. They all spoke, however, not only as if they knew her quite well, but as if she had done each of them personally some terrible wrong. Lady Montdore was not popular in the county, and the reason was that she turned up her nose at the local squires and their wives as well as at the local tradesmen and their wares, ruthlessly importing both her guests and her groceries from London.

It is always interesting, and usually irritating, to hear what people have to say about somebody whom they do not know but we do. On this occasion I positively squirmed with interest and irritation. Nobody asked for my opinion, so I sat in silence, listening. The dominant thought of the discussion was that Lady Montdore, wicked as hell, had been envious of Polly, her youth and her beauty, ever since she grew up, had snubbed her and squashed her and kept her out of sight as much as possible, and that, furthermore, as soon as Polly got an admirer Lady Montdore had somehow managed to send him about his business, finally driving her into the arms of her uncle as the only escape from an unhappy home.

'Now I happen to know for a fact that Polly' (they all called her Polly, though none of them knew her) 'was on the point of getting engaged to Joyce Fleetwood, only just the other day, too – he stayed at Hampton for Christmas and it was all going like a house on fire. His own sister told me. Well, Lady Montdore got rid of him in double quick time, you see.'

'Yes, and wasn't it just the same with John Coningsby? Polly was madly in love with him, and no doubt he'd have come up to scratch in the end, but when Lady Montdore twigged what was going on she had him out on his ear.'

'And in India too, it happened several times, Polly only had to fancy a young man for him to vanish mysteriously.' They spoke as if Lady Montdore were an enchantress in a fairy tale.

'She was jealous, you know, of her being supposed to be such a beauty (never could see it myself, don't admire that flatfish look).'

'You'd think she'd want to get her off all the quicker.'

'You can't tell how jealousy is going to take people.'

'But I've always heard that Dougdale was Lady Montdore's own lover.'

'Of course he was, and that's exactly why she never imagined there could be anything between him and Polly. Serve her jolly well right, she ought to have let the poor girl marry all those others when she wanted to.'

'What a sly little thing though, under the very noses of her mother and her aunt like that.'

'I don't expect there's much to choose between them. The one I'm sorry for is poor old Lord Montdore, he's such a wonderful old man and she's led him the most awful dance you know for years, ever since they married. Daddy says she utterly ruined his career, and if it hadn't been for her he could have been Prime Minister or anything.'

'Well, but he was Viceroy,' I said, putting in my oar at last. I felt thoroughly on Lady Montdore's side against these hideous people.

'Yes he was, and everybody knows she nearly lost us India – I believe the harm she did there was something terrible. Daddy has a great friend, an Indian judge, you should hear his stories! Her rudeness –!'

'Of course, lots of people say Polly isn't Lord Montdore's child at all. King Edward, I've heard.'

'It doesn't seem to make much difference now whose child she is, because he's cut her out of his will and some American gets it all.'

'Australian, I heard. Imagine an Australian at Hampton, sad when you come to think of it.'

'And the whole thing is that old woman's fault, the old tart. That's all she is when you come to think of it, needn't give herself such airs.'

I suddenly became very furious. I was well aware of Lady Montdore's faults, I knew that she was deplorable in many ways, but it seemed to me wrong of people who had never even met her and knew nothing at first hand, to speak of her like this. I had a feeling that they did so out of an obscure jealousy, and that she only had to take any of these women up and bestow a flicker of her charm upon them for them to become her grovelling toadies.

'I hear she made a ghastly scene at the wedding,' said the don's wife whose Daddy knew an Indian judge. 'Screamed and yelled and had hysterics.'

'She didn't,' I said.

'Why, how do you know?'

'Because I was there.'

They looked at me curiously and rather angrily, as though I ought to have spoken up sooner, and changed the subject to the eternal ones of children's illnesses and servants' misdeeds.

I hoped that at my next dinner party I should be meeting the noble, thoughtful, intellectual women of my Oxford dream, if indeed, they existed.

After this Norma Cozens took a fancy to me for some reason, and used to drop into my house on her way to or from the huge walks she went for every day with the Border terriers. I think she was the crossest person I ever met, nothing was ever right for her, and her conversation, which consisted of lectures, advice, and criticism, was punctuated with furious sighs, but she was not a bad old thing, good-natured at heart, and often did me little kindnesses. I came to like her in the end the best of all the dons' wives; she was at least natural and unpretentious and brought her children up in an ordinary way. Those I found impossible to get on with were the arty-crafty ones with modern ideas, and ghastly children who had never been thwarted or cleaned up by the hand of a nanny. Norma was a type with which I was more familiar, an ordinary country hunting woman, incongruous, perhaps, in academic circles, but with no nonsense and certainly no nastiness about her. Anyhow, there she was, self-constituted part of my new life, and accepted by me as such without question.

2

A more difficult and exacting relationship was the one which now developed between me and Lady Montdore. She haunted my house, coming at much odder and more inconvenient times than Norma (who was very conventional in such ways), and proceeded to turn me into a lady-in-waiting. It was quite easy; nobody has ever sapped my will-power as she did, and like Lord Montdore, but unlike Polly, I was quite completely under her thumb. Even Alfred lifted his eyes for a moment from pastoral theology and saw what was going on. He said he could not understand my attitude, and that it made him impatient.

'You don't really like her, you're always complaining about her, why not say you are out when she comes?'

Why not, indeed? The fact was that I had never got over the physical feeling of terror which Lady Montdore had inspired in me from childhood, and though with my reason I knew now what she was, and did not care for what I knew, though the idol was down from its pedestal, the bull-fighter back in his ready-made suit, and she was revealed as nothing more or less than a selfish old woman, still I remained in awe of her. When Alfred told me to pretend to be out when she came I knew that this would be impossible for me.

'Oh, no, darling, I don't think I could do that.'

He shrugged his shoulders and said no more. He never tried to influence me, and very rarely commented on, or even appeared to notice, my behaviour and the conduct of my life.

Lady Montdore's plan was to descend upon me without warning, either on her way to or from London, or on shopping expeditions to Oxford, when she would take me round with her to fetch and carry and check her list. She would engage all my attention for an hour or two, tiring me out, exactly as small children can, with the demands she made of concentration upon her, and then vanish again, leaving me dissatisfied with life. As she was down on her own luck, but would have considered it a weakness to admit it even to herself, she was obliged to bolster up 'all this', to make it seem a perfect compensation for what she had lost by denigrating the circumstances of other people. It was even a help to her, I suppose, because otherwise I cannot account for her beastliness, to run down my poor little house, so unpretentious, and my dull little life, and she did so with such conviction that, since I am easily discouraged, it often took days before everything seemed all right again.

Days, or a visit from some member of the Radlett family. The Radletts had the exactly opposite effect, and always made me feel wonderful, owing to a habit known in the family as 'exclaiming'.

'Fanny's shoes –! Where? Lilley and Skinner? I must dash. And the lovely new skirt! Not a new suit, let's see – not lined with silk – Fanny! You are lucky, it is unfair!'

'Oh, dear, why doesn't my hair curl like that? Oh, the bliss of Fanny altogether – her eyelashes! You are lucky, it is unfair!'

These exclamations, which I remember from my very earliest childhood, now also embraced my house and household arrangements.

'The wallpaper! Fanny! Your bed – it can't be true. Oh, look at the darling little bit of Belleek – where did you find it? No! Do let's go there. And a new cushion! Oh, it is unfair, you are lucky to be you.'

'I say, Fanny's food! Toast at every meal! Not Yorkshire pudding! Why can't we live with Fanny always – the heaven of it here! Why can't I be you?'

Fortunately for my peace of mind, Jassy and Victoria came to see me whenever there was a motor car going to Oxford, which was quite often, and the elder ones always looked in if they were on their way to Alconleigh.

As I got to know Lady Montdore more intimately I began to realize that her selfishness was monumental, she had no thoughts except in relation to herself, could discuss no subject without cleverly edging it round to something directly pertaining to her. The only thing she ever wanted to know about people was what impression did she make on them, and she would do anything to find this out, sometimes digging traps for the unwary, into which, in my innocence, I was very apt to tumble.

'I suppose your husband is a clever man, at least so Montdore tells me. Of course, it's a thousand pities he is so dreadfully poor – I hate to see you living in this horrid little hovel, so unsuitable – and not more important, but Montdore says he has the reputation of being clever.'

She had dropped in just as I was having my tea, which consisted of a few rather broken digestive biscuits with a kitchen pot on a tray and without a plate. I was so busy that afternoon, and Mrs Heathery, my maid of all work, was so busy too, that I had dashed into the kitchen and taken the tray myself, like that. Unfortunately, it never seemed to be chocolate cake and silver teapot day when Lady Montdore came, though, such were the vagaries of my housekeeping while I was a raw beginner, that these days did quite often, though quite unaccountably, occur.

'Is that your tea? All right dear, yes, just a cup, please. How weak you have it – no no, this will do quite well. Yes, as I was saying, Montdore spoke of your husband today at luncheon, with the Bishop. They had read something of his and seem to have been quite impressed, so I suppose he really is clever after all.'

'Oh, he is the cleverest man I ever met,' I said, happily. I loved to talk about Alfred, it was the next best thing to being with him.

'So of course, I suppose he thinks I'm a very stupid person.' She looked with distaste at the bits of digestives, and then took one.

'Oh no, he doesn't,' I said, inventing, because Alfred had never put forward any opinion on the subject one way or another.

'I'm sure he must, really. You don't mean to tell me he thinks I'm clever?'

'Yes, very clever. He p'r'aps doesn't look upon you as an intellectual –'

Crash! I was in the trap.

'Oh, indeed! Not an intellectual!'

I could see at once that she was terribly offended, and thrashed about unhappily in my trap trying to extricate myself; to no avail, however, I was in it up to the neck.

'You see, he doesn't believe that women ever are intellectuals hardly hardly ever, perhaps one in ten million – Virginia Woolf perhaps –'

'I suppose he thinks I never read. Many people think that, because they see me leading this active life, wearing myself out for others. I might prefer to sit in a chair all day and read some book, very likely I would, but I shouldn't think it right, in my position, to do so – I can't only be thinking of myself, you see. I never do read books in the daytime, that's perfectly true. I simply haven't a moment, but your husband doesn't know, and nor do you, what I do at night. I don't sleep well, not well at all, and at night I read volumes.'

Old volumes of the *Tatler*, I guessed. She had them all bound up from before the war, and very fascinating they were.

'You know, Fanny,' she went on, 'it's all very well for funny little people like you to read books the whole time, you only have yourselves to consider, whereas Montdore and I are public servants in a way, we have something to live up to, tradition and so on, duties to perform you know, it's a very different matter. A great deal is expected of us, I think and hope not in vain. It's a hard life, make no mistake about that, hard and tiring, but occasionally we have our reward – when people get a chance to show how they worship us, for instance, when we came back from India and the dear villagers pulled our motor car up the drive. Really touching! Now all you intellectual people never have moments like that. Well,' she rose to leave, 'one lives and learns. I know now that I am outside the pale, intellectually. Of course, my dear child, we must remember that all those women students probably give your husband a very funny notion of what the female sex is really like. I wonder if he realizes that it's only the ones who can't hope for anything better that come here. Perhaps he finds them very fascinating – one never sees him in his own home, I notice.' She was working herself up into a tremendous temper now. 'And if I might offer you a little advice, Fanny, it would be to read fewer books, dear, and make your house slightly more comfortable. That is what a man appreciates, in the long run.'

She cast a meaning look at the plateless digestives, and went away without saying good-bye.

I was really upset to have annoyed her so stupidly and tactlessly, and felt certain that she would never come and see me again; funnily enough, instead of being relieved by this thought, I minded.

I had no time to brood over it, however, for hardly was she out of the house than Jassy and Victoria bundled in.

'Not digestives! Vict. – look, digestives! Isn't Fanny wonderful, you can always count on something heavenly – weeks since I tasted digestives, my favourite food, too.'

Mrs Heathery, who adored the children and had heard their shrieks as they came in, brought up some fresh tea and a Fuller's cake, which elicited more exclamations.

'Oh, Mrs Heathery, you angel on earth, not Fuller's walnut? How can you afford it, Fanny – we haven't had it at home since Fa's last financial crisis – but things are better you know, we are back to Bromo again now and the good writing-paper. When the loo paper gets thicker and the writing-paper thinner it's always a bad sign, at home.'

'Fa had to come about some harness, so he brought us in to see you, only ten minutes though. The thing is we've got a funny story about Sadie for you, so are you listening? Well, Sadie was telling how some people, before their babies are born, gaze at Greuze so that the babies shall look like it, and she said "You never know about these things, because when I was a little girl in Suffolk a baby was born in the village with a bear's head, and what do you think? Exactly nine months before a dancing bear had been in that neighbourhood." So Vict. said "But I can quite understand that, I always think bears are simply terribly attractive", and Sadie gave the most tremendous jump I ever saw and said, "You awful child, that's not what I mean at all". So are you shrieking, Fanny?'

'We saw your new friend Mrs Cozens just now and her blissful Borders. You are so lucky to have new friends, it is unfair, we never do, really you know, we are the Lady of Shalott with our pathetic lives we lead. Even Davey never comes now horrible Polly's marriage is over. Oh, by the way, we had a postcard from horrible Polly, but it's no use her bombarding us with these postcards – we can never never forgive.'

'Where was it from?'

'Seville, that's in Spain.'

'Did she sound happy?'

'Do people ever sound unhappy on postcards, Fanny? Isn't it always lovely weather and everything wonderful, on postcards? This one was a picture of a glorious girl called La Macarena, and the funny thing is this La Macarena is the literal image of horrible Polly herself. Do you think Lady Montdore gazed a bit before H.P. was born?'

'You mustn't say horrible Polly to me when I love her so much.'

'Well, we'll have to see. We love her in a way, in spite of all, and in a few years, possibly, we might forgive, though I doubt if we can ever forget her deep, base treachery. Has she written to you?'

'Only postcards,' I said. 'One from Paris and one from St Jean de Luz.'

Polly had never been much of a letter-writer.

'I wonder if it's as nice as she thought, being in bed with that old Lecturer.'

'Marriage isn't only bed,' I said, primly, 'there are other things.'

'You go and tell that to Sadie. There's Fa's horn, we must dash or he'll never bring us again if we keep him waiting, and we promised we would the very second he blew. Oh, dear, back to the fields of barley and of rye, you are so lucky to live in this sweet little house in a glamorous town. Good-bye, Mrs Heathery – the cake!'

They were still cramming it into their mouths as they went downstairs.

'Come in and have some tea,' I said to Uncle Matthew, who was at the wheel of his new big Wolseley. When my uncle had a financial crisis he always bought a new motor car.

'No thank you, Fanny, very kind of you but there's a perfectly good cup of tea waiting for me at home, and you know I never go inside other people's houses if I can possibly avoid it. Good-bye.'

He put on his green hat called a bramble, which he always wore, and drove away.

My next caller was Norma Cozens, who came in for a glass of sherry, but her conversation was so dull that I have not the heart to record it. It was a compound of an abscess between the toes of the mother Border terrier, the things the laundry does to sheets, how it looked to her as if the slut had been at her store cupboard so she was planning to replace her by an Austrian at 2s. a week cheaper wages, and how lucky I was to have Mrs Heathery, but I must look out because new brooms sweep clean, and Mrs Heathery was sure not to be nearly as nice as she seemed.

I was very much mistaken if I thought that Lady Montdore was now out of my life for good. In less than a week she was back again. The door of my house was always kept on the latch, like a country-house door, and she never bothered to ring but just stumped upstairs. On this occasion it was five minutes to one and I plainly saw that I would have to share the little bit of salmon I had ordered for myself, as a treat, with her.

'And where is your husband today?'

She showed her disapproval of my marriage by always referring to Alfred like this and never by his name. He was still Mr Thing in her eyes.

'Lunching in college.'

'Ah, yes? Just as well, so he won't be obliged to endure my unintellectual conversation.'

I was afraid it would all start over again, including the working herself up into a temper, but apparently she had decided to treat my unlucky remark as a great joke.

'I told Merlin,' she said, 'that in Oxford circles I am not thought an intellectual, and I only wish you could have seen his face!'

When Mrs Heathery offered the fish to Lady Montdore she scooped up the whole thing. No tiresome inhibitions caused her to ask what I would eat, and in fact I had some potatoes and salad. She was good enough to say that the quality of the food in my house seemed to be improving.

'Oh, yes, I know what I wanted to ask you,' she said. 'Who is this Virginia Woolf you mentioned to me? Merlin was talking about her too, the other day at Maggie Greville's.'

'She's a writer,' I said, 'a novelist really.'

'Yes, I see. And as she's so intellectual, no doubt she writes about nothing but station-masters.'

'Well, no,' I said, 'she doesn't.'

'I must confess that I prefer books about society people, not being myself a highbrow.'

'She did write a fascinating book about a society person,' I said, 'called *Mrs Dalloway*.'

'Perhaps I'll read it then. Oh, of course, I'd forgotten – I never read, according to you, don't know how. Never mind. In case I have a little time this week, Fanny, you might lend it to me, will you? Excellent cheese, don't tell me you get this in Oxford?'

She was in an unusually good temper that day. I believe the fall of the Spanish throne had cheered her up, she probably foresaw a perfect swarm of Infantas winging its way towards Montdore House, besides, she was greatly enjoying all the details from Madrid. She said that the Duke of Barbarossa (this may not be the name, but it sounded like it) had told her the inside story, in which case he must also have told it to the *Daily Express*, where I had read word for word what she now kindly passed on to me, and several days before. She remembered to ask for *Mrs Dalloway* before leaving, and went off with the book in her hand, a first edition. I felt sure that I had seen the last of it, but she brought it back the following week, saying that she really must write a book herself as she knew she could do much better than that.

'Couldn't read it,' she said. 'I did try, but it is too boring. And I never got to that society person you told me of. Now have you read the Grand Duchess's *Memoirs*? I won't lend you mine, you must buy them for yourself, Fanny, and that will help the dear duchess with another guinea. They are wonderful. There is a great deal, nearly a whole chapter, about Montdore and me in India – she stayed with us at Viceroy's House, you know. She has really captured the spirit of the place quite amazingly, she was only there a week but one couldn't have done it better oneself, she describes a garden party I gave, and visits to the Ranees in their harems, and she tells what a lot I was able to do for those poor women of India, and how they worshipped me. Personally, I find memoirs so very much more interesting than any novel because they are true. I may not be an intellectual, but I do like to read the truth about things. Now in a book like the Grand Duchess's you can see history in the very making, and if you love history as I do (but don't tell your husband I said so dear, he would never believe it), if you love history, you must be interested to know the inside story, and it's only people like the Grand Duchess who are in a position to tell us that. And this reminds me, Fanny dear, will you put a call through to Downing Street for me please, and get hold of the P.M. or his secretary – I will speak myself when he is on the line. I'm arranging a little dinner for the Grand

Duchess, to give her book a good start, of course, I don't ask you dear, it wouldn't be intellectual enough, just a few politicians and writers, I thought. Here is the number, Fanny.'

I was trying at this time to economize in every direction, having overspent myself on doing up the house, and I had made a rule never to telephone, even to Aunt Emily or to Alconleigh, if a letter would do as well, so it was most unwillingly that I did as she asked. There was a long wait on the line before I got the Prime Minister himself, after which Lady Montdore spoke for ages, the pip-pip-pips going at least five times, I could hear them, every pip an agony to me. First of all she fixed a date for her dinner party, this took a long time, with many pauses while he consulted his secretary, and two pip-pip-pips. Then she asked if there were anything new from Madrid.

'Yes,' she said, 'badly advised, poor man [pip-pip-pip] I fear. I saw Freddy Barbarossa last night (they are being so brave about it, by the way, quite stoical. Yes, at Claridges) and he told me . . .' here a flood of *Daily Express* news and views. 'But Montdore and I are very much worried about our own special Infanta – yes, a close friend of ours – oh, Prime Minister, if you could hear anything I should be so more than grateful. Will you really? You know, there is a whole chapter on Madrid in the Grand Duchess's book, it makes it very topical, rather splendid for her. Yes, a near relation. She describes the view [pip-pip-pip] from the Royal Palace – yes, very bleak, I've been there, wonderful sunsets though, I know, poor woman. Oh, she hated them at first, she had special opera glasses with black spots for the cruel moments.

'Have you heard where they are going? Yes, Barbara Barbarossa told me that too, but I wonder they don't come here. You ought to try and persuade them. Yes, I see. Well, we'll talk about all that, meanwhile, dear Prime Minister, I won't keep you any longer [pip-pip-pip] but we'll see you on the tenth. So do I. I'll send your secretary a reminder, of course. Good-bye.'

She turned to me, beaming, and said, 'I have the most wonderful effect on that man, you know, it's quite touching how he dotes on me. I really think I could do anything with him, anything at all.'

She never spoke of Polly. At first I supposed that the reason why she liked to see so much of me was that I was associated in her mind with Polly, and that sooner or later she would unburden herself to me, or even try and use me as go-between in a reconciliation. I soon realized, however, that Polly and Boy were dead to her; she had no further use for them since Boy could never be her lover again and Polly could never now, it seemed, do her credit in the eyes of the world; she simply dismissed them from her thoughts. Her visits to me were partly the outcome of loneliness and partly due to the fact that I was a convenient half-way house between London and Hampton and that she could use me as restaurant, cloakroom, and telephone booth when in Oxford.

She was horribly lonely, you could see that. She filled Hampton every week-end with important people, with smart people, even just with people, but, although so great is the English predilection for country life, she generally managed to get these visits extended from Friday to Tuesday, even so she was left with two empty days in the middle of the week. She went less and less to London. She had always preferred Hampton, where she reigned alone, to London, where she faced a certain degree of competition, and life there without Polly to entertain for and without Boy to help her plot the social game had evidently become meaningless and dull.

3

It was no doubt the dullness of her life which now deflected her thoughts towards Cedric Hampton, Lord Montdore's heir. They still knew nothing about him beyond the mere fact of his existence, which had hitherto been regarded as extremely superfluous since but for him the whole of 'all this', including Hampton, would have gone to Polly, and, although the other things she had been going to inherit were worth more money, it was Hampton they all loved so much. I have never made out his exact relationship to Lord Montdore, but I know that when Linda and I used to 'look him up' to see if he was the right age for us to marry it always took ages to find him, breathing heavily over the peerage, pointing, and going back and back.

. . . having had issue,

Henry, b. 1875, who m. Dora, dau. of Stanley Honks Esq. of Annapolis, Nova Scotia, and d. 1913 leaving issue, Cedric, heir pres., b. 1907.

Just the right age, but what of Nova Scotia? An atlas, hastily consulted, showed it to be horribly marine. 'A transatlantic Isle of Wight' as Linda put it. 'No thanks.' Sea breezes, in so far as they are good for the complexion, were regarded by us as a means and not an end, for at that time it was our idea to live in capital cities and go to the Opera alight with diamonds, 'Who is that lovely woman?' and Nova Scotia was clearly not a suitable venue for such doings. It never seemed to occur to us that Cedric could perhaps have been transplanted from his native heath to Paris, London, or Rome. Colonial we thought, ignorantly. It ruled him out. I believe Lady Montdore knew very little more about him than we did. She had never felt interest or curiosity towards those unsuitable people in Canada, they were one of the unpleasant things of life and she preferred to ignore them. Now, however, left alone with an 'all this' which would one day, and one day fairly soon by the look of Lord Montdore, be Cedric's, she thought and spoke of him continually, and presently had the idea that it would amuse her to see him.

Of course, no sooner had she conceived this idea than she wanted him to be there the very next minute, and was infuriated by the delays that ensued. For Cedric could not be found.

I was kept informed of every stage in the search for him, as Lady Montdore could now think of nothing else.

'That idiotic woman has changed her address,' she told me. 'Montdore's lawyer has had the most terrible time getting in touch with her at all. Now fancy moving, in Canada. You'd think one place there would be exactly the same as another, wouldn't you? Sheer waste of money, you'd think. Well, they've found her at last, and now it seems that Cedric isn't with her at all, but somewhere in Europe, very odd of him not to have called on us in that case, so now, of course, there'll be more delays. Oh, dear, people are too inconsiderate – it's nothing but self, self, self, nowadays, nothing –!'

In the end Cedric was traced to Paris ('Simply extraordinary,' she said. 'Whatever could a Canadian be doing in Paris? I don't quite like it.') and an invitation to Hampton was given and accepted.

'He comes next Tuesday, for a fortnight. I wrote out the dates very carefully indeed, I always do when it is a question of a country-house visit, then there is no awkwardness about the length of it, people know exactly when they are expected to leave. If we like him he can come again, now we know that he lives in Paris, such an easy journey. But what do you suppose he is doing there, dear, I hope he's not an artist. Well, if he is we shall simply have to get him out of it – he must learn to behave suitably, now. We are sending to Dover for him, so that he'll arrive just in time for dinner. Montdore and I have decided not to dress that evening, as most likely he has no evening clothes, and one doesn't wish to make him feel shy at the very beginning of his visit, poor boy.'

This seemed most unlike Lady Montdore, who usually loved making people feel shy; it was well known to be one of her favourite diversions. No doubt Cedric was to be her new toy, and until such time as, inevitably I felt, just as Norma felt about Mrs Heathery, disillusionment set in, nothing was to be too good for him, and no line of conduct too much calculated to charm him.

I began to think a great deal about Cedric, it was such an interesting situation and I longed to know how he would take it, this young man from the West, suddenly confronted with aristocratic England in full decadence, the cardboard earl, with his nobility of look and manner, the huge luxurious houses, the terrifying servants, the atmosphere of bottomless wealth. I remembered how exaggerated it had all seemed to me as a child, and supposed that he would see it with very much the same eyes and find it equally overpowering.

I thought, however, he might feel at home with Lady Montdore, especially as she desired to please, there was something spontaneous and almost childlike about her which could accord with a transatlantic outlook. It was the only hope, otherwise, and if he were at all timid, I thought, he would find himself submerged. Words dimly associated with Canada kept on occurring to me, the word lumber, the word shack, staking a claim (Uncle Matthew had once staked a claim, I knew, in Ontario in his wild young poker-playing days, with Harry Oakes). How I wished I could be present at Hampton when this lumber-jack arrived to stake his claim to that shack. Hardly had I formed the wish than it was granted, Lady Montdore ringing up to ask if I would go over for the night, she thought it would make things easier to have another young person there when Cedric arrived.

This was a wonderful reward, as I duly remarked to Alfred, for having been a lady-in-waiting.

Alfred said, 'If you have been putting yourself out all this time with a reward in view, I don't mind at all. I objected because I thought you were drifting along in the wake of that old woman merely from a lazy good-nature and with no particular motive. That is what I found degrading. Of course, if you were working for a wage, it is quite a different matter, so long, of course,' he said, with a disapproving look, 'as the wage seems to you worth while.'

It did.

The Montdores sent a motor car to Oxford for me. When I arrived at Hampton I was taken straight upstairs to my room, where I had a bath and changed, according to instructions brought me by Lady Montdore's maid, into a day dress. I had not spent a night at Hampton since my marriage. Knowing that Alfred would not want to go, I had always refused Lady Montdore's invitations, but my bedroom there was still deeply familiar to me. I knew every inch of it by heart. Nothing in it ever changed, the very books between their mahogany bookends were the same collection that I had known and read there now for twelve years, or more than half my life: novels by Robert Hichens and W. J. Locke, *Napoleon, The Last Phase* by Lord Rosebery, *The House of Mirth* by Edith Wharton, Hare's *Two Noble Lives*, *Dracula*, and a book on dog management. In front of them on a mahogany tallboy was a Japanese bronze tea-kettle with embossed water-lilies. On the walls, besides the two country-house old masters despised of Davey, were a Morland print, 'The Higglers preparing for Market', a Richmond water-colour of the 'old lord' in a kilt and an oil painting of Toledo either by Boy or Lady Montdore. Their styles were indistinguishable. It was in their early manner, and had probably hung there for twenty years. This room had a womb-like quality in my mind, partly because it was so red and warm and velvety and enclosed, and partly because of the terror with which I always used to be assailed by the idea of leaving it and venturing downstairs. This evening as I dressed I thought how lovely it was to be grown-up, a married woman, and no longer frightened of people. Of Lord Merlin a little, of the Warden of Wadham perhaps, but these were not panicky, indiscriminate social terrors, they could rather be classed as wholesome awe inspired by gifted elders.

When I was ready I went down to the Long Gallery, where Lord and Lady Montdore were sitting in their usual chairs one each side of the chimneypiece, but not at all in their usual frame of mind. They were both, and especially Lady Montdore, in a twitter of nerves, and looked up quite startled when I came into the room, relaxing again when they saw that it was only me. I thought that from the point of view of a stranger, a backwoodsman from the American continent, they struck exactly the right note. Lord Montdore, in an informal green velvet smoking-jacket, was impressive with his white hair and carved, unchanging face, while Lady Montdore's very dowdiness was an indication that she was too grand to bother about clothes, and this too would surely impress. She wore printed black-and-white crêpe-de-chine, her only jewels the enormous half-hoop rings which flashed from her strong old woman's fingers, and sat as she always did, her knees well apart, her feet in their large buckled shoes firmly planted on the ground, her hands folded in her lap.

'We lit this little fire,' she said, 'thinking that he may feel cold after the journey.' It was unusual for her to refer to any arrangement in her house, people being expected to like what they found there, or else to lump it. 'Do you think we shall hear the motor when it comes up the drive? We generally can if the wind is in the west.'

'I expect I shall,' I said, tactlessly. 'I hear everything.'

'Oh, we're not stone deaf ourselves. Show Fanny what you have got for Cedric, Montdore.'

He held out a little book in green morocco, Gray's poems.

'If you look at the fly-leaf,' he said, 'you will see that it was given to my grand-father by the late Lord Palmerston the day that Cedric's grandfather was born. They evidently happened to be dining together. We think that it should please him.'

I did so hope it would. I suddenly felt very sorry for these two old people, and longed for Cedric's visit to be a success and cheer them up.

'Canadians,' he went on, 'should know all about the poet Gray, because General Woolf, at the taking of Quebec –'

There were footsteps now in the red drawing-room, so we had not heard the motor after all. Lord and Lady Montdore got up and stood together in front of the fireplace as the butler opened the door and announced 'Mr Cedric Hampton'.

A glitter of blue and gold crossed the parquet, and a human dragon-fly was kneeling on the fur rug in front of the Montdores, one long white hand extended towards each. He was a tall, thin young man, supple as a girl, dressed in rather a bright blue suit; his hair was the gold of a brass bed-knob, and his insect appearance came from the fact that the upper part of the face was concealed by blue goggles set in gold rims quite an inch thick.

He was flashing a smile of unearthly perfection; relaxed and happy he knelt there bestowing this smile upon each Montdore in turn.

'Don't speak,' he said, 'just for a moment. Just let me go on looking at you – wonderful, wonderful people!'

I could see at once that Lady Montdore was very highly gratified. She beamed with pleasure. Lord Montdore gave her a hasty glance to see how she was taking it, and when he saw that beaming was the note, he beamed too.

'Welcome,' she said, 'to Hampton.'

'The beauty,' Cedric went on, floating jointlessly to his feet. 'I can only say that I am drunk with it. England, so much more beautiful than I had imagined (I have never had very good accounts of England, somehow), this house, so romantic, such a repository of treasures, and above all, you – the two most beautiful people I have ever seen!'

He spoke with rather a curious accent, neither French nor Canadian, but pecu-liar to himself, in which every syllable received rather more emphasis than is given by the ordinary Englishman. Also he spoke, as it were, through his smile, which would fade a little, then flash out again, but which never altogether left his face.

'Won't you take off your spectacles?' said Lady Montdore. I should like to see your eyes.'

'Later, dear Lady Montdore, later. When my dreadful, paralysing shyness (a disease with me) has quite worn off. They give me confidence, you see, when I am dreadfully nervous, just as a mask would. In a mask one can face anything – I should like my life to be a perpetual *bal masqué*, Lady Montdore, don't you agree? I long to know who the Man in the Iron Mask was, don't you, Lord Montdore? Do you remember when Louis XVIII first saw the Duchesse d'Angoulême after the Restor-ation? Before saying anything else you know – wasn't it all awful or anything – he asked if poor Louis XVI had ever told her who the Man in the Iron Mask was. I love Louis XVIII for that – so like *One*.'

Lady Montdore indicated me. 'This is our cousin – and a distant relation of yours, Cedric – Fanny Wincham.'

He took my hand and looked long into my face, saying, 'I am enchanted to meet you' as if he really was. He turned again to the Montdores, and said, 'I am so happy to be here.'

'My dear boy, we are so happy to have you. You should have come before – we had no idea – we thought you were always in Nova Scotia, you see.'

Cedric was gazing at the big French map table. 'Riesener,' he said, 'this is a very strange thing, Lady Montdore, and you will hardly believe it, but where I live in France we have its pair – is that not a coincidence? Only this morning, at Chèvres, I was leaning upon that very table.'

'What is Chèvres?'

'Chèvres-Fontaine, where I live, in the Seine-et-Oise.'

'But it must be quite a large house,' said Lady Montdore, 'if that table is in it?'

'A little larger, in every dimension, than the central block at Versailles, and with much more water. At Versailles there only remain seven hundred *bouches* (what is *bouche* in English? Jets?). At Chèvres we have one thousand five hundred, and they play all the time.'

Dinner was announced. As we moved towards the dining-room Cedric stopped to examine various objects, touched them lovingly, and murmured,

'Weisweiller – Boulle – Caffieri – Jacob. How is it you come to have these marvels, Lord Montdore, such important pieces?'

'My great-grandfather (your great-great-grandfather), who was himself half French, collected it all his life. Some of it he bought during the sales of royal furniture after the Revolution and some came to him through his mother's family, the Montdores.'

'And the boiseries!' said Cedric, 'first quality Louis XV. There is nothing to equal this at Chèvres, it's like jewellery when it is so fine.'

We were now in the little dining-room.

'He brought them over too, and built the house round them.' Lord Montdore was evidently much pleased by Cedric's enthusiasm, he loved French furniture himself but seldom found anybody in England to share his taste.

'Porcelain with Marie-Antoinette's cypher, delightful. At Chèvres we have the Meissen service she brought with her from Vienna. We have many relics of Marie-Antoinette, poor dear, at Chèvres.'

'Who lives there?' asked Lady Montdore.

'I do,' he replied carelessly, 'when I wish to be in the country. In Paris I have an apartment of all beauty, *One's* idea of heaven.' Cedric made great use of the word one, which he pronounced with peculiar emphasis. Lady Montdore had always been a one for one, but she said it quite differently, 'w'n'. 'The first floor of the Hotel Pomponne – you see that? Purest Louis XIV. Tiny, you know, but all one needs, that is to say a bedroom and a bed-ballroom. You must come and stay with me there, dear Lady Montdore, you will live in my bedroom, which has comfort, and I in the bed-ballroom. Promise me that you will come.'

'We shall have to see. Personally, I have never been very fond of France, the people are so frivolous, I greatly prefer the Germans.'

'Germans!' said Cedric earnestly, leaning across the table and gazing at her through his goggles. 'The frivolity of the Germans terrifies even *One*. I have a German friend in Paris and a more frivolous creature, Lady Montdore, does not exist. This frivolity has caused me many a heartache, I must tell you.'

'I hope you will make some suitable English friends now, Cedric.'

'Yes, yes, that is what I long for. But please can my chief English friend be you, dear dearest Lady Montdore?'

'I think you should call us Aunt Sonia and Uncle Montdore.'

'May I really? How charming you are to me, how happy I am to be here – you seem, Aunt Sonia, to shower happiness around you.'

'Yes, I do. I live for others, I suppose that's why. The sad thing is that people have not always appreciated it, they are so selfish themselves.'

'Oh, yes, aren't they selfish? I too have been a victim to the selfishness of people all my life. This German friend I mentioned just now, his selfishness passes comprehension. How one does suffer!'

'It's a he, is it?' Lady Montdore seemed glad of this.

'A boy called Klugg. I hope to forget all about him while I am here. Now, Lady Montdore – dearest Aunt Sonia – after dinner I want you to do me a great great favour. Will you put on your jewels so that I can see you sparkling in them? I do so long for that.'

'Really, my dear boy, they are down in the strong-room. I don't think they've been cleaned for ages.'

'Oh, don't say no, don't shake your head! Ever since I set eyes on you I have been thinking of nothing else, you must look so truly glorious in them. Mrs Wincham (you are Mrs I hope, aren't you, yes, yes, I can tell that you are not a spinster), when did you last see Aunt Sonia laden with jewels?'

'It was at the ball for –' I stopped awkwardly, jibbing at the name, which was never now mentioned. But Cedric saved me from embarrassment by exclaiming,

'A ball! Aunt Sonia, how I would love to see you at a ball, I can so well imagine you at all the great English functions, coronations, Lords, balls, Ascot, Henley. What is Henley? No matter – and I can see you, above all, in India, riding on your elephant like a goddess. How they must have worshipped you there.'

'Well, you know, they did,' said Lady Montdore, delighted, 'they really worshipped us, it was quite touching. And of course, we deserved it, we did a very great deal for them, I think I may say we put India on the map. Hardly any of one's friends in England had ever even heard of India before we went there, you know.'

'I'm sure. What a wonderful and fascinating life you lead, Aunt Sonia. Did you keep a journal when you were in the East? Oh! please say yes, I would so love to read it.'

This was a very lucky shot. They had indeed filled a huge folio, whose morocco label, surmounted by an earl's coronet, announced 'Pages from Our Indian Diary. M. and S.M.'

'It's really a sort of scrap-book,' Lord Montdore said, 'accounts of our journeys up-country, photographs, sketches by Sonia and our brother-in – that is to say a brother-in-law we had then, letters of appreciation from rajahs –'

'And Indian poetry translated by Montdore – "Prayer of a Widow before Suttee", "Death of an old Mahout", and so on, touching, it makes you cry.'

'Oh, I must read it all, every word, I can hardly wait.'

Lady Montdore was radiant. How many and many a time had she led her guests to 'Pages from Our Indian Diary', like horses to water, and watched them straying off after one half-hearted sip. Never before, I guess, had anybody so eagerly demanded to read it.

'Now, you must tell us about your life, my dear boy,' said Lady Montdore. 'When did you leave Canada? Your home is in Nova Scotia, is it not?'

'I lived there until I was eighteen.'

'Montdore and I have never been to Canada – the States, of course, we spent a month once in New York and Washington and we saw Niagara Falls, but then we were obliged to come home, I only wish we could have gone on, they were quite touchingly anxious to have us, but Montdore and I cannot always do as we should like, we have our duties. Of course, that was a long time ago, twenty-five years I should think, but I dare say Nova Scotia doesn't alter much?'

'I am very very happy to say that kindly Nature has allowed a great sea-fog of oblivion to rise between me and Nova Scotia so that I hardly remember one single thing about it.'

'What a strange boy, you are,' she said indulgently, but she was very well suited by the fact of the sea-fog, since the last thing she wanted would have been long-winded reminiscences of Cedric's family life in Canada; it was all no doubt much better forgotten, and especially the fact that Cedric had a mother. 'So you came to Europe when you were eighteen?'

'Paris. Yes, I was sent to Paris by my guardian, a banker, to learn some horrid sort of job, I quite forget what, as I never had to go near it. It is not necessary to have jobs in Paris, one's friends are so very very kind.'

'Really, how funny. I always thought the French were so mean.'

'Certainly not to *One*. My needs are simple, admittedly, but such as they are they have all been satisfied over and over again.'

'What are your needs?'

'I need a very great deal of beauty round me, beautiful objects wherever I look and beautiful people who see the point of *One*. And speaking of beautiful people, Aunt Sonia, after dinner the jewels? Don't, don't, please say no!'

'Very well, then,' she said, 'but now, Cedric, won't you take off your glasses?'

'Perhaps I could. Yes, I really think the last vestige of my shyness has gone.'

He took them off, and the eyes which were now disclosed, blinking in the light, were the eyes of Polly, large, blue, and rather blank. They quite startled me, but I do not think the Montdores were specially struck by the resemblance, though Lady Montdore said,

'Anybody can tell that you are a Hampton, Cedric. Please never let's see those horrid spectacles again.'

'My goggles? Specially designed by Van Cleef for me?'

'I hate spectacles,' said Lady Montdore firmly.

Lady Montdore's maid was now sent for, given the key of the safe from Lord Montdore's key-ring and told to bring up all the jewel cases. When dinner was over and we got back to the Long Gallery, leaving Lord Montdore to his port, but accompanied by Cedric, who was evidently unaware of the English custom which keeps the men in the dining-room after dinner and who followed Lady Montdore like a dog, we found the map-table covered with blue velvet trays each of which contained a parure of large and beautiful jewels. Cedric gave a cry of happiness and got down to work at once.

'In the first place, dear Aunt Sonia,' he said, 'this dress won't do. Let me see – ah, yes' – he took a piece of red brocade off the piano and draped her in it very cleverly, pinning it in place on one shoulder with a huge diamond brooch. 'Have you some *maquillage* in this bag, dear? And a comb?'

Lady Montdore rummaged about and produced a cheap lipstick and a small green comb with a tooth out.

'Naughty, naughty you,' he said, carefully painting her face, 'it cakes! Never mind, that will do for now. Not pulling your hair, am I? We've got to show the bone structure, so beautiful on you. I think you'll have to find a new coiffeur, Aunt Sonia – we'll see about that – anyway, it must go up – up – like this. Do you realize what a difference that makes? Now, Mrs Wincham, will you please put out the top lights for me, and bring the lamp from that bureau over here. Thank you.'

He placed the lamp on the floor at Lady Montdore's feet and began to hang her with diamonds, so that the brocade was covered with them to her waist, finally poising the crown of pink diamonds on the top of her head.

'Now,' he said. 'Look!' and he led her to a looking-glass on the wall. She was entranced by the effect, which was indeed very splendid.

'My turn,' he said.

Although Lady Montdore seemed to be almost solid with diamonds the cases on the tables still held many huge jewels. He took off his coat, his collar and tie, pulled open his shirt and clasped a great necklace of diamonds and sapphires round his neck, wound up another piece of silk into a turban, stuck a diamond feather in it and put it on his head. He went on talking all the time.

'You really must pat your face more, Aunt Sonia.'

'Pat?'

'With nourishing creams. I'll show you. Such a wonderful face, but uncultivated, neglected and starved. We must feed it up, exercise it and look after it better from now on. You'll soon see what a lot can be done. Twice a week you must sleep in a mask.'

'A mask?'

'Yes, back to masks, but this time I mean the sort you paint on at night. It goes quite hard, so that you look like the Commandeur in *Don Juan*, and in the morning you can't smile, not a glimmer, so you mustn't telephone until you've removed it with the remover, because you know how if you telephone smilelessly you sound cross, and if it happened to be *One* at the other end, *One* couldn't bear that.'

'Oh, my dear boy, I don't know about this mask. What would Griffith say?'

'If Griffith is your maid she won't notice a thing, they never do. We shall notice, though, your great new beauty. Those cruel lines!'

They were absorbed in each other and themselves, and when Lord Montdore came in from the dining-room they did not even notice. He sat for a while in his usual attitude, the fingers of both hands pressed together, looking into the fire, and very soon crept off to bed. In the months which had passed since Polly's marriage he had turned into an old man, he was smaller, his clothes hung sadly on him, his voice quavered and complained. Before he went he gave the little book of poems to Cedric, who took it with a charming show of appreciation and looked at it until Lord Montdore was out of sight, when he quickly turned back to the jewels.

I was pregnant at this time and began to feel sleepy very soon after dinner. I had a look at the picture papers and then followed Lord Montdore's example.

'Good night,' I said, making for the door. They hardly bothered to answer. They were now standing each in front of a looking-glass, a lamp at their feet, happily gazing at their own images.

'Do you think it is better like that?' one would say.

'Much better,' the other would reply, without looking.

From time to time they exchanged a jewel ('Give me the rubies, dear boy.' 'May I have the emeralds if you've finished with them?') and he was now wearing the pink tiara; jewels lay all around them, tumbled on to the chairs and tables, even on the floor.

'I have a confession to make to you, Cedric,' she said, as I was leaving the room. 'I really rather like amethysts.'

'Oh, but I love amethysts,' he replied, 'so long as they are nice large dark stones set in diamonds. They suit *One* so well.'

The next morning when I went to Lady Montdore's room to say good-bye I found Cedric, in a pale mauve silk dressing-gown, sitting on her bed. They were both rubbing cream into their faces out of a large pink pot. It smelt delicious, and certainly belonged to him.

'And after that,' he was saying, 'until the end of her life (she only died just the other day), she wore a thick black veil.'

'And what did he do?'

'He left cards on all Paris, on which he had written *"mille regrets"*.'

4

From the moment that the Montdores first set eyes on Cedric there was no more question of his having come to Hampton for a fortnight; he was obviously there for good and all. They both took him to their hearts and loved him, almost at once, better than they had loved Polly for years, ever since she was a small child; the tremendous vacuum created by her departure was happily filled again, and filled by somebody who was able to give more than Polly had ever given in the way of companionship. Cedric could talk intelligently to Lord Montdore about the objects of art at Hampton. He knew an enormous amount about such things, though in the ordinary sense of the word he was uneducated, ill-read, incapable of the simplest calculation, and curiously ignorant of many quite elementary subjects. He was one of those people who take in the world through eye and ear; his intellect was probably worth very little, but his love of beauty was genuine. The librarian at Hampton was astounded at his bibliographical knowledge. It seemed, for instance, that he could tell at a glance whom a book had been bound for and by whom, and he said that Cedric knew much more than he did himself about eighteenth-century French editions. Lord Montdore had seldom seen his own cherished belongings so intelligently appreciated, and it was a great pleasure to him to spend hours with Cedric going over them. He had doted on Polly; she had been the apple of his eye in theory, but in practice she had never been in any respect a companion to him.

As for Lady Montdore, she became transformed with happiness during the months that followed, transformed, too, in other ways, Cedric taking her appearance in hand with extraordinary results. Just as Boy (it was the hold he had over her) had filled her days with society and painting, Cedric filled them with the pursuit of her own beauty, and to such an egotist this was a more satisfactory hobby. Facial operations, slimming cures, exercises, massage, diet, make-up, new clothes, jewels reset, a blue rinse for her grey hair, pink bows and diamond daisies in the blue curls; it kept her very busy. I saw her less and less, but each time I did she looked more unnaturally modish. Her movements, formerly so ponderous, became smart, spry, and bird-like; she never sat now with her two legs planted on the ground, but threw one over the other, legs which, daily massaged and steamed, gradually lost their flesh and became little more than bone. Her face was lifted, plucked and trimmed, and looked as tidy as Mrs Chaddesley Corbett's, and she learnt to flash a smile brilliant as Cedric's own.

'I make her say "brush" before she comes into a room,' he told me. 'It's a thing I got out of an old book on deportment and it fixes at once this very gay smile on one's face. Somebody ought to tell Lord Alconleigh about it.'

Since she had never hitherto made the smallest effort to appear younger than she was, but had remained fundamentally Edwardian-looking, as though conscious of her own superiority to the little smart ephemeral types, the Chaddesley Corbetts and so on, Cedric's production of her was revolutionary. In my opinion it was not successful; for she made the sacrifice of a grand and characteristic appearance without really gaining in prettiness, but no doubt the effort which it involved made her perfectly happy.

Cedric and I became great friends and he visited me constantly in Oxford, just as Lady Montdore used to before she became so busy, and I must say that I greatly preferred his company to hers. During the later stages of my pregnancy, and after the baby was born, he would come and sit with me for hours on end, and I felt completely at ease with him; I could go on with my sewing, or mending, without bothering about what I looked like, exactly as if he were one of my Radlett cousins. He was kind and thoughtful and affectionate, like a charming woman friend; better, because our friendship was marred by no tinge of jealousy.

Later on, when I had got my figure back after the baby, I began to dress and make myself up with a view to gaining Cedric's approbation, but I soon found that, with the means at my disposal, it was not much use. He knew too much about women and their accessories to be impressed by anything I could manage. For instance, if with a great effort I changed into silk stockings when I expected him, he could see at once that they were Elliston, 5s. 11d., all I could afford, and it really seemed more sensible to stick to lisle. Indeed, he once said to me,

'You know, Fanny, it doesn't matter a bit that you're not able to dress up in expensive clothes, there'd be no point in it anyway. You are like the Royal Family, my darling. Whatever you wear you look exactly the same, just as they do.'

I was not very much pleased, but I knew that he was right. I could never look fashionable, even if I tried as hard as Lady Montdore, with my heather-hair and round salubrious face.

I remember that my mother, during one of her rare visits to England, brought me a little jacket in scarlet cloth from Schiaparelli. It seemed to me quite plain and uninteresting except for the label in its lining, and I longed to put this on the outside so that people would know where it came from. I was wearing it, instead of a cardigan, in my house when Cedric happened to call, and the first thing he said was,

'Aha! So now we dress at Schiaparelli, I see! Whatever next?'

'Cedric! How can you tell?'

'My dear, one can always tell. Things have a signature, if you use your eyes, and mine seem to be trained over a greater range of objects than yours, Schiaparelli – Reboux – Fabergé – Viollet-le-Duc – I can tell at a glance, literally a glance. So your wicked mother the Bolter has been here since last I saw you?'

'Might I not have bought it for myself?'

'No, no my love, you are saving up to educate your twelve brilliant sons, how could you possibly afford twenty-five pounds for a little jacket?'

'Don't tell me!' I said. 'Twenty-five pounds for this?'

'Quite that, I should guess.'

'Simply silly. Why, I could have made it myself.'

'But could you? And if you had would I have come into the room and said Schiaparelli?'

'There's only a yard of stuff in it, worth a pound, if that,' I went on, horrified by the waste of money.

'And how many yards of canvas in a Fragonard? And how much do planks of wood cost, or the skin of a darling goat before they are turned into commodes and morocco? Art is more than yards, just as *One* is more than flesh and bones. By the way, I must warn you that Sonia will be here in a minute, in search of strong tea. I took the liberty of having a word with Mrs Heathery, the love of whose life I am, on my way up, and I also brought some scones from the Cadena which I deposited with her.'

'What is Lady Montdore doing now?' I said, beginning to tidy up the room.

'Now, this very minute? She is at Parker's buying a birthday present for me. It is to be a great surprise, but I went to Parker's and prepared the ground and I shall be greatly surprised if the great surprise is not *Ackerman's Repository*.'

'I thought you turned up your nose at English furniture?' I said.

'Less and less. Provincial but charming is now my attitude and *Ackerman's Repository* is such an amusing book, I saw a copy the other day when Sonia and I went over to Lord Merlin's, and I long to possess it. I expect it will be all right. Sonia loves to give me these large presents, impossible to carry about; she thinks they anchor me to Hampton. I don't blame her, her life there must have been too dull for words, without me.'

'But are you anchored?' I said. 'It always seems to me that the place where you really belong is Paris – I can't imagine you staying here for ever.'

'I can't imagine it either, but the fact is, my darling, that the news from Paris is not too good. I told you, didn't I, that I left my German friend Klugg to look after my apartment and keep it warm for me? Now what do I hear? The baron came last week with a *camion* and took all the furniture, every stick, leaving poor Klugg to sleep on bare boards. I dare say he doesn't notice, he is always quite drunk by bedtime, but for waking up it can't be very nice, and meanwhile I am mourning my commodes. Louis XV – a pair – such *marqueterie*, such bronzes, really important pieces, *objets de musée* – well, often have I told you about them. Gone! The baron, during one fatal afternoon, took everything. Bitter work!'

'What baron?' I asked.

I knew all about Klugg, how hideous and drunken and brutal and German and unlettered he was, so that Cedric never could explain why he put up with his vagaries for a single moment, but the baron was a new figure to me. Cedric was evasive, however. He was better than anybody I have ever known at not answering questions if he did not want to.

'Just another friend. The first night I was in Paris I went to the Opera, and I don't mind telling you, my darling, that all eyes were upon me, in my box, the poor artistes might just as well not have been on the stage at all. Well, one of the eyes belonged to the baron.'

'Two of the eyes, you mean,' I said.

'No dear, one. He wears a patch to make himself look sinister and fascinating. Nobody knows how much I hate barons, I feel exactly like King John whenever I think of them.'

'But Cedric, I don't understand. How could he take your furniture away?'

'How could he? How, indeed? Alas, he has, and that is that. My Savonnerie, my Sèvres, my sanguines, all my treasures gone and I confess I am very low about it, because, although they cannot compare in quality with what I see every day round me at Hampton, one does so love one's own things which one has bought and chosen oneself. I must say the Boulle at Hampton is the best I have ever seen – even at Chèvres we had no Boulle like that. Sensational. Have you been over since we began to clean the bronzes? Oh, you must come. I have taught my friend Archie how to unscrew the bits, scrub them with ammonia, and pour boiling water on them from a kettle so that they dry at once with no moisture left to turn them green. He does it all all day, and when he has finished it glitters like the cave of Aladdin.'

This Archie was a nice, handsome boy, a lorry-driver, whom Cedric had found with his lorry broken down near the gates of Hampton.

'For your ear alone, my darling, it was a stroke of thunder when I saw him. What one does so love about love is the time before they find out what *One* is like.'

'And it's also very nice,' I said, disloyally, 'before *One* finds out what they are like.'

Archie had now left his lorry for ever, and gone to live at Hampton to do odd jobs. Lady Montdore was enthusiastic about him.

'So willing,' she would say, 'so clever of Cedric to think of having him. Cedric always does such original things.'

Cedric went on, 'But I suppose you would think it more hideous than ever, Fanny. I know that you like a room to sparkle with freshness, whereas I like it to glitter with richness. That is where we differ at present, but you'll change. Your taste is really good, and it is bound to mature one day.'

It was true that my taste at this time, like that of the other young people I knew who cared about their houses, favoured pickled or painted furniture with a great deal of white, and upholstery in pale cheerful colours. French furniture with its finely chiselled ormolu (what Cedric called bronzes), its severe lines and perfect proportions was far above my head in those days, while Louis XIV needlework, of which there was a great amount at Hampton, seemed dark and stuffy. I frankly preferred a cheerful chintz.

Cedric's word with Mrs Heathery had excellent results, and even Lady Montdore showed no signs of despising the tea which arrived at the same time as she did. In any case, now that she was happy again, she was much more good-natured about the attempts of the humble, such as myself, to regale her.

Her appearance still gave me quite a jump, though by now I really should have been getting accustomed to her flashing smile, her supple movements, and the pale blue curls, a little sparse upon the head, not unattractively so, but like a baby's curls. Today she was hatless, and wore a tartan ribbon to keep her hair in place. She was dressed in a plain but beautifully made grey coat and skirt, and as she came into the room, which was full of sun, she took her coat off with a curious, swift, double-jointed movement, revealing a piqué blouse and a positively girlish waist-line. It was warm spring weather just then, and I knew that she and Cedric did a lot of sunbathing in a summer-house specially designed by him, as a result of which her skin had gone rather a horrid yellow, and looked as if it had to be soaked in oil to prevent it from falling into a thousand tiny cracks. Her nails were varnished dark red, and this was an improvement, since formerly they had been furrowed and not always quite clean. The old-fashioned hoops of enormous diamonds set in gold which used so stiffly to encircle her stiff fingers were replaced by square-cut diamonds in clusters of cabochon emeralds and rubies, her diamond earrings too had been reset, in the shape of cockle shells, and more large diamonds sparkled in a fashionable pair of clips at her throat. The whole thing was stunning.

But although her aspect was so much changed, her personality remained the same, and the flashing (brush) smile was followed by the well-known up-and-down look.

'Is that your baby making that horrid noise, Fanny?'

'Yes. He never cries as a rule but his teeth are upsetting him.'

'Poor thing,' said Cedric, 'couldn't he go to the dentist?'

'Well, I've got your birthday present, Cedric. It can't be a surprise though, because it's all over the floor of the motor. They seemed to think, at Parker's, that you would like it – a book called *Ackerman's Suppository* or something.'

'Not *Ackerman's Suppository* – not really!' said Cedric, clasping his hands under his chin in a very characteristic gesture. 'How kind you are to me – how could you have guessed? Where did you find it? But, dearest, it's bad about the surprise. Birthday presents really ought to be surprises. I can't get Sonia to enter into the true spirit of birthdays. Fanny, what can *One* do about it?'

I thought *One* had done pretty well. Lady Montdore was famous for never giving presents at all, either for birthdays or at Christmas, and had never even relaxed this rule in favour of the adored Polly, though Lord Montdore used to make up for that by giving her several. But she showered presents, and valuable presents too, on Cedric, snatching at the smallest excuse to do so, and I quite saw that with somebody so intensely appreciative this must be a great pleasure.

'But I have got a surprise for you, as well as the books, something I bought in London,' she said, looking at him fondly.

'No!' said Cedric. I had the feeling he knew all about that, too. 'I shan't have one moment's peace until I've wormed it out of you – how I wish you hadn't told me.'

'You've only got to wait until tomorrow.'

'Well, I warn you I shall wake you up for it at six. Now finish your tea, dear, and come, we ought to be getting back, I'm in a little bit of a fuss to see what Archie has been up to with all those bronzes. He's doing the Boulle today and I have had a horrid idea – suppose he has reassembled it into a lorry by mistake? What would dearest Uncle Montdore say if he suddenly came upon a huge Boulle lorry in the middle of the Long Gallery?'

No doubt, I thought, but that both Lord and Lady Montdore would happily have got into it and been taken for a ride by Cedric. He had completely mesmerized them, and nothing that he could do ever seemed otherwise to them than perfection.

5

Cedric's advent at Hampton naturally created quite a stir in the world outside. London society was not at first given the chance to form an opinion on him, because this was the year following the Financial Crisis – in fact, Cedric and the Crisis had arrived at about the same time, and Lady Montdore, though herself unaffected by it, thought that as there was no entertaining in London it was hardly worth while to keep Montdore House open. She had it shrouded in dust-sheets except for two rooms where Lord Montdore could put up if he wanted to go to the House of Lords.

Lady Montdore and Cedric never stayed there, they sometimes went to London, but only for the day. She no longer invited large house parties to Hampton. She said people could talk about nothing but money any more and it was too boring, but I thought there was another reason, and that she really wanted to keep Cedric to herself.

The county, however, hummed and buzzed with Cedric, and little else was talked of. I need hardly say that Uncle Matthew, after one look, found that the word sewer had become obsolete and inadequate. Scowling, growling, flashing of eyes and grinding of teeth, to a degree hitherto reserved for Boy Dougdale, were intensified a hundredfold at the mere thought of Cedric, and accompanied by swelling veins and apoplectic noises. The drawers at Alconleigh were emptied of the yellowing slips of paper on which my uncle's hates had mouldered all these years, and each now contained a clean new slip with the name, carefully printed in black ink, Cedric Hampton. There was a terrible scene on Oxford platform one day. Cedric went to the bookstall to buy *Vogue*, having mislaid his own copy. Uncle Matthew, who was waiting there for a train, happened to notice that the seams of his coat were piped in a contrasting shade. This was too much for his self-control. He fell upon Cedric and began to shake him like a rat; just then, very fortunately, the train came in, whereupon my uncle, who suffered terribly from train fever, dropped Cedric and rushed to catch it. 'You'd never think,' as Cedric said afterwards, 'that buying *Vogue* magazine could be so dangerous. It was well worth it though, lovely Spring modes.'

The children, however, were in love with Cedric and furious because I would not allow them to meet him in my house, but Aunt Sadie, who seldom took a strong line about anything, had solemnly begged me to keep them apart, and her word with me was law. Besides, from my pinnacle of sophistication as wife and mother, I also considered Cedric unsuitable company for the very young, and when I knew that he was coming to see me I took great care to shoo away any undergraduates who might happen to be sitting about in my drawing-room.

Uncle Matthew and his neighbours seldom agreed on any subject. He despised their opinions, and they in their turn found his violent likes and dislikes quite incomprehensible, taking their cue as a rule from the balanced Boreleys. Over Cedric, however, all were united. Though the Boreleys were not haters in the Uncle Matthew class, they had their own prejudices, things they 'could not stick', foreigners, for example, well-dressed women and the Labour Party. But the thing they could stick least in the world were 'aesthetes – you know – those awful effeminate creatures – pansies'. When, therefore, Lady Montdore, whom anyhow they could not stick much, installed the awful effeminate pansy Cedric at Hampton, and it became borne in upon them that he was henceforth to be their neighbour for ever, quite an important one at that, the future Lord Montdore, hatred really did burgeon in their souls. At the same time they took a morbid interest in every detail of the situation, and these details were supplied to them by Norma, who got her facts, I am ashamed to say, from me. It tickled me so much to make Norma gasp and stretch her eyes with horror that I kept back nothing that might tease her and infuriate the Boreleys.

I soon found out that the most annoying feature of the whole thing to them was the radiant happiness of Lady Montdore. They had all been delighted by Polly's marriage, and even those people who might have been expected wholeheartedly to take Lady Montdore's side over it, such as the parents of pretty young daughters, having said with smug satisfaction, 'Serve her right'. They hated her and were glad to see her downed. Now, it seemed, the few remaining days of this wicked woman, who never invited them to her parties, were being suitably darkened with a sorrow which would surely bring her grey hairs to the grave. The curtain rises for the last act, and the stalls are filled with Boreleys all agog to witness the agony, the dissolution, the muffled drum, the catafalque, the procession to the vault, the lowering to the tomb, the darkness. But what is this? On to the dazzling stage springs Lady Montdore, lithe as a young cat, her grey hairs now a curious shade of blue, with a partner, a terrible creature from Sodom, from Gomorrah, from Paris, and proceeds to dance with him a wild fandango of delight. No wonder they were cross.

On the other hand, I thought the whole thing simply splendid, since I like my fellow-beings to be happy and the new state of affairs at Hampton had so greatly increased the sum of human happiness. An old lady, a selfish old creature admittedly, who deserved nothing at the end but trouble and sickness (but which of us will deserve better?) is suddenly presented with one of life's bonuses, and is rejuvenated, occupied and amused; a charming boy with a great love of beauty and of luxury, a little venal perhaps (but which of us is not if we get the opportunity to be?), whose life had hitherto depended upon the whims of barons, suddenly and respectably acquires two doting parents and a vast heritage of wealth, another bonus; Archie the lorry driver, taken from long cold nights on the road, long oily hours under his lorry, and put to polish ormolu in a warm and scented room; Polly married to the love of her life; Boy married to the greatest beauty of the age, five bonuses, five happy people, and yet the Boreleys were disgusted. They must indeed be against the human race, I thought, so to hate happiness.

I said all this to Davey and he winced a little. 'I wish you needn't go on about Sonia being an old woman on the brink of the grave,' he said, 'she is barely sixty, you know, only about ten years older than your Aunt Emily.'

'Davey, she's forty years older than I am, it must seem old to me. I bet people forty years older than you are seem old to you, now do admit.'

Davey admitted. He also agreed that it is nice to see people happy, but made the reservation that it is only very nice if you happen to like them, and that although he was, in a way, quite fond of Lady Montdore, he did not happen to like Cedric.

'You don't like Cedric?' I said, amazed. 'How couldn't you, Dave? I absolutely love him.'

He replied that, whereas to an English rosebud like myself Cedric must appear as a being from another, darkly glamorous world, he, Davey, in the course of his own wild cosmopolitan wanderings, before he had met and settled down with Aunt Emily, had known too many Cedrics.

'You are lucky,' I said. 'I couldn't know too many. And if you think I find him darkly glamorous, you've got hold of the wrong end of the stick, my dear Dave. He seems to me like a darling Nanny.'

'Darling Nanny! Polar bear – tiger – puma – something that can never be tamed. They always turn nasty in the end. Just you wait, Fanny, all this ormolu radiance will soon blacken, and the last state of Sonia will be worse than her first, I prophesy. I've seen this sort of thing too often.'

'I don't believe it. Cedric loves Lady Montdore.'

'Cedric,' said Davey, 'loves Cedric, and furthermore he comes from the jungle, and just as soon as it suits him he will tear her to pieces and slink back into the undergrowth – you mark my words.'

'Well,' I said, 'if so, the Boreleys will be pleased.'

Cedric himself now sauntered into the room and Davey prepared to leave. I think after all the horrid things he had just been saying he was afraid of seeming too cordial to him in front of me. It was very difficult not to be cordial to Cedric, he was so disarming.

'I shan't see you again, Fanny,' Davey said, 'until I get back from my cruise.'

'Oh, are you going for a cruise – how delicious – where?' said Cedric.

'In search of a little sun. I give a few lectures on Minoan things and go cheap.'

'I do wish Aunt Emily would go too,' I said, 'it would be so good for her.'

'She'll never move until after Siegfried's death,' said Davey. 'You know what she is.'

When he had gone I said to Cedric,

'What d'you think, he may be able to go and see Polly and Boy in Sicily – wouldn't it be interesting?'

Cedric, of course, was deeply fascinated by anything to do with Polly.

'The absent influence, so boring and so overdone in literature, but I see now that in real life it can eat you with curiosity.'

'When did you last hear from her, Fanny?' he said.

'Oh, months ago, and then it was only a postcard. I'm so delighted about Davey seeing them because he's always so good at telling. We really shall hear how they are getting on, from him.'

'Sonia has still never mentioned her to me,' said Cedric, 'never once.'

'That's because she never thinks of her, then.'

'I'm sure she doesn't. This Polly can't be much of a personality, to have left such a small dent where she used to live?'

'Personality –' I said. 'I don't know. The thing about Polly is her beauty.'

'Describe it.'

'Oh, Cedric, I've described it to you hundreds of times.' It rather amused me to do so, though, because I knew that it teased him.

'Well,' I said, 'as I've often told you before, she is so beautiful that it's difficult to pay much attention to what she is saying, or to make out what she's really like as a person, because all you want to do is just gaze and gaze.'

Cedric looked sulky, as he always did when I talked like this.

'More beautiful than *One*?' he said.

'Very much like you, Cedric.'

'So you say, but I don't find that you gaze and gaze at *One*, on the contrary, you listen intently, with your eye out of the window.'

'She is very much like you, but all the same,' I said firmly, 'she must be more beautiful because there is that thing about the gazing.'

This was perfectly true, and not only said to annoy poor Cedric and make him jealous. He was like Polly, and very good-looking, but not an irresistible magnet to the eye as she was.

'I know exactly why,' he said, 'it's my beard, all that horrible shaving. I shall send to New York this very day for some wax – you can't conceive the agony it is, but if it will make you gaze, Fanny, it will be worth it.'

'Don't bother to do that,' I said. 'It's not the shaving. You do look like Polly but you are not as beautiful. Lady Patricia also looked like her, but it wasn't the same thing. It's something extra that Polly has, which I can't explain, I can only tell you that it is so.'

'What extra can she possibly have except beardlessness?'

'Lady Patricia was quite beardless.'

'You are horrid. Never mind, I shall try it, and you'll see. People used to gaze before my beard grew, like mad, even in Nova Scotia. You are so fortunate not to be a beauty, Fanny, you'll never know the agony of losing your looks.'

'Thank you,' I said.

'And as talking about pretty Polly makes us both so disagreeable let's get on to the subject of Boy.'

'Ah now, nobody could say that Boy was pretty. No gazing there. Boy is old and grizzled and hideous.'

'Now Fanny, that's not true, dear. Descriptions of people are only interesting if they happen to be true, you know. I've seen many photographs of Boy, Sonia's books are full of them, from Boy playing Diabolo, Boy in puttees for the war, to Boy with his bearer Boosee. After India I think she lost her Brownie, in the move perhaps, because "Pages from Our Indian Diary" seems to be the last book, but that was only three years ago and Boy was still ravishing then, the kind of looks I adore, stocky and with deep attractive furrows all over his face – dependable.'

'Dependable!'

'Why do you hate him so much, Fanny?'

'Oh, I don't know, he gives me the creeps. He's such a snob, for one thing.'

'I like that,' said Cedric. 'I am one myself.'

'Such a snob that living people aren't enough for him, he has to get to know the dead, as well – the titled dead of course, I mean. He dives about in their Memoirs so that he can talk about his dear Duchesse de Dino, or "as Lady Bessborough so truly says". He can reel off pedigrees, he always knows just how everybody was related, royal families and things I mean. Then he writes books about all these people, and after that anybody would think they were his own personal property. Ugh!'

'Exactly as I had supposed,' said Cedric, 'a handsome, cultivated man, the sort of person I like the best. Gifted, too. His embroidery, really wonderful, and the dozens of *toiles* by him in the squash court are worthy of the Douanier himself, landscapes with gorillas. Original and bold.'

'Gorillas! Lord and Lady Montdore, and anybody else who would pose.'

'Well, it is original and bold to depict my aunt and uncle as gorillas, I wouldn't dare. I think Polly is a very lucky girl.'

'The Boreleys think you will end by marrying Polly, Cedric.' Norma had propounded this thrilling theory to me the day before. They thought that it would be a death blow to Lady Montdore, and longed for it to happen.

'Very silly of them, dear, I should have thought they only had to look at *One* to see how unlikely that is. What else do the Boreleys say about me?'

'Cedric, do come and meet Norma one day – I simply long to see you together.'

'I think not, dear, thank you.'

'But why? You're always asking what she says and she's always asking what you say, you'd much better ask each other and do without the middleman.'

'The thing is, I believe she would remind me of Nova Scotia, and when that happens my spirits go down, down, past *grande pluie* to *tempête*. The house-carpenter at Hampton reminds me, don't ask me why but he does, and I have to rudely look away every time I meet him. I believe that's why Paris suits me so well, there's not a shade of Nova Scotia there, and perhaps it's also why I put up with the Baron all those years. The Baron could have come from many a land of spices, but from Nova Scotia he could not have come. Whereas Boreleys abound there. But though I don't want to meet them I always like hearing about them, so do go on with what they think about *One*.'

'Well, so then Norma was full of you just now, when I met her out shopping, because it seems you travelled down from London with her brother Jock yesterday, and now he can literally think of nothing else.'

'Oh, how exciting. How did he know it was me?'

'Lots of ways. The goggles, the piping, your name on your luggage. There is nothing anonymous about you, Cedric.'

'Oh, good.'

'So according to Norma he was in a perfect panic, sat with one eye on you and the other on the communication cord, because he expected you to pounce at any minute.'

'Heavens! What does he look like?'

'You ought to know. It seems you were quite alone together after Reading.'

'Well, darling, I only remember a dreadful moustachioed murderer sitting in a corner. I remember him particularly, because I kept thinking, "Oh, the luck of being *One* and not somebody like that".'

'I expect that was Jock. Sandy and white.'

'That's it. Oh, so that's a Boreley, is it? And do you imagine people often make advances to him, in trains?'

'He says you gave him hypnotic stares through your glasses.'

'The thing is, he did have rather a pretty tweed on.'

'And then, apparently, you made him get your suitcase off the rack at Oxford, saying you are not allowed to lift things.'

'No, and nor I am. It was very heavy, not a sign of a porter as usual, I might have hurt myself. Anyway, it was all right because he terribly sweetly got it down for me.'

'Yes, and now he's simply furious that he did. He says you hypnotized him.'

'Oh, poor him, I do so know the feeling.'

'Whatever had you got in it, Cedric? He says it simply weighed a ton.'

'*Complets*,' Cedric said, 'and a few small things for my face. Very little, really. I have found a lovely new resting-cream I must tell you about, by the way.'

'And now they are all saying, "There you are – if he even fixed old Jock, no wonder he has got round the Montdores".'

'But why on earth should I want to get round the Montdores?'

'Wills and things. Living at Hampton.'

'My dear, come to that, Chèvres-Fontaine is twenty times more beautiful than Hampton.'

'But could you go back there now, Cedric?' I said.

Cedric gave me rather a nasty look and went on,

'But in any case I wish people would understand that there's never much point in hanging about for wills – it's just not worth it. I have a friend who used to spend months of every year with an old uncle in the Sarthe so as to stay in his will. It was torture to him, because he knew the person he loved was being unfaithful to him in Paris, and anyhow, the Sarthe is utterly lugubrious, you know. But all the same, he went pegging away at it. Then what occurs? The uncle dies, my poor friend inherits the house in the Sarthe, and now he feels obliged to live a living death there so as to make himself believe that there was some point after all in having wasted months of his youth in the Sarthe. You see my argument? It's a vicious circle, and there is nothing vicious about me. The thing is, I love Sonia, that's why I stay.'

I believed him, really. Cedric lived in the present. It would not be like him to bother about such things as wills; if ever there was a grasshopper, a lily of the field, it was he.

*

When Davey got back from his cruise he rang me up and said he would come over to luncheon and tell me about Polly. I thought Cedric might as well come and hear it at first hand. Davey was always better with an audience even if he did not much like its component parts, so I rang up Hampton, and Cedric accepted to lunch with pleasure and then said could he possibly stay with me for a night or two?

'Sonia has gone for this orange cure – yes, total starvation except for orange juice, but don't mind too much for her, I know she'll cheat. Uncle Montdore is in London for the House and I feel sad, all alone here. I'd love to be with you and to do some serious Oxford sightseeing, which there's never time for when I've got Sonia with me. That will be charming, Fanny, thank you, dear. One o'clock, then.'

Alfred was very busy just then and I was delighted to think I should have Cedric's company for a day or two. I cleared the decks by warning Aunt Sadie that he would be there, and telling my undergraduate friends that I should not be wanting them around for the present.

'Who is that spotty child?' Cedric had once said, when a boy who had been crouching by my fireplace got up and vanished at a look from me.

'I see him as the young Shelley,' I answered, sententiously, no doubt.

'And *I* see him as the young Woodley.'

Davey arrived first.

'Cedric is coming,' I said, 'so you mustn't begin without him.' I could see he was bursting with his news.

'Oh, Cedric, it is too bad, Fanny, I never come without finding that monster here, he seems to live in your house. What does Alfred think of him?'

'Doubt if he knows him by sight, to tell you the truth. Come and see the baby, Dave.'

'Sorry if I'm late, darlings,' Cedric said, floating in, 'one has to drive so slowly in England, because of the walking *Herrschaften*. Why are the English roads always so covered with these tweeded stumpers?'

'They are colonels,' I said, 'don't French colonels go for walks?'

'Much too ill. They have always lost a leg or two and been terribly gassed. I can see that French wars must have been far bloodier than English ones, though I do know a colonel, in Paris, who walks to the antique shops sometimes.'

'How do they take their exercise?' I asked.

'Quite another way, darling. You haven't started, about Boy, have you? Oh, how loyal. I was delayed by Sonia, too, on the telephone. She's in all her states – it seems they've had her up for stealing the nurses' breakfast – well, had her up in front of the principal, who spoke quite cruelly to her, and said that if she does it again, or gets one more bit of illicit food, she'll have her holiday. Just imagine, no dinner, one orange juice at midnight, and woken up by the smell of kippers. So naturally, the poor darling sneaked out and pinched one, and they caught her with it under her dressing-gown. I'm glad to say she'd eaten most of it before they got it away from her. The thing is she started off demoralized by finding your name in the visitors' book, Davey. Apparently she gave a scream and said, "But he's a living skeleton, whatever was he doing here?" and they said you had gone there to put on weight. What's the idea?'

'The idea,' said Davey, impatiently, 'is health. If you are too fat you lose and if you are too thin you gain. I should have thought a child could understand that. But Sonia won't stick it for a day, no self-discipline.'

'Just like *One*, poor darling,' said Cedric. 'But then, what are we to do to get rid of those kilos? Vichy, perhaps?'

'My dear, look at the kilos she's lost already,' I said, 'she's really so thin, ought she to get any thinner?'

'It's just that little extra round the hips,' said Cedric, 'a jersey and skirt is the test, and she doesn't look quite right in that yet – and there's a weeny roll round her ribs. Besides, they say the orange juice clears the skin. Oh, I do hope she sticks it for a few more days, for her own sake, you know. She says another patient told her of a place in the village where you can have Devonshire teas, but I begged her to be careful. After what happened this morning they're sure to be on the look-out and one more slip may be fatal, what d'you think, Davey?'

'Yes, they're madly strict,' said Davey. 'There'd be no point, otherwise.'

We sat down to our luncheon and begged Davey to begin his story.

'I may as well start by telling you that I don't think they are at all happy.'

Davey, I knew, was never a one for seeing things through rose-coloured spectacles, but he spoke so definitely and with so grave an emphasis that I felt I must believe him.

'Oh, Dave, don't say that. How dreadful.'

Cedric, who, since he did not know and love Polly, was rather indifferent as to whether she was happy or not, said,

'Now, Davey dear, you're going much too fast. New readers begin here. You left your boat –'

'I left my ship at Syracuse, having wired them from Athens that I would be arriving for one night, and they met me on the quay with a village taxi. They have no motor car of their own.'

'Every detail. They were dressed?'

'Polly wore a plain blue cotton frock and Boy was in shorts.'

'Wouldn't care to see Boy's knees,' I said.

'They're all right,' said Davey, standing up for Boy as usual.

'Well, then, Polly? Beautiful?'

'Less beautiful' (Cedric looked delighted to hear this news) 'and peevish. Nothing right for her. Hates living abroad, can't learn the language, talks Hindustani to the servants, complains that they steal her stockings –'

'You're going much too fast, we're still in the taxi, you can't skip to stockings like this – how far from Syracuse?'

'About an hour's drive, and beautiful beyond words – the situation, I mean. The villa is on a south-easterly slope looking over olive trees, umbrella pines and vineyards to the sea – you know, the regular Mediterranean view that you can never get tired of. They've taken the house, furnished, from Italians and complain about it ceaselessly, it seems to be on their minds, in fact. I do see that it can't be very nice in winter, no heating except open fireplaces which smoke, bath-water never hot, none of the windows fit, and so on, you know. Italian houses are always made for the heat, and of course, it can be jolly cold in Sicily. The inside is hideous, all khaki and bog oak, depressing if you had to be indoors much. But at this time of year it's ideal, you live on a terrace, roofed in with vines and bougainvillea – I never saw such a perfect spot – huge tubs of geraniums everywhere – simply divine.'

'Oh, dear, as I seem to have taken their place in life, I do wish we could swop over sometimes,' said Cedric. 'I do so love Sicily.'

'I think they'd be all for it,' said Davey, 'they struck me as being very homesick. Well, we arrived in time for luncheon, and I struggled away with the food (Italian cooking, so oily).'

'What did you talk about?'

'Well, you know, really, it was one long wail from them about how difficult everything is, more expensive than they thought it would be and how the people – village people, I mean – don't really help but say yes yes the whole time and nothing gets done, and how they are supposed to have vegetables out of the garden in return for paying the gardener's wages but actually they have to buy everything and as they are sure he sells the vegetables in the village they suppose that it is their own that they buy back again: how when they first came there wasn't a kettle in the place and the blankets were as hard as boards and none of the electric light switches worked and no lamps by the beds – you know, the usual complaints of people who take furnished houses, I've heard them a hundred times. After luncheon it got very hot, which Polly doesn't like, and she went off to her room with everything drawn and I had a session with Boy on the terrace, and then I really saw how the land lay. Well, all I can say is I know it is wrong, not right, to arouse the sexual instincts of little girls so that they fall madly in love with you, but the fact is, poor old Boy is taking a fearful punishment. You see, he has literally nothing to do from morning to night, except water his geraniums, and you know how bad it is for them to have too much water; of course, they are all leaf as a result. I told him so. He has nobody to talk to, no club, no London Library, no neighbours, and of course, above all, no Sonia to keep him on the run. I don't expect he ever realized what a lot of his time used to be taken up by Sonia. Polly's no company for him, really, you can see that, and in many ways she seems dreadfully on his nerves. She's so insular, you know, nothing is right for her, she hates the place, hates the people, even hates the climate. Boy at least is very cosmopolitan, speaks beautiful Italian, prepared to be interested in the local folk-lore and things like that, but you can't be interested quite alone and Polly is so discouraging. Everything seems rot to her and she only longs for England.'

'Funny,' I said, 'that she should be quite so narrow-mindedly English when you think that she spent five years in India.'

'Oh, my dear child, the butler was grander and the weather was hotter but otherwise there wouldn't be much to choose between Hampton and Viceroy's House. If anything, Viceroy's House was the less cosmopolitan of the two, I should say, and certainly it was no preparation for Sicilian housekeeping. No, she simply loathes it, so there is the poor fellow, shut up month after month with a cross little girl he has known from a baby. Not much cop, you must admit.'

'I thought,' said Cedric, 'that he was so fond of dukes? Sicily is full of heavenly dukes, you know.'

'Fairly heavenly, and they're nearly always away. Anyhow, he doesn't count them the same as French or English dukes.'

'Well, that's nonsense, nobody could be grander than Pincio. But if he doesn't count them (I do see some of the others are a bit unreal) and if he's got to live abroad, I can't imagine why he doesn't choose Paris. Plenty of proper dukes there – fifty to be exact – Souppes told me so once, you know how they can only talk about each other, in that trade.'

'My dear Cedric, they are very poor – they can't afford to live in England, let alone Paris. That's why they are still in Sicily, if it wasn't for that they'd come home now like a shot. Boy lost money in the crash last autumn, and he told me that if he hadn't got a very good let for Silkin they would really be almost penniless. Oh, dear, and when you think how rich Polly would have been –'

'No cruel looks at *One*,' said Cedric. 'Fair's fair, you know.'

'Anyway, it's a shocking business and only shows where dear old sex can land a person. I never saw anybody so pleased as Boy was when I appeared – like a dog let off a lead. Wanted to hear every single thing that's been going on – you could just see how lonely and bored he feels, poor chap.'

But I was thinking of Polly. If Boy was bored and lonely she was not likely to be very happy either. The success or failure of all human relationships lies in the atmosphere each person is aware of creating for the other, what atmosphere could a disillusioned Polly feel that she was creating for a bored and lonely Boy? Her charm, apart from her beauty, and husbands, we know, get accustomed to the beauty of their wives so that it ceases to strike them at the heart, her charm used to derive from the sphinx-like quality which came from her secret dream of Boy; in the early days of that dream coming true, at Alconleigh, happiness had made her irresistible. But I quite saw that with the riddle solved, and if the happiness were dissolved, Polly, without her own little daily round of Madame Rita, Debenhams and the hairdresser to occupy her, and too low in vitality to invent new interests for herself, might easily sink into sulky dumps. She was not at all likely to find consolation in Sicilian folk-lore, I knew, and probably not, not yet, anyhow, in Sicilian noblemen.

'Oh, dear,' I said. 'If Boy isn't happy I don't suppose Polly can be either. Oh, poor Polly.'

'Poor Polly – m'm – but at least it was her idea,' said Davey, 'my heart bleeds for poor Boy. Well, he can't say I didn't warn him, over and over again.'

'What about a baby?' I asked, 'any signs?'

'None that I could see, but after all, how long have they been married? Eighteen months? Sonia was eighteen years before she had Polly.'

'Oh, goodness!' I said. 'I shouldn't imagine the Lecturer, in eighteen years' time, will be able –'

I was stopped by a well-known hurt look on Davey's face.

'Perhaps that is what makes them sad,' I ended, rather lamely.

'Possibly. Anyhow, I can't say that I formed a happy impression.'

At this point Cedric was called to the telephone, and Davey said to me in a lowered voice,

'Entirely between you and me, Fanny, and this is not to go any further, I think Polly is having trouble with Boy.'

'Oh, dear,' I said, 'kitchen-maids?'

'No,' said Davey, 'not kitchen-maids.'

'Don't tell me!' I said, horrified.

Cedric came back and said that Lady Montdore had been caught red-handed having elevenses in the Devonshire tea-rooms and had been given the sack. She told him that the motor would call for him on its way, so that she would have a companion for the drive home.

'There now,' he said gloomily. 'I shan't have my little visit to you after all, and I had so been looking forward to it.'

It struck me that Cedric had arranged the orange cure less with a view to getting rid of kilos than to getting rid of Lady Montdore for a week or two. Life with her must have been wearing work, even to Cedric, with his unflagging spirits and abounding energy and he may well have felt that he had earned a short rest after nearly a year of it.

6

Cedric Hampton and Norma Cozens met at last, but though the meeting took place in my garden it was none of my arranging; a pure chance. I was sitting, one afternoon of Indian summer, on my lawn, where the baby was crawling about stark naked and so brown that he looked like a little Topsy, when Cedric's golden head appeared over the fence, accompanied by another head, that of a thin and ancient horse.

'I'm coming to explain,' he said, 'but I won't bring my friend, I'll attach him to your fence, darling. He's so sad and good, he won't do any harm, I promise.'

A moment later he joined me in the garden. I put the baby back in its pram and was turning to Cedric to ask what this was all about when Norma came up the lane which passes my garden on her afternoon trudge with her dogs. Now the Boreley family consider that they have a special mandate, bestowed from on high, to deal with everything that regards the horse. They feel it to be their duty no less than their right, and therefore the moment she saw Cedric's friend, sad and good, standing by my fence, Norma unhesitatingly came into the garden to see what she could do about it. I introduced Cedric to her.

'I don't want to interrupt you,' she said, her eye upon the famous piping of the seams, brown today, upon a green linen coat, vaguely Tyrolean in aspect, 'but there's a very old mare, Fanny, tied up to your fence. Do you know anything about it – whom does she belong to?'

'Don't, dear Mrs Cozens, tell me that the first horse I have ever owned is a female!' said Cedric, with a glittering (brush) smile.

'The animal is a mare,' said Norma, 'and if she is yours I must tell you that you ought to be ashamed of yourself for keeping her in that dreadful condition.'

'Oh, but I only began keeping her ten minutes ago, and I hope that when you see her again, in a few months' time, you simply won't know her.'

'Do you mean to say that you bought that creature? She ought to go straight away to the kennels.'

'The kennels? But why – she's not a dog!'

'The knacker, the horse-butcher,' said Norma impatiently, 'she must be destroyed, put down immediately, or I shall ring up the R.S.P.C.A.'

'Oh, please don't do that. I'm not being cruel to her, I'm being kind. That horrid man I bought her from, he was being beastly, he was taking her to the knacker. My plan was to save her from him, I couldn't bear to see the expression on her poor face.'

'Well, but what are you going to do with her, my dear boy?'

'I thought – set her free.'

'Set her free? She's not a bird, you know, you can't go setting horses free like that – not in England, anyway.'

'Yes I can. Not in Oxford perhaps, but where I live there is a *vieux parc solitaire et glacé*, and it is my intention to set her free there, to have happy days away from knackers. Isn't knacker a hateful word, Mrs Cozens?'

'The grazing at Hampton is let,' said Norma. It was the kind of detail the Boreleys could be counted on to tell you. Cedric, however, took no notice and went on,

'She was being driven down the street in a van with her head sticking out at the back, and I could see at once that she was longing for some nice person to get her out of this unpleasant situation, so I stopped the van and bought her. You could see how relieved she felt.'

'How much?'

'Well, I offered the man forty pounds, it was all I had on me, so he kindly let me have her for that.'

'Forty pounds!' cried Norma, aghast. 'Why, you could get a hunter for less than forty pounds.'

'But my dearest Mrs Cozens, I don't want a hunter, it's the last thing, I'd be far too frightened. Besides, look at the time you have to get up – I heard them the other morning in the woods, half-past six. Well, you know, I'm afraid it's "up before seven *dead* before eleven" with *One*. No, I just wanted this special old clipper-clopper, she's not the horse to make claims on a chap, she won't want to be ridden all the time as a younger horse might, and there she'll be, if I feel like having a few words with her occasionally. But the great question now, which I came to tease practical Fanny with, is how to get her home?'

'And if you go buying up all the horses that are fit for the kennels, however do you imagine hounds are going to be fed?' said Norma, in great exasperation. She was related to several Masters of foxhounds and her sister had a pack of beagles, so no doubt she was acquainted with all their problems.

'I shan't buy up all the horses,' said Cedric, soothingly, 'only this one, which I took a liking for. Now, dear Mrs Cozens, do stop being angry and just tell me how I can get her home, because I know you can help if you want to and I simply can't get over the luck of meeting you here at the very moment when I needed you so badly.'

Norma began to weaken, as people so very often did with Cedric. It was extraordinary how fast he could worm his way through a thick crust of prejudice, and, just as in the case of Lady Montdore, the people who hated him the most were generally those who had seen him from afar but never met him. But whereas Lady Montdore had 'all this' to help in her conquest of disapproval, Cedric relied upon his charm, his good looks and his deep inborn knowledge of human, and especially female, nature.

'Please,' he said, his eyes upon her, blinking a little.

I could see that he had done the trick; Norma was considering.

'Well,' she said at last, 'there are two ways of doing it. I can lend you a saddle and you can ride her over – I'm not sure she's up to it, but you could see –'

'No, Mrs Cozens, no. I have some literary sense – Fauntleroy on his pony, gallant little figure, the wind in his golden curls, all right, and if my uncle had had the sense to get me over from Canada when I was younger we should have seen that very thing, I've no doubt. But the gloomy old don on Rosinante is quite another matter, and I can't face it.'

'Which gloomy old don?' asked Norma, with interest. 'But it makes no odds, she'd never get there. Twenty miles, now I come to think of it – and I expect she's as lame as a cat.'

She went to the fence and peered over.

'Those hocks –! You know, it honestly would be kinder – Oh, very well, very well. If nothing I can say will make you understand that the animal would be far happier dead, you'll have to get the horse-box. Shall I ring up Stubly now, on Fanny's telephone, and see if he can come round at once?'

'No! You wouldn't do that for me? Oh, dearest Mrs Cozens I can only say – angel! What a miracle that I met you!'

'Lie down,' she said, to the Borders, and went indoors.

'Sexually unsatisfied, poor her,' said Cedric, when she had gone.

'Really Cedric, what nonsense. She's got four children.'

'I can't help it. Look at all those wrinkles. She could try patting in muscle oil, of course, and I shall suggest it as soon as I get to know her a little better, but I'm afraid the trouble is more deep-seated. Of course, I feel certain the Professor must be a secret queer – nobody but a queer would ever marry Norma, to begin with.'

'Why? She's not at all boyish?'

'No, dearest, it isn't that, but there is a certain type of Norma-ish lady which appeals to queers, don't ask me why, but so it is. Now supposing I arranged for her to come over every Tuesday and share a facial with Sonia, what do you think? The competition would be good for both of them, and it would cheer Sonia up to see a woman so much younger, so much more deeply haggard.'

'I wouldn't,' I said. 'Norma always says she can't stick Lady Montdore.'

'Does she know her? Of course, I doubt if anything short of a nice lift would fix Mrs Cozens, but we could teach her "brush" and a little charm to help the Waynflete Prof. to do his work a bit better, or failing that, and I fear it's rather a desperate hope, some nice Woodley might come to the rescue. No, darling, not *One*,' he added, in response to a meaning look from me. 'The cuticles are too desperately anaphrodisiac.'

'I thought you never wanted to see her because she reminded you of Nova Scotia?'

'Yes, I thought she would, but she is too English. She fascinates me for that reason, you know how very very pro-English I am becoming. The cuticles are rather Nova Scotian but her soul is the soul of Oxfordshire and I shall cultivate her after this like mad.'

Some half an hour later, as Cedric went off, sitting by the driver of the horse-box, Norma, panting a little from her efforts with the mare who had stubbornly refused at first to get into it, said,

'You know, that boy has some good in him after all. What a shame he couldn't have gone to a decent public school instead of being brought up in those shocking colonies.'

To my amazement, and great secret annoyance, Cedric and Norma now became extremely friendly, and he went to see her, when he was in Oxford, quite as often as he did me.

'Whatever do you talk about?' I said to him, crossly.

'Oh, we have cosy little chats about this and that. I love Englishwomen, they are so restful.'

'Well, I'm fairly fond of old Norma, but I simply can't imagine what you see in her, Cedric.'

'I suppose I see whatever you see,' he replied, carelessly.

After a bit, he persuaded her to give a dinner party, to which he promised to bring Lady Montdore. Lord Montdore never went out now, and was sinking happily into old age. His wife being provided with a companion for every hour of the day, he was not only allowed but positively encouraged to have a good long nap in the afternoon, and he generally either had his dinner in bed or shuffled off there immediately after dinner. The advent of Cedric must have proved an absolute blessing to him in more ways than one. People very soon got into the habit of asking Cedric with Lady Montdore instead of her husband, and it must be said that he was much better company; they were going out more now than when Cedric first arrived, the panic caused by the financial crisis was subsiding and people had begun to entertain again. Lady Montdore was much too fond of society to keep away from it for long, and Cedric, firmly established at Hampton, weighed down with many large expensive gifts, could surely now be shown to her friends without danger of losing him.

In spite of the fact that she was by way of being unable to stick Lady Montdore, Norma got into a perfect state over this dinner party, dropping in on me at all hours to discuss the menu and the fellow guests, and finally imploring me to come on the morning of the day to make a pudding for her. I said that I would do so on one condition, she must buy a quart of cream. She wriggled like an eel not to have to do this, but I was quite firm. Then she said would the top of the milk do? No, I said, it must be thick rich unadulterated cream. I said I would bring it with me and let her know how much I had paid for it, and she very reluctantly agreed. Although she was, I knew, very wealthy, she never spent a penny more than she could help on her house, her table, or her clothes (except her riding-clothes, for she was always beautifully turned out in the hunting-field and I am sure her horses lived on an equine substitute for cream). So I went round, and, having provided myself with the suitable ingredients, I made her a crème Chantilly. As I got back to my own house the telephone bell was pealing away – Cedric.

'I thought I'd better warn you my darling that we are chucking poor Norma tonight.'

'Cedric, you simply can't, I never heard anything so awful, she has bought cream!'

He gave an unkind laugh and said,

'So much the better for those weedy tots I see creeping about her house.'

'But why should you chuck, are you ill?'

'Not the least bit ill, thank you, love. The thing is that Merlin wants us to go over there for dinner, he has got fresh *foie gras*, and a fascinating Marquesa with eyelashes two inches long, he measured. Do you see how *One* can't resist it?'

'*One* must resist it,' I said, frantically. 'You simply cannot chuck poor Norma now, you'll never know the trouble she's taken. Besides, do think of us, you miserable boy, we can't chuck, only think of the dismal evening we shall have without you.'

'I know, poor you, won't it be lugubrious?'

'Cedric, all I can say is you are a sewer.'

'Yes, darling, *mea culpa*. But it's not so much that I want to chuck as that I absolutely know I shall. I don't even intend to, I fully intend not to, it is that something in my body will make me. When I've rung off from speaking to you, I know that my hand will creep back to the receiver again of its own accord, and I shall hear my voice, but quite against my will, mind you, asking for Norma's number, and then I shall be really horrified to hear it breaking this dreadful news to Norma. So much worse, now I know about the cream, too. But there it is. But what I rang you up to say is, don't forget you are on *One's* side – no disloyalty Fanny, please, I absolutely count, dear, on you not to egg Norma on to be furious. Because so long as you don't do that you'll find she won't mind a bit, not a bit. So, solidarity between working girls, and I'll promise to come over tomorrow and tell about the eyelashes.'

Oddly enough, Cedric was right and Norma was not in the least put out. His excuse, and he had told the truth, merely adding a touch of embroidery by saying that Lady Montdore had been at school with the Marquesa, was considered quite a reasonable one, since dinner with Lord Merlin was recognized at Oxford as being the very pinnacle of human happiness. Norma rang me up to say that her dinner party was postponed, in the voice of a society hostess who postpones dinner parties every day of the week. Then, lapsing into more normal Oxford parlance, she said,

'It's a bore about the cream, because they are coming on Wednesday now, and it will never keep in this weather. Can you come back and make another pudding on Wednesday morning, Fanny? All right, and I'll pay you for both lots together, if that suits you. Everybody is free and I think the flowers may last over, so see you then, Fanny.'

But on Wednesday, Cedric was in bed with a high temperature, and on Thursday he was rushed to London by ambulance and operated upon for peritonitis, lying between life and death for several days, and in the end it was quite two months before the dinner party could take place.

At last, however, the date was fixed again, another pudding was made, and, at Norma's suggestion, I invited my Uncle Davey to come and stay for it, to pair off with her beagling sister. Norma looked down on dons quite as much as Lady Montdore did, and as for undergraduates, although of course she must have known that such things existed, since they provided her husband and mine with a livelihood, she certainly never thought of them as human beings and possible diners-out.

It would never formerly have occurred to me that 'touching', a word often on Lady Montdore's lips (it was very much of her day), could come to have any relation to herself, but on the occasion of Norma's dinner, the first time I had seen Lady Montdore with Cedric since his illness, there was really something touching about her attitude towards him. It was touching to see this hitherto redoubtable and ponderous personage, thin, now, as a rake, in her little-girl dress of dark tulle over pink taffeta, with her little-girl head of pale blue curls, dark blue ribbons and a swarm of diamond bees, as she listened through her own conversation to whatever Cedric might be saying, as she squinted out of the corner of her eye to see if he was happy and amused, perhaps even just to be quite sure that he was actually there, in the flesh; touching to see with what reluctance she left the dining-room after dinner; touching to watch her as she sat with the rest of us in the drawing-room waiting for the men to return, silent, or speaking at random, her eyes fixed upon the door like a spaniel waiting for its master. Love with her had blossomed late and strangely, but there could be no doubt that it had now blossomed, and that this thorny old plant had very much altered in character to accord with the tender flowers and spring-time verdure which now so unexpectedly adorned it. During the whole of the evening there was only one respect in which she behaved as she would have done in her pre-Cedric days. She piled wood and coal, without so much as a by your leave, on to the tiny fire, Norma's concession to the fact that winter had begun, so that by the end of the evening we sat in a mellow warmth such as I had never known in that room before.

The men, as they always do in Oxford, remained an inordinate length of time over their port, so long, in fact, that Lady Montdore, with growing impatience, suggested to Norma that they might be sent for. Norma, however, looked so absolutely appalled at the idea that Lady Montdore did not press it any further, but went on with her self-appointed task as stoker, one spaniel-eye on the door.

'The only way to make a good fire,' she said, 'is to put on enough coal. People have all kinds of theories about it, but it's really very simple. Perhaps we could ask for another scuttle, Mrs Cozens? Very kind. Cedric mustn't get a chill, whatever happens.'

'Dreadful,' I said, 'him being so ill, wasn't it?'

'Don't speak of it. I thought I should die. Yes, well, as I was saying. It's exactly the same with coffee, you know, people have those percolators and things and get the Bolter to buy them special beans in Kenya, perfectly pointless. Coffee is good if it is made strong enough and nasty if it is not. What we had just now would have been quite all right if your cook had put in three times the amount, you know. What can they be talking about in the dining-room? It's not as if any of them were interested in politics.'

At last the door opened. Davey came in first, looking bored and made straight for the fire. Cedric, the Professor, and Alfred followed in a bunch, still pursuing a conversation which seemed to be interesting them deeply.

'Just a narrow edging of white –' I heard Cedric say, through the open door, as they came down the passage.

Later on I remembered to ask Alfred what could have led up to this remark, so typical of Cedric but so untypical of the conversation in that house, and he replied that they had been having a most fascinating talk on burial custom in the High Yemen.

'I fear,' he said, 'that you bring out the worst in Cedric Hampton, Fanny. He is really a most intelligent young man, interested in a large range of subjects, though I have no doubt at all that when he is with you he confines himself, as you do, to remarks in the nature of "and did you notice the expression on her face when she saw who was there?" because he knows that general subjects do not amuse you, only personalities. With those whose horizon is a little wider he can be very serious, let me tell you.'

The fact was that Cedric could bring out edgings of white to suit all tastes.

'Well, Fanny, how do you like it?' he asked me, giving a twitch to Lady Montdore's tulle skirt. 'We ordered it by telephone when we were at Craigside – don't you die for television – Mainbocher simply couldn't believe that Sonia had lost so much weight.'

Indeed, she was very thin.

'I sit in a steam barrel,' she said, looking fondly at Cedric, 'for an hour or two, and then that nice Mr Wixman comes down twice a week when we are at Hampton and he beats and beats me and the morning is gone in a flash. Cedric sees the cook for me nowadays, I find I can't take very much interest in food, in my barrel.'

'But my dear Sonia,' said Davey, 'I hope you consult Dr Simpson about all this? I am horrified to see you in such a state, really much too thin, nothing but skin and bones. You know, at our age, it's most dangerous to play about with one's weight, a terrible strain on the heart.'

It was generous of Davey to talk about 'our age', since Lady Montdore was certainly fourteen years older than he was.

'Dr Simpson!' she said derisively. 'My dear Davey, he's terribly behind the times. Why, he never even told me how good it is to stand on one's head, and Cedric says in Paris and Berlin they've been doing it for ages now. I must say I feel younger every day since I learnt. The blood races through your glands you know, and they love it.'

'How d'you know they love it?' said Davey, with considerable irritation. He always scorned any régime for health except the one he happened to be following himself, regarding all others as dangerous superstitions imposed on gullible fools by unscrupulous quacks. 'We understand so very little about our glands,' he went on. 'Why should it be good for them? Did Dame Nature intend us to stand on our heads – do animals stand on their heads, Sonia?'

'The sloth,' said Cedric, 'and the bat hang upside down for hours on end – you can't deny that, Davey.'

'Yes, but do sloths and bats feel younger every day? I doubt it. Bats may, but I'm sure sloths don't.'

'Come on, Cedric,' said Lady Montdore, very much put out by Davey's remarks, 'we must be going home.'

Lady Montdore and Cedric now installed themselves at Montdore House for the winter and were seen no more by me. London society, having none of the prejudices against the abnormal which still exists among Boreleys and Uncle Matthews in country places, simply ate Cedric up, occasional echoes of his great success even reaching Oxford. It seemed that such an arbiter of taste, such an arranger of festivities, had not been known since the days of the beaux, and that he lived in a perfect welter of parties, dragging Lady Montdore along in his wake.

'Isn't she wonderful? You know, she's seventy – eighty – ninety –' her age went up by leaps and bounds. 'She's a darling, so young, so delicious, I do hope I shall be just like her when I'm a hundred.'

So Cedric had transformed her from a terrifying old idol of about sixty into a delicious young darling of about a hundred. Was anything beyond his powers?

I remember one icy day of late spring I ran into Mrs Chaddesley Corbett, walking down the Turl with an undergraduate, perhaps her son, I thought, chinless, like her.

'Fanny!' she said. 'Oh, of course, darling, you live here, don't you? I'm always hearing about you from Cedric. He dotes on you, that's all.'

'Oh,' I said, pleased, 'and I'm so very fond of him.'

'Couldn't like him more, could you? So gay, so cosy, I think he's a perfect poppet. As for Sonia, it's a transformation, isn't it? Polly's marriage seems to have turned out to be a blessing in disguise for her. Do you ever hear from Polly now? What a thing to have done, poor sweet. But I'm mad about Cedric, that's all – everybody in London is – tiny Lord Fauntleroy. They're both dining with me this evening, I'll give them your love, shall I? See you very soon, darling, good-bye.'

I saw Mrs Chaddesley Corbett perhaps once a year, she always called me darling and said she would see me very soon, and this always left me feeling quite unreasonably elated.

I got back to my house and found Jassy and Victoria sitting by the fire. Victoria was looking very green.

'I must do the talking,' Jassy said, 'Fa's new car makes poor Vict. sick and she can't open her mouth for fear of letting the sick out.'

'Go and let it out in the loo,' I said. Victoria shook her head vehemently.

'She hates being,' said Jassy, 'anything rather. We hope you're pleased to see us.' I said that I was, very.

'And we hope you've noted how we never do come nowadays.'

'Yes, I have noted. I put it down to the hunting.'

'Stupid you are. How could one hunt, in this weather?'

'This weather only began yesterday, and I've heard of you from Norma, hunting away like anything up to now.'

'We don't think you quite realize how bitterly offended we feel over your behaviour to us the last year or two.'

'Now, now children, we've had this out a thousand times,' I said firmly.

'Yes, well, it's not very nice of you. After all, when you married we rather naturally expected that your home would open up all the delights of civilized society to us, and that sooner or later we should meet, in your salon, the brilliant wealthy titled men destined to become our husbands. "I loved her from the first moment I saw her, the leggy little girl with the beautiful sensitive face, who used to sprawl about Mrs Wincham's drawing-room at Oxford." Well, then, what happens? One of the richest *partis* in Western Europe becomes an *habitué de la maison* and are we thrown at his head by our cousin, naturally ambitious for our future, does she move heaven and earth to further this splendid match? Not even asked to meet him. Spoilsport.'

'Go on,' I said, wearily.

'No, well, we're only bringing it up' – Victoria here fled the room, Jassy took no notice – 'in order to show our great magnanimity of soul. The fact is that we know

a very interesting piece of news, and in spite of your Counter-Honnish behaviour
we are going to tell it to you. But we want you to realize that it is pretty noble of
us, when you take everything into account, his flashing eyes, his floating hair, only
seen in the distance, it is such a shame, and I must wait for Vict. to come back or
it would be too unfaithful, and can we have some tea, she's always starving after.'

'Does Mrs Heathery know you're here?'

'Yes, she held Vict.'s head.'

'You don't mean to say she's been sick already?'

'It's always thrice – once in the car and twice when we get there.'

'Well, if Mrs Heathery knows, tea will appear.'

It appeared simultaneously with Victoria.

'Fanny's loo! The bliss! It's got a carpet, Jassy, and it's boiling warm, one could
stay there all day. Crumpets! Oh, Fanny!'

'What's this news you know?' I asked, pouring out milk for the children.

'I like tea now, please,' said Jassy, 'which shows how long since you saw us. I like
tea and I almost like coffee. So the news is, Napoleon has left Elba and is on his
way back.'

'Say it again.'

'Dense. Nobody would think that you were a hostess to the younger cosmopolitan intellectual set, noted for her brilliant repartee.'

'Do you mean Polly?' I said, light suddenly dawning.

'Very bright of you, dear. Josh was out exercising this morning and he stopped
at the Blood Arms for a quick one, and that's what he heard. So we came dashing
over to tell you, Fanny, in sickness and in health, so does one good turn not deserve
another, Fanny?'

'Oh, do stop being such a bore,' I said, 'and go on telling. When?'

'Any day now. The tenants have gone and the house is being got ready, Lady
Patricia's sheets and things, you know. She's going to have a baby.'

'Who is, Polly?'

'Well dear, who do you think? Not Lady Patricia. So that's what she's coming back
for. So are you admitting that it was handsome of us to come over and tell you?'

'Very handsome,' I said.

'So will you invite us to luncheon one day soon?'

'Any day you like. I'll make chocolate profiteroles with real cream.'

'And what about closing our eyes with holy dread?'

'Cedric, if that's what you mean, is in London, but you can close them at Jack
Boreley,' I said.

'Oh, Fanny, you brute. Can we go upstairs and see dear little David?'

7

The weather now became intensely cold, and much snow fell. The newspapers
came out every day with horror stories of sheep buried in snowdrifts, of song-birds
frozen to the branches on which they perched, of fruit trees hopelessly nipped in

the bud, and the situation seemed dreadful to those who, like Mrs Heathery, believe all they see in print without recourse to past experience. I tried to cheer her up by telling her, what, in fact, proved to be the case, that in a very short time the fields would be covered with sheep, the trees with birds, and the barrows with fruit just as usual. But though the future did not disturb me I found the present most disagreeable, that winter should set in again so late in the spring, at a time when it would not be unreasonable to expect delicious weather, almost summer-like, warm enough to sit out of doors for an hour or two. The sky was overcast with a thick yellow blanket from which an endless pattern of black and white snowflakes came swirling down, and this went on day after day. One morning I sat by my window gazing idly at the pattern and thinking idle thoughts, wondering if it would ever be warm again, thinking how like a child's snowball Christ Church looked through a curtain of flakes, thinking too how cold it was going to be at Norma's that evening without Lady Montdore to stoke the fire, and how dull without Cedric and his narrow edging of white. Thank goodness, I thought, that I had sold my father's diamond brooch and installed central heating with the proceeds; then I began to remember what the house had been like two years before when the workmen were still in it, and how I had looked out through that very same pane of glass, filthy dirty then, and splashed with whitewash, and seen Polly struggling into the wind with her future husband. I half wanted and half did not want Polly in my life again. I was expecting another baby and felt tired, really, not up to much.

Then, suddenly, the whole tempo of the morning completely altered because here in my drawing-room, heavily pregnant, beautiful as ever, in a red coat and no hat, was Polly, and of course, all feelings of not wanting her melted away and were forgotten. In my drawing-room too was the Lecturer, looking old and worn.

When Polly and I had finished hugging and kissing and laughing and saying 'Lovely to see you' and 'Why did you never write?' she said,

'Can I bend you to my will?'

'Oh, yes, you can. I've got simply nothing to do, I was just looking at the snow.'

'Oh, the heaven of snow,' she said, 'and clouds, after all those blue skies. Now the thing is, Fanny, can I bend you until late this afternoon, because Boy has got an utter mass of things to do and I can't stand about much, as you see. But you must frankly tell me if I shall be in your way, because I can always go to Elliston's waiting-room – the blissful bliss of Elliston after those foreign shops, I nearly cried for happiness when we passed their windows just now – the bags! the cretonnes! the horror of abroad!'

'But that's wonderful,' I said, 'then you'll both lunch here?'

'Boy has to lunch with someone on business,' said Polly, quickly, 'you can go off then, darling, if you like, as Fanny says she can keep me, don't bother to wait any more. Then come back for me here when you've finished.'

Boy, who had been rubbing his hands together in front of the fire, went off rather glum, wrapping a scarf round his throat.

'And don't hurry a bit,' she called after him, opening the door again and shouting down the stairs. 'Now, darling Fanny, I want to do one final bend and make you lunch with me at Fuller's – don't speak, you're going to say "Look at the weather", aren't you? but we'll ring up for a taxi. Fuller's! You'll never know how much I used to long for Dover sole and walnut cake and just this sort of a day, in

Sicily. Do you remember how we used to go there from Alconleigh when you were getting your house ready? I can't believe this is the same house, can you, or that we are the same people, come to that. Except I see you're the same darling Fanny, just as you were the same when I got back from India. Why is it that I, of all people, keep on having to go abroad? I do think it's too awful, don't you?'

'I only went just that once,' I said, 'it's very light, isn't it?'

'Yes, horrible glare. Just imagine if one had to live there for ever. You know we started off in Spain, and you'll never believe this but they are two hours late for every meal – two hours, Fanny – (can we lunch at half-past twelve today?), so of course, by then, you've stopped feeling hungry and only feel sick, then when the food comes it is all cooked in rancid oil, I can smell it now, it's on everybody's hair too, and to make it more appetizing there are pictures all round you of some dear old bull being tortured to death. They think of literally nothing all day but bulls and the Virgin. Spain was the worst of all, I thought. Of course, Boy doesn't mind abroad a bit, in fact he seems to like it, and he can talk all those terribly affected languages (darling, Italian! you'd die!), but I truly don't think I could have borne it much longer, I should have pined away with homesickness. Anyway, here I am.'

'What made you come back?' I said, really wondering how they could afford it, poor as Davey said they were. Silkin was not a big house, but it would require three or four servants.

'Well, you remember my Auntie Edna at Hampton Court? The good old girl died and left me all her money – not much, but we think we can just afford to live at Silkin. Then Boy is writing a book and he had to come back for that, London Library and Paddington.'

'Paddington?' I said, thinking of the station.

'Duke, Muniment room. Then there's this baby. Fancy, if one had to have a baby abroad, poor little thing, not a cow in the place. All the same, Boy doesn't much want to settle down here for good, I think he's still frightened of Mummy, you know – I am a bit, myself – not frightened, exactly, but bored at the idea of scenes. But there's really nothing more she can do to us, is there?'

'I don't think you need worry about her a bit,' I said, 'your mother has altered completely in the last two years.'

I could not very well say my real thought, which was that Lady Montdore no longer cared a rap for Boy or for Polly, and that she would most likely be quite friendly to them now, it all depended upon Cedric's attitude, everything did nowadays, as far as she was concerned.

Presently, when we were settled at our table at Fuller's, among the fumed oak and the daintiness ('Isn't everything clean and lovely – aren't the waitresses fair – you can't think how dark the waiters always are, abroad.') and had ordered our Dover soles, Polly said that now I must tell her all about Cedric.

'Do you remember,' she said, 'how you and Linda used to look him up to see if he would *do*?'

'Well, he wouldn't have *done*,' I said, 'that's one thing quite certain.'

'So I imagine,' said Polly.

'How much do you know about him?'

I suddenly felt rather guilty at knowing so much myself and hoped that Polly would not think I had gone over to the enemy's camp. It is so difficult for somebody who is as fond of sport as I am to resist running with the hare and hunting with the hounds whenever possible.

'Boy made friends, in Sicily, with an Italian called Pincio, he is writing about a former Pincio in his new book, and this wop knew Cedric in Paris, so he told us a lot about him. He says he is very pretty.'

'Yes, that's quite true.'

'How pretty, Fan, prettier than me?'

'No. One doesn't have to gaze and gaze at him like one does with you.'

'Oh, darling, you are so kind. Not any longer though, I fear.'

'Just exactly the same. But he is very much like you, didn't the duke say that?'

'Yes. He said we were Viola and Sebastian. I must say I die for him.'

'He dies for you, too. We must arrange it.'

'Yes, after the baby – not while I'm such a sight. You know how cissies hate pregnant ladies. Poor Pinchers would do anything to get out of seeing me, lately. Go on telling more about Cedric and Mummy.'

'I really think he loves your mother, you know. He is such a slave to her, never leaves her for a moment, always in high spirits – I don't believe anybody could put it on to that extent, it must be love.'

'I'm not surprised,' said Polly. 'I used to love her before she began about the marrying.'

'There!' I said.

'There what?'

'Well, you told me once that you'd hated her all your life, and I knew it wasn't true.'

'The fact is,' said Polly, 'when you hate somebody you can't imagine what it's like not hating them, it's just the same as with love. But of course, with Mummy, who is such excellent company, so lively, you do love her before you find out how wicked she can be. And I don't suppose she's in all that violent hurry to get Cedric off that she was with me.'

'No hurry,' I said.

Polly's blank blue look fell upon my face. 'You mean she's in love with him herself?'

'In love? I don't know. She loves him like anything, he makes such fun for her, you see, her life has become so amusing. Besides, she must know quite well that marriage isn't his thing exactly, poor Cedric.'

'Oh, no,' said Polly. 'Boy agrees with me that she knows nothing, nothing whatever about all that. He says she once made a fearful gaffe about Sodomites, mixing them up with Dolomites, it was all over London. No, I guess she's in love. She's a great, great faller in love, you know, I used to think at one time that she rather fancied Boy, though he says not. Well, it's all very annoying because I suppose she doesn't miss me one little bit, and I miss her, often. And now tell me, how's my Dad?'

'Very old,' I said. 'Very old, and your mother so very young. You must be prepared for quite as much of a shock when you see her as when you see him.'

'No, really? How d'you mean, very young? Dyed hair?'

'Blue. But what one chiefly notices is that she has become thin and supple, quick little movements, flinging one leg over the other, suddenly sitting on the floor and so on. Quite like a young person.'

'Good gracious,' said Polly, 'and she used to be so very stiff and solid.'

'It's Mr Wixman, Cedric's and her masseur. He pounds and pulls for an hour every morning, then she has another hour in a hay-box – full-time work, you know, what with the creaming and splashing and putting on a mask and taking it off again and having her nails done and her feet and then all the exercises, as well as having her teeth completely rearranged and the hair zipped off her arms and legs – I truly don't think I could be bothered.'

'Operations on her face?'

'Oh, yes, but that was ages ago. All the bags and wrinkles gone, eyebrows plucked and so on. Her face is very tidy now.'

'Of course, it may seem odd here,' said Polly, 'but, you know, there are hundreds and hundreds of women like that abroad. I suppose she stands on her head and lies in the sun? Yes, they all do. She must be a sight, scene or no scene, I utterly can't wait for her, Fanny, when can we arrange it?'

'Not for the moment, they're in London now, fearfully busy with the Longhi Ball they are giving at Montdore House. Cedric came to see me the other day and could talk of nothing else – he says they won't be going to Hampton again until it's over.'

'What is a Longhi Ball?'

'You know, Venetian. Real water, with real gondolas floating on it, in the ballroom. "O sole mio" on a hundred guitars, all the footmen in masks and capes, no light except from candles in Venetian lanterns until the guests get to the ballroom, when a searchlight will be trained on Cedric and your mother, receiving from a gondola. Fairly different from your ball, Polly? Oh, yes, and I know, Cedric won't allow any Royalties to be asked at all, because he says they ruin everything, in London; he says they are quite different in Paris where they know their place.'

'Goodness!' said Polly, 'how times have changed. Not even old Super-Ma'am?'

'No, not even your mother's new Infanta. Cedric was adamant.'

'Fanny, it's your duty to go to it – you will, won't you?'

'Oh, darling, I can't. I feel so sleepy after dinner when I am pregnant, you know, I really couldn't drag myself. We shall hear about it all right, from Cedric.'

'And when does it take place?'

'Under a month from now, the sixteenth, I believe.'

'Why, that's the very day I'm expecting my baby, how convenient. Then when everything's all over we can meet, can't we? You will fix it, promise.'

'Oh, don't worry, we shan't be able to hold Cedric back. He's fearfully interested in you, you're Rebecca to him.'

Boy came back to my house just as we were finishing our tea, he looked perished with cold and very tired but Polly would not let him wait while some fresh tea was made. She allowed him to swallow a tepid cup and dragged him off.

'I suppose you've lost the key of the car, as usual,' she said unkindly on their way downstairs.

'No no, here it is, on my key-ring.'

'Miracle,' said Polly, 'well then, good-bye, my darling, I'll telephone and we'll do some more benders.'

*

When Alfred came in later on I said to him,

'I've seen Polly, just imagine, she spent the whole day here, and oh, Alfred! she's not a bit in love any more!'

'Do you never think of anything but who is or is not in love with whom?' he said, in tones of great exasperation.

Norma, I knew, would be just as uninterested, and I longed very much for Davey or Cedric to pick it all over with.

8

So Polly now settled into her aunt's house at Silkin. It had always been Lady Patricia's house more than Boy's, as she was the one who lived there all the time, while Boy flitted about between Hampton and London with occasional visits to the Continent, and it was arranged inside with a very feminine form of tastelessness, that is to say, no taste and no comfort either. It was a bit better than Norma's house, but not much, the house itself being genuinely old instead of Banbury Road old and standing in the real country instead of an Oxford suburb; it contained one or two good pieces of furniture, and where Norma would have had cretonnes the Dougdales had Boy's needlework. But there were many similarities, especially upstairs, where linoleum covered the floors, and every bathroom, in spite of the childlessness of the Dougdales, was a nursery bathroom, smelling strongly of not very nice soap.

Polly did not attempt to alter anything. She just flopped into Lady Patricia's bed, in Lady Patricia's bedroom whose windows looked out on to Lady Patricia's grave. 'Beloved wife of Harvey Dougdale' said the gravestone, which had been erected some weeks after poor Harvey Dougdale had acquired a new beloved wife. 'She shall not grow old as we that are left grow old.'

I think Polly cared very little about houses, which, for her, consisted of Hampton and the rest, and that if she could no longer live at Hampton she could not take much interest in any other house anywhere else. Whatever it was in life that Polly did care for, and time had yet to disclose the mystery, it was certainly not her home. She was in no sense what the French call a *femme d'intérieur* and her household arrangements were casual to the verge of chaos. Nor any longer, alas, was it Boy. Complete disillusion had set in as far as he was concerned, and she was behaving towards him with exactly the same offhand coldness that had formerly characterized her attitude towards her mother, the only difference being that whereas she had always been a little frightened of Lady Montdore it was Boy, in this case, who was a little frightened of her.

Boy was busily occupied with his new book. It was to be called *Three Dukes*, and the gentlemen it portrayed were considered by Boy to be perfect prototypes of nineteenth-century aristocracy in their three countries. The Dukes in question were Paddington, Souppes and Pincio, all masters, it seemed, of the arts of anecdote, adultery, and gourmandise, members of the Paris Jockey Club, gamblers and sportsmen. He had a photograph, the frontispiece for his book, of all three together taken at a shoot at Landçut. They stood in front of an acre of dead animals and, with their tummies, their beards, their deerstalker's hats and white gaiters, they looked like nothing so much as three King Edwards all in a row. Polly told me that he had finished Pincio while they were in Sicily, the present man having put the necessary documents at his disposal, and was now engaged upon Paddington with the assistance of the duke's librarian, motoring off to Paddington Park every morning, notebook in hand. The idea was that when that was finished he should go to France in pursuit of Souppes. Nobody ever had the least objection to Boy 'doing' their ancestors. He always made them charming and endowed them with delightful vices, besides which it gave a guarantee, a hall-mark of ancient lineage, since he never would take on anybody whose family did not go back to well before the Conquest, in England, or who, if foreign, could not produce at least one Byzantine Emperor, Pope, or pre-Louis XV Bourbon in their family tree.

The day of the Montdore House ball came and went, but there was no sign of Polly's baby. Aunt Sadie always used to say that people unconsciously cheat over the dates when babies are expected in order to make the time of waiting seem shorter, but if that is so it certainly makes the last week or two seem endless. Polly depended very much on my company and would send a motor car most days to take me over to Silkin for an hour or two. The weather was heavenly at last, and we were able to go for little walks and even to sit in a sheltered corner of the garden, wrapped in rugs.

'Don't you love it,' Polly said, 'when it's suddenly warm like this after the winter, and all the goats and hens look so happy?'

She did not give me the impression that she was very much interested in the idea of having a baby, though she once said to me,

'Doesn't it seem funny to have talcum powder and things and boring old Sister waiting about, and all for somebody who doesn't exist?'

'Oh, I always think that,' I said, 'and yet the very moment they are there, they become such an integral part of your life that you can't imagine what it was like without them.'

'I suppose so. I wish they'd hurry up. So what about the ball – have you heard anything? You really ought to have gone, Fanny.'

'I couldn't have. The Warden of Wadham and Norma went – not together, I don't mean, but they are the only people I've seen so far. It seems to have been very splendid, Cedric changed his dress five times, he started with tights made of rose petals and a pink wig and ended as Doris Keane in Romance and a black wig, he had real diamonds on his mask. Your mother was a Venetian youth to show off her new legs, and they stood in a gondola giving away wonderful prizes to everybody – Norma got a silver snuff-box – and it went on till seven. Oh, how badly people do describe balls.'

'Never mind, there'll be the *Tatler*.'

'Yes, they said it was flash flash all night. Cedric is sure to have the photographs to show us.'

Presently Boy strolled up and said,

'Well, Fanny, what d'you hear of the ball?'

'Oh, we've just had the ball,' said Polly, 'can't begin all over again. What about your work?'

'I could bring it out here if you like.'

'You know I don't count your silly old embroidery as work.'

Boy's face took on a hurt expression and he went away.

'Polly, you are awful,' I said.

'Yes, but it's for his own good. He pretends he can't concentrate until after the baby now, so he wanders about getting on everybody's nerves when he ought to be getting on with Paddington. He must hurry, you know, if the book is to be out for Christmas, he's still got Souppes to do. Have you ever met Geoffrey Paddington, Fanny?'

'Well, I have,' I said, 'because Uncle Matthew once produced him for a house party at Alconleigh. Old.'

'Not the least bit old,' said Polly, 'and simply heavenly. You've no idea how nice he is. He came first to see Boy about the book and now he comes quite often, to chat. Terribly kind of him, don't you think? Mamma is his chief hate so I never saw him before I married – I remember she was always trying to get him over to Hampton and he would never come. Perhaps he'll be here one day when you are, I'd love you to meet him.'

I did meet him after that, several times, finding his shabby little Morris Cowley outside Silkin when I arrived. He was a poor man, since his ancestor, the great duke, left much glory but little cash, and his father, the old gentleman in spats, had lavished most of what there was on La Païva and ladies of the kind. I thought him friendly and very dull, and could see that he was falling in love with Polly.

'Don't you think he's terribly nice?' said Polly, 'and so kind of him to come when I look like this!'

'Your face is the same,' I said.

'I really quite long for him to see me looking ordinary – if I ever do. I'm losing hope in this baby being born at all.'

It was born, though, that very evening, took one look, according to the Radletts, at its father, and quickly died again.

Polly was rather ill and the Sister would not allow any visitors for about ten days after the baby was born, but as soon as she did I went over. I saw Boy for a moment in the hall, he looked even more gloomy than usual. Poor Boy, I thought, left with a wife who now so clearly disliked him and not even a baby to make up for it.

Polly lay in a bower of blossom, and the Sister was very much in evidence. There should have been a purple-faced wailing monster in a Moses basket to complete the picture and I felt its absence as though it were that of a person well known to me.

'Oh, poor –' I began. But Polly had inherited a great deal of her mother's talent for excluding what was disagreeable, and I saw at once that any show of sympathy would be out of place and annoy her, so instead I exclaimed, Radlett-fashion, over two camellia trees in full bloom which stood one each side of her bed.

'Geof. Paddington sent them,' she said. 'Do admit that he's a perfect love, Fanny. You know, Sister was with his sister when she had her babies.'

But then whom had Sister not been with? She and Boy must have had some lovely chats, I thought, the first night or two when Polly was feverish and they had sat up together in his dressing-room. She kept on coming into the room while I was there, bringing a tray, taking away an empty jug, bringing some more flowers, any excuse to break in on our talk and deposit some nice little dollop of gossip. She had seen my condition at a glance, she had also realized that I was too small a fish for her net, but she was affability itself and said that she hoped I would come over every day now and sit with Lady Polly.

'Do you ever see Jeremy Chaddesley Corbett at Oxford?' she asked. 'He is one of my favourite babies.'

Presently she came in empty-handed and rather pink, almost, if such a thing were possible with her, rattled, and announced that Lady Montdore was downstairs. I felt that, whereas she would have bundled any of us into our coffins with perfect calm, the advent of Lady Montdore had affected even her nerves of iron. Polly, too, was thrown off her balance for a moment and said faintly,

'Oh! Is Mr – I mean my – I really mean, is Boy there?'

'Yes, he's with her now. He sent word to say will you see her – if you don't want to, Lady Polly, I can say quite truthfully that you may not have another visitor to-day. You really ought not to, the first day, in any case.'

'I'll go,' I said, getting up.

'No, no, no, Fanny, you mustn't, darling. I'm not sure I will see her but I couldn't possibly be left alone with her, sit down again at once, please.'

There were voices in the garden outside.

'Do go to the window,' said Polly, 'is it them?'

'Yes, and Cedric is there too,' I said, 'and they're all three walking round the garden together.'

'No! But I must, I must see Cedric – Sister, do be a darling, go down and tell them to come up at once.'

'Now, Lady Polly, no. And please don't work yourself up, you must avoid any excitement. It's absolutely out of the question for you to see a stranger today – close relations was what Dr Simpson said, and one at a time. I suppose your mother must be allowed up for a few minutes if you want her, but nobody else and certainly not a strange young man.'

'I'd better see Mummy,' Polly said to me, 'or else this silly feud will go on for ever, besides, I really can't wait to see her hair and her legs. Oh, dear, though, the one I long for is Cedric.'

'She seems to be in a very friendly mood,' I said, still looking at them out of the window, 'laughing and chatting away. Very smart in navy blue with a sailor hat. Boy is being wonderful. I thought he might be knocked groggy by her appearance, but he's pretending not to notice, he's looking at Cedric all the time. They are getting on like mad.'

Most astute of him, I thought privately. If he hit it off with Cedric he would, very soon, be back in Lady Montdore's good graces, and then perhaps there could be a little modification of Lord Montdore's will.

'I die for the sailor hat, come on, let's get it over. All right then, Sister, ask her to come up – wait – give me a comb and a glass first, will you? Go on with the running commentary, Fanny.'

'Well, Cedric and Boy are chatting away like mad, I think Boy is admiring Cedric's suit, a sort of coarse blue tweed, very pretty, piped with scarlet. Lady Montdore is all smiles, having a good look round. You know the way she does.'

'I can just see it,' said Polly, combing her hair.

I did not quite like to say that Lady Montdore at this very moment was peering over the churchyard wall at her sister-in-law's grave. Boy and Cedric had left her there and were wandering off together towards the wrought-iron gates which led to the kitchen garden, laughing, talking, and gesticulating.

'Go on,' said Polly, 'keep it up, Fanny.'

'There's Sister, she is floating up to your mother, who is simply beaming – they both are – I never saw such smiles, goodness, how Sister is enjoying it! Here they come. Your mother looks so happy, I feel quite sentimental, you can see how she must have been missing you, really, at the bottom of her heart, all this time.'

'Nonsense,' said Polly, but she looked rather pleased.

'Darling, I do so feel I shall be in the way. Let me escape now through Boy's dressing-room.'

'Oh, on no account whatever, Fanny. Fanny, you'll upset me if you do that – I absolutely insist on you staying here – I can't face her alone, beams or no beams.'

Perhaps it had occurred to her, as it now did to me, that Lady Montdore's beam would very likely fade at the sight of Polly in Lady Patricia's room, unchanged in almost every respect, in the very bed where Lady Patricia had breathed her last, and that her repugnance for what Polly had done would be given a new reality. Even I had found it rather unattractive until I had got used to the idea. But over-sensibility had never been one of Lady Montdore's failings, and besides, the great flame of happiness that Cedric had lit in her heart had long since burnt up all emotions which did not directly relate to him. He was the only person in the world now who had any substance for her.

So the beam did not flicker, she positively radiated good humour as she kissed Polly first and then me. She looked round the room and said,

'You've moved the dressing-table, it's much better like that, more light. Lovely flowers, dear, these camellias – can I have one for Cedric's button-hole? Oh, from Paddington, are they? Poor Geoffrey, I fear he's a bit of a megalomaniac, I haven't been over there once since he succeeded. His father now was very different, a charming man, great friend of ours, King Edward was very fond of him, too, and of course, Loelia Paddington was perfectly lovely – people used to stand on chairs, you know. So the poor little baby died, I expect it was just as well, children are such an awful expense, nowadays.'

Sister, who came back into the room just in time to hear this remark, put her hand to her heart and nearly fainted. That was going to be something to tell her next patients about; never, in all her sisterhood, can she have heard its like from a mother to an only daughter. But Polly, gazing open-mouthed at her mother, taking in every detail of the new appearance, was quite unmoved; it was too typical of Lady Montdore's whole outlook on life for somebody who had been brought up by her to find it odd or upsetting. In any case, I doubt if she minded much about the baby herself; she seemed to me rather like a cow whose calf has been taken away from it at birth, unconscious of her loss.

'What a pity you couldn't have come to the ball, Fanny,' Lady Montdore went on. 'Just only for half an hour, to have a look. It was really beautiful. A lot of Cedric's friends came from Paris for it, in most striking dresses, and I am bound to say, though I have never liked the French, they were very civil indeed and so appreciative of anything one did for them. They all said there hadn't been such a party since the days of Robert de Montesquiou and I can believe it – it cost £4,000, you know, the water for the gondolas was so heavy, for one thing. Well, it shows these foreigners that England isn't done for, yet, excellent propaganda. I wore all my diamonds and I have given Cedric a revolving diamond star (goes by clockwork) and he wore it on his shoulder – most effective, I must say. We thoroughly enjoyed every minute and I wish you could read the letters I've had about it, really touching, people have had so little pleasure the last year or two and it makes them all the more grateful, of course. Next time we come over I'll bring the photographs, they give a wonderful idea of what it was like.'

'What was your dress, Mummy?'

'Longhi,' said Lady Montdore, evasively. 'Veronica Chaddesley Corbett was very good as a prostitute (they were called something different in those days) and Davey was there, Fanny, have you heard from him? He was the Black Death. Everybody made a real effort, you know – it's a terrible pity you girls couldn't have come.'

There was a pause. She looked round the room and said with a sigh,

'Poor Patricia – well, never mind, that's all over now. Boy was telling us about his book, such an excellent idea, *Three Dukes*, and Cedric is very much interested because young Souppes, the son of the Prince des Ressources, whom we used to see at Trouville, is a friend of his. Chèvres-Fontaine, which Cedric used to take every summer, belongs to his first cousin. Isn't it a curious coincidence? So of course, Cedric can tell Boy a great many things he never knew about them all, and they think later on they might go to Paris together to do some research, in fact, we might all go, wouldn't that be amusing?'

'Not me,' said Polly, 'no more abroad for me, ever.'

At this point Boy came into the room and I discreetly left it, in spite of a furious look from the bed. I went into the garden to find Cedric. He was sitting on the churchyard wall, the pale sunshine on his golden hair, which I perceived to be tightly curled, an aftermath of the ball, no doubt, and plucking away with intense concentration at the petals of a daisy.

'He loves me he loves me not he loves me he loves me not, don't interrupt my angel, he loves me he loves me not, oh, heaven heaven heaven! He loves me! I may as well tell you, my darling, that the second big thing in my life has begun.'

A most sinister ray of light suddenly fell upon the future.

'Oh, Cedric,' I said. 'Do be careful!'

I need not have felt any alarm, however, Cedric managed the whole thing quite beautifully. As soon as Polly had completely recovered her health and looks, he put Lady Montdore and Boy into the big Daimler and rolled away with them to France. The field was thus left to a Morris Cowley which, sure enough, could be seen day after day in the drive at Silkin. Before very long, Polly got into it and was taken to Paddington Park, where she remained.

Then the Daimler rolled back to Hampton.

'So here we all are, my darling, having our lovely cake and eating it too, *One's* great aim in life.'

'Yes, I know,' I said, 'the Boreleys think it's simply terrible.'

The Blessing

To Evelyn Waugh

Part One

I

'The foreign gentleman seems to be in a terrible hurry, dear.'

And indeed the house, though quite large, what used to be called a family house, in Queen Anne's Gate, was filled with sounds of impatience. Somebody was stamping about, moving furniture, throwing windows up and down, and clearing his throat exaggeratedly.

'Ahem! Ahem!'

'How long has he been here, Nanny?'

'Nearly an hour I should think. He played the piano, very fast and loud, for a while, which seemed to keep him quiet. He's only started this shindy since John went and told him you were in and would be down presently.'

'You go, darling, and tell him he must wait while I change out of these trousers,' said Grace, who was vigorously cleaning her neck with cotton wool. 'Oh, the dirt. What I need is a bath.'

The drawing-room door was now flung open.

'Do I see you or not?' The voice was certainly foreign.

'All right – very well. I'll come down now, this minute.'

She looked at Nanny, laughing, and said, 'He might go through the floor, like Rumpelstiltskin.'

But Nanny said, 'Put on a dress dear, you can't go down like that.'

'Shall I come upstairs?' said the voice.

'No, don't, here I am,' and Grace ran down, still in her A.R.P. trousers.

The Frenchman, tall, dark and elegant, in French Air Force uniform, was on the drawing-room landing, both hands on the banister rail. He seemed about to uproot the delicate woodwork. When he saw Grace he said 'Ah!' as though her appearance caused him gratified surprise, then, 'Is this a uniform? It's not bad. Did you receive my note?'

'Only now,' said Grace. 'I've been at the A.R.P. all day.'

They went into the drawing-room. 'Your writing is very difficult. I was still puzzling over it when I heard all that noise – it was like the French Revolution. You must be a very impatient man.'

'No. But I don't like to be kept waiting, though this room has more compensations than most, I confess.'

'I wouldn't have kept you waiting if I'd known a little sooner – why didn't you . . .'

He was no longer listening, he had turned to the pictures on the walls.

'I do love this Olivier,' he said. 'You must give it to me.'

'Except that it belongs to Papa.'

'Ah yes, I suppose it does. Sir Conrad. He is very well known in the Middle East – I needn't tell you, however. The Allingham Commission, ah! cunning Sir Conrad. He owes something to my country, after that.' He turned from the picture to Grace looking at her rather as if she were a picture, and said, 'Natoire, or Rosalba. You could be by either. Well, we shall see, and time will show.'

'Papa loves France.'

'I'm sure he does. The Englishmen who love France are always the worst.'

'The worst?'

'Each man kills the thing he loves, you know. Never mind.'

'You've come from Cairo?' she said. 'I thought I read Cairo in your letter and something about Hughie? You saw him?'

'The fiancé I saw.'

'And you've come to give me news of him?'

'Good news – that is to say no news. Why is this picture labelled Drouais?'

'I suppose it is by Drouais,' said Grace with perfect indifference. Brought up among beautiful things, she took but small account of them.

'Indeed? What makes you think so?'

'Are you an art dealer?'

'An art deal-ee.'

'But you said you had news. Naturally I supposed it was the reason for your visit, to tell this news.'

'Have you any milk chocolate?'

'No, I'm sure we haven't.'

'Never mind.'

'Would you like a cocktail – or a glass of sherry?'

'Sherry, with delight.'

'Did you enjoy Cairo? Hughie says it's great fun.'

'The museum is wonderful – but of course no pictures, while the millionaires, poor dears, have wonderful pictures, for which they've paid wonderful prices (from those ateliers where Renoirs and Van Goghs are painted on purpose for million-aires), but which hardly satisfy one's cravings. Even their Corots are not always by Trouillebert. You see exactly how it is. So this afternoon I went to the National Gallery – shut. That is war. Now you will understand what an oasis I have found in Sir Conrad's drawing-room, though I must have a word with him some time about this Drouais, so called.'

'I'm afraid you won't see many pictures in London now,' said Grace. 'Papa has sent all his best ones to the country, and most people have shut up their houses, you know.'

'Never mind. I love London, even without pictures, and Englishwomen I love.'

'Do you? Don't we seem terribly dowdy?'

'Of course. That's what make you so amusing and mysterious. What can you possibly do, all day?'

'Do?'

'Yes. How do you fill those endless eons of time when Frenchwomen are having their hair washed, trying on hats, visiting the collections, discussing with the *lingère* – what is *lingère* in English?'

'Underclothes-maker.'

'Hours they spend with the underclothes-maker. What a funny word – are you sure? Anyhow, Frenchwomen always give one to understand that arranging themselves is full-time work. Now you English, like flowers in a basket, are not arranged, which is quite all right when the flowers are spring flowers.' He gave her another long, approving look. 'But how do you fill in the time? That is the great puzzle.'

'I'm afraid,' she said, laughing, 'that we fill it in (not now, of course, but before the war) buying clothes and hats and having our hair washed. Perhaps the results were not quite the same, but I assure you that great efforts were made.'

'Please don't tell me. Do leave me in the dark, it makes you so much more interesting. Do let me go on believing that the hours drift by in a dream, that those blind blue eyes which see nothing, not even your father's pictures, are turned inward upon some Anglo-Saxon fairyland of your own. Am I not right?'

He was quite right, though perhaps she hardly knew it herself. She thought it over and then said,

'Just before the war I used to have a terribly thrilling dream about escaping from the Germans.'

'One must always escape from Germans. They are so very dull.'

'But now my life is as flat as a pancake, and I can hardly bear it. I quite – almost – long for bombs.'

'I am sorry to have to say that when life is flat it is your own fault. To me it is never flat.'

'Are you never bored?'

'I am sometimes bored by people, but never by life.'

'Oh how lucky.'

'Perhaps I'll take you out dancing. But where? The night clubs here must be terrible.'

'It depends on who you go with.'

'I see. Like all night clubs everywhere. So, I pick you up at eight? I love the black-out. I am trained to be a night bomber – I have flown behind the German lines dropping delightful leaflets, so of course I can find my way by the stars. This gives me confidence, sometimes misplaced I am obliged to own. Then we'll dine at the Connaught Hotel, where I'm staying, and where they have a very good *plat sucré*. What is *plat sucré* in English? – don't tell me, I know, pudding.'

'How d'you know such wonderful English?'

'My mother was. Still it is rather wonderful, isn't it? I can recite the whole of the *Excursion*, but not now. So eight o'clock then.'

'I'll be quite ready,' said Grace.

The Frenchman ran downstairs and out of the house, and she saw him from the window running towards St James's Park. Then she went up to her room, pulled a lot of clothes from various drawers and cupboards, laid them on her bed, and hovered about wondering what on earth she should wear. Nothing seemed somehow quite suitable.

Nanny came in. 'Good gracious! The room looks like a jumble sale.'

'Run me a bath, darling. I'm going out to dinner with that Frenchman.'

'Are you, dear? And what's his name?'

'Bother. I never asked him.'

'Oh well,' said Nanny, 'one French name is very much like another, I dare say.'

2

His name was Charles-Edouard de Valhubert. About a month later he said to Grace, 'Perhaps I will marry you.'

Grace, in love as never before, tried to keep her head and not to look as if about to faint with happiness.

'Will you?' she said. 'Why?'

'In ten days I go back to the Middle East. The war will begin soon, anything may happen, and I need a son.'

'How practical you are.'

'Yes. I am French. *Mais après le mariage – mince de – nettoyage, – La belle-mère! – on s'assied dessus!*' he sang. He was forever singing little snatches of songs like that. 'But you won't have a *belle-mère*, unfortunately, since she died, poor dear, many years ago.'

'I must remind you,' said Grace, 'that I am engaged to somebody else.'

'I must remind you that your behaviour lately has not been the behaviour of a faithful fiancée.'

'A little flirtation means nothing at all. I am engaged, and that's that.'

'Engaged. But not married and not in love.'

'Fond.'

'Indeed?'

'You really did see Hughie in Cairo?'

'I saw him plain. He said, "Going to London are you? Do look up Grace." Not very clever of him. So I looked up. He is very dull.'

'Very handsome.'

'Yes. So perhaps on Wednesday?'

'Wednesday what?'

'The marriage? I will now go and call on your father – where can I find him?'

'At this time of day he'll be at the House.'

'How little did I ever think I should end up as the son-in-law of the Allingham Commission. How strange is one's fate. Then I'll come back and take you out to dinner.'

The next day Sir Conrad Allingham went to see Mrs O'Donovan, a widow with whom he had had for many years a loving friendship. Sir Conrad preferred actually making love, a pastime to which he devoted a good deal of energy, with those whose profession it is, finding it embarrassing, never really able to let himself go, with women whom he met in other circumstances. But he liked the company of woman to an extent rare among Englishmen, and often went to chat for an hour or so with Mrs O'Donovan in her light sunny little house which looked over Chelsea Hospital. She was always at home, always glad to receive a visitor, and had a large following among the more intellectual of the right-wing politicians. Her regard for Sir Conrad was special; she spoke of him as 'my Conrad' and was out to other callers when he came to see her. It was said that he never took a step without asking her advice first.

He said, without preamble, 'Have you seen Charles-Edouard de Valhubert?'

'Priscilla's son?'

'Yes.'

'Is he in London?'

'He's been in London several weeks, courting Grace so it seems.'

'Conrad! How extraordinary! What's he like?'

'Really, you know, irresistible. Came to see me at the House yesterday – wants to marry her. I knew nothing – but nothing. I thought Grace was buried in that First Aid Post, and, of course, I've been busy myself. Rather too bad of her really – here I am presented with this *fait accompli*.'

'Well, but what about Hughie?'

'What indeed? Mind you, my sympathies with Hughie are limited – he ought to have married her before he went away.'

'Poor Hughie, he was longing to. He thought it wouldn't be fair.'

'What rubbish though. He leaves a position utterly undefended, he can't be surprised if it falls into – well, Allied hands. I never cared for him, as you know, quite half-baked and tells no jokes. However, she didn't ask my advice when she became engaged to him, nor did she ask it before breaking the engagement (if, indeed, she has remembered to do so). Clearly it doesn't matter what I think. So much for Hughie. He has made his exit all right.'

'I can see that you're pleased, really.'

'Yes and no. Valhubert is quite a chap I will say, tall, attractive (very much like his father to look at, much better dressed). He is clearly great fun. But I don't like the idea of Grace marrying a Frog, to tell the truth.'

'Conrad! With your love for the French?' Mrs O'Donovan loved the French too. She had once spent several months in Paris as a child; it had touched her imagination in some way, and she had hankered to live there ever since. This love was one of the strongest links between her and Sir Conrad. They both belonged to the category of English person, not rare among the cultivated classes, and not the least respectable of their race, who can find almost literally nothing to criticize where the French are concerned.

'Only because of Grace's special character,' he said. 'Try and picture her mooning about in Paris society. She would be a lamb among wolves; it makes me shudder to think of it.'

'I'm not sure – after all she's a beauty, and that means a great deal more in France than it does here.'

'Yes, with the men. I'm thinking of the women. They'll make short work of our poor Grace, always in the clouds.'

'Perhaps her clouds will protect her.'

'In a way, but I'm afraid she's deeply romantic, and Valhubert has a roving eye if ever there was one. Don't I remember that Priscilla was very unhappy? There used to be rumours –'

Mrs O'Donovan delved in her mind for everything she had known, long ago now and buried away, about Priscilla de Valhubert. Among other things she brought to the surface was the memory that when she had first heard of Priscilla's engagement she had felt exactly what she was feeling now, that it was really rather unfair. Mrs O'Donovan was as much like a Frenchwoman as it is possible for any

Anglo-Saxon to be. She spoke the language faultlessly. Her clothes, her scent, the food she ate, the wine she drank, all, in fact, that makes life agreeable, came from France. There was a *bidet* in her bathroom; she had her afternoon rest on a chaise-longue; she hardly read a word of anything but French; her house was a centre for visiting Frenchmen; the cheese appeared before the pudding at her table, and her dog, a poodle, was called Blum.

In London she was considered the great authority on everything French, to all intents and purposes a Frenchwoman, and she had therefore, quite naturally, come to have a proprietary feeling with regard to France. So it had seemd unfair then that Priscilla, just as it seemed unfair now that Grace, ordinary, rather dull English girls, should marry these fascinating men and sink back with no further effort to the enjoyment of all the delights of French civilization.

Mrs O'Donovan had never wanted to marry any particular Frenchman, and had been exceedingly happy with her own husband, so that this feeling was nothing if not irrational. All the same, as jealousy does, it stung.

'Yes, very unhappy,' she said, 'partly because she never felt comfortable in Paris society (she never quite learnt French) but chiefly, as you say, owing to the terrible unfaithfulness of Charles-René, which really, I believe, killed her in the end.'

'Oh – killed her,' said Sir Conrad. 'I don't suppose she died of love all the same. French doctors, more likely. When did Charles-René die?'

'Years ago. Fifteen years I should think – very soon after Priscilla. Is old Madame de Valhubert still alive? And Madame Rocher?'

'No idea – never knew them.'

'Madame Rocher des Innouïs is, or was, Madame de Valhubert's sister. Madame de Valhubert herself was always a kind of saint, as far as I can remember, and Madame Rocher was not. I knew them when I was a child, they were friends of my mother.'

'Oh well,' said Sir Conrad testily, 'nobody tells me anything. Nothing was said about any relations. I just talked with the chap for half an hour, mostly about my Drouais, which, according to him, is by some pupil of Nattier. Terrible rot. I did ask him why he wanted to marry her. They won't have many interests in common, unless Grace makes an effort to educate herself at last.' Grace's dreamy illiteracy always exasperated her father.

'What did he say?'

'He said she is so beautiful and so good.'

'And so rich,' said Mrs O'Donovan.

'It can't be that, my dear Meg. The Valhuberts have always been immensely rich.'

'Yes, but nobody, and especially no French person, ever minds having a bit more, you know.'

'I don't somehow feel it's that. Wants a son before he gets killed, more likely. The marriage, if you please, is tomorrow.'

'Tomorrow?'

'Yes, well, what can I do? Grace is of age – twenty-three, time she did marry, in fact – and in love, radiant with love, I must say. Valhubert is more than old enough to know his own mind, twenty-eight it appears, and is off to the war. They have decided, without asking me, that they will marry tomorrow. It remains for me to make a settlement and look pleasant.'

In spite of all this peppery talk, Mrs O'Donovan, who knew him so well, could see that 'her' Conrad was not really displeased at the turn of events. He always rather liked the unexpected, so long as it did not interfere with his personal comfort, and was infinitely tolerant towards any manifestation of love. He had taken a fancy to Valhubert, who, since he was off to the war, would not be removing Sir Conrad's housekeeper and companion for months, possibly years to come. He who was so fond of Paris would be glad to have a solid family foothold there when the war was over, while the incompatibility of the couple, as well as Grace's broken heart, were, after all, only matters for speculation.

'Where are they to be married?' she asked. 'Shall I come?'

'I hope so indeed, and to luncheon afterwards. Twelve o'clock at the Caxton Hall.'

Mrs O'Donovan, who was, of course, a Roman Catholic, was shocked and startled. 'A civil marriage only? Conrad, is that wise? The Valhuberts are an intensely Catholic family, you know.'

'I know. I did think it rather odd. But Grace is not a Catholic yet, though I suppose in time she will become one. Anyway,' he said, getting up to go, 'that's what they've arranged. Nobody asked my advice about any of it, naturally. When I think how I used to turn to my dear old father – never moved a step without his approval –'

'Are you sure?' she said, laughing. 'I seem to remember a river party – something about the Derby – a journey to Vienna –'

'Yes, yes, I don't say I was never young. I am speaking about broad outlines of policy –'

Grace went out and bought a hat, and dressing for her wedding consisted in putting on this hat. As the occasion was so momentous she took a long time, trying it a little more to the right, to the left, to the back. While pretty in itself, a pretty little object, it was strangely unbecoming to her rather large, beautiful face. Nanny fussed about the room in a rustle of tissue paper.

'Like this, Nan?'

'Quite nice.'

'Darling, you're not looking. Or like this?'

'I don't see much difference.' Deep sigh.

'Darling! What a sigh!'

'Yes, well I can't say this is the sort of wedding I'd hoped for.'

'I know. It's a shame, but there you are. The war.'

'A foreigner.'

'But such a blissful one. Oh dear, oh dear, this hat. What is wrong with it d'you think?'

'Very nice indeed, I expect, but then I always liked Mr Hugh.'

'Hughie is bliss too, of course, but he went off.'

'He went to fight for King and Country, dear.'

'Well, Charles-Edouard is going to fight for President and Country. I don't see much difference except that he is marrying me first. Oh darling, this hat. It's not quite right, is it?'

'Never mind, dear, nobody's going to look at you.'

'On my wedding day?'

But when Charles-Edouard met them at the registry office he looked at her and said, 'This hat is terrible, perhaps you'd better take it off.'

Grace did so with some relief, shook out her pretty golden hair, and gave the hat to Nanny, who, since it was made of flowers, looked rather like a small, cross, elderly bridesmaid clasping a bouquet.

They went for their honeymoon to Sir Conrad's house, Bunbury Park, in Wiltshire, and were very happy. When, during the lonely years which followed, Grace tried to recall those ten short days, the picture that always came to her mind was of Charles-Edouard moving furniture. The central block of the house having been requisitioned by soldiers, he and Grace occupied three rooms in one of the wings, and Charles-Edouard now set himself the task of filling these rooms with objects of art. He seemed not to feel the piercing cold of the unheated hall, with its dome and marble floor, where most of the furniture had been put away, but bustled about in semi-darkness, lifting dust sheets, scrambling under pyramids of tables and chairs, opening cupboards and peering into packing cases, like a squirrel in search of nuts. From time to time, with a satisfied grunt, he would pounce upon some object and scurry off with it. If he could not move it alone he made the soldiers help him. It took eight of them to lug the marble bust of an Austrian archduke up the stairs into Grace's bedroom. Nanny and the housekeeper clearly thought Charles-Edouard was out of his head, and exchanged very meaning looks and sniffs while the archduke was making his painful progress. One of Marie Antoinette's brothers, bewigged and bemedalled, the Fleece upon his elaborately folded stock, he now entirely dominated the room with his calm, stupid, German face.

'He looks dull,' said Grace.

'But so beautiful. You look too much at the subject – can't you see that it's a wonderful piece of sculpture?'

'Come for a walk, Charles-Edouard, the woods are heavenly today.'

It was early spring, very fine and dry. The big beeches, not yet in leaf, stood naked on their copper carpet, while the other trees had petticoats of pale green. The birds were already tuning up an orchestra as if preparing to accompany those two stars of summer, the cuckoo and the nightingale, as soon as they should make their bow. It seemed a pity to spend such days creeping about under dust sheets.

'Nature I hate,' said Charles-Edouard, as he went on with his self-appointed task. So she walked in the sunny woods alone, until she discovered that if she could propose an eighteenth-century mausoleum, Siamese dairy, wishing well, hermit's grotto or cottage orné as the object for a walk, he would accompany her. He strode along at an enormous speed, often breaking into a run, seizing her hand and dragging her with him. '*Il neige des plumes de tourterelles*', he sang.

Her father's park abounded in follies, quite enough to last out their visit. What did they talk about all day? She never could remember. Charles-Edouard sang his little songs, made his little jokes, and told her a great deal about the objects he found under the dust sheets, so that names like Carlin, Cressent, Thomire, Reisener and Gouthière always thereafter reminded her of their honeymoon. Her room became transformed from a rather dull country house bedroom into a corner of the Wallace Collection. But he hardly talked about himself at all, or his family, or life in Paris, or what they would do after the war. A fortnight from their wedding day he left England and went back to Cairo.

Grace soon realized that she was expecting a child. When the air raids began Sir Conrad sent her to live at Bunbury, and here, in a bedroom full of works of art collected by his father, Sigismond de Valhubert opened his eyes upon the calm, stupid face of an Austrian archduke.

3

'He is a little black boy – oh, he is black. I never expected you to have a baby with such eyes, it doesn't seem natural or right.'

'I don't know,' said Grace. 'I think one gets tired of always gazing into these blue eyes. I like this better.'

'Such a funny sort of name, too,' Nanny went on, 'not like anything. If he'd had been called after his father he could have been Charlie, or Eddy, but Sigi –! Well, I don't care to say it in the street, makes people look round.'

'But you're so seldom in streets, darling.'

'Salisbury. People stop and look at him as it is.'

'That's because he's such a love. Anyway, I think he's a blessing.'

And so of course did Nanny, though she would have thought him an even more blessed blessing had he resembled his mother more and his father less.

Grace stayed on at Bunbury. She had not meant to, she had meant to go back to London and the A.R.P. as soon as Sigi was weaned, but somehow, in the end, she stayed on. She fell into various country jobs, ran a small holding, and looked after the baby as much as Nanny allowed. Sir Conrad went down to see her at week-ends, and sometimes she spent a few days with him in London. So the years of the war went by calmly and rather happily for Grace, who never much minded being alone. She had a placid, optimistic nature, and was never tortured by anxious thoughts about Charles-Edouard, or doubted that he would return safely in due course. Nor did she doubt that when, in due course, he had safely returned, their marriage would be one of Elysian happiness.

Her father and Mrs O'Donovan selected many books for her to read, in preparation for a French life. They told her she ought to be studying the religious writings of the seventeenth, the drama and philosophy of the eighteenth, the prose and politics of the nineteenth centuries. They sent her, as well as quantities of classics and many novels and *mémoires*, Michelet in sixteen morocco volumes and Sainte-Beuve in sixteen paper ones; they sent her Bodley's *France* and Brogan's *Third Republic*, saying she would feel a fool if she did not understand the French electoral, judicial, and municipal systems. Grace did make spasmodic efforts to get on with all this homework, but she was too mentally lazy and untrained to do more than nibble at it. In the evenings she liked to turn on the wireless, think of Charles-Edouard, and stitch away at a carpet destined to be literally laid at his feet. It was squares of petit point, in a particularly crude Victorian design of roses and lilies of the valley and blue ribbons. Grace thought it too pretty for words.

She lived in a dream of Charles-Edouard, so that as the years went on he turned, in her mind, into somebody quite divorced from all reality and quite different from the original. And the years did go on. He came back for three hectic days in July 1940 which hardly counted, so little did Grace see of him, and after that seemed to go farther and farther away, Fort Lamy, Ceylon, and finally Indo-China. When the war ended he was not immediately demobilized, his return was announced again and again, only to be put off, so that it was more than seven years after their wedding when at last the telephone bell rang and Grace heard his voice speaking from Heath Row. This time he was unannounced; she had thought him still in the East.

'Our Ambassador was on the plane with me, and he is sending me straight down in his motor,' he said. 'It seems I'll be with you in an hour or two.'

Grace felt that, whereas the seven years had gone in a flash, this hour or two would never never end. She went up to the nursery. Sigi was having his bath before bedtime.

'Don't let him go to sleep,' she said to Nanny. 'Guess what, darling – his father will be here presently.'

Nanny received this news with the air of one resigned to the inevitable fact that all things, especially good things, have their term. She gave a particularly fearful sniff and said, 'Well, I only hope he won't over-excite the poor little fellow. You know what it's like getting him off, evenings, as well as I do.'

'Oh, Nanny, just for once, darling, it wouldn't matter if he stayed up all night.'

She left the nursery and wandered down the drive to the lodge, where she sat on one of the stone stumps that, loosely chained together, enclosed grassy mounds on either side of the gates. There was no traffic on the little road outside the park, and beyond it, bordered by clumps of wild rose bushes, the deep woods were full of song. It was high summer now, that week when cuckoo and nightingale give their best, their purest performances. The evening was warm, but she felt glad of a cardigan; she had begun to shiver like a nervous dog.

At last the motor drove up. Charles-Edouard sprang out of it and hugged her, and then she remembered exactly what he was like as a real person, and the other, dream Charles-Edouard, was chased into the back of her mind. Not quite chased away, she often thereafter remembered him with affection, but separated from reality.

They got back into the motor and drove up to the house.

'You are looking very beautiful,' he said, 'and very happy. I was afraid you might have become sad, all these years and years down here, away from me.'

'I longed terribly for you.'

'I know. You must have.'

'Don't tease, Charles-Edouard. But if we had to be separated I would rather have been here than anywhere. I love the country, you know, and besides, I had plenty to do.'

'What did you do?'

'Oh, goats and things.'

'Goats must be very dull.'

'No, really not. Then of course there was Sigi. Are you excited for him?'

'Very very much excited.'

'Come then, let's go straight up to the nursery.'

But outside Grace's bedroom Charles-Edouard caught her hand and pointed sternly to the door. 'I must see if the archduke is still there,' he said, and they went in.

Grace said presently, 'If you had been killed in the war, it would have finished me off.'

'Ah! Would you have died? That's very nice.'

'Yes, I couldn't have gone on living.'

'And would it have been a violent death by poison or a slow death by misery?'

'Which would you prefer?'

'Poison would be very flattering.'

'All right then, poison. Now come on, let's go to Sigi.'

In the day nursery Nanny's face was a picture of disapproval. 'Funny thing,' she said, 'I thought I heard a car quite half an hour ago. Time he went off to sleep, poor mite.'

They went through into the night nursery. Sigi was standing on his bed. He had black, silky curls and clever little black eyes, and he was always laughing.

'Have you ever seen me before?' he said to his father.

'Never. But I can guess who you are.'

'Sigismond de Valhubert, a great boy of nearly seven. Are you my papa?'

'Let me present myself – Charles-Edouard de Valhubert.' They shook hands.

'What are you?'

'I am a colonel in the French Air Force, retired. And what are you going to be?'

'A superman,' said the child.

Charles-Edouard was much gratified by this reply. 'Always the same old story,' he said, '*l' Empereur, la gloire, hommage à la Grande Armée*. I shall have a lot to tell you about the Marshal of France, your ancestor. Do you know that at home we have a standard from the battlefield of Friedland?'

Sigi looked intensely puzzled, and Grace said, 'I'm afraid his superman isn't Napoleon, not yet at least, but Garth.'

'Goethe?'

'Oh dear – no. Garth. It's a strip – I can't explain, I'll have to show you some time. It's rather horrible really, but we don't seem able to do without it.'

'Garth, you know, in the *Daily*,' Sigismond said. His grandfather had forbidden him to call it the *Mirror* so he compromised with the *Daily*. 'When I'm big I'm going to have a space ship like Garth and go to the –'

'But what do you know, Sigismond? Can you count? Can you read, and can you name the forty Kings of France?'

'Forty?' said Grace. 'Are there really? Poor little boy.'

'Well eighteen are Louis and ten are Charles. It's not as bad as it sounds. I always forget the others myself.'

'Isn't he a darling?' said Grace, as they went downstairs.

'A darling. Rather dull, but a darling.'

'He's not dull a bit,' she said indignantly, 'though he may be a little young for his age. It comes from living all alone with me in the country, if he is.'

'So perhaps tomorrow I take you both home to France.'

'Tomorrow? Oh no, Charles-Edouard, not –'

'We can't stay here. I've seen all the leaning towers and pavilions and rotundas and islands and rococo bridges, I've moved the furniture and rehung the pictures. There's nothing whatever to do, and we have our new life to begin. So –?'

'Oh darling, but tomorrow! What about the packing?'

'Don't bother. We're going straight to Provence, you'll only want cotton dresses, and you must have all new when we get to Paris, anyhow.'

'Yes, but Nanny. What will she say?'

'I don't know. The plane is at twelve, giving us time to catch the night train to Marseilles. We leave here at nine. I've arranged everything and ordered a motor to take us. I suppose you've got the passports as I told you to last year?'

'But Nanny –' wailed poor Grace.

Charles-Edouard began to sing a song about sardines. '*Marinées, argentées, leurs petits corps decapités . . .*'

4

Charles-Edouard, Grace, Sigismond, and Nanny arrived at Marseilles in a torrid heat wave. Grace and the child were tired after the night in the train, but Charles-Edouard and Nanny were made of sterner stuff. His songs and jokes flowed like a running river, except when he was actually asleep, and so did Nanny's complaints. These were a recitative of nursery grievance in which certain motifs constantly recurred. 'No time to write to Daniel Neal – all those nice toys left behind – the beautiful rocking-horse Mrs O'Donovan gave us – his scooter with rubber tyres and a bell – poor little mite, grown out of his winter coat, how shall we ever get another – what shall I do without my wireless? – the Bengers never came, you know, dear, from the Army and Navy – shall we get the *Mirror* there and my *Woman and Beauty*? Oh, I say, I never took those books back to Boots, what will the girl think of me – that nice blouse I was having made in the village –' Then the chorus, much louder than the rest. 'Shame, really.'

They were met at the station by Charles-Edouard's valet, Ange-Victor, in a big, rather old-fashioned Bentley. Ange-Victor was crying with joy, and it seemed as if he and Charles-Edouard would never stop hugging each other. At last they stowed the luggage into the motor, Grace and Sigi crammed into the front seats beside Charles-Edouard, with valet and nurse behind, and he drove hell for leather up the narrow, twisting, crowded road which goes from Marseilles to Aix.

'I'm a night bomber, have no fear,' he shouted to Grace as she cringed in her corner clasping Sigi. The hot air rushed past them, early as it was, the day was already a scorcher. Charles-Edouard was singing '*Malbrouck s'en va'-t-en guerre et ne reviendra pas.*'

'But I am back,' he said triumphantly. 'Never never did I expect to come back. Five fortune-tellers said I should be killed.'

And he turned right round, in the teeth of an enormous lorry, to ask Ange-Victor if Madame André, in the village, still told the cards.

'Shall I tell your fortune now?' said Grace. 'If you don't drive much more carefully there will soon be a widow, a widower, an orphan, and two childless parents in this family.'

'Try and remember that I am a night bomber,' said Charles-Edouard. 'I have driven aeroplanes over the impenetrable jungle, how should I have an accident on my old road I've known from a baby? Here we turn,' he said, wrenching the motor, under the very bonnet of another lorry, across the road and down a lane to the left of it. 'And there,' he said a few minutes later, 'is Bellandargues.'

The Provençal landscape, like that of Tuscany which it so much resembles, is marked by many little hills humping unexpectedly in the middle of vineyards. These often have a cluster of cottages round their lower slopes, overlooked by a castle, or the ruin of a castle, on the summit. Such was Bellandargues. The village lay at the foot of a hill, and above it, up in the blue sky, hung the castle, home, for many generations, of the Valhubert family.

As they drove into the village it presented a gay and festive appearance, all flags for the return of Charles-Edouard. A great streamer, with '*Vive la Libération, Hommage à M. le Maire*', was stretched across the street; the village band was playing, and a crowd was gathered in the market-place, waving and cheering. Charles-Edouard stopped the motor. M. Mignon, the chemist, made a long speech, recalling the sad times they had lived through since Charles-Edouard was last there, and saying with what deep emotion they had all heard him when he had spoken on the London radio in July 1940.

'Hm. Hm.' Charles-Edouard had a certain face which betrayed, to those who knew him well, inward laughter tinged with a guilty feeling. His eyes laughed but his mouth turned down at the corners. He made this face now, remembering so well the speech at the B.B.C.; how he had been exchanging looks as he delivered it with the next speaker, on the other side of a glass screen. She was a pretty little Dutch girl, and he had taken her out to tea, he remembered, before going back to Grace. M. Mignon made a fine and flowery peroration, Charles-Edouard spoke in reply, the village band then struck up again while he and Grace shook hundreds of hands. Great admiration was lavished upon Sigi, pronounced to be the image of his papa; he jumped up and down on the seat, laughing and clapping, until Nanny said he was thoroughly above himself and pinned him to her lap.

'Well,' said Grace, when at last they drove on, 'if you never thought you'd be son-in-law to the Allingham Commission, it certainly never occurred to me that I should marry a mayor.' She turned round and said, 'Wasn't that delightful, Nan?'

'Funny-looking lot, aren't they? Not too fond of washing, if you ask me. Fearful smell of drains, dear.'

The road up through the village got steeper and steeper, the side alleys were all flights of steps. Charles-Edouard changed down into bottom gear. They bounced through a gateway, climbed another slope, came out on to a big, flat terrace, bordered with orange trees in tubs, and drew up at the open front door of the castle. The village was now invisible; far below them, shimmering in the heat and punctuated with umbrella pines, lay acre upon acre of vivid green landscape.

As she got out of the motor Grace thought to herself how different all this was going to look in a few weeks, when it had become familiar. Houses are entirely different when you know them well, she thought, and on first acquaintance even more different from their real selves, more deceptive about their real character than human beings. As with human beings, you can have an impression, that is all. Her impression of Bellandargues was entirely favourable, one of hot, sleepy, beautiful magnitude. She longed to be on everyday terms with it, to know the rooms that lay behind the vast windows of the first floor, to know what happened round the corner of the terrace, and where the staircase led to, just visible in the interior darkness. It is a funny feeling to visit your home for the first time and have to be taken about step by step like a blind person.

An old butler ran out of the door, saying he had not expected them for another half-hour. There was more hugging and crying, and then Charles-Edouard gave him rapid instructions about Nanny being taken straight to her rooms and a maid sent to help her unpack.

'And Madame la Marquise?' he said.

The butler replied that Madame la Marquise must be in the drawing-room. He said again that they had arrived before they were expected.

'Come, then,' Charles-Edouard said, taking Sigi by the hand. 'Come, Grace.'

'Go with the butler, Nan,' said Grace. 'I'll be up as soon as I can.'

'Yes, well, don't keep Sigi too long, dear. He's filthy after that train.'

Her words fell on air, Grace was pursuing husband and son into the shadows of the house and up the stairs. Somewhere a Chopin waltz was being played, but Grace did not consciously hear it, though she remembered it afterwards.

'Wait, wait, Charles-Edouard,' she cried. 'Who is this Marquise?'

'My grandmother.'

'Charles-Edouard, dearest, stop one minute, I didn't know you had a grandmother – oh, do stop and explain –'

'There's nothing to explain. In here.' He held open a door for her. Grace walked into a huge room, dark and panelled, with a painted ceiling. Furniture was dotted about in it; like shrubs in a desert the pieces seemed to grow where they stood, following no plan of arrangement, and dotted about among them were human figures. There was an old man painting at an easel, an old lady at a piano playing the Chopin waltz, while another old lady, in the embrasure of a window, was deep in conversation with an ancient priest. She looked quickly round as the door opened, and then ran towards Grace.

'So soon?' she cried, 'and nobody downstairs to meet you? It's that wretched stable clock, always slow.' She kissed Grace on both cheeks, and then again, saying, 'A beauty! What a beauty! Well done, Charles-Edouard,' she said, hugging him. 'This is wonderful happiness, my child.'

Now there was a perfect hubbub of greetings and introductions. 'Tante Régine – M. le Curé, how are you? Yes, yes, I quite realized that,' said Charles-Edouard when M. le Curé began to explain that he had not been down in the village because M. Mignon was in charge of the welcome there. 'Grace, this is M. de la Bourlie, and this is M. le Curé, Grace, who has been M. le Curé here – for how long?'

Madame de Valhubert said, 'M. le Curé arrived here, a young priest, the same summer that I arrived, a young bride. We shall have seen sixty grape harvests together this year.'

Tante Régine became rather fidgety while her sister was speaking, and said to Grace in an aside, 'But I am much younger, I was always the baby – fifteen – twenty years younger than Françoise.'

Their faces were the same, soft, white faces with black eyes, but while Madame de Valhubert's was framed in soft white hair and her clothes were very much like those of a nun, Madame Rocher, painted and powdered, had her red hair cut in the latest way and wore such a beautiful, simple, desirable cotton dress that Grace could look at nothing else in the room.

'Dear Tante Régine, I'm very much pleased to see you,' said Charles-Edouard. 'And Octave?'

Octave was her late husband's nephew, the present holder of his title, whom Madame Rocher had brought up and then, because he bored her, had pushed into the army. The old Marquis had left her every penny of the enormous fortune which came to him through his mother, so she was able to behave in a very high-handed manner with his relations.

'Oh poor Octave, no luck at all, as usual,' said Madame Rocher. 'He is still with his regiment, still only a captain. Of course, if it hadn't been for this wretched war he would be at least a colonel by now.'

'Hm. Hm,' said Charles-Edouard, bursting with inward laughter. 'And I, in spite of this wretched war, am a colonel, do you know that? Grandmother, did you know that I am a colonel?'

'Yes, yes, we know a great deal about you here. Little Béguin, who was invalided home after the Libération, was full of your exploits.'

'Indeed I did splendidly,' said Charles-Edouard, laughing. 'I am a colonel and I have a son – where is this son, by the way?'

He dragged Sigi out from behind a curtain, where he was hiding in a most unusual state of shyness.

'Sigismond, come and kiss the hand of your ancestress. Now that you are a French boy we should like to see some manners, please.'

Sigi became quite scarlet with embarrassment, but the old lady, taking two boxes of sweets from a table, held them out to him and said, 'You can kiss my hand another time, darling, but now choose which you'll have, a chocolate or a marron glacé. A little bribery never spoils anything,' she said to Charles-Edouard as Sigi carefully made his choice. 'Well?'

'Well, I do love chocolate, certainly I do, but I suppose I ought to choose the one with the silver paper on account of the poor lepers.'

'What, my child?'

'You see Nanny – well you haven't met her yet – she keeps a silver-paper ball, and when it weighs a pound she sends it up and one poor leper can live on that – oh for years, probably. They hardly need anything at all Nanny says, quite contented with a handful of rice from time to time, but it's ages now since Nanny sent up, silver paper is so terribly rare in these days. She will be pleased.'

'But this child has saintly thoughts!' cried Madame de Valhubert. 'M. le Curé, did you understand? The little one is already planning for the lepers. It is wonderful, so young. How he does look like you, Charles-Edouard, the image of what you were at that age, though I don't remember that you had such gratifying pre-occupations.'

'Yes, isn't he the very picture,' said Charles-Edouard, 'but I'm afraid he's not as brilliant as I was. Now if you will excuse us perhaps I'll show Grace the rest of the house before luncheon, and take St François Xavier up to his nursery.'

Outside on the staircase, Nanny was hovering with a face of leaden reproach. She pounced upon Sigi and hurried him off, muttering her recitative under her breath. She was very slightly in awe of Charles-Edouard, and would only let herself go, Grace knew, when alone with her. The words 'unbearably close, here' were just distinguishable, a look of terrifying malice flashed in the direction of Charles-Edouard, and she was gone. Grace absolutely dreaded the day when she would be obliged to have it out with him about Nanny. She had known, as a child, that her father and mother used to have it out at intervals, until her mother, by dying, had saddled Sir Conrad with Nanny for ever. She gave Charles-Edouard a nervous, laughing look, but he did not notice it; he put his arm round her waist, and they went slowly up the stairs.

Then she went back to what she had been wondering as they came out of the drawing-room. 'But why didn't you tell me about your grandmother – well, really, all these people?'

'I have one very firm rule in life,' he said, 'which is never to talk to people about other people they have never seen. It is very dull, since people are only interesting when you know them, and furthermore it can lead to misunderstandings. You and my grandmother, having no preconceived ideas about each other –'

'You haven't got a wife hidden away in some other room, I hope?'

'No wife.'

'Oh good. But of course it's just like in *Rebecca*. By degrees I shall find out all about your past.'

'Oh my past! It's such a long time ago now.'

'So tell me more, now I've seen them. Who is the old man?'

'M. de la Bourlie? He is my grandmother's lover.'

'Her lover?' Grace was very much startled. 'Isn't she rather old to have a lover?'

'Has age to do with love?' Charles-Edouard looked so much surprised that Grace said,

'Oh well – I only thought. Anyway, perhaps there's nothing in it.'

He roared with laughter, saying, 'How English you are. But M. de la Bourlie has visited my grandmother every single day for forty-six years, and in such a case you may be sure that there is always love.'

'He doesn't live here, too?'

'No. He has a beautiful house in Aix. He generally comes over in the afternoon, but today, of course, he has come early, dying of curiosity to see l'Anglaise. They all must be, we shall have the whole neighbourhood over. It will be very dull. Never mind.'

'Why don't they marry?' said Grace.

'Who? Oh my grandmother. Well, but poor Madame de la Bourlie.'

'Poor her anyway. In England, when there is a long love affair like that people always end by marrying.'

'And in America if you hold a woman's hand you are expected to go round next day with the divorce papers. The Anglo-Saxons are very fond of marriage, it is very strange.'

'I've never seen a pale green wig before.'

'He's worn that wig ever since I was a little boy. He has been a tremendous lady-killer in his time, wig and all.'

'And when I am old like your grandmother, will you love me still?'

'It depends.'

'How horrid. Depends on what?'

'It all depends, entirely, on you.'

'Charles-Edouard, was the reason you didn't tell me about your grandmother because you thought I wouldn't like the idea of sharing my house with another woman?'

Charles-Edouard looked immensely surprised. 'It never occurred to me for a single minute,' he said. 'It's not your house, exactly, but a family house, you know. But we shall hardly ever be here.'

'Oh! I thought it was my new home?'

'One of them. Our real home is in Paris, and there my grandmother, though she lives in the house, has a separate establishment. You will love her, you know. For one thing, French people (and you are French now) always love their relations, and then my grandmother is a saint.'

'Yes,' said Grace, 'I see that. I know I shall. It was so charming the way she gave those chocolates to Sigi when she saw he didn't want to kiss her hand. But how sad, Charles-Edouard, to have this lovely house and not to live in it?'

'Oh dearest Grace, for living the country is really impossible. It is too dull. I am obliged to come down here on business, but I could never never live here.'

'What business?'

'I must explain that, whereas in England the country is for pleasure and the town for business, here it is the exact opposite. We French have all our pleasure in Paris, where we have nothing to do except amuse ourselves, but we work really hard in the country. I have a lot of work when I am here, local business, since I am the mayor, and much family business, looking after my property.'

They had reached a wide landing, arranged like a room, with old-fashioned, chintz furniture. Two great windows from floor to ceiling were open upon an expanse of pale blue sky. Charles-Edouard led her through one of them on to a balcony, and, waving at the green acres far below, he said,

'There grows the wealth of the Valhubert family.'

'D'you mean that vegetable? But what is it? I was wondering.'

'Vegetable indeed! Have you never been in the country in France before! How strange. These are vineyards.'

'No!' said Grace. She had supposed all her life that vineyards were covered with pergolas, such as, in Surrey gardens, support Miss Dorothy Perkins, heavy with bunches of hot-house grapes, black for red wine, white for champagne. Naboth's vineyard, in the imagination of Grace, was Naboth's pergola, complete with crazy paving underfoot.

However she did not explain all this to Charles-Edouard, but merely said, 'I've never seen one before. I thought they would be different, somehow.'

Grace's bedroom was at the top of the house. It was a large, white-panelled room with many windows, from most of which, so high up was it, so hanging in the firmament, nothing was visible but sky. But on one side two French windows opened on to a tiny garden of box hedges and standard roses, which looked like a stage set forming part of the room itself.

'Very English,' said Charles-Edouard, 'you will feel at home here.'

It had been arranged by his mother with old-fashioned chintz and embroidered white muslin.

'The garden!' said Grace. 'I never saw anything so lovely.'

'Every floor of this house has a terrace. It is built on the side of a hill, you see. Here are your bathroom and dressing-room, and here are my rooms. So we are all alone together.'

'Literally in heaven,' said Grace, with a happy sigh.

'Now perhaps I'll take you to the nursery; we go down again and up this little staircase. Here we are.'

'Oh, what a lovely nursery – isn't it lovely, Nan, much the biggest we've ever had, and so light – and what a view!'

This was Grace's technique with Nanny. She would open an offensive of enthusiasm, hoping to overcome and silence the battery of complaints before Nanny could begin firing them off. It almost never worked, she could see it not working now, though for the moment she was shielded by the presence of Charles-Edouard. Nanny remained silent and went on with what she was at, grimly unpacking toys from a hamper.

'I'll come back,' said Charles-Edouard. 'I want a word with Ange-Victor.'

Grace's heart sank, but she rattled bravely on. 'You've got a garden, too, isn't it delightful? I love it being surrounded by those pretty red roofs against the sky, like Kate Greenaway. Look at the plants growing out of them, what are they, I wonder? Doesn't it all smell delicious? I long for you to see my bedroom; it is so pretty. Tell you what, darling, I'll get you a garden chair, then you'll be able to sit out here of an evening.'

Nanny looked over her shoulder to make sure that Charles-Edouard had gone, and then spoke. 'Horribly draughty I should think, with all those roofs. Smutty, too, I dare say. Aren't the stairs awful? I shan't be able to manage them many times a day, in this heat. Well, I've been trying to unpack, but there's nowhere to put anything, you know – shame, really – no nice shelves for our toys. No mantelpieces, either, for my photographs and the ornaments. Funny sort of rooms, aren't they? Not very homey. I'd like to show you the bathroom and lavatory, dear – nothing but a cupboard – no window at all, really most insanitary – it would never be allowed at home.'

'How fascinating,' said Grace, 'look, it's built in the thickness of the wall, this big bathroom.'

'Perhaps it may be. Then what is that guitar-shaped vase for, I wonder? Oh, well, it'll do to put the things to soak. Not very nice, is it? Leading out of our bedroom like that?'

'Never mind, in this lovely weather you can leave everything wide open – it's quite different from England.'

'Different!' a deep sniff, 'I should say it is.'

'Look at the swing! How amusing! That will quite make up to Sigi for leaving his rocking-horse behind.'

'Yes, well it's a funny place for a swing, in our bedroom.'

'It's all so huge, isn't it? And like being out of doors, with these great windows everywhere. Heavenly, really. Look, here's a cupboard, darling – the size of a room, too. Hadn't you noticed it? You can put everything here – and see, there's a light for it. That is nice.'

'Just smell inside, dear – horribly musty, I'm afraid. Then I was wanting to speak to you about these roofs – the little monkey will be up on them in no time. My goodness! I knew it! Come down this instant, Sigi, what did I tell you? You are not to climb on those roofs – what d'you think you're doing? It's most dangerous.'

'I'm Garth on the mountains of the moon.'

Charles-Edouard reappeared, saying, 'Oh, do be Napoleon crossing the Alps. This Garth is really too dull. The roofs are quite safe, Nanny, I lived on them when I was his age, mountaineering and exploring. I must get out my old *Journal des Voyages* for him, since I suppose he is rather young for Jules Verne?'

Nanny having retreated into the nursery, 'don't know how you can stand the glare,' Charles-Edouard pulled at the neck of Grace's cotton dress and implanted a kiss on her shoulder.

'Ugh! You soppy things,' said Sigismond, 'I don't like all this daft kissing stuff.'

'You'll like it all right one day,' said Charles-Edouard. 'That big bell means luncheon time. Good appetite, Sigi.'

As they went back through the nursery a man-servant was laying the table on a thick, white linen tablecloth. 'Good appetite, Nanny,' said Charles-Edouard. Nanny did not reply. She was looking with stupefied disapproval at a bottle of wine which had just been put down in front of her.

5

Very hungry, accustomed to English post-war food, Grace thought the meal which followed the most delicious she had ever eaten. The food, the wine, the heat, and the babel of French talk, most of which was quite incomprehensible to her untuned ear, induced a half-drunk, entirely happy state of haziness. When, after nearly two hours, the party rose from the table, she was floating on air. Everybody wandered off in different directions, and Charles-Edouard announced that he was going to be shut up in the library for the afternoon with his tenants and the agent.

'Will you be happy?' he said, stroking Grace's hair and laughing at her for being, as he could see, so tipsy.

'Oh I'm sleepy and happy and hot and sleepy and drunk and happy and sleepy. It's too too blissful being so drunk and happy.'

'Then go to sleep, and when I've finished we'll do whatever you like. Motor down to the sea if you like, and bathe. I'm sleepy myself, but the *régisseur* has convened all these people to see me – they've been waiting too long already – I must go to them, so there it is. See you presently.'

'All right. I'll go and have a little word with Nanny and then a lovely hot sleep. Oh the weather! Oh the bliss of everything! Oh how happy I am!'

Charles-Edouard gave her a very loving look as he went off. He thought he was going to like her even more in France than in England, and was well satisfied to have come back accompanied by this happy beauty.

Alas for the hot, tipsy sleep! Nanny sobered and woke her up all right, her expression alone was a wave of icy water. Grace did not even bother to say 'Wasn't the luncheon delicious? Did you enjoy it?' She just stood and meekly waited for the wave to break over her head.

'Well, dear, we've had nothing to eat since you saw us, nothing whatever. Course upon course of nasty greasy stuff smelling of garlic – a month's ration of meat, yes, but quite raw you know – shame, really – I wasn't going to touch it, let alone give it to Sigi, poor little mite.'

'Nanny says the cheese was matured in manure,' Sigi chipped in, eyes like saucers.

'I wish you could have smelt it, dear, awful it was, and still covered with bits of straw. Makes you wonder, doesn't it? Well, we just had a bite of bread and butter and a few of Mrs Crispin's nice rock cakes I happened to have with me. Not much of a dinner, was it? Funny-looking bread here, too, all crust and holes, I don't know how you'd make a nice bit of damp toast with that. Poor little hungry boy – never mind, it's all right now, darling, your mummy will go to the kitchen for us and ask for some cold ham or chicken – a bit of something plain – some tomatoes, without that nasty, oily, oniony dressing, and a nice floury potato, won't you, dear?'

These words were uttered in tones of command. An order had been issued, there was nothing of the request about them.

'Goodness, I've no idea what floury potato is in French,' said Grace, playing for time. 'Didn't you like the food, Sigi?'

'It's not a question of like it or not like it. The child will eat anything, as you know, but I'm not going to risk having him laid up with a liver attack. This heat wave is quite trying enough without that, thank you very much, not to mention typhoid fever, or worse. I only wish you could have smelt the cheese, that's all I say.'

'I did smell it, we had it downstairs – delicious.'

'Well it may be all right for grown-up people, if that's the sort of thing they go in for,' said Nanny, with a tremendous sniff, 'but give it to the child I will not, and personally I'd rather go hungry.' This, however, she had no intention of doing. 'Now, dear,' she said briskly, 'just go and get us a bite of something plain, that's a good girl.'

'I'm so dreadfully starving, Mummy, I've got pains in my tummy. Listen, it rumbles, just like Garth when he'd been floating for weeks on that iceberg.'

Sigi looked so pathetic that Grace said, 'Oh all right then. I don't know where the kitchen is, but I'll see what I can do. I think it's all great rubbish,' she added in a loud aside as she slammed the nursery door behind her.

She wandered off uncertainly, hardly able, in that big, complicated house built at so many different dates, on so many different levels, to find her way to the first-floor rooms. At last she did so, looked into the drawing-room, and was almost relieved that there was nobody there. Her mission seemed to her absurd, and really so ill-mannered, that she quite longed for it to fail. She assumed that everybody except Charles-Edouard would be happily asleep by now, and only wished that she were too. Loud French voices came from the library, apart from them the house was plunged in silence. She stood for a moment by the library door but did not dare to open it, thinking how furious Sir Conrad would be at such an interruption. The dining-room was empty; no sign of any servant. She went through it, and found a stone-flagged passage, which she followed, on and on, up and down steps, until she came to a heavy oak door. Perhaps this led to the kitchen; she opened it timidly. A strangely dark and silent kitchen, if so, with cool but not fresh air smelling of incense. She stood peering into the gloom; it was quite some moments before she realized that this must be a chapel. Then, not two yards from her, she saw Madame de Valhubert, a lace shawl over her head, praying deeply. Grace shut the door and fled, in British embarrassment, back to the nursery.

'I can't find the kitchen, or one single person to ask,' she said, in a hopeless voice. Nanny gave Grace a look. 'Where's Papa then?'

'At a meeting. Well Nan you do know, we should never have dared disturb my papa at a meeting, should we? I don't see how I can. Are you sure you haven't any food with you, to make do just for now?'

'Nothing whatever.'

'No groats?'

'Groats isn't much of a dinner. The poor little chap's hungry after all that travelling. We didn't get much of a dinner yesterday if you remember, in that aeroplane, expecting every moment to be our last.'

Sigismond now began to grizzle. 'Mummy I do want my dinner, please, please Mummy.'

'Oh all right then,' said Grace, furiously. There was clearly nothing for it but to set forth again, to summon up all her courage and put her head round the library door. Abashed by the sudden silence that fell and the looks of surprise and interest on eight or ten strange masculine faces, she said to Charles-Edouard, who was the furthest from her so that she had to say it across the whole room, 'I'm so sorry to interrupt, but could I possibly have a word with you?'

He came out at once, shut the door, put his arms round her, and said, 'You were quite right to come. It was very dull in there, and now we'll go to your room.'

'Oh no,' said Grace. 'It wasn't for that.'

'How d'you mean? it wasn't for that. What is "that", anyway?' he said, laughing.

'Oh don't laugh at me, it was terrible going in there. I was so terribly frightened, but I had to. It's about Nanny.'

'Yes, yes, I know. We must have a long talk about Nanny, but not now. First we go upstairs – what must be must be, and quickly too.'

'No, first we go to the kitchen and ask for a floury potato for Nanny, who is waxy, in a bait, I mean, because they've had no luncheon.'

Grace, by now, was really rather hysterical.

'Had no luncheon!' cried Charles-Edouard, 'this is too much. I must find my grandmother.'

'Oh they had it all right, they just couldn't eat it.'

'What d'you mean, Grace? I'm sure they had the same as we did. You said yourself it was delicious.'

'Yes, of course it was, and I'm furious with Nanny for complaining, but the fact is Nannies never can bear new food you know, it's my own fault, I ought to have remembered that. Now dear, dearest Charles-Edouard, do come to the kitchen and help me to find something she can eat.'

'Very well. And tomorrow we send her back to England.'

There. Grace's heart sank.

'But who would look after poor little Sigi?'

'M. le Curé must find him a tutor. This child is quite unlettered, I had a long talk with him in the train. He knows nothing, and can't even read.'

'But of course not, poor little boy. He isn't seven yet!'

'When I was five,' said Charles-Edouard, 'I had to read all Dumas, *père*.'

'I've noticed everybody thinks they themselves could read when they were five.'

'Ask M. le Curé.'

'Anyway you must have been too sweet for words,' said Grace. 'I only wish I'd known you then.'

'I was exceedingly brilliant. Now here is the kitchen, and here, by great good luck, is M. André, the head chef. Will you please explain exactly what it is that you do want?'

While some of the household slept (though sharp attacks of insomnia characterized that afternoon) and Madame de Valhubert prayed, Madame Rocher des Innouïs and M. de la Bourlie took themselves off to a little garden, deeply shaded by an ilex tree, to have a nice chat about Grace. One summer long ago they had conducted a violent love affair under the very noses of Madame de Valhubert, Madame de la Bourlie, M. Rocher, and Prince Zjebrowski, the lover of Madame Rocher. It had really been a *tour de force* of its kind; they had succeeded in hoodwinking all the others, none of whom had ever had the slightest suspicion of it. After that they had remained on cosy, rather conspiratorial terms.

'We must begin by saying that she is beautiful – more beautiful, perhaps, than Priscilla.' Madame Rocher spread out the ten yards of her Dior skirt and settled herself comfortably with cushions. 'But not, as anyone can see, a society woman. Of good family, yes perhaps, but perfectly green in worldly matters. She told me, at luncheon, that she has hardly been out in society since the war, but spent all those years looking after goats. Of course the English are very eccentric, you don't know that, Sosthène, you have never crossed the Channel, but you can take it from me that they are all half mad, a country of enormous, fair, mad atheists. Why did she look after goats? We shall never know. But looking after goats can hardly be considered as a good preparation for life with Charles-Edouard, and I am bound to say I feel uneasy for her. They are not married religiously, by the way.'

'Oh! How do you know?'

'I asked her.'

'What an extraordinary question to ask.'

'After all, I am Charles-Edouard's aunt.'

'I meant what an extraordinary idea. It would never have occurred to me that they might not be.'

'It occurred to me. I know England, Sosthène. We went every year for the Horse Show, don't forget.'

'Shall you tell Françoise?'

'Of course not, on no account, and nor must you. It would upset her dreadfully.'

'Speaking frankly then, nothing matters very much?'

'I don't agree at all. It's true that they can easily be divorced, and that Charles-Edouard will be able to marry again without waiting for an annulment, but before that happens he will have made her totally miserable. Charles-Edouard is a good, warm-hearted boy, he won't be able to help making her miserable, but he will suffer too. Oh dear, what could have induced him to marry an Englishwoman – these English with their terrible jealousy – it will be the story of Priscilla all over again, you'll see.'

'But the English husbands then, how do they manage?'

'English husbands? They go to their clubs, their boat race, their Royal Academy – they don't care for making love a bit. So they are always perfectly faithful to their wives.'

'What about the Gaiety Girls?'

'I don't think they exist any more. You are behind the times, my poor Sosthène, it is the gaiety boys now, if anything. But they have no temperament. Now Charles-Edouard cannot – he really cannot – see a pretty woman without immediately wanting to sleep with her. What foolishness, then, to go and marry an Anglo-Saxon.'

'You talk as if Latins are never jealous.'

'It is quite different for a Frenchwoman, she has ways and means of defending herself. First of all she is on her own ground, and then she has all the interest, the satisfaction, of making life impossible for her rival. Instead of sad repining her thoughts are concentrated on plot and counterplot, the laying of traps and the springing of mines. Paris divides into two camps, she has to consider most carefully what forces she can put in the field, she must sum up the enemy strength, and prepare her stratagem. Whom can she enlist on her side? There is all society to be won over, the hostesses, the old men who go to tea parties, and the families of those concerned. Then there is the elegance, the manicurists, the *masseuses*, the *vendeuses*, the *modistes*, the *bottiers*, and the *lingères*. A foothold among the tradesmen who serve her rival's kitchen may prove very useful; we must not, of course, forget the fortune-tellers, while a concierge can play a cardinal role. The day is not long enough for all the contrivances to be put on foot, for the consultations with her women friends, the telephoning, the messages, the sifting and deep consideration of all news and all fresh evidence. Finally, and not the least important, she has her own lover to comfort and advise her. Ah! Things are very different for a Frenchwoman. But these poor English roses just hang their lovely heads and droop and die. Did Priscilla ever defend herself for a single moment? Don't you remember how painful it was to us, for years, to see how terribly she suffered? And now I suppose we are condemned to live through it all over again with this Grace.'

M. de la Bourlie thought how much he would have liked to appropriate to himself one of these loving, faithful and defenceless goddesses. When Madame de la Bourlie finally succumbed to a liver attack, he thought, why should he not take a little trip to London? But then he remembered his age.

'So hard to believe that we are all over eighty now,' he said, peevishly.

'Yes, it must be, but what has that to do with Charles-Edouard? Poor boy, he has certainly made an unwise marriage. All the same I rather like this Grace, I can't help it, she is so lovely, and there is something direct about her which I find charming. I also think her tougher, a tougher proposition than poor Priscilla was, more of a personality. There was never any hope for Priscilla, and I'm not quite so sure about Grace. If I can help her I will. Should I try to prepare her a little while she is here? Warn her about Albertine, for instance? What do you advise?'

'I don't think it ever does much good, to warn,' said M. de la Bourlie, thinking how furious he would be, in Charles-Edouard's place, if somebody were to warn his exquisite new wife about his intoxicating old mistress.

'No good at all,' agreed Madame Rocher, 'you are quite right. And then it's not as if it were only Albertine. I'd have to warn against every pretty woman and every *jolie-laide* at every dinner and every luncheon that they go to. I'd have to warn against Rastaquouères and Ranees, Israelites and Infantas, Danes and Duchesses, Greeks and Cherokee Indians. I'd have to give her a white list and a black list, and now, I suppose, since he has just come back from Indo-China, a yellow list as well. No, it would really be too exhausting, the young people must work it out for themselves – everybody has storms and troubles at their age no doubt, and there is no point in getting mixed up in them. All the same, I do wish so very much that Charles-Edouard could have married a good, solid, level-headed little French woman of the world instead of this beautiful goat-herd.'

The long summer days went by, slowly at first and then gathering speed, as days do which are filled from dawn to dusk with idleness. Grace spent most of the morning on the terrace outside her bedroom sewing away at her carpet. Charles-Edouard liked to see her doing it; her fair, bent head and flashing, white hands made such a pretty picture, but he decided that the day the carpet was finished it would have to be overtaken by some rather fearful accident, a pot of spilt indelible ink, or a spreading burn. Charles-Edouard was not one to cherish an object, especially so large and ugly an object as this was going to be, for reasons of sentiment.

After luncheon there was the siesta, and then Charles-Edouard and she would often drive down to the sea for a bathe. He had countless friends and acquaintances on the coast to whose villas they could go and from whose rocks they could swim, but Grace's complete lack of suitable clothes protected her from a really social life, from dinner parties, and visits to the Riviera. For this she was thankful. She liked the sleepy existence at Bellandargues, though Charles-Edouard complained of its dullness. His crony there was Madame Rocher, who poured into his ears an endless saga, her own version of all that had happened to all his friends since he had last seen them in 1939. It sounded simply terrific to Grace, whenever she overheard any of it. Madame Rocher was bored herself, longing to be off to yachts and palazzos and villas at which various impatient hosts and hostesses were said to be awaiting her. But this year she had decided to obey her doctor, and to stay quietly at Bellandargues for at least a month. She kept herself amused by the overwhelming interest she took in all that happened in house, village, and neighbourhood. When Grace and Charles-Edouard went off on their bathing expeditions she was able to tell them a great deal about their hosts, and what they were likely to find in the way of a household.

'Is it today you go to the English Lesbians? The nephew of the old one is there, I believe – if he is her nephew. They've just bought a refrigerator, what extravagance!'

'The Italian *ménage à trois*? Have you explained to Grace that *she* only like boys of sixteen and *they* get them for her? An excellent cook, I hear, this year.'

'Those two pederasts? Poor people, they are being horribly blackmailed by an ex-convict who lives in the village. But their rocks have never been nicer.'

And so on.

'Your aunt sees life through a veil of sex,' Grace said to Charles-Edouard when, for the third or fourth time, the company, represented to her by Madame Rocher as steeped in lurid vice, had turned out to be an ordinary, jolly house party.

'And who's to say she's wrong?'

'Well, I do think to call Mrs Browne and Lady Adela the English Lesbians is going rather too far. Anybody can see they've never heard of such a thing, poor darlings.'

'Then it's time somebody told them. More fun for them, if they know.'

'Charles-Edouard! And that dear old Italian lady with her two nice friends and all their grandchildren. I can't believe it!'

'One must never entirely discount Tante Régine's information on these subjects.'

One day when they were going to see an intensely pompous French duke and his wife, Madame Rocher hissed through the window of the motor at Grace, 'Reds.'

'Dear Tante Régine, come now!' Even Charles-Edouard was laughing.

'That family have always been Orleanists, my dear boy, and you very well know it. Impossible to be more to the Left.'

As they drove back in the beautiful evening light Charles-Edouard said, 'Shall we go to Venice? You could buy some clothes in Cannes on our way.'

Grace's heart sank. 'I'm happy here – aren't you, Charles-Edouard?'

'The evenings here are so terrible,' he said. 'I can get through the day, but the evenings –!'

'I love them,' she said, 'they must have been exactly the same for hundreds of years.'

She dreaded leaving Bellandargues, she felt she could cope with life there. The world that awaited them outside its walls was so infinitely complicated, according to Madame Rocher.

'Very well,' said Charles-Edouard, 'if you like it so much we'll stay until we go to Paris. I like it all right except for after dinner.'

Certainly the evenings were not very gay. The party repaired for coffee and *tisane* to a small salon where they chatted or played bridge until bedtime. Hot night noises floated in through the open windows. 'Why do French ducks quack all night?' Grace had asked. 'Those are frogs, my dearest, our staple diet you know.' Sometimes Madame Rocher played Chopin. It really was rather dull. Then Charles-Edouard discovered that she knew how to tell fortunes by cards, after which there was no more Chopin and no more gossiping. Grace was left at the bridge table while Charles-Edouard bullied Madame Rocher in a corner.

'Come on, Tante Régine, to work, to work!'

'But I've told you all I can.'

'That was yesterday. Today some new and hitherto unknown factor may have changed the whole course of my existence. Come, come!'

Madame Rocher, completely good-natured, would take up the cards and go on to the end of her invention. 'No wonder those five fortune-tellers said you would be killed in the war – they simply had to, to get rid of you.'

'Once more, Tante Régine – do I cut in three this time?'

'That's it, flog the poor old horse till it drops.'

'I passed by Madame André's cottage this afternoon, and made her tell the cards.

She is much more dramatic than you, Tante Régine – dark ladies and fair ladies – wicked ladies of all sorts about *chez* Madame André.'

'Yes, but I am handicapped by the presence of your wife,' said Madame Rocher, laughing.

'Oh!' said Grace, from the bridge table, 'you mustn't be. I'm not a bit a jealous person. I don't know what it is to be jealous.'

Madame Rocher raised her eyebrows, Madame de Valhubert and M. de la Bourlie looked sadly at each other across the table, and M. le Curé said, 'I declare a little slam.'

'That's very naughty, M. le Curé,' said Grace, 'now we shall be two down.'

6

'It's about this Mr Labby, dear.'

Charles-Edouard, who always got things done at once when he had decided upon them, had produced a young abbé to give Sigismond his lessons, and of course M. l'Abbé and Nanny were, from the very first, at daggers drawn. That is to say, Nanny's dagger was drawn, but it hardly penetrated the thick, black, clerical robes of the priest, who seemed quite unaware of her existence. That was his weapon.

'Oh Nan! But he seems nice, don't you think? So gentle. And Sigi loves him.'

Indeed that was partly the trouble. Sigi was always running off to be with M. l'Abbé, adored his lessons, had asked for longer hours, and Nanny was jealous.

'That's as may be,' she said darkly, 'you never can tell with these foreign clergymen, but it's his little brain I'm thinking of. Their little brains are so easily taxed. I wish you could hear him scream of a night. He's nothing but a bundle of nerves, all on edge – awful dreams he has, poor little fellow. I was wondering if these lessons aren't too much for him.'

'No, darling, of course not. We all learnt to read, you know. I was reading *The Making of a Marchioness* when Mummy died, I remember it so well.'

It was a memory that she always found rather disturbing. The little girl, with her nose in the book, had felt that she ought to feel sad, and yet all she wanted was to get on with the story. Sir Conrad had come into the nursery, tears pouring down his cheeks, at the very moment when Emily Fox-Seaton was setting out for the fish, and Grace had been distinctly annoyed by the interruption. Later on in life she had pondered over this apparent heartlessness with some astonishment. Did little children, then, not feel sorrow, or was it that the book had provided her with a refuge from the tragic, and perhaps embarrassing, reality?

She did not remember feeling sorrow at the loss of her mother, though she had often been seized with a physical longing for the soft lap and scented bosom of that intensely luxurious woman.

'I was only six – do you admit, Nanny?'

'Practically seven, and girls are always more forward.'

'Besides, you know, he simply must learn French.'

Nanny sniffed. 'He's learning French quick enough from that Canary. Another thing I wanted to talk to you about, when he's with Canary and all those other little devils they go off together goodness knows where, and I wouldn't be surprised if they bathe in the pond.'

'I expect they do.' Grace had, indeed, often seen them at it, and very pretty they looked popping naked in and out of the green water of a Renaissance fountain on the edge of the village. 'But it doesn't matter. Sigi's papa says he always bathed there when he was a child. It's perfectly safe.'

'Oh, perfectly safe until the poor little chap gets poliomyelitis and spends the rest of his life in a wheel chair. I wish to goodness he'd never taken up with that Canary, he's a perfect menace.'

Canari, the little yellow-headed son of Mignon the chemist, was Sigi's friend. 'M. l'Abbé is teaching me to pray. I prayed for a friend and I got Canari.'

Every afternoon, at the hottest time of the day, Sigi would race down to the vineyard to meet Canari and his band of *maquisards*. He was seen no more until Nanny rang the bell for Dick Barton, when he would race back up the hill. Nanny now had a powerful wireless installed, which turned the nursery into for ever England with six o'clock news, nine o'clock news, Music While you Work, and Twenty Questions. The *Daily Mirror*, too, had begun to arrive, bringing Garth in person, and so had *Woman and Beauty*, since when the nursery front had been distinctly calmer.

'But we mustn't worry too much, Nanny darling. Sigi is a little boy, growing up fast now, he's bound to dash off, you know, that's what little boys are like. I think it's a lovely life for him here, I only wish we could stay for ever.'

'You love M. l'Abbé, don't you, Sigismond?' said Grace, next morning. He always sat on her bed while she had her breakfast, a great bowl of coffee with fresh white bread, served on old Marseilles china. It was in many ways her favourite moment of the day; she drank her coffee looking at the hot early morning sky through muslin curtains; everything in the room was pretty, and the little boy on the end of her bed, in a white cotton jersey and red linen trousers, the prettiest object of all.

'I love M. l'Abbé and I revere him, and I've got a new ambition now. I wish to be able to converse with him in Latin.'

'French first, darling.'

'No, Mummy, the Romans were civilized before the Gauls, M. l'Abbé says. He tells some smashing stories about these Romans, and I've a new idea for Nanny. Supposing we got her into an arena with a particularly fierce bear?'

'Oh, poor Nanny. Where will you find the bear?'

'One of our *maquisards* comes from the Pyrenees, and they've got three bears there, wild, to this day. I showed him a picture of Garth digging a cunning pit, covered with leaves and branches –'

'Not Garth still?' said Charles-Edouard, coming in with the morning's letters. 'Run along, Sigi,' he said, holding the door and shooing him with a newspaper.

'Why do you always say run along, Papa?' He dragged through the door, looking crestfallen.

'It's what my mother used to say to me. "Run along, Charles-Edouard." The whole of my childhood was spent running along. I did hate it, too. Off with you! That was another.' He shut the door and gave Grace her letters.

'If you didn't like it,' she said, 'I can't think why you inflict it on the poor little boy. I don't think he sees enough of us, and he never sees us together.'

'That's not the point. The point is that we see quite enough of him,' said Charles-Edouard. 'There is nothing so dull as the conversation of small children.'

'It amuses me.'

'It does sometimes amuse women. They've got a childish side themselves, nature's way of enabling them to bear the prattle. And while we are on the subject, M. l'Abbé tells me that Nanny won't leave them alone at lesson time, she's always fussing in with some excuse or other. It's very annoying. Perhaps you'd speak to her about it?'

'I do know. I was afraid you'd be cross.'

'Well, speak.'

'Yes, I'll try. But you know what it is with Nanny, I'm dreadfully under her thumb. She thinks M. l'Abbé is taxing his little brain.'

'But his little brain has got to be taxed, it's there for that. Let Nanny wait till he's reading for his *bachot* if she wants to see him taxed – going on to twelve and one at night – poor little green face – rings under his eyes – attempted suicide – breakdowns –'

'Oh, Charles-Edouard, you are a brute,' said Grace, quite horrified.

He laughed, and began kissing her arm and shoulder.

'All this loony kissing again,' Sigi appeared in the window, 'over the pathless Himalayas, that's where I've come.'

'Yes, I wondered how long it would be before you found the way,' said Charles-Edouard.

'Shall I tell you something? I've just seen the *Daily*, and Garth has renounced the love of women.'

'Oh, he's like that, is he?'

'He's an Effendi now. What's an Effendi, Papa?'

'Talk about taxing his brain,' said Charles-Edouard.

'Well I know, but if it wasn't for Garth and Dick Barton he'd never go near the nursery, and poor Nanny would have a stroke looking for him on the roof and in the vineyards all day.'

'Now, Sigismond, just go back over those trackless paths, will you?'

'In other words, run along and off with you. All right, if I must.'

'M. l'Abbé talks about teaching him Latin.'

'Yes?' Charles-Edouard was opening his letters.

'Seems rather a waste of time?'

'Latin is a waste of time?' he said, putting a letter in his pocket and looking at Grace with surprise. 'Surely he must learn it before he goes to Eton?'

'Well it won't be the right pronunciation. Do we want Sigi to go to Eton?'

'Why not, for a bit? Then he can be top in English when he goes to St Cyr.'

'But I don't think they can go to Eton for a bit. Oh dear, I thought the thing about being French was you had your blessing always at home.'

'Do we always want him at home?'

'I do. Anyway, you have to be put down for Eton before your parents are married now – long before you are conceived, so I think this dream will come to nothing.'

Charles-Edouard, who was still reading his letters, said, 'Brighton College then, it's all the same.'

'Please can I come to the sea with you?'

'Not today, darling. We're lunching with some grown-up people.'

'It is unfair. I want to take a photograph of a huge, frightened wave.'

'But today it will be flat calm. Next time there's a mistral we'll take you.'

'I'm so hot. I do so want to bathe.'

'Don't you bathe in the fountain, with Canari?'

'I'm *brouillé* with *le chef*.'

'Not *brouillé* with Canari?'

'Yes I am. It was *convenu* that the *maquisards* should come here and be *chasseurs alpins* on the roof one day and the next I should spend with them doing sabotage in the village. Well, they came here, and yesterday I went down to the village and he was under the lime trees with *les braves*, and he said, *"va-t-en. On ne veut pas de toi."'*

'But why, Sigi?'

'I don't know. But I don't care, not a bit. I want to go to the sea and swim under water and spear an octopus.'

'When you are older.'

'When shall I be older?'

'All in due course. Run along now and find M. l'Abbé.'

'He is reading his *bréviaire*.'

'Well, Nanny then. Anyway, run along, darling.'

That night, at dinner, Madame de Valhubert said, 'Do you know our poor little *maquisard* spent the whole afternoon by himself in the salon? He looked the picture of woe. In the end Régine and I had to play cards with him for very pity.'

'It's that wretched Canari,' said Grace, 'he has sent him packing, and nobody knows why. Oh, I do hope they'll make it up soon, or the poor duck will have no more fun at all. I feel quite worried. Couldn't you go down and speak to M. Mignon, Charles-Edouard, and find out what it is?'

Charles-Edouard laughed, looked round the table at the others, who were all smiling, and said, 'Alas, my influence with Mignon is but limited, I fear.'

'But why? He made that nice speech.'

'That was the *solidarité de la libération*. It just held long enough for him to make the speech. Now we are back among all the old feuds again. A very good sign that peace is really here.'

'M. le Curé, couldn't you do something?' said Grace.

At this there was a general laugh. M. le Curé lifted his hands, saying that Grace did not quite grasp the situation. M. Mignon, he said, was a Radical Socialist. If Grace had not spent the years of the war so idly, stitching dreams into an ugly carpet or leading goats to browse on blackberries, if she had taken the advice of her father and concentrated instead upon Messrs Bodley and Brogan, whose works lay among a huge heap of unopened books behind the back stairs, these

words would have meant something to her, and what was to follow would have
been avoided. But as she looked completely blank Charles-Edouard began to
explain.

'Not only is M. Mignon, *père*, a Radical Socialist of the deepest dye – Canari
doesn't go to our school, I would have you observe, but to the *Instituteur* – but he
is actually a Freemason.'

'Well, in that case, it's a pity my father's not here to have a word with him. They
could wear their aprons, and do whatever it is together.'

Charles-Edouard tried to kick Grace under the table, but she was too far for him
to reach her. She went blandly on.

'Papa is one of the top Freemasons, at home, you know. Couldn't we tell M.
Mignon that? It might help.'

Silence fell, so petrifyingly cold that she realized something was very wrong,
but couldn't imagine what.

Madame de Valhubert's black eyes went with a question mark to Charles-
Edouard. Madame Rocher and M. de la Bourlie exchanged glances of mournful
significance; M. le Curé and M. l'Abbé gazed at their plates and Charles-Edouard
looked extremely put out, as Grace had never seen him look before. At last he said
to his grandmother, 'Freemasons are quite different in England, you know.'

'Oh! Indeed?'

'The Grand Master, there, is a member of the Royal Family – is that not so,
Grace?'

'I don't know,' said Grace. 'I don't really know much about them.'

'With the English anything is possible,' said Madame Rocher. 'What did I tell
you, Sosthène?'

'Oh no, but all the same,' muttered the old man, 'this is too much.'

There was another long silence, at the end of which Madame de Valhubert rose
from the table, and they all went into the little salon. The evening dragged much
worse than usual, and the party dispersed for the night very early indeed.

'What have I done?' said Grace in her bedroom.

'It's not your fault,' said Charles-Edouard, crossly, for him, not knowing that it
was entirely her fault for neglecting the information Sir Conrad had put at her
disposal, 'but I must beg you never again to speak of Freemasons before French
people. Take a lover – take two – turn Lesbian – steal valuable boxes off your
friends' tables – anything, anything, but don't say that your father is a Freemason.
It will need ten years of virtuous life before this is forgiven, and it will never be
forgotten. *La fille du francmaçon!* Well, I'll see my grandmother in the morning and
try to explain –' He was laughing again now, but Grace saw that he was really very
much embarrassed by what she had done.

Madame de Valhubert having rushed to the chapel, Madame Rocher went down
with M. de la Bourlie to his motor, and they stood for a moment on the terrace
together.

'You see!' she said, 'daughter of Freemasons! What did I tell you? No wonder
she was married by a mayor, all is now plain as daylight. Can they, I wonder, really
be considered decent people in England? I must find out. Poor Charles-Edouard,
I see his path beset by thorns. Terrible for the Valhuberts, especially as they have
had this sort of trouble in the family once – well not Freemasonry, of course, but

that dreadful Marshal. All so carefully lived down ever since. No wonder Françoise is upset – she will be on her knees all night, I feel sure.'

M. de la Bourlie was greatly shocked at the whole affair. Even were he not over eighty, even were Madame de la Bourlie not still alive, a beautiful English wife now ceased to be any temptation to him. He had learnt his lesson.

Grace's blunder had one good result however. Sigi got back into the Canari set, from which he had been expelled, had he but known it, on grounds of clericalism. His adherence to M. l'Abbé had been doing him no good among the *maquisards*.

M. le Curé was unable to keep the extraordinary pronouncement of young Madame de Valhubert to himself; he told one or two gossips, and the news spread like wild-fire, causing the greatest possible sensation in the village. The Catholics, adherents of the M.R.P. and so on, were very much shocked, but the rest of the population was jubilant. The daughter of a Freemason was an unhoped-for addition to the Valhubert family. Nanny, whose resistance to M. l'Abbé stiffened every day, came to be regarded as the very champion of anti-clericalism. The position of Charles-Edouard remained anomalous, a certain mystery seemed to surround his opinions, and nobody knew exactly where he stood. On one hand there was the Freemason wife, on the other it was he and nobody else who had summoned M. l'Abbé to teach his child. Since he was popular, jolly, and a good landlord, since his war record was above reproach, and they knew, from his own voice on the radio, that he had been one of the very first to join General de Gaulle, he tended to be claimed as one of themselves by all sections of the community while they awaited further evidence from which to draw further conclusions.

Charles-Edouard did manage to convince his grandmother that Freemasonry in England was regarded by decent, and even royal, families as perfectly correct. It took some doing, but finally he succeeded.

'Very well then,' she said. 'I believe you, my child. But as we are on disagreeable topics, why this marriage by a mayor? Why not a priest?'

'Ah!' he said. 'You know?'

'Yes, I know.'

'The fact is I was not quite sure. I married this foreign woman after a very short courtship, I was off to the war, perhaps for years, she was engaged to somebody else when I first met her, and might have – I didn't think so, but there was no proof – an unstable character. And she was a heathen. The English, you know, are nearly all heathens, like Freemasonry, it is a perfectly respectable thing to be, over there. Should she have got tired of waiting and gone off with somebody else, I didn't want to be debarred for ever, or at any rate for years, from a proper marriage. If she, or her father, had made the least objection to the civil marriage, if they had even mentioned it, I would have got a priest, but the subject was never raised. It was very odd. They regarded the whole thing as perfectly normal and natural. Sigismond has been baptized, by the way. I wrote and asked for that, and it was immediately done, just as if I had asked for him to be vaccinated.'

'And now?' said Madame de Valhubert.

'Grace is still a heathen, but you can see for yourself that she is a soul worth saving. In due course we shall convert her; it will be time enough then to be married in church.'

'Charles-Edouard, you have brought home a heathen concubine instead of a wife! You are living in mortal sin, my child.'

'Dearest grandmother, you know me well enough to know that I am generally living in mortal sin. We must trust, for my soul, to the mercy of God. As regards Grace, all will turn out for the best, you will see.'

Grace would have been intensely surprised if she could have overheard this conversation. They both spoke as if he had picked up the daughter of a cannibal king in darkest Africa, whereas she thought of herself as a perfectly ordinary Christian. Something of this occurred to Charles-Edouard.

'Please, grandmother, if you speak with Grace about this, don't say that she is only a concubine. She wouldn't like it. Trust me – I'm sure everything will be all right, meanwhile you can look upon us as fiancés.'

'Very well,' said the old lady. 'I won't say a word on any religious subject. It is your responsibility, Charles-Edouard, and you know as well as I do where your duty lies in this matter.'

'But,' she thought to herself, 'there are other things I must have out with her before they go back to Paris.'

'I suppose Charles-Edouard must seem very English to you, dear child,' she began, next time she found herself alone with Grace.

'English?' Grace was amused and surprised. For her Charles-Edouard was the forty kings of France rolled into one, the French race in person walking and breathing.

'Indeed at first sight he is very English. His clothes, his figure, that enormous breakfast of ham and eggs, his aptitude for business. But you know him very little, dearest, as yet. You have been married (if one can call it a marriage) for seven years and yet here you are, strangers, on a honeymoon, with a big child. It's a very odd situation, and not the least curious and wonderful part is that you are both so happy. But I repeat that so far you have only seen the English side of your husband. He is getting restless here (I know him so well) and very soon, probably at a day's notice, he will take you off to Paris. When you are there you will begin to see how truly French he is.'

'But he seems so French to me already. How can he seem even more so in Paris? In what way?'

'I am giving you a word of warning, just one. In Paris you and he will be back in his own world of little friends all brought up together. I advise you to be very, very sensible. Behave as if you were a thousand years old, like me.'

'You think I shall be jealous. Tante Régine thinks so too, I can see. But I never am. It's not part of my nature. I'm not insensitive, it isn't that, I can mind things quite terribly, but jealous I am not.'

'Alas, my dear child, you are in love, and there is no love in this world without jealousy.'

'And I may not have known Charles-Edouard for long, but I do know him very well. He loves me.'

'Yes, yes, indeed he does. That is quite plain. And so do we all, dear child, and that is why I am talking to you like this, in spite of everything. I tell you too that if you are very sensible he will love you for ever, and in time everything will be regulated in your lives and you will be a truly happy couple, for ever.'

'That's what Charles-Edouard tells me. All right, I am very sensible, so he will love me for ever. Don't I look sensible?'

'Alas, I know these practical, English looks and how they are deceptive. So re-assuringly calm on the surface, and underneath what a turmoil. And then the world reflected in distorting glasses. Latin women see things so clearly as they are; above all they understand men.'

'I never know quite what it means, to understand men.'

'Don't you, dear? It's very simple, it can be said in a few words. Put them first. A woman who puts her husband first seldom loses him.'

'Well I dare say,' said Grace with some indignation, 'that a woman who lets her husband do exactly as he likes, who shuts her eyes to every infidelity, and lets him walk over her, in fact, would never lose him.'

'Just so,' said Madame de Valhubert, placidly.

'And do you really advise that?'

'Oh I don't advise, the old must never advise. All I do say is remember that Charles-Edouard is a Frenchman – not an Englishman with a French veneer, but a deeply French Frenchman. If you want this to become a real marriage, a lifelong union (I don't speak of a sacrament), you must follow the rules of our civilization. A little life of your own, if you wish it, will never be held against you, so long as you always put your husband first.'

Grace was thoroughly shocked. 'I could have understood it if Tante Régine had spoken like that – would have expected it in fact, but your grandmother!' she said to Charles-Edouard.

'My grandmother is an extremely practical person,' he said, 'you can see it by the way she runs this house. You can always tell by that, with women.'

The next day Charles-Edouard made one of his sudden moves and whirled Grace off to Paris. Nanny and the little boy were left behind to follow in a week or two, escorted by the faithful Ange-Victor.

7

The Valhuberts' Paris house was of a later date than any part of Bellandargues, and had only been finished a month or two before the Revolution. It stood on the site of a Louis XIII house whose owner, planning to receive Marie Antoinette there, had pulled it down and built something more fashionable, to be worthy of her. The intended fête for the Queen never took place, and in the end it was Josephine, not Marie Antoinette, who was received as guest of honour in the round, white and gold music room. This was an episode in their family history very much glossed over by future Valhuberts, and most of all by Charles-Edouard's grandmother. The truth was that the eldest son of Marie Antoinette's admirer, a soldier born and bred, had not been able to resist the opportunity of serving under the most brilliant of all commanders. He had joined the revolutionary army, had risen to the rank of General before he was thirty, and was killed at the battle of Friedland shortly after receiving his Marshal's bâton.

'Most fortunately,' Charles-Edouard said when recounting all this to Grace, 'or he would certainly have ended up as a Duke with some outlandish title. I prefer to be what I am.'

'Perhaps he would have refused.'

'Perhaps. But I've yet to hear of anybody refusing a dukedom.'

The family, after his death, had once more embraced a cautious Royalism, and a veil was drawn over this unfashionably patriotic outburst. Old Madame de Valhubert always pretended that she knew nothing of it, and, if anybody mentioned the Marshal, would say that he must have been some very distant relation of her husband's. All his relics, his portrait in uniform by Gros, the eagle which it had cost him his life to recapture, his medals, his sword, and his bâton were hidden away at Bellandargues in a little outhouse, locally known as *le pavillon de la gloire*, and even Charles-Edouard would not have dared bring them back into the salon during the lifetime of his grandmother.

'It will be the same with me,' he said. 'Sigi's great-grand-daughter-in-law will hide away my Croix de Lorraine, my *médaille de la résistance*, and the badge of my squadron, and say that I was some distant relation of her husband's. They are terrible, French families.'

The house, long, three-storied, lay between courtyard and garden. Old Madame de Valhubert, when in Paris, occupied one of the lodges in the courtyard. 'She moved in there during the war, after the Germans had looted the main block, and now she likes it so much that she has stayed on.' The other lodge housed the servants. The ground floor of the house itself consisted of five enormous drawing-rooms leading out of each other, the middle one being the famous round music room, masterpiece of the brothers Rousseau. Over this, the same shape and almost as elaborately decorated, was Grace's bedroom. These rooms were on the garden side, facing due south and with a wide view of trees.

'What an enormous garden, for a town,' said Grace.

'It used to be three times as long, but some of it was taken, alas, in the time of Haussman to make the horrible rue de Babel, well named. However we can't complain, many houses in this neighbourhood suffered more – many wonderful houses either lost their gardens altogether, or were even pulled down. Paris was only saved from complete ruination by the fall of Napoleon III. Bismarck really saved us, funnily enough!'

As Charles-Edouard had quite openly joined the Free French under his own name, everything he possessed was confiscated during the war and would have been taken off to Germany had it not been for the initiative of Louis, his old butler, who had piled pictures and furniture in the cellar, built a wall to hide them, and, to make this wall convincing, put a wash basin with brass taps against it.

'We had so little time,' he said, when explaining all this to Grace and Charles-Edouard, 'that we had to connect the taps with an ordinary bucket of water hung up on the other side of the wall. Oh how we prayed the Germans wouldn't run them very long. All was well, however. They came, they tested the taps for a minute, just as we hoped they would, and went away again. Oh what a relief!'

'And they never requisitioned the house?'

'They didn't like this side of the river – too many dark, old, twisting streets; they felt more comfortable up by the Étoile in big, modern buildings. They just carted off everything they could see, and never came back again. Fortunately, as I've been here so long I knew which were the best pieces (we didn't dare hide everything). Later on we installed ventilation in the cellar, and the things were miraculously well preserved through those long, terrible winters. In all this we were helped by M. Saqué the builder – M. le Marquis will perhaps go and thank him.'

'Very probably I will,' said Charles-Edouard, more touched than he cared to admit by this recital. He loved his furniture and objects, and specially loved his pictures. He showed them to Grace before he even allowed her to go upstairs. It was a charming collection of minor masters with one or two high spots, an important Fragonard, a pair of Hubert Roberts, and so on. He was always adding to it, and had bought more than half the pictures himself.

The weeks which followed, spent by Grace alone with her husband in the empty town during unfashionable September, were the happiest she had ever known. Charles-Edouard, rediscovering, after seven long years, the stones of Paris, for which he had an almost unhealthy love, walked with her all day in the streets, and sometimes, when there was a moon, after dinner as well. Grace was a good walker, even for an Englishwoman, but he was indefatigable, and sometimes, as when they went to Versailles for the day, she had to cry for mercy. He was wonderful company. He knew the long, intricate histories of all the palaces of the Faubourg St Germain and exactly where to find each one, hidden behind huge walls and carriage door-ways.

'You could ring the bell there and have a peep,' he would say, 'nobody knows you as yet – but I shall remain here, out of sight.'

So Grace would ring, put her head round the wicket, apologize to the concierge, and be rewarded by a transparency of stone and glass and ironwork, placed, like her own house, between courtyard and trees. When the ground floor was the width of one room these trees would be visible through the two sets of windows.

'Well, did you like it?'

'Oh wonderful – I can't get over it, Charles-Edouard!'

'Please do not demonstrate in front of these policemen. Please remember that I am a well-known figure in this neighbourhood. Did you notice the sphinxes in the courtyard?'

Grace never noticed any details of that sort; her eye was quite untrained, and she was content to take in a general impression of beauty, to which she was very receptive. Unlike her husband, however, she really preferred natural beauty to things made by man.

'I am loving it, oh I am loving it. I didn't know Paris was like this. When I was at school here it was different – rue de la Pompe and Avenue Victor Hugo (the hours we spent in the Grand Magazin Jones!) in those days. And even so I was always happy here, but now –! I suppose it's got something to do with you as well, my happiness.'

'Something!' said Charles-Edouard. 'Everything.'

'How lucky I am! I could never have loved anybody else half as much.'

'I know.'

'Still, I wish you wouldn't say "I know" like that. You might say that you're lucky too.'

'I'm awfully nice,' he answered, 'never could you have found anybody as nice as I am. Admit that you amuse yourself when you are with me. Now look – the Fountain of Bouchardon, so beautiful. But how foolish to put those horrible modern flats just there.'

'You ought to have a Georgian Society,' said Grace. 'Do you think you're really the whole reason for my happiness?'

'Almost certainly.'

'Oh dear, I hope not, so dangerous when it all depends on one person. Perhaps the Blessing has a bit to do with it too.' But she knew that if so it was a very minor bit, much as she loved the pretty little boy.

'Look, the gateway of the Hôtel de Bérulle, is it not a masterpiece of restraint and clever contrivance? See how a coach would be able to turn out of this narrow street, and drive in.'

'Oh yes, how fascinating!'

'Please do not demonstrate –'

But he was really delighted at the way she was taking to everything French. He saw that, in spite of her bad education, she showed signs of a natural taste which could easily be developed. As for Charles-Edouard, art was a religion to him. If he had a few moments to spare he would run into the Louvre as his grandmother would run into church for a short prayer. The museums were awakening one after another from their war-time trance, and Charles-Edouard, intimate with all the curators, spent hours with them discussing and praising the many improvements.

Grace said, 'How strange it is that you, who really take in everything through the eyes, should hate the country so much.'

'Nature I hate. It is so dull in the country, that must be why. But Art I love.'

'And pretty ladies you love?' she said, as he turned to peer at a vision in black and white flashing by in a little Rolls-Royce. September was nearing its close and the pretty ladies had begun to trickle back into town, filling Grace with apprehension.

'Women I love,' he said with his guilty, interior laugh. 'But also I am a great family man, and that will be your hold over me.'

But how to have a hold, she thought, unless one's own feet are firmly planted on the ground? And how can they be so planted in a strange country, surrounded by strangers at the very beginning of a strange new life?

In due course Nanny and Sigi arrived on the night train from Marseilles, and that afternoon Grace took them across the river to the Tuileries Gardens. Nanny was in a wonderfully mellow mood, delighted to have got away from the heat of Provence, from Canari, and, temporarily, at any rate, from M. l'Abbé. (He was coming to Paris after Christmas, when the lessons would be resumed.) Delighted, too, to be in a town again, where a child is so much easier to control than in the country. She entirely approved of the fact that the door to the street could only be opened by the concierge, and that the garden was surrounded by walls high as the ramparts of a city. No means of escape here for little boys. She was not even entirely displeased with the nursery accommodation; arranged for Charles-Edouard by his English mother it was like an old-fashioned nursery in some big London house, and had none of the strange bleakness of the rooms at Bellandargues.

Her smiles, however, always on the wintry side, soon vanished when she was confronted with the goat carts, the donkeys, the Guignol, and the happy crowd of scooting, skating children in the Tuileries Gardens. Sigi had, of course, no sooner seen the goat carts than he was in one.

'We shall never get the little monkey away from these animals – is there nowhere else for us to go, dear, more like Hyde Park? I'm not going to stand the whole winter in this draughty-looking square waiting for him to ride round hour after hour.'

'Oh no, darling, you mustn't. We must ration him. But don't you think this is a charming place for children, more fun really than Hyde Park?'

Grace had been so much looking forward to bringing Sigi here and watching him enjoy all the treats that she had overlooked the certain disapproval of Nanny.

'Grace! I'm surprised to hear you say such a thing! Think of the Peter Pan monument, and the Dell! Goodness knows what he'll pick up from all these children. Anyway there's to be no question of him going inside that filthy-looking theatre, or whatever it is. I hope that's quite understood, dear.'

'Of course, Nan, just as you say.'

Nanny took Grace's arm and said in a low voice, 'Isn't that Mrs Dexter over there?'

'Grace!'

'Carolyn!'

'I was just going to ring up your house and see if you were back. We've come to live here, isn't it lovely! I spoke to your papa on the telephone on our way through London and he gave me your number, but we've been so busy flat-hunting. Yes, now we've found a lovely one – only miles from you I'm afraid – up by the Parc Monceau. Is this Sigi? Seven, I suppose – he looks more. Poor little Foss will be rather young for him, but Nanny will be pleased to see you, Nanny, it will make all the difference. Which day can you come to tea? Then we must get together, Grace, and meet each other's husbands! Isn't it exciting?'

Carolyn Broadman was a lifelong friend of Grace. Their fathers had been friends and they had been at the same school. Carolyn was a little older and much cleverer, she was the head girl at school, revered by the others, many of whom had been passionately in love with her. She was tall, with curly, auburn hair and particularly piercing bright blue eyes. This colouring constituted her claim to beauty; her features were not very good, though her figure was excellent. She moved with more than the hint of a swagger, and Sir Conrad always called her Don Juan. She had certainly been one at school, coldly gathering up the poor little hearts laid at her feet and throwing them over her shoulder. Grace had not seen her since the war, but knew that she had married an enormously rich, important American whom she had met in Italy. As was to be expected she had become a female General in the war – were there such things as female Marshals she would, no doubt, have been one.

'Come back to tea now,' said Grace, 'and meet Charles-Edouard.'

'Darling I can't. I'm just off to our Embassy where they've got a cocktail party for some Senators – I must pick up Hector at his office and then go home and change for it. I promised I'd go early and help.'

So they chatted for a few minutes more and then parted with many plans for meeting again soon.

'Nice to see a clean English skin,' said Nanny, as they wandered back across the Pont de Solferino.

Charles-Edouard was in the hall, evidently on his way out.

'Well,' he said, 'what are the news?'

'I took Sigi and Nan – run along up darling, it's tea-time – to the Tuileries Gardens and who d'you think we met? An old friend of mine called Carolyn Dexter. Wasn't it funny?'

'Beautiful?'

'I don't know if you'd think so. Beautiful colouring.'

'That means red hair I suppose. Not my type.'

'And a wonderful figure, and she's terribly clever. She's married to a very important American called Hector Dexter.'

'So, go on. What did she tell you?'

'Well, they live up by the Parc Monceau. We must all meet some day soon.'

'Go on. What else?'

'Nothing else.'

'Ha! So you stood together in the Tuileries gazing into each other's eyes without a word?'

'You do tease me. We chattered like magpies.'

'But what about?'

'She was just off to a cocktail party at the American Embassy.'

'This is all very dull.'

'Don't be such a bully, Charles-Edouard.'

'You must tell me stories about what happens during your day, to amuse me. Do go on.'

'They have a little boy, but younger than Sigi, and Nanny is longing to go and meet their English nanny –'

Charles-Edouard's attention was wandering. '*Quand un Vicomte rencontre un autre Vicomte,*' he sang, '*Qu'est-ce qu'ils se racontent? Des histoires de Vicomtes.*' He picked up his hat.

'Are you going out?'

'Yes.'

'Back to tea?'

'No.'

Grace had her tea in the nursery, that day and subsequently. Charles-Edouard was never in at tea-time because he now resumed an afternoon habit of many years' standing, he visited Albertine Marel-Desboulles. She was one of the little friends, all brought up together, about whom Madame de Valhubert had wanted to warn Grace, and quite the most dangerous of them. She and Charles-Edouard had had the same nurse as children (passed on to Charles-Edouard's mother by Albertine's, since Albertine was older). When he was eighteen and she a young married woman they had had a short but enthusiastic love affair; this had simmered down to a sentimental friendship in which love, physical love at any rate, still played a part. Charles-Edouard found her more entertaining than anybody; she was certainly quite the reverse of dull, always having something to recount. Not plain slices of life served up on a thick white plate, but wonderful confections embellished with the aromatic and exotic fruits of her own sugary imagination, presented in just such a way as to tempt the appetite of such sophisticated admirers as he. She had endless tales to spin around their mutual friends, could discuss art and objects of art with his own collector's enthusiasm as well as with imaginative knowledge, and, what specially appealed to Charles-Edouard, would talk by the hour, also with imaginative knowledge and with collector's enthusiasm, about himself. She was an accomplished fortune-teller. Like a child who knows where the sweets are kept, Charles-Edouard always went straight to the Japanese lacquer commode, in the right-hand corner of whose top drawer lay packs of cards.

'How many years since I have done this?' she said, shuffling and dealing, her long, spidery fingers bright with diamonds.

'You said I would be killed in the war, I remember,' said Charles-Edouard.

'I said I couldn't quite see in what circumstances you would be coming back. Suppose I had told you it would be complete with an English wife and a son, that would indeed have been a *coup* for me. Unfortunately I didn't foresee anything so improbable. Please cut the cards. However, I see her now, clear as daylight, surrounded by old maids, not another man in her orbit. She must be very faithful. Nice for you to have this faithful wife. Good. Cut the cards. Yes. Now here we have a surprise, not that it surprises me very much. Not English, and not your wife, but a sparkling beauty, a brilliant. There is an enormous amount of interesting incident round you and your relationship with this brilliant. Cut the cards. This is for you. Yes, here you are and with all your talents, your charm, your wit, your good nature, watching yourself as you live your life, and fascinated by the spectacle.'

'Ah!' said Charles-Edouard, 'this is very nice. How I love being rubbed the right way.'

'Cut three times. I am bound to tell you that there will be a few little tiresomenesses, to do with the brilliant. You won't be careful enough, or you'll be unlucky – there'll be a torrent of tears, but they won't be your tears, so never mind. Cut the cards. Nothing different – you again, between the brilliant and the wife. I can't tell any more today.'

She leant her head on her hand and looked at him with blue, lollipop eyes, which seemed out of place among her pointed Gothic features. Everything about her was long and thin, except for these round, blue eyes; she was an exceedingly odd-looking woman.

'So! How do you find marriage?'

'Rather dull,' said Charles-Edouard, 'but I rather like it, and I love my wife. She is original, she amuses me.'

'And lovely?' said Madame Marel.

'She will be, when she is arranged. No doubt you will see her at the Fertés on the tenth.'

'Yes indeed. We shall all be there, all agog. You haven't changed much, Charles-Edouard, except that you are better looking than ever.'

'Ah!' said Charles-Edouard. He got up and locked the door.

'No need to do that,' she said, smiling. 'Pierre would never let anybody else in when he knows you are here.'

Presently Charles-Edouard, lying relaxed among the cushions of an enormous sofa, said, 'So tell me, since all these years what have you become?'

'Oh it's a long story – or rather a long book of short stories.'

'Yes, I expect it is. And now –?'

'Nothing very much. I have an Englishman who is madly in love with me – I don't believe I've ever been loved so violently with such really suicidal mania, as by this Englishman.'

'Ah, these English, they are terrible.'

'You may laugh, but it is no joke at all. The evidences of his love simply pour into the house – I don't know what the concierge can think, it is full-time work carrying them across the courtyard. Flowers, telegrams, letters, parcels, all the day.'

'Does he live here?'

'Better than that, in London. But he flies over to see me at least once a week, and then the tears, the scenes, the jealousy, the temperament. It is wearing me out, and I ought really to get rid of him.'

'Why don't you?'

'Because of the bourgeois thrift I learnt from my dear husband. Never throw anything away, it might come in useful. Besides, I do love to be loved.'

'And what is his name?'

'It's not an interesting name – Palgrave, Hughie Palgrave.'

'It is interesting to me, however,' said Charles-Edouard, 'since Hughie Palgrave was once engaged to my wife.'

8

As soon as she had some presentable clothes Charles-Edouard began taking Grace to see his relations. 'Very dull,' he said, 'but what must be, must be.' So at 6.30 every day they would put themselves into a little lift which shook and wavered up to the drawing-room of some old aunt or cousin of the family. These lifts, these drawing-rooms and these old ladies differed very little from each other. The rooms were huge, cold and magnificent, with splendid pieces of furniture arranged to their worst advantage and mixed up with a curious assortment of objects which had been collected during the course of long married lives. The old ladies were also arranged to their worst advantage, and covered with a curious assortment of jewellery. Prominent upon a black cardigan they generally wore the rosette of the Legion of Honour.

'We might be going in for a literary prize,' said Charles-Edouard, as for the fifth time they tottered up in the fifth little lift.

'Why might we?'

'This is how you win a literary prize in France. First you write a book – that is of no importance, however. Then you go and see my aunts, treat them with enormous deference, and laugh loudly at the jokes my uncles make over the *porto*.'

'I don't understand.'

'No wonder. All the literary prizes here are given by my aunts.'

'And won by other aunts?'

'Not usually. Their works, of an unreadable erudition, are crowned by the Academy. That is different, though my aunts have great power there also, and have managed to insert my uncles under the cupola all right.'

'Does Tante Régine give prizes?'

'Heavens no! She is in quite a different world. You will find her (she's coming back next week, by the way) at all the parties, the dress collections, the private views, the first nights. It's another product altogether. The Novembre de la Fertés, my grandmother's and Tante Régine's family, have never gone in for intellect – nor have the Rocher des Innouïs. All these clever old girls are Valhubert relations – their cradles were rocked by Alphonse Daudet and the Abbé Liszt. Ah! *Ma tante! Bonjour mon oncle.* So, this is Grace.'

'Grace! Sit here where we can see you, dear child, and tell us – so cut off from England for so long – all about Mr Charles Morgan.'

The rest of the company consisted, as usual, of earnest, dowdy young women, following in the footsteps of their elders, of old men so courtly in manner that they seemed dedicated to eternal courtship, and one or two bright, overgrown boys. They put Grace on a high-backed needlework chair facing the window, sat round her in a semi-circle, and plied her with weak port wine, biscuits, and questions. They passed from Mr Charles Morgan, about whom she knew lamentably little, to Miss Mazo de la Roche, about whom she knew less. They gave her to understand that one of the most serious deprivations caused by the war had been that of Les Whiteoaks, Les Jalna. Then they fired questions at her from all sides, wanting to know about English novelists, dramatists, lesser country houses, boy scouts, gardens, music, essayists, and the government of Britain, until she felt like an ambulating Britain in Pictures. Their knowledge of England was quite astonishing, very much like the knowledge some astronomer might have of the moon after regarding it for many a long night through a telescope.

Grace felt that they were trying to place her. Not, as Tante Régine was always trying, to place her in English society, to find out whom she knew and if her family was really, in spite of the Freemason father, quite respectable, but in another way. Some of them had read Sir Conrad's *Life of Fouquet.* They pronounced it honourable, and assumed, from the fact of its existence, that Grace must have been brought up in intellectual circles. They wanted to place her views and inclinations, her turn of mind. They wanted to know if she was Oxford or Cambridge, whether she preferred *The Times* or the *Daily Telegraph*, what she felt about Shakespeare and Bacon. Their questions were not at all hard to answer, but she felt that by her answers to these, possibly deceptively, simple questions, she was being forever judged.

She found it a great strain, and had said so to Charles-Edouard after the last tea-party.

'But that is what French people are like,' he had replied, shrugging his shoulders. 'In France you are always in a witness box. You'll get used to it. But you must sharpen your wits a little, my dearest, if you want a favourable verdict.'

The old uncles did not play much part in all this. They were still, after a lifetime of marriage, lost in admiration at the brilliance of their wives, quite wrapped up in whatever these wonderful women were doing. So when they met each other out of doors, which happened continually, as they all lived in the same neighbourhood and all had Scotties to exercise, they would shout across the street, 'Good morning, and how is Benjamin Constant going on' (or whoever it was that the other's wife was known to be studying just then). 'Splendidly, splendidly. And the old stones of Provins?'

With Grace they were charming, making her feel that she was a pretty woman and that therefore nothing she said would ever be held against her. However, she was shrewd enough to see that it was the aunts who counted. These aunts were a great surprise to Grace. She had hitherto supposed that, with the exception of a few very religious people like Madame de Valhubert, all Frenchwomen, of all ages, were entirely frivolous and given over to the art of pleasing. From which it will be deduced that the works of Mauriac and Balzac, like those of Brogan and Bodley, lay mouldering, their pages uncut, in the great heap behind the kitchen stairs at Bunbury.

'Are you happy?' Charles-Edouard said, as they walked home. It was some days, he had noticed, since Grace had said how happy she was, of her own accord.

'I am perfectly happy,' she said, 'but I can't feel at home yet.'

'You felt at home at Bellandargues, why not here?'

'Bellandargues was the country.' She found it hard to explain to Charles-Edouard how different was life in Paris from anything she had ever known, so complicated and artificial that her only refuge of reality was the nursery. The other rooms in her house, with their admirable decoration and gold-encrusted furniture, so rich that to enter one of them was like opening a jewellery box, belonged to the Valhuberts past, present, and future, but she could not feel as yet that they belonged to her. The smiling servants maintained the life of the house undirected by her; the comings and goings in the courtyard, the cheerful bustle of a large establishment, would all go on exactly the same if she were not there. In short she played not the smallest part in this place, which was, nevertheless, her home.

Charles-Edouard had quite fallen back into his pre-war existence. He spent the morning telephoning to friends whose very names she did not know; in the afternoon he ran from one antiquary to another; he was out a great deal, and always out at tea-time.

Every fortnight or so he went for the inside of a day to Bellandargues to perform his mayoral duties, and very occasionally he stayed there the night. 'I do hate to sleep out of Paris,' he used to say, and did so as seldom as he possibly could.

Grace herself was quite busy, an unaccustomed busyness, since it was all concerned with clothes. Madame Rocher's *vendeuse* had taken charge of her, and kept her nose to the grindstone, making her get more and more dresses for more and more occasions; big occasions, a ball, Friday night at Maxims, the opera, the important dinner party; little occasions, the theatre, dinner at home alone, or with one or two friends, luncheon at home, luncheon in a restaurant; and odd occasions, luncheon or dinner in the country (nothing so lugubrious as a week-end party was envisaged), and the voyage.

'Could I not travel in my morning suit?'

'It is always better to travel with brown accessories.'

'I am perfectly happy,' she repeated, 'only not quite at my ease yet. Perhaps a little homesick.'

But more than ever passionately in love with Charles-Edouard.

The first big occasion to which Grace went in Paris was a dinner given for her by the Duchesse de la Ferté. At this dinner Grace's preconceived ideas about the French, already shaken by the *porto* parties, were blown sky high. She knew, or thought she knew, that Frenchwomen were hideously ugly, but with an ugliness redeemed by great vivacity and perfect taste in dress. Perfect taste she took to mean quiet, unassuming taste – 'better be under- than over-dressed' her English mentors such as Carolyn's mother used to say. Then she imagined that all Frenchmen were small and black, at best resembling Charles Boyer, her own husband's graceful elegance being easily accounted for, in her view, by his English blood.

So all in all she was unprepared for the scene that met her eyes on entering the Fertés' big salon. The door opened upon a kaleidoscope of glitter. The women, nearly all beauties, were in huge crinolines, from which rose naked shoulders and almost naked bosoms, sparkling with jewels. They moved on warm waves of scent, their faces were gaily painted with no attempt at simulating nature, their hair looked cleaner and glossier than any hair she had ever seen. Almost more of a surprise to Grace were the men, tall, handsome, and beautifully dressed. The majority of both men and women were fair with blue eyes, in fact they had the kind of looks which are considered in England to be English looks at their best. Grace saw that these looks in the women were greatly enhanced by over-dressing, always so much more becoming, whatever Carolyn's mother might say, than the reverse. That the atmosphere was of untrammelled sex did not surprise her, except in so far as that sex, outside a bedroom, could be so untrammelled.

Madame de la Ferté took Grace by the arm and led her round, introducing her to everybody. She was so much fascinated by what she saw that the terrible up and down examination accorded to a newcomer to the herd went on without her even being aware of it, and it was a long time before she realized how underdressed, under-painted, and under-scented she must seem. The jewels, however, which Charles-Edouard had forced her to put on against her own inclination, were second to nobody's. Her face, too, though lacking the sparkle of the French faces, had no rival in that room for beauty of line and structure.

The party waited some time for the arrival of a young Bourbon and of a certain not so young woman who, to underline the fact that she was now his mistress, liked to arrive late in queenly fashion. The affair was being discussed by the group round Grace, the rapid quality of whose talk, so precise, so funny, so accomplished, so frighteningly well-informed, positively paralysed her. Her own brain seemed to struggle along in the rear. Charles-Edouard, swimming in his native waters, was happy and animated as she had never seen him.

A moment before the arrival of the Prince, his mistress came in on her husband's arm. She curtsied lower than anybody, murmuring, 'Monseigneur!'

'They left the luncheon together, they must have been in bed the whole afternoon.'

'I don't think so. She had a fitting at Dior.'

When the late arrivals had shaken hands with the company they all went in to dinner. Grace sat beside her host, the brother of Madame de Valhubert and Madame Rocher. He seemed a thousand years old, very frail, and wore a shawl over his shoulders. Opposite her was Charles-Edouard, between his hostess and a majestic old woman who had swept in to dinner holding in one hand the train of her dress and in the other a large ebony ear-trumpet. During the hush which fell while people were finding their places and settling down she said to Charles-Edouard, in the penetrating voice of a deaf person, but with a very confidential look as if she thought she was whispering:

'Are you still in love with Albertine?'

Charles-Edouard, not at all put out, took the trumpet and shouted into it, 'No. I'm married now and I have a son of seven.'

'So I heard. But what has that to do with it?'

Grace tried to look as if she had heard nothing. She was wondering desperately what she could talk about to M. de la Ferté when, greatly to her relief, he turned to her and said that he had just read *Les Hauts de Hurlevent* by a talented young English writer.

'I wondered if you knew her,' he said. 'Mademoiselle Émilie Brontë.'

This was indeed a lifeline. 'I really know her sister Charlotte better.'

'Ah! She has a sister?'

'Several. They all write books.'

'But no brothers?'

'One brother, but he's a bad lot. Nobody ever mentions him.'

'This Mademoiselle Brontë tells of country-house life in England. It must be very strange – well of course one knows it is. They do such curious things, I find. I should like to read other books by her talented family.'

'I wonder whether they've been translated.'

'No matter. My concierge's son knows English, he can translate them for me.'

M. de Tournon, on Grace's other side, was handsome, blond, and young, and when the time came for them to talk he opened the conversation in English, saying, 'You are new to Paris life, so I am going to explain some very important things to you, which you may not have understood, about society here.'

'I wish you would,' she said gratefully.

'Footnotes, as it were, to the book you are reading.'

'Just what I require.'

'We will begin, I think, with precedence, since precedence precedes everything else. Now in England (and here I break off to explain that I know England extremely well; let me give you my credentials, Mary Marylebone and Molly Waterloo are two of my most intimate friends). Now what I am going to explain first is this. Please do not imagine that social life is easy here, as it is in England. It is a very very different matter. I will explain why. In England, as we know, everybody has a number, so when you give a dinner it is perfectly easy to place your guests – you look up the numbers, seat them accordingly, and they just dump down without any argument. *Placement*, such a terrible worry to us in France, never bothers you at all.'

'Are you sure,' said Grace, 'about these numbers? I've never heard of them. *Placement* doesn't bother us because nobody minds where they sit, at home.'

'People always mind. I mean the numbers in the beginning of the peerage. I subscribe to your peerage, such a beautiful book, and then I know where I am with English visitors. I only wish we had such a thing here, but we have not, and as a result the complications of precedence are terrible. There is the old French nobility and that of the Holy Roman Empire (Lorraine, Savoy, and so on). These are complicated enough in themselves, but then we have the titles created by Napoleon, at the Restoration, by the July monarchy and Napoleon III. There are the Bourbon bastards and the Bonaparte bastards. I think you have no special place for your big bastards in England?'

'I don't think there are any.'

He looked at her with pity and reeled off some well-known English family names. Grace saw that she was doing badly in this witness box.

'Mrs Jordan alone had about eighteen children,' he said. 'After all, royal blood is not nothing. But to come back to France. Suppose you have asked three dukes to dinner, which do you put first? You ring up the protocol – good, but the dukes meanwhile ring you up, each putting forward his claim. Then, my dear, you will positively long to be back in England, where you can have any number of dukes and members of the Academy at the same time. Where do you place Academicians, in England?'

'R.A.s?' said Grace. 'I don't know any.'

'Indeed! Now here, when you get to the dining-room, those of your guests who think themselves badly placed, if they don't leave at once, will turn their plates in protest and refuse the first course (though if it looks very delicious they may take it when it is handed round again).'

'Goodness!' said Grace, 'so what is the solution?'

'Do not ask more than one duke at a time.'

'But supposing they are friends?'

'Never will they be friends to that extent. But it shows how you are fortunate over there, you could ask all twenty-six – am I not right in saying there are twenty-six?'

'I haven't the faintest idea,' said Grace.

'I think so. You could ask all twenty-six to the same dinner without making a single enemy. Unimaginable. To go on with our lesson. Whereas in England the host and hostess sit at the ends of the table, here they face each other across the middle, the ends being reserved for low people, those who have married for love and so on. Two years of love, we say here, are no compensation for a lifetime at the end of the table.'

'Might not the end be more amusing?'

'No. It is not amusing to be with one's near relations and the people other people have married for love. Because near relations of the house go to the end, you and Charles-Edouard would be there tonight, except that this dinner is being given in your honour. Juliette, as you see, is there; as you also see, she is far from liking it.'

The young woman he indicated was the prettiest of them all, and the most dressed-up. She wore white tulle with swags of blue taffeta which matched her eyes, her skin looked as if a light were shining through it, and her hair fell on her shoulders in fat, chestnut curls. She was very lively and very young, hardly more than a child.

'Who is she?'

'Juliette Novembre de la Ferté, daughter-in-law of the house. The other end is her husband, watching with his jealous eye, poor Jean, and much good will it do him. She is the great success of the year.'

'How old is she?'

'Eighteen? – nineteen? Very soon she will have to begin her family, poor dear.

Jean will have to take her to the country if he wants the necessary number, and wants them to be his.'

'Necessary number?'

'Yes, hasn't Charles-Edouard explained? We all have to have six nowadays if we are to prevent everything – but everything – being taken away in taxation. So most of us took advantage of the war years and just devoted ourselves to pro-creation. My wife and I have four (we prayed for twins – in vain, alas). Very soon we shall have to make up our minds again. Oh, how we were bored, I never shall forget it. We had our house full of Germans, how they were middle-class and dreary.'

Grace, who regarded Germans as frightening rather than dreary, was very much surprised, and more so when he went on:

'There was one not so bad, a Graf, who sang little lieder after dinner, a charm-ing baritone. But we had moments of grave disquietude, you know, caused by the *maquisards*. They were well-intentioned, but so tactless – at one moment we thought they would kill our baritone, and then, only think, there might have been a battle!'

'In wars,' said Grace, 'you rather expect battles.'

'Not in one's own château, my dear! How we were relieved when the Germans went away – just packed up one day and went – and we saw two nice young Guards officers of good family, Etonians, coming up the drive. Because please don't think I was on the side of the Germans. Why, when I saw them swarming over the hill (we lived in the unoccupied zone), I put out my hand and took down my gun. There and then I made a vow never to shoot again until they were out of France.'

'You mean, never to shoot birds again?'

'And rabbits and pigs, yes. You may not think much of this vow, but I live for shooting, it is my greatest joy.'

'Then why didn't you join the *maquis* and shoot the Germans?'

'Oh no, my dear, one couldn't do that.'

'Why not?'

'For many reasons. My brother-in-law joined a *maquis*, dreadful people, he soon had to give that up. They weren't possible, I assure you.'

'Well they may not have been possible, but they were on our side, and I love them for it.'

'Oh! my dear, we were all on your side, so you must love us all in that case.'

After dinner Charles-Edouard made a bee-line for Juliette Novembre. Grace heard him say, 'If you were Juliette de Champeaubert how is it I don't remember you? Jeanne Marie is one of my very greatest friends.'

'Oh, I've only just been invented,' she said gaily, 'but before I was invented I used to hang out of the window, waiting to see you get into that pretty black motor you had in those days. My governess used to pull me back by my hair.'

'No! But that's awfully nice,' said Charles-Edouard. 'Come – I want to see my uncle's Subleyras again.'

They went off together into another room. Somebody said, 'It was quite indi-cated that those two would take to each other – she might be made for Charles-Edouard.'

M. de Tournon brought his wife over to Grace. He wanted her to see for herself this uncouth girl Charles-Edouard had so oddly married, in order to be able to talk about her when they got home. Madame de Tournon was Italian, more really beautiful and more elegant than Juliette Novembre but with much less sparkle.

'I am a cousin of yours now,' she said. 'Let's all sit here. So tell me what you have been doing in Paris since you arrived – there haven't been any dinners so far, have there? We only got back ourselves last night – we came back for this.'

'Really I've done very little. I've bought some clothes.'

'Is that Dior? Yes, I could see. But are they making these high necks now?'

'I had it altered – it seemed too naked.'

'Oh no, my dear,' said Madame de Tournon, 'you've got beautiful breasts, so why hide them up like that? It spoils the line. What else?'

'I've met Charles-Edouard's aunts.'

Madame de Tournon made a little face of sympathy. 'Any cocktail parties?'

'There have been one or two, but I never go to them, I hate them. Charles-Edouard goes. I don't terribly like lunching out either,' she went on. 'If I had my way I'd never go out before dinner-time.'

The Tournons looked at each other in growing amazement as she spoke.

'But listen,' cried Madame de Tournon, 'nobody can dine out more than eight times in a week. But if one lunches every day and goes to, say, three cocktails, as well as dining out, one can go to forty houses in a week. We often have, haven't we, Eugène?'

'Sometimes more, in the summer. I wish you could see us in July, fit for a nursing home by the time we get to the seaside.'

'Where do you go to the seaside as a rule?' asked Grace, thinking of them on the sands of some French Eastbourne with their four tots.

'Always Venice. Say what you like, it's the only place in August.'

'But is it fun for the children?'

They stared at her. 'We don't take the children to Venice – poor little things, what on earth would they do there? Besides, the children don't need a change, they don't have an exhausting season in Paris, they lead a perfectly healthy outdoor life in the Seine et Marne.'

Charles-Edouard and Juliette only reappeared when a general move was being made to go home. In the hall, as they were putting on their coats, Juliette flourished a hand for Charles-Edouard to kiss, saying, 'Good-bye for the present then, wickedness, I will consider your proposition.' She and her husband then got into the lift which took them to their own apartments.

'What proposition?' said Grace, in the motor.

'No proposition.'

'Oh dear! Need we dine out very often?'

'What d'you mean?'

'Let's dine together, alone, in future.'

'It would be very dull,' said Charles-Edouard.

'Such a terrible man I sat next to.'

'Eugène? He's a friendly old thing.'

'You can't think what he's like when he talks about the war.'

'I know. I saw him at a picture dealer's the other day and we had it all. But you mustn't be too hard on old Eugène – he joined up quite correctly in '39 and fought quite bravely in '40. His father was killed quite correctly in 1917. These Eugènes are not so rotten, it is the State of Denmark.'

The Tournons, meanwhile, were discussing Grace.

'My dear, the lowest peasant of the Danube knows more than she – just fancy, she had never heard of the English order of precedence, didn't know how many dukes there are in England, and didn't seem to think any of it mattered.'

'And did you hear what she said about taking the children to Venice? She must be backward, I'm afraid.'

'Allingham. What is this name? I must write at once to Molly Waterloo and ask her if they are people one can know. Poor Charles-Edouard – I pity him really.'

'Everything will be all right. Madame Rocher told my mother they are not married religiously.'

Madame Rocher had gone to Venice the week after Grace and Charles-Edouard left Bellandargues, and there she had managed to do quite a lot of harm to Grace, not wilfully at all, not intending mischief, but because she was utterly incapable of holding her tongue on any subject of general interest. Interest was very much centred, at the moment, on Charles-Edouard and his marriage.

Everybody thought it a pity that he, with his name and his fortune, should have married an English Protestant. When it transpired that she was the daughter of a Freemason, the general disapproval knew no bounds, a Bolshevist would have been as gladly received. Those who were informed on political subjects pointed to the dire results, for France, of the Allingham Commission, and it was freely hinted that Grace was very likely in the pay of the Intelligence Service. Rather soon, however, the pendulum swung back in her favour. Older, cosmopolitan Frenchmen, writers, diplomats, and the like, who did not only live for society and yet had great influence with the Tournons of the world, had known the charming, cultivated, francophile Sir Conrad, and had read his books. They said he was by no means to the Left in politics, a rigid Conservative, in fact. Silly old Régine must have got the Freemason story all wrong, so like her, for it could not possibly be true. As to the Allingham Commission, the prime mover in that was a terrible villain called Sparks, paid by Arabs, in whose hands poor Sir Conrad had been as putty, and furthermore the results of the Commission, while annoying to the French government of the day, had not in the long run done any harm to France. It was absurd to say that the Allinghams were not the sort of people you could know; even Eugène de Tournon was quite impressed when he saw in his peerage who Grace's mother had been.

The highbrow aunts, who, dowdy as they seemed, counted for a good deal in society, weighed in on her side, saying that, though not an intellectual, she was very nice and well brought up. Her beauty, too, was in her favour. At last the nine days' wonder came to an end, and Grace was accepted. She was a new girl, she must watch her step, but the general feeling was that she would do.

She and Charles-Edouard now dined out nearly every day, and after all these dinners Charles-Edouard would sit with Juliette Novembre, as far removed from the rest of the company as possible, until it was time to go home.

9

Carolyn Dexter and Grace saw a good deal of each other, sitting on nursery fenders, and at first this was a comfort to Grace because of her need to feel at home somewhere. She felt at home with Carolyn. But as time went on Carolyn often irritated her dreadfully. Since marriage with the important Mr Dexter the swagger and self-assurance which had made her so fascinating to the other girls at her school had deteriorated into bossiness. She was forever telling Grace what she ought to do and whom she and Charles-Edouard ought to see, and was also forever enlarging upon the faults of the French. She had a particular grievance against the world of Parisians which was led by such young couples as the Tournons and the Novembre de la Fertés, not, oddly enough, on the grounds of their really frightening frivolity, but because they so seldom invited herself and her husband to their houses. In view of the importance of Mr Dexter and the fact that she was the niece of a former British Ambassador to Paris, she had expected immediately to be asked everywhere, but, except for big, official parties, the Dexters moved almost entirely in an Anglo-American world. Mr Dexter did not mind this at all. When he said, as he continually did, that he despised the French, he meant it. He had no wish to meet any, except those he was obliged to work with. But Carolyn was not quite so honest. If the French annoyed her it was very largely by ignoring her presence in their town.

Carolyn thought that Grace ought to give a dinner party for her, and said so in her extremely outspoken way. Grace replied, with perfect truth, that, for the moment, she and Charles-Edouard were taken up with his many relations. Carolyn did not accept this as easily as some people would have, and often returned to the charge.

'I hear you dined last night with the Polastrons. Are they relations of your husband?' she said, before even saying hullo to Grace, who had come to tea.

'Yes, I think so.'

'How are they related?'

'Perhaps they're not. But anyway, great old friends.'

'Great old friends, but not related. I thought you were only seeing relations at present?'

'Well, but Carolyn – I leave it all to Charles-Edouard, you know.'

She felt instinctively that Charles-Edouard would find the Dexters very dull.

'Let's have a cocktail,' said Carolyn. 'I'm exhausted. I've had an awful afternoon struggling with the garage people to do something about my car. Promised for yesterday – you know the sort of thing. Really I'm fed up with these wretched French.'

'I thought you loved France. You always used to.'

'I love France, but I can't say I love the French, nowadays. They are quite different, you know, since the war. Everybody says the same.'

Grace somehow felt sure that they were not quite different at all. She really did love them. She loved the servants in her house for their friendly efficiency, their faithfulness to Charles-Edouard; she loved the highbrow aunts, now that she was getting to know them, for being so clever and so serious, and she loved the gay young diners for being so pretty and so light-hearted. She even loved their snob-bishness, it seemed to her such a tremendous joke, so particularly funny, somehow, nowadays. She was beginning to love the critical spirit of all and sundry. It kept people up to the mark, no doubt, and had filled her with the desire to improve her mind and sharpen her wits. She longed to make a better appearance in the box, and be a credit to Charles-Edouard. And she loved the people in the streets for smiling at her and noticing her new clothes.

'I don't say I hate them,' said Carolyn, 'but they irritate me, and I see their faults.'

'What faults?'

'Oh, you're sold to the French, Grace, it's hardly worth talking to you about them. Faults! They hit you in the eye if you're not blind. Never punctual – don't get things done – not reliable (you should hear Hector) – dirty – the dirt! Look at the central heating here – just gusts of hot dust, impossible to keep anything clean. Then the butchers' shops – after living in America you feel ill to see them – flies all over the meat –'

'I like that,' said Grace. 'Meat can't be too meaty, for my taste.'

'Ugh! Anyhow, you can't like the rudeness –'

'Nobody's ever rude to me. They smile when they see me, even strangers in the street.'

'Trying to pick you up. And what about those dreadful policemen!'

'I always think they look like young saints, in their capes.'

'Saints! I must tell that to Hector, he'll roar.'

'I've never had anything but niceness from them – over Nanny's identity card and so on.'

'I expect your husband gives them enormous bribes.'

'Of course he doesn't.'

'I suppose even you will admit the French would do anything for money.'

'Perhaps they may – it's never crossed my path, but you may be right. Perhaps they are more frank and open about it than other people.'

'Frank and open is the word. They always frankly and openly marry for money, to begin with.'

'Charles-Edouard didn't.'

'Are you – Oh well there may be exceptions, and I suppose he wouldn't need to. But at the time when our grandfathers were marrying actresses for love their contemporaries here were all marrying Jewesses for money. I was thinking of dozens of examples last night in bed.'

'I think they were quite right. Just look at it from the point of view of their grandchildren. Honestly now, which would you prefer as a grandmother – a clever old Jewess, who has brought brains and money and Caffieri commodes into the family, or some ass of an actress?'

'I can't understand you, Grace, you used to seem so very English at home.'

'Yes, well now,' said Grace rather sadly, 'I'm nothing at all. But I would love to have been born a Frenchwoman, and I can't say more, can I?'

'Oh, you'll change your tune, I bet. By the way, I've been meaning to tell you – we quite often see Hughie.'

'Hughie! Does he live here too?'

'He was here with a military mission, now he's back in England, but he keeps coming over. Hector sees him at the Travellers and brings him in for a drink, most weeks. He's terribly in love with a Frenchwoman here, a Madame Marel-Desboulles. Hector thinks it's a disaster for him, he has heard all about this Madame Marel and says she's no good.'

'Marel – Marel-Desboulles. Don't I know her?' Grace said vaguely.

The names and faces of the French people she met had not yet clicked into place, they floated round her mind separately, many names and many faces, all wonderfully romantic and new but not adding up into real people. So the name Marel-Desboulles had a familiar ring but no face, while the brilliant woman who played conversational ping-pong with Charles-Edouard, across a dinner-table, sometimes across a whole roomful of people all delighted by the speed and accuracy of the game, volley, volley, high lob with a spin, volley, cut, smash, had not yet acquired a surname. Grace only knew her as Albertine.

'He wants to marry her.'

Carolyn looked at Grace to see if she minded, but she hardly even seemed interested.

'And will he?'

'I don't think so. He says she is very Catholic, and talks all the time of going into a convent – poor Hughie says he'll kill himself if she does. But Hector says nobody at the Travellers thinks there's much danger of that. What happened about your engagement to Hughie, Grace? I never really knew.'

'Oh, just that we were engaged, and he went to the war and I married Charles-Edouard instead. I'm afraid I didn't behave very well.'

'Pity, in a way.'

'I can't agree.'

'I meant nothing against your husband. I hear he is charming. I only meant pity to marry a Frenchman.'

Grace longed to retaliate with 'well then, what about marrying an American' but she knew that, while it is considered nowadays perfectly all right to throw any amount of aspersions on poor old France and England, one tiny word reflecting anything but exaggerated love for rich new America is thought to be in the worst of taste. She was also, by nature, more careful of people's feelings than Carolyn. So she said, mildly, that she could not imagine any other sort of husband.

The two nannies clung to each other like drowning men, and Sigi was now taken every day for air and exercise to the Parc Monceau instead of the Tuileries Gardens. He was very cross about this, and complained bitterly to his mother.

'Pascal and I are so fond of each other. I never knew such an obliging goat, and now I never see him. It's a shame, Mummy.'

'Why don't you meet Nanny Dexter in the Tuileries sometimes for a change?' Grace said to her Nan.

'Oh no thank you, dear. We don't like those Tuileries. It's the draughtiest place in Paris. I only wish you could feel the stiff neck I caught there the other day, waiting for the little monkey to finish his ride. I don't think all those smelly animals are very nice, if you ask me, and the children there are a funny lot too. Some of them are black, dear, and one was distinctly Chinese. The Parc Monceau is a much better place for little boys.'

'Oh well, Nan, it's just as you like, of course, but when I went there I thought it fearfully depressing, such thousands of children, like a children's market or something, and all those castor-oil plants. Hideous.'

'Still you do see a little grass there,' said Nanny, 'and decent railings.'

'I hate the silly little baby Parc Monceau,' piped up Sigi, 'and I loathe dear little Foster Dexter aged four. Under the spreading chestnut tree, I loathe Foss and Foss loathes me.'

'Very stupid and naughty, Sigismond. Foster's a dear little chap – so easy too. Nanny Dexter has never had one minute's trouble with him since he was born, and they've been all over the place – oh, they have travelled! I must say Mrs Dexter's a marvellous mummy.'

'In what way?' Grace asked, with interest. She tried her best to be a marvellous mummy too, but her efforts never received much acknowledgement.

'Well, she has tea in the nursery every day.'

'But, Nanny, so do I – nearly every day.'

'And gives little Foss his bath often as not, and, what's more, every Saturday and Sunday Mr Dexter gives him his bath. He is a nice daddy, Mr Dexter.'

Unfortunately Grace was stumped by this. Nobody could say that Charles-Edouard was that sort of nice daddy; he never went near the nursery. He liked the idea of Sigi, and was delighted when people said the child was his living image, but a few minutes of his company at a time were more than sufficient. He was such a restless man that a few minutes of almost anybody's company at a time were more than sufficient.

Grace said to Charles-Edouard,

'You know my friend Carolyn?'

'The beautiful Lesbian?'

'No, no, Carolyn Dexter.'

'You said she was a Lesbian at school.'

'I said we were all in love with her, that's quite different. Besides, people are all sorts of things at school – Carolyn used to be a Communist then – we used to point her out to visitors as the school Communist – and look at her now! Marshall Plan up to the eyes. Anyway, can we dine there on Thursday? – I'm to let her know.'

'You keep our engagements, it's for you to say.'

'We are quite free, but I wanted to know if you'd like it.'

'Who will be there?'

'Well, it sounded like this, but I may have got it wrong. The Jorgmanns of *Life*, the Schmutzes of *Time*, the Jungfleisches, who are liaison between *Life* and *Time*, the Oberammergaus who have replaced the Pottses on the Un-American Activities Committee, European branch, the Rutters, who are liaison between the French Chamber of Commerce, the Radio-Diffusion Française and the *Chicago Herald Tribune*, and an important French couple, the Tournons. Are the Tournons important really?'

'Of course they are, in their way, but it won't be those Tournons. It will be what we call *les faux Tournons* – he is *chef de cabinet* to Salleté, very dull, but she is rather nice.'

'Carolyn says these are all people you ought to meet.'

'Why ought I to meet them?'

'Now darling, do be serious for once. It's all that Aid and so on. They might like you, and it's so terribly important for them to like French people because of the Aid. Carolyn's always saying so, and she's very clever, as I've told you. She says what happens is that the important Americans who come here meet all the wrong sort of French. Then they go back to the middle of America and tell the people there, who hate foreigners anyway, that the French are undependable, and so nasty it would be better to cut the Aid and concentrate on Italy, where they are undependable too but so nice, and specially on Germany, where they are dependable and so wonderful, and leave the nasty French to rot. All because they meet the wrong sort. And all this is very discouraging to Hector Dexter, who is dying to help and aid the French more and more.'

'Well of course Hector Dexter would lose his job if they cut the Aid, that's very plain.'

'There you are, being French and cynical, just like Carolyn always says. And as if it would matter to Mr Dexter whether he lost his job or not. He's far too important.'

Indeed the word important seemed, at that time, to have been coined only for Mr Dexter, and his name never occurred either in print or in conversation without it. It seemed that he was one of the most, if not the most, important of living men.

'My dear child, do you really think, when a great country like America has settled on a certain policy with regard to another great country like France, it can be deflected from it by the Jungfleisches, meeting the wrong sort of French person?'

'Carolyn says it can.'

'And what makes you think I'm the right sort of French person for them to meet?'

'Well look at what you did in the war.'

'But the Americans hate the people who were on their side in the war. It's one thing they can never forgive. I'm surprised you haven't noticed that. Never mind,' he said, seeing her face fall. 'We'll go, and I'll do my best to be nice, I promise you.'

10

The Dexters invited their guests at eight, but only sat down to dinner at nine. The intervening hour was spent drinking cocktails while Hector Dexter talked about the present state of France.

'I have known France all my life. I came here as a kid; I came during my vacations from college; I came on my honeymoon with my first wife, the first Mrs Dexter, and I was here during World War II. So I am in some sort qualified to make my diagnosis, and I have made my diagnosis, and my diagnosis is as follows, but first I would like to tell you all a little story which I think will help me to illustrate the point I am going to try if I can to make.

'Well, it was just before the Ardennes counter-offensive; we were up in this little village near the frontier of Belgium, or no, maybe it was near the frontier of Luxembourg – it makes no odds really and doesn't affect my story. Now there was this *boulanger* in the village, and I think now I will if I may describe the state of the village. Well it had been bombed by the U.S. air force, precision bombed, if you see what I mean; it had then been bombed by the Luftwaffe quite regardless I am sorry to say (sorry because I am one who hopes very soon to see the Germans playing a very very important part in the family of nations), bombed, then, quite regardless of civilian property and military objectives. It had then been shelled by U.S. infantry and taken and occupied; it had then been shelled and retaken and reoccupied by the Reichswehr, and I am sorry to say that when it was reoccupied by the Reichswehr certain atrocities took place which I for one would rather forget. It had then been shelled and retaken and occupied by the U.S. infantry. And the rain was falling down day and night. I dare say you can picture the state of this village at the time of which I am telling you. But it so happened that the habitation of this *boulanger* was still intact. It had been damaged, of course, the windows were blown in and so on, but the walls were standing, a bit of roof was left and the big oven had suffered no impairment. So I went and asked him if he would care to have some U.S. army flour so that he could bake bread for those civilians who were left in the village. But this little old *boulanger* simply said what the hell, though he said it in French of course, what the hell, the Boches will be back again this evening and I don't see much point baking bread for the Boches to eat tonight.

'Now this little story is symbolical of what I see around me and of what we Americans in France are trying to fight against. There is a malaise in this country, a spirit of discontent, of nausea, of defatigation, of successlessness around us, here in this very city of Paris, which I for one find profoundly discouraging.

'Now my son Heck junior is here temporarily with us, my son by the first Mrs Dexter, an independent, earning, American male of some twenty-two summers. He trained to be a psychiatrist. In my view, everybody nowadays, whatever profession they intend eventually to embrace, ought to have this training. Now he has a column.'

Charles-Edouard, gazing all this time at Mrs Jungfleisch, who happened to be very pretty, and wondering if there were another room he could sit in after dinner with her (but he knew really that the flat was not likely to have a suite of drawing-rooms), was startled out of his reverie by the word column.

'Doric?' he asked with interest, 'or Corinthian?'

But Mr Dexter, in the full flood of locution, took no notice.

'And my son walks in the streets of this town – he is not here with us tonight because he prefers to eat alone using his eyes and his ears in some small, but representative bistro – and he claims that he can sense, by observing the faces of the ordinary citizens, and by various small actions they perform in the course of their daily round, he claims to observe this malaise in every observable walk of life, and I am sorry to say, sorry because I am very deeply sincere in my wish and desire to help the French people, that what my son senses as he goes about this city is entirely reflected in this column.'

And so on. Grace thought it exceedingly clever of Mr Dexter to keep up such a flow, but she could see it was not quite doing for Charles-Edouard. If only he were more serious, she thought sadly, he could be just as wonderful, or more so, but he never seemed to care a bit about the things that really matter in the world. Even during the war he had done nothing, when she was with him, anyhow, but make love, sing little snatches of songs, roar with laughter, and search for objects of art on which to feast his eyes. And yet he must have a serious side to his nature since he had been impelled to leave all these things he cared for and to fight long years in the East. She knew that he could have been demobilized much sooner if he had wished, but that he had refused to leave his squadron until they all came home. She longed for him to get up and make a speech even cleverer than Mr Dexter's, in defence of his country, but he only sat laughing inside himself and looking at pretty Mrs Jungfleisch.

At last they went in to dinner. Grace, who was by now accustomed to an easy flow of French chat from her dinner partners, was completely paralysed when Mr Rutter opened the conversation by turning to her and saying, 'Tell me about yourself.' She was looking, as she always did, to see if Charles-Edouard was happy; it distressed her that he had been put as far as possible from pretty Mrs Jungfleisch. He too clearly did not admire Carolyn, who was talking to him about Nanny, a subject that did not bring out the best in him.

'Myself?' she said, and fell dumb.

However, Hector Dexter now tapped his plate for silence.

'I'm going to call on each person here,' he said, 'to say a few words on a subject with which we are all deeply preoccupied. I mean, of course, the A-bomb. I think Charlie Jungfleisch can speak for the ordinary citizen of our great United States of America, as he is just back from there. Aspinall Jorgmann will tell us what they are saying behind the Iron Curtain (Asp has just done this comprehensive six-day tour and we all want to know his impressions), Wilbur Rutter can speak of it as it will, or may, affect world prosperity, M. Tournon represents the French government at this little gathering, and M. de Valhubert –'

'Perhaps I will listen without joining in,' said Charles-Edouard, much to Grace's disappointment, 'as an amateur of *pâte tendre*, you will understand, I find the whole subject really too painful. My policy with regard to atom bombs is that of the ostrich.'

'Just as you like,' said Mr Dexter. 'Then I call on Charlie. There is one thing we here in Europe are very anxious to know, Charlie, and that is what, if any, air-raid precautions are being taken in New York?'

'Well, Heck, quite some precautions are being taken. In the first place the authorities have issued a very comprehensive little pamphlet entitled "The Bomb and You" designed to bring the bomb into every home and invest it with a certain degree of cosiness. This should calm and reassure the population in case of attack. There are plenty of guidance reunions, fork lunches, and so on where the subject is treated frankly, to familiarize it, as it were, and rob it of all unpleasantness. At these gatherings the speakers stress that the observation of certain rules of atomic hygiene ought to be a matter of everyday routine. Keep a white sheet handy, for example, since white offers the best protection against gamma rays. Then the folks are told what to do after the explosion. The importance of rest can hardly be over-estimated; the protein contents of the diet should be increased – no harm in a glass of milk as soon as the bomb has gone off. If you feel a little queer, dissatisfied with your symptoms, send at once for the doctor. You follow me, it is elementary, of course, but these things cannot be too much emphasized. If the folks know just what they ought to do in the case of atomic explosion, such explosion is robbed of half, or one-third, its terrors.'

'Thank you, Charlie,' said Mr Dexter. 'I for one feel a lot easier in my mind. There is nothing so dangerous as a policy of *laisser-aller*, and I am very glad that the great American public, if I may say so, M. de Valhubert, without offending your feelings, is not hiding its head in the sand, but is looking the Bomb squarely in the eye. Very glad indeed. And now I shall call on Asp for a few words. Tell us what they are thinking in the Russian-occupied countries, Asp.'

'Well, I have just had six very very interesting days in Poland, Czechoslovakia, Rumania, Bulgaria, the East or Russian-occupied part of Germany, and the East or Russian-occupied part of Austria, and I'm here to tell you that these countries, if not actually preparing for war, which I think they are, are undeniably being run on a war-time basis.'

'And did you talk with the ordinary citizens of these countries, Asp?'

'Why, no, Heck. For reasons of which I suppose you are all cognizant I did not, but I saw the key men and key women of our embassies and missions in these countries, and I gleaned enough material for three, or two, very very long and interesting articles which I hope you will all be reading for yourselves –'

And so it went on. Fortunately some more very important people came in after dinner, so Grace and Charles-Edouard were able to slip away without looking too rude. Charles-Edouard never managed to have a word with Mrs Jungfleisch, who had settled down to a cosy chat with Mr Jorgmann about conferences, vetos, and what Joe Alsop had told her when she saw him in Washington. Pretty Mrs Jung-fleisch, like Mr Dexter, was deeply concerned about the present state of the world, and had no time for frivolous Frenchmen who preferred *pâte tendre* to atom bombs.

Charles-Edouard was particularly nice to Grace about this dinner, and insisted on asking the Dexters back the following week. The two couples dined alone together, rather quickly, and went to *Lorenzaccio*. If Charles-Edouard had suffered from boredom at the Dexter dinner, he had more than his revenge on Hector, who really could hardly sit still at *Lorenzaccio*, and said, quite rudely, in the entr'acte, that whoever would take this play to Broadway was heading for a very very serious financial loss indeed.

'But my dearest,' said Albertine, 'dinner with the wife's best friend and the best friend's husband is a classic. I could have warned you about that, as much a part of married life as babies, nannies, and in-laws. Of course a jolly bachelor like your-self had never envisaged such developments.'

'I wish I understood Americans,' said Charles-Edouard. 'They are very strange. So good, and yet so dull.'

'What makes you think they are so good?'

'You can see it, shining in their eyes.'

'That's not goodness, that's contact lenses – a kind of spectacle they wear next the eyeball. I had an American lover after the liberation and I used to tap his eye with my nail file. He was a very curious man. Imagine, his huge, healthy-looking body hardly functioned at all by itself. He couldn't walk a yard; I took him to Versailles, and half-way across the Galerie des Glaces he lay on the floor and cried for his mother. He couldn't do you know what without *lavages*, he could only digest yoghourt and raw carrots, he couldn't sleep without a sleeping draught or wake up without benzedrine, and he had to have a good strong blood transfusion every morning before he could face the day. It was like having another automaton in the house.'

'You had him in the house?'

Albertine, who hated too much intimacy, had never done this with any of her lovers.

'For the central heating, dearest,' she said apologetically. 'It was that very cold winter. Americans have no circulation of their own – even their motors are artificially heated in winter and cooled in summer. I never shall forget how hot he kept this room – my little thermometer sprang in one day from *"rivières glacées"* to *"vers à soie"*, and even then he complained. Finally it reached Sénégale, all the marquetry on my Oeben began to spring, and I was obliged to divorce him. We were married, by the way.'

'Married?' Charles-Edouard was quite astounded.

'Yes, he could do nothing in bed without marriage lines. I tried everything, I even got an excellent aphrodisiac from the doctor. Useless. We had to go to the Consulate together, and after that he was splendid. The result is I've got an American passport, which never does any harm.'

'And what has become of him now?'

'Oh he's got the cutest little wife and the two loveliest kids, and he sends me boxes of cleansing tissues every Christmas.'

II

Madame de Valhubert died suddenly the very day she was to have left Bellandargues for Paris. She made the journey all the same, and was buried in the family grave at the Père La Chaise. Charles-Edouard was very sad, cast down as Grace had never seen him. He said they must go into mourning in the old-fashioned, strict way which has been greatly relaxed in France since the war; it was a tribute, he said, that he owed to his grandmother. So Grace was no longer subjected to an enormous dinner party, reception or ball nearly every day, and this was a great comfort to her. Not a truly social person, these parties, as soon as they had ceased to frighten, had begun to bore her, and she envisaged almost with horror the endless succession there would be of them to the end of her life. She was very much happier now that, for the moment, they were ruled out. She did not have much more of her husband's company than usual; he continued to spend whole days at the sale-rooms in the Hôtel Drouot and with the antique dealers, and was still always out at tea-time. They never spent an evening at home together quietly; the moment he had swallowed his dinner he would drag Grace to a film, a play, or a concert.

Charles-Edouard's long absences from his house had never surprised her or struck her as needing an explanation. She had been brought up in the shadow of Parliament, Brooks's, White's, and Pratt's; her own father was practically never at home, and she supposed that all men were engaged, for hours every day, on some masculine business, inexplicable, at any rate never explained, but quite innocent and normal.

But although she saw rather little of him it seemed to her that Charles-Edouard was cosier, more at home with her now, than when they had first arrived in France. It had never even occurred to her that she was, perhaps, more in love than he was. In her eyes, all the evidence pointed to a great deal of love on his side. He was very nice to her, he made love continually, and she had not enough experience to look for any of the other signs that indicate the condition of a man's heart. Now that they were no longer going out she never saw Juliette, and assumed that Charles-Edouard never did either. This was certainly a relief, though the affair had annoyed rather than worried her. It seemed to her that it was too open to matter, she had taken it half as a joke, and teased him about it.

So Grace regarded herself as a perfectly happy woman whose marriage was entirely satisfactory, with one very small reservation.

'You know, Charles-Edouard,' she said to him, 'I can't help thinking it's a pity you never set eyes on our Blessing. I often wonder whether I see enough of him, but you are an absolute stranger to the poor little boy. Sigi,' she called, hearing him outside on the stairs, 'come in here. Who is this gentleman?'

'Papa!'

'Yes, quite right, but how did you guess?'

He looked his mother up and down. 'I say, Mummy, you are getting Frenchified.'

'Don't you think we all are, now we live in France?'

'Nanny isn't, and Nanny Dexter isn't, and Mrs Dexter isn't.'

'Well, perhaps not. Are you just going out?'

'Oh yes, boring old Parc Monceau as usual.'

'Does he go to the Parc Monceau?' said Charles-Edouard. 'This is very foolish. Why not the Tuileries, or the Luxembourg, or the beautiful garden of the Musée Rodin? I should hate it if my childhood memories were of the Parc Monceau.'

'His little friend goes there.'

'My little friend indeed! Nanny's little friend. I loathe him. Anyway, I like grown-up people.'

'Ha!' said Charles-Edouard. 'How I agree with you, so do I. Will you chuck the Parc Monceau today and come for a walk with me instead?'

'With delight. And Mummy too?'

Grace thought it would be much better if they went off alone, without her, and said, 'I can't, darling. I've got to try on a hat. Go with Papa and I'll be here for tea when you get back.'

'Always hats! Wouldn't be much good in a tight fix with interior tribes, you and your old hats.' He was not displeased, however. His experience of walking with two grown-up people was that they chatted away together up there in the air while you were left to look for francs in the gutter.

'I think you underestimate the value of hats,' said Charles-Edouard. 'They can have a very civilizing influence on interior tribes. Look at Mummy –'

'Oh shut up, Charles-Edouard.'

'Cut the necking,' said Sigi.

'Where does the child learn this sort of language?'

'It's what I tell you. If he was more with us –'

'Where shall we go, Papa?'

'Promenons-nous dans le bois
Pendant que le loup n'y est pas.'

'No, not *dans les bois*. A street walk.'

'The most beautiful walk in the world then. Across the Beaux Arts bridge, through the Cour Carrée, under the Arc du Carousel (averting the eye from Gambetta) and across the Place de la Concorde. How would that be?'

'Then we could have a word with Pascal on the way?'

'Who is Pascal?'

'My goat.'

'Ah no. No words with goats.'

They set off hand in hand, Charles-Edouard dragging the child along at a furious speed. At the Arc du Carousel Charles-Edouard began reciting '*A la voix du vainqueur d'Austerlitz* – when you know that by heart,' he said, 'I'll give you a prize.'

'What sort of prize?'

'I don't know. A good sort.'

'How can I learn it?'

'It's written up there on the arch. At your age I used to read it every day. Oh how I loved the Emperor, at your age.'

'How can I read it when we never come here?'

'You must come. You must refuse the Parc Monceau and come.'

'But Papa –'

'No excuses. Nothing so dull.'

Sigi waved at Pascal with his free hand, but was dragged on.

'You are too old for goats. I'll show you some horses. There, the flying horses of Coysevox, are they not wonderful?'

'Look, look, Papa! Mrs Dexter in her lovely new Buick.'

'Come on, she's not my type. What is a Buick?'

'Papa! It's a motor, of course.'

'Ha! You know Buick and you've never heard of Coysevox. What a world to be young in. Now here are the *chevaux de Marly* – are they not beautiful?'

'Can I get up there and ride on one of them?'

'Ride on the *chevaux de Marly*? Certainly not, what an idea.'

They hurried on to Charles-Edouard's destination, the shop of an art dealer who had written to him about a pair of vases. Here Sigi was put to sit, kicking his heels, on one of those stools which, at Versailles, were kept exclusively for dukes. 'So now,' said the dealer, 'you are *duc et pair de France*.'

Charles-Edouard began an exhaustive examination of everything in the shop: the vases, a tray of jewelled boxes, an ink-stand which had belonged to Catherine the Great, a pair of cherubs said to be by Pigalle, and so on. He always asked the price of everything, like a child in a toy shop, and roared with derisive laughter when he was told. He was the flail of the dealers, his technique being to arrive with the words, loudly enunciated before the other customers, 'Why don't you burn all this rubbish and get some decent stock?' But they respected his knowledge and his love of beautiful things.

Sigi gazed out of the plate-glass window. It was very dull being *duc et pair de France* for so long. In a window across the road there was a great heap of mattresses, as in the story of the Princess and the pea. The sight of these mattresses, combined with the endless aeons of inactivity so terrible to a child, filled him with a great longing to jump up and down on them.

Presently Madame Marel came into the shop. Charles-Edouard, who had forgotten that he had half arranged to meet her there, was a little bit put out at being found with Sigi. He knew that all would be reported to Grace.

'How are you, my dear Albertine? Here are the vases – not bad, what do you say? But the price is the funniest thing I ever heard. M. Dupont does love to make me laugh. Now what of this bronze? I am thinking of it most seriously. I do love Louis XIV bronze, so delightfully solid, so proof against housemaids. Once you fall into Louis XV you are immediately in the domain of restored *terre cuite* and broken china, of things which must go behind glass in any case. I love them too, far too much, but there is something comfortable about this old satyr. As soon as M. Dupont has mentioned its real price I shall buy it – at present he is in the realms of romance. Such an imaginative man, such an artist in figures, M. Dupont. So – this is Sigismond.'

Sigi, rather unwillingly, but forced to it by a severe look from his father, kissed her hand.

'This is Sigi? Now all is explained – he is well worth it. Have you been here long? Very long? Poor little boy, not very amusing for you, sitting on that *tabouret* and thinking of what, I wonder? What were you thinking of, Sigismond?'

'The mattresses over there. I would like to jump and jump and jump and roll and roll and roll on them.'

'Already?' she said. 'How like your father. I'll tell you what, darling, shall we go over there and jump while he goes on breaking poor M. Dupont's heart? Shall we? Come on.'

'No, Albertine, certainly not. I am a well-known figure in Paris, please try and remember. It is quite out of the question.'

'He wants to so badly.'

'But this child has the most peculiar ambitions. On the way here he wanted to chat to a goat and to ride on the *chevaux de Marly*.'

'What a lovely idea, and how well I can understand it. Why don't we arrange it for him?'

'Try not to be foolish, Albertine. Flirt with the child if you can't help it, but keep within reason.'

'Your father has this pompous side to his nature, you know. When one comes up against that there's nothing to be done. Will you come to tea with me one day, if I collect some little friends?'

'He loathes little friends.'

'So much the better, he can come alone. There are lots of things in my house to amuse you – things that you wind up which do tricks. A dancing bear, a drinking monkey, a singing dog. Will you come?'

'Oh yes please,' said Sigi. He took greatly to this lady who was so nice to him and who smelt so delicious.

'Today?'

'Not today,' said Charles-Edouard rather hastily. 'I'm taking him home now, he has been out long enough. Say good-bye, Sigismond.'

Madame Marel said, in French, which she presumed the child would not understand, 'Then come straight on to me – tea will be ready and I've got many things
to tell you.'

'Did you enjoy your walk with Daddy?' Grace asked as they sat down to tea. The
two nannies had at last found an English grocer, so their tables were laden now
with (for export only) such delicacies as Huntley and Palmer's biscuits, good
black Indian tea, Tiptree's strawberry jam, Gentleman's Relish, and rich fruit
cake.

At luncheon, chutney, Colman's mustard, and horseradish sauce made it possible to swallow the nasty foreign-looking meat swimming in fat, and hardly a day
went by without a sago pudding or castle cakes with Bird's custard.

Grace never went to the nursery without feeling rather like the maiden in the
fairy story whose husband allowed her to have one room in the castle lined with
nettles to make her feel at home again.

'I enjoyed it very much indeed. We saw Pascal in the distance, but he didn't see
me.'

'You didn't have a drive?'

'Papa was in such a hurry. Then we saw Mrs Dexter in her Buick but she's not
his type, then we saw the *chevaux de Marly* but he was in too much of a hurry to
let me ride on them, then we saw a huge heap of mattresses and I wanted to jump
and jump up and down on them, but Papa wouldn't let me even though the lady
we met said he ought to because it would be very amusing, and she said it was just
like Papa, wanting to jump and roll on the mattresses.'

'You met a lady?'

'Yes, she smelt heavenly and Papa has gone to tea with her. I think she is his
type.'

'A pretty lady?'

'Very Frenchified.'

'So on the whole you had a good time?'

'Smashing,' said Sigi with conviction, his hour of restless boredom on the *tabouret*
quite forgotten.

When Charles-Edouard got back he found Grace in the little library next door
to her bedroom where she generally sat when she was alone. She was tucked up
on a chaise-longue looking pretty and comfortable and a little fragile, since she
was expecting a child.

'Who was it you met on your walk? She's made a great hit with Sigi, he said she
smelt too delicious.'

'Yes. I wish I knew what scent she uses, but it has always been a state secret.
Albertine Marel-Desboulles.'

'Marel. Oh! Isn't that the woman Hughie's in love with?'

'Exactly. She tells me she has fourteen English suitors, it's very amusing.'

'Not very amusing for poor Hughie. He's terrified that she'll go into a convent,
according to Carolyn. Do you think it's likely?'

Charles-Edouard roared with laughter. 'Convent indeed! Never, in a long life,
have I heard anything so funny.'

'Where does she live?'

'Just round the corner in the rue de l'Université, in that house you always look at with the two balconies.'

'Oh, the lovely house. Does she live there?'

'As you would know if you ever listened to what I say. She has extraordinary furniture, and the most famous collection of old toys in the world. Her husband's family made all the toys for the French court from the time of Henri II to the Revolution.'

'Does she live with her husband?'

'He is dead. He was vastly rich and he died.'

'And she's an old friend of yours?'

'Since always. We had the same nurse.'

'Take me to see her one day?'

'Perhaps – I'm not sure. Albertine is not very fond of women.'

Three or four days later Grace was driving home at tea-time when she saw Charles-Edouard leaning against the great double doors of Madame Marel's house. He had evidently just rung the bell. A small side door flew open and he disappeared through it. For the first time since her marriage Grace felt a jealous, heart-sinking pang. By the time he came in, some two hours later, she was so nervous that she thought it better to speak.

'But Charles-Edouard,' she said, 'you went to tea with Madame Marel again today?'

Charles-Edouard always acted on the principle with women, of telling the truth and then explaining it away so that it sounded highly innocent.

'Yes,' he said carelessly. 'It's an old habit of all my life. I go there every day, at tea-time.'

'Then you are in love with her?'

'Because I go to tea?' He raised his hand and shook his head reassuringly, but with his inward, guilty laugh.

Grace was not reassured. 'Because you go there every day. That's why you never come and have tea with us, in the nursery.'

'Only partly why.'

'When you told me about M. de la Bourlie visiting your grandmother every day you said in such a case there is always love. I remember so well, they were your very words, Charles-Edouard.'

'Now listen, my dearest Grace. As life goes on each person develops many different relationships with many different people, and each of these relationships is unique in quality. My relationship with you is perfect, is it not?'

'I thought so,' she answered sadly.

'If you think so it is so. Is it spoilt if I have another relationship, much less intense, much less important, but also perfect in its way, with Albertine Marel? Be frank now. You didn't mind me being alone for hours with my grandmother; you wouldn't mind if I went to a club, or spent hours with some old school friend, a man. You are not sad because the hours are not spent with you, you realize we can't be together every minute of the day; you mind because Albertine is a still desirable woman. And yet we are old school friends – nursery friends, in fact, and we share a great interest and hobby, that of collecting. I will tell you something very seriously, Grace. If you don't empty your mind and heart of sexual jealousy, if you let yourself give way to that, you will never be happy with me. Because I really cannot help liking the company of women. Do you understand what I have said?'

'It sounds all right,' said Grace.

'Try and remember it then.'

'Yes, I'll try.'

'Are you happy again?'

'Yes. But, oh dear, how nice it would be if you had tea here with us every day.'

'In the nursery? With Nanny? Are you mad?'

12

On Madame de Valhubert's birthday, in February, Charles-Edouard, Grace, and Sigismond went to the Père La Chaise with a bunch of spring flowers for her. It was beautiful weather, a respite between two particularly sharp spells of winter. The sun shone, the birds sang, and the blue gnomes who keep order in the streets of the dead were all beaming cheerfully. Even the floating widows looked as if they did not much object to being left alone a few more years above the ground.

'Have a good look at everything, Sigi,' said Charles-Edouard, 'you will be longer here than anywhere on earth.'

'Oh the funny little houses,' said the child, running from one to another and looking in, 'can I come and live in one?'

'All in good time. So, we'll pay some visits as we go.'

They climbed the long, steep hill, Charles-Edouard pulling Grace up by the hand.

'Many friends. Here are the Navarreins. The first ball I ever went to was in their house. M. de Navarrein was a link with the past, one of those things I never can remember. Let me see, his father was kissed by somebody whose great-great-grandfather had been held in the arms of *le grand Condé*. You know, it all depends on everyone concerned having children when they are ninety, really rather disgusting. There's the beautiful tomb of the Grandlieus – Madame de Grandlieu was my godmother, and she gave me the praying hands by Watteau which are over my bed.'

'Oh look,' said Grace, 'poor little Laetitia Hogg – younger than Sigi. What was she doing in Paris, and why did she die, I wonder?'

'One of those questions which are posed in graveyards. James and Mary Hogg must have loved her, since they bought her this tomb in perpetuity. Ha! the Politovskis, I'd not noticed them here before.' He went up to read the inscription, and began to laugh loudly. 'Oh no! This is too much! I've never heard such a thing! They've given themselves an S.A.R.! It's perfect, I can't wait to tell Tante Régine, what rubbish really. *"Il conquit Naples et resta pur."* Maybe he did, though not very likely, but even that doesn't entitle him to be a Royal Highness. Langeais and his wife, so charming, Sauveterre (poor Fabrice, give me one flower for him, how he would have laughed to see me here with wife and child). We've already passed enough friends to collect a large dinner party, a large amusing dinner party. *Hélàs*, where are they all now, I wonder?'

'Having large, amusing dinner parties somewhere else,' said Grace, suddenly seeing herself as doomed to eternal dinner parties, 'wishing you were there and wondering what I'm like.'

'Yes indeed. *L'Anglaise!* Intelligence Service. *Fille de francmaçon,*' said Charles-Edouard with his inward laugh. 'Here we are, this is the Avenue of the Marshals of France, our future home. Sigismond will spend some melancholic moments here, I hope, before it is his turn. Is it not beautiful up on this cliff, are we not lucky to be so well placed? Mind you, it is not the smart set, but at least we are not among presidents of the Republic, actors, duellists, and English pederasts. We have this pretty view and we have *la gloire*. Not bad, is it?'

'I feel sad,' said Grace, 'it reminds me of your dear grandmother's funeral.'

'I was very sad. Tired, and very sad. But there is only one thing I clearly remember of that whole day, the look of terrible triumph on the face of Madame de la Bourlie.'

'Oh surely not, at her age?'

'Age cannot blunt the hatred of a lifetime.'

They put their flowers at the base of a stone pyramid. It was a fine Empire tomb with bas-reliefs of battles and battle trophies.

'Poor Grandmère, she can't be very much pleased with the neighbours – Masséna, Lefebvre, Moscowa, Davout – not at all for her, I'm afraid. Come here, Sigismond, can you read this?'

'*Famille* Valhubert,' he spelt it out.

'This is your little house.'

'Can't I have one with a lace table-cloth and a door?'

'No. You will lie here with Grandmère and all of us.'

'Yes, but supposing I am killed in a stratospheric battle with the Martians?'

'That I should applaud. You may or may not become a Marshal of France, but you should always die in battle if you can, or you may live to be shot by your fellow-countrymen, like poor Ney over there, who was not fortunate enough to be killed by the enemy like Essling and Valhubert. I hope you are paying attention to what I am telling you, Sigismond. And now who would you like to see? I can offer you painters, writers, musicians, cooks (Brillat-Savarin, the French Mrs Beeton, is here), and all the great bourgeois of Paris. The nineteenth-century Russians, *rastaquouères* of their day, with huge, extravagant tombs, Rumanian princes in miniature Saint Sophias, domed and frescoed. Auguste Comte, the founder of positivism, might interest Sigi? But you look very tired, my dearest, and I think we had better walk gently back to the motor.'

The following day Grace had a miscarriage. They said she had perhaps walked too fast up the hill. It was not serious, quite early in her pregnancy, but it pulled her down, depressed her spirits, and she was a long time in bed. This was not a bad place just then. Late snow had fallen, it lay in the garden, white and brown, under a low, dark sky.

But her room gave a sunny impression, yellow with spring flowers. The mimosa was changed three times a day so that it should be always fluffy. People were very kind; Ange-Victor said that Madame Auriol herself would not have had more inquiries, flowers and books poured into the house, and so, when she was well enough to receive them, did visitors. Among those who came, and found Grace by chance alone, was Albertine Marel-Desboulles.

'I never see you,' she said, smiling with all her great charm at Grace. 'Before Madame de Valhubert died I used to have the pleasure of that lovely face to look at over the dinner-table – those huge, boring dinners in the autumn. Now, though we live so near, you have vanished again. But I have met the entirely delightful Sigismond.'

'I know. He told me. He thought you were heavenly.'

'When I heard you were ill I decided to call on you. Charles-Edouard and I are the oldest friends in the world – foster-brother and sister in a way, since we had the same nanny – well, to cut short all these explanations, here I am. How pretty you have made this room. I know it of old because here we used to put our coats when Madame de Valhubert gave her famous music parties.'

'I didn't know Madame de Valhubert was musical.'

'Oh well, music was not the only object of the parties, but the house has this music room and Régine Rocher had a Polish lover who played Chopin, so it all fitted in rather conveniently. As I was saying, then, we used to come up here with our coats – it was a hundred years ago – and in those days there was an Empire dressing-table with a marble top, very ugly, I can see it now, and on this slab of horrid grey marble there were hair-pins and safety-pins and *papier à poudre* for our shiny noses. I must explain that this was thought very old-fashioned and a great joke even then. I am old, but not so old that I have ever not owned a powder puff. It was freezing up here, agony to take off our coats, so we only stayed a moment, I don't suppose anybody ever used the *papier à poudre*. Then we would go to the music room, where the Polish lover was fiercely thumping away with passionate glances at Régine, and Charles-Edouard couldn't be stopped from talking. He would sit next the prettiest woman, which sometimes happened to be me, and talk at the top of his voice, while Régine got more and more furious. But dear Madame de Valhubert, who literally never knew one note from another, not that it would have made much difference if she had, was quite delighted to see him enjoying himself so much.

'So I've known this room a long time, but it's never been as pretty as now. I can see that you are one of those women with a talent for living in a house, which is quite different from the talent for arranging houses, and far more precious.'

Of course Grace was completely won over. Presently the door opened again and the pretty head of Juliette Novembre, in a sable hat with violets, peeped round it.

'I've brought you a camellia – can I come in, or are you talking secrets?' she said, like a child.

'Oh please please come in.'

'Just look at her, *la jolie*,' said Albertine, 'what a seasonable hat.'

'I love my little bit of rabbit. How are you?' she said to Grace. 'Isn't it horrid? I had one last year.'

Albertine said, 'I'm longing to hear about the ball, Juliette.'

'Yes, but why didn't you come? We were all wondering.'

'I was discouraged. My new dress wasn't ready, and I do hate autumn clothes in the spring. So after dinner I went home. But as soon as I had sent the motor away

I longed very much for the ball. I couldn't go to bed, I sat in my dressing-room until three consumed by this longing to be at the ball. Isn't it absurd, really! But to me a ball is still a miracle of pleasure. I see it with the eyes of a Tolstoy and not at all those of a Marcel Proust, and really, I promise you, it is terrible for me to miss one, even at my age. So now, torture me, tell us exactly what it was like.'

'Divine, a *bal classique* – no fancies, no embroideries. The prettiest women, in their prettiest clothes, a very good band, sucking pig for supper, wonderful champagne, in that house where everybody always looks their best. I loved it; I stayed to the end, which was after six. But nothing dramatic, Albertine, no fight, no elopement, nothing to tell really, hours and hours of smiling politeness.'

'I knew it, what I love the most. You have twisted a knife in my heart,' cried Albertine. 'Perhaps I ought to have gone, even in an old dress. But there – a ball to me is such a magical occasion that I cannot enjoy it wearing just anything. For days I have been seeing myself at that ball wearing my new dress, and when I found it couldn't be ready in time (nobody's fault, influenza in the workrooms), I didn't want to spoil the mental picture by going in another dress. Don't you understand?'

'Oh yes,' said Juliette. 'I'm just the same. I can't think of any occasion – a tea party even – without seeing an exact picture of how I shall look at it, down to shoes and stockings. I often wonder how social life – or life at all – can be much pleasure to people who don't care about dress. I'd hardly get myself out of bed in the morning if I hadn't something pretty and rather new to put on, and never get myself to a party. Now take all one's old relations, they love going out, but why? How can they enjoy it, really?'

'Oh their enjoyment comes from thinking of all the money they have saved by not dressing. They look at Régine Rocher and they add up what her clothes must have cost (you'll find they know, too, to a penny) and they feel as if somebody had given them a present of the amount.'

'Poor you, all that mourning,' Juliette said to Grace.

Like Albertine, she was out to please. They chatted away and Grace enjoyed herself. It was the enjoyment of frivolous, cosy, feminine company, of which she was very much starved. Carolyn, her only woman friend in Paris, could neither be described as frivolous nor cosy. She had many virtues, Grace knew that she was loyal and would be a rock in times of trouble, but she was not much fun, too restless and discontented. These two, rattling on with their nonsense, seemed to her perfectly fascinating, and she quite forgave Charles-Edouard for liking to be with them, it seemed so natural that he should.

Presently she sent for Sigi, who arrived hand in hand with his papa. Juliette became extremely animated, almost fidgety, making up to both father and son. Grace thought 'it's rather charming now, she's still only like a little girl, but at forty she will be terrible'. Albertine went to the chair on which she had put her things, produced a long, beautifully made wooden box, and gave it to Sigi.

'A present for you, darling. Open it.'

'What is it?' he said, pink and excited.

'It's called a kaleidoscope. Take it out. It was made for the poor little Dauphin,' she said to Grace.

'Oh you shouldn't! How good of you.'

Charles-Edouard took it from Sigi. 'You shut one eye, like Nelson, and see the stars. So.'

'Is it a telescope?'

'Better, you make your own stars as you go along. Venus – can you see? Shake it. Mars. Shake it. Jupiter as himself. Shake it. Jupiter as a swan.'

'Charles-Edouard, you'll muddle him.'

'Now here's another star you can see with the naked eye,' he said, pointing to Juliette. 'Doesn't she twinkle? She'll tell us all the gossip of the heavens. So, Juliette, tell.'

'Nothing to tell. I lead the life of a good little girl who does her lessons.'

'Ah yes? What lessons?'

'In the morning I sing, coloratura, "Hark, hark the lark"; in the afternoon I paint a snowy landscape; and when it is night I go to the Louvre and see the statues lit up.' She looked at Charles-Edouard with huge, innocent, blue eyes.

'Hm, hm,' he said, clearly rather annoyed. Grace felt again that horrid pang or twinge of jealous uneasiness that she had had on seeing Charles-Edouard outside Albertine's house in the rue de l'Université. Only that morning he had promised to take her, when she was well again, to see the statues lit up, saying how beautiful was the Winged Victory, white in the black shadows and then black against a white wall. She could not help noticing his present embarrassment, and was quite sure that he must have been to see the statues with Juliette. Her feeling of not being able to blame him for liking to be with this pretty wriggler, this flapper of eyelids and purser of lips, suddenly gave way to a feeling that she blamed him very much, and indeed could hardly bear it.

Meanwhile Sigi was entranced with the kaleidoscope.

'Please,' he said, 'can I take it to bed when I go?'

'But this child is his father over again,' cried Albertine. 'The moment he sees something pretty he wants to take it to bed with him.'

Two large tears rolled down Grace's cheeks. She felt, all of a sudden, most exceedingly tired.

Sir Conrad now came over to visit Grace, though he refused to stay with her, preferring the freedom of an hotel. When in Paris he liked to submit himself to the rather strenuous attentions of a certain Hungarian countess, an old friend of before the war; after visiting her establishment he needed a restful morning, and did not feel up to much family life before luncheon-time.

Charles-Edouard introduced him to Madame Rocher, and this was a stroke of genius, they could have been made for each other. She came out of mourning and gave a large dinner party for him, at which he charmed everybody. The rumours about the Allinghams not being people to know were now for ever scotched. He and Madame Rocher embarked upon a shameless flirtation, and were soon on such intimate terms that she even taxed him with being a Freemason. Sir Conrad, who was of course perfectly aware of the implications of this in France, roared with laughter, did not make any definite statement but let it be understood that his daughter had, of course, been joking, and a very good joke too. Madame Rocher, who was no fool, began to see that Charles-Edouard must have been quite right in what he had said about English Freemasons. Henceforward she addressed Sir

Conrad as *Vénérable*, referred to him as *le Grand Maître*, and all was merry as a marriage bell.

He liked Charles-Edouard more than ever. It would have surprised and gratified Grace to know that they had long, interesting discussions on political subjects when they were alone together, during which Charles-Edouard showed himself quite as serious, if not quite as long-winded, as Hector Dexter. One evening Charles-Edouard, though protesting that he himself only cared for society women, took his father-in-law round the brothels. These, having lately been driven underground by the ill-considered action of a woman Deputy, had become rather difficult for a foreigner to find.

Sir Conrad, who had never had many topics on which he could converse with his daughter, now found fewer even than when she was living with him.

'Are you happy?' he asked her, before leaving.

'Very happy.'

'Take care of yourself, darling. You don't look well.'

'I was quite ill. I shall be all right in a week or two.'

'Nanny hasn't changed much.'

'Oh dear, no.'

'Well, sooner Charles-Edouard than me is all I can say. Must you keep her? Couldn't you get a governess soon, or a tutor or something?'

'Papa! Nanny! – I couldn't possibly do without her.'

'No, no, I suppose not. And as she seems to have the secret of eternal youth (sold her soul to the devil, no doubt) I suppose Sigi's children won't be able to do without her either. If we were savages she would undoubtedly be the chieftainess of the tribe.'

Back in London, Sir Conrad went straight off to see Mrs O'Donovan and recount his visit.

'It's such a pity you didn't come,' he said, 'next time you really must. Grace would love to put you up, she asked me to tell you.'

'I don't believe I shall ever go back to Paris,' she said. 'I've known it too well and loved it too much. I couldn't bear to find all my friends old and poor and down at heels.'

'If it's only that,' he said with a short laugh, 'I've never seen them so prosperous, all living in their own huge houses, thousands of servants, guzzle, guzzle, guzzle, swig, swig, swig, just like old days.'

'Are they really so rich? But why?' she said querulously, as if they ought not to be.

'I suppose I don't have to enter into the economic reasons with you. You know as well as I do why it is.'

'In any case you can't deny they are all ten years older.'

'But the point is you'd think they were twenty years younger. They've all had Bogomoletz. That is something we must look into, you know. You get the liver of a newly killed young man (killed on the roads, of course, not on purpose) pumped into your liver, and the result is quite amazing.'

'My dear Conrad –'

'Or if you jib at that you can press unborn chickens on to your face before going out.'

'Thank you very much if by you, you mean me. *I* get one Polish egg a week on my ration.'

'Remarkable what your cook manages to do with that one Polish egg, I must say. Hens must lay enormous eggs in Poland, or are they ostriches? But to go back to your friends, none of them looks a day more than forty. I can't think why you're not pleased, you're supposed to love the French so much.'

'I think it's frightfully annoying, after all they've been through. Now I want to hear a great deal about other things. What is the exact situation at present.'

'Situation?'

Sir Conrad had come back in a very uppish mood, she thought, like a child after a treat.

'The political situation, of course. What does Blondin say, for instance?'

'My dear Meg, I didn't see Blondin, or any of them. I was entirely given over to pleasure and fun. But you know what the silly fool says as well as I do, since I am well aware that, like me, you see all the French papers.'

Mrs O'Donovan sighed. She did wish her English political friends could be a little more serious about the terrible state of the world. Sir Conrad, she thought, might well take a leaf out of the book of that important, well-informed Mr Hector Dexter whom she had met the day before at a dinner party, and who had told her some interesting, if rather lowering, facts about present-day French mentality.

Sir Conrad was not unconscious of these critical thoughts, he knew Mrs O'Donovan too well for that, but he was still a little drunk with all the pleasure and fun he had been having, so he went carelessly on,

'I want you to help me give a big, amusing dinner for Madame Rocher des Innouïs next month if she comes, as I hope she will, to stay at the French Embassy.'

'Régine Rocher,' said Mrs O'Donovan, faintly, 'don't tell me she's got the liver of a newly run-over young man.'

'I should think she's got everything she can lay her hands on. Anyhow she's remarkably pretty for what Charles-Edouard says is her age. He says she spends £8,000 a year on clothes, and the result, I'm obliged to tell you, is top-hole.'

'Simply ridiculous, I should imagine.'

Mrs O'Donovan, who was generally the driest of blankets, was proving such a wet one on this occasion that Sir Conrad took himself off to the House. Here he had a sensational success with all his traveller's tales about Bogomoletz and embryo chickens, not to mention detailed descriptions, unfit for the ears of a lady, of the goings-on *chez* Countess Arraczi.

13

'Our visit to London,' said Hector Dexter, 'was an integral success. I went to learn about the present or peace-time conditions there and to sense the present or peace-time mood of you Britishers, and I think that I fully achieved both these aims.'

The Dexters and Hughie Palgrave were dining with Grace. Charles-Edouard had told her earlier in the week that he was obliged to dine alone with Madame de la Ferté to talk family business.

'My uncle is so old now, he really makes no sense at all, and Jean is no use to her either. Nobody knows whether he is a case of arrested development or premature senile decay; she is having him injected for both, and the only result so far has been a poisoned arm. Why don't you ask some friends here to keep you company?'

Grace jumped at the idea of having the Dexters without Charles-Edouard. Although he never said they bored him, and indeed professed to admire Carolyn, whom he always referred to as *la belle Lesbienne*, she could somehow never bring herself to suggest inviting them again when he was there. As for Hughie, there would clearly be an awkwardness if he were to meet Charles-Edouard. She herself saw him quite often at the Dexters, and once a certain embarrassment between them was over they had become good friends again. They had never been much more than that, never passionate lovers.

'It's not the first time you've seen London, is it?' Grace said.

'No, Grace, it is not. I was in London during World War II and I will not pause now to say what I felt then about the effort which every class of you Britishers was putting forward at that time because what I felt then is expressed in my well-known and best-selling book *Global Vortex*. This time I found a very different atmosphere, much more relaxed and therefore much more difficult to sense, harder to describe.'

'Whom did you see?'

'We saw a very representative cross-section of your British life. We were in London and had a good time there, many very pleasant lunch parties and dinner parties and cocktail parties being given for us. We spent some nights with Carolyn's relatives in the North and had a good time there and some nights with some other relatives of Carolyn's near Oxford and had a good time there too.'

'So now what was your general impression, Heck?'

Hughie revered Hector, who seemed to him quite the cleverest man he had ever met. His own ambition was to go into politics as soon as he could get a seat to contest, and he liked picking Hector's brains on international subjects, or rather, allowing Hector's brains to flow over him in a glowing lava of thought.

'I must be honest with you, Hughie, my impression is not quite satisfactory.'

'Oh dear, that's bad. In what way?'

'An impression, I am sorry to say, of a great deal of misplaced levity.'

'Levity? I never see much levity at home; nothing much to levitate about, I shouldn't have said.'

'I must explain a little further. My government expects and gets, reports from me on the political equilibrium, stability, and soundness of the various countries I visit. At first sight this stability, equilibrium, and soundness seem very great in Britain. At first sight. But there is a worm, a canker in this seemingly sound and perfect fruit which I for one find profoundly disquieting. I refer to the frivolous attitude you Britishers have adopted, just as it has been adopted here (the difference being that nobody expects the French to be serious whereas we do most certainly expect it of you Britishers), the frivolous attitude towards – we are all grown-up and I guess I can speak without embarrassing anybody – sexual perversion.'

'Have we adopted a frivolous attitude?' said Hughie. 'The poor old dears are always being run in, you know.'

'I think I will put it this way. I think it cannot be generally understood and realized in Britain, as we understand and realize it in the States, that morally and
politically these people are lepers. They are sickly, morbose, healthless, chlorotic,
unbraced, flagging, peccant, vitiated and contaminated, and when I use the word
contaminated I use it very specifically in the political sense. But I think you British
have absolutely no conception of the danger in your midst, of the harm these
perverts can do to the state of which they are citizens. You seem to regard them
as a subject for joking rather than as the object of a deep-seated, far-reaching purge.'

'But they're not in politics, Heck – hardly any, at least.'

'Not openly, no. That's their cunning. They work behind the scenes.'

'If you can call it work.'

'For the cause of Communism. The point I am trying to make is that they are
dangerous because politically contaminated, a political contamination that can, in
every traceable case, be traced to Moscow.'

'I say, hold on, Heck,' said Hughie. 'All the old queens I know are terrific old
Tories.'

'I am bound to contradict you, Hughie, or rather I am bound to put forward
my argument, and you are going to see that it is a powerful argument, to persuade you of the exact opposite of what you have just said and to persuade you
that what you have just said is the exact opposite of the truth as known to my
government. We Americans, you may know, have certain very very sure and
reliable, I would even say infallible, sources of information. We have our Un-
American Activities Committee sections, we have our F.B.I. agents, we have
countless very very brilliant newspaper men and business men all over the world
(men like Charlie Jungfleisch and Asp Jorgmann); we have also other sources
which I am not at liberty to disclose to you, even off the record. And our sources
of information inform us that nine out of every ten, and some say ninety-nine
out of every hundred, of these morally sick persons are not only in the very
closest sympathy but in actual contact with Moscow. And I for one entirely
believe these sources.'

Hughie was unconvinced. 'But my dear Heck, in Russia you go to Siberia for
that. I've got a friend of mine who's awfully worried about it in case they come –'

'Maybe you do, maybe you don't. There are some very curious anomalies, things
you would hardly credit, Hughie, but of which our agents are cognizant, going on
in that great amorphous blob of a country today. But I am not concerned with the
pervert in Russia, my concern is with the pervert in Western Europe because my
professional concern at the moment is with Western Europe, more especially in
its moral and ethical aspect.'

'Then what about the pervert in America?' said Hughie.

'And I am very very glad to say that this very unpleasant problem does not exist
in the States. We have no pederasts.'

'How funny,' said Grace, 'all the Americans here are.'

She was thinking of various gay, light-hearted fellows whom she met with
Charles-Edouard and his friends. Mr Dexter was displeased with this remark and
did not reply, but Hughie said,

'Perhaps they have a bad time at home and all come here, like before the war
one used to think all Germans were Jews. But honestly you know, Heck, what

you've just said makes no sense, and the more one thinks of it the less sense it makes.'

'I will make one more attempt to explain my meaning to you, Hughie, and then we must go. If a man is morally sick, Hughie, he is morally sick, if he is sick in one sense he will be sick in another, and if he is sexually sick he will be politically sick as well.'

'But, poor old things, they're not sick,' said Hughie, 'they just happen to like boys better than girls. You can't blame them for that, it's awfully inconvenient, and they'd give anything to be different if they could. But I don't see that it's any reason for calling them Bolshevists. I probably know more about them than you do, having been at Eton and Oxford, and if there's one thing they're not it's Bolshevists. Anything for a quiet life is their motto. I'm afraid, old man, you've got the wrong end of the stick there, and if this is what your infallible sources are telling you, I should advise a comb-out of the sources.'

The Dexters now got up to leave. The Jungfleisches, they explained, were giving a party for important people, and they had promised to be there early.

'Poor old Heck,' said Hughie when they had gone. 'He does see things in black and white. Funny, really, for such a clever man. I can't help remembering how all over the Russians he used to be, in Italy. He bit my head off the other day for reminding him, but it's true.'

'Like Carolyn,' Grace said, laughing, 'she used to be our school Communist. I know it was she, though now she pretends I've been mixing her up with another girl. She gets furious when I tease her about it.'

Hughie said, 'Let's go and have a glass of wine somewhere before bedtime, shall we?'

Grace felt tired, as she often did now, but it seemed rather a shame to send him away so early, and she consented.

'Just for an hour then,' she said.

They went to a White Russian night club, a stuffy, dark, enclosed room with music from the Steppes. Cossacks, in boots and white blouses, have keened here night after night for thirty years over a life that has gone for ever. The hours of darkness seem too short for them to express the whole burden of their desolation, so that any reveller who will sit up and listen to the wails and whimpers of their violins until late into the next day becomes their brother and their best beloved. Whereas in other night places the band may be anxious to catch the last metro and go home, these Russians would rather anything than that a lack of customers should drive them out to the first metro. The little room has come to represent Holy Russia to them, and when they leave it in the morning exile begins again. It is really a place designed for lovers or for drunkards, people who like to sit all night engulfed in sound rather than for those who want an hour of sober chat.

Hughie had come to unburden himself about Albertine, and he had to talk very loud so as to be heard over the scream of the violins. From time to time the noise suddenly dropped to a dramatic hush, intended to represent the lull in a storm, and then Hughie's powerful English voice would ring out into the silence so that he was embarrassed, and Grace wanted to giggle. As soon as he had lowered it a gusty crescendo would swallow up his next sentence. It was a very fidgety way of confiding.

'Of course she'll never want to marry me, I know. I don't allow myself to think of it. She is far above me, far too clever and wonderful. She knows everything, not only all French literature but English and German too – she has even read Mrs Henry Wood, for instance. I wish you could hear her reciting – by the hour, it's extraordinary. When I think of all the years I've wasted – but I never guessed there was somebody like that just round the corner or I would have tried to educate myself a bit. You can't be surprised she rather looks down on me, as it is. So now I'm trying terribly hard to make up for lost time, just in case one day she might think of marrying me. Not very likely, I know, but in life things do sometimes happen. For instance she might be ruined and need a home, or have a fearful accident and be disfigured, or lose a leg –'

The words 'lose a leg', falling into one of the pools of sudden silence, echoed round the room so that Grace could not help laughing.

'Lose a leg?' she said.

Hughie laughed himself, saying, 'Oh well, of course it sounds ridiculous; it's one of those things which I sometimes think of. After all Sarah Bernhardt did, it can happen, and then she'd need somebody to push her about. The worst of it is such hundreds of people do want to marry her, she'd be unlikely to choose me. There's another terrible worry. She talks of going into a convent. I wake up in the night and think about it. Supposing one day I were to call at her house only to be told "Madame Marel-Desboulles is no more. Pray for Soeur Angélique"?'

Grace laughed again, and said, 'You've been reading Henry James – so do I, in the hopes of understanding them all better. But I don't think Albertine is another Madame de Cintré, nor do I think she'll ever marry again. I guess you'll be able to go on like this for years, if it's any consolation to you.'

'It's very much better than nothing, of course. So, as I say, I read a lot to try to educate myself, but I must have let my mind go badly and it's an awful strain. Have you ever tried the *Mémoires* of Saint-Simon? Heavy weather, I can tell you. Then I try and see as many clever people as I can. That's why I go such a lot to the Dexters.'

'D'you think them so very clever?'

'Carolyn is brilliant of course, she takes me sight-seeing and we go to lectures. As for old Heck, well, if he is a bit muddle-headed about some things, he's got the gift of the gab, hasn't he? I wish I could talk like that, on and on.'

'I always think he talks as if he doesn't quite know English.'

'Really, Grace, what an idea. All those words – I'm English, but I don't know what half of them mean. Albertine would like me much better if I could put on an act like Hector, I'm sure she would. But when I'm with her I seem to get so tongue-tied.'

At this moment a large party of people got up to go. The violinists came forward, still playing, to try and persuade them to stay. They surrounded them, playing with all their souls. But the people, though smiling, were firm, and made a passage through the deeply bowing, still playing Cossacks. When they had gone, and the violinists had returned to the band, Grace suddenly perceived, in a very dark corner, hitherto obscured by these other people, the figures of Charles-Edouard and Juliette. Their backs were turned, but she could see their faces in a looking-glass. They were evidently enjoying themselves enormously, heads close together, laughing and chattering sixteen to the dozen. Grace was particularly struck, stricken to the heart indeed, by Charles-Edouard's look, a happy, tender, and amused expression, which, she thought, she herself used to evoke at Bellandargues but which she had not seen of late.

She felt weak, as if she were bleeding to death. 'I'm so sorry,' she said, 'but I think I might faint. Could we go home please, Hughie?'

'Goodness,' he said, 'you are white, Grace.' He hurried her to the motor, full of self-reproach. 'I should never have suggested this, you're not strong enough yet.'

'Don't worry, it's nothing, I promise. I feel better already. I'm just a little tired, that's all. Don't come in,' she said, when they arrived at her house. 'My maid always waits for me – she's old-fashioned; I'm so lucky. Good night, Hughie.'

When Charles-Edouard got back, not very late, she was in bed, crying dreadfully.

'Why do you weep?' he said, with great solicitude.

'Because you're in love.'

'I am in love?'

'With Juliette.'

'Why do you say this?'

'I was at the Russian place. I saw you.'

Charles-Edouard looked very much taken aback. 'But you never go to night places.'

'I know. I hate them, but Hughie wanted to –'

'Ha! You've been out with Hughie?'

'I told you we were all going to dine here, me and Hughie and the Dexters. Well the Dexters went on to a party after dinner so Hughie and I – Oh Charles Edouard, you're in love with her?'

He raised his hand, shook his head, and replied, 'Not at all.'

'Then why were you looking so happy?'

'Would I look happy if I were in love with Juliette? It would be very inconvenient, after all she is my cousin's wife. No, I look happy because I am happy – happy in my life and with you, and then I do love to go out with a pretty woman.'

'Why did you pretend you were going to dine with Tante Edmonde?'

'But my dear Grace, it was no pretence at all. I did dine there. It so happens that Juliette also was dining with her mother-in-law. Jean has gone to Picardy; she was alone in her flat so she dined downstairs. When I had finished talking with my aunt I took her out for half an hour before bedtime. I didn't want to come back here and find your dinner still going on.'

'Oh!' This sounded so reasonable. 'Oh dear, I'm sorry to make a scene and I do apologize.'

'For what? The rights of passion have been proclaimed once and for all in the French Revolution.'

'The worst part of the whole thing,' said Grace, tears beginning to well into her eyes again, 'is that what I minded so terribly was your look of happiness. I am supposed to love you and yet I mind you looking happy. When you were sad, when your grandmother died, I was sorry, of course, but I could easily bear it – now I find that what I can't bear is for you to look happy. What can it mean, it doesn't make sense.'

'That, I'm afraid,' said Charles-Edouard, 'is love.'

'But what can I do! I can't live with somebody whom I would rather see sad than happy. Perhaps I'd better go back to England?'

'No. Do stay.'

Grace laughed. 'You say that as if you were asking me for a week-end.'

'Do stay, for good.'

'I can't bear to make scenes, I'm ashamed of myself, it is dreadful.'

'You won't have to very often.'

'I shall begin to imagine all sorts of things whenever you go out.'

'That would be the greatest pity – imaginative women are terrible. Now let's calmly consider what did happen this evening. What did you actually see? Juliette and me, sitting quite properly at a table in a perfectly proper establishment. I was not looking unhappy, but then I have no reason to, I'm not a White Russian violinist. So! That is what you saw. Then your imagination got to work, and what did you imagine? That I had told you a lie, sneaked off to dine in a loving intimacy with Juliette and then taken her to a night club. Knowing me as you do, you might have thought it more probable that, if I were in love with Juliette, I would go straight to bed with her, but no! We choose the night club where we can be seen by all and sundry, and where in fact you see us, staying perhaps an hour, not more. I take her home, but only to the door. My aunt's concierge, like ours, has to get out of bed to let people in, so there could be no question of me going upstairs with Jean's wife; the whole of Paris would know it tomorrow if I did. I say good night in the street and come back here – it is still not one o'clock. I don't think any of this indicates the existence of a great and guilty passion for Juliette. You must be more reasonable, dearest. Shall I give you a piece of advice, quite as useful in love as in warfare? Save your ammunition, and only shoot when you see the whites of their eyes. Now in this particular case I would have you observe that I spent exactly the same sort of evening as you did. We both dined with a few rather dull people, and then went out with the least dull of them for an hour or so before bed.'

'Hughie isn't as pretty as Juliette.'

'Hughie is very handsome, and you know it. But I haven't come near to seeing the white of his eyes yet. I shan't shoot this time, and nor must you.'

Grace was completely reassured. She went happily to sleep.

14

A few days later Grace lunched with Carolyn, and the talk was all of a certain guide who took personally conducted tours into the private houses of Paris. Carolyn said that she had followed one of these tours every day that week.

'I've been into such wonderful houses, which I would never have seen otherwise,' she said. 'He gets permission to visit anything that is *"classé"*, and of course that means anything worth seeing. His lectures, too, are good and informative. Yesterday we went to Mansard's own house in the Marais.'

She described it to Grace. Carolyn was at her best on the subject of old Paris and really knew a great deal about it. She liked the monuments of the town better than its denizens who still threw her into a fever of irritation.

'Now I asked you not to be late,' she said, 'because this afternoon M. de la Tour is taking us to see a very famous private house, one of the hardest to get into, the Hôtel de Hauteserre in the rue de Varenne. I simply must go, and you'd better come too, Grace. It's a chance we shan't have again for ages, and I believe the *boiseries* are unique.'

Grace had nothing much to do and was, like Hughie, forever trying to scrape up a little culture. Besides, she thought, it might be something for Charles-Edouard with his perpetual 'What are the news?' She never had enough to tell him about her day. 'So, what did *la belle Lesbienne* recount? Or did you sit, as usual, gazing at each other in silence?' As her talk with Carolyn was never anything that could possibly interest him, being all about nannies, the Parc Monceau, and mutual friends at home, and as Grace had no talent for cooking up such plain food with either the spice of malice or the sauce of funniness, she was always obliged to leave it that they had gazed in silence. 'Very strange, this dumbness.'

After luncheon Carolyn drove her across the river to the rue de Varenne. Her exasperation with the French always reached boiling-point when she was driving a motor. As they went she told Grace about a dishonest mechanic who had put back her spare wheel unmended (she was never happier than when some little thing of this sort occurred, another stick with which to beat them), and punctuated her story with, 'Look at that! Did you ever see such driving? I shan't give way; I'm in my rights and he knows it. Disgusting. Oh get on. What a place to park. What people, really!'

It was one of those Paris afternoons when, by some trick of the light, the buildings look as if they are made of opaque, blue glass. Grace wondered how much Carolyn really did love the stones of Paris. She seemed not to notice, as they went by, the blue glass façade of the Invalides surmounted by its dome powdered with gold, but only the bad driving in the Esplanade.

Now when they arrived at their destination Grace saw that it was none other than the Ferté house. She had never known that its old name was Hôtel de Hauteserre, to her it had always been 83 rue de Varenne or the house of Tante Edmonde. She laughed, and said to Carolyn, 'But I know this house by heart – it belongs to Charles-Edouard's old great-uncle; we lunch or dine here every week of our lives. I don't think there's much point in me going in.'

'Nonsense,' said Carolyn, 'you'd better come along as you're here. M. de la Tour will tell you all about it, and very likely show you lots of things you hadn't ever suspected.'

Grace thought again that it would be something funny to tell Charles-Edouard, and that the idea of her sight-seeing in that house would be sure to amuse him. So she paid 100 francs at the door and went in with Carolyn. There was quite a crowd of people, and the guide was just beginning his lecture.

'This house,' he said, 'was built in 1713 by Boffrand for the famous – I should perhaps say notorious – Marquise de Hauteserre, who created a record by keeping the Régent as her lover for eighteen weeks. He was by no means her only lover, and they were, in fact, numberless. I am glad to be able to announce that when we have seen the state rooms, which are of an extraordinary beauty, we are to be allowed the great privilege, hardly ever accorded to tourists, of seeing Madame de Hauteserre's own bedroom. Madame la Duchesse has given me the key; she knows that we are all serious students of French art and not mere gaping sightseers.'

'Have you seen it?' whispered Carolyn to Grace.

'No.'

'There – what did I tell you?'

'This bedroom,' the guide continued, 'has an erotic ceiling, a thing rare in France though not uncommon in Italy, by Le Moine; a Régence bed of wonderful quality, and *boiseries* by Robert de Cotte. When I tell you that all this is quite unrestored, you will easily realize that what you are about to see is unique, of its sort, in Paris.'

They went upstairs into the reception rooms of the first floor which Grace knew so well, gold and white, blue and white, gold and blue with painted ceilings. The lecturer went at length into the history of every detail; they were nearly an hour examining these three rooms, and Grace began to feel tired. At last, in the Salon de Jupiter, where the Fertés usually sat after dinner, the lecturer went to a little door in the wall, which Grace had never noticed there. Taking a large key from his pocket he unlocked this door, saying, 'And now for the famous bedroom of Madame de Hauteserre.'

Grace happened to be standing beside him, and together they looked in. It was a tiny room decorated with a gold and white trellis; an alcove contained a bed, and on the bed, in a considerable state of disarray, were Juliette and Charles-Edouard.

The guide quickly slammed and relocked the door. He turned to the crowd, saying, 'Excuse me, I had quite forgotten, but of course the *boiseries* and the ceiling have gone to the Beaux Arts for repair.'

Nobody but Grace and the guide had seen into the room; greatly to her relief the tourists accepted his statement without dispute, if rather crossly. They had certainly had their money's worth in this beautiful house, although they had been looking forward to the erotic ceiling as a final titbit. Carolyn, still gazing at a panel in the Jupiter room, said, 'Oh never mind, we've really seen enough for one day. Shall I give you a lift home, Grace?'

Grace got into the motor, talked away quite naturally, thanked Carolyn for the afternoon, and went into her house as if nothing had happened. She lay on the day bed in her library, saying to herself, 'This is the end.' But, as with some physical blow, she had not yet begun to feel any pain.

Presently Charles-Edouard came in.

'I looked for you in the nursery,' he said.

'Aren't you having tea with Madame Marel?'

'Not today. I never do on Wednesday, it's her day for receiving. Where do we dine? Oh yes, of course, I remember, Tante Régine. That's sure to be great fun. So, what are the news? Don't tell me, I can guess. You lunched, in an impenetrable silence, with la Dexter. Such a curious friendship, I find.'

'And after luncheon we went sight-seeing.'

'Indeed? Where?'

'The Hôtel de Hauteserre.'

Charles-Edouard looked at her, startled, and then said, quite angrily for him,

'Really, Grace, you are too extravagant. What could have induced you to pay 100 francs to see the house of your uncle, which you know perfectly well already? No – this is not sensible, and I'm very cross with you. Why, 100 francs was a dowry when my grandmother was young.'

'You pay for the lecturer. He shows all sorts of unexpected things.'

'I will take you over it one day. I know much more about it than any lecturer.'

'You would never show me what he did, this afternoon.'

'Ha!' said Charles-Edouard. He went to the window and looked out of it.

'This is very annoying,' he said presently.

'I thought so too. I've seen the whites of their eyes, Charles-Edouard.'

'Imbecile of a lecturer. He should know better than to come bursting into bedrooms like that.'

'Yes. Being French you'd think he would.'

'Perhaps I'll give up Juliette.'

'You needn't bother. I'm going back to England.'

'Do stay,' said Charles-Edouard.

'For the week-end?'

'No. For ever.'

'It's no good, Charles-Edouard. I'm too English; your behaviour makes me too miserable, and I can't bear it any more.'

'But my dear, that's nothing to do with being English. All women are the same; indeed if you were Spanish I dare say you would have killed me by now, or Juliette, or both. No, we've been particularly unlucky. This unspeakable lecturer, paid 100 francs to open bedroom doors in the middle of the afternoon! What could have induced Tante Edmonde to let him, she is out of her mind. I know what it is of course, she hopes to get off taxes by allowing the public into her house, but what a shortsighted action! Half that crowd must have been Treasury spies, nosing about to see how many signed pieces she owns, and the rest of course were burglars making out lists of all the objects in the glass cases. I blame her terribly. Then I'm bound to say it was a little bit your own fault, wasting 100 francs and a whole afternoon in a house where you dine at least once a week. Bad luck, and bad management.'

'In fact everybody's fault but yours.'

'No, no, I blame myself most, for being so careless.'

'Oh dear! How cynical you are.'

'Not at all. I see things in the light of reality.'

'Yes. Well I also must try to be a realist. After this I could never again be happy with you because I should never again have an easy moment when you were out of my sight, never. You are wonderful at explaining things away until one happens to have seen with one's own eyes, but from now on the explanations won't be any good. So I shall go back to Papa.'

'And when do you leave?'

'Tomorrow. I shall take Sigi.'

'Yes, you must. And Nanny, too, perhaps?'

'And Nanny, too. And please excuse me to Tante Régine. I've got a headache, and there's a great deal of packing to be done.'

*

'Nanny, we're going home to England tomorrow.'

'What, all of us?'

'You and me and Sigismond.'

'Mm.' The tone was one of disapproval. 'Tomorrow, dear? And what about the packing?'

'The train isn't till 12.30 and there's Marie to help you. You must manage somehow, darling, please.'

'But how long are we going for?'

'For good. Now don't look sad, it will be London, not Bunbury. So think – Hyde Park every day, Daniel Neal, steam puddings, Irish stew –'

'Irish stew indeed. My sister says you never see a nice neck, these days. And Sigi's Papa?'

'He's not coming.'

'Mm.'

'Do be pleased, darling. I thought at least somebody would be.'

'Well dear, I've always said little boys ought to have a mummy and a daddy.'

'That can't be helped. And think of the hundreds who don't.'

'I'm wondering how I'm ever to get all his toys packed up in the time. Funny thing, one never gets any notice of these journeys.'

'Send Marie out to buy an extra hamper if there's no room.'

Next day there had to be a special motor to take Sigi's luggage; he had exactly twice as many items as his mother.

'Anybody would suppose that he was a famous cocotte,' said Charles-Edouard, who went to the station exactly as if he were seeing them off for a little change. Sigi skipped about on the platform, getting in everybody's way and saying, 'Can I ride on the engine, please, Papa?'

'Certainly not. And I hope you'll have learnt to read before I see you again.'

'Will you give me a prize if I can?'

'Perhaps. If you can read everything, and not only the little bit out of the *Journal des Voyages* you already know by heart.'

'What sort of prize?'

'A good sort.'

'Can I ride on the *chevaux de Marly* for my prize?'

'You can only ride on the *chevaux de Marly* when you know *A la voix du vainqueur d'Austerlitz* by heart.'

'How can I learn it, in England?'

'I can't imagine. Anyhow you can learn to read. Shall I tell you what will become of you if you can't read when you are grown up?'

'All grown-up people can read,' said the child, conclusively.

'Good-bye, Grace,' said Charles-Edouard. 'Do come back soon.'

'For a week-end?'

'No. For good.'

He kissed her hand and left them. He was quite surprised at how much he minded their departure.

15

'What's all this about?' said Sir Conrad when Sigi, Nanny, and their baggage had been deposited in the nursery and he had Grace to himself. 'I'm delighted to see you, it goes without saying, but why such short notice? Is it not rather hysterical?'

'Yes, well, you may call it so. I've left Charles-Edouard.'

'You've left your husband?'

'Yes.'

Sir Conrad was not surprised, since this sudden run for home could hardly, he knew, mean anything else.

'And are you going to tell me why?'

He did not doubt what the reason would be, broadly speaking, but was curious as to the details.

Grace told him at some length about her life in Paris.

'I could bear it when he went to tea every day with Madame Marel, though I didn't like it; I could even bear his terribly open flirtation at every party we went to, with Juliette Novembre, but what happened yesterday afternoon at the Hôtel de Hauteserre is more than I can endure or forgive.'

'What did happen?'

But when she told him Sir Conrad annoyed her very much indeed by bursting into a hearty laugh.

'I say, what bad luck! Now don't look so cross and prim, darling, I quite see it was horrible for you, and I'm very sorry, but I can't help thinking of Charles-Edouard too. You must admit it was bad luck on him, poor chap.'

'Perhaps it was. But lives can't be built entirely on luck.'

'No good saying that, as they always are. Luck, my darling, makes the world we live in. After all, it was by luck you met Charles-Edouard in the first place (bad luck for Hughie); by luck that he came back from the war safe and sound; by luck that you had that clever little Sigi – by luck, indeed, that you got your mother's large blue eyes and lovely legs and not my small green eyes and bow legs. Luck is a thing you can never discount. It may be unfair, it generally is, but you can't discount it. And if Charles-Edouard is having, as he seems to be, a run of bad luck you ought to be there, sympathizing with the poor chap. It doesn't seem right to go off and leave him all alone. I hoped I'd brought you up better than that.'

'You're talking as if he had lost all his money at the races.'

'Oh well, not quite so bad, thank goodness.'

'And as if you're on his side.'

'We must try and see his side of the question, I suppose.'

'I don't think you need, you're my father.'

'Now listen, my darling child. I love you, as you know, and only desire your happiness. This is your home, available for you whenever you need it. You can always come here, and even bring Nanny if you must, so please don't think I want to send you away. Quite the contrary, I like to have you here, it's a great pleasure. But it's my plain duty, as your father, to try to make you see things as they are, and, above all, to try and make you see Charles-Edouard as he is. I'm very fond of Charles-Edouard, and I presume that you are too, as you married him.

'Now he is a man who likes women in the French way of liking them, that is he likes everything about them, including hours of their company and going to bed with them. I suppose you would admit that this is part of his charm for you. But you hardly ever find a man, or anyhow a young man, with his liking for women who can be faithful to one woman. It's most exceedingly rare.'

'Yes, Papa, all this may be true about Charles-Edouard. But with me it's a question of how much I can stand, and I can't stand a life of constant suspicion and jealousy. Juliette, Albertine, the women he looks at in the street, the way he flirts with everybody, everybody, even Tante Régine, the way he kisses their hands, the way he answers the telephone when they ring up – oh no, it's too much for me, I can't.'

'My dear child, I always thought you had a healthy outlook on life, but this is positively morbid. You really must pull yourself together or I foresee great unhappiness for you in the future.'

'I shan't be unhappy a bit if I can marry an ordinary, faithful, English husband.'

Grace had been sustained during her journey by the mental picture of an idealized anglicized Charles-Edouard, whom she was to meet and marry in an incredibly short space of time. This vision had come to her when the light airiness of Northern France, with its young wheat, pink roads and large, white, rolling clouds, had been exchanged for the little, dark, enclosed Kentish landscape, safe and reassuring – home, in fact. She had looked out of the window at the iron grey sky pressing upon wasteful agriculture, coppices untouched by hand of woodman, tangles of blackberry and gorse, all so familiar to her eyes, and she was comforted by the thought that she could be an English countrywoman once more, gardening, going for walks, playing bridge with neighbours, a faithful English Charles-Edouard, tweeded and hearty, by her side. She would be quite happy, she thought, living in an oast-house, or a cottage with a twist of smoke on the edge of Mousehold Heath, or a little red villa with glass veranda in the Isle of Wight – anything, anywhere, so long as it was safe in England and she safely married to this tower of strength and reliability, this English Charles-Edouard.

'I'm afraid an ordinary faithful English husband will seem very plain pudding after the extraordinarily fascinating French one you are throwing away so carelessly,' said her father. 'People like Charles-Edouard don't grow on every tree, you know. The fact is women must choose in life what sort of a man it is that they do want – whether what is called a good husband, faithful to his wife but seldom seeing her, going off to the club and so on for his relaxation, or one that really loves women, loves his wife, probably, best and longest, but who also and inevitably feels the need for other relationships with other women.'

'Is that the sort of husband you were, Papa?'

'Yes, I'm afraid so. And as I never had a quarter the bad luck of poor Charles-Edouard, and as your mother was either entirely unsuspicious or else very very clever, it was a perfect success, and we were happy. But I didn't care to risk it again after her death, so here I am unmarried.'

'Don't you feel lonely sometimes?'

'Often. That's why I can't help being pleased to see you and the little boy back again, though I suppose if I had any moral sense whatever I'd send you off with a flea in your ear. May I ask what you are planning next?'

'Really, Papa, I hadn't thought.'

'You should try to think before you act, my dear child. Do you want a divorce?'

'Don't let's talk about it now, I'm so tired. Divorce sounds so horrible.'

'Yes, well, leaving your husband is rather horrible.'

'But I suppose it will come to that.'

Sigi now put in an appearance, to say 'Grandfather –'

'Yes, Sigi?'

'You know adultery –?'

Sir Conrad raised an eyebrow and Grace quickly intervened, saying, 'Really Nanny is too naughty, she will teach him these dreadful words out of the Bible. Adultery is for when you're older, darling.'

'Oh I see. A sort of *pas devant* thing?'

'Yes, that's just it. So Nanny must be pleased to be back in her own old nursery again?'

'Not a bit. Fluff under the carpet – she doesn't know what the girls are coming to these days. One thing she will say for Paris, the housemaids there did know their work. And she's just rung up her sister – offal is a thing you never see in London now. So Nanny's in a terrible dump. Grandfather –'

'Now what?'

'Are there cartridges again, and can I learn to shoot?'

'We'll have to talk to Black about that, when we go to Bunbury.'

'Oh good. Can you have a word with Nanny before dinner, Mum?'

Grace, who had been expecting this summons, sighed deeply and went upstairs.

Part Two

I

The days of 'run along, Sigismond' were now in the past; nobody ever said it to him again. Grace, lonely and wretched, concentrated herself on the little boy, he was with her from first thing in the morning to his bedtime. He would arrive with her breakfast tray, open her letters, answer her telephone, and play with the things on her dressing-table. From time to time, in a desultory manner, she gave him reading lessons.

'You simply must be able to read books by the time you see Papa again,' she said.

'And when shall I see him again?'

'I expect it will be after the summer holidays.'

'Shall I go and stay with him?'

'I expect so.'

'In Paris, or Bellandargues?'

'Paris. He's not going to Bellandargues this year.'

'And you too?'

'We'll see when the time comes.'

'I say, Mummy, are you divorced?'

'Certainly not, darling. What do you know about divorce?'

'Well I've told you about Georgie in the Park? His mummy and daddy are divorced and he says it's an awfully good idea – you have a much better time all round, he says, when they are.'

'Goodness, darling –!'

'Actually his mummy and daddy have both married again, so he's got two of each now, and he says the new ones are smashing, really better than the original ones. You ought to see the things they give him, they're so lovely and rich. So shall you be marrying again, Mummy?'

'You seem to forget that I'm married already, to Papa.'

'Nanny told her sister she thought perhaps Mr Palgrave. She always thought it would have been better, in the first place.'

'Don't fidget with that necklace, Sigi, you'll wear out the string.'

'Do you know what Mr Palgrave gave me last time I saw him?'

'No, what?'

'Eleven bob.'

'What a funny sum.'

'Yes, well, Nanny always takes 10 per cent for her old lepers. I told him that and he very nicely made it up. I need a lot of money.'

'Why do you?'

'Because I'm saving up for a space ship when it's invented. Mum, when can I have a bike?'

'When we go to the country perhaps.'

'And why don't you marry Mr Palgrave?'

'Because not.'

'Nanny says it's nicer for little boys to have a mummy and a daddy, but I expect it's best of all when they have two mummies and two daddies.'

'Shall we get on with the reading?'

They went for the summer holidays to Bunbury. At first Grace thought she would find it unbearable to be in the place so impregnated now with memories of Charles-Edouard, where they had spent their honeymoon, where she had lived all those years dreaming of him, and where he had come to find her after the war. But her father wanted to go there, it would be good for Sigismond, and it was, after all, her home, the home of her ancestors; it would belong to her when Sir Conrad died. Memories of Charles-Edouard were not the only ones connected with it. And, in any case, her thoughts were of him all day, wherever she was.

'One thing I must ask you,' she said to Sir Conrad. 'Will you give orders for the Archduke to be taken out of my room?'

'Certainly I will,' he replied. 'The proper place for that Archduke is the hall – I never could understand what he was doing upstairs. And while we are on the subject, I should very much like to see my Boucher back in the drawing-room, if you don't mind.'

In the end Grace's room became less like a corner of the Wallace Collection and more like an ordinary country-house bedroom. It was really more convenient.

Nanny, in so far as she was ever pleased by anything, was pleased to be back at Bunbury. Just as Grace had spent the war years dreaming of Charles-Edouard, so Nanny had spent them dreaming of Hyde Park and what fun it would be, now she had a baby once more, taking him there. But when at last, on their return from Paris, she had achieved this objective, the dream, as dreams so often do, had turned to ashes. The Park, she found, had lost its old character. Not only had the railings disappeared, the beautiful fleur-de-lis railings which used to surround it, the stout stumps of Rotten Row, the elegant Regency railings of the flower beds, and the railings on which children loved to walk a tight-rope at the edges of the paths, but so, to a very great extent, had the nannies. Increasing numbers of little boys, it seemed, while they had a multiplicity of mummies and daddies, had no nannies at all. They were no longer wheeled about in prams, morning and afternoon, as a matter of course, but when they needed fresh air they were hung out of windows in meat safes. As soon as they could toddle they toddled off to nursery schools, where they were taught to sing little songs, given a great deal of milk to drink, and kept strictly out of the way of their harassed parents. So Park society was not what it had been. There was no wide range of choice, as in the past, and the few nannies who were left clung together, a sad little bunch, like the survivors in an autumnal poultry yard, most of whose fellows had already gone to the pot. Nanny had few friends among them and pronounced them to be, on the whole, a very inferior type of person. But at Bunbury she had congenial gossips, the old housekeeper, the groom's wife, Mrs Atkin the butler's wife, and Mrs Black, to whom she was able to boast and brag about her year in France until they stretched their eyes. Anybody who knew how terribly she had complained during the whole of her sojourn there, or who could have heard her comments to Nanny Dexter on every aspect of French civilization, would have been amazed by the attitude she now assumed over the clanking cups of tea with her cronies.

'Say what you choose, France is a wonderful country – oh it is wonderful. Take the shops, dear, they groan with food, just like pre-war. I only wish you could see the meat, great carcasses for anybody to buy – the offal brimming over on to the pavement – animals like elephants. They could have suet every day if they knew how to make a nice suet pudding. But there is one drawback, nobody there can cook. They've got all the materials in the world but they cannot serve up a decent meal – funny, isn't it? It's the one thing I'm glad to be back for, you never saw such unsuitable food for a child – well I ended with a spirit lamp in the nursery, cooking for ourselves. There now – I wish you could have seen our nursery, a huge great room looking out over the garden, with a real English fireplace. Then I wish you could have seen the château, it is different from Bunbury – oh it is. Abroad, and no mistake. Like a castle in a book, at the top of a mountain, you quite expect to see knights in armour coming up on their horses. And warm! Well, imagine the worst heat wave you ever knew in your life, the summer of 1911 for instance, and double that. No, I didn't mind a bit, it simply didn't affect me, though the poor mite got rather peaky. You don't know what heat can be, in this country.'

Sir Conrad gave Sigi a little gun, and with it a great talking to on the handling of guns in general and the manners of a sportsman in particular.

'And just remember this,' he said in conclusion, 'never never let your gun pointed be at anyone. That it may unloaded be matters not a rap to me! And Black is going to keep it for you in the gun-room; he'll teach you to clean it and so on, and you may only use it when you are with him.'

So Sigi never left Black's side all the long summer days, trotting happily about the woods and pooping off at magpies and other vermin.

'There's something I do regret,' he remarked to his mother. 'I would like to show my gun to Canari. It's small, but you could kill a man with it if you got the vital spot. Now Canari isn't a silly little baby mollycoddle, like dear little Foster Dexter, or dear little Georgie in the Park. Canari is a *maquisard*, a brave, a dragon, and he would never sack me out of his *bande* again if I had this gun. They're terribly short of equipment in Canari's *maquis*, it's a shame.'

Grace could hardly bear to think of lovely Bellandargues shut up and empty all the summer and that, for the first time in living memory, the big salon would no longer be the scene of a conversation piece like that which was discovered when Charles-Edouard had first held open the door for her to walk in, and repeated thereafter every day of her visit; Madame Rocher at the piano, M. de la Bourlie at his canvas, and Madame de Valhubert deep in earnest talk with M. le Curé.

She had an uneasy feeling of guilt, exactly as if it were all her own fault and not that of Charles-Edouard.

Also she longed very much for the heat and light of Provence. They had come home to a typical English summer. Rain poured all day on to the high trees out of the low clouds, clouds which lifted and parted towards nightfall so that a pallid ray of north-western sunshine illumined the soaking landscape, a pallid ray of hope for the morrow.

'It's lovely now – we must go out. Don't you think the weather may have turned at last?'

The next morning those who, suffering in their bodies, or, like poor Grace, in their hearts, and who therefore slept little at a time, would awake with the birds to such a glorious glitter of sunshine from cloudless sky upon wet leaves that summer, it would seem, must be there at last. This happened nearly every morning to Grace, who would presently doze off again, rather happier. But long before breakfast the rain would be blowing in fine white sheets across her window, the promise of early morning quite forgotten. She would go down, later on, to the drawing-room, glad to find a little fire.

Charles-Edouard, she knew, had gone to Venice this year. He had taken a palazzo on the Grand Canal and was entertaining many Paris friends, among others Madame Rocher, the Novembre de la Fertés, and Albertine Marel-Desboulles. This had been a great blow to poor Hughie. He had cherished a hope all the summer that Albertine might have gone with him for a motor tour in Sweden. But as soon as the Venetian party offered itself, with Charles-Edouard and all her friends, the motor tour became, for various good reasons, impossible. Furthermore she discouraged Hughie from following her to Venice, saying vaguely that she would be taken up with the film festival. So he often came now to spend a day or two at Bunbury. He was trying to stand for Parliament, but had had no luck so far with the Selection Committees, partly of course, he said, because he was so stupid, and partly because he had no wife. He longed more than ever to be married to Albertine, even though he felt sure that in that case it would be her they would want as candidate and not him. He could just imagine the kind of speech she would make, bringing her point of view, inspired, sensible, and well expressed, to bear on all the problems under discussion.

'I, the soul of the French bourgeoisie, my solid legs planted on the solid earth, I Albertine Labé, descended from generations of timber merchants, who have always given good measure for good money, I have the gift of seeing things clearly and truthfully as they are. I cannot pretend. I feel the truth, I feel it here in my heart and here in my bowels as well as knowing it here in my brain. It is a power, this seeing and feeling and knowing truth, and it has been bred in me by my ancestors the merchants.'

'And I tell you, I, Albertine Labé, bourgeoise, that it is this power of truthfulness and of knowing truth which is needed if we are to rebuild your England, rebuild my France, and rebuild our Europe.'

Just the stuff for the Selection Committees, he thought. There was another line of talk which ran, 'I who loathe the bourgeoisie, I who would rather burn charcoal in the woods than buy or sell anything whatever it might be, I who would rather freeze to death out of doors in the cruel winter of my native Lorraine than sit over a warm fire in a back shop, I, Albertine Labé de Lespay, aristocrat, child of knight and warrior, whose ancestors never touched money or even carried it on their persons because they thought it the dirtiest of dirt, I tell you that I know the truth, I know it here and here and here, and it is this truth, this virtue, this hatred of gold that is needed if we are to rebuild etc. etc.'

The second statement, actually, had more foundation in fact, since Albertine did not possess one drop of bourgeois blood, and her ancestors, a line of powerful princes, had only been timber merchants to the extent of owning vast forests in Lorraine. But the trend of the modern world had not escaped her notice, and the timber merchants were ever increasingly brought into play. Hughie was much too much dazzled by her to notice any discrepancy; both these statements had, at different times, bowled him over, as he assumed that they would bowl over the Selection Committees. He was unable to imagine anybody, even an English Conservative, standing up against the charm and brilliance of this extraordinary woman. With her by his side, to inspire and teach him, it seemed that no goal in the world would be unobtainable.

'Of course I'm glad to think of her in Venice,' he said, not gladly though, to Grace, as they sat over the little drawing-room fire, summer rain fiercely beating on the windows. 'She loves Italy so much, she needs the beauty. Then there is the important work she does there, with the films.'

'What work? She's frightfully rich, she doesn't need to work.'

'She doesn't need to, she does it for her country, for France. She is a moving power in the French film industry with her taste and knowledge and influence. No film is ever made there without first being submitted to her, you know. She has an infallible instinct. Yes, I love to think of her in Venice, but I do wish she would write to me. She won't, of course. "What is writing?" she said once. "Just a scratch of metal upon paper." Well, look at it that way and what is it?'

Grace, whose heart was also in Venice, and who would also have welcomed a scratch of metal upon paper, or even upon a postcard, sympathized with Hughie, but did not quite enjoy his interminable eulogies of Albertine, who seemed to her one of the many causes of her own wretchedness. She wondered if he was aware that Charles-Edouard went to tea with her every day, but was too polite and tactful to mention it.

'Don't you think young people nowadays manage their lives much worse than we used to?' Sir Conrad said to Mrs O'Donovan, who had come down for a little country air. 'Surely you and I would have been more competent than either of those two in the same circumstances, and less gloomy? I'm tired of all the despondency in this house; it's getting me down. Why on earth don't they pack up and go off to Venice and have it out finally with these Frogs?'

'Just imagine having anything out finally with Madame Marel,' she replied. 'As for Grace, you mustn't be too hard on her. I think she has received a terrible shock, and is still suffering from it. To see a thing like that with your own eyes can have really grave results, psychologically.'

'Oh, nonsense, Meg. She ought to have another baby, that's all.'

'Having a baby is not a sovereign cure for everything, although all men, I know, think it is.'

'Anyhow, she's in a thoroughly tiresome state of mind. I can't find out what it is she does want – divorce or what. She says one thing one day and another the next, and it's time something was settled, in my view.'

'What does he think, do you know?'

'Yes, I do. I've had a long letter from him. As I've often told you, I never understood why he wanted to marry her in the first place, but whatever the reason may have been it still seems to hold good, and he wants her back again.'

'Have you told her?'

'It wouldn't be any use me telling her in her present mood; he must come and tell her himself. But meanwhile she goes on havering and wavering about shall she or shan't she divorce until I'm tired of discussing it with her. She's grown up, and she must decide for herself which it is to be.'

'It really doesn't make a pin of difference,' said Mrs O'Donovan. 'They weren't married in church, and therefore neither Charles-Edouard nor anybody else in Paris counts them as being properly married at all.'

'I suppose it would only make a difference if one of them wanted to marry again. The whole thing is thoroughly tiresome and annoying. Well, after the holidays I'll run over to Paris and have a word with Charles-Edouard, that will be best. I'll tell him he must come and fetch her back if he wants her – I don't believe she'd ever resist him in flesh and blood. She'd much better stick to him, this fidgeting about with husbands is no good for women, it doesn't suit them. Hullo, Sigi, I didn't know you were there –'

'It's too wet to go out and too early for Dick Barton, and Mummy and Mr Palgrave are talking about Madame Marel, as usual. If you go to Paris I wish you'd take me.'

'Why?'

'Because I want to learn the words of *A la voix du vainqueur d'Austerlitz*, and nobody knows them here.'

'Oh I do,' said Mrs O'Donovan. 'I used to read them every morning of my life when I was a little girl with a hoop in the Tuileries Gardens. I'll teach them to you if you come along to my bedroom before dinner.'

2

That night Sigi was woken up by a tinkle of breaking glass under his open window. He nipped out of bed and looked down. The pantry window was underneath his and he saw a bit of broken glass shining on the gravel beside it; there seemed to be a light on in the pantry. Nanny was snoring away undisturbed in the next room, so it must be very late he knew; well after midnight. He crept out of his room and down the back stairs, feeling his way by the banisters. Sure enough there was a light shining under the pantry door. He put his eye to the keyhole and saw a man examining the door of the silver cupboard, big and heavy like that of a safe. Now Sigi, owing to a great friendship formed in early babyhood with Atkin the butler, knew all the little ways of this silver cupboard. He opened the pantry door and walked in. The burglar, a small, fair young man, turned quickly round and pointed a revolver at him.

'I don't care for these manners,' said Sigi, in a very governessy voice. 'Surely you know that never never should your gun pointed be at anyone. That it may unloaded be matters not a rap to me.'

'It's not only unloaded,' said the burglar, 'but it's not a gun at all. It's a dummy. You get into a terrible mess, in my trade, if you go carrying guns about.'

'Are you a burglar?'

'Yes, I try to be.'

'I think it's very careless of you not to wear gloves. What about the finger-prints?'

'I know. I simply cannot work in gloves – never could – can't drive a car in them, either. I'm not very good at my work as it is – look at this wretched door, I don't know how you'd open it.'

'Why do you do it then?'

'The hours suit me – can't get up in the morning, and everything you earn, such as it is, is tax free, with no overheads. There's a good deal to be said for it. I expect I shall improve.'

'How about prison?'

'Haven't had any yet. I'm so fearfully amateurish that nobody ever thinks I can be serious, and when I get caught they simply think it must be a joke.'

'Where I live it's not a joke at all, burgling. They come with machine-guns and wearing masks and they generally kill off the whole family and the concierge before they begin.'

'That must make it much easier.'

'Yes. Sometimes they only sausage them.'

'They what?'

'Tie them up like sausages, brr round and round, and gag them and put them in a cupboard, where they are found next day more dead than alive.'

'Where do you live then?'

'Paris. I'm a French boy.'

'You talk pretty good English for a French boy.'

'Yes, and I talk pretty good French for an English boy. Would you like me to open the silver cupboard for you?'

'Why? Do you know how to?'

'Of course I do. Mr Atkin showed me. You blow on it, see. Like that.' The door swung slowly open. 'I always feel on the side of burglars because of Garth. So you go on and I'll keep *cave*.'

The burglar looked at him uncertainly. 'I suppose I'd better make sure,' he said, half to himself, and before Sigi realized what was happening he found himself gagged and trussed up.

'There you see. English burglars sausage people too sometimes,' said the young man, putting Sigi gently on the floor. 'I'm sorry, old fellow, it won't be for long, but really to leave you keeping *cave* would be carrying amateurishness too far.'

Sigi was perfectly outraged. 'All right then,' he said to himself.

The burglar went into the cupboard and began to examine its contents. Sigi waited a moment, then he rolled under the pantry table and kicked a certain catch he knew of. The cupboard door clanged to, and the burglar was trapped. Then Sigi began to roll and wriggle through the green baize swing-door into the dining-room, through the dining-room door, which luckily was open, into the hall, where he lay kicking the big gong until Sir Conrad appeared at the top of the stairs.

'Good gracious,' he said, when he saw Sigi rolling and wriggling like a little eel. 'My dear child,' he said, untying him, 'whatever have you been up to?'

'Ugh! That tasted awful. Grandfather, grandfather, I've got a burglar, in the silver cupboard.'

'What do you mean?'

'Yes, I promise. I did it with Mr Atkin's patent catch – he's in there now. Come and see.'

'I say! Good boy!'

'And he's got a dummy gun.'

'Never mind. He won't dare use that. Go and get Atkin for me, will you?'

'Mr Atkin – Mr Atkin – Grandfather wants you – I've got a burglar in the silver cupboard! Mummy, Mummy, I've caught a burglar! Nanny, Nanny, I've got a burglar. I did it all by myself.'

Nanny, hurrying into her dressing-gown, said, 'Tut-tut, all this excitement in the middle of the night is very bad for little boys. You're coming straight back to bed, my child.'

But Sigi was off again in a flash, down to the pantry, where Sir Conrad was sitting on the edge of the table talking to the burglar and surrounded by quite a little crowd. Hughie now put in an appearance.

'Hullo, Hughie,' said the burglar.

'Oh! Hullo, Ozzie. It's you, is it?'

'That your nipper?'

'No. I wish he were.'

'Wouldn't mind having him for a partner. The child's an expert.'

'I was your partner till you sausaged me,' Sigi said furiously.

'The milk train,' said Sir Conrad, looking at the pantry clock, 'leaves at 6.15. Perhaps you'd better be off, it's more than an hour's walk. Or would you suggest that I should send you in the motor?'

'I wouldn't hear of it,' said the burglar. 'Good-bye,' he said, rather in the manner of one who, leaving a party first, says a general good-bye in order not to break it up. He climbed out through the open window and was gone.

'Grandfather! He was my burglar – I caught him, and now you've let him go. It is unfair.'

'Yes, well you couldn't keep him as a pet, you know.'

'I wanted to see the coppers put the bracelets on and drag him off in a Black Maria.'

'Sigismond, will you come back to bed this instant, please?'

'You were a very good, clever boy,' said Sir Conrad, 'and tomorrow I'll get you a bike with three speeds.'

'I don't want any old bike at all.'

'There you are, these high jinks always end in tears. Now come along, and look sharp about it.'

'Really Papa,' said Grace, when a dejected Sigi had padded off with Nanny, 'I'm not sure you ought to have turned him loose on the community like that, you know.'

'Oh, my dear child, he hadn't done any harm. On the contrary, he spoke very nicely of my article on Turenne in the *Cornhill*, before you came down.'

3

The long, cold, light summer came to an end. As soon as autumn began, warm, mellow, and golden, the Bunbury household removed itself to Queen Anne's Gate.

It was now agreed between Charles-Edouard and Grace, through the medium of Sir Conrad, that they had better be divorced. Sir Conrad told Grace that the situation must be regularized one way or the other.

'You must choose,' he said, 'between going back to France and living with your husband – far the best solution, in my view – or divorcing the poor chap. It's too unsatisfactory to spend the rest of your lives married and yet not married, impossible, really. Besides, I want to make certain financial arrangements for you. I know you never think about money, you've never had to, so far, but you might as well know that I can't live on my income any more. I'm eating up my capital like everybody else, and before it's all gone I propose to make some over to you and some to Sigismond, in the hopes that you'll be able to keep Bunbury when I am dead. Now I must have a word with Charles-Edouard about all this. We had better arrange the divorce at the same time.'

'Oh – oh –!'

'Darling Grace, you know what I think about it, don't you? But if you really can't live with him you'll have to make up your mind to it, I'm afraid. It has to be one thing or the other.'

'Papa, I couldn't just go back like that, it's not so easy. For one thing he hasn't asked me to.'

'He didn't ask you to go away. He assumes that you will go back when you feel like it. He wants you to, I know.'

'It was he who made it impossible for me to stay. If he really wants me he must come over and ask me, beg me, in fact, show that he is serious, and promise –'

'Promise what?' Sir Conrad gave her a very unsympathetic look. How could Charles-Edouard promise what she would want him to? He thought his daughter was being utterly unreasonable.

Grace burst into tears and left the room.

Sir Conrad went to Paris. Charles-Edouard was most friendly, and they had long talks on many subjects of interest to them both, including the future of Sigi.

'One can't tell, of course, what things will be like by the time he inherits,' said Sir Conrad, 'but it seems to become increasingly difficult for anybody to live in two countries. I wonder if he'll ever be able to keep Bellandargues and Bunbury. Oh dear, the ideal thing would have been if Grace had had this other child and I could have settled Bunbury on him, or her. Now I suppose I must wait and see if she marries again, or what happens. I would so much like to have it all tied up before I get too old. I'm quite against leaving these decisions to a woman, specially Grace, who is so unpractical.'

'That wretched miscarriage was the beginning of all our troubles,' said Charles-Edouard. 'She was set on having that child; disappointment I think more than the actual illness pulled her down and made her nervous. Really so unlucky. Pregnant women, after all, don't have this tiresome mania for sight-seeing.'

'She is in a very nervous state indeed now,' said her father.

'Shall I go to London and see what I can do?'

'You can try, it would be the only way, and I suppose you'll succeed if she consents to see you. But I'm not at all sure, in her present mood, that she will. It's as if the whole thing had been too much for her, though presumably, in time, she'll become more reasonable.'

'Very well, I'll try. I'll say I've come to fetch the boy for a visit, then it will be quite natural to have a word with her between two trains. It won't be like a formal interview, which might put her off. I think I ought to be able to persuade her of how very much I long for her, as it's quite true.'

'I'm sure she longs for you. What an idiotic situation, really.'

'But in case this all goes wrong, and since you are here, perhaps we'd better begin to arrange about a divorce. It means nothing whatever to me, as I've certainly no intention of marrying again, but if we are to live apart I'd rather be divorced, I'm tired of people asking where my wife is. So perhaps we'll visit my lawyer. I've had to make a change, such a nuisance, but the old one of all my life was a terrible collaborator and you don't realize what that means. Two hours of self-justification before one can get down to any business. There's no bore like a collabo in all the wide world. So, this afternoon then?

'By the way, Tante Régine is coming to luncheon. When I told her you were here she screamed like a peacock and rushed off to buy a new hat.'

The hat was very pretty, and Madame Rocher was in a cheerful bustle between, she said, the autumn collections, which were simply perfect this season (for some forty-five seasons now they had appeared simply perfect in her eyes) and the Bal des Innouïs. This was a famous charity ball which she organized every other year in aid, not to put too fine a point on it, of her late husband's relations. The Rocher des Innouïs were an enormous tribe, as fabulously poor as she was fabulously rich, and she had devised this way of assisting them at a minimum cost to herself. With the proceeds of the ball she had built, and now maintained, the Hospice des Innouïs which, situated on a salubrious slope of the Pyrenees, not only provided a delightful setting for the old age of the Rocher relations, but also kept them far away from the Hôtel des Innouïs. 'If I must entertain them,' she would say, 'I'd much rather do so at the Hospice than at home.' So strong are family ties in France that, had they lived within reach of Paris, Madame Rocher would have received visits from all at least once a week; as it was she descended upon them every summer laden with boxes of chocolates, kissed them tremendously several times on each cheek, and vanished away again in a cloud of dust and goodwill.

The ball was always great fun, an intensely elegant occasion, and Madame Rocher would cut the photographs of it out of *Match* and papers of that sort and send them to be pinned up on the walls of the Hospice. She often said how much she wished her dear cousins could have been there to see for themselves what they were missing.

'We have been in despair,' she said to Charles-Edouard and Sir Conrad, 'to know what to have as our motif this year. We've already had birds, flowers, masks, wigs, moustaches, sunshades, kings, and queens. Now that darling, clever Albertine has got an entirely new idea; everybody is to suggest their own *bête noir*; not to be her, you understand, but to wear something that suggests her. It is very subtle – nobody but Albertine could have conceived it.'

'What a pretty idea,' said Charles-Edouard. 'Who is your *bête noir*, Tante Régine?'

'That I keep as a secret weapon. I said to M. Dior this morning "If my dress is not delivered tomorrow, Dior, it will be you". Most efficacious. And the lovely Grace – will she be back in time for it?'

All Paris was eaten with curiosity as to the situation between Charles-Edouard and Grace. He had given out that she was paying a long visit to her father, and had never dropped the smallest hint, even to his most intimate friends, even to Albertine, that there was any sort of a breach. She was always said to be expected back in a week or two. So rumours were rife, some saying that she had eloped, and others that she had a disfiguring illness, but the great majority headed by the Tournons maintained that she must have gone into a home for persons of retarded intellect. 'A bit late,' they said, 'but modern science can do wonders. And,' they said, 'it will need to.'

Charles-Edouard was getting tired of this 'coming back soon', which made him look a fool, and he knew that Sir Conrad's visit would already have set tongues wagging. 'The lovely Grace,' he now told Madame Rocher, 'wishes to divorce.'

'Very English, and all in the best Freemason tradition,' she said. 'So now you will have her tied to your apron strings once more, *mon cher Vénérable.*'

Having made this excellent joke she could hardly wait to get home to her telephone and scatter the news that Charles-Edouard was a marriageable unit once more. She was going to have great fun. The little girls of all her friends and relations would have to be lined up and looked over, an occupation she would very much enjoy. Like horses, their pedigrees would have to be carefully considered; certain strains were better avoided altogether, Bourlie blood, for instance, had never been know to do a family much good, while certain others always seemed fatal in combination. A substantial dowry, while not absolutely necessary, never spoilt anything. She imagined the excitement of the various mammas, and thought how amusing it was going to be to see the discomfiture of those who had recently married their daughters to less eligible husbands. In short, Madame Rocher foresaw some very agreeable hours ahead of her.

'Good-bye, *cher Vénérable*, all my best wishes to the Grand Orient,' she cried, waving a pink glove from the window of her motor.

'Well, Papa?'

'Well, darling. Charles-Edouard was most reasonable, as I knew he would be. I like him more every time I see him.'

Grace thought her father looked old and sad, and she had a pang of conscience. This was all her fault.

'You look tired, Papa.'

'Yes, I am. The fact is we had a bit of a night out, last night.'

'I see.' Really it was too bad, at this moment of crisis in her life, that her father should regard the man she was going to divorce merely as a dog to go hunting with.

'Naturally you never spoke about me, at all!'

'Oh, indeed we did. We spent hours with the lawyer, we arranged all about the divorce, the money, and Sigi, every detail.'

Grace realized that she must have been entertaining, subconsciously, a hope which these words laid low, though what hope, exactly, she did not feel quite sure.

'Sigi? What about him?'

'You are each to have him six months of the year, to be divided up as seems most convenient, until he is ten, when he will live with his father during the term and with you during the holidays.'

'He's to go to school in France?'

'He's a French boy, my dear. I've got a letter for you from Charles-Edouard.'

She took it with, once more, a feeling, a flicker of hope. It was the first time she had seen Charles-Edouard's writing on an envelope since she left him. It was very formal, ending up *affectueusement et respectueusement*, and was merely to ask whether the little boy could now go to Paris for a while. She handed it to Sir Conrad, who said, 'Yes. If you consent, Charles-Edouard will come over himself next week to fetch him.'

'Oh of course I do. Only I won't see Charles-Edouard, Papa.'

'That's entirely for you to say, my love.'

'No, no, no – it wouldn't do at all.'

But she knew that if Charles-Edouard really wanted her back he would insist on seeing her, and that if he did so his cause was won. Everything would be different once they had seen each other. Life without him, here in London, had become so grey and meaningless that she was beginning to feel she would put up with almost anything, even the constant jealousy and suspicion she so much dreaded, to be with him once more in Paris. Surely, she thought, he would not bother to come himself for Sigi unless he wanted to see her, and if he wanted to see her it could only be for one reason.

The days went by. Charles-Edouard was definitely expected, Nanny's opposition to another move had been overcome, and Grace's will to resist was evaporating. She kept up a façade of resistance, she did not pack her things, or prepare to leave in any practical way, but the citadel was ready to surrender.

He came over in the ferry, and was to return, an hour or so later, by Golden Arrow. When he arrived at Queen Anne's Gate, Grace (it was the last remaining gesture of independence) was still in bed. She never got up early, and, in case by some horrible chance Charles-Edouard did not ask her to go with them after all, she did not want to look as if prepared there and then to step into the train. In fact she calculated that she could easily be ready in time; her maid could bring the luggage later. She had had her bath, and was very carefully made up.

Sir Conrad's motor had gone to the station to meet Charles-Edouard. She heard it arrive; she heard his voice, and heard the front door slam. 'There's Papa,' she said to Sigismond. 'You run downstairs and ask him if he'd like a cup of coffee in here before you go. Hurry –!'

Sigi was off in a flash. 'Papa – Papa – are we going on the boat? Is there a storm? Can I stay on deck all the time?'

'Very likely you can. Where's your mummy? I want to see her.'

But Sigismond did not favour this idea at all. He wanted to travel, as he had been told he would, alone with his papa, attention concentrated on him, Sigi. If Papa went upstairs, if he saw Mummy, that daft kissing stuff would begin, 'Run along, Sigi', and who knows? Grown-up people are so unaccountable, Mummy might quite well decide to come back to Paris with them, and it would be 'Go to Nanny, darling' all day and every day as of old. Life had become considerably more fun with Mummy and without Papa; it would be considerably more fun to go back to Paris with Papa but without Mummy.

'Mummy's in bed and asleep,' he said.

'Asleep – so late – are you sure?'

'Quite quite sure. She went out dancing last night – she expected to be out till any hour, and strict orders are she is not to be called.'

'And your grandfather?'

But Sir Conrad was away, shooting in the North.

Charles-Edouard considered what he should do.

Nanny appeared on the stairs, the footman was sent to fetch a taxi, Sigi's luggage being far too much for one motor, and the footman and Nanny went off to Victoria to register the heavy things.

'Now listen, Sigi,' said Charles-Edouard when they had gone, 'you run up to your mummy's room, say I'm here (wake her up if she's asleep) and ask if I can see her for a moment.'

'All right.' Sigi ran up, but not to his mother's room. He waited on the landing for a minute and then skipped downstairs again, curling up bits of his hair with one hand, as he always did when telling lies though nobody had ever noticed the fact, and saying, 'No good. The door's locked and she's written up "don't disturb". I tell you, she wants to sleep till luncheon.'

'Come on then,' said Charles-Edouard, taking Sigi by the hand, 'we'll walk to the station. I need a little air.' He felt furious with Grace, deeply hurt and deeply disappointed.

The front door slammed again and Grace was left alone in the house, Sigi had not even said good-bye to her.

'Well,' said Charles-Edouard, settled in the train with a large English breakfast before him and Sigi opposite. 'Come on now, what are the news? What have you been doing in England?'

'Oh, Papa, I've had the whizz of a time. I caught a burglar all by myself – I cunningly trapped him in the silver cupboard – and I've saved up nearly £5 out of tips, and Grandfather is investing it at 2 1/2 per cent compound interest, and I've got a gun and I shot an ill thrush, it was kinder really, and I've got a bike wot fair mops it up.'

'You've got a what which does what?'

'*Un vélo qui marche à toute vitesse*,' he kindly explained.

'Good gracious! And I have to compete with all this?'

'Yes, you have. But it's quite easy – I only want to ride on the *chevaux de Marly*.'

'Is that all. Which one?'

'I don't mind.'

'Ah! But do you know the words?'

The little boy shut his mouth tight and laughed at his father with shining black eyes.

'Sigismond. Do you?'

'I shall say the words when I am on the horse, and not before.'

'Then I fear,' said Charles-Edouard, 'that these words will remain for ever unspoken.'

In the Customs shed at Dover there was quite an excitement. The woman next to them was asked to hand over a coat she was carrying on her arm. From its pockets the Customs officer drew several pound notes. He then began to search her luggage, and produced pound notes from everything he touched, like a conjurer; from books and sponge bag and hot-water-bottle cover and bags and pockets and shoes, everything capable of containing a pound note seemed to do so. The poor lady, white and sad, was then led away. Sigismond looked on, perfectly fascinated.

'She won't catch the boat,' said Charles-Edouard with the smugness of one who, having an English father-in-law, was under no necessity to conduct any illicit currency operations.

'Won't she really, Papa? Why?'

'She's a silly fool, breaking a silly law in a very silly way.'

'So will she go to prison?'

'No, not for pound notes. Gold would have been more serious. I expect she'll miss the boat, that's about all,' said Charles-Edouard. 'Come come, up that gangway with you.'

4

As soon as Madame Marel was back in the rue de l'Université from her summer holiday, which had included a long visit to Vienna after Charles-Edouard's Venetian party had broken up, Hughie rushed over to Paris. He only stayed there two days, returning to London in a thoughtful frame of mind, the very day that Sigi left with his father.

Grace rather wondered what could have happened, but she said nothing and she was not a woman to ask for confidences. As she now felt lonely without her little boy, and as Hughie seemed to be at a loose end, they began to see a great deal of each other. Nearly every week he drove her down to his country house for a few days.

This house, Yeotown Manor, in Hertfordshire, was like a large, rambling cottage. Part of it was really old, a little old manor, but most of the low, dark, inconvenient rooms, the huge beams, the oak doors with wooden bolts and latches, the linen-fold panelling and inglenooks, while quite genuine of their sort, had a certain false air owing to the fact that they had been added to the structure by Hughie's mother out of old cottages which she had bought and carved up to serve her purpose. It had no beauty but a certain cosy charm, to which Grace was susceptible at that time since it was so completely English, so much the antithesis of anything she had known in France. Nothing in it reminded her of either of her French homes, or of Charles-Edouard. She was dreadfully saddened now by such memories, and only longed to put them from her.

Hughie always had a few people at week-ends, and perpetual games of bridge went on day and night. Thump thump thump went the radiogram, thumping its way through great heaps of jazz records from breakfast to bedtime, while Hughie and his guests sat by electric light at green baize tables, drink at their elbows, ashtrays filling all round them, shuffling, dealing, playing, and scoring.

At this time Grace was happier there than anywhere. She had always liked gambling, and now she flew to it as to a drug. Also she missed Charles-Edouard less acutely when she was with Hughie, whose masculine presence calmed her nerves. He had become very much more attentive to her of late; indeed, had she not known about Albertine, she would have supposed that he was courting her again. Onlookers, Mrs O'Donovan for instance, and Carolyn Dexter, assumed that it would only be a matter of months before they married.

Time passed, and a morning came when Grace woke up at Yeotown feeling, if not quite happy, at least without a stifling blanket of unhappiness. This blanket had hitherto weighed upon her like something physical, so that there had been days when she had hardly been able to rise from under it and get out of bed. But on this particular morning it seemed to have gone. Through latticed windows the sun shone on a bank of beeches and on the few golden leaves which still clung to their branches. The sky was very blue, her room was warm, her bed intensely comfortable. When she rang the bell Hughie's housekeeper herself came in with the breakfast tray, followed by a housemaid with all the Sunday papers. The serv-ants there were very fond of Grace and spoilt her as much as they could, hoping that she would marry Hughie. The breakfast was a delight, as it always was in that house, pretty to look at, piping hot, and carefully presented. Grace thought, not for the first time, that it would be difficult for somebody who led such an intensely comfortable life as she did to be quite submerged in unhappiness. There were too many daily pleasures, of which breakfast in bed was by no means the least. Perhaps too, she thought, this English life, so much more suitable for her than a French one, would in the end bring her more happiness. Here she was within her depth, she could do the things which were expected of her, and was not always having to try to learn and understand and do new things. It would have taken her years, she knew, to be able to tell at a glance whether an object was Louis XV or Louis Philippe, First or Third Empire; years before she could bring out suitable quotations from Racine or Apollinaire, write phrases in the manner of Gide and Proust, or even make, in good French, the kind of joke, naïve and yet penetrating, that is expected from an English person. Accomplishments of this sort seemed to be a necessity in France, the small change of daily intercourse. It had all been, quite frankly, a most terrible effort. The English, on the other hand, take people as they are, they don't expect that the last ounce of energy will be expended on them in the natural order of things, and are, indeed, pleased and flattered at the slightest attempt to entertain them.

She often had these moments of thinking that what had happened was really all for the best, but they never lasted very long. Today the reaction came as soon as she went downstairs. Thump thump thump went the radiogram, gobbling its waxen meal. Hughie was already shuffling the cards, the Dexters, who made up the party, already had glasses in their hands, and tedium loomed. The only hope was to get quickly to the game, but even that magic did not always work.

Hector Dexter had just made a tour of the Industrial North, and was telling, with his usual wealth of word and detail but with an unusual note of humanity, of life as it is lived in the factories. In these terrible, dark, Victorian buildings, he said, where daylight is never seen, the people sit at the same table going through the same motions hour after hour, day after day, with music while you work in the background. As Grace dealt the cards it occurred to her that week-ends at Yeotown were not unlike that. You sat by electric light at the same table hour after hour, going through the same motions, with music while you work, thump thump thumping in the background, life passed by, the things of the mind neglected, the beautiful weather out of doors unfelt, unseen. 'One club, two no trumps. Three spades. Four spades. Game and rubber. I make that one a rubber of 16 – pass me the washing book, old boy.'

'Luncheon is served,' said the butler.

A break, while you go to the canteen. Her life in Paris may have been difficult and exacting, she may have been a flustered witness ever in the box, ever trying not to give the game away to a ruthless cross-examining counsel, but it may also have been a more satisfactory existence than this. At least she had felt alive, she had been made to use whatever mind she possessed, and there had seemed to be point and purpose to each day. It had never merely been a question of getting through such hours as remain before the grave finally closes.

During luncheon Hector Dexter went on talking about his tour. 'I'm afraid I must be perfectly frank,' he said, 'and tell you that in my opinion this little old island of yours is just like some little old grandfather clock that is running down, and if you ask me why is it running down I must reply because the machinery is worn out, deteriorated, degenerated and decayed, while the men who work this machinery are demoralized, vitiated, and corrupt, and if you ask me why this should be so I will give you my viewpoint on the history of Britain during the past fifty years.' His viewpoint on this subject was then exposed, in great detail. Hughie listened to him with rapturous interest, wondering how anybody could achieve so much knowledge and such a flow of words – oh would that he could pour out its like before the Selection Committees. He had another in front of him that week. Grace felt more than ever as if she were a factory hand, in the kind of factory where people come and chat to the workers on subjects of general interest. 'We are lucky enough to have here today the important Mr Hector Dexter, who is going to talk to us about some of our problems, their roots in the past, and how they may be solved in the future.'

By the time they were drinking their coffee he had more or less finished with the roots, which were very dull and into which the word 'vision' came a great deal, and was warming up to the remedy.

'Now you will ask me if I can see a remedy for this state of things, a state of things, mind, which I do not only observe and take cognizance of in your country but which I have observed and taken cognizance of in all the European countries, that is to say all those countries in Europe west of the so-called Iron Curtain, to which I am sent by my government in order to form my views in order to acquaint my government of those views which I have formed. Now what you need in this little old island, and what is needed in all the countries of Europe west of the so-called Iron Curtain, and even more I imagine, though I do not speak with personal experience, in all the countries of Europe east of the so-called Iron Curtain as well as in the backward lands of the Far East and the backward lands of Africa, is some greater precognition of and practice of (but practice cannot come without know-ledge) our American way of living. I should like to see a bottle of Coca-Cola on every table in England, on every table in France, on every –'

'But isn't it terribly nasty?' said Grace.

'No, ma'am, it most certainly is not. It tastes good. But that, if I may say so, is entirely beside the point which I am trying, if I can, to make. When I say a bottle of Coca-Cola I mean it metaphorically speaking, I mean it as an outward and visible sign of something inward and spiritual, I mean it as if each Coca-Cola bottle contained a djinn, and as if that djinn was our great American civilization ready to spring out of each bottle and cover the whole global universe with its great wide wings. That is what I mean.'

'Goodness!' said Hughie.

'I say,' said Grace, who was getting rather fidgety, 'oughtn't we to have another rubber before tea?'

Grace did all she could to avoid being left alone with Carolyn, but to no avail. Carolyn came into her bedroom while she was dressing for dinner and was quite extraordinarily tactless; she seemed not to have any consideration whatever for her friend's feelings.

'Well,' she began. 'So what happened, exactly? Didn't I tell you, it's not possible for an English girl to settle down with a French husband and be happy. What finally drove you away?'

'Nothing, Carolyn. I'm not finally driven away. I haven't been very well since my miscarriage, so I've been quietly at home with Papa.'

'Oh bunkum! I know you're going to divorce, Madame Rocher has told everyone so. I don't blame you, Grace, on the contrary, you're quite right. But now there's the problem of Sigi. You really must try and get him away from his father. I think it's my duty to tell you that Charles-Edouard is ruining that child. They're never apart, according to Nanny; he takes him to visit all his mistresses, has him down to dinner, keeps him up far too late and gives him wine. Nanny is quite in despair. You ought to see a lawyer and try and get a court injunction to stop it, you know.'

'But Sigi is a French boy. It's only right for him to be brought up at least half in France; Charles-Edouard won't do anything that's bad for him.'

'My dear Grace! I think it's your positive duty to get him away and bring him up yourself. Don't you lie down under it, show a little backbone.'

'I don't want to bring him up entirely myself. A boy needs his father.'

'Yes well, I'm coming to that. What we all hope is that you'll do as you ought to have done in the first place, marry Hughie. You're made for each other. Then he'll be a father to the boy, who couldn't have a better one. Hughie is through with the frogs for ever, he told Heck, no more sand in his eyes. He'll arrange for Sigi to go to Eton, and make a man of him.'

'Charles-Edouard used to be rather in favour of Eton – more than I was in fact.'

'Rather in favour! What a way to talk about Eton.' Carolyn's family, the Boreleys, were passionate Etonians.

'You're sending Foss there?' said Grace, hoping to change the subject. She couldn't bear discussing Sigi and Charles-Edouard, who were so much in her heart at the moment, with Carolyn. She had been half pleased and half tormented to hear from Nanny of Charles-Edouard's odd new passion for the child.

'It's a little different for us,' said Carolyn. 'Foss is an American boy and Heck thinks an Eton accent would do him a lot of harm when the time comes for him to get a job.'

'I wouldn't lie down under that,' said Grace. 'Show a little backbone, Carolyn.'

'Simply absurd, Grace. You don't seem to realize the unique position of the Union of States to which Hector and I belong. You can't compare them with any other country, because in a very few years they will be the absolute rulers of the world.'

'Oh. So we're going to be ruled by Foss, are we?'

'Yes, in a way. It's a privilege for a young man to be brought up there, as Foster will be. But France is finished and done for, and that's the difference.'

'It may be finished and done for, but it's far the most agreeable country to live in.'

'Well I notice you didn't stay there very long,' said Carolyn, triumphantly having the last word.

There was a tinkle of cowbells, meaning that dinner was ready, and they went downstairs.

Early on Monday morning the Dexters drove away in their huge, sick-coloured motor from which issued puffs of heat and high strains of coloratura. They were to visit some more factories on their way to London.

Hughie said he would motor Grace up in time for dinner. He took her for a long walk and asked her to marry him.

'But what about Albertine?' she said, in great surprise. 'I don't think I want another husband who goes to tea at the rue de l'Université every day. Charles-Edouard always did, you know; how I hated it.'

'You needn't worry about that. I shall never see her again as long as I live.'

'Why? Has something happened?'

'Yes. When I went over to Paris in October she played me a thoroughly low and dirty trick which I shall never forgive. But it did have one good result, it showed me quite clearly that you and I ought never to have got mixed up with all these foreigners; we ought to have married in the first place. The sooner we do so now, forget all about these people and settle down to an ordinary English life, the better.'

'I often think that,' said Grace. 'What was it, Hughie?'

'I haven't told you before because it involves your husband, Grace, but now I hear you are divorcing anyhow, so I can. Well. I hadn't seen her since the summer, as you know; she was away for ages, first Venice and then Vienna. I spoke to her on the telephone as soon as I arrived. She was terrifically loving, I was to go round at six, take her to a varnishing, and then dine with her.

'I was there on the stroke of six, as you can imagine, and Pierre showed me into the little salon there is under her dressing-room, saying she was changing and would be down at once. I could hear her upstairs, getting ready as I supposed, walking to and fro. I imagined her at her dressing-table, going over to the cupboard, trying on one hat, changing it, perhaps changing her dress again. I'd so often seen it – she takes hours to get ready, and then she changes everything again, and so on. I was feeling most awfully romantic, so I got a bit of paper and wrote a little poem about her in her dressing-room and hearing the tap tap of her heels overhead. Fearful rot, of course, but I began longing to show it to her, and finally I thought "why not, I'll go upstairs and find her."

'I went into the dressing-room, but it was Maria, her Italian maid, who was walking up and down. I didn't think much of this, I thought Albertine must be in her bedroom and I went through, and sure enough there she was – in bed with your husband. Never had such a shock in my life. She must have told Maria to walk to and fro to keep me quiet downstairs. You see? Not very nice, was it? But I think that kills two birds with one stone; it kills Albertine for me and it ought to kill Valhubert for you.'

Grace tried not to laugh. The story did not upset her at all. Could she possibly, she thought, be coming round to the point of view of her father and Charles-Edouard on these matters?

'Very French,' she said.

'Yes, and I wish you could have heard her trying to explain it away on the telephone afterwards – very French too. "Come now, Hughie, Charles-Edouard is my foster-brother, we had the same nurse and drank the same milk, how could there be anything between him and me? We were having a little rest after luncheon."'

'Course I just rang off.'

'Poor Hughie!'

'Funny thing is I honestly didn't mind, in fact it was really, after the first shock, a great relief. You see, I'm too English, just as you are, Grace, to cope with people like that. It's unsuitable, we shouldn't attempt it. And it showed me something else too, that it's you I love, Grace. What I felt for Albertine was simply infatuation.'

'I always wish I knew the difference between infatuation and love,' said Grace.

'You are infatuated with your husband, but it can't last, it's not built on anything solid and very soon you'll begin to love me again. You like this place, don't you, and our life here, it suits you, and you like being with me. Then if I take up politics you'll like that; you're used to it, with your father, and you'll be a great help to me. You loved me all right before you met Valhubert, and I'm sure you will again, and you'll like having some real English children with blue eyes and things, more natural for you. Besides, we've both had the same experience now, it makes us understand each other as an outside person never would. So, when the divorce is over, Grace –?'

'Let's wait a bit,' said Grace. 'No hurry, is there? I'm pleased and touched to have been asked, but I can't say, yet. It all depends, very much, on Sigismond.'

'He'll be all for it, you'll see,' said Hughie with confidence. 'I'll think of every sort of amusing thing for him to do when he gets back.'

5

It did not take Sigi very long to notice that life in Paris alone with Charles-Edouard was a very different matter from family life there with a mummy you only saw at tea-time and a daddy you hardly ever saw at all. It was much more fun. He was with his father morning, noon, and night, and all the things they did together were delightful. They went to the antique shops and museums; Sigi learnt about marquetry and china and pictures and bronzes and was given a small cabinet to house an ivory collection of his own. They went to the Jockey Club, and though Sigi was left sitting, like a dog, in the hall, he didn't mind that because he collected small, but regular, sums in tips from various members who thought he looked bored and wanted to see him smile.

'Shall I belong to the Jockey Club when I'm grown up?'

'If I remember to do for you what my father did for me,' said Charles-Edouard, 'and get you in before you've made too many enemies among husbands. Husbands can be most terrible black-ballers. But it's very dull.'

'Then why do we come so often?'

'I don't know.'

On the rare occasions when Charles-Edouard was at home in the evening Sigi dined downstairs with him, and this was the greatest treat of all. He was given a glass of wine, like his father, and made to guess the vintage. When he got it right Charles-Edouard gave him 100 francs.

'In England,' said Sigi, 'little boys don't have dinner.'

'No dinner?'

'Supper. And sometimes only high tea.'

'What is this, high tea?'

'Yes well, it's tea, you know, with cocoa and scones, and eggs if you've got hens and bacon if you've killed a pig, and marmalade and Bovril and kippers, and you have it late for tea, about six.'

'How terrible this must be!'

'Oh no – high tea is absolutely smashing. Until you come to supper-time, and then I must say you do rather long for supper.'

Nanny sat talking with the Dexter nanny, who had come round for her evening off. They had been obliged to put Sigi to bed in the middle of their nice chat, which they both considered an outrageous bore. He now lay in the next room, on the verge of sleep but not quite off, and a certain amount of what they were saying penetrated his consciousness. It was all mixed up with noise from the B.B.C., which ran on in that nursery whatever the programme. Young, polite, rather breathy English voices were playing some sort of paper game; their owners hardly seemed to belong to the same race as the two nannies, so dim their personalities, so indefinite their statements.

'The Marquee never used to look at him when Mummy was with us. Funny, isn't it? It's as much as I can do now to get him up here for the time it takes to change his shoes – thoroughly spoilt he's getting – out of hand. More tea, dear?'

'Thanks, dear. But it's always like that with separated couples, in my opinion. I've seen it over and over. Because, you know, each one is trying to give the child a better time than the other.' At these words Sigi woke right up and began listening with all his ears. 'Nothing can be worse for the children.'

'I know. Shame, really. Well I told Mummy – I don't care for these youths on the wireless much, do you?'

'Not at all. There seems to be nothing else nowadays, youth this and youth that. Nobody thought of it when I was young.'

'Yes well, as we were saying. If you ask me I rather expect they'll come together again, and I'm sure it's to be hoped they will. I know Mummy was awfully upset about something, but I don't suppose he's worse than most men, except for being foreign of course, and I think it's their plain duty to make it up for the sake of the poor little mite. That's what I shall tell Mummy when I see her again, and I shall warn her plainly that if he goes on like this, getting his own way with both of them as he does now, he'll become utterly spoilt and impossible. No use saying anything to the Marquee, he's always in such a tearing hurry, though I must say I'd like to give him a piece of my mind about these dinners – the poor little chap comes to bed half drunk if you ask me.'

It was while listening to this conversation that Sigismond first made up his mind, consciously, that his father and mother must never be allowed to come together again if there was anything he could do to prevent it.

Charles-Edouard always took Sigi with him now when he went, at five o'clock, to see Albertine. She gave them an enormous tea, after which Sigi would play with her collection of old toys and automata. The most fascinating, the one of which he never tired, was a toy guillotine. It really worked, and really chopped off the victim's head, to the accompaniment of sinister drums and the horrified gestures of the other dolls on the scaffold. Besides this there were many varieties of musical box, there were dancing bears, smoking monkeys, singing birds, and so on, and while Albertine told the cards Sigi was turned loose among them, with tremendous injunctions from Charles-Edouard to be very very careful as they were very very precious.

'Why are they more precious than other toys?'

'Because they are old.'

'Are old things always precious?'

'Yes.'

'In that case Nanny must be very precious.'

'Always this young man between you and the blonde lady you think about so much.'

'Could it be Hughie?' Charles-Edouard was very much puzzled. He knew that Grace was seeing a good deal of Hughie now, but had never given the matter a serious thought. 'Did he ever come back again, by the way, Albertine? What happened?'

'He was furious, I've never known a man so angry. I rang him up twice and explained everything, but each time he rang off without even saying good-bye. These English –!'

'How did you explain it?' said Charles-Edouard, very much amused.

'I told him the truth.'

'No wonder he rang off in a rage.'

'My dearest, you know as well as I do that there is never only one truth and always many truths. I told him that you, Charles-Edouard de Valhubert, and I, Albertine Labé de Lespay, had drunk the same milk when we were little, young babies.'

'What milk?'

'Come now, Charles-Edouard, we had the same nurse!'

'Old Nanny Perkins didn't have one drop of milk when I first knew her, and wasn't that amount younger when she was with you!'

'We had the same nurse, therefore, to all intents and purposes, we drank the same milk. We are foster-brother and sister – how could he think of us as anything else? The Anglo-Saxon mind reduces everything to sex, I've often noticed it. Cut three times. Very odd indeed – here is the young man again, keeping you apart. Surely surely she cannot love Hughie?'

'Oh yes she does,' Sigi piped up from his corner. 'He is the love of her life.'

'This is very strange,' said Charles-Edouard, genuinely surprised that anybody in a position to be in love with him could fancy Hughie.

Albertine was not displeased. 'Come here, Sigi, and tell us how you know.'

'When Mr Palgrave is coming to see her, she looks like this,' he said, and did a lifelike imitation of his mother as she had looked after the front door had slammed that morning when Charles-Edouard came to fetch him away. He opened enormous eyes and smiled as if something heavenly were about to happen. 'She thinks the world of Mr Palgrave, and so do I. He gives me pounds and pounds.' He was twisting his hair into curls as he spoke.

'Go on with the cards,' said Charles-Edouard, very much put out.

'Cut then. But why did you not have an explanation with her when you were in England?' she said in Italian, so that Sigi would not understand.

'She was in her room and refused to see me.'

'Unlike you not to gallop up the stairs.'

'In what way unlike me? I would have you observe, Albertine, that I have never forced my way into a woman's bedroom in my life.'

'Take four cards. What a curious thing – intrigues and misunderstandings, just like a Palais Royal farce, with this real old-fashioned villain plotting away in the background. Fancy Hughie being so wicked, it makes him more interesting, all of a sudden. I must send him a Christmas card. What do you want for Christmas, Sigi?'

'I want to ride on the *cheval de Marly*.'

'This child has an obsession.'

'And what else?'

'Nothing else.'

'Be very careful, Sigismond. Consider it well. Do you really want to wake up with an empty stocking, to find a tree loaded with no presents, to spend the whole day unpacking no parcels?'

'Well, what will you give me?'

'You must say what you want first. It's always like that. Then we have to consider whether we can afford it.'

Sigismond became very thoughtful and hardly spoke another word the rest of the evening.

'M.P.'s daughter divorces French Marquis,' Sigi, chanting this loudly, came into his father's bathroom. Charles-Edouard was shaving at the time.

'What do you know about this – who told you?'

'I heard Nanny clicking her tongue at the *Daily*, so I went and looked over her shoulder and saw it. I can read quite well now, you see, how about a prize?'

'You couldn't read a word of *Monte Cristo* last night.'

'I can only read if it's in English, and printed, and I want to. At first the marriage was a happy one – who are the other women, Papa? I know, Madame Marel and Madame Novembre.'

'Be quiet, Sigi. These are things you must not say.'

'*Pas devant?*'

'*Pas du tout*. If you do you'll be punished.'

'What sort of punishment?'

'A bad sort. And you'll never never be allowed to ride on the *chevaux de Marly*.'

'O.K. And if I don't speak, when can I ride?'

'I don't know.'

'So now you can't be married to Mummy again, can you?'

'Yes I can. Tomorrow, if she likes.'

'Oh!' His mouth went down at the corners.

'Why, Sigi? Don't you want us to be?'

'It wouldn't be the slightest good wanting, I'm afraid. My mummy is quite wrapped up in Hughie now.' His hand went to his hair and began twisting it.

'Mr Palgrave.'

'He lets me call him Hughie.'

'How very unsuitable. But is she?' said Charles-Edouard. 'Is she really, Sigi? He is very dull.'

'That's nothing. Look how dull is Mr Dexter, and yet Mrs Dexter is quite wrapped up in him, the nannies always say so.'

'What is all this wrapping up, Sigi?'

'*Emballé*. Like you are with Madame Novembre.'

'Hm. Hm. Get ready to go out and I'll take you to see Pascal.'

'Well if I can't ride on you know what, I suppose that dreary old Pascal will have to do.'

Now that Charles-Edouard's divorce was in the papers, great efforts were made, in many directions, to marry him, and nobody tried harder than his two mistresses.

Albertine, shuffling the cards, said, 'I have been noticing a very different trend in your fate. It seems to become more definite, more inescapable, every time I take up the pack. You have turned a corner, as one sometimes does in life, and a new landscape lies at your feet. For some days the cards have left the atmosphere of Palais Royal and have pointed to a grave decision – two grave decisions in fact – which lead to extraordinary happiness, to a journey and to advancement. Anybody who knew the rudiments of fortune-telling would see these bare facts, they repeat and repeat themselves; it now remains to interpret them, and that, of course, is more difficult. Cut the cards. There now. It looks very much like service to your country in some foreign land.'

'Indo-China?' Charles-Edouard looked puzzled. 'I'm rather old, now, it's only the regular army they want. Still, I suppose there would be something for me, though I can't say I'm absolutely longing to go back.'

'Oh I don't mean that, not military service. All the same, have you never thought that now your marriage is over it might be a good thing to go away for a while? To change your ideas?'

'But Albertine, I never go away from Paris, you know that very well. I go to Bellandargues when I must, but otherwise I can't be got as far as St Cloud even. What are you thinking of?'

'Let me tell you, calmly and clearly, what I see. Cut the cards. I will lay out the whole pack. Now. I see you in a foreign land, a civilized one, among white people, and I see you negotiating, treating, making terms, and driving bargains, for France.

'There is a word for somebody who does all those things – ambassador. Why should you not, in fact, become an ambassador?'

'Me? Albertine, you must be mad!'

'So mad, my love? After all, you have been in the foreign service – there are still broken hearts in Copenhagen I believe.'

'Oh that Copenhagen – dinner at 6.30 – never shall I forget it. But if you remember, I resigned because I can't bear to be away from Paris. I was away seven years during and after the war, and that is enough for my lifetime, thank you very much.'

'I don't believe it. I believe you would like to serve your country once more, to put this time at her disposal, as well as your great courage, your charm and eloquence, and gift for languages. You have extraordinary gifts, Charles-Edouard.'

'Well, but who is going to make me an ambassador all of a sudden?' he said, rather more favourably.

'I could help you there. I am on very good terms with the Foreign Minister, and, even more important, with Madame Salleté. I am practically certain it would be arranged. And that brings us back to the cards. You understand that you would need to be married for such an assignment; an unmarried ambassador (and especially if that ambassador were you, dear Charles-Edouard) is in a position to be gravely compromised. It wouldn't do at all. Salleté wouldn't consider it for a single moment. Now the cards, ever since they have taken on this new direction, as you might call it, have been pointing to re-marriage. An older wife, not only nearer your own age but older, mentally, than our poor dear Grace. A Frenchwoman, of course, who would be able to play her part; a widow, whom you could marry in church. Above all,' she said, lowering her voice, 'somebody who would be able to help you with the education of our beloved little Sigismond.'

Charles-Edouard saw just what she meant. 'Ah yes,' he said, 'but the fact is that I am obliged to remain in Paris precisely on Sigi's account. Presently he must go to the Condorcet as I did, while living here with me.'

'You don't feel that a cosmopolitan education is more precious for a boy of today?'

'Sigi will be bilingual whatever happens. I think he ought to go to school in France. And besides, I don't, I really don't, think I could accept any favour from Salleté.'

Albertine was much too clever to press her point. 'Think it over,' she said, calmly, 'and now, cut three times.'

Charles-Edouard did think it over, and soon began to feel that marriage with Albertine was perhaps not such a bad idea. He got on very well with her, old friend of all his life; she never failed to amuse him, they talked the same language, understood the fine shades of each other's character and behaviour; they knew the same people and had identical tastes. Albertine owned several pictures that Charles-Edouard had always coveted; he would give a great deal to see her big Claud Lorraine on his own walls, not to mention her Louis XIV commode in solid silver. No need for a quick decision, his divorce was not yet absolute, but some time, he thought, he might find out how Sigismond felt about it.

Juliette's approach was more direct. She rolled lazily over in Madame de Hauteserre's bed (the door now bolted as well as locked), her eyes, which always became as big as saucers after making love, upon the erotic ceiling, and said, 'So I hear you have your divorce at last. What now, Charles-Edouard?'

'I'm tired. Perhaps I'll sleep for a few minutes.'

'No. Don't sleep. I want to talk. What are your plans?'

'No plans.'

'Charles-Edouard! But you must marry again.'

'No more marriage.'

'But my dearest, you'll be lonely.'

'I'm never lonely. It's people who can't amuse themselves who feel lonely, another word for bored. I am never bored, either.'

'Shall I tell you what I think?'

'No. Tell me a story, to amuse me.'

'Presently. I think you and I ought to go and see M. le Maire together.'

'And what about poor Jean?'

'I'm perfectly sick of poor Jean. He's the dullest boy in Paris.'

'I thought you wanted to be a duchess?'

'I will renounce it for your sake. I will be divorced and give up being a duchess, Charles-Edouard, and all for you.'

'How would you get an annulment?'

'There may be grounds for that.'

'It would take years and years.'

'But I thought we might be married by M. le Maire, as you were with Grace.'

'Yes, and a terrible mistake too. I will never be married again, except in church. No,' he said sleepily, 'of all the women in the world you are the one I would soonest marry, but, alas, it cannot be.'

'Why not?'

'Because of Sigismond. From now on my life must be dedicated to him.'

'But the poor child needs a mother. And little sisters, Charles-Edouard, darling, pretty little girls, surely you'd like that?'

'Well now, perhaps I would,' said Charles-Edouard. He turned over, laid his head between Juliette's breasts and went to sleep.

As it became increasingly obvious that the key to Charles-Edouard's heart was held by his little boy both Albertine and Juliette now proceeded to pay their court to Sigismond. Juliette employed exactly the same technique of seduction and cajolery as with his father; Albertine's approach, while she never neglected the uses of sex, was rather more subtle.

Juliette gave the little boy treat after treat. She took him to all the various circuses, to musical plays, to the cinema, and even to see the clothes at Christian Dior. Greatest treat of all, and a tremendous secret, she would drive him out of Paris in her pretty little open motor, and when they came to the straight, empty, poplar-bordered roads which lead to the east she would change places with him and let him take over the controls.

'Look, look, Madame Novembre, *cent à l'heure*,' he would cry in ecstasy as the speedometer went up and up. She bore it unflinchingly, though sometimes very much frightened.

After one of these clandestine outings they were drinking hot chocolate with blobs of cream in her pretty, warm little boudoir at the rue de Varenne. The mixture of camaraderie and sex in Juliette's approach to Sigi made her almost irresistible and the little boy was fascinated by her, though rather sleepy now from the cold afternoon air. Presently she said, 'We do have a good time together, eh, Sigismond?'

'Oh we do!'

'You'd like it to go on for ever, wouldn't you?'

'Yes please, I would.'

'For ever and ever. It easily could, you know. I could become your *maman* and live in the same house – would you like that?'

'Mm,' he said, his nose in the chocolate.

'Then you could drive my motor every day, not only sometimes, like now. We'd do all sorts of other lovely things, specially in the summer.'

'Could we have a speed-boat on the river?'

'Yes, that would be great fun.'

'And a glider perhaps.'

'Surely.'

'And I very much long for a piebald rat.'

'Well –' she said with a slight shudder, 'why not?'

'And what else?'

'Let's see what would be nice. Perhaps – little brothers and sisters?'

Sigi took his nose out of the chocolate and gave her a very sharp and wide-awake look. He finished the cup, put it down on the table and said, 'I think it's time to go home.'

Juliette realized at once that she had made a blunder, though she did not know quite how fatal it was going to be to her ambitions, and nor could she know that her words would be underlined that very evening by the two nannies.

'That Madam November,' Sigi overheard, from his bed, 'is a perfect menace. She gets hold of the child, and the things they do – thoroughly unsuitable – dress shows, and awful sorts of films, and he says (not that I quite believe it, mind you, but you never know) that she lets him drive her car. Anyway she fills his little head with rubbish and spoils him, oh she does spoil him. If you ask my opinion it's the Marquee she's after and that's the way she's setting about it, and quite likely it would be all for the best if she got him. Because then little Master Grown-up would be back in the nursery for good, sure as eggs is eggs, no more high jinks, and the young person occupied with her own children likely as not.

'That child's getting ruined between the lot of them, and I don't mind who knows it. I can't do a thing with him any more.'

'Yes well,' said Nanny Dexter, 'none of it's any surprise to me.'

'Papa,' said Sigi next morning.

'Hullo! You're early today.'

'Yes I've got something very important I want to talk about.'

'Well?'

'You know how you're wrapped up in Madame Novembre?'

'So you always tell me.'

'Were you thinking of marrying her?'

'Why, Sigismond?'

'Because she's not at all the type of person I would like to have as my *maman* – not at all.'

'Nothing,' said Charles-Edouard, 'could be further from my thoughts.'

But this was not perfectly true. The idea of marriage with Juliette had been occupying his mind of late, chiefly because, as he said to one of his men friends, it was so dreadfully tiresome always going to bed in the afternoon. However if Sigi felt like that about it the question would arise no more.

6

Albertine played upon the little boy's social sense, already very much developed.

'I have three invitations for you, darling, two parties and luncheon at the Ritz.'

'You know, Madame Marel, I'm very tired of parties. Always that silly old conjurer, he's getting on my nerves with his doves and rabbits. Can't I go to a ball?'

'You want to go to a ball now, do you? But for several reasons that is impossible. Firstly, how would you dress? Secondly, you are too small for dancing with grownup people, and thirdly, as it is not the custom for boys of your age to go to balls you'd find that you would not enjoy yourself at it. You must wait for balls until you are older.'

Sigi's mouth went down at the corners and he looked very glum. He was not accustomed, now, to being refused things.

'What can we do?' Albertine said to Charles-Edouard when he had gone home. 'The poor little boy looked so sad. I must think this over.'

She thought it over, and presently had an idea of genius. She would give a ball for Sigi, a fancy-dress ball, 'Famous parents with their famous children', which would be the most sensational of the season. Her first intention was that parents with their children only would be allowed, no famous child admitted without a famous parent, and, far more testing, no famous parent without his or her own famous child. But this rule led to such shrieks down the telephone from Albertine's many bachelor friends that she was finally obliged to relax it in favour of uncles and aunts. Further she would not budge; nobody, she said, would be allowed in without either their own child or their own nephew or niece.

Never before had children been at such a premium. A great deal of sharing out took place in families. 'If I have Stanislas and you take Oriane that still leaves little Christophe to go with Jean'; fleets of aeroplanes were chartered to bring over nephews and nieces for the many bachelors from Chile, Bolivia, and the Argentine who live in France, while legal adoptions were hurried through at a rate never previously known in the department of the Seine. The Tournons, and others who, like them, had had several children in order to avoid taxation, now sent to the country for them, and these little strangers suddenly found themselves the very be-all and end-all of their parents' existence.

As was to be expected, the Tournons were positively dramatic in their approach to the ball; indeed one night, shortly before it was to take place, Madame de Tournon woke up screaming from a nightmare in which her nursery had caught fire before her very eyes and all her now priceless brood had perished in the flames. M. de Tournon calmed her with difficulty, promising to go out as soon as the shops opened and buy the latest form of fire-escape. Even so this dream, which had been a particularly vivid one, recurred to her at intervals for several days. She was dreadfully shaken by it, and never felt quite comfortable again until the ball had begun.

Of course the great question was how should they go to it. What famous couple, fair husband dark wife, with three boys and one girl, was famous enough for the Tournon family? They racked their brains, they refused all their invitations in order to stay quietly at home, thinking. At last Eugène de Tournon said that they would never have any truly original idea in the hurly-burly of a town, and that the absolute peace and quiet of the country were essential to any such act of creation. So away they went. They had not seen the country, except through the windows of some fast-moving vehicle, for several years, and they came back to Paris saying that people ought to go there more, it really was rather pretty. Their friends were relieved to hear that the journey had been a success, the great inspiration having come to them as they walked down a forest glade – Henri II, Catherine de Medicis, the three little kings and la Reine Margot. Almost every other family of four children had had the same idea. Indeed there was very little originality in the choice of characters; parents with only sons were Napoleon, Eugénie, and the Prince Imperial; mothers with only daughters Madame de Sévigné and Madame de Grignan; uncles with only nephews (of which there seemed to be dozens) Jerome or Lucien with l'Aiglon; families of a boy and a girl Louis XVI, Marie Antoinette and their children, and so on. Charles-Edouard decided upon Talleyrand and Delacroix, chiefly because Sigismond looked so charming in the black velvet coat and big, floppy bow tie of the artist. Albertine, in a wonderfully elaborate dress made of fig leaves, was Eve the Mother of All.

Madame Rocher des Innouïs alone was allowed to break the hard and fast rule about blood relations, but then she was a law unto herself, nobody in Paris, not even Albertine, would think of giving a party without her. She sent for two little orphans from the Hospice des Innouïs. 'After all,' she said, 'I am Tante Régine to everybody at the Hospice.' Two ugly little boys arrived, one very fat and one very thin. After some thought she dressed them in deer-stalkers, white spats and beards as Edward VII and the Tsar of Russia, going herself as the Queen of Denmark, 'Mother-in-law of Europe'. When they arrived Albertine murmured rather feebly, 'I said aunts, not mothers-in-law,' but of course she let them pass.

She was not so lenient, however, to Madame Novembre. Juliette had no possible excuse for being asked, except a niece, the daughter of her only sister who had married a Czech and gone to live in South Africa. This wretched spoil-sport refused to deliver up her child, even on the receipt of several long, explanatory telegrams from Juliette. It must be said that the probability of such a refusal had been taken into the fullest consideration by Albertine when making her plans.

Juliette now became perfectly frantic, and told her husband there was nothing for it, they must adopt a child. But at this the worm turned. Jean Novembre may not have been very bright in the head, but he was impregnated with a deep respect for his own family tree. Never, he said, would he bestow the great name of Novembre de la Ferté, not to speak of the proportion of his income which, by the laws of adoption, he would be obliged to settle, on some little gutter-snipe, simply in order to allow Juliette to go to a ball. He said it was unreasonable of her to expect such a thing; he also pointed out that she was the one who had consistently refused to have children of their own, which he wanted very much.

'Everybody's doing it,' said Juliette.

'The *rastaquouères* and Israelites may be, and who cares? Paris can easily support the presence of a few more Montezumas and Montelevis, it makes no difference to anybody. But Novembre de la Ferté is quite another matter. It's entirely your own fault, Juliette. You have always mocked at Isabella de Tournon for having all those children – I tell you she's a clever woman, and now you see who has come best out of the affair.'

Finally Juliette was reduced to borrowing her concierge's child, a loathly specimen whom she hoped to pass off as the South African niece. Albertine was not deceived for a moment by this manoeuvre, and Madame Vigée Lebrun and her daughter entered the house only to make an ignominious exit. 'Take that hideous child away this instant, Juliette. I know perfectly well who it is – I see it picking its nose every time I come into your courtyard. Off with you both and no argument. A rule is a rule; I refuse to make any exceptions.'

Very fortunately, three (really) famous (real) musicians, all excellent mimics, happened to be arriving at this moment. For weeks afterwards they re-enacted the scene, in high falsetto, at every Paris gathering. It became longer and more dramatic every time they did it, and was finally set to music and immortalized in the ballet 'Novembre approche'.

A pair of young mothers now became the centre of interest. They had risen from their lying-in much sooner than the doctors would otherwise have allowed. (French doctors are always very good about recognizing the importance of social events, and certainly in this case had the patients been forbidden the ball they might easily have fretted themselves to death.) One came as the Duchesse de Berri with l'Enfant du Miracle, and the other as Madame de Montespan and the Duc du Maine. The two husbands, the ghost of the Duc de Berri, a dagger sticking out of his evening dress, and Louis XIV, were rather embarrassed really by the horrible screams of their so very young heirs, and hurried to the bar together. The noise was indeed terrific, and Albertine said crossly that had she been consulted she would, in this case, have permitted and even encouraged the substitution of dolls. The infants were then dumped down to cry themselves to sleep among the coats on her bed, whence they were presently collected by their mothers' monthly nurses. Nobody thereafter could feel quite sure that the noble families of Bregendir and Belestat were not hopelessly and for ever interchanged. As their initials and coronets were, unfortunately, the same, and their baby linen came from the same shop, it was impossible to identify the children for certain. The mothers were sent for, but the pleasures of society rediscovered having greatly befogged their maternal instincts, they were obliged to admit that they had no idea which was which. With a tremendous amount of guilty giggling they spun a coin for the prettier of the two babies and left it at that.

The famous parents and their famous children were now lined up for the entrée. Each group, heralded by a roll of drums, entered the ballroom by a small stage. Here they posed a few moments for the photographers, after which they joined the crowd on the ballroom floor. Very soon the famous parents dumped their famous offspring at the buffet and left them there while they went off to dance, flirt, gamble, or gossip with other famous parents. The children happily stuffed away with cream and cake and champagne, all of which very soon combined with the lateness of the hour to produce a drowsy numbness. Every available sofa, chair, and settee now bore its load of sleeping babies; they lay on the floor round the edges of the rooms, under the buffet, and behind the window curtains. The grown-ups, all set for a jolly evening, waltzed carelessly among their bodies.

Presently two incongruous, iron-clad figures appeared, clicking their tongues, the Dexter and Valhubert nannies in search of their charges. They peered about, turning over an occasional body, and looking like nothing so much as two tragic mothers after some massacre of innocents. Sigi was found in the arms of the Reine Margot; Foss had crept into a corner and been terribly sick. Of course Carolyn knew that she ought never to have allowed him to come, she felt most extremely guilty about it; but the fact was that this ball had had the effect, in Paris, of a bull-fight in some small Spanish town – that is to say, disapprove of it as you might, the atmosphere it produced was such that it was really impossible to resist going to it. Bearing away the little bodies, their faces glowing with a just indignation, the two English nannies vanished into the night.

Charles-Edouard spent most of his evening with Madame de Tournon, whom he had always rather fancied but whom he had never so far courted because she was Juliette's greatest friend. He detested scenes and drama in his private life, and would go to almost any lengths, within reason, to avoid them.

Madame Rocher set her cap at Hector Dexter. She was organizing a gala at the Opéra in June, to provide the Hospice des Innouïs with some new bath-chairs and other little comforts for the aged.

The Dexters were just the people to rope in for this gala, a big box, she thought, and possibly a row of stalls as well. Having been told that one certain way to the heart of every American was through his mother, she said,

'Your mother was a Whale, I believe, Mr Dexter?'

'Why yes, indeed, Madame des Innouïs, that is so.'

'My late husband, who knew America, was entertained there by the Whales; he has often and often told me that their house was an exact copy, but ten times the size, of – let me see – was it Courances or Château d'O? – one of those houses entirely surrounded by water anyhow.'

'This is another branch of the Whale family, Madame Innouïs. There are hundreds of Whales in the States since this family is a very very large and extensive one and I have a perfect multiplicity of aunts and uncles and cousins and other more distant relatives, spread over the whole extent of the U.S.A. and all originating as Whales.'

'How delightful.' Madame Rocher's attention was wandering. She longed to join the group round Janvier, Cocquelin and Daudet, the musicians, who were doing their imitation of Juliette's gate-crashing, Janvier leading in Daudet, Cocquelin as the outraged Albertine – not the polished affair it afterwards became but none the less funny for that – to the accompaniment of happy shrieks from their audience. First things first, however. She turned again to Mr Dexter, saying, 'And have you any children yourself?'

'I am glad to be able to tell you yes, Mrs Innouïs. I have a son and a daughter by my first wife, the first Mrs Dexter, and a son by my second wife, and a son, who is here this evening costumed as George Washington, by my third wife, who is also here, costumed as George Washington's mother, I myself being costumed as you can see, as George Washington's father. My eldest son, Heck junior, is not perhaps quite brilliant, but he is a very very well-integrated, human person. My daughter,

Aylmer, is married, and happily married I am glad to say, to a young technician in a very prominent and important electrical concern. My son by my second wife is now at Yale, having a good time. In the States, Madame Innouïs, we believe in all young folk being happy, and we do all we humanly can to further their happiness.

'Now here in Europe a very different point of view seems to prevail. Here so many of the entertainments and parties seem to be given by old people for other old people. Now I am over forty, Madame Innouïs, but many and many's the time, in French houses, when I have been the youngest person present, and I've never yet, at any parties, seen really young folks, college boys and girls or teen-agers. How do your French teen-agers amuse themselves, Madame Innouïs?'

'They are young, surely that is enough,' she said indignantly. 'Surely they don't need to amuse themselves as well.'

'But in the States, Madame Innouïs, we think it our duty to make sure that precisely while they are young they are having the best years of their lives. Now in what way do the young folks here spend these best years of their lives, Madame Innouïs?'

'I believe they are entirely nourished on *porto*,' said Madame Rocher enigmatically. She decided that she must get away from Mr Dexter come what might, and even if it had to be at the expense of that big box and two rows of stalls. She made a sign of command to Eugène de Tournon, who sprang forward, gave her his arm, and took her to supper.

'Many people don't realize at all,' she said, 'what I go through in order to support those dear good creatures at the Hospice. Champagne please, at once. He called me Madame Innouïs.'

'But everybody knows, Tante Régine, that you are a saint, an absolute, literal saint.'

'Yes indeed, Tante Régine,' said Charles-Edouard, at whose table they sat down, 'we shall find you on the ceiling one of these days, I've always thought that.'

'And where is our adorable little Sigi?' she asked, as a very tipsy Grand Dauphin tottered past the table, followed by Mademoiselle de Blois who, with that high whine peculiar to French children, was demanding another glass of champagne. The innocents were beginning to come to life again.

'That old dragon of a Nanny came and took him away. So stupid. As if one night out would do him any harm.'

'Poor little things.' Madame Rocher surveyed them through her lorgnette. 'I'm glad it's not me growing up now. What a world for them! Atom bombs, and no brothels. What will their parents do about that – after all you can't very well ask your own friends, can you? I suppose they'll all end up as pederasts.'

'Far the best thing to be, if you can fancy it,' said Charles-Edouard. 'Just imagine – no jealous husbands, what, Eugène? None of the terrible worries that make our lives so distracting. No pregnancies, no abortions, no divorce – I envy them.'

'Blackmail?'

'Blackmail indeed! They've only got to write a journal clearly stating what they are. You can't blackmail a man by threatening to tell the world what he has told the world already.

'Now supposing I were to write a journal making it quite plain how much I have loved women – to begin with nobody would buy it, and to go on with it would have a terrible effect on the husbands and I should be in worse odour than ever before. It's really most unfair.'

Charles-Edouard got up to shake hands with Mr and Mrs Dexter, saying, since they were clearly going to, anyhow, 'Do come and sit here. We are talking about brothels, pederasts, and blackmail.'

'You don't surprise me at all,' said Carolyn.

The Dexters, having now lived two years in Paris, had become quite accepted as part of French society, and were asked everywhere. But Carolyn still could not get to like, or be in the least amused by, the French.

'I am very very happy to be able to tell you,' said Mr Dexter, settling into his chair, 'that when our ancestors left little old Europe and shook its dust off their feet in order to found our great United States of America, those three things are three of the things they left behind them here on your continent.'

'Well then, perhaps you can tell us,' said Madame Rocher, 'how, in a country where there are no brothels, do the young men ever learn?'

'I am very very happy to be able to tell you, Madame Innouïs, that the young American male is brimming over with strong and lustful, but clean desire. He is not worn out, old, and complicated before his time, no ma'am, he does not need any education sentimental, it all comes to him naturally, as it ought to come, like some great force of nature. He dates up young, he marries young, he raises his first family young and by the time he is ready to re-marry he is still young. And I am now going to give you a little apercoo of our American outlook on sex and marriage.

'We, in the States, are entirely opposed to physical relations between the sexes outside the cadre of married life. Now in the States it is usual for the male to marry at least four, or three times. He marries first straight from college in order to canalize his sexual desires, he marries a second time with more material ends in view – maybe the sister or the daughter of his employer – and much later on, when he has reached the full stature of his maturity, he finds his life's mate and marries her. Finally it may be, though it does not always happen, that when he has raised this last family with his life's mate and when she has ceased to feel an entire concentrated interest in him, but is sublimating her sexual instincts into other channels such as card games and literature, he may satisfy a longing, sometimes more paternal than sexual, for some younger element in his home, by marrying the friend of one of his children, or, as has occurred in certain cases known to me personally, of one of his grandchildren.

'In the States we just worship youth, Madame Innouïs, it seems to us that human beings were put on this earth to be young; youth seems to us the most desirable of all human attributes.'

'In that case I very much advise you to go in for Bogomoletz. The wonders it has done for me! Why, my hair, which was quite red, has positively begun to go black at the roots.'

'My faith, Madame Innouïs, is pinned to this diet I follow. Perhaps you would care to hear of it. Well it was entirely invented by a very very good friend of mine and its basis is germ of wheat oil, milk fortified with powdered milk and molasses, and meat fortified with yoghourt. Now in my case this diet, very carefully followed over a period of months, has succeeded in strengthening, beyond belief, the tissues of certain very very important organs –'

'The usual conversation of the over-forties, I see,' said Albertine, joining them. 'Let me just warn you all not to brush your faces. Little Lambesé was told to brush his face, to induce circulation or some rubbish, and he is still in his room, poor boy, marked as if he had encountered a savage beast.'

'After all, the face is not a suède shoe,' said Madame de Tournon. 'Is that why he's not here? He told me he was coming as a famous aunt.'

'Yes, and he wouldn't have been the only one.'

'I think it's very hard luck, and I'm sorry,' said Madame Rocher. 'Now supposing I make more money than I expect to at the Gala des Innouïs I will try and give Lambesé a Bogo; if anybody deserves one it is he.'

'I thought the lift had been such a great success, and if so why did he brush?'

'He thought nothing of it,' said Madame Marel. 'If you want that extra radiance, he was told, brush – brush. He did have some particular reason for wanting it – he brushed – and there he was looking like Paul in *Les Malheurs de Sophie.*'

It was past six when the ball ended. The famous parents gathered up their famous children, wilting and dishevelled, as accessories to fancy dress always are by the time a party is over, and carried them away. The last to leave was Henri II, with the three little Valois kings and la Reine Margot, but without Catherine de Medicis.

'Where is my wife?' he said to everybody he saw.

'And where,' said Albertine, more in sorrow than surprise, 'is Charles-Edouard?'

7

The next day, after luncheon, Charles-Edouard and Sigi set out to walk to the Jockey Club, both feeling the need for a little fresh air after their various excesses of the previous night. They crossed the Place de la Concorde as only Frenchmen can, that is to say they sauntered through the traffic, chatting away, looking neither to right nor to left and assuming that the vehicles whizzing by would miss them, even if only by inches. (A miss is as good as a mile might be taken as their motto by French pedestrians.) The skirts of their coats were sometimes blown up by passing motors, but they were, in fact, missed, and reached the other side in safety.

'So what did the Reine Margot tell you?'

'She isn't really the Reine Margot, she's Jeanne-Marie de Tournon.'

'And what did she tell you?'

'Nothing at all – it's easy.'

Sigi was sometimes quite as obstinate as his mother when it came to 'What are the news'.

'Ha!' said Charles-Edouard. 'So you lay together on that sofa, hour after hour, gazing into each other's eyes and saying nothing at all. How very strange!'

'She lives in the country all the year round. She is dull. I was dull when you first knew me and I lived always in the country.'

'Are you not dull now?'

'I am not. I can read and write and do difficult sums and I'm excellent company.

I know all about the Emperor and I can say the words of – oh Papa, Papa, do look –'

Some workmen were engaged upon Coustou's horses. The right-hand one was being cleaned and the other, with the arm of its groom over its back, still had a long ladder poised against the stone mane.

'Papa! Can I?'

Charles-Edouard looked round. There was nobody very near them, and no policeman nearer than the Concorde bridge.

'Do you know the words?'

'Yes. You'll hear, when I'm up there.'

'On your honour, Sigi?'

'*Honneur,*' he cried, taking off his coat, '*à la Grande Armée!*'

He nipped up the ladder and, clambering with the agility of a monkey on to the horse's back, began to chant: '*A la voix du vainqueur d' Austerlitz l'empire d' Allemagne tombe. La confédération du Rhin commence. Les royaumes de Wurtembourg et de Bavière sont crées. Venise se réunit a la couronne de fer, et l'Italie toute entière se range sous les lois de son libérateur. Honneur à la Grande Armée.*'

The motors in the Champs Elysées and Place de la Concorde began to draw into the side and stop while their occupants got out to have a better view of the charming sight.

'It must be for the cinema,' they said to each other. '*C'est trop joli.*'

And indeed the little boy, with his blue trousers, yellow jersey, and mop of bright black hair on the white horse, outlined against a dappled sky, made a fascinating picture. Charles-Edouard laughed out loud as he looked. Then, as several whistling policemen arrived on the spot, he decided to allow Sigismond to deal alone with the situation as it developed. He hailed a taxi and went home. It was quite another half-hour before Sigi dashed into the house with a very great deal to tell.

Photographers, it seemed, had appeared; a man with a megaphone had told him to stay where he was. The crowd, led by Sigi, had begun to sing his favourite song, *Les Voyez-vous, les hussars, les dragons, la garde*. The firemen had arrived in a shrieking red car, had swarmed up more ladders to the horse, had carried him down and borne him home in triumph, shooting across red lights in the boulevard.

'So these words have not remained unsaid after all, Papa, you see.'

'If his mummy had been here,' come floating into the night nursery, 'none of this would ever have happened. That Madam Marel would never have given that wicked ball (poor little mites, I can't get them out of my head lying about in great heaps all over the shop), and the Marquee would never have taken him for a walk – once in a blue moon was how often we saw the Marquee when Mummy was here. Allowing him to ride up on that horse indeed; it's a mercy he didn't fall off and crack his little skull.'

Next morning Charles-Edouard drank the several cups of black coffee and ate the several slices of ham which constituted his so-called English breakfast, with Sigi, on the floor beside him, busily cutting photographs of himself out of half a dozen newspapers brought in by Ange-Victor.

'Now guess what I'm going to do,' said Charles-Edouard. 'Ring up Mummy and tell her all about it and see if she'd like to have you over there for a bit.'

'Oh good,' said Sigi. 'Can I go tomorrow?' He was longing to see his mother, boast to her about what Nanny called the high jinks of the last two days, and see what she could do, now, to amuse him.

'Yes, unless you think she'd like to come over and pay us a visit instead? What do you say, Sigismond? We can always try to persuade her, can't we?'

If Charles-Edouard had seen the look Sigi gave him he might have interpreted it correctly, but he had already taken up the telephone (he seldom sat out of reach of this instrument) and was dialling the foreign exchange number.

'I want a personal call to London,' he said, giving Grace's name and number. He then went off to have his bath. 'Sit by the telephone, Sigismond, and call me at once if it rings.'

Sigi perched on his father's bed, reflecting.

As soon as the water began to run loudly in the bathroom next door he lifted the receiver and cancelled the call to London. When the water stopped running Charles-Edouard heard 'That you, Mummy? We're coming back tomorrow. Yes, Nanny and me, on the Arrow. Yes. Unless you'd like to pay us a visit here, Papa says? Oh! Mum!' a tragic, reproachful note in the voice. 'Won't you even speak to him? Here he is, out of his bath – oh! She's cut off,' he said, handing the receiver to Charles-Edouard, who, indeed, only heard a dialling tone. He slammed it down furiously and went back to his bath, saying 'Go and tell Nanny to pack, will you?'

Sigi went slowly off, twisting his hair until it was a mass of tangles.

In London Grace cried over her coffee. 'Paris wants you' to her had meant that in a minute or two she might hear the voice of Charles-Edouard. But when her telephone bell rang again and she answered it with beating heart it was only to hear: 'Sorry you have been troubled. Paris has now cancelled the call.'

8

Grace now had two suitors, Hughie Palgrave, and a new friend, Ed Spain. Ed Spain was a leading London intellectual, known to his contemporaries as the Captain or the Old Salt, which names he had first received at Eton, on account, no doubt, of some long-forgotten joke. He had a sort of seafaring aspect, accentuated later in life by a neat beard; his build was that of a sailor, short and slight, and his keen blue eyes looked as if they had been concentrated for many years on a vanishing horizon. In fact he was a charming, lazy character who had had from his schooldays but one idea, to make a great deal of money with little or no effort, so that he could lead the life for which nature had suited him, that of a rich dilettante. When he left Oxford somebody had told him that one sure road to a quick fortune was the theatre. With his small capital he had bought an old suburban playhouse called, suitably enough, the Royal George, and had then sat back awaiting the success which was to make him rich. It never came. The Captain had too much intellectual honesty to pander to his audiences by putting on plays which might have amused them but which did not come up to his own idea of perfection. He gained prestige, he was said to have written a new chapter in theatrical history, but certainly never made his coveted fortune.

However he soon attracted to himself a band of faithful followers, clever young women all more or less connected with the stage and all more or less in love with the Captain, and these followers, by their energy and devotion, kept the Royal George afloat. He called them My Crew, and left the management of his theatre more and more in their hands as the years went on, a perfect arrangement for such a lazy man. The Crew were relentlessly highbrow, much more so, really, than the Captain, whose own tastes, within the limits of what was first-class of its kind, were catholic and jolly. The Crew only liked plays written by sad young foreigners with the sort of titles (*This Way to the Womb, Iscariot Interperson*) which never seem to attract family parties out for a cheerful evening. Unfortunately these are the mainstay of the theatre world. The Crew, however, cared nothing for so contemptible a public. Their criterion of a play was that it should be worthy of the Captain, and when they found such a work they did not rest until they had translated, adapted, and produced it at the Royal George.

They took charge, too, of the financial side of the venture, which they ran rather successfully on a system of intellectual blackmail. Nobody in a certain set in London at that time, no clever Oxford or Cambridge undergraduate, would dare to claim that he was abreast of contemporary thought unless he paid his annual subscription, entitling him to two stalls a month, to the Royal George. These subscriptions, payable through Heywood Hill's bookshop, ensured a good, regular income for the theatre, but would not necessarily have brought in an audience but for the Captain's own exertions. Nobody minded forking out a few pounds a year to feel that they were in the swim, but the agony of sitting through most of the plays was hardly endurable. However, if the theatre was quite empty for too many performances the Crew was apt to get very cross; it was the Captain's job to see that this did not happen. He let it be understood that those who wished to keep in his good graces must put in an occasional appearance at the Royal George.

As he was one of the most amusing people in London, as his presence was a talisman that ensured the success of any party (so long as he was well fed and given what he considered his due in the way of superior French wines, otherwise he had been known to sulk outrageously) this exacting tribute was paid from time to time by his friends and acquaintances. There was no special virtue, however, in going to a first night, since the house was always full on these occasions. First nights at the Royal George were very interesting affairs, and the Captain himself allocated all the seats for them. M. de Tournon's anguish over the placing of dukes at his dinner-table found its London counterpart in the Captain's anguish over the placing, on these first nights, of the grand young men of literature and the arts. His own, or Royal box, only held four. Neither he nor the Crew were ever likely to forget the first night of *Factory 46* when Jiři Mucha, Nanos Valaoritis, Umbro Apollonio, Chun Chan Yeh, and Odysseus Sikelberg had all graciously announced their intention of being present. The situation was saved by Sikelberg getting mumps, but only at the very last minute.

Grace and her father went with Mrs O'Donovan, who was what she called '*abonnée*', to the first night of *Sir Theseus*. Naturally they were not in the Royal box, full, on this occasion, of darkies, but they were well placed, in the second row of the stalls. The Captain, who often saw Sir Conrad at White's, came and sat with them for part of the time, a signal honour. *Sir Theseus* was, in fact, *Phèdre*, written with a new slant, under the inspiration of modern psychological knowledge, by a young Indian. Phaedra was the oldest member of the Crew and really rather a terror, only kept on by the Captain because she was such an excellent cook. She was got up to look, as Sir Conrad said, like a gracious American hostess, with crimped blue hair and a housecoat. When she bore down upon Hyppolitus, whose disgust at her approach, as he cowered against the backcloth, had nothing to do with histrionic art, Sir Conrad said in his loud, politician's voice, 'She's got young Woodley on the ropes this time.' The Captain loved to laugh, as he did at this, though really he half-hated the sort of joke which implied that art might not be sacred. He half-loved and half-hated, too, the sort of person represented by Sir Conrad. If the Captain had known in which direction he wanted to set his compass, life would have been that much easier for him. However on this occasion, attracted by the beauty and elegance of Grace, he invited her father to bring her and Mrs O'Donovan back to his house for supper after the play.

The Captain lived in a large, rambling, early nineteenth-century house, built to be an hotel or lodging-house, on the river, hard by the Royal George. This he shared with such members of the Crew who were able and willing to do housework. They lived in attics and cellars which no servant would have considered for a single moment, but which the clever Captain had invested with romance. 'Les toits de Paris' he would murmur, craning through a leaky skylight and squinting at *les toits de Hammersmith*, while the cellars, damp and dripping, were supposed to be the foundations of a famous convent, 'the English Port Royal'. He reserved for himself big, sunny rooms on the first floor furnished in the later manner (much later, some said) of Jacob. Here an excellent supper, withdrawn from oven and hay-box by Phaedra with the assistance of Oenone, was served to quite a large party, consisting mostly of critics and fellow highbrows, such as the editors of *Depth* and *Neoterism*. The Indian author of *Sir Theseus* lay on the floor reading a book and never spoke to anybody.

'What really wonderful champagne,' said Sir Conrad.

'I'm so glad you like it.' The Captain was pouring out two sorts of wine, a Krug 1928 for some and an Ayala for others. This had nothing to do with meanness; he really could not bear to see the bright, delicious drops disappear into a throat that would as soon receive any other form of intoxicant. There were many such throats among them on this occasion.

Presently those members of the Crew who had been engaged upon the more mechanical jobs at the theatre began to arrive. They looked very much alike, and might have been a large family of sisters; their faces were partially hidden behind curtains of dusty, blonde hair, features more or less obscured from view, and they were all dressed alike in duffel coats and short trousers, with bare feet, blue and rather large, loosely connected to unnaturally thin ankles. Their demeanour was that of an extreme sulkiness, and indeed they looked as if they might be on the verge of mutiny. But this appearance was quite misleading, the Captain had them well in hand; they hopped to it at the merest glance from him, emptying ash-trays and bringing more bottles off the ice. The Royal George, if not always a happy ship, was an intensely disciplined one. Like the Indian, however, the Crew added but little to the gaiety of the party. They sat in silent groups combing the dusty veils over their faces and thinking clever thoughts about *The Book of the It, The*

Sheldonian Synthesis, *The Literature of Extreme Situations* and other neglected masterpieces.

The Captain was very much struck by Grace with her French name and Paris clothes, a year old, but all the easier for that on an English eye. He knew about the General de Valhubert killed at Friedland because this General had been a great friend, indeed one of the few known friends, of General Choderlos de Laclos. He took Grace to his library and showed her what he said was his greatest treasure, General de Valhubert's own copy of *Les Liaisons Dangereuses*. It was bound in red morocco with the Valhubert coat of arms, a stag and a rose tree, and the General had written a sort of journal, or series of notes, during one of his campaigns, all over the margins. It was a collector's piece of rare interest. That coat of arms, so familiar to Grace, who during her short and happy life in France had seen it every day on china, silver, carpets, books, and linen, gave her a dreadful pang.

'How strange. It must have been stolen from Bellandargues,' she said, looking sadly at the book.

'Thrown away, more likely. No respectable French family would have cared to have *Les Liaisons Dangereuses* lying about their house, in the nineteenth century.'

'Oh yes, that's it, of course. And then my husband always said they were really ashamed of the Marshal, though in another way pleased to have had a Marshal of France in the family. All very complicated.'

'French people are complicated. Did you like the play?' he asked.

'Yes, though I like the real *Phèdre* better.' It was Charles-Edouard's favourite play, she remembered.

'The real *Phèdre* is wonderful poetry, but, as my friend Baggarat has shown us this evening, it is psychologically quite unsound. Racine's *Phèdre* has two psychological weaknesses – the first is that we can never believe in Hyppolite's love for Aricie, and the second we cannot understand why he should recoil in such horror from this fascinating woman who loves him.'

'Except that she was as old as the hills.'

'How do you know? My guess is that she was half-way between the ages of Thésée and Hyppolite, and still very attractive. But if Hyppolite was homosexual, everything is explained – he adores Hara-See the dancing boy, he loathes the idea of making love to a woman. I think my friend Baggarat has done a very fine piece of work, valuable for the future of the theatre.'

Grace was impressed. She liked the Captain very much, she liked his jolly, careless, piratical look, she thought his house most original and charming, and she was quite prepared to like the Crew. But the Crew despised her and made no effort to conceal the fact. They could not be the clever girls they were without seeing life a little bit through Marx-coloured spectacles, and to them Grace was the very personification of the rich bourgeoisie. They despised the rich bourgeoisie. Her presence in the house made them uneasy, superstitious, it was as though Jonah had come aboard the Royal George.

They sat in a sulky, silent group, combed their hair over their faces and watched the Captain through it. To their distress they saw that he was putting himself out to be as agreeable to Grace as if she had been Panayotis Canellopoulos in person. Why? What could he see in this spineless creature, who, unable to get on with her husband, had run back to her father like a spoilt child? When the various members of the Crew had been unable to get on with their husbands they had struck proudly out on their own, taken rooms near the Deux Magots, hitch-hiked to Lithuania, or stowed away to the Caribbean. She was the sort of woman, with no self-respect, whom they positively execrated. They combed and watched, but if they harboured mutinous thoughts, they still hopped to it at a look from the Captain. In those days it seemed unthinkable that actual rebellion should ever break out on that ship while the Captain was at the helm.

The Captain soon fell in love with Grace, if that can be called love which has nothing physical in its composition. He was not attracted to her physically, she was too clean, too tidy, and too reserved for him; impossible to conceive of cuddling or rumpling Grace. Her stiff Paris dresses, lined with buckram and padded petticoats, in themselves precluded such cosy goings on. He could not even imagine her sitting on his lap. But in every other way he loved her; he loved her elegance, her sad, romantic look, and the serious attention which she bestowed upon everything he said. Above all he loved his own mental picture of what life with her would be like if they were to marry. He imagined a small eighteenth-century villa not too far from London, where great luxury would prevail. Large, delicious, regular meals would arrive with no effort to himself, none of the expense of spirit which it cost him to keep Phaedra up to the mark; he would have a gentleman's library, a first-class cellar, intellectual friends would come and stay, he would be able to chuck the Royal George and write a masterpiece. Later, when Sir Conrad was dead, they would live at beautiful Bunbury. Sex would not play much part in all this. The French husband, it was to be hoped, would have satisfied her in that respect for ever, and after all people could live together very happily without it. He knew many cases. They would just have to sublimate their sexual desires, it was really quite easy.

Grace, too, had made a mental picture of what marriage with the Captain would be like, as women always do when they become aware that a man's thoughts have turned in that direction. Her picture was not so very different from his. As with his, sex was left out. They would live together like brother and sister, she thought, a long, quiet, cultivated life. She saw them as the Wordsworths, in a larger, warmer house, nearer to London and without Coleridge; as Charles and Mary Lamb without the madness; as Mr and Mrs Carlyle without the liver attacks. Visits to Paris came into this picture, since she could not imagine life always away from France, and revenge of some sort on Charles-Edouard for making her so very unhappy. She began to see a great deal of the Captain, whose intentions became increasingly clear.

Sir Conrad was not enthusiastic about either of his possible sons-in-law as such. Hughie was a nice, good creature, of course, but so boring, with his political pretensions. Sir Conrad thought that politics should be transacted, lightly, by clever men, and not ponderously by stupid ones. The Captain, whose company he very much enjoyed, seemed to him altogether too bohemian for marriage.

'Don't you think,' he said to Mrs O'Donovan, 'that there may still be a chance of her marrying Charles-Edouard again? They both adore the boy, surely it's only reasonable to think that they ought to make some sacrifices on his account. After all, so little is wanted – a little discretion from Charles-Edouard and a little toleration from Grace. Mind you, it all depends on Grace. I happen to know that Charles-Edouard would take her back tomorrow, he still wants her.'

'It all depends,' said Mrs O'Donovan rather severely, 'on Grace taking a more Christian view of the duties of a wife. I have been able to forgive her behaviour up to now on account of the shock she must have received, but she has got over that. She is certainly planning to marry again, and is making up her mind whether it shall be Hughie or the Captain. This ceremony, if you can call it that, in a registry office naturally meant nothing to her and marriage as a sacrament is quite outside her experience.'

'Yes, well, you're a Papist, Meg, so that's how you look at it. I think it all comes from a sort of silly pride. Anyhow it's most exceedingly tiresome. That wretched Carolyn with her mania for sight-seeing. I never could stand her, even as a child. The sort of woman who always manages to put her foot in it. Well she managed that time to some tune, it's enough to make you cry. Just when everything was going like a marriage bell. Grace was so happy with Charles-Edouard, and furthermore so happy, which is rare for an Englishwoman, living in Paris. She loved it.'

'Is that rare?' she said with a sigh. 'I know I should love it.'

'Most English people hate living in France. I always think it's got a great deal to do with French silver. They don't realize it's another alloy, they think that dark look means that it hasn't been properly cleaned, and that makes them hate the French. You know what the English are about silver, it's a fetish with them. I've so often noticed it. In the other war the silver at Bombon used to put up the backs of all our generals; they never could talk about anything else after a meal there with old Foch.'

'I like that rich, dark silver,' said Mrs O'Donovan.

But then she liked everything French, indiscriminately and unreasonably, and her life in England, though it was all she had ever known, seemed to her a perpetual exile, so insistent was the beckoning from over the Channel.

9

Grace, called to the telephone in the middle of a rubber of bridge at Yeotown, came back and said to Hughie, 'Most mysterious – Sigi and Nanny have arrived in London. I think I must go back.'

'Don't do that. I'll send the motor for them. They'll be here by dinner-time.'

Dinner had begun when the little boy burst into the room and threw himself into his mother's arms, saying 'D'you know what, Mum – I rode on a *cheval de Marly.*'

'No!'

'Yes I did – look!' He fished some very tattered newspaper cuttings out of one pocket, but somehow forgot to fish a letter from Charles-Edouard out of another. Charles-Edouard had written coldly but clearly stating that, in his view, it was their absolute duty to their child to re-marry as soon as possible. He had done so without much hope of moving Grace, but he wanted her to know quite definitely, to read in black and white, his views on the subject, and to make it clear that their continued estrangement was her own responsibility.

'My darling Sigi – however did you get up there? But first say how d'you do please to Mr and Mrs Fawcett and Hughie, and thank Hughie very very much for sending his motor. No – you don't kiss people's hands in England.'

'Please always kiss mine,' said Mrs Fawcett, 'I love it, Sigismond.'

'Don't muddle him, Virginia, he must learn the difference.'

'Well, Mummy, I got up a ladder the workmen had left. Papa allowed me to and then he went home and left me there, and I rode for ages, it was so lovely up in the sky, and there was an enormous crowd to see me and I recited to them. Well first I said the words, that was for Papa, then we had *Waterloo, morne plaine*, then we all sang *Les voyez-vous*, and then the pompiers came and we had the *Marseillaise*, all the verses, then they carried me down and took me home.'

'I never heard such a thing,' said Grace, with a look at Hughie which clearly said 'Now what? We can never compete with this.' 'Ask Hughie if you may dine here with us as a great great treat.'

'Wouldn't be any treat at all in Paris, I always dine with Papa and have a glass of Bordeaux and 100 francs if I can tell the vintage.'

'You can have a glass of Bordeaux here,' said Hughie, 'only we call it claret, and half a crown if you can tell the vintage.'

He poured it out.

'Quite an honourable wine,' said Sigi, 'but not *grand cru*. I can only tell when it's *grand cru*.'

This remark having gone down, he saw, rather badly, Sigismond settled to a hearty meal.

Presently Hughie said to him, 'What do you do all day in Paris, Sigi?'

'In Paris,' said Sigi, 'I have two great friends. One is Madame Novembre de la Ferté, who gives me treats, allows me to drive her motor, and so on, and the other is Madame Marel, who gives me my lessons. They both give me very very expensive presents.'

'But doesn't M. l'Abbé give you your lessons any more?'

'He did for a while, but he's gone away. So now I have lessons with Madame Marel. I like it far better. I know masses of poetry by heart and we go to the *jardin des plantes*.' Sigi was curling up bits of hair with one hand. 'And what d'you think we saw the turtles doing? Yes, but it wasn't her fault, they only do it once every three years – bad luck really. You ought to have heard them bellowing.'

'Well,' said Hughie, 'that doesn't amount to much. You've ridden a stone horse and driven a car – which you'll do every day of your life when you're grown up – and learnt poetry and heard turtles bellowing.'

'They weren't only bellowing,' said Sigi. 'Expensive presents, too – and a ball.'

He spoke very crossly. He was tired after the journey, more than half asleep, and felt that he had not done himself justice or made it sufficiently clear that nobody in Paris could think of anything from morning till night but how best to keep him amused. However he was reassured by Hughie's next words.

'What about learning to ride a real horse so that you can go hunting next winter?'

'O.K. Can I begin tomorrow?'

'No. Tomorrow is Sunday. You can begin on Monday.'

Grace left Sigi in the dining-room and went up to see Nanny.

'High time we did get back, in my opinion. Such goings on, dear. The Marquee does spoil him – oh he does, lets him do anything he says. That Madam November too and that Madam Marel – they fill his head with the most unsuitable ideas between them. Did he tell you about the ball?'

'He did say something. He's half-asleep, I think.'

'You'll hear it all, no doubt. I never saw such an exhibition in my life, those poor little mites, in ridiculous clothes for children (though I must say Sigi looked sweet) kept up I believe, some of them, till six in the morning. Nanny Dexter and I – the servants didn't want to let us in, but we weren't having any of that – we went and fetched our two away quite early on. Sigi was sound asleep, but poor little Foss, oh he was sick. I wish you could have seen the stuff he kept on bringing up. She hasn't got his little tummy right yet. The usual rush over the packing, of course, and nobody to meet us at Victoria, dear.'

'But Nanny, nobody knew you were coming.'

'There now. The Marquee said he'd rung up and everything was arranged – oh well, French you know!'

Sigismond was very sleepy indeed, but not too sleepy to burn his father's letter to his mother in the empty nursery grate, with a match he had brought upstairs with him on purpose, while Nanny was running his bath.

The fact that Hughie now began to pay court to Sigismond just as, in Paris, Albertine and Juliette had paid court, and with the same end in view, that of becoming his step-parent, was clear as daylight to the little boy. Like his mother he had been quite doubtful whether the high level of amusement to which he had lately become accustomed could be maintained in England. Greatly to his surprise he found that it was positively surpassed. It so happened that Sigi had a natural aptitude for all forms of sport, and therefore very much enjoyed practising them. Hughie, an excellent athlete, gave up hours a day to coaching him; he played tennis, squash, and cricket with him, and taught him to ride. So of course Sigi loved being at Yeotown and very much approved of Hughie, whose stock, in consequence, soared with Grace. Visits to Yeotown became more and more frequent and prolonged, and very soon Sigi was quite ready to consider Hughie as an auxiliary papa. He realized that his mother could never have put on such a good show by herself.

Hughie said to Grace, 'This child must go to Eton – I'm sure they'd make a cricketer of him. Seems waste of excellent material for him to go to some French school where they do nothing but lessons.'

'But he was never put down for it,' said Grace.

'I can fix that, I'm sure. A word with Woodford. The boy is exceptional, you see.'

'Oh dear, I wonder whether Charles-Edouard would allow it. He did once seem to think of it, I remember.'

'It's my opinion that child can do anything he likes with his father. If he wants to go he'll go, it all depends on that.'

Hughie was one of those to whom Eton is bathed retrospectively in a light that never was on land or sea. He talked much of it to Sigi, who began to imagine himself as Captain and Keeper of this and that, and inclined very favourably to the idea. At last Hughie suggested that the three of them might go down for the day, take out his own nephew, Miles Boreley, and let Sigismond have a look round.

'We'll go down next Thursday, I'll ring up Miles's tutor now and arrange it. Once the child has seen it for himself the thing's a foregone conclusion – there'll be no holding him – he'll be as good as there.'

Miles Boreley was a sad little boy. He stood waiting for them at the Burning Bush, top hat crammed on to large red ears, mouth slightly open, large, red hands hanging down. Though very plain, he had a disquieting look of his handsome uncle Hughie. They left the motor and walked with him towards Windsor. He said he had engaged a table for luncheon at a restaurant there.

It was one of those summer days when the cold of the Thames valley eats into the very bone, though the boys who slouched about the street with no apparent aim in view, looking like refugees in a foreign town, did not seem to notice it. Sigi's bright little eyes, which missed nothing, darted from one to another. He was amazed by their archaic black clothes and general air of ill-being. Hughie, bathed in the light that never was, glanced at him from time to time, wondering if the magic had already begun to work. Had he known his Sigi better he would have been quite well aware that it had not. The corners of the mouth were drooping in a very tell-tale way.

They were shown their table in the restaurant and were settling themselves round it when Miles, looking with disfavour at the seat of his chair, asked if he could have a cushion. The waitress quite understood, and went off to get him one.

'Been in trouble, old boy?' said Hughie.

'Only been beaten by the library.'

'Bad luck. What for?'

'Changing the times sheet, as usual.'

'Oh I say, you shouldn't do that, you know.'

'You're telling me.'

'Beaten?' said Sigi. His blood ran cold.

'Yes, of course. Aren't you ever beaten?'

'Certainly not. I'm a French boy – I wouldn't allow such a thing.'

'What a sissy!'

'But do you like being beaten?'

'Not specially. But I shall like it all right when it's my turn to beat the others.'

Hughie said, 'When I got into the library I used to lay about me like Captain Bligh. I had a lot of leeway to make up – we had an awful time at m'tutor's from a brute called Kroesig. But I got my own back. How's the food this half, Miles?'

'Well you literally can't see it, there's so little. We buy everything at the sock shop now. M'tutor is married,' he explained for the benefit of Grace and Sigi, 'and Mrs Woodford has got three children and a fur coat, all paid for by the housebooks, of course, and is saving up for more.'

'More children or more fur coats?'

'More of everything. She's literally the meanest miser you ever saw.'

'Yes, married tutors can be the devil,' said Hughie. 'Mine was a bachelor and I'm bound to say he never starved us, but m'dame used to steal our money.'

'Steal it!' said Grace. 'What a shame.'

'Well that's what we used to say. Rather like Miles and the fur coats, you know.

These Eton rumours shouldn't be taken too seriously, they would none of them stand up to scientific investigation.'

Sigi looked relieved. 'What about the beating?' he said. 'Is that a rumour too?'

'Just take a look at my behind,' said Miles. 'I'll show you after. That will stand up to any amount of scientific examination, as you'll see.'

A family party now came in. A woman, looking incredibly old to be the mother of children in their teens, was followed by two little girls and a stocky boy with a square of pink elastoplast on the back of his neck. They hurried through the restaurant and went upstairs.

Miles's mouth opened wider; he turned quite pink.

'Badger-Skeffington,' he said.

'No!' said Hughie, craning round to look. But they had disappeared.

'Badger-Skeffington!' said Grace, laughing hysterically. She was thinking that, wonderful as it seemed, some man must have gone to bed with that old lady only a few years before, since the youngest little girl was not more than twelve.

'What are you laughing at?' said Hughie.

'Such a funny name.'

'It may seem funny to you, but I can tell you, you haven't heard it for the last time. That boy is an extraordinary athlete; it's years since they've had such a boy here. Tell them, Miles.'

'Keeper of the Field, Keeper of Boxing, Captain of the XI. They'll be having a black-market lunch up there,' he said enviously. 'Badger-Skeffington's mother is a most famous black-marketeer.'

'Are you sure? She doesn't look a bit like that.'

'Didn't you notice how they were all weighed down with baskets and things? Tons of beefsteak, I expect, pots of cream, pounds of butter. That's why they go upstairs, so that nobody shall see what they are unpacking. They bribe the police with huge sums, it's well known.'

'Miles! I expect they have a farm.'

'So likely, in Ennismore Gardens. That's why Badger-Skeffington always wins everything – Daddy says he's literally full of food, like a French racehorse. They're *nouveaux riches*, you know.'

'Now hold on, Miles, that's not true. I often see Bobby Badger at my club, he's frightfully poor, it was a fearful effort to send the boy here at all, I believe.'

'Yes, I know, Uncle Hughie, the point is they are *nouveaux riches* and frightfully poor as well. There are lots like that here. Their fathers and mothers give up literally everything to send them.'

'Oh dear, how poor everybody seems to be, in England,' said Grace. 'It's too terrible when even the *nouveaux riches* are poor.'

'Yes, and while we are on the subject I would like to know exactly why it is they are all so stinking rich in France,' said Hughie, stuffily. He was rich himself, but his capital seemed to be melting away at an alarming rate. 'It seems quite sinister to me.'

'Quite easy really. The French have always looked after their estates. They have foresters in their forests, not just gamekeepers, and their vineyards are a gold mine. In England, when I was a child anyhow, landed estates simply drained away the money – I remember quite well how my father and uncles used to talk as if it was a most tremendous luxury, owning land. There was never any idea of making it pay.'

'H'm,' said Hughie. Were he clever, like Albertine, had he the gift of the gab, like Heck, he would have been able, he thought bitterly, to prove to Grace the undoubted fact that the French are rich because they are wicked, while the English are poor because they are good. As he was neither clever nor gabby he was obliged to leave the last word with her. It was most annoying.

Some friends of Hughie's now came in, accompanied by two charming little boys. They said 'hullo', looked with interest at Sigi, and went through to another room. 'See you later, perhaps.'

'They look rather nice,' said Grace to Miles. 'Do you know them?'

'Who, Stocker?'

'Yes.'

'Yes, he's in my house.'

'Is he nice?' she persevered.

'He's just a boy.'

'Yes, I see. And the other?'

'The other one is a tug. We must only hope Badger-Skeffington doesn't see him. Badger-Skeffington is the scourge of the tugs.'

'What is a tug?' said Sigi.

'Somebody a bit brighter in the head than the rest,' said Grace, to tease Hughie. He was suddenly very much on her nerves. They had been too much lately at Yeotown, she thought, and decided they must have a few days in London, though no doubt Sigi would complain dreadfully at being dragged away from his riding and all the games.

After luncheon they went with Miles to his house, and there they followed him through a rabbit warren of passages and up and down little dark staircases. A deathly silence reigned.

'How empty it all seems,' said Grace. 'Where's everybody?'

'Having boys' dinner.'

'Very late.'

'Yes, well, it doesn't make much difference. Late or early there's literally nothing to eat.'

Miles's room, when they finally got to it, was extraordinarily bare and bleak. The walls were beige, the window curtains orange, and a black curtain hung from ceiling to floor in one corner. Over the empty fireplace there was a valedictory poem, illuminated and framed, on the closing of the Derby racecourse.

> There'll be no more racing at Derby
> It rings indeed like a knell, etc., etc.

It was terribly cold, colder than winter. Grace sat on the only chair, huddling into her fur coat, and the others stood round her as if she were a stove.

'Is this your bedroom?' Sigi said, taking in every detail.

'Yes, of course.'

'Is there a bed?' If he had been told that Miles slept on a heap of rags on the floor, like the concierges in Poland, he would not have been at all surprised.

'Here, of course,' said Miles scornfully. He lifted the black curtain to disclose an iron instrument against the wall. 'You pull it down at night, and the boys' maid makes it. And now, Uncle Hughie, if you'll excuse me, I must go off and do my time. Will you wait here or what?'

'I'm so terribly cold,' Grace said imploringly to Hughie. 'Couldn't we go home?'

'Well, rather bad luck on Miles when we've come to take him out. His time won't last more than three-quarters of an hour, you know.'

'Give him two pounds, he won't mind a bit,' she whispered.

'Oh I say, Uncle Hughie, thanks very much. Are you going, then?' he said, in tones of undisguised relief. 'Good-bye. Will you excuse me? – I shall be late.' He clattered away down the passage.

'Really, Grace – two pounds! I usually give him ten bob.'

'I'll go shares,' she said, 'put it on the bridge book. Worth it to me, I was dying of cold simply.'

The visit to Eton finished off Hughie's chances of marrying Grace for ever. Sigismond had seen a red light, and immediately took action.

'Mummy!'

'Hullo – you're early this morning!'

'Well yes, I've got something rather important to say. You know Hughie?'

'Yes.'

'Were you thinking of marrying him?'

'Why, darling?'

'The Nannies always say you will.'

'Would you like me to?'

'That's just the point. I would not.'

'Oh – Sigi –!'

'No use pretending, I would not.'

'Very well, darling. I promise I'll never marry anybody you don't like. And now just go and tell Nanny to pack, will you? We're going up to London after luncheon.'

Sigi gave his mother a nice hug and trotted off. He was not at all dissatisfied to find himself later in the day on the road back to London. The riding and the games had been great fun, but if they were to lead to the prison house, whose shades he had now seen for himself, they simply were not worth it.

10

All this time the Captain had been going on with his pursuit of Grace, and of course he too had seen that, if there were a way to her heart, that heart so curiously absent, it would be through Sigismond.

'Bring him to *Sir Theseus* on Thursday afternoon,' he said.

'My dear Captain – is *Phèdre* very suitable for little boys?'

'*Exquise* Marquise, what about the Matinée Classique at the Français – is it not full of little boys seeing *Phèdre*?'

'All right then,' she said. It was a comfort to her to be with somebody who knew about the Matinée Classique and other features of French life. Hughie, in spite of all his efforts to educate himself in the Albertine days, had never really got much further than the Ritz bar, and now his love for everything French had turned to unreasonable hatred. Whenever Grace spoke to him of France he would say horrid little things which annoyed her. Like many large, bluff, and apparently good-natured men, Hughie had a malevolent side to his character, and knew exactly how to stick a pin where it hurt. He was always exceedingly catty about the Captain, who spoke, however, rather charmingly of him.

'Why does he hate her so much?' asked Sigi, as Hyppolitus recoiled in homosexual horror before the advancing Phaedra.

'Because she's his stepmother.'

'Oh. If Papa married Madame Marel would she be my stepmother and would I hate her?'

'Sh – darling, don't talk so loud, it's rude to the actors.'

She couldn't very well have said it was disturbing to the audience. A beautiful, hot day, one of the very few that summer, had not been helpful in filling the Matinée Classique with little scholars of modern psychological drama, and the theatre was empty. Three or four members of the Crew sat about, balefully watching Grace through their hair; the Captain, who always said he preferred to see his plays from the back of the gallery, an excellent alibi, was having a guilty sun-bath on the roof of his house.

'Mum?' Sigi was wriggling about, bored.

'Yes?'

'Where's Hyppolitus's own mummy?'

'I'm not sure, I think she's dead, we must ask the Captain.'

'Mummy? Sir Theseus what?'

'You must ask the Captain that too.'

'Well – what's happened to Hyppolitus now?'

'Darling, try and pay attention. Didn't you hear Theramenus saying how he had fallen off his bicycle and been run over by a lorry?'

'Coo! Phaedra is upset and no mistake.'

'Don't say coo. I'm always telling you.'

'Mummy, why has Sir Theseus adopted Hara-See?'

'I suppose he feels rather lonely, now everybody seems to be dead.'

'Will he have to make over some of his money to Hara-See?'

'I don't know. Here's the Captain, you must ask him.'

The Captain took them backstage and showed them the machinery, switchboard, and so on, all of which interested Sigi a great deal more than the play. After this he was allowed the run of the Royal George, to the displeasure of the younger members of the Crew, who had seen through their hair exactly how the land lay. Phaedra, however, took a great fancy to Sigi and spoilt him.

The Captain's courtship, meanwhile, was not making much real progress. He was hampered in it by Grace's failure to attract him sexually, by a shyness and feeling of discomfort in her presence that he never seemed to get over. While it may be possible to do without sex in married life, he began to realize that it is very difficult to propose to a beautiful young woman without ever having had any physical contact with her. A little rumpling and cuddling bridges many an awkward gulf. In fact it now seemed to him as if the impossibility of cuddling Grace was endangering his whole heavenly scheme. He blamed her bitterly for it. Why should she be so stiff and remote? Why not unbend, make things easier for him? It was very hard. He had thought so much, during many a wakeful night, of all that marriage with her would bring. The laurels of Madame Victoire, the griffins and castles of Madame de Pompadour, the dolphins and the fleur-de-lis; Château Yquem, Chambolle-Musigny, Mouton Rothschild. He could feel, he could see, he could taste them. Sometimes he thought that he would break down and cry like a child if all this and much more were to elude his grasp, simply because of his inability to grasp the waist of Grace.

Nothing was going well for the Captain at this time. Subscriptions to the Royal George were falling off at a disquieting rate, various creditors were pressing their claims, *Sir Theseus* could obviously not be made to run much longer, and, worst of all, the Crew was in a chronic bad temper. Only old Phaedra was nice to him now, but her varicose veins had got worse and the doctor said she must give up the kitchen while she was playing this long and arduous role. So he was at the mercy of the others for his comforts, and they gave expression to their feelings through the medium of housework. Smash and burn were the order of the day. His home life had never been so wretched.

It now became imperative to find another play with which to replace *Sir Theseus*. The Crew pushed their hair out of their eyes and read quantities of manuscripts, many of them in the original Catalan, Finnish, or Bantu, and wrote résumés of them for the Captain to see. He had told them, and indeed in their hearts they knew it, that this time they must put on something which would sell a few seats. 'For once,' he said, 'try and find a play with a plot. I believe that would help. Something, for once, that the critics could understand.'

One bright spot in the Captain's life just then was how well he was getting on with Sigismond. The little boy hung about the theatre, thoroughly stage-struck, and told his mother, who of course repeated it, that he revered the Captain second only to M. l'Abbé.

The Captain, on his side, was entranced. Knowing as he did no children of that age, Sigi appeared to him a perfect miracle of grace and intelligence. He kept begging to be given a part in a play, and the Captain thought that, if something suitable could be found, it would be from every point of view a good idea. The child had received a great deal of publicity for having ridden the *cheval de Marly*, he was very pretty, possibly very talented, and the whole thing would bring the Captain into continual contact with Grace. Sitting with her in his box on the first night, both feeling rather emotional, it might suddenly become possible for him to take her hand, to press her knee, even to implant a kiss on a naked shoulder when nobody was looking.

Now it so happened that a certain member of the Crew had been teasing the Captain for quite a long time to put on a play she had translated from some Bratislavian dialect, and of which the protagonist was a little boy of ten. The Captain had read her translation, which, he thought, probably failed to convey the fiery poetry and political subtleties of the original. In English it seemed rather dreary. But now this play was being very much discussed on the Continent. It was put on in Paris, where it had a mixed reception, and was said to have run clandestinely for several months in Lvov. The Captain, with Sigi in mind, decided to have another look at it.

It was called *The Younker*. An old Communist, whose days had been spent wringing a livelihood from the bitter marsh land round his home, lay on his bed, ageing. He lay alone because, so ungovernable was his temper, no human dared approach him. His dog, a famous mangler, lay snarling by the empty hearth. His only son had married a foreign Fascist woman; for this he had turned him out. The son had gone to the foreign Fascist woman's land and there had died. The old man kept his savings in gold in a pot under his bed, and it came upon him that he would like to give this pot, before he died and before the Party got it, to his son's son, and that he would like to see this child before his old eyes failed. The younker arrived. He was a manly little fellow, not at all awed by his grandfather's ungovernable rages, or by his grandfather's dog, the mangler. Indeed he went everywhere with his little hand resting on its head. He brought love into that house, and presently he brought his mother, the Fascist woman, and she made the bed, which had never been made before. And by degrees this child, this innocent, loving little creature, bridged even the great political gap between his mother and his grandfather. They joined a middle-of-the-road party and all ended in happiness.

The Captain began to see possibilities in this play if it could be altered and adapted according to an idea he had, and put on with Sigi in the name part. The great difficulty would be to get round the Crew; if only he could achieve that he foresaw a box-office success at last.

He called a conference on the stage after the Saturday matinée. The Crew sat about in high-necked sweaters, shorts, and bare, blue feet, their heads bowed and their faces entirely obscured by the curtain of hair. Though he did not know it, they were in a dangerous mood. They had hardly set eyes on the Captain of late, either at home or in his theatre; he had been, they knew, to many parties, in rich, bourgeois houses, with Grace. Rumour even had it that he had been seen in Sir Conrad's box at the Ascot races. None of this had done him much good with his Crew.

The Captain began by saying that it was quite essential for the Royal George to have a monetary success. If it did not, he pointed out, they would no longer be able to satisfy their serious public with plays that they alone were brave enough to produce. They would, in fact, be obliged to shut their doors and put out their lights and close, leaving a very serious gap in the intellectual life of London. The Crew knew that all this was so. They sat quite still listening. The Captain went on to praise Fiona very highly for her translation of *The Younker*. He said he had been re-reading it, that it was very good, that he thought it would do. He then branched off into a disquisition on the psychology of audiences through the ages.

'The two greatest dramatists of the modern world,' he said, 'are Shakespeare and Racine.'

There was no sign of life from the figures round him; faceless and dumb, bowed immovably over their bare, blue feet, they waited for him to go on. The Captain knew that had he said Sartre and Lorca there would have been some response, a tremor, perhaps, parting the silky blonde curtains, or a nodding of the veiled heads. No such tremor, no such nodding, occurred. He began to feel nervous, to wonder whether he was going to fail in what he was attempting. But he had never failed, as yet, to master his Crew, and he thought all would be well.

'Now Shakespeare and Racine,' he went on, nervously for him, 'understood the psychology of the playgoer, and they both knew that there are two things that audiences cannot resist. The first (and if we are to take a lesson from these great men, as I think we should, this will give scope to Ulra when designing her set) is the appeal of the past. The second, I am afraid, discloses a weakness in human nature, a weakness which exists as strongly today as it did in the seventeenth century. Not to put too fine a point on it, audiences like a lord. Shakespeare knew what he was about, that can't be denied. You'll hardly find a single commoner in Shakespeare's plays, and when they do occur he doesn't even trouble to invent names for them. 1st gravedigger, 2nd soldier, and so on. You'd think he might have written some very penetrating studies of the burghers of Stratford, he must have had plenty of copy. Not a bit. Kings and lords, queens and ladies made up his dramatis personae. Webster the same. And who's to say they're wrong? "I am Duchess of Malfi still" makes us cry. "I am Mrs Robinson still" wouldn't be at all the same thing.'

The Crew did not raise a titter at this joke, and the Captain had an uneasy feeling it had probably been made before. He hoped he was not losing his grip, and hurried on,

'As for Racine, his heroes and heroines are usually Imperial.

'Now I say that what was good enough for the Globe and the Théâtre Royal is good enough for the Royal George. Supposing, Fiona dear, that you were to rewrite *The Younker*, to set it in an English country house in the nineties, to change the violent old Communist into a violent old Earl? Write the part of the boy for our adorable little Sigismond – he should prove a tremendous attraction. If you do all this, as only you can, Fiona, if Ulra makes a really amusing set for it – a Victorian castle, Ulra, in the Gothic style, lace collar, velvet suit for the Younker – I think I can prophesy certain success. I think we could count on six months with the house packed. After that we shall be able to go on with what we are trying to do in this theatre, don't be afraid that I've lost sight of that. I won't keep you now,' he looked at his watch, 'I have to go to London, but I will be home for dinner.' They always dined after the evening performance in the Captain's house. 'We can talk it over then –'

Not a movement, the curtained figures sat as in a trance. He did not quite like it, but was not seriously alarmed; he had weathered too many a storm in that ship with that Crew, those hearts of oak.

When the Captain arrived home rather late for dinner the house was in darkness, and empty as the *Marie Céleste*. There were signs of recent human activity, a meal had evidently just been eaten and not cleared away, but nobody was there.

The Captain supposed that his Crew must have gone on shore. They sometimes did so of an evening and always, on these occasions, left some delectable titbit sizzling in the oven for him. But the kitchen was in darkness, the oven cold and bare. He peered into the bedroom usually occupied by Ulra to see if a sulking figure were not perhaps lolling on the bed. If so it must be stirred up, made to minister to his needs. Not only was there no sulking figure, but nylon hairbrush and broken comb had vanished from the dressing-table, crumpled underclothes no longer brimmed from half-open drawers, duffel coats and ragged ball dresses no longer bulged behind the corner curtain, there were no old shoes lying about on the deal floor and no old hats on the deal shelf. Ulra had clearly gone, and taken all her belongings. Down in the Port Royal, up beneath the Toits de Paris, the same state of affairs existed in every bedroom. The Captain's heart sank within him. This was desertion. Mutiny he could have dealt with, his dreaded cat o' nine tails, sarcasm, had but to be seen by the Crew for them to come to heel, but desertion was far more serious. They had almost certainly, he knew, gone off in a body to join the staff of Neoterism.

The Captain passed a sleepless night, during which he decided that there was only one course left for him to take. He must go and see Grace and persuade her to marry him. Not a bad thing, perhaps, to do it on an impulse, though he would have preferred to lead up to it with the triumphant success on the boards of Sigismond. He must try and whirl her to a registry office before either she or he had any more chance of thinking it over. Thinking it over was no good now, the time had come for action. Breakfastless, feeling rather sea-sick, the Captain set out for Queen Anne's Gate.

Now it so happened that on this particular day Grace had woken up sadder and more hopeless than at any time since leaving Paris. Her divorce had just become absolute, and she had finished her carpet. She had made a sort of bet with herself that before these two things happened there would have been a sign from Charles-Edouard; none had come. The weather, which always affected her spirits, remained terrible, as it had been so far the whole summer. Day after day it was a question of putting on winter clothes and crowning them, for no other reason than that the month was June, with a straw hat, through which the cold wind whistled horribly. She was putting on one of these hats to go out to a dull luncheon when her maid came in and said that the Captain was downstairs. This news cheered her up.

'Give him a glass of vodka – I'm just coming.'

The Captain was already pouring vodka down his throat in great gulps like a Russian and feeling much more confident that all would yet be well. The door opened, and, instead of Grace, Sigismond appeared.

'Good morning, Old Salt,' he said, too cockily for a child of his age the Captain thought, irritated. He must get rid of him, he had got to see Grace alone while the action of the vodka on his doubly empty stomach (no dinner, no breakfast) was having its excellent effect.

'And when do I go into rehearsal, Cap?'

This was too much for the Captain's nerves. He took Sigi by the shoulder, propelled him to the door, gave him a sharp push and said,

'It's your Mummy I want to see, not you. Run along to Nanny, there's a good boy.'

Sigi gave him a very baleful glance. Aware that he had done himself no good, the Captain felt about in his pocket. He had a shilling and a fiver, and if one seemed too little the other seemed immeasurably too much. He fished out the shilling, which Sigi pocketed without a word, going furiously upstairs. Nobody had ever insulted him with so small a coin in his life before.

Grace appeared. She looked very pretty and was pleased to see the Captain, quite approachable, he thought. He took the plunge.

'I've come on an impulse, to ask you to marry me, Grace.'

'Good heavens, Captain!'

'I suppose you think I ought to lead up to it, pave the way, break it like bad news. I don't. We're both grown-up people, and I think if I want to marry you the easiest thing is to say so straight out.'

'Yes. I expect you're quite right.'

'And please don't think it over. I hate the sort of people who are forever thinking things over, horrid, calculating thoughts. Say yes now – and I'll go off and get a licence.'

Grace was seriously tempted to do so. She was feeling furious with Charles-Edouard, with his attitude of 'come back whenever you like but don't expect me to bother about you, or make it any easier for you', and with his manner of conveying it to her, indirectly, through Sir Conrad. Why did he never telephone, write, or make any direct approach? It was intolerable. She felt it would punish him if she were to marry the Captain, brilliant, sparkling, friend of Paris intellectuals, much more than if she were to marry someone like Hughie. Hughie could only be a stopgap, the Captain might well be a great new love.

'I don't want to think it over,' she said, 'but I shall have to consult Sigismond.'

The Captain was very much taken aback. 'Consult Sigi?'

'Oh Captain, if Sigi didn't like it I could never do it, you know. I've given him my word never to marry without asking him first.'

'It's mad. Little boys of that age change their ideas every few minutes – he might say yes one day and no the next, it would mean nothing at all. According to whether – well for instance according to whether one had last tipped him with a shilling or five pounds. Sigi is very fond of me, you must have noticed that for yourself. I shan't turn out to be a Mr Murdstone, I can assure you – I am good-natured and I love children. I tell you this, so it must be true. What people say about themselves is always true. When they say "Don't fall in love with me, I shall make you very unhappy" you must believe them, just as you must believe me when I tell you that both you and Sigi will have happy lives once you are married to me. Quiet, uneventful, but happy.'

'Oh I do, Captain, I do believe it. I've known it really for a long time.'

As Grace said this she looked positively cuddlable, and the Captain was about to press her to his bosom when she saw the time, gave a tremendous jump, said she was half an hour late for luncheon already and fled – shouting from the staircase 'Come back at tea-time.'

'Tell me something, Sigi. You love the Captain, darling, don't you?'

'Shall I tell you what I think of the Captain?'

'Yes, that's what I'm asking you.'

'I think he's a bloody bastard, so there.'

'Sigismond – go to bed this instant. Nanny – Nanny –' Grace was running furiously upstairs, 'Please put Sigismond to bed without any supper and without Dick Barton. I won't have it, Sigi, you're not to speak of grown-up people like that, do you understand? Oh no, it's too much,' and she burst into tears. She had quite made up her mind that she was going to marry the Captain and now this consolation was to be denied her.

Sigi, rather puzzled and very cross, received pains and penalties, but he had hit his target first. That night the Captain left London, alone, for France. The Royal George had gone down, without her crew complete. Her new owner, having repainted, furbished up, and rechristened her, more in the spirit of the age, The Broadway, opened triumphantly that autumn with a dramatization of *Little Lord Fauntleroy*.

II

Madame Rocher des Innouïs, as old ladies sometimes do, now got an idea into her head, and decided that she would not rest until she had seen it carried out. The idea was that Grace and Charles-Edouard must be brought together again, must be married properly this time, that Grace must be converted, that they must have more children, and do their duty by the one they had already. The present situation had become impossible. Charles-Edouard quite clearly had no intention of marrying any of the nice, suitable girls vetted and presented by his aunt, and was now in trouble with half the husbands of Paris. Grace, according to information received by Madame Rocher through the French Embassy in London, was contemplating remarriage with some very unsuitable sailor, and the child was being outrageously spoilt on both sides of the Channel. Bad enough that a Valhubert should be written about and photographed in *Samedi Soir*, it now seemed that his mother contemplated putting him on the London stage, while Sir Conrad, whom Madame Rocher loved but whom she did not trust a yard, was no doubt initiating him into the terrible rites of Freemasonry. Charles-Edouard's heir was on the way to becoming a publicity-monger, an actor, and a Nihilist; what must poor Françoise be thinking?

Madame Rocher took action. She arrived in London to stay with the French Ambassador, sent for Grace, and weighed in at once with what she had to say.

'Grace, my child, it is your duty to return to Paris and marry Charles-Edouard. Picture this unfortunate man, lonely, unhappy, reduced to pursuing the wives of all his friends, forced to go to bed at the most inconvenient times, and always with the risk of his motive being misunderstood. He may find himself trapped into some perfectly incongruous marriage before we know where we are. Then think of your little boy, brought up like this between the two of you, no continuity in his education. Nothing can be worse for a child than these six months of hysterical spoiling from each of you in turn. You are very reasonable, Grace dear, surely you must understand where it is that your duty lies.

'I know the English are fond of duty, it is their great speciality. We all admire you so much for having no black market, but what is the good of no black market if you will not do your duty by your own family, Grace? Have you thought of that?'

Grace, sick to death of living alone, longing night and day for Charles-Edouard, was unable to conceal from Madame Rocher's experienced eye the happiness these words gave her, and that in her case duty and inclination were the same.

'But Charles-Edouard never asks me to go back,' she said. 'I'm always hearing from my father that he wants me, but I've never had a direct communication from him. It makes it rather difficult.'

Madame Rocher gave a sigh of relief. The day, she saw, was won.

'It is perhaps not so very strange,' she said. 'Charles-Edouard has never been left before by a woman. He fully understands the technique of leaving, one might say he has brought it to a fine art, but being left is a new experience. No doubt it puzzles him, he is not quite sure how to deal with it. Could you not take the first step?'

'Oh Tante Régine! Yes, perhaps. But then what about Juliette and Albertine?'

'Back to them again? You are behind the times, my dearest. Juliette is quite finished. But let's try and be sensible about it. Charles-Edouard was sleeping with you, I suppose?'

Grace became rather pink, but she nodded.

'Well then, that's all right. Why not look upon these others as his hobby? Like hunting or racing, a pursuit that takes him from you of an afternoon sometimes, amuses him, and does you no harm?

'There's another thing I wanted to tell you. Of course one never can say for certain, and people vary in this respect, but very often at Charles-Edouard's age a man does begin, all the same, to settle down with his own wife. If you go back to him it would not surprise me in the least to see a very different Charles-Edouard five or ten years from now.

'Tea with Albertine, yes I expect so, she is one whom people never quite get out of their systems, I'm afraid, and Charles-Edouard had her in his long before he ever met you. But the Juliettes of this world have their little day, it is soon over, and sometimes they are not replaced. I think Charles-Edouard is a particularly hopeful case because of the great love he has of his home. Consider the hours and the energy he expends on it, rearranging his furniture and pictures, adding to his collections, pondering over almost insignificant details of the lighting, and so on. Think how much he hates to leave it, even for a short holiday at Bellandargues or in Venice. He goes away, complaining dreadfully, for a month while the servants have their holiday and is back before the dust sheets are off.

'All this can be very much on your side if you can manage to make him feel that you are part of his home, its goddess, in fact. I had a cousin, a terrible Don Juan, whose wife retrieved him, really, with her knitting. She sat through everything with this eternal ball of wool and click of needles – how we used to mock at her for it. But it was not stupid. In the end it became a symbol to him I think, a symbol of home life, and he so turned to her again that when they were old he seemed never to have cared for anybody else. Could you not try to see this whole problem rather differently, Grace? More like a Frenchwoman and less like a film star?'

Grace felt that she could, and knew that she longed to, since this different vision was clearly essential if she were to go home to Charles-Edouard.

'Yes, Tante Régine,' she said. 'I will try, I promise you. But Charles-Edouard must come and fetch me.'

'Oh – that! I shall have a word with him, and I can promise he'll be here next week. So all is settled then – good. And now, when do I see my dear Vénérable?'

'Ah well, the Vénérable dies for you. He rang up the Embassy to find out your plans – it seems they are taking you to the Ballet tonight, so he hopes that you will dine with us tomorrow. He's out shopping this very moment, trying to find some-thing fit to offer you.'

'Wearing his apron, no doubt. But please tell him not to trouble. I love your English cuts, sirloins and saddles – you see how I remember, and I haven't been here since 1914. I love them just as they are. That excellent roast meat, those steak and kidney puddings, what could be more delicious? At eight o'clock then tomor-row?' She kissed Grace most affectionately on both cheeks.

Grace went home, a warm feeling at her heart. Everything was going to be all right now, she knew.

The dinner party for Madame Rocher consisted of an M.P., Clarkely by name, member of the Anglo-French Parliamentary Committee, Sir Henry and Lady Clarissa Teazle, owner of one of the big Sunday papers and his wife, noted francophiles, and, of course, Mrs O'Donovan. Madame Rocher arrived in full Paris fig. Her breasts were contained (but only just, it seemed that they might spring out at any moment, and then how to coax them back again?) in pale blue glass bubbles embroidered on yellow silk; her pale blue skirt, carved, as it were, out of hundreds of layers of tulle, was rather short, and when she sat down it could be seen that she wore yellow silk breeches also embroidered at the knee with bubbles. Mrs O'Donovan and Lady Clarissa could not take their eyes off bosom and knees, and exchanged many significant glances.

'What a joy,' Madame Rocher cried effusively, 'to see dear Meg. Why do you never come to Paris now? I know more than one who still dies of love for you there. Nobody,' she said to the company at large, 'certainly no foreigner, has ever had so much success in Paris as Madame Audonnevent.'

All the English guests had been chosen because they spoke excellent French, but they did not get much opportunity to air this accomplishment, since Madame Rocher was determined to practise her English, and, furthermore, never drew breath the whole evening.

Her theme was the delight, the ravishment, the ecstasies into which she had been thrown by her two days in London.

'This morning,' she said, 'I got up at eight, and imagine! I was ready for the opening at nine.'

'The opening?'

'Of the shops. Oh those shops! I have already bought all my hats for the Grande Semaine.'

'No! Where?' said Mrs O'Donovan, hoping for the name of a talented little French modiste, kept perhaps in some secret mews by the ladies of the French Embassy.

'My dear, can you ask? D. H. Heavens, of course – in the basement. I never saw such beauties – the straw! the workmanship! the chic! I have got Christmas presents for all my friends – how they will be thrilled – of your famous English scent, the Yardley – so delicious, so well presented, such chic bottles. Then all my cotillon favours for the bal des Innouïs at the Woolworth – oh the joy just to wander in the Woolworth. The very names of the shops are a poem – the Scotch House – I bought a hundred mètres of tartan to cover all my furniture, many country beréts, and a lovely fur bag, in the Scotch House, while as for the Army and the Fleet! The elegance! I shall come over once a month now for the elegance alone.

'At Oopers I ordered a new Rolls-Royce, of cane-work – you see the chic of that. From time to time, when I get a little tired, for all this shopping does tire me rather,

I go to the Cadena Café and order a *café crème* and sit very happily watching your English beauties. They are a refreshment to the eye. I notice how sensible they are, they scorn the *demi-toilette*, and quite right too, there is nothing worse. They come out with no make-up, hardly having combed their hair even, to do their shopping. Then, of course, they go home and arrange themselves properly. Now I admire that. All or nothing, how I agree.

'So I had no time for luncheon as you can imagine, but who cares when you can have a bun and a cup of tea? The afternoon I spent in fittings!'

'Fittings?' Mrs O'Donovan and Lady Clarissa were stunned by this recital.

'Junior Miss, my dear. All my little dresses for the plage. Don't ask me what Dior will say when he hears of Junior Miss. I'd rather not think. No thank you, no wine – when I am in England I drink nothing but whisky.'

Mr Clarkely, more interested in French politics than English elegance, began asking a few questions about the Third Force, saying that he had made friends, through his Committee, with many of the Ministers, but Madame Rocher merely cried,

'Don't talk to me of these dreadful people – they think of nothing, day and night, but their stomachs and their mistresses.'

'Really?' said Mr Clarkely. 'Are you sure?' It had not been his impression at all.

'On what do you suppose they squander their salaries – those huge augmentations for which they are always and forever voting?' (Madame Rocher would have complained very much if she had found herself compelled to dress on the amount annually earned by a French Minister.) 'Stomachs, dear sir, and mistresses. The vast sums that dreadful Dexter gives them for tanks and aeroplanes, what d'you suppose happens to them? My nephew, a commandant, tells me there are no tanks and no aeroplanes and hardly even a pop-gun. Why? Because, my dear sir, these sums are spent on the stomachs and the mistresses of your friends.'

Mr Clarkely was very much surprised. 'Surely not so and so,' he said, mentioning a certain prominent Minister noted for his dyspeptic austerity of life and devotion to work.

'All – all! Don't mention their names or I shall have an attack! All, I tell you, all! They take the best houses to live in, they have fleets of motors, they spend the day eating and drinking and all night the relays of mistresses are shown up the *escalier de service*. It has ever been so, but let me tell you that the scandals of Wilson and Panama, of the death of Félix Fauré even, are nothing, but nothing, to what goes on today. Give us back our King, my dear sir, and then speak to me of politics,' she said, rather as if her King were kept a prisoner in the Tower of London. 'More whisky, Vénérable, I pray.'

Mrs O'Donovan whispered to Mr Clarkely, 'It's no use asking that sort of French-woman about politics – ask me. I know a great deal more than she does.'

But Mr Clarkely went to tea once a week at St Leonard's Terrace and had been told what Mrs O'Donovan knew already. He had hoped for something more direct from the horse's mouth.

'Is she really so royalist?' he turned to Grace. Madame Rocher was telling Sir Conrad her summer plans and begging him to go with her to Deauville, Venice, and Monte Carlo.

'Like all the Faubourg,' said Grace, 'she has a photograph of the King on her piano, but I don't think she'd raise a finger to get him back. My husband says the French hate all forms of authority quite equally.'

After dinner Madame Rocher took Sir Conrad aside, saying, 'And tell me, *mon cher Vénérable*, how goes the Grand Orient? You know,' she said, breathing a scented whisper (not Yardley's) into his ear, 'that I have designs on one of your adherents?'

'I am most glad to hear it,' he replied, delightfully drowning in the great billows of sex that emanated from her in spite of her seventy-odd years. 'Come in here a minute and we will discuss ways and means together.'

I2

Madame Rocher's journey turned out not to have been really necessary. The night of Sir Conrad's dinner party Sigismond was very sick and feverish; in the morning the doctor came, and said he must have his appendix out at once. He was taken by ambulance to a nursing home to be prepared for the operation, deeply interested in the whole affair.

'Shall I die? And go to the Père La Chaise? And see l'Empereur, like in Le Rêve? Well, I forgive Nanny for everything. Can I see the knife? I shall have a scar now, like Canari! oh good! When are you going to do it?'

'Not until tomorrow morning,' said the nurse, 'and don't get so excited.'

'Better give him something to keep him quiet,' said the doctor, after which Sigi became intensely drowsy. Grace sat with him until evening, when Nanny came, prepared to spend the night in the nursing home. As there seemed no point in them both being there and as Nanny insisted on staying, Grace went back to Queen Anne's Gate. Charles-Edouard was getting out of a cab just as she arrived.

It seemed quite natural to see him, she felt no embarrassment or constraint, and nor, quite obviously, did he.

'*Ravi de vous voir, ma chère Grace*,' he said, kissing her hand in his rapid way.

She opened the door with her key and they went into the house together.

'So how is he? And when is the operation? I was out when your father telephoned or I could have been here sooner.'

'It doesn't matter,' she said, 'he's been asleep more or less all day and the operation isn't till the morning. There's no danger, and no need to worry.' She sat down rather suddenly, feeling giddy.

'You look tired.'

'Yes. I was up most of the night, and I've been at the nursing home ever since without much to eat. I shall feel better after dinner.'

The butler came into the hall. He looked uncertainly at Charles-Edouard's bag, left it where it was and said, 'Sir Conrad won't be back from the House until late.'

'Perhaps we could have dinner at once then, please.'

Charles-Edouard was delightful at dinner; he told her all the Paris gossip.

'I'm so very pleased to see you,' he said from time to time, and towards the end of the meal, 'You don't know how much I've missed you.'

'Oh Charles-Edouard, I've been ill from missing you.'

'I thought I would open Bellandargues this summer. Sigi can get over his operation there. Won't you come?'

'For a week-end?'

'For good. Let's go upstairs.'

They went up. When they got to the drawing-room Grace opened the door, but Charles-Edouard took her hand and pointed further up.

'Charles-Edouard, we can't. We're not married.'

'We never have been married,' he said.

They went together into her bedroom.

'But I think we had better be,' he said, later on, 'and properly this time. For the sake of the child.'

Grace repeated happily and sleepily 'For the sake of the child.' Then she woke up a little more and said, 'But why, Charles-Edouard, did you never make a sign? A whole year and no sign?'

'No sign? When you refused to see me although I'd come all the way from Paris – when you told Sigi nothing would induce you to speak to me on the telephone – when you never answered the long letter I gave him for you. No sign? What more could I have done?'

So then it all came out. All poor Sigi's major acts of iniquity and minor acts of trouble-making were revealed before the horrified gaze of his parents.

'We seem to have given birth to a Borgia,' said Charles-Edouard at last.

'Rubbish!' Grace said indignantly, 'he's a dear, affectionate little boy. The whole thing was entirely our own fault for leaving him too much alone when we were happy and depending too much on him when we were lonely. We've been thoroughly selfish and awful with the poor darling from the very beginning, I see it all now. He only did it because he loves us and wants to be with us. When we were together we left him out and made him jealous, so of course he thought the best plan would be to keep us apart.'

'It's terrible all this jealousy. First you and then the child. What am I going to do about it?'

'You must try to be nicer, Charles-Edouard.'

'I must anyhow try to be more careful.'

'One thing, he did stop us marrying anybody else.'

'Were we seriously considering such a step?'

'I was, twice.'

'How extraordinary. Confess you would never have amused yourself so much as you do with me.'

'Amusement is not the only aim of marriage,' said Grace primly.

'Are you quite sure?'

They decided never to let Sigi realize that they knew all, but to keep a firm lookout for any underhand dealings in the future.

When Sir Conrad got back, very late, he found Charles-Edouard's suitcase still in the hall, the drawing-room empty and dark. He nodded to himself, and went happily to bed.

Next morning Sigismond, still very much interested, was lifted on to a trolley, 'Like the pudding tray at the Ritz,' he said, and was wheeled away. The last thing he knew was the surgeon's enormous eye gazing into his.

The very next minute, or half a lifetime later, he opened his eyes again. He was back in his bed. He saw the nurse and smiled at her. Then he saw his father and mother. They were holding hands. His mother leant over him. 'How d'you feel, darling?' Suddenly the full significance of all this became hideously apparent. He shut his eyes again with a shudder.

'He's not quite round,' said the nurse, 'he hasn't seen you yet.'

'Oh yes I have,' said Sigi, 'and I'm going to be sick.'

As soon as Sigismond was well enough to travel they all left for Paris on the Golden Arrow, complete with Nanny, the usual mountain of luggage, and Grace's carpet, a huge roll done up with straps.

'It will do for your bedroom at Bellandargues,' said Charles-Edouard.

'I meant it for your bedroom in Paris.'

But Charles-Edouard raised his hand, shook his head, and said, very kindly but firmly, 'No.'

Madame Rocher, who was already back in Paris and delighted by this turn of events, rang up Charles-Edouard the day before their journey. 'I've got Fr Lanvin,' she said, 'he'll marry you on Thursday morning at eleven, and then Grace must be converted by him. He's far the best and quickest, he did the Princesse de Louville in no time.'

But Albertine, whom Charles-Edouard rang up to make quite sure that all Paris should know the facts of the case, begged him to go to her priest. 'Fr Lanvin is quite all right, I'm sure, but I think you need somebody of a different calibre. Fr Strogonoff is so gentle and understanding, and then he specializes in foreign converts –'

'Yes, I'm sure, Albertine, but you see my aunt has made the appointment now, I think we'd better keep it. We can always change, if Grace doesn't like him.' Grace thought it was just the way people go on about their dentists.

'What?' said Charles-Edouard, still on the telephone. 'No! Are you sure?'

He was listening with all his ears. Grace could hear Albertine's voice, quack, quack, quack, down the receiver, but could not hear what she was saying. Charles-Edouard seemed entranced by whatever it was.

'Oh how interesting. Go on. Yes. What a sensation! Don't you know any more? Don't cut off – wait while I tell Grace. The Dexters,' he said to Grace, 'have flown to Russia. They've been Communist spies from the very beginning, and they've gone. It will be in the papers tomorrow. Salleté has just told Albertine the whole story. Well then, Albertine dearest, good-bye, and we'll count on you Thursday at eleven. Saint Louis des Invalides. Nobody at all except Tante Régine and my father-in-law. Good-bye.'

'So –?' said Grace, all agog.

'Well, it seems the Americans have been rather suspicious of your friend Heck for quite a long time. At last they had enough evidence to arrest him – he must have got wind of it and he flew to Prague the day before yesterday. The latest information is that he has turned up in Moscow.'

'And Carolyn?'

'With Carolyn and little Foss.'

'Rather a comfort,' said Grace, 'to think that little Foss won't be ruling the world after all.'

'Rather a comfort,' said Charles-Edouard, 'to think that we shall never have to listen to Hector's views on anything again.'

'Poor Carolyn, will she like living in Russia? One thing, the Russians can't get on her nerves more than the French used to. So I was quite right, you see, she was a Communist at school. No wonder she got so cross when I reminded her.'

'And it seems that his real name is Dextrovitch.'

'He told me his mother was a Whale.'

'She was. His father, Dextrovitch, became an American just before he was born. They say they have evidence now that Hector has been a Bolshevist all his life, his father brought him up to be one. It's a most interesting story really. The father saw his two brothers shot by the Tsarist police, he escaped to America, married this rich Whale, and had Hector.'

'Can you beat it,' said Grace. 'Where's Papa – do let's go and tell him.'

Of course the journey to Paris was greatly enlivened for Grace, Charles-Edouard, and Nanny by the Dexter story, which now filled all the newspapers. Hector Dexter, it seemed, was worth at least ten atom bombs to the Russians. He had held jobs of the highest responsibility for years, had always been *persona grata* at the White House, where he knew his way about better than anybody except the President himself, had never been denied access to any information anywhere, and was one of the most brilliant of living men. Great stress was laid upon how deeply he was beloved by his countless friends (good old Heck) in London, Paris, and New York. Many of these refused to believe that he had gone to Russia of his own accord, but were quite certain that the whole family must have been kidnapped, putting forward as evidence that Carolyn had left her fur coat behind. 'I suppose they've never heard of Russian sables,' Charles-Edouard said when Grace read this out to him.

Asp Jorgmann and Charlie Jungfleisch were interviewed in Paris. 'Whatever Heck may have done,' they said, 'he remains a very very good friend of ours.'

But the French Ambassador to London, who was on the train and with whom Charles-Edouard went to sit for a while, told him that his American colleague regarded it as worth quite a lot of atom bombs to be relieved of good old Heck's company for ever. 'He's supposed to have gone straight off for a conference with Beria. Well, I feel awfully sorry for Beria.'

'Perhaps he won't mind as much as we do; we're always told the Russians have no sense of time,' said Charles-Edouard.

'It does seem strange, dear, such a good daddy. And fancy Mrs Dexter too. What will Nanny Dexter say?'

'You must ring her up the very minute we arrive and see if she's still there.'

Sigi sat by his mother in a fit of deep sulks, his mouth down at the corners, his clever little black eyes roving to and fro like those of an animal cornered at last. When the train was nearly at Dover the clever little black eyes suddenly had their attention fixed. The Bunbury burglar was walking up the Pullman on his way, no doubt, to the Trianon bar. Charles-Edouard was asleep in his corner, and Grace half-asleep in hers.

'Where are you going, Sigi?' she said, as he slipped out of his seat.

'Just to stretch my poor scar.'

'Well don't be long, we're nearly at Dover. You'll be able to lie down on the boat,' she said, 'poor darling.'

He sidled off, and found his burglar alone in the bar, drinking whisky.

'Good Lord,' said the burglar. 'It's you! Where are you off to?'

'Paris. I'm a French boy, like I told you. And I'm going home with my father and mother, but leaving my appendix in London.'

'Oh dear. They ought to have given it you in a bottle.'

'Are you coming to Paris too?'

'I hope so. If nothing awkward happens on the way.'

Sigi got very close to him and said confidentially, 'Have you got anything you'd rather I carried through the Customs for you? My papa travels to and fro the whole time, they all know him, he never has anything opened.'

The burglar looked at him and said, 'Whose side are you on now?'

Sigi began twisting up his curls. 'On your side, like I was last time, if you remember, until you sausaged me. But although it was very treacherous, what you did, I do feel I owe you a good turn to make up for shutting you in the cupboard.'

'Mm,' said the burglar doubtfully. They were passing through Dover Town station, sea and cliffs were in sight, seagulls mewed, and passengers began to fuss.

'White horses,' said Sigi. 'Poor Nanny.'

At last the burglar said, 'All right. If you like to give me a hand with this.' He passed him a small leather writing-case.

'Coo!' said Sigi. 'Heavy, isn't it?'

'Heavy because full of gold.'

'Can I see?'

'No. We're arriving. Be a good boy, bring it to me on the boat, cabin 11, can you remember? Then I'll give you a bit for a keep-sake.'

'Oh here he is. You shouldn't wander off like that, darling, we were quite worried.' The train stopped with a bump.

'What's that satchel, dear?' Nanny asked as they went towards the Customs shed.

'I'm looking after it for Papa —'

'That makes eighteen pieces then — I'd only counted seventeen. Where is that porter going?'

Charles-Edouard told Grace and Nanny to go on board. 'I'll see to the luggage.' He gave Grace their tickets. 'And it's cabin No. 7.'

'Eighteen pieces of luggage, sir.'

'Thank you, Nanny. Run along, Sigi.'

'No, no,' said Sigi, 'this is the part I enjoy.'

Charles-Edouard laughed and said to Grace, 'We saw some idiot taken away last time, for smuggling, I suppose he hopes for the best again.'

'I do. Very much indeed.'

A huge heap of luggage, mostly, of course, belonging to Sigi, was piled on to the counter in the Customs shed. Charles-Edouard stood by, with his back to the counter, talking to a friend who was in the Ambassador's party. They were both roaring with laughter still about the Dexters.

Sigi put his little writing-case on top of the other things and said, confidentially, to the Customs man, 'If I were you, officer, I would take a look inside that.'

'These all your things, sir?' The officer leant forward and spoke rather loudly to Charles-Edouard, who replied, half-looking round, 'Yes, yes, all mine', and went on talking with his friend. The officer, who knew Charles-Edouard by sight, began chalking the cases as he passed them.

Sigi, getting very fidgety, said, 'You mustn't mark that one without opening it first.'

The officer laughed. 'What are you up to? Smuggling?'

'Not me, my papa. Oh do look – do look inside.'

The officer good-naturedly snapped open the case, which seemed at first sight to contain coffee in half-pound bags. Still laughing, he took one out. Then his face changed. He tore open the bag and gave a loud whistle. Charles-Edouard was saying to his friend 'See you in a few minutes then.' The friend went on out of the shed and Charles-Edouard turned to the Customs officer who said, 'Excuse me, sir, is this your case?'

'I think so. If it's with the others,' he said, rather puzzled at the sudden gravity of the man's expression.

'Then I'm afraid I must ask you to follow me.'

'Follow you. Why?'

'This way, sir, please.'

'Yes, but why?'

'Your case is full of gold coins,' said the officer, showing him.

'*Nom de nom*,' said Charles-Edouard, very much taken aback. 'But wait a moment, that's not my case, I've never seen it before.'

'You've just said it was yours, sir.'

'Sigi – does this case belong to you?'

'Oh no, Papa, you gave it to me to hold, don't you remember?' Sigi was wildly twisting up his hair.

Two Englishwomen said to each other, 'Shame, making the child smuggle for him.'

Charles-Edouard gave Sigi a very searching look and said, 'Sigismond, what is all this? Now will you please go on board this minute, go to cabin 1, find M. l'Ambassadeur and ask him to come here.'

Sigi ran off and Charles-Edouard followed the Customs man into a back office.

When Sigi got on to the ship he made no effort to find cabin 1 or the Ambassador. Since he had time to get rid of, and did not want to run into his burglar, he made his way to the ladies' room, where, as he knew he would, he found Nanny lying down with her skirt off and occupying the entire attention of the stewardess, who stood over her with a bottle of sea-sick tablets. 'Not as bad as all that,' the stewardess was saying, 'bumpier this side. You go right off to sleep, dear, that'll be the best.'

'And what about the little monkey?'

'I'll be all right,' said Sigi. 'I'm just waiting for the boat to start and then I'll go and find Mummy. I've got some very interesting news for Mummy, but only when we've started.'

'Won't be long now,' said the stewardess, looking at her watch.

Meanwhile the Ambassador's servant had arrived in his cabin, saying, 'M. le Marquis de Valhubert is in trouble with the Customs and it doesn't look as if they will allow him to travel.'

The Ambassador did not hesitate. He had a word with the ship's captain and

immediately went on shore again, accompanied by an officer who took him straight
to the room where Charles-Edouard was talking with several Customs men.

'What is all this about?' said the Ambassador, in English.

Charles-Edouard said furiously, 'My child, who seems to be a member of the
criminal classes, has planted a case full of gold coins on me. Don't ask me how he
got them. I'm in a very awkward position indeed.'

The Ambassador said to the senior official, 'It's absolutely out of the question
that M. de Valhubert should be smuggling gold. You need not consider it even as
a possibility. There must be a mistake.'

'Yes, sir, we feel sure there is. But we must find out where all this gold comes
from. Where is the little boy?'

'He went off to find you,' Charles-Edouard said to the Ambassador.

'I haven't seen him. My valet told me you'd been delayed, that's why I came.'

'It was most good of you, *mon cher*, I'm exceedingly grateful.'

'I could do no less.'

Another official now put his head round the door.

'Mr Porter, please, one moment.'

Mr Porter, went out, and was back again almost at once.

'I think we've got to the bottom of it,' he said. 'A man has just been arrested on
board. If I might have your name and address, sir, you've time to catch the boat,
I'm very glad to say.'

Charles-Edouard gave him his card and hurried on board with the Ambassador.

Sigi's timing had gone a little bit wrong, and he had arrived in his mother's cabin
rather before he meant to. Charles-Edouard, from outside, heard a well-known
voice piping, 'He has always been wrapped up in Madame Novembre – it doesn't
surprise me in the least. They're made for each other, and now they've gone off
together – oh yes, Mummy, I saw them, I tell you, in her Cadillac.'

Charles-Edouard burst open the door, saying, in a voice which neither Sigi nor
Grace had ever heard, and which turned Sigi to stone with terror, 'Sigismond'.
This was followed by a tremendous box on the ears. The three of them stood
looking at each other for a moment. Then Charles-Edouard, mastering his temper,
said, 'What you need, my child, is a family of little brothers and sisters, and we
must try to see that you get them. And now, please run along and find Nanny.'

Don't Tell Alfred

To Anna Maria Cicogna

I

On the day which was to be such a turning-point in my life, I went to London by the 9.07. I had planned to do a little shopping; somebody had told me of Chinese robes in the sales, perfect for dinner at home since they would cover up everything. I was also going to see my naughty boy, Basil, a perennial worry to me; Aunt Sadie begged me to look in on Uncle Matthew and there was something I had long wanted to put to him. I had appointments to lunch with the one and to have tea with the other. It was a Saturday because that was Basil's half-holiday – he was cramming for the Foreign Office. We were to meet at a restaurant, then go back to his lodgings, what used to be called 'rooms' and is now called a 'service flat'. My idea was to do a little, surely much needed, tidying up there, as well as to collect some dirty clothes, and bring them back with me to have them washed or cleaned. I took a large canvas hold-all to contain them and the Chinese robe, if I bought it.

But, oh dear, I don't think I've ever looked such a fool as I did in that Chinese robe, with my brown walking shoes, enormous beneath the hem, hair untidy from dragging off a hat, leather bag clasped to bosom because it had £28 in it and I knew that people snatched bags at sales. The assistant earnestly said think of the difference if I were carefully *coiffée* and *maquillée* and *parfumée* and *manicurée* and *pedicurée*, wearing Chinese sandals (next department, 35/6) and lying on a couch in a soft light. It was no good, however – my imagination could not get to work on all these hypotheses; I felt both hot and bothered; I tore the robe from me and fled from the displeasure of the saleswoman.

I had made my plan with Basil some days before, on the telephone. Like all the children he is quite incapable of either reading or writing a letter. I was rather more worried about him than usual; last time he had come to Oxford his clothes had been distinctly on the Teddy side while his hair combed (or rather pulled) over his forehead and worn in a bob at the back gave him a curiously horrible look. This, no doubt, is now the fashion and not in itself a cause for alarm. But when he was alone with me he had spoken about his future, saying that the prospect of the Foreign Service bored him and that he thought he could put his talent for languages to better account in some other career. The sinister words 'get rich quick' were uttered. I was anxious to see him again and ask a few questions. It was a blow, therefore, though not a great surprise, when he failed to turn up at the restaurant. I lunched there alone and then went off to find his service flat. The address he had given me, in Islington, turned out to be a pretty old house, come down in the world (soon no doubt to come down altogether). There were five or six bells at the front door with cards attached; one bell had no card but somebody had scribbled Baz on the wall beside it. I pressed it, without much hope. Nobody came. I went on pressing at intervals.

A sharp lad in Teddy costume was lounging in the street, eyeing me. Presently he came up and said, 'If it's old Baz you're after, he's gone to Spain.'

Rain, rain, go to Spain. 'And when will he be back again?'

'When he comes for the next batch. Old Baz is a travel agent now, didn't you know? Joined up with his Grandad – some people are lucky in their relations. Baz herds them out to the Costa Brava, goes into hiding while they live it up there and brings back the bodies a week later. Or that's the general idea – he's only just started the work.'

Travel agent – Grandad – what did the child mean? Was not this a line of talk intended to keep me here until a man who was walking up the street should be out of sight? There was nobody else about, this dread Teddy, armed, no doubt, with blades, was clearly after my bag and the £28. I gave him a nervous, idiotic smile. 'Thank you very much,' I said, 'that's just what I thought. Good-bye and thank you.'

Upper Street was near and very soon I was in a good old No. 19 sagely ambling towards Piccadilly. This sort of thing always happened when I tried to see Basil. Oh well, one must put oneself in his shoes. Why should he want to spend his Saturday afternoon with a middle-aged mother? What a bore for a young man, on his own for the first time, to have to watch this elderly woman messing about in his room and taking away his suits. All the same, it was not like him to throw one over quite so callously; what could have happened? How could I find out? Meanwhile here I was in London on a Saturday afternoon with nothing to do until tea-time. We were passing the National Gallery, but I felt too dispirited to go in. I decided to walk off my bad temper in the Park.

Though I have lived in London for longish periods at various times in my life, I have never been a Londoner, so that its associations to me are more literary and historic than personal. Every time I visit it I am saddened by seeing changes for the worse: the growing inelegance; the loss of character; the disappearance of landmarks and their replacement by flat and faceless glass houses. When I got off my bus at Hyde Park Corner, I looked sadly at the huge hotel where Montdore House used to be, in Park Lane. When first built it had been hailed as a triumph of modern architecture, but although it had only stood there for three years it had already become shabby, the colour of old teeth, and in an odd way out of date. I stumped off towards Kensington Gardens. Somebody had told me that Knights-bridge Barracks were soon to go, so I said good-bye to them. I had never looked at them very carefully – I now saw that they were solid and well built in a pretty mixture of brick and stone. No masterpiece, but certainly far better than the glori-fied garage that would replace them. Wendy's Wishing Well is horribly altered, I noted, and what has happened to the trees in the Broad Walk? However, Kensing-ton Palace is still there, though probably not for long, and eccentric old men are still sailing boats on the Round Pond, which has not, as yet, been dried and levelled and turned into a car park.

Presently, drops of rain began to fall. It was half-past three. Uncle Matthew never minds one being early; I decided to make for his mews at once. If he were in he would be pleased to see me, if not I could wait for him in a little sheltered place where the dustbins are kept.

Uncle Matthew had handed over Alconleigh to his only surviving son, Bob Radlett, keeping a small Regency house on the estate for himself. Aunt Sadie was delighted by this exchange; she liked being nearer the village; the new house got sunshine all day and it amused her to do it up. Indeed, newly painted from top to toe and containing what little good furniture there had been at Alconleigh, it had become a much more desirable residence than the other. But hardly had they moved into it than my uncle fell out with Bob: the eternal story of the old king and the young king. Bob had his own ideas about shooting and estate management; Uncle Matthew disagreed violently with every innovation. His son-in-law, Fort William, his brother-in-law, Davey Warbeck, and such neighbours as were on speaking terms with Uncle Matthew had all warned him that this would happen; they had been invited to mind their own business. Now that they had been proved right he refused to admit the real cause of his chagrin and persuaded himself that Bob's wife, Jennifer, was to blame. He pronounced his intense dislike for her; her vicinity, he said, was not to be endured. Poor Jennifer was quite inoffensive, she only wished to please and this was so obvious that even Uncle Matthew, when asked to explain the reason for his hatred, found himself at a loss. 'Meaningless piece of flesh,' he would mutter. Undeniable; Jennifer was one of those women whose meaning, if they have one, is only apparent to husband and children, but she certainly did not deserve such a torrent of hatred.

Of course Uncle Matthew could not remain in a place where he risked setting eyes on this loathed daughter-in-law. He took a flat in London, always known as The Mews, and seemed strangely contented in a town which he had hitherto regarded as a plague spot. Aunt Sadie remained peacefully in her nice new house, able to see a few friends and entertain her grandchildren without any fear of explosions. Uncle Matthew, who had been fond of his own children when they were young, took a very poor view of their progeny, while my aunt really liked them better, felt more at her ease with them, than she ever had with their parents.

At first domestic troubles raged in The Mews. There was no bedroom for a servant; daily women were found but Uncle Matthew pronounced them to be harlots; daily men smelt of drink and were impertinent. Luck favoured him in the end and he arrived at a perfect solution. One day, driving in a taxi to the House of Lords, he spied a pound note on the floor. On getting out, he handed it and his fare, plus, no doubt, an enormous tip (he was a great over-tipper), to the cabby, who remarked that this was a nuisance because now he would be obliged to take it round to the Yard.

'Don't you do any such thing!' said Uncle Matthew, rather oddly, perhaps, for a legislator. 'Nobody will claim it. Keep it for yourself, my dear fellow.' The cabby thanked him warmly, both for the tip and the advice, and they parted on a chuckling note, like a pair of conspirators.

The next day, by chance, Uncle Matthew, having rung up his local shelter (or, as it is probably now called, Drivers' Rest and Culture Hall) for a cab to take him down to the House, got the same man. He told my uncle that, though he had quite seen the good sense of his advice, he had nevertheless taken the pound to Scotland Yard.

'Damned fool,' said Uncle Matthew. He asked him his name and what time he started his day. The name was Payne and he was on the streets at about half-past eight. Uncle Matthew told him that, in future, he was to put his flag down when he left his garage and drive straight to The Mews.

'I like to get to Victoria Street every morning in time for the Stores to open so that would suit us both.' The Stores (Army and Navy) had ever been a magnet to my uncle; Aunt Sadie used to say she wished she could have a penny for each pound he had spent there. He knew most of the employees by name and used to take his constitutional in the magic precincts, ending up with a view from the bridge, whence he would note the direction of the wind. No sky was visible from The Mews.

Presently Payne and my uncle came to a very suitable arrangement. Payne would drop him at the Stores, return to The Mews and put in a couple of hours doing housework there. He would then go back for Uncle Matthew and drive him either to his club or home, in which case he would fetch him some hot luncheon from the Rest and Culture Hall, where according to my uncle, the cabbies do themselves exceedingly well. (I often feel pleased to remember this when waiting in a bitter wind for one of them to finish his nuts and wine.) For the rest of the day Payne was allowed to ply his trade on condition that between every fare he should ring up The Mews to see if anything were wanted. Uncle Matthew paid him, then and there, whatever was on the clock and a tip. He said this saved accounts and made everything easier. The system worked like a charm. Uncle Matthew was the envy of his peers, few of whom were so well looked after as he.

As I was walking along Kensington Gore a cab drew up beside me, Payne at the wheel. Taking no notice of his fare, who looked surprised and not delighted, he leant over to me and said, confidentially, 'His Lordship's out. If you're going to The Mews now I'd best give you the key. I'm to pick him up at St George's Hospital after taking this gentleman to Paddington.' The fare now pulled down the window and said furiously, 'Look here, driver, I've got a train to catch, you know.'

'Very good, sir,' said Payne. He handed me the key and drove away.

By the time I arrived it was raining hard and I was glad not to be obliged to sit on the dustbin. Although we were already in July the day was turning chilly; Uncle Matthew had a little fire in his sitting-room. I went up to it, rubbing my hands. The room was small, dark and ugly, the old business room at Alconleigh in miniature. It had the same smell of wood fire and Virginia cigarettes and was filled, as the business room had always been, with hideous gadgets, most of which my uncle had invented himself years ago and which, it was supposed of each in turn, would make him rich beyond belief. There were the Alconsegar Ash Tray, the Alconstoke Fire Lighters, the Alconclef Record Rack and the Home Beautifier, a fly trap made of fretwork in the form of a Swiss chalet. They vividly evoked my childhood and the long evenings at Alconleigh with Uncle Matthew playing his favourite records. I thought with a sigh what an easy time parents and guardians had had in those days – no Teddy boys, no Beards, no Chelsea set, no heiresses, or at least not such wildly public ones; good little children we seem to have been, in retrospect.

Tea was already laid out, silver hot-dishes containing scones and girdle cakes and a pot of Tiptree jam. You could count on a good tea, at The Mews. I looked round for something to read, picked up the *Daily Post* and fell upon Amyas Mockbar's Paris Page. Provincials like myself are kept in touch with fashionable and intellectual Europe in its last stronghold of civilized leisure by this Mr Mockbar who, four times a week, recounts the inside story of Parisian lives, loves and scandals. It makes perfect reading for the housewife, who is able to enjoy the chronicle without having to rub shoulders with the human horrors depicted therein; she lays down the paper more contented than ever with her lot. Today, however, the page was rather dull, consisting of speculations on the appointment of a new English Ambassador to Paris. Sir Louis Leone, it seemed, was due to retire after a mission of unusual length. Mockbar had always presented him as a diplomatic disaster, too brilliant, too social and much too pro-French. His beautiful wife was supposed to have made too many friends in Paris; reading between the lines, one gathered that Mockbar had not been among them. Now that the Leones were leaving, however, he was seized with an inexplicable tenderness for them. Perhaps he was saving his ammunition for the new Sir Somebody whom he confidently tipped as Sir Louis's successor.

I heard the taxi crawling into The Mews. It stopped, the door slammed, the meter rang, my uncle rattled some half-crowns out of his pocket, Payne thanked him and drove off. I went to meet Uncle Matthew as he came slowly up the stairs.

'How are you, my dear child?'

It was comfortable to be my dear child again; I was so accustomed to seeing myself as a mother – poor, neglected mother today, left to have her luncheon all alone. I looked at myself in a glass while Uncle Matthew went to the little kitchen to put on a kettle, saying 'Payne got everything ready, there's only the tea to make.' No doubt there was something in my appearance which made 'my dear child' not too ridiculous, even at the age of forty-five. I took off my hat and combed my hair which was as springy as ever, turned up all over my head and was neither faded nor grey. My face was not much lined; my eyes looked bright and rather young. I weighed the same as when I was eighteen. There was an unfashionable aspect about me which came from having lived most of my life in Oxford, as much out of the world as if it had been Tibet, but no doubt some such drastic treatment as a love affair (perish the thought) or change of environment could still transform my appearance; the material was there.

'Very civil of you to come, Fanny.'

I saw Uncle Matthew but seldom these days and never really got accustomed to finding him old, that is to say, no longer in the agreeable, seemingly endless autumn of life but plunged in its midwinter. I had known him so vigorous and violent, so rampageous and full of super-charged energy that it went to my heart to see him now, stiff and slow in his movements; wearing spectacles; decidedly deaf. Until we are middle-aged ourselves, old age is outside our experience. When very young, of course, everybody grown up seems old while the really old people with whom we come into contact, never having been different during the few years – short to them, endlessly long to us – of our acquaintance, seem more like another species than members of our own race in a different condition. But the day comes when those we have known in the prime of life approach its end; then we understand what old age really is. Uncle Matthew was only in his seventies, but he was not well preserved. He had gone through life with one lung, the other having been shot away in the Boer War. In 1914, on the reserve of officers, he had arrived in France with the first hundred thousand and spent two years in the trenches before being invalided home. After that he had hunted, shot and played lawn tennis as though he had been perfectly fit. I can often remember, as a child, seeing him fight to get his breath – it must have been a strain on the heart. He had known sorrow too, which always ages people. He had suffered the deaths of three of his children and those his three favourites. Having lost a child myself I know that nothing more terrible can befall a human being; mine, having died as a baby, left no gap comparable with the disappearance of Linda and the two boys he was so proud of.

When he came back with the tea, looking like some old shepherd of the hills who had invited one to his chimney-corner, I said, 'Whom were you visiting at St George's?'

'Why, Davey! I though you couldn't have known he was there or you would have come.' Davey Warbeck was my uncle, widower of Aunt Emily who had snatched me from my own, unmaternal mother and brought me up.

'Indeed I would have. Whatever is he in for now?' There was no terror in my voice as I asked; Davey's health was his hobby and he spent much of his life in nursing homes and hospitals.

'Nothing serious. It seems they have got a few human spare parts, frozen, don't you know, from America. Davey came up from the country to give them the once over. He says it was hard to know what to choose, they were all so tempting. A few yards of colon, some nice bits of membrane, an eye (but where could he put it? Even Davey would look rather odd with three) – finally he picked on a kidney. He's been after a suitable one for ages – he's having it grafted. It's to give the others a chance. Now who else would have thought of that? Wonderful fella – and all for nothing, don't you know? We pay – health service.'

'It sounds rather terrific – how did he seem?'

'Strong as a bull and having the time of his life. Doctors and nurses so proud of him – exhibit A. I asked if they couldn't give me a new lung but they wouldn't touch it. Kill me stone dead they said, with my heart in the state it is. You want to be in the pink, like Davey, to have these graftings.'

'Delicious girdle cake.'

'Comes from the Shelter – they've got a Scotch cook there now. Davey's been telling me about your mother's new husband. You know how he likes to be in on things – he went to the wedding.'

'No – how could he! Weren't the papers awful?'

'I thought so too, but he says not nearly as bad as they might have been. It seems to have been a thick week, luckily for us, with all these heiresses running to leper colonies and the Dockers docking at Monte Carlo. What they did put in they got wrong, of course. Have you seen him, Fanny?'

'Who? Oh, my mother's husband? Well no, she has rather stopped asking Alfred and me to meet her fiancés. They've gone abroad now, haven't they?'

'To Paris, I believe. He's only twenty-two, did you know?'

'Oh dear, I can easily believe it.'

'She's as pleased as Punch, Davey says. He says you must hand it to her, she didn't look a day over forty. It seems your boy Basil was at the wedding – he introduced them in the first place.'

'Goodness! Did he really?'

'They both belong to the same gang,' said Uncle Matthew, adding rather wistfully, 'we didn't have these gangs when I was young. Never mind, though, we had wars. I liked the Boer War very much, when I was Basil's age. If you won't have wars you must expect gangs, no doubt.'

'Does my stepfather, aged twenty-two (oh, really, Uncle Matthew, it is past a joke. Why, he is the boys' step-grandfather, you realize?), does he do any work or is he just a criminal?'

'Davey said something about him being a travel agent. That's why they've gone abroad, most likely.'

The words of that Teddy boy came back to me. 'Old Baz is a travel agent . . . he's joined up with his Grandad.' I became very thoughtful. What was I going to tell Alfred when I got home?

I said: 'At least that sounds fairly respectable?'

'Don't you believe it. A chap in the House was telling me about these travel agents. Bandits, he said. Take people's money and give them ten days of hell. Of course, going abroad in itself would be hell to me. Now how many would you say that makes, Fanny?'

'What, Uncle Matthew?'

'How many husbands has the Bolter had now?'

'The papers said six –'

'Yes, but that's absurd. They left out the African ones – it's eight or nine at least. Davey and I were trying to count up. Your father and his best man and the best man's best friend, three. That takes us to Kenya and all the hot stuff there – the horsewhipping and the aeroplane and the Frenchman who won her in a lottery. Davey's not sure she ever married him, but give her the benefit of the doubt: four. Rawl and Plugge five and six, Gewan seven, the young man who writes books on Greece – relatively young – old enough to be the father of this one – eight and the new boy nine. I can't think of another, can you?'

At this point the telephone bell rang and my uncle picked up the receiver. 'That you, Payne? Where are you now – East India Docks? I'd like the *Evening Standard*, please. Thank you, Payne.' He rang off. 'He can take you to the station, Fanny. I suppose you're catching the 6.05? If you wouldn't mind being a bit on the early side so that he can be back here in good time for the cocktail party.'

'Cocktail party?' I said. I was stunned. Uncle Matthew loathed parties, execrated strangers and never drank anything, not even a glass of wine with his meals.

'It's a new idea – don't you have them at Oxford? You will soon, mark my words. I rather like them. You're not obliged to talk to anybody and when you get home, it's bedtime.'

Timidly, without much conviction, but feeling it my duty to do so, I now broached the subject which was the reason for my visit. I asked him if he would like to see Fabrice, Linda's child whom Alfred and I had adopted. He was at school with our Charlie; they had been born on the same day and in the same nursing home; Linda had died; I had survived and left the home with two babies instead of one. Aunt Sadie went to Eton sometimes and took the boys out but Uncle Matthew had not set eyes on his grandson since he was a baby, during the war.

'Oh, no, my dear Fanny, thank you very much,' he muttered, embarrassed, when he understood what I was trying to say. 'I don't set great store by other people's children, you know. Give him this and tell him to keep away, will you?' A pocket book lay beside him – he took out a fiver. This unlucky idea of mine was a cold spoon in the soufflé; the conversation lapsed and I was thankful when Payne arrived with the *Evening Standard*.

'Eighteen and six on the clock, m'lord.'

My uncle gave him a pound and two half-crowns. 'Thank you, Payne.'

'Thank you – much obliged, m'lord.'

'Now, Payne, you'll take Miss Fanny to Paddington – no scorching, I beg, we don't want her in the ditch, we are all very fond of Miss Fanny. While you are there, would you go to Wyman's, present my compliments to Mr Barker of the book-stall and see if he could oblige me with a ball of string? Come straight back, will you? – we are going to Lord Fortinbras in Groom Place. I am invited for six-thirty – it wouldn't do to miss the beginning.'

When I arrived at Oxford I was startled to see Alfred waiting for me on the platform. He never came to meet me as a rule – I had not even said what train I would take. 'Nothing wrong?' I said. 'The boys – ?'

'The boys? Oh dearest, I'm sorry if I frightened you.' He then told me that he had been appointed Ambassador to Paris.

2

It may be imagined that I got little sleep that night. My thoughts whizzed about, to begin with quite rational; more and more fantastic as the hours went on; finally between sleeping and waking, of a nightmare quality. In the first place, of course, I was happy to think that my dear Alfred's merits should have been publicly recognized at last, that he should receive a dazzling prize (as it seemed to me) to reward him for being so good and clever. Surely he was wasted in a chair of Pastoral Theology, even though his lectures on the pastoral theme made a lasting impression on those who heard them. During the war he had filled a post of national importance; after that I had quite expected to see him take his place in the arena. But (whether from lack of ambition or lack of opportunity I never really knew) he had returned quietly to Oxford when his war-work came to an end and seemed fated to remain there for the rest of his days. For my part, I have already told* how, as an eager young bride, I had found University life disappointing; I never reversed that opinion. I was used to being a don's wife, I knew exactly what it involved and felt myself adequate; that was all. The years rolled by with nothing to distinguish them; generations of boys came and went; like the years I found that they resembled each other. As I got older I lost my taste for the company of adolescents. My own children were all away now: the two youngest at Eton; Basil – oh where was he and when should I confide my fears about him to Alfred? Bearded David, the eldest, was a don at a redbrick university, living with the times, or so he informed me. In moments of introspection I often thought that a woman's need for children is almost entirely physical. When they are babies one cuddles and kisses and slaps them and has a highly satisfying animal relationship with them. But when they grow up and leave the nest they hardly seem to belong any more. Was I much use to the boys now? As for Alfred, detached from all human emotions, I thought it more than likely that if I were to disappear he would go and live in college, as happy as he had ever been with me. What was I doing on earth at all and how was I going to fill in the thirty-odd years which might lie ahead before the grave?

* In *Love in a Cold Climate*

Of course I knew that this state of mind is common among middle-aged, middle-class women whose children have gone into the world. Its causes, both psychological and physiological, are clearly understood nowadays and so is the fact that there is no remedy. What can't be cured must be endured. But Alfred's miraculous appointment might effect a miraculous cure. I had often longed to leave behind me a token of my existence, a shell on the seashore of eternity. Here was my chance; Alfred might become one of those plenipotentiaries whose names are ever remembered with gratitude and respect, and some of the credit might be mine. At the very least I would now have a little tiny place in history as one of the occupants of a famous house.

All this was rather cheerful, if high-falutin', midnight stuff. But by the early hours doubts and terrors were crowding in. I knew little enough about Paris or diplomatic life, but I did know, like everybody else, that Sir Louis and Lady Leone, whom we were to replace, held a glittering court there, reminiscent of the great embassies of olden days. Lady Leone was universally admitted to be more beautiful, charming and witty than any other woman in public life. Absurd to think that I could compete with her – how could I fill her place even adequately? Not only had I no training, not the very slightest knowledge of diplomacy, but I had certain decided disabilities. I can never remember people, for instance, either their names or their faces or anything at all about them. I am a poor housekeeper. When I first arrived in Oxford as a young bride I had resolved not to be as other dons' wives in this respect; to begin with my dinners were decidedly better than theirs. However, my dear Mrs Heathery never improved beyond a certain point, I had four hungry boys to shovel down the vitamins and a husband who never noticed what he ate. After the end of coupons, other people's food improved, mine did not. I had never presided over a large household or had more than three servants (one of them a daily) in my life. What would the domestic side of the Embassy be like, mismanaged by me? Visiting Ministers, or worse, visiting Royalty, would complain and this would be bad for Alfred. My clothes – better to draw a veil. So, with my absent-mindedness and ghastly food and ghastly clothes I should become the Aunt Sally of diplomatic life, a butt and a joke.

I only wished I could go to sleep for a bit and forget the whole thing. Yes, a joke. I began to see myself in farcical situations. This silly habit of kissing everybody – quite new since the war. My ex-undergraduates and other men friends kiss when they see me; it has become an automatic gesture. Mental picture: a party in some official building, very pompous and grand. Out of pure distraction I kiss the President of the Republic.

I suffer from weak ankles and sometimes topple over unexpectedly. When this happens in the Turl nobody minds; I am picked up by some friendly young chap, go home and change my stockings. Mental picture: the Arc de Triomphe, military music, wreaths, television cameras. Flop, down I come, extinguishing the Eternal Flame. Now I really must wake myself up properly from these half-nightmares, undermining my morale. I stood at the window and, watching the sun's first rays as they fell upon Christ Church, I let myself get very cold. Then I went back to my warm bed, and fell into a dreamless sleep.

In the morning when I told Alfred some of these unnerving thoughts (not the kissing and falling-down ones however) he said, 'I specially didn't want you to lie in bed working yourself up, that's why I never mentioned your side of the business last night. I'm glad to say Philip is in England and I've told him to come and have luncheon with you today. You'll be able to talk it all over with him and get these worries out of your system. I must go to London for a few hours.'

'Oh, of course we shall find Philip in Paris – I'd quite forgotten he was there. I say, what a comfort!'

'Yes, and a great comfort to me, too. Meanwhile do remember that the social side is quite unimportant. As I told you last night mine is intended to be a serious mission – sobriety, security the keynotes. The *ci-devants* have had their day with the Leones, I intend to concentrate on the politicians and people of real importance. And by the way, dearest, perhaps your – shall I say – flightier relations could be discouraged from paying us too many visits?'

'Yes, darling, I quite agree. But the boys –'

'The boys! Why of course it will be their home whenever they want to come. Nice to have a healthy youthful element, which has been lacking there of late.'

This was clearly not the moment to mention my worries about Basil. Anyhow, the holidays were about to begin, when he was supposed to be leaving the crammer to work on his own in some quiet place. I decided to wait and see what happened.

Philip Cliffe-Musgrave sauntered in at one o'clock. Ten years younger than me, he was by far my favourite of all the undergraduates who had passed through our hands, so to speak. Owing to the war, he had come late to Oxford, a man, not a boy. He had, I thought, been slightly in love with me and I might easily have returned this slight love had not the example of my mother, the Bolter, for ever discouraged me from such adventures which begin so cheerfully and finish so shoddily, I had noticed. However, we had trodden the pleasant path of a loving friendship and I had remained extremely fond of him. He was an elegant creature, the best-dressed man I have ever seen, and one of those people who seem to have been born with a knowledge of the world. Alfred thought him very brilliant.

'Well,' we said now, looking at each other and laughing.

'*Madame l'Ambassadrice*. Too interesting for words. There have been the wildest rumours about Sir Louis's successor, but truth is certainly stranger than fiction. The dinners I shall be asked to when it gets out that I actually know you!'

'Philip, I'm terrified!'

'No wonder. They'll gobble you up, all those smart women. At first, that is. I think you'll defend yourself in the long run.'

'You are horrid – Alfred said you would reassure me.'

'Yes, yes, I'm only teasing.'

'Be careful – I'm in a delicate state. Such a lot of things I want to ask; where to begin? Do the Leones know?'

'That they are leaving? Oh yes.'

'I mean about us?'

'When I came away, three days ago, he had been told it was a possibility. They'll be pleased, I think. That is, it will kill her to leave the Embassy but if she has to hand it over she'd rather it were to someone like you.'

'Oh. Dreary, d'you mean?'

'Different. And above all not the wife of a colleague. You don't know what the jealousy between wives is like, in that service. As for Sir Louis, he is a typical career diplomat. He despises the amateur and is certain that Alfred will make an unholy mess of the job. This, of course, will soften the blow of leaving quite considerably.'

'Philip, do tell me – why have they chosen Alfred?'

'Up to their clever tricks, you know.'

'Now what's coming?' I said, uneasily.

'Don't be so nervous. I only mean that when the war was comfortably over, the Entente doing all right, the allies in love with each other – not the rulers but the people – everybody busy with their own internal affairs, they sent Sir Louis to captivate the French. And oh, how he succeeded – they eat out of his hand. Now that we are running into choppy seas they send Alfred to puzzle them.'

'And will he puzzle them?'

'As he does everybody. His whole career has been one long mystery if you come to consider it. What was he doing with Ernie Bevin during the war? Have you ever understood? Nobody else has. Did you know that he lunches at No. 10, alone with the P.M., at least once a week? Bet you didn't. Or that the well-informed regard him as one of those people who really govern the country?'

'Alfred is very secret,' I said reflectively. 'I often think that's why I'm so happy with him. Plate glass is such a bore.'

'I shall be very much interested to see him at work. No doubt he will keep Bouche-Bontemps and his merry men in a state of chronic perplexity which may be very useful.'

'Who is Bouche-Bontemps?'

'My poor Fanny, you'll have to mug up the political situation a bit. Surely you must have heard of him – he's the French foreign minister.'

'They change so often.'

'Yes, but there are a few old faithfuls who reappear like the soldiers in *Faust* and he is one.'

'I know about M. Mendès-France.'

'Only because he's called France. Everybody in England has heard of him because the *Daily Post* goes on about Mr France, which makes it nice and easy.'

'I know about General de Gaulle.'

'Yes, well you can forget him, for the moment at any rate.'

'To go back to the Leones. She minds leaving dreadfully?'

'All Ambassadresses mind. They are generally carried screaming from the house – *"encore un instant, M. le Bourreau"* – poor Pauline, yes, she is in despair.'

'And you'll hate to lose her?'

'Yes. I adore her. At the same time, Fanny, as it's you, I shall be on your side.'

'Need there be sides? Must we be enemies?'

'It is never otherwise. You'd better know the form. By the time you arrive she'll have had an enormous send-off at the Gare du Nord – the whole of Paris – flash-lights, flowers, speeches, tears. All her world will have heard – not directly from her but by a sort of bush telegraph – what brutes you and Alfred are. I suppose I shall swim against the tide, but I shan't exhaust myself – a few languid strokes – because it will turn so quickly. The point is that, until you arrive, Parisian society will curse upon your name and wish you dead, but from the moment you set foot in the Embassy you will become entirely delightful. Soon we shall hear that the Leones never really quite *did*, in Paris.'

'How cynical you are.'

'That's life, I guess. Mind you their friends will continue to love them, give dinners for them when they go back and so on. But people are always attracted by power and high office; a house like the Embassy, to which the rulers of the earth gravitate, is worth more to its occupant than the prettiest face, the kindest heart, the oldest friendship. Come now, Fanny, you know enough of the world to know that, I suppose. In this case you are the beneficiary. Soon it will be as though Pauline had never been there – Pauline Leone. Pauline Borghese never leaves and she is on the side of the sitting tenant.'

'Why Pauline Borghese?'

'It was her house, you know. We bought it from her, furniture and all, after Waterloo.'

'Oh, dear. You haven't really reassured me very much. There's another thing, Philip – clothes. Of course there's always Elliston's Petite Boutique but it's so expensive.'

'I shouldn't worry. As soon as you arrive, you'll make an arrangement with one of the dressmakers there. Aren't you rather rich now, Fanny?'

'Richer, yes we are. My father left me quite a lot – I was surprised. But what with the boys and so on I never feel I ought to spend much on myself.'

He then told me about the running of an embassy and calmed my fears in that direction. According to him, the comptroller and the housekeeper do the work. 'You will only need a social secretary – some nice quiet girl who won't get married at once.'

'I'd thought of that. My cousin Louisa Fort William has got the very one, Jean Mackintosh.'

'Yes, I know her. Not a ball of fire, is she? By the way, whom d'you think I saw at a cocktail party last night? Lord Alconleigh.'

'No! Do tell me what he was doing?'

'He was standing with his back to the wall, a large glass of water in his hand, glaring furiously into space. The rest of the company was huddled together, rather like a herd of deer with an old lion in the offing. It was impressive – not altogether cosy, you know.'

Alfred's appointment was well received by the responsible newspapers, partly no doubt because many of their employees had been at Oxford and known him there. It was violently opposed by the *Daily Post*. This little paper, once considered suitable for schoolroom reading, had been bought by a press peer known to the world as Old Grumpy and now reflected his jaundiced view of life. It fed on scandal, grief and all forms of human misery, exposing them with a sort of spiteful glee which the public evidently relished, since the more cruelly the *Daily Post* tortured its victims the higher the circulation rose. Its policy, if it could be said to have one, was to be against foreign countries, cultural bodies, and the existing government, whether Conservative or Labour. Above all, it abominated the Foreign Office. The burden of its song on this occasion was, what is the point of maintaining an expensive foreign service which cannot produce a trained man to be Ambassador in Paris but has to fall back on a Professor of Pastoral Theology.

The French papers were perfectly friendly, if puzzled. The *Figaro* produced a leading article by a member of the Académie Française in which the word pastoral was wilfully misunderstood and theology left out altogether. The Knight on horseback (Alfred) coming to the Shepherdess in her orchard (Marianne) was the theme. No mention of the Knight's wife and boys (Alfred was a Knight now; he had been to London and seen the Queen).

I received many letters of congratulation, praising Alfred, praising me, saying how well we were suited to the work we should have to do and then going on to speak of some child or friend or protégé of the writer's who would like to join our establishment in almost any capacity. Louisa Fort William, ever practical, cut out the praise and offered me Jean. Alfred knew this Jean, who had been up at Oxford, and did not include her among my flightier relations. With his approval I wrote and engaged her to be our social secretary.

At Oxford, Alfred's colleagues and their wives took but little account of our news. This was no surprise to me. Nobody who has not lived in a university town can have any idea of its remoteness from the world. The dons live like monks in a cloister, outside time and space, occupied only with the daily round; ambassadors to Paris do not enter their ken or interest them in the very least. To be Warden or Dean would seem to them a far greater thing. At this time, it is true, there were some rich, worldly dons whose wives dressed at Dior, and who knew about Paris and embassies, a tiny minority on the fringe of the University – in every way; they did not even live in the town itself as we did. They regarded Alfred as a bore; he disregarded them; their wives disregarded me. These Dior dons were not pleased by our appointment; they laughed long and loud, as kind friends informed us, at the idea of it and made witty jokes at our expense. No doubt they thought the honour would sit better upon them; how I agreed with them, really!

After twenty-five years of university life my outlook was more akin to that of the monkish than to the Dior type of don, but, though I had little first-hand experience of the world, I did know what it was. My cousin Linda had been in contact with it and my mother had always been of it, even during her wildest vagaries. Lady Montdore, though she saw real life through distorting glasses, had had the world and its usage at her fingertips; I had not been a sort of lady-in-waiting to her for nothing. How I wished she were still alive to see what fate had brought to me – like the Dior dons she would have mocked and disapproved but unlike them she would have been rather impressed, no doubt.

Our summer holidays passed as usual. Alfred and I went to stay with Davey Warbeck, in Kent, and paid one or two other visits. Our youngest boys, Charlie and Fabrice, were hardly with us at all. They were invited by a boy called Sigismond de Valhubert, who was at their house at Eton, to stay in Provence, after which all three went shooting in Scotland. Bearded David sent postcards from the Lakes – he was on a walking tour. As for Basil, he might have been dead for all I knew; I weakly told Alfred that he had gone to Barcelona to rub up his Spanish. Very soon we came to the last days of August and of our monotonous but familiar Oxford life.

3

I shall never forget my first impression of the Embassy. After the hurly-burly of our reception at the Gare du Nord, after the drive through Paris traffic which always unnerves those not accustomed to it, the large, beautiful, honey-coloured house, in its quiet courtyard, seemed a haven of delight. It has more the atmosphere of a country than a town house. For one thing, no town noises can be heard, only the rustle of leaves, the twittering of birds, an occasional mowing-machine, an owl. The French windows on the garden side fill the rooms with sunshine and air in amazing quantities. They open to a vista of trees; the only solid edifice in sight is the dome of the Invalides, a purple shadow on the horizon, hardly visible through summer leaves. Except for that and the Eiffel Tower, on the extreme right hand of this prospect, there is nothing to show that the house is situated in the centre of the most prosperous and busy capital on the continent of Europe. Philip took us straight up to the first floor. At the top of the fine staircase there is an antechamber leading to the yellow drawing-room, the white and gold drawing-room, the green drawing-room (to be our private sitting-room) and Pauline Borghese's bedroom, so recently vacated by the other Pauline. These rooms all face south and open into each other. Behind them, looking north over the courtyard, are the Ambassador's dressing-room and library and the social secretary's office. Well-wishers had filled the house with flowers; they made it look very beautiful, glowing in the evening light, and also reassured me. Many people seemed prepared, at any rate, to like us.

I believe it would have been normal for me to have paid a visit to the outgoing ambassadress soon after our appointment was announced. However, the said ambassadress had set up such an uninhibited wail when she knew she was to leave, proclaiming her misery to all and sundry and refusing so furiously to look on the bright side (a happy and respected old age in a Kensington flat), that it was felt she might not be very nice to me. Her attitude seemed rather exaggerated until I saw what it was that we were usurping; then I understood. Lady Leone had reigned in this palace – the word reign is not too much, with her beauty, elegance and great funniness she had been like a queen here – for five whole years; no wonder she left it all with death in her heart.

As for me, my fears fell away and so did my middle-aged gloom. The house seemed to be on my side; from the very first moment I set foot in it I was stimulated, interested, amused and ready for anything. When I woke up next morning to find myself in Pauline's bed, the bed of both the Paulines, opening my eyes on the dark red walls and mahogany furniture, a curious contrast to the light gaiety of the rest of the house, I thought, 'This is the first day, the beginning.' Then I wondered how I should feel on the last day, the end. I was deeply sorry for Lady Leone.

Alfred appeared, in high spirits. He was going to have breakfast in his library. 'Philip will come and talk to you while you have yours. He says you must never get up too early. You'll have a tiring life here; try and be quiet in the morning.' He dumped a lot of papers on my bed and went off. There was nothing much about us in them – a small flashlight photograph in the *Figaro* – an announcement in *The*

Times that we had arrived – until, at the bottom of the heap, I came to the *Daily Post*. The whole of the front page was covered with an enormous photograph of Alfred, mouth idiotically open, apparently giving the Hitler salute. My heart sank; horrified I read:

> The mission of the former Pastoral Theologian, Sir Alfred Wincham, to Paris has begun with an unfortunate incident. As M. Bouche-Bontemps, who had interrupted his holiday to meet Sir Alfred at the Gare du Nord, came forward with a gesture of welcome, our envoy rudely brushed him aside and confabulated, at length, IN GERMAN, with a tall fair young man in the crowd . . .

I looked up from the paper. Philip was standing by my bed, laughing.

'Is this all right? One always used to see Pauline before she got up – it seemed a good moment.'

'Oh dear,' I said, 'you'll miss that lovely face under the baldaquin.'

'This is different,' he sat down on the end of the bed, 'and in some ways nicer. So, I see you've got to the incident.'

'Philip!'

'Don't say it has upset you. It's nothing to what there will be – the *Daily Post* man here, Amyas Mockbar (you mustn't forget that name), is preparing the full treatment for you; you're on Old Grumpy's black list.'

'But why are we?'

'The English Ambassador here always is; besides, Lord Grumpy personally dislikes Alfred, who seems unaware of his existence.'

'He is unaware. There's one blessing, Alfred only reads *The Times* and I shan't mind what the *Daily Post* says.'

'Don't you be too sure. Mockbar has a wonderful knack of making people mind. I've had to give up seeing him and I mind that – he's such a jolly old bird, there's nothing more enjoyable than drinking whisky with old Amyas at the Pont Royal bar.'

'But this incident,' I said.

'You see, you are minding already.'

'Yes, because it's entirely invented.'

'Not entirely – he never entirely invents, that's where he's so devilish.'

'Alfred talked to a German at the Gare du Nord?'

'While you were being introduced to Madame Hué, Alfred spied poor old Dr Wolff of Trinity peering at him under the arc lights. Of course, being Alfred, he darted off – then he came straight back and explained the whole thing to Bouche-Bontemps. The incident was of no consequence, but it wasn't entirely invented.'

'But Dr Wolff isn't a tall, fair, young German – he's a tiny little old dark one.'

'Mockbar never sees things quite like other people, his style is strictly subjective; you'll have to get used to it.'

'Yes, I see.'

'There are a lot of things you'll have to get used to here, but I think he is the worst. What have you done about a social secretary?'

'I've got Jean Mackintosh coming next week. I wanted to settle myself in first and Alfred thought you'd lend me a hand until then, though I know you are far too important.'

'Certainly I will. It amuses me and I can help you as I know the form. There's no other work at present – total lull on the international front and all the ministers are away. Bouche-Bontemps is off again tomorrow. So let's get down to it. First, here's a list of the people who have sent flowers; you'll want to thank them yourself. Then Alfred thought you had better see the arrangements for this week – rather hectic, I'm afraid. You have to polish off the colleagues – visit them, you know – and there are eighty embassies here so it takes a bit of doing.'

'Are there so many countries in the world?'

'Of course not – the whole thing is great nonsense – but we have to keep up the fiction to please the Americans. There's nothing the millionaires like so much as being ambassadors; at present there are eighty of them, keenly subscribing to party funds. We have to tag along. In small countries like the Channel Islands practically all the male adults are ambassadors, nowadays.'

I was looking at the list of names he had given me. 'I only know one of the people who have sent flowers – Grace de Valhubert.'

'She's still away,' said Philip. 'How do you know her?'

'Her boy and my two are friends at school. They've just been staying down in Provence with her. If they have kindly said they will come here for Christmas it's chiefly on account of Sigismond.'

'Sweet Sigi, fascinating child,' said Philip with a good deal of feeling. 'I may as well tell you, Fanny, since we are such old friends and anyhow you're sure to find out, that I'm in love with Grace.' I felt a small, stupid pang when he said this. No doubt I would selfishly have preferred him to concentrate on me, as he used to when he was at Oxford.

'With what result?'

He said bitterly, 'Oh, she keeps me hanging about. She probably rather likes to show her husband, whom she is madly in love with, that somebody is madly in love with her.'

'Silly old love,' I said, 'bother it. Let's go on with the list. Who is Mrs Jungfleisch?'

'Mildred *Young fleesh*. The Americans have begun to copy our tiresome habit of not pronouncing names as they are spelt. She says you know her.'

'Really? But I never remember –'

'Nor you do. She's always going to Oxford so I expect you have met her.'

'With the Dior dons probably, though I hardly ever see them – not their cup of tea at all.'

'I suppose not.'

'There, you see yourself how I'm not. So how shall I manage here where people are twice as frightening?'

'Now – now!'

'Mrs Jungfleisch is a *femme du monde*, I suppose?'

'Yes, indeed. I've known her for years – we went to the same charm school in New York when I was with U.N.O.'

'You went to a charm school? I always thought you were charm personified!'

'Thank you. Mildred and I went to see if we couldn't pick up a little extra warmth of manner, but as you so kindly suggest we found we were too advanced for the course.'

'The person who needs it is me.'

'Wouldn't be any good to you, because of not remembering who people are. A memory for names and faces is the A.B.C. of charm, it's all built up on the pleased-to-see-you formula, but you must show that you know who it is you're being pleased to see.'

'I know so few Americans,' I said. 'Do you like them, Philip?'

'Yes, I'm paid to.'

'In your heart of hearts?'

'Oh, poor things, you can't dislike them. I feel intensely sorry for them, especially the ones in America – they are so mad and ill and frightened.'

'Shall we see a lot of them here? – I suppose so. Alfred has been told he must collaborate.'

'You can't avoid it, the place teems with them.'

'Any friendly ones?'

'Friendly? They make you long for an enemy. You'll like some of them though. They fall into three categories, the ones here. There are the business men trying to make a better position for themselves at home as experts on Yurrup. They are afraid there may be a boom in Yurrup. Of course they don't want to miss anything if there is. For instance, there's the art market – all these old antique objects to marry up to the dollar. (Art is booming so they love it, they even call their children it.) There are dollars in music too – Schu and Schu can be quite as profitable as Tel and Tel. Art and music are only to be found in Yurrup; they come over prospecting for them – at the same time they don't want to be left out of things at home, so they play an uneasy game of musical chairs between Yurrup and the States, hurtling to and fro in rockets, getting iller and madder and more frightened than ever.'

'Frightened of what?'

'Oh, somebody else being in on something first; falling down dead; a recession – I don't know, dreadfully fidgety. Then there are literally thousands of officials who are paid to be here. One never sees them, except for a few diplomatic colleagues. They are dreadfully unhappy; they huddle together in a sort of ghetto – terrified of losing their American accent.'

'What a funny thing to mind losing.'

'It would be ghastly for them if they did. They'd be branded for ever as un-American. Finally we have the Henry James type of expatriates who live here because they can't stick it at home – perfect dears. A bit on the serious side perhaps, but at least they don't jabber on about art and dollars – it's the future of mankind with them. Mildred is in that camp – camp commandant you might say.'

'Shall I like her?'

'You won't get the chance. She adores Pauline and is preparing to be very cold and correct with you.'

'Then why does she send me flowers?'

'It's an American tic. They can't help doing it – they send them to friend and foe alike. Whenever they pass a flower shop their fingers itch for a pen to write down somebody's name and address.'

'I'm all for it,' I said, looking at the Jungfleisch sweet-peas on my dressing-table. 'Lovely, they are –'

*

After a few days in the Embassy I began to suspect that something was afoot. Of course in a new house one cannot account for every sight and sound; even allowing for this I sensed a mystery. From my bedroom I distinctly heard a gathering of people making merry, some sort of party which went on every evening until the early hours; I would wake up in the night to shriek upon shriek of laughter. I thought the noise must come from the next house until I discovered that this is a block of offices belonging to the American government. Surely their employees did not laugh all night? By my bed there was a telephone with a line direct to the public exchange, not through the Embassy, and a discreet little buzzing bell. This sometimes rang and when I answered it I would hear confused phrases like 'Oh Lord – I forgot', '*C'est toi, chérie? Oh pardon, Madame, il y a erreur*' – or merely '*Aïe!*' before the line went dead. Twice Alfred's *Times* arrived late with the crossword puzzle already done.

The courtyard always seemed to be full of elegantly dressed people. I presumed they had come to write their names in our book (whose pages, according to Alfred, read like a dramatis personae of the whole history of France). Why, then, were they so often grouped on the little outside staircase in the south-west corner of the courtyard? I could have sworn that I saw the same ones over and over again, people with famous faces known even to me; a bejewelled dressmaker like a puppet in a film cartoon, face composed of brown golf balls; a Field-Marshal; a pianist with a guilty look; an ex-king. A pretty young woman, vaguely familiar to me, seemed to live in the courtyard, constantly up and down the little staircase with flowers, books, or gramophone records; sometimes she was carrying a huge picnic basket. Catching my eye one day she blushed and looked away. Mockbar, whom I had now met, was often in the Faubourg peering through our gateway. No mistaking him; he had the bucolic appearance of some little old groom, weather-beaten face, curved back, stiff bandy legs, wildly flailing elbows and an aureole of fuzzy grey hair.

'I wonder if you would like to make a statement?' he said, rolling towards me as I was walking home from the dressmaker one afternoon.

'Statement?'

'On the situation in your house.'

'Oh you are kind, but no, thank you very much, you must ask my husband.' I went indoors and sent for Philip.

'Philip,' I said, 'I'm a paper. Would you like to make a statement?'

'Statement?'

'On the situation in my house.'

He gave me a whimsical look, half-amused, half-worried.

'Who has the rooms on the right-hand side of the courtyard – did I see them when you showed me round?'

'Yes, it's time you knew,' he said. 'The fact is, Pauline has dug herself in there and we can't get her to leave.'

'Lady Leone? But she did leave. I saw her on a newsreel, in floods. How can she still be here?'

'She left the Gare du Nord all right, but she had the train stopped at Orry-la-Ville and came straight back, still holding Bouche-Bontemps' roses. She said she was very ill, possibly dying, and forced Mrs Trott to make the bed in the entresol for her. There's a sort of little flat where the social secretary used to live. Naturally she's not ill in the least. She has the whole of Paris in there day and night – I wonder you haven't heard them.'

'I have. I thought it was the Americans next door.'

'Americans never shriek like that.'

'Now I understand everything. But Philip, this is very bad for Alfred. Such an absurd situation, at the beginning of his mission.'

'That's what the F.O. thinks. They tell us to get her out – yes, but how? I've just been on to Ashley again. You see, at the beginning one thought it was a lark – that in a day or two she'd get tired of it. So the idea was not to bother you. But now the Parisians have joined in the joke and it's the fashion to go and see her there. People are pouring back from their holidays so as not to be left out. The smart resorts are in despair – nobody left to be photographed on the beaches. So, of course, she's having the time of her life and quite honestly I don't see how we shall ever induce her to go. We're all at our wits' end.'

'Can't we tell the servants not to feed her?'

'They don't. Mildred brings her food, like a raven.'

'The one with picnic basket? We could stop her coming – tell the concierge not to let her in?'

'Very difficult – it would be awfully embarrassing for him to have to bar the way. He's known her for years.'

'Yes, I see, and of course we can't very well kidnap her. Then could we bribe her? What does she like best in the world?'

'English top policy makers.'

'What, M.P.s and things?'

'Ministers, bankers, the Archbishop, Master of the Belvoir, editor of *The Times* and so on. She likes to think she is seeing history on the boil.'

'Well, that's rather splendid. Surely these policy makers must be on our side? Why don't they lure her to England – luncheon at Downing Street or a place for the big debate on Thursday?'

'I see you don't understand the point of Mildred. They worship her in the House – they can hardly bear to have a debate at all until she's in her place there. She's the best audience they've ever had. As for luncheon at Downing Street, why, she stays there when she's in London.'

'Oh, bother – !'

'And now I come to think of it, she isn't really the clue to our problem.'

'You said she brought the food.'

'I know. Food means nothing to Pauline.'

'Still, she can't live without it.'

'The point is, she can. She's forever going off to Tring for the starvation cure. It's a mystery to me, this starving. People on rafts begin eating each other after a week; Pauline and Mildred are sometimes at Tring for a whole month – not a nibble out of each other's shoulders.'

'Oh dear, we don't want her here for another month. Surely the policy makers must stand by their employees, Philip, and lend a hand? Have you spoken to any of them?'

'They are doing what they can. The P.M. had a word with Sir Louis at Brooks' last night. No good at all. Sir Louis just sat with his hand over his nose heaving with giggles in that endearing way he has,' said Philip affectionately. 'But after all, what can he do? Apart from the fact that it amuses him to death –'

'Some important person ought to come over and see her – tell her she's being unpatriotic and so on. She is, too.'

'We've tried that. Moley came between two aeroplanes. He arrived very strict, but he didn't keep it up. He said she lay there like a beautiful stag dying in the forest, and he hadn't the heart to be cross.'

'Why do you think she's doing it?'

'Oh, I don't think there's any very profound reason – it amuses her – she's got nothing else to do – and if it teases you she can easily bear that. She thinks Alfred got the job by plotting against Sir Louis.'

'You know he didn't.'

'Didn't he? In any case, Sir Louis wouldn't have stayed on – it was time for a change.'

'I saw Mockbar in the street.'

'He'll go to town on it all right.'

'Has he seen Lady Leone?'

'Certainly not. Even Pauline draws the line somewhere.'

'We shall have to tell Alfred before Mockbar's piece appears.'

'He knows. It's he who has been saying don't tell Fanny.'

Distant, derisive laughter assailed my ear. The evening was drawing on; the entresol was waking up. I felt quite furious.

'How is the Quai d'Orsay taking it?'

'Thrilled. Hughie has given out that no wives are to join in, but I'm not sure I didn't see –'

'Who is Hughie?'

'Jacques-Olivier Hué, head of the protocol. Always known as Hughie.'

I was getting more irritated every minute. I have a sense of humour, I hope; this situation was clearly very funny; it was maddening not to be able to join in such a good joke, to be on the stuffy, official side against all these jolly bandits. I said, spitefully, 'As far as Alfred can make out, your friend Sir Louis simply lived for pleasure when he was here.'

'Ambassadors always go on like that about each other,' said Philip. 'One's predecessor is idle and one's successor is an intriguer. It's a classic of the service. But Sir Louis was an excellent ambassador, make no mistake about it.'

'Oh all right,' I said. 'Let's try and keep our tempers. If we think it over calmly there must be a solution.'

A long silence fell between us. At last I said, 'I'm going to speak to Mrs Jungfleisch.'

'You can now if you want to – she's sitting in her car in the courtyard, reading the New Deal.'

'Why isn't she in there shrieking with the others?'

'I tell you, she's a very serious girl – she puts aside certain hours every day for historical study. Besides she says the room is too hot – twenty people in that tiny room on a day like this – it must be the Black Hole of Calcutta.'

'Then why not go home and read the New Deal there?'

'She likes to be in on things.'

'The cheek of it!' I said.

I stumped out into the courtyard, opened the door of Mrs Jungfleisch's Buick and boldly got in beside her. She was very fair and pretty with a choir-boy look, accentuated by the big, white, pleated collar she wore and straight hair done with a fringe. She turned her calm, intelligent blue eyes upon me, put down a document she was reading and said, 'How d'you do? I am Mildred Jungfleisch. We did meet, ages ago, at Oxford.'

I was agreeably surprised by her voice which was not very American, rather more like that of an Englishwoman who has once lived in the United States. Although I knew about the charm school prospectus being too elementary for her and guessed that this was the fully qualified charmer's voice, specially warm, for soothing an irate ambassadress in the grounds of her own embassy, it worked. Feeling decidedly soothed, I said: 'Please excuse me for getting into your motor without an invitation.'

'Please excuse me for sitting in your courtyard without an invitation.'

'I want to talk to you.'

'I'm sure you must, Lady Wincham. It's about Pauline, of course?'

'Yes – how long do you think she intends to stay?'

'Pauline is utterly unpredictable. She will leave when she feels inclined to. Knowing her as I do, I guess she'll still be here at Christmas.'

'With you still feeding her?'

'I'm afraid so.'

'If my husband were a private person, none of this would matter. As things are, I intend to get rid of Lady Leone.'

'How?'

'I don't know.'

'In my experience of Pauline it is impossible to deflect her from her purpose.'

'Aha! She has a purpose?'

'Please do not misunderstand me, Lady Wincham. Her purpose is a simple one, she wants to have a good time. She has no desire to upset you, still less to damage the embassy or embarrass the Foreign Office. It all began because she had a sudden impulse to stop the train at Orry-la-Ville and spend one last night in this house which she worships – you can have no idea what she feels about it.'

'I quite understand, on the contrary. People do get like that about houses and this one is so very extraordinary.'

'You are under the spell already! Then she found she was having fun. She rang up a few friends, for a joke; they came around. It started to be the thing to do; one signs your book and then one goes in to see Pauline. Excuse me, please, there's the Nuncio – I think he's looking for her door.'

She got out of the motor, put the prelate on his way and came back again.

'Philip tells me that you are a very responsible person,' I said. 'Couldn't you explain to her that if she goes on like this she will undo all the good she and Sir Louis have done during their brilliant embassy?'

The honest choir-boy eyes opened wide. 'Indeed, Lady Wincham, I have told her. I've even pointed out that only one person, in the end, can reap an advantage from her action.'

'And who is that?'

'Why, Mr Khrushchev.'

I felt this was going rather far; still it was all on the right side.

'Unfortunately Pauline has no public conscience whatever. I find many European women are like that. They do not give a thought to the great issues of our time, such as the delicate balance of East and West – they will not raise a finger to ease the path of N.A.T.O., U.N.E.S.C.O., O.E.E.C. or the World Bank. Pauline is frankly not interested.'

'So there's nothing you can do?'

'Regretfully, no.'

'All right,' I said, 'I may look rather mousy but I must tell you that I very often get my own way. Good-bye.'

'Good-bye, Lady Wincham. Awfully nice to have seen you.'

4

'We must send for Davey,' I said.

This uncle of mine by marriage had long filled the same role in our family as the Duke of Wellington in that of Queen Victoria. Whenever some apparently insuperable difficulty of a worldly nature arose, one consulted him. While Alfred and I had been staying with him, we had of course talked of little else than our appointment and Davey had urged me not to forget that he understood the French. He had once lived in Paris (some forty years ago), had frequented salons and been the darling of the hostesses. He understood them. He had never liked them much, 'cross, clever things', and indeed, before the Nazis had taken over, during the decadent days of the Weimar Republic, he had greatly preferred the Germans. It was a question of shared interests; his two chief ones, health and music, were catered for better in Germany. As soon as the healthy, musical race began to show other preoccupations, Davey left Berlin and all the delightful Bads he was so fond of and which did him so much good, never to return. He always said thereafter that he did not understand the Germans. But he continued to understand the French.

I don't know what magic wand I expected him to wave, since Lady Leone and Mrs Jungfleisch were not French and he had never claimed to understand them. True, he was a childhood friend of Lady Leone's but that was no reason why he should prove more persuasive than the head of the Foreign Office. It would, however, be a comfort to have him with me as I felt sure he would be on my side, more sure than I was about Philip whose loyalties must, in the nature of things, be rather divided. After my talk with Mrs Jungfleisch I had a long discussion with Alfred as a result of which I telephoned there and then to Davey.

'It's an S.O.S.,' I said. 'I'll explain when I see you.'

'You have run into storms,' said Davey, hardly bothering to conceal his glee, 'even sooner than I had expected. I'll let you know as soon as I've got a place on an aeroplane.'

The next morning, one read in Mockbar's page:

DUKES

Four French Dukes, three ex-Ministers, nine Rothschilds, and countless Countesses crossed the courtyard of the British Embassy yesterday evening. Were they going to pay their respects to our envoy, Sir Alfred Wincham? They were not.

ALONE

The former Pastoral Theologian and Lady Wincham sat alone in the great suite of reception rooms on the first floor, waiting for callers who never came. The cream of Parisian society, meanwhile, was packed into a tiny room off their back staircase.

TWO AMBASSADRESSES

It is no secret to anybody here that an unexpected and awkward situation exists at the Embassy where we now seem to have one ambassador and two ambassadresses. Lady Leone, wife of the last envoy, is still living there. Lady Wincham, though a woman of charm, cannot compete with her brilliant predecessor; she is left out in the cold. The Corps Diplomatique is wondering what the upshot will be.

I went to Orly to meet Davey. Although he was now past the middle sixties, his appearance had hardly changed since the day, nearly thirty years ago, when I first saw him with my sharp little girl's eyes at Alconleigh looking, as I thought, unlike a captain and unlike a husband. (On the second count, at any rate, I had been completely wrong. Nobody ever had a happier marriage than my dear Aunt Emily.) If his face had become rather like a portrait by Soutine of that other younger face, his figure was perfect. Elegant and supple, waving the *Daily Post*, he darted out of the group of arrivals from London. 'A pretty kettle of fish!' he cried cheerfully. 'Must see my luggage through the customs – wait for me in the motor.'

Then, getting in beside me, he said, 'Mind you, it's not a new situation, far from it. Lady Pickle kept the key of the Embassy garden in Rome and gave a garden party there weeks after the Betteridges had arrived. Sir George looked out of the window and saw her receiving the whole of the Embassy black list. Lady Praed opened a junk shop in the Faubourg here and nabbed people as they were going into the Embassy. Lady Pike went back to Vienna and then I seem to think she lived in a tree like a bird. English ambassadresses are usually on the dotty side and leaving their embassies drives them completely off their rockers. Alfred's statement is out in the evening papers – perfect, very dignified.' Alfred had said that Lady Leone not being well enough to travel, he was, of course, delighted to lend her the secretary's flat until she was better. 'You needn't worry, Fanny, the sitting ambassador holds all the cards – he can't help winning in the end.'

'If he doesn't win soon it may be the end,' I said.

'Yes, it's time she went. I lunched at Boodle's just now – Alfred's enemies are beginning to crow – you may imagine. *Daily Post* in great demand there.'

'We utterly count on you, Davey.'

'Quite right. As soon as we get back I must have a very strong cocktail and then I'll go straight to Pauline.'

'Good,' I said. 'I've got an ambassadress from some invented country (the real ones are all away still) coming to call on me at six. That fits in very well and we'll see you at dinner.'

As I sat with a little rat of a woman in black velvet with jet sleeves (dressed for the *thé dansant* I thought until I remembered what an old-fashioned notion that was), I heard the usual irritating sounds of distant laughter, punctuated now by Davey's well-known and rather specially piercing shriek. He was evidently enjoying himself. I found it even more difficult than usual to concentrate on the *thé dansant* lady's domestic problems. 'The Americans get them all because they don't mind what they pay.'

Davey reappeared in a black tie, at dinner-time.

'Nobody to meet me?' he said, seeing three cocktail glasses only.

'I thought you would be tired after the journey.'

'Now that I've got this extra kidney I'm never tired. No matter.'

'Whom would you like to see – anybody special? A lot of people are still away but Philip could find somebody for tomorrow, I expect, and of course, Davey, you must ask your own friends while you're here.'

'Well, tomorrow –' a little shade of embarrassment perhaps – 'I said I'd take pot luck with Pauline.'

'Don't tell me poor Mrs Jungfleisch has got to stagger here with a pot for a whole dinner party now?'

'Only for Pauline and me. The others will dine at home and look in after.'

'Perhaps you'd like my chef to send something up?' I said, sarcastically.

'Now, Fanny, don't be cross and suspicious. This is only a little exploratory operation – if I'm to effect a cure I must know all about the case, mustn't I?'

'Mm. Who was there?'

'They came and went – awfully elegant and pretty and funny, one must hand them that. I'd forgotten about French clothes being so different. They think it was very brave of you to beard Mrs Jungfleisch in her own motor.'

'She was in my own courtyard. Do they talk about me?' I said, not best pleased.

'My dear, you are topic A. They know absolutely everything you do, which dressmaker you've got an arrangement with, what the arrangement is, what clothes you have ordered ("*ça, alors!*"), what impression Alfred makes at the Quai ("*évidement ce n'est pas Sire Louis*") and so on. When they heard I was your uncle they were all over me. Thought to be a new feather in Pauline's cap, getting somebody who is actually staying with you and a relation to boot. By the way, Philip Cliffe-Musgrave – I suppose he is on your side? If you ask me he has been in communication with the enemy.'

'That's inevitable under the circumstances.' Alfred now appeared and we went in to dinner.

The next morning was spent trying to get in touch with Davey's Paris friends of olden times. He had lost his foreign address book, it seemed. I sent for Philip to assist; he looked carefully at the names but said he had never heard of any of them in spite of having had four years of intensive social life all over France. None of them were in the telephone book. 'That doesn't mean anything,' said Philip, 'you wouldn't believe how many people here aren't. There is the pneumatique, you see, for urgent messages.'

He and Davey sat on my bed surrounded by books of reference. 'To begin with,' said Philip, 'we'd better consult Katie.' Katie was Miss Freeman of the Embassy telephone exchange, a great dear, soon to become a key figure in our lives. He took my telephone and said, 'Have a look at your list, Katie, will you, see if you've got any of these people and ring me back.' He read out the names of Davey's friends. A few minutes later the bell rang and Philip answered. 'None? Not even on G.P.O.? Thanks, Katie.'

'What is G.P.O.?' I asked.

'Garden Party Only. It runs into thousands. If they're not on that it means they've never set foot here. Now we must start on these directories.'

At this point Davey took his list back and jettisoned several mysterious figures, saying he had not really known them so very well or even liked them so very much. He could die happy without having seen them again. But he absolutely clung to three who must be found at all costs. They were a Marquis, an Academician and a doctor. We began with the Marquis who was neither in the *Bottin Mondain* nor the *Cahiers Noirs de la Fausse Noblesse* nor the *Dictionnaire des Contemporains*. Two fellow Marquises whom Philip rang up had never heard of him (though they said of course the name was that of a famous family) nor had George at the Ritz bar.

'What are his hobbies?' said Philip.

'He used to be the greatest living expert on Russian genealogies.'

'Try Père La Chaise,' said Philip.

'Not at all, he's quite alive, he sent me a *faire part* of his granddaughter's marriage just the other day.'

'What address on the *faire part*?'

'I lost it. I can only remember the church – St François Xavier.'

Philip rang up the Curé of St François who gave him an address in Picardy. A telegram was duly dispatched there.

'That's one,' said Philip. 'Now, what about this alleged Academician?'

'Do you mean to say his name means nothing to you?'

'No, and furthermore I'll take a huge bet he's not in the Académie Française. I know those old Forty by heart and oh how I despise them. There they are, supposed to be looking after the language, do they ever raise a finger to check ghastly misuses of it? The French wireless has started talking about Bourguiba Junior – Junior – I ask you – why not Bourguiba Fils?'

'That's awful, but what could the Forty do?'

'Make a fuss. Their prestige is enormous. But they don't care a bit. Anyway, as I was saying –'

'But I've got a photograph of him in his uniform – I sent a pound to help buy his sword – I know he is a member.'

'What's his subject?'

'He's the greatest living expert on Mauretanian script.'

'Aha!' said Philip. 'Then he'll be of the Académie des Inscriptions. English people always forget there are five academies under the same cupola and mix them up.'

Davey was displeased at being thus lumped together with ignorant English people but Philip was quite right. A pneumatique was sent off to the Institut de France.

As for the doctor, he seemed to have found the perfect hideout. 'Docteur Lecœur,' said Davey impatiently, 'the greatest living expert on the *vésicule bilière*.'

I asked what that was. 'It's a French disease we don't have in England,' said Philip, rather too spry.

Davey shot him a look of great dislike. 'It's not a disease at all, it's a part of the body. We all have it. You ought to see the stones that came out of mine.'

Philip giggled annoyingly. He then rang up several famous doctors and the École de Médecine; nobody had ever heard of this greatest living expert.

'He used to live in the rue Neuve des Petits Champs.'

'Doesn't exist any more.'

'Pulled down? Those lovely houses?'

'Not yet, thank goodness. Only rechristened.'

'Oh, it is too bad. What about the "Ballad of Bouillabaisse"?

> "A street there is in Paris famous
> For which no rhyme our language yields,
> Rue Neuve des Petits Champs its name is,
> The New Street of the Little Fields."

How cruel to give it a new name. The Academicians might well have protested about that.'

'Not they!'

'I wonder if Docteur Lecœur isn't still there? D'you know, I think I'll go round and see – I must have a little walk anyhow. Where is the best chemist?'

He went off in slight dudgeon. Philip said, 'The English so often have these unknown French friends, I've noticed. Collaborators one and all, mark my words. And talking of that, has it occurred to you that your uncle isn't perfectly sound? He seems to be keenly fratting with Pauline in her entresol.'

'The only person in Paris who isn't is me,' I said. 'I'm feeling thoroughly out of it.'

Philip looked guilty. 'Oh well,' he said, 'that's the whole morning wasted. How thankful I shall be when Miss Mackintosh arrives.'

I was sorry that he and Davey were not quite hitting it off. I never saw my uncle again all day. Alfred and I had to lunch with the American Ambassador, who was passing through Paris between two holidays, and my evening was again taken up with ambassadresses from improbable lands which I could certainly not have pinpointed on a globe; as I discussed the disappearance of the genus footman with them I again heard those shrieks which undoubtedly meant that Davey was keenly fratting in the entresol. I began to be very downhearted indeed.

To add to my trials, the morning post brought news that good, clever, plain Jean Mackintosh, not attractive to men, unlikely to get married, whose sensible support was going to facilitate my task in such a variety of ways, was now not coming. She had married, suddenly, not sensibly at all, a member of the Chelsea Set; Louisa wrote to tell me this news, evidently thinking herself more to be pitied than I was.

'Her godmother left her £4,000 and a tiara. It seems this Chelsea setter is always marrying or deed-polling people for little things like that. Oh Fanny!'

Jean, I knew, was her favourite child. She ended up a perfect wail of despair: 'P.S. I am sending you Northey instead but it won't be the same.'

I had a feeling it would not be at all the same. I racked my brains to remember what I could about Northey, whom I had not seen since the early days of the war when Louisa and I were living at Alconleigh with our babies. A flaxen-haired toddler, she used to be brought to the drawing-room at tea-time and made to sing loud, tuneless songs, 'S'all I be p'etty, s'all I be rit?' We all thought her tremendously sweet. Louisa once told me that she was conceived in the Great Northern Hotel – hence her curious name. My children knew her well as they often stayed with the Fort Williams in Scotland; I seemed to have noticed that their verdict was rather scornful. 'Northey is old-fashioned.' 'Northey, brimming as usual.'

'Brimming?'

'Yes, her eyes are always brimming over with tears.'

'What about?'

'Everything.'

Basil could have given me an account of her, he was good at describing people. Naughty Baz, in Spain, in Spain. I had at last received a sheet of paper from him, dirty and crumpled, having spent many a week in a trouser pocket, with a Barcelona postmark, on which was written, 'I shan't be able to lunch Saturday, all news when we meet. Love from Baz.'

I wondered if I should not do well to put off this Northey, in spite of the fact that I had no other candidate and was beginning to feel the need of a secretary. Then my eye fell on the envelope of Louisa's letter and I saw that she had scribbled something almost illegible on the back of it, by which I understood that the child was already on her way, in a cattle boat going from Glasgow via I couldn't read what.

'Good luck to her,' said Philip, when I told him this. 'What time do you think your uncle left the entresol last night?' he added sourly.

'About half-past three,' I said. 'I heard them. Mrs Jungfleisch brought champagne, by the sound of it.'

'I've been talking to Mildred, she says it was absolutely hilarious – Pauline and Mr Warbeck are wonderful together, telling tales of the 1920s. If I were you I should put a stop to all this, it's only prolonging the agony. Mildred says Pauline, who had been getting rather bored, has taken on a new lease of life.'

'We must give him time, Philip. He's only been here two days – I'm sure he'll fix it in the end, he is so clever.'

'Hm – I feel very doubtful.'

So, in my heart of hearts, did I.

Davey now appeared, bright and bustling, not at all like a man in the late sixties who had been up until half-past three. 'Sorry I'm late. Docteur Lecœur has just been round to give me an injection of bull's brains.'

'Oh, so you found him then.'

'He's dead. But his son carries on in the same old house, with the same concierge. Paris is extraordinary the way nothing changes. If I hadn't lost that address book I would have found all those nice friends of mine, or at least their children.'

'And what about the Marquis and the Academician?'

'Both away. Hope to see me next time I come. Anyhow, Lecœur was the important one – goodness, I felt exhausted this morning – the lives you lead here – I wasn't in bed till four!'

'I heard you shrieking,' I said, reproachfully.

'I wished you'd popped down. Pauline was at the peak of her form. We had the life cycle of the Bolter, among other things, and now of course they are all longing to meet you.'

Philip looked at me significantly.

I said, 'I hope you had a good dinner?' Davey was fussy about food.

'Not very. Coarsely mashed potatoes – there's no excuse for that, nowadays. However, enough of this frivolity, agreeable as it has been. I was quite right to go into the thing thoroughly and in fact I only thought of the solution to our problem late at night after several glasses of wine.'

'You have thought of a solution?'

'Yes. It's very simple but none the worse for that, I hope. As Philip so truly says, one can't starve Pauline out and one certainly can't lecture her out. We must bore her out. The problem is how to stop all these Dukes and Rothschilds and countless Countesses from going to visit her. Now I suppose the social life here is built up on "extras", those men in white coats who go from party to party handing things round?'

'Indeed it is,' said Philip, 'more so every day.'

'You must get hold of one who is seen at all the big receptions. IS SEEN are the operative words. He must know everybody by sight, but above all they must be well aware he does. Post him at the steps to the entresol, paper and pencil in hand, and tell him to write down the names of Pauline's visitors – he might ask them as they go in – it must be very much underlined, what he is up to. At the same time, Philip, you must put it about on the grape vine that those who are found frequenting the entresol will not be invited to anything here during The Visit. I think you'll find that will do the trick all right.'

Philip gave a great shout of laughter – Davey joined in and they rocked to and fro. 'Wonderful,' Philip said.

'I think it's rather neat myself.'

'But what Visit?' I was considerably unnerved.

'Not necessary to specify,' said Philip, who now showed the true niceness of his character by accepting Davey's scheme with whole-hearted appreciation, 'the word Visit, with a capital V, is magical in Paris. To the *gens du monde* it is as the din of battle to the warrior. They will never risk missing it, like brave Crillon, simply in order to have a few more jolly evenings with Pauline. Hitherto it has been a sign of social failure not to be seen in the entresol – from now on it will be social death to go there. I'd have given anything to have thought of your scheme myself – what a genius you are. The decks will be cleared in half an hour.'

'It must be properly organized,' said Davey.

'Yes, indeed. We won't allow it to go off at half-cock, that would never do. First I'll ring up the greatest gossips I know. Then I'll go and engage M'sieur Clément. He's our boy, he rules the concierges of the Avenue du Bois with a rod of iron and is the king-pin of that neighbourhood. All Paris knows him by heart. So I've got a busy day, better get on with it. I congratulate you keenly,' he said to Davey and went off.

Davey said complacently, 'I hope now you are sorry that you suspected me of changing sides.'

'Davey – I humbly apologize.'

'Not that I mind. But you realize how it was. I had to find out what sort of people she was seeing. There are many amusing and delightful people here who wouldn't care a rap about a Visit or even expect to be invited if there is one. Docteur Lecœur, for instance. Those friends of hers, however, would. As I told you before, I understand the French.'

5

Davey's plan could not be put into operation for a day or two. When M'sieur Clément understood what he was being hired to do he demanded an enormous bribe. He pointed out that Lady Leone's acquaintances all employed him in one capacity or another; if they suspected him of betraying them to *les Anglais* he might lose the many lucrative engagements and transactions on which his living depended. Philip, after a long session with him, came back to report and explained this to Davey and me but said that in fact no Parisian, especially not those who lived in M'sieur Clément's district, would dare get on the wrong side of him. He had been king of the black market during the war and was now indispensable for things like difficult railway and theatre tickets and for his ability to produce any requirement, from unlimited whisky to a trained nurse, not to speak of other, more sinister commodities, at a moment's notice. Undoubtedly very thick with the police, he knew all about the private lives of a vast section of the community. Philip had suggested to him that he would not really be risking very much by undertaking our assignment and had said that we, for our part, were obliged to take into account the remuneration he would receive from people wanting him to keep dark the fact that they had been about to visit Lady Leone. After long, hard bargaining and double bluffing on both sides, Philip got him down to £500. They shook hands on this. M'sieur Clément, wreathed now in smiles, said it might seem rather expensive but he guaranteed that the work would be impeccable. Philip then flew to London and, with some difficulty, persuaded the powers that be to disburse this amount from the secret funds. All these negotiations had to take place without the knowledge of Alfred who would certainly never have allowed them for a single minute.

At last the stage was set. Davey, Philip, and I were the audience, established behind muslin curtains at Philip's bedroom window. His flat, which was over one of our lodges, had good views both of the courtyard and the street and was therefore in a commanding position. One could see and not be seen.

'I haven't been so excited since chubb-fuddling days with Uncle Matthew,' I said to Davey.

M'sieur Clément, a lugubrious individual with a bottle nose, had posted himself by the staircase of the entresol. For some reason he was not only dressed in inky black from head to foot but the sheets of paper which he held ready for the guilty names were black-edged like those put out, for the congregation to sign, at a French funeral. No doubt, in fact, pinched from one, according to Philip, since M'sieur Clément was, of course, a beadle. (Another of his part-time jobs was that of executioner's assistant.)

Presently a group of Lady Leone's gossips sauntered elegantly into the courtyard. There were five or six of them, all seemed to have arrived together and they were deep in talk. A tall, commanding man began to recount something, the others clustered round him, savouring his words. Two more people came in from the street; they joined the group, shook hands and were evidently put into the picture, after which the teller continued his tale. Suddenly, looking round as if to illustrate some point, his eye fell on M'sieur Clément. He stopped short, clutched the arm of a young woman and pointed; they all turned and looked. Consternation. Hesitation. Confabulation. Flight. Never had chub been more thoroughly fuddled; they flapped off, mouths open, and disappeared into the main stream of the Faubourg.

After this, incidents succeeded each other. A well-known pederast fainted dead away on seeing M'sieur Clément and was heaved, like Antony to the Monument, into the entresol. Women screamed; very few kept their heads and demanded to sign our book. Nobody else went near Lady Leone. Gradually, the intervals between visitors became longer; at eight o'clock, when the entresol was usually at its liveliest, a whole hour had gone by without a single soul coming through our gate.

'It's done the trick,' Philip said, 'all the telephones in Paris must be engaged. I'd better go and give the old fiend his ill-gotten gains and then we can dine. Good work!' he said to Davey.

'I must say I never saw £500 so easily earned.'

'M'sieur Clément would reply, like Whistler, that we are paying for the knowledge of a lifetime.'

Lady Leone was now deserted by her friends, except for faithful Mrs Jung-fleisch, but greatly to my disappointment she showed no signs of leaving us. She lay on in her bed, perfectly contented, according to Davey, with her embroidery, the crossword puzzle and a very loud gramophone. When I suggested that we might take the gramophone away, since it did not belong to her at all but had been presented to the Embassy by a visiting rajah long ago, Davey and Philip made me feel like some cruel gaoler trying to remove the last solace of a lovely, unfortunate, incarcerated princess. It was less irritating, certainly, for me to hear strains of Mozart or the war speeches of Sir Winston Churchill, which she was inordinately fond of and which she played at full blast, than shrieks of laughter; at least Lady Leone could not be discussing me and my mother with a gramophone. The sting of her presence had been drawn by Davey's clever manoeuvre – now that nobody went near her any more the fiction of illness could be maintained. Alfred's face was saved. All the same it annoyed me that she should still be under my roof and so did the fact that Davey was in the habit of slipping downstairs for a game of scrabble before dinner. However, both he and Philip were rather reassuring. They said she was bored and restless; furthermore Mrs Jungfleisch was anxious to go to London for a debate at Chatham House. Their view was that Lady Leone would not be with us much longer, that she was merely biding her time in order to make a suitable exit. 'Pauline won't sneak out unobserved, you can be very sure. I expect she is hiring the Garde Républicaine to conduct her with trumpets and drums.'

I had various preoccupations at this time, still without a secretary, Philip much busier than he had been at the beginning. The days seemed too short for the hundred and one things which I must see to, among others our first entertainment, a cocktail party for the Dominions' Ambassadors. I was terrified at the thought of it, nightmares crowding in. I had not felt so nervous since the first dinner party I gave at Oxford, many years ago, for Alfred's professor. This was rather unreasonable since I had very little to do with the organization. Philip made out the lists and Major Jarvis, our comptroller, saw to the drink and the food of which there was to be a mountain. 'How can people eat anything at all between an enormous luncheon and an even more terribly stuffing dinner?' I asked.

'You'll see how they can. Are you going to do the flowers, Lady Wincham?'

The day came. I bought a lot of pink carnations (my favourite flowers) and stuck them into silver bowls. They looked so pretty, I was quite amazed at my own cleverness. Then I went upstairs and put on my cocktail dress. Nobody could have said that it looked pretty; hideous it was and very strange. My maid, Claire, pronounced it to be 'chic', but without much conviction. I had never liked it, even when worn by a wonderfully elegant Indo-Chinese mannequin, and had only been persuaded into ordering it because my vendeuse, in urging it on me, seemed to have the backing of a prominent English writer on fashion.

'Make no mistake,' asserted this pundit (photograph appended), with her usual downright authority, 'waists have gone for good.'

Having no wish to make a mistake over a dress which cost what had formerly been my allowance for a whole year, I had plumped for this waistless creation and oh! how I loathed it. However, there was nothing to be done; I was in it now, I must hope for the best and only try not to see myself in a glass.

The party was to take place in the state rooms on the ground floor. I went down and found Philip and Davey in hilarious mood, having had, I thought, good strong cocktails. I hurried towards them. They were kind enough not to remark on my dress but began making silly criticisms of the flowers.

'So like you, Fanny – why didn't you ask us first?'

'Carnations dumped in vases simply don't do any more. Haven't you ever heard of Arrangements? Don't you know about the modern hostess and her clever ways? Still-lifes – imaginative – not only flowers but yards of red velvet, dead hares, pumpkins, wrack from the seashore, common grasses from the hedgerow and the Lord knows what rubbish! Or else Japanesey, one reed by itself cunningly placed is worth five dozen roses, nowadays.'

I did know what they meant. Once, asked to the house of a Dior don, with other wives (women in Oxford have no identity, they are lumped together as wives), I had noticed a lot of top-heavy old-man's-beard in an urn surrounded by cabbages on the floor, and thought it all looked like a harvest home. People were saying, 'Utterly divine, your Arrangements.'

'Did Lady Leone go in for them?'

'Yes, indeed. Her feeling for colour and sense of form were the despair of all the hostesses here.'

'Shall I tell you something? – I intend to stick to pink carnations.'

Alfred joined us, saying, 'What's that dress, Fanny?' in a falsetto voice he sometimes used to denote that he was being quizzical.

'It's the fashion.'

'We are not here to be fashionable, you know.'

There were voices in the hall now, our guests were beginning to arrive; Alfred
and I stood by the fireplace waiting to come forward effusively when they were
announced. Philip had suggested that warm American rather than cold English
manners might be adopted on this occasion and that we must do our best to look
as if we were pleased to see the people.'

'I can't say it, it wouldn't seem a bit real.'

'Don't force yourself then, but do just bare the gums.'

So there we were, preparing to simper, under the eyes of King George and Queen
Mary, bad copies of bad portraits. I felt them disapproving of the fashionable dress,
of the grins and of the whole notion of a cocktail party but approving of the carnations. Nobody came into the room. I felt perfectly idiotic planted there like a
waxwork, horrible dress and artificial smile. There were clearly a lot of people in
the hall; a curious silence had fallen on them. Davey and Philip went over to the
door; when they got there they looked left towards the entrance and then, as though
following the gaze of others, they sharply turned their heads to the staircase. They
remained quite still, looking up it, with a stupefied expression.

'What is this all about?' said Alfred, going over to join them. He too stood eyes
to heaven, with his mouth slightly open. I followed him. The hall presented a scene
like a picture of the Assumption: a mass of up-turned faces goggling at the stairs
down which, so slowly that she hardly seemed to be moving, came the most beautiful woman in the world. She was dressed in great folds of white satin; she sparkled
with jewels; her huge pale eyes were fixed, as though upon some distant view, over
the heads of the crowd. Following her, two of my footmen were carrying a large
gramophone; then came Mrs Jungfleisch, elegant in white linen, a basket on her
arm. All the time, more guests were arriving. When Lady Leone got to the bottom
of the stairs they divided into two lanes; she shook hands, like a royal person, with
one here and there as she sailed out of the house for ever.

6

Charming Northey, how to describe her? Can this creature of *commedia dell'arte*
really have resulted from the copulation on a hard, brass, hotel bed, trains rumbling
below, of dear old Louisa and terribly dull John Fort William? Some pretend that
the place of conception, that of birth, and also the Christian name have a bearing
on personality. Northey, product of King's Cross and Hill View Clinic, Oban, and
with that name, must be a living refutation of this theory. Nothing of the north-
erner about her, no vague mistiness, no moments of absence; she was not
romantic nor did she yearn after the unknown. She was the typical product, one
would have said, of an ancient civilization beneath cerulean skies. Impossible to
believe that she had a Scotch father, old enough to be her grandfather, and Pictish

ancestors; yet surely good Louisa – oh no, perish the thought! She was incapable of inventing such a wealth of detail to cover up a sin. I incline to think that Northey must have been a changeling; that carelessness occurred in Hill View Clinic, Oban, by which the child of some noble Roman lady and a strolling player was exchanged for Louisa's brat. Physically she bore no resemblance whatever to the other Mackintoshes who all had solid frames, ginger heads and freckles. She was like a small exquisite figure in enamelled glass, with hair the colour of a guinea; her eyes the liveliest and most expressive I ever saw, not very large, brilliantly blue. In moments of excitement or distress they became diamond-shaped. When she talked she used her whole body in the concentrated effort of expressing herself, gesticulating, wriggling, as babies and puppies do. Her little thin hands never lay still in her lap. Furthermore, there was something indescribably lovable about her, she radiated affection, happiness, goodwill towards men. From the first moment we set eyes on her Alfred and I were her slaves.

She exploded into our household as we were dining alone together, tired and depressed, after the Dominions party. Davey had gone off saying that his friend the Marquis was now in Paris; it seemed that Philip was obliged to dine with his London stockbroker; both, I suspected, had really joined Lady Leone at Mrs Jung-fleisch's. I thought the party had been a total flop, though I heard afterwards that it was the most successful ever given at the Embassy in the sense that those who had missed it were wild with fury while those who had been present were sought after by the whole of Paris and supplied with free meals for weeks. But as Alfred and I could not discuss the great topic of the evening with our guests we were naturally the last people they wanted to talk to. They were longing to compare notes with others who had witnessed Lady Leone's exit, to buttonhole newcomers who had not and tell them about it, above all to leave as soon as they decently could and get on to the telephone. Everybody was very polite; indeed I was finding out that diplomats are diplomatic, it is one thing you can say for them. After the frank and outspoken rudeness I was accustomed to in Oxford this made a pleasant change. There were, too, moments of encouragement as when somebody said, 'Ah! The Irish Ambassador! That is a feather in Sir Alfred's cap – he never came to the Leones.'

The Ambassador of the Channel Islands praised my carnations, a major export, so he told me, of his country. A marvellous-looking Othello of a man gorgeously draped in pale blue taffeta (slightly marred by boots sticking out below, as my walking shoes had stuck out from beneath the Chinese robe) had invited me to go lion shooting in his. But the party had had a restless undercurrent and was certainly not much fun for the hosts.

So now it was over and we were dining. All of a sudden Northey was there, in the doorway, an inquiring look on her face. 'It's me,' she said.

'Darling!'

'I'm so sorry, I had to ask them to pay the taxi. No money at all. The station-master had to lend me a ticket. Yes I did, but I lost it.'

'Nothing matters now you're here. You must have had a beastly journey.'

'Oh Cousin Fanny (oh, you are kind, may I really), oh Fanny –' the soft skin of her forehead crumpled like tissue paper, her eyes took on a diamond-shaped, tormented expression which was to become very familiar to me and they brimmed.

I saw exactly what Basil had meant about the brimming. 'You can't, you can't imagine. There were sweet bullocks on board. You don't know the sadness – the things they do to them. Their poor horns had been cut off – imagine the pain – and all because they get a pound more for them without horns and that's because then they can pack them tighter. I'd like to drop a hydrogen bomb on Ireland.'

'And kill millions of cows and all the birds and animals and the Irish also who are so charming?' Alfred said, gently.

'Charming!'

'Oh yes, they are. They have to export these bullocks in order to live. They have no industries, you see.'

'I hate and loathe and execrate them.'

'Darling, you mustn't be so worked up.'

'But I must be. These little creatures are put in the world for us to look after them. We are responsible. How do we treat them? They don't sleep you know, cows, they never have a moment of forgetting. Their comfort is to chew the cud – nobody feeds them properly on the journey – not enough water – fourteen hours in the train after the boat, with no water in this weather. And when they get to the – you know – dreadful place, does anybody give them water there?'

These things have worried me all my life; as I despise myself for not having the strength of character to do more than give an occasional pound to the R.S.P.C.A., I try to put them out of my mind.

'Come and have your dinner, dearest.'

'No, I couldn't,' she said, when the butler put a plate of consommé before her, 'nothing made of meat – I won't prey on them – never again.'

Alfred said, 'But if nobody ate meat the whole race of cows and sheep and pigs would become extinct. They have happy little lives you know and death is never agreeable, it won't be for us, either. It's the price we all have to pay.'

'Yes, but not torture. That's too much. Fanny, do promise you'll never have cruel food here.'

'What is cruel food?'

'For instance, lobsters and Irish horses and foie gras. A Frenchman on board told me what they do to sweet geese for pâté de foie gras.'

'Very wrong and stupid of him.'

'He told to make me care less about the bullocks.'

'This journey has been a nightmare. Now you must forget it.'

'But if people always forget these things they go on and on. All right, I suppose I'm boring you.'

'You're not boring us,' said Alfred, looking at her with love, 'but we don't like to see you so upset.'

'But you understand why, don't you? There we were, all travelling together – I used to go and chat to them, they looked so sad and good, poor little creatures – then I come to this lovely house and you, while they –' she was eating the remains of a cheese soufflé now, evidently very hungry. 'The captain of the *Esmeralda*,' she said, with her mouth full, 'was a most unpleasant person. He was ghastly to the bullocks and he offered to – you know – to hug me. But the sweet Frenchman who was there got me off.'

'Weren't there any women on board?'

'Only me.'

'And this Frenchman – he didn't want to hug you himself?'

'M. Cruas? He might have liked to but he didn't offer. He *is* kind. So is the station-master. When we got on shore and I looked for my ticket, quelle horrible surprise – there it wasn't. M. Cruas is poor, you know, so he couldn't buy me one, he could only carry my luggage to save porters. So the station-master lent. Can we pay him back at once, Sir Alfred – oh you are kind, may I really? Alfred? He knows about us because Lady Leone never has a ticket, or any money, or a passport – just a basket he says. Sacrée Lady Leone. Why sacred I wonder?'

'It only means that blooming Lady Leone,' said Alfred, in his falsetto. 'How's your French, Northey?'

'Very nice. M. Cruas is a teacher, so he taught me.'

'Did you not learn it at school?' An embarrassed, pouting wriggle was the answer to this. 'You went to school, I suppose?'

'I went. Only I didn't stay.'

'Why not?'

'It was too dread.'

'You'll have to learn quickly you know or you won't be any good to Fanny.'

'Yes. I've thought of that. So M. Cruas will come here and go on with the lessons.'

Alfred said to me afterwards, 'Your cousin Louisa is a fool. Imagine letting that child go alone on a cattle boat and sending her to a school where she was so unhappy she had to leave. I've no patience with such people. The poor little thing seems to have been utterly mismanaged.'

Implacable where his own contemporaries were concerned, Alfred had infinite indulgence for the young; in fact I sometimes thought he was too much on their side – hoodwinked by them. It was plain to see that Northey would twist him round her little finger.

Presently Philip came in. Perhaps he felt sorry for us, all alone as he thought, dwelling on that horrid party. When he saw Northey, he said, 'Don't tell me, I'm going to guess. I suppose this must be the wonderfully efficient young lady who is going to make life easier for all of us? Northey, in fact. How d'you do? How was the cattle boat?'

Alfred and I began talking simultaneously to change the subject. Northey made a sad little noise like a kitten but went on eating; the food, and the sight of Philip (that, perhaps most of all, she was gazing at him as if she had never seen a young man before) seemed to be taking the edge off her sorrow.

'This is Philip,' I said, 'he is busy, he mustn't be put upon, but in real emergency you'll find that he will come to the rescue.'

'Each for each is what we teach,' said Northey, looking at him from under her eyelashes. Oh bother, I thought, silly old love, again. Why does he have to be in it already, with Grace? Like all happily married people I am inclined to make matches; Philip and Northey seemed, on the face of it, such an ideal couple.

'What would a real emergency be?' she asked him.

'Let me think. Well, if you invited the Tournons to the same dinner party as les faux Tournons, that would be a pretty kettle of fish.'

'Please explain.'

'There is a couple here called M. et Madame de Tournon – social butterflies, pretty, delightful, perfectly useless. They are the real Tournons. Then there are M. et Madame Tournon. He is a deputy, a brilliant young man who specializes in finance, hard-working, ambitious, a parliamentary under-secretary. His wife is a prominent physicist. In spite of the fact that he is almost bound to become Prime Minister, while she may well end up with the Nobel prize, they are known to the whole of Paris as the false Tournons. Now if you had the two couples here together, protocol would demand that the false Tournons, elected by the people, should take precedence of the others. Thereupon the real Tournons would turn their plates upside down and say, *"il y a erreur"*. I suppose you have understood every word? What a look! Never mind, in six months' time all this will be second nature to you.'

'You know, Philip,' said Alfred, 'I don't wish to fill this house with the ornaments of society.'

'No, sir. If I may be allowed to make an observation, all ambassadors begin by saying that. The fact is, however, that if you don't have a sprinkling of them the others don't care to come. By the way, I really looked in to tell you that Bouche-Bontemps has just telephoned. He wants to know if he can see you tomorrow.'

I liked M. Bouche-Bontemps very much, felt natural and at my ease with him. 'He's a dear,' I said.

'Yes. The old-fashioned kind – a jolly Roman Catholic. All the up-and-coming young men seem to be Protestants – makes them so priggish.'

'I thought the old ones were free-thinkers?'

'It's the same as far as jollity goes.'

'Let's ask him to luncheon, shall we?' I said.

'Tomorrow? I don't know if he could with this crisis impending.'

'Of course, there's a crisis. I've been too much occupied with our own to take much notice.'

'All the same it might just suit him. I'll go and see.'

'What crisis?' said Northey, following him out of the room with her eyes.

'One of your duties here will be to read the papers,' said Alfred. 'You can read, I suppose?'

'I can read and I have a certain native intelligence. Don't be sarcastic with me, I beg.'

'Well, then, there's a parliamentary crisis going on and it looks as if this government may fall.'

'Then there'll be a general election? You see, I know about politics.'

'The point is that there will not. Fanny must give you some books to read about the state of France.'

Philip came back and said the Foreign Minister would be very much pleased to lunch, but he had business to do with the Ambassador and must see him alone.

'Northey and I can eat in the Salon Vert,' I said, 'and you can have your secrets in the upstairs dining-room. But do bring him in for a cocktail first, if you think he has time.'

'They always have time in the middle of the day,' said Philip. 'They can be up all night and start intriguing again before breakfast but the hours between one and three are sacred. That's why they are all so well – one never hears of a French politician dying – they live for ever, haven't you noticed?'

★

'I've come to say good-bye,' said Davey, arriving with my tray in the morning.

'Davey, don't go. It's so comfortable to feel you're here. Why don't you stay on in some capacity – comptroller? I think Major Jarvis is leaving us. Take his place – oh do!'

'Sweet of you, Fanny, but I couldn't live with the French. I understand them too well. Besides, I have fish to fry at home. New curtains for the drawing-room. And I can't live for ever without Mrs Dale. Tea-time at home is delightful – blinds are drawn at the witching hour of 4.30 and I have her on the wireless.'

'We've got a wireless; you can have her here.'

'I've tried. She doesn't sound the same.'

'I wanted you to see Northey.'

'I have. We had our breakfast together just now. Rocks ahead there. So, I'm off. When you're next in trouble send for me, won't you? See you very soon in that case.'

When the Foreign Minister saw Northey he said we must all lunch together. He could do his business with Alfred in two minutes on his way out – he had never meant that the charming Ambassadress should be excluded from their talk. Mees Nortee was no doubt aware that her job demanded enormous discretion and indeed he could see by her face that she was a serious woman. During luncheon he addressed himself to her in a tender, avuncular, bantering tone of voice.

'So you are studying French. But why? Everybody here speaks English. And reading books on the state of France by English experts? I know these experts. They are all in love with Arabs.'

'No,' said Alfred firmly, 'respectable, married men.'

'The English who specialize in French affairs fill me with misgivings. Why are there so many of them and why must they concentrate on my poor country – are there no others in the world whose state is worth considering? Why not the state of Denmark for a change?'

'You ought to be flattered,' said Alfred. 'The publishers know they can sell any amount of books about France – in fact France, like Love, is a certain winner on a title-page.'

'Ah! So Mees Nortee is to learn about France and Love. I shall teach her, I know more than the English experts.'

'You are kind,' said Northey, 'because I can see that these books are a bore. No pictures, no talk and such terribly long sentences.'

'You told me you could read,' said Alfred.

'Like all of us she can read what interests her. When you have been here for a year, Mees, you will probably find yourself enjoying books about the state of France – though what this state will be by then, who can say?' He sighed deeply. 'Now, we will begin our lesson. Your uncle, the Ambassador here, has two bones to pick over with the French government, whenever there is a government. There are Les Îles Minquiers, a very nice point. You will hear more of them in due course – hats off to the Intelligence Service! And there is the European Army, known as C.E.D. or E.D.C., nobody can ever remember why. One of your uncle's assignments is to persuade us to merge our army, which is overseas, fighting, with that of the

Germans which is non-existent. This merging is desired by the Americans who see everything in black and white – with a strong preference for black.'

'M. le Ministre –' said Alfred sharply.

'Your protest is registered, M. l'Ambassadeur. The English are really indifferent, they don't care, but whenever they can please the Americans without it costing anything they like to do so. Armies have never meant much to them in times of peace – one army – another army – zero they think, anyhow, in the face of the Bomb. At the same time they have never been averse from weakening the Continental powers. All their Generals and Field-Marshals tell them that a European force would be quite unworkable so they say come on, the Americans want it, it rather suits us, let's have it. Now, if it were a question of commerce, M. l'Ambassadeur, I believe the nation of shopkeepers would sing a very different song? Suppose we wanted a European market, Excellency, what would you say to that?'

This lesson seemed to be more for the benefit of Alfred than of Northey who, crumpled forehead, looked extremely puzzled.

Alfred said, 'My American colleague tells me that you are going to accept the European Army, however.'

'Your American colleague has a beautiful wife whom everybody wants to please. No Frenchman can bear to see somebody so exquisite looking sad for a single moment. So wherever she goes, in Paris or the provinces, the deputies and mayors and ministers and IGAMEs say "of course" to whatever she tells them. And she tells them, most beguilingly, that they are going to accept the European Army. We shall never accept. This government, as you see, is tottering. It will fall during the night, no doubt. But no French government could pass such a measure. We may be weak – nobody can say we are very strong at present – but we have an instinct for self-preservation. We shall appear to be about to give way, over and over again, but in the end we shall resist.'

'And over the Minquiers,' said Alfred, 'you will appear to resist, but in the end you will give way?'

'You have said it, M. l'Ambassadeur, not I.'

'And then what about Europe? If the C.E.D. fails?'

'It will be built up on a more peaceful and workable foundation. My great hope is, that when the time comes, you will not oppose it.'

After luncheon M. Bouche-Bontemps said, 'Shall I take Mees to the Chambre? She could then see the state of France in action.'

'Oh, you are kind. The only thing is, M. Cruas said he would come at five.'

'Who is M. Cruas?'

'He teaches me French.'

'Ring him up. Say you have another lesson today.'

'He's poor. He hasn't got a telephone.'

'Send a pneumatique,' said the Minister, impatiently.

He had a word on the staircase with Alfred and then left the house accompanied by Northey, who hopped, skipped and jumped across the marble paving of the hall, Alfred said, like a child going to a pantomime. I saw no more of her that day. Philip, in and out of the Chambre, reported during the evening that she seemed perfectly entranced, determined to stay to the end. The government fell in the early hours and Northey slept until luncheon-time.

'So what was it like?' I said, when she finally appeared.

'Terribly like that dread school I went to. Desks with inkpots and a locker. From where I sat you could see there are lollipops in the lockers and when they are pretending to listen to the lecturer or read lesson books they are really having a go at the illustrated mags. All the same they do half-listen because suddenly all the Madames get up and stamp and roar and shout and the master has to ring a bell and shout back at them.'

I had a vision of ghastly women, Erinyes, *tricoteuses*, obstructing the business of the Chambre. 'Madames? Women deputies?'

'No, Fanny,' said Northey as one explaining a well-known fact to a child. 'Madames are the Social Republicans, so called because their party head-quarters are in the rue Madame. The Republican Socialists, whose H.Q. is in the rue Monsieur, are called les Monsieurs. They are each other's worst enemies. You see how sweet M. Bouche-Bontemps was quite right and going is better than reading.'

'What was the debate about?'

'Really, Fanny, I'm surprised that you should ask me that. Have you not seen your *Figaro* this morning? I hear that it is very well reported. Pensions for remarried war widows, of course.'

'Are you sure?'

'Quite sure. There was a nice person in the box called Mrs Jungfleisch who told me all about it. And an Englishwoman married to one of the deputies – a marquis I suppose because when he got up to speak the Communists chanted "*imbécile de Marquis*" and he became quite giggly and lost his place.'

'That must be Grace de Valhubert,' I said, pleased to think that she was back in Paris.

'Yes. She knows Fabrice and Charlie and she sent you her love. She talks with such a pretty French accent and Fanny! her clothes! Sweet M. Bouche-Bontemps came and took me out to dinner. He said if he fell he would be able to devote himself to my education. Well, he has fallen, so – Philip brought me home,' she added, nonchalantly.

I thought I understood now why she had stayed so late.

7

Now that the French were comfortably without a government, Alfred received instructions from the Foreign Office to make strong representations at the Quai d'Orsay about Les Îles Minquiers. These islands, which were to occupy his waking thoughts for many a long month to come, are described in Larousse as dangerous rocks near St Malo and given no independent notice in the *Encyclopaedia Britannica*. There are three of them and at high tide they are completely submerged. During the liberation of France, General de Gaulle found time to have a tricolour run up, at low tide, on the Île Maîtresse or middle island. Never has the adage 'let sleeping dogs lie' been more justified. This flag was immediately spotted by the Argus-eyed Intelligence Service and the Admiralty found time to send a frogman, at high tide, to haul it down again. Now that the attention of Whitehall was drawn to the existence of the Minquiers, some busybody with a turn for international law began to study the complicated question of their ownership. It transpired that the Traité de Brétigny (1360) which gave Normandy to the Kings of France, and Calais, le Quercy, le Ponthieu, Gascony, etc., to the English crown, made no allocation of the Minquiers. They were not covered by the various Channel Island treaties and have existed throughout history as a no-man's-land. As they are within sight, when they can be seen at all, of the French coast, no doubt they were always assumed to be part of France, but nobody seems to have minded one way or the other. It was bad luck for Alfred that the government which appointed him to Paris should be determined to paint the Minquiers pink on the map; nothing could have been more calculated to annoy the French at that particular juncture.

'But what is the point of these islands?' I asked as Alfred was about to leave for the Quai d'Orsay.

'Islands are always rather desirable – the Royal Yacht Squadron would like them to be English; our fishermen could use them, I suppose. The Foreign Secretary says the question must be settled now in the interests of Western solidarity. I must say, I'm not delighted to have to make a nuisance of myself at such a time.'

The President of the Republic, M. Béguin the outgoing Prime Minister, and the heads of the parties, one of whom was M. Bouche-Bontemps, had been up for several nights trying to resolve the crisis; tempers were beginning to be frayed. The English newspapers were pointing out the impossibility of relying on an ally who never seems to have a government. In decidedly gloating tones they inquired: will France be represented at the Foreign Ministers' Conference next week or shall we, as usual, see an empty seat? Can the Western Alliance afford these continual tergiversations? The people of England look on with dismay; they have but one desire, to see our French friends strong, prosperous and united.

The French papers urged the political parties to settle their differences with the least possible delay since 'nos amis britanniques' were clearly about to make use of the situation to further their own sinister schemes. The two old neighbours are not always displeased by each other's misfortunes, nor do they trust each other not to take advantage of them.

'And you will notice when you have lived here for a bit,' said Grace de Valhubert, 'that it is the English who are the more annoying. The French never sent arms to the Mau-Mau, that I heard of.'

Grace counted herself as a sort of supernumerary English ambassadress; like most people who have been accredited for years to a foreign country she could only see one side of every question and that not the side of her own, her native land. Everything French was considered by her superior to its English equivalent. She was inclined to talk a sort of pidgin English, larded with French words; she slightly rolled her r's; at the same time her compatriots in Paris noted with glee that her French was by no means perfect. She was a bit of a goose, but so good-natured, pretty and elegant that one could not help liking her. It was the fashion to say that she had a terrible time with her husband but when I saw them together they always seemed to be on very comfortable terms. She was evidently quite uninterested in Philip.

She had come to call on me, sweet and affectionate, bringing me flowers. 'So sorry not to have been here when you arrived but I always stay at Bellandargues as long as I can. It's what I like best in the world. Anyway, who knows that I would have resisted the entresol? Too awful if you hadn't been able to ask me when next there is a Visit!'

'Oh Grace, the rules would be quite different for you!'

I took her to my room to see the fashionable dress I hated so much. She transformed it instantly by putting a belt on it, after which it became the prettiest I had ever had. 'Never believe that we have seen the last of the waist – the English have been saying it ever since the New Look went out – wishful thinking I suppose. An Englishwoman's one idea is to get into something perfectly shapeless and leave it at that.'

I thought of the Chinese robe.

'As a matter of fact,' she went on, 'if you're like me and get fond of your clothes and want to wear them for years the first rule is to stick to the female form. Everything that doesn't is dated after one season. Perhaps I'd better take you to my dressmaker – he's in the Faubourg – very nice and convenient for you – his clothes are more ordinary and far more wearable. I always think Dolcevita really wants to make one look a figure of fun.'

I thanked her for this advice, on all of which I acted. 'Come back to the Salon Vert and we'll have some tea.'

'You've moved the furniture about – it's better like this,' said Grace, looking round the room. 'It never seemed very much lived in. Pauline used that gloomy bedroom more.'

I poured out the tea and said I hoped the boys had behaved themselves at Bellandargues.

'We never saw them except at meals. They were very polite. Do you know about Yanky Fonzy?'

'I don't think so – is he at school with them?'

'He's a jazz biggy,' said Grace, 'he sends them. All that lovely weather they were shut up with a gramophone in Sigi's room being sent by Yanky. Haven't you seen their shirts with Yank's the Boy for Me printed on them? It's a transfer from Disc.'

'What does that mean?'

'I don't know, I'm quoting.'

'How did your husband take it?'

'Don't ask,' said Grace, shutting her eyes. 'However, it's entirely Charles-Edouard's own fault for insisting on Eton instead of letting the child go to Louis-le-Grand like everybody else. Then he'd never have heard of this ghastly Yanky.'

'Any news of him since they all arrived in Scotland?'

'*Silence de glace*. But as a matter of fact I have never received a letter from Sigismond in my life – I wouldn't know his writing on an envelope if I saw it. I pity the women who fall in love with him. When he first went to Eton I gave him those printed postcards: I am well, I am not well – you know, *rayer la mention inutile*. Of course he never put one in the box. Steamed off the stamps, no doubt. Afterwards he said the only thing he wanted to tell me was that his fag-master had stolen £5 from him and he couldn't find that on the list. They went back yesterday, didn't they?'

'Day before, I think.'

'I rang up my father in London this morning – thick fog over there, needless to say – look at the glorious sun here, it's always the same story – yes, so I begged him to go down and see them. No good worrying, is it? Charles-Edouard doesn't in the least. He says if Sigi is ill they'll have to let one know and when he's expelled he'll come home. He'll be obliged to, if only to worm some money out of us.'

'I suppose so, at that age. Later on they don't seem to need money and then they vanish completely.' I was thinking of Basil.

'What d'you hear of the crisis?' said Grace.

'Can you explain why the government fell at all? It seems so infinitely mysterious to me. War widows or something?'

'They were already bled to death on foreign affairs. The pensions for remarried war widows only finished them off. It's always the same here, they never actually fall on a big issue – school meals, subsidies for beetroot, private distilling, things of that sort bring them down. It's more popular with the electorate (they like to feel the minorities are being looked after) and then the deputies don't absolutely commit themselves to any major policy. *C'est plus prudent.*'

'Does your husband like being in the Chambre?'

'He gets dreadfully irritated. You see he's a Gaullist; he can't bear to think of all these precious years being wasted while the General is at Colombey.'

'Nobody seems to think he'll come back.'

'Charles-Edouard does, but nobody else. I don't think so, though I wouldn't say it, except to you. Meanwhile all these wretched men are doing their best, one supposes. M. Queuille has failed – did you know? – it was on the luncheon-time news. Charles-Edouard thinks the President will send for M. Bouche-Bontemps now.'

The telephone bell rang and Katie Freeman said, rather flustered, 'I've got M. Bouche-Bontemps on the line.'

'But the Ambassador is in the Chancery.'

'Yes, I know that. It's Northey he wants and I can't find her – she's not in her office and not in her room. He's getting very impatient – he's speaking from the Élysée.'

'Let me think – oh I know, I believe she's trying on something in my dressing-room.' She had borrowed two months' wages from me, bought a lot of stuff and had turned my maid, Claire, into her private dressmaker. 'Just a moment,' I said to Grace, 'it's M. Bouche-Bontemps.' I went to look and sure enough, there was Northey being pinned into a large green velvet skirt. 'Come quickly, you're wanted on the telephone.'

She gathered up the skirt and ran into the Salon Vert. 'Hullo, oh, B.B.?' she said. 'Yes, I was working – not in my office – my work takes many different forms. That would be lovely. Ten o'clock would be best – I'm dining with Phyllis McFee but then I'll say I must go to bed early. Ten, and you'll pick me up? Oh, poor you, you must really? Never mind, soon be over.' She rang off.

Grace looked very surprised at this conversation.

'B.B. has to see the President now, which is a bore he says. But when that's over he'll take me to Marilyn Monroe.'

'That means he's going to refuse,' said Grace. 'The crisis will go on and the English will bag the Îles Minquiers, you mark my words. It's intolerable.' She said to Northey, 'You must come and dine one evening and we'll go dancing. I'll arrange something as soon as the household is a bit organized.'

'The utter kindness of you,' said Northey and trotted back to Claire.

'What a darling!'

'Oh, isn't she! You can't imagine how much I love her – so does Alfred.'

'And Bouche-Bontemps, it seems.'

'He's very kind to her. Don't look like that, Grace, he's a grandfather.'

'Mm,' said Grace.

'And she's as good as gold.'

'All right, I believe you.'

'Yes, you must. I sometimes think I would swap all my naughty boys for one daughter like Northey.'

'I've got three little girls, you know, but they are babies. The eldest is only six. I wonder – they are heavenly now, but people say girls can be so difficult.'

These words of Grace's soon came true. Adorable as she was, Northey was by no means an easy proposition. She was now in love, for the first time (or so she said, but is it not always the first time and, for that matter, the last?) and complained about it with the squeaks and yelps of a thwarted puppy. Her lack of reticence astounded me. When dealing with the children, I always tried to think back to when my cousins and I were little; any of us would have died sooner than admit to unrequited love, even in a whisper to each other, in the Hons' cupboard, while the grown-ups never had the smallest idea of what went on in our hearts. But with Northey there was no question of concealing the worm, the canker and the grief; she displayed them. The loved one himself was not spared.

'Oh, Philip, I worship you.'

'Yes, I know.'

'Shall I chuck B.B. and dine with you instead?'

'No, thank you. I'm dining out.'

'Chuck!'

'No fear. It's a most amusing dinner.'

'The pathos! Well, if you won't take me out to dinner you might throw me a civil word.'

'If you go on like this, I'll throw something blunt and heavy. I must explain, m'lord, that my life had been made a purgatory. My work was suffering, I gave way to an uncontrollable impulse – it may have been wrong; it was inevitable. Fanny will be a witness for the defence, won't you?'

The fact that every Frenchman who saw her fell in love made her no easier to deal with and considerably complicated my task as ambassadress. Instead of a nice, sensible, methodical secretary ever at my elbow to help and support me I had this violent little fascinator flitting about the house, bewailing her lovelorn condition to anybody who would listen, or paralysing Alfred's private line as she wailed down it to one of her new friends. They were not spared the desperate state of her heart any more than we were. How could sobriety and security, the keynotes of our mission, be maintained under these circumstances? Northey created a circumambience of insobriety and doubtful security. Nothing could have been more unfortunate than her choice of followers. Such personages as the first Vice-President of the Chambre, the Secretary-General of the Élysée, an ex-Minister of Justice, the Ambassador of the Channel Islands, the Governor of the Bank of France, the Prefect of the Seine, not to speak of the outgoing Foreign Secretary who looked like being the next Prime Minister, could hardly be treated as ordinary young dancing partners. Difficult for Alfred to insist that they must not come to the house until they were invited or that they should at least limit themselves to the usual hours for calling on young ladies. They were all busy with the crisis, so they came when they could or else lengthily telephoned.

Perhaps unwisely, we had given Northey the entresol recently vacated by Lady Leone, with its own entrance to the courtyard. At all hours of the day and night one was apt to see French government or C.D. motors there whose owners were not transacting business with Alfred, while motor-bicyclists dressed like Martians continually roared up the Faubourg to stop at our concierge's lodge with notes or flowers or chocolates for Northey. She had taken to the social and political life of Paris with an ease more often exhibited nowadays by pretty boys than by pretty girls. Philip, who knew that esoteric world better than anybody else in the Embassy, said it was almost incredible how quickly she was picking up its jargon and manners. While I was still feeling my way through a thick fog, not knowing who anybody was, summoning small talk with the greatest difficulty, Northey seemed completely at home with the different groups which make up French society.

In one respect, however, she remained the same little Scotch girl who had arrived on the cattle boat. Her passion for animals was in no way modified and, as might have been foreseen, she began to accumulate pets which she had rescued from some misfortune.

'Yes, I saw this group of children in the Tuileries. Now I've always noticed that if you see children clustered round something and looking down at it fixedly it's going to be a creature and they are going to be cruel to it. Sure enough, they had got hold of this sweet torty. They kept picking her up and waving her about and putting her down again. You know how it's dread for a tortoise to be waved because she naturally thinks she is in the clutches of an eagle. So cruel, to bring them here from Greece – thousands of them – and wave them about all the summer and then leave them to die in the winter. Ninety per cent die, I read. Oh Fanny, the world! Anyway I bought her from those ghastly children for 1,000 francs, which I luckily had on me (we must have a little talk about money) and now she can be happy until the cold weather. Just look at the way she walks though, anybody can see her nerves are in ribbons.'

'Would you like to see my cat? She's old. She's bandaged up like this because her abscesses keep breaking out. The Duke's vet comes every morning when he has finished with the pugs and gives her penicillin. How d'you mean, kinder? Can't you see she's enjoying her life? She lies there purring, quite happy. Could I borrow a little money? Yes, well, penicillin is expensive, you know. You are kind – I'm keeping a strict account.'

Then she went for a walk on the quays and saw a badger asleep in a cage on the pavement outside an animal shop. 'The cruelty – they hate daylight – they live all day in a sett and only come out when it's dark. Imagine keeping it like that – why bring it here from its wood, poor little creature? So I came back for Jérôme and the Rolls-Royce and borrowed some money from Mrs Trott (darling, could you pay her for me if I promise to keep a strict account?) and together we lugged Mr Brock into the motor, huge and heavy he is, and brought him to the Avenue Gabriel, through that gate, and he's in the garden now. Do come and look –'

'Oh Northey, was that a good idea? As it's broad daylight in the garden – I don't see much difference.'

'Oh, the dear fellow will manage somehow.'

He did. The next morning there was an enormous, banked-up hole like an air-raid shelter in the middle of the lawn.

She was wildly unrealistic about money; each for each, her favourite adage, was evidently the keynote of her faith in such matters. She borrowed from any and everybody out of whom she could wheedle the stuff and then made Alfred or me pay them back, saying, 'I'm keeping a strict account. I've had my wages now until June of next year.'

'Dearest,' I said one day, 'what about M. Cruas? Ought we not to pay him for his lessons?' He came every afternoon for at least an hour, so Northey told me; he was evidently a good teacher as her French progressed amazingly.

'No, Fanny, it's not necessary, he comes for love. But if you have got a few thousand francs to spare, Phyllis McFee and me did a little recce in Main Street and saw un cocktail, prix shock, which is just my affair. Sharpen your wits, darling, it's French for a cheap afternoon dress.'

This Phyllis McFee was a Scotch friend of Northey's, from Argyllshire, who also had a job in Paris. So far I had not met her. I was glad that Northey had somebody to run round with, other than elderly cabinet ministers.

'Oh you are kind, now I can go and buy it. So I've had my wages until August I think – anyway I keep a strict account you know, it's all written carefully down.'

It could not exactly be said that Northey's work suffered from all these distractions, she had such a genius for delegating it. 'Each for each is what we teach' meant that Alfred and I, Mrs Trott the housekeeper, Jérôme the chauffeur, Major Jarvis and Philip did practically all her various jobs for her. Our reward was 'You are kind, oh the kindness of you.' But quite apart from extraneous calls on her time and attention, she was not cut out to be a secretary, nobody has ever been less of a career woman. She lived, quite frankly, for pleasure.

'I see what my boys mean when they say she is old-fashioned,' I observed to Philip, 'she is as frivolous as a figure of the twenties.'

'Thank goodness for that anyway. These new ones make me despair of the female sex. I belong to the old world, that's what it is, I talk its language – I'd sooner marry a Zulu woman of my own age than one of these gloomy beauties in red stockings.'

Quite good, I thought, as far as it went, but I was sorry to see that Philip showed no sign of falling in love with Northey. He burned for Grace and I feared that when that flame died down for want of fuel it would never be relit by Northey whom he regarded as a charming, funny little sister. I told her so. She had discovered that Grace was his love (enlightened, probably, by one of the followers, hoping to further his own suit) and came, eyes like diamonds, to communicate her dismay.

'Horrible, horrible Grace, how could he?'

I thought it better to be astringent, not too sympathetic. 'Last time we talked about her you said she was so fascinating.'

'Never! Idiot, rolling her *r*'s and dressing up French. Besides, she's as old as Time.'

'As old as Philip.'

'It's different for a man as you know very well. Fanny, I can't understand it.'

'I'm afraid we never understand that others may be preferred to ourselves.'

'Has Alfred ever preferred anyone to you?'

'Yes, and very boring it was.'

'But you managed?'

'As you see. I think it's a good thing, really, that you know about Philip and Grace.'

'Why is it? I was much happier before.'

'Because now you won't go on harbouring dangerous illusions.'

'More dangerous for me to despair.'

'Don't despair, but don't be too hopeful, either. Remember that it would be a miracle if Philip fell in love with you, under the circumstances.'

'Well, there are miracles. Why shouldn't God do something for me?'

'Yes, I only say don't count on it.'

Philip, overhearing these words as he came into the Salon Vert, said, 'If you're after a miracle St Expédite is your boy. He's a dear little Roman saint who deals with lost causes and he hangs out at St Roch. Only he doesn't like it if you begin asking before the cause is really lost; you must be quite sure before you bother him. I thought we might get him on to the European Army soon. What do you want a miracle for, Mees?'

'It was love and love alone that made King Edward leave his throne.'

'Oh, love! Don't tell me you're keenly running after Bouche-Bontemps?'

'You know I'm not, you brute.' Brimming. 'You know quite well who it is.'

'By the way, I'd forgotten! That is a lost cause, I can tell you and I should know. There, there, mop them up. Are you going to the Chambre to see the old boy present his ministry?'

'Of course. I'm his Egeria.'

'Don't be up until five again,' I said.

'No. He's going to make one of his nutshell speeches – not more than two hours – he says they'll have thrown him out by midnight.'

'Oh, that's how it is?' said Philip. 'I wasn't sure. Excellent. Then we can get on with the Îles Minquiers.'

'I wish I understood about these islands,' said Northey.

'So do I,' said Philip.

'Why do our papers keep saying the French should be urged to give them up for their own sake?'

'Because we want them.'

'If it's good for us to have them, why is it good for the French to get rid of them?'

'In the first place they almost certainly belong to us. Then there's our altruism. In our great, true, sincere love for the French, knowing they will be better without the islands (and a great many other places as well) we are willing to take the responsibility for them off their shoulders. Now, put that in your pipe and stop asking questions. I'm a civil servant, policy is nothing to do with me, I am there to obey orders. I may add that I wish to heaven the bloody thing could be settled and forgotten – it's poisoning my existence.'

The telephone bell rang. 'Answer,' I said to Northey, 'and ask who it is.'

'Hullo – oh – yes, he's here – who is it? Quelle horrible surprise! It's for you, an affected foreign voice,' she said loudly, handing the receiver to Philip.

'Grace? Oh, don't pay any attention, she's not quite all there, you know. *The Times*? No, I haven't. There's a leader? Well, it won't be the last, they've got to fill that space every day – ghastly for them. And a letter from Spears? Not a bit surprised. But, Grace, I've told you it's nothing to do with me. I don't approve or disapprove, I'm not meant to have an opinion. No, I won't resign, it never does any good and then one is unemployed. Do you want me to leave Paris? And all because of a few rocks which honestly don't matter either way. We'll talk about it presently. Yes, of course I will, I'd love to.' He rang off and said to me, 'We're both dining there, aren't we, Fanny? She wants me to take her to the Chambre later on.'

'You said you'd pick me up and take me,' Northey brimmed.

'But we will. Grace won't mind a bit.'

'I mind.'

'Ah! Then you'd better tell them to send the Presidential motor, with its moon, for you.'

'Very funny and witty.'

'Jérôme can take you, darling. Send him on to the Valhuberts', that's all.'

'It's because – I don't like going in there alone. I know.' She took the telephone and said, 'Katie, love, put me through to the Bureau of the Assemblée, will you? I'll speak in my own room.'

8

Alfred had gone to London for a day or two, so Philip took me to the Valhubert dinner. I was beginning to lose my fear of such social occasions now that I knew some of the people likely to be present. They were all very nice to me. I was dazzled by the French mode of life; they keep up a state in Paris which we English only compete with in country houses. A Paris dinner party, both from a material point of view and as regards conversation, is certainly the most civilized gathering that our age can produce, and while it may not be as brilliant as in the great days of the salons, it is unrivalled in the modern world.

The Hôtel de Valhubert, like the Hôtel de Charost (the English Embassy), lies between a courtyard and a garden. It is built of the same sandy-coloured stone and, though smaller and of a later date, its ground plan is very similar. There the resemblance ends. The Embassy, having been bought lock, stock and barrel from Napoleon's sister, is decorated and furnished throughout in a fine, pompous, Empire style very suitable to its present use. The Hôtel de Valhubert is a family house. The rooms still have their old panelling and are crammed with the acquisitions of successive Valhuberts since the French revolution (when the house was sacked and the original furnishings dispersed). Beautiful and ugly objects are jumbled up together, and fit in very well. Grace's flowers were perfection; no yards of velvet, no dead hares, not a hint of harvest home, pretty bouquets in Sèvres vases.

After praising my dress, which was, I thought myself, quite lovely and which came from her dressmaker, Grace introduced me to various people I did not know already. 'It's pouring in London tonight,' she said, 'I've just had a word with Papa. He'd been to Eton and taken the boys out – you'll be glad to hear they are all three alive. He says he never saw such rain!'

Mrs Jungfleisch said the weather had been perfect when she was in London, much better than in Paris.

'Come off it, Mildred. You see London through rose-coloured specs, though I notice you don't go and live there.'

I had not met Mrs Jungfleisch since she came down my staircase, in white linen, actively participating in the rapine of the gramophone. She showed no signs of embarrassment but said, 'Nice to see you again.' I felt as if I had behaved badly in some way and had now been forgiven.

At dinner I sat next to Valhubert and we talked about the children, a ready-made topic whenever he and I saw each other.

'Poor Fabrice,' he said, speaking of my Fabrice's father. 'He was my hero when I was a little boy and as soon as I grew up we were more like brothers than cousins. I must say the child has a great look of him. I was telling my aunt – naturally she is anxious to see him – will you allow me to take him down there when he comes for Christmas? It could be to his advantage, she is rich and there is nobody left of the Sauveterre family. She might adopt him – no – you wouldn't care for that?'

'I don't think I would mind. After all, she is his grandmother. In another five years I suppose he will have gone out of my life. These boys seem to vanish away as soon as they are grown up.'

'And then what do they do?'

'I wish I knew. Alfred and I have always acted on the principle with them of never asking questions.'

'Like the Foreign Legion?'

'Exactly. Now I sometimes wonder if it has been a good plan. We have no idea what goes on; the two elder sons might be dead for all we see or hear of them.'

'Where are they – in diplomacy?'

I began telling him about Beard and Ted, but I could see that he was not listening. He was interested in his own Sigi and in his cousin's Fabrice while accepting our Charlie as inseparable from the others. Bearded professors, whiskered travel agents (if that was what Basil had become) were out of his ken. I knew that my encounter in the street with Basil's accomplice would have seemed strange and dreadful to any man of my own generation; I had never told Alfred of it.

'Aren't you going down to the House?' I said, to change the subject. I knew that the session began at nine o'clock.

'My father-in-law always says down to the House – I like it very much. Yes, presently I will. There's no hurry, we know to a minute what is happening. Jules Bouche-Bontemps at this moment is launching a pathetic appeal – no, pathetic is not the translation, it is one of those trap words which mean different things in the two languages. Rousing, perhaps, a rousing call, or a moving speech. (Nobody will be roused or moved by it, but let that pass.) I could make this speech for him if he fell ill in the middle, I know it as well as he does and so does the whole of his audience. He will begin by saying that our divisions suit nobody except certain allies who had better be nameless. Here we shall have a long digression on Les Îles Minquiers, their history and moral attachment to France. (Those islands are a bore, I can't listen to anything which concerns them, it is too dull.) This will be put in so that if we lose them – and who, except, of course, Grace, cares if we do? – he will be able to say that it is the fault of my party and les Madames who are all preparing, as he very well knows, to vote against him. He will pretend to be deeply shocked by the unholy alliance between les Madames and the Gaullists, all playing London's game. Well, that's a change from Moscow's game, isn't it, which he generally accuses us of playing? Then he will move on to next week's railway strike. The rotting vegetables and stranded tourists will also be the fault of ourselves and Mesdames. Of course all these gloomy prophecies and reproaches and upbraidings will have not the slightest effect and he knows it. He knows to a vote where he will be at the end of the session, that is to say out, not in, so he really might save himself the trouble of making this speech. But he is fond of speaking, it amuses him, and above all it amuses him to publish the iniquities of his fellow-countrymen. Do you like him?'

'Oh yes – very much.'

'I love him – I really love old Bouche-Bontemps.'

Philip leant across the table and said to me, 'All French politicians love each other, or so they say. You see, they never know when they may want to join each other's governments.'

Everybody laughed. Conversation became general, people shouting remarks at each other in all directions. I like this lively habit which enables one to listen without the effort of joining in, unless one has something to say. When the babel died down again I asked M. Hué, my other neighbour, what would happen if the crisis went on.

'René Pléven, Jules Moch and Georges Bidault, in that order, will try and form governments and they will fail. Anglo-French relations will deteriorate; social troubles will multiply; North Africa will boil. In the end even the deputies will notice that what we chiefly need is a government. They will probably come back to Bouche-Bontemps who will get in with the same ministers and the same programme they will have rejected tonight. Is it true that Sir Harald Hardrada is coming over to give a lecture?'

'So Alfred tells me.'

'That's bad.'

'Oh – I was looking forward –'

'I don't mean the lecture. There is nothing on earth more enjoyable than listening to Sir Harald. But it is a storm signal – the first in a sequence of events only too well known to us at the Quai d'Orsay. Whenever your government is planning some nasty surprise they send over Sir Harald to lull our suspicions and put us in a good humour.'

'What's the subject of the lecture?' Valhubert asked me.

'I think I heard it was to be Lord Kitchener.'

The two Frenchmen looked at each other.

'Nom de nom – !'

'We always think we can tell what is coming by the subject, you see. How well I remember "A Study in Allied Solidarity". It was intensely brilliant – delivered in

Algiers just before the Syrian affair. "Lord Kitchener" can only mean good-bye to Les Îles Minquiers. Well, if it's that, it's no great surprise. Let's hope the Intelligence Service is not preparing something much worse.'

'Talking of the Service,' said Valhubert, 'when do I meet the irresistible Mees Nortee?'

'Oh, poor Northey, so she's a spy, is she?'

'Of course. And such a successful one. It was devilish work sending her.'

'Well, you'll be able to see for yourself at our dinner party next week.'

'Good. Can I sit next to her?'

'Certainly you can't,' said Philip.

'Why not? If it's an official dinner, I get the *bout de table* anyway.'

'No – we have other candidates – me for one – it's a big dinner and you'll be well above the salt.'

'I thought the English never bothered about protocol?'

'When in Rome, however, we do as the Romans do – eh, Hughie?'

'Put me next to Mees –'

'After dinner,' said Philip, 'you may have a tête-à-tête with her on a sofa. It's as far as I can go.'

As we left the dining-room Valhubert and two or three other deputies took themselves off, leaving a preponderance of Anglo-Saxons. Philip looked sadly across the room at Grace. I noticed that when she was present Philip became unsure of himself in his anxiety to please her and, as a result, lost much of the charm which lay in his lounging, bantering, casual, take-it-or-leave-it manner. It was rather pathetic to see him sitting bolt upright, hands folded on his knees like a small boy. Presently Mrs Jungfleisch moved over to join him. She began questioning him about what all the Americans in Paris seemed to call the Eels. I listened with half an ear. I had got M. Hué again and he was telling a long, probably funny story about Queen Marie of Rumania. It was the kind of thing I often have trouble in listening to; this time, I had a feeling he had told it to me before and that I had not listened then, either.

Mrs Jungfleisch was saying, 'This parochial squabble over a few small rocks hardly seems to fit into the new concept of a free and balanced world community, does it?'

'Does it?' Philip spoke mechanically, his eyes on Grace.

'A certain absence of rationalism here?'

'To say the least of it.'

'If there are no inhabitants, how does auto-determination apply?'

'It can't.'

'But the modern concept of sovereignty is built up, surely, on auto-determination?'

'That's what we are told.'

'Another query which comes to mind. Where there are no inhabitants how can one know whether the Eels are French- or English-speaking?'

'One can't.'

'And yet language is a powerful determinant of the concept of sovereignty?'

'It's a question of law, not of language.'

'The French say they will soon have a Bomb.'

'Makes no odds. They won't drop it on London because of the Îles Minquiers.'

'I don't believe I have a perfectly comprehensive grasp of this problem from the point of view of you Britishers. Could you brief me?'

'I could. It would take hours. The whole thing is very complicated.'

I saw that Philip was longing for the party to break up so that he could drive Grace to the Chambre, having her alone with him for a few minutes in his motor. I was dying to go to bed. Although it was rather early I put on my gloves and said good night.

9

Bouche-Bontemps' ministry was rejected by the Assembly. '*L'homme des Hautes-Pyrénées*', as the French papers often called him, as if he were some abominable snowman lurking in those remote highlands, made his pathetic or rousing or moving oration to about three hundred and fifty pairs of dry eyes and flinty hearts. The two hundred and fifty who were sufficiently moved to vote for him were not enough to carry him to office. It was rather annoying for Alfred and me, because, shortly before M. Béguin fell, we had invited him and most of the members of his cabinet to a dinner party. Now it looked as if our first big dinner would be given to a lot of disgruntled ex-ministers.

The railway strike duly occurred. As always in France, the human and regional element played a part here. The northern workers came out to a man; their meridional colleagues, more whimsical, less disciplined, by no means as serious, brought quite a lot of trains into Paris. This caused a bottleneck; tourists on their way home from late holidays got as far as the capital and could get no further. Amyas Mockbar said:

STRANDED

Thousands of Britons are stranded in strike-torn Paris. They are camping round the idle stations, foodless, comfortless, hopeless. What is the British Embassy doing to alleviate their great distress? Organizing a lorry service to take them to the coast where British ships could rescue them? Arranging accommodation? Lending them francs with which to buy themselves food? Nothing whatever.

DINNER PARTY

Miss Northey Mackintosh, niece and social secretary to Ambassadress Lady Wincham, told me today: 'My aunt is far too busy arranging a big dinner party to bother about the tourists.' N.B. Estimated cost of such ambassadorial entertainments, £10 a head.

'Did you tell him?' I asked, handing her the *Daily Post*. I was having my breakfast and she was perched on the end of my bed. She came every morning at this time for orders – those orders which were carried out by anybody but herself.

'Quelle horrible surprise! Of course I didn't tell him – would I have said my aunt when you are my first cousin once removed?'

'But do you see him, darling?' I knew that she did. Philip had met them walking up the Faubourg hand in hand looking, he said, like Red Riding Hood and the grandmother.

'Poor little Amy, he's a good soul,' said Northey, 'you'd love him, Fanny.'

'I doubt it.'

'Can I bring him here one day?'

'Certainly you can't. Whenever he sees Alfred or me he writes something utterly vile about us. You ought to be furious with him for this horrible invention. And now I must scold you, Northey. It's partly your fault for mentioning a dinner party at all, though of course I know quite well you didn't say those words. When one sees inverted commas in the paper these days it means speech invented by the writer. If you must go out with him, which I greatly deprecate, please remember never to tell him anything at all about what goes on here.'

'Oh the pathos! It's Lord Grumpy who forces the poor soul to write gossip. What interests him is political philosophy – he says he wants to concentrate on the Chambre but Lord Grumpy drags him back to the Chambre *à coucher*. You see, he's a witty soul!'

'I wonder if he's really such a good political journalist? It's rather a different talent from gossip writing, you know.'

'Oh, don't tell poor little Amy that – he might commit –'

'I only wish he would commit –'

'He's a father, Fanny.'

'Many revolting people are.'

'And he has to feed his babies.'

'So do tigers. One doesn't want to be their dinner, all the same.'

'Fanny,' wheedling voice.

'Mm?'

'He wants to do a piece on Auntie Bolter. He says when she got married he had a thick week with the Dockers and the Duke of Something and couldn't do her justice. He'd like to know when she's coming to stay here so that he can link her up with you and Alfred.'

'Yes, I expect he would love that. Just the very thing for a political philosopher to get his teeth into – now, Northey, please listen to me,' I said, in a voice to which she was quite unaccustomed. 'If we have trouble with Mockbar and if it turns out to be your fault I shall be obliged to send you back to Scotland. I am here to protect Alfred from this sort of indiscretion.'

Northey looked mutinous, her eyes brimmed and her mouth went down at the corners.

The door now burst open and a strange figure loomed into the room. Side whiskers, heavy fringe, trousers, apparently moulded to the legs, surmounted by a garment for which I find no word but which covered the torso, performing the function both of coat and of shirt, such was the accoutrement of an enormous boy (I could not regard him as a man), my long-lost Basil.

'*Quelle horrible* surprise!' said Northey, not at all displeased at this diversion from her own indiscretions, past and future.

Basil looked from one to the other. When he realized that we were both delighted to see him, the scowl which he had arranged on his face gave way to a particularly winning smile.

'Well, Ma,' he said, 'here I am. Hullo, Northey!'

'This is very exciting. I thought I'd lost you for ever.'

'Yes, I expect you did. What about breakfast – I could press down some bacon and eggs – in short I am starving. I say, this is all very posh, isn't it! Cagey lot of servants here, Ma – I had to show them my passport before they would let me in.'

'Have you caught sight of yourself in a glass lately?' said Northey, taking the telephone to order his breakfast.

'They must have seen a Ted before – how about *les blousons noirs*?'

'Not in embassies, darling, it's another world.'

'And what's this?' said Northey, fingering an armband he wore inscribed with the words: 'Grandad's Tours'.

'That's magic. Open sesame to the whole world of travel.'

'Where have you come from, Baz?'

'This minute, from the Gare d'Austerlitz. Actually from the Costa Brava.'

'Begin at the beginning, miserable boy. Do remember I've seen and heard nothing of you for three whole months.'

'Why, that's right, nor you have.'

'Not since you cut our luncheon that day.'

'But I wrote and put you off.'

'Six weeks later.'

'I wrote at once – I'm afraid there was posting trouble. Well, it's like this. You know old Grandad? Yes, Ma, of course you do, Granny Bolter's new old man.'

'I've never seen him.'

'Still, you know he exists. Actually, Granny met him with me – old Grandad and me have been matey for an age – he was the brains of our gang. I can tell you, Granny's got a good husband this time, just what she deserves. You can't think how well they get on.'

I had always noticed that, while my children regarded everybody over the age of thirty as old sordids, old weirdies, ruins, hardly human at all, the Bolter, at sixty-five, was accepted as a contemporary. She had an astonishing gift of youth due, perhaps, to a combination of silliness with infinite good nature and capacity for enjoyment. Physically she was amazing for her age; it was easy to see that her heart had never been involved in any of her countless love affairs.

Basil went on in his curious idiom, which consisted in superimposing, whenever he remembered to do so, cockney or American slang on the ordinary speech of an educated person. 'Old Grandad found that Granny's money is earning a paltry four or five per cent on which she pays taxes into the bargain. Now that's not good enough for him, so 'e scouts round, see, and finds out about this travel racket – oh boy, and is racket the word? 'E lays down a bit of Granny's lolly for premises and propaganda and now he's all set for the upper-income group – tax free of course – and I'm on the band-wagon with him and soon I'll be about to give you and Father the whizz of an old age. Grandad's the brainy boss and I'm the brawny executive; the perfect combination. So you see now why I couldn't lunch that day – I had just embarked on my career.'

'Which is?'

'I'm the boy wot packs in the meat.'

'Here's your breakfast.'

'Thanks very much. It's many a day since proper food crossed my palate. Ever been to Spain? Don't! Well, to go on with my exposey – Grandad assembles the cattle and I herd it to and fro. In plain English, Grandad, with many a specious promise and hopeful slogan – "No hurry, no worry if you travel the Grandad way" and so on – gets together parties of tourists, takes their cash off them and leaves me to conduct them to their doom. Ghastly it is – fifteen to a carriage across France and worse when we change for the peninsula. Then, when they finally disembark, more dead than alive after days without food or sleep, they have to face up to the accommodation. "Let Grandad rent you a fisherman's cottage" says the prospectus. So he does. The beds are still hot from the honest fisher folk prized out of them by yours truly! That's when the ruminants begin collapsing – disappointment finishes them off. Anyhow the old cows drop like flies when the temperature is over a hundred – Britons always think they are going to love the heat but in fact it kills them – we usually plant one or two in the bone-orchard before we start for home. I keep a top hat over there now, for the funerals, it looks better. Lucky I'm tough, you need to be for this work, I can tell you!'

'I wonder they don't complain?'

'Complain! But what's the good, they've got to go through with it once they are caught up in the machine. There's no escape.'

'How I should hate you!' said Northey.

'They hate all right – the point is they utterly depend. They can't speak any language bar a little basic British and they've got no money because Grandad bags whatever they can afford for the trip before they leave. So they are at my mercy. You should see the letters they write when they get home about "your tall, dark courier", threatening my life and everything. Bit too late then of course, I'm far away, packing in the next lot.'

'Whatever induces them to go in the first place, without making a few inquiries? It seems perfectly mad!'

'Ah! There you have the extraordinary genius of me Grandad. He literally mes-merizes them with his propaganda. All built up on smoothing the path of sex. "Let Grandad take you to the Land of Romance, Leisure and Pleasure." "Will you hear a Spanish lady, how she wooed an Englishman?" See the sort of thing? We've got a plate-glass window at the office, with life-sized dummies of a señorita riding behind a caballero. Inside it's lined with wedding snaps of people who have mar-ried Spanish grandees during Grandad tours (no funeral snaps of course). There's something in it, mind you, some of the girls do sleep with customs officers.'

'On those horrid tables?' said Northey, interested.

'But how do they have time?' I asked. 'I always seem to be in too much of a hurry to sleep with people at the customs.'

'Next time you must try Grandad's way – *no hurry*. The trouble is you travel soft. You don't know what a journey can be like when you go cheap – it beats imagination. The Leisure, the Pleasure! The waits are endless, whole days some-times – hours to spare at every frontier you come to. Of course the douaniers, being in uniform, get the pick. The older ladies are obliged to pay waiters and beach attendants and such like.'

'I thought they had no money?'

'They tear off their jewels.'

'Well then, just tell the programme. You go sight-seeing or what?'

'Nothing whatever. The British female goes abroad for romance and that's that.'

'Ay de mi!' said Northey, 'how true!'

'And the men? Aren't Spanish women very much guarded?'

'The men usually arrive dead beat. They take the journey worse than the women do and fury tires their hearts. They just have the energy to strip and peel. I don't think they would ever manage – you know, in the state they are in. Besides, their emotions and energies, if any, are concentrated on revenge.'

'And how do you spend your time?' I vaguely hoped for an account of advanced lessons in Spanish.

'Me? I lie on my face on the beach. It's safer. Once we've arrived at the place and they've seen where they've got to doss down and when they've smelt the food, redolent of rancidol, which they are expected to press down, the younger male Britons have only one idea. Señoritas be blowed – they just want to kick my lemon – give me a fat lip, see? So I lie there, camouflaged by protective colouring. My back is black, but my face is white; they don't connect the two and I am perfectly all right providing I never turn over. When the day comes for going home they need me too much to injure me.'

'Goodness, Basil!'

'You may well say so. Where's Father?'

'He's been in London – back any time now. Look, darling, I haven't told him about your summer – I didn't know anything for certain – so let him think, what I rather hoped myself, that you were polishing up your pure Castilian. He might not like the idea of you – well –'

'Carting out the rubbish?'

'Oh dear, no, he wouldn't like it. But I don't think we need tell him. Now the holidays are over and you'll be going back to your crammer I think we might, without being deceitful, forget the whole thing?'

'Only I'm not going back to the crammer. That wasn't a holiday, Ma – funny sort of hol that would be – no, it's my career, my work, my future.'

'Lying on your face in the sand is?'

'Yeah.'

'You're giving up the Foreign Service?'

'You bet.'

'Basil!'

'Now listen, Mother dear, the Foreign Service has had its day – enjoyable while it lasted no doubt, but over now. The privileged being of the future is the travel agent. He lives free, travels soft – don't think he shares the sufferings of his people, he has a first-class sleeper, the best room in the hotel. Look at me now, washed, shaved, relaxed and rested. I only wish you could see my victims at this moment! Haven't taken their clothes off for days. Some of them stood the whole way last night while I lay at my ease. Even during a railway strike you've only got to exhibit the armband and the officials will do anything for you. You see we hold the national tourist industries in the hollow of our hands. There's nothing they dread more than a lot of unorganized travellers wandering about their countries exhibiting individualism. They'd never force a tourist on his own into those trams and hotels – he'd go home sooner. But you can do anything with a herd and the herd must have its drover. As he keeps the tickets and the money and the passports (no worry) even the most recalcitrant of the cattle are obliged to follow him. No good jibbing when the conditions are ghastly because what is the alternative? To be stranded without hope of succour. So the authorities need us; the tourists need us; we are paramount. Oh, it's a wonderful profession and I'm lucky to have the family backing which got me into it.'

My blood ran cold at these words. I have seen the promise of too many young men fade away as the result of taking a wrong step after leaving their university not to feel appalled at the prospect of this brilliant boy, easily my favourite child, thus jeopardizing his future. There is no sadder spectacle than that of a lettered beachcomber, a pass to which Basil seemed to have come in three short months.

'And your first in history,' I said, 'your gift for languages – all to be wasted?'

'It's no good, Ma, you'll have to be realistic about this. The world isn't like it was when you were young. There's more opportunity, more openings for a chap than there were then. You can't really expect me to swot away and get into the Foreign Service and put up with an aeon of boredom simply to end my days in a ghastly great dump like this? I love Father, you know I do, and I don't want to hurt your feelings, but I've no intention of wasting the best years of my life like he has and nothing you can say will persuade me to. So now, having partaken of this smashing breakfast, for which I'm truly grateful, I must wend my way back to the hungry sheep who will look up, poor brutes, and not be fed.'

'They must be fed. Where are they?'

'Sitting on bursting canvas bags at the Gare du Nord – at least I hope so. I put them into the metro, before taking a cab myself, and told them where to get out and that I'd be along. I said to meet at the bus stop of the 48 because I believe the crowds at the station are terrific and one sheep looks very much like another. I expect they'll be there now for days – only hope this fine weather will go on.'

'You horrify me. Can't we do something for them?'

'They're all right. Singing "Roll out the Barrel" like Britons always do at waits – wish they'd learn a new tune.'

'How many are there?'

'In my party? About twenty-five. You don't need to bother about them, Ma, honest.'

'Please go straight to the Gare du Nord and bring them here. I'll have breakfast for them in the garden, ready by the time they arrive.'

A wail from Northey. 'No, Fanny, you're not to – they'll petrify my badger.'

'Surely he's blacked out in his air-raid shelter?'

'He'll smell them down there and tremble. A badger's sense of smell is highly developed – people don't understand about creatures.'

'Don't you take on,' said Basil, 'they smell like badgers themselves. He'll be thrilled – he'll think his mates have arrived.'

'Go at once, Baz,' I said.

'But, Ma, this strike will probably last for days. You'll get awfully tired of "Roll out the Barrel".'

'Yes. As soon as you've brought them there you must see about a lorry to take them to the coast.'

'No fear. All our profit would melt away – Grandad would kill me.'

'I'll pay.'

'You're soft. Another thing – have I got to face all those posh butlers with that lot in tow?'

'Northey can go with you and bring you in through the Avenue Gabriel. It's nearer for the metro. Get the key of the garden, dearest, from Mrs Trott as you go out and tell Jérôme to be ready to help Baz find a lorry. Go on, Basil, twitch your mantle blue.'

I was not at all surprised when Basil's Britons turned out to be entirely delightful, very different indeed from the furious, filthy, haggard, exhausted, sex-starved mob which anybody not knowing Basil and not knowing England might have expected from his description. They were, in fact, sensible, tidy and nicely dressed, covered with smiles and evidently enjoying this adventure in a foreign land. There were rather more women than men, but it was unimaginable that any of them could have gone to bed with customs officers or waiters or indeed that they should commit fornication or adultery under any circumstances whatever. They looked more than respectable. I was glad to be confirmed in my suspicion that Basil's account of his own tough and unmerciful behaviour was an invention, to startle Northey and me. The Britons were full of his praises and when he explained that I was his mother they crowded round to tell me what a wonder boy or miracle child I had produced. They had no idea that they were in an embassy – not that they would have been impressed had they known it, since the English are less conscious than any other race of diplomatic status; they evidently thought I kept a hotel in Paris. 'Nice here,' they said, 'we must tell our friends.' Any strangeness in their situation they would put down to being abroad. 'Very nice,' they said of the breakfast, which they ate with the relish of extreme hunger.

When they had finished they told me, in detail, how splendid Basil had been. Hundreds of Britons, it seemed, many of whom had paid much more for the trip than they had, were left behind at Port-Vendres; Basil had literally forged a way through the mob, and, using his gigantic strength in conjunction with his mastery of languages, had lifted and pushed and shoved and lugged and somehow inserted every single member of his party on to a train already full to suffocation.

'Now all the others who were on it are stifling at that horrid Gare du Nord while here we are in these nice grounds.'

'Masterly organization,' said an elderly man of military aspect. 'He'll do well in the next war – a genius for improvisation – marvellous linguist – I think you should be proud of him. I could have done with more like him in the Western Desert. Now he's gone off to get a lorry to take us to the coast. What initiative! We are all going to subscribe for a memento when we get home.'

I said, 'You must be so tired.'

'Oh no.' A cheerful woman like a W.V.S. worker spoke up. 'After the holiday we've had, a night or two in the train seems nothing. Yes, forty-eight hours we've been since leaving. Quite an adventure!'

'And I suppose it wasn't too comfortable in Spain?'

'You don't go abroad for comfort exactly, do you? I always say, plenty of that at home. One likes to see how the foreigners live, for a change. There's no end to what they'll put up with. The toilet arrangements! You'd never believe!'

'Excuse me, but is that a badger's sett?'

'You are clever!' said Northey, twinkling and sparkling at the poor man whose head was turned there and then.

'Are there many badgers in this part of Paris?'

'I've never seen another but there may be. Do you have them where you live?'

'Oh no, not in the Cromwell Road. I knew what it was from the TV. I see you have a redstart, now that's a delightful bird.'

'Yes, and an owl at night. But we haven't got a TV.'

'Shame,' said the Briton. 'They don't seem to go in for them abroad we've noticed. Still, with so much nature about you hardly need one. That's what I have mine for, the nature. I didn't know Paris was like this, wouldn't mind living here myself.'

As Northey and I went back to the house we met Alfred. 'I was looking for you. Who are all these people?'

'Sweet Britons,' said Northey.

'Stranded by the railway strike,' I added. He seemed satisfied with this explanation. 'How was London?'

'Worrying. I'll tell you later – I must go to the Chancery now. Are we lunching in? Oh, thank goodness –'

I told Northey to see that the Britons got off all right, to have some sandwiches made up for them and to say good-bye to Basil for me. My business now was to protect Alfred, tired and preoccupied as he seemed, from the sight of his son in such a garb.

The Britons had a little nap on the grass. Then they began a sing-song. We had 'Lily Marlene', 'Colonel Bogey' (whistling only) and 'Nearer my God to Thee'. The noise was not disagreeable, thinly floating on a warm breeze. Just before luncheon-time I heard female voices sounding a cheer in the Avenue Gabriel.

Northey came running, to announce that they had gone, in a car.

'What, all twenty-five in one motor?'

'Car is French for charabang. Basil sends his love and he'll probably be back next week. He seems to think the Embassy can be his Paris H.Q. in future, if you're lucky. He's cooking a lot of schemes, I note. Then faithful Amy turned up.'

'You don't mean Mockbar?' I was horrified.

'Good little soul, indeed I do. But don't worry. I told Baz you wouldn't like to have him hanging about in the garden and he got rid of him in a tick.'

'How did he? That's a formula worth knowing.'

'It's not one you can use very often though. He pretended the Britons were all radioactive. Amy buggered off before you could say *canif*.'

'I absolutely forbid you to say that word, Northey. No, not *canif*, you know quite well. Wherever did you pick it up?'

'The Captain of the *Esmeralda*. He was a most unpleasant person, but I rather liked some of his expressions.'

'Well, I beg you won't use that one again.'

'All the same, do you admit it's perfect for describing the exits of Amy?'

I dreaded the *Daily Post* after that. Sure enough:

RADIOACTIVE

Some two score radioactive Britons sought the protection of our Embassy in Paris yesterday. Did Sir Alfred Wincham send for scientific aid? Are they now receiving treatment at a clinic?

DUMPED

No British officials went near them. They were hustled into a lorry by our amateur envoy's son Mr Basil Wincham and dumped at the coast. All efforts to get in touch with them subsequently have been fruitless. Where is this dangerous lorry-load now? Have the sanitary authorities been informed? If they went home on a British ship were the necessary precautions taken to see that their fellow-travellers were not contaminated? This whole incident seems to typify the slack and unprofessional outlook which permeates our Paris mission today.

I was quite terrified, envisaging awful developments. After a consultation with Philip we decided not to tell Alfred until something happened, knowing that he would never look at the *Daily Post* of his own accord. Nothing happened at all. The powers that be in England knew better than to believe an unsupported statement by Mockbar; the French were unaware of his existence and of that of the *Daily Post*. Philip said that even if their sanitary authorities should raise the question he could easily deal with them. 'You know what the French are, they don't quite believe in modern magic. They all go to fortune-tellers (M. de Saint-Germain is booked up for months), they read the stars every day and make full use of spells. But they don't get into a state about things like radioactivity.'

Old Grumpy, having failed to make any mischief for us, had to drop the story because Basil and his Britons, merged among thousands struggling home on Channel steamers, were never identified and therefore could not be interviewed.

In London, Alfred had submitted his own views on the likelihood of the French ever accepting the European Army; they were in direct contradiction to those of his American colleague. The Cabinet would naturally have preferred to be told what they wanted to hear and Alfred's prognostications were not well received. He was merely instructed to stiffen his attitude and informed that London regarded the C.E.D. as inevitable and essential. He was also informed that our government were going full steam ahead over the Minquiers and that he must make this perfectly clear in Paris. The Foreign Secretary announced that he would be coming over to see his opposite number, as soon as he had one. I believe that Alfred heartily wished himself back in Oxford, though he did not say so to me.

10

M. Moch, M. Pléven and M. Bidault all tried to form governments and all duly failed. Then Bouche-Bontemps tried again and was accepted by the Chambre the very day before our dinner party. Alfred and I were delighted. For one thing, he had become a friend and it was most fortunate for us to have him to help and even sometimes guide us while we were still finding our feet; besides which our dinner was, we thought, saved. Bouche-Bontemps was taking the direction of foreign affairs himself, anyhow for a while, so that the government was virtually the same as that which had been in power before this long crisis. M. Béguin was now Vice-Président instead of Président du Conseil, and one or two minor ministries were given to new men, belonging to groups hitherto in opposition. This procedure, known as *dosage* and frequently resorted to during the Fourth Republic, had ensured the extra votes necessary to put Bouche-Bontemps in.

I told Northey and requested Philip to come to my bedroom early on the morning of the dinner in order to talk over dispositions. Philip appeared, punctual as always. 'Isn't this a mercy!' I said. The morning papers hailed the end of the crisis, giving Bouche-Bontemps a friendly reception. In fact a naïf and optimistic reader, like myself, would suppose that a long term of stable government lay ahead. *The Times*, in a leading article, compared Bouche-Bontemps to Raymond Poincaré; the *Daily Telegraph* said he was the strongest man thrown up by the Fourth Republic so far and shared many characteristics with Clemenceau.

Philip looked sceptically at the headlines. 'You can thank the General for this. If he were not sitting like the rock of ages at Colombey we should never have a government here at all. As it is they are obliged to come to these little temporary arrangements simply in order to keep King Charles in exile. This ministry won't last six weeks. Hullo – have you seen Mockbar?'

'No – don't tell me – better not shake my nerve – !'

'Not too bad. It's headed: Paris Dinner Muddle. "Confusion – bungling – secrecy – lack of organization are casting a shadow over our amateur envoy's first official dinner." And so on. Zero, in fact. The old boy's losing his grip – he'll get the sack if he can't do better than that. Where's Mees – I thought she was to come for orders?'

'Naughty girl. I suppose she's overslept as usual.'

'She's not in her room – I banged as I came up the back stairs – nor in the bath, I banged there, too.'

'Are you sure? How very odd. I wonder if Katie knows anything?'

Katie knew everything, as she always did, in her cage and told what she knew with evident enjoyment. Philip listened in to her account with the earphone. It seemed that while Alfred and I had been out the evening before, rushing from the National Day of Iceland to a party for the Foreign Minister of Bali, ending up at a concert at the Costa Rican embassy, a hamper of live lobsters had arrived for me. They were a present from M. Busson, a deputy with a seaside constituency, one of the people invited to our dinner. The chef, overjoyed, unable to get hold of me, had informed Northey, saying that the menu would now have to be

altered. It would then have been Northey's plain duty to send interim acknow-
ledgment and thanks to M. Busson. No such thing. On seeing the dear lobsters,
which were lurching about on the kitchen floor, she flew into a *fantigue*. She
made Katie put her through to the Ministère de la Marine where, strange to say,
she had no friend, and asked to speak to the Chef de Cabinet. Presenting Alfred's
compliments she inquired at what point the Seine became salt. The answer was
Rouen. She then ordered Jérôme for 8.30 a.m. When the time came she forced
the furious chef to cram the lobsters back into their hamper, and made the footmen load them on to the Rolls-Royce (not in the boot, for fear of smothering
the darlings, but inside, on the pretty carpet). By now she was well on the way
to Normandy where the sweet creatures would duly be put back in their native
element.

'Thank you, Katie.' I rang off and looked at Philip, suppressing a giggle as best
I could. He shook his head, not very much amused.

'This Northey!' he said. 'In the first place the French navy, a thoroughly Anglo-
phobe institution, will immediately assume that we are up to some monkey work.
Why should Alfred want to know where the Seine becomes tidal, all of a sudden?
In the second place Busson, who is the new Minister of Atomic Energy, is the leader
of a small but powerful group in the Chambre. He is also a famous gourmet. He
will be angry and disappointed when his lobsters fail to appear this evening – he
may never forgive. In the third place, I think it's too irresponsible of Mees to go
off like this on the one day when she might be some slight use to you!'

The telephone bell rang: Katie again. 'I forgot to say, she took a follower. At least
I expect he is one by now –'

'Who?'

'The Chef de Cabinet. She arranged to pick him up at the side door of the
Ministry in the rue St Florentin.'

'That's quite a good thing,' I said to Philip, 'at least he'll see for himself she's
not spying.'

'My dear, they are madly suspicious of Mees – all the ones who aren't in love
with her, that is. The sweet lobsters won't reassure them, I can tell you.'

'What time should you say she'll be back?'

'Who knows? Rouen is nearly 100 miles, I think. The Chef de Cabinet will spin
it out as long as he can, no doubt. Oh well – it's not as if she'd be much use here,
one can't trust her even to put cards round the table, let alone work out the seating.
I should have had to do it for you in any case. I'll get on to old Hughie, presently.'

'Let's put M. Busson next to Northey so that she can explain about the lobsters
in her own words – ?'

'And make an enemy for life? He has never been a minister before, he wouldn't
at all relish sitting next to your social secretary. We must make her apologize to
him before dinner – lucky she's so irresistible to French politicians. Now – business.
Let's see who we've got. I suppose I shall have to have Mees – no hope of Grace
for me, eh? Talking of Grace, why not ask her to come and give you a hand with
the flowers and things? I know she'd love to.'

'Philip, what a good idea!'

'Yes, I'm going to telephone now – she'll turn up trumps, you'll see.'

*

He was quite right. Grace came for me in her motor after luncheon and took me to St Cloud to pick flowers for the party. Valhubert had a property there, just outside the park, an ancient garden on the site of a hunting-lodge which the Germans had destroyed in 1870. Here he grew flowers and fruit for his own use. It was a melancholy, romantic spot, especially in the autumn when the dark green leaves of the adjacent woodlands were flecked with yellow and the old fruit trees covered with apples and pears and peaches. Impossible to imagine that one was only ten minutes away from Paris. The flowers that were visible all grew in tubs and stone vases, while those for cutting were planted in regular rows, like vegetables, behind a hornbeam hedge. 'Charles-Edouard hates to see flowers growing in the earth,' Grace explained. 'Look how the hot summer has brought out the orange blossom and even ripened a few oranges; very rare, in this climate.' Wearing a dark grey linen dress with broderie anglaise collar and cuffs she looked exactly right there, as she always did whatever the circumstances. She gave me a pair of secateurs with which to cut the old-fashioned roses, lilies, hollyhocks, tuberoses, carnations, fuchsias and geraniums. 'We'll make a lovely mixture,' she said. 'Don't they smell better than those you buy in shops?'

'And no nursing-home flowers,' I said. 'That's rare at this time of year.'

'Those horrible gladioli, we don't dream of allowing them. Aren't English autumn flowers too loathsome!'

'Nursing homes here have them too.'

'Not quite such brutes. The English are forever building themselves up as being so good at growing flowers, best gardeners in the world and all that, and what does it boil down to *en fin de compte*? Michaelmas daisies and chrysanths, *sentant le cimetière*.' Grace was off on her hobby-horse now. 'Have you ever noticed it's just those very things the English pride themselves on most which are better here? Trains: more punctual; tweeds: more pretty; football: the French always win. Doctors: can't be compared, nobody ever dies here until they are a hundred. Horses, we've got M. Boussac. The post, the roads, the police – France is far better administered –'

I felt quite furious. 'Well, come on, Fanny,' she said, 'I'm waiting for the answer – you're the Ambassadress, you're meant to know it –'

'It isn't fair. You've got these things all ready to trot out, and I suppose facts and figures to bolster them up if I begin to query them. Before I see you next I shall do a bit of prep, but for the moment my mind is a blank. Oh! I know – justice. Better and much quicker at home – admit?'

'We hurry people to the gallows all right. Fluster them up in the witness box and then swing them. Give me a dear old *juge d'instruction*, plodding away, when I'm in trouble –'

'No, Grace, we don't hang them any more.'

'Not even murderers?'

'Specially not them.'

'What are you telling me? I don't care for this news at all! Do you mean people can murder one as much as they like and nothing happen to them?'

'Yes. Unless you're a policewoman. I'm not sure they are meant to poison one either or perhaps it's shooting that's not allowed. I can never remember. But don't worry. If they know nothing will happen they don't murder so much.'

'Are you sure?'

'Yes, it was all in the papers. I say – I've thought of something else – the papers are better at home –'

'Are they? I can't say I ever see them except when Mockbar has a go at us, then some kind friend cuts it out and sends it. He's a delightful writer, such polish, such accuracy!'

'You take in *The Times*,' I said. 'I know you do. Try and be more truthful, Grace –'

'My father sends it, but we hardly ever open it. I keep it for covering the furniture in the summer.'

'I've thought of something else – digestives.'

'All right, I'll give you digestives and I'll give you Cooper's Oxford and if you're very good potted shrimps as well. Now that's rather typical. The only subject we agree on is food, which is not supposed to be an English talent at all. It's the things they pretend to be good at which are such flops.'

'It's THEY now, is it!' I said.

'Don't be angry, Fanny. After all, Charles-Edouard and the children are French –'

'That's no reason for downing the English.'

'I don't down them – not really, but they annoy me with their pretended superiority. And oh, how they chill me! Not only the climate –'

'Same as here.'

'Nonsense, darling, there's no comparison – but also the hearts. I was noticing that yesterday. I had to go to a wedding at the Consulate – cold as charity it was. Gabble gabble gabble – gabble gabble gabble – may I give you my best wishes? Over. Think of the difference between that and a wedding in a *mairie*! When the bride and bridegroom come in, M. le Maire, in his sash of office, throws up his arms like General de Gaulle: *"Mes enfants! Voici la plus belle journée de votre vie –"'*

'Yes, Grace. I dare say, but people must be themselves you know. Can you imagine poor Mr Stock throwing up his arms like General de Gaulle and saying "My children, this is the most beautiful day of your lives"? It would be simply ridiculous if he did.'

'Ridiculous, because he hasn't got a heart. That's what I complain of.'

'Anyhow it wouldn't have sounded very convincing at yesterday's wedding when you think that the Chaddesley-Corbetts are both nearly seventy and have been divorced I don't know how many times.'

We snipped away in silence. Presently Grace asked how the Minquiers were getting on.

'Nothing new, I think. Mr Gravely comes here next week to see M. Bouche-Bontemps. Partly about the Eels, I suppose.'

'Oh, does he? Bringing Angela?'

'No. Wives mustn't come too often because of foreign currency. It seems she was here in the summer.'

'So she was. Isn't it mad of the Treasury the way they drive these important politicians to the brothels just for the sake of the few pounds it would cost to bring their wives with them!'

'Darling! He's sixty, looks like an empty banana skin and is only coming for the inside of a week –'

'Some chaps can't stand more than twenty-four hours, you know.'

The Chef de Cabinet did indeed spin it out. Grace and I had done the flowers and done the table and she had gone home to dress when Northey reappeared. She seemed quite unaware of having done wrong and I saw no point in scolding as that particular misdeed was unlikely to recur. Besides, I was longing to hear about her day as much as she was longing to tell. The sweet lobsters having been returned to their native element the Chef de Cabinet had told Jérôme to make a little detour of about fifty miles which took them to a three-star restaurant. Here they ordered luncheon and then went for a walk in beautiful woods. The Chef de Cabinet, no doubt in an emotional state, had lost his head and ordered *homard à l'armoricaine*. When Northey discovered that this was French for lobster, and the cruellest sort at that, she was furious; she cried and sent him to Coventry for half an hour. They made it up again, ordered a different luncheon and got rather tipsy while it was being cooked. Back in Paris at last, the Chef de Cabinet, unable to endure the parting, put it off by taking her to see Notre Dame. 'Though really,' said Northey, 'when you know the outside you can guess what the inside is going to be like and he made me miss my fitting at Lanvin –'

'Fitting at Lanvin?'

'Didn't I tell you? M. Castillo has offered me Cecil Beaton. Oh, sharpen your wits, Fanny – Cecil Beaton, that heavenly dress with the bobbles –'

II

Our guests assembled under the gaze of King George and Queen Mary. When there is a large dinner at the Embassy it takes place in a banqueting-hall added on to the ground floor by Pauline Borghese. Though by no means beautiful, it is of an earlier date and therefore less catastrophically hideous than its equivalent at the Élysée which so torments the ghost of poor little Madame de Pompadour. The eighteenth-century dining-room on the first floor, with Flemish tapestries painful to a French eye, where we usually had our meals, only holds about twenty people.

When M. Busson arrived, Philip grabbed Northey by the shoulder and steered her towards him, saying that she had something to explain. She took him into a corner and I could see her launching into a pantomime, partly French, partly English, mostly dumb show, tortured expression and flying hands. He looked puzzled, though fascinated, and then amused. Finally, to my relief, he burst out laughing. He gathered his colleagues round him and gave a rapid résumé of Northey's statement. 'And now,' he ended up in English, 'these succulent crustaceans are no doubt swimming away to Les Îles Minquiers.'

'Swimming!' said Northey, scornfully. 'I have yet to see a lobster with fins.'

M. Béguin, who was always rather grumpy and more so now that he was no longer Président du Conseil, remarked sourly that these succulent crustaceans were more likely to be boiling away, at this very moment, in peasant cottages. Far better for them, he explained in his cold, clipped voice, had they been cooked at the Embassy, because the cottage saucepans would be smaller, the cottage fires weaker and the agony more prolonged.

Northey was unmoved by this argument. 'I could see on their sweet faces when they were bug – I mean making off – that they would never let themselves be caught again,' she said, comfortably.

Bouche-Bontemps said, 'Perhaps Mees is quite right, who knows? The Holy Office forbade the boiling alive of heretics – they tried it once, in Spain, and even Spanish nerves gave way at the sight. Ought we really to subject living creatures to such terrible cruelty in order to have one or two delicious mouthfuls?'

'M. *le Président*,' said Northey, '*je vous aime*.'

'It is reciprocal.'

M. Béguin looked like a Nanny whose charges have gone too far in silliness. He said something to M. Hué about the frivolity of *les britanniques* being beyond endurance. M. Hué, a good-natured fellow, replied that while naturally deploring the waste of delicious lobsters, he found the whole thing funny, touching and *plutôt sympathique*. M. Béguin raised his eyes to heaven. His shoulders, too, went up until it seemed as if they would never come down again. He looked round for a partisan, saw that Madame Hué's gaze was also fixed to the ceiling and that she was clearly on his side. They went off together to a sofa where they sat talking very fast, throwing malignant glances in the direction of Northey.

The Valhuberts now arrived, raising the level of looks and elegance. I introduced him to Northey and had the satisfaction of seeing that this well-known ravager of the female heart fell there and then victim to the charm of Mees. The evening seemed to have begun extremely well; most of the guests, if not all, were there and were getting on famously. I am always struck by how easily a French party slides down the slipway and floats off to the open sea. People arrive determined to enjoy themselves instead of, as at Oxford, determined (apparently) to be awkward. There are no pools of silence, all the guests find congenial souls, or at least somebody with whom to argue. Even M. Béguin's disapproval had that positive quality which facilitates the task of a hostess; it led to lively talk and a reshuffling of the company.

At this point, Northey was supposed to count the guests and let me know if they were all there. However she was so completely surrounded by ministers that I could not catch her eye to remind her of her duty. Philip, with a resigned wink in my direction, performed it for her. 'That's it,' he said, presently.

The door opened. I supposed that dinner was going to be announced and vaguely wondered why by that door and not the one which led to the dining-room. For a moment nothing happened. Then my bearded son David came crab-wise into the room, pulling after him a blue plastic cradle and a girl attached to its other handle. He was dressed in corduroy trousers, a duffel coat, a tartan shirt and sandals over thick, dirty, yellow woollen socks. The girl was tiny, very fair with a head like a silk-worm's cocoon, short white skirt (filthy) swinging over a plastic petticoat, a black belt, red stockings and high-heeled, pointed, golden shoes.

In the silence which fell as this curious group came into the room I heard a voice

(M. Béguin's I expect) saying something about *'cet individu à mine patibulaire'* and another (Charles-Edouard de Valhubert probably), *'pas mal, la petite.'*

I am always pleased when my children turn up. The sight of them rejoices me, I rush forward, I smile and I embrace. I did so now. David and the girl dumped the cradle on a precious piece by Weisweiller. He kissed me warmly (oh horrid, scrubbing-brush beard) and said, 'Ma, this is Dawn.'

Alfred's reactions were not as immediately enthusiastic as mine. With him it is not so much a physical instinct as a matter of principle that makes him welcome the boys whatever the circumstances of their arrival. Our house is their home, their shelter from the stormy blast. If they are naked they must be clothed; if hungry, fed; if the police of five nations are hot on their heels they must be hidden. No questions must ever be asked. Now he came forward and shook hands with his son, giving him a stern, grave, penetrating look. 'This is Dawn, Father.'

'How do you do?'

Alfred led Dawn and David round the room, introducing them, while I held a hurried consultation with Philip about fitting them in to our dinner.

He said, 'Do you really think it's a good idea? They are so travel-stained –'

Unfortunately I knew my David far too well to think that the stains had anything to do with travel.

'We can't possibly send them out when they have just arrived,' I said. 'Alfred wouldn't hear of it.'

'There's no room for them here. The table only holds fifty – it would take at least an hour to put in another leaf and re-do it.'

'Oh dear, oh dear,' I considered a moment. 'In that case, Philip, I'm most dreadfully afraid, and too sorry, that you'll have to take Northey out to dinner. Go to the Cremaillere – on the house of course. Do you mind?'

'Yes,' said Philip, displeased at this turn of affairs. Though he had not been able to arrange the seating so that he would be next to Grace (he was between Northey and Mrs Jungfleisch) he had been placed exactly opposite her so that he would be able to look at her all the time and occasionally lean over and exchange a remark. 'I mind but I bow to the inevitable.'

'What a funny little person,' I said, 'who do you imagine she is?'

'An heiress, by the look of her.'

'How too splendid that would be. Northey – come here – Philip is going to take you to dine at the Cremaillere to make room for David and the young lady.'

'Oh goody gum trees!' said Northey, eyes shooting out electricity.

'Yes, darling. And before you go, will you give that baby to Mrs Trott and ask her to keep an eye on it and also say I want two bedrooms got ready. Then come straight back after dinner, won't you?'

'We will,' said Philip.

Northey picked up the cradle, swung it round her, performed a pirouette and said, 'Come on, worshipful, let's bugger –'

The spontaneous sound of discontent rising from a dozen French throats as Northey left the room was silenced by the announcement of dinner. When at last I had got the women through the dining-room doors – all holding back politely and saying *'passez – passez'* to each other – I led David and the young lady to the places designed for Philip and Northey.

'Why do you put me next my wife?' he said angrily. 'This seems most unusual.'

'But, dear duck, I'm not a fortune teller. How am I expected to know that she is your wife?' I said to Dawn: 'Please forgive me, but we can't do the table all over again. You must simply try and imagine that you are at a city banquet.'

She looked at me with huge, terrified, grey eyes, and I saw, what the extraordinary clothes had hitherto prevented me from realizing, that she was very pretty. I also noticed that she was pregnant.

I went to my place between Bouche-Bontemps and Béguin. They were already plunged in a violent political discussion; seeing that I was not really present in the spirit they continued it across me. David had Mrs Jungfleisch on his right. We had asked her because Philip had asserted that it was impossible to give a dinner party in Paris without her; how thankful I felt now that she had accepted. With a lack of inhibition which no European woman would have exhibited under the circumstances, she went straight to the point. I strained my ears and listened as hard as I could; this was made possible by the fact that, except for my two neighbours, everybody else was doing likewise.

'Your wife is quite beautiful,' she said, 'is she a model?'

'No. She's a student.'

'Indeed. And what does she study?'

'Modern languages.'

'How old is the baby?'

'I'm not sure. Not old at all.'

'Are you staying here long?' I held my breath at this.

'No. We are on our way to the East.'

'I envy you that. Provins and Nancy are at their best in the fall. Such interesting towns. Try and go to Cirey, it's well worth it, and just outside Paris don't forget to stop your car at Grosbois –'

'We haven't got a car. We are walking.'

'Walking to Provins? With the baby?'

'The baby? Oh yes, he's coming too. Not to Provins, to China.'

'My! That's quite some walk. China – let me see now – after Provins and Nancy – don't miss the Place Stanislas – you can take in Munich and Nuremberg and Prague. I envy you that. Lemberg, they say, has charm. After Moscow there is the holy city of Zagorsk, the tomb of St Serge in solid silver. Are you looking for a special school of architecture or just going haphazard? By the way, I suppose you have your visas for China. I heard it was none too easy –'

David said they had no visas for anywhere. They were looking for Truth, he added.

'Aren't you afraid you may end up in gaol?'

He said, loftily, that Truth flourished in gaols, specially in Eastern ones.

'We are the bridge,' he added, 'between pre-war humanity with its selfishness and materialistic barriers against reality and the new race of World Citizens. We are trying to indoctrinate ourselves with wider concepts and for this we realize that we need the purely contemplative wisdom which comes from following the Road.'

Mildred Jungfleisch now had her clue. As soon as she realized that David was not on an ordinary House and Gardens honeymoon, but was in search of Truth, she knew exactly where she was and how to cope. She dropped the Place Stanislas and Grosbois and brought out such phrases as 'Mind-stretching interpretation of the Cosmos', 'Interchange of ideas between sentient contemporary human creatures', 'Explode the forms and habits of thought imposed by authority', 'I once took a course in illogism and I fully realize the place it should hold in contemporary thought', 'Atmosphere of positive thinking – change is life'.

One saw why she was such an asset in society; she could produce the right line of talk in its correct jargon for every occasion. She never put a foot wrong. David was clearly both delighted and amazed to find so kindred a spirit at his parents' table; they talked deeply until the end of dinner. Their neighbours lost interest in the conversation as soon as it moved from personal to eternal issues (the highlight having been the disclosure that David did not know the age of his own baby) and the usual parrot-house noise of a French dinner party broke out. As for the student of modern languages, she never opened her mouth. M. Hué, who was next her, tried all sorts of gambits in French, English, German, Portuguese and Norwegian. She merely looked as if she thought he was about to strike her and held her peace.

I now tried to put these children out of my mind for the present and do my duty as a hostess.

'What does *patibulaire* mean?' I asked M. Bouche-Bontemps. I thought M. Béguin had the grace to look embarrassed; he turned hurriedly to his neighbour.

'*Patibulum* is Latin for a gibbet.'

'I see exactly.'

M. Bouche-Bontemps was very kind and tactful. Instead of abruptly wrenching the conversation in an obvious manner from the subject which was clearly preoccupying me, he began talking about difficult young persons of former days. In seventeenth-century England there were the Ti Tyre Tu, educated gangsters who called themselves after the first line of Virgil's first eclogue. In the 1830s, 'the same length of time from Waterloo as we are from Dunkirk', young Frenchmen called Bousingos, like the Ti Tyre Tu, wore strange clothes and committed lurid crimes. I could have wished he had left out the lurid crimes, but I saw the connexion.

'I don't know about England,' he said, 'but in France mothers are frightened of making their children frown. They love them so much that they cannot bear to see a shadow on their happiness; they never scold or thwart them in any way. I see my daughter-in-law allowing everything, there's no authority outside school and the children do exactly as they like in their spare time. I am horrified when I see what it is that they do like. They never open a book, the girls don't do embroidery, the boy, though he is rather musical, doesn't learn the piano. They play stupid games with a great ball and go to the cinema. We used to be taken to the Matinée Classique at the Français and dream of Le Cid – that's quite old fashioned – it's The Kid now. How will it end?'

'I think you'll find they will grow out of it and become like everybody else.'

'Who is everybody else, though – you and me and the Ambassador or some American film actor?'

'You and me,' I said firmly. 'To our own children we must be the norm, surely. They may react from our values for a while but in the end they will come back to them.'

'But these grandchildren of mine are getting so big – they don't seem to change. They still throw that idiotic football at each other as soon as their lessons are over.'

'Good for the health, that's one thing.'

'I don't care. I don't want them to win the Olympic games. Furthermore healthy children are generally stupid. Those wise old monks knew what they were doing when they founded the universities in unhealthy places. I hate health – the more over-populated the world becomes the more people bother about it. *Hünde, wollt ihr ewig leben?* says I!'

'To your own grandchildren?'

'Specially to them!'

'I don't believe you.'

'I am very serious, however. This is a moment in the history of the world when brains are needed more than anything else. If we don't produce them in Western Europe where will they come from? Not from America where a school is a large, light building with a swimming-pool. Nor from Russia where they are too earnest to see the wood for the trees. As for all the rest, they may have clever thoughts about Karl Marx and so on, but they are not adult. If the children of our old civilization don't develop as they ought to, the world will indeed become a dangerous playground.'

I said, 'My two grown-up boys were perfect when they were little, very, very brilliant, longing to learn, all for Le Cid as opposed to The Kid. They both did well at Oxford. Now look at them. Bearded David there, with a first in Greats if you please, is walking to China in search of Truth. In other words he has given way to complete mental laziness. The other one, Basil, even cleverer, my pride and joy, lies on his face all day on a Spanish beach. How do you explain that?'

'I think they've got a better chance than my poor grandchildren because at least they have some furniture in their heads already.'

'If you ask me they'll all come out of these silly phases. They are nothing new – my cousins and I were quite idiotic when we were young. The only difference is that in those days the grown-ups paid no attention, while we concentrate (too much probably) on these children and their misdoings. How old are yours, by the way?'

'They must be quite seven, eight and nine by now.'

He was very much surprised when I laughed.

'At their age,' he said, 'I was reading the great classics in my spare time.'

'We all think that about ourselves, but it isn't always quite true!'

As soon as we left the dining-room, David took his wife away. He explained that they had an important rendezvous at the Alma. 'We are several days late – we must go at once.'

'But you'll come back for the night?'

'Possibly, or we may sleep there.'

'Where?'

'Under the bridge, where we are meeting our friend.'

'Oh, don't do that. You must be tired.'

'The great Zen Master, Po Chang, said when you are tired, sleep. We can sleep anywhere.'

'And the baby?'

'He'll come too. He sleeps all the time. Good night, Ma.'

'Shall we see you tomorrow?'

'Possibly. Good night.'

Philip and Northey reappeared. Valhubert sprang from his chair beside Madame Hué and in a rapid and skilful manoeuvre he whisked Northey to an unoccupied sofa. They sat there for the rest of the evening, laughing very much. Grace, half-listening to Philip who had made a bee-line for her, looked at them imperturbably, quizzically, even, I thought. At the usual time and in the correct precedence, the guests came and thanked us for a delightful evening and went their way. I have seldom felt so exhausted.

12

I sat on my bed, looking at Alfred.

'Do we laugh or cry?' he said. 'Did you see the baby?'

'Not really. It seemed to be asleep. I saw the cradle all right.'

'Whose do you think it is?'

'Oh, surely theirs?'

'It's yellow.'

'Babies often are.'

'No, darling. I mean it's an Asiatic baby.'

'Heavens! Are you quite sure? I thought it was our grandchild.'

'It may be. A throw-back. Had you a Chinese ancestor of any sort, Fanny?'

'Certainly not. Perhaps you had?'

'I doubt it. The Winchams, as you know, were yeomen in Herefordshire, in the same village since the Middle Ages. If one of our ancestors had gone to the East and brought back an exotic wife it would have become a thrilling legend of the family – don't you think? The little young lady didn't look Mongolian, did she?'

'Not a bit. How very mysterious. Well, if they're taking it to China that will be coals to Newcastle, won't it?'

For two days we saw nothing of David, Dawn or the cradle; on the third day they turned up again. Alfred and I were having our tea in the Salon Vert. 'It looks as if they've gone for good,' I was saying. 'Weren't we nice enough to them?'

'I don't see what more we could have done.'

'I suppose not. I have this guilty feeling about David, as I've often told you, because of loving him less than the others.'

'One must see things realistically, my darling. You love him less because he is less lovable – it's as easy as that.'

'But may it not be because I loved him less from the beginning – I lie awake, trying to remember –'

'He has always been exactly the same,' said Alfred, 'he was born so –'

Then they sidled, crabwise, cradle between them, through the door.

'Oh good, oh good,' I said, 'there you are. We were beginning to be afraid you had gone East.'

David pressed his beard into my face and said, 'On the contrary we went back a little – West – to Issy-les-Moulineaux. But now we are really on the road. We've just called in to say good-bye.'

I rang for more tea cups and said to Dawn, hoping to bring her into the conversation, 'Issy-les-Moulineaux is such a pretty name. What's it like when you get there?'

She turned her headlamps on to me, dumb, while David scowled. He despised small talk and civilized manners.

'It's just a working-class suburb,' he said. 'Nothing to interest anybody like you. We went to see a practising Zen Buddhist who's got a room there.'

'And where did you stay?'

'In his room.'

'For three whole days?'

'Was it three days? How do I know? It might have been three hours or three weeks. Dawn and I don't use watches and calendars since we have no [voice of withering scorn] "social engagements"!'

'I thought you said he lived under a bridge.'

'He used to, but they have turned the embankment into a road. Imagine motor cars speeding through your bedroom all night. He says the French are becoming simply impossible –'

The baby now began to scream. 'I expect he wants changing,' said David.

Dawn got up and bent over the cradle as if to do so there and then. 'Come upstairs,' I said. We each took a handle and went to the lift. 'I got this room ready for you hoping you would stay for a night or two. It's called the Violet Room. Mrs Hammersley and Mr Somerset Maugham were born here, imagine –'

She smiled. She was a duck, I thought – I did so wish she could speak. When she picked up the baby I saw that Alfred was quite right, it was as yellow as a buttercup, with black hair and slit black eyes, certainly not European: a darling little papoose of a baby.

'The pet!' I said. 'What's its name?'

At last the pretty mouth opened. "Chang.'

I saw that a canvas bag with a broken zip fastener had been deposited on a folding table meant for luggage. 'I'll send my maid, Claire, to unpack for you.' She shook her head vehemently.

'She's not frightening a bit and she'd love the baby – very well, if you'd rather not. Have you got what you need, dearest?' She nodded. 'Come down again when you are ready.'

I went back to the Salon Vert. David was saying, 'Zen forbids thought' and Alfred was looking sad, no wonder, at these words which were the negation of his whole life's work. 'It does not attempt to be intelligible or capable of being understood by the intellect, therefore it is difficult to explain.'

'It must be.' (Falsetto.)

'The moment you try to realize it as a concept, it takes flight.'

'Mm.' (On a very high note.)

'Its aim is to irritate, provoke and exhaust the emotions.'

To my utter amazement, Alfred now lost his temper. During twenty-six years of married life I had never seen that before. He said, furiously, 'You have succeeded in irritating, provoking and exhausting my emotions to a point at which I must tell you that, in my view, most Asiatics are incapable of thought. Zen must be simply perfect for them. But you are not an Asiatic; you have studied the great philosophies –'

'Please, Father, say Asian.' David had not even noticed the effect he was having on Alfred.

'I suppose, alone with you and your mother, I may be allowed to use the correct –'

'Not if it hurts my feelings. You see, our baby is one –'

'Adorable!' I said.

'Oh my dear boy, I beg your pardon a thousand times. Well, I've got some papers to read so perhaps I'll go back to the Chancery. Good-bye for the present.'

'He's called 'Chang, Dawn told me,' I said as the door shut on Alfred.

'We named him after the great Zen Master Po Chang. We dropped the Po. You have heard of him?'

'I seem to know the name – I'm awfully ignorant though, about all that.'

'It was Po Chang who placed a pitcher before his followers and asked them "What is this object?" They made various suggestions. Then one of the followers went up to it and kicked it over. Him Po Chang appointed to be his successor.'

'Oh of course! Well, anyhow, I thought the baby a perfect angel.'

'He's everything to us.'

This rule about never asking questions, though I knew it to be sound and would never break it, sometimes made life rather difficult. I was dying to know the origins of baby 'Chang but how could I find out?

'You must have one of your own,' I hazarded.

'We are going to – that's why we got married.'

'When you've got two babies, which makes a family, will you not settle down?'

'The wheel of birth and death, in the face of eternity, is of no more importance than sleeping or waking. Do you not know that new bodies are only created so that we can work out our own Karma?'

'Oh, do shut up and talk sensibly,' I said.

'To talk in terms that you would understand, Ma, I can't approve, I never have, of your way of life. I hate the bourgeoisie. In Zen I find the antithesis of what you and Father have always stood for. So I embrace Zen with all my heart. Do you see?'

'Yes. I wonder why you feel like that?'

'It seems almost incredible that people like you should still be living in the 1950s.'

'You can't expect us to commit suicide in order to fall in with your theories.'

'Oh, I don't mind you being alive, it's the way you live. Basil feels as I do. I've implored him for years to cut the umbilical cord and now at last he has.'

'That's your doing, is it? Thanks very much. He lies on his face on hot sand, instead of reading for his exam. It seems appalling waste of time to me.'

'Time does not exist. People who have clocks and watches are like bodies squashed into stays. Anything would be better than to find oneself in your and Dad's stays when one is old. Dawn and I are looking for an untrammelled future. Where is she?'

'If you go to the room above this one you'll find her.'

He went. Presently I heard his heavy footfall over my head. When David was a child Uncle Matthew used to say he walked like two men carrying a ladder. Greatly relieved, I telephoned to the Chancery. I got Philip. 'Just tell Alfred,' I said, 'that old Zennikins has gone and he can come back and finish his tea.'

Alfred kissed the top of my head. 'To think he took a first in Greats!'

'Let me pour you out another cup – that's cold. I remember, when the boys were little, you used to say if they don't revolt against all our values we shall know they are not much good.'

'That was not very clever, was it?'

'You were very clever – you took a first in Greats yourself. Another thing was: "I hope when they see me coming into a room they will look at each other as much as to say: here comes the old fool. That is how children ought to regard their father."'

'How very odd of me. I've quite forgotten.'

'Yes, one forgets –'

'Hot news,' Northey said, next day. 'David and Dawn are drinking whisky with sweet Amy in the Pont Royal bar. 'Chang has been dumped with the men's coats.'

'How do you know?'

'I've just seen them.'

'And what were you doing at the Pont Royal bar?'

'I was meeting Phyllis McFee, the friend of my far-distant youth in Caledonia stern and wild.'

'Northey, it's not a suitable place for young girls. Please find somewhere else to meet her – why not here? What's the good of giving you that pretty room – ?'

'You're saying all this because you don't like clever little Amy.'

'No, I do not.'

The answers to all the questions we had so discreetly not asked now became available to us in the *Daily Post*.

ZEN BUDDHISTS AT PARIS EMBASSY

Bearded, sandalled, corduroyed, and piped, accompanied by wife Dawn and baby 'Chang, David Wincham, the eldest son of our envoy to France (formerly Professor of Pastoral Theology, Sir Alfred Wincham), is staying with his parents on his way East, where he plans to join a Zen community. During a Parisian tea-ceremony yesterday David outlined his projects.

EXPECTING

'Dawn and I were married last week. We are expecting our first baby in two months. Dawn's father, the Bishop of Bury, disapproves. He wanted her to finish her studies and he was against our adopting little 'Chang, the child of our Zen Master.'

WORLD CITIZEN

'Yes, 'Chang is a Chinese name; our child is a World Citizen. Dawn's father is against World Government. He does not understand Zen nor does he realize the importance of the empty or no-abiding mind. He thinks that people ought to work; Dawn and I know that it is sufficient to exist.'

So David, Dawn, and 'Chang are existing very comfortably at the expense of the taxpayer. I asked when they expect to leave for the East. 'In seven hours, seven days, seven weeks, or seven years. It's all the same to us.'

'If it's seven years,' said Philip, 'your successor will have to give them the entresol.'

As a matter of fact, we heard no more about going East; they settled quite contentedly into the best spare room over the Salon Vert. It seemed that the long maturing of the Sacred Unsubstantiality could come to pass quite as well in the Hôtel de Charost as in a Siberian gaol – better, perhaps, because they were not certain to find a Zen Master in the gaol whereas there was this excellent one at Issy-les-Moulineaux. Dawn felt tired and was not anxious to recontemplate the wisdom of the road. David told Mildred Jungfleisch all this and she kindly passed it on. No explanations were vouchsafed to me or Alfred, but the portents seemed to indicate a good long stay. I bought an Empire cradle which I set up in the Salon Vert and banned the blue plastic one from any of the rooms inhabited by us. This was the only step I took to assert my personality.

13

Valhubert joined the throng of Northey's suitors. No doubt this was inevitable, but it worried me since he was in quite a different category from the others: a man of the world, experienced seducer, with time on his hands; I thought he would make mincemeat of the poor child. Besides I was very fond of Grace, my most intimate friend in Paris. She was obviously changing her mind about Northey; I never seemed to hear her say 'What a darling' any more. The other followers were rather a nuisance; they took up far too much of Northey's time and attention and doubled the work of our telephone exchange but I did not think them dangerous. I used to have long confabulations on the subject with Katie, who, fond of Northey and in a commanding position, was invaluable to me. She was sensible in a particularly English way in spite of having lived abroad for years. She had been at the Embassy longer than anybody else, since before the war, during which she had worked with the Free French.

'Of course, I don't listen,' she said, 'but sometimes I can't help hearing.'

'Do listen as hard as you can, Katie. It's so important for me to know what she's up to. I'm responsible for her, don't forget.'

'You needn't worry – she doesn't care a pin for any of them; she drags in the name of Philip whenever possible. They must be sick of being told that she worships him, poor things. Of course, the ones who can use the secret line, but I feel it's exactly the same. She's so transparent, isn't she!'

'What do the French think of it all, I wonder?'

'The worst, of course, but then they always do. If she had no followers at all they would say she's a Lesbian or has got a lover in the Embassy. You can't count what they think.'

'Tell me something, Katie. Does she often speak to Phyllis McFee?'

'Who?'

'A Scotch girl who is working here in Paris –'

'Never, as far as I know.'

'That's funny. When she doesn't want to do anything she always drags in Phyllis McFee as an excuse.'

'She's probably shut up in some office where she can't use the telephone.'

'Well –' I said, 'I wonder!'

I did not ask Katie about M. de Valhubert but I knew that he was constantly on the line. I also noticed that Phyllis McFee, whose name had hitherto cropped up at regular but reasonable intervals, now seemed to be Northey's inseparable companion.

'Northey, aren't you rather behind-hand with my letters?'

'Not bad – about twelve, I think.'

'Why don't you sit down and finish them after dinner, then they would be off your mind?'

'Because tonight, actually, Phyllis McFee and me are going to Catch.'

'Catch?'

'That's French for all-in wrestling.'

'Darling, it's really not suitable for two girls to go alone to all-in wrestling.'

'We shan't be alone. Phyllis McFee and me have got admirers. We shall be escorted.'

'How can you bear to watch it?'

'I adore it. I love to see horrible humans torturing each other for a change instead of sweet animals. L'Ange Blanc, the champion, has got the fingers of a doctor, he knows just where it hurts the most –'

'Funny sort of doctor. But there's still the question of the letters. They can't be put off indefinitely.'

'I say, Fan, you know how you're not dining out?'

'You want me to do them? But what do I pay you for?'

'You won't be paying me anything at all until November the twenty-eighth next year. I've borrowed until then. Fanny – each for each?'

'Oh, very well. Bring me your little typewriter and I'll do them in bed.' Only young once; we did not have these boring jobs at that age. Indeed when we were that age, Polly Hampton, my cousins and I, it was as much our duty to go out with young men and enjoy ourselves as now it was Northey's to write twelve letters. I only wished I could be certain that Phyllis McFee was really going to be of the party and that the escort was not Valhubert. As I wrote my letters I resolved that I would have to speak to Northey; the Foreign Legion policy of no questions may be quite all right with boys; girls are a very different proposition, giddy, poor things, hopelessly frivolous, wayward and short-sighted. Although I hate all forms of interference between human beings I felt, nevertheless, that I had a duty to carry out.

I was busy just then. Mr Gravely, the Foreign Minister, came and went. I saw little of him as the dinner which Alfred gave in his honour was for men only. He seemed a dry old stick. I said to Philip, 'I do love Grace's idea of him being driven to the brothels because his wife didn't come!'

'She's not far wrong. All English politicians want to do dirty things as soon as they get to Paris. Only of course they don't want to be seen by Mockbar. It's a nuisance that the only night club which is fairly respectable should happen to be called Le Sexy. La Tomate sounds quite all right but we really could not let them go there – no, I couldn't possibly tell you. Ask Mees –'

Contrary to all known precedent, Mr Gravely did not fall in love with Northey, in fact he hardly noticed her. He gave her various odd jobs to do for him, speaking in a dry, official, impersonal voice which so took her by surprise that she actually did them all herself, quite efficiently.

The night he left we dined at home. Alfred seemed tired and depressed; the visit had probably added to his difficulties. I had not yet had an account of it. David and Dawn had gone to share a bowl of rice with a friend – they never could say they were dining out, like anybody else. However, when we got to the dining-room we found that my social secretary was honouring us, a very unusual occurrence.

'Your cows, Northey,' said Alfred, 'are a nuisance.'

'I know – isn't it splendid! B.B. has stopped them, Fanny, I quite forgot to tell you. You see what can be done, by making a fuss!'

'Again I say, they are a nuisance. The Irish Ambassador was so friendly to me, everything seemed perfect between us. Now he has been called home by his government for consultation. It's very serious for the Irish – one of their main exports has vanished overnight. They all think it's due to the devilish machinations of the English.'

'So it is and serve them right for being so cruel!'

'All poor peasant communities are cruel to animals, I'm afraid – and not only the Irish. If they can't export cattle to France they'll be even poorer. It's not the way to make them kinder. The result will probably be that they will send the unhappy beasts to other countries where the journey will be longer and the slaughter-houses more primitive.'

'B.B. doesn't think so. He says there are no other practicable markets.'

'You know you should use your, apparently absolute, power to make the French eat frozen food. If they would do that these journeys could all be stopped and the beasts could be killed at home.'

'They won't,' said Northey, 'they call it frigo and they loathe it. B.B. says they are quite right – it's disgusting.'

'All very well – they'll have to come to it in the end.'

After dinner she said she was simply exhausted. 'I must dree my weird to bed – oh the pathos of the loneliness!' She trotted off to her entresol. We too went early to our rooms. Before I went to bed I heard a little cheeping noise, very far off, rather like a nest of baby birds, which meant that Northey was on the telephone. I could just hear her when all was quiet in the house. As I went to sleep she was still at it. I woke up again at three in the morning; she was still piping away.

When she came for her orders next day I said, 'Northey, I don't want to be indiscreet, but were you telephoning practically half the night?'

'The agony of clutching the receiver all those hours! My arm is still aching!'

'Who was it? M. Bouche-Bontemps?' She looked surprised that I should ask but replied, nonchalantly, 'No, poor duck, he is too busy nowadays. It was Charles-Edouard.'

Just as I thought. It was evidently time that I should intervene, unless I were going weakly to let things take their course. I went on, very much against my own inclination, 'Whatever was it all about?'

'My investments.'

'Indeed! Have you investments – ?'

'Yes. He has forwarded me my wages until Alfred's sixtieth birthday by which time you will retire and I shall be out of a job. Now he is advising me how to place the money. He says it's very important because nobody else will ever employ me and I am facing a penurious old age. So I have bought Coffirep, Finarep and Rep France. You can't imagine how they whizz. *Les reps sont en pleine euphorie*, the *Figaro* said, yesterday.'

'I don't think you ought to let M. de Valhubert talk to you all night. Grace might not like it.'

Northey's face closed up in a mutinous expression. 'Who cares?'

'I do, for one. But it's not that, darling, I worry about you. I'm so dreadfully afraid you will fall in love with Charles-Edouard.'

'Fanny! Hoar antiquity!'

'No hoarier than most of your followers – they all seem to be over forty and Bouche-Bontemps –'

'But I'm not in love with any of them. Is this a talking-to?'

'I suppose it is a sort of one.'

'*Quelle horrible* surprise! You never scold me. What's come over you?'

'I'm not scolding, I'm trying to advise. There are sometimes moments in people's lives when they take a wrong direction. I feel that both Basil and David have – but men can more easily get back to the right path than women. You ought to reflect upon what you want, eventually, and steer towards that. Now, as M. de Valhubert has noticed, you don't seem to have professional ambitions, so I suppose you are after marriage?'

'Perhaps I would prefer to be a concubine –'

'Very well. In that case the first rule is don't enter a seraglio where there is a head wife already.'

'I see your mind is still running on Charles-Edouard.'

'All this midnight telephoning makes it run.'

'But Fanny, if I wanted to hug Charles-Edouard I would do it in bed, not on the end of a telephone line.'

'I don't say you do want to hug, yet. I'm simply afraid that presently you may.'

'I've often told you I'm in love with Worshipful.'

'Yes, often, indeed! Do you think it's true?'

'St Expédite is covered with candles – why do you ask me that?'

'If you want to marry Philip you're setting about it in a very funny way.'

'I never said I wanted to marry him. Why shouldn't I be his concubine?'

'Philip isn't a Pasha, he's an ambitious English Civil Servant. The last thing he would do would be to saddle himself with a concubine – drag her round after him from post to post, can you imagine it! He'd very soon get the sack if he did. The only thing he might do would be to marry you.'

'Fanny – you said it was hopeless –'

'You are making it quite hopeless by your behaviour.'

'How ought I to behave?'

'Be more serious. Show that you are the sort of person who would make a splendid Ambassadress – pay more attention to your work –'

'Now I see exactly what you are getting at –'

'Our interests happen to coincide. And go slow with the followers.'

'I don't understand why, as I don't hug –'

'I might believe that but nobody else will. With Frenchmen love leads to hugs.'

'They're not in love.'

'What makes you think so?'

'They wouldn't mind a hug or two, I must admit, and they do sometimes very kindly offer, but they're not in love. I know, because as soon as somebody is I can't bear him. There was somebody at home – oh, Fanny, the horror of it!'

'Dear me, this is very inconvenient. How are we ever going to get you settled?'

'With Worshipful of course, who you say never will be –'

Alfred came in. 'Bouche-Bontemps seems to be on the telephone for you,' he said to Northey, 'in the library. They made a mistake (Katie's day off) and put the call through to me – his secretary was very much embarrassed.' As Northey skipped away, delighted, no doubt, at being delivered from a tiresome lecture, he shouted after her, 'Ask him if his government will survive the debate on the national parks, will you?'

'No. I'm not the Intelligence Service! Ask your spies –!'

'Is that rather cheeky? Never mind. I say, Fanny, our son Basil has appeared. He is dressed [falsetto] like *"O Richard, O mon Roi!"* What do you think this portends?'

'I hardly care to tell you. He has left the crammer, given up all idea of the Foreign Service and has become a travel agent.'

'Good God,' said Alfred, 'Basil too?'

'But he's not quite as bad as poor darling David,' I hastened to say, 'because there is no bogus philosophy, no wife, no adopted baby involved and at least he has work and prospects of a sort. He doesn't do nothing all the time. Oh, how I wish I knew where we went wrong with those boys –!'

'Perhaps it's the modern trend and not exactly our fault.'

'Where is he now?' I asked.

'Having breakfast with the Zen family in the dining-room. David has come down in his dressing-gown today – he looks ghastly. They started nagging away at each other – I couldn't stand it, I took my coffee to the library.'

'Nagging about what?'

'It seems [falsetto] that Beards never get on with Teds. Well, I must go, I'm due at the Affaires Étrangères.'

'The Eels?'

'Oh yes indeed – the Eels, the European Army, Guinea, Arms to Arabs – I've got a horrible morning ahead.'

'And the young man who pirated Dior's designs?'

'No, Mr Stock copes with that, thank goodness. See you presently.'

My next visitor was Basil. I saw what Alfred meant: with his loose garment, tight trousers and hair curling under at the back he had the silhouette of a troubadour. Although I vastly preferred his appearance to that of David (he was quite clean, almost *soigné* in fact) I wished so much that they could both be ordinary, well-dressed

Englishmen. I felt thankful that we had been able to send the two youngest to Eton; presumably they at least, when grown up, would look like everybody else.

Basil plumped on to my bed. 'I say, old David's gone to seed, hasn't he? Of course one knows he's holy and all that – still – !'

'How long since you saw him?'

'About a year, I should think.'

'He told me it was he who advised you to take to the road, or whatever it is you have taken to?'

'The coffee-and-jump, did he just? What a build-up! It's true, he used to bang out long saintly letters in that weird old Bible script of his but naturally I never read them.'

'I worry about you boys. What are you up to, Baz?'

'Well, it's like this. The Spanish season is over, thanks be. I've brought over a flock of the bovines on the hoof – turned them out to graze in the Louvre this morning – this afternoon I shall be flogging them down to Versailles. But these little tours are peanuts; we want to keep the racket going until Grandad can get the hustle on his new phenangles. And oh boy! Is he cooking up some sleigh-rides!'

My heart sank. If I did not quite understand what Basil was saying I felt instinctively against phenangles and sleigh-rides. They were not likely to denote a kind of work that Alfred would approve of. 'Could you talk English, darling?'

'Yes, Mother dear, I will. I gets carried away when I thinks of me ole Grandad. Well then, with Granny Bolter's capital (she sends her love incidentally) he is building a fleet of telly-rest coaches. Get the idea? The occupational disease of the British tourist is foot and mouth. Their feet are terrible, it makes even my hard heart bleed when I see what they suffer after an hour or two in a museum. By this evening several of them will be in tears. There are always some old bags who flatly refuse to get out of the bus towards the end of a day; they just sit in the car-park while their mates trail round the gilded saloons to see where the sneering aristocrats of olden times used to hit it up. Sometimes gangrene sets in – we had two amputations at Port Bou – very bad for trade – just the sort of thing that puts people off lovely holidays in Latin lands. The other trouble, mouth, is worse. Britons literally cannot digest Continental provender – it brings on diarrhoea and black vomit as surely as hemlock would. The heads I've held – I ought to know. After a bit they collapse and die in agony – no more foreign travel for them. So I reports all this to ole Grandad and 'e strikes 'is forehead and says, "Now I've got a wizard wheeze" and just like that, in a flash, this man of genius has invented the telly-rest coach. When they gets to the place they've come to see – the Prado, say, or some old-world hill town in Tuscany, they just sits on in the coach and views the 'ole thing comfortable on TV while eating honest grub, frozen up in Britain, and drinking wholesome Kia-ora, all off plastic trays like in aeroplanes. If they wants a bit of local atmosphere, the driver can spray about with a garlic gun. You wait, Ma, this is going to revolutionize the tourist trade. Grandad has got a board of experts working out the technical details and we hope to have the first coaches ready by next summer. We reckon it will save many a British life – mine among others, because they will no longer need a courier.'

'Ah! So then what will you do?'

'Specials. Millionaires and things like that. We've got an interesting special coming off next month which I'm partly here to see about. Grandad wants to capture the do-gooders market, he thinks it has enormous possibilities for the future – you know, all those leisured oldsters who sign letters to *The Times* in favour of vice. Now they and their stooges are forever going abroad, to build up schools the French have bombed, or rescue animals drowning in dams, or help people to escape from Franco gaols. They've got pots of money and Grandad thinks no harm in extracting a percentage.'

'I don't think it's right to cash in on people's ideals, Basil, even if you haven't got any yourself.'

'Somebody's got to organize their expeditions for them. Now me Grandad has thought of a particularly tempting line-up, see – an atom march. These do-gooders are not like ordinary Britons, they have feet of sheer cast iron and love a good long walk. But they've had Britain. They've done John o' Groat's and all that and they know every inch of the way to Aldermaston. So me Grandad thinks they might like to walk to Saclay, where the French atom scientists hang out – make a change. If that's a success they can go on to the great atom town in the Sahara. We call it A.S.S. – they start at Aldermaston as usual – Saclay – Sahara. Well, Ma, I wish you could see the provisional bookings. It is a smashing pisseroo old Grandad's got there. He's busy now, working out the cost. He'll make them pay a sum down, quite substantial – you see it's a different public from our Spanish lot, ever so much richer. Then the idea is to have some treats on the side which they'll pay extra for – interviews with atom ministers and such like. I thought Father would come in useful there?'

'I wouldn't count on it.'

'Oh well then, Northey can –'

'What can I do?' She reappeared, with Philip. 'Hot news,' she said. 'Bigman's going to fall again (that's French for Président du Conseil) – not national parks, Sunday speed limit – so we shall see more of him. Goody gum trees.'

'It's gum drops, not gum trees,' Basil said, scornfully.

'Oh Lord,' said Philip, 'not another chap in fancy dress? What have you come as, may one ask? Really, Fanny, your children! Do you know, the Ambassador has just been obliged to go to the Quai in a taxi because David sent Jérôme with the Rolls-Royce to fetch his Zen Master?'

'No! It's too bad of David – I can't have him doing that sort of thing. Go upstairs, Northey, and tell him to come here at once, will you?'

'Wouldn't be any use – they'll be Zenning away with the door locked by now. They go back to bed after breakfast to empty their minds again. Suzanne can never get in to do the room until luncheon-time. The mess is not to be believed. Have you been up there, Fanny?'

'I had a feeling I'd better not.'

'I went to have a chat with Dawnie yesterday when David was out. It's rather fascinating. You'd never think so much deep litter could come out of one canvas bag. Then they've stuck up mottoes everywhere: "How miraculous this is: I draw water and I carry fuel" (it would be, if they did) and a picture of a hoop saying "The man and his rice bowl have gone out of sight."'

'When you chat with Dawn what does she talk about?'

'I do the talking. She looks sweet and says nothing. She can explain about the ten stages of spiritual dish-washing but she hasn't much ordinary conversation. I love her and adorable 'Chang. If only David would bugger off and leave them both behind –'

'Northey, if you say that word again I shall send you straight back to Fort William.'

'Northey,' said Basil, 'do you know any atom ministers?'

'Yes, there's a dear one called Busson in the rue de Varennes, terribly excited about his old bomb. He's going to poop it off in 1960.'

'Is he indeed?' said Philip. 'Thanks for the tip, Mees. At last you've produced the solid fruit of all that spying you do.'

'I read it in *Aux Écoutes*, to tell you the truth.'

Basil said, 'Could you get permission for a few people to see him?'

'What sort of people?'

'Britons.'

'Rather,' said Philip. 'He simply dotes on Britons, he's always hanging about here, under the Union Jack, keenly waiting for one.'

'Witty,' said Northey. 'Yes, Baz, I expect so. You must put it in writing. You can get permission for anything in France if you send up a written request. Come to my office and I'll type it out for you.' She gave Philip a long look under her eyelashes which would have transported any of the followers and left the room with Basil.

When they had gone, I said to Philip, 'Oh! the children! What a worry they are. Basil has got some horrible new scheme on foot. Never mind. Meanwhile I've decided that somehow or other I must get rid of the Davids.'

'Now you've mentioned it – I didn't like to – but how?'

'So far I haven't thought of a way. After all, our house is their home. We can't turn them out if they don't want to go, Dawn so pregnant and that darling 'Chang, and let David drag them off to China. Then it's no good arguing with him, he has studied philosophy and knows all the answers.'

'Besides, he's such a humbug. All that rot about time meaning nothing – turns up sharp enough for meals, I notice, and the Guru is on the dot when Jérôme goes for him – won't miss a lift if he can help it.'

'Yes – yes,' I said rather impatiently. Poor David, it was too easy to criticize and laugh at him and really got us no further.

'Need your house be his home now that he is married?'

'I suppose the boys never seem grown up to me. Yes, I like them to feel that it is. Nothing would matter if it didn't upset Alfred, but he has got such a lot of worries now and I can see that David is fearfully on his nerves. I must protect him – I must try and get them to go back to England. David can always earn a living there with his qualifications.'

'What are they using for money?'

'A tiny little pittance I give him.'

'Can't you cut it off and say he must find work?'

'His pathetic allowance? No, really I don't think I could.'

'One doesn't have to be a fortune-teller to see they'll be here the full seven years.'

'I'm not sure, Philip. I often get my own way – Lady Leone left quite quickly, did you notice? Oh!' I said, sitting up in bed and seizing the telephone. 'Davey! We must get him over – I'll ring him up now this very minute!'

14

Davey arrived post-haste, in the early afternoon of the following day. 'Quite right to send for me. Oh – this room?' he said displeased, when I had taken him upstairs. He had had the Violet Room before but it was now occupied by David and Dawn and I had been obliged to change him over. I sat on his bed. 'I'll tell you the reason. It's all to do with why I asked you to come.'

'Don't begin yet. I must go for a walk. The thing about having three kidneys is that you need a great deal of exercise. Until you have had it you are apt to see things out of proportion.'

'That won't do. We are all trying to keep a sense of proportion. Can I come with you? I'd love a walk. Is there anywhere special you'd like to go to?'

'Yes, there is.' He opened his medicine chest and took out a piece of glass. I looked at it, fascinated, wondering what part of his anatomy it could be destined for.

'My housemaid broke this off a candelabra I'm fond of. I want to see if the man in the rue de Saintonge who used to blow glass is still there. I last saw him forty years ago – Paris being what it is I'm quite sure we shall find him.'

'Where is the rue de Saintonge?'

'I'll take you. It's a beautiful walk from here.'

It was indeed a beautiful walk. Across the Tuileries, through the Cour Carrée, and the Palais Royal and then past acres of houses exactly as Voltaire, as Balzac, must have seen them, of that colour between beige and grey so characteristic of the Île de France, with high slate roofs and lacy ironwork balconies. Though the outsides of these houses have a homogeneity which makes an architectural unit of each street, a glimpse through their great decorated doorways into the court-yards reveals a wealth of difference within. Some are planned on a large and airy scale and have fine staircases and windows surmounted by smiling masks, some are so narrow and dark and mysterious, so overbuilt through the centuries with such ancient, sinister rabbit-runs leading out of them, that it is hard to imagine a citizen of the modern world inhabiting them. Indeed, witch-like old women, gnome-like old men do emerge but so, also, do healthy laughing children, pretty girls in stiletto heels and their prosperous fathers, Legion of Honour in button-hole. Most of the courtyards contain one or two motor cars – quite often D.S.s or Jaguars – mixed up with ancient handcarts and pedal bicycles. The ground floors are put to many different uses, shops, workshops, garages, cafés; this architecture has been so well planned in the first place that it can still serve almost any purpose.

Davey and I walked happily, peering and exclaiming and calling to each other to come and look. I said, 'Bouche-Bontemps and the other Frenchmen I see always talk as if old Paris has completely gone; Théophile Gautier died of grief because of what Haussmann did here; a book I've got, written in 1911, says that Paris has become an American city. Even so, it must have far more beautiful old houses left than any other capital in the world. We have walked for half an hour and not seen one ugly street.'

'What I think sad about modern buildings,' Davey said, 'is that when you've seen the outside you know exactly what the inside will be like.'

'Northey said that, about Notre Dame. But I admit she was in a hurry to get to Lanvin.'

The rue de Saintonge itself is inhabited by artisans. Its seventeenth-century houses, built originally for aristocrats and well-to-do burgesses, have not been pulled down (except for one block where the Département de la Seine has perpetrated a horror) but they have been pulled about, chopped and rechopped, parcelled and reparcelled by the people who have lived and worked in them during the last two hundred years. Here are the trades which flourish in this street:

Workers in morocco, fur, india-rubber, gold, silver and jewels; makers of buttons, keys, ribbons, watches, wigs, shoes, artificial flowers and glass domes; importer of sponges; repairer of sewing-machines; great printer of letters; mender of motor cars; printer; midwife. There may be many more hidden away; these put out signs for the passer-by to read.

At the end of the street we came to Davey's glassblower, still there, covered with smiles. He and Davey greeted each other as if it were only a week instead of forty years since they last met. The piece of glass, produced from Davey's pocket, was examined. It could be copied, quite easily, but there would be a delay of perhaps two months.

'That has no importance,' said Davey, in his perfect, literary French, 'my niece here is our Ambassadress – when it's ready you will send it round to her.'

More smiles, compliments, protestations of love: 'How we thought of you, when London was bombed.'

'And how we thought of you, during the Occupation. Thousands of times worse to have them marching about the streets than flying about overhead.'

'Yes, perhaps. My son deported – my son-in-law murdered – *c'est la vie* – !'

Back in the Tuileries Gardens we sat down in order to begin our, what statesmen call, discussions about David. I described the arrival of the Holy Family and their subsequent behaviour. Davey was very much interested. 'My dear! The unkind French! So how did they take it?'

'Sweet and polite as they always are, to me anyhow.'

'I wish I could have heard what they said to each other, afterwards. Of course I saw Mockbar's account of the Zen Buddhists and paid no attention, but for once there seems to have been a grain of truth in his ravings. I say, look at that statue of an ancient Gaul. What can he be doing?'

'He seems to be eating a Pekinese – or perhaps he's kissing it?'

'No – it's his own beard, but why is he holding it up like that with both hands?'

'Most peculiar.'

'You might have let me know that my godson was married.'

'Nobody let anybody know. The Bishop of Bury saw it in the paper – Alfred rang him up and they mourned together. Oh, Dave, isn't the modern world difficult!'

'Ghastly. No standards of behaviour any more.'

We sat sadly looking at the Gaul.

Presently Davey said, 'I expect I know what we shall have to do for David. It must be the old, old pattern of emotional unstability and absence of rationalism plus a serious defection of the glands. He will almost certainly have to have a series of injections and a course of psychotherapy. I count on the Jungfleisches to find us a good man – where there are Americans there are couches galore. Madness is their national industry. What's the joke?'

'In other words, send for the doctor. Davey, how like you – !'

'No, Fanny. Did I order doctors for Pauline? Did I get rid of her?'

'All right, I admit. And there may be something in what you say. But I'm wondering if he will cooperate. He's become so difficult.'

'He'll be delighted to. He is evidently an exhibitionist – that is shown by the beard, the pipe, the strange clothes and Chinese baby. The more attention paid to him the better pleased he'll be. Say what you like about the modern world, we must give three cheers for science. Look at me! If I'd been born fifty years sooner I'd have been pushing up the daisies by now.'

'Very likely, since you would have been a hundred and sixteen. Uncle Matthew always says you are the strongest man he has ever met.'

'It is too bad of Matthew when he knows quite well how delicate I am.' Davey was seriously annoyed. He rose to his feet and said he must go home and have a rest before dinner.

'We've asked some people to meet you.'

'Oh dear! You always seem to dine alone, so I made a little plan with Mildred. One can count on interesting conversation there.'

As Davey and I came to the Place de la Concorde we saw that there was something going on. A mob of men in mackintoshes, armed with cameras, were jostling each other on the roadway outside the Hôtel Crillon. Mockbar leant against the wall by the revolving door of the hotel. I never can resist a crowd. 'Do let's find out who it is they are waiting for,' I said.

'It can only be some dreary film star. Nothing else attracts any interest nowadays.'

'I know. Only, if we don't wait we shall hear afterwards that something thrilling occurred and we shall be cross.' I showed him Mockbar. 'There's the enemy. He looks more like a farmer than a gossip writer.'

'Lady Wincham – how are you?' It was the *Times* correspondent. There was a moment of agony when I could remember neither his name nor Davey's. I feebly said, 'Do you know each other?' However my embarrassment was covered by the noisy arrival of policemen on motor-bicycles.

'Who is it?' I shouted to the *Times* man.

'Hector Dexter. He has chosen Freedom. He and his wife are expected here from Orly any minute now.'

'Remind me –' I shouted.

'That American who went to Russia just before Burgess and Maclean did.'

I vaguely remembered. As everybody seemed so excited I could see that he must be very important. The noise abated when the policemen got off their bicycles. Davey said: 'You must remember, Fanny – there was a huge fuss at the time. His wife is English – your Aunt Emily knew her mother.'

More police dashed up, clearing the way for a motor. It stopped before the hotel; the journalists were held back; a policeman opened the door of the car and out of it struggled a large Teddy-bear of an American in a crumpled beige suit, a coat over his arm, holding a brief-case. He stood on the pavement, blinking and swallowing, green in the face; I felt sorry for him, he looked so ill. Some of the journalists shouted questions while others flashed and snapped away with their cameras. 'So what was it like, Heck?' 'Come on, Heck, how was the Soviet Union?' 'Why did you leave, Heck? Let's have a statement.'

Mr Dexter stood there, silent, swaying on his feet. A man pushed a microphone under his nose. 'Give us your impressions, Heck, what's the life like, out there?'

At last he opened his mouth. 'Fierce!' he said. Then he added, in a rush, 'Pardon me, gentlemen, I am still suffering from motion discomfort.' He hurried into the hotel.

'Suffering from what?' said Davey, interested.

'It means air sickness,' said the *Times* man. 'I wonder when we shall get a statement. Dexter used to be a tremendous chatterbox – he must be feeling very sick indeed to be so taciturn all of a sudden.'

A large pink knee loomed in the doorway of the motor. It was followed by a woman as unmistakably English as Dexter was American. She merely said 'Shits' to the snapping and flashing photographers. Using the *New Statesman* as a screen she ran after her husband. Her place was taken by a fat, pudding-faced lad who stood posing and grinning and chewing gum until everybody lost interest in him. I saw that Mockbar's elbows were getting into motion, followed by the rheumaticky superannuated stable-boy action of his lower limbs, the whole directed at me. 'Come on,' I said to Davey, 'we must get out of this, quick –'

Philip was invited to the Jungfleisch dinner as well as Davey and next morning he came to report. The return of the Dexters had been, of course, the sole topic of conversation. When it transpired that Davey had actually witnessed it he became the hero of the evening.

'They are puzzled, poor dears,' said Philip.

'Who – the Jungfleisches?'

'All the Americans here. Don't know how to take the news. Is it Good or Bad? What does it mean? How does Mr Khrushchev evaluate it? What will the State Department say? The agony for our friends is should they send flowers or not? You know how they can't bear not to be loved, even by Dexter – it's ghastly for them to feel they are not welcoming old Heck as they ought to – at the same time it was very, very wrong of him to leave the Western Camp and it wouldn't do for them to appear to condone. The magic, meaningless word Solidarity is one of their runes; old Heck has not been solid and that's dreadfully un-American of him. But one must remember old Heck has now chosen Freedom, he has come back to the Western Camp of his own accord and they would like to reward him for that. So they are in an utter fix. In the end it was decided that Mildred must have a dinner party for policy makers; Jo Alsop, Elsa Maxwell, Mr Gallagher and Mr Shean are all flying over for it – but most of them can't get here before the end of the week. We shan't know any more until they have been consulted. Meanwhile there's the question of the flowers. Either you send at once or not at all; what are they to do? Davey suggested sending bunches with no cards, so that presently, if they want to, they can say, "Did you get my roses all right, Heck?"'

'Isn't Davey wonderful?'

'It went down very badly. They were sharked.'

★

Davey got to work on his godson. Dr Lecœur came and took many tests, David cooperating quite satisfactorily. The Americans at Mrs Jungfleisch's dinner had been unanimous in recommending Dr Jore, head psycho-analyst to N.A.T.O. David brought him to the Salon Vert to have a word with me before taking him up to see his patient. He wanted to get the background first. He was a gangling young man, perhaps really much older than he looked. Davey seemed to like him; I tried to put prejudice out of my mind and do the same. When I had told him all I knew about my son, going back to babyhood, even trying to remember how I had taught him to use a pot ('I suppose I smacked him'), Dr Jore cleared his throat.

'As I see it then, Mrs Ambassadress, though of course I may be wrong since no system of psychiatry is as yet I believe infallible, the human element playing, as it must play in all human affairs, its part, since we are only endeavouring towards daylight and though I think I may say that the system by which I personally am guided is now very largely perfectioned, the foregoing reservation must be very distinctly borne in mind. With this reservation, then, very distinctly borne in mind, what I am about to say may be deemed to approximate the facts as they most probably are. Your son, Mrs Ambassadress, in addition to a condition of aboulia which is probably due to oily terlet training, and which may be possible to combat but which is likely to be difficult, stubborn and lengthy, in short not easy, to overcome, your son has an anoetic Pull to the East. Period.'

'A Pull to the East?' I said.

'Please let Dr Jore speak,' Davey said, sternly.

Dr Jore slightly bowed and went on. 'Perhaps I could put this matter rather more succinctly by stating a paradigm which I believe to be unconfutable. Human beings, in my view and in the view of others more qualified than I, are roughly divided (in respect of what I am about to enucleate, to the best of my endeavour and without having had access to my case), human beings, then, fall into two roughly definable categoremia: those who are subject and liable to a Pull to the East and others, I am happy to say an appreciably larger grouping, who are subject and liable to a Pull to the West. Perhaps I could explain this matter more readily comprehensibly if I were to state that those on the continent of Europe who feel a very compelling wish and desire to visit England, Ireland and the Americas feel little wish or desire to go to Russia, China and the Indias, whereas those forcibly attracted to China, Russia and the Indias –'

'Don't want to go to America.'

'Please let Dr Jore finish what he is saying,' Davey said peevishly. 'It's so interesting, Fanny –'

'Of course,' I said. 'If you go far enough East you come to the West. If you could manage to push my son a little further we might get him to Hollywood. Then he could join up with Auden and everybody,' I said to Davey, 'and Jassy could keep an eye on him. That might be a solution?'

Davey sighed deeply. 'And now, perhaps, we could be allowed to hear what the doctor has to say?'

Dr Jore had shut his eyes while I spoke. He opened them again. 'Mrs Ambassadress, ma'am, you have put your finger on the very heart of the matter.'

I looked triumphantly at Davey who said 'Ssh.'

'This is a point which has by no means escaped the learned professor who was the first to proclaim this doctrine of Oriental versus Occidental attraction. Now this attraction (whether towards the Orient or East or towards the Occident or West) occurs in the persons subjected to its magnetism in greater or lesser degrees and we practising psychiatrists find it possible to cure or check it according to its strength. May I explain myself? If the pull, whether to the East or to the West (a pull to the West, of course, is very much more desirable than its converse, and rarely needs to be cured, though in a few, very extreme, cases it should be checked), if the pull, then, is very strong it is comparatively easy to cure. If it is overwhelmingly strong the patient has only to be encouraged to follow it and in these days of jet travel he will find himself back where he started in a surprisingly short time. Period. In the case, however, Mrs Ambassadress, of your son, the pull, by all the evidence which I have been able to garner, is weak. It has pulled him over the English Channel and across Normandy as far as Paris. Here it seems to have left him. Where there is so little for me to combat, the case is difficult. Therefore when your uncle suggested that I should work in collaboration with a physician I gladly agreed to do so. I feel that by super-adding the action of certain glands it should be possible to augment the will-power of your son, thus giving myself a basis on which to proceed. I must now touch upon another and more serious aspect of the Pull. Should the patient yearn towards the manners, customs and ways of thought of the Eastern Lands – should he sit on the floor eating rice; should the muezzin call for him in the Champs Élysées; should he dream of military deploys in the Red Square and think the bronzes of Démé-Jioman superior to those of Michelangelo – then, what I might call the jet treatment will not be sufficient. Then we must wean him back to the manners, customs and ways of Western Civilization and this we must do by means of his subconscious. Here the silent, long-playing gramophone record during sleep has its role, super-added to a daily personal collocution with myself or one of my assistants. Period.'

Dr Jore shut his eyes again and there was silence. I did not dare to break it. At last Davey said, 'Excellent. That is precisely the conclusion I had come to myself. Now I think you should see your patient in his own surroundings – I'll take you up to his room.'

Dr Jore was with David for about an hour, after which he went to Davey's room for an uninterrupted consultation. David came rocketing down to me.

'I see that you and Uncle Davey think I'm mad.'

'Oh, no, darling – whatever makes you say that?'

'Then why have you called in this ghastly Yank?'

'Davey – you know what he is – thought you weren't looking very well.'

'He's quite right there. I don't feel a hundred per cent. But isn't Dr Lecœur coping with that? Why should I need an alienist?'

'You must ask Davey,' I said weakly. 'He's your godfather, he has taken you on, it's nothing to do with me.'

'You told this doctor about teaching me to pee into a pot, didn't you?'

'He asked.'

'Yes, well, another time please let him ask. After all, this was most private between you and me, I call it wildly indiscreet of you to discuss it with a stranger. Another thing, Ma, if Dr Jore comes here every day like he says he's going to he will drive me mad. Really, properly barking. I am quite serious.'

'I must say I see your point.'

'I heard him telling Davey he's going to empty my mind and refurnish it with contemporary Western ideas. Now my Zen Master empties my mind and fills it with the ancient unlearning of the East. It can't be right for them to go on empty-ing and filling it in competition with each other?'

'I must say it doesn't sound right. You wouldn't think of giving up the Zen Master?'

'I don't like talking to you about Zen – I know you think it's funny – you're laughing now, Ma, aren't you? That's what makes it difficult to confide in you, you laugh at everything.'

'Darling, never at you,' I said, guiltily.

'In that case I'm the only one. You're nothing but a mocking materialist, like all your generation. If your children are not well-balanced you have only yourself to blame.'

'Oh dear. Do you think that you and Basil are different from other people because I mocked?' I was very much disturbed at this notion.

'Different from other people – different from whom? You go about the world with your eyes shut. If you opened them you would see thousands of people exactly like me and Basil – Beards and Teds abounding in every direction. Next time you go driving in that awful great hearse of yours, just look out of the window. You'll see that we're not as different from other people as all that –'

'Then in what way do you think you are unbalanced?'

'I lack self-confidence and will-power. That's what Dr Jore thought.'

'And you don't feel that he can help you?'

'I've told you, Dr Jore would drive me into a bin. Only two people can help me. Dawn is one and the Zen Master is the other. They understand. I could never give them up, either of them.'

'No, darling, you shan't. I absolutely agree about Dr Jore – he's a bore.'

'There you are, with your scale of false values! You divide human souls into bores and non-bores, don't you? I'm a bore and Basil isn't, that I've always known. You ought to be considering where everybody stands in the universal scheme instead of laughing at them and saying they are bores.'

'Anyway, in this case our different methods bring us to the same conclusion. I say Jore is a bore; you say Jore's standing in the universal scheme is low: we both say Jore must go.'

At this David became more agreeable. He kindly admitted that though I was regrettably frivolous I was not without a certain comprehension. He harrowed my face with his beard and we parted on the best of terms.

Davey was more hurt than surprised when I told him that he must get rid of Jore. In my view, I explained, he was calculated to give anybody who had to see much of him a nervous breakdown and I refused to have one of my own children handed over to him. 'David can't bear him,' I said, 'so I'm sure he wouldn't be much good.'

'He's far better than the Zen Master,' said Davey, who, unlike me, had been allowed to meet this legendary figure.

'That I can easily believe. However, David doesn't think so; people must be allowed to go to hell their own way.'

'It's the greatest pity he has taken against Jore. I thought his diagnosis quite amazing – he hit the nail on the head in one. Mildred says he is intensely brilliant; the Supreme Commander has him every afternoon.'

'How can he bear the dissertation?'

'You must remember, with Americans, that they are fighting to express themselves in a language they've never properly learnt. They need the dissertation; the kind of shorthand that we talk would be useless to them.'

The next evening, Davey was good enough to dine in. We were waiting for Alfred and sipping cocktails.

'Why does one never see Northey?' Davey was asking, upon which the door opened and the pretty face looked round it.

'I say, what's happened to David? He fell on me like a stallion just now, in my office.'

'Oh good,' said Davey. 'Dr Lecœur's super-adding gland injection must have begun to work.'

'Really, Davey, I call that rather inconvenient!' I said. 'What about all the young women in the Chancery? I'm supposed to be responsible for their morals, you know.'

'This is Paris. They must be used to dealing with satyrs.'

'In the Bois, perhaps, but not in the Embassy. Is it necessary to turn the poor fellow into a satyr?'

'Please, Fanny, I must ask you not to interfere any more with my treatment of David.'

'Oh, very well. Do you dine with us, darling?'

'Not really. I'm after *France Soir*. Goody gum trees, the Bourse has found her vigour again – but Ay de mi, the Reps have reacted unfavourably to M. Bourguiba's speech. Now there will be a pause for introspection, mark my words. The worry of it!'

'Where's Baz?' I said.

'Buggered. He'll be coming back next week.'

'Buggered!' said Davey, faintly.

'Now, Davey, you tell her she mustn't.'

'It's all right, I know I mustn't and I'm trying desperately hard not to.'

'Is he bringing the atom marchers next week?'

'No, ruminants until the end of the month. He's been very busy organizing the march – he spent hours yesterday with precious Amy, seeing about the publicity. Anything for me to do, Fanny? Don't say yes, there's a darling, but lend me your little mink jacket, I'm so tired of my bunny.'

'Very well, on condition you reform your language. What are you up to?'

'Phyllis McFee and me are going to the Return of the Cinders with M. Cruas. He's poor, he can't take us to a proper theatre. *Le Retour des Cendres*, Fanny, sharpen your wits – the body of Napoleon coming back to the Invalides. So I go and get the jacket – you are lucky to be so kind – good night –'

'They were talking about her at Mildred's,' Davey said. 'It seems she is in full fling with Valhubert.'

I could not help remarking, 'One can always be sure of some good conversation there –'

'Fanny, be serious. Aren't you worried about it?'

'More worried about Valhubert than the others certainly – but no, you know, not really. Northey is a good little child.'

'There are certain women who go through life in a cloud of apparent innocence under cover of which they are extremely unchaste.'

'Yes. My mother for one. But if Northey's like that I don't see what we can do about it. I did scold her for talking half the night to Valhubert on the telephone – she replied that if there was anything wrong between them she would have been in bed with him, not just chatting. Very true I should think.'

'Yes, there's something in that. How much does she remind you of Linda?'

'On the face of it, very much indeed. But there are differences. She's not nearly so concentrated. When Linda was in love she never bothered about followers – they only cropped up when she was out of love with one man and not yet in with another.'

'But is Northey in love?'

'Oh yes, hasn't she told you? She's meant to be madly in love with Philip – I suppose she is, but sometimes I can't help wondering. She never moons about as Linda used to (do you remember the games of patience, the long staring out of the window, the total distraction from real life?). Northey lives in an absolute rush, with at least twenty different admirers. When she has half an hour to spare I think she does go and have a word with St Expédite about Philip.'

'St Expédite,' said Davey, 'how that takes me back! He's a good saint, if ever there was one – I must go and see him again, but only for old sake's sake, alas! At my age one doesn't have these desperately hopeless desires. So she's in love with Philip – how perfect that would be. Doesn't he fancy her – why not?'

'He adores Grace, unfortunately. But I've begun to think, just lately, that he's getting fonder than he knows of Northey and that finally it may all come right.'

'That makes it important to scotch the Valhubert business now at once. Remember, being in love with Prince André didn't stop Natasha from making a fool of herself.'

'I know. Cressida too. Young women are very silly.'

'I think you ought to have a word with him.'

'What, with Valhubert? Davey, the terror! I really don't think you can ask me to do that!'

'Alfred then? It might be easier for him?'

'Oh no, no! Don't tell Alfred – he has enough to worry him. The children are my affair – I never allow him to be bothered by them if I can possibly help it. How late he is, by the way. What can he be doing?'

'Philip told me he had gone to a football match, but surely that must be over by now?'

When at last Alfred appeared he seemed quite worn out. 'I'm sorry to be late – I had to get quickly into a bath – I was simply soaked with rotten eggs at the France versus England. Lord, how I do hate sport. Then I had an endless visit from the Irish Ambassador about those wretched cows.'

15

For a long time now Charles-Edouard de Valhubert had been urging me to go with him and visit the old Duchesse de Sauveterre at her country house, the Château de Boisdormant. He said she wanted to talk about her grandchild, little Fabrice. We had twice made plans to do this; for one reason or another they had come to nothing; at last a day was fixed which suited all of us. Grace, who was expecting a baby and felt rather sick, decided to stay at home. I had always felt nervous at the idea of a long motor drive alone with Valhubert, who intimidated me, but since my talk with Davey I positively dreaded it. If it was really my duty to speak about Northey, now would be the time. However, sitting in the front seat of a new Jaguar, with Valhubert at the wheel, I soon found that the physical terror far outweighed the moral.

'Have I not a style of my own, in driving?' he said, weaving up the rue Lafayette. 'I don't take the outer boulevards, they are too ugly.'

The style consisted in never slowing down. I began to pray for the traffic lights to go red and stop him; my foot was clamped to an imaginary brake until the muscles hurt. The terror increased when he began to imitate the style of other drivers; the young chauffeur of a Marshal of France, the old chauffeur of an American hostess, the driver of a police car (hands never on the wheel) and M. Bouche-Bontemps. He kept looking at me to see if I were laughing, which, indeed, I was; finally his eyes never seemed to be on the road at all. 'Oh please, do be yourself!' I said, and wished I had not as he spurted forward.

Once outside Paris and past Le Bourget I calmed down. He was in full control of the machine, though he went much too fast. We chatted away enjoyably and I realized that he was not at all frightening, much less than he seemed to be when one met him at a Parisian party. When we passed the cross-roads at Gonesse he recited the names of all the people he knew who had been killed there in motor car accidents, after which silence fell, because of my inability, since I had not known any of them, to aliment the conversation. Thinking that now was my chance, I bravely forced myself to say, 'I worry about Northey.'

'I love this little girl.'

'Yes. That's exactly why I worry.' I was astounded at my own courage.

'Ah – no!' He looked vastly amused and not at all embarrassed. 'I don't love her – I mean I like her very much.'

'It's not you I worry about. She might love. She tells me she thinks of being a concubine.'

He roared with laughter. 'Not in my harem, I can assure you. Why, she is only two years older than Sigi – and half his mental age.'

'That's no protection, surely?'

'With me it is. I don't happen to be attracted by children – not yet – no doubt that will come, one of the horrors of senility. And I dislike the sensation of doing wrong.'

'I thought it added to the amusement?'

'Greatly, if one is cocufying some old prig one was at school with. But to seduce

Northey would do her harm and also lead to trouble. I love Mees and I hate trouble. No, we must marry her to Philip – I'm working for that. If he thinks I am courting her and if she seems to cool off him, that, human nature being what it is, may do the trick. He has sighed after Grace quite long enough, it's a bore. Like this I hope to kill two birds with one stone.'

I was not completely reassured but there was nothing more I could say. It was another beautiful day. (When I look back on our first months in France we seem to have enjoyed an uninterrupted Indian summer.) Valhubert and I were now crossing the Seine-et-Marne country where everything is on an enormous scale. Avenues of poplar trees rush over vast horizons and encircle the globe; down the roads bordered by them the largest, whitest of horses draw ancient wagons loaded with beetroots the size of footballs; each farm with its *basse-cour*, kennels, cow-byres, stables, barns and sheds occupies enough space for a whole village. The land breathes of prosperity; the predominating colour at that time of year is gold.

'This is the battlefield of the Marne,' he told me, 'where thousands of young men were killed in 1914, on days like this, almost before they could have realized they were at war. The Uhlans, mounted, with their lances, the Cuirassiers glittering in polished armour, went into action on horseback. Those battles were more like a military tournament than modern warfare – to read of them now is reminiscent of Agincourt or Crécy. One can't believe they happened in living memory and that there are still many people we know who took part in them.'

We came to a village of whitewashed houses with red and navy-blue roofs clustered round a twelfth-century church. 'I have an uncle who was wounded here at St Soupplets. When he came to, in hospital, they said "You were in the Battle of the Marne." He was perfectly amazed. He remembered seeing a few Germans round that inn across the road there – and then he was knocked down by a bullet, but he had no idea he had been in anything as important as a battle.'

'Stendhal's description of Waterloo is rather like that – casual and unfrightening.'

'I love this country so much but now it makes me feel sad to come here. We must look at it with all our eyes because in ten years' time it will be utterly different. No more stooks of corn or heaps of manure to dot the stubble with light and shade, no more peasants in blue overalls, no more horses and carts, nothing but mechanicians driving tractors and lorries. The trees are going at a fearful rate. Last time I came along this road it was bordered by apple trees – look, you can see the stumps. Some admirer of Bernard Buffet has put up these telegraph poles instead.'

'It is still very beautiful,' I said, 'I never saw the apples trees so I don't grieve for them as you do. When I go to the country I always wonder how any of us can bear to live in towns – it seems perfect madness.'

'I'm sure you didn't feel like that when you were Northey's age.'

'Now I come to think of it, when I was Northey's age I did live in the country and my only idea was how to get to London.'

'Of course it was. Young people need urban life, to exchange thoughts and see what goes on in the world – it's quite right and natural. By degrees the tempo slows down and we take to peaceful pleasures like gardening or just sitting in the sun. Very few young people are sensitive to beauty, that's why there are so few poets.'

'Yes. But now it seems almost unbearable to think what one is missing by being in a town as the days and months go by. So dreadful only to know the seasons by the flower and vegetable shops.'

'I call that rather ungrateful. Your embassy is in a forest.'

'I know. Our Oxford house is not, however.'

'When were you born?'

'In 1911.'

'And I the year after. So we remember the old world as it had been for a thousand years, so beautiful and diverse, and which, in only thirty years, has crumbled away. When we were young every country still had its own architecture and customs and food. Can you ever forget the first sight of Italy? Those ochre houses, all different, each with such character, with their *trompe-l'œil* paintings on the stucco? Queer and fascinating and strange even to a Provençal like me. Now, the dreariness! The suburbs of every town uniform all over the world, while perhaps in the very centre a few old monuments sadly survive as though in a glass case. Venice is still wonderful, though the approach to it makes me shudder, but most of the other Italian towns are engulfed in sky-scrapers and tangles of wire. Even Rome has this American rind! "*Roma senza speranza*", I saw in an Italian paper; all is said.' He sighed deeply. 'But like you with the apple trees, our children never saw that world so they cannot share our sadness. One more of the many things that divide us. There is an immense gap between us and them, caused by unshared experience. Never in history have the past and the present been so different; never have the generations been divided as they are now.'

'If they are happy and good in the new world it doesn't much matter,' I said.

'Will they be happy? I think modern architecture is the greatest anti-happiness there has ever been. Nobody can live in those shelves, they can't do more than eat and sleep there; for their hours of leisure and their weeks of holiday they are driven on to the roads. That is why a young couple would rather have a motor car than anything else – it's not in order to go to special places but a means of getting away from the machine where they exist. The Americans have lived like that, between earth and sky, for a generation now and we are beginning to see the result. Gloom, hysteria, madness, suicide. If all human beings must come to this, is it worth struggling on with the world? So,' he said, narrowly missed by a D.S. which, at a hundred miles an hour and the law on its side, hurtled at us from a right-hand turning, 'shall we put an end to it all?'

'No,' I said hurriedly, 'we must wait and see. I have a few things to leave in order when I go – Northey – the boys. It may not be as bad as we fear. There may be less happiness than when we were young – there is probably less unhappiness. I expect it all evens out. When would you have liked to be born?'

'Any time between the Renaissance and the Second Empire.'

I trotted out the platitude, 'But only if you were a privileged person?'

He said, simply, 'If I were not, I wouldn't be me.'

Very true. Such men as Valhubert, my father, Uncle Matthew would not have been themselves had they not always been kings in their own little castles. Their kind is vanishing as surely as the peasants, the horses and the avenues, to be replaced, like them, by something less picturesque, more utilitarian.

I said, 'Perhaps the Russians will explore some nice empty planet and allow people like us to go and live on it.'

'No good to me,' said Valhubert, 'I wouldn't care a bit for oceans on which Ulysses never sailed, mountains uncrossed by Hannibal and Napoleon. I must live and die a European.'

We whizzed down the ancient roads leading to the Holy Roman Empire in silence now, each thinking his own thoughts. I was no longer frightened by the speed, but exhilarated, enjoying myself. Up in the sky two parallel white lines drawn by two tiny black crosses showed that young men in aeroplanes were also enjoying themselves on this perfect day. At last a signpost marked Boisdormant showed that we were nearing our destination.

'Madame de Sauveterre – ?' I said. 'Just tell me –'

'You have never seen her?'

'Such years ago. I used to stay with an old woman called Lady Montdore –'

'The famous one?'

'Yes, I suppose she was. When I was about eighteen I met Sauveterre and his mother there. It's the only time I ever saw him.'

'Poor Fabrice! He was the most charming person I have known, by very far.'

'So was my cousin Linda.'

'*Le coquin!* You say he hid her in Paris for months and nobody had any idea of it.'

'She wasn't divorced. Besides, she was terrified that her parents would find out.'

'Yes. And the war had only just begun and didn't seem serious, then. Life appeared to be endless in front of one. Also I think Fabrice had somebody else – another reason for secrecy. Always these complications!'

'Were you very intimate?'

'Oh, very. His mother is my great-aunt – Fabrice was much older than me, twelve years at least – but as soon as I was grown up we became bosom friends. It was an adoration on my side. Hard to think of him as dead, even now.'

'His mother –' I said, coming back to the point.

'She's a worldly old woman as you will see. Fabrice was the only meaning to her existence. Now that he has gone she lives for money and food, torn between miserliness and greed. Enormously rich, no family, no heir. That's why it's important that she should see the boy.'

'Good of you to take so much trouble. You must remember he may not play up. Children are unpredictable – at his age old people are a bore and money hardly seems to exist.'

'He has good manners and he looks like his father. I'll be very much surprised if he doesn't win her over.'

We were now on a little white, untarred country lane winding between rank hedgerows. The crop of berries that year was rich and glistening; I thought I had not seen so white a road and such scarlet berries since I was a child. Presently we came to a park wall of stones covered with peeling plaster – perched up in one corner of it like a bird's nest there was a little round thatched summer-house.

'Is it not typically French, all this?' said Valhubert. 'What makes it so, I wonder? The colour of that wall, perhaps?'

'And that ruin on the hill, with a walnut tree growing out of it; and the trees in the park, so tall and thin and regular –'

An avenue of chestnuts led from the lodge gates to the house, their leaves lay in the drive, unswept. A flock of sheep, watched by a shepherd with a crook, were cropping away at long dark green grass. The house, an old fortress built round three sides of a square, was surrounded by a moat, the turrets at its corners were entirely covered, even to their pointed roofs, with ancient ivy so that they looked like four huge mysterious trees. Valhubert stopped the engine, saying, 'I don't trust that drawbridge. I think we'll walk from here.'

The oldest butler in the world opened the front door long before we reached it. He greeted Valhubert in the way of a servant with somebody he has known and loved from childhood, hurried us upstairs into a round white drawing-room, inside one of the ivy trees, sunny and cheerful, and vanished at the double.

'She'll be down in exactly a quarter of an hour,' said Valhubert. 'Grace thinks she can't bear to begin painting her face until she actually sees us arriving for fear we should have an accident on the road and then all the powder and paint and eye black would be wasted. She and Oudineau are hard at it now. He's her lady's maid as well as butler, caretaker, wood-man, chauffeur, gardener and gamekeeper. Nobody has ever been so much *à tout faire*. The exquisite luncheon we are about to eat (you'll see how it's worth the journey for that alone) will have been fished, shot and grown by Oudineau and cooked by his son. This Jacques has an enormous situation in Paris, but he is obliged to drive down here and do the cooking when my aunt has guests. I must say it only happens once in a blue moon.'

'Is he a chef, in Paris?'

'By no means! He directs an enormous electrical concern – Jacques Oudineau will produce all the atomic plant of the future. He's immensely powerful and very attractive, one meets him dining out everywhere – that's his Mercedes, parked by the kitchen garden.'

'What a charming room this is!'

'Yes – there's nothing so pretty as a *château-fort* – redecorated in the eighteenth century. This panelling is by Pineau. Look at those heaps of illustrated papers – they go back fifty years and more. One day Grace and I were waiting for her to come down and we began looking at them (I am particularly fond of Matania – orgies – galley-slaves – jousting and so on). Literally showers of banknotes came tumbling out of them, all obsolete. Yes, she's a miser in the true sense of the word.'

Presently our hostess appeared looking, I thought, exactly the same as she had some twenty-seven years ago, at Hampton. She had then been in her fifties; she was now in her eighties; she had seemed old then and not a day older now. She must once have been pretty, with little turned-up nose and black eyes, but almost before middle age, probably, she had become stout; there was something porcine in her look. It was hard to imagine that she could have given birth to the irresistible Fabrice. Almost on her heels, Oudineau reappeared and in a voice of thunder announced, "*chesse est servie.*'

We lunched, in a narrow room with windows on both sides, off Sèvres plates which must literally have been worth their weight in gold. 'They belonged to Bauffremont – you know them very well, my dear Charles-Edouard. I never allow Jacques Oudineau to wash them up; he is quite a good cook, but a most unreliable boy in other ways.'

The luncheon was indeed worth the journey. We began with brochet. Why is brochet so good and pike so nasty, since the dictionary affirms that they are one and the same? Then partridges, followed by thick juicy French cutlets quite unlike the penny on the end of a brittle bone which is the English butcher's presentation of that piece of meat. They were burnt on the outside, inside almost raw. Boiled eggs suddenly appeared, with fingers of buttered toast, in case anybody should still be famished. Then a whole brie on bed of straw; then chocolate profiteroles. I was beginning to get used to such meals, but they always made me feel rather drunk and stupid for an hour or two afterwards.

When she tasted the salad, Madame de Sauveterre said 'Vinegar!'

'Jacques is in despair, Madame la Duchesse, he forgot to bring a lemon.'

'It's inadmissible. This boy always forgets something. Last time it was the truffles. He has no head. Thank goodness I haven't got shares in his concern.'

'Thank goodness I have,' said Valhubert, 'since they double every year.'

The Duchess asked a hundred questions about the Embassy, specially wanting to know what had become of all the English people she had known there in the past.

'*Et cette adorable Ava – et la belle Peggy – et ce vieux type si agréable du Service, Sir Charles?*'

When she saw how little I could tell her about any of them she put me down for what I am, provincial. Valhubert, however, knew all the answers. He told her that she had met me already, at Hampton, after which she got on to Lady Montdore and her circle. Here I did better.

'Yes, she died before the war, of heart failure while having an operation in Switzerland.'

I did not add that it was an operation for leg-lifting which Cedric, the present Lord Montdore, had persuaded her to undergo against a great deal of medical advice. He said that he utterly refused to be seen with her at the Lido again until it had been done. Her heart, worn out by dieting and excessive social life, had stopped under the anaesthetic. As this happened at a very convenient moment for him, the whole affair seemed fishy and many people openly said that he had murdered her. Soon afterwards the war broke out and he fled to America. 'Darling, you can't really imagine ONE going over the top?'

Indeed it was an unlikely conception. However, having killed Lady Montdore and failed to kill Germans, he was badly received in England when he returned there after the war. He had very soon gone back and settled in his native continent.

'The present Montdore? Yes, he lives in the West Indies. I miss him very much. Polly? She is happy, has thousands of children and has completely lost her looks.'

'Fabrice always said she would. And Lady Montdore's lover – *ce vieux raseur* – I forget his name?'

'Boy Dougdale? He has become one of our foremost biographers.'

'Now tell me about yourself, *charmante Ambassadrice*. I hear you have two boys at school with that little monster of Charles-Edouard's? I don't know much about young people as I never see any, but one hears such tales –'

'Does one?' said Charles-Edouard, amused. 'What sort of tales penetrate to Boisdormant, *ma tante?*'

'You would know how true it is,' she said to me, 'but I am told the boys and girls nowadays are against birth?'

'Against birth?'

'Against being born.'

'My aunt means they don't care whether they belong to good families or not, any more.'

'Oh, I see.' I had supposed she meant something to do with birth control. 'But do you think young people ever cared about such things?'

'When I was young we did. In any case it is shocking to be against. The grand-children of a friend of mine actually started a newspaper against birth – horrible, I find, and so of course one of the girls married somebody who wasn't born –'

'Yes,' said Valhubert, with a quizzical look in my direction, 'it won't do. We can't have these goings-on in society, though I must say the unborn young man is rather solid for a disembodied spirit.'

'You laugh now, Charles-Edouard, but when your daughters are grown up you will see these things in a very different light. Tell me more about your boys, Madame l'Ambassadrice, I hear that one of them is called Fabrice?'

'He is the child of my cousin who is dead. I have adopted him.'

Suddenly we both found that we could not go on with this conversation. We looked at Valhubert who came to the rescue. 'When all three of them come over for the Christmas holidays I'll bring them here for a few days.'

'Yes, you must. Old Oudineau can teach them to ride bicycles – children like that very much, I find. Do you heat the Embassy with coal or mazout?'

16

When we got back to the Embassy Philip was crossing the courtyard. Charles-Edouard refused a cup of tea; he said Grace would be longing to hear about our day and he thought he had better get back. He drove straight off. Philip came into the house with me. I said, 'I like Valhubert very much.'

'The thing about lady-killers is that they kill ladies,' he replied, grumpily. 'That ass of a Northey is dining with him again tonight.'

'Oh, Philip – alone?'

'I've no idea. Did you see the papers this morning?'

'Hardly. I was in a rush.'

'Didn't see Mockbar?'

I stood still. We were half-way up the stairs. 'Now what?'

'He has found out that the famous Frenchman who won your mother in a lottery is none other than poor old Bouche-Bontemps. He says he is able to reveal that the French premier is one of the ex-stepfathers of Ambassadress Lady Wincham.' Philip pulled a newspaper cutting from his pocket. 'Here we are – able to reveal, yes – Her sixty-three-year-old mother, he goes on – yes, listen to this, it's stirring stuff – ex-Lady Logan, ex-Mrs Chaddesley-Corbett, ex-Viscountess Tring, ex-Madame Bouche-Bontemps, ex-Mrs Rawle, ex-Mrs Plugge, ex-Señora Lopez, ex-Mrs Chrisolithe, is now married to Pimlico man "Grandad" Markson, 22, organizer of Grandad's Tours. Interviewed in London, Mrs Markson said she had lost touch with husband number four. "We were madly in love," she said. Asked if it was true that M. Bouche-Bontemps won her in a lottery, she said, "I think it was a tombola."'

'So?'

'Bouche-Bontemps is frantic, I've had him on the telephone a dozen times. He says he remembers keenly living with this lady, out of her head, but pretty and funny, and he thinks they were together for two or three months but he certainly never married her.'

'Goodness!' I said, 'that seems to put him in an awkward position, doesn't it? Like when are you going to stop beating your wife? If he married the Bolter it's bad but if he didn't marry her it's worse?'

'No, no. You don't understand the French, as Davey would say. If he married her that's the end of his career but if he only lived with her nobody here would think anything of it. Can't you ring her up and find out?'

'Dear me! But I'm afraid she says [I was looking at Mockbar's piece] husband number four. Come on, we'll put a call through now.'

It was not necessary, however. In the Salon Vert there was a telegram on top of my afternoon letters. 'Never married him darling it was deed-pollers gave no interview have taken it up with Grumpy who promises denial tomorrow in *Daily Post* Bolter.'

'Oh well,' said Philip when I handed him this. 'That will make it much better. If they really deny it in the *Daily Post* the French papers won't copy it. They are far keener on accuracy than ours.'

'Don't you think Mockbar has gone too far? Might he not get the sack?'

'Not he! Much more likely to get a rise so that he can fatten his brats until the next jump in the cost of living forces him to make another scoop.' He lifted up the receiver. 'Katie, get the Président du Conseil for Lady Wincham, will you?'

'Is that my stepfather?' I said and was nearly blown over by a burst of laughter. 'Listen – I've had a telegram from my mother which Philip thinks will make everything all right. She says the paper is denying a marriage. It was only deed-poll she says.'

'Deed-poll,' said Bouche-Bontemps suspiciously, 'what is this?'

'What's deed-poll in French?' I asked Philip and repeated after him. '*Acte unilatéral* but you don't have it here like we do. You know – it means she took your name.'

'Did she? There was certainly no *acte*. But why should she take my name?'

'For the neighbours, I expect.'

'But, *chère Madame l'Ambassadrice*, it was at Harrar! The neighbours were Abyssinians – never mind, go on.'

'Anyhow, the point is there will be a denial tomorrow. Oh dear, I'm so sorry – though it's not exactly my fault.'

'But nothing matters as long as I am not supposed to be *bigame* – what is it in English? – bigamous. That would be very annoying – the Hautes-Pyrénées would not like it and nor would my late wife's family les Pucelards (*textiles Pucelard*) from Lille. The only person who would be delighted is my daughter-in-law who hates me, it would quite compensate her for being married to a bastard. Now, of course, I shall be labelled Intelligence Service but as the only Frenchman of whom that is never said is General de Gaulle I suppose I can bear it. *Sacrée Dorothée* – is she really your mother? How strange! No women could be less alike – though I now see a striking resemblance between her and Mees.'

'Oh don't! I always try not to!'

When I had finished talking to Bouche-Bontemps I went to find Northey. Her room was full of newborn wails. 'Mélusine has had six lovely babies, clever girl.'

'I thought you said she was old?'

'Yes. They are miracle-children.'

'So now what? Hadn't somebody better bucket them at once? Before she has got fond of them?'

'Fanny!'

'I know. But darling duck, we can't keep them here.'

'In this enormous house? I saw a dead rat in the courtyard only yesterday.'

'It was a visiting rat then. There aren't any in the house and we've got a perfectly good cat in the kitchen.'

'Sweet Minet. Very well, if you are so unwelcoming I shall give them away.'

'Yes. You must. Did you enjoy the Return of the Cinders?'

'It was lovely. We all shouted *Vive l'Empereur* – a bit late, but never mind.'

'I hear you are going out with M. de Valhubert again?'

'On business, Fanny. I must have a long serious talk about the *porte-feuille*. If the *assainissement de notre place* goes on like this all my profits will disappear and then what will my old age be like? Can you afford to pension me off? I'm getting seriously annoyed about it.'

'You talk worse pidgin than Grace. Do try to keep to one language at a time. I suppose you read Mockbar this morning?'

'Clever little soul. By the way, Davey asked me to say good-bye.'

'Davey has buggered off?'

'Fanny! Never mind, I won't tell Alfred. Yes. He says he can feel himself getting cancer of the lungs at every breath he takes in Paris.'

'What nonsense! Among all these trees! There's no smell of petrol here.'

'He says it's the scentless fumes, heavier than air, which do all the damage.'

'I must say that's a bit too much. He turns David into a sex-maniac and then leaves us to bear the brunt.'

'He'll bravely come back, when he's decarbonized, to see about David. Meanwhile Docteur Lecœur has given him a calming injection so the idea is that all our virtues are saved for the present. Katie had a ghastly time with him last night – she says it was the nearest thing – that beard and those feet, how can poor Dawnie? Why are Zen-men's feet always so awful?' She shuddered.

'I wish Docteur Lecœur would give Mockbar a calming injection.'

'No, Fanny, he's courting. It would be too unfair.'

'Courting whom?'

'Phyllis McFee, for one.'

'Tell me something, Northey. Does Phyllis McFee really exist?'

Wide-eyed, injured look. 'How d'you mean, does she really exist?'

'You haven't invented her, by any chance?'

'She's my old friend of for ever. (The poor make no new friends – oh don't! That wretched Bourse!) Surely I'm allowed the one?'

'Then I can't understand why you never bring her to see me?'

'She works.'

'What at?'

'World Something.'

'Not in the evening surely?'

'Specially then because, you know, the World is round so it's later in America. When that great throbbing, teeming, bustling heart of little old New York begins to beat, Phyllis McFee, relaxed, efficient, smiling (not to grin is a sin), suitably dressed in her latest Mainbocher, immaculate hair-do, neat ankles and red nails, must be on the Transatlantic line. She has no time to waste on people like you.'

'Bring her to luncheon one day?'

'She's far too busy. She can't do more than *un queek dans un drog* which is French for luncheon in a chemist's shop. Just imagine, scrumptious grub all among the cotton wool – takes thinking of – admit –'

'All right then, don't bring her. I don't mind. She seems to work a good deal harder than some people we know.'

'Is that a hint? Not very kind, Fanny. As a matter of fact, Phyllis McFee has ambitions, she wants to hug her boss (which would be French for employer if it didn't happen to mean bruise). I don't.'

'Another person I never see, while we are on the subject of invisible beings, is M. Cruas.'

'He's timid. He wouldn't like to be seen by you. And speaking as your secretary, quite as much up to date, thorough and efficient as Phyllis, may I remind you that you and Alfred have got the National Day of the North Koreans, after which you dine early with the Italians to go to a lovely play, at the Théâtre des Nations, about refrigerators. Some people have all the luck – !'

Feeling myself dismissed, I went up to my bedroom and tried to forget my manifold worries in a long, hot, scented bath.

It took us some time to get from the North Korean to the Italian Embassy. Between the hours of seven and eight all the Americans who live in Paris bring out motor cars the size of lorries, shiny, showy and horribly cheap-looking, and sally forth to meet each other, drink whisky and rub up their accents. This also happens to be the time when the Parisians are on the move from work-place to home; the streets become almost impassable.

As we drove towards the Alma, at about one mile an hour, Alfred said, 'You seem preoccupied, darling. Is there something on your mind?'

'Something! About a ton of different things –'

'Such as?'

'Mockbar, to begin with. I suppose you didn't see it –'

'Yes, I did. Philip put it under my eyes. Anything sillier I have seldom read. Bouche-Bontemps says it's quite untrue and he must know. Really – if that's all –'

'Oh, how I wish it were. Northey worries me dreadfully.'

'Northey? Why?'

'Any little girl as attractive as she is must be a worry until one has married her off. The followers –'

'Safety in numbers, surely.'

'There are one or two whom I don't think safe.' I did not want to specify Valhubert to Alfred without more proof than I had that he was really a danger.

'Can you wonder they follow? The other day – it was after your luncheon party – she took Madame Meistersinger downstairs. I'd just been seeing off the Burmese and then had gone into Mrs Trott's room to telephone. When I came out the hall was empty – the footman was putting the old woman into her motor and behind their backs, at the top of the steps, Northey was going through a sort of pantomime of ironical reverences. Oh I can't describe how funny it was! Of course she had no idea anybody was watching. It made me realize that one might be terribly in love with that little creature.'

'We all are,' I said, 'except Philip. One does so long for her to have a happy life, not like the Bolter.'

Alfred now said something extraordinary: 'Deeply as I disapprove of your mother and her activities I don't think she could be described as unhappy.'

I looked at him in amazement. We were all so much accustomed in my family to deploring the Bolter's conduct that one took for granted the great unhappiness to which it must have, if only because it ought to have, led.

'You should try and see things as they are, Fanny. Whether her behaviour has been desirable or not is a different proposition from whether it has made her unhappy. I don't think it has; I think she is perfectly happy and always was.'

'Perhaps. Still, you wouldn't want that sort of happiness for Northey, I suppose. My prayer is that she will marry Philip and settle down.'

'I agree. I don't want it for her. But neither do I want her to marry him because, if she does, mark my words, she won't settle down. She will bolt.'

'Alfred, why do you say that?'

'Philip wouldn't hold her. Not enough fantasy, no roughage. Although vastly superior in every way to Tony Kroesig he is in some sort not the contrary of him. Just as Tony didn't do for Linda, so Philip wouldn't for Northey.'

'I see in a way what you mean – they are both rich, conventional Englishmen – but really it's very unfair to Philip.'

'I'm extremely fond of him, I only say he's not the husband for her.'

'I wonder! Luckily it's out of our hands – something they must settle for themselves. Are you beginning to be interested in people in your old age, darling?'

'Old age?' Falsetto.

'Well, I really think it must be that. You used utterly to despise me when I made these sort of speculations.'

'I'm interested in the children and I count Northey as one.'

'I sometimes wish she was our one and only – no, of course I don't mean that, but I could wish that David and Baz hadn't reached these difficult stages just when you and I have our hands full. We can be of so little use to them, under the circumstances.'

'I don't know. We seem to be lodging David and his family, providing medical attention and everything. Basil comes and goes as he likes – what more could we do? I think it's just as well we are busy; it takes our minds off them. Useless for us to worry and we have no cause to reproach ourselves. They are only suffering from growing pains I think – nothing very serious.'

'I do reproach myself for not having sent them to Eton. If we had they might have turned out so differently.'

'I don't agree. Eton produces quite as large a percentage of oddities as other schools. In any case we weren't rich enough, then. We did our best for them, and that's that.'

'We must count our blessings. How I'm looking forward to going over on St Andrew's Day and taking out the little boys. They are perfect.'

'Perfect?' Falsetto again.

'I mean like other people.'

'Oh. So it's perfect to be like other people, is it? Grace tells me they think of nothing but jazz.'

'That's a phase.'

'So are the eccentricities of Basil and David, no doubt . . .'

'My point is that going to Eton will have minimized the danger of such extreme phases in the case of Charlie and Fabrice.'

'*Unberufen*,' said Alfred, as we drove into the courtyard of the Hôtel de Doudeauville.

17

The word '*unberufen*' rang so unaccustomed on the lips of Alfred that it stuck in my mind. Whether it was the result of old age or of having a new position in the world, he seemed to be mellowing; the Alfred of a year ago would have conducted our conversation in the motor on different, sterner lines and would not have said '*unberufen*'. However, when, the next day before luncheon, Katie told me that there was a personal call for him from Windsor, I knew that he must have unberufened in vain. He had gone to the railway carriage in the forest of Compiègne to celebrate the Armistice; I said that I would take the call. No doubt some sort of worst had occurred; I prayed, wrongly, weakmindedly, that it would prove to be a moral and not a physical worst. For a few seconds there was a muddle on the line: *"allo Weendzor – parlez Weendzor*,' during which time an amazing amount of horrible speculations managed to pass through my head. The moment I heard the housemaster's voice, decidedly peevish but not sad, I was reassured: Charlie and Fabrice were obviously still with us on this earth. He did not beat about the bush or try to prepare me for bad news; he told me that the boys had left.

'Run away?' I said, perhaps too cheerfully, in my relief.

'People don't exactly run away any more. The snivelling boy dragged off the stagecoach by an usher is a thing of the past.'

I laughed hysterically at this piece of light relief, put in perhaps to steady my nerves.

'No, you could hardly call it that. In any case, running away is a spontaneous action with which one can have a certain sympathy. This was a premeditated, indeed an organized, departure. They asked to speak to me after early school and announced it, quite politely I must say. Then all three got into a Rolls-Royce, apparently hired for the purpose, and drove off –'

'All three?'

'Valhubert was with them.'

'Oh, he was, was he! And did they give a reason?'

'The excuse was the food – in other words, no excuse at all because I think I may say the food in my house is excellent. I eat it myself. They pretended that poor little Billy last half – you remember the tragedy – threw himself into the weir on purpose because of it. Nothing could be more far-fetched. They said the choice was between a suicide pact and immediate departure.'

'Naughty!' I stifled a giggle.

'I need hardly tell you that I shall be unable to take them back again after this. The drama was played out in public – half the school saw them go. It seems they stopped in Slough for Fabrice to say good-bye to his mistress and three children.'

'Rubbish,' I said irritably. 'I've heard about this mistress in Slough all my life – ever since my cousins were at school. And the King of Siam's seven wives living over the post-office. Typical Eton tales.'

'That may be. I'm only telling you to show the effect of all this on the other boys and the impossibility of my overlooking their conduct.'

'Oh yes, I see, and I quite realize. Does M. de Valhubert know?'

'Not yet. I shall ring him up now.'

'Just tell me where they've gone, will you?'

'I have no idea.'

'No idea! Didn't you ask them?'

'Certainly I did not.'

My irritation turned to fury. What did we pay the wretched man for? With incredible frivolity he had allowed these children we had put in his care, while we were serving our country overseas, to vanish into the blue. All very well for him to be so light-hearted about it; he had got rid of them for good. My troubles were just beginning, but that evidently left him cold.

'Then there's nothing more to say?'

'Nothing, I'm afraid.' We rang off.

I told Katie to keep the line clear until Madame de Valhubert should ring up. Presently I asked her, 'What's become of Northey? I haven't seen her this morning.'

'She was up all night with the kittens. Mélusine doesn't seem to have any milk – too old probably – so it's the fountain-pen filler. Poor Northey's trying to get some sleep; I've taken over for her. Every two hours, and one of them isn't sucking properly. I think this is Madame de Valhubert now – that was her butler's voice –'

'Fanny – you are *au courant*?'

'Yes, indeed. That idiot rang us up first. I'm simply furious –'

'Old Tartuffe! Did you ever hear anything so shameful!'

'It's a disgrace, Grace. I shall tell Alfred he's not to pay a penny for this half.'

'No, don't let's. The boys have never cost him much at any time – Sigi lived on mercy parcels I had to send from Hédiard. The wretch! Calmly telephoning to say he let the boys leave without even having taken the trouble to find out where they were going! I expect they are all being murdered by a sex maniac in the fog at this very minute, poor little things –'

'Oh well, I expect not –'

'You know what England is, darling. I was wondering if couldn't *porter plainte* against the school?'

'What does Charles-Edouard say?'

'He's down in his *circonscription* for the Armistice – and I suppose Alfred has gone to Compiègne? What ought we to do? So dreadful to think of those children all alone in London.'

'We aren't even sure they've gone to London.'

'Knowing Sigi I think they have. Who will feed them?'

'I've a good mind to go over now and see what they are up to,' I said.

'You can't. There's a fog as usual. Didn't you notice, no English papers? Look at it here, such a heavenly day –'

'In any case it wouldn't be much good for me to wander round London looking for them like Thomas à Becket's mother, without a clue as to where they are. I suppose we must wait and consult with our husbands when they get back. We'll keep in touch, but let's anyhow meet tomorrow and talk it over. I should think we'll know more by then.'

'You're an optimist!' said Grace. '*À demain* then, unless there's any news before.'

However, at tea-time she rang up again. 'Almost too irritating,' she said, 'I've just telephoned to my father on the chance he might know something and sure enough he gave them all luncheon at Wilton's. Of course the wicked old man is on their side – he would be. Like all Englishmen he's a schoolboy himself really. What a race! He says they ate everything within sight. They showed him menus of all the meals they've had this half which they kept as *pièces justificatives* and he says he can't think how they stuck it as long as they did. Naturally no mention of the mercy parcels. Clever of Sigi, that was, the way to my father's heart has always been through his stomach.'

'Little brutes!' I said. I had transferred some of my rage with the housemaster to the boys, as, I noticed, had Grace.

'The maddening thing is,' she went on, 'he admits he gave them money.'

'How much?'

'He pretends he can't remember – a few pounds he says. If I know Papa, he'll have had at least £50 on him and if I know Sigi, he'll have wheedled it all. So now goodness alone knows when we shall hear any more of them. They were still alive at luncheon-time, apart from that the situation is worse than if he hadn't seen them.'

'Didn't you ask where they were staying?'

'Naturally I did. He only said not with him. Trust him not to make himself uncomfortable in any way!'

At this point Katie cut in, saying, 'Do we take a reversed charge call from London?'

'Oh yes,' I said, 'that's always one of the boys. I'll ring you up presently, Grace.'

'Ma?' It was Basil. 'Look, Ma, it's like this. Old Charles and Fabrice and Sigi are here.'

'Basil, you are a faithful boy. I've been so worried!'

'Oh, so you knew they'd left the booby-hatch, did you?'

'Yes, their tutor rang up this morning and of course Sigi's mother and I have been in the most fearful state wondering what had happened to them.'

'I suppose you thought the robins had covered them with leaves! Your capacity for worry beats anything I ever heard of. Anyway, knowing you, I thought I'd better ease your mind. They are quite alive and nobody has interfered with them, not yet.'

'So what are they going to do?'

'Live it up here. They've gone to a pop show now this minute to see their idol, Yanky Fonzy.'

'Have they got much money?'

'There you are, being your old bourgeoise self. Money! Didn't you know it doesn't count in the modern world? Everybody's got the stuff nowadays. As a matter of fact, they seem to be quite specially well fixed for it – they've pooled Charles's savings, Fabrice's camera and what Sigi's old ancestor gave them just now.'

'Where are they living?'

'Me Grandad has set them up in a shack he happened to own.'

'Then quickly give me the address – I've got a pencil. Good. Any telephone number?'

'I'm not allowed to give it. They don't want the O.C.s beefing down the line – specially Sigi doesn't.'

The O.C.s, I knew, meant the old couples, in other words us and the Valhuberts. 'Aren't they afraid the O.C.s may arrive and beef in person?'

'Not really. They reckon Father's too busy – Sigi's mother is pregnant – Sigi's father wouldn't demean himself and if you come over they can cope.'

'Oh indeed! Let me tell you, Baz, I've seldom been so furious.'

'That's not reasonable of you, Ma. I don't see 'ow you could expect them kids to go on wasting the best years of their lives in that ole cackle factory.'

'Anyway, darling, it was awfully good of you to telephone –'

Alfred surprised me by taking the news very badly indeed. I said, 'I don't know why you should mind this more than you did about David and Baz. After all, they are intellectuals, far more brilliant than the little boys, it is dreadfully sad that they should have become so peculiar. But yesterday you said it was only a phase, growing pains. So it is with the others, probably.'

'I mind less about David and Basil precisely because they are cleverer. They have got their degrees. When they see the futility of their present state they can return to more rewarding occupations. Also there is something in their heads. We may feel annoyed with them for not following the path we had hoped they would, but as human beings they are perfectly entitled to decide for themselves what they wish to do. These boys are only in the middle of their lessons – I don't see how the gap in their education is ever to be filled. There is no philosophical basis for their conduct; it comes from sheer irresponsibility. You know what I feel about education.'

I could see that Alfred, whatever he might say, had counted as much as I had on magic Eton to produce two ordinary, worthy, if not specially bookish young men and was disappointed as well as disturbed by this new outbreak of non-conformism.

The Valhuberts came round and the two stricken families held a conference. Charles-Edouard was in a rage, with Grace crowing over him annoyingly, I thought.

'Of course, poor Charles-Edouard is angry with me for being right all along. Such a pity to send the child to Eton, when we could have kept him here and fed him up and had him taught by the Jesuits at Sainte-Geneviève.'

'My dear Grace, they would never have taken Sigi at Sainte Geneviève. That's a school for clever boys. Franklin, perhaps – not sure. No. I sent him to Eton for the education, not for the instruction. Sigi has the brain of a bird, as even you must admit. I wanted him to be at least a well-dressed bird with good manners. Besides I can only stand a limited amount of his company. Now he'll be back on our hands all the year round unless I can persuade them to take him at Les Roches.'

'If he runs away from Eton he would never stay at Les Roches. It will have to be the Jesuits – you must go and see the Superior at Franklin.'

'When you do, will you be so good as to ask him to recommend a tutor for our two?' said Alfred. 'I suppose we shall have to have them here where we can keep an eye on them; they can at least get a proper grounding in French before they cram for Oxford.'

'Have them here?' I said, quite as much dismayed at the prospect as Valhubert was. It seemed to me we had enough on our hands already, what with the holy Zen family, Northey's caravan of followers and Basil's Cheshire-cat appearances and wild-cat schemes.

'What else can we do?' said Alfred. 'That school they call the Borstal Boys' Eton might take them – think of the friends they would pick up there!'

'Gabbitas and Thring?'

Alfred buried his head in his hands.

Grace now said, with perfect truth, that we were looking too far ahead. We must get them away from London and the shack found for them by my stepfather, under our own influence again, before making these elaborate plans. It was decided that we had better wait until it was reasonable to suppose that they would have run out of cash and that then one of us should go over and bring them back.

'But what about your father, Grace? If he goes on supplying them they won't ever run out.'

'I'm thankful to say he has now left London for a round of shoots and he'll be away at least a month.'

It then became evident, just as the little brutes had foreseen, that I should be the one deputed to go after them. The only alternative was Valhubert and he said himself that he was too angry and would be sure to lose his temper at the mere sight of them. The words 'if you do, they can cope' rang a mocking chime in my ears, but I had no choice; I accepted the mission.

So we planned for our sons, hoping to undo the harm they had done themselves. It never occurred to us that they would refuse to cooperate. We were soon to learn our mistake.

We let the rest of November go by; then I sent them a telegram, reply paid, asking them to dine with me at the Ritz the following day. They were kind enough to accept the invitation quite promptly. Alfred said this showed they were starving and should easily be caught, like animals in the snow.

'The gilt will be off the gingerbread by now – they'll have begun to see what it's like to be alone in London with no money. It was far better not to go at once.'

On St Andrew's Day I arrived at the Ritz. When I had unpacked and had a bath I was still about half an hour too early for our appointment; there was nothing else to do so I went downstairs, sat on one of those little sofas below the alcove, where I have perched at intervals all my life, and ordered a glass of sherry. Never possessing a London house of my own I have always found the Ritz useful when up for the day or a couple of nights; a place where one could meet people, leave parcels, write letters, or run into out of the rain. It now remains one of the few London interiors which have never changed a scrap; the lace antimacassars are still attached to the armchairs with giant hairpins; the fountain tinkles as it has for fifty years; there is the same sound of confident footfall on thick carpet and the same delicious smell of rich women and promising food. As in the Paris Ritz the management has been clever enough not to touch the decoration designed by M. Meuwes, the excellent architect employed by M. Ritz. I have been told that the late Lady Colefax once refused a commission to redecorate the ground floor, saying that it would be wrong to alter any of it.

I sipped my sherry and reflected on the enormous length of human life and the curious turns it takes, a train of thought always set off by a place with which I have been familiar at irregular intervals for many years. Some people, I know, feel aggrieved at the shortness of life; I, on the contrary, am amazed at how long it seems to go on. The longer the better. Paris had cured me of my middle-aged blight exactly as I had hoped it would; if I was sometimes worried there I never felt depressed, bored, and useless, as at Oxford. I managed the work far better than I had expected to. I had neither kissed the President nor extinguished the Eternal Flame nor indeed, as far as I knew, committed any major gaffe. As I am not shy, and most of the people I met were engaged in responsible, therefore interesting, work I found no difficulty in conversing with them. Philip had provided me with one or two useful gambits. ('I suppose you are very tired, M. le Ministre' would unloose floodgates.)

Alfred was an undoubted success with the French, whatever Mockbar might say. He was more like their idea of an Englishman, slow, serious, rather taciturn, than the brilliant Sir Louis, who had been too much inclined to floor them on their own ground. Such worries as I had all came from the children; Alfred's were more serious. He was obliged to press the European Army upon the French although personally convinced by now of its unacceptability. The Îles Minquiers, too, were still giving him a lot of uncongenial work. However, Mr Gravely seemed quite satisfied with the way these things were shaping. The Americans had assured him that the European Army was almost in the bag. He thought he had himself persuaded M. Bouche-Bontemps to give up the Minquiers and that it was only, now, a matter of time before they became British Isles.

Two men coming out of the alcove and passing my sofa roused me from these thoughts. 'When I got to the factory,' one of them said, 'they told me that seven of the girls were knocked up – well, pregnant in fact. It's the new German machine.'

'You don't surprise me at all,' said his friend, 'these new German machines are the devil.'

I have overheard many a casual remark in my life; none has ever puzzled me more. As I pondered over it I saw three figures ambling towards me from the

Arlington Street entrance. They were dressed as Teddy boys, but there was no mistaking the species. With their slouching, insouciant gait, dead-fish hands depending from, rather than forming part of, long loose-jointed arms, slightly open mouths and appearance of shivering as if their clothes, rather too small in every dimension, had no warmth in them, they would have been immediately recognizable, however disguised, on the mountains of the Moon, as Etonians. Here were the chrysalises of the elegant, urbane Englishmen I so much longed for my sons to be; this was the look which, since I was familiar with it from early youth, I found so right, and which I had missed from the tough premature manliness of the other two boys. Charlie and Fabrice had changed their clothes but not yet their personalities; what a relief!

18

'We didn't think we were late?'

'You're not. I was early.'

'Pretty dress, Mum. We've brought you some flowers.'

'Oh, you are nice. Thanks so much – roses!' (But this was rather sinister. Roses are expensive on St Andrew's Day; they must still have got some money.) 'My favourites! Give them to the porter, Charlie, will you, and ask him to have them put in a vase for me. There – let's go and dine.'

I thought the boys were feeling quite as much embarrassed as I was and I counted on food to unbutton us all. They ordered, as I knew they would, smoked salmon and roast chicken and then politely tried to put me at my ease.

'Did you have a good journey?'

'Was it a Viscount?'

'Have you seen the new Anouilh in Paris?'

'Have you read *Pinfold*?'

I said yes to everything but was too much preoccupied to enlarge on these topics. General conversation was really not possible under the circumstances; I ordered a bottle of wine and bravely plunged. 'Perhaps you'll tell me now what this is all about?'

Charlie and Sigi looked at Fabrice who was evidently the spokesman. 'Are you furious with us?' he said.

'I'm more worried than furious. Your fathers are very angry indeed. But why did you do it?'

'The ghoulishness of the food –' Sigi said, in a high wail.

'It's no good telling me about the food,' I said firmly, 'because I know perfectly well that had nothing to do with it. I'd like the real reason, please.'

'You must try and put yourself in our place,' said Fabrice, 'wasting the best years of our lives (only three more as teenagers – every day so precious, when we ought to be hitting it up as never again), wasting them in that dark creepy one-horse place with Son et Lumière (the head beak) and all the other old weirdies yattering at us morning and night and those ghoulish kids mouldering in the same grave with us.

It's a living death, Mum; we've been cheesed off for months. In the end it became more than flesh and blood could stand. Do you blame us?'

I was uncertain how to say what must be said. 'What's that you've got on your jersey, Charles?'

'Yank's the Boy for Me. Do you like it?'

'Only rather. Who is Yank?'

'Who is Yank? Yanky Fonzy of course, the Birmingham-born Bomb. I should have thought even you would have heard of Yank – that lanky Yank from Brum – the toughest guy that breathes. He's a disc star.'

'And he's the boy for you?'

'Oh definitely. Of course he's a man's man, you might not dig him like we do, lots of girls don't and hardly any oldsters. But we're his fans, the screamin' kids who follow him round the Beat Shows. Boy! does he wow us!'

'Oh,' I said, flummoxed.

'You ought to come and see for yourself,' said Sigi. *'Tout comprendre c'est tout pardonner!'*

'Do you think I would understand though?'

'If you saw you would,' said Fabrice. 'Yank, coming right into the attack – treating the kids like a man squeezing an orange. That ole mike is putty in his hands; he rolls on the floor with it – uses it as a gun – throws it around, spins it, snarls into it. Then, sudden, dramatic, he quiets down into a *religioso*: "I count them over, every one apart, my Rosary." From that it's Schehera-jazz: "Pale hands I loved beside the Shalimar." "Oh Shenandoah, I long to hear you." Ending up with the patriotic stuff: "Shoot if you must this old grey head but spare my country's Flag, she said." Something for everybody, see?'

'Oh Mum, do try and realize how it makes jolly boating weather seem like a rice pudding.'

'Perhaps I do. But all this has no connexion with real life, which is very long, very serious and for which, at your age, you ought to be preparing.'

'No. The whole point is that we are too old, now, to be preparing. This is life, it has begun, we want to be living.'

'Dearest, that's for your parents to decide. As we support you we must be allowed to have a say in your activities, I suppose?'

'Ah! But I'm just coming to that. Teenagers are definitely commercial nowadays. It's not like we were back in history – David Copperfield. The modern Copperfield doesn't have to tramp to Dover and find Aunt Betsy – no – he is rich – he earns £9 a week. That's what we are making; not bad for a start?'

'£9 a week?' I was very much taken aback. Starving animals in the snow, indeed! This was going to make my task difficult if not impossible. 'For doing what, may I inquire?'

'Packing.'

'That's nearly £500 a year!'

'Definitely.'

'What do you pack?'

'Shavers – you know, razors.'

'Do you like it?'

'Does anybody like work?'

I snatched at this opening.

'Oh, indeed they do, when it's interesting. That's the whole point of lessons, so that one can finally have work which is more enjoyable than packing.'

'Yes, that's what we've heard. We don't believe it. We think all work is the same and it's during the time off that you live your life. No use wasting these precious years preparing for jobs that may be far worse than packing when we shall be old and anyway not able to feel anything, good or bad. As it is we get two days off and our evenings. In between we are inspired by Yank.'

'But my dear children, you can't go on packing for the rest of your lives. You must think of the future.'

'Why must we? All you oldies thought and thought of the future and slaved and saved for the future, and where did it get you?'

'It got your father to Paris.'

'And what good does that do him? How many days off does he get? How does he spend his evenings? Who is his idol?'

'In any case it's now we want to be enjoying ourselves, not when we are rotting from the feet up at thirty or something ghoulish.'

'Just tell me,' I said, 'were you unhappy at Eton? People hardly ever are, in my experience.'

They looked at each other. 'No – not exactly unhappy. It was this feeling of waste we had.'

'It wasn't the Perthshire Set?' I knew that when they first arrived they had been teased (according to their own statements, discounted by me, positively martyrized) by Scotch boys larger and older than they, one of whom was Sigi's fag-master, who were alleged to have stolen their money and borrowed and broken such treasures as cameras, besides inflicting dire physical torments on them.

'Ay, the gret black monolisks fra' Pitlochry,' said Fabrice, 'a' change heer for Ballachulish.' The others were shaking with laughter at what was evidently an ancient and well-loved joke. 'Nu – now we are na' longer wee bairnies they canna scaith us.'

'You didn't leave because of them?'

'They are still ghoulish (in Pop now) but no, definitely not.'

'And you haven't been beaten this half?'

'Oh definitely. I was beaten for covering a boy with baby-powder and Sigi was for holding a boy's head under the bath water.'

'Sigi!' There was such horror in my voice that he looked quite startled and quickly said, 'But I didn't hold it for as long as they thought.'

'Mum – nobody minds being beaten, you know.'

'Speak for yourself, Charlie,' said Fabrice, making a face.

'Of course it's rather ghoulish pacing up and down one's room before. But not nearly enough for running away. Our reasons were positive, not negative.'

The others agreed. 'Definitely. It was the feeling that life was passing us by and we weren't getting the best out of it.'

'Packing and rocking and rolling aren't the best, either. They will stop wowing you very soon and then where will you be?'

'By then nothing will matter any more. Our teens will have gone and we shall be old and we shall die. Isn't it sad!'

'Very sad but not quite true. You will get old and die, but after the end of your teens until your death beds there will be endless years to fill in somehow. Are you going to spend them all, all those thousands of days, packing shavers? Is it for this that you were created?'

'You see, you haven't understood, just like we were so afraid you wouldn't.'

'Why don't you come back with me to Paris in the morning?'

They looked at each other uncomfortably. 'You see, we think London is a better town to live in at our age. Paris isn't much good for teenagers.'

'Definitely less commercial.'

'So you won't come?'

'You see, we've signed on for our work.'

It was evidently no good pursuing the subject so we spoke of other things. They asked how Northey was. 'By the way,' I said, 'she's a teenager but she's perfectly happy in Paris; she loves it.'

They said, scornfully but quite affectionately, that she had never acted like a teenager.

'Act is the word,' I said, beginning to lose my temper, 'acting and showing off. If you had to leave Eton why couldn't you have gone at the end of the half instead of having a scene with your tutor and hiring a Rolls-Royce to take you, in full view of everybody? So vulgar, I'm ashamed of you. And how I wish you knew how babyish you look in that silly fancy dress.'

'This dinner party is going downhill,' said Fabrice.

'Definitely,' said Sigi.

'Ghoulish,' said Charlie.

'Yes. I think I'm tired after the journey.' I looked at my children and thought how little I knew them. I felt much more familiar with David and Baz. No doubt it was because these boys had always been inseparable. As with dogs, so with children, one on its own is a more intimate pet than two or three. The death of my second baby had made a gap between David and Basil; I had had each of them in the nursery by himself. I suppose I had hardly ever been alone with either of the other two in my life; I was not at all sure what they were really like.

'Don't be tired,' said Fabrice. 'We thought we'd take you to the Finsbury Empire. It's not Yank unfortunately (he's in Liverpool) but quite a good pop show.'

'Darling – no, I can't anyhow. I promised I'd ring up Sigi's mother and tell the news. She's expecting a baby, Sigi.'

If I'd hoped to soften him with this statement I was disappointed. 'I know!' he said furiously. 'It really is too bad of her. What about the unearned income? There'll be nothing for any of us if she goes on like this.'

'Lucky you're so good at packing.' I felt I had scored a point.

As soon as the children had finished their pudding I paid the bill and said good-bye to them. There seemed to be no point in prolonging the interview only to hear, as I was already sick of hearing from David and Baz, what a ghastly (or ghoulish) failure Alfred and I had made of our lives; how we had wasted our youth and to what purpose? It was true that I was tired and, in fact, deeply depressed and upset. I had been unable to touch my dinner; I longed to be alone and lie down in the dark. First, however, I telephoned to Grace. (Alfred I knew was dining out, I would speak to him in the morning.) She was not surprised to hear about the crooner.

'It went on the whole summer at Bellandargues – lanky Yank the Boy from Brum, till I could have killed them. You didn't quite take it in when I told you. It's an absolute mania. But then, Fanny, aren't they getting hard up?'

'I'm coming to that,' I said, just as Fabrice had, 'hold everything, it's far the worst part. They've got a job – they're quite all right for money and I'd just like you to guess what they are earning.'

'Perhaps – I don't know – they couldn't be worth £3 a week?'

'Nine.'

'Pounds a week? Each? But it's perfectly insane! We shall never get them back now.'

'Exactly.'

'But what do they get it for?'

'Packing, Grace. They pack all day, five days a week, in order to have their evenings free for the Birmingham-born Bomb.'

There was a long pause while she digested this fact. Then she said, 'My dear, the person who gives Sigismond £9 a week to pack for him must be out of his mind. I only wish you could see his box when he comes back from school!'

The next day at Orly the lively face of Northey was in the crowd waiting for friends by the entrance. There was something about the mere sight of that child which made my spirits rise, as that of my own boys, alas, no longer did. She had hopped into the Rolls-Royce when she saw it leaving the Embassy. 'Anything to down tools for an hour or two,' she said, frankly, adding, 'hot news!'

'Don't, Northey!'

'Good news I mean – Coffirep has had children. Oh dear, I'm so over-excited – !'

'Dearest – is that the badger?'

'Fanny, do sharpen your wits and concentrate on my life. Coffirep is my shares – so I'm rich, my old age will be nice, oh do be pleased!'

'I can't tell you how delighted I am, specially about it not being the badger.'

'As if he could all alone, poor duck. In the spring I'll get him a sweet little wife – I'm sure he's made a breeding chamber down there, we don't want him to feel disappointed. Oh, I was dying to tell somebody. Alfred didn't properly listen (he's in a do about the boys); Philip only said he wished he knew if there really is any marketable oil in the Sahara; the holies don't care about money, or so they say. (I note they always make me pay the cab if we go in one.) And Charles-Edouard is shooting, which he calls hunting, in Champagne. It's very dull having nobody to take an interest – thank goodness you are back.'

Not another word about the boys; she was either being tactful or was too much occupied with her own affairs – the latter I suspected. She babbled on until we got home. When we drove into the courtyard I saw a group of people, who were obviously not followers, waiting by Northey's entrance.

'Mr Ward,' she explained, 'has very kindly allowed me to put up a notice in W. H. Smith offering my kittens to good homes. It gives me a lot of extra work, taking up references and so on; they have to be rather special people as you may imagine. They must promise not to – you know – castrate; they must live on the ground floor with a garden (I go myself and see), and above all they must not be related to any scientist, chemist or furrier. The kits aren't ready to leave me and Katie yet; this is only for when they are.'

Of course Mockbar duly informed the world that Envoy's Sons had left Eton because the headmaster had threatened to thrash them and were now employed by the London firm of such-and-such in their packing department. Mockbar hardly annoyed me any more nor even extracted a wry laugh; I was getting used to his style and the observations which punctuated all our doings. His paragraphs no longer made me tremble for Alfred's career. Six million people read them, so one was told, and evidently regarded them as enjoyable fiction. He was too often obliged, by the solicitors of some victim, to withdraw a statement for the public to place much reliance in his word.

A few days later Charles-Edouard left hurriedly for London. To my secret rage and disgust he returned that same evening with Master Sigismond in tow. Grace informed me of this, adding, 'He cracked the whip, darling. Thank God I married a Frenchman. Whatever you may say, they do have some authority in the family!'

'The thing is, Alfred can't go over just now; I don't feel I ought to worry him by suggesting that he should. He's having a difficult time, he's busy.'

'He must be. The English! Words can't express what I feel! They are being quite simply too awful. I'm sure Sir Alfred can't approve. Having that Niam on an official visit! Fanny, it's the limit. He has eaten simply hundreds of Frenchmen and now he's got a loan from Stalin – yes, I know, but they're all Stalin to me, I can't keep learning their new names – so that he can catch and eat hundreds more.'

'Nonsense, Grace. In a profile of Dr Niam I read somewhere, they said he is a vegetarian and very pro-French at heart.'

'At stomach they mean. Oh good, I've made a joke, I must tell Charles-Edouard. I've been too pregnant, lately.'

'They say he's firmly attached to the Western World and has a great sense of humour.'

'Oh, do shut up. Are the English our allies or are they not?'

How I wished I knew what whip, cracked by his father, had brought Sigismond to heel. Cracking whips seemed to be something of which neither Alfred nor I was capable. When our boys refused to listen to reason we were done for. It was beginning to be borne in on me that as parents we were a resounding failure. While all three boys had been in full revolt I could just bear it; now that Sigi had returned to parental authority, the evil conduct of our two was stressed. Surely we, too, ought to be able to find some way of mastering them?

'Hot news!' said Northey. 'Guess why Sigi is here?'

'I thought M. de Valhubert went over and cracked a whip?'

'Yes, well, if you really want to know, he went over because Sigi was in bad with the police. He was caught nicking shavers.'

'Doing what, dearest?'

'They were packing shavers – you knew that, didn't you? And were getting £9 a week, which, incidentally, makes skilled secretarial work in embassies seem rather underpaid but let that pass. Clever Sigi discovered that if you nick a few every day (no, Fanny, *don't* keep asking what things mean, sharpen your wits and listen) you can bump up the screw to quite a pound more. But as he's not used to stealing, so far, he was caught and there was a fearful rumpus. Charles-Edouard had to go and buy him off or he'd have gone to a remand home or something. Can you beat it!'

I felt a glow of superiority. 'Poor Grace,' I said, 'how dreadful.'

'By the way, the old foreign lady is not to be told.'

'Ah! Quite right – of course she mustn't be. So is Charles-Edouard furious?'

'Not a bit. He thinks it's most frightfully funny and he's delighted to have Sigi delivered into his hands. Now he'll be obliged to go to the strict Jesuits after all.'

'I shouldn't think even the strictest Jesuits will do that boy much good – he'll come to a bad end all right.'

Northey bashed me out of my complacency with: 'Charlie and Fabrice have got the knack of it now.'

'The knack of nicking?'

'Yes. Sigi says he invented a foolproof method on the way over and rang them up to tell, very kindly. They'll get lovely and rich, he says, in no time.'

19

Holy David had been looking decidedly better since Docteur Lecœur took him in hand, even slightly cleaner. His interest in secular or non-Zen affairs seemed to be reviving; he came with me to the Louvre one day and saw one or two plays with Dawn. I had become devoted to her, which shows that speech is not an essential factor in human understanding. (Northey said who ever thought it was? Think of creatures and how well we get on with them in silence.) I was very hopeful that if the improvement in David continued at this rate he would go back to his university and resume his career.

Then he told me, casually, one day, that he and Dawn were about to resume their journey to the East. I was sorry, indeed, that it should be East rather than West but to tell the truth I felt such a surge of relief that at first I hardly cared which direction they were taking. David's presence in the house was not convenient. The servants and the whole of Alfred's staff disliked him. English statesmen and important officials who came and went in a fairly steady stream cannot have relished the sight of his gowned form and naked feet at breakfast. He was on his father's nerves. Whenever Mockbar was short of a story he fell back on Envoy's Son for some spiteful little paragraph. How heavenly to think that the Zen family was on the move at last! Concealing joy, I said, 'You'll tell me when you would like Jérôme to take you to the station?'

'Not the station, the road. Send us to Provins; after that we will fend for ourselves.'

'With Dawn in her present condition? Oh no, David, that's not possible.'

'Pregnant women have astonishing powers of survival. That has been proved in every great exodus of history. All the same, I think I will leave little 'Chang here.'

The surge of relief subsided, the joy was extinguished. I might have guessed there would be a snag somewhere. 'No, you can't,' I said, putting up what I really knew would be a perfectly ineffectual resistance. 'Who's going to look after him?'

'Mrs Trott and Katie simply love him.'

'We all simply love him; that's not the point. Neither Mrs Trott nor anybody else here has time to nurse little 'Chang. He's your responsibility; you adopted him; nobody asked you to! Why did you, anyway?'

'We wanted a brother for our baby so that they can be brought up together. It was very bad for my young psychology to be three years older than Basil; Dawn and I don't intend to repeat that mistake of yours.'

'But if he's here and your baby is in the East?'

'As soon as our baby is born it must join little 'Chang. I shall send it to you at once so that they can unfold their consciousness together.'

'So I've got to bring up your family?'

'It will be a boon to you. Middle-aged women with nothing to do are one of the worst problems that face the modern psychologist.'

'But I've got far, far more to do than I can manage already.'

'Cocktail parties – trying on clothes – nothing to get your teeth into. You must try not to be so selfish. Think of poor Dawn, you really can't ask her to carry half the cradle like she used to. 'Chang has put on pounds and pounds and she doesn't feel very well.'

'Leave her here. I'd love to keep her. Then she can have her baby under proper conditions, poor duck.'

'I didn't marry Dawn in order to leave her. I need her company all the time.'

She now appeared with the World Citizen, making furious Chinese noises, in her arms. I thought she looked very frail.

'Dawnie, David has just told me he is on the move again. Why don't you stay comfortably here with little 'Chang and all of us, at any rate until after the baby?'

I had forgotten about the dumbness; her huge eyes projected their gaze on her husband's face and he spoke for her. 'You see she has no desire whatever to stay comfortably here. Dawn has never had such a bourgeois reaction in her life.'

I went to my bedroom and rang up Davey. I begged him to come and save the situation. He was uncooperative and unsympathetic; said that it was impossible for him to move for the present. 'My drawing-room curtains have gone wrong – much too short and skimpy. They must all be made again and I must be here to see to it. That's the sort of thing your Aunt Emily used to do – everything in the house was perfect when she was alive. I do hate being a widower; it really was too bad of her to die.'

'Davey, you haven't understood how serious it is about David.'

'My dear Fanny, I think you are being rather ungrateful to me. You asked me to get rid of him; he is going, is he not?'

'I know – but –'

'If he is going East and not West that is entirely your own fault for not insisting on Dr Jore. I told you that a psychiatrist was needed in conjunction with a physician. Docteur Lecœur strengthened his will-power by working on his glands and correcting his inertia. Dr Jore would have altered the trend of his thought. By rejecting Jore you abandoned him to the Zen Master – the Temple Bells are calling and the flying-fishes play. Another time perhaps you will allow me to know best.'

'I wouldn't mind so much if it weren't for Dawnie. I think he'll kill her, poor little thing.'

'Oh no he won't. Women are practically indestructible, you know.'

'Then think of Alfred and me beginning nurseries all over again. Chinese ones at that.'

'Very tiring for you,' said Davey. 'I must go now or I shall miss the Archers.' He rang off.

David and Dawn left that afternoon. The Rolls-Royce took them to Bar-le-Duc and only returned the next day. David had borrowed money from every single person in the Embassy; all, pitying the plight of Dawn and probably confident of being paid back by me (as of course they were), had produced as much as they had available. It amounted to quite a tidy sum. Mrs Trott found a solid peasant girl from Brittany to look after 'Chang.

'Hot news!' Northey said to Alfred. 'Faithful Amy has had orders from Lord Grumpy to give you treatment number one.'

'Oh, indeed?' Falsetto. 'And how does this differ from that which I have been receiving?'

'Differ? So far you have only had number three, watered down at that by precious Amy on account of loving us all so much.'

'He loves me?'

'Oh yes – he's always saying I like that man. He reveres you. It's very distressing for him to be obliged to write all these horrid and not quite true things about us here when he would give his eyes to be part of the family.'

'Part of the family? In what capacity, may I ask?'

'Perhaps you could adopt him?'

'Thank you. We've got 'Chang and the badger, I don't think we want any more pets.'

'Poor soul.'

FAILURE

It is no secret that Sir Alfred Wincham has proved a failure in Paris and that Whitehall now wishes to replace him with a more dynamic personality. Sir Alfred's well-known aptitude for university intrigue has not carried him very far along the twisting paths of French foreign policy. More professional talent, it is felt, is needed at a time when Anglo-French relations have never been worse.

FRIENDSHIP

In view of M. Bouche-Bontemps' old friendship with Lady Wincham's mother (first revealed in this column) French political circles feel that the Embassy has an unfortunate preference for his party, the L.U.N.A.I.R. Members of opposition parties are never received there any more. Sir Alfred is out of touch with French public opinion.

RANGOON

Well-informed circles are speculating on Sir Alfred's future, and rumour has it that he may shortly be posted to Rangoon.

Northey and Philip raced each other to my bedroom the morning these delightful paragraphs appeared. She dumped 'Chang on my bed. I always had him for a bit after breakfast and found him delightful company; a contented, healthy baby, easily amused and anxious to please. I thought, when I was with him, that his generation may be on the way to rejecting the anti-charm which is the fashion now, may even develop a sense of humour and seek to attract rather than repel. If my grandchild turned out to be half as nice as the World Citizen I would not be at all sorry to have the two of them for keeps.

'At last Mockbar has overreached himself,' Philip said. 'I think it's actionable; Alfred must speak to his lawyer and we might even get rid of him, who knows?'

'Then the poor little soul will starve,' said Northey.

'No matter.'

'Fanny, you brute. What about his babies?'

'They'll survive,' I said. 'Are Anglo-French relations really so bad, Philip?'

'That part I'm afraid is true. Not Alfred's fault (quite the contrary) but boiling up for a first-class crisis. We are determined to get those bloody islands and to help the Americans re-arm the Germans.'

'Seems mad, doesn't it?'

'Not if we really need them as allies.'

Northey said, 'I wish I knew why people want the Germans on their side. I have yet to hear of them winning a war.'

'They'd be all right with French generals.'

'I wish the whole thing could be settled. The Bourse is strongly disconcerted by all these elements.'

'You can't wish it more than I do,' said Philip.

'I must dree my weird. Shall I leave 'Chang? I've got a lot of work.'

'Yes, leave him. Your work has been very satisfactory of late; you're a good girl and I'm pleased with you.'

'It's the well-known cure for a broken heart,' she said with a tragic look at Philip.

'Go on,' he said, 'I like it.'

I asked her, 'Darling, what are you up to tonight?'

'Docteur Lecœur.'

'*Lecœur soupire la nuit le jour, qui peut me dire si c'est l'amour?*' said Philip.

'Yes, it is.'

'And I suppose,' he went on, 'that every time you pass the Palais Bourbon, the statues of Sully and l'Hôpital get up and bow to you?'

'Yes, they do. It's the English who don't appreciate me. Good-bye all.'

We looked at each other when she had gone, laughing. 'Northey!'

He said, 'The diplomatic hostesses here are furious with Mees because she has got Tony de Lambesc in tow – yes, Fanny – that small, fair chap one sees everywhere. They regard him and me as the only sortable bachelors in this town – we have to do all their dinner parties. There are hundreds of unattached Frenchmen who would like to be asked, but you know what those women are, too timid to try anybody new. They might have to deal with unexpected dialogue and that would never do. The conversation must run on familiar lines, according to some well-worn old formula. Suppose somebody mentions Prince Pierre – of course the correct move is, he simply worships his daughter-in-law! Now a stranger might say do you mean the explorer? or worse still, Prince Pierre in *War and Peace*? and the whole party would feel a wrong turn had been taken – they might even have to begin using their brains. That would never do. They like a gentle game of pat-ball and have no desire for clever young polytechnicians hitting boundaries. Lambesc and I know the right answers in our sleep. But now he's always either taking Mees out or hoping to. He waits till the last moment, praying she'll be chucked; it's no use asking him a week ahead. The only hope is to ring him up at half-past eight and get him to come round, disgruntled, there and then. It has upset social life dreadfully. Time Mees got married, that's what it is.'

'Yes, but to whom?'

'Who is there? Bouche-Bontemps is a bit old – that Chef de Cabinet (always forget his name) is too ugly – Cruas is said to be poor –'

'Would that matter?'

'With Mees? She would ruin a poor man in no time.'

'Does Cruas exist? I've still never seen him, have you?'

'Somebody has taught her French; she rattles away at a hundred miles an hour. Then Lecoeur is too busy – Charles-Edouard too much married (worse luck) – the Ambassador to the Channel Islands has a *fort des balles* he adores – Amyas now, what about him? An eligible widower –'

'I'm against,' I said, 'though I may be prejudiced.'

'Then there's Lambesc, but he has his scutcheon to gild.'

I said boldly, 'Why don't you marry her?'

'Well, you know, I might. In spite of the carry-on, I can't imagine life without Mees, now I'm used to her. I suppose she is the last of the charmers. The horsetail girls don't seem to be interested in any of the things I like, least of all sex. They join up with the Teds and the Beats and wander about Europe with them, sharing beds if it happens to suit; three in a bed if it's cheaper like that (shades of Sir Charles Dilke) and probably nothing happens! Sex is quite accidental. Is there a baby on the way or isn't there? They hardly seem to notice. Now Northey is a wicked little thing but at least she is out to please and my word how she succeeds!'

'She's not wicked at all. I even think she is virtuous.'

'Anyway, she's a human being. Very likely I shall end by proposing to her.'

'Only, Philip, don't leave it too long or she'll fall in love with somebody else, you know!'

20

Sir Harald Hardrada now came to give his lecture. It was very brilliant and a great success, Sir Harald being one of the few living Englishmen who, even the French allow, has a perfect mastery of their language. As they detest hearing it massacred and really do not like listening to any other, foreign lecturers are more often flattered than praised at the end of their performance (not that they know the difference). We all went to the Sorbonne where the lecture took place and then Mildred Jungfleisch gave a dinner party. The company was: Sir Harald, M. Bouche-Bontemps, the Valhuberts, the Hector Dexters, an American couple called Jorgmann, Philip and Northey, Alfred, and me. The Dexters had been given a clean bill by the State Department, to the enormous relief of their compatriots in Paris. Having had enough, it seemed, of political activities, Mr Dexter was now acting as liaison between leading French and American art dealers.

Mrs Jungfleisch lived in a cheery modernish (1920) house near the Bois de Boulogne. Its drawing-room, painted shiny white and without ornament of any sort, had an unnaturally high ceiling and stairs leading to a gallery; the effect was that of a swimming-bath. One felt that somebody might dive in at any moment, the Prime Minister of England, perhaps, or some smiling young candidate for the American throne. Almost the only piece of furniture was an enormous pouf in the middle of the room on which people had to sit with their backs to each other. As Americans do, she left a good hour between the arrival of the guests and the announcement of dinner, during which time Bourbon (a kind of whisky) could be imbibed.

Bouche-Bontemps had come to the lecture. He and Sir Harald were old friends. They now sat on the pouf, craning round to talk to each other.

'Excellent, my dear Harald! Nothing could have been more fiendishly clever than your account of Fashoda – you haven't got the K.C.V.O. for nothing! I very much liked the meeting between Kitchener and Marchand on the Argonne front – some time you must read the page from Kipling where he describes the naïf joy of the French poilus as they witnessed it. They thought the hatchet had been buried for ever and that if we won the war, *les Anglais* would become real friends and leave us our few remaining possessions. Never mind –'

'Like all the French,' Sir Harald said urbanely, to the company at large, who were twisting their necks to be in on this conversation. 'M. le Président has the work of our great Imperial protagonist by heart.'

'We defend ourselves as best we can,' said Bouche-Bontemps, 'poor Marchand, I knew him well.'

'Were you already living at Fashoda with the Bolter when he arrived?'

'No. Precocious as I may have been, at six months old I was still living with my parents.'

'You can't imagine how fascinated we all were to learn that the famous Frenchman in her life was none other than yourself. I had always pictured an old douanier with a beard and a wooden leg.'

'Not at all. A jolly young ethnographer. Dorothée – *tellement gentille* –'

'I'd no idea you had this African past, Jules. Whatever were you doing there?'

'In those days I was passionately fond of ethnography. I managed to get on to the Djibouti-Dakar mission.'

'Oh! You rogue! Everything is becoming as clear as daylight. So it was you who took away the Harar frescoes?'

'Took away? We exchanged them.'

'Yes. Kindly tell Mrs Jungfleisch here and her guests what it was you exchanged them for?'

'A good exchange is no robbery, I believe? Harar acquired some delightful wall-paintings in the early manner of your humble servant and the gifted mother of your ambassadress. Oh! How we were happy and busy, painting these enormous frescoes – perhaps the happiest days of my life. Everybody was so pleased – the Fuzzie-Wuzzies greatly preferred our bright and lively work to the musty old things which were there before.'

'We don't say Fuzzie-Wuzzies,' said Sir Harald.

'Indeed?'

'No. Like your foreign policy, all this is old-fashioned.'

'*Hélas!* I am old-fashioned, and old as well. *C'est la vie, n'est-ce pas, Mees?*'

'When are you going to fall again?' said Northey. '(Golly, my neck is aching!) We never see you, it's a bore.'

'With the assistance of the present company it should be any day. What are you preparing for us, Harald?'

Sir Harald became rather pink and looked guilty.

Hector Dexter, who had pricked up his ears at the word frescoes, said, 'And where are the Harar paintings now, M. le Président?'

'Safe in the cellars of the Louvre, thanks to me, where no human eye will ever behold them.'

'I have a client in the States who is interested in African art of unimpeachable provenance. Are there no more ancient frescoes at Harar or in its environs?'

'No,' said Sir Harald, 'the Frogs swiped the lot.'

'We don't say Frogs any more,' said Bouche-Bontemps, 'it's old-fashioned, like taking away other people's islands.'

There was a little silence. Ice clicked in the glasses, people swallowed, Mrs Jungfleisch handed round caviar. Sir Harald turned from Bouche-Bontemps to the opposite side of the pouf and said, 'Now, Geck, we want to hear all about Russia.'

Hector Dexter cleared his throat and intoned: 'My day-to-day experiences in the Union of Soviet Socialist Russia have been registered on a long-playing gramophone record to be issued free to all the members of the North Atlantic Treaty. This you will be able to obtain by indenting for a copy to your own ambassador to N.A.T.O. I was there, as you may know, for between nine and eight years, but after the very first week I came to the conclusion that the way of life of the Socialist Soviet citizen is not and never could be acceptable to one who has had cognizance of the American way of life. Then it took me between nine and eight years to find some way of leaving the country by which I could safely bring Carolyn here and young Foster with me. It became all the more important for me to get out because my son Foster, aged now fifteen, is only ten points below genius and this genius would have been unavailing and supervacaneous, in other words wasted, behind the Iron Curtain.'

'Why? There can't be so many geniuses there?'

'There is this out-of-date, non-forward-looking view of life. They have not realized the vast potentialities, the enormous untapped wealth of the world of Art. They have this fixation on literature; they do not seem to realize that the written word has had its day – books are a completely outworn concept. We in America, one step ahead of you in Western Europe, have given up buying them altogether. You would never see a woman, or a man, reading a book in the New York subway. Now in the Moscow subway every person is doing so.'

'That's bad, Heck,' said Mr Jorgmann, heavily.

'Why is it bad?' I asked.

'Because books do not carry advertisements. The public of a great modern industrial state ought to be reading magazines or watching television. The Russians are not contemporary; they are not realist; they exude a fusty aroma of the past.'

'So young Foster is going into Art?'

'Yes, Sir. By the time my boy is twenty-one, I intend he shall recognize with unerring certainty the attribution of any paint on any canvas (or wood or plaster), the marks of every known make of porcelain and every known maker of silver, the factory from which every carpet and every tapestry –'

'In short,' said Sir Harald, 'he'll be able to tell the difference between Rouault and Ford Madox Brown.'

'Not only that. I wish him to learn the art trade from the beginning to the end; he must learn to clean and crate and pack the object as well as to discover it and purchase it and resell it. From flea-market to Jayne Wrightsman's boudoir, if I may so express myself.'

'I should have thought that sort of talent could have been used in the Winter Palace?'

'There is too much prejudice against the West. The Russians do not possess correct attitudes. It was an unpleasant experience to discuss with individuals whose thinking is so lacking in objectivity that one was aware it was emotively determined and could be changed only by change of attitude. Besides, hypotheses, theories, ideas, generalizations, awareness of the existence of unanswered and/or unanswerable queries do not form part of their equipment. So such mental relationships as Carolyn here and I and young Foster Dexter were able to entertain with the citizens of Soviet Socialist Russia were very, very highly unsatisfactory.'

'But, Geek,' said naughty Sir Harald (I remembered that the Russian alphabet has no H), 'one doesn't want to say I told you so – not that I did, only any of us could have if you'd asked our advice – why on earth did you go?'

'When I first got back here some four or three weeks since, I could have found that question difficult, if not impossible, to answer. However, as soon as I arrived here in Paris I put myself in the hands of a brilliant young doctor, recommended to me by Mildred: Dr Jore. I go to him every evening when he has finished with the Supreme Commander. Now Dr Jore very, very swiftly diagnosed my disorder. It seems that at the time when I left this country some nine or eight years ago I was suffering from a Pull to the East which, in my case, was so overwhelmingly powerful that no human person could have resisted it. As soon as Dr Jore sent his report to the State Department they entirely exonerated me from any suspicion of anti-American procedure, deviation from rectitude, improbity, trimming or what have you and recognized that I was, at the time when I turned my back on the West, a very, very sick man.'

'Poor old Heck,' said the Jorgmanns.

'Another Bourbon?' said Mrs Jungfleisch.

'Thank you. On the rocks.'

Sir Harald asked, 'And how does he set about curing a Pull to the East?'

'In my case, of course, I have already undergone the most efficacious cure, which is a long sojourn there. But we must prevent any recurrence of the disease. Well, the doc's treatment is this. I lie on his couch and I shut my eyes and I force myself to see New York Harbour, the Empire State building, Wall Street, Fifth Avenue and Bonwit Teller. Then very, very slowly I swivel my mental gaze until it alights on the Statue of Liberty. All this time Dr Jore and I, very, very softly, in unison, recite the Gettysburg Address. "Four score and seven years ago our fathers –"'

'Yes, yes,' said Sir Harald, almost rudely, I thought, breaking in on Mr Dexter's fervent interpretation. 'Very fine, but we all know it. It's in the *Oxford Book of Quotations.*'

Mr Dexter looked hurt; there was a little silence. Philip said, 'Did you see anything of Guy and Donald?'

'When Guy Burgess and Donald Maclean first arrived we all shared a dacha. I cannot say it was a very happy association. They did not behave as courteously to me as they ought to have. The looked-for Anglo-Saxon solidarity was not in evidence. They hardly listened to the analysis of the situation, as noted and recounted by me, in Socialist Soviet Russia; they laughed where no laughter was called for; they even seemed to shun my company. Now I am not very conversant with the circumstances of their departure from the Western camp, but I am inclined to think it was motivated by pure treachery. I am not overfond of traitors.'

'And how did you get away?'

'In the end very easily. After nine or eight years in the U.S.S.R., the Presidium having acquired a perfect confidence in my integrity, I was able to induce them to send me on a fact-finding mission. On arrival here, as I explained to them, the accompaniment of wife and son lending a permanent appearance to my reintegration in the Western Camp, I would easily persuade my compatriots that I had abandoned all tendency to communism. When their trust in me was completely re-established, I would be in a position to send back a great deal of information, of the kind I knew they wanted, to the Kremlin.'

'*Nom de nom!*' said Valhubert.

Bouche-Bontemps shook with laughter: '*C'est excellent!*'

Alfred and Philip exchanged looks.

The Jorgmanns exclaimed, 'That was smart of you, Heck!' Mrs Jungfleisch said, 'And now don't you want to go and dine?'

We all stood up and, like so many geese, stretched our necks. That hour on the pouf had been absolute agony.

The day after Sir Harald's lecture, Alfred had to communicate a very stiff note indeed to the Quai d'Orsay on the subject of the Îles Minquiers. The French were invited immediately to abandon their claim to these islands which, said the Note, was quite untenable, against their own interests, and was undermining the Western Alliance. Simultaneously an anti-French campaign of unprecedented violence was launched in London. Bludgeon and pin were brought into play. Dr Niam duly paid his official visit which was reported in a manner calculated to infuriate the French. Bouche-Bontemps was rudely taken to task in Parliament and the newspapers for the criminal obstinacy with which he was refusing to make a united Europe. At U.N.O. the English voted against the French on an important issue. After these bludgeonings came the pinpricks. The newspapers said that Spanish champagne was better than the real sort. Tourists were advised to go to Germany or Greece and to miss out expensive France. Women were urged to buy their clothes in Dublin or Rome. Several leading critics discovered that Françoise Sagan had less talent than one had thought.

When some softening up on these lines had been delivered the campaign settled down to its real objective, the Îles Minquiers. Facts and figures were trotted out, heads were shaken over them and judgement severely passed. It transpired that after a thousand years of French administration, the islands had no roads, no post office, no public services. They sent no representative to Paris; there was no insurance against old age; the children were not given vitamins or immunized against diphtheria; there was no cultural life. The fact that there were no inhabitants either was, of course, never stated. The kind-hearted English public was distressed by all these disclosures. As a gesture of solidarity with the islands, an expedition was organized to go and build a health centre on the Île Maîtresse (Grandad cashed in on this). The Ambulating Raiments were immediately dispatched there. These baleful bales are full of ghastly old clothes collected at the time of the Dutch floods. Since then they have been round the world over and over again, bringing comfort to the tornadoed, the scorched, the shaken, the stateless, the volcanoed, the interned, the famished, the parched, the tidal-waved; any communities suffering from extreme bad luck or bad management are eligible for the Raiments, which are so excellently organized that they arrive on the scene almost before the disaster has occurred. There is a tacit understanding that they are never to be undone, indeed nobody, however great their want, would dare to risk the vermin and disease which must fly out from them as from Pandora's Box. The recipients take their presence as a sort of lucky sign or sympathetic visiting card. (It is only fair to say that in cases of great distress the Raiments are often followed up by a gift of money.) There was just time to have the bundles photographed, at low tide, on the rocks of the Île Maîtresse before they had to be dispatched to Oakland, California, where a gigantic fire had wiped out acres of skyscrapers.

The French sharply resented all these insults. Their press and wireless, which are at least as clever as ours when it comes to throwing vitriol, now revealed terrifying depths of hatred for their old crony over the way. M. Bouche-Bontemps' government, given up for lost, came unscathed through a debate on vegetables out of season which in normal times would have annihilated it. None of the opposition parties wanted to take over in the middle of such a crisis. When the full perfidy of Albion had been exposed for a few days, French opinion was stirred, flickered, then blazed into fury. Individual citizens began to give expression to the public feeling. The shop called Old England was rechristened New England. The windows of W. H. Smith were smashed. English decorations and medals, signed photographs of King Edward VII and Northey's kittens were deposited at the Embassy accompanied by disagreeable messages. Anglo-French sporting events were called off. Import licences for Christmas puddings were withheld. Grace was beside herself, of course. She announced that she was going to empty the English blood from her veins and have them refilled from the blood bank of the VIIth arrondissement.

Alfred sent an alarmed report to the Foreign Office but was told that these waves of ill feeling come and go and are not to be taken seriously. Philip, however, said that he had never seen the two old ladies so cross with each other.

21

At no season does Paris look more beautiful than early in December. There is a curious light, particular to the Île de France and faithfully interpreted by the painter Michel, which brings out all shades, from primrose to navy blue, implicit in the beige and grey of the landscape and buildings. The river becomes a steely flood which matches the huge clouds rolling overhead. As this is not, like harvest time or the first warm days of spring, one of those seasons that induce an almost animal craving for field and forest, you can sit by the fire, look out of the window and peacefully enjoy the prospect. I was doing exactly this in the Salon Vert one afternoon, reflecting with satisfaction that for the rest of that week we had no social engagements (they had fallen off notably of late). I had been writing to Aunt Sadie, to give her news of us all, specially of her granddaughter Northey, my pen was poised while I searched for some little titbit to end up with.

I became conscious of a clamour outside, an unidentified noise which had perhaps been going on for some time, heard by my ears but not realized by my brain. I went over to the window, looked down at the garden and was very much startled by what I saw there. A large crowd was stamping about on the lawn, pushed forward by an ever-increasing multitude milling in from the Avenue Gabriel; between it and the house, like idle maids flicking dusters, a few policemen were half-heartedly manipulating their capes. For the moment they were holding the crowd in check; one felt that a really determined push would easily submerge them. When the fishwives surged into Versailles, the Queen's first instinct was to find her husband; so, now, was mine. Like Louis XVI on the same occasion, Alfred was frantically looking for me. We wasted several minutes missing each other in the huge house; I ran through to the Chancery – he had left it; he found the Salon Vert empty; finally we met in Northey's office off the anteroom at the top of the stairs.

'Go to the nursery, darling,' I was telling her, 'and fetch 'Chang. There's a riot or something in the garden. We'd better all stay together.'

Alfred said, 'The French have had enough and I don't altogether blame them. I wrote in my last dispatch that it would end like this; now it has. Not a bad thing perhaps, it will shake both the governments into seeing sense. Meanwhile I hope these hooligans will bear in mind that the person of an Ambassador is sacred and the territory of an Embassy inviolable.'

'They haven't remembered about the territory. They are completely ruining all our nice new shrubs – just come and see.'

We went back to the Salon Vert and looked out at the rioters.

'I shall lodge a complaint. The police force is inadequate, in my view. What are they shouting? It sounds like a slogan.'

'Listen – no, I can't make it out.' They seemed to be shouting two words and stamping in unison.

Philip ran in, breathless, having come from his own flat. 'The Faubourg is full of demonstrators,' he said. 'Good Lord – the garden too! We are completely surrounded in other words. They are shouting *"Minquiers Français"*, do you hear?'

'That's it, of course,' said Alfred. '*Minquiers Français, Minquiers Français*. I only hope this will show the Foreign Office there are limits of ineptitude beyond which they should not go. Another time perhaps they will listen to the man on the spot.'

I said, 'They are nearly up to the veranda now – ought you not to let Bouche-Bontemps know?'

'All in good time,' said Alfred, 'no need to panic. We are his responsibility.'

Northey appeared, 'Chang in her arms, grumbling about her badger.

'Pity we can't all be safely down there with him,' I said.

'I've just had a word with B.B.,' said Northey, 'he is the absolute, utter limit. Shrieking with laughter if you please. He says we may have to stand a long siege and he hopes we've got plenty of Spanish champagne. He can't get the police to do much, he says, it's only a crowd of children.'

'Yes, they do look young – I was thinking that. Why should these boys and girls mind about the Îles Minquiers?'

'Agitators. You can work up a crowd on any subject.'

'B.B. is delighted. He says the teenagers here are supposed to think of nothing but jazz – look at them now! Riddled with patriotism.'

'So he's not going to rescue us?'

'Not he!'

'Then who will? What about N.A.T.O?'

'We only know one thing for certain about N.A.T.O. – it can't get a force into the field in less than six weeks.'

'Anyhow,' said Philip, 'this is the Supreme Commander's time for Dr Jore – nobody's allowed to interrupt them, they'll be in full flood of Gettysburg at this very minute – can't you hear it? "Foor-scoor and savan eers ago oor faethers brourt fourth –"'

'Don't tell me the Supreme Commander has a Pull to the East?'

'Of course. All Dr Jore's patients have.'

Alfred said, 'You must try and check this latent anti-Americanism, Philip – I've already spoken to you about it.'

'Yes, sir.'

'Now I'm going to the Chancery to do some telephoning. You take Northey and Fanny to your flat, will you? The rioters can come through the veranda any minute, those feeble policemen aren't going to stop them.'

'*Minquiers Français – Minquiers Français –*' rose ever more insistent from the garden.

'I do wish they would leave off stamping, they are ruining the lawn.'

'The French government will be obliged to make good any damage.'

'Come on,' said Philip. 'Alfred's quite right, you'll be better over there. Besides, I want to see what's happening in the Faubourg.'

We crossed the courtyard, went into Philip's flat and looked out of his dining-room window at the street which was jammed as far as the eye could see with young people stamping and shouting '*Minquiers Français*'. I was glad to notice quite a large force of policemen looking, I thought, very much amused, but keeping the crowd away from our gate and exhibiting more authority than those in the garden.

'Oh do look!' said Northey. 'There's good little Amy – the brave soul.'

'I don't see him?'

'Yes, in the ancient bibelot shop, pretending to be a Dresden figure.' She leant out of the window and waved at Mockbar who looked sheepish and seemed not to see her. Then she shouted '*Aimée!*' whereupon he began scribbling in his note-book.

'He's ashamed of you,' said Phillip. 'Anyway I'm glad to see he's on the job all right. For once we need all the publicity we can get; it's the only way to stop this silly bickering – give Bouche-Bontemps and our Foreign Minister a bit of a jolt. They don't want actual war, one supposes.'

'Can't see that it's B.B.'s fault.'

'He'd much better let the thing go to The Hague and be settled once for all.'

Suddenly the shouting and stamping and clapping subsided and a rather sinister silence fell on the crowd. Philip said, anxiously, 'Don't like this much, I hope they're not waiting for a signal.'

Almost as he spoke, the crowd came violently, terrifyingly to life. It surged in the narrow street as if it must burst apart the houses; the slogan took on a blood-curdling note. 'Chang began to scream at the top of his voice; the din was deafening. The police now joined hands and forced the rioters away from the entrance to our courtyard; to my horror I saw that the huge wooden gates were slowly opening.

'Look,' said Northey, 'the gates – a traitor – !'

'Good Lord,' said Philip and made as though to go downstairs.

'Don't leave us –' I was frightened for the baby who might so easily be hurt if the mob poured in and overwhelmed us. I looked out again. The police seemed to be in control. In the middle of the screaming crowd a London taxi, escorted by policemen, was crawling up the street. It was driven by Payne; Uncle Matthew, deeply interested, craned from the window; on its roof, dressed from head to foot in shiny black plastic material, were our boys, Fabrice and Charlie, with another boy, a stranger to me, dressed in shiny white. This child was waving a guitar at the crowd as though he thought the screams and shrieks were meant for him. The more the people cried *Minquiers Français* the more he grinned and waved in acknow-ledgement. With a superhuman effort, the police cleared a passage for the taxi, got it into the courtyard and shut the gates behind it. We all ran downstairs.

Uncle Matthew was being helped out of the cab by Charlie and Fabrice. The other boy was fidgeting about, snapping his fingers. He looked cross and impatient.

'Excitable lot, these foreigners,' said my uncle, 'how are you, Fanny? Here are your spawn, safe and sound thanks to Payne. We found them in the aeroplane or at least they found me, I didn't know them from Adam of course. They recognized me and hopped into the cab. Do you know, we flew it over – now your stepfather thought of that, very competent fellow.'

'This is Yanky Fonzy, Mum,' said Fabrice, indicating the third lad. He was an unprepossessing hobbledehoy, with pasty face, sloppy look about the mouth and hair done like Queen Alexandra's after the typhoid. 'Didn't the kids give him a wonderful reception – you heard them screaming, "Yanky Fonzy, Yanky Fonzy"? It's never been like this in London.'

'D'you mean that terrifying riot was all about him?' I said.

'It only was a riot of enthusiasm,' said the youth. 'The kids are never nasty or out for manslaughter. They buy my discs and support me. Why are they shut away from here? Where can I go and wave to them? Why are the arrangements breaking down? Where's my French agent?' He fired these questions at each of us in turn, snapping his fingers. He seemed in a thoroughly bad humour.

This curious new light having been thrown on the situation, Philip burst into a loud laugh and went into the house, no doubt, I supposed, to find Alfred.

'He's not much to look at,' said Uncle Matthew, indicating Mr Fonzy, 'and his clothes would frighten the birds, but I'm bound to tell you he whacks merry hell out of that guitar. We had tunes the whole way here.'

I took Charles by the arm and led him out of earshot of the others. 'Just tell me what this means? Your packing job – have you left it?'

'Definitely. Chucked it.'

'Tell me truthfully, Charlie, you haven't been nicking shavers?'

'Oh no, Mum, hardly at all. But even you wouldn't want us to go on packing for the rest of our lives? It turned out to be rather ghoulish and there's no future in it whatever. No, we've moved on. We're in the Showbiz now where there are fortunes to be picked up. Actually we are Yanky's publicity agents. Grandad arranged it for us – he's a smashing old forebear! It was he who thought of arriving like that with the weirdie in the taxi – oh boy, what a gimmick! Yank's Continental debew has started with a real explosion, hasn't it? – there must be thousands of kids round this dump.'

Fabrice came over to us. 'I say, Mum, the kiddos are yearning for Yank, you know. They may easily turn ghoulish if you keep him shut up in this yard for ever.'

'Definitely,' said Charles.

'But how did they know he was coming?'

'That's all done by Sigi, our Paris agent. First-class organization!'

The hobbledehoy was now behaving like a prima donna.

'Where can I go and be with my fans? What's happening here? They'll turn dangerous if they don't see me soon. I say, you kids, something has gone wrong. Please send me my Paris agent at once.'

'Here I am.' Sigi appeared out of the blue.

'Well done, Sigi,' said Fabrice, 'jolly spiffing show.'

'So far,' said Yanky, 'but we must keep up the tempo. Where are the kids now? I want to be with them.'

'They've all gone round to the other side of the house,' said Sigi. 'There's a huge garden and a balcony where you can do your act. I've just been rigging up the mike. Come on, no time to waste. Excuse us,' he said to me, ever polite, kissing my hand, 'but if they don't see him soon they will rush the place.' He ran into the house, followed by the other boys.

I turned to Uncle Matthew, feeling I had not made enough fuss of him in all the commotion. 'How d'you do, Payne?'

'Payne's just had a word with your porter,' said Uncle Matthew, 'it seems the street is clear now so I think we'll be on our way. I never meant to bother you at all – Paris isn't on our itinerary – we came here to oblige those boys.'

'Now you are here, do stay. Where are you off to, anyhow?'

'Ypres,' said my uncle. 'Payne and I thought we'd like to see old Wipers again. A fellow in the House told me there's a sector they've preserved exactly as it was. We had the time of our lives in those trenches when we were young, didn't we, Payne?'

'To tell the truth, m'lord, I'd just as soon see them in present circumstances.'

'Nonsense! It will all seem very dull, though better than nothing no doubt.'

'But there's no hurry, is there? Don't go yet. Now you are here, stay for a few days.'

'Oh my dear child, but where?'

'Here, with us, of course.'

'You haven't got room?'

'Darling Uncle Matthew – in that enormous house? Jérôme, our chauffeur, will show Payne where to put the cab and fill it up and everything.'

'Well, that's very civil of you, Fanny. I do feel rather tired. Will there be a cocktail party?'

'Yes, indeed, nearly every evening. I know we've got some people coming presently.'

Uncle Matthew gave me a superior look, saying, 'I thought you'd find out about them sooner or later. Well, that's splendid. If I could see my room I'll go and sit down for a few minutes, then I'll be ready for anything.'

'Take your grandfather up in the lift,' I said to Northey. 'I think we'll give him the Violet Room. Then will you send Jérôme out to look after Payne, please? I must go and see what those boys are up to.'

On the stairs I was overtaken by Philip. 'That unspeakable Sigi,' he said.

'Where's Alfred?'

'He's gone to the Quai to complain – he went out by the Chancery as soon as the street began to clear. Now listen, Fanny –'

'Yes, but hurry. I must go and stop it all –'

'This is very important though. Don't tell Alfred. I don't believe those journalists in the Faubourg have understood – I hope that at this very moment they are whizzing back stories of a riot about the Minquiers. Alfred has already informed the F.O. If we can keep up the fiction, this so-called riot will have a splendid effect. Both sides will feel they have gone too far and there'll be a beautiful reconciliation.'

'That would be perfect but I'm afraid it's too good to be likely. They are all in the garden still, according to Sigi.'

'Yes, they are, I've just been through to have a look. The boy is crooning and the fans are swooning and so on. But the only people there who look like journalists all belong to jazz papers – they won't get anything into the general news and they don't even know that they are in the Embassy garden. Now I'm off to the Crillon to see the press boys there. So sealed lips, eh? – and shoo Yanky off, that's your job.'

'Yes, indeed. But Philip – you'll have to square Mees or good little Amy will know all. She's taken 'Chang to the nursery I think.'

'Right, I'll do that first.'

I ran on up to the yellow drawing-room where I found the boys making a perfect exhibition of themselves. The French windows were wide open; on the little balcony Yank Fonzy was bellowing into a microphone; behind him on the parquet my boys and Sigi were stamping and clapping while the huge crowd of children in the garden had lost all control. The scene was vividly evoked afterwards in *Le Discophile* and I cannot do better than to quote: '*L'atmosphère fut indescriptible. Ce jazz-man chanta avec une passion qui n'appartient qu'aux grands prédicateurs. On dansait, on entrait en transes, on se roulait au sol tout comme les convulsionaires de Saint Médard. Le gazon était lacéré, les arbustes déchiquetés – affligeant spectacle.'*

I pounced forward and very crossly dragged Master Yanky back into the room, then I disconnected the microphone and slammed the windows on the afflicting spectacle. He was so much surprised at this unaccustomed behaviour that he put up no resistance; in any case his body felt as if it were made of dough. Sigi opened the windows again, went on to the balcony and shouted, '*Tous au Vél d'Hiv*': a cry which was taken up by the crowd and had the effect of clearing the garden. Chanting '*Yanky Fonzy – Yanky Fonzy*' the fans made off in the direction of the river.

'I'm sorry, Madame l'Ambassadrice,' ever polite, 'but it was the best way to get rid of them.'

'And what next?' I said. I was almost too angry with Sigismond to be able to speak to him, but it must be said that he was the only one of the boys in control of himself. The others were still rolling and stamping about like poor mad things, well and truly sent.

'Please don't worry at all, we are going now. I'll take Yanky, Charlie and Fabrice to the Club to meet the Duke. After that we're joining up with the kids at the Vélodrome d'Hiver, where there is the great Yanky Fonzy Pop Session you have no doubt seen advertised on all the kiosks.'

'The Club? The Duke?' I had a horrid vision of Yanky in white leather and my boys in black leather bursting in on the Duc de Romanville at the Jockey Club.

'Le Pop Club de France. We've got a rendezvous with Duke Ellington there.'

'Now listen to me, Sigi, I'm not going to have that boy to stay.'

'No, no.' Sigi laughed inwardly, reminding me of his father. 'He has got the honeymoon suite at the George V. I went there to see that everything was all right, which is why I was a bit late. You can't imagine what the flowers and chocolates are like. I managed to nick some and gave them to the concierge for you.'

'Too good of you. And now be off, I beg, and don't use this house any more for your disreputable activities.'

'Count on me, Madame l'Ambassadrice,' he said, with his annoying politeness.

22

As six o'clock struck, a remarkable demonstration of English punctuality occurred in the Salon Vert. Uncle Matthew stood at the ready by the fireplace, while a procession, of a sort very familiar to me by now, came across the Salon Jaune. Few days ever passed without this sort of influx. First there was Brown, the butler. Two fine, upstanding men, older than they looked, as could be seen by grey flecks in the hair, but without a line on their faces or, obviously, a care in the world, marched close on his heels. Conservatives I knew they were, from one or other of the Houses of Parliament. Two elderly wives panted and limped after them in an effort to keep up, one arm weighed down by those heavy bags which Conservative women affect and in which they conserve an extraordinary accumulation of rubbish and an extraordinarily small amount of cash. Two or three boys, of a demeanour already described, which proclaimed that they had but recently left Eton, trailed along behind them, then two or three pretty, cheerful, elegant schoolgirls who seemed to view their relations rather objectively. They were probably about to be confided to 'families' and I would be asked to keep an eye on them. They looked, and no doubt were, ready for anything and I only hoped that I should not be held responsible when anything overtook them.

Simultaneously Alfred, whom I had not seen since the riot, came through the door which led to his own room and library. I had just time to say, 'Alfred, here's Uncle Matthew who has come for a few days. Imagine, he has brought our two little boys – they all arrived in the middle of the excitement!' when the Conservative wives, breaking into a rapid hobble, managed to catch up with Brown and precede their husbands through the double doors.

'We've brought the whole family!' Loud English voices, familiar since all time. 'Thought you wouldn't mind! Let me see now, I don't think you know my sister-in-law, do you?'

I didn't think I knew any of them, though on the telephone, when they had asked to come, there had been something about having met at Montdore House in the old days; I tried to look welcoming but I was dying for a word with Alfred. 'What would you like to drink?'

'My dear! Liquid fire if you've got it! Vodka – just the very thing! We are utterly, completely, and absolutely whacked! Well, the shops all the morning, only to have a look of course – the prices! Then luncheon, that set us back considerably. Then we went to see Myrtle's Madarm – now here's the name (you know, I couldn't remember it yesterday on the telephone).' Delving among the alluvial deposits in the bag and bringing out a crumpled piece of paper. 'Comtesse de Langalluire – that's a tongue-twister if ever there was one! You've never heard of her? I say, I only hope there's nothing fishy. The flat (Boulevard Haussmann) is none too clean and when we arrived Madarm had gone to the police; one of the girls had escaped.'

'No, Mum, she hadn't escaped at all in the end. You know quite well, she'd only gone out to lunch and forgotten to say.'

'So we saw the Monsewer – a sinister little hunchback.'

'The concierge was sweet.' Myrtle was evidently determined to be confided to Madarm whatever happened.

'There was a son who looked quite idiotic and rather frightening.'

'Yes, but I shan't see anything of him as I'll be out all day at the Sorbonne.'

'However, when Madarm herself arrived we thought she seemed rather nice.'

'She had a crew cut,' said one of the boys.

'Her face was sensible, I thought.'

While all this was going on, the Conservative husbands were expressing amazement at finding Uncle Matthew, whom they knew quite well but who clearly did not know them from Adam.

'This is Lord Alconleigh, Peggy.'

'How d'you do? I'm a great friend of Jennifer's.'

'For pity's sake! What on earth do you see in her?'

'It seems you had a spot of trouble here this afternoon?' the other M.P. was saying to Alfred.

'No harm was done; personally I think it will have a good result. Both sides will have to be more conciliatory – both have been to blame. This may clear the air.'

'Can't see the point of making bad blood over those islands, myself. Massigli tells me they are submerged most of the time.'

'There has never been a more pointless quarrel,' said Alfred, firmly. 'Now I hope the question will be sent up to The Hague and that we shall hear no more about it.'

When everybody was happily chattering, Alfred murmured to me, 'Did you say Charlie and Fabrice are here?'

'Uncle Matthew brought them.'

'How splendid of the old boy. Where are they now?'

'Gone to a concert, with Sigi.'

'Good. That's very good news. Now we must take serious steps – get them into a lycée if we can –'

Brown reappeared, announcing 'Madame la Duchesse de Sauveterre and Monsieur le Marquis de Valhubert.'

'We've just heard about your riot,' said Charles-Edouard, 'we called to see if you were alive. When the concierge said you were at home we came up. Tante Odile is in Paris for a few days.'

'How kind you are.' I was frantic inside because of not knowing what names to put to the loud Conservative voices. To my relief, Alfred did the introducing. When he got to Uncle Matthew, I said, 'My uncle saw more of the riot than any of us because he arrived when it was at its worst and drove through the thick of it, escorted by policemen –'

'I call that very brave,' said an M.P.

'My dear fellow, they were a perfectly harmless lot – just a pack of children. I didn't think much of it – if that's the best they can put on –'

'Never underestimate a French crowd,' said the Duchess. 'I speak with knowledge. Three of my grandmothers perished in the Terror.'

'Three!' said Uncle Matthew, much interested. 'Did you have three grandfathers as well? What happened to them?'

'We say grandmothers when we mean ancestresses,' Charles-Edouard explained.

The Duchess said, 'Oh, various things. One of them was murdered in the Jacquerie, and the best housemaid I ever had was shot dead in the Stavisky riots. So don't talk to me of a French crowd being harmless.'

Uncle Matthew seemed to be struggling to remember something and came out with, 'Joan of Arc – didn't she have a sticky end? I suppose she was a relation of yours?'

'Certainly, if she was a d'Orléans, as most people think nowadays.'

'Really?' said Charles-Edouard, with his inward laugh. 'Why do they?'

'*Voyons, mon cher! La Pucelle d'Orléans!* Did she not sit at the King's table? That simple fact alone is all the proof I need. For a woman who was not born to sit at the table of a King of France would be a greater miracle than any voices, let me tell you.'

'My aunt takes no account of historical characters unless they happen to be relations of hers. Luckily they nearly all are. Charles X was a great-grandfather so that arranges the legitimate royal lines of every country except Russia, while her Murat grandmother brings in Napoleon and the Marshals.'

Madame de Sauveterre asked Alfred to show her his library which had been redecorated during the time of Sir Louis Leone. She said she had seen coloured photographs of it in a magazine which Jacques Oudineau had brought down to Boisdormant. 'He knows I like picture papers so he brings me all the ones he has finished with when he comes to see his father. You wouldn't believe how extravagant he is – *abonné* to everything under the sun and you know the price they are nowadays. People are getting much too rich, it can't be a good thing.'

'I want to see Jacques Oudineau,' said Charles-Edouard. 'I hear he has got a Moreau l'aîné he wouldn't mind selling –'

Uncle Matthew began telling the Conservatives about Yanky. 'Teenage Beats,' I heard him say. 'You must remember the name, Yanky Fonzy, and ask for his records because he gets money for every one they sell. Of course, I'm not saying he's Galli-Curci –'

I took Valhubert by the arm. 'I must have a word with you.' In a loud voice I added, 'Come in here, the National Gallery has sent us a large, dull picture and I want you to advise me where to hang it.' We went into the yellow drawing-room. 'Have you seen Grace this evening?'

'Not yet. When we got back from the country my concierge said there had been this riot so I drove straight on here to see what it was all about.'

I told him everything. He shook with laughter, especially when I got to the Club and the Duke. 'But my dear Fanny, what now? What does Alfred say?'

'You do realize we must never tell him about the riot not being real. He would look the most awful fool if it got out – I haven't told Grace by the way –'

'No, better not. Pity to spoil her fun – an anti-English riot is just her affair – she must be thrilled!'

'She is naughty! Philip says if we can keep up the fiction there's some hope of making them all see sense. As for the boys, Alfred doesn't know the full horror. When these people have gone I shall have to explain about Yanky and the Showbiz. Oh, Charles-Edouard, *children!*'

'Don't worry. They'll soon be off our hands, in prison.'

'Here's Philip, oh good. So what's up?'

'It's wonderful. I've been with the press boys ever since I saw you. The best hoax of all time. Simply nobody has twigged. The stories will be amazing, you'll see.'

The newspapers played up exactly as Philip had hoped they would. The reputable ones stated, quite soberly, correctly as far as it went, that several hundred students had gathered outside the British Embassy shouting slogans and that after about half an hour they had dispersed of their own accord. These reports were accompanied by editorial comment to the effect that if there was a serious misunderstanding between France and England it was time that it should be cleared up. Perhaps the English had not used the most tactful of methods in pressing their rightful claim to the Minquiers Islands. No doubt it had been necessary to entertain Dr Niam (now in Pekin) but the timing of his visit had been unfortunate. As for the European Army, while we in England realized its desirability and inevitability, we had not shown much comprehension of French difficulties in this respect. All in all, we should do well to keep in with our friends since our enemies were legion. The French papers were even more conciliatory, digging into the history of the

Entente and saying that so solid an edifice was not to be shaken by a few students exhibiting bad manners.

The Grumpy group reported the affair in their own inimitable style:

According to Mockbar, a fearful mob, baying for British blood, had milled in the Faubourg utterly uncontrolled by the police who looked as if they would join in for tuppence. It reminded him of the worst days of the Commune. No mention of sheltering among the ancient bibelots; heroic Mockbar had swayed to and fro in the thick of young devils who, had they guessed he was a Briton, would have scuppered him then and there. While, inside the Embassy, women wailed and babies wept ('That's you and 'Chang, Northey,' I said), the Ambassador had escaped by a back door and taken shelter at the Quai d'Orsay. His First Secretary was drinking at the bar of a nearby hotel.

Lord Grumpy's editorial said: British lives are threatened, British property is menaced. Where? Behind the Iron Curtain? In barbarous lands across the seas? Not at all. These things occurred in Paris. How did our Ambassador the Pastoral Theologian respond to the outrage? Was he at his post? We think there should be a full inquiry into the events of this black day in the history of British diplomacy. If Sir Alfred Wincham has failed to do his duty, he should go.

Lord Grumpy's remarks, as usual, gave much pleasure. They were read with delight and absolutely unheeded by several million Englishmen. Later in the week, Alfred went home to report on the, now vastly improved, situation and to see, with the Foreign Office experts, what could be done to re-establish the Entente. This was made easier by the fact that Junior across the Atlantic was annoying Mother and Auntie with behaviour learnt, it must be said, at their knees. Under a cunning pretext of anti-colonialism, the Americans were scooping up trade in a part of the world where hitherto French and English interests had been paramount. The quarrel over the Eels began to look silly; as soon as the newspapers had lost interest in them and gone on to more important subjects, the dispute was quietly submitted to The Hague Court where the islands were judged to belong to England. In harmony with the spirit of the age, we then granted them full independence.

During the Anglo-French honeymoon which now began, Basil disembarked his atom marchers at Calais. They were all in fancy dress, the men in kilts, the women in trousers; the weather was clear and sparkling and not too cold; the whole expedition was permeated from the start with a holiday atmosphere. Since atom objectors do not exist in France, literally the only public matter on which all Frenchmen are united being the desirability of a Bomb of one's own, the French immediately assumed that the march was a congratulatory gesture to unite Aldermaston with Saclay. The word *jumelage* was freely used by the newspapers; the two establishments were henceforward twin sisters, friends for ever. When the Britons got off their boat they were met with flowers, flags, speeches and wine; from the moment they landed they hardly drew a sober breath. None of them knew any French so, cleverly prompted by Basil, they concluded that the reception meant that the whole population felt as they did; in a joyful Kermesse they danced rather than marched across Normandy. They were not allowed to pay for a meal, a drink or a bed; Basil and his Grandad, who had extorted huge sums for the all-in trip, garnered a rich profit. At Saclay the Atom Minister himself, sent by Northey, was there to greet them. There were more flowers, more flags, stronger wine and longer speeches. The Britons were cordially invited to go to the Sahara and witness the first French atomic explosion whenever it should take place. In a happy haze of drunken misapprehension, they were then driven in official motors, with a circus turn of motor-bicyclists escorting them, to Orly and sent home free by Air France.

'Never, since the war, have Anglo-French relations been so cloudless,' said *The Times*. The *Daily Telegraph* said, 'Sir Alfred Wincham's wise and subtle manoeuvring in a difficult situation has been triumphantly successful.' Lord Grumpy said the cunning French had twisted the lion's tail once more and that their valet, Wincham, ought to be sent, forthwith, to Rangoon. Plans and projects for The Visit were now put into operation.

23

'I wouldn't mind the boys calling me Dad,' said Alfred (who did mind, however, and had made great efforts, successful with David and Baz, to be called Father), 'if only they wouldn't pronounce it Dud.'

It was the morning after the riot; Grace and Charles-Edouard had come round for another conference on what could be done with the children. Our two had had breakfast with Alfred; there had been a long, perfectly fruitless argument on lines which were becoming all too familiar. In a sincere effort to use language that Alfred could understand they explained that members of the Showbiz were the aristocracy of the modern world; that Yanky was its King and that as Yanky's gentlemen-in-waiting they had the most covetable position of any living teenagers. Alfred asked what their plans were for the immediate future. 'Driftin' with Yank to Russia,' was the reply. (Driftin', it seems, is Showbiz for touring.) They were to drift through France, Switzerland, and Czechoslovakia, possibly taking in the Balkans; their final objective was Moscow. 'So lucky we all opted to learn Russian at school.'

'And wherever we appear,' Fabrice said, 'the kids will go screaming, raving mad because in those countries everybody has Yanky's discs which they buy on the black market. You should see the fan-mail he gets from iron teenagers.'

Alfred then spoke, in the tongue of our ancestors. He summoned up all his wisdom, all his eloquence, he drew tears from his own eyes as he argued his case for civilization. They listened politely for an hour. When they were quite sure he had finished and that they were in no way interrupting him they replied that his fate had been an example to them. They couldn't help noticing that he had led a sorrowful existence year after year, growing old without having known any pleasure, fun, or enjoyment and that as a result he had landed up in this deplorable, antiquated giggle-academy, the English Embassy at Paris.

'When I left the room,' he said, after telling us all this, 'I heard Charlie say to Fabrice "Poor Dud, he's had it!" I think that pretty well sums up their attitude. We are duds, Valhubert, and we've had it. Yes, even you.'

'I don't know why you should say even me. Specially me, I should have thought.'

'You are a man of action and as such they might have had a certain respect for you. Of course they know quite well that you had a good war, but I'm afraid that means nothing to them because what were you fighting for? They don't care a fig for liberty, equality, fraternity, or any of our values – still less for their King and Country. The be-all and end-all of their existence is to have a good time. They think they could have rocked and rolled quite well under Hitler and no doubt so they could.' Alfred buried his face in his hands and said despairingly, 'The black men affirm that we are in full decadence. Nothing could be truer, if these boys are typical of their generation and if they really mean all the things they told me just now. The barbarians had better take over without more ado. We made the last stand against them. At least we have that to be proud of. But you have fought in vain, my life's work has come to nothing – this job the most pointless part of it, very likely.'

'My dear Ambassador,' said Valhubert, 'you take it all too tragically. Young persons in prosperous circumstances live for pleasure. They always have and no doubt they always will. When I think what Fabrice and I were like, right up to the war! Between women and hunting, we never had a serious thought. Of course when we were Sigi's age, our noses were pressed in the direction of a grindstone by force of economic sanctions. If we could have earned £9 a week packing shavers do you really think we would have stayed at the lycée another hour? And I bet we'd have found some watertight method of nicking, by the way.'

'I'm sorry, Valhubert, but I cannot agree with you. Many adolescents, even rich ones, have a love of learning for its own sake. I know, because as a don I have had hundreds of civilized rich young men through my hands.'

'But with these boys you must face the fact that they are not, and never will be, intellectuals. Hard for you, I know – still two out of four in your family took firsts, quite an honourable percentage. The other two never will, in a hundred years. In the end they will probably be the most conformist all the same.'

'But nowadays no respectable career is open to people without degrees.'

'To speak practically. Sigi will be very rich – I have never had to work so I can't exactly blame him if he doesn't, can I? Little Fabrice only has to play his cards well enough to refrain from throwing them in Tante Odile's face to be in the same circumstances.'

'But Charlie must earn his living.'

'Don't you see, darling,' I intervened, 'the point is that he can. He was making this huge amount in London, and now, at sixteen, he is one of the kings of Show-biz!' I trust that a note of pride could not be detected as I said these words.

'You torture me. Have we brought a human soul to this stage of development only to see him promoting pop sessions?'

'But, dearest, how can we prevent it? Charles-Edouard is quite right. We can't do more for the boys now (any of them) than look on at their vagaries with toler-ance and provide a background when they need one.' Twinge of conscience here. Had I been nice enough to David?

Valhubert said, 'Exactly. They are grown up. Each man in the last resort is responsible for himself. Let them be – let them go. Sigi tells me they are drifting off tomorrow with Yanky Fonzy, taking 20 per cent of his earnings, plus their expenses and anything else they can nick. All right. Count it as the Grand Tour; they'll see the world; it's better than packing. When they come back, if they are eighteen by then, they can go to the wars like everybody else. Only do send Fabrice this afternoon to see Tante Odile.'

'How French you are, Charles-Edouard,' said Grace, laughing.

'Hot news!' This was Northey, coming in with my breakfast. 'The Bomb from Brum has buggered!'

'Already? And the boys never came to say good-bye?'

'The point is, he has left them behind. There was the most terrific bust-up yesterday at Le Pop Club and he has gone.'

'Can it be true? What has happened?'

'It was all about the publicity. You see when Yank saw those kids in Main Street – biggest outdoor reception even he has dreamed of – he thought he'd never had it so good. He expected to hit the headlines on the front pages. Grandfather in the taxi, he thought, gave that little extra something that journalists love, then the crowds, the police, Alfred going to the Quai (I must say it wrung my withers not telling the dear little soul about it).'

'If you had, Northey –'

'Yes, well, I didn't, did I? So Yank thought the boys were geniuses and honestly, Fanny, in a way they were. You've got to hand it to Sigi – he mobilized that enormous crowd – then the Vel d'Hiv was a whizz, every teenager in Paris must have been there and the receipts broke all records. At the Club they were congratulating Yank on his wonderful agents and he was so pleased he kept signing travellers' cheques, giving them to the boys. Of course he could hardly wait to see the papers. Came the Dawn – *quelle horrible* surprise! As you know, sweet Amy and the rest of them barked up the wrong tree – Yank might have stayed in London for all they knew and the bitter thing was his wonderful riot was put down to those silly old islands. His name wasn't mentioned in the news at all – no photographs of him with the screaming kids – taxi gimmick thrown away. A few paragraphs in the entertainment pages saying that he had arrived in Paris and sang from a balcony in the Avenue Gabriel. There'll be a story in the jazz papers of course, but he always has them on his side and this time he'd counted on the dailies. In short, Sigi did marvels, but he only warned the jazz journalists and he got all of them in the garden. He never thought of telling the others – he had no idea, of course, that there would be such a mob of kids in Main Street. So the whole thing has fallen as flat as a pancake. Yank says that's what comes of dealing with bloody amateurs; he telephoned to London for his old agent he's always had and as soon as he arrived they drifted off –'

'Northey! It's too interesting and unexpected! So how are the boys taking it?'

'If you ask me, they are relieved. They had begun to see that Yanky is a most unpleasant person. And Fanny, it's my opinion they've had about enough of earning their own livings. They admit now that the shavers were a tremendous bore – it seems you are shut up in a horrible sort of place which brings on headaches. Driftin' would have been rather fun, but not with Yank. He has put them right off the Showbiz – and they didn't much care for the people at the Club (except for the Duke, who is heaven). They were all on Yanky's side and made the boys feel inferior. Then one of their friends at Eton has asked them to a boys' shoot in Jan which they long to accept. Apparently it's a spiffing house to stay in, where the oldies know their place. They'd like to become ordinary again, you know – they'd really give anything to go back to Eton.'

'Well, that's out of the question – silly little fools. We shall have to see what can be done with them – Condorcet probably, before they cram for Oxford. Meanwhile it's almost the Christmas holidays and they can go to their old shoot. Oh, darling, you don't know what a weight off my mind this is!'

At dinner that evening the boys were studiously normal. They wore dinner jackets, their hair, which had been standing on end, was now watered and brushed in the usual way; they were clean. They gave us looks which I well remembered from their early nursery days and which I could remember bestowing, myself, on the grown-ups; looks which said if all can be forgotten and forgiven we will be good again. They called Alfred Father, and asked him to explain about the C.E.D. They asked me what books I had been reading – I quite expected them to say 'Have you been abroad lately?' a favourite gambit with people they hardly knew. They were sweet and attentive to Uncle Matthew and told him about the shoot they were going to. His old face lit up because it had once belonged to a relation of his and he had shot there many a time in the past.

'Who has got it now?'

'The father of our friend Beagle. He has made nine (you know, the big ones, millions, I mean), since the war.'

'Like blissful Jacques Oudineau,' said Northey, half to herself.

'Has he indeed? You want to look out, in the Sally Beds, not to shoot up the hill. Feller peppered me there once good and proper. Where's young Fonzy this evening?'

Sheepish looks. 'Gone to Moscow,' said Northey.

'What's he want to do that for? Payne and I had our luncheon at a place where the cabmen eat. They haven't got proper shelters; this is a restaurant. Dangerous good snack. We got talking with a Russian there who seemed heartily dissatisfied with his government – you'd hardly believe the things he told us. Now young Fonzy is a very civil chap. He gave me a lot of his records, signed. Of course the signature doesn't make the smallest difference – I mean you can't hear it – but he meant it kindly no doubt.'

'What have you been doing all day, Uncle Matthew?'

'After luncheon we went to the museum. Saw old Foch's coat and a lot of dummy horses and some pictures of battles we liked very much. Then I came back to see if there would be a cocktail party but you were out.'

'Oh bother, yes – it was a National Day we had to go to.'

'It didn't matter. I was rather tired you know, really.'

After dinner he said it was bedtime and he'd better say good-bye. 'We have an early start – I shan't come and disturb you in the morning, Fanny – I know you've never been much use before seven and I want to be off at half-past five. Many thanks. Payne and I have enjoyed ourselves.'

'Come again,' I said.

*

All three boys were invited to stay at Boisdormant. Before they left I screwed up my courage to have a long-postponed talk with Fabrice. This was a moment I had always dreaded, when I must tell him who his father was. He knew that my cousin Linda was his mother and presumably thought that her husband, Christian Talbot, whose surname he bore, was his father. He had never seen Christian or exhibited any interest whatever in him and since he had asked no questions I had not raised the subject. I found it, for some reason, deeply embarrassing to do so.

'Fabrice, darling, you're sixteen now –'

'Definitely.'

'Which is really grown-up. In fact you have taken charge of your own life; you're not a child any more. So I suppose I can talk frankly to you –'

'If this is a pi-jaw hadn't I better fetch Charlie?'

'No, it isn't. One doesn't pi-jaw with one's fellow grown-ups. I simply want to talk about your parents. Now I've always told you that my darling cousin Linda was your mother.'

'Definitely. And my father was the son of this old woman we are going to stay with.'

'Yes, but how did you know?'

'Mum, you are a scream! Of course I've known since I was nine – from the very first moment I saw Sigi at Easterfields. He had heard the nannies telling each other when he was meant to be asleep.'

I suppose my feelings on hearing this must have been the same as those of a mother who finds that her girl has been conversant with the facts of life since childhood. Thankful, really, not to have to enter into difficult explanations, I felt slightly aggrieved to think that Fabrice had kept such important knowledge from me all these years and not best pleased at the way in which he had found it out.

'Everything's always arranged by Sigi,' I said, crossly. 'Never mind. So, darling, be very nice to your grandmother, won't you?'

'Then she might adopt me and leave me a lot of money?'

'Oh dear! How cold-blooded you are –'

But I knew that at sixteen people put on a cold-blooded air partly because they are terrified of betraying sentiments which might embarrass them. Fabrice would be incapable now of saying that Alfred and I were his heart's father and mother; that would come much later, if at all.

He went on, 'Sigi thinks we might make a syndicate for getting what we can out of her. She can take the place of Yanky in our lives.'

'Good luck to you!' I said. 'I expect that Duchess is capable of looking after herself – just like Yanky. You boys aren't quite as clever as you think you are –'

'Don't be ghoulish, Mum.'

They stayed a week at Boisdormant and came back in tearing spirits, having greatly enjoyed themselves. Oudineau had taken them out shooting every day and Jacques Oudineau, who kept a little aeroplane at a nearby aero-club, had allowed them to flop out of it in parachutes to their hearts' content. In the evenings they had listened with real, not simulated, interest to the Duchess's endless tales of her family and the history of Boisdormant. They were taking notes of episodes suitable to be incorporated in the Son et Lumiére and other attractions for tourists which they planned to produce there the following summer. Jacques Oudineau would see to the technical details, Sigi was to be publicity agent in Paris while our boys, collaborating with Basil and Grandad, would supply an endless stream of Britons. Beautiful Boisdormant was clearly destined to wake up one day and find itself the French Woburn. As these activities were not likely to get the boys into much trouble and could easily be combined with their lessons, I could only feel thankful at the turn their lives had taken. Jacques Oudineau, young and dynamic, seemed to have gained a far more complete ascendancy over them in one week than Alfred and I during their whole lives; they could only talk of him. He had decreed that they must now work very hard and pass all the exams with which the modern child is plagued; then he would take them into his business and they would be happy ever after. As for the Duchess, according to Valhubert she found that Fabrice more than came up to her expectations. As soon as she saw Uncle Matthew, she said, she realized that the family was *bien*. Fabrice himself then won her heart by looking like her late son and exhibiting perfect manners. Her will, it seemed, had already been altered in his favour.

24

After Christmas, Philip was posted to Moscow. It seemed to me that everybody had either gone or was going there. M. Bouche-Bontemps, in a fur hat, was conferring with Mr K. at the Kremlin; the French papers were full of lines and sidelines on Russia, no photograph without its onion dome. On Boxing Day, David and Dawn had their baby in a snowstorm between Omsk and Tomsk, causing the maximum amount of trouble to Alfred's colleague in Moscow; telegrams flew back and forth. They were illegally on Soviet territory; it was not easy to get permission for them to stay there until David should be out of danger. (The other two had risen above the experience but it had nearly killed him.) However, the kind Ambassadress took them all in; knowing by experience how difficult it would be to budge them again, I felt sorry for the Ambassador. Yanky Fonzy was enjoying a triumphant season at the Bolshoi. Basil and Grandad had just got their visas and were going to Moscow to negotiate a long-term exchange of tourists.

It was more of a blow than a surprise to learn that we were to lose Philip. We had always known that he was due for a move and that he had only been left at Paris long enough to see us comfortably into the Embassy before becoming Counsellor somewhere else. When he came to tell me his news I said, 'Talk about a Pull to the East – I feel as if I were living in the last act of *The Three Sisters*. All we get back from Moscow is Hector Dexter, a very poor exchange for you and Northey.'

'How d'you mean, me and Northey?'

'I naturally suppose you'll be taking her. You're not going to leave her here with a broken heart, Philip – don't tell me that?'

'Oh, dearest Fanny, do I really want the whole of the Praesidium milling round my dacha? Not to speak of faithful wolves and sweet Siberian crows in one's bedroom?'

'As soon as she's married, with a baby, all that will stop, I've seen it so often. How is your love for Grace?'

'Very hopeless, what with one thing and another. My own fault for telling Mees about St Expédite. Every time I go to St Roch, there she is keenly putting up candles. It's quite ridiculous – the saint doesn't know which way to turn, as Mees said herself, last time we met there.'

'Chuck the whole thing and marry her.'

'What a matchmaker you are.'

'It's time the poor duck was settled. Besides, think how lonely you'd be in Moscow, without any of us.'

'Good for trade,' said Philip, 'promotion, important post and so forth, but I can't say I greatly look forward to it. I would certainly find it much jollier if I had Mees there. But what would you do without her yourself?'

'It won't be the same, but I can have sister Jean now. The Chelsea setter has already found another girl with more money and a larger tiara, and Jean is looking for a job.'

'Oh dear – how I hate taking irrevocable decisions!'

'Go on, Philip. No time like the present. She's in her office – go and propose to her this very minute.'

'All right. So long as you realize that it's entirely your responsibility.' He kissed me on both cheeks and went off.

I was now seized by misgivings. Left to himself, would not Philip have havered and wavered and in the end gone away without coming to a decision? I had induced him to propose, deliberately ignoring the wise reflections of Alfred, although I knew that there was a great deal of truth in them. On the face of it, Philip had the makings of an excellent husband. Attractive, kind, clever, gay, and amusing, never boring, he was also very rich. Nevertheless something was missing, some sort of intensity or ardent flame which, had it existed, might well have won over Grace, or, in the old Oxford days, me myself. Furthermore, he had been in love with us as he was not with Northey. She had fallen in love at first sight, so she loved an image which she had invented and which might easily be rubbed away in daily wear and tear. On the other hand, I told myself, there are no rules for successful marriage. Northey and Philip seemed rather suited, she so lively, he so orthodox; her superabundant vitality, the maternal instinct she lavished on creatures, would turn into their proper channel when she had babies; she was accustomed, now, to Embassy life.

Another factor, I must say, weighed with me. Mockbar had, of late, taken Northey as the heroine of his page. It was no secret now to the readers of the *Daily Post* that the Marquis de Valhubert, who had escorted the world's most beautiful women, was her 'friend'. His British-born wife was expecting her fifth child in March; Mockbar gave the impression that, after this happy event, Valhubert would announce his engagement to Northey.

'Really, darling,' Grace said, 'I shall have to find out what sort of thing the bridegroom's wife is expected to wear at a wedding.'

'Poor soul,' was Northey's reflection, 'he has found out the truth about the riots and he is minding. Hard put to it to mollify Lord Grumpy, just as the children are getting to the age of a glass of wine with their food, you know. However, there's hot news today. M. Cruas is engaged to Phyllis McFee!'

I wondered why these characters were suddenly being liquidated. M. Cruas may have been based on fact; Phyllis McFee was certainly a figment of Northey's imagination; both played a useful part in what Philip called 'the carry-on'. During the last week or two they had been unusually busy – hardly a day without one or other being invoked. It seemed rash of her to make such a clean sweep; I felt a little uneasy. 'Is it wise to get rid of them both at a blow?' I asked.

'Much as I shall miss the beloveds, I have their happiness to consider. Each for each is what we teach. They are buggering off on a long, long honeymoon in Asia Minor.'

Everything considered, was it not my duty to Louisa to get this wayward creature married if I could?

Northey stood in the doorway. Her eyes were like blue brilliants; she radiated happiness. She stood quite still and said, 'It's me, Fanny! I'm engaged!'

'Darling – yes, I know. I can't tell you how delighted I am!'

'You know?'

'Philip told me.'

'But I've only just told him.'

I saw that I had been tactless, of course she would not like the idea of Philip having discussed the matter beforehand.

'He was looking everywhere for you and I suppose he felt so happy that he couldn't resist telling me.'

'Oh yes, I see – he did very kindly offer. Only think, Fanny, two short weeks ago I would have accepted.' She shuddered.

'But, darling, I don't quite understand. I thought you said you were engaged?'

'Yes. I'm engaged to Jacques Oudineau.'